P9-DVN-718

". . . And Ladies of the Club"

"...AND LADIES OF THE CLUB"

HELEN HOOVEN SANTMYER

G. P. Putnam's Sons
New York

 Published on the same day in Canada
by General Publishing Co. Limited, Toronto.

Library of Congress Cataloging in Publication Data

Santmyer, Helen Hooven, date.
"... and ladies of the club."

Reprint. Originally published: Columbus, Ohio : Ohio
State University, c1982.
I. Title.
PS3537.A775A82 1984 813'.52 84-2094
ISBN 0-399-12965-0

Printed in the United States of America

Thirteenth Impression

“. . . And Ladies of the Club”

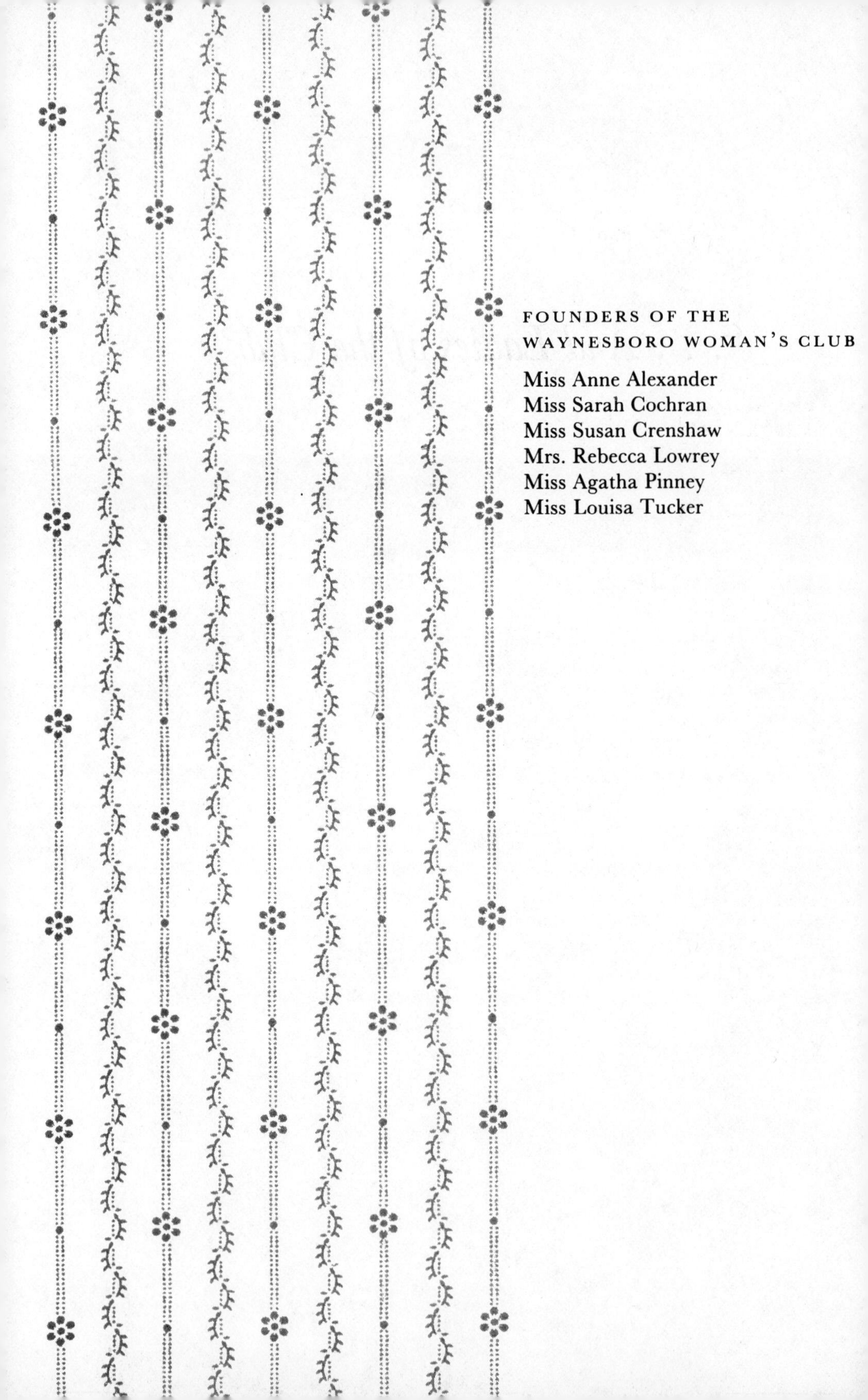

FOUNDERS OF THE
WAYNESBORO WOMAN'S CLUB

Miss Anne Alexander
Miss Sarah Cochran
Miss Susan Crenshaw
Mrs. Rebecca Lowrey
Miss Agatha Pinney
Miss Louisa Tucker

* 1868 *

"The formation of the Waynesboro Woman's Club was first proposed in the early summer of 1868."

The Waynesboro Female College in the eighteen fifties and sixties was a fitting subject, along with the Court House, the churches, the "gentlemen's mansions," for a steel engraving of the sort then fashionable. The two College buildings were well back from the street behind an iron fence and a wide, deeply shaded campus. A brick wall led from the gate; it divided midway in its course, one branch leading straight to the dormitory, the other turning right to the classroom building. From the gate the two looked to be identical: severely rectangular façades, entrance doors deeply recessed above a half-dozen granite steps with iron handrails, the windows of three floors set in exact pairs, one pair above another up to the wooden cornices and the brackets supporting the wide overhang of almost flat roofs. But one of these College buildings, as an engraving must have shown, was larger than the other: the classroom hall was cubical, with one chimney towering above each corner of the roof; the dormitory had much more depth than width, and along the edge of the roof on both sides, front to back, stood rows of double chimneys, evidence of coal fireplaces in every room. The house where the owner of the school lived with his family was back and behind and out of sight of any possible engraver, unless he wandered down the side street that it faced. But it was not worth an artist's pencil—rather small and rather shabby, and fortunately out of sight of the school's front gate. As a matter of fact, the College buildings were themselves clearly to be seen only part of the year, concealed as they were behind low-hanging branches of primeval trees; an artist who wanted a little human life in his picture could have included, in among the tree trunks, the figures of young ladies in hoop skirts playing croquet.

This scene would surely have been included in any set of engravings of "The Beauties of Waynesboro." In the middle years of the century, there were families in southern Ohio long enough established to have grown prosperous who considered it a matter of course that their daughters should have the conventional education of the day. Waynesboro girls were usually day school pupils; the dormitory housed the boarding school students who came "from away." In the sixties and seventies, the Waynesboro Female College, though small, was a flourishing institution.

For various Waynesboro ladies one day of that remote historical period seemed to mark the beginning of an era. June seventeenth, in the year 1868, was Commencement Day at the College. Ordinarily the College's graduation exercises were held in the auditorium of the Methodist church; each of ten or twelve girls read an essay in which she expressed her convictions as to the fundamental virtues, or solved the profounder problems to be met with in life; the school sang; the minister preached; the musicians among the pupils performed on the piano, singly or by twos, and parents and elderly kinfolk enjoyed for some uninterrupted hours the feelings of pride and gratification to which they were entitled. In 1868 the exercises were held on the College lawn, beneath the trees, where a larger audience could gather than the church would hold. An audience larger than usual had been invited because the town's most distinguished citizen, late a Brigadier General of Volunteers and now the district's representative in Congress, had consented to make the commencement address. Those townspeople who would not otherwise have been there, those who had no connection with the school or its pupils, were grateful for the innovation. Commencement at the Female College was distinctly an occasion that was a privilege to attend. Local parents of day school students attributed the departure from custom not to Professor Lowrey, who was a dry little man of few words and unpretentious tastes, but to Miss Tucker, the teacher of mathematics, who had come to Waynesboro from Massachusetts and was generally believed to be as fertile in new and exasperating ideas as other Bostonians of the day.

All families of graduates would have been displeased had the presentation of commencement essays by their authors been omitted: no parent would have been satisfied without a public demonstration of an acquired education. Most of the morning therefore was given over to this display of learning, moral sentiments, and seriousness of purpose; when shortly before noon the orator rose to make his speech, of all the essayists only the valedictorian was still to be heard from.

While General Deming spoke, the midsummer sun crossed the zenith. Under wide boughs the shade lay pleasantly on bonneted heads and gloved hands; only here and there a patch of sunshine fell on a summer frock, or moved lazily across a bit of ribbon, and made them brighter. The group of men and women before the platform seemed larger than it was, perhaps: the chairs were spaced apart to give room for ballooning skirts and petticoats, and every row was broken by trunks and twisted roots of elm and maple tree; yet even so there lay between the farthest chairs and the fence a wide stretch of green separating the invited from the uninvited audience. Outside the gate the idle and curious had collected, and the genuinely interested, who were black men, most of them. They leaned on the pickets and peered over them, shuffled their feet now and then, and sighed, or exchanged glances with one another, but did not speak. They listened intently and soberly to the orator on the platform. There was no difficulty in hearing what he said. The General was a florid, bearded man, heavyset, not particularly broad-shouldered, not tall, but thick through the chest. There were powerful lungs behind his voice, so that in spite of its hoarseness, it would have carried above wind and rain and battle, and on a quiet June morning reached ears for which it was not aimed. Or perhaps the loafers beyond the fence were within the range of his intentions.

"The Republican party," he told them, "declares that every man, white or black, in the late rebel states, shall have his rights. The Democratic party wants the white men in those states to have all the rights of citizens and the freedmen none."

This was one of the sentiments that caused the Negroes to look at one another, nod, and draw nearer to the fence, that they might not miss a word. But they were so far from the speaker that he could not possibly have felt their sympathy, and besides, as he must have reflected, they still could not vote, not yet, even in Ohio. His eyes passed from one to another of the ladies and gentlemen before him. Their faces were amiable, resigned, and slightly bored, like the faces in a schoolroom where the teacher repeats a lesson learned so long ago that there can be no further interest in it. He may have resented this rather patronizing acquiescence; he continued:

"Be warned, my friends. You must understand precisely what the coming election means. It is to decide whether the loyal states or the Rebels won the late war. The Democrats hope that our party is so divided on fundamental issues that it cannot possibly win in November. On the one hand, President Johnson and his supporters would withdraw all troops from the South forthwith, and welcome back into the Union without more ado the erstwhile Rebel states. But those of us who are called "Radicals" would continue to occupy those states until the rights of the freedmen are guaranteed. The northern Democrats were halfhearted or worse during the war. Today that party does not pretend to have suffered a change of heart, nor do the Rebels. Be not deceived: defeat never converts. It is to the defeated what persecution is to the persecuted. The cause becomes daily more precious, and devotion to it a more sacred duty. The course of the Southern States since the surrender shows this ever more clearly. Now, united with Northern Democracy, it deploys on the open field. It flaunts its black flag in the sunshine. It demands repudiation of the country's debts, disgrace, anarchy. It is not dismayed, it is merely embittered by the result of the war. Its purpose in this election is the same as it was at Bull Run and Andersonville, although the means are different. Let the country lift its eyes, let it behold the years from Sumter to Appomattox, and let it answer!"

In response to this eloquence, a few men in the audience tightened their jaws, a few women, angry-eyed, nodded; but the greater number looked somehow embarrassed, a little ashamed for the speaker. The man on the platform was quick to feel his audience's lack of interest, and the cause of it. His guests said "But enough of that," and his laugh was rueful.

"You must forgive my misplaced fervor. My mind has been full of these things to the exclusion of all else. I have but now returned from the Republican Convention in Chicago, where we nominated as our candidate for the Presidency that greatest of all living Americans, General Grant. Those scenes of enthusiasm linger in my memory. I know that when I was asked to speak at the Commencement Exercises of the Waynesboro Female College, I was not expected to dwell long on questions of state for the benefit of those who have no voice in their settlement. But young ladies, let me remind you of one thing." He turned toward the row of girls behind him.

Until this moment they had been heedless of the presence of this man in front of them. They sat quite stiff, "primly still," with their gloved hands in their laps, their wide-brimmed hats shading their faces, as they studied the audience scattered on the grass before the platform. Their demeanor had suggested not impatience but a composed excitement—a deliberately tasted relish of the situation. Their eyes had said to those who faced and watched them, "Here we are at last; look at us, not at him, this is our moment, not his; his words are nothing, yet serve to give us time—time to make the most of this hour, of this sun that shines for us, time to look around and notice who is here to see us thus briefly enthroned." Their glances had brushed over Professor Lowrey in his chair on the other side of table from the speaker; he had taught them history and Paley's *Evidences of Christianity,* and reflected in their faces were tolerance, amusement, and something of pity: "You are old, you know a lot, you may be wise, but you are old." At his wife, in the front row of chairs, they had looked and looked away, half-friendly, half-contemptuous: "You don't understand us, you were wrong a thousand times, yet you are a person and we like you." Their eyes ranging along the line of teachers beside Mrs. Lowrey said, "You disapproved of laughter and high spirits, you thwarted us when you could, yet perhaps someday even these things—" They passed over the two ineffectual little gentlemen who came up from Cincinnati twice a week to teach them music and modern languages, and studied instead, with a puzzled, cool curiosity, the straight-backed fair young woman in the chair on the aisle: "You are beautiful and we are young, and the young love beauty and are weak before it; we meant to love you but could not, and even now we don't know why."

So long as the girls did not look beyond their teachers, their expressions were as alike as their figures, dressed as they were in white, their thin waists, tight bodices and spare, childish shoulders rising from an amplitude of ruffled skirt as the stems of flowers rise from a rosette of leaves. But when their eyes searched over the farther audience for parents, brothers and sisters, friends and acquaintances, the unity of the group was broken, and each became something other than a schoolgirl, a part of some other whole than a graduating class. In the place of honor, in the center of the line, sat the valedictorian, who had not yet spoken; if she still suffered from a sense of strain that for the others had passed, she gave no sign of it. She was a slight girl with an undistinguished snub nose, a wayward childish mouth, and black eyes too large for her face. Those eyes had selected almost at the beginning of the General's speech two men to watch, in the center of the audience, and had rested on them with unabashed tenderness. The older of the two was tall and square-built, with gray mustache and imperial, wearing a frock coat; a tired-looking man, now relaxed and sunk in upon himself, he had returned her regard as steadily, with a kind of unsurprised, unruffled pride. The younger man was shorter and slighter; his lips and chin were shaven, but close-clipped sideburns emphasized his hollow cheeks and the harsh lines about his mouth. When he forgot himself and his situation, his face was gloomy and rather bitter; but when his restless eye turned for a moment to the girl on the platform, he smiled, grimaced, and winked at her, with an impudent schoolboy mischievousness.

He smiled, too, and nodded to the girl next in the row of chairs, a tall girl with golden hair and fair skin, and a mature and generous figure. She had a curious air of dignity, broken now and then by a gleam of mirth in her eyes, as though dignity were forced upon her as a consequence of her height and conspicuous position; it was not assumed easily or without lapses. She lifted the nosegay she held in a salute to a middle-aged couple in prominent seats near the platform, a pair handsome in a restrained, unostentatious way, the man bearded, spectacled, and a little compressed-looking in his tight broadcloth, the woman dressed richly but quietly, her every ruffle in place. Neither acknowledged the girl's unseemly recognition of their presence. Rebuffed, she lifted her eyes from them to the farther chairs. She nodded almost imperceptibly to the young man with the shadowed eyes, but her regard stopped a longer while on another youth who sat alone and apart, in front of a maple tree, his chair tilted a little to rest against the trunk. Her unhurried consideration of his appearance could amost be checked, item by item: it moved from his shoulders, too broad for the camp chair, to his bare head, his hair bleached to straw-color, and back again to his face, his flaxen mustache, his cheek and jawbones, his skin burnt to copper-color. Her concentration drew his eyes to hers; their faces remained blank, yet they said to each other "You are a stranger, and strangers are invisible—yet—wait—"

Not until the orator had turned to them with his "Young ladies," had they really looked at him. Now, when they did, their eyes went blank and stubborn, holding him off: "Let us alone, Let us forget the war. Our lives begin today. The future is ours, it lies ahead, a certain promise. The war is over and done with. It had nothing to do with us, and we have heard more than enough about it."

He spoke against that rebuff. "Let me remind you: the hand that rocks the cradle is mightier than the hand that wields the sabre. What your mothers and sisters were in the hour of the nation's need, you must be when you take your places in the world. God grant that your husbands and your sons will never be called to the stricken field to fight for the flag! But in the years of peace, there are other battles to be fought, less spectacular but no less important, and you must understand the principles at stake. The first of these battles is upon us. Let nothing minimize the importance of electing General Grant in November. You want peace." He turned to his larger audience for his peroration. "We all want peace. But let me say to you that if the friends of peace, demanding conditions for reconstruction and equal rights for all men, be not as sleepless, as untiring, and as wary as their enemies, peace will be indefinitely postponed."

When he had finished, he bowed thrice, to his audience on the grass, to the girls, to Professor Lowrey; then, under cover of the applause, murmured across the table to the schoolmaster: "Will you pardon me a moment while I slip out and speak to my friends outside the gate? I fear they will not linger through the rest of the proceedings. I know," and his smile was deprecating, "that most of them have no vote—as yet—but after all, they are my constituents, as surely as the gentlefolk here."

Released, he strode with a fine martial swing across the platform, down the steps, and around the chairs toward the gate. The "gentlefolk" dismissed him from their attention when he had passed; only the young man tilted against the maple tree sat up and turned to watch, with a considering air, the tatterdemalion but able-bodied Negroes who crowded to the gate to shake the General's hand, humbly, with a proper solemnity and appreciation of the high honor shown them.

On the platform Professor Lowrey stepped forward, his hands clasped behind him under the tails of his coat, and spoke briefly, his tones dry, a little sardonic. "I am sure we are grateful to General Deming for his eloquent exposition of the—er—crisis which confronts the country, and of our duty as citizens in that—crisis. The young ladies who today pass into a wider scene from the—er—somewhat cloistered walls within which they have labored have need to remember that they too are citizens, if not voters, of the Republic. You have had an opportunity to hear from their own lips with what—er—devotion to the high ideals inculcated in them they approach their new duties, their ampler opportunities. From one more of them, who by her high standing in the school has won the coveted honor of delivering the Valedictory, we have still to hear. I take great pleasure in presenting at this time one of yourselves, fellow-townsmen of Waynesboro, the daughter of one of your most esteemed citizens. Introduction would be superfluous were there not many here who do not know Waynesboro and Waynesboro's daughters. Our Valedictorian, Miss Anne Alexander."

While the audience applauded, he turned to peer nearsightedly at the row of girls. When Miss Alexander rose from the chair behind his, he bowed formally, and she curtsied, blushing like a child. Quickly she stepped to the edge of the platform. She walked like one too newly promoted to the extravagance of the latest fashion to be unaware of her petticoats, yet she managed them with a conscious skill: flounces and ruffles drawn back and looped up to her waistline, topped in back by a mammoth flat bow. The contrast between this spread of skirt and the bodice tight about her ribs and breasts and across her shoulders accentuated her slimness, as the elaborate coiffure—curls, bangs and braids, beneath a pancake hat—exaggerated the smallness of her face. Her eyes saved that face from being merely childish and insignificant; excitement made them seem larger even than they were, and they glowed with a friendly confidence in the bond, a shared loved of merriment, between her and her audience.

She ducked her head toward Professor Lowrey, as she had been taught, and murmured his name, toward her classmates, "Fellow graduates," and to her audience, "Ladies and Gentlemen," and then proclaimed with a solemn gesture, "'And now a long farewell to all our greatness—'" paused, and added, apologetically, "In these words I had planned to begin my valedictory. According to the little Latin I have learned, 'Valedictory' means saying goodbye. Farewells are always sad, but because no one wants to be sad at a time like this, I had planned to make little jokes about our melancholy state of mind. I did not know that my trifling remarks would follow so unsuitably a speech about the duties of citizenship, but I must go on now with the words I have been practicing for weeks in front of the looking glass." Her audience laughed with her, indulgently. "I hope you will not begrudge us 'one last lingering look behind,' before we take up our new responsibilities. And so I say again, 'And now a long farewell to all our greatness.' But I want to assure you that if we seem unduly impressed with the position we hold today, it is because we know it is but fleeting. We realize that we shall never be so great again. Never again shall we be head of the school, reverenced by all, and with only the Gods on Olympus"—she lifted her hand to indicate Professor Lowrey, and threw him a sidelong mischievous glance—"ranking above us. Our opinions have been respected, our persons admired, our peculiarities imitated. Doors have been held open for us, we have walked first in every procession. Now those days have come to an end, and we go forth to start in another world at the foot of the ladder.

"But do not think that we have not earned our place. There are fourteen of us, and we have gone through school together. We came here as children. We were children in the school when Fort Sumter was fired on, but not so small that we cannot remember it. We remember when the Waynesboro regiment marched away, and when other regiments passed through our depot and we helped to distribute cakes and doughnuts to them. We remember when our fathers and brothers and uncles and cousins went off to the war. For four years there was not a battle fought where the life of some soldier dear to some one of us was not in danger.

"Because we have memories like this to share, our class has a greater bond to unite it than many classes have. You will understand why it faces the end of its schooldays with a sad seriousness. There is another reason: we feel a greater sense of responsibility than most classes have to bear. While the war was being fought, while the questions that rose afterward were being settled, we were in school; the burden was on other shoulders. Now it is time to say, 'The war is over and done with. The country is united and at peace. Let us make it greater than it has ever been.' It is we—not just we fourteen, of course, but all who are newly facing the world—who will have to do this if it is to be done. Those who are older—even only a little older—have the war too much on their minds." Her voice faltered for a moment; she gazed steadfastly at the remote and indifferent sky. "They cannot forget it. And those who are younger—if we wait for them it may be too late." And then, as if she suspected that what she was saying might sound like bombastic nonsense, she laughed apologetically. "I hadn't meant to be so serious, or to expose ourselves to your laughter by solemn words about our intentions. I had meant to make a jest of them. It is the part of the Valedictorian to speak of the future as well as the past. It does not matter how extravagant my prophesies are because no one will know whether they come true or not. We shall be scattered, this time next week, from the Alleghenies to the Great Plains. We have made many plans for visits back and forth, but I am sure we shall not all be together again, for me to be reminded how I guessed wrong. So let us pretend that our hopes have been accomplished, and I will tell you what they are. First comes Emma Austen, of Fort Wayne, Indiana, who spoke to you a while ago on 'The Rights of Women,' who would like to leave off hoops because they are a nuisance, and cut off her hair because it is a bother. She plans, somehow, to study law. Emma will be a Judge before she dies."

In this facetious strain, she outlined the future life of each of her classmates. It did not matter that her voice hardly could have been audible as far as the last rows of chairs. Her audience was not critical. When she ceased speaking and turned toward her seat, the applause was more spontaneous than that which had followed General Deming's oration.

Professor Lowrey stepped behind the table on which the diplomas lay, tied up with scarlet ribbons; he pronounced the girls' names, and one by one they went to him, curtsied, received their diplomas, and returned to their chairs. After the last he faced the audience once more.

"The exercises will be brought to a close by the singing of the 'Star-Spangled Banner,' after which the Reverend Mr. Otis will pronounce the benediction. Will you then please make your way to the other side of the campus, where an *al fresco* luncheon will be served, honoring the graduating class and their guests."

The crowd remained standing for the benediction; after the "Amen" it began to break its lines, to form in groups and move toward the platform, either to welcome daughters to the family bosom or to find General Deming and express concurrence with his sentiments. The girls filed down the steps, diplomas clutched tight in gloved hands, crinolines managed warily, with heedful eyes on the trailing skirt ahead. Anne Alexander stopped at the edge of the platform for a last look about her, and then touched the shoulder of the girl just in front, on the top step, the same tall fair girl who had sat beside her earlier.

"Sally, look at Miss Tucker. She's lying in wait for the General."

The only one of the group of teachers who was still, by other standards than the girls', a young woman, and by any standards a handsome one, had drawn Mrs. Lowrey away from their colleagues and led her to intercept the General as he returned from his handshaking at the gate. The two girls above them watched the introduction. "I begged for this," Miss Tucker said. To the ears familiar with its every inflection, her voice was audible above all the babel around them. "I feared that if I postponed my congratulations on your timely address, I should not have another opportunity."

General Deming, indubitably pleased, stood bowing over her hand until she withdrew it. The girls saw this with something like contempt. Anne said, "Well, I never! Old Teapot in action!" Miss Tucker was known to the school by that nickname because she had brought a teapot to Ohio with her, so certain had she been that the western wilderness lacked all such amenities. Sally shrugged her shoulders and went on down the steps. "After all, she's from Massachusetts—she probably believes all that about giving the vote to colored men. We're going to eat luncheon together, aren't we? Papa and Mama are in the central aisle."

They parted at the foot of the steps, to search in the throng for their families. Sally moved diagonally across the lawn, between and around groups and knots of people. She knew where her parents were, approximately, and she wandered vaguely in that direction while her eyes were intent on finding the sunburned young man who had leaned against the maple tree. He was alone when she discovered him, but she saw him joined by a plump girl with pigtails and skirts above her ankles. "Minna Rausch. But she's only a child," Sally thought. "Her brother?"

She came to where Mr. and Mrs. Cochran waited for her, and surrendered her attention, apparently to her father's congratulations ". . . Rejoice that Anne did not foresee for you a future in the law courts." Through his pompously humorous sentences, she watched Minna and the young man as they moved purposefully between the empty chairs. She thought, "He's seen someone he knows—it's Dock Gordon." Her father's words were still flowing about her ears. ". . . Glad to know you harbor the proper sentiments in regard to the duties of women . . . your essay . . . The Full Life . . . creditable . . ." She cut his fluency short.

"We must find the Alexanders, Papa. We're to have lunch with them, and I'd like a chance to speak to John Gordon. You remember, he's here for Anne's Commencement."

"Since your mother has asked them all to dine with us, I do remember it." He was a little tart; he was unused to being interrupted so unceremoniously. But Commencement had gone to Sally's head. He offered his arm to his wife, and they followed after their daughter where she led them toward a group of three standing apart from the crowd—Anne, her father, and the morose-looking young man who had sat with him. Nearer to them than the Cochrans were Minna Rausch and the sunburned stranger, but Sally came on quickly enough to overhear the greeting.

"Howdy, Cap'n Gordon! Is this the home town of the Forty-sixth Ohio? Or are you practicing here?"

"Captain Rausch!" The dark face, puzzled for a moment, came suddenly to life. "I'm glad to see you. Didn't know you, at first, in civilians. Yes, this is my home town. I'm not practicing. I'm selling insurance in Cincinnati, and came up today for the Commencement."

"Had enough of sawing bones, did you? This is my little sister Minna. She's in school here. I stopped off on my way home to get her—she's too young to go on the sleeping cars alone."

The Rausches were introduced by John Gordon to Anne and Dr. Alexander: "I learned all the medicine I ever knew in his office."

"I owe you something, then, sir," Captain Rausch said to the older man. "Cap'n Gordon saved my life at Vicksburg. Remember the Duckport hospital, Cap'n?"

Anne murmured a sympathetic "Wounded?" then without awaiting a reply added, "Here are the Cochrans."

Again there were introductions, but before Sally had a chance to do more than repeat Captain Rausch's name, General Deming, with Miss Tucker on his arm, paused in his triumphal progress through the crowd to speak to Mr. Cochran and Dr. Alexander.

"An auspicious day for parents."

"Your speech—a very necessary reminder, General, of what in our peaceful town we are all too likely to forget. But forgive me if, as a banker," Mr. Cochran cleared his throat, made a deprecatory gesture, "I wish that you could have been more explicit as to the party's attitude toward gold redemption."

"Oh, Papa! How vexatious!" Sally murmured the words to no one, or to Captain Rausch, at her side. "Now we'll never get rid of the old wind-bag."

Stately Miss Tucker, whose air toward the General had become almost proprietary in the few minutes she had been with him, overheard, and reproved her with an incongruous archness.

"Sally Cochran! I am *really ashamed* for you. Waynesboro's most distinguished citizen, and your brilliant representative in Congress!"

Sally stared at her as one stares at an old acquaintance who affects suddenly a manner startlingly out of character. The General turned to the two younger men.

"Soldiers, of course? To be sure, I can't miss the signs, you know, after leading a brigade of our gallant fellows. Ah, Captain John Gordon, of course. Oh Doctor, I should say. How does civilian practice seem after service in the Medical Corps? Measles and chickenpox rather tame, eh?"

John did not again explain that he was not practicing, but in as few words as possible presented his companion.

"'Captain Rausch,'" the General repeated. "That has an *echt Deutsch* sound. You 'fit mit Sigel,' perhaps?" He was bland, patronizing.

"No, sir." The tones were blunt, almost contemptuous. "Sixth Iowa. In General Sherman's command, from Shiloh to Goldsborough. My regiment and Captain Gordon's were brigaded together. That's how we knew each other."

"Ah, you were fortunate. General Sherman is a great soldier—a very great soldier. We were all three no doubt companions in arms from Chattanooga to Atlanta. My brigade was in General Thomas's command."

He bowed his approval of the younger men, turned to make a parting remark on the senior members of the group, and then, with Miss Tucker on his arm, marched away.

"Who the devil is he?" Captain Rausch watched the triumphal procession of the two through the crowd.

"One of our political brigadiers. I never heard that he distinguished himself particularly, on any 'stricken field.' He's back in Congress now, where he belongs. Electioneering today, of course."

"There's a plague of generals in the land, like grasshoppers. Bound to be for a few years. They can't do much harm, only talk like fools, like today. All this to-do about the South springing to arms again. When I last saw the South three years ago, they'd gotten their fill of fighting."

"Yes. Grant'll be elected."

"Of course. I wish your General had talked less about getting him in and more about what he'll do when he is in."

"What's it matter to us? We don't have to be reconstructed."

"Oh, reconstruction!" Captain Rausch dismissed the tiresome subject. "I mean finances. Gold redemption or repudiation. You aren't interested? Then your heart isn't in the insurance business."

"I don't know that it is." John considered. "It's just something to do. You're in business? Meat-packing, isn't it?"

"My father is a packer, in Burlington. I've been selling farm machinery in Iowa. But I'd rather go into manufacturing."

"I see." John was plainly indifferent. They turned again to the girls, and Sally resumed her broken conversation with Captain Rausch as she led the way toward the luncheon tables.

"This is very lucky for me," he told her. "If I hadn't seen Captain Gordon, I don't suppose it would have occurred to Minna to introduce me to you and Miss Alexander, in spite of all she's told me about you."

Sally looked beside her at Minna's shocked face, and laughed without embarrassment. "What a fib! You never listened to a word of Minna's tales about her school."

"If I had known—I am afraid Minna lacks the descriptive gift." But he did not continue in this vein; he was too seriously interested in other matters. "Tell me," he said, abruptly, "have you many niggers in Waynesboro? I saw them, outside, listening."

"Yes. But they can't vote. Ohio said 'no' to that last year."

"They soon will. It's plain politics. The Republicans can't hold the South without the nigger vote, and they'll never vote there until they vote everywhere."

"Aren't you a Republican?"

"Certainly. But that doesn't make me give highfalutin reasons for what's plain political expediency. The Republicans who really think the nigger's a man and a brother are mostly confined to New England."

"I suppose so. But there are some in Waynesboro. Real Radicals. Oh, well." Sally was plainly bored with the subject.

"I know," he agreed. "We heard enough about them from the platform. I just wondered, if there are many niggers, what they find to do in a town like this."

"'Do'? Work, you mean? It's the women that work, mostly. The men are janitors, or stable hands, or do odd jobs; cut grass, shovel the snow in the winter. Why?"

"It's a possible labor supply." As if that were a full explanation, he dropped the subject while they moved along beside the table looking for eight empty chairs together. When they had found them and were about to sit down, Mrs. Lowrey passed on her way toward the foot of the long trestle table. After she had seen them, she hesitated, with a blank, reminded air, then returned and said, "I should be obliged to you, Sarah and Anne, if you would come in to my office for a moment after lunch. At two-thirty? Yes, I should think I would be free by that time. There's a subject I want to discuss with you. If you haven't any other engagements—" She left them before they could agree or disagree. They looked at each other in consternation.

"But she can't be going to give us demerits. We're through with all that. It's just her manner. She can't help it."

"As if we hadn't better things to do," Sally grumbled.

They turned back to their places at the table, and Anne explained to John. "And I was looking forward to seeing you, for a visit, I mean."

"It's all right, Anne. You needn't think about me. I must drive out to the farm this afternoon to see my sister." Then he turned to Sally, to tease her. "I expect your schoolmarm has heard rumors that you called General Deming a 'wind-bag.'"

The Methodist minister rose to ask the blessing; they hushed and bowed their heads. Sally's mind was busy during the interval of silence; after the "Amen" when everyone relaxed and started to talk and the waitresses began to pass behind the table with platters of fried chicken, she leaned forward so that she could catch her mother's eye beyond the intervening persons.

"Just think, this is the first time Dock and Captain Rausch have met since they were discharged from the army. But they'll not have much time together, if Dock has to go into the country this afternoon and the Rausches leave for Chicago tonight."

Mrs. Cochran laughed; Sally's hints were hardly subtle. "Of course, Miss

Rausch and the Captain must have dinner with us, with John and the Alexanders. We should be delighted."

Minna looked frightened, but her brother accepted the invitation without consulting her. Their train did not leave until eleven. "And perhaps," he added, "if the young ladies are not 'kept in' too long by Mrs. Lowrey, they will join Minna and me in a stroll, later? I'd like to see more of Waynesboro while I'm here."

After luncheon Anne and Sally went into the dormitory and knocked, rather timidly, at the closed office door. The trepidation long associated with that threshold could not at once be outgrown. But their uneasiness subsided when, invited from within to enter, they found awaiting them only Miss Pinney and Miss Crenshaw. Miss Pinney was a thin, ingratiating little spinster who taught the primary children and could not be concerned with any peccadilloes of theirs. Nor was Miss Crenshaw an intimidating person. She had taught them what Latin they knew and some Greek; in four years they had grown used to her long face with its grim features and bilious color; they no longer saw it; when they looked, they saw "poor old Crenny," who was funny being Cicero and thundering against Catiline in the Roman Senate, and even funnier fumbling with the pages of Virgil, turning them over hastily, and bidding her class leave those passages untranslated. Miss Crenshaw was now giving up teaching; their last year had been her last, too; retired to a dreary old age, she would continue to live alone in her cottage down on Chillicothe Street. Perhaps it was because she had no further connection with the Female College that she sat, now, with her back to the window. It was wide open, and on the lawn below schoolgirls, their teachers, their families, still moved to and fro. Names affectionately spoken, farewells and promises for the future, all were audible; but instead of watching them, or listening, Miss Crenshaw sat and stared at the engraving, hung above the mantel, of the Coliseum in Rome.

The girls, too, seated themselves to wait for Mrs. Lowrey; they looked about them and for the first time, not without bewilderment, saw what had been a court of justice as an ordinary room, rather shabby, more than a little untidy. Tall bookcases, in the corner between the windows, were so stuffed with books and pamphlets that the glass doors would not quite close. The coal grate was empty and unscreened, its bars rusty and its fender unpolished. The flat felt-covered desk was littered with papers, ledgers, pens, and ink bottles. Behind it was a swivel chair. The other chairs in the room were of an ecclesiastical pattern, upholstered with horsehair.

Of these chairs the girls had chosen the two closest together; while they braced themselves in them, they engaged the two older women in a labored conversation until Mrs. Lowrey came in. She entered breathlessly, as if carried on a high wind, her thin cheeks flushed and her hair disheveled. She gave the girls a quick mischievous look, and chuckled at their blank faces.

"Did you think I had reserved one last scolding for you? There may be occasions still when I think it wouldn't come amiss, but your behavior is no longer my responsibility. No, I asked you to join us for a moment this afternoon because I thought you might be interested in what we have been discussing." She glanced out the window as she passed it on her way to the desk. "I think we need not wait for Miss Tucker."

Miss Tucker followed, however, close on her heels, with a quiet dignity and no accompanying breeze. "I beg your pardon for my tardiness. I wished to exchange a few opinions with General Deming before he went away. One has so few opportunities to discuss matters of moment with those who play a part in them."

Mrs. Lowrey, her head bent, looked up through her eyelashes with what might almost have been amusement. "Ah, yes, General Deming, so distinguished," she murmured. "You weren't late, really; I just came in myself." She turned to the girls to answer the question in their eyes. "It won't take me a moment to say what I wanted to say to you. For some time we ladies at the College"—she indicated her colleagues with a gesture—"have been discussing the possibility of organizing a literary club in Waynesboro, a *woman's club*, not a 'female circle,' to meet at intervals and promote an interest in culture—in letters, in poetry—at least in a small group. Some of us regret that Waynesboro is too small to afford us the pleasure of the Lyceum lectures. The only substitute in our power would be a club whose own members would be the ladies of Waynesboro. That is why we asked you to come in this afternoon." She paused and added a little doubtfully, "There are the Ballards and the Misses Gardiner—" She waited for their response.

"A *literary* club, Mrs. Lowrey?" Sally sounded a little doubtful.

"Yes. Purely literary. All controversial subjects would be barred. I know what you are thinking. The Ballards"—she hesitated before the unseemliness of personalities, then took the plunge. "As we all know, the Ballards are deeply concerned in various movements for reform—are just now, in fact, delegates to the State Convention of the Woman Suffrage Association. But they are also very deeply interested in things of the mind; I think they would not begrudge us one afternoon a fortnight. And they are very keen, very able women. Then there is Miss Reid, who will be back with us next year in Miss Crenshaw's place. As you know, she is to be graduated from Oberlin this month: she would join such a club, I am sure. And perhaps she would be the best one of us to interview the Ballards, as she and Miss Thomasina Ballard are intimate friends."

"Yes." Miss Tucker nodded gravely. "She is really a *student*, and could convince them that we intend to undertake this work *seriously*, not as a *frivolous pastime*." It was incisiveness, not affectation or excitability, that italicized Miss Tucker's speeches. She did not look now toward the befurbelowed and ringleted girls, but they acknowledged the cut: they glanced at each other and away.

"Yes. And you young ladies,"—Mrs. Lowrey's eyes twinkled—"you may think the prospect deficient in entertainment. But you will find time hanging heavy on your hands next year; there are not many young people in Waynesboro, and your home duties will not be onerous. And besides," and she laughed, a little ruefully, "having labored for many years to instill in you some understanding of the beauties of literature, I should like to see you develop that knowledge."

The two girls had long since exchanged their opinions, in silence, by lifted brows, almost imperceptible grimaces, nods, and becks. Anne had at first indicated a stubborn negative, and had widened her eyes at Sally to express amazement at her acquiescence; but she had allowed herself to be outnodded, and now let Sally speak for them both.

"Thank you, Mrs. Lowrey. It is very kind of you, and it is flattering to be considered. I am afraid that we are not so well acquainted with literature as we should be, but we will not fail to do our best when our turn comes. Yes, we should like to be members."

Anne, her head lowered, smiled wryly. The drawing-room manners of her mother sat oddly on Sally, but Sally was going to be a Young Lady now, and she must support her.

"Yes, Mrs. Lowrey," she said, "it would be a great honor, and one that we will work hard to deserve."

Only Miss Tucker lifted her brows, perhaps skeptically. Mrs. Lowrey resumed where she had left off. "Then there are the Misses Gardiner. I do not know them myself. I believe they are rather aloof, and have not many friends in Waynesboro. But they might be interested in a club of this kind. Their father was a distinguished lawyer, and they are reputed to have the largest library in the town next to Judge Ballard's."

"They are members of our church," Anne volunteered. "But of course while I lived at the College, I had to go to the Methodist church. I don't really know them, only just to bow to."

"Mamma calls on them, I believe." Sally was hesitant.

"Oh? I wondered if she wouldn't know them. No doubt you will now accompany your mother on her calls. Sometime between now and the first of October you might acquaint them with our plans, and invite them to join us. Would you do that?

"Yes, Mrs. Lowrey."

"We shall plan to have our first meeting in the autumn. We can organize, and elect officers when all interested are present."

Mrs. Lowrey rose to indicate that her purpose with them had been accomplished. The girls hesitated no longer than politeness required before they made their escape. Outside the office door, in the hall, Anne whispered to Sally, "What possessed you?"

"How could we refuse?" Sally frowned a little as she marshaled her arguments. "This club might turn out to be important in the town, and if we'd once refused, we'd never be asked again. And we can always withdraw if we don't like it. Besides, to refuse would give Old Teapot a chance to say 'I told you so.' She thinks we're not serious-minded."

Anne stopped beside the foot of the staircase and leaned against the newel post to laugh. "Oh, Sally! You'll be the death of me. We *aren't* serious-minded."

"Why did you say 'yes' then?"

"I couldn't miss the chance of seeing you in action. How you behave, I mean, in a circle of serious minds. And we've always done everything together. Besides, it will be fun to tell Mrs. Lowrey what we really think of her English poets—Wordsworth, for instance—in a place where she'll have to be polite about our opinion."

They went on to the outer door, and down the steps to the path where the Rausches, brother and sister, awaited them. Anne had fallen behind, and she thought as she watched him that Captain Rausch did not even look to make sure that she was there. Smiling, his head back, the sun on his fair hair, his eyes were all for Sally as she stepped close to him and they started toward the gate side by side. Without a word Anne fell in with Minna behind them. The arrangement irked her a little. She was tired from the strain of the long morning, she was not dressed for walking, and she was disappointed because John was not with her. She had nothing to say to Minna; they had never shared anything but the daily commonplaces of boarding school life. The child could hardly be so stupid as not to realize why, now, Sally was pretending; but no one would deliberately belittle herself in the eyes of an older brother. Minna would not tell the Captain that the two older girls were not, really, friends of hers; she would pretend that this sudden intimacy was not new. And Sally, the minx, was counting on it. Anne, with a smile half-mocking, half-admiring, watched the tall strong young couple ahead of her.

Her incipient crossness was not averted by the course of their walk; past the Cochran house halfway down the Market Street hill, to the iron-fenced Court House square. By that time Sally and Captain Rausch were chatting easily, paying no attention to the Court House or its rear entrance behind a stand of sycamore trees, not to the hole in the ground on the opposite Market Street corner, where stone masons were laying the foundation of the prospective City Hall-cum-Opera House, nor to the Presbyterian church on the third corner, across Main Street. Still talking, they turned left under the elm trees along the side of the square, turned right at the Main and Chillicothe crossing, without as much as a glance at the impressive portico of the Court House with the clock tower rising above it. Anne wondered at Sally's ignoring of what might possibly be called a "beauty of Waynesboro," but she said nothing, and with Minna plodded along behind them west on Chillicothe Street, with the town's "good stores" on their side, and across the wide street, various barber shops, small groceries, and the Hoffmann beer parlor. With no indication of interest they walked around the jutting steps of Dr. Alexander's office, crossed a narrow side street, passed Miss Crenshaw's cottage, and the square unadorned brick building that was the town's public school, and continued through the "goose pasture" where the Irish lived.

They led the way, serenely unconscious of the girls behind them, across the railroad track and on and up the cobbled ramp to the wooden bridge over the towpath and the canal.

As they paused at the railing to look down at the dark sluggish stream, Anne and Minna came up and joined them in contemplation of the slow-moving water, an almost compulsive act for anyone standing on a bridge. Only Captain Rausch was studying the wider scene: the road that continued on a level with the bridge, crossing a strip of land perhaps as wide as the length of a city block to an iron bridge on stone piers, its framework criss-crossing high above the wide but shallow river, whose far bank was lined as far as could be seen up and down the stream, by an earthen levee. The road crossed the levee and disappeared, presumably down another ramp.

Anne, whose crossness had not been mitigated by the long dusty walk in her white slippers and her Commencement dress, said, "Is this your idea of a beauty spot to exhibit to a visitor?"

"It's the one beauty spot Captain Rausch wanted to see."

"I suppose it is—picturesque."

"Oh, picturesque." The tall young man smiled down at her, then turned again to Sally. "There are no levees along the canal? Anyway, this bit of land in between is higher—quite a bit higher. I can see. It is never flooded?"

"Not that I can remember. The canal is much deeper than the river, and if need be, the locks can be opened. The river does flood the far bank sometimes, so we need that levee."

From where they stood they could see patches of sand above the water rippling over the shallows.

"Is this strip of land an island?"

"Oh, no. The river makes a wide bend to Waynesboro. They say that Wayne's army forded it here; that's how the town got its name. Of course, that was long before the canal was dug."

"And over there is the ropewalk your father was talking about at lunch?" He pointed upstream. A hundred feet or so from the bridge an unpainted wooden building, long and low like a warehouse, was half-visible behind the scrubby willows lining the bank. Beyond and behind it a cobbled yard could be guessed at, and a few small frame buildings, hardly more than sheds. A long way beyond, in full view from the bridge, a cobbled ramp led down to a landing on the canal's bank.

"The canal is still used, I suppose?"

"Oh, yes. Not for passengers, since the railroad, but for freight. It is so much cheaper."

Anne said, "Isn't it quiet for a factory? Do they still make rope?"

"By hand, start to finish. Papa says their day is done—they haven't the capital to buy machinery."

"Didn't he say two old Dutchmen started it and still own it? By 'Dutchmen' I suppose he meant Germans?"

"No, when Papa says 'Dutch', he means it, though Germans do get called that in these parts."

"Would you ladies excuse me for a moment? I should like to go down and speak to them."

He swung around the end of the bridge to the canal bank. They watched him brush through the weeds that crowded the towpath, and disappear in the darkness of an open door.

"Your brother," Sally sighed with mock resignation, "thinks more of manufacturing than the delights of female companionship."

Minna flushed, but answered promptly, with stolid German seriousness. "I guess he's more interested in rope than anything. He wants to make it himself, or string or something. I heard him talking to Uncle Otto once, in Cincinnati."

"Oh, I see." Sally's eyes widened; she whistled softly between her teeth.

They waited patiently until he returned. He vouchsafed nothing as to his purpose or its accomplishment; he had evidently dismissed the matter from his mind, for on the walk up Chillicothe Street he showed a proper visitor's interest in the streets and houses that they passed.

Anne parted from them at the steps to Dr. Alexander's office, went inside and along a dark hall to a side door opening on the brick path to the stable yard, passed it to an alley gate, crossed the alley to another gate that led to the Alexander back yard and on into the house by way of the side porch door. She found Captain Gordon waiting for her in the sitting room. Her "Oh, John! I'm sorry!" had as much disappointment as contrition. "They walked me all the way down to the old ropewalk and back, in this!" She indicated her ruffles. "Not exactly a suitable walking costume." She took off her pancake hat and laid it and her gloves on the round center table. "It was hot, too." Handkerchief in hand, she pushed up the heavy braid of hair surmounting her fringe until it looked like a coronet. Indicating by a gesture that he was to return to his chair, she herself took a stiff one without arms, and spread her skirts around her.

"Was your sister home? How was she?"

"Same as ever." John scowled as he relaxed in the depths of the armchair. "She's queerer'n Dick's hat-band. Tramping around in boots. Skirts clinging to her knees, looking like a scarecrow." He laughed brusquely; he would not pretend that a visit to Kate was anything but an unpleasant duty. Everyone in Waynesboro knew how eccentric his sister was, running the farm like a man, never coming to town if she could avoid it, making no friends, paying no calls, never going to church, or wearing hoop skirts and bonnets. Her father had willed his land to John and his money to Kate; but when John had progressed from Dr. Alexander's office to the Ohio Medical College, with the avowed intention of leaving the farm behind him forever, she had bought the place, and for ten years it had been hers to do with as she pleased. She was a competent farmer, and even something of a genius with hired hands and livestock, but that made her seem no less peculiar. John said now, "Let's not talk about Kate."

He smiled at Anne, delighted by her ribbons and ruffles, her conventional femininity, and somewhat amused by it, too, because she seemed to him like a little girl who had borrowed her mother's clothes for dressing up. She was so prim, sitting straight in the stiff chair, her feet hidden, her hands clasped in her lap, her eyes veiled. It seemed no time at all since her hair had hung in a tangled mane down her back and she had worn grass-stained pinafores and pantalettes, and had haunted her father's library, interrupting him and her brother Rob at their books, staring over their shoulders with morbid curiosity at the diagrams of worse-than-naked human figures.

"It seems good to be in this house again," he said, after a moment, and thought, "although it's so different, with Rob gone, and your mother gone and those of us left so much older. When did you open it up?"

"It still has an unlived in smell, doesn't it? Though Martha came down last week and aired and cleaned it, and brought Papa's things over from that flat above the office. So that the minute Commencement was over we could come home. You remember Martha?"

"Vaguely. She was here when I came home on furlough. A slip of a girl, black as coal."

"She was young when she came to us. When Mamma took sick. She worked for us through the war years, and only left when Papa got the silly notion of having me stay at the college as a boarder, and moving himself into that flat. She went to the Allens on the understanding that she would come back to us when I was through school. Silly. We could have stayed right here. With Martha here, I could have kept house for Papa easy as not. Of course, with the Cochrans traveling abroad all this last year, and Sally boarding at the College too, it was fun. Anyway, I think Papa kind of enjoyed living like a bachelor again, being as untidy as he pleased, and eating with his friends at the hotel."

They were silent for a minute; then Anne rose, crossed to the table to pick up her hat and gloves, and said, "I must go fix up a bit for dinner at the Cochrans'. If you would like to wash, use Rob's room; there is water there, and soap and towels."

He followed her upstairs. On the threshold of Rob's room, as he paused, he thought, "I could have told her why the Doctor was glad to close the house." Of course, after Rob had died, and then Mrs. Alexander, her father had wanted Anne out of a house that would be beyond her power to make cheerful. He had probably hoped to preserve her gift of lightheartedness, and so had sent her to board at the Female College these last few years. As a child, she had adored Rob, but she could not have been more than twelve or thirteen when he died. She probably hadn't now the poignant memories of her brother that he, John Gordon, had. Rob and he, reading the medical books, helping the doctor in the office; Rob rebelling one day and going to read law with Judge Ballard instead. Then the war, and Rob and he together again in the same company. And now, Rob gone and he here in this room, in his stead. Rob's room was so familiar to him: he had used that washbowl and pitcher so often—had so often and so long ago brushed his hair before that mirror hung over the chest of drawers. As quickly as possible he had made himself presentable and went downstairs to find Dr. Alexander ready and waiting in the sitting room. Anne did not keep them long, and the stableman-coachman had the carriage at the front gate. For such an occasion one rode even a few blocks instead of walking.

The two Rausches were ahead of them, deposited on the stone carriage steps inside the curb by the hack they had taken from the row lined up in front of the hotel. Minna was familiar with what was visible from the street of the Cochran place: the big yard, the tall trees, the surrounding iron fence with two gates, the one that opened on the walk up to the front door and the double one, usually left open, to the driveway past the steps at the end of the porch. But because she had never been particularly interested, she had never really noticed the house. Now going through the gate ahead of Ludwig, waiting while he paid the cab driver, looking ahead up the steep flagstone path, she felt its intimidating effect, and hung back to take Ludwig's arm.

Built in the same decade as the Female College in much the same style, the Cochrans' was undoubtedly a "gentleman's mansion": a massive square brick house at the top of a slope, it stood well above street level, its upper stories half hidden by tree tops. Like the College buildings, it had a wide cornice with brackets supporting the overhang of the roof; unlike them, a wide veranda crossed the front of the house, with cast-iron supports in a grape and leaf pattern under its roof, and around the roof's edge a railing in the same pattern. Front steps led across the veranda to the deeply recessed double front door; at one end other steps descended to the driveway, which continued around the corner of the house, past the kitchen wing to the stable.

While Minna hung back, half behind Ludwig, he marched up the walk and the steps, bold as brass, and bold as brass rang the doorbell.

The door was opened immediately by a colored houseman in a white jacket (Reuben, who on any social occasion was promoted temporarily from coachman): he ushered them to the parlor door, where the three Cochrans awaited them. After the polite remarks proper to the occasion, Mr. Cochran said, "We are hopeful, my wife and I, that we can have an evening of music after dinner. I have asked Sarah to put out her sheet music and books of songs. Perhaps you will have time to look them over before the Alexanders come." The three young people went obediently to the piano where the songs had been spread out. The round-eyed Minna, standing at her brother's side as they turned over such favorites as "The Blue Juniata," "When I Saw Sweet Nellie Home," "Rocked in the Cradle of the Deep," lost some of her awe: those songs were not what at home she had learned to consider music; she now wondered as much at Ludwig's solemn consideration of their merit as she had before at his ease in such surroundings. She ceased to pay attention as the other two flipped through the songbooks, humming a bit, talking a bit, laughing quite a lot. She gave her mind instead to a scrutiny of the Cochran parlors; from the piano, close to the front windows, she had a full view of the two rooms and could store details in her memory to recount at home.

Everything was dark and rich, with a depth to the richness: the gold-patterned wallpaper, the walnut woodwork, the flowered carpet. The sides of the double door between the rooms as well as the long windows were hung with maroon chenille draperies, looped back and up with the cord and tassel, the extra length spread in half-circles on the roses of the carpet. Each room had its fireplace, with a peacock screen, a mantelpiece of black marble veined with green, and a mirror above as long as the width of the mantel, with elaborately carved frames of misted gold leaf. Twin chandeliers hung far below remote and shadowy ceilings, six-branched, with a stiff-legged heron standing rigid at the top of each branch, in his bill one end of the chain that held suspended a prismed lamp. There were walnut-and-horsehair sofas and marble-topped stands, a couple of heavy tapestry armchairs, and on the walls vast dark engravings with wide walnut frames. The rosewood piano, under Minna's elbow, gleamed with a high polish; it was open, and the mother-of-pearl inlay behind the keyboard glittered when it caught the light and reflected it.

Minna had put on a dark merino frock suitable for traveling; in it she felt unnoticeable, a mere child, and could stare freely at everything, coming at last to Sally's bright figure, in high relief against her background. Sally wore her Commencement gown still, with its flounces and laces and bows; her fair hair had been dressed anew with even more elaboration of braid and ringlet than in the morning, and she had added to her costume a gold chain about her neck, a pair of wide bracelets on either arm, and earrings set with black onyx.

The massive jewelry helped establish the effect of maturity suggested by her figure, her height, her nobility of carriage, and, for the moment at least, her dignity of manner. She had at first been gracious to Ludwig, but she had passed from that to the easy friendliness of the afternoon. She had been kind to Minna, with a kindness that multiplied the years between them. But when she heard the Alexanders at the door, she was turned young again by the voices abrupt and impulsive. She pushed the sheets and books of music into an untidy heap, said, "We'll try some of them after dinner," and crossed the room eagerly to meet her other guests. When the houseman brought in sherry and biscuits on a tray, and offered her, in her turn, a glass, she was still not grown-up, and looked questioningly at her father, flushed and surprised.

"Take it," he commanded her, from where he stood teetering on his heels in front of the empty fireplace. "Aren't we celebrating your entrance into womanhood? Eh, Doctor?"

"Yes. Drink it, Anne, and be thankful. Although it's a pity to waste it on them. I suppose this is what you brought back with you from Europe?"

Mr. Cochran's brief account of his tour abroad concluded with a justification of it. "Mrs. Cochran wanted to go, and Sally wanted to board at the school—and I could leave the bank, then. The public mind was not concerned last year with financial questions, it was fixed on the impeachment trial. I couldn't have gone this fall, with an election impending."

They had hardly touched on that all-important topic before they were summoned to dinner; therefore in the dining room, at the table, they discussed at length—or the men did, while the women listened with accustomed patience—politics, gold redemption of government bonds, reconstruction, and the resumption of specie payments. Mr. Cochran spoke with authority, Dr. Alexander and John Gordon with the disinterested cynicism of the uninvolved, and Ludwig Rausch with the eagerness of the novice.

"If the citizens of the country can be made to realize the situation," the banker assured them, "and vote accordingly, so that we may have an administration sworn to uphold the country's credit, there will be such a development of industry, railroads, agriculture, as we have never seen."

"Then you think that if Grant is elected, it would be an opportune time for a man to start out for himself?"

"Captain Rausch is thinking," Sally explained to her father, "of starting a factory in Waynesboro."

"But I haven't said so." He turned to Sally, amazed, and not altogether pleased.

"You are, aren't you?" Her radiant smile, her triumph at having guessed his secret, teased him out of thinking her officious.

"It's hardly got to the point of serious thinking. You see, sir," and he turned again to Mr. Cochran, "since the War I've been selling agricultural implements in Iowa, Nebraska, Kansas. All that flatland is being homesteaded now, grassland is being plowed up, because with mechanical reapers and binders it can be planted and harvested without the farmhands that aren't there. I know pretty well what the new machines can and can't do. Binders still use wire, and snippets of it get into the grain and straw, and eventually into the stomachs of the livestock. The farmers complain, naturally. Soon someone will invent a binder that uses twine. Then, every harvest, there'll be hundreds of thousands of feet of it used by those machines to bind the grain. There's always someone to come up with what will satisfy a felt need. Is that not so? Then more grasslands will be ploughed, more wheat harvested, and more twine used. In the meantime," he added more slowly, "if a man had a ropewalk, he'd be ready, and until then, he could be making rope."

"And might be making rope all his life. But why not? It will always be needed." Mr. Cochran nodded his head approvingly. "And there's ropewalk here."

"Yes. Why here, I wonder? In the beginning, I mean?"

"Hemp, American hemp. The farmers around here and in Kentucky raise it, but not so much as they used to; I've an idea most help is imported nowadays. I'm afraid the Waynesboro mill's out-of-date."

"Yes. There's machinery now, I understand, for part of the process, at least." Then modesty or caution brought the young man to a pause. "This notion of mine—I expect it's silly to talk about dreams. Particularly," and he looked around at the silent table, "such dull dreams, at such a time. I'm sorry. We ought to be talking about what the young ladies are going to do next, not me."

"There's not much doubt, is there," and Dr. Alexander looked from Sally to his daughter, opposite, next to John, "about what young-ladies-out-of-school are going to do next?"

Anne made a face at him, impudently, across the table. "If you were to guess from now till Doomsday, you'd never guess what Sally and I are going to do next." Three parents looked rather frightened, but did not respond to her challenge. She reassured them. "We're going to help organize a club—a woman's literary club." And she laughed suddenly, irrepressibly, as if she saw it as wholly ridiculous. "We're going to meet around at each other's houses and tell each other what we think of Shakespeare and Milton."

Her father nodded. "Well, that's harmless; it ought to keep you out of mischief."

"Harmless?" Mrs. Cochran, who up to this point had had little to say, leaned forward. "I don't know, Doctor. It sounds like Woman's Rights to me. Just who is to belong to this club, Sally?"

Sally told her, and explained that Mrs. Lowrey had summoned them to her office that afternoon in order to invite them to join. "And it is to be purely literary, Mamma. All controversial subjects barred."

Sally's earnestness amused the two fathers, who expressed their agreement as to the foolishness of the women with winks and nods. "I shouldn't worry about it, if I were you," Mr. Cochran advised his wife. "A dozen women can't meet every other week for a whole winter and remain on speaking terms. It won't last long enough to make a blue-stocking out of Sally."

The men might have lingered indefinitely over their empty dessert plates, making the most of this new pretext for teasing their daughters, but the servant brought in a message for the doctor; and when he begged to be excused, they all rose with him and went together into the hall.

Mr. Cochran was urbane, regretful. "Of course, with gentlemen of your profession it must be expected. But you do make the most unsatisfactory guests. The best part of the evening is to come: we are to have some music now, I believe."

"If I'm not too late, I'll come back. And if I don't, Anne, don't keep the Cochrans up. John, take her home at bedtime."

In the parlor again Mrs. Cochran chose one of the armchairs, and Mr. Cochran perched uneasily on a narrow haircloth sofa; Sally twirled the piano stool, and Ludwig found the ballads they had chosen before dinner. When they had worked their way through those, Ludwig sang "Kennst du das Land" and "Der Erlkönig," while Sally played; then he took his turn at the piano and with his sister went through the German lieder of their childhood, the shy Minna now as unselfconscious as a bird. Mrs. Cochran asked for

"Old Black Joe"; John and Anne joined the others at the piano, and from that beginning they worked their way through Stephen Foster and made the easy transition to songs of the war. On "John Brown's Body" and "Tramp, tramp, tramp," they let their voices out and shouted with a wholehearted abandon while Ludwig thundered on the piano, the pictures trembled on the walls, the bronze herons tottered on their stiff legs, and the lights swung on their chains. When Dr. Alexander returned they were singing "Kingdom Comin'":

De win' blows cold, but I's done with toil,
An I's lef' de cotton patch—

They turned to smile at the doctor from the piano but continued without a break to the end:

Den fling away de plow an' hoe
Dis am de jubilee:
De rain may come, de win' may blow,
But bless de Lord I's free.

He waited until they had finished, then said, "Time for us to go, Anne," and the group dissolved, shook hands, bade each other good-night or good-bye, and went into the hall for hats and shawls.

In the carriage Anne felt all at once too weary even for conversation, and the men too had little to say. It was not until they were back in the Alexander house, after they had heard Zeke close the stable door, that the doctor spoke the words to John that Anne had been expecting all day to hear in one form or another. He had dropped heavily into the leather armchair by the fire-place, and looked up at John standing by the fender filling his pipe.

"I'm getting to be an old man, I guess. I'm tired—tired. When are you coming back, John, to do my work for me?"

John moved uneasily, spilling crumbs of tobacco on the hearth. He said, "Oh, Anne, see what I did. I'm sorry—" but nothing more.

"Haven't got over it yet, eh?" The older man looked up at him shrewdly, good-humoredly. "Give yourself more time, then. But don't forget everything you ever knew."

"I've tried to." John was stubborn. But under Anne's reproachful eye, he could not say more. He went to the foot of the stairs with the doctor, who was ready for bed. John's train back to Cincinnati passed through Waynesboro at four-thirty in the morning, and he would spend the hours until then at the station hotel. But when the doctor had gone, he returned to the parlor for a moment and stood over Anne's chair.

"Does he really want me to come back?" he asked her. "Or is it that it was promised that I should be his partner, and he thinks he can't go back on it?"

"He wants you back. He needs you."

"But Rob—" John pulled a chair closer and sat down to face her. "How can he pretend to have forgotten?"

"Rob? What has poor Rob to do with it?" She was confused and sorrowful.

"He was in my regiment. He was brought to my field hospital. He died. How could his father think of me, still, as a doctor?"

"Oh, John! All these years, you've thought that!" The confusion cleared from her mind. She understood what had made him behave like a sensitive schoolboy toward her father: John had hardly dared meet his eye, lest he see reproach in it. "You needn't have. It isn't as if Papa weren't a doctor himself. He knew. I remember it, that day when word came that Rob had been wounded—how he had been wounded. Papa told Mamma that she mustn't hope—that there couldn't be any hope. He said, 'Our only comfort is that he'll have John there beside him, to make it easier—that much of home'." Her eyes were wide and dim as she looked back for a moment; then she closed them, shook her mind free of what it had looked back upon, opened them again, and gazed at him with a profound gratitude as she added, "You should know what it meant to Papa, to all of us, that Rob was in your hospital, that you could be with him. How could you be so morbid?"

"'Morbid'?" He smiled briefly, not bitterly but with condescension. "You believe we should forget the war. Wasn't that what you said this morning?" Forget it, he thought, when everything that had happened since, everything that ever would happen, however long they lived, would be nothing but make-believe, in comparison. But he mustn't say that to a woman; a man must live as if there had been no war, and a woman who would share his life must be persuaded to believe he had put it all behind him. "Don't you see, Anne—that's what I've been trying to do, forget it?"

"I know." She nodded gravely. "I remember what you said, when you came back. You had had 'enough of butcher's work to last a lifetime.' But you never told me what it was like."

"No. Do you think you want me to?" He was almost angry at her persistence. "Cutting off arms and legs and tossing them into tubs, like slaughter-house offal. Because if we didn't, wounds would gangrene. How comfortable to be a woman," he mocked her, "and never know the smell of gangrene. In that hospital in Louisiana, there was plenty of it. The Surgeon, you see, stayed with the regiment and crossed the river to Vicksburg with the army, so they gave me, his assistant, the hospital, with only convalescent wounded to help. And I couldn't do anything, except watch the men die. I didn't know enough."

"They didn't all die. There's Captain Rausch." She was thinking, "And you were only a boy. When you and Rob went to the war, I believed you were men, but you were only boys."

"Oh, Rausch!" He was scornful. "A case of dysentery. I couldn't have killed him."

"He's very agreeable, isn't he? I like him."

"Oh, Rausch is all right." He welcomed the change of subject. "It looked like Sally took quite a shine to him."

"She never set eyes on him till today."

"I know. But it doesn't take her long to make up her mind, and once it's made up, I've never known her not to get what she wants. And I've known Sally, like I've known you, since she wore pantalettes."

"She used to come here—how we plagued you and Rob. Sally's not likely to let go of an idea. She called you 'Dock' then, and she calls you that now, and always will, if you never write another prescription."

"I know. She can't see that other people may change their minds."

"They might change them once, and then back again, if they weren't stubborn. John, I really wanted to know what it was like—the war—so I could tell you that private practice isn't like that. You know it isn't. It's mostly measles and scarlet fever, and Tommy doubling up with cholera morbus in the middle of the night from eating green apples."

He rose, sighing, and stood over her with a hand on the back of the chair. It was late, and he should go, but he must have this out with her.

"Do you want me to come back? I mean, are you asking me to come back?"

She stiffened, and said "No" shortly, then added, more slowly, "I'd like you to, of course, for Papa's sake. But what I want hasn't anything to do with it. It's your life. Do whatever you want most." She let her voice trail away to nothing because she saw how taken aback he looked, and it made her certain of what lay, perhaps unknown to himself, behind his abrupt unkind question. He had made up his mind, but he had not yet admitted it to himself; he wanted to be persuaded. "Would you like to sell insurance all your life?" she asked him, willing to oblige, willing to go to any length short of begging him to come back because she wanted him there. "It would be such a waste. All that knowledge, so hard come by, shut up in your head, when there's so much need for it. Even in the army, where everything else was wasted—talent and ability—even in the army, when they found you'd almost finished at Medical College, didn't they give you a furlough, so that you could get your M.D. and go back as Assistant Surgeon?"

"How eloquent!" he laughed at her. "Then you think I ought to come back?"

She shook her head. "There's no 'ought' about it. I'm not trying to persuade you against your own judgment." Because he had laughed, she added, with a youthful unwillingness to let her acuteness remain undisclosed, "You want me to, don't you? Because if I did, and you gave in, and hated it afterward, you could blame me, and say 'I knew best, but I let her have her way.'"

He said, "No, I'll make up my own mind. I just wanted to know how you felt about it." He turned away, toward the hall, as if he had finished, but beside the hatrack, with his hat in his hand, he continued. "I'll be back soon. When I know, as you put it, what I want to do with my life."

She said good-night to him at the door. If the day had ended less than memorably—if she was disappointed, having thought, perhaps, "At Commencement time, when he sees that I'm grown up—," she gave no sign of it. She took the night lamp from the hall table in one hand, with the other lifted her skirts before her, to clear a way for her feet, and went upstairs humming softly, under her breath

Dis am de jubilee:
De rain may come, de win' may blow,
But bless de Lord I's free.

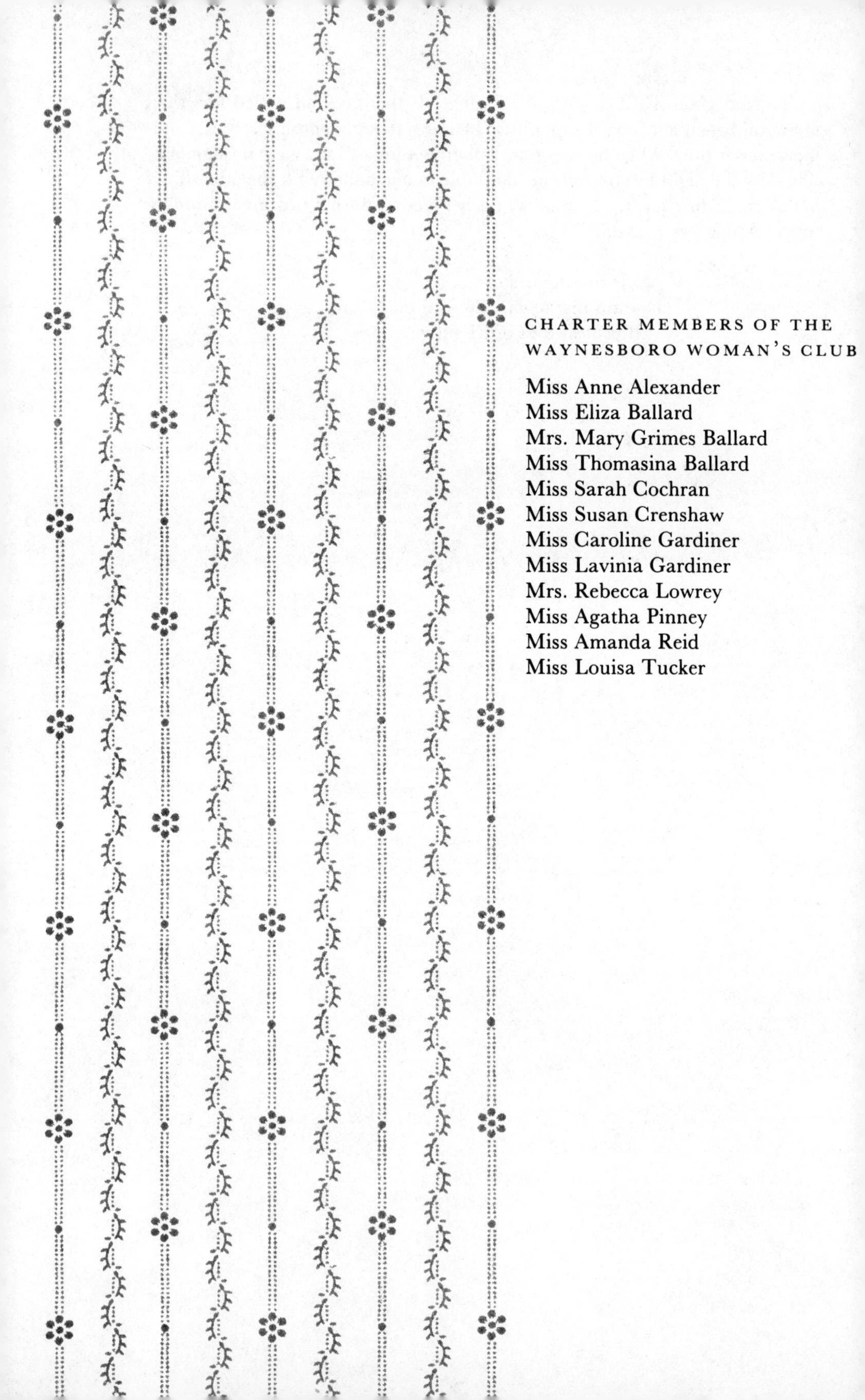

CHARTER MEMBERS OF THE WAYNESBORO WOMAN'S CLUB

Miss Anne Alexander
Miss Eliza Ballard
Mrs. Mary Grimes Ballard
Miss Thomasina Ballard
Miss Sarah Cochran
Miss Susan Crenshaw
Miss Caroline Gardiner
Miss Lavinia Gardiner
Mrs. Rebecca Lowrey
Miss Agatha Pinney
Miss Amanda Reid
Miss Louisa Tucker

* 1868 *

"Six other Waynesboro ladies were consulted."

The summer of 1868 passed rapidly, as summers had done before and have done since, for women busy with the small matters of their households. Gardening, pickling, preserving, making jelly for the winter sped the brief mornings; calls and less formal visiting back and forth, picnics, drives, and, since it was an election year, barbecues and parades quickened the long sunny afternoons and warm evenings. August had almost gone before Anne and Sally reminded one another, shamefacedly, that they had promised to ask Miss Lavinia and Miss Caroline Gardiner whether they would join a Waynesboro woman's club.

In the months since Commencement, nothing had been said to either of the girls to keep the proposed club in their minds. The College buildings had been closed. Miss Tucker had gone back to Boston for her vacation; Miss Pinney and Miss Crenshaw had withdrawn into the obscurity that awaited them outside the schoolroom door. Professor and Mrs. Lowrey had been overwhelmed in June by the annual descent upon them of their married daughter and her irresponsible, undisciplined children. It was only now, the summer ended, that the Lowreys were alone, except for their younger daughter, still at school in the Female College. When the newspaper reported the departure of the Tylers, Anne and Sally realized that they must not let an unfulfilled promise hang longer over their heads: they must call on the Misses Gardiner to invite them to join a Waynesboro woman's club. It loomed as a formidable undertaking. Hopefully, they would go to Mrs. Lowrey first to make sure she still wanted the club she had proposed.

For their call they arrayed themselves with care, Anne in a wine-red surah that brought a little color to her cheeks, Sally in an apple-green calling costume, both frocks fluted, draped, and puffed, adorned with braid and buttons in the newest mode as interpreted by the Waynesboro dressmaker. They were correctly bonneted and gloved; each carried her calling-card case, one of tortoise shell, one of mother of pearl, and they felt more absurd than impressive as they drove up the hill in the Cochran victoria, behind the Negro coachman, the few blocks to the gate of the Female College. Perhaps it was the necessity they felt to reject this absurdity, to explain their state as a bit of play-acting, that led them to greet with overemphatic fervor a young woman whose hand was on the latch of the gate as they descended from the victoria.

"Amanda Reid!" Sally swept toward her. "Oh, Amanda, it's pleasant to see you back!"

"Amanda!" Across the gate Anne extended her hand. "You're all ready to begin teaching Latin, aren't you? With a man's degree: it's wonderful. Tell us, is Mrs. Lowrey home? Have you seen her? We promised to call on the Gardiners to ask them to join her club—d'you know about it? That's why we're all fixed up like this." She turned her hands over and back to show how they were pinched in their tight gloves. "We haven't heard anything more about the club since Commencement Day, so we thought maybe we had better ask Mrs. Lowrey."

Amanda smiled briefly at this childish babble. She was a fairly tall but slight young woman wearing a drab poplin frock and a shapeless bonnet. Her face was grave and colorless, her square jaw emphasized by the bonnet strings tied beneath it. She had a jutting, prominent nose, straight brows, and uncompromising eyes, light and clear. She said, "I have just seen Mrs. Lowrey. There is to be a club. I hand't heard about it until this afternoon. Now I am on my way to the Ballards to ask if they will join. I think Mrs. Lowrey supposes you have already been to the Gardiners."

"Then we'd better go on without seeing her," Anne sighed.

"Did you say you were going to the Ballards'? Do let us take you out there before we make our call." Sally opened the gate, and now gestured toward the victoria. "We can all three squeeze in."

"I can walk. It's on my way home." Amanda shrank from contrast with the wine-red, the apple-green.

"Why should you, though? Do come, and give us an excuse for postponing our errand for another half-hour."

"Is that what you want?" Amanda laughed, and climbed after Anne into the victoria. "You don't want to go to the Gardiners'?"

"We'd rather have a tooth pulled, wouldn't we, Anne?" Sally was still poised hesitantly on the curbstone. "We don't really know them. My mother does, and Dr. Alexander is their doctor and they are Presbyterians, but that may not stop them from turning us out. Isn't that the way you feel about going to the Ballards'?"

"I know them too well. Thomasina and I have been friends all our lives. Otherwise I might. They work for so many important causes, they may think a literary club is a waste of time."

Instead of following the other girls, Sally looked over her shoulder toward the school, withdrew a little from the curb, and said, "Are many of the girls back? College opens on Monday, doesn't it? If you'll excuse me for about two minutes, I'd like to see who is here."

Without awaiting their permission she went on through the gate. Anne began to fill in the "two minutes" with the polite questions demanded of her by the circumstances: when had Amanda got back, was she going to like teaching at the College, what did it feel like to have a B.A.? Amanda was more than a little bewildered. This blithe disregard by Anne and Sally of all the great sum total of things that they did not have in common with her had shaken and startled her. She had been surprised, half an hour earlier, by Mrs. Lowrey's mention of these girls as members of a possible club. They had not entered into her picture of Waynesboro except as part of the background, children who had come after her in the school, and who by this time would be young-ladies-in-society. She would never have known them intimately in the natural course of things. When Mrs. Lowrey had named them, she had felt a need to calculate her resources for an encounter, as if they could meet only as mere acquaintances. Instead, it had been assumed that between them and her an old friendship was now to be resumed. The four or five years' difference in age had shrunk to nothing, and if these girls were aware that any other more fundamental disparities existed, they gave no sign of it.

She answered Anne's questions with half her mind; her attention was only fully caught when a buggy stopped behind them on the brow of the hill and a gentleman alighted from it. He dropped a weight to the curb, with the hitching strap fastened to it, crossed the path, and entered the College gate. Anne broke off midway in what she was saying to exclaim, "What's he doing here? I thought he was to speak at the barbecue this afternoon, out at the Jacobses' farm."

"General Deming!" Amanda was equally amazed. "He's wasting his time here. There are only three voters on the premises."

Then Anne began to laugh. "I know: is Miss Tucker back? He was wonderfully taken with her last Commencement time. There's no one so easily caught as a vain old bachelor, is there?"

"Is he vain? I don't know. Why 'caught'? Why not Miss Tucker? It seems to me eminently suitable." Amanda could not wholly keep disapproval out of her voice. Anne—both these girls—were frivolous and given to thoughts of beaux, so that they saw matrimony in prospect everywhere.

"Oh, suitable." Anne laughed. "But she hasn't a drop of warm blood in her veins." Then she nudged Amanda's arm and began to talk about the weather. The General and Miss Tucker had come down the dormitory steps. He escorted her to the gate, his hand hovering at her elbow, opened it for her, and led her through. They bowed toward the victoria and passed out of sight behind it. Not until they had got into the buggy and started down the hill again did Anne return to the subject. "I know: he's taking her out to the Jacobses' to hear his speech."

"I'm quite sure you misjudge her," Amanda said severely. "She is high-minded, liberal, and well-educated. If she and General Deming are friends, it is only natural: they have many views in common."

"Perhaps," Anne conceded. "Only it would be a lark if they did. It's so hard to imagine Teapot Tucker—"

"Why do you join the same club, if you dislike her so much?"

"Well, there isn't any other club, is there? Besides—I know you're much too good to believe this, Amanda—but it's fun sometimes, to dislike people. I can't be indifferent. I expect you can: that's why you stick up for her. But I either like them or dislike them. Of course, it's nicer to like them. But—"

"But what?" Amanda smiled at her. This frankness was softening: it is difficult not to respond to the fact, even if only implied, that you are liked.

"But you can't be hurt through the people you dislike, can you?"

"What an extraordinary idea! You aren't a very good philosopher, I'm afraid." She meant "Christian," but didn't say it. "Harboring dislike hurts you. Real injury can only come from one's self."

"I didn't mean 'injury' when I said 'hurt.' I meant—well, 'grieved,' I suppose."

They were still exchanging personalities, disguised as ethics, when Sally returned. She got into the victoria, squeezing Amanda over, and told Reuben to drive them to Judge Ballard's. The horse was turned in the narrow street, and headed down the hill. Anne said abruptly, "Did he come?"

"No. Who? What do you mean?" Sally blushed. "Most of the girls are back."

"Of course. But did Captain Rausch come?"

"Oh, Captain Rausch. I did see Minna for a minute. He brought her as far as Columbus, and went on to Cincinnati to see his uncle on business. But she says he's coming up later."

"Beaux," Amanda thought again, and let the dialogue go on without really listening to it. This sort of thing, she supposed, was what the town's social life was made up of, but she hadn't expected it to be a part of her Waynesboro. She hadn't thought much about what she did expect, while she was away; and she had prolonged her absence, working all summer in the Oberlin library. But that morning, when she had awakened in her bedroom, in her mother's house, she had faced the prospect of four years of teaching at the Female College, and she had braced herself, as she realized now, sitting in the Cochran victoria and laughing at nonsense she did not even hear.

Looking back, she had tried to think why her mood had been unreasonable and full of un-Christian hostility. Though glum and awkward at the uncongenial tasks, she had helped her mother and the cook in the kitchen. After twelve o'clock dinner she had retreated to her bedroom, but had not dressed to go out until the "theologues," whom her mother boarded, had eaten their meal and returned to the Seminary. She did not dislike them: they were earnest young men, called of God, and she respected them for their calling and for the learning it demanded of them. But if she had been ready to leave the house when they took their hats down from the rack in the hall, she would have had to walk along with them, and anyone who had seen her would have said, "There's Amanda Reid, just like all the other Reformed Presbyterian girls, looking over the students before she picks one. Her degree hasn't changed matters much."

"Amanda Reid, B.A." She was continuously aware of that "B.A." It stood for so much achievement, so much endeavor, so much sacrifice. She regretted that it had been necessary to accept her widowed mother's help. Having given it, Mrs. Reid felt entitled to obedience, or, at least, compliance with her wishes. Her own sacrifice lay ahead of Amanda and not behind: she was to teach in the Female College on half-salary until the money the Lowreys had lent her had been repaid. They alone, except for the Ballards, had sympathized with her ambitions, and out of their meager savings they had let her have what she needed, and had given her this opportunity to pay it back, slowly, without making her feel like a debtor. She was immensely grateful, but she could not look forward to the years of drudgery with pleasure. She had long believed, with a faith that today seemed to her heartbreaking, that all that was necessary to enable women with brains to lead really important lives, important to themselves and the world, was education; that from the eminence labeled "B.A." one could look around a wide horizon and choose one's destiny. But hers, for four years, was not open to choice. Four years was a long time, and in those years there would be nothing. She had always believed too in that other argument for education, and as a last resort, she had that to fall back on: if one could fill one's mind with history and philosophy, with all poetry, in Greek and Latin and English, then one would have resources enough to make a refuge from the exigencies of life. She had told herself, that noon in her bedroom, that this at least she must cling to. She must not begin to doubt whether simply to know would be enough if one were alone in a town with one's knowledge.

She had waited, in this sad humor, in her cramped little room, where the roof sloped to within a few feet of the floor and the windows were set so low beneath the eaves that it was necessary to stoop to look out. Not that there was much to see: a street that had dwindled away to a country road, here on the uttermost edge of town, treetops, trunks, a picket fence, an unkept yard, and three times a day a flock of sober young men coming in, two by two, singly or in knots, three times a day going out, two by two. Depressed by the spectacle, she had risen from the window sill and had put on, hurriedly and carelessly, her poplin dress over a crinoline of an outdated shape, and a black bonnet with ribbons as limp as strings.

She had slipped down quietly to the landing, but she had not escaped without her mother's reproaches. The narrow staircase creaked under as firm a footfall as Amanda's. Mrs. Reid had come out to stand by the newel post. With a weary gesture she had pushed the strayed hair back from her flushed cheeks; she always gave the impression of having that instant straightened from leaning over a cookstove, just as the house smelled perpetually of cheap food. And as her physical strength was exhausted by cooking for them, so was her store of good nature spent on her boarders. With Amanda she was always querulous. That afternoon she had covered the whole range of her complaints: "Going out, just when I had a minute to sit down." Then when Amanda had explained her errand at the College, "It's a shame. You could have found a better place than that. You get a pittance from the Lowreys and I go on keeping boarders. I'm sure they've taken advantage of you." And finally, "Must you wear that shabby frock uptown? I wonder you don't even leave off hoops." At that Amanda lost patience. "I can't help being shabby, but I don't have to be queer. I must prove that a woman can learn something without being a monstrosity!" And her mother had laughed at her: "As if strong-minded women can ever be anything but monstrosities."

It was this attitude of her mother's that had sent Amanda out to face her world armed by antagonism. She realized it now, looking back at her day while she sat in the Cochran victoria and in it was carried around the corner of Market Street to Main and slowly down Main Street hill. The Ballard house was at the edge of town where Main Street became a country road. She had time to realize that there had been no necessity for that armor, and reviewed with an aloof amusement her defiant attitude of an hour ago. She listened with half an ear to the banter of the cheerful overdressed girls beside her, while she went back over what she had felt and thought on the long walk from her mother's house on Linden Street.

At first she had half-regretted the poplin, whose only virtue was that it didn't show the dust; in it she indeed looked like a schoolteacher. But she had brought back all her summer muslins soiled, and the laundress wouldn't come until Monday. She had picked her way carefully, through the grass that edged the road. Then she had begun to look ahead to her Latin classes (and perhaps even Greek), had wondered about her students, had forgotten the dust and tramped steadily through it, regardless, past the cottages scattered here and there behind picket fences: past empty stretches of pasture, where ironweed and goldenrod grew high and flowered in autumnal brilliance. This far end of Linden Street was not built of brick and stone as in the heart of the town. Amanda could not, now, while she drove behind the Cochran coachman, remember her resentment against brick and stone without an inner contemptuous smile for her irrationality. She had gone so far as to make an enumeration, a catalogue. Stone: the Court House, the bank, the Methodist church. Brick: the College, the railroad depot, the jail, the other churches, a number of homes. Linden Street climbed a hill (the same hill they were now descending, on Main Street), and at the foot of the slope it became definitely a part of the town, with brick houses, big yards, shrubbery, iron fences. Climbing the hill, you could not see the next house until you reached its gate, just as you could not see anyone on the path above you because of the trees' branches hanging so low. Anyone walking down the hill came into view feet first, from beneath the thick-leaved boughs. It had turned out to be no one she knew whose feet she had seen coming toward her; she had been ashamed of the relief she had felt. She should have washed one of her muslins: washed, boiled, starched, and ironed yards and yards of muslin. No! Better the poplin than such a waste of time. She had not slipped obscurely up Maple Street, which ended at the Lowreys' gate, behind the College, but had gone a square farther, out of her way, and turned onto Market Street at the corner opposite Dr. Alexander's, and so had approached the College by its front gate.

Dr. Alexander's was a brick house, painted gray, with a long porch whose roof was curved like the roof of a pagoda, and whose pillars were broad bands of ironwork, a confusion of arabesques and grapevines. Market Street was flat and straight past the Alexanders', past the Presbyterian church, past the back of the Court House square and the front of the sheriff's house and the jail. Then it began to climb. Two hills to walk up, every day, between home and the College. The Cochran house, halfway up the hill, that was brick, too.

Then, at the College, she had encountered Kitty Lowrey, and had received the first sympathetic welcome to her new life. She had not thought about Kitty beforehand, and if she had, she would have thought of her as a child. But Kitty evidently had been looking forward to her return. Now, in the victoria, thinking of their meeting, she laughed; and when Anne and Sally turned to look at her inquiringly, she said, "You didn't see Kitty Lowrey this afternoon? When I went to the College, there was a maid scrubbing the steps, with her head tied up in a kerchief, on her knees beside the scrub-bucket. I asked for Mrs. Lowrey before I saw it was Kitty, and she said, "Norah, to you, Miss. Mrs. Lowrey's plumb tuckered out. She's went home to rest."

Anne said, "The Lowreys are all alike," while she laughed; but Sally added, "Kitty's not so irresponsible as the others. She'd rather do the scrubbing herself than leave it undone."

"Yes. She said that every time you want an Irish woman there's either a wake or a wedding." Amanda thought how the thin, mischievous face had lighted while they talked, and she went on, "Kitty must be sixteen, I suppose? She says she's to be in my Virgil class." It was the recollection of the ardor, the anticipation, that had shone in Kitty's face that now made Amanda smile almost tenderly. "She's getting ready for her Oberlin examinations, in another year. I talked to her only a minute, as I had to see her mother."

Amanda had found Mrs. Lowrey on the sofa in her sitting room, and had sat down beside her for a long conversation about the school and about Amanda's classes. The talk had been concluded by an account of the proposed woman's club.

Mrs. Lowrey had sat up, put her feet on the floor, and pushed her untidy hair out of her eyes, sighing, "I hope you'll like teaching, but you won't find it as congenial as Oberlin. I envy you the quiet you had, and the books. Here there is nothing but turmoil: inevitable where there's a school full of children. But we have a plan: we women hope to provide ourselves with some food for the mind, a quiet hour when we can think and talk."

As she explained, Amanda had listened with increasing interest and hope.

"I'll see the Ballards," she had promised. "Thomasina will like it. I don't know about Mrs. Ballard and Eliza. Who else is there?"

"The Gardiners, perhaps. Sarah Cochran said she would ask them. She and Anne will join us."

Amanda's enthusiasm had been chilled, then. "I shouldn't have thought—I mean—those girls aren't intellectual, are they? I shouldn't have expected them to be interested. They seem so frivolous: they belong to the dancing, card-playing set."

"Waynesboro is too small for sets," Mrs. Lowrey had chided her, maternally. "I think you will find the two young ladies have their serious side. They have adequate intelligence. At any rate, they will come to realize—they no doubt have long lives ahead of them in which to learn it—that there are times when the resources of the mind are the only stay and consolation, next of course to religion."

Amanda had agreed, a little doubtfully. Then, departing, she had been met at the gate by those very girls with so unaffected an acceptance of her, with such forthright friendliness, that she had not been able to think that they were pretending, or even that they were weighing her with judgment suspended. The contrast between what she had expected of them and what she had found was confusing, but she felt herself wanting to respond, wanting to forgive frivolity in so pleasant a guise.

The horse continued on its way out toward the end of Main Street. Riding, Amanda had no time to appraise the houses they passed, as she had done on Linden Street on her way into town. But having reviewed in her thoughts the day as she had suffered it, she could not after all throw to the winds all reservations, all guardedness, nor accept quite without testing it this assumption of friendship. She was confirmed in her caution by the tone in which the two girls began to discuss the Ballard house as they approached it.

The Ballards were as far from the Court House square as the Reids' when Amanda or Thomasina wanted to visit, she had only to cut across a vacant lot or two between their respective back fences. But the Ballard house, which was new, was not so familiar to the other girls; and when they began to talk about it, it was in a tentative fashion.

"Everyone agrees that it's elegant inside," Anne ventured.

"It is. I called there this summer. They're on Mamma's calling list, however much she disapproves of them. Walnut woodwork, inlaid with holly. And everything." Sally's descriptive powers were leashed. "They are building lots of these villa-type mansions in the East, Papa says."

Amanda led them on. "You don't like it?"

"I expect it's just that we're not used to it," Anne assured her, cheerfully. "You know how Waynesboro is. We look so askance at anything the least bit new and different. And it wouldn't seem so—well, odd—if it were anyone but Judge Ballard. The house is so unlike him, somehow. But it must have cost a mint of money, so it's probably what he wanted."

They had come to the fence corner of the Judge's land, and between the trees could get a glimpse of raw brick walls, of gleaming white stone trim, and of long round-topped windows. As they approached the gate, each of the three studied the house and judged according to her own standards its architectural devices: a mansard roof, many-windowed and covered with slates in a varicolored pattern; a porte-cochere, and a side veranda; a square tower in front, in the middle, that rose above the rest of the house to end in a high, steep, four-sided slope of roof. This roof was crowned with an iron railing that had a lightning rod at each of four corners; around its lower edge there was a stone parapet, and behind the parapet were dormer windows, one to a side. The tower windows of the third and second floors had each its own narrow little balcony. Beneath the lower balcony was the front door, set deep within a vestibule and approached by stone steps with broad stone balustrades. A brick path led from Main Street to this front door; a driveway ran from another gate past the side veranda and under the porte-cochere and on to the stable.

Amanda did not at once descend from the carriage when it stopped. Instead she stared at the house and said, slowly, "I really believe that Mrs. Ballard and the girls don't care much for it. It's too big: it's a burden, if you don't like housekeeping. But of course they would never let the Judge guess, after he had it built to please them."

"But did he?" Anne laughed. "The town thinks he built it for a joke: made it large and elaborate, so that it would keep Mrs. Ballard busy. Oh, of course," she added hastily, apologetically, "no one really believes it. No one would play a joke so expensive as that. And besides, we know he likes his wife to join him in advancing his causes."

"He had his fun out of it, anyway," Sally insisted. "A man like Judge Ballard couldn't possibly put up anything like that and not think it a joke." She nodded toward the Negro boy, in iron, who stood behind the curbstone, one hand dangling a ring for hitching straps; his iron pantaloons were painted a bright blue, his open jacket was yellow, and his hat straw-colored and tilted jauntily back over a mop of impossibly kinky hair.

"I don't know. D'you think so?" Amanda asked doubtfully. "After all, he gave the best years of his life to the abolition cause."

"And you think that hitching post is a kind of symbol?" It was Anne who asked, but both girls looked at Amanda curiously, respectfully.

"Something of the sort." She gathered her skirts in her hand and descended from the victoria, with Reuben's helpful hand at her elbow. When she had thanked them for the drive, the horse was turned and started back toward town. It was not until they were certain they were out of hearing that the girls permitted themselves to laugh.

"Poor Amanda. She can't see a joke. But, Anne, we oughtn't to have said all that about Judge Ballard. I know Papa thinks he has a sense of humor, but maybe he hasn't. Maybe he did build that house to please them."

"There isn't anyone in town who doesn't know that Mrs. Ballard hasn't any interest in her home," Anne said crisply. "Her husband surely knows it. But he may have hoped the girls would like it."

"Perhaps they do. Poor Thomasina ought to, anyway—she's the only one who's ever there," Sally said carelessly as the horse slowed to a walk at the foot of the hill. The girls dismissed the Ballards from their consideration and began instead to rehearse what they would say to the Misses Gardiner.

Back at the Ballards', only the younger daughter was at home. "Poor Thomasina" was a martyr to hay fever in the summer and to asthma in the winter. She had been left alone that afternoon by her mother and sister, and because the house had seemed empty, forlorn and unlived in, she had spent the early hours on the croquet ground, knocking the balls around in a desultory fashion. Thomasina's habitually wistful expression sat rather oddly on her own particular version of the Grimes features. Mrs. Ballard had been a Grimes, and her daughters "took after" her: they had long faces, like horses, with rather broad noses soft at the tips. Thomasina's nose was so continually in torment that it had become shapeless. She had vague blue eyes, a diffident smile, and abundant soft taffy-colored hair that she wore bundled anyhow into a net behind her ears. She read much poetry and wrote a little; she would have gone to Oberlin with Amanda had not her asthma forbidden it, and she loved her friend no less dearly because she had been left behind on the path to achievement.

When she heard the carriage in the gutter, she tossed aside her mallet and went toward the gate; she and Amanda met on the brick path.

"Dear Amanda." Thomasina kissed her on the cheek, then took her arm and led her toward the house. Although the taller of the two, there was distinctly the impression conveyed in her attitude of respect almost amounting to veneration. "I've been hoping you would come, but when I saw the victoria I thought it was callers. Whose was it?"

"Cochrans'." Amanda explained how she had encountered the girls at the College gate.

"Let's not go inside. It's like a tomb. Let's sit here on the steps." They sat down opposite each other, their backs against the hard balustrades, and faced each other, smiling.

"It's pleasant to find you here. Thomasina. Waynesboro, without you—" Amanda sighed. "But I didn't come to visit, today, I came on an errand. Mrs. Lowrey sent me. Have you heard about her woman's club? She wants to know if you and Eliza and your mother will join."

"Oh, I know. Sally Cochran told me about it, then made me promise not to say anything until we'd been officially asked to join. She seemed to consider it a humorous idea. I don't see why."

"I'm afraid neither she nor Anne Alexander take anything very seriously. They are rather thoughtless and light-minded, aren't they? I admit one can't help liking them," Amanda concluded, rather reluctantly.

"They weren't brought up to think, as you and I were. I like them, too, and I think the club may help them. I should enjoy it very much, I know. I haven't said anything to the others, after promising I wouldn't. We'll ask them when they get back. They're at the Republican rally, out at the Jacobs farm: Papa and General Deming and some other men are speaking. I stayed home because it makes my hay fever so much worse to go into the country. And I'm so glad I did, or I might have missed you. Now I have you all to myself. Tell me about your summer, and your Commencement."

For an hour or more they talked, sitting there on the hard steps. Then, just as Amanda was thinking of her mother and supper for the students, the Ballard carriage turned in the driveway gate and stopped under the porte-cochere. Thomasina took Amanda into the house through the front door, and the two parties met in the hall. When the necessary polite speeches of greeting and congratulations had been made, Mrs. Ballard led the way into the sitting room, where they sat down in semi-obscurity in the shuttered gloom, and Amanda explained again the errand she had come on.

"An excellent thing for the community," was Mrs. Ballard's verdict. "An hour or two in a fortnight when a few chosen spirits can withdraw from the heat of public conflict or the distresses of family life, or the drudgery of the schoolroom, and in peace and quiet consider the fruits of genius." She nodded, sighed, and added, dropping the public lecture cadence for one more natural and emphatic, "Women should be able to do that sort of thing, whatever their political or denominational differences. Men can. I don't know—I'm afraid the Misses Gardiner will decline. Just after the war, knowing what an ardent abolitionist their father had been, I went to enlist them in the fight for universal suffrage. I found them extremely antipathetic, and I fear I let them see that I was disappointed in their attitude."

The Judge, who had followed the ladies into the room, said now, austerely, "Differences in regard to controversial matters should not interfere with plans for a literary club." He went from window to window and opened the shutters, then sat down close to the empty fireplace in a corner whence he could see them all. "I knew the Gardiner ladies, slightly, when I was their father's partner, and we were both working for abolition. The daughters do not have the reformer's temperament. Had it not been for their father, they would not have been abolitionists. They would have stayed in Virginia and kept their slaves. I always felt certain that they resented, secretly, perhaps without quite knowing it, his having entertained views that removed them from their old home, and that made their old friends hostile. Of course, they were young when their father freed his slaves and moved up here—that was twenty years ago—but they have lived so apart, I should think they would welcome a chance like this. They are cultured ladies, you know: they were well-educated by their father, who inculcated in them a love of literature." He paused to clear his throat and peer around the room at his listeners. Amanda rose. She knew he hadn't finished, but she should have been home long ago. He got to his feet, said good-bye, and waited until she had gone out, with Thomasina following after her; then he resumed his chair, crossed his knees, hooked his thumbs over his watch chain, and continued to an audience composed of his wife and elder daughter his lawyer's summation of the evidence available and his conclusions drawn from it in the case of the Gardiners.

"As a student of human nature, I should like to understand those two ladies better." He dropped his head forward; his bushy white eyebrows hung over his eyes. "They are two spinsters, in their forties, rather badly off, living very quietly. With those handicaps they have managed to impose themselves on the town as beings apart, aristocrats, uninvolved in the hurly-burly of life; they are spoken of with bated breath, and approached by other ladies only in the most ceremonious fashion, carrying out the ritual of the afternoon call, and not approached in any way by other people."

"They attend the Presbyterian church most faithfully," his wife reminded him.

"So I understand. Driven in a hired carriage by a Negro coachman, helped down by their nephew, who is an old man at sixteen or seventeen, conducted by him to their pew—and when church is over, the same process reversed."

"You mean you wonder how they have managed to make their impression?" Eliza interrupted, abrupt and scornful. "That's easy. The town thinks they're rich."

Her father shook his head. "Too many other people know that isn't true. They have that house and a dwindling capital with an orphaned nephew to educate. Their father surrendered most of his wealth when he freed his slaves. No. They simply let people alone, and the people turned around and built up the legend of the aristocratic Virginians. A bit ridiculous, when you think that the town was founded, back in the seventeen-nineties, by Virginians, although those pioneers were not slaveholders, and therefore, not aristocrats. No, that isn't what I want to know." He was serious now. "I want to know why they have so lived that it has become next to impossible to conceive of their taking part in the concerns of the town. What does such a life offer them?"

"It happened by accident, I suppose," his wife replied. "They were brought up apart from what you call the 'hurly-burly,' and then they lost the other members of their family, who might have linked them to the town: their sister-in-law in childbed, their brother in the war, their father before the war was over."

"People don't 'just happen' to be different from other people, without any assignable cause." He lifted his eyes from his watch chain and glanced at her quizzically, smiling. "Almost always one can put one's finger on that cause. I suspect that with the Gardiners, their being so set apart and looked up to, even held in awe, is a sort of compensation for them—for the contempt they suffered, back in the Shenandoah Valley, when they were girls, because their father was an abolitionist. They were cast out by their kin, ostracized by their old friends—they had lost most of what they cared for long before Mr. Gardiner sold his plantation and came up here with his slaves to free them. Now they are in a position to do the casting out; they may join your club to strengthen that position. It was quite clever of Mrs. Lowrey to send those young girls to ask them. The girls will hold their breath with awe, and it will have a very flattering effect. After they've joined, whether it will be good for them or not will depend on you other women. I should like to see them humanized. Mr. Gardiner was a very good friend of mine. Speak to them in the same tone of voice you use with Mrs. Lowrey—don't take them more seriously than you take her—and you may prevent their pride from becoming arrogance."

"It is not my custom," Mrs. Ballard reminded him, severely, "to treat anyone with veneration who has done nothing to deserve it." Then, seeing that the Judge had said all that he had to say, she rose and went to her desk to look over her mail. Eliza went into the hall to look for her sister, and the Judge retired to his study, where he could read in peace for an hour before dinner and smoke his cigar.

Anne and Sally had rung the Gardiner doorbell some time earlier, not altogether speechless with awe but a little dry in the mouth and more than ready to admit that they wished their strange errand were accomplished. A colored maid admitted them, received their cards on a silver tray, and conducted them to the parlor. They sat down gingerly on two of the light French chairs of gold and ivory, upholstered in faded green damask and, while they waited, looked about them. The room was colder and emptier than the parlors to which they were accustomed; woodwork and mantelpiece were painted white, the chandelier was brass and crystal, there were sconces at intervals on the pale walls, and they too were hung with prisms. There was a center table, round, mahogany, with a pedestal base and claw feet; bare except for a candelabra. Against the back wall and in the corner beyond the mantel stood tall mahogany bookcases. In front of one of them, almost hidden by the jut of the fireplace and the chair beside it, Douglas Gardiner was sitting on an ottoman with a book on his knee. He had not risen, but did, with rather a contemptuous expression, when he saw himself discovered. Anne, suspecting he had been in an agony of hope that he might somehow escape unobserved, rose too from her chair and stepped toward him. His figure was slight, immature. He had a club foot; Anne moved quickly to save him a painful exposure of the infirmity about which, she knew, he was sensitive.

"You don't remember me, I'm afraid. Dr. Alexander is my father."

"Of course I remember Miss Alexander." Tight-lipped, he bowed over her hand.

"Do you remember Miss Cochran, too?"

He bowed again, in her direction. Anne returned to her chair, and he seated himself, stiffly, in the one beside the fireplace.

"I was surprised to see you because I supposed you had gone back to school."

"I have finished with school. I enter Princeton this fall."

"Oh, Princeton! How very agreeable that will be." Anne, ashamed of the weakness of her conversational effort, relapsed into silence. His aunts entered the room, and the three young people rose again. His eyes begged them for release. Miss Lavinia rescued him. When she had greeted the two girls and said, "You know my nephew, I believe," she turned to him. "Douglas, will you be good enough to ask Lutie to bring in cakes and blackberry cordial?"

With his book under his arm, he made his escape. Anne and Sally returned to their chairs. The Misses Gardiner were alike slender, with pale skins and light brown hair streaked with grey, both dressed unfashionably but with a certain faded elegance—lace at their throats, and round cameo brooches, tight basques, and circular hoop skirts without bustles. There was a faint question in their manner, a pause between sentences, as though they were too polite to ask for a reason for the call, but knew there must be one. The colored maid brought in a tray of wine glasses and a plate of cookies. Anne thought that when they had drunk the cordial, fifteen minutes would have passed and they would be expected to go. Sally had once or twice drawn a deep breath and opened her mouth, tentatively, only to close it again. Anne braced herself to get it over with, although in doing so she knew she risked their pleasant reception as ladies calling. "We came on an errand," she explained, "sent by our elders. Perhaps they thought if you wanted to say 'no' you wouldn't mind saying it to us, and they don't want you to say 'yes' unless you would really like to—"

The two colorless faces had chilled, grown blank. The sisters had not moved in their chairs, but gave the impression of having withdrawn.

"She makes it sound dreadful, doesn't she?" The ice broken, Sally spoke lightly, but she gave Anne a reproachful glance. "It is just that several ladies in Waynesboro have been planning to organize a woman's literary club, and hope very much that you would both like to become members." She explained in detail. When she had finished, Miss Lavinia asked for the names of the ladies.

"I do not believe that we know them, do we, Caroline?" She turned to her sister. "Except you two. Mrs. Ballard we have met."

"We have heard nothing but good of the ladies of the Female College." Miss Caroline began where Miss Lavinia left off. A blind man might not have known that there were two of them. "They are no doubt very interesting. I am not sure that we should be capable of taking a place among them."

"If they think we deserve a place," Anne laughed frankly, "there couldn't be any question about you."

"But you are much closer to your books than we are. I am afraid that Caroline and I have forgotten most of the *belles lettres* we once knew and loved. You will forgive us if we don't decide offhand? My sister and I will discuss the matter and let you know. Or perhaps Mrs. Lowrey? We can send Douglas around with a note."

Their purpose accomplished, the girls did not dally. Lutie conducted them to the front door. Inside, when the two sisters heard it close, they continued to sit still, questioning each other with a steady look. Miss Caroline spoke first. "It was yesterday," she said softly, with something of wonder in her voice, as though it had been enough for Miss Lavinia to wish for a miracle, "you said it was a pity, for Douglas's sake, that we didn't have more acquaintances in Waynesboro."

"More influential acquaintances," Miss Lavinia reminded her. "Miss Cochran and Miss Alexander are very pleasant, in the somewhat free-and-easy western way. But they are too young. What could they do for Douglas? You know very well," she continued, rather tartly, as though she resented being made to speak out, "why I made that remark about more acquaintances. We have the money to send Douglas to college and support him for a few years while he reads law in some office. After that he must make his own way. Unless we have friends to help him. He may not want to come back to Waynesboro, but if there were an advantageous opening for him— But can you think that any friendship we might establish with the teachers of a Female College could advance his fortunes any?"

"No." There was a pause, and then Miss Caroline ventured, thoughtfully, "Our father was a friend of Judge Ballard, and for a short time, his partner. The Judge has his law firm still listed as Ballard, Gardiner, and Merrill.

"And no one in Waynesboro could do more for a young lawyer than Judge Ballard. We should have foreseen the necessity long ago." Miss Lavinia sighed. "It was foolish of us, but we couldn't be so—such dissemblers—as to pretend to approve of woman suffrage."

"At any rate, we have a chance, now, to undo that error. For Douglas's sake. He can take a note to Mrs. Lowrey in the morning, to say that we accept her invitation to become members of the club."

The Misses Gardiner had reached this decision almost before Sarah and Anne had closed the gate behind them. The girls had gone down the short brick path very sedately, their heads held high and confidently, feeling ten years older than when they had gone in. Somehow they had been, by their call, established in their place as grown-up young ladies, a place they had hitherto seemed to occupy on sufferance. They had not needed to say much—Anne only "It wasn't unpleasant, after all," and Sally, "Mother always said they were agreeable, with truly aristocratic manners," and Anne again, "Do you think they will join? I do, I believe maybe we'll enjoy being members of the woman's club." She laughed. "It is beginning to make me feel important."

CHARTER MEMBERS OF THE
WAYNESBORO WOMAN'S CLUB

Miss Anne Alexander
Miss Eliza Ballard
Mrs. Mary Grimes Ballard
Miss Thomasina Ballard
Miss Sarah Cochran
Miss Susan Crenshaw
Miss Lavinia Gardiner
Mrs. Rebecca Lowrey
Miss Agatha Pinney
Miss Amanda Reid
Miss Louisa Tucker

1868

"The formal organization of the Club was effected . . ."

The first meeting of the Waynesboro Woman's Club was held on the afternoon of October 7, 1868, at Mrs. Lowrey's house. The very weather that day was a benison on the undertaking. Over the College paths the low-hanging boughs of the maple trees were a ceiling of rose and gold, lighted by the sunshine that sifted through the leaves; the sky was blue overhead and faintly amethystine in the distance. A dark line of woods edged the horizon wherever it could be seen from the hilltop, in the gaps between roofs, chimneys, steeples, and nearer trees. The grass across the level of the school grounds was thick and green as it had not been since spring, and the air, cool and sweet and scented, was perceptible and a stimulant to high spirits. It was Wednesday, and the school's half-holiday. Girls walked arm-in-arm on the paths, played croquet in the dappled sun and shade, or sat in the dormitory behind open windows and fluttering curtains, whence the sound of high young voices and quick laughter came remotely but clearly to those outside and below.

Of the ladies chosen to become members of the Club, Sarah Cochran was the first to enter the gate and come up the brick walk, beneath the eyes of the curious girls; if she was not set apart from them by any great superiority in age, she was certainly by her dress and carriage: she walked light-footed, her head up, drinking the wine of the air, but with a dignity enhanced by the stiffness of her hoops, and draperies drawn up to her bustle, and the spread fullness of her apple-green skirts. She did not turn at once toward the Lowrey door, but went instead along the dormitory path, her eyes lifted as she passed them to the open windows overhead. Purposely she had allowed herself a few minutes to spare in which she might say how-do-you-do to Minna Rausch.

The dormitory hall was empty; she let slip her dignity, and sped up the wide stairs with a swish of silken skirts, flashed around the balustrade and down the corridor. She half-expected to find that Minna and her roommate had gone out, but she could at any rate leave a note of greeting; and so when her knock at Minna's door went unanswered, she opened it, uninvited, and paused on the threshold. Before she could move further, she was caught off balance and knocked to one side by a pillow that hurtled through the air into her face. The pillow dropped to the floor; Sally clung for an instant, breathless and angry, to the door jamb, with her flat hat over one ear and all her braid loosened. Then she straightened up, said "Minna" angrily and looked into an apparently untenanted room. Two narrow beds, neatly and precisely made, a wardrobe and chest of drawers, a washstand. Then a stifled sound of mirth drew her eyes to the top of the wardrobe, which towered to within a few feet of the high ceiling: above its cornice the curved line of a huddling back and shoulder was plainly in view.

"Minna! What on earth are you doing up there?"

"It isn't Minna. It's me." The voice was shamed, contrite; but when the shoulder twisted up and back and a face came into view over the corner of the wardrobe, it was not only streaked with dust and cobwebs, but was crimson with suppressed laughter.

"Kitty Lowrey! I might have known," Sally said, bitterly.

"I'm sorry." The sharp chin came to rest on the edge of the cornice. "I thought it was Minna. I wouldn't have rumpled you so for worlds. You're all dressed up, too. For Mamma's new Club, I suppose."

The last statement was made in so bitter and scornful a voice that Sally's attention was distracted from her injury. "Yes. Why not? What's the matter with the Club?"

"Nothing, except Mamma ought to know she's got enough to do running this school, without taking on anything else outside. Of course, she doesn't run it really. Miss Tucker does—but suppose we lose her." Kitty squirmed into a more comfortable position: crossed her arms on the cornice, and rested her chin on them, prepared to be talkative even in so unconventional a situation.

"What do you mean: 'lose her'? She's joining the Club."

"Don't pretend you don't know, Sally Cochran. She's making a dead set at General Deming. Thinks she would like Washington, I suppose. She couldn't be in love with that pompous humbug."

Sally crossed the room to the chest of drawers, where a mirror hung, and took off her hat so that she could pin up the tumbled masses of her hair. "Why should you care? No one likes her very much."

"Oh, 'likes her'—that doesn't matter. She lives here in the dormitory, and runs it. Do you remember what it was like before she came? Mamma over at our house trying to keep Ellen's boys from carrying on like Comanche Indians, and no one here but Miss Crenshaw and Miss Pinney?"

"I didn't board here then."

"Neither did I," Kitty sniffed, "but I know what it was like, and so must you. Like Lowood in *Jane Eyre*. Papa's mind on the schoolroom, and Mamma's never on the same thing two minutes handrunning. A thievish cook, and never enough to eat. Cornmeal mush for breakfast and supper and fried mush for dinner with butter or molasses but not both. If Miss Tucker goes, it'll be like that again, and here's Mamma starting something new to take up her thoughts."

"Mrs. Ballard will run the Club," Sally said, and dismissed the subject. "Now will you tell me why you're up there and what you're doing?" She backed off to a corner of the room, whence she could see the absurdly skimpy and diminished figure, in petticoats and without hoops, curled on the top of the wardrobe.

"I'm waiting for Minna. The pillow was for her. She had permission to go out for a walk with her brother, and she didn't even invite me into the parlor to meet him, and I'm supposed to be her best friend."

"Oh, Minna's brother is here?"

"Yes. He came up from Cincinnati on the one o'clock train with that beau of Anne Alexander's—what's his name?—Gordon."

Sally turned to the door, in a hurry now to be gone, but Kitty stopped her on the threshold by saying, in a meek voice, "Would you mind giving me back the pillow?"

"You'll get pins and needles sitting up there, and serve you right, too."

"Not with the pillow to sit on. It's quite comfortable. And I brought a book up with me. I'm truly sorry I hit you." She drew the corners of her mouth down and rolled her eyes, to express contrition.

Sally laughed and tossed the pillow up to her. Her annoyance had been dispelled by the last bit of information she had got from Kitty. Outside Minna's door she picked up her skirt and, as quietly as possible but swiftly, raced headlong down the stairs and out the door. In the public eye again she dropped her skirts and slowed to a walk as she crossed the grass, cater-cornered, to the Lowrey house. If she could only reach Anne before the meeting—it would be dreadful to sit all afternoon with good news locked in your bosom. By the time the maid had admitted her and conducted her to the parlor door, she had caught her breath, so that she could have whispered to Anne without panting, but she was too late. The ladies had assembled, and were seated in a rigid semicircle before Mrs. Lowrey, who stood behind a marble-topped oval table with a notebook in her hand. Anne was in a chair between Amanda Reid and little Miss Pinney; she looked very demure and prim, and raised her eyebrows at Sally. Sally, blushing and confused, looked away toward Mrs. Lowrey, who had paused and who now, with a nod, indicated an empty chair. Sally crept into it, rebuked and ashamed.

Mrs. Lowrey smiled a little, and perhaps as a sort of apology to the young lady for having made her feel like a tardy schoolchild, explained in a few words just how much progress had been made.

"We have decided that our first step must be the election of officers. Then the President can appoint a committee to draft a constitution and another to decide on a program." She turned from Sally to look at the circle that faced her. "Have you any suggestions as to how we should proceed with the business of the election?"

All the ladies, a little ill at ease, looked at one another or at the floor. Sally, who had got over her embarrassment, let her eyes follow Mrs. Lowrey's around the room. Miss Crenshaw was beside the window; the bright light of the October afternoon showed the yellowish tinge in her cheek that deepened almost to green at the corners of her mouth; her dark-circled eyes were hard, like agates: stony, remote, and bleak. There was no response in them to anything that Mrs. Lowrey had said; she might as well not have been there. Sally thought that Miss Crenshaw had got past caring where she went or what she did: she continued to go through the motions of daily life after she had lost interest in them because they were a habit, and easy, requiring no thought. Why was it that she wanted not to think? Surely not just because she had retired. Sally puzzled for a minute, and then, uncomfortable, shifted her eyes. Between Miss Crenshaw and Miss Pinney sat the two Misses Gardiner, as aloof, delicate, and without animation as two figures in porcelain. Miss Pinney stared at the toe of her own shoe while she traced with it the line of the pattern in the carpet; she was like a shamefaced and bashful child who might be called on for a recitation. Anne looked slyly amused: she watched Mrs. Lowrey with a kind of mischievous expectancy. Sally knew why. Mrs. Lowrey was always flustered by a class of stubborn and tongue-tied pupils, and she showed symptoms now of a similar loss of control. She opened her mouth, closed it, opened it again, and said, weakly, "Has no one any suggestions?"

Still no one spoke. Beside Anne, Amanda's square face was solemn, and her eyes bright with enthusiasm: but she kept silence. The three Ballards, beyond Amanda, were a little restless, as though they were telling themselves they couldn't wait too long while giving the other ladies their chance; only Thomasina's washed-blue eyes, on Mrs. Lowrey, were unhappy, as if she suffered with the chairwoman in her ineptitude. Next to Sally Miss Tucker was trim, grave, and cold, by her stillness withdrawing herself from this awkward moment. The silence grew intolerable, but just as Mrs. Lowrey, despair in her eye, looked to Mrs. Ballard for rescue, and said, "Shall we have nominations from the floor, and a written ballot?" help came from an unexpected quarter.

"Madam Chairman." A rocker squeaked on the floor. Miss Caroline Gardiner leaned forward a little, and spoke softly in Mrs. Lowrey's direction, watching her older sister's face, as if it were there that she hoped for approval. "Most of us have had no experience in organizations of this kind. Would it not be wise to make the one of us President who knows most about it? Can't we vote unanimously to elect Mrs. Ballard to the office?"

Mrs. Lowrey looked relieved and taken aback, at the same time; Miss Lavinia Gardiner was startled. Only Mrs. Ballard preserved her impassivity as they all waited. After an instant's pause Mrs. Lowrey stammered, "Did you wish to make that a motion?"

Miss Caroline nodded, and Miss Tucker murmured, "I second." Mrs. Lowrey straightened her shoulders and said, in a firmer voice, "It is moved and seconded that Mrs. Ballard be elected president by acclamation."

There was a faint chorus of "ayes" that sounded like a sigh of relief. Mrs. Lowrey exchanged places with Mrs. Ballard, who took the chair amidst a polite patter of applause. In her capable hands matters moved expeditiously. The method of her election had been so simple that it was applied to the other officers: no one cared, really, who they were, and so the first person mentioned was selected: Miss Tucker, Vice-President; Miss Reid, Recording Secretary; Miss Cochran, Corresponding Secretary and Treasurer. That business concluded, Mrs. Ballard returned the favor accorded her by appointing Miss Lavinia Gardiner chairman of a committee to draw up a constitution and report in two weeks' time. Then she said, "I understand that Miss Tucker and Mrs. Lowrey have been working on a tentative program for the year. I shall ask them to serve as a committee to carry it on to completion. I wonder if Miss Tucker would like to report now on what they have in mind for the next meeting?"

Miss Tucker rose, half-turned to face her audience. "Madam President, ladies: We thought it would be wise to emphasize from the start the non-controversial character of the Club, and choose for the first year a subject whose study must be without prejudice. How would you enjoy working on 'English Poets of the Nineteenth Century'?" She paused. There was a gratifying buzz of approval. "To assign a different poet to each member for an essay is a harder matter," she resumed, "since we have as yet no clues to individual tastes and sympathies. We decided, therefore, to proceed alphabetically." She looked along the chairs beside her. "We are asking Miss Alexander to prepare an essay for the next meeting on the poetry of Mr. Robert Browning."

Anne's jaw dropped. She looked for an instant distracted. Then she closed her mouth firmly and nodded. Sally alone understood the gleam in her eye, the irrepressible twitching of her lip, and wondered if the poetry of Mr. Browning would prove a non-controversial subject.

When the meeting was shortly thereafter adjourned, Anne and Sally did not behave like schoolgirls and rush into each other's arms, but they managed to drift toward each other while they said things like, "You honor us, Mrs. Ballard, serving the Club as President," and "A lovely afternoon, Miss Gardiner, and a most enjoyable meeting, wasn't it?" Together they reached Mrs. Lowrey and in turn shook her hand and thanked her for her hospitality; together they went out the door and were alone at last on the path across the College grounds.

"What a pity," Sally teased, "that it had to be Mr. Browning instead of Wordsworth."

"Mr. Browning will serve quite as well as a declaration of independence. Now tell me why you came in late and panting? What had you been up to?"

"I went over to see Minna. She wasn't there. She was out with her brother. Kitty Lowrey told me. He came up from Cincinnati today with John."

"John? John is in town?" Anne stopped dead, then with her hand on Sally's elbow, started more rapidly down the walk. "Bother Mr. Browning, and the Club, too. What a way to spend an afternoon, if John is at our house."

"It wasn't so bad," Sally insisted. "Mrs. Ballard will make a good President. I was afraid it would be Miss Tucker, then we might as well have been back in school. Kitty thinks she's going to marry General Deming. If she does, she'll have to go to Washington. There's only one member of the Club who bothers me."

"I know," Anne said softly. Her step slowed again, until she had almost stopped. "Miss Crenshaw. You can't look at her without knowing she thinks her life is over. She's just filling in the time."

"I wonder if it is almost over. Anne, do you suppose she has a *growth?*"

They stared at each other. The dread that comes to stand at every woman's shoulder made its presence felt, for one instant. The air struck cold to their bones, and the sunshine was dimmed. "I don't know," Anne said, "but imagine: if she has, living all alone, and facing *that.* She looks dreadful—her eyes—as if that might be what she's trying not to see."

Silently, each busy with the effort of imagining herself in that older woman's place, they walked out of the schoolyard and down the hill. At the Cochran's gate they parted, and Anne, her mind turned to the prospect of seeing John, went on more quickly home.

She did not find him in the house. She walked through the empty rooms from front door to kitchen, where she came upon Martha dozing peacefully in the rocking chair beside the window, chin sunk on ample bosom, carpet slippers on the floor, bare feet tucked under her calico skirt. Anne went on tiptoe past her to the back porch, down the steps, and along the brick path that led to the back gate and the shortcut across to the doctor's offices.

A side door (the family entrance) opened into a passage as long as the house, with a flight of stairs on the outer wall, three doors in the inner wall, and another outside door at the end. This front door, where patients came in from the street, was unlatched and had been pushed back by the wind, so that the daylight revealed all too clearly the tracks on the worn carpet, whose pattern had been obliterated in an oblique line across to the waiting room. That door was also open, and from within voices were audible, lowered, half-frightened. The two other doors were discreetly closed. The doctor's office was behind the third door; there he had his patient's chair and all his paraphernalia; the room was inviolably private and the door from the hall kept locked. The central door, unlocked, opened on a smaller room, half public, half the doctor's own; it was furnished as a study, his desk littered with books and papers; it was permeated with a flavor distinctly its own of drugs, tobacco, coal smoke, and the crumbling leather of worn armchairs and sofa. Here Anne, as she had expected, found John, sunk deep in one of the chairs, close to the hearth, where a handful of coals burned fitfully, with a gaseous splutter.

When he heard the door, he dropped his newspaper to the floor, got up, laid his pipe on the mantel, and went to meet her. She held out her hand.

"Oh, John! I heard you were here. I was afraid I'd missed you. Our Club—remember?—had its first meeting this afternoon. If I'd known, I wouldn't have gone."

"There's always tomorrow. I've come up to stay."

"You mean until the election? I thought you'd want to vote."

"Oh, yes. I'll vote. But I meant I've come back to live, and go to work again with your father."

"Oh." Anne's heart stopped and began again with a slow hard beat; she felt suddenly hollow, and sat down on the end of the couch. "I'm so glad." Then with all a woman's contrariness and dislike of responsibility, she added, "I hope not just on account of anything I said the last time I saw you?"

"No. At least, I knew you were right. My life doesn't seem very valuable to me, but that's no reason for not trying to put it to some use."

"You've seen Papa?"

"Yes. I'll go on his rounds with him until I've got my hand in again, then he'll make me his partner. He's offered me the rooms upstairs to live in. I brought all my traps up with me; I don't have to go back for them."

Anne said, for the second time that afternoon, and more emphatically than before, "Bother Mr. Browning!" and explained her predicament. "And only two weeks to do it in. Do you think I must read everything he has written? Anyway I shan't begin tonight. You'll have supper at our house, of course."

"I'm afraid not. I came up with Ludwig—Captain Rausch—and promised to meet him at the hotel for dinner. He's come on business, not only to escort his sister to school. He intends, if he can, to buy that old ropewalk down by the canal. Has his plans for it all worked out."

"You mean he's coming to Waynesboro to live? Oh, good!" She stopped herself from saying "Sally will be pleased," though the words hung on her tongue: how Sally felt at this point was Sally's secret and should not be made the subject of gossip. John saw nothing in what she said beyond the surface meaning: "Yes, he's a good fellow—he'll be an asset to the town."

"You can bring him to supper, too. There'll be enough, I'm sure. I'll run along and tell Martha." As she glanced at the clock on the mantelpiece, the door to the inner office was opened, and her father escorted a woman across the room, said good-bye at the opposite door, then turned for a word with the young people before he invited another patient in.

"John has told you? Can't we arrange to take him in as a boarder? That would be like old times. She isn't much of a cook," he added, "but Martha is teaching her. Fix it up with him, Anne." He laid a hand for an instant on John's arm, then turned back to the waiting room door and said, rather gruffly, "Who's next? Miss Armstrong?" as Anne and John went out into the hall.

He left her at the outside door to go and find Ludwig at the hotel. Anne went on into the house, but it was too late then for her to make any attempt to disprove her father's unkind words about her cooking: she let Martha set the table with cold meat, with maple syrup for fried mush, with pickles, jelly, cake, and pie, and tried not to think of the last meal Captain Rausch had had in Waynesboro, at the Cochrans'. The men were uncritical, and ate their fill; but Ludwig must have remembered the previous dinner, because they had hardly returned to the parlor before he begged to be excused: he felt he should pay his respects to the Cochrans. John suggested that they accompany him, for the walk, as far as Sally's gate, and Anne obediently put on her bonnet and cloak.

It was a clear, frosty October night, and the stars shone brilliantly through the thin-leaved boughs; but in spite of the cold, they walked slowly, Ludwig with the long rolling stride of the western soldier, John with a shorter step, to keep pace with Anne, between the two men. She stayed in the center of the path, her eyes lowered, searching the shadows on the walk, where the roots of trees had lifted the bricks and thrust them at angles from the level to trip the unwary. They were silent, except for Ludwig's bumblebee humming of some German tune, and the street was quiet; there were no falling stars, no thunder-on-the-left, no presage in the air. It was not until, when they had bade good-night to Ludwig at the Cochran gate and John said, brusquely, in a choked voice, "Let's go on to the top of the hill," that Anne knew that he had brought her out, not just for want of something better to do, but because the time had come. Meekly, and without a word, she laid her hand on the arm he held out for her. They turned toward the crown of the hill, where the fence of the College across the street was barely visible in the dark of the trees and the night.

"I wanted a chance to talk to you, outside your father's house. There we can't help being bound by the past—all we remember—what we were, and I was, when I was young and expected to do so much." John had begun to speak slowly, groping his way, then he gave up trying to find the right words, and let the first ones that came to mind serve his purpose. "Out here, we can drop all that; there's just you and me." He ended lamely, "If you see what I mean. I can't put it clearly."

"Put what clearly?" Not that she didn't know what he wanted, she thought, her heart beating wildly, but what he wanted to say was another matter. He might say anything, John might, and what he said would have to be dealt with, first.

He did not at once answer; they came to the top of the hill, and there he turned to face her. "What I want to ask you is what I amount to in your life. Not your brother's friend, or your father's pupil, or the soldier you wrote letters to because he was a soldier, but *me*."

"You know, don't you?" She said it ruefully, almost resentfully. "But I don't think you should ask me that first. What if I were to say 'Everything,' and you were to say 'That's all I wanted to know'?"

He interrupted her pitiful attempt to jest and relax the strain of the moment. "If I ask you to marry me, and you say 'yes,' it won't be just because you're afraid that 'no' would be betraying the past?"

"You mean am I so fond of you, just because you've been a part of my life so long, that I couldn't hurt you by saying 'no' even if I didn't care for you, like a wife?"

"Something like that."

They both laughed, and she said, "This is the queerest proposal a girl ever had. You are proposing to me, aren't you?"

"Yes."

"You know what I would say."

"I thought I did. But I didn't want you to say it for any but the one reason. I've known you so well, for so many years. When you were little—and I don't suppose you've changed much—you adored Rob and me in the same way, and you wouldn't do anything to distress either of us. You see, I know I'm taking advantage of you. It isn't fair. You're only eighteen, and just out of school; I'm twenty-eight, and have nothing to offer you."

"John," she said, in a small voice, "are you alone somewhere arguing with yourself, or are you talking to me?"

"I'm talking to you." He drew a long breath. "I love you so much, Anne, that without you I'd have so much less than nothing that it won't bear thinking of. Will you marry me, and trust me to make something of my life?"

"Thank you, John. That's better."

"Don't laugh."

"I'm not laughing. I feel like Christian when his burden rolled away. I've been so afraid you wouldn't—didn't—it was like a shadow in the background, and it's gone. I'm free—free to love you, without being frightened of how much." She put her hands on his upper arms and pressed against him, looking up into his face, set at liberty by the dark to say what she wished to say. "Not as I loved Rob—not as a sister. Don't think I don't know the difference." He embraced and kissed her, but when he let her go again, she slipped her hand down his coat sleeve from his elbow, twined her fingers in his, and began again where she had left off, speaking with a happy confidence. "I didn't know the difference when I first decided I was going to marry you, when I was about ten. It's only these last few years, since the war, since I've grown up—and then I realized it wasn't mine to say. If you didn't want me, then I should have to be an old maid, because I couldn't marry anyone else, not after all these years of imagining how I'd get your breakfast in the morning and put your slippers on the fender every night."

He laughed, too, at that, and they kissed each other again, joyfully, then turned and went back down the hill, hand in hand. It was not until they reached her father's gate that Anne thought of the doctor, and that he would have to be told; she said "Papa?"

"I spoke to him."

In the ten feet between gate and doorstep, she considered and decided against asking John to come in; she had no dread of her father, and there was no point in dragging John in to hear whatever parental advice convention required of Dr. Alexander. They parted at the door; she went into the house, stopped long enough in the dimly lighted hall to hang her wraps on the rack, and then with a firm step crossed to the sitting room door, where she stayed on the threshold for a moment, to get her breath, to stop her heart's racing, until she could speak.

Her father was in his leather chair by the hearth. He glanced up when she came to the door, laid his book face down across his knee, took his pipe from his mouth to cuddle its bowl in the palm of his hand. He said, "I see John has spoken to you. He asked me today if he might. You accepted him, of course?"

She looked abashed. "How did you know—'of course'?"

"I'm not blind. You've been waiting for it ever since you've known him." From beneath lowered brows he watched her gravely as she crossed the room and came to stand beside him, one hand over his shoulder, on the back of the chair.

"You've no objections, have you, Papa?"

"No. No. I'd like to ask you, though: you haven't persuaded him against his will, have you, to come back into practice? I mean: hinted that you wouldn't marry him unless he did?"

"Of course not." Then she added, with solemnity, "I'd have married him if he were a hod-carrier. No, I've better sense than that: do you think I want him to hate me?"

"Oh? Then you suspect he may not be successful as a doctor?"

"No, I didn't mean that." She spoke slowly, as if preparing to explain what she did mean; but the suggestion in her father's question caught and checked her. She went round in front of him, pushed his slippered feet from the hassock where they rested, and sat down on it, facing him. "No, I was only afraid he mightn't like doctoring, not that he wouldn't be a good doctor. Why? Do you think—I've heard you say he knows more about medicine than you do."

"Oh, so he does," her father grunted. "All the newfangled notions. But knowledge isn't everything. Nor sympathy, nor kindness. John lets himself be haunted by the suffering he sees, and that won't do in a doctor. Because it isn't in a man not to dodge suffering if he can. And when a doctor begins to withdraw, like a snail into its shell, refusing to face the things he must face, then he isn't going to be much good. A doctor, if he's going to help his patients, must be *there*, like a rock, for them to lean on, not looking the other way; he's got to be ruthless and callous. John may develop the necessary callosity, with time: then he will be a good doctor; or he may learn to conceal and control his weakness: then he'll be a good doctor. But not, I'm afraid, a good husband. Unless you do more than your part."

"You mean, 'a good husband, or a good doctor, but not both'?"

"John has a—shall we say 'difficult'?—temperament. If he forces himself to behave as a doctor should—if he assumes a strength he doesn't have, for the sake of his patients—there will be times when the tension will break. At home. Unless he deliberately looks elsewhere for something to break it."

"Are you warning me that John may take to drink, or something like that?

Or are you simply trying to tell me that he isn't an easy person to live with? I know that."

"Oh, you do." He smiled at her for the first time, and then, also for the first time, spoke somewhat ironically. "Then you know that if you want to make him happy all you have to do is be patient, be devoted, but never make a noise about your devotion either, and hold your tongue. Don't say it, whatever it is, if you're feeling cross."

"Yes, Papa." She was meek as a little girl, but looked amused.

"Be tolerant. All men have their vagaries, if not their vices. Don't reproach and don't whine."

"I never whine."

"No, I don't think you do. Give John lots of rope." Then he chuckled. "This is queer advice for a man to give his daughter. But after all, I'm a doctor. I've seen so many lives made unhappy by self-righteous women. And John is almost a son to me. I want you both to be happy."

Anne, embarrassed by his easy use of words like "happy" and "devoted," words not often on the tongues of men so self-contained as her father, contented herself with nodding and murmuring "I know."

"I'm hoping for the impossible," he continued, bluntly. "That's something you don't know, yet. But you have a gift for loving people. That has always been easy for you, and it is in your power to make him as happy as it is possible for a man like John to be, who is by temperament moody and unstable, and who is still suffering the nervous traumatism consequent to the war." He saw perhaps, in her face, that she had had enough; he leaned over to empty his pipe into the fireplace and rolled about in his chair to reach the tobacco pouch in his pocket. Anne rose from the hassock, took from the vase on the mantel a long paper spill, and from the dying fire lit it and gave it to him.

"Is that all, Papa? Because I think I'll go to bed now."

"It's all," he said doubtfully, "if I've made myself clear. It boils itself down to this. If you want John to be happy, don't stand in the way—don't let anything stand in the way—of his being a successful doctor. Fortunately, being a doctor's daughter, you know he'll not be able to call his soul his own; still less can you call it yours."

"Yes. I know all that. For a doctor, no single hour in the day can be counted on as his, to eat, or sleep, or wash, even. Just the same, I'm glad he is a doctor."

She went upstairs to bed, with very little of her father's subtler implications lingering in her ears; what his talk dissolved into was the conviction that she mustn't fuss with John when he didn't get home to meals on time, nor when he had to go out in the middle of the night and leave her alone, nor when he was gloomy. She wilfully closed her mind to anything more disturbing than these trivialities because she was unused to having her father talk to her so freely, exposing her and John and himself so without reserve, and she shrank from it in distaste when she might well have been frightened. Instead, she was supremely happy, and rejected what might make her less so.

The next two weeks were so full that there would have been no time for sober reflection on her future with John. Most important were those few hours when she could be with him, when he was not in her father's office, or out on the twice-daily round of house calls. Less exciting, but still fun enough, were those visits with Sally, beginning with the first one, when Anne told of her approaching marriage, each visit covering in rapid chatter plans for the wedding, for the wedding journey, for the house and housekeeping.

Subdued to a secondary excitement because of the crisis in her personal life was the forthcoming election, with mass meetings at the Armory, and a culminating election eve parade, which she and Sally and Sally's father and mother watched from the Cochran gate, and which the two girls applauded with an unladylike fervor, when they identified John and Ludwig marching together, with oilcloth capes over their uniforms, their sheepish expressions lighted grotesquely by their torches, in glimpses, as the flames rose and fell and the smoke glowed with a rosy light and yet obscured features and blurred outlines and made of the procession a phantasmagoria, noisy, lurid, and smelling of the pit.

Election day, in Ohio and a few other states, for governor and the local officials fell on the thirteenth of October; when those votes were counted and the Republicans everywhere were elected, there could be no doubt that General Grant would carry Ohio in November, and suspense went out of the atmosphere, a universal fever collapsed and could be forgotten, like the air let out and lost from a burst balloon, and everyone could give his mind again to his personal life. Anne's constant awareness of the delights of acknowledged love had never been suspended, but she had postponed until after the Ohio election any paper-and-pencil work on her essay for the Woman's Club. She had salved her conscience by reading, every night in bed, the poetical works of Mr. Browning, but somehow she had never got through more than a few stanzas before the lamp chimney began to smoke. Every afternoon after the election she took her papers and pencils and the 1868 edition of the poems, borrowed from Mrs. Lowrey, and sat down to work at the center table in the sitting room. Before she could get more than a quotation or two copied down, in her neat tiny writing, the fire would call for attention; then, almost without volition, she would bundle books and papers into her arms, move to the hearthrug, and squat there, cross-legged, in the center of her spread skirts, with the tablet on her knee. In that place, and that position, long ago her favorite for reading, and for writing letters to Rob before he died and to John, she could forget her physical surroundings and concentrate on the making of an essay. It would have been out of the question for her to have forgotten all the while that she was triumphantly, openly, in love, and it was therefore only natural that the poetry that got past her eyes to her mind was that which was an affirmation or denial of the validity of love, romantic or passionate. The essay that she composed contained but little more than her own emotional response to those poems that most harmoniously fitted in with her mood, or most severely cut across it. In spite of her intention, as stated to

Sally, to belittle the poets whom she had been forced to admire in the classroom, she could not fail to be convinced by one who could say

> Love that was life, life that was love,
> A tenure of breath at your lips decree,
> A passion to stand as your thought approve,
> A rapture to fall where your foot might be.

She wrote down what occurred to her with little second thought, and, by the evening before the Club was to meet, she had a few pages, neatly copied, that she could stand up and read to the ladies. Then, when it was too late, she blushed for the childishness of her statements, but she told herself that to have given more time to it would have been a waste; she didn't care a snap of her fingers really for any of their opinions.

The Misses Gardiner had invited the Club to meet with them. It rained on Wednesday, and John left the office long enough to drive Anne up the hill. He was still amused by the idea of a Woman's Club, and Anne, who sat silent in the curtained buggy, was glad that the day was raw and cold enough to explain her shiverings; she would not have had him know that she was shaken suddenly, at the last moment, by stage fright. He helped her from the buggy, her gloved hand limp in his, just as the Cochran carriage drew up behind him, with Mrs. Lowrey, Miss Pinney, and Miss Tucker in it, besides Sally. The Ballards had brought Amanda and Miss Crenshaw with them; the Club assembled punctually in the Gardiners' gold and crystal drawing room.

Anne had thought that she would be called upon at once to read her essay, and so would shortly be done with it, but she had reckoned without the President's love of parliamentarianism for its own sake. Mrs. Ballard naturally did not forgo an opportunity to exercise the art in which she had been schooled. The minutes of the last meeting were read and approved. The proposed constitution was presented: "Name, the Waynesboro Woman's Club (not the *Ladies'* Club nor the *Female* Club, Mrs. Ballard emphasized); object: the mutual benefit to be obtained by its members in intellectual pursuits. Officers, . . . method of their election . . . membership not to exceed twelve . . . dues . . . new members: a name proposed for membership to be presented to the Secretary in writing and voted upon two weeks after presentation. The vote shall be by ballot, and three negatives shall exclude the proposed person from membership . . . meetings shall be held fortnightly at the homes of members on alternate Wednesday afternoons—this, as Mrs. Ballard explained in an aside, 'will permit the teachers of the College to be present, since it is the school's half-holiday.' That Wednesday evening is Prayer Meeting night need not disturb anyone: Club meetings will not be so long as prevent anyone's attendance at her church." Each article was discussed separately, and separately voted upon. The proceedings dragged interminably, particularly to one who sat clutching in a clammy hand an essay of which she was heartily ashamed. When the constitution had been adopted and Mrs. Ballard had handed it over to the secretary to be copied into the minutes, the chairman of the Program Committee was called upon for a report. Miss Tucker rose and with a few explanatory phrases, distributed hand-written copies of the list of subjects with which the members of the Club would occupy themselves for the Club year. Under the general heading "English Poets of the 19th Century," each lady had been assigned a topic, and a date for its discussion.

When Miss Tucker had been thanked and complimented by the President, Mrs. Ballard flashed a look at Anne that made her feel sick and hollow beneath the bones of her stays, and asked the secretary to read the program for the day. Amanda rose from the chair beside the President's table and announced, "'The Poetical Works of Mr. Robert Browning,' Miss Alexander." Her expression was resigned: it said "We expect little, but are willing to listen"; it was not conducive to assurance on the part of the essayist.

"Madam President, and Ladies of the Club." Anne's voice did not tremble, but once she began to read, she raced through her pages so precipitately that she was soon breathless. She was mortified at being so obviously rattled, but she could not help it. They were too close to her, these women: she could not look over their heads, forget them, and so state without embarrassment what she really believed. And unfortunately that was what she had written, on those afternoons she had spent on the floor between the fender and the coal scuttle, simply because it had been easier and quicker and sooner done with than if she had tried to be literary. She was miserable, now, because she had said so much about love; she should have remembered the audience she was writing for, and not have expected these women to understand love as she understood it, and as Mr. Browning understood it.

Only when she came near the end did her voice strengthen and her pace slow down, so that her ideas seemed to be presented with conviction instead of apologetically. She even paused to look up at Sally for a bright-eyed instant, as if to say, "Here is what I promised: a defiance of all their beliefs." She read the first stanza of *Rabbi Ben Ezra* and stated flatly that she believed no word of it. Mr. Browning had written it at an age when he was least justified in speaking on such a subject with what seemed like authority. "He was fifty-two when it was published, and it seems to me that a man of fifty-two is not really old, but only in advanced middle-age. However, he may be old enough to have forgotten what it is like to be young. We who read *Rabbi Ben Ezra* in our youth cannot but cry 'no' in contradiction to the poet. We know that we shall never again feel so fervently as we do now, never pursue our ambitions with so much ardor, never lose with so much devotion, never be so willing to put our lives, without reservations, at the service of our friends, our families, and our country. On the other hand, Mr. Browning only knows old age as we know it: by observation. Can it be that he sees it with a less realistic eye than we see it because he approaches it so much more nearly? He may have persuaded himself, but he cannot persuade us, that 'the best is yet to be.' Old age may have its compensations, but they can be but mild, suited to a time when the blood is running sluggish and cold, and the most that life can offer is a corner at the hearth where one may keep warm, a chair at the dinner table, and a minor place in the affections of one's descendants." Anne read this in a firm voice, but she was contrite, as youth in its less hard moments is contrite at having attacked the false tenets with which its elders comfort themselves against their fate. She perhaps exaggerated her power to disturb their confidence: it did not occur to her that they might be amused at her presumption, while they retained their beliefs unshaken. At any rate, she was not so bold as to close on that note and leave so defiant a challenge ringing in the air. She had reserved an incontestable point for her peroration:

"However much we may think the poet is wrong about old age, it seems to me we may all agree with him and be grateful for the things he has said about death. Death, he believes, is not a horror to be shrunk from in a cowardly fashion: it is merely the last struggle of all to be faced by mortal man, and to be faced courageously, even triumphantly, with immortality the recompense. You all know *Prospice*. You will all remember, as I do, its first publication in the June, 1864, issue of *Atlantic Monthly*. I was a mere child at the time, and don't know how I happened to read it, but I did, and remembered it, and in the months that followed it seemed to me something to cling to. When the summer became one long, horrible battle—The Wilderness, Spottsylvania, Cold Harbor—it was a poem that echoed in my mind:

> I am nearing the place
> The power of the night, the press of the storm,
> The post of the foe;
> There he stands, the Arch-Fear in a visible form.

She read the poem to the end. When she had finished she looked blankly at Mrs. Ballard for a second, brought to earth too abruptly, and then with a bent head, sank limply again into her chair.

Mrs. Ballard permitted no awkward pause in which disagreement or hostility might go looking for words, and so be expressed more cogently than a regard for urbanity could desire.

"Thank you very much, Miss Alexander. You have given the ladies of the Club some new points of view from which to consider the work of the poet. I think that we may all forgive you," and she smiled benignly, "for your very youthful attitude toward *Rabbi Ben Ezra*. You cannot be expected, yet, to 'welcome each rebuff'; nor have you reached an age to appreciate 'What I aspired to be, And was not, comforts me,' since I suppose you no doubt still expect to accomplish your aspirations." She nodded to Anne, and beamed, and then turned to Miss Tucker. "Do you not agree with me that we may be grateful to Miss Alexander?"

Miss Tucker said "Madam President" so gravely that Anne held her breath and awaited a rebuke. She could not know what an acknowledged maturity and equality would do for her, any more than she could have foreseen, inexperienced as she was, the establishment of a standard of courtesy that would make the Club possible.

"The Program Committee has every reason to be grateful to Miss Alexander for being willing to undertake so vast and difficult a subject on such short notice. It is not to be wondered at that she should have been unable to deal with more than a part of the poet's work, nor that she should have chosen that part which treats of love." Miss Tucker smiled briefly, not looking at Anne. "Probably no other member could have interpreted those particular poems with so much sympathy, and so we may congratulate ourselves that we asked Miss Alexander to write this essay. Later, when we have a study of 'Present-Day Philosophies as Revealed by the Poets,' I hope that we shall hear something of other aspects of Mr. Browning's work."

Amanda Reid started to speak, remembered herself in time, said "Madam President," paused until her application to the chair had been acknowledged. "I see that is to be my subject. It could hardly be adequately dealt with without a consideration of Mr. Browning's philosophy, among others. But I hope that we shall have further papers devoted to him exclusively. I agree that Miss Alexander's presentation of certain of his works has been very interesting and rewarding. But there are many other points in regard to him worthy of an afternoon's discussion. His life, his education, his sources, the use he made of them." Amanda turned to Anne, her manner impersonal, her eye coldly judicial. "Please do not understand me to imply that all this should have been included in the afternoon's essay. I offer it as a suggestion to future program committees."

When the meeting adjourned a few minutes later, after the reading of the program next to follow, and the ladies crossed the hall to the Gardiner sitting room for their cloaks and shawls, Anne caught Amanda by the elbow, and circled her until they stood face to face.

"Amanda: I was ashamed before I ever read that paper, but I want to say I hadn't known how much I did leave out. I didn't look up all those things because I didn't think of it. I didn't know how to go about writing an essay for the Club—" and she laughed at herself. "So I wrote what I thought about the poems I happen to like. But next time—I really value your good opinion, you see, because you know so much. Next time will you help me?"

"Nonsense!" Amanda looked at her directly, frankly. Her eyes said, "Frivolous!," her tongue, shrewdly, "It isn't knowing a lot that matters, it's putting your mind to it. And I liked what you said about *Prospice*. As for *Rabbi Ben Ezra*: you read but one stanza, didn't you, for fear you wouldn't be justified in what you meant to say? You didn't read 'All that is, at all, Lasts ever, past recall.' He means that when you're old, you still have your youth, as well as what you've gained: an intensified knowledge of God, and a willingness to submit: 'Earth changes, but thy Soul and God stand sure'."

"Yes, but Amanda—" Then Anne gave it up; it was easier for her to talk about love than about God and the soul. Embarrassed, she added, "I mustn't stop now; John's outside waiting for me, in the rain."

In the door to the hall, Sally stopped her and drew her toward the foot of the staircase, away from the chatter in the Gardiner sitting room, where the ladies were picking up their wraps. She had nothing to say to Anne about her essay; indeed, she had hardly listened to it; she had been too intent on the author, too watchful of Anne's face. She deprecated the candor and delight her friend had displayed, in every glance of her eye, every smile, every inflection of her voice, the state of her emotions. She went around looking, Sally told herself, like a hound-dog saved from starvation and given a good home. She was as afraid for her as if Anne were laying herself open to injury. If John saw her looking like that—it was safer not to reveal one's self so completely.

"You're a wretch, Anne," she said, now. "I haven't seen you since the election."

"I've been writing this essay. It wasn't good, either. It was humiliating to have Miss Tucker make excuses for me. But just think," a sudden light broke on her, "I have finished for the year. I can put my mind on other things."

"On John, I suppose that means."

"He's out there now. I saw him from the window. I'll come up to your house in the morning."

"But wait," Sally held to her arm. "I've a piece of news I must tell you. After the election Captain Rausch bought the old rope factory. He's going to put in some machines and manufacture rope."

"And live in Waynesboro?" Anne still did not conceal her desire to be gone, but she made an effort to be enthusiastic. "I'm so glad. It will be very pleasant to have him here."

"You take it coolly enough!" You might as well, Sally thought, expect to make an impression on a fever patient in a delirium.

"No. I'm delighted, really. For your sake," Anne added mischievously, as if with a sudden awareness of Sally, her reality, and the reality of her interests. "But I must go now—" and went back to the parlor to make her formal adieux to the Misses Gardiner.

Sally followed her, half-amused and tolerant, half-provoked. Love swept all other interests from your consciousness, of course she knew that—the name "Ludwig" thundered into her mind and left it blank for a second, then she thought how silly it was of Anne, to be so swept off her feet by something she'd always, really, expected to happen. Ludwig had come like a comet into her life—if *he*—that would be different.

She had been thinking of Anne all through the meeting: thinking how she would give a party for her when she came back from her honeymoon. Not a reception. Anne's mother's friends could do that. A Christmas party for the Club members and their families. It mightn't mean much to Anne, unless she had come down to earth by that time, but it would to Miss Pinney and Miss

Crenshaw and perhaps the Gardiner sisters. She mustn't call it a Christmas party, though, or Amanda wouldn't come. Reformed Presbyterians thought any recognition of Christmas "Popish." They could act charades. Or, if that wasn't cultural enough, tableaux. Famous Masterpieces of Art. Now, as she saw Anne dart through the door and down the steps into the rain, holding her shawl high over her Sunday bonnet, she thought, "the first Club bride"; that would be her excuse for the party, and for inviting the old ladies.

The "old ladies," as she called them in her mind, had collected in the sitting room doorway, waiting for her to lead them back to the carriage that had brought them there. She went to tell them that she was ready, and to say good-bye to Miss Lavinia and Miss Caroline Gardiner.

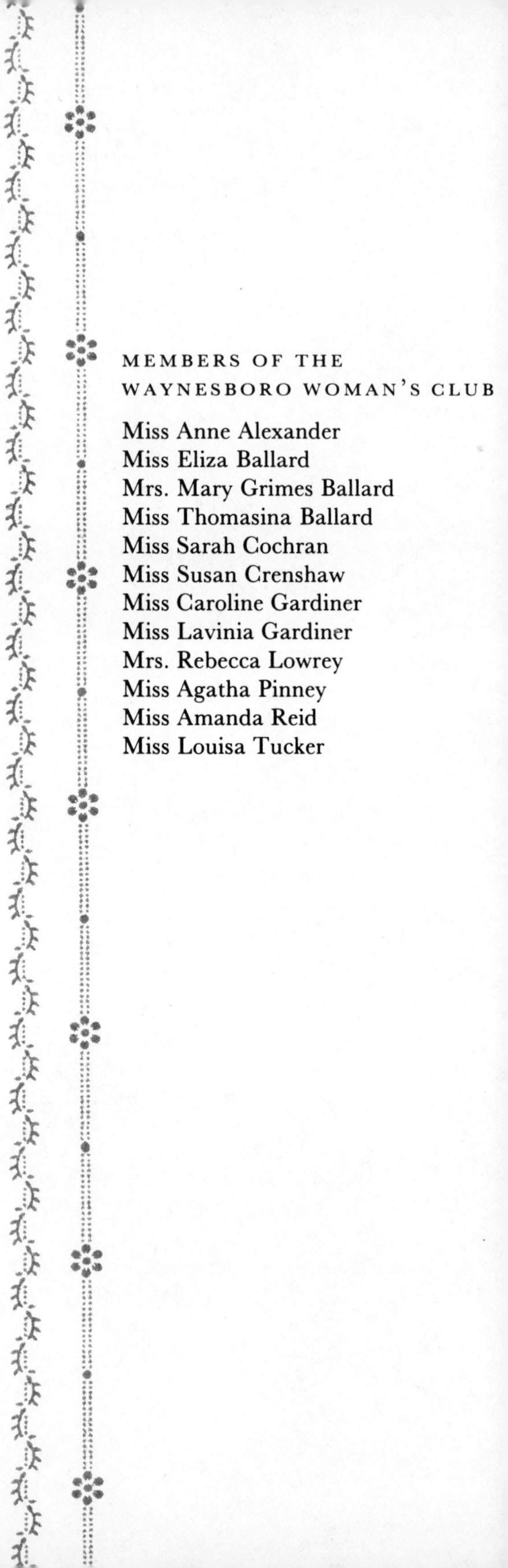

MEMBERS OF THE
WAYNESBORO WOMAN'S CLUB

Miss Anne Alexander
Miss Eliza Ballard
Mrs. Mary Grimes Ballard
Miss Thomasina Ballard
Miss Sarah Cochran
Miss Susan Crenshaw
Miss Caroline Gardiner
Miss Lavinia Gardiner
Mrs. Rebecca Lowrey
Miss Agatha Pinney
Miss Amanda Reid
Miss Louisa Tucker

✻ 1868 ✻

"At the Club party, 1868, tableaux were the order of the evening."

Anne and John at once made plans for their wedding. They would be married while he was still Dr. Alexander's assistant and not yet his partner; when, presumably, there would be patients to consider him "their" doctor, and be peevish and apprehensive if they had to accept instead the services of the older man. If he went away now, John could be gone from the office long enough for the honeymoon trip that Anne, who had never been far from home, had set her heart on. They could see Niagara Falls, Albany, the Hudson River, New York, Philadelphia, and Washington with part of the money John had saved since the war. With what remained they could set up housekeeping. For a wedding present Anne's father transferred to her the title to the Alexander house; he would move again to the rooms over the office where he had lived since he had sent Anne to board at the College. She suspected that he could not be happy now in the house where he had spent all the years of his married life, where daily sight and use of the familiar shabby furniture would remind him of his losses, bring back the happier years when she and Rob were children and their mother young and strong; or, perhaps, she thought sometimes, it might just be that he preferred to grow old alone, without the interference of women, in untidy comfort, with his books and tobacco. At any rate, she did not doubt that he was glad to be rid of the house; she had not tried to dissuade him from his intention, but accepted with gratitude the gift that made her feel at last completely grown-up, with a woman's responsibilities: property to manage, a household to look after, a husband to make comfortable.

Anne did not indulge in the customary last parade of girlhood. John would have hated it. They had a quiet wedding at home one afternoon. The house was immaculate (she and Martha had seen to that), but no attempt had been made to decorate it. The Presbyterian minister stood in the parlor with his back to the fireplace; Anne came to him on her father's arm, John crossed the room with Ludwig at his side, and they were married there in the presence of a few friends of Anne's parents, one or two of John's companions in arms, the three Cochrans, Professor and Mrs. Lowrey, and John's sister. Instead of white satin, a veil, and orange blossoms. Anne wore her traveling costume, a pearl grey corded silk. The color was becoming to her, but made her look almost somber in the half-light of the November afternoon. John, too, was solemn, but rather more apprehensive than stern and self-confident.

Or so Sally Cochran thought, watching them. The ceremony, or lack of it, was not to her taste. Had she been in Anne's place, she would not have forgone the pageantry of a church wedding. She loved pageantry for its own sake, and in Anne's case it would have held everyone's attention, and prevented any of those present from thoughts of how incongruous the joining of these two families was. Anne had only her father, to be sure, and John, in Waynesboro, only his sister. But surely Anne could not accept without misgivings the addition of Kate Gordon to her family. Sally, sitting close to the side window, was across the parlor from Kate, who stood facing the long mirror between the two windows that opened on the porch. That end of the room was fairly light, and Kate's face and figure were clearly reflected in the mirror. Sally studied her with close attention, partly because she was interesting looking, and partly because the other women present were all so well known to her. But Kate had so often been the subject of gossip; she had scandalized the town by her masculine proclivities. She ran the garden, marketed the produce, and raised both cattle and hogs. Sally had sometimes seen her on Saturday afternoons, her clinging skirts (no crinolines) spattered with mud, likely as not striding about the streets with a buggy whip in her hand. Kate Gordon arrayed for her brother's wedding was therefore an amazing spectacle. Sally stared and felt reassured on Anne's account: the woman couldn't be completely eccentric, after all. She had on a fashionable frock, a dark brown, matching her eyes and hair, that mitigated the leatheriness of her skin; a long underskirt with a six-inch pleated flounce, and over it a princess overdress, tight in sleeve and bodice, down to her knees in front and extravagantly draped; the ruffles and bows softened her angularities and emphasized the slimness of her waist and the uprightness of her carriage. Her bonnet concealed the roughness of her hair, gloves the cracks and scars on her hands. The only disquieting thing was her expression, half-amused and half-disdainful, as if she were saying, "You see that even I can do this sort of thing: put on the absurdities decreed by fashion and assume the airs of a woman of the world; but what fools you are to take this ability to behave like other people with seriousness, as if it were important."

Afterward—after the wedding supper, which Sally and Ludwig ate at the bride's table—when John and Anne had gone upstairs and the guests waited in the lower hall for them to come down again and say good-bye, Sally had another, and a different, glimpse of Kate. She was close to the lamp table, erect against the door frame, her hands clasped behind her. Amusement and disdain had gone from her face. In the bright lamp light that flared up across it, it was hard like stone. Her cheeks were flat, and slanted sharply in from her cheekbones; her nose was thin and curved. Her mobile full-lipped mouth was stiff and sullen, her eyes desperate. As if, Sally thought, wherever she looks, even at a wedding, she sees and can't help seeing the skeleton beneath the flesh. Startled by the bleak lucidity of the woman's gaze, Sally jerked her eyes and thoughts away, and went to the newel post to wait for the bride and groom to come downstairs. When they did, she was there to give Anne one last impetuous hug; if she could, she would have gone with her to the door and prevented any glimpse of the death's-head that waited lurking there. But Kate had come to herself: she kissed John warmly, Anne tenderly, and said in her husky voice, "Have a good time, children, and be happy together." Anne responded with an affectionate embrace. However, when the door had closed behind them, Kate Gordon said good-night to Dr. Alexander with rude brusqueness, ignored the rest of them, and went out, through the kitchen, to fetch her own horse from the doctor's stable. Sally stared after her, then shrugged her shoulders and dismissed her from her mind. After all, Anne and John loved each other: even while Anne kissed her friends good-bye, John's hand had been tight about her wrist, and after her final embrace of her father, she had turned to her husband with a shamelessly open look of adoration. What could a sister-in-law matter, who lived several miles away, in the country?

In the weeks that followed, Sally had no time for thinking of Anne's future happiness. The Gordons' wedding trip lasted for a month, but Sally missed Anne less than she had supposed she would, less than she protested in the letters she sent East after the bridal couple. Ludwig Rausch had begun to court her, in the wholehearted sentimental fashion of an honest German, and Sally, who had looked on him with approval from the moment when she had seen him for the first time as the most conspicuous person in a crowd of several hundred, did nothing to discourage him. He spent almost every evening at the Cochrans'. Mr. Cochran, who had studied Ludwig shrewdly, with a banker's eye, was not averse to leaving them alone in the front parlor, to play the piano or not as they chose. Mrs. Cochran was not so complacent. Ludwig's parents were immigrants, and he himself had been born in Germany. To her, an immigrant was an immigrant, whether he came penniless to settle on homestead land, or whether, like Mr. Rausch, he was a "48-er" who came because participation in an abortive revolution had made his homeland impossible for him. His foreign birth was her only complaint against Ludwig. It did not trouble her, nor Sally either, that he brought with him to their parlor, faintly, the tarry odor of the ropewalk. At that time, and in that community, young men were expected to start out for themselves and make their own way; Ludwig's behavior in setting to work to learn at first-hand the business he had bought was considered wholly commendable.

He had incorporated the mill as Rausch Cordage Company, Rope and Twine, and had sold stock to his father and uncle, keeping for himself the majority interest. He retained in his employ the two old Dutchmen from whom he had bought the ropewalk, making them foremen to oversee the laborers, whom he also continued to employ. He was quickly on easy terms with them; the majority were Negroes, the minority mostly Irishmen and like himself veterans of the war. For some time the laborers had been troubled about the security of their jobs, since the business had so clearly been going downhill. Now they were relieved of that uncertainty, and were intent on proving their worth to the new owner. Ludwig as boss was easy to like, particularly after he had collected them one noon in the cobbled yard and made a speech in which he told them that when he could afford it, he intended to put in machinery to do away with most hand labor, but that any one of them who needed and wanted to work would be retained and taught how to run the machinery. "And," he had concluded, "it won't be tomorrow that machines can be installed. This plant isn't the U. S. Mint." Reassured, they laughed willingly at even so feeble a joke.

In the meantime, under the tutelage of the Roseblooms, he set about learning the processes that went into the making of rope by hand. He opened bales of hemp, delivered by canal boat from Cincinnati; he shook it out ready for the hatchelers, and thereby learned to distinguish varieties and grades of fiber. Standing by the workmen, he learned the steps involved in the preparation of the hemp for the spinners: he helped in the tarring shed, taking directions from the Negroes who boiled the tar in cauldrons and kept it at the right temperature for the yarn to be drawn through it. Finally, he joined the spinners: the skilled workers, top of the order in the mill. With them he stepped backward down the long walk, twisting threads of fiber into yarn, as it came from the wheels the wheel boys turned. Yarns, tarred or untarred, were twisted into strands, and the strands into rope. Finally one triumphant day, applauded by the other spinners, he stood at the end of the walk and held up for all to see the last few feet of the twelve hundred coiled on the floor: rope with no kinks or uneven twists in it. He had acquired the skill of the experts. He had homework to do, also: the relation of size and hardness of twist was worked out in formulas; Ludwig studied the mathematics of his new business in his boardinghouse room at night, after he had left the Cochrans.

The distinction between different kinds of rope and line and twine was explained to him by his willing teachers, in the noon hour, while they lunched: when it was fine and sunny, on the canal bank; when it was rainy and cold, inside the hemp house, with bales of hemp for chairs and tables. The old men brought their lunch with them when they came to work: Ludwig had his from the Hoffmann beer parlor. Frederica Hoffmann sent it down in the hands of a boy: rye bread sandwiches with cheese or liverwurst or bloodwurst, and a pail of lager. Sometimes as they ate and afterward as they smoked, the old men told stories of their youth in Bremen, or Ludwig recounted his adventures in the war; but mostly the time was a lesson hour when he learned the difference between hawser and cable, shroud and boltrope, between tacks and sheets, between leadline, logline, houseline, and marline. The nautical terms, with all their associations, were fascinating to the inland-bred young man, but he did not delude himself into thinking that he could make cordage for sailing ships in southern Ohio, even if the sailing ships were not doomed to be superseded entirely by steam. Ludwig knew exactly what market he stood a fair chance of supplying. A farmer's reaper and binder would use twine to tie up their cut wheat into sheaves, and the more land homesteaded in the plains, the more wheat to be reaped. In the meantime he could make belt and transmission rope for the factories springing up everywhere, drilling rope for oil wells in Pennsylvania and Ohio, and hawsers or cables for the riverboats—barges, flatboats, showboats, passenger boats—that crowded the Ohio. This last market he knew he could reach without difficulty through his uncle, who was a wholesale hardware merchant in Cincinnati. The canal, although neglected since the railroads had been built, was still serviceable; hemp was delivered by barge, and Ludwig sent his rope down to the city on the same horse-drawn canal boats, in charge of a man and boy who tied up at night and slept on the coils of rope.

Ludwig's day was a long one. Like his men, he worked from six to six, but he made the most of every opportunity for becoming acquainted in Waynesboro; at his rooming house, at the hotel where he went for breakfast and supper when he was not at the Cochrans', and at the Hoffmann beer parlor, where he foregathered occasionally in the evenings with the Germans newly come to town. Seated with two or three of them at a table covered with a red-checked cloth, he discussed politics and the state of the country, and teased the Hoffmann girls, the sisters of the owner, as they came and went with foaming steins. But when he could be, he was with Sally, and his courtship progressed as smoothly as his rope-making.

Sally, however much in love, was not one to sit dreaming all day long in anticipation of the few evening hours when her suitor could be with her. Immediately after Anne's wedding she had begun to plan for what she called to herself her Christmas party. First she suggested to Mrs. Lowrey that they should honor the Club bride, and Mrs. Lowrey sounded out the older members, who, when they found that they would be involved in nothing more than attendance at the Cochran home, were enthusiastic. Sally appointed a committee, Amanda and Thomasina Ballard, to work out a program with her. She had not been sure that Amanda would cooperate in anything so theatrical as tableaux, but she made her approach a tactful one, an appeal to Amanda's superior knowledge. Amanda disclaimed almost scornfully any acquaintance with art (the tableaux were to represent "Famous Pictures"), but when Sally begged her to apply the eye of a scholar to the costumes and make sure they were as like those of the original paintings as possible, and were historically correct, she agreed to help. Amanda was not so reluctant as she had tried to make them believe. Her Waynesboro parties had been mostly church sociables, where the girls played Spin the Plate and Going to Jerusalem with the theological students, and generally behaved like children. Sally, on the other hand, might have been expected to give a ball for Anne and John: there were young people enough in Waynesboro who did dance to make such entertainments frequent and popular. The fact that she had instead chosen to spend an evening on as cultural a program as "Famous Pictures" in tableaux showed that the Club was having a beneficent effect on her native lightmindedness. Amanda could hardly refuse to encourage her. When Sally told her that she looked exactly like Holbein's portrait of Sir Thomas More, Amanda could not see why she should not pose as so famous a scholar and writer, even if he had been a Catholic.

Thomasina was pleased and touched when Sally asked for her help. She was more than willing to spend her days making costumes, although she was no seamstress. It took her as long to put in one conscientious hem as it did Sally to make a frock. But Sally never seemed to notice her slowness, and Thomasina enjoyed, as she had perhaps enjoyed no other time in her life, the long afternoons in the Cochran sewing room, with the gray November skies lowering outside the windows and a fire on the hearth within, and pretty Sally, flushed, disheveled, but competent, assembling one costume after another, driving the sewing machine furiously by fits and starts, and by fits and starts chattering about Waynesboro people and their own schooldays and occasionally breaking out with the irrepressible name, Ludwig. Even when Amanda came down from the College, after classes were over, they still discussed only their plans for the tableaux, as if there were nothing of importance going on in the country, no problems to be solved; and Thomasina found a vacation from national reform movements rather pleasant.

She was deputed to ask her sister Eliza to pose in a couple of the tableaux. Eliza consented, chiefly out of indifference and reluctance to hurt Thomasina's feelings, although she was sarcastic about the program and derisive of her own or Thomasina's likeness to any picture ever painted. Miss Tucker was approached by Amanda, and agreed to appear as Gainsborough's Sarah Siddons. Plans were made for Anne in her absence, and costumes basted together for her that could be tried on when she returned. The other ladies of the Club, with their families, would compose the audience. Sally sent around written invitations to Mrs. Reid, Judge and Mrs. Ballard, Professor and Mrs. Lowrey, Miss Pinney, Miss Crenshaw, the Misses Gardiner and Mr. Douglas Gardiner, Dr. Alexander, and to Anne and John. "Tableaux," the invitations said, and "To honor Dr. and Mrs. Gordon."

Anne and John came home on the day that the Cochran coachman delivered Sally's invitations. After dinner, on the same day, Sally, escorted by Ludwig, went down to the Gordons' to spend the evening. John had gone to keep office hours with Dr. Alexander, but Ludwig was no one to feel uncomfortable in feminine society. Anne had so long since accepted him as Sally's prospective husband, and had felt so at home with him since the beginning of their acquaintance, that it was possible now for her to ignore him almost entirely, and to describe as she would have done to Sally alone the wonders of her tour of the East. She talked of her travels, while Sally discussed her coming party and the tableaux, and in spite of the confusion that resulted, they were soon straight again with each other, and could pick up their intimacy at the point where they had left off.

Ludwig interrupted with statement or question only once or twice, as when he asked whether the Gordons had, in Washington, taken advantage of their opportunity to hear "*our* legislators." He spoke the words in a tone that made Anne laugh, suggesting as it did that he would have avoided legislators like the plague.

"Yes, we did. We went to the Capitol and sent our card in to General Deming, and he came out and went with us to the visitors' gallery, and pointed out the notables. But there wasn't much going on of any importance. An Ohio man made a speech. Mr. Garfield. You've heard of him, I expect."

"Of course. He was a General. So many of our Congressmen were," Ludwig murmured.

"He spoke very eloquently, but it was only something about the Indian Bureau. We should have been there the next day, when the President's message was delivered, and the Senate called it "offensive," and adjourned without reading it. They're a disgrace to the country: Congress and President both. It'll be a blessing when General Grant is inaugurated. And that reminds me, Sally: General Deming told us Congress would adjourn for the holiday recess and he'd be coming home. I never knew him to come home for Christmas before, did you? It's to see Miss Tucker, I guess. You'd better invite him to your party."

"Of course. And we can peek through the curtains at him while she poses."

And on the next day Reuben, the coachman, left at the General's house to await his return another of Sally's written invitations.

The last-minute preparations for the evening of tableaux were taken in hand by Ludwig. He built a frame for the living pictures, with brackets along its lower edge for lamps with reflectors, like footlights, which he cut from sheets of tin. He set the frame in place between the parlors, far enough behind the double door that the maroon draperies could be drawn across it without risk of being scorched by the lamps. With a Teutonic contempt for Waynesboro's lack of enthusiasm for Christmas, he went into the country with John on his rounds one afternoon to find a shapely spruce tree and sharp-scented branches of evergreen and bright-berried vines. He decorated the Cochran house with his own hands, trailing bittersweet across the mantel in the parlor, thrusting pine boughs behind the pictures, and standing his Christmas tree in the space between the piano and the front window. He persuaded Sally, in spite of her misgivings, to string popcorn and cranberries to hang on the tree, and he made a star of gold paper to fasten at its tip, and candle-holders of tin for every branch. For the first time in her life, Mrs. Cochran was hardly consulted about a party to be given in her own house. She did not approve of the candles, but Ludwig promised to blow them out when the company had seen the tree. For that purpose he took his stand by the piano while Sally's guests arrived, and beamed with approval at everyone who exclaimed in admiration at the sight of the lighted spruce against its dark background. Sally had been afraid that the ladies would not take kindly to such a departure from Waynesboro custom, but even the most rigid Reformed Presbyterian of them all, Amanda's mother, only looked startled at first, and then unaware, as if by pretending to ignore such heathenishness she could absolve herself from the charge of condoning it.

When the guests were seated, Ludwig blew out the candles and tiptoed from the room and down the hall to the back parlor, where he took his stand beside the frame, to light the lamps and adjust them as needed.

The program was an unqualified success. Mrs. Ballard made an introductory speech in which she recounted the story of the origin and intention of the Club. Politely she welcomed the gentlemen, and hoped they would be able to applaud the efforts of the female sex to amuse and edify them; politely, the gentlemen did applaud when she had finished, but they looked a little smug and amused: all of them, from white-bearded, bushy-browed Judge Ballard down to Douglas Gardiner, as if they remembered that Ludwig Rausch was hidden behind a corner somewhere, where he could render the female sex any assistance necessary.

The tableaux were eight in number: Eliza Ballard as Stuart's full-length Washington, wearing a scornful expression quite foreign to the subject; Amanda, in her Oberlin gown and a cap copied by Sally from the picture, as Holbein's More, her square jaw and jutting nose making her really something like the portrait; Sally as Romney's Parson's Daughter, wild-haired and mischievous, but hardly so elfin as the original; Anne as Rembrandt's Son Titus, dark in a kind of dark gloom behind dimmed lights, in the shadow of a wide plumed hat, looking more like the masterpiece she represented than any of the others; Miss Tucker as Sarah Siddons, in full panoply of plumes, muff, and ribbons, was regally majestic, even haughty, and decidedly the hit of the evening; Anne again as Reynolds's Nelly O'Brien, this time in a blaze of light that revealed her as more Anne than Nelly; Eliza as Gainsborough's William Pitt, no more closely resembling the second statesman than the first; and, finally, Thomasina as one of Mme Vigée LeBrun's self-portraits, in a mobcap and ruffles, with palette and brushes, looking if not beautiful, at least happy and amused, as she indeed had been, by Sally's comforting assertion that no doubt Mme Vigée LeBrun had flattered herself.

This program was interspersed with music, and concluded with the reading of some verses, "A Happy New Year," by Miss Thomasina Ballard. When the applause had died away, the Negro houseman came to the door to announce that supper was served in the dining room. The Cochran table had been drawn to its fullest length. The whole party, with a little crowding and keeping elbows close, was able to sit around it to hot baked ham, candied sweet potatoes, beaten biscuits, and mince pie. It was an oddly mixed group that had come together for this midnight meal. Miss Pinney and Miss Crenshaw were shabby and undistinguished, and nothing could make them seem otherwise; but while Miss Pinney was humble and propitiatory, Miss Crenshaw was stiffened by some kind of pride that nothing could break, not even whatever disease it was that gnawed at her vitals and that she concealed, as the Spartan boy concealed the wolf. Mrs. Lowrey was untidy and careless, but her intelligence and her nervous vigor redeemed her from the commonplace; at any gathering at any time, her presence was felt. The Ballard women were richly, stiffly, and quietly dressed. The mother had presence and was obviously a leader, the elder daughter was blunt in manner, while her sister had taken on their color to some extent, but was betrayed by her eyes' timidity. Amanda Reid wore black taffeta with a high neck and a round collar pinned at her throat. The Misses Gardiner had on ancient ball dresses and were elegant if not fashionable in their hoop skirts, one in apricot, the other in pale blue. Beside the regality of Miss Tucker in her green silk, they were washed out almost to invisibility. Anne wore the evening gown that was part of her trousseau, without jewels except for a pair of bracelets. Only Sally was in full fig, her white arms and shoulders bare, her golden hair a fall of curls behind, a maze of braids above, her "garnet set" of earrings, necklace, and bracelets sparkling in the light as she turned in her chair from one to another of her neighbors. But in spite of the disparity between one and another of these women, they were oddly at their ease together; after a few meetings of their club, they had already grown accustomed to each other, and each other's limitations, whether they were of the purse or the imagination. From this circle the only other two women present were set apart, spoken to with an almost exaggerated politeness, as if some special effort must be made to prevent their feeling like outsiders. If one could have judged them by their expressions, neither Mrs. Reid nor Mrs. Cochran would have chosen to be there: Mrs. Reid sat with bowed shoulders and lifted chin, her angry eyes darting from one to another person, from one to another corner of the room as if storing up items of complaint and criticism. Mrs. Cochran, at the foot of the table, sat upright and remembered to smile when she spoke, but she looked bewildered, as if she were wondering what this queer assemblage could be doing in her house.

There was no link between the men to make them feel at home with one another. Douglas Gardiner was a boy, and although he looked older than his years, he made no attempt to conceal a boy's discomfort at being there. John and Ludwig were almost openly amused by the spectacle of such a gathering in the Cochran dining room. Professor Lowrey looked shrunken and wizened, but his eyes were bright and mirthful. Dr. Alexander seemed tired and bored, Mr. Cochran bored but friendly, hospitable but condescending. Judge Ballard was the only one of any distinction of appearance, with his authoritative carriage, his white imperial and thick brows; beside him General Deming was coarse, florid, and overfed. The General was obviously not a man of any sensitiveness of perception: he could not have been expected to know of the Club's ban against controversial subjects, but had he had any feeling for atmosphere, he would not have burst out, as he did during a pause in the conversation, with a challenge to debate. His comments on the success of the evening were concluded with the observation that such a program as they had witnessed was a demonstration of woman's equality with man, and an argument in favor of giving the sex the suffrage that it had begun to demand. As he spoke, the General looked around the table, and it was accident that brought his eye to rest on Douglas Gardiner just when he asked the rhetorical question: "Do you not agree with me?"

"On the contrary. To me, sir, such an occasion seems an argument against it." There was a suggestion of mockery in Douglas's cool tones, even, as he continued, of sarcasm. "How could the ladies find time to entertain us so agreeably if they took up the burden of governing the country?"

"Am I to understand," the General leaned forward and boomed at him jovially, "that you do not believe in suffrage for women? And you can say so, here in the presence of these great workers for that cause?" He indicated, with an oratorical gesture, the Ballard women, whose grave, solid, equine faces were impassive as they listened and waited.

"I do not, sir. And if I did, I shouldn't believe that the present time of confusion, with Reconstruction only half-accomplished, was the moment for it. If an amendment giving the vote to women came before the house, would you vote 'yes'?"

Douglas's aunts, their cheeks colored faintly, looked half-frightened, half-pleased at this effrontery; they watched not General Deming but Judge Ballard as the argument continued.

The General cleared his throat. "I should vote," he declaimed, "as my party caucus decided would be right, and expedient. I agree with you that this is hardly the time to take up the question of suffrage for women, while we are still in the midst of the fight for the enforcement of the Fourteenth Amendment."

"Oh, as to that," said the boy audaciously, "I don't believe in giving the nigger the vote, either."

"What!" The General leaned back in his chair and glared at his opponent with mock portentousness, like a tame bear more amused than angered by the snapping of an impudent puppy at his heels. "Your grandfather would turn over in his grave. He devoted his life to freeing the bondsman, and you, by denying the Negro the vote, would degrade him to his old position." He turned from Douglas, looked at Ludwig and John. "Can you soldiers sit there and listen to him without argument, after risking your lives in the bloodiest war in history, in order that the Negro might be set free?"

This, too, was perhaps intended for a rhetorical question, but John blurted out, "I didn't fight to set the nigger free."

"But that was the root of the matter, wasn't it?" General Deming protested, reasonably. "What did you think you were fighting for?"

"God knows."

The blunt words were uttered in too sullen a voice to have been meant for humor, but in the shocked silence that followed, Ludwig began to laugh, the deep, hearty laughter of an unconstrained man.

"What an Anglo-Saxon you are, Dock! Your tongue could be torn out before you'd confess publicly to an emotion. It would be impossible for you to say, out loud, that you loved your country. But I," he tapped his coat lapel and nodded his blond head, "I am what you would call a 'sentimental German.' I can tell you why he fought, and I, and all of us, in the western armies. Not for the niggers." Then Ludwig turned serious. He thumped the table with his fist, and all the glassware jingled. "To save the country. To stop its being torn limb from limb. To keep the flag flying over the whole of it. I'm not sure I know," he added more quietly, "what the flag meant to boys like Dock, in '61. It was their fathers' fathers', bone of their bone. Of course they fought for it. Even I, and thousands like me, from the old countries: it meant enough to us to take us into the army. I was a little fellow when we came here, eight or nine. But I can remember in Germany learning to respect the flag of America. The flag of a country where there were no princes, and a free people governed itself. We learned to hope that so might Germany be, some day. Then after '48, when my father and men like him were in danger, it was the flag of a country where he could be safe, and his children could grow up free and unafraid. Under the flag we found a home. By '61 it was my flag, my country. Do you think that I could bear to see lost that old dream of a free country governed by a free people, and the country itself torn to bits, and the flag in the dust? Of course I went to war. So too did Dock. Oh, by '61 when the war began, I knew that it was still a dream only half-fulfilled: the free country and the free people; and the struggle for its fulfillment didn't end with the war. That's why, when Dock says 'God knows,' like he did, it sounds as if he thought the war hadn't been worth fighting, when it's only that he doubts whether the country has been saved, in spite of all the bloodshed, because those of its saviors who have been governing it haven't been so very wise. But now, in a few more months," and he beamed happily at them all, around the table, "General Grant will be President. Then there will be no more 'God knows.' On that we all agree, not so? When General Grant is President, the country will be safe and at peace and united again?"

Triumphantly, his head up, he smiled at them. With gratitude, or amusement, or admiration, they looked back at him, and clapped their hands. Sally cried gaily, "Bravo, Ludwig!" and loved him for his boyishness. John's eyes twinkled at his friend; he said "Thank you, Captain Rausch, for the favorable interpretation," and admired Ludwig's artfulness, sounding so ingenuous and being in fact so tactful.

When the murmur of agreement dropped to silence, and it seemed as if the time had come for the party to push back its chairs and go, Mr. Cochran rose in his place and held his hand up, palm out, to keep the rest of them seated.

"As you know," he said, "my daughter invited you here tonight to do honor to her friends, our friends, the bride and groom, Dr. and Mrs. John

Gordon. I regret that you feel that we must not drink a toast to their happiness in the good old-fashioned way. But I am sure you all join me in the wish, at any rate." He paused for a spatter of applause, then resumed. "We had another purpose in this assembling together of my daughter's friends. Mrs. Cochran and I take great pleasure in announcing Sarah's betrothal to Captain Ludwig Rausch. As you know, Captain Rausch has purchased a business in Waynesboro and expects to make his home here. I am sure that you will unite with me in hoping that this new association will be fortunate for both him and Waynesboro, and that Captain and Mrs. Rausch will have a long and happy married life in our community."

The proper exclamations were made, the conventional reproaches: "You might have told us." But no one there could have been much surprised: the wedding had been counted on as a certainty for some time. The genuine amazement was in the response to what followed. After the exchange of some inaudible remarks between Miss Tucker and Professor Lowrey, and between him and General Deming across her plate, the Professor pushed back his chair and rose in his turn.

"We should be grateful for such good news." The dry little man had a reluctant air, as if he had been drawn into something distasteful to him. In his attempt to make the comments that would be expected of him, he overshot the mark. "It is always a pleasure to see our young people joining hands and going forth together to find their lives' happiness. Mrs. John Gordon had the honor to be the Waynesboro Woman's Club's first bride. Miss Cochran will be a close second. I take this opportunity to felicitate Captain Rausch on his good fortune. I have the honor to announce another betrothal tonight between a young lady to whom I stand, I might say—at any rate, in Waynesboro—*in loco parentis*, and a gentleman whom we all delight to honor: Miss Louisa Tucker and General Deming."

There was an instant of silence, then an outburst of congratulation; under its cover Anne and Sally dared look at each other, and by lifted brows and twisted lips express their mirth at the picture of Miss Tucker and the General as "young people joining hands and going forth together." Afterward, when all had risen from the table and they went together to Miss Tucker to wish her happiness, their faces were solemn, almost religious, in the fear that she might suspect their laughter. She accepted their friendly speeches with condescending graciousness: they need have had no fear of wounding her. Her betrothal removed her altogether from her present sphere: Washington would henceforth be her home, and what picture she presented to the eyes of two country girls, one married to a young apprentice doctor, and the other engaged to an immigrant, she would not have thought worth her conjecture.

Nevertheless, the two girls did think the prospect of her marriage delightfully comic. When everyone had gone, Dr. Alexander, Anne, and John lingered with Ludwig and the Cochrans in the drawing room. The chairs had been put back in their places, and the extra ones returned to where they belonged. The half-dozen people stood poised uncertainly before the hearth, until Mr. Cochran asked them to sit down. "We'll have the sherry out, now, and drink our toasts."

"To General Deming and his bride," Sally laughed and drew Anne down beside her on the horsehair sofa. "Hand in hand." The two of them were spent with a mirth incomprehensible to their elders.

"It seems to me most suitable," her mother reproached Sally coldly. "Of all the ladies and gentlemen you asked here tonight, General Deming and Miss Tucker appeared to me the least peculiar, the most worth cultivating."

"I never cared much for General Deming," Sally said, inconsequently, "but she will lead him a dance."

"He very nearly spoiled your party tonight," Anne's eyes danced, "but Ludwig, gallant soldier, leaped into the breach."

"Yes." John for an instant laid a hand on Ludwig's arm before he passed him to put his glass on the mantelpiece. "You saved me from saying something that might really have spoiled Sally's party. You're very skillful at distracting people's attention. You ought to go into politics."

"Politics, indeed." Sally got up from the sofa, and went to stand beside Ludwig. "He meant every word of it, didn't you?"

"I see." John smiled at her quizzically. "The essential thing in a politician is that he mustn't mean it."

"Douglas Gardiner was as bad as the General." Anne intervened because she wasn't sure how Sally would take John's teasing. "It was almost impertinent of him, I thought."

"Ah, that boy." Ludwig was interested. "Tell me about him. He is both bold and intelligent. Now he might someday be a politician."

"He's too cold," Sally said. "He could never move an audience."

"I don't agree. He's young, and he's lame. Because he's lame, he's angry at the world, and looks to avenge himself on it. No one who could be so hurt and angry is cold. He will love a woman someday and forget that he has a grudge against life."

"That poor cripple? Oh, Ludwig, I hope not."

John interrupted them to say good-night. "Don't you see what you've done to Ludwig, Sally? He wants everyone to fall in love. He'll get over it. When he's been married as long as I have, he'll be sufficiently engrossed in his own affairs to forget everyone else's."

And Sally, watching as John took Anne's shawl from her hands and bundled her into it, wondered that she could have been uneasy about Anne and the happiness of her marriage. At any rate—and she slipped her hand under Ludwig's arm and for a second, unrestrained even by the presence of her parents, her physician, and her friends, stood with her shoulder close behind his and leaned her weight against him—she felt no misgivings as to her own future and Ludwig's, if they could be together; they loved each other and there would be no shadow on that love.

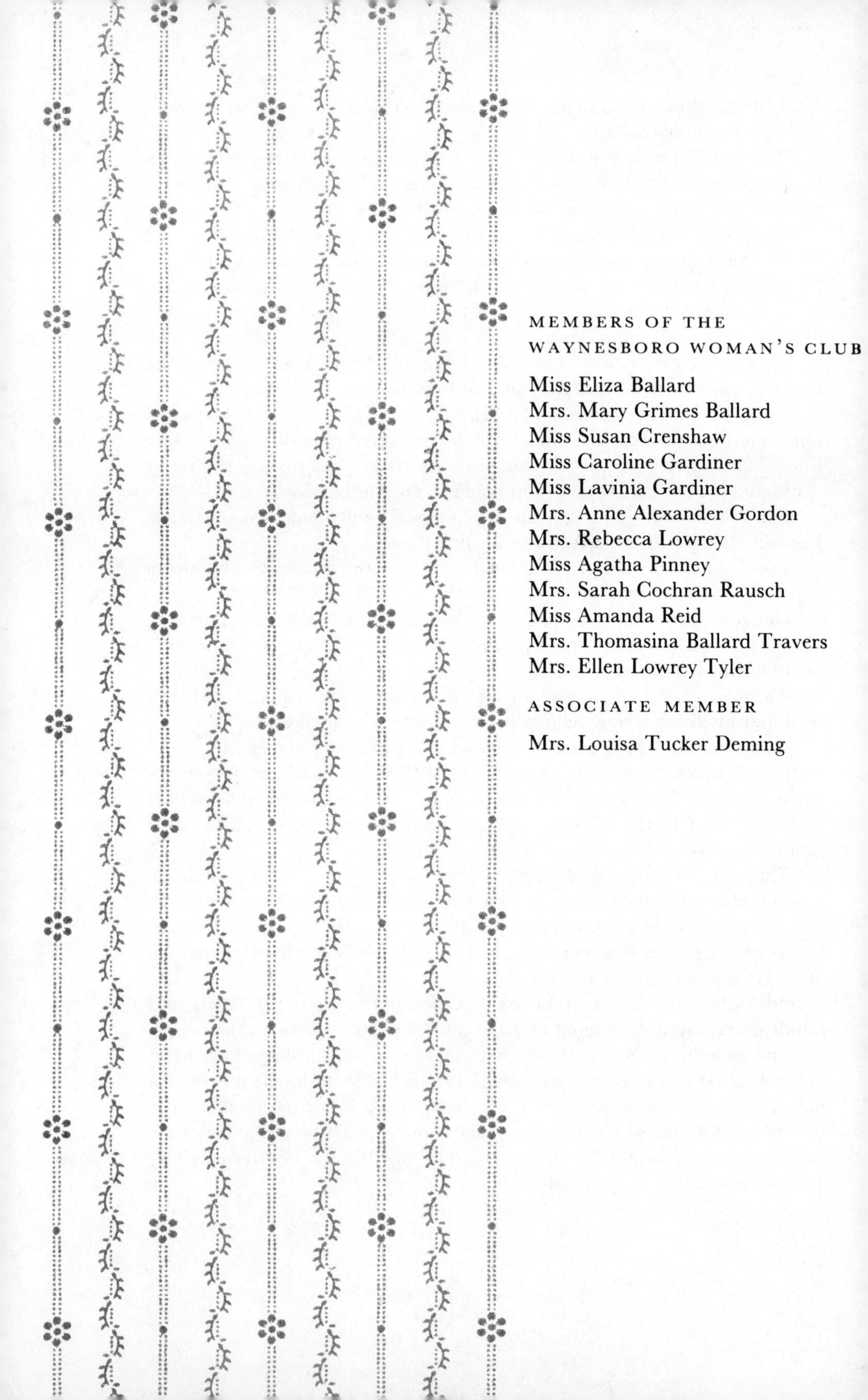

MEMBERS OF THE
WAYNESBORO WOMAN'S CLUB

Miss Eliza Ballard
Mrs. Mary Grimes Ballard
Miss Susan Crenshaw
Miss Caroline Gardiner
Miss Lavinia Gardiner
Mrs. Anne Alexander Gordon
Mrs. Rebecca Lowrey
Miss Agatha Pinney
Mrs. Sarah Cochran Rausch
Miss Amanda Reid
Mrs. Thomasina Ballard Travers
Mrs. Ellen Lowrey Tyler

ASSOCIATE MEMBER

Mrs. Louisa Tucker Deming

✻ 1869 ✻

"The first year of the Club's existence was a momentous one in the lives of several of its members."

The Woman's Club held its first meeting of the new year, 1869, on the sixth day of January, at the home of Mrs. John Gordon.

Anne had made a zealous effort to prepare for the ladies. Until now she had had no opportunity to offer the hospitality of her home; in the Club's honor (and with Martha's help), she had had the sitting room and parlor turned topsy-turvy, the windows cleaned, the furniture polished. With her own hands (not trusting Martha that far) she had carried to the kitchen her mother's treasures from the parlor whatnot—the conch shell, the millefiore paperweight, the porcelain figures, the bottle of water from the river Jordan—and with her own hands had washed and dried them. When all these had been set back on the shelves, when the rooms were spotless, when she had given her husband and her father their midday dinner and dismissed them, she was so tired that her knees ached, and her back was so stiff that she could hardly rise from her chair; but when she looked about her room, and saw Martha, with her starched white apron, in her place at the door, she was satisfied that her work was good, and that she would be recognized as a housekeeper. When the ladies came, she was able to greet them with conventional graciousness, sure that however much she felt like an actress in a new part, no one who shook hands with her could guess it.

Whether or not she had deceived them into thinking of her as one of the town's matrons, or Anne Gordon instead of Anne Alexander, she was not sure. She was not allowed to forget her status as the Club bride. When Thomasina had read her rather ecstatic paper on Tennyson, and had laid down the last page on the table beside her, she did not return to her chair, but said quickly, before her mother could take charge of the meeting, "I have a few lines which I should like to read to you, if you will bear with me. They are called 'Verses to Our Bride,' and were composed in honor of Mrs. John

Gordon." Thomasina paused to gasp for breath. Her asthma always troubled her, and the Club had grown so used to her affliction that they hardly noticed it, until now when it was aggravated by embarrassment. Anne shifted uneasily in her chair, and wished that Thomasina would sit down, and wondered what gratification the poor girl could get out of such torture. But the poetess added, "I wrote this for the party given by Miss Cochran in the bride's honor, but hadn't quite the courage to read it, with gentlemen present." Then with trembling fingers she unfolded a sheet of paper, and read.

All the ladies present listened soberly, but accepted the verses with varying judgment. The older members regarded Thomasina with the uncritical pride bestowed on a prodigy in whom one has a personal interest. Anne did not look up because she was self-conscious: she considered the sentiments expressed pretty but not applicable to John and her and the humdrum life they led. Not humdrum to themselves, of course, but no one, certainly not a poor plain creature like Thomasina Ballard, had any business making guesses about *that* side of her married life. Sally was amused by the poem, and thought it was like Thomasina to be so highfalutin, and wondered if she would take it upon herself to act as poet laureate to the Club: if she did, she would be kept fairly well occupied, for there would be two more weddings in the spring. Eliza Ballard had no use for poetry, her sister's or anyone's; and Amanda, who loved the poetess as she loved no one else there present, believed the subject sentimental, and the thoughts foolish and the language trite. After the Club had voted that the secretary should copy "To Our Bride" in the minutes, and Thomasina had shyly offered the paper to her, Amanda read the verses again and was confirmed in her opinion. If outspoken candor had not been a quality of her nature, and if, on the other hand, she had not felt for Thomasina a kind of rueful tenderness, it is probable that she would have copied the lines in the minute book without comment, and that there, though they would have been obscurely immortalized, they would have had no influence on anyone's life or the course of future events. But Amanda had hurt Thomasina's feelings, and wanted to make amends in some way. She therefore sought a wider publication for "To Our Bride," something their author would never have been so bold as to do.

Because Thomasina, wholly modest, revered and respected Amanda as much as she loved her, she was inept enough to select her for questioning in her human desire for praise. Amanda said, "You know I care most for poetry about nature, or that has some philosophical content. I never read love poetry, nor epithalamia, and I think most contemporary poetry is singularly *mindless*. You read too much of it, Thomasina: you're being corrupted by the *Keepsake* sort of thing: you should go back to your Latin for a while and wash all the pretty adjectives out of your head."

To her honest astonishment she saw Thomasina take the words as a blow—saw her head jerk, her features twitch, her eyes blink. "I'm sorry I sounded so dreadfully unappreciative," Amanda added quickly. "I suppose it is an error to hold everything to an absolute, to one's highest standards. I wasn't comparing your poem to what one of us might have written, but to Horace and Virgil." Such apologies as she could make she did, and Thomasina was grateful; but Amanda knew the wound was unhealed, and felt that she must do something, somehow, that would be curative. She bundled the minute book under her arm with an intent frowning face and went out from among the chattering ladies with only a brief good-bye to Anne.

Sally Cochran lingered in Anne's sitting room when the others all had gone. Ludwig had promised to stop for her, on his way from his rooming house to the Cochran dinner table. She did not expect him at once: he was preparing to buy his first machinery for the ropewalk, and was engrossed in specifications, descriptions, and drawings, or perhaps was entertaining some representative from one of the manufacturers who were trying to sell him the machines. Sally explained that he might be delayed, and that she and Anne would have time for a gossip; she began to rattle off a description of her trousseau: a bridal gown from Shillito's in Cincinnati, fifteen yards in the skirt pattern ("Ludwig says how can he get close enough to put a ring on my finger?"), Chantilly lace sacque, Lyons velvet cloak, while llama shawl, fur jacket. The wedding cake was being sent up by Ludwig's uncle: he had got some Bavarian friend of his to bake it, and it would be a masterpiece in three tiers, with arches and columns, bridal couples, cupids and roses, all done in icing.

Sally was to be married in church; her only regret was that it couldn't have been some other church than her parents'. She said, "I wish we were Presbyterians, too. Mamma sets so much store on what is genteel, and elegant—wouldn't you think she'd see there's nothing elegant about that poky, unfashionable little Baptist church? But Papa's its mainstay—maybe he likes knowing it couldn't get along without him."

Anne was shocked. She said severely, "You ought to be ashamed, if that's all you care for your religion." She could no more conceive of being disloyal to her church than to her country.

Sally laughed at her. "Oh, what do denominations matter?" She considered Anne's habit of piety, of reading a Chapter every night before she went to bed, of saying her prayers, of never speaking lightly of her church—one of her childish traits, sometimes endearing, sometimes provoking. "So long as it's Protestant, one's like another, isn't it?"

Anne did not undertake to enlighten her, but said, "Maybe it's just as well you feel like that. Ludwig might want you to go to his church."

Sally looked taken aback, almost frightened. "I don't know if he's a church member or not. I guess it won't matter to him." But she decided to find out, when he came and she had him alone.

It was dark when he rang the bell and she went out to join him. The street lamps were not yet lighted, but the snow on the ground made it possible to see. There was a lantern in the vestibule of the Presbyterian church, at the

Main Street end of the block. The church door was open, and as they approached it they saw the janitor on the step, silhouetted against the light, broom in his hand. Sally called attention to his labors.

"Getting ready for prayer meeting." Then she continued, as if the sight of the church had brought it to her mind. "That's Anne's church, and John's too, though he doesn't go. Ludwig, when we're married, would you like me to go to your church?" Her hand was under his elbow: she walked close to him, and spoke meekly.

"My church?" he repeated blankly. "I have no church."

"Aren't you a Lutheran?" Sally hardly dared admit her relief. The Baptist church was bad enough.

"My mother is, and devout. But my father, like all the Revolutionaries, is a freethinker, and he taught me—would it distress you very much"—he looked sideways, apprehensively, at the profile so close to his shoulder yet so impossible to read in the dark—"if I'm something of a freethinker, too?"

"No, I'm not distressed. So long as you don't mind if I still attend my church." Her smile, which he couldn't see, was sweet and submissive, but her sigh, which he heard, was so patently one of relief that after a moment he began to laugh.

"Ach, Sally, what a fraud! You were afraid you would be expected to turn Lutheran and perhaps sit in the same pew with the Hoffmann girls and work at church festivals with Mrs. Klein."

"Don't be horrid. I wasn't really. I know they're good respectable people, in spite of the beer parlor and the butcher shops and the market gardens; but I should feel so strange. I've always been a Baptist." She committed herself definitely to an unfashionable church, but there were worse possibilities. "And it would mix things up so. The Ballards are friends of ours, and they're trying to put the Hoffmanns out of business."

"You don't expect me to like that?"

"No. And if Papa serves wine at home, why should I say the Hoffmanns shouldn't serve beer?"

"Are you a good Baptist?" His tone was grave, but his lip twitched. "I thought they neither drank, played cards, nor danced."

"Any church is what its congregation makes it," Sally said carelessly. "Look at Waynesboro. The Presbyterians and Reformed Presbyterians say the same Catechism, I guess, and believe the same about foreordination and—and all that, but they're at opposite poles. The Reformed Presbyterians haven't moved a step from the Scotch Covenanters, and the Presbyterian is the most liberal church in town, with the gayest members. As for the Baptists, Papa practically pays the minister's salary, so they don't criticize us. Then there's the Methodists; they don't shout and sing so much, here, because the Ballards aren't shouters, but it's the reformingest church in this town." Then, reminded by her reference to the Ballards of the meeting she had attended that afternoon, she began to describe it to him. "Thomasina Ballard read a poem in Anne's honor. I thought it was right pretty—I know I couldn't have written it. But Amanda Reid looked like she'd taken a dose of quinine, and she's one of those people that must tell the truth though the heavens fall, so I expect Thomasina's feelings were hurt."

But if Sally accused Amanda in her own mind or to Ludwig of being callous to injured feelings, she was wrong. Amanda, having injured her only friend, had already planned what recompense she could make. That same night, after she had copied "To Our Bride" in the minute book, she wrote it out again on a sheet of foolscap paper, headed by the underscored title "To a Bride," and on Thursday took it with her when she went to the College for her first class. After school that afternoon she stopped at the office of the *Waynesboro Torchlight.*

The *Torchlight* was published in a ramshackle two-story frame building across the street from the public square, whence, as those were accustomed to say who were inclined to be cynical about local politics, an eye could be kept on the main door of the Court House. Mr. William Bonner, owner and editor of the *Torchlight*, was a rather formidable character, and it was unlikely that anyone would approach the Court House for a nefarious purpose in full view of his window. Of course, there were other entrances, around the corner and out of sight of Mr. Bonner, but it was remarkable how much he contrived to know.

In 1861 Mr. Bonner had enlisted, with the other young men of the town. He was taken captive at Chickamauga, and had not been freed until the end of the war. After his release he was famous for a while as the only soldier of the Union Army who had survived more than a year's imprisonment in Andersonville. He had returned to Waynesboro on his discharge, and the town was shocked and horrified at what the years in prison had done to him. He was a man built on a generous scale, big-boned and tall; he had gone into the army weighing well over two hundred pounds, and had returned to his home a skeleton beneath a leathery livid skin. He had "lived on his fat," the town said, and feasted him with genuine patriotic ardor. He did not regain much of the lost flesh; he was still gaunt and emaciated. And it was not only the fat of his body that had been burned away by those years; other superfluities had been fined away from his mind. He was down to the bare truth, naked and unadorned, without illusion and without hope. Hope, that is, for his country and mankind; it was beyond knowledge what his views of and for himself were. He had at least had confidence enough to have fathered two more children in addition to the two born before the war, and was certainly making and putting by money in substantial amounts. He had bought the *Torchlight* with the soldier's pay that had accrued to him during his captivity; it was then a feeble bankrupt little sheet unable in a literate community to compete with the *Cincinnati Commercial* and the *New York Tribune*. Four years later the *Torchlight* was flung daily on the porch of practically every house in town, and a weekly edition was mailed to every farm in Shawnee County. Often there was nothing much in it, but one never knew when there might be. Mr. Bonner conducted the paper with no respect for his community's prejudices and with a bitter regard for what seemed to him the truth. He was in favor of Negro suffrage, and of the punitive policies toward the South of the Radical Republicans; such views were explained by his experiences. He was against woman suffrage, temperance, foreign missions, and the churches; such vagaries were considered by his readers mere perversity, and were passed over lightly. His columns of local news induced everyone to subscribe to his paper and made half of his subscribers afraid to open it. What he knew he told. He employed no euphemisms: in his column of court news, when men beat their wives or died in drunken brawls or committed suicide, he printed the information; he scorned to resort to innuendo when divorce or other cases involving women reached the court; he dealt with corruption and venality in Waynesboro in the brutal, heavyhanded, and sometimes effective way of his contemporary *Harper's Weekly*, although he had no Nast on his limited staff. In one matter he subscribed to the country-newspaper fashion of the time: he printed a poem every day on his editorial page.

In the summer of 1868 he had bought a cylinder press for the paper and had installed it on the ground floor of the *Torchlight* building, where it clattered and banged and shook the walls and made it impossible for anyone to hear. Amanda, poem in hand, had gone into the pressroom in her ignorance, and had been bewildered by the noise and the sight of men in inky overalls where she had expected to find Mr. Bonner. She backed out breathlessly, and then—too late to prevent her making a fool of herself, she thought, scornfully—she saw a narrow doorway with a signboard nailed to its frame that read "Editorial offices" above a pointing hand. She followed the finger up a flight of dirty stairs so narrow that she had to squeeze her skirts out of shape to save them from brushing the wall; at the top she drew a deep breath and plunged without knocking through the first door she saw. Two youths were standing stoop-shouldered at two high desks; the nearest one stared at her insolently, and spat into the cuspidor just behind the railing where she stood. Amanda's square chin went up; her brows drew together.

"I should like to see Mr. Bonner."

"Tell me," he grinned at her. "I'll see it gets in the paper."

But the farther youth leaned from his desk to open a door beside him; he said, "Bill, lady to see you," and motioned Amanda to pass through the gate in the railing and into the inner room.

She had climbed the stairs in some trepidation, but the rudeness she had encountered made her angry and therefore less timid; she went into Mr. Bonner's office with her face stern, her shoulders back.

He sat facing the door, his feet on the desk; he had no doubt questioned the "lady." When she entered, he lifted his feet, then slowly and rather lazily gathered himself together and stood up. He said "Good afternoon," and "What can I do for you?"

Amanda wasted no breath on preliminaries. "You print a poem every day on your editorial page. Would you use a poem by a Waynesboro person if it seemed to you good enough?"

"Perhaps." He smiled briefly. "Let me see: you're Amanda Reid, aren't you? And you had the courage to go through Oberlin and take a degree? I congratulate you." He held out an inky hand, which perforce she took, although reluctantly. She had come on business with the editor of the *Torchlight*, not as Amanda Reid to call on Mr. Bonner the atheist. He continued. "And now you're writing poetry? May I see your work?"

As she took out the sheet of paper and gave it to him, she explained that it was not hers. He read the verses through at a glance, laughed a little, scratched his fingers in his short rough beard, and said, "Do you think this is good poetry?"

She shook her head. "No. And I told her so. She was hurt. That is why I am doing this: because its publication might restore her self-esteem. But I don't think the poems you publish are good, either. This is just like them."

"You are honest, Miss Reid. They aren't good. It's my one concession to the town's taste: so many lines of pap a day. Who wrote this? I must know, if I'm to print it."

When she told him, he whistled through his teeth and looked at her oddly, mischievously. She remembered then, for the first time, all the *Pro Bono Publico* letters Mrs. Ballard had written to the *Torchlight*, from time to time, on the subject of temperance and woman suffrage, and the answer by him, signed "Ed.", that had been printed in the paper. It would seem a kind of joke, to him, to publish Thomasina's poem; but Amanda didn't care, for to Thomasina he wouldn't be a person at all, but an *editor*.

"I'll print it, Miss Reid, if I have the poet's permission. I will get into communication with her."

In due time "To a Bride" appeared on the editorial page of the *Torchlight*, in the poet's corner, signed modestly "TB." Thomasina pretended to be indifferent, but was in fact transparently delighted. Amanda had gone to her at once that same afternoon to confess what she had done. "I was afraid I didn't know enough about poetry to criticize it," she said, "so I took it to an editor. That's the only way to find out what a poem's worth." Thomasina was more than satisfied: she was touched and grateful; she would never have been bold enough to do so herself. Her family's reception of the printed verses was a little chilling, but after all, they had done so many important things that one little poem in a country newspaper couldn't seem of moment to them: Thomasina told herself that she must keep a sense of proportion. She mustn't let other people—members of the Club, old school friends and teachers, even comparative strangers—flatter her by seeming impressed: it was nothing, really. She was quite stern with herself, saying in her mind "It is nothing," until she could receive the congratulations of acquaintances without turning awkward and flushing to the tip of her nose. By Sunday she had almost conquered her self-consciousness, until she was thrown into confusion by Mr. Samuel Travers.

Mr. Travers was the organist of the Methodist church. Sunday after Sunday the Ballards had sat in the congregation, so far to one side that the only view they had of the organist was of his back, and his face in the mirror that hung over his keyboard. Thomasina knew no more of him than that he was youngish, round-faced, brown-haired, that he played acceptably and that he had come to Waynesboro to earn his living by giving music lessons. She was amazed when he came panting up the aisle after church, while her father was still talking to the pastor. But instead of voicing his congratulations, he touched her elbow, shyly, and said, "Come into the Sunday school room a minute, will you? I want to speak to you."

She followed him, blushing and stumbling, into the barrack-like room beside the auditorium, where the chairs were grouped in knots or scattered in crooked rows. They stopped inside the door.

"I beg your pardon, Miss Ballard—I—I'm afraid I've been presumptuous. But I did hope for a chance to speak to you."

He looked like a scolded boy, Thomasina thought; his mouse-colored hair was so untidy, his round cheeks so pink, his eyes so appealing. She smiled, and he went on, "I scarcely know you, and the compliments of anyone as unimportant as I can't mean much. But I wanted to say how much I liked your little verses. And I thought maybe," he added precipitately, "if you don't like the idea you can say 'no,' you'd give me permission to set them to music."

"Oh, I didn't know you were a composer." Thomasina was ashamed of the condescension she had felt: she looked at him with a dawning respect.

"I fear I'm not. I've only composed a few songs, so far. It's an ambition of mine. I don't mind admitting it to you, a fellow artist; but I keep it quiet for fear of being laughed at, and I must earn my living. Who would send children to a music teacher who was the town joke? But your verses *sing* themselves in my mind: I think I could set them to music, if you would permit it."

"It's an honor to be asked. Of course you may. When you've finished it," and the blood came hotly to her face and made it an ugly mottled color, "you must promise to come and play it for me."

"Thank you. I'm complimented to be asked." He bowed over her hand and stood aside for her to rejoin her family.

Thomasina told them, once they were all in the carriage and on their way home, the substance of her conversation with Mr. Travers. The Judge said nothing, but looked at his daughter with something in his eyes dreadfully like pity. Mrs. Ballard said, "How very flattering," almost as remotely as if Thomasina were no relation to her. Eliza was contemptuous.

"That little imitation of a man! You *asked* him to call? No man worth his salt ever spent his life at the piano."

"For all you know, he may be another Beethoven." Indifferently

Thomasina had watched Mr. Travers play the organ, Sunday after Sunday; now she was stung to his defense.

"The world doesn't need another Beethoven just now. What it needs—"

Her father said mildly, "A Beethoven wouldn't come amiss in any century, Eliza. Don't be extravagant."

But Eliza returned to the attack later, when the sisters were in their bedrooms with the door open between them. "Can't you see the man's a *nobody?* What he wants is to scrape acquaintance with you, and worm his way into Waynesboro society."

"Then he chose the wrong person. No one in town goes fewer places, or knows fewer people, or has less fun."

"He may not know that. Besides, I didn't suppose that you aspired to get *fun* out of life."

"I don't. And I don't think Mr. Travers does, either: I believe he cares for music and poetry. Oh, I know my poetry isn't good, Eliza, but maybe it's better than you think, because you don't like poetry."

"I think it's silly, like some people I know."

But whether Eliza and her mother thought her silly or not, Thomasina received Mr. Travers warmly when he came. He brought his composition with him. They spent a long evening at the piano in the big music room over the sitting room and the Judge's study. He played the tune he had composed, and sang it for her, and then they sang it together. In Thomasina's ears her limping verses had taken on new life: they seemed no longer hers; she could sing them without self-consciousness. She was so delighted that she told Mr. Travers "yes" when he asked if she hadn't other poems hidden away in her desk. She went to her room for her notebook, and let him take it away, to select what he could use for other songs.

Mr. Travers could write a tune in a week or ten days. As the spring progressed, his visits at the Ballards' assumed regularity. In Thomasina's eyes he became a modern representative of the troubadours. She could no longer sit in church and watch with impersonal vagueness while he played the organ. To the contempt of her sister, the disapprobation of her mother, the uneasiness of her father, she was indifferent or blind to them all. Her parents refrained from comment: they did not conceal their feelings, but neither did they express them.

Eliza thought Thomasina fatuous and trivial, all too ready at the first slight temptation to yield her life's more serious purposes; and shaken by Thomasina's indifference to her opinion, she was stung into making more and more outrageous remarks, and even, finally, into making them to other people if Thomasina was within earshot. After a Club meeting, late in February, when Sally's wedding invitations, just delivered, were the chief topic of acclaim, Eliza, with Thomasina's elbow in her hand, paused as the ladies crossed Mrs. Lowrey's doorstep to depart and scatter, and said to Sally, "It's as well you didn't wait any longer, or you mightn't have had the pleasure of being the Club's second bride." Thomasina's exclamation of distaste might have made the hint clear, but Sally thought the remark referred to Miss Tucker's approaching nuptials and paid no heed. It was not until some months after Sally and Ludwig were married that Thomasina's affair became generally known and she the object of sympathetic or derisive attention.

Sally's wedding in March crowded the small old-fashioned Baptist church to the doors; the most modish bonnets in Waynesboro rose above the partitions of the box pews, and their wearers stared with almost as much curiosity at the whitewashed walls, the pulpit, and the baptistery with its casket-sized font, as they did at the bridal procession. Sally wore the fifteen-yard wedding gown, with a train that swept the aisle from pew to pew, a lace veil, and orange blossoms; but Ludwig was not flurried by her splendor, and had no difficulty in slipping the ring on her finger. Minna Rausch, awed to a state of stupefaction, was the bridesmaid. Ludwig's parents came to Waynesboro and stayed at the Cochrans'; his uncle and aunt and innumerable cousins were there from Cincinnati. After the lavish and elegant wedding reception, Sally and Ludwig took the train for Chicago; they spent a week there, and then went on to Burlington for another week with the Rausches.

By the first of April they were home, and had set up housekeeping in the smallish house at the foot of the Linden Street hill, which Mr. Cochran had bought for them as a wedding present. It was understood that in time the Cochran house would be theirs, since Sally was an only child, and that eventually they would be under obligation to move in with Sally's parents when they had grown so old as to need them. In the meantime Sally and Ludwig could be independent in the Linden Street house, and perhaps might be granted years enough to bring up there the children they expected to have. Sally hired a young Negro girl to help with the housework, and herself set about learning to cook.

Ludwig had determined to start mechanizing his mill; he would not appeal to his father-in-law, but by borrowing enough from a Cincinnati bank, and adding it to what he had accumulated, he could buy a few machines, put up a building for housing them, and another for offices. Business was good in the spring of 1869, after General Grant's inauguration. The new President's choice of cabinet members had not met with universal approval; but the important posts were in capable hands, and citizens of the state of Ohio had been gratified by the appointment of their onetime Governor, the former General Cox, to be Secretary of the Interior. The first act of the new Congress had been the passage of a bill pledging the government to pay off its five twenty-six percent bonds in gold rather than in greenbacks: this evidence of a sound money policy on the part of the new administration set the wheels of industry flying. Ludwig had no fears of being unable to repay his bank loan.

By May the new buildings for Rausch Cordage Company were well under way. First completed was the office building: a one-story two-room brick cube, just beyond the canal bridge, facing Chillicothe Street. The foundation stones lifted it a few feet above the ground; a couple of granite steps with iron handrails led to a door under the gold-lettered sign. Inside a small vestibule opened on the left to Ludwig's office, which had also a side door to the cobbled mill yard, and another, on the right, to a room for a bookkeeper and whatever other clerical staff might come to be needed. As soon as the plaster dried, Ludwig installed in his office a flat desk and revolving chair, and a cabinet for his files: he moved all the papers that had piled up in his cubby hole at the end of the ropewalk and took possession.

As spring advanced, it became evident that Waynesboro's small boys, fishing in the river or swimming in the canal, felt free to include the mill yard as a part of their playground, racing back and forth across it and generally making nuisances of themselves. Ludwig in self-defense had an eight-foot-high, solid board fence put around three sides of his property: past the canal to the office corner around to the canal again and to the ramp; it was interrupted only by the wide double gate, a few yards from its beginning, that gave access to yard and building, and by a second at the top of the canal ramp. Happily for the boys, the posts could not be set solidly in sand or mud: the fence was put far enough back from both river and canal bank to leave room for their aquatic sports. As it turned out, the gates were generally left open, the one on Chillicothe Street for wagons and workers coming and going, the other for loading or unloading barges; by canal was still the cheapest way to move freight.

The new mill building was going up beyond the hemp house, a brick two-story structure as unadorned as a shoe box except for the two rows of windows on both long sides. In time, Ludwig hoped, the second floor would be needed for additional preparation machinery; in the meantime it would serve as a warehouse and only the first floor used for the preparation machinery. He was following what seemed to him a logical plan. Until he could buy the new machines for spinning hemp and forming strands and laying rope, those processes could be carried on in the old ropewalk as they always had been. Getting the hemp ready for spinning was a long process and a slow one when hand labor was used; the new machines would be faster. A small steam power plant would keep the machinery moving by means of transmission ropes. It was not in the beginning an efficient layout, since the prepared fiber had to be taken all the way across the yard to the spinners; but boys with wheelbarrows could do that, and someday another building, along the river-side of the mill and at right angle to the first one, would house the rope-making machines Ludwig could not afford to buy now.

When all was finished that could be finished, when the machinery could be put in motion by a newly hired mechanic, Ludwig declared a holiday for the spinners, and a day of celebration for all concerned, from bricklayers to Mr. Cochran and Sally, who had been hearing so much about rope that she insisted on seeing Ludwig's achievement with her own eyes. On the eventful morning the yard was crowded with visitors as well as laborers: when the steam whistle was sounded, running up the scale and down again, the wheel boys burst into a cheer that all joined in. The Rausch Cordage Company, Rope and Twine, was on its way.

The first brief session of the newly elected Congress had ended in March of 1869, before Ludwig's great day. General Deming, when he came home from Washington, had the satisfied bearing of one who has shared in a creditable performance. His fellow townsmen were glad to give him their approval when he appeared in public: only Mr. Bonner watched cynically from the window of the *Torchlight* office, and put a paragraph in the paper about the approaching marriage of the lovely and learned Miss Tucker to the ex-Brigadier and present Representative, "now at the summit of his career." The General had no great ambitions, he told his betrothed, but no one liked being informed that he had got as far as he could go, although he supposed the fellow'd meant to be complimentary.

The marriage could not take place until after the end of the school year. It was celebrated on Commencement afternoon, on the College lawn, "where they had first met." The invitation to be married at the College pleased the General; his vanity was flattered by the obvious reluctance of the Lowreys to lose their teacher, and by the gloom of Kitty Lowrey, who looked at him with hatred in her eyes. He felt like the hero of a romance: he had won for his wife a lady used to the adoration of old and young yet willing to accept in its stead his isolated devotion. He was but slightly dashed by the extreme matter-of-factness of the parting, after his wedding, of Mrs. Lowrey and the bride: flustered questions, "What shall I do about having the chimneys swept?"; and solemn admonitions: "Don't let the dormitory cook rob the kitchen"; "Don't let your grandchildren turn the schoolrooms topsy-turvy."

The wedding was witnessed and the wedding supper eaten by an even larger company than had seen the Rausches married: the College pupils were there, and the General's most prominent allies and supporters from the whole Seventh District. All members of the Woman's Club were present, except Anne Gordon.

Anne was "not going out" that summer. She was sorry to miss such an outstanding festivity as the Tucker-Deming wedding, but she was well pleased to be "in a family way," and having a baby was worth withdrawing from the world for a season. There was enough to do at home to keep her busy, she told John, and she amused him by the sentimental fervor with which she set about restoring her mother's garden. She dug the grass roots out of the flower beds, and nursed the columbines and garden heliotrope and purple flags back to their ancient vigor. She had Jonah, the Negro stable hand and handyman, prune back the rose that grew on the trellis at the end of the porch, and was rewarded by its abundant blooms in early summer. She put a red bud in John's buttonhole every morning, when he was ready to go out the front door, black bag in hand, to the horse and buggy brought around to the hitching post by Jonah.

On the morning after the Tucker-Deming wedding, she lingered in the side yard to cut roses for the dining room, thinking as she worked that Sally would be along in a little while to tell her about it. She heard the huckster down the street calling "Fresh rhubarb," and she gathered up the roses and went into the house for her purse. She couldn't very well do her marketing uptown now; besides, the huckster, a German youth named Fritz Klein, was a favorite with Anne. She had been one of his earliest patrons, and he was grateful. He had come to Waynesboro with his family a year before; his father had rented a farm on the edge of town, and Fritz sold from house to house the garden truck the other Kleins had raised.

Anne went out to the curbstone when the lazy rawboned horse stopped there. Fritz jumped down from his seat; together they picked out the best strawberries and asparagus; when she had paid him he did not at once return to his place on the wagon, but stopped instead to talk, with wide exuberant gestures on his soil-stained hands. She stood to listen, nodding and smiling in friendly fashion.

"I haf news for my customers, I hope you vill say 'Glück auf!'" His face was round and radiant, high-colored; his eyes shone. "I haf already yet in zis new country a bride chosen—Frederica Hoffmann." He paused for her congratulations, then resumed, "Und iss zat not all. Soon I vill grocery haf, und no more go round, so, mit a horse und vagon." He lifted a hand to dismiss the patient horse sleeping between the shafts. "Ya," he insisted, delighted as a child by the amazement she had simulated for his pleasure. "I haf a store rented, by Chillicosee Street. Not far from ze Herr Doctor's office. Und zere vill die gnädige Frau come und buy mein Vater's sparrowgrass und berries. Some day," he puffed out his chest and tapped it, "vill I a sign mit goldt letters haf, und vill caviar sell, und anchovies und pickled herring und oysters. Aber nun I must mit Klein's fresh fechtaples start, und flour und cornmeal und potatoes und molasses, all vass folk most need. You vill by my store come buy, nicht wahr? Die Frau Doktorin iss my best customer. Aber nein, natürlich, die Frau goes not now on ze street. I vill to you come, und fresh fechtaples bring."

Anne blushed at his unembarrassed reference to her condition, but accepted his offer gratefully. "By the time I see your store, you'll be selling caviar, I expect. I hope you and Frederica will be happy. Where are you going to live?"

"Ve start poor, like in ze store. Ve go to housekeeping in ze rooms ofer it."

When Fritz had bowed his goodbye, Anne turned away with a lighthearted feeling: it was good to be alive in a June world where the humblest were happy and full of hope. Fritz was honest and a hard worker; he would be rich some day. And Frederica was a pretty girl, and now she could forget her brother's beer parlor, where she had been helping.

Anne had closed the gate behind her, and Fritz had drawn away across the street, when his place at the curb was taken by another horse and a buggy. Anne looked over her shoulder. Kate Gordon. She put her armful of vegetables down on the step, and returned to the gate. Beside Kate, sitting so far back that her face was in the shadow of the buggy's hood, there was a girl; only her skirt was in the sun, a bright print spread over hoops that crowded Kate's sharp knees against the whip-socket. This was the girl, then, Anne thought; John had said something, and had sounded cross and brotherish when he said it, about a neighbor's daughter living with Kate, helping with the housework.

Anne waited inside the fence, but Kate made no move to get down. She called "Howdy," and sat still.

"I'm glad to see you. Aren't you coming in?"

"Haven't time this morning." Kate's face was taut and did not relax; her tone was brusque. "Come here a minute, will you?"

Anne opened the gate and went out again, willingly enough, but when she saw how Kate's eyes widened almost as if with horror at the sight of her ungainly body, her face burned, and she said "What is it?" almost resentfully.

"Is John home? I stopped at his office, but he wasn't there."

"Home at this hour? No, he's making his calls. Did you want to see him professionally? He'll be in his office this afternoon."

"Not for myself." Kate's lip curled contemptuously. "I'm never ailing. For Esther. Do you know Esther Jacobs?" Anne nodded to the girl, who shrank farther into the corner. "She has a cough I don't like. But I can't waste a whole day in town. Ask John, will you, to stop in the next time he comes past the farm?"

Hardly waiting for Anne's promise, she lifted the reins, and slapped them on the horse's back. Anne, watching the buggy down the street, supposed John would be provoked: Kate had that effect on him, but he would go out to see her that afternoon. The effect Kate had on her was different, for some reason more oppressive: she made the sun seem dimmer.

Anne started for the house again, but stopped once more because she saw Sally coming in Linden Street. She waved her hand and waited. Sally crossed Market Street on a long diagonal that brought her to the hitching post; she stamped the dust from her slippers, opened the gate, and took Anne's arm.

"How are you? Who was that driving away? Kate Gordon? She's odd, isn't she—but I suppose she doesn't bother you much."

The two young matrons went into the house together. Sally stopped in the sitting room; Anne went to the kitchen, turned flowers and vegetables over to Martha, and returned.

"You go on with what you were going to do. I just came to tell you about the wedding."

"I'm sewing." She picked up her sewing basket from the table. "By hand. John thinks I shouldn't use the machine now. I'm obliged to you for coming: I hated to miss it."

"I'll hem one of those for you. Aren't men geese! The sewing machine, indeed! And you needn't be obliged to me, because I depend on you to do as much for me when I get in the same pickle." Sally grimaced as she stripped off her gloves and picked up a diaper.

Her account of the wedding was circumstantial and vivid. She concluded it by sending the bridal couple off to New England on their wedding journey, and then added, "Do you suppose they'll be here much? I heard her say they expected to make their home in Washington."

"Surely he won't sell his house. He won't be Representative forever. I wonder if she'll resign from the Club."

"And if she does, who we'll ask in her place. Listen, Anne: did you ever hear that Thomasina has been going with that young Mr. Travers who plays the organ at their church?"

"I remember he set that poem of hers to music. Why?" Anne looked up from her sewing, eager-eyed. She rather liked Thomasina, but one couldn't always refuse to laugh at one's friends.

"Eliza said something yesterday, at the wedding. She can be cruel, don't you think? But Thomasina didn't hear her, so it didn't matter. Mrs. Lowrey made a joke about an epidemic of weddings in the Club, and wondered if this would be the last, and Eliza said, short and sharp, 'When there's an infection in the air, Thomasina's sure to catch it, whether it's measles or love.'"

For a minute they were silent; then Anne said, "D'you suppose she'd marry him, a penniless music teacher no one knows anything about? Of course, he may not be penniless, but if he isn't, would he be here giving children music lessons? And what future is there for him here? Maybe that's why he wants Thomasina. I'll ask John what he knows: he hears everything, but you have to ask or he won't tell."

As she spoke, she anticipated the noon meal and a gossip with John and her father over the coffee cups. But after Sally had gone home, a country boy brought a message to the door: John had been called to a lying-in case half-a-dozen miles from town, and couldn't get home for dinner, probably not even for supper. Dr. Alexander came in at noon, ate, and went back to his office; he returned from his late afternoon round of calls for supper with Anne, and then crossed the back yards again to his office. Anne, when he had left her, took her knitting out to the little square porch between dining and sitting room. When dusk deepened in her corner, she folded her hands over the long needles and the afghan she was making and gave herself up to enjoyment of the quiet June night and to vagrant thoughts of the time when the voice of her child would be sounding among those who were playing games in the street. She had forgotten the things she had planned to tell John, and ask him, before he finally came home. It was nine o'clock when she heard him come in the kitchen door; he called, and when she answered he came to the porch, passed her chair with a hand on her shoulder, sat down on the top step, and took out his pipe. She would have risen, with a murmur about supper, but he stopped her.

"I ate at the Crawfords'. The baby was born at six. We were more than ready for supper when Mrs. Crawford's mother finally got it served up. I made a few calls after that or I wouldn't have been so late."

"It was long. Did she have a bad time?"

"Nothing out of the way. It was her first, and took longer. Your father looked in on us once, and went away again. He wouldn't have left me in charge if she hadn't been coming along all right. Lord, I'm tired, though." He added the last with a groan, but Anne would not be diverted from the suggestion that, casual as it had sounded, had rather startled her.

"What do you mean?" she asked him, sharply. "Doesn't he trust you with bad cases?"

"All ready to take him to task on my account, aren't you?" He chuckled. "You needn't. He's protecting me. He turns simple afflictions over to me, and keeps the cases he knows will be fatal. He doesn't say so, of course, but it's for the sake of my reputation. I'm to be the doctor who never lost a case."

"That's hard on him, isn't it?" Anne was mollified and rather relieved, yet at the same time shocked, to discover that she had more faith in her father as a physician than in John.

"Not particularly. People feel safer in his hands, and if they're turned over to me, they know there's nothing much the matter. Sometimes, though, I wish—there's one case I'm troubled about. You know medical knowledge does advance, and I went to medical school years after he had started to practice. It used to be believed that it helped a woman with phthisis to have a child; now we know it's fatal."

Anne's mind catalogued, hastily, the young women whom she knew to be her father's patients. "Flora Allen?" she asked.

"You know, then?"

"I know the Allens because they come to our church. I know she's got consumption, and is promised to the Wilkinson boy. You think she oughtn't to marry him?"

"I know she oughtn't, but your father is urging it. He says she'll die anyway, but if she marries and has a child, it may make her better for a while. I say pregnancy would be fatal and she needn't die, if she had nothing to do or worry about, and plenty to eat, and stayed outdoors day and night, summer and winter."

"And Papa won't let you try it?"

"No. He says if I encouraged them to hope and she died, I should be a long time living it down. He means well, but I've got to stand by and see that girl lose her only chance."

"If you can't do anything, it isn't your responsibility. Why don't you and Papa tell the Allens and the Wilkinson boy what you think, and let them decide?" They would do what her father said, Anne thought, but John wouldn't worry if he'd given the girl her chance. But he laughed at her.

"And you a doctor's daughter! You should realize that we must seem to know what we're doing, even when we don't. If we lose the faith of our patients, the battle's lost."

"Maybe they'd have more faith if they knew you were telling the truth."

"The first time they saw us look dubious they would call in someone else. Don't worry, it *is* my responsibility: but I'll try talking to your father again." He sighed and changed the subject, and they chatted indifferently for a while before he rose to go to bed. She got up, too, and waited while he emptied the ashes from his pipe on the roots of the honeysuckle, and they went into the house together. Their bedroom had once been her parents'; the front windows overlooked the street, the porch roof, and a strip of yard. One door led from the hall, another opened on the upstairs porch over the one where they had been sitting. Because it was hot on the second floor, John set this door wide open. A chance breeze drifted through, fluttered the curtains, and carried with it the fragrance of the June night. John, quickly in bed, not so sleepy as he was tired, lay on his back while Anne brushed her hair and then, her elbows propped on the chest of drawers, read her evening psalm in the circle of light from the coal-oil lamp. He watched her, and, through the open door, the moonlight on the porch floor, making a pattern in shadow of the railing and the honeysuckle leaves, and slanting in across the doorsill to light a square patch of the bedroom matting.

When Anne finally came to lie beside him, he said, "It smells sweet tonight. What is it?"

She sniffed, delicately. "Essence of moonlight, I expect."

"Ridiculous," he said fondly, and took her arm in his hand. She lay on her back, knees up, laughing at him. Her hair was in two long braids over her shoulders. In her long-sleeved, high-necked nightgown, with its fluted ruffles around her wrists and neck, and with the tent of the sheet concealing her misshapen body, she looked like a teasing sleepy child.

"Tell me," he insisted. "what it is that smells so sweet?"

"Honeysuckle, mostly, on the porch out there. White petunias in the bed by the dining room windows. And white clover in the grass, because Jonah hasn't mowed the lawn this week, and the hundred-leaf roses by the fence. But I'm not sure," she added prosaically, "that you can smell the roses up here. But there are lots of them. I gave Sally a bunch, when she was here, to take home. She came around to tell me about the wedding."

"So the General's hitched. I don't know Mrs. General at all, but from her manner I'd expect her to lead him by the nose. He's all bluster and no backbone."

"I know. She's a perfect lady, New England style, but when she's displeased, it's like having an icicle down your back."

"Sally say the wedding was very elegant?" John yawned, and locked his fingers together under his head. He wasn't particularly interested.

"I guess so. Kate was here too, this morning. I forgot to tell you."

"Kate? What'd she want?" His hands came down, and he propped himself on an elbow.

It was funny, Anne thought, that the mention of Kate should be so startling. What had she ever done, after all, that he should always be on edge about her? "She brought that girl in to see you—the one that lives with her. And she hasn't time to come again, so will you please stop at the farm? The girl has a cough."

"Oh, Lord," John groaned. "Again?"

"'Again'? Has she been sick before?"

"Another girl, I mean. Kate's always finding an ugly duckling in one of her neighbors' families that she can make over into a swan. And when she's done it—taken the girl and bought her clothes and sent her to school—then her swan falls in love with a neighborhood gander, and Kate turns her out, and is sick with rage and disappointment. I should think she'd have given up hope by now."

"Hope of what?" Anne was bewildered as much by the disgust of his tone as by what he said.

"Undying gratitude and devotion, I suppose," John said drily. "I'll go see the girl tomorrow and tell Kate what a fool she is. And neither of them will be any better off."

In this dark humor he sighed. Anne said hurriedly, "Speaking of ugly ducklings, have you heard that Thomasina Ballard is being courted by that young Mr. Travers who plays the Methodist organ?"

"Something about it," John admitted. "They're saying uptown that when he came he asked who was the richest girl in Waynesboro. But that's ridiculous. The Judge can't have much besides his salary. He used to be the attorney for the railroad before he was Judge, but he spent a pile on his house."

"Maybe Mr. Travers is looking for a comfortable home."

"Maybe he's in love."

"With Thomasina? I like her, but she's not the sort a man—No—but she's such a trusting soul, I hope she never finds him out. Maybe she never will. He seems like a meek little man who would know his luck and not presume on it." Anne was talking principally to herself; she was amazed that John beside her should be shaking with mirth. She said, "I don't see what's so funny about that."

"Oh, woman! Lordy, Lordy! All you know is that the man's calling on her occasionally, and already you're worrying for fear she'll find out he married her so as to have some standing in the town."

"Just the same, John Gordon, I feel sorry for her. Poor Thomasina!"

"Poor Thomasina" at any other time in her life would have winced at the knowledge that such an epithet was commonly coupled with her name; it is humiliating to be pitied. But had she heard it that summer, she would have laughed. She was innocently and completely happy. Samuel Travers called to see her two or three nights a week, and she spent enchanted evenings with him at the piano upstairs in the music room. Her sister's sneers and her mother's silent contempt were shut away by closed doors. Samuel played for her the tunes he had composed and sang her pretty verses, and when he had done, he whirled the piano stool about and talked to her without a hint of reservation. With his round face alert and eager, his mousey hair hanging untidily over his eyes, he confided in her all his ambitions.

He said such things as "I have never dared to whisper my hopes to anyone else, but you are so sympathetic," or "I will not always be giving music lessons in Waynesboro, you wait and see." Thomasina would hold her breath: she did not want to wait and see, she wanted to be with him at his triumph. She told herself that she had no illusions about Samuel: she knew now that he would never be a second Beethoven; but his songs were beautiful, and there was room in the world for another Schubert.

Whenever the Judge, a member of the State Supreme Court, came home from circuit-riding to spend a Sunday with his family, Mrs. Ballard and Eliza reported the progress of the affair that was so distasteful to them. He would listen in silence with lifted eyebrows and would watch dubiously his self-conscious daughter in her uncharacteristic abandon, as she ran up or down the stairs, or as she jumped from her chair at the sound of the doorbell. He saw that the advent of her annual siege of hay fever had little effect on her spirits. He said finally to his wife, "I like to see Thomasina happy—if I could only be sure it would last."

"She's a fool," said the downright Mrs. Ballard. "If we don't stop it now, it'll be too late when she finally comes to her senses."

"If she never comes to her senses, she will be happy. But if you are so disturbed, why don't you take her away for her hay fever?"

No one with hay fever ever rebelled against seeking relief from it, and Thomasina could see, when her mother suggested a trip to Michigan, that her family might be tired of hearing her choke and sniffle, and she agreed to go. If Eliza and her mother were willing to give up the annual Woman's Suffrage Convention, she could not complain of a few weeks' separation from Mr. Travers. She did not guess that she was expected to forget him. She prepared for the trip with a light heart. It wasn't even as if her father would be left at home alone, for his district was a large one, and riding circuit would be easier for him if he made no attempt to get back to Waynesboro. The Ballard place was closed, except for the rooms over the stable occupied by the German couple who did the work on the place.

Mrs. Ballard and her daughters spent August and most of September in Michigan. Concerned as they always were with national events, they read the newspapers assiduously, but their interest did not extend to the financial pages. Only when the rapid increase in the price of gold became headline news did they begin to discuss what it meant. Mrs. Ballard could explain it to the satisfaction of her daughters and herself: the Republicans were pushing for a bill in Congress that would provide for the redemption of greenbacks in gold; if it passed, the government would have to supplement the Treasury reserve with gold bought at the market price. Speculators were buying gold in the belief that such a bill would pass. That was all logical enough: what would have seemed to them preposterous was the fact that two men were trying to corner the supply of gold, but what they understood very well was that the financial soundness of the country was in question. Then on Friday, 24 September, the price of gold rose to 162. The government, finally convinced of the threat, released four million in Treasury gold to the market. The day when the price of gold dropped would be remembered as Black Friday. The attempt to corner gold collapsed, and the gamblers were ruined.

The Ballard women were frightened: however little they understood about money speculation, they were sure that honorable men who had made what seemed a good investment could have been as cruelly hurt as the rascals. Judge Ballard was an honorable man, but as they knew, not a stranger to the Cincinnati stock market. They packed their trunks and valises and took the train home.

When they alighted at the Waynesboro depot, both Judge Ballard and Mr. Travers were there to meet them. Mrs. Ballard abhorred the practice of coercing foolish daughters; Thomasina's correspondence with her suitor had been free from interference or supervision. She got down from the train first and kissed her father; she called herself wicked because she could almost be glad that he looked so worn and downcast, and had surely lost money. Her mother would be too busy bolstering him up to pay any attention to her. Afterward, while Eliza and Mrs. Ballard were greeting the Judge with more restraint, she had a moment to speak to Mr. Travers, and invite him to the house after dinner. She knew that he wouldn't be taken into the carriage with them now, and indeed her family swept past him with the slightest of acknowledgments.

His presence on the platform had been proof enough, however, that Thomasina's absence had had no effect on their devotion. The Judge admitted to his wife in their bedroom that his plan had been unsuccessful. "But it was the only chance," he insisted, "and since it didn't work, we may as well accept the inevitable with a good grace."

"He's a good Christian, but a nonentity," Mrs Ballard said severely. "I hoped our daughters would marry men of distinction. If you accept him, can you afford to support him as well as Thomasina, and any children they may have?"

"I'm a poorer man than I was a month ago. Is that what you're hinting at, Mary? But I can still support my family and any likely additions to it."

That night he sat in his library until after Mr. Travers had gone, thinking that perhaps Thomasina, or both of them, would come to him there; but Thomasina, when she had closed the front door behind her caller, went on upstairs to bed. She was not at the breakfast table the next morning, but when Johann brought the carriage around to the veranda steps and the Judge went out the side door to get in it, he found her waiting for him in the porte-cochere.

"Papa, are you going to the Court House? Couldn't you walk this morning—just once? I do so want to speak to you."

He responded to the desperate pleading in her eye, told Johann to put the horse up unless the other ladies wanted to drive, and turned away with Thomasina toward the gate. Beside him, she burst hurriedly into an explanation. "I wanted to see you alone, where Eliza—where there's no one to interrupt, or overhear."

They closed the driveway gate behind them and went forward into the dust of Linden Street.

"I didn't mean to speak to you like this. I told Samuel that I wouldn't, that he must do it, so he's coming to your office this morning. But then I got frightened and thought maybe if you weren't prepared you would be—would be—"

"Cruel to your young man?" he finished for her, with a bright oblique glance of his keen eye.

"Oh, Papa, I know you couldn't be really cruel, but he's so sensitive."

"The prerogative of musicians, I believe. Well, Thomasina: for what am I to be prepared? Now, don't squirm like that, there's a good girl."

At his tone Thomasina drew herself up, and with a semblance of dignity announced, "Mr. Travers has asked me to marry him. Have you any objections?"

"You answered him, I presume, without waiting to find out?"

"Yes, I did." Thomasina was stubbornly defiant. "I've been brought up to believe that women have as much right to dispose of their lives as men. I know Mamma and Eliza won't approve. I can't help that. But I hoped you—I don't want to do anything displeasing to you." She weakened, dropped her voice, turned tearful. "I owe you too much, and believe me, Papa—"

"Never mind that," he said in the tones of one to whom emotional exhibits were distasteful. "I shall not interfere. I hope that you will be happy. May I ask whether Mr. Travers believes that he can support a wife? Where do you plan to live?"

"At his boardinghouse, until he sells his music, his songs."

"Tch—let's keep to the present. There's more space for him in our house than for you in a single room."

"No, Papa, I'd rather not. Eliza and—Eliza would make it too difficult. She despises him. We'd rather have our own home."

"A boardinghouse is no home. Our house can be arranged to give you a separate apartment, quite apart from the rest of us. The music room could, I suppose, be your parlor, and one of the bedrooms be used as a dining room, and the back room made into a kitchen. Your mother and I and Eliza need only two bedrooms on the other side of the hall. We could even manage to put another staircase in the back hall, with an outside entrance on that side of the house."

"You're very kind." Thomasina could not be angry at her father, but she knew the proposed arrangements had been discussed behind her back: he couldn't have reacted so promptly otherwise. She was as angry as she could possibly be at Eliza, who so plainly wanted her and her Samuel pushed to one side, out of sight. "Dear Papa, I am grateful."

"Nonsense. I am only sorry I cannot give you a house. The music room—I suppose he intends to continue teaching?—I am afraid will have to double as your parlor or sitting room. I would do more if I could. But I have had some losses."

"I know: like everyone else. That wicked Mr. Gould! We'll pay you rent for our part of the house. Samuel would rather, I know."

"We'll discuss that later. And as to whether you want a kitchen or not. You know nothing about cooking. If I were your Samuel, I think I should elect to eat with the family."

"Eliza—"

At sight of the shadow on her face, he took that part of her burden on his own shoulders. "Leave Eliza to me. I'm sure we shall all like Mr. Travers when we know him better."

They had come to the beginning of the brick sidewalk, and the Judge stopped to flick the dust off his shoes and the cuffs of his trousers with his silk handkerchief. Thomasina held out her hand for it and said, "Let me." For a moment he lost patience with her. "Don't be abject," he thundered, in his courtroom voice. Then as she recoiled he added hastily, "Don't worry. I'll be gentle with your young man, and I'll handle Eliza."

Thomasina went home reassured, and with good reason. There was no further open objection to Mr. Travers on the part of her family. Without much argument the date of her wedding was set for the end of October, and the invitations were issued before the first Club meeting after the summer vacation. At that meeting there was no official recognition of the coming event, no reference to "our Club bride." The President was the bride's mother, who was displeased by the whole idea. She kept her eyes averted from her daughter and proceeded briskly with what business must be brought before the meeting before the day's program could be advanced. The ladies were asked to vote to instruct the corresponding secretary to write a note congratulating Mrs. Anne Gordon on the birth of a son. The secretary was then invited to read any communications she had received: she responded with a letter from Mrs. Deming, tendering, with great regret, her resignation from the Club: General Deming, for the present, at least, intended to live in Washington. The ladies accepted the resignation, but voted to make Mrs. Deming an Associate Member.

When all other business was concluded, Miss Reid was called upon to present her essay. The Club in this second year of its existence was devoting its energies to a study of American Men of Letters, and Amanda had been given the first subject: The Philosophy of Mr. Emerson. She had been shaken with disappointment at the eager and total defection of Thomasina. A friend in love, and particularly one who could be in love with a mediocre being like Mr. Samuel Travers, was a friend lost. For Amanda the only life that could hold any satisfaction would be the life of a scholar. Her paper on Emerson was the first fruit of that consecration: she pursued every idea to its source, and worked it out in all its ramifications deliberately and thoroughly. It was not easy for the ladies to concentrate without fidgeting on the long involved path she followed to her conclusions.

Two at least of those present, Thomasina and Sally Rausch, did not try. Thomasina was too full of more important emotions to care, just then, what Mr. Emerson believed, and she felt cut off from her old admiration of Amanda by Amanda's attitude toward her marriage. Eliza had reported, triumphantly, that Amanda wished she had never taken "To a Bride" to the *Torchlight* office, and Thomasina had felt a loss, however unimportant in comparison with her great gain, and a pain of desertion and betrayal. At the meeting she kept her thoughts and her eyes turned resolutely away from Amanda. She noted how small the meeting seemed, even with Mrs. Lowrey's married daughter there as a guest: Anne was absent still, Mrs. Deming was gone, and Sally, she suspected, wouldn't be coming much longer, although of course she couldn't be so rude as to stare. She hoped the Club wouldn't dwindle to nothing, because she enjoyed it.

Something like this was running at the same time through Sally's vagrant thoughts. With Anne absent it seemed very dull to be shut up for an afternoon with old women—the Gardiner sisters, Mrs. Lowrey, and the other teachers, all dried up and withered, like forgotten potatoes turned up on the bottom of a bushel basket—and premature old maids like Amanda and Eliza Ballard.

Sally considered the full-blown and slightly frowzy figure of the Lowreys' elder daughter, and wondered if she had brought her children to Waynesboro to stay. As usual, they had been at the Lowreys' all summer: the children had run wild not only on the College grounds but all over the neighborhood. Once before Mrs. Tyler had stayed at her parents' house until her husband wrote from Chicago telling her to come home at once or not at all; on that occasion she had packed her trunk, collected her children, and departed. The story had been told in the school by Kitty Lowrey, who did not get along well with her sister Ellen. There had been trouble, too, between Ellen and Miss Tucker because Ellen had tried to interfere with Miss Tucker's management of the school. But now Miss Tucker was Mrs. Deming, and in Washington, Kitty was away at Oberlin, and Ellen Tyler and her children were still in Waynesboro in October.

If she had come to stay, if she had left her husband, the Club would soon know it because her name would be proposed for membership, in Mrs. Deming's place. Sally thought if that happened she would have to hurry with her plans for the Christmas party: have them all made before there was any need for consultation. Mrs. Tyler had an alert and dictatorial eye. Sally hoped to have another party this year; it had been fun, a year ago, and there was a long time ahead of her when she couldn't entertain or go out. She would have it at her mother's, since her own house was too small. At the next meeting she would speak to Amanda and ask her to help again.

In the two weeks that passed between Club meetings, a scandalized Waynesboro learned that Mrs. Tyler had left her husband for good; she also had quarreled with and dismissed the new teacher at the College, hired in Mrs. Deming's place, and had herself taken over those classes. Of course, the dismissed teacher had to be paid part of her salary, but Mrs. Tyler needn't be paid anything; it would all be in the family, and might in the end prove an economy, although there would be those extra mouths to feed. If, said the town, doubtfully, Mrs. Tyler could teach the young ladies their algebra.

It was no surprise to the Club members when, at the next meeting, its President announced, "A name has been proposed for membership to be voted on two weeks from this afternoon. Will the secretary please read the name."

After adjournment Sally caught Amanda by the door and kept her for a minute in the hall. "Will you help me with a party again this winter? We had such a successful one last year." Then she added, carelessly, "I'd like to get all the plans made before Mrs. Tyler's a member."

Amanda stiffened. "You would prefer her not to be a member? You can vote against her."

Of course, Sally thought, Amanda proposed her name; she's so devoted to the College and to Mrs. Lowrey, she would do it for her sake. She said, "I won't vote against her. No one will. And hurt Mrs. Lowrey's feelings? I don't dislike her personally, it's just that she has so many ideas. I know she's a brilliant woman and all that, but at my own party, even if it is for the Club, I'd like to make the plans myself. You will help me, won't you? Thomasina won't want to give up much of her time, and Anne is all taken up with her baby."

Mrs. Tyler was duly elected to membership in the Club, but nothing was said to her about a party, where there would again be tableaux to be stage-managed. Alone Amanda and Sally made their plans and their costumes, and coaxed the other younger members to be present at rehearsals. The tableaux were to represent scenes from the works of the poets studied the previous year. Except for the absence of the Demings and the addition of Mrs. Tyler and Mr. Samuel Travers, the company was the same that had been invited a year ago. Again the program was completely successful, and the gentlemen carried their capacity for enjoyment into the dining room with them, where Sally had provided a bountiful supper. She had every reason for congratulating herself on the success of the evening. But what most pleased her mischievous spirit was the progress she was making in opposition to the illiberal prejudices of half the Club. They would still blanch at any suggestion of play-acting, but perhaps, in another year, the tableaux could be enlivened by lines spoken by the characters represented. Would that be acting? After that, they could give dialogues, then someday a real play: that was Sally's program for the Club's future. If only Mrs. Tyler didn't interfere and take the Christmas party out of her hands, and if there weren't too many babies, hers and others, to take up time and occupy the mind.

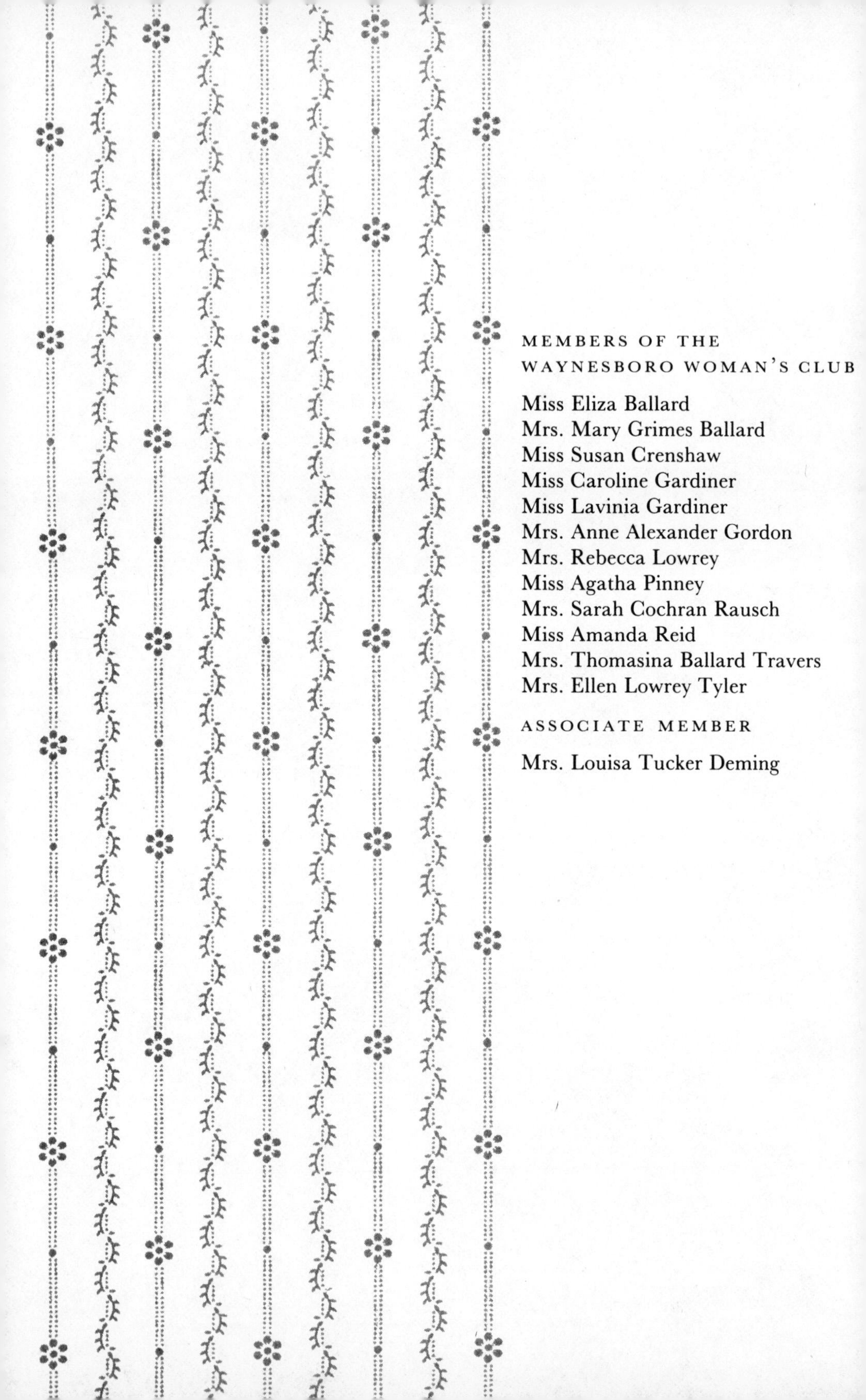

MEMBERS OF THE
WAYNESBORO WOMAN'S CLUB

Miss Eliza Ballard
Mrs. Mary Grimes Ballard
Miss Susan Crenshaw
Miss Caroline Gardiner
Miss Lavinia Gardiner
Mrs. Anne Alexander Gordon
Mrs. Rebecca Lowrey
Miss Agatha Pinney
Mrs. Sarah Cochran Rausch
Miss Amanda Reid
Mrs. Thomasina Ballard Travers
Mrs. Ellen Lowrey Tyler

ASSOCIATE MEMBER

Mrs. Louisa Tucker Deming

✻ 1870 ✻

"The Club sponsored a Lecture Course."

Fortunately, Mrs. Tyler had no interest in parties or anything of so little consequence. Before the new year had well begun, that energetic matron was deep in plans of real importance to the community. Anne and Sally called her, to each other, "Mrs. Jellyby," but in fact they would have liked her better, and resented her less, had she resembled more closely that famous fictional character. Ellen Tyler gave no thought to the improvement of the morale and customs of remote heathen tribes: all her schemes were for the advancement in culture and information of her immediate neighbors. Her children, like Mrs. Jellyby's, were neglected, but they were far from forlorn; they seemed rather to flourish in their freedom from parental oversight and admonition.

The Tyler boys attended the Reverend Mr. Wainwright's day school. The girls were in the primary department of the Female College, where Miss Pinney was no match for them, and only sighed with relief when they took it into their heads to depart from the schoolroom and pursue their pleasures elsewhere. Sometimes curiosity and a love of troubling others took them into advanced classrooms. Teachers who were strong-minded enough ignored them; their mother blandly assumed that if they dropped in to observe her demonstrations of complex problems at the blackboard, it was because they longed to know algebra; and therefore she made them welcome. Only Amanda fought them off: behind a locked door she taught her classes their Latin grammar. Fortunately, her schoolroom was on the second floor, and the little Tyler girls could not climb up on the window sill outside and make faces, or press their noses against the glass, to peer in at the cob-webby busts of Caesar and Cicero, and the dark engravings of Roman ruins. Amanda did not hold Mrs. Tyler culpable for the misbehavior of her children: rather, she sympathized, as if they were an affliction for which their mother had been nowise responsible. Children were one of the awful and inescapable consequences of marriage. Amanda had washed her hands of Thomasina Ballard Travers, who, although she showed no sign of pregnancy, was still completely besotted about her husband. Amanda turned instead to the woman who had obviously had enough of marriage, who had cast off as many of her bonds as she decently could. Amanda became Mrs. Tyler's most active and able lieutenant in her campaign for the improvement of Waynesboro.

The Opera House, so long under construction, had finally been completed. The mayor, two policemen, and a drunk-and-disorderly prisoner moved into their offices, courtroom, and jail on the first floor. The theater upstairs was dedicated to the public with a road company performance of *Fanchon the Cricket*, with Maggie Mitchell. On the afternoon that followed this gala occasion, the *Torchlight* in a long article described at length the sumptuous attractions of the new playhouse: the red carpet in the aisles, the scenic drop curtain, the Corinthian columns upholding the balcony, the portrait of the Bard of Avon at the top of the proscenium arch. The reporter was not parsimonious, either, in his use of adjectives in the paragraph given to an account of those who had gone to see Maggie Mitchell. "The brilliance of the acting was matched by the distinction of the audience. The elite of Waynesboro filled the orchestra seats of the house. Our town may take rank with the greatest cities of the state in appreciation of the Thespian art—"

This was accurate enough, as newspapers go, yet far more than half the town got all its knowledge of the Opera House, and of *Fanchon the Cricket*, from the columns of the *Torchlight*. Many respectable citizens curled their lips scornfully at the word "elite." Others—the Reformed Presbyterians, the Methodists, most of the Baptists—believed that Satan had been given a new toehold in Waynesboro. Most Presbyterians, all the few Episcopalians, and the handful of freethinkers, were play-goers. Lutherans and Catholics had no prejudices against the theater, but few of them were comfortable in the company of the town's "elite." The Cochrans, the Rausches, the Gordons, and the Gardiners were present at Maggie Mitchell's performance. The Ballards, the Lowreys, and the Reids stayed at home.

The Reformed Presbyterians ignored the Opera House. They could pass it without seeing it, so long as their young people were not tempted, or, being tempted, did not fall. They cared not at all how many plays were performed there for the pleasure of those not of the elect, who could attend them without further endangering their already doomed immortal souls. But that was not the Methodist temperament, and Mrs. Tyler was a Methodist. With contempt and something of indignation, she read in the *Torchlight* a list of the entertainment booked for the season. She resented the use of a community building for the enjoyment of less than half of that community. Some nourishment should be provided for those who demanded another kind of fare, intellectual, moral, and sober, and she proposed to see that it was spread before them.

First she ascertained from the mayor that the auditorium could be rented by any organization for any decent purpose; next she wrote the manager of a Lyceum Bureau and found that it was not too late to secure speakers for that season, and finally she suggested to the Club that it sponsor a series of lectures in Waynesboro, to be given in the new Opera House.

The ladies of the Club, a little flustered at having a prearranged lecture course thrust upon them, agreed dazedly to Mrs. Tyler's plan before they realized they would be responsible for the sale of tickets. Then some of them were amazed and confounded. The Misses Gardiner would not lower their dignity by hawking tickets from door to door; they purchased one each, and felt that they had done their duty. Miss Crenshaw and Miss Pinney cried off on the grounds of lack of time or strength. Sally took four for her own family, but could not sell any: her own Christmas party would be her last public appearance before late spring. Anne got rid of her share to the Presbyterian Ladies Aid and the members of her Sunday school class. The Ballards, Amanda, and Mrs. Tyler sold the rest. Amanda appeared before her mother's boarders at dinner one evening and browbeat the theological students into subscribing, and Mrs. Ballard and Eliza and Mrs. Tyler moved among the Methodists. As a matter of fact, Mr. Bonner's commendatory articles in the *Torchlight* created a demand for the tickets, and their sale required no special effort. The country had been educated in the preceding decades to believe that culture could be acquired painlessly by listening to Lyceum lectures.

The first lecturer was Theodore Tilton. The town would have gone just to see him had he been stricken dumb before arrival. Mrs. Ballard with accustomed poise introduced him to the audience; he acknowledged the introduction with suitable gallantry: In all his long experience as a lecturer, he had never before had the honor and pleasure of being introduced by a woman. He was followed a month later by Wendell Phillips; in April, General Lew Wallace spoke on "Turkey and the Turks." In May it would be the turn of Anna Dickinson, who would talk on "Woman's Rights." To bring Anna Dickinson to a town so essentially conservative as Waynesboro was considered a daring undertaking. Mrs. Ballard and Mrs. Tyler, who were Miss Dickinson's enthusiastic admirers, were afraid she would face an auditorium of empty seats; and they exacted promises from all the Club members that they would attend, with their husbands or whatever friends, male or female, they could persuade to join them.

Sally had from the first declared frankly to Anne that she was glad she had an excuse not to go to the lectures; she liked seeing notables, but not having to listen to them, and Sally in her youth was not one to pretend to an interest she did not feel. But Anne thought there must be something worth hearing in what so many people liked, and she was interested in the famous or the notorious, to see them and hear them and think what made them so. Besides, it was stultifying to think only, day in, day out, of your husband and your baby; and little Johnny was six months old and could perfectly well be left with Martha for an evening now and then. Even if Anne went to sleep at every lecture, she would go, she insisted stoutly, because the Club was doing it, and she was a member of the Club.

John went with her to the earlier lectures; he did not rebel until Anna Dickinson loomed on the horizon. He felt no interest in the woman who had set the country on its ears; he was indifferent to woman's rights, unable to take the subject seriously enough to be on one side of the question or the other. Over his objections Anne secured his promise to go, but on the evening of the lecture, when he came to the supper table, he asked Anne if she couldn't persuade her father to escort her to the Opera House that once.

Dr. Alexander grimaced and held up his swollen misshapen hands in protest. "I and my rheumatics have come to the place where no woman can beguile us into a hard seat for a whole evening."

Anne said, "I know better than to try." She lowered her eyes from his hands in pity. Her father was not much over sixty; it was not right that he should be so crippled, or look so white and haggard. But that was a familiar worry; she thrust it into the background of her mind. John looked haggard, too; she had known even before he spoke that something had happened that had shaken him and left him wretched. But if it was one of his patients, he would not tell her if she asked. He had not yet grown able to shed his patients' disasters, which were also his. She said: "You don't either of you have to go: I can go with one of the neighbors. Or I can give both tickets away, and stay home with you, if you'll stay home and rest, and let Papa take the office calls."

"I wish I could. But I've got to go out."

Dr. Alexander looked oddly at the young man; Anne saw the glance.

"If it's a patient Papa knows about, couldn't he go? You come to the lecture, and get your mind off your work for a change."

"It's my case."

They said no more at the moment. When supper was over, he followed Anne into the hall and upstairs, according to the custom that took them both to the baby for a few moments' play before John returned to the office for the evening. But although they could hear from the upstairs hall Martha's rocker swinging over the floor in the baby's room, while she sang to him, John went directly into their bedroom. When Anne returned in a few moments, satisfied that her child was safely asleep, she found him flung face down on the bed.

With slow fingers she unbuttoned her basque, while she watched him; then she went to the dresser, took down her braids, and began to brush out her fine hair, which still had golden highlights where beams from the lamp touched it. When he turned his head so as to be able to watch her, she could stand it no longer. She came and stood over him, barearmed, the hair brush in her hand.

"Did you have a hard day, John?"

"Oh, hard—" he groaned. After a moment's silence he broke out, abruptly. "There was a row out at Kate's this afternoon."

"At Kate's?" She sat down quickly on the foot of the bed, obscurely frightened. "What kind of a row?"

He turned over and sat up then, his feet over the side of the bed, his elbows on his knees, his hands in his hair.

"Mr. Jacobs had to send for me." He lifted his head and looked at her, almost accusingly. "I told you how it would be. You remember the Jacobs girl? The one Kate had living with her? Kate met her in the woods this afternoon with a young farmhand, and flew off the handle. I don't know what she accused her of—everything, I guess. The girl went home to her father's and had hysterics in the kitchen, and Kate followed her, screaming and carrying on."

"John! How awful!" Anne, horror-stricken and ashamed, went limp against the bedpost. "But why? I can't see—Kate always seems so—so self-controlled—as if she cared for nothing."

"I know. Until something like this happens and she goes all to pieces."

"What did you do?"

"It was an hour and a half before they found me and I could get there. She'd left the Jacobses' by that time. I suspect they'd put her out; the things she'd said, and the way she'd said them, made them think she'd taken leave of her senses. They were frightened out of their wits. I found her sitting on a stump in the woods. She'd got hold of herself, and let me take her home. I couldn't get anything out of her. I didn't try, much. Just persuaded her to go to bed, and gave her a bromide to take when she'd got there. I stopped at the tenant's and asked Mrs. Allen to go up and sleep in the house with her. But I must go back and make sure she's sleeping."

"Couldn't you have given her laudanum enough to be sure?"

"Laudanum? I'd never give Kate laudanum. She's the last person—it's a dangerous drug."

"Oh, I know, if you get the habit. But Papa gives it, doesn't he? I often smell it in the office."

"That's the old-fashioned way." He managed to smile at her, but he was startled. He had known for a long while, but hoped that Anne would never know, why Dr. Alexander liked to live alone; he wanted to sleep, and sleep in peace, now that there was someone else to take night calls, and there was only one way he could be sure of sleeping when his rheumatism was bad. "Laudanum is just one of the things we disagree on, prescribing it as if it were no more than lemonade."

"John, if it were anyone but Kate, and you had given her a sleeping draught, and made sure there was someone in the house, would you go back tonight?"

"No, I suppose not."

"Surely, early in the morning would be better."

Anne was interrupted in her attempt to dissuade him from returning to Kate that night. The doorbell rang. When John had gone downstairs to answer it, she shamelessly hung over the stair rail to listen, her heart beating with a painful, thick rapidity. But it was only one of the Tyler boys come to summon the doctor for another of the Tyler boys who had fallen off the Lowreys' porch roof and broken a wrist. Dr. Alexander had sent him over from the office to get Dr. Gordon.

"All right, Bob," John assured him. "I'll go to the office for splints and then be right along. Keep him quiet until I get there." He called up to Anne, "If I do go to the country, I expect I'll not get back before you go. Shall I meet you at the Opera House?"

"I'll leave your ticket at the ticket window for you; if you're early, come on inside. If you're late, I'll come home with the Wilsons; they go right past here."

Anne dressed with the effort and slowness of a convalescent; she could not rid herself of a sick feeling at the end of her breastbone. But she forced herself, when she had closed the door behind her, to set off briskly in the sweet May twilight, to greet cheerfully and vigorously such acquaintances as she encountered at the Opera House door, on the stairs, and in the aisle. And then, after all, John came in before the lecture began, sheepish and shamefaced, in the wake of Mrs. Tyler, who leaned over the empty aisle seat to speak to Anne before she made way for him to slip into it.

"Your husband was going to play truant. But I brought him right along when he'd finished setting Danny's arm. I know too much about men and their excuses. 'A case in the country,' indeed! He couldn't tell me one single convincing thing about it. So I sent Bob to tell his man he wouldn't need the horse after all. And," added the unblushing outspoken matron, "we told the usher where to find him in case some inconsiderate woman chooses tonight to have a baby."

John muttered something under his breath. Mrs. Tyler proceeded down the aisle. Anne, unaccountably relieved, as if she had won a reprieve from some unnameable disaster, laughed at him.

"You're weak-kneed."

"What could I do? Everything I said made my case seem more fictitious. If I'd only told her in the beginning my sister was ill, but I didn't want to even mention her name. And now that I am here," he settled himself in his seat with a wiggle, "I hope I can stay. No babies tonight, thank God! Sally Rausch ought to wait a couple more weeks, and there's no one else."

But just when Miss Dickinson had got well under way, the usher came down the aisle, touched John on the shoulder, and whispered, "You're wanted, sir."

John reached under his seat for his hat and without a word, only a despairing look, departed. Anne, at sight of his face, knew with a certainty beyond any reason that it was Kate—that he knew it was Kate. As he stepped into the aisle and away from her, she had the impulse to follow and push ahead of him, to shield him from anyone's glance. His expression, his pallor, his fixed eyes, were a kind of nakedness in public.

Kate had done something awful. Not letting herself think what the awfulness might be, Anne sat through the rest of the lecture, not knowing why, but quite unable to rise and go. What she was doing there, held immobile while a strange woman's voice went on and on, a disparate fragment of her mind kept asking in vain. She was caught in a nightmare. Fantastic, ominous, became the rows of people before her in the shadowy dress circle, the edge of the balcony looming over her head, pressing down; hypnotic the row of footlights so that the figures behind them became the unreal fabric of a dream, while out there, somewhere, on the farm, in the blackness of night in the shadows of the trees, Kate lay dead. She could see the carved profile, like old yellow ivory, eyes closed against the sky, the hair fallen back from the temples.

When the lecture ended and the applause died, she behaved automatically, saying, "Good evening," agreeing, "Yes, very" to "Wasn't it interesting?" She forced her way between thrusting elbows as quickly as she could and fled. She felt as though there were no bones in her knees, as if she were walking on air and must fall headlong if she paused or stopped. She knew that her father would have come to meet her. She saw him at once, took his elbow, and led him to the curb to cross the street to the Court House square, where there would be comparative solitude and shelter under the elms from the flaring gas streetlight on the corner.

"Don't run, Anne. I can't go so fast."

She hesitated, slowed her steps, but stumbled as she crossed the dusty street that moved in waves beneath her feet. She was glad to take her father's arm when they reached the rough pavement under the elms, for she had begun to tremble.

"Stop and take a deep breath, Anne. You're all right. It must have been a long lecture. I've been waiting forever."

The prosaic sanity of his tone, almost impatient, as if he had dealt with enough hysterical females to be bored by them, steadied her so that she could go on, even cross Main Street when they came to it.

"John asked me to meet you."

Poor Papa. He thought he had to tell her. "You've seen John? How is he?" But that was ridiculous, she mustn't leave out the things that needed to be said; she must tell her father what she knew. "Kate is dead?"

"Yes."

They got across Main Street, and were under the low-hanging boughs of the maple trees of their own block, passing the church among the couples and groups going home from the lecture; they must walk along as if they were only two others of them, and speak low, so that no one could hear. The tree roots had broken the pavement where they walked. Anne had begun to tremble again, and each uplifted edge of brick threatened to stop her progress. She clung to her father's arm and felt with a cautious foot for breaks that at other times she could step over without thinking, even in the dark, she knew them so well.

"Papa—she killed herself?"

"Yes. Who told you?"

"No one. I just knew. The way John knew when they came for him."

"Nonsense, my dear. Like all women, your imagination leaped to the worst. Sh—not here, Anne. I'll tell you about it."

They reached the house at last. The lamp was burning in the sitting room, steady and sane. Anne took off her gloves and bonnet and stood for a moment with her fingers pressed to her eyeballs. Then she looked up at her father, standing beside her.

"When, Papa? When?"

"When? What does that matter? I don't know. As soon as John had left her, I suppose. He'd given her a sleeping draught that never took effect."

"John wanted to go back and didn't, and I was afraid. I thought—"

"I see. No, he couldn't have got back in time, even if he'd gone right from supper. Besides, it's hopeless trying to prevent a suicide." He turned her Boston rocker around from the fireplace and pressed her into it. "Sit down, my dear. Let me feel your hands."

They were cold, Anne knew. She was cold all over. She was not surprised when her father turned to the dining room.

"I'll bring you a little brandy. That will help."

"In a minute, Papa. Tell me first. What did she—what did she do?"

"The hired man found her when he brought the horses back from ploughing. He'd worked late. She'd hanged herself in the barn. He came in for John, and found me; we went to the Opera House for him. We didn't tell the usher, nor John until we'd got him in the buggy, so how you could think he knew—"

"Oh, he knew. I suppose, in a way, he'd been expecting it." Her teeth had begun to chatter. Her father went on to the dining room, returning with the brandy. Her hand shook so that he kept the glass and held it to her lips.

"I ought to be out there with him," she said. "Will you take me out?"

"John sent me to tell you to go to bed. He'll be out there all night. You're not to wait up for him because he won't be back."

"I want to go."

"What for? The coroner's probably out there now."

"Coroner? Of course, I didn't think. How awful! Poor Kate. *Why* do you suppose?"

"Don't distress yourself more than you can help. Kate was an unhappy woman—not quite sane, I think—and she wouldn't have grown any happier. Nor would John. She would always have been a threat to his peace of mind. Of course, I wouldn't say this to him." He stooped over, put his hands on her shoulders, drew her to her feet. "Go on to bed, Anne, and when you're ready, I'll bring you a sedative. If you don't sleep, you'll be of no use to John tomorrow."

Heavily she climbed the stairs; she was no longer trembling, but leaden with misery. Before she got into bed, she went into the next room for the baby. She must nurse him before she slept. Even as she crossed the threshold with him in her arms, he wakened enough to turn his face to her breast. When he had finished and was asleep again, she put him on her bed. This one night she would keep him with her. When she called to her father, he brought her the dose he had prepared, and the last thing she heard was the sound of his steps as he paced the hall outside her door, waiting for her to sleep.

The next morning when John came in, Anne had his breakfast ready in the oven, his coffee on the stove. It was very early. The baby was still sleeping, and she hoped that he would not waken until she had said whatever should be said to John; because she loved him so completely, she had prayed before dressing that she would know what his need was.

She kissed him wordlessly when she met him at the door. Together they entered the sitting room. John sank into his deep leather chair while Anne knelt beside him in the circle of her skirts to change his shoes for slippers.

"Papa said I was to tell you, first thing, that you weren't to worry about the patients you were to see this morning. He'll make your calls. Now—" She put her hand on the arm of his chair and struggled to her feet, made awkward by the encumbering petticoats. "Don't stir till I've brought you a cup of coffee. After that you must eat some breakfast."

She poured the coffee in the kitchen, and brought in the cup and saucer. He took the cup in an unsteady hand, but he emptied it like a man dying of thirst, hot as it was. As she took it from him, he spoke for the first time. "Kate hanged herself in the barn." He was not looking at her; his eyes were on the empty fireplace.

"I know. Papa told me." Then she added, because she could not help it, "But why, John? Why?"

"Because that girl ran away from her. I shouldn't have left her yesterday. I thought it was just hysterics, and that she would be all right."

"It wouldn't have made any difference, would it? I mean, if it hadn't been yesterday, it would have been today or some other time. That's what Papa said, if a person's bent on suicide—" She started for the dining room with the coffee cup in her hand. "Come on and eat, John. I have your breakfast all ready."

He followed her. It was not until he had given up his valiant attempt to finish his plate of chops and fried potatoes that she asked him what the coroner had said.

"What could he say? She killed herself."

"Did he know why, I mean? Did he think she wasn't—wasn't—"

"Sane? Oh, she was sane. I told him so." Then he noticed her fleeting expression of horror, and added, "I know most people think suicide in a family's a kind of disgrace. But you're a doctor's daughter, Anne; don't you know a taint of insanity is worse? The coroner didn't know about the Jacobs girl; he will, because country people talk, and I don't know what he'll think then. He thinks now that she was sane but unhappy. I showed him the note she left. Oh, she was sane—sane enough to know there's only one thing to do if you're doomed to be unhappy."

"She left you a note?"

He drew the paper from his pocket and gave it to her. She unfolded it and read the words written in Kate's heavy, uncontrolled handwriting.

> Good-bye, John. Don't let them say I'm crazy, I'm not. It's just that I like life less and less as I grow older. And it's not only being unhappy yourself, but making everyone around you miserable, too. So I'm going.
>
> Don't ever blame yourself, or think you could have done something. You've done everything anybody could do. Please forgive me the trouble this will cause you. But it will soon be over and done with. And you can forget me, I was going to say, but I hope you won't forget me altogether. Forget the last twenty years and remember me when I was twelve and you were seven or eight.
>
> I think if there is a Heaven everyone will be the age they were when they were most themselves. So that is how old I'll be, twelve. Driving cows to pasture, running wild in the woods, wading in the creek and catching minnows. Remember me like that, I was happy then and it was still good to be Kate Gordon.
>
> Good-bye, John and Anne. I have left the farm to young John.
>
> "Kate"

Anne put the note on the table when she had finished reading it. "I wish I'd known Kate when she was little." Tears filled her eyes and ran down her cheeks. She fumbled in the pocket of her apron for a handkerchief, as she began really to cry with long shaking sobs.

"Don't, dear. She was queer even then, sullen and quiet in the house, all shut up inside herself, but outdoors like a wild deer, quick and light on her feet, and shy."

Anne choked back her sobs, "I wonder if she was right—about Heaven, I mean. I always sort of took it for granted that you began there where you left off here. Anyway, unless you lived to the end of your days, how would you know when it was, that you were most yourself? But I don't believe I want to think it would be when I was an old lady."

"Dear Anne!" John smiled, rather sadly, to be sure, but still an unforced genuine smile. He rose from the table, drew her up beside him, and held her in his arms for a long moment. "Dear Anne! You'll make a nice old lady, I feel sure, but you couldn't be more yourself than now, at this instant, when you're young and I love you."

She had won his attention for the moment, but she could not keep his mind on her, the baby, his patients, away from Kate and tragedy. All day his face was that of a man haunted by a nightmare, unable to shake off the terrors of the dark. He did not rise from his chair in the sitting room when the boy brought the evening *Torchlight*. Anne saw his face change at the noise it made, the thud against the door. She went for the paper, carried it into the kitchen and thrust it into the stove unopened: no one wanted to see the words she knew were there in print: "Dead by her own hand!"

At the funeral John had hold of himself; he had managed to wipe all expression from his face, and was white and rigid as stone. Anne was not less afraid for him than she had been, when she watched him standing above the closed coffin, seeing nothing. The farmhouse parlor was full of Kate's neighbors, thwarted of their sight of her by the coffin lid, but satisfying their curiosity by their long oblique glances at John. Anne could not hate them; she knew that they were genuinely sorry and sympathetic, but she could hardly breathe the air they had made heavy-scented and cloying with their vases full of peonies and syringa.

After they were home again, the lawyer came to tell them that Kate had left the farm in trust to young John, with her brother and Mr. Cochran as trustees. When he had gone, there was a great emptiness and stillness in the house; an illogical and causeless emptiness, since Kate had rarely been there in the flesh. John could not endure the silence, the blank waiting for night and another day; without a word to Anne he took up his hat and went through the side porch door and across the yard to the office. Anne climbed the staircase alone, to find her baby, to take him up, to nurse him, sitting down on the edge of the bed. When he had finished, she put him beside her and let him lie there, kicking his heels in the air. She watched him without any lessening of her dread. Somewhere within her mind words were saying themselves, over and over, "Dear God, what am I to do with John? Dear God—" and beneath that sentence an echo: "Isn't it sane, if you know you're doomed to be unhappy?" She was moved to roll over on the bed and crouch there, her back bowed, her head bent into the pillow, her knees drawn up beneath her chin. She had so crouched when, as a child, she had given way to her woes. But now she resisted the impulse that would express her despair, that would be a childish surrender to it. For John's sake she must not be helpless. Resolutely she got up, took the baby back to his own room, and washed and dressed him in fresh ruffles.

While she was still there, she thought she heard carriage wheels outside, and the squeak of a gate on its hinges. The doorbell rang, and Martha went to answer it. She had not made up her mind whether to go down or not, to receive condolences, when she recognized Sally's voice. With the baby in her arms, she went downstairs.

"Sally, how good of you! But should you have let her come, Ludwig?"

"Nonsense!" Sally said brusquely, letting go of the shawl she had held to conceal her figure; and moving to the foot of the stairs, she kissed Anne and the baby. "Isn't he a darling? Ludwig, do you suppose we'll have one as nice?"

Ludwig, laughing, took Anne's hand. "She wants before it is born to hear how perfect her child is!"

They went into the sitting room, Sally talking as she went. "I wanted to come before the funeral, but Ludwig was afraid I'd be upset." She drew down the corners of her mouth in mock scorn. "But he saw I was getting more upset worrying about you, so he promised to bring me when he got home from the mill. That's why we're so late. He borrowed Papa's horse and buggy, so that I wouldn't have to walk up the hill."

Ludwig did not sit down with the two women; he asked for John and, when told that he was at the office, said that he would look for him there, and he took the family shortcut, out the side door and through the back yards. In the sitting room Anne put the baby on a quilt on the floor; for a brief moment they watched him roll and squirm, and then they went to sit side by side on the sofa beneath the window. Anne was pleased that Sally had come; she sat now with her arm through Sally's and held Sally's hand on the sofa between them. And yet she was afraid of what Sally might say; she had somehow, sometime, been made aware that Sally considered Kate Gordon a menace to their peace, hers and John's. A little breathless, she began to speak quickly.

"It's good of Ludwig. I hope he can make John think of something else. He's taking it hard."

"Dock always does take things hard, doesn't he? And this must have been an awful shock. Kate was all the family he had left around here. I'm sorry for him. But after all, haven't you always known in your heart Kate would do something awful sometime?"

"I don't know. Anyway, that wouldn't have made it any easier when it came."

"Wouldn't it?" Sally was thoughtful, frowning. She was not going to be put off what she meant to say; she believed in cauterizing a wound. "I should think it might. Suspense is so nerve-wracking." With an anxious, searching look, she brought it out. "Now it's over and done with. You and Dock are past the worst."

"Sally, you're not saying we ought to be glad?"

"Glad! Of course not. I mean if it *had* to happen—and it was bound to happen Kate being what she was—then isn't it best that it should be now? While Johnny's a baby. By the time he's old enough to hear about it, it will be an old story that doesn't matter any more."

"That it's best for Johnny, and any other children we may have, yes. But it's John I'm worried about."

"He'll be past the worst of it in a little while. He has his work to keep him busy, and it's work that he has to put his mind on. At least I hope it is. I'm going to be needing him any day now."

That was all the consolation Sally had to offer. The commonsense words did not leave Anne the happier. However much Sally might deprecate suicide, she could not see in Kate's death anything but the removal of a menace. Anne, without argument, let her conclude her visit. Not for anything in the world would she have put into words, even to Sally, that the shadow of a suicide hanging over her family seemed to her a greater menace than any living woman. She told herself her fear must never be put into words. Such fears were best kept unspoken, lest the voice's echo give them a reality they might not otherwise have. But she was not strong enough, after all, to hold her tongue.

For several days John remained queer, rigidly constrained, remote from her as if she had no reality for him. He followed the routine of his life, but Anne suspected that his patients were no more than automata to him, to be dealt with accordingly. She was glad when the night came on which Ludwig summoned him, just at suppertime. Sally, in trouble, in need of him, would waken and rouse him.

John spent the most of that night at the Rausches'. He had with an effort shaken himself free from his preoccupation to concentrate on the task before him. But Sally was young and superbly strong and healthy, and presently he found himself doing what had to be done without its engaging more than half his mind. He kept seeing Kate's swollen congested face on the pillow instead of Sally's; it was Kate whom he heard cry out. When it was over at last, and he called Ludwig in for a moment before Sally dropped deep as a stone into the sleep of exhaustion, when the midwife had bathed the baby and Ludwig had carried it across the hall to show to its grandparents, John was worn out, almost uncertain on his feet not so much from the ordeal ended as from the effort to keep his mind clear.

When Mrs. Cochran took the baby back to the nurse, Ludwig went to the dining room for brandy and glasses, and poured drinks for the three men. Ludwig was in understandably high spirits, but John heard his banter and boasting without paying much attention to it. He said, "What are you going to name her?" while he swirled the glass in his hand, and stared morosely at the pale liquid. He thought that if enough brandy would make him forget for a while, he would drain the bottle. But it was not so much forgetfulness he wanted as release. Release from himself, from being John Gordon. What he wanted was to lie down in the arms, on the breast, of some kind promiscuous soul to whom he would be merely man, not John Gordon. His wife could not give him that kind of release; she loved him too much for that; he looked into her eyes and saw himself mirrored there. He wanted to escape from himself for a night or a week. There was a house down by the railroad where promiscuity was walled in, and identities left outside the walls. But Anne, who loved John Gordon, whom he loved—

He rose and put his glass on the table, congratulated Ludwig and Mr. Cochran, picked up his bag, and went home. He let himself in as quietly as possible, laid hat and bag on the table in the hall, took up the lighted lamp that stood there, and went into the dining room. There he poked about in the sideboard until he found a bottle of brandy; with it and a glass he sat down at the table.

While he was still there, slumped in a chair, with the glass almost untasted on the table before him, Anne came downstairs to find him. She had put on a trailing robe, all beruffled around the neck and down the front; with the night lamp in one hand and the robe caught up in the other, with her hair in two braids over her shoulders, she looked half-eager, half-frightened, altogether childish. John smiled at her, hoping she could not see the effort it cost him. "Put down that lamp and bring a glass and we'll toast the new young Rausch."

"I heard you come in, and I couldn't imagine why you didn't come to bed. I couldn't wait any longer to hear the news. How's Sally? Is it a boy or a girl?"

She held out a glass, and he poured a tablespoonful of brandy into it.

"Right as rain. She had an easy time of it, comparatively."

"I know what that means. Men make me tired. And the baby?"

"A girl, to be named Elsa for Ludwig's mother. Drink for her, Anne—a long life and a happy one."

He drained his glass and set it on the table. "If there is such a thing."

Anne's eagerness was quenched. She forgot Sally. John hadn't been much distracted after all. Sudden futile silly tears filled her eyes. She brushed them away, like a child, on her ruffled sleeves and said, "John—"

He looked up at her, and then away from the love and compassion in her face. "Go back to bed, Anne. I'll be up in a minute."

Instead, because she could no longer help herself, she went down on the floor beside him, her back against the edge of the dining table, her breast against his knees. She put her head down and wept. It was for only a moment. Before he had spoken or recovered from his amazement, she lifted her head, sat back a little and looked at him.

"I'm sorry, John, to be such a fool, but I couldn't bear it one more instant."

"Bear what?" He had his arm around her; he held her close, so that her head was tight against him.

"John, if I swear never to ask you to make me another promise so long as we live, will you promise me just one thing?"

She felt the start he made, drew back from his arm to look, and saw something like consternation in his eyes. Had he, then, thought of that end for himself sometime? Did he know what she had been thinking? She went on speaking hurriedly. "Promise me, even if you're unhappy—however unhappy you are—you'll never—" she dropped her eyes, and even then could not quite say it; she mumbled the rest, "you'll never do what Kate did?"

"Kill myself? For God's sake." Surprise flattened his voice, made it unduly loud. When he went on, it was more quietly. "My poor darling! What have you been thinking?" Anne could feel the slow relaxation of his body. "Of course I won't. I promise, darling. I give you my solemn word of honor. I'll live it out, whatever comes. Why did you think—?"

"Oh, I don't know. You can be so awfully unhappy. And you said it was sane, if a person was unhappy, to—Oh, never mind. I'm sorry, but just the same, thank you for promising." The burden had rolled off her mind; she could even laugh a little in a dubious fashion. "I was so frightened. You were frightened too, John, for fear I was going to ask you for a promise you didn't want to give. What did you think—?"

He was confused. "I don't know." He put his hand on the brandy bottle. "I thought maybe when you found me here you thought I'd taken to secret drinking, and were going to ask me to sign the pledge."

"Oh, John!" She did laugh, then, her head thrown back, childish again, perhaps a little hysterical. "I wasn't brought up a Ballard to think a drink now and then a sin. I know," she added contemptuously, "that a little brandy after a night's hard work doesn't make a man a drunkard. Now I have your promise, I'll keep my word too." She got to her feet and stood smiling down at him. "I won't ask you to give up any of your minor vices."

John put the brandy bottle away, and they went upstairs together. He was wondering whether promising not to do something he'd never been tempted to do set him free to indulge in the other "minor vices" without violating his conscience.

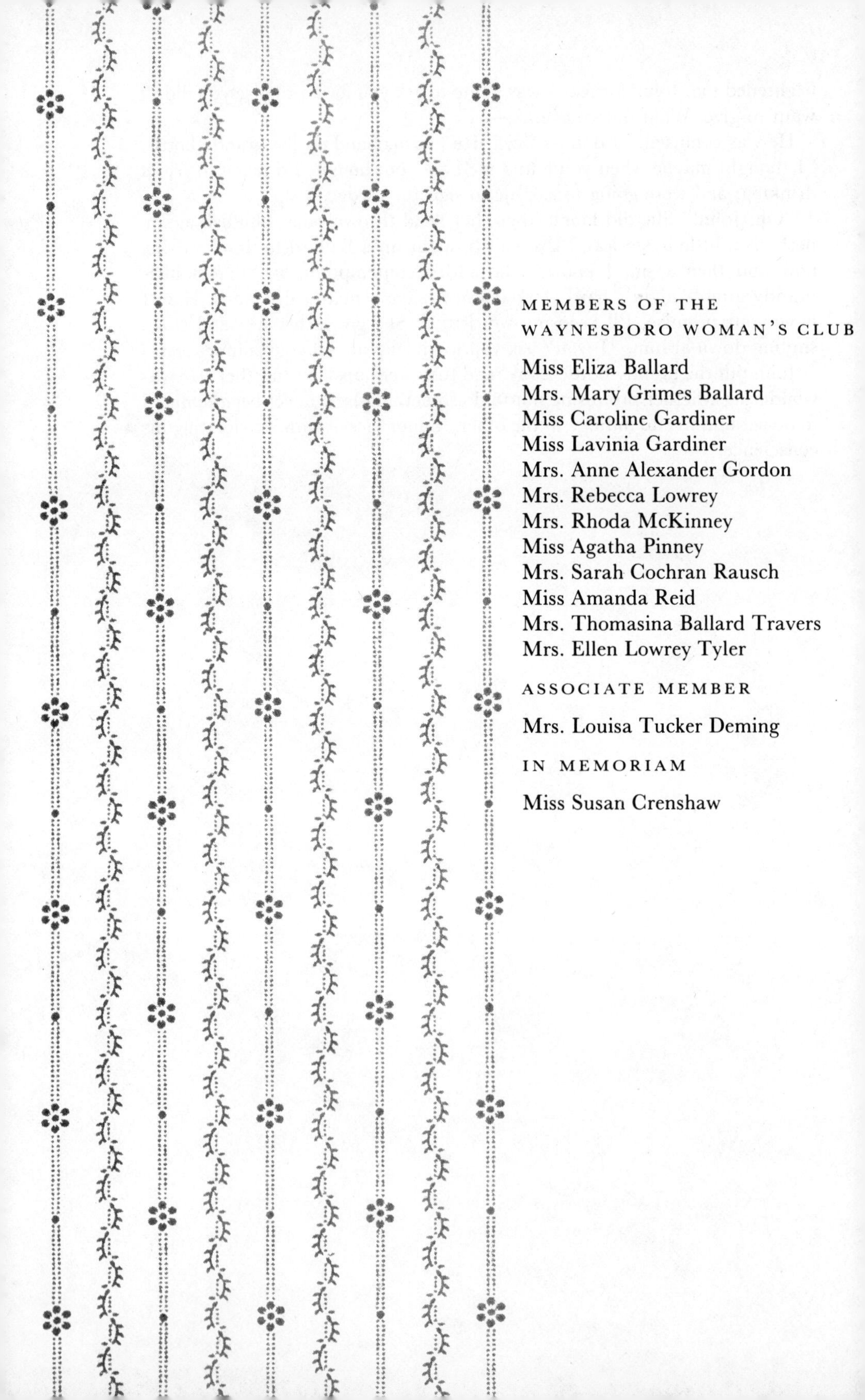

MEMBERS OF THE
WAYNESBORO WOMAN'S CLUB

Miss Eliza Ballard
Mrs. Mary Grimes Ballard
Miss Caroline Gardiner
Miss Lavinia Gardiner
Mrs. Anne Alexander Gordon
Mrs. Rebecca Lowrey
Mrs. Rhoda McKinney
Miss Agatha Pinney
Mrs. Sarah Cochran Rausch
Miss Amanda Reid
Mrs. Thomasina Ballard Travers
Mrs. Ellen Lowrey Tyler

ASSOCIATE MEMBER

Mrs. Louisa Tucker Deming

IN MEMORIAM

Miss Susan Crenshaw

* 1872 *

"For the first time the Grim Reaper . . ."

On Wednesday, the first of May, 1872, the Liberal Republicans met in convention in Cincinnati. On the same afternoon the Waynesboro Woman's Club held its regular meeting at the home of its President. The greater event was not without its influence on the lesser one.

In 1872 the Ballard house, comparatively new by Waynesboro standards, was the showplace of the town, so elaborate was its architecture. Built of brick with granite trim, it had roofs of different heights, shingled with slate in variegated patterns. The impressive double front door was seldom open, unless the family was in the yard playing croquet or sitting under the trees; but only those who came on errands or expected to make but a brief stay approached the house from this direction, after tying their horses to the negro-boy hitching post outside the iron fence. The customary entrance for visitors was a driveway that ran along the left side of the house, near the property line, and led to a wide porte-cochere and beyond to the turn-around and stables. It was at the porte-cochere that Johann stood to greet company arriving on horseback or in carriages.

Inside the house two halls of equal width intersected one another at right angles near the center of the building both upstairs and down. One, the front hall, began at the front door and ended just beyond the free-standing staircase that climbed in leisurely fashion to the upstairs hall and gave access to the family bedrooms and the music room above the parlor. The second or back hall ran between the porte-cochere and a smaller entrance on the opposite side, which opened onto a brick wall that led to the street. The parlor, which one could enter from either hall through doors that were usually permitted to stand open (thereby lending an air of spaciousness and elegance), offered a striking example of Victorian grandeur in which the plain Mrs. Ballard, the severe Eliza, and the vaguely apologetic Thomasina were incongruous figures. Indeed, though the Club had met there often enough to have grown accustomed to the splendid room, it had remained impossible to get used to the Ballard women at home in all its splendor.

The parlor contained a marble fireplace, whose mantel was adorned by a pair of Sèvres vases and a clock of rose Pompadour porcelain. Tall arched windows on either side were hung in tamboured lace curtains and gold broché draperies. The windows of the deep bay that faced on Main Street had white Holland blinds with tasseled pulls, and in the bay stood a fernery. The draperies that hung at the sides of this embrasure were also of gold broché, and the material was repeated in the upholstery of two plump and deeply tufted armchairs, the long sofa that stood against the opposite wall, and the love seat next to the front hall door. A pier glass between this door and the bay window was framed by Corinthian columns and an overhanging cornice; and between the sofa and the second door stood a massive cabinet with a bowed front, filled with Dresden figurines. Overhead two crystal chandeliers fell from the ceiling, and a striped beige moquette carpet lay underfoot.

Thomasina's marriage had changed the Ballard house somewhat. An upstairs apartment had been fashioned out of the bedrooms, and the privacy of the married couple had been ensured by the addition of two partitions, one upstairs in the front hall, just beyond the stairway; and the second downstairs in the back hall, just past the door into the dining room. A new, narrow, and steep stairway had been built for the use of the couple living upstairs and the pupils who came to take piano lessons with Samuel. A door had been cut in the downstairs partition, but this was kept locked. The house no longer had the old spaciousness, but had taken on a closed look. The front staircase led nowhere but to the large music room over the parlor.

The ladies, on that May afternoon, sat on stiff chairs that were widely spaced to provide room for their full skirts. From the Club's beginning it had been taken for granted that a meeting was a formal occasion, not to be denigrated by anything less than one's best afternoon costume. It would have been an insult to assume that one's second- or third-best would do for an afternoon spent with that particular group. The Ballards, who believed in dress reform, set an example by their attire: no bustles, no ruffles, no draped overskirts or wasp waists. Mrs. McKinney, the wife of the Presbyterian minister and Mrs. Ballard's guest, was seated next to her and wore the blue bombazine that was her Sabbath day costume. The teachers from the Female College wore their usual dark poplins, skirts draped over modest bustles, tight basques, with touches of lace at the throat and lace cuffs under bishop sleeves. The Gardiner sisters could still draw upon the preserved riches of their girlhood: the heavy corded silks, the taffetas, the mousselines de laine. Miss Caroline, with the town dressmaker's help, had made an attempt to change a round hoop skirt to one with a more fashionable silhouette, but Miss Lavinia, so proud as to prefer being considered eccentric rather than poor, clung to her round crinolines (and would do so for the rest of her life; when the time came that the Gardiners were once more "well-fixed," her new dresses were made in the old fashion: she could not bring herself to admit that the hoop skirts had not always been a matter of preference). Only Sally and Anne did credit to the place and occasion: Anne in a nut-brown faille with a draped overskirt and a tassel-trimmed postilion basque; Sally in a reseda green cashmere with a polonaise, tight above the waist, then full and long, over a bustled skirt, trimmed with ruffles and pleated ruchings. Her fair braids and curls were pinned chignon fashion on the back and top of her head, so that her little green hat brim, curled up at the sides, was thrust forward over her nose, its streamers and flowers trailing down over the chignon behind. In spite, however, of whatever satisfaction she must have derived from her turn-out, Sally was in a temper: her social smile was frozen and signified nothing. An air of constraint stiffened all the members that afternoon, not only Sally. There were questioning glances from eye to eye, and the fixed expressions of amiability on several faces did not conceal their emotions.

When the roll was called, silence followed the naming of Miss Crenshaw. Her absence needed no explanation. She had for a long while been rather a *memento mori*, so thin, so jaundiced had she grown, so despairing, and then so resigned had been the look in her eyes. Now Miss Pinney, after too long a pause, spoke for her: "Miss Crenshaw sends her regrets. She was feeling very unwell when I last called." And she added stoutly, her vague blue eyes held wide open to prevent her tears falling, "She is not, however, confined to her bed." Then she could not help it: the tears overflowed and trickled down her cheeks. There was no one among her audience who did not grieve with her.

The presence of Mrs. Ballard's guest was a clear indication that Mrs. McKinney would be proposed as a candidate for the vacant membership when poor old Crenny—the idea was repellent particularly to Sally Rausch, and perhaps to the Gardiners, who did not care much for reformers of any stripe, since reform had been thrust upon them in their youth. And Mrs. McKinney was a Reformer. None knew her well, since her husband had so recently been called to the Presbyterian church. Anne did not really know her, but she had not felt moved to like one who moved down the church aisle to the ministerial pew with the sweeping irresistibility of the figurehead of a ship under way, her impressive bust seeming to cleave the waves, her skirts fluttering behind like a swirling wake. She had a solid, square, heavy face and a firm repressive smile that deepened the lines from nose to mouth, from mouth to chin. Her eyes behind her steel-rimmed spectacles were, when turned upon the young, judgmatical and upon occasion disapproving; that the same eyes could be and often were kind and friendly meant nothing to those upon whom the kind glances were not bent. On that afternoon, she sat stiffly in her chair next to the fireplace, bolt upright, her eyes bent on her gloved hands folded in her lap, while the members looked away from her politely, and thought about her until their minds slipped away to even more uncomfortable things.

The subject for the essay of the afternoon was "Mr. Howells, Our Ohio

Author," the essayist, Miss Eliza Ballard. Eliza, who by temperament preferred realism to sentimentalism, and who had read what Stendhal and Balzac she had been able to get her hands on, was fairly contemptuous of Mr. Howells. She read her paper with a vigor that perhaps emphasized her contempt unduly. It was in reality not so much the novelist she was angry with as her sister and brother-in-law, and when she heard in the pauses between her own words the faint tinkling notes from the piano, upstairs, on the other side of the house, where Samuel was dealing with one of his pupils, her voice scolded him in the words with which she attacked *Their Wedding Journey*. She had requested Thomasina to suggest that the afternoon music lessons be postponed. "The ladies should not have to stumble over grubby children on our doorstep," she had said. Thomasina had refused. "You know very well that Samuel's pupils are not 'grubby'; they come here scrubbed till they shine. And they use the side door on the other side of the house, and the private staircase Papa put in for us, so there will be no stumbling over them! Besides, his pupils are as important to him as your paper is to you." Now, the tinkling notes went on, and Eliza's tone became more and more acid as she rebuked Mr. Howells for looking at the world with too kind an eye.

Anne thought, "No wonder Eliza's an old maid, if she despises agreeable people as much in real life as she does in books." Other members of the Club, with whom *Their Wedding Journey* was a universal favorite, were hurt by the implied criticism of their judgment; they even moved in their chairs, restlessly, as a way of expressing disagreement. Then they let their minds wander to the thoughts that had been waiting on the threshold all afternoon. When the Club had been organized, it had been clear that since its membership was to be composed of women of such diverse tastes and opinions all controversial subjects must be barred from discussion, and meetings limited to purely literary programs; they had prided themselves on their ability to ignore their differences.

But until now it had not occurred to them that there might ever be serious political disagreements among them. Even in 1868 there had been factions in the party; Radicals fought for postponement of Reconstruction until certain that the equality and the right to citizenship of the freedmen were assured. The Ballards, the Lowreys, the Demings had been of that persuasion. Moderates and ex-soldiers like Ludwig and John, who were entirely convinced of the South's readiness for peace and a return to the Union, were indifferent to the Fifteenth Amendment, and were tired of all the to-do over Reconstruction. But the Republican party was the party of all the ladies; it had supported the war and saved the Union, and they had no intention of deserting it. And once Grant had been nominated and elected, differences would be forgotten.

By 1872 the whirligig of time had done its work. It had become evident that however wrong the Radicals might have been about Reconstruction, they were right, at least in the eyes of all conservative men and certainly in those of a rising young manufacturer, in their financial policy. Supporters of sound money would stick with the party and vote to give Grant a second term. On the other hand, some one-time Radicals could not stomach corruption in high places: they became Liberal Republicans ("come-outers") and would nominate their own man for the Presidency. It remained to be seen in that spring of '72 whether women whose menfolk had suddenly become political opponents, even enemies, could continue to gather together amicably, as men seemed to be able to do.

Ludwig, newcomer to the town though he was, had become one of the local leaders of the party and a member of the County Central Committee; this responsibility had been awarded him partly on account of his zeal, partly on account of his influence over his German friends and over the Negroes, who were many of them his employees (and in Ohio Negroes could now vote). In the spring of 1872 he was supporting General Grant and the rest of the ticket. Comments highly infuriating to Sally Rausch had been attributed to Mrs. Ballard and Mrs. McKinney, to the effect that it was scandalous that Waynesboro should be controlled by that upstart Ludwig Rausch and his beer-swilling cronies, and that the district should be represented by a man of questionable integrity like General Deming, against whom nothing definite was known, but who was certainly involved in the hanky-panky going on in Congress and round about President Grant. Judge Ballard, who had once been the most radical of Republicans, had said nothing indiscreet about local men, but to him the corruption of the national government seemed so dangerous and so contemptible that he was willing to take part in the Liberal Republican movement, even though its success would mean a too-hasty settlement of Reconstruction and an end of the attempt to win equality for the Negro.

Criticism of General Deming must have been embarrassing to the Lowreys, who had encouraged their Miss Tucker to marry him, and even to Mrs. Tyler and Miss Pinney, who were involved in all the Lowrey loyalties. The Misses Gardiner were indifferent to political questions, but were committed to at least a tacit support of the Ballards, since the Judge had promised their nephew a place in his office, and a chance to read law there when he had finished at Princeton. Amanda and the Ballard women were of course wholeheartedly with the Judge; indeed, Mrs. Ballard, presiding at the Club meeting, gave the impression of one held against her will to attend to trifles while world-shaking events were taking place elsewhere.

Outwardly decorous and attentive as the older ladies, inwardly Anne began to seethe with temper as soon as she let her mind slip from attention to Eliza's crisp accents. She dared not let herself look too often at Sally, because she knew that Sally was seething too, and would consider the presence of Mrs. McKinney almost a personal affront. Ludwig had been attacked by name; Sally had that to pretend to be unconcerned about. Anne did not think that she could have done it. The attacks on General Grant were enough to make her angry—so angry that she could feel the blood rising in her neck, beating full and hard under and in her ears. She could not help the feeling that whoever defamed General Grant defamed his soldiers, and among them John. She gave herself a brief, fleeting smile as this went through her mind, because John would have laughed at her; she knew that however loyal he was to General Grant, it was General Sherman whom he loved, and he had indulged in some forcible exclamations from time to time when he read newspaper accounts of Washington affairs. But it was natural that he should not feel as she did. She knew better than he what the war had done to him. He had come a long way toward recovery since they had first been married—a long way toward peace of mind and a capacity to forget his patients when he had treated them. But still when he had a sad or serious case on his mind, he was apt, in the night, to struggle awake from nightmares, smothered and strangling, to be unable to sleep again until he had gone to the porch for fresh air to wash the smell of gangrene out of his lungs. He was unable still to dissociate death and the smell of gangrene. Anne's thoughts slipped to Miss Crenshaw and, even more obliquely, to her own father, who was not well—oh, worse than "not well," growing feebler every day—then to the point she was trying to make clear in her own mind: that the war should have injured John was endurable, so long as the war seemed not only necessarily but also worthily won, and its winners, the generals, recognized as heroes. But if its greatest general was besmirched—somehow besmirching became retroactive—John had been led by a man not worth following, and all that it had cost him had been paid for nothing. Anne did not believe the newspaper articles of defamation. It was necessary to her not to believe them, to believe that no matter how much other men might abuse their power General Grant at least was above reproach. Therefore, the vile accusations hurled against him, by Democrat and Liberal Republican alike, were false, and she was justified in her anger.

When the Club meeting adjourned, finally, and Eliza had been congratulated on a paper that had seemed to them "a new way to look at fiction," and a "different point of view," "a criticism so original, dear": then, their obligations discharged, the ladies drifted to the hall door and across to the family sitting room for their wraps. There was very little of the usual casual visiting back and forth. Someone asked Mrs. Ballard when she expected her husband home, and she said, "Not until the convention has adjourned." Some asked Anne about her father's health, and she breathed deep to break the catch at her heart before she answered: she had been concerned, but she had not realized that his "breaking" would be noticeable to outsiders; of course everyone knew that rheumatism had stopped his making house calls, but inquiries were too compassionate to be comfortable.

With Amanda, she and Sally went down the brick path to the gate. It was chilly for the first of May, so chilly that it seemed a miracle the apple trees could be in bloom; but the sun was shining, and it was a good day to walk. Sally, since her marriage, had ceased to use the Cochran carriages, and Ludwig and John had need of their horses and buggies; Anne and Sally had grown accustomed to walking to Club meetings except in extremely bad weather. They took it slowly, the long walk from the Ballards', for, as Anne and Amanda both knew, Sally was again pregnant, though it did not yet show, except in her general plumpness and her seeming serenity—cowlike serenity, Amanda thought. Amanda, out of respect for her Sabbath-day boots and her best dress, did not take the vacant-field-and-back-fence way to her house, but accompanied the others along the first cross street to Linden, where she must turn back as Anne and Sally went in the opposite direction to the Rausch cottage. So long as the three of them were together, politics was not mentioned; indeed, even after Amanda had left them, there was not much for Anne and Sally to say, since each knew so well what the other thought. Anne did ask for Ludwig's opinion of the convention.

"He's worried to death. He thinks that if those people in Cincinnati nominate a good man, it'll be nip and tuck in November. And he respects Judge Ballard. He hasn't said so, but I think he wishes the Republicans didn't have to run President Grant again."

"Oh, Sally! Surely Ludwig doesn't believe all those lies!"

"Of course not," Sally said stoutly. "But they do stick. How about John?"

"John would never vote against Grant."

"It's the things they say about Ludwig that rile me. And they roll off him like water off a duck's back. Anne, do you know what I think? I think Mrs. Ballard's going to propose Mrs. McKinney for the Club in poor old Crenny's place. If she does, I vow I'll resign. Whatever your church was thinking of—"

"We had never seen her. She wasn't with him when he came candidating."

"Anyway, maybe by that time we'll have the Demings home to stay, and she'll want to come back into the Club."

"You don't think we'll send a *Democrat* to Congress? The Seventh District? Why, General Deming thinks he has a life job."

"I know. But there's been a lot of talk. Maybe the other counties in the district will nominate someone else. Where does it come from, all the money the Demings spend? And that junket last year on the new railroad, all the way to California, and the newspapers' hints about 'railroad congressmen.'"

"I declare, Sally, you're as bad as Mrs. McKinney, yourself."

"I never did think much of General Deming. But for goodness' sake, forget it, Anne. You understand, these are all my private opinions, not Ludwig's. He would be scandalized to hear me talk so. And why do you care about General Deming?"

"I don't really. I wouldn't put anything past *him*," Anne said cheerfully. "And wouldn't old Teapot be in a fine taking if there were a scandal!" And they both laughed at the idea.

When they reached the Rausch gate, the front door was opened by slim black Cassie, trained now to Cochran standards: a model nurse-housemaid-cook. Little Elsa let go of her hand and started down the path; Sally went inside the gate to stoop and kiss her. At two, Elsa was a sturdy blonde child with clear, very blue eyes and soft bright hair held back from her face by a round comb.

"Mamma's come," she called back to Cassie, "and"—she peeped around her mother—"Johnny's mamma."

Anne stood smiling, outside the gate, while Sally smoothed the little girl's hair, looking from the pair of them to the house, thinking how happy Sally was, endowed with everything she wanted: Ludwig, Elsa, another baby coming, the house—a quaint house, old-fashioned, with its high-pitched roof and the three peaks in it, a large one in the center, over a door to the porch roof, a smaller one on each side over a round-tipped window, all the eaves fringed with an elaborate lacework of white-painted wood. The window frames were white and set off by shutters. The brick walls were ivy-covered, and altogether the house looked like one of the engraved illustrations for a *Harper's Weekly* love story, as if no one could ever be unhappy in it.

Sally turned from the child to invite Anne in.

"It's dinnertime, Sally, and here comes Ludwig now."

Ludwig, when he saw the group at the gate, stopped his horse at the hitching pose, instead of going on to the driveway that led back to the stable. He tied the horse and joined them while Elsa was struggling to unlatch the iron gate. He reached over from outside, picked her up, and swung her to his shoulder.

"Schönes Mädchen!"

"Papa! Mamma! Papa has me."

"So I see."

Ludwig, laughing, reached over the gate and put a big finger on the tip of Sally's hat, pulling it farther over her nose.

"Schönes Mädchen, tell your mamma never before has there been so absurd a bonnet."

"And I just got through telling Anne how worried you were."

"Worried? Niemals! Where have you been, looking like fashionplates, both of you? Oh, yes, don't say it. I do remember: your Club. Are you on the way home, Anne? If you can squeeze your fal-de-rals into my buggy, Elsa and I will drive you up the hill. Kiss me, Sally, I'll be back directly."

"Not on the street, you goose!" But she lifted her face to him over the gate, serene in the knowledge that the great maple trees above and around her were springing into leaf; he gave her a hearty smacking kiss before he lifted Elsa into the buggy and turned to help Anne.

In front of the Gordons' Johnny was swinging on their gate, his eyes watching the street from between its iron-vined posts; he was not tall enough to be able to see over its top, even standing on the crosspiece. When the buggy stopped at the carriage step, he let the gate click shut and continued to watch them gravely, even when Elsa pointed her fat forefinger and shouted, "Johnny!"

"No lady ever points a finger," her father said. "And you can't have Johnny now, Mamma's waiting for us."

He had started to climb down, to come around the buggy to help Anne alight, when John came out on the porch and called to him.

"Sit still, Ludwig. I'm coming."

At the gate Johnny slipped his hand into his father's and went onto the carriage step, still regarding solemnly and wordlessly the occupants of the buggy.

Elsa pointed her finger again, "My Uncle Dock."

"So it is, mein liebes Mädchen, but don't point. She's so pleased to recognize a friend." He apologized for her, as John, with a hand under Anne's elbow, helped her to the carriage step and thence to the ground; Ludwig tightened the reins, but held the horse for a moment, as John spoke.

"What news, Ludwig, from the Convention?"

"None. So far as I know, they're just milling around, still. Come spend the evening with us sometime, you two, and we'll drink confusion to all Come-Outers in Hoffmann's finest lager."

Anne grimaced, John laughed, they waved good-bye to Ludwig and Elsa, and turned into the house, the little boy in his sashed frock and pantalettes between them, swinging on their hands.

At dinner (the evening meal, since John had little time at noon) while Anne looked to the needs of her son, perched on the chair beside her on a couple of his grandfather's thick outdated medical books, she made a tale of her afternoon's outing for her husband and father; she spoke gaily even while she remembered the solicitous inquiry for Dr. Alexander, and tried not to show in her face the compassion she felt at the sight of his awkward fumbling with his silverware, as if knife and fork were too heavy for his stiff swollen hands.

It was not until he had said good-night to them and gone back to his solitary rooms over the office—not until Martha had come in from the kitchen to the sitting room, to take the child to bed—that she asked her husband about Miss Crenshaw. She was standing, having risen to kiss Johnny good-night and hand him over to Martha at the door, and had returned to the hearth to poke the coal fire that had been lighted in the grate, her back to John: "They asked about Papa, too. Do you think he looks so bad?" She hoped that her offhandedness would make it easy for him, as if, being unconcerned herself, he must perforce be unconcerned, too.

But he put down the evening paper he was reading, rose, put his pipe on the mantelpiece, and took the poker from her.

"You have a master-hand with a fire—a positive genius for putting it out. Let me build that up for you before I go back to the office. If it goes out, you'll be cold."

She sat down on the edge of her rocker while he rebuilt the fire. It was not until he had gone back to his chair and picked up his paper again that he answered her question.

"He doesn't look very good—it's the rheumatism—he suffers from it, but it won't kill him."

"So long as he isn't helpless. He would hate it so. And Miss Crenshaw?"

"You must know, Anne. You've seen her."

"She won't be out again?"

He shook his head.

"How long?"

"No one could tell you that. But I'll make it as easy for her as possible."

"Oh, John! And what has she had out of life, to have made it worth all this?"

He answered gently. "You don't know, Anne. Perhaps her life has seemed a happy one to her. That's something no one can judge or estimate, or measure, for another. She talks a good deal, now, about her childhood."

"You aren't—it isn't worrying you?"

"That I can't do anything for her, you mean?" He spoke more shortly, "No, no one would. I don't like seeing anyone die of cancer, but there isn't a doctor living who could have saved her."

"But sometimes—" She dropped whatever she had started to say, and shifted the subject slightly. "Sally is all put out. She thinks Mrs. Ballard is just waiting for Crenny to die to invite Mrs. McKinney into the Club. We think that's why Mrs. Ballard had her at the meeting today."

"I'd already guessed you didn't care much for your minister's wife." His eyes twinkled at her, over the top of the paper.

"I don't like reformers. They have a kind of itch. What's the matter with Waynesboro the way it is? I never minded when Mrs. Ballard was thinking of nothing but Woman Suffrage."

"You know you believe in that, as a matter of fact."

"I think I have as much right to vote, and know as much, as all those colored men. But Sally's against it because Ludwig is."

"Ludwig's getting to be a behind-the-scenes politician, and politicians don't want an incalculable element coming into the picture. What has Mrs. B. got on her mind now?"

"Temperance. Now that Mrs. McKinney's got hold of her."

"I hear Sheldon & Edwards have taken the keg of whiskey out of the store."

"Yes, old C. P. is such a good Presbyterian—he's an elder, even—of course he did, when the McKinneys got after him. It was a backwoods idea, anyway, having that keg in a dry-goods store, with a tin cup hanging, for anyone to take a drink who wanted it. But those women will be going after the Hoffmanns next, and what will you and Ludwig do then?"

John snorted. "There's no harm in the Hoffmanns. It's a curious notion those temperance reformers have, that to stop drunkenness you must begin with the saloonkeepers. They'll never get anywhere until they begin with the drunkards. Find out what they're running away from and why. I see more of the mischief drunkenness can do than the Ballards ever did."

"Of course, drunkenness is loathsome. Only, I don't want to feel ashamed every time you come in smelling of beer."

"You'd better not. But don't worry about the Hoffmanns for awhile anyway. Now that Judge Ballard's gone over to the new party, the reformers won't do anything to antagonize the Germans."

"D'you think the Liberals have got a chance?"

"No. High-flying idealists, without anyone to pull them together." He rose, knocked his pipe out in the grate and put it in his pocket. "I must go. Don't poke the fire out again." He ruffled her head with a quick hand as he passed her and went out the side door to the porch.

At the Rausches', after dinner, politics were discussed at much greater length, and more seriously. Sally was enjoying one of those stretches of mental leisure that come but seldom to wives and mothers, when there is no worry haunting the brain, no problem to be solved. Concern with politics was a recreation, a game in which she could participate only as an onlooker; but being married to one of the players, she could at least learn the rules and might some day be able to give advice. When they left the dinner table, they went to the fireplace end of the long living room. Ludwig picked up the evening paper, while Sally rocked Elsa on her lap. In the dining room behind them, with only a wide uncurtained opening between, they could hear Cassie clearing the table, the soft clink of silver on china, the brittler sound of plate on plate; not until she had gone into the kitchen, letting the door swing shut behind her, did they speak.

"Is there anything in the paper about the Cincinnati Convention? Have they done anything?"

"Yes, plenty in the paper. But no, they haven't done anything. Milling around, not even able to get organized. Cranks and idealists in the limelight, and some pretty shrewd ambitious men—disappointed men—there to see what they can get out of it."

"Do you think they have any chance at all? Surely not."

"They might. They are right about many things."

"But here? In Waynesboro?"

"There will be Judge Ballard's influence to fight, with the niggers and the church people, and Carl Schurz's with the Germans."

"But you can persuade the Germans: they like you."

"They may like Schurz better, and common honesty in government."

"Anne thinks all this talk about dishonesty in government is a libel cooked up against General Grant and his cabinet by men who want their places."

Ludwig laughed. "Anne is a law unto herself. Loyalty with her is a vice, she carries it to such an extreme." He folded the newspaper, rose, and took it to Sally. She held it in one hand over the arm of her chair while he lifted Elsa from her lap and carried her back to his place; he gave himself over to amusing the child until Cassie came in from the kitchen and bore her off to bed.

Sally let the paper slide to the floor beside her. "At any rate, you have Mr. Bonner on your side, and he's a host in himself."

"Yes, he's not ready to put an end to Reconstruction: he'd like to see every rebel state made to feel the conqueror's heel for quite a while yet. That's Andersonville, and I don't know that I blame him. but I don't think harping on that strain will help us much now."

"Is it just loyalty that is keeping you in the party, Ludwig?"

"What is it that is troubling you, meine Liebe? The things they say about me and the 'lower element'?"

"I'm not thin-skinned, even if the things they say about you make me furious. I just wondered, though, since you seem to agree with them."

"Loyalty is a part of it. Grant was my general too long for me not to vote for him. But it isn't Grant I'm working for primarily. Men, honest and dishonest, come and go; we can get rid of the dishonest ones in time without breaking up the party. It is the party I work for because I believe in its principles. A protective tariff. D'you think I could sell any rope without it? A sound currency. Resumption of specie payments, the gold standard. Our Radical Repuclicans have been wrong over and over again about Reconstruction, but that is bound to be settled for good before many more years. The other questions will never be settled permanently. There will always be a debtor class to clamor for inflation, and farmers to want free trade, and they can't see for their own headaches that if the country's money is no good, nothing is any good, or the farmers, that if industry and labor go smash, there'll be no one able to pay for what they produce. I want the party kept in power because I think it's for the good of the country."

When Sally asked him what he thought the Liberal Republican platform would be, he snorted contemptuously.

"The good God only knows. All the cranks in the country are there, but they are cranks along different lines. Free trade—but Greeley and his friends are high tariff men. Greenbackers—but Schurz and Adams are for gold resumption. The only thing they all want is honesty in government, and the South taken back into the Union without more ado. And even so, there are sure to be some politicians among them who see a chance for success and won't be too great sticklers for honesty."

"It's their assumption that *all* the honesty is on their side that infuriates me. And Ludwig, when Miss Crenshaw dies, Mrs. Ballard is going to want that unspeakable McKinney woman in the Club."

Ludwig threw back his head, shouting with laughter. "Sally, Liebste—so it is that you are angry about! But I thought that in your so-literary Club you rose above personalities."

"Oh, men make me tired." But Sally smiled at him.

"You aren't going to start a feud in the Club, are you? Listen, Liebe, if you are going into politics with me, there are some things you must learn from men. That you can be personal friends with your political enemies. That you can catch more flies with sugar than vinegar."

"I can *pretend*," Sally said scornfully, "but don't you think I'll ever like Mrs. McKinney, because I never shall. One thing sure," she added, with satisfaction, "the McKinneys'll never have any influence over your German friends, with the temperance bee in their bonnets."

"It's not the McKinneys that worry me. I'm afraid you'll have to get used to my spending my evenings—some of them, at any rate—with the 'lower element' they talk about. At the Hoffmanns'. That's where they foregather. By the way—this is interesting—have you seen that new fellow Lichtenstein around town?"

"The lawyer who has an office up over Thirkields' Drug Store? Weighs, I should think, three hundred pounds? I've seen him sitting at the bottom of that narrow flight of steps that goes up to his office, and wondered if he had to rest before he started up, or was afraid he couldn't squeeze between the walls. Why? Do you know him?" Her voice wws startled as if she had to face the possibility that Ludwig's avocation might involve him with questionable characters. "He's grotesque, like something out of Dickens. I can't imagine his having clients."

"His figure is his misfortune. But not three hundred pounds. And however uncouth his appearance, it's misleading. There are a good many Germans who will trust him as a lawyer. He doesn't speak English well because he's lived these last years with an uncle in Over-the-Rhine Cincinnati, still speaking German, of course; but as soon as he was admitted to citizenship, and to the bar, he moved up here, a widower with a small son, to establish a law practice. I hope his accent doesn't set him apart from other than German clients. He has a fine education—Wittenberg—and a brilliant mind. He's the only man in town who can give Dock Gordon a trimming at chess. There's a board kept set up for them on a table at Hoffmann's, although it isn't often Dock has time to play. I play a practice match with Lichtenstein now and then, but that's all it is for him, practice. Everyone who comes in there likes and respects him. If I could get him to help. Don't look so, Sally, bitte schön. I do not ask you to be friends with him, only with the ladies of your Club."

"After they're in the Club, maybe," Sally agreed grudgingly. "But I wish I could think of someone else to be in it besides Mrs. McKinney." And with the air of one studying a weighty problem, her brows knit and her lips compressed, she took out her sewing from the basket on the table.

As the week went on, the anxiety of Ludwig and of other regular Republicans was considerably mitigated by the lack of direction and the sounds of confusion that prevailed at the Liberal Republican convention. And the worst of their fears were dismissed when the news came that Horace Greeley had been nominated for President. It seemed like some kind of cosmic joke, and was to seem more of one when the Democrats later that summer, seeing some slight chance to defeat the incumbent party, also chose him for their candidate. The man who had been during the war the oracle of the Republicans, particularly of country and village Republicans in the Middle West, who had once been more rabid against the South than any soldier, who was still the highest of high-tariff men, had been chosen to represent the liberals, the inflationists, the free-traders, and the reconstructed states of the South. But what was comedy to much of the nation, and to almost all Waynesboro, was tragedy to Liberals who had supported other candidates, and most certainly to Judge Ballard.

He came home from Cincinnati by the evening train after the last day of the Convention. He had not thought it worthwhile to telegraph his family of his arrival; the carriage, of course, had not been sent for him, and he took a hired hack for the long ride from the railroad station to his house at the other end of town. He was very tired, and the ride on the cars had not been restful; even the slow, rattling hack, with its smell of straw and horse blankets, racked his bones, but he expected to be able to pull himself together and make the best of things before the girls, if they were still up, at least until he and his wife were together in their massive, high-pillowed bed, with the lamps out.

Mrs. Ballard and Eliza, reading in the sitting room, were the first to hear the horses' hooves and the wheels on the gravel of the drive and under the porte-cochere. They started for the side hall. Then Thomasina came to the head of the side stairs just as the outer door opened.

"It *is* Papa," she called over her shoulder, and came running down as the driver of the hack set her father's valise inside the door. Her husband followed more slowly, with his irritating air (irritating to the Judge, at least) of being not quite sure that he was considered one of the family.

"Well, Thomasina," her father said, checking her embrace, "I have not been to the North Pole." He paid the driver and closed the door behind him. "Leave the valise there," he added to the over-helpful Samuel, "I'll pick it up on my way to bed. Come along to the study. I suppose you all want me to tell you how it happened."

"You can wait, Thomas, if you are very tired."

"Now, Mary, you never make all this to-do when I come home from riding circuit. I am frequently tired on those occasions, too. Not but what a cup of tea would be welcome, Thomasina."

Presently they were all in his small study behind the sitting room; the lamp had been lighted and a match set to the fire laid in the grate; Thomasina had brought in the tea equipage and had lighted the spirit lamp. It would take a while for the water to boil; as they waited she asked him the question the others would not have asked—not before Samuel—if they had had to wait all night.

"How did it ever happen, Papa? I thought you had plans all made."

"I still don't know. I fear that I am not an adept politician, but better politicians than I am are nonplussed, too. Judge Stanley Matthews—"

"Are you terribly disappointed?"

He looked at his probing daughter with some wonder, but it was Eliza who answered her sister first. "You don't know your A-B-C's," she snapped. "What else have we been talking about, since you heard—"

"Yes, certainly I was disappointed. But your mother and I have worked many years for many causes, and we know that there are disappointments more often than not. But discouragement—even seeming hopelessness—has never induced us to give up. Another time—"

Thomasina, her heart wrung by his look of desperate exhaustion, broke in with a lamenting "Oh, Papa! It does seem as if the wicked flourish like the green bay tree!"

He smiled with the rueful amusement his daughter so often provoked. "It is hardly so bad as all that. Mr. Greeley does not have horns or cloven feet."

"Mamma thinks he does." Thomasina busied herself making the tea. Mrs. Ballard nodded, her mouth a grim, straight line.

"I have not forgiven, and cannot forgive, his treason to the Woman's Rights movement. He promised, and betrayed his promise. It is a pity, after all the hard work that you and Judge Matthews and the others have done, to have such a—well, to put it mildly—*weather-cock* thrust upon you."

"Yes. Yes, as you know, Mr. Greeley was not my choice for the nomination." He sipped his tea, put the cup down on the desk beside which he was sitting, wiped his white mustache and imperial. "But what we say about him must not go beyond this room. For I must exert my best efforts in the endeavor to elect him. He is at least incorruptible."

"But Papa—" He knew what Thomasina would say. He had always held that though it was right that a judge should use what influence he had to advance a cause he believed in, it was quite different—and improper—for a judge to enter actively into the campaign for the election of one man or another. His earlier expectation that he would not speak openly until he was alone with his wife he now felt to have been wrong. His daughters were grown, his son-in-law perfectly trustworthy, if not very forceful, and his situation—the family situation—should be made clear to them all.

"Don't remind me, Thomasina, of what I have so many times expressed as my firm conviction. It is still my conviction. But I am thinking of resigning from the bench." His endeavor to speak matter-of-factly was betrayed by a sigh audible in the hush that followed his words. All who heard it saw him for an instant as a man who was growing old, almost ready to give up.

His wife least of all could bear to see him so. "Thomas, you will feel differently when you are rested. I know that there are moments when one's life seems to have been wasted—all one's strength given for nothing—but fortunately such moments pass."

"It is not that, Mary. There was some personal disappointment for me in the outcome of the convention, in addition to my disappointment for the country. If things had happened otherwise—if Cox and Judge Matthews had had their way—there was a suggestion, almost a promise, that if we carried the election I should be appointed to the next vacancy in the Federal District Court. Now there is no chance of that."

"Won't Mr. Greeley listen to their advice, if he is elected?"

"He won't be elected."

"But why should you resign?"

"Like a petulant child, you think? It is not that. But the salary of a State Supreme Court judge is hardly enough for us to live on. I believe that it would be wise for me to devote myself to reviving my law practice."

A shocked silence followed. This time it was Eliza who broke it.

"But Papa—don't misunderstand me: it was good of you to build us this house—but we don't have to have it; we'd as lief go back to Spring Street. Rather, if it's a burden to you."

"I do not consider it a burden." He spoke shortly. "Thomasina, pour me another cup of tea, will you?"

She took his cup and held it under the spigot of the urn. Her hands moved, her thin wrists turned, in the pool of light from the lamp on the table. Something, a movement, a whisper of sound, bereft him suddenly of all sense of reality. The richly furnished, dimly lighted study, where a few coals burned so comfortably in the grate, became a dream, and into the dream seeped remembrances, old and sad, that he had thought long exorcised. He saw again his father's thin intent face, bent above heavy books in candlelight. The crowded little house in Cincinnati, its very scent. The day his father's body was brought home. His father was dead—his brilliant father; a state supreme court judge at thirty-five—dead of consumption at thirty-eight, having collapsed in his tavern room in the little country town where court was being held. A sorrowing escort of lawyers had brought the body to Cincinnati, and had done what they could. But there was little they could do that day or afterward. There was no money—no money at all for the widow and her six children. The children had been parceled out, after the funeral, among the relatives; but because he was the youngest, he had been permitted to go with his mother to her married sister's, and had grown up seeing her made a drudge in the household, while he was a helpless, grudgingly accepted, useless burden. His mother's only solace had been having him with her to listen to praises of his father.

"Your tea, Papa."

"Thank you." He took the cup. The room came back into focus, hard and clear; it was there once more, solid plaster and woodwork. "How swift the mind," he thought, "looping backward through the years, to and fro, covering a lifetime in the moment it took to fill a cup with tea." He said, "I suppose that in spite of my self-deception, saying that I built the house for you, it means more to me than to anyone. You have heard the story of my boyhood, but perhaps I never told you how, when I was small, I promised myself that some day I would build my mother a house of her own—a truly splendid house, not just an aggregation of four walls and a roof—to get her away from Aunt Deborah's. For her sake and my father's, I also vowed that I would attain what she had dreamed of for him: a seat on the Supreme Court. Well, my mother died before I was grown, and I never reached the Supreme Court. I know now that that wás an idle dream. But I built the house."

They all listened to him wide-eyed. Thomasina clutched Samuel's hand in hers, under her skirt on the sofa. Her love for her father had never been unmixed with awe; he had seemed to her always a being of clay superior to hers, a man who could never be an object of compassion. After this, however much he might shut himself away behind the distinction of his appearance and the cold gravity of his manner, he would not be without feeling to her. What Eliza felt, as her eyes clung to the Judge's face, was a sudden surprising upsurge of love for the house they had never wanted. But it was not in Eliza to give expression to an emotion. It was Mrs. Ballard who finally broke the long silence.

"At least, Thomas," she said gently, "there is no need to be precipitate. Mr. Greeley may be elected, he may make you a Federal judge. And as for the idle dreams: you might well have been on the Supreme Court by this time, if you had pursued your career single-mindedly, with that in mind. Instead you gave time, energy, devotion to causes that seemed to you right: sacrificed your career for abolition."

"I am past sixty, Mary. Let us not delude ourselves. But I did not mean to frighten you. When I accepted a seat on the bench, I had what I believed enough capital saved from my practice for us to live on. I had had for some years a handsome annual retaining fee from the railroad, for one thing. But unfortunately, as you know, some of my investments have proved unsound." Even in this moment, when his reserve had been broken down by his weariness and need for understanding, the Judge could not have brought himself to use the word "speculation." "However, I still have some funds invested. Let us keep the house"—he paused to stroke his imperial; those who listened knew that the moment of confidence had come to an end—"even if I do have to return to private practice. Fortunately, I have kept my office, and my partnership with Merrill all these years. At any rate, my affairs are of no importance compared to those of the nation. We must try to elect Mr. Greeley, and if we fail, we must choose a better man next time."

"Do you think we can accomplish anything in Waynesboro?"

"Frankly, no."

Mrs. Ballard brought her fist down on her knee. "I've about come to agree with Mrs. McKinney. The place to begin to reform the world is in one's own community. One bad effect of a defeat now will be that the same men will be left in control locally."

"Captain Rausch?" Thomasina liked Sally, wanted to be free to like Ludwig. "Is he really so bad an influence?"

"The temperance cause will not move forward in Waynesboro if he can prevent it," Mrs. Ballard insisted. "Besides, it makes me angry when I think how very hard we worked, against what violent prejudices, to forward the abolition movement, to get the Fifteenth Amendment passed, and now—why, Ludwig Rausch never wanted the Negroes to be given the vote, but today they will all vote as he tells them, rather than as you advise, simply because he is their employer."

"Quite true, but be fair to him, Mary. He believes that Republican principles make for prosperity and upon his mill's prosperity depends the Negroes' livelihood. And that he should look at government from the point of view of the industrialist is as natural as that I should not. Let us not allow politics to interfere with our friendly associations with those who differ from us."

As the summer began, Ludwig was not so sure as Judge Ballard (who did not wait for the election but resigned from the bench in midsummer) that Greeley would be defeated—not even after the Democrats had swallowed the bitter pill and joined the Liberals in nominating him, and all the Republican papers had jeered at them for "eating crow." While Greeley, in spite of his age, was campaigning strenuously about the country, while he and Carl Schurz (the latter in truth but halfheartedly) were making speeches to great crowds in other Ohio towns, Ludwig was hard at work convincing the men of Waynesboro that they should continue their support of General Grant.

Most of his work of persuasion was done in the evening at the Hoffmanns', where the Germans sat all evening around square tables with red-checked cloths, their beer and bowls of pretzels in front of them. Other townsmen too drifted in for a stein of beer on hot summer evenings, teasing the Hoffmann girls at the pumps, stopping to watch a chess game in progress, talking politics with Ludwig.

He had become friendly with Herman Lichtenstein as the weeks passed. The new citizen might be "grotesque" in build, but there was a child-like candor, an open friendliness, in the broad face, the clear blue eyes, that won an honest liking from Ludwig. Lichtenstein had come to America with a passionate fervor for democracy, but that democracy, as represented by Waynesboro, seemed to him endangered by its inadequate educational system. He was looking forward to marriage with the second Hoffmann sister, and to the establishment of a family; all the ardor that overflowed from his bountiful love for his motherless son Rudolph and his promised bride was devoted to pleading the cause of the schools.

"Verstehen Sie—Ich weiss," he said to Ludwig. "You need not to sink about ze schools. Ihre Kinder to school here vill not go." He spoke slowly, sputtering his gutterals over his thick tongue. "Aber ve who no money haf—ve dip-pend on ze State, nicht wahr? Und vat do we haf?"

Ludwig laughed. He knew what the Waynesboro schools were like, outwardly at least: two drab, shabby brick buildings.

"Nothing, educationally speaking. And the schools should be good enough for anyone's children. All our children should go to school together—that is the foundation of democracy. My children should go there with yours. I do believe that. I tell you, Lichtenstein, we'll put you on the school board, and you get the schools in shape by the time my Elsa's old enough to go. She's two now."

Ludwig was jesting, but when he saw that astonished honest face light up, he knew that here was a man he must not hurt. He knew, too, that here was a man who could be a crusading zealot. Ludwig lifted his stein and grinned across the top of it.

"Gesundheit! Of course you understand, you must be elected. Having your name on the ticket isn't everything. But I'll drive a bargain with you: your influence with your friends for General Grant, for mine with my friends for you."

Sally, when this conversation was faithfully reported to her by her husband, hardly knew whether to be annoyed with Ludwig for having become involved with unpresentable people of Mr. Lichtenstein's sort, or amused at what seemed to her his adroitness in using them. That he would seriously attempt to elect Mr. Lichtenstein to the school board she did not believe; and still less did she think that if he did try it, he might succeed. Members of the school board were reelected from year to year, almost automatically: they were nonentities of good family with a steadfast regard for the taxpayer's pocketbook. Sally only hoped that Mr. Lichtenstein would not be too disappointed, nor ever realize that Ludwig had made a one-sided bargain with him.

For some reason the State Republican Committee decided to open the campaign for Ohio votes in Waynesboro and Shawnee County: perhaps because the Seventh District was as surely Republican as any in the state, and enthusiasm developed there might be contagious. The date chosen was in the middle of August; Ohio held its state election in October, the conventions, state and local, were all over, and the August date was chosen that there might be two full months for campaigning. It might have been an unfortunate time; the County Fair had just ended, and the country folk had worked off their exuberance there; it was dry and hot; the streets of Waynesboro were ankle-deep in dust. But Ludwig was an excellent organizer; he had committees in every crossroads hamlet in the county and all the townships, and encouraged them to vie with each other, rousing their competitive spirit: Oak Grove would not let itself be outdone in the daylight parade by Maple Corners, nor Maple Corners by Monroe township. The State Committee did its part, and assembled a list of notable names for the morning of speechmaking; neighboring cities as well as the district's villages would send delegations for the torchlight procession. The notables—fortunately, Ludwig said—would not have to be entertained overnight; they could make their speeches in the morning and depart, or stay if they wanted to, but he would not be responsible for them after they had been fed at the noon barbecue. Governor Noyes was all right, and Mr. Cochran, who was acquainted with him, could ask him to spend the night at his house, if he liked; but in all the town only Judge Ballard knew Senator Wade, and now they were on opposite sides of the fence. As for Ben Butler, Ludwig didn't know who would take him in, unless it was General Deming.

"I never believed half the things they said about General Butler," Sally remonstrated with him, "after all, Rebels—"

"The silver-spoon business? Nonsense, of course. He made the southern women angry, and he will be defamed for a hundred years for his governing of New Orleans, when really, he was just tactless. But he's not one of our most incorruptible politicians."

Whatever the county's opinions of Ben Butler's morals, or Senator Ben Wade's fierce Radicalism in Congress, it assembled in full strength to hear them speak: seldom had there been an opportunity in Waynesboro to see so many famous men all at once. Farmers brought their families into town as soon as the chores had been done; town boys had scarcely the patience to finish their breakfasts, so sure were they that they were missing something memorable and exciting. Their parents were more restrained, but soon after the dishes had been washed, they too were hunting a place to stand in the crowded space within the Court House fence. Long before the speeches were to begin, the square was packed solid, and latecomers had to thrust their way as best they could to the iron fence, where they could cling and not be torn away, but might be pressed to suffocation. Speech-making began at ten o'clock, when the great men were led out from the Court House south door on the bunting-draped platform that had been built on a level with the portico. General Deming was present to perform the introductions; Mr. Bonner and Ludwig, already flushed with the heat, were on the platform. Those of the audience who had come late and were of necessity outside the fence had a certain advantage: after an hour or so of listening, it was possible for them to drift away, by judicious and not too violent use of elbows, without attracting attention. Almost all, however, stayed to the bitter end, in spite of heat, sweat, tobacco-chewing neighbors, and crying children: they enjoyed oratory, the more oratorical the better, and the former General Butler was a famous silver-tongue.

The last syllable spread through the stale, hushed air not long after noon; the speakers turned back into the Court House; applause and cheers dwindled and died; the crowd crumbled along its edges, moved convulsively from its center, and began streaming away through all the gates of the square. The barbecue was to be held in the "circus lot" on the south edge of town; farmers collected their families and loaded them back into the wagons or carryalls in which they had come to town; townspeople walked through the heat, or, more sensibly, figuring they would not be missed, went home for noon dinner.

The district parade was set for two o'clock. Ludwig had played effectively upon pride and jealous apprehensions; it was a good parade: every hamlet's and township's veterans marching in uniform, on horseback or afoot; every village's prettiest girls in decorated wagons: Oak Grove's all in white, all carrying tiny flags, seated in rows of tiered benches running lengthwise of the wagon; Maple Corner's standing, grouped around a golden-haired Columbia with a shield; Georgetown's on kitchen chairs in a row around a lath-and-paper model of the Court House, carrying banners—white banners black-lettered on one side, "U. S. Grant, Ohio's Greatest Son," on the other, "U. S. Grant, The Georgetown Boy." (After all, although Georgetown was not in the Seventh District, it was not so very far away; even if President

Grant had left there many years ago, still he was after a fashion a product of the region.) There were other floats; there were bands; there was dust kicked up by the marching feet and the trampling horses. Even when the parade was over, the dust hung level a few feet above street and pathway, a yellowish cloud. Most of the country people went home after their part was done, there were always the cows to be milked. Some, who had trustworthy hired men, had brought picnic baskets, and as the sun went down, returned with them to the scene of the noon barbecue, or, too tired for that effort, made themselves at home on the benches and the grass of the Court House lawn.

General Butler and Senator Wade had taken an afternoon train out of Waynesboro, but Governor Noyes was entertained at dinner by Mr. and Mrs. Cochran. General Deming was there, and Mrs. Deming, and Mr. Bonner and his wife; but Sally was no longer appearing in public, and Ludwig was busy meeting the trains that brought in the delegations from Cincinnati, Dayton, and Columbus, which were to march in the torchlight procession. By late afternoon these visitors and all the white Republican males of Waynesboro who were still on their feet assembled at the Court House, and were ranged in line in full view of the sated picnickers, who lolled on the grass or leaned on the iron fences. The parade could not begin until it was dark, but it would take until nightfall to get them in line.

It was deep dusk, and order had still not been wrought out of confusion when General Deming and Mr. Bonner came down Market Street hill on horseback, followed by the Cochran stableman with Ludwig's horse. Those three were to be the marshals of the parade. Ludwig finished barking his orders to the men who were to march, placed one band at the head of the column, another in the middle, took the horse from Reuben, and swung into the saddle. It was not quite deep-dark, but the flaring torches and the transparencies were lighted, the band struck up, and they were off, up Chillicothe Street into the East End, where the gaping Negroes grinned and shouted; from the top of Chillicothe Street through to Market; down to its end, past the Female College, past the Cochrans', past the Presbyterian church and the Gordons' and around the corner to Linden; north on Linden, down Linden Street hill, past Ludwig's. He saw the light in his house, and under cover of the noise the band made, he leaned over and shouted to General Deming, "I'm going to drop out here for some food. Gott, I'm starved!"

The General shouted back, "Don't blame you. You missed a damn good dinner."

"You know the route? Out Linden to the last cross street, through to Main. I can slip through the alley yonder and join you on Main Street, on your way back."

The General lifted his arm in salute; Ludwig wheeled his horse, kicking and dancing, and walked him back through the soft, churned dust to his gate; he took the horse down the driveway and tied him to the redbud tree, lest, at the hitching post, he be startled by the noise, the torches, the smoke.

As he stepped onto the porch, Sally spoke from its far shadowy corner.

"That you, Ludwig? What's the matter?"

"I'm famished. Ask Cassie to bring me something, will you, if it's only a hunk of bread. I have only a few minutes till they come back, in Main Street."

She passed him, on her way to the door, patting his arm as she went. His eyes more accustomed now to the darkness, he could see that she had not been alone. "That you, Mother Cochran?"

"Yes, along with Anne, and Johnny and Elsa."

"How does the parade look from here?" He turned, himself, to look over the porch railing, across the lawn to the street.

"It's splendid, Ludwig. Who are the men with the white capes and the white high hats? A Cincinnati delegation? The children want to go hang on the gate, but we wouldn't let them."

"Why not? Run along, Kinder, but stay inside the fence."

The marching men outside were singing:

I dreamed a dream the other night
  When all around was still,
I thought I saw old Horace Greeley
  Coming down the hill.

There was a ruffle of drums, a banging of cymbals, and then the chorus:

O, Horace Greeley
  You've surely lost your way,
And Grant will bring you to account,
  On next election day.

All the little boys in the gutter, streaming along with the torchbearers, caught it up and repeated it shrilly. Elsa and Johnny clung to the gate, entranced. The band music swelled, crashed, broke—the band had passed. The Waynesboro men came on, marching like the soldiers they had been, their transparencies held steady, but half-obscured by the smoke. There was something hellish about the scene: the tramping feet, the flaring unsteady lights, the dust that rose and mingled with the smoke, the black-caped figures obscurely seen through the leaves of the trees. But torchlight parades were an old story to those on the Rausch porch: they were concerned only as to the impression it gave of overwhelming strength. Sally brought a plate of roast beef and bread; Ludwig made a sandwich and stood at the railing munching it. The last contingent of marchers passed; the slowest of the small boys, or the weariest, went trailing after it. The sound of the band died away out toward the end of Linden Street. Ludwig sat down to rest for a moment, resisting sternly the temptation to go into the house, take off his shoes, and stretch out on the bed. Then he heard someone speak to the two children still hanging on the gate. It was a familiar voice. He peered between the trees and could just make out a bulky figure, dark against the smoke.

He lifted his voice in an easy soldier's shout, "Lichtenstein? Was ist?"

"Stellen sie sich vor" came the grumbling reply, "Zey go—ze Reiter, sie sagen—zey say: 'Pass ze word down ze line' to turn left on Main Stret, zey vill go zu beangstigen ze old Yudge."

Ludwig by that time was at the gate; he exchanged a few sentences in swift fierce German with Mr. Lichtenstein: then he picked up the two children and returned, with one under each arm, to the porch.

He was still swearing in German, to himself (it sounded like swearing) as he came up the porch steps and deposited the wriggling children.

"Those fools!" he exclaimed. "Bonner, I suspect, or maybe Deming. As soon as I dropped out, they passed the word along the line to turn left on Main Street instead of right. They're going past the Ballards for some kind of demonstration. To frighten him, Lichtenstein says—to jeer, I rather imagine. But—"

"Can't you stop them? You have a horse."

"I'll try. But by the time I catch them, they'll be going the wrong way on Main Street, and I can never get them to about face without breaking up the parade. Poor Lichtenstein! As soon as the word reached him, he dropped out of line and came back to warn me, but he's not very fast on his feet."

Ludwig dashed for his horse and set off after the parade, but he was not in time: he met the leaders already on the way back toward town. General Deming saluted as Ludwig came up and wheeled his horse to ride beside him.

"Took us longer than you figured, eh? We went out to pay our respects to Judge Ballard. Three groans for a Greeleyizer!"

Ludwig fell into his place without a word. If General Deming was too stupid to see that there might have been hope of winning Judge Ballard back into the fold some later year, and that they—particularly he, Deming—might then need his support, what was the use of explaining? It was done now. He rode out the parade with them, to its traditional breaking-up place: "Five Points," where the "Goose-Pasture" began. There the Irish Democrats were waiting to stone the transparencies; but to Ludwig the ensuing fight seemed to lack its usual zest, perhaps because the Irish were only half-hearted about Greeley, perhaps because his conscience was as sore as if he, personally, had stood in the road and jeered at Judge Ballard; after all, he was responsible for the procession; the Ballards would certainly blame him. The Judge, who must know that political demonstrations were that and nothing more, might not be unduly hurt; but his womenfolk would be, and they were friends of Sally's.

He was partly right, partly wrong. The Ballards had stayed at home all day. However queer it seemed to be, opposing old allies like Senator Wade, they could not now applaud; they would therefore not go to the Court House to listen. The day had seemed long, odd, as if they had been quarantined, were plague-stricken; but when dark fell, the evening was just like any other; the day was over; they relaxed around the sitting room lamp. Of course the torchlight procession was going on, but in the dark they would not be missed. Thomasina alone could not sit down to read; she was listening for the band, which they could surely hear, with all the windows open to the summer night. She had seen the route as printed in the *Torchlight*, and knew where the procession was to come through from Linden and turn back on Main Street. This sitting at home while others paraded was not new to Thomasina; on other election years she had been left at home when the time came for the torchlight procession because the dust and smoke so aggravated her hay fever. She sat in a straight chair in the big bay window that matched the one on the parlor side of the house; it gave her a fair view of Main Street for a short way toward town. She hoped to get a glimpse of the parade, even though it was the enemy's; when she finally heard the band she rose and stood in the window, watching. The others paid no attention to her until she said, "Why, they're coming this way! The paper didn't say—"

Her father came to stand at her shoulder. "Paying me the honor of a visit, no doubt," he said, drily.

"Oh, Papa, how awful! What will they do?"

"Nothing—just let us know they are there. Bring me the field glasses out of my desk drawer, will you, Samuel? Then let us turn the lamp out, so they will not have the satisfaction of seeing us watch them."

Samuel brought the glasses to the Judge. The room was darkened. Plain now to the naked eye was the approaching procession, the figures of two horsemen looming against the phantasmagorical light of the torches.

Mrs. Ballard had remained contemptuously in her chair. "Why pay them any attention? It is one of young Rausch's bright ideas, I suppose."

The Judge had lifted the glasses to his eyes. "I just wondered whether so old a friend as Senator Wade could be with them. But the horsemen—I think—yes, Deming and Bonner. I don't see Rausch."

"Hasn't the courage to let himself be seen, I suppose."

The horsemen reached the gate and went on; they rode far enough out past the Judge's gate for the whole procession to crowd up behind them into the space before the Ballard fence. Then they left-faced, the bands ceased playing, a bass drum boomed, and the line of men groaned deeply, once, twice, thrice. After a long pause, the drum crashed again, the line left-faced once more, waited for the marshals to ride past them to what had become the new head of the line, and then all marched off again.

Judge Ballard put his field glasses back in their case. He knew that Thomasina, beside him, was weeping. He put a hand on her shoulder. "My child, that was a comparatively mild demonstration. Remember, I have, in my time, been pelted with rotten eggs—mobbed, even."

"I know, but this is so awful, Papa, because they're all your old friends. How can they be so heartless?"

"Most of them are strangers from the cities, and the Waynesboro men mean nothing by it; they'll have forgotten it by the time the election is over."

Eliza struck a match and relighted the lamp. "Is Thomasina sniveling? Don't be such a goose!"

"Did you like it?" Thomasina came from the bay window to stand by her mother's chair.

"No. But you weep now, and in a week will be wondering why Mamma and I don't like Ludwig Rausch."

"Eliza," her father rebuked her, "men cannot take politics so vindictively and continue to live comfortably in the same town. Women must learn to be more tolerant."

"If women were as tolerant as men, the world would never move," Mrs. Ballard said tartly. "But I am glad that Senator Wade did not demean himself by joining them. I should hate to see the old ties with him made meaningless."

The Judge did not think it worth while to say again that the "old ties" could not be so easily broken, but when he returned from his office on the following day, he did try to persuade them that so far as Ludwig Rausch was concerned, there was nothing to forgive.

He introduced the subject as he carved the evening's roast of beef. "It seems that it wasn't until Rausch dropped out of the parade that they took it into their heads to come out here. He had no dinner, too busy organizing the various delegations, and when the procession passed his house he dropped out to get a bite to eat. When he heard what was about to happen, he started in pursuit, but was too late."

"Who told you all this? Did he come in to apologize?"

"No. Mr. Lichtenstein came in to see me."

"Why should you believe him? He's one of them, the saloon loafers."

"Mary, you are being unduly severe. I have no reason to question Mr. Lichtenstein's integrity. He's rather an uncouth young man, but I feel perfectly sure he is honest. He told me that such a demonstration had been discussed before the parade and Rausch had vetoed it, on the grounds of the respect due me, and respect due 'an honest difference of opinion.' And so after Rausch dropped out of the parade, and the word as to the change of plans, passing down the line, reached Lichtenstein, he too dropped out. It was he himself who went back and told Rausch, and he saw him take his horse and start off. Of course, he was too late."

"Then I suppose he asked Mr. Lichtenstein to apologize to you?"

"No. When the parade finally broke up, Mr. Lichtenstein asked him if he shouldn't come to me and explain, and he said no, that it would be better if I held him responsible rather than those who actually were. Better for the party in the long run."

"Who?"

"Deming, I suppose. And Bonner. I never thought Deming was a very farseeing man; I believe that young Rausch is. He sees that if the Liberal Republicans are badly beaten in November, it may be the end of them."

"Then you will go back to the Republicans?"

"There or nowhere. And young Rausch doesn't want me to be an enemy to Deming."

"We must see to it that the Liberal Republicans are not beaten."

General Deming spent the summer in Waynesboro campaigning for General Grant and himself. His wife was not with him; she had taken her year-old child and gone for the summer to her kin in Massachusetts. Little Julia, he explained, was not very strong and they feared the Ohio summer would be too much for her. The General slept at home, but ate at Mrs. Forrest's boardinghouse, and did no entertaining in the residence he had rebuilt and lavishly redecorated before his marriage.

The ladies of Waynesboro were not surprised that the child should be frail. After their first astonishment a year ago at the news of its birth, they had settled down to feeling slightly scandalized that a pair as old as the Demings should have produced a child. Waynesboro mothers commended the General's fatherly devotion, shown not only in his willingness to conduct his campaign without wifely support but also by his frequent trips to Boston, in the intervals of speech-making. Of course, he had railroad passes, but in such hot weather it could not be pleasant to spend so much time in the cars. At home he worked vigorously for himself and his party's ticket, denying as campaign libels all the charges that had been flung at the administration. In September the New York *Sun* began to print accusations that had hitherto been whispered about members of Congress and Credit Mobilier stock, and General Deming's name was on the list of those involved. But when Blaine and other Congressional leaders made vigorous denials, when it became known in Waynesboro that the General had sworn to Ludwig Rausch that he had never owned a share of stock he had not paid for, his constituents were satisfied—some were even convinced—and all were faintly flattered that their representative was important enough in the national picture to have been included in the list of the vilified.

When Club meetings began in the fall, the ladies were not thinking of the election. Their chief concern all that long hot summer was the slow dying of Miss Crenshaw. She still lived alone in the clapboard-covered log cabin that had been her parents', on Chillicothe Street a block below Dr. Gordon's office. A young Irish girl did her housework, and took care of her, after a fashion, but her friends had not the heart to leave her alone in the last months of her life with no other company than Rose Tobin's. They took turns in going to her: every afternoon one member of the Club stopped in and, if there were no caller there from her church or from among her neighbors, would stay for an hour or so. Before the summer was over Sally had to give up her turn; her pregnancy had so advanced that it was no longer decent for her to appear on the street. But the others, even the Misses Gardiner, performed their Christian duty nobly until the end, until Miss Crenshaw died, late in October. And not one of them ever forgot those afternoons. The house edged the sidewalk, so that anyone passing by could look in through the lace curtains; there was an excuse, therefore, for having the green outer shutters closed, and inside in the dim light, when one sat beside the horsehair sofa where Miss Crenshaw lay, the ravages of her disease were not quite so painfully impressed upon the eye. But on hot afternoons the room grew foul and close, choking, so that sometimes one must press a handkerchief over mouth and nose. On some days Miss Crenshaw was stupefied with morphine; at other times, less heavily drugged, she talked and talked. Listening to her there in the twilit room, not seeing her except dimly, it was difficult to believe that she was so near to death. Her morphine-clouded mind had turned back to her childhood, and she told one member of the Club after another about the days when the house had been a long cabin in the woods, those years before the War of 1812. It was not always quite clear to her audience how much of all she told she herself had experienced and how much she remembered of the tales of others; but she always came back to what quite plainly had meant most to her in her long life: her mother had been a New England girl, educated in the best of academies of late-eighteenth-century Connecticut, and she was quite capable of teaching her children, cut off from the world there in the cabin in the woods, not only the fundamental three R's, but Latin, Greek, and mathematics. In her weak voice Miss Crenshaw related with pride how her brothers had been prepared for college—for the recently established Miami University—right there in that parlor when it hadn't been a parlor but the one room of a log cabin. In her praise of her mother and brothers was mingled her own delight, naïve as a young girl's, in her own love of books and learning, and in her ability to keep up with her brothers in Latin and algebra, even after they had gone off to college.

However often one came to Miss Crenshaw's, and whether one stayed all afternoon or for only a few minutes, one never heard her speak of death. She dismissed as briefly as possible an initial inquiry as to how she felt. She had found her refuge—the past—and she clung to it, and the women who listened to her repetitious anecdotes were proud of her, proud that she was going down to her end with the knowledge of that end plain to be seen in the bleakness of her eyes, but never to be heard from her lips. And because Miss Crenshaw had never been really close to any of the women except Miss Pinney and Mrs. Lowrey, she became to the others rather other than an individual: Woman, Dying of Cancer.

Except for the afternoons that Anne spent with Miss Crenshaw and the days she took Johnny with her to play with Elsa while she and Sally gossiped together and sewed baby clothes, she stayed at home, putting up fruit and vegetables for the winter, making jam, telling stories to the child and watching her father. Dr. Alexander looked old and ill; he who had been so alert and dependable, so wise, was now slow and feeble, his hands crippled, his knees stiff, his eyes clouded. John watched him too, and was glum and brusque about the house; and Anne saw him watching, but said nothing. She didn't want to confirm her fears by putting them into words, or having John put them into words for her.

And then one morning a week or so after the day of the Republican jamboree, Dr. Alexander had an attack of angina in the office. John came in from his rounds to find his father-in-law lying exhausted on the office sofa. By that time the attack had passed, and there was little John could do for him, beyond telling him to stay there. After a while the older man fell asleep; John left him and went across the back yards to the house. He found Anne in the kitchen with Martha, making apple jelly, while Johnny played at her feet with his Noah's ark. When his father appeared in the door, the boy scrambled to his feet and went to meet him. Absently John smoothed the soft brown hair, "Not now, son. You stay here with Martha. I want to talk to your mother. Can you come out on the porch a minute, Anne?"

She went with him, not even stopping to take off her sticky apron.

"What is it? Is Papa all right?"

"He is all right now. But I found him on the sofa in the office. He had a heart attack."

"Oh, John! How bad?"

"This time, I'm afraid, pretty bad. He's had lesser attacks before. He didn't want me to tell you. It's angina."

Anne sat down on the porch step. The little boy came out of the kitchen and climbed into her lap. She dropped her cheek to his head.

"Oh, John! I've been so worried. But people sometimes live for years with angina, don't they? If they're careful?"

"Yes. But he can't stand many attacks like this last one."

"He mustn't stay over there in those rooms alone."

"No. Nor climb stairs. We can turn the study into a bedroom for him. But we can't interfere with his habits."

"You mean laudanum?"

"He has taken it so long for the severe pain that he needs to take more and more to find relief."

Dr. Alexander moved back into his daughter's house, bringing with him his books, his saddlebags, his instruments. He not only gave up his practice entirely, he seemed even to have ceased thinking about it. He asked John few questions. Rainy days he spent dozing on his bed, or sitting in his deep leather chair by the empty grate, with a volume of Dickens open on his knee; on sunny days he moved to the side porch and a chair in the shade of the honeysuckle vines, with his grandchild for company. He liked having the little boy somewhere at hand. Like Miss Crenshaw he was dreaming back over his childhood and youth. He told Johnny about sleeping in the loft of his grandfather's log cabin, when the snow sifted through the cracks in the slab roof and lay unmelted on his bed, and about how, when he was a baby, his father had gone off to Detroit to fight in the War of 1812, and how the old musket was still hanging in the attic. When Anne, knowing that these stories were beyond the comprehension of a child of three, took up her sewing or her knitting and went to sit with them, then her father talked about his youth, when he had been taught medicine by old Dr. Templeton, riding horseback beside him for fifteen or twenty miles through the woods, reciting anatomy and physiology all the way, except when they stopped at some cabin or lonely farmhouse to treat a patient and he was given a chance to show how well he had learned his lesson. Once Dr. Alexander asked Anne if she remembered the cholera epidemic.

She had heard many times about the cholera epidemic; she did not say so. "That was in '49, wasn't it, Papa? I wasn't born until '50."

"Of course. It was Rob who was a child then. Little Susy and Rachel had died of scarlet fever the year before. The sisters you never saw."

"I know, Papa."

"The epidemic was the worst thing that ever happened here. The railroad was being built. All those strapping young Irishmen came down with cholera."

"And you turned your own stable into a hospital for them."

"It was the only thing to do. But I sent your mother and Rob into the country to stay with her people."

"You were a hero, Papa."

"Hero? Oh, no. They couldn't be left along the right of way where they collapsed. But so many died. A doctor can't do much, Anne, if it's cholera, but just stave it off."

Sometimes Dr. Alexander would talk to Johnny about his son Rob, killed in the war. Then Anne, sitting on the top step if they were on the porch, would look up at him, laughing, and would rack her brain to remember the merrier escapades of Rob's boyhood. Her whole being seemed numb with a dull pain, so that she was a little surprised at being able to laugh; but she managed it, and Johnny would laugh, too, often not knowing why. She was surprised, remembering what had after all not been many years ago, at how long a time it seemed to have lasted, her childhood and Rob's, when her mother and father had seemed forever fixed and stable and not to be changed, and they had all been happy. Back of that lay her father's childhood, which had also continued for a measureless time, and had also been happy. She thought, "At the end, it means more than religion, to have had a happy childhood. Memory of it serves to hold off pain and fear; it is an unfailing resource." With yearning tenderness, she knew that she must make a childhood like that for Johnny and for whatever other children she might have, because if one's childhood was happy, one had no reason to fear life, and those who had not feared life could face death with acceptance when they must.

In September her father had another very bad attack, fortunately on Sunday, when John was home. While Dr. Alexander was still in bed recovering slowly from the desperate exhaustion in which the attack had left him, Anne spent as much of the day as she could and all her evenings beside him, sick at heart, and wondering at herself that she could behave so normally, reading to him, reviewing the trivial incidents of her day involving Johnny, Martha, John, even Fritz Klein delivering the groceries. But one night he interrupted her.

"What time is it, Anne? I want to talk to you a minute before John gets back from the office and comes in to give me my—my sedative for the night. Sit down there on the bed a minute."

Obediently she moved from her chair to the foot of the bed, and sat facing him, where he could watch her as he spoke.

"You have been happy with John, haven't you? Somehow, until these last few weeks, I've seen so much more of him than I have of you."

"Of course, Papa. I should think you could see." She was startled, not at the atmosphere of deathbed confidences, but at the form that they were taking. "Papa" she flushed, slowly. "You know that I love him with all my heart."

"Yes, I know that." He spoke slowly, with long pauses to recruit his strength. "But one can love and still not be happy. I suppose if Rob had lived, I should not be so much concerned about John. And you, of course. But I am so close to him, sometimes I think I see him more clearly than you do. John is still—in a way—a casualty of the war. He hasn't altogether gotten over it, and there are times when he wants to escape being John Gordon. And you are always there, saying—oh, not with your tongue, I don't mean, but with all your being—'John, John.'" He broke off and watched her for a moment. Her eyelids were lowered. She whispered, "Yes, I know I do, I even say it—" She flushed again, and clenched her hands in her lap.

"A great love, Anne, like yours, makes demands: not selfishly, but just by being. And few men can live up to such demands. Particularly one who is still suffering from the effects of the war. All I want to say, Anne, is that should John ever make you unhappy, don't turn from him because you are hurt. Remember he has been worse hurt. Give him time until all the horrors he has lived through are forgotten. For my sake, Anne. John's the only son I have. And great love carries with it great responsibility."

"Papa, I'm not sure what you mean. John has never made me unhappy—never for a moment, except when I've been unhappy for him, like when Kate died. And of course I won't turn against him. It's inconceivable."

He smiled briefly. "I suppose I sound out of my right mind. Well, perhaps I am. And maybe I've been wrong, putting ideas in your head."

"My head has no room for ideas that John and I could ever be unhappy together." She smiled at him. She had been troubled for a moment, but then she thought, "It's the laudanum. And sick people get these morbid notions." And her worry for him crowded out of her mind all that he had said.

She missed most of the Club meetings that fall. She hardly realized that Greeley was coming to Waynesboro—or rather, that his train was going to stop there—until she heard about it afterward.

Between Republicans who had gathered at the depot to jeer and heckle,

Liberal Republicans who had gone to shake his hand or at least to applaud, and Irish Democrats who did not like Mr. Greeley much, but were ready to fight the Republicans anyway—between them all, they made that hour the liveliest Waynesboro had known for many a year: respectable citizens had their noses bloodied, and the Irish howled so that Mr. Greeley could not make himself heard. Judge Ballard, whose dignity was considerably ruffled in the melee, swore off politics forever. And Ludwig, whose eye was blacked, perhaps had his vision colored thereby, for he was discouraged as to the outcome of the campaign, actually thinking that if Greeley could attract such crowds everywhere he appeared, perhaps he did have a chance. But the state election a few days later was carried by the Republicans, and so successfully that the party workers ceased to worry. The national election was almost an anticlimax. President Grant was reelected, and so was General Deming; the usual bonfire was burned at the crossing of Main and Chillicothe streets, and the campaign was over. But not quite, in its consequences, for in a month or so Mr. Greeley died, heartbroken and worn out by his speech-making tours, heaping coals of fire on the heads of all who had abused him.

Herman Lichtenstein was elected to the school board, to the town's astonishment, Sally's consternation, Ludwig's huge amusement, and his own great and touching delight. His broad face was illumined with a light of consecration and of zeal, and so patently vulnerable was he in his ardor that Ludwig felt it incumbent upon him to utter a word of warning.

"You are all set to make things hum now, eh? But don't forget you have only one vote on the board, and if you antagonize the mossbacks, the cause of education won't advance much. Stir up a hornet's nest, you'll be beaten next time you run, and you can't accomplish much in one term." Ludwig grinned. "There's plenty of time before your children will be ready for school."

"Nun—iss zere only ze kleiner Rudy, aber schnell." He winked ponderously. "Nun—ze ozer Kinder must I not forget. Ze gr-r-reatest tact vill I exercise. For zis year vill I listen und smile, und nod ze head, so—und zen ve shall see."

Ludwig, in those days of late October and early November, was walking on air. He had made a success of his first test of political responsibility: the ropewalk, in spite of his distractions from it, was doing increasingly well, although he had not yet enough capital set aside for the further improvements he planned. Best of all, Sally, the week after the election, bore him a son. She wanted to name the baby for him, but he insisted that it should be called Ernest. "For my father we name this one. The next one Charles, for your father. After that a little Ludwig, if you like." Then, feeling a little sheepish because in his great joy it was so easy to forget the oaths he had sworn on the morning the baby was born, he added, "But maybe for you one daughter and one son is enough? I would not ask more of you, meine liebste Sally." He smiled down at her where she leaned, rosy-cheeked against her pillow, two golden plaits over her shoulders.

"Oh, Ludwig," she laughed at him. "It was not so bad, truly. I'll be ready for little Charles in a couple of years, then little Ludwig. And then please may I have another little girl to play with Elsa?"

In the same week that Sally's baby was born, Miss Crenshaw died. Sally was unable to attend either the funeral services or the Memorial meeting held by the Woman's Club at Mrs. Lowrey's. She was determined, however, to be out and about in time to blackball Mrs. McKinney, whose name was proposed for membership at the next meeting after the Memorial service. "Couldn't wait for Crenny to grow cold," she grumbled to Anne, who had dropped in after the meeting. "I'm going to blackball her."

"It wouldn't do any good. It takes more than one vote," Anne reminded her, "and I couldn't blackball my own minister's wife, I just couldn't."

"I'm going to vote against her, if I'm the only one. Anyone who said the things she said about Ludwig."

Ludwig at that moment came into the bedroom where they were sitting by the fire, Anne in her best winter afternoon polonaise and walking skirt, Sally comfortable in her negligee, the baby asleep in his crib, Elsa playing on the hearth at their feet. Ludwig often came home early on those ugly, early-dark November afternoons, just to make sure that his son was still there, alive and happy. He hung over the crib long enough to see that the baby was sleeping; then he drew another chair to the fire and took Elsa on his lap.

"Whose Schöne Elsa are you?" he demanded, tickling her neck with his mustache.

She gurgled with laughter, flung her arms around his neck, shouted, "Papa's Shaney! Papa's Shaney!"

"Hush, you two. You'll wake the baby."

"At his age? His ears aren't dry yet. What were you two good wives discussing when I came in? I heard my name."

"Mrs. McKinney. I'm going to blackball her for the Club."

Ludwig was immediately serious, "Oh, no, Sally, no. Never kick your opponent when he's down. We've beaten the Liberals. Now let's forget it."

"Your enemies are my enemies," she insisted stubbornly.

"That's what I'm trying to tell you, Sally: they aren't my enemies. This election has killed the Liberals as a party. Now we must make it easy for them to come back and be good Republicans again. What was said during the campaign is water under the bridge. Besides, I like Judge Ballard, and he's a bitterly disappointed man. And we do need him in the party, to help clean things up a bit."

"Clean things up?"

"The party. Don't pretend you don't know it needs it. You go to your Club and vote for Mrs. McKinney, and like her. You like all those other women." His tone was that whoever could like them could like anyone. Anne and Sally both laughed.

"I like some of the things about them. But I won't belong to a Club that is used to make reforms I don't believe in."

"It can't be used," Anne said. "It's in the constitution. And Mrs. Ballard and Mrs. McKinney, and Mrs. Tyler, I suppose, wouldn't be enough to make closing the saloons a Club project."

"Very well. But I think for the Christmas party this year I will dramatize some scenes from Dickens, the Jellybys and the Turvey-drops. Will you help me?"

"I don't see how I can promise, with Papa so sick. I don't suppose I'll even be there."

Anne's father died early in December. Sally and Ludwig went sorrowfully to the funeral; Sally's heart ached for Anne, shut in the dining room with the "family," John, and such cousins of the old doctor's as were still able-bodied enough to attend the funeral. Then her mind drifted away from Mr. McKinney's long-winded eulogy, mulled over the question of the Christmas party, and decided that she must give it up this year. Time was short for one thing, and no one was in the mood for merrymaking.

The Woman's Club was, on the surface at any rate, all ready to start the New Year in a spirit of amiable oneness.

MEMBERS OF THE
WAYNESBORO WOMAN'S CLUB

Miss Eliza Ballard
Mrs. Mary Grimes Ballard
Mrs. Louisa Tucker Deming
Miss Caroline Gardiner
Miss Lavinia Gardiner
Mrs. Anne Alexander Gordon
Miss Katherine Lowrey
Mrs. Rebecca Lowrey
Mrs. Mary McCune
Mrs. Rhoda McKinney
Miss Agatha Pinney
Mrs. Sarah Cochran Rausch
Miss Amanda Reid
Mrs. Thomasina Ballard Travers
Mrs. Ellen Lowrey Tyler

IN MEMORIAM

Miss Susan Crenshaw

✻ 1873–1874 ✻

"For the only time in its history, members of our Club were arraigned in police court."

The Demings returned to Waynesboro when the Forty-second Congress adjourned after Grant's second inauguration. The Forty-third would not meet in regular session until December. Congressmen went home that spring to face an electorate angered by the last-minute "Salary Grab" Act and ashamed of their representatives involved in the Credit Mobilier affair. As far back as 1869 there had been whispers and then newspaper accusations of graft and bribery in connection with the building of the Union Pacific Railroad. Blaine and Garfield in self-defense had demanded an investigation. The long-drawn-out inquiry, still going on in Washington, eventually found few Congressmen guilty of anything but stupidity. Nevertheless, the spring of '73 was not a happy time for Republican Congressmen, going home to face their constituents. General Deming, genuinely bewildered but shaken by the consequences of actions that had never seemed to him dishonest or against the interests of his country, might not have appeared in his district during those intervening months between the two sessions of Congress had not his wife insisted upon it.

"It is exactly *now*," she had said firmly, "that you must prove to your constituents that you have done nothing of which you are ashamed."

"But I haven't!" he protested stubbornly, his face red and angry at the thought of all he had endured. "A few years ago, everyone wanted transcontinental railroads; now that they've got one, they've turned around like a pack of curs on the fellows that financed it. Of course they made a good thing out of it—it wouldn't have gotten done, otherwise."

"I know." Mrs. Deming sighed. She had listened more than once to the arguments which her husband would have liked to use in answer to his official inquisitors. "Even the Investigating Committee recognized that you have not been worse than foolish. If party leaders like Blaine and Garfield can shrug the whole thing off, so can you. But to stay away from Waynesboro would make the people who know you suspect the worst."

"People who know you are always ready to suspect the worst. But there isn't a damn one of them wouldn't have jumped at a chance to get Credit Mobilier stock if Mr. Ames had offered it to him for half its value. Damn it all, I paid for that stock with the dividends as they came in—I beg your pardon, my dear."

She nodded to him forgivingly across the table. They were having breakfast together in Washington. "There are occasions when I can see it must be a great temptation to use strong language."

The conversation preceded Congress's passage of the act to raise salaries retroactively. General Deming was as astonished as his fellow Representatives at the storm of vituperation that followed. On the cars, going home, his mind kept gnawing away at his troubles; they were present in the background of his consciousness even when he took little Julia and held her on his knee to show her the houses and barns, the horses and cows that swung past the Pullman car windows. Julia was a small-boned, fair child, with eyes of light clear blue, and her mother's clean-cut features. She was only two, but even at that age was fastidiously dainty, and sat contentedly in her father's lap, avoiding all contact with the sooty window sill and the grimy plush seats. She knew her father was aware of her being there, and felt no need to demand acknowledgment of her presence; for long miles she sat quietly on his broad thigh, her head against his watch pocket, looking out of the window, or smiling at her mother on the opposite seat.

The General, too, occasionally let his eyes rest on his wife. She was a woman to be proud of; prosperity became her, and in her restrained but elegant traveling costume, she looked aloof, haughty, and aristocratic. She and her husband spoke very little on the trip; they had talked the situation to tatters, and could only wait now to see what could be rescued of his career. It seemed to the General that she had somehow, in some vague way, failed him in his trouble. He felt, obscurely, that she might even be a little contemptuous of him for being upset and unhappy. Would she have been better pleased had he been shrewder and more aware of what he was doing, and prepared for a storm should it be discovered? But she hated even the suggestion of corruption. Not the least among the causes of his bewilderment was the fact that he hardly admitted to conscious thought that his wife, who despised stupidity almost as much as she hated corruption, had shown no surprise when he had discovered himself as stupid. Perhaps she would as lief have Waynesboro think him crooked? He shifted uneasily in his seat, and the child tipped her head back to look up, her blue eyes serene and trusting. His arm tightened about her. At least Julia was too small to know: in that lay his chief comfort. It would all blow over; before she grew up, he would have lived it down. Fortunately, he had been reelected for another term before the storm had burst; he might have a chance of vindication before '74. He knew what the men who had voted for him were saying now: they were pointing at his house and whispering "boodle." Before his marriage, he had rebuilt his parents' simple frame house for his bride, adding a round tower at one corner, with a pointed roof and a lightning rod, a bay-window at the end of the living room, overlooking the side yard, and a wide veranda across the front, from the bulge of the tower to the corner of the house. He knew how it looked now, gleaming with white paint, the green shutters bright in the sun. In his mind's eye he saw the neighbors pointing, and whispering, "341% paid on that Credit Mobilier investment."

He caught Louisa's eye and smiled sheepishly. "Not the least of all this is that Waynesboro will never believe to the end of my life that I haven't got millions salted away somewhere. Actually, dividends from C. M. stock hardly paid for remodeling the house. And today the shares aren't worth what I paid for them."

"Don't brood, George." Then because she saw, suddenly and for the first time, how weary and flushed he looked, how grievously hurt, she added, gently, "They'll forget all about it in a week or two. The Republican party isn't going to repudiate its leaders, and if they can live it down, so can we. Let's forget it, please."

Once they were settled in the house in Waynesboro, forgetting was easier than the General had feared: no one seemed to have noticed their arrival, except Mr. Bonner in his paper:

> Our esteemed Representative, General George Deming, has returned to Waynesboro with his family, having accomplished his duties as a member of the 42nd Congress with the brilliance we have come to expect of him. We tender our congratulations, particularly for his share in the final act of Congress, by which the servants of the Republic have been, and in the future will be, more amply recompensed for their sacrifices, and by which they will be freed from any necessity to take part in speculations on the stock market. We hope that in the next Congress, General Deming will play an even more honorable and conspicuous part.

The General had become somewhat hardened to newspaper abuse, and he might have been able to pretend that he did not recognize the *Torchlight*'s paragraph for sarcasm. But Mrs. Deming, who had really believed that in her husband's own town they would have to face no overt criticism—that no one would dare, that they were above and out of reach of that sort of thing—was so furious when she read it that her nose looked pinched, and white lines stood out around her mouth.

"I suppose we *must* expect this kind of vulgar mockery, but surely there is something we can do. Can't you talk to Judge Ballard?"

He stared at her in astonishment. "Ballard! Don't you remember that he got out of the party because he thought it was riddled with graft? Have you forgotten that I was in that torchlight procession, not a year ago, that expressed its contempt for 'Come-Outers' in general and him in particular? Why, he's probably saying 'I told you so' to everyone who will listen. No. I think myself we'd better let sleeping dogs lie, but if it will make you happier, I'll go see young Rausch, or Bonner, with a horsewhip." He laughed uneasily, but her expression of contemptuous anger was not altered.

"I cannot see what a young upstart like Ludwig Rausch could have to do with *your* career. However, you know best. I shall go call on the Lowreys. Apparently they have no intention of coming *here* to welcome me home."

"But surely, my dear, you are not on such formal terms with the Lowreys that you must sit here in your parlor waiting for them to make the first visit. I should suppose they were too busy with the school for much calling."

Before Louisa Deming set out on the following afternoon, she debated for a moment as to whether or not to take Julia in the carriage with her: the child might break the ice and offer a refuge of small talk; but on the other hand, both Mrs. Lowrey and Mrs. Tyler were profoundly indifferent to small children, and Julia might be turned over to the young Tylers to get her out of the way. Julia's mother decided to go alone while she was arraying herself carefully in her most correct, unostentatious afternoon costume. General Deming ordered the buggy brought around, and he himself drove her to the college, helped her down, and opened the gate for her before he went on his way to the Rausch mill.

As she started up the walk, she saw at once the marks of deterioration: the school was slipping downhill. She straightened her shoulders unconsciously, straight though they had been before. She felt the unacknowledged satisfaction in another's trouble that is common to the proud: the satisfaction in knowing yours is not the only misery in the world, and therefore not so conspicuous as you had feared.

The day was wet and bleak, which perhaps accounted for the depressed look of the grounds, muddy beneath leafless trees, with even a last filthy patch of snow here and there. But the dormitory had grown shabby: the shutters were faded, the ironwork rusty. The windows were unwashed; the steps to the school building were tracked with mud. She went up them and through the vestibule to the office, where Mrs. Lowrey used always to be at this hour. But the office was empty. There was a low murmur of voices from upstairs, where classes were being held, but she saw no one on the ground floor. She went out again and across the campus to the Lowreys' house.

Mrs. Lowrey herself came to the door, her hair an untidy bird's nest, her skirt falling straight about her lank figure, and her bustle tied around her waist outside it.

"Louisa! Ah, my dear: how delightful." They kissed in the hall. "Come into the parlor and sit down. I'll send someone for Ellen. If you'll excuse me just a moment." She caught sight of herself sideways in the long pier glass between the front windows, and laughed as she lifted her hands in horror. "I declare, I am hopeless. I had to slip over to the dormitory a moment ago, and I just put my bustle on under my coat. You know how shocked the girls would be if I appeared without one!—and I forgot it when I came in—make yourself comfortable, and I shall be back in a moment."

Mrs. Deming went into the dark, unaired parlor and took a seat on the sofa whose horsehair upholstery was broken along the edges, and hence more than ordinarily prickly. The shabby room, with its worn grosgrain carpet and knobby walnut furniture, the murky mirror over the mantel, and ash-filled cold grate, fortified her self-possession. She sat composed, her gloved hands clasped about her card case, until Mrs. Lowrey returned. The older woman had changed into more formal attire, and had combed her hair, but her manner was still distraught. She sat down on the sofa beside Mrs. Deming, and laid a thin-veined hand for an instant on the gloved ones.

"I fear I am growing old, my dear: I seem to be in a continual flurry. Ah, but we miss your calm hand at the helm. I sent one of Ellen's children to the dormitory for her. She is living there now as matron. Until she comes, tell me about yourself: how are General Deming and the baby?"

Mrs. Deming acknowledged the courteous inquiries. "They are well. And you? And Mr. Lowrey? And Kitty?"

"Oh, Kitty! So disappointing to us. She wants to be married when she has finished at Oberlin in June. Young Sheldon Edwards: you know, Sheldon and Edwards, the dry goods store: that family. The boy's at Oberlin, too."

"I remember him, vaguely: a pale, blond young man. What an unlikely choice for Kitty. She was such a tomboy. I should never have suspected her of a romantic tendency."

Mrs. Lowrey cocked an eyebrow. "Romantic? Oh, no. Kitty is extremely clear-sighted, with a yearning for peace and orderliness. You know"—with seeming irrelevance—"she never did get along well with her sister. But Kitty, bless her heart, has a conscience. Nothing but marriage would excuse her desertion of us. And anyway, I think she'll come back to teach for a year or two, if we need her."

"The school—you don't mind my asking? Isn't it doing well?"

"Of course I don't mind. In whom else should I confide? You were our mainstay, once. No. The school is falling off. We no longer attract the class of girls who used to attend. The brighter ones are going to the new women's colleges and universities that can grant them degrees. Others are going to the new public high schools. So many parents now seem indifferent to their religious training. And of course we never were a fashionable boarding school for rich men's daughters." Mrs. Lowrey laughed at the very idea. "No, what students we have are mostly farmers' daughters. But we may get along if Kitty will take Amanda's place as classics teacher for a while. We wouldn't have to pay her a salary."

"Amanda is leaving? I should have thought loyalty would keep her."

"So it would, if we were to permit it. As it is, she taught another year after she had repaid all she owed us. But when Mr. Fletcher offered her more than we could afford to pay, we insisted she take it." Then, to enlighten Mrs. Deming's bewilderment, she added, "Mr. Fletcher is the new superintendent of schools."

"The *public* schools?"

"Yes. We have had a revolution here. There is to be a high school, when the town authorizes a bond issue. A very good thing," she said briskly, "though hard on us."

"And Amanda is going to teach mill-hands' children and the little Germans? A sad way to waste her brains, I should think."

"Her mother is very difficult—refuses to leave. A pity. She might go far in her profession. But the 'little Germans' are bright enough and docile: she'll find them easier to teach than our girls. But we shall miss her. As we still miss you, Louisa."

"Thank you. My years here were very pleasant. In some ways," and she smiled coolly, "much pleasanter than this last year has been. Obscurity has its compensations. But the family of a man in public life learns not to take abuse too seriously."

"Oh, that Bonner." Mrs. Lowrey laughed as she destroyed whatever hopes Mrs. Deming might have cherished that the *Torchlight* paragraph had not been recognized as sarcasm. "I shouldn't pay him any attention." She looked at her hands, clasped loosely in her lap, to spare Louisa and to conceal her own curiosity. She herself might have avoided embarrassing subjects, but it was like Louisa to want to establish firm ground under her feet and to assume that her friends would respect whatever attitude she chose to assume.

"A man's most valiant services," Mrs. Lowrey murmured encouragingly, "so soon forgotten by an ungrateful public."

"Ah, it isn't the public so much. My husband is convinced in his heart, I think—although he's never said so, since *Amnesty* seems to be the order of the day—that the Democrats are having their revenge for our winning the war by blackening the characters of the men who saved the country."

Mrs. Lowrey, however unimpeachable her intellectual integrity, would yet have let this pass, had she not thought that so strong a line was dangerous for the Demings.

"Well, yes, perhaps. But you know I'm not quite sure but the less said the better. It isn't the Democrats who are investigating, is it? After all, a good many Republicans, like the Ballards—but of course the General can take care of all that, in his own way."

She then changed the subject. "You have had my letters about the Temperance Crusade that is sweeping the state? We are getting organized for our effort. Although we have been a little slow, we have decided not to 'go out' until April. March is such a chancy month, and it would not help to have our crusaders come down with pneumonia after kneeling in the slush. I know your opinion as to the vileness of the liquor trade. I hope you will join us."

Mrs. Deming, naturally antipathetic to any public demonstration, had already made up her mind to join the Crusade as one way of helping her husband with the church people. She said, "You know that I believe wholeheartedly in your cause. Of course I will join you." Having done her best for him, she rose to go. "The General has no doubt been detained, and I mustn't keep you any longer. It is so pleasant to be in a small town again, where one *can* walk. Washington is really very tiresome. I am not sure that I shall return with the General next year. Little Julia would be better off here, I believe, and it is not as though Washington were a cosmopolitan city, with great advantages."

"I am sorry that you must go now, without seeing Ellen. But if you remain in Waynesboro—it would please your friends to have you here again, Louisa. I hope you would like to be restored to active membership in the Club."

"Yes. I think so. I have been much interested in the copies of the programs I have received."

They moved to the door, where Mrs. Deming made her farewells briskly. She was not one to linger on a threshold uttering last-minute postscripts.

The General in the meantime had driven across town, into the West End, to the Rausch Cordage Company. He stopped at the office hitching post, but sat still for a moment, studying the steps to the door, the iron balustrades, and the crisp gold lettering of the sign overhead, the tall board fence that cut off any view of the mill yard except through its half-open gate; he caught only a glimpse of someone crossing the cobbled yard against a background of brick wall. There was much audible: a clatter, as of barrels rolled on paving stones, the squeak of a barrow, a broken measure of song inside somewhere. A warm smell of tar was borne along black smoke that flattened and fanned out beneath the strong March wind. A reminiscent smell, the General thought—southern pine woods on fire. A possible approach? Better not; these young fellows seemed to want to forget the war as quickly as possible: their victory, their responsibilities. He puffed a bit as his foot groped for the round step of the buggy, and he let himself down in his stiff middle-aged fashion.

Ascending the few steps, he pulled open the heavy door, and let it swing shut behind him. From the vestibule he could see that the office on the left was empty; in the one on the right there was only a milk-and-water youth in an alpaca jacket, who slipped off his high stool at the ledger-covered desk and came to question the General. He said, "You want to see Mr. Rausch?" and crossed Ludwig's office to the yard door, and called to one of the ever-present boys. Presently Ludwig appeared, and the General, in the yard door watching, saw him there for a flash in the afternoon sunlight—tall, broad-shouldered, dressed like a workman, his yellow hair tousled, his mustache almost invisibly blond, his face flushed—and was contemptuous of himself for being at the mercy of this work-soiled young man. He had avoided the bank and Mr. Cochran, and Bonner at the *Torchlight*: by Judge Ballard he had been greeted distantly, with ceremony but no warmth (and that had hurt); but his future was not in the hands of any of those men as it was in young Rausch's. "Young Rausch," coming in the door just then in blue overalls and thick brogans that tracked tar and oil over the threshold, was an incongruous element, out of place in General Deming's picture of himself and his career.

Ludwig welcomed his visitor, closed the door to the vestibule, indicated a chair, and sat down himself behind his desk. His office was in keeping with overalls and brogans: the battered desk, covered with letters, papers, and tarred samples of rope; the squeaking swivel chair behind it. The room's other chair, which he offered his guest, was a rough Windsor with a cane seat.

"Well, General: what can I do for you?"

"I have not forgotten our last conversation, and I know you haven't either." The General chewed moodily on his cigar. "I came to repeat what I said to you then. I bought and paid for by Credit Mobilier stock; I considered it an investment, nothing more nor less. And no one ever asked me to use my influence as a Representative."

Ludwig looked at him levelly for a moment, and then grinned. "I believe you, sir."

General Deming took the cigar from his mouth, stared at it, stared at Ludwig. "Then, by God, Rausch, you're the only fella in Waynesboro that does."

"Yes, I shouldn't be surprised if that's true."

The older man's face darkened. "D'you think I'm called on to resign?"

Ludwig felt sorry for him; he looked so weary and so hurt. "No, sir. Then they'd be sure you were guilty of something. Last fall you were elected for another term. Stick it out."

"That would be the wisest course for me, of course—selfishly speaking. But"—he wheezed a little, sucking for air—"if the good of the party—"

"No. For the good of the party, face it down. Garfield will. Blaine will. They weren't guilty, either, of anything but being damn fools."

The General laughed, a hollow effort. This brusque young man could make him uncomfortable, after all. But how easy to say "damn fools" if you were young and making money. "Yes, all of us: 'damn fools.' D'you think I can live it down by '74, or is this going to be my last term?"

"Oh—well, of course, that's hardly for me to say. It's early days yet. The district convention will decide on the Congressional candidate next year. I'm only county chairman; there's five other counties in the district."

"But your voice will have some weight in the convention." The General put his cigar in his mouth and his hands on his knees to hide the tremor the cigar had magnified. "What do you advise?"

"Wait and see. There's another session of Congress ahead." Ludwig fiddled with some papers on his desk. "But if you want my honest opinion, I'm not sure you wouldn't be well out of it. There are things going on in the government—it's gotten to the place where we're all expecting the worst. There's sure to be a Democratic Congress elected in '74; the trend's that way, and all this hullabaloo is going to help it. And when the Democrats get in, there'll be investigations that'll make the Credit Mobilier look like small punkins. I wouldn't want to be there, myself, even if I weren't guilty of anything but being a Republican."

"You don't think the ol' Seventh District—?" The General attempted a bearish playfulness.

"I don't know. It's safe in a presidential year. Oh, I think it's safe anyway. But the Germans don't like corruption, and they don't like Reconstruction. The farmers don't like corruption, nor the tariff, except the wool-growers, and luckily there's a lot of sheepmen in Ohio. However, I think we'd carry the county for you, if you were the nominee. The trouble'd be in the District Convention. The other county chairmen keep reminding me we've had the Representative for four terms, now. Boone County, particularly, is getting restive. They want to put up Liddell of Whitewater. You know him: he's state senator, now, from this district."

"Yes. A good man." The General sat heavily for a moment, silent. He had been discussed then, and his successor proposed. "Well, we'll let it ride a while. But you can count on my doing whatever is best for the party."

Both men were sure that the General's career as Congressman would come to an end with the completion of the coming term. There was nothing more to be said on that subject.

"How is the factory doing, my boy? You seem busy."

"Yes. But business is slowing down." Ludwig smiled. Perhaps it made the old duffer feel better to "boy" him. "Boom times are coming to an end. But we're one of the few rope manufacturers west of the Alleghenies, you know, sir. That helps. Would you like to see the plant? We're laying a ten-inch hawser now for one of the Great Lakes' shipyards."

He rose, and the General lumbered to his feet and went with him, first to the cobbled ramp from the canal landing, then to the small, square building just beyond. "The hemp house. Hemp is brought here from the barges. Not American hemp, now. They've quit growing it. We have to import." Opening the door, he indicated the piled bales of hemp. From that point he showed the General no mercy; he took him through all the stages of the preparation process, assuming that any male must be as interested as he himself in the various machines. They came finally to the hatchelors, where the honey-colored hemp came down off the heckling pins like a waterfall, the fibers as straight and smooth as a woman's hair.

"Manilla hemp," Ludwig explained, "used for big rope. Other kinds haven't that color. Manilla costs more, but it doesn't have to be tarred—goes from the spinners to the forming mill."

Outside again, Ludwig pointed to a three-sided shed on the river side of the yard. There, in the half-dark, the tar-tank bubbled over a fire box, tended by Negroes whose bare torsos gleamed blue-black in a queer, smoky, fire-shot light. One of the Negroes kept the fire going, while at one end a boy tossed a junk of yarn into the tank and at the other a Negro laborer drew it toward him indolently and slowly, with a long hooked pole; when it finally came under his nose he hooked it out, and with the same easy indolence flung it over a rack behind him.

"Smells like North Carolina in '65," the General said. "Is it tarred for water-proofing? How long is it in the tank? Does a Negro like that guess at it, or does he have some way of measuring time?"

"Fifteen feet a minute through the tar is the right rate, in a tank that length." Ludwig laughed. "Just about natural speed for a nigger like Aaron. But he does have some way of knowing time: he sings or hums, or taps a foot. And when he's been at the job long enough, he just knows. He's the envy of the other niggers: tarring is the perfect job; warm, slow-moving."

The two men stood aside to let a Negro with a loaded wheelbarrow pass. "The actual rope-making begins with the spinning of the yarn." Ludwig led the way across the cobbles to the rope walk, unchanged since he had bought it, where the spinning of yarn, the forming of strands, the laying of rope, were still done by hand. Ludwig and the General watched for a moment. "Here we used skilled labor," Ludwig explained. The men backed down the length of the shed as boys turned the wheels that twisted the fibers fastened to them, the spinners all the while keeping the strands from kinking and adding new fiber from the bundle hung at their waists as the strands running through their fingers showed signs of coming to an end.

This process bored the watching General; Ludwig could see that he wanted to get away. "I hope I haven't kept you too long. I forget that not everyone shares my interest."

"Not at all, not at all. I believe you said something about a big rope?"

Ludwig, itching to get back, led the way to the far side of the long shed, where the most skilled workers, under the eyes of a Roseboom brother, were laying the hawser. They were concentrated with a kind of fierce intensity on what they were doing, but when Ludwig and the General entered, and Roseboom spoke to them, they looked up with welcoming grins or slight gestures, and the tension relaxed. General Deming, at Ludwig's elbow, was as interested in the young man's easy relations with those at work as he was in the work itself.

"That rope's as thick as my forearm," he said.

"Hawser," Ludwig corrected automatically, and he enlightened his companion on the difference between rope-lay, cable-lay, shroud-lay, right- and left-lay. "This is the biggest hawser we've ever had an order for. That's why we're all so excited." Ludwig looked proudly at his workers, who without pausing looked proudly back, grinning at the boss. "We'd best leave them to get it done, I guess."

The General was tired: Ludwig's enthusiasm made him feel old and a little grumpy. Perhaps it was awareness of middle-age and failure that made him say, as they paused at the office door to look back, "Well, my boy, you have the makings of a right nice little business here." And perhaps it was the grumpiness that made him, a few moments later, throw cold water over Ludwig's confidence in the future, or it might have been a felt compulsion to be in his turn informative, to give the impression of being on confidential terms with men who dealt with the really important affairs of the country.

"Trouble is," Ludwig said, scowling across the yard from his office door, "the plant is so higgledy-piggledy. Except for the new building I showed you, makeshift sheds, not in the right places. Too much waste motion, carrying fiber and yarns and cordage back and forth. Soon as I can swing it, there'll be a new mill for ropemaking machinery to take the place of the old walk." Seated again in the office, he explained. There was room enough on the river side of the yard to put up a new building adjacent, but at right angles to, the preparation mill. The railroad main line was not far away: if business ever warranted it, a siding could be laid down. He still shipped to Cincinnati by canal, but most of his product went north now, to Lake Erie, and to ship that distance by canal was far too slow: finished rope was hauled by drays to the freight depot and moved by rail to the lake ports. "All this won't happen tomorrow, I know. I'd have to borrow, and the way business is slacking off, I don't see my way, right now."

"I dunno. I'm afraid easy times are over. I'd wait, if I were you. If things went smash, borrowed money would be harder to pay back."

"You think we may be in for a real depression?"

Perhaps General Deming was gratified by Ludwig's startled expression; he stood a moment longer by the desk. "God knows, I'm no financial genius. I've proved that, I reckon. But there's a funny feeling in the air—men are looking over their shoulders. And it's common sense to be a little wary. We've pushed railroad building too far. Mind you, I wanted the U.P. built—the country needed to be tied together. I thought it was a great thing, and still do. But once it was finished, all the speculators in the country who'd said it couldn't be done jumped into railroad building. And Congress helped them, with land grants, and they sold bonds; but if their roads don't do business, how're they going to pay interest on the bonds? And where's the business coming from? They lay thousands o' miles o' track through wilderness—there isn't any business there."

"But they're selling the lands they got from Congress. And all the people homesteading—there'll be crops."

"In time, maybe. If that land can grow crops. Lord! I crossed it, remember, in '69, when they drove in the golden spike. Anyway it won't be settled for a while, and if the roads go bankrupt, so will iron and steel, because all this iron and steel they're making is for the roads. . . . Well, I may be wrong; I hope so. But if I were you I'd hold off for a while." He shook his head lugubriously as he took his leave.

Home again, he himself drove the buggy into the stable, and alighting, noted ruefully the damage to his shoes. Louisa wouldn't be pleased. He sent the stable boy to the kitchen for another pair, and left the tarred ones to be cleaned.

He found his wife and child in the sitting room awaiting him. Julia left her mother at once and came to him to be lifted on to his knee. He had that satisfaction at least, he thought, as he put one arm about her and with the other hand pressed her bright head against his watch pocket; Julia did not doubt or question. All that she asked was that he be aware of her. She rested against him silently while he talked, only twisting her head back to look at him when he seemed by the laxness of his hands to have forgotten her. Then he would embrace her again, she would let her head fall back once more, and would smile a little to herself as she watched her mother.

"What I have been through in the interests of my career, Louisa! I now know all the ins and outs of the manufacture of rope. All to no use, I'm afraid. They're through with me. Of course, he turned down my offer to resign."

"You offered to *resign*?" Mrs. Deming sat up straighter, if possible, in her chair, leaned forward a little.

"Oh—a gesture, my dear. They would never demand that sacrifice—but so far as next term is concerned, it seems Boone County wants to run Liddell, of Whitewater."

"Who said so?"

"Why, young Rausch. That's who I was talking with."

Mrs. Deming's face was perfectly white and still; it might have been cut with a chisel. Once upon a time her pupils would have said "Ol' Teapot's boiling."

"Ludwig Rausch! A German immigrant! A boy who came to this town without a penny, married the banker's daughter, and set himself up."

"No, Louisa. He's the duly chosen chairman of the County Republican Central Committee."

"But it's not the Committee's opinion he's passing on to you. It's his. Oh, you know these young soldiers; anyone who was a high-ranked officer is an enemy."

"No, no, Louisa. That's hardly fair. Rausch isn't my enemy. He didn't come here penniless, either: his family's pretty well fixed, and he was able to buy that mill."

"But it is not right that he should presume to dictate to you as to your career."

"But he wasn't—he was only explaining, advising." The General was astonished; he had never seen his wife so angry. Queer, what roused women: he wouldn't have supposed she cared so much about his career. "And anyway, it's a long way off. There's a session of Congress between now and then: anything can happen."

"I mean to see it does happen. You are the town's first citizen, now. Judge Ballard's day is past, and there's no one else. Whether you are reelected in '74 or not—" And she went on to tell him how on the moment's inspiration she had said to Mrs. Lowrey that she would stay in Waynesboro and not go back to Washington in December. "They'll take me back into their Club: it's in the constitution," she said with satisfaction. "An Associate Member can always ask to be reinstated as an Active Member."

"There are no votes in your Club, my dear. And even if those women could tell their husbands what to do, there aren't more'n a dozen of them."

"But they count. Your rehabilitation with that group would do much for you. I promised to take part in the Temperance Crusade, too—that may help."

The General flushed. He did not like the word "rehabilitation."

"And Sarah Cochran Rausch is a member of the Club."

She spoke with such hint of meaning in her voice that the General was terrified.

"Oh, look here, my dear! No feuds—that wouldn't help."

"Feuds! Certainly not. But I flatter myself I can handle that young woman; don't forget: I *taught* her."

"But can she handle Rausch?"

"She and the bank? Don't be absurd, George. And don't worry, all will turn out well, I feel sure."

Whether the General was reassured or not, he did not say, but turned his attention to his child.

In the meantime Ludwig, left alone in his office, meditated on the General's warning. After all, booms must end sooner or later, postwar booms particularly. In that early spring of '73 the country seemed to be heading into what Ludwig hoped would be only a mild and brief recession. Rausch Cordage Company was still receiving orders, as the correspondence on his desk served to prove. It might be wise, however, to postpone any capital investment until any recession had blown over. He would at least ask his father-in-law's advice when he and Sally and the children would be at the Cochrans' for Sunday dinner.

He was not too surprised to find that Mr. Cochran was pessimistic: he had to an exaggerated degree the banker's cautious nature. But a few weeks later, although little had been said or printed about "hard times coming"—perhaps in the hope that what was not spoken of would not happen—there was foreboding in the air. Ludwig shared his misgivings with no one but Sally, to whom he had to explain the postponement of his building plans. He sold stock and bought government bonds; he knew that Mr. Cochran was calling what loans he could and preparing the bank for a storm. This seemed particularly wise after the panic in May on the Vienna Bourse, which stopped the sale in Europe of American securities. Crops promised to be large that year, but if they could not be sold abroad?

In that same spring everyone came to recognize the necessity for frugality. There was not much talk about it or undue lamentation among the Woman's Club members. They all wore last season's dolman, redingote, or polonaise, and smiled at them no more than they did at Miss Gardiner's hoops, to which they had become accustomed. What did create comment, soon after the Demings' return to Waynesboro, was Mrs. Deming's announcement at a Club meeting, which she had attended as an Associate Member, that she would not go back to Washington with the General, but would stay at home with little Julia. It was much more economical to live in Waynesboro, she explained, and kept a bland countenance as she searched for a face that might be reflecting the all too likely thought, "All that Credit Mobilier stock—they must have plenty." However, no one smiled in any but the kindest way, and all expressed delight at the prospect of her return to active membership.

This desire of Mrs. Deming to be taken back into the fold did confront the ladies with a problem. Even the most enlightened bluestocking would have agreed that thirteen is a most uncomfortable number, and besides, there was Kitty Lowrey, soon to be an Oberlin B. A., ready to come home and begin teaching at the Female College. Mrs. Ballard therefore appointed a committee to work out a revision of the constitution that the ladies could vote on at the next meeting. Mrs. McKinney was appointed chairman, Mrs. Rausch and Mrs. Gordon members. Since no alteration was suggested other than the change in the number of members, one meeting of the committee would be sufficient, and its chairman could report a fortnight hence. Having dealt with that problem, Mrs. Ballard went on to speak of the Temperance Crusade to be undertaken shortly, which any of the ladies were invited to join.

The committee meeting on altering the constitution was held at Mrs. McKinney's house, by her invitation. The Woman's Club had never met there. Anne was of course familiar with the manse, since Mrs. McKinney was her minister's wife, but Sally had never been inside it. She thought she had never seen a room more suited to its owner's personality: it was rather grim, all horsehair and tortured walnut, glass-fronted bookcases full of black theological tomes, a walnut-topped table with lamp and Bible, and a large sepia "Christ in the Temple" over the mantel.

Mrs. McKinney welcomed and seated them, side by side on the horsehair sofa, smiled the odd compressed smile that dug her chin into her collar and swelled her jowls, and set about making a social occasion of the meeting, introducing the subject closest to her heart: times were hard but sometimes people were more easily moved when the world's affairs were going awry. She and Mr. McKinney, the Ballards, and various other leading church people were so very much moved by the Temperance Crusade sweeping the state. The ladies of Hillsboro and Washington Court House, under the leadership of Mr. Dio Lewis, had done such wonderful work in closing the saloons. She did hope that in April the Woman's Club would join other organizations in sponsoring a crusade in Waynesboro.

Tact and discretion were not a part of Mrs. McKinney's being. Or, Anne thought wildly, did Mrs. Ballard really believe, and Mrs. McKinney, that she and Sally would Crusade, or that Sally had forgotten who had called Ludwig a "ward heeler"? But while she was still struggling, mouth open, to think of something to say, Sally took the situation into her capable hands.

"The Club constitution forbids its participation as a Club in anything of a controversial nature. But perhaps you had thought of revising the constitution in that section, too?"

It was Mrs. McKinney's turn to look startled. "Oh, no, certainly not. There was no authorization to do so. It simply hadn't occurred to me that *temperance* could be considered a 'controversial matter' by the ladies of the Club."

"Oh, temperance! Of course not. I thought you meant total abstinence, and driving out the saloons. Of course, what individual members of the Club do is their own concern. But for that sort of crusade to be successful, don't you want women whose husbands drink up all their wages, and beat them, and abuse the children, to make the saloonkeepers' consciences hurt?"

"The saloonkeepers wouldn't be moved by our hymn-singing, I'm afraid." Anne managed not to smile, although the whole notion seemed to her truly mirth-provoking. "They know our husbands don't beat us."

This was received coolly by Mrs. McKinney, and the committee meeting would certainly not have established any bonds between the three women had chance not intervened.

The little colored maid came to the parlor door. She was a child from the County Home, taken by the McKinneys and given a home in return for help in the kitchen. She bobbed an awkward curtsey.

"Please, ma'am. Tom's at de back do'—he finished he wo'k. He ask to see you, Ma'am, befo' he go." And she mumbled something unintelligible about coal.

Mrs. McKinney rose, reluctantly it seemed, as if she would have preferred seeing her guests on their way first. But they had not settled on whether Club membership should be increased to fourteen or fifteen.

"I'm sorry I must ask you to excuse me for just a moment. My husband is out, or I should call him in to play host."

She had scarcely gone, leaving the parlor door open, before a plaintive voice called from upstairs, and kept calling: "Rhody! Oh, Rhody!"

Sally and Anne looked at each other, more than a little startled. They knew, as did everyone in town, that the Reverend Mr. McKinney's senile mother lived with them at the manse; story had it that she was locked up somewhere in the attic—a suspicion based on the popular novels of the day, added to the fact that no one had ever seen her. When the voice sounded again so much more clearly that its owner must have come to stand at the head of the staircase, Anne rose uncertainly, hesitated, said, "She might fall down the stairs," and stepped into the hall, stopped with her hand on the newel post, and looked up.

"Mrs. McKinney has been called to the kitchen. Is there anything I can do?"

A tiny little old lady sat on the top step. She was neatly dressed in a gray calico printed over with black and white flowers; she wore a bonnet and carried a shawl over her arm. She peered down at Anne vaguely.

"Who are you? I don't know you, do I? You ain't George's girl?"

"No, I'm Mrs. Gordon. The doctor's wife."

"Doctor?" The voice was frightened. "I don't know no doctor. Nor I ain't ailing."

"Of course not. I'm just calling on Mrs. McKinney. I thought I'd tell you she was busy."

"If she's busy, then mebbe you can come along up here and help me."

The old lady made a feeble attempt to rise, clutching the banisters, but started to topple, and sank down again. Anne flew up the stairs, helped her to her feet, and drew her away from the edge of the landing. She would have resisted going down the hall to the front bedroom, but the blue-veined hand on her arm was insistent.

"George won't come until tomorrow, now. It's too late. It's getting dark." She nodded toward the hall window. It was indeed true: the clouded, gloomy day was drawing to a close. "I must get my bed to rights before bedtime."

Anne hesitated again at the bedroom door. "I don't know Mrs. McKinney well enough to be upstairs in her house. Now you're safe, I'd better go back. She mightn't like it."

"Rhody?" The old lady blinked up at her out of glazed blue eyes. The bonnet with its ribbons tied under her chin fell back from the crown of her head. "Rhody never scolds. She's been very good to me, Rhody has. Only, I want to go home."

In the open door Anne stood astonished. The bureau was bare. The china from the washstand was piled in a wicker clothes basket. The spool bed was stripped not only of bedding, mattress, and springs, but even of the slats, which had been tied in a bundle and propped against the wall. The mattress was rolled up and tied, the bedding folded and piled on a chair, the springs tilted against the foot of the bed.

"I thought George would surely come today, but something must have kept him. I won't worry—" and she mumbled vaguely: "Rhody always says not to worry. He'll come tomorrow, certain. But you must help me fix my bed for tonight."

Anne, wondering at the philosophical calm with which the old woman accepted disappointment, carried the bundle of slats to the bed, untied it, and was fitting them into place, when Mrs. McKinney entered.

"Rhody, you do think it's too late for George today, don't you? I asked her—what did you say your name is, child?—to help me. You didn't come when I called."

"I'm sorry, Mother. I didn't hear you. Yes, it's too late for George, now. We'll get the springs and mattress back on the bed for you, then you can make it, and set the room to rights."

Together she and Anne got the bed put together again. Then Mrs. McKinney drew Anne from the room.

"She'd rather make her own bed. She'll be all right now. I'm sorry."

Anne misunderstood. "I'm sorry she was disappointed, but she took it well, not worrying. I hope nothing happened to George. He is her son?"

"Oh, my dear: I thought you realized." Mrs. McKinney stopped to look at Anne, her hand on the banisters. "George *was* her son. He's been dead twenty years. But he lived on the homeplace, and the poor old soul wants to go home."

They moved on slowly to the end of the hall and down the stairs. "Every morning after breakfast she gets ready for George to come and move her. Packs everything up, and strips the bed. Where she finds the strength is a mystery. Then she pulls her rocker to the window and watches for George. All day long. When it begins to get dark, she decides something has happened, and she puts it all back again till next day. Only by that time she hasn't got strength left to manage the slats and springs and the mattress. That's why she called."

"How—how sad! And how hard for you."

Mrs. McKinney smiled, tucked her chin in, shook her head. "Not really. She's perfectly satisfied to sit in her window and watch, and she's sure if George doesn't come today, he'll come tomorrow. And taking the bed apart and putting it together again gives her something to do."

The two of them returned to the parlor where Sally was waiting. The committee then finished its business promptly, and the two young women made their farewells. They went silently through the gate and silently started up the street. They were walking as far as the Gordons', where Ludwig would stop for his wife as he drove home from the mill.

Anne was feeling considerably chastened as she told Sally what had occurred upstairs. "I'm ashamed of myself," she said meekly, in conclusion. "Mrs. McKinney's a *really good* woman. Kind. I wouldn't have believed it. Imagine! How hard to live with that day in, day out—and she's always cheerful."

"She's dignified about it, too," Sally was beginning to set more store by dignity than Anne ever would. "And that's why she's never had the Club—she'd rather have died than ask us not to mention it."

"We won't, of course." And they didn't, except to their husbands.

Perhaps even more than they realized, the incident altered their feelings toward Mrs. McKinney. However much, that year and later, they were to disagree with and oppose her, they never ceased to feel for her a deep respect, which in time came to be the mildly affectionate regard one feels for a cousin or a lifelong neighbor who may not be congenial but is still made dear by association and shared experience. A long time later, young women of another generation, seeing genuine regret at the Club farewell tea for Mrs. McKinney, were to wonder whether having been fellow members so long had made sentimental hypocrites of their elders, or whether ladies of so diverse character and outlook had truly felt some bond. By that time, of course, the Reverend Mr. McKinney's senile mother had been dead for years, and forgotten by Waynesboro.

The report of the committee on the revision of the constitution was read at the next Club meeting, at Mrs. Lowrey's, and accepted unanimously by its members. The membership would be increased to fifteen. After adjournment there was muted discussion as to whose name should be presented as candidate for fifteenth member. Thirteen and fourteen would be Mrs. Deming and Kitty Lowrey. There was some discussion of the literary capacity of this or that minister's wife. Sally protested that there was nothing in the amendment that said there must be fifteen members: it might be well to give themselves a little time. She was still protesting as she started to walk home with Anne and Amanda Reid: surely there were other women in town besides ministers' wives who would make good Club members. But in naming over the possibilities—her mother's friends, like Mrs. Sheldon and Mrs. Edwards and various other merchants' wives—Mrs. Torchlight Bonner, as Sally called her, Mrs. Keyes, the wife of the other banker—she admitted they seemed hardly suitable. Amanda, who had no antipathy to ministers except that which sprang from too close an acquaintance with them in their embryo state, wanted to propose the name of Mrs. Fletcher, the wife of the superintendent of schools. She was a plain, pleasant middle-aged woman whose intellectuality, if it existed at all, had probably been acquired after marriage, but no one could possibly have objected to her on any other ground than dullness. Unfortunately, Amanda must have been "got at" between that meeting and the next one, at the Rausches', for Mrs. Ballard, presiding, read three names from slips of paper that had been handed her, and Mrs. Fletcher's was not among them. Proposed instead was Mrs. Mary McCune, the wife of the minister of the First Reformed Presbyterian Church. The Reids' church. Of course Amanda had given up Mrs. Fletcher and agreed. Sally kept her face smooth and social and said nothing, although the constitution provided for two weeks' time between the proposing of a name and the voting on it, for the purpose of discussion and consideration. But already the Club membership had established the convention whereby candidates for membership were rejected—if they were to be rejected—before their names were proposed, never after they had been read out in meeting.

So that it was not until the Club was adjourned and Sally was helping the ladies find their wraps in her parlor bedroom that she said firmly, but *sotto voce*, to Amanda, "What possessed you? Mrs. McCune! That pretty, helpless, beaten little thing, who daren't have an opinion that isn't her husband's. She'll never be present, she has a baby every year. And she certainly isn't intellectual."

Mrs. McKinney, who was standing too close not to have heard, perhaps had her own estimates of Sally's intellectual powers.

"Do you know anyone more suitable, Mrs. Rausch? The wife of one of your husband's German friends? I understand they're very learned men. Mrs. Lichtenstein, perhaps?"

Red flamed in Sally's cheeks, but she managed to laugh. "I'm afraid I'm not acquainted with Mrs. Lichtenstein. But for all I know, she may be very charming. And I don't doubt that she is intellectual." Sally choked a bit over this falsehood, having in her mind's eye, from Ludwig's description, a vivid picture of Rosa Hoffmann, now the second Mrs. Lichtenstein, at work in her brother's beer parlor, carrying foaming mugs and bowls of pretzels to the customers. But she continued, bravely, "Mr. Lichtenstein is so very brilliant. He's the only man in town can beat Dock Gordon at chess." (Anne can just share this humiliation with me, she thought.) "And he cares so very much about education."

Afterward, when all the others had gone, she said to Anne, "Wait till I tell Ludwig! He insists on making friends of all these people." She had almost forgotten her original grievance. But when Ludwig was told in due time, he not only refused to see why she had been embarrassed but proposed that she call on Mrs. Lichtenstein to see for herself what she was like, and Sally was not certain enough that he was joking to care to continue the discussion.

The ladies whose names had been presented to the Club were by unanimous vote invited to become members, and Mrs. Deming to be welcomed back. Regardless of the deepening depression affecting the country, most of the Club ladies, along with a great number of churchwomen, continued to busy themselves with plans for an April Temperance Crusade, which they hoped would drive the saloons from Waynesboro.

Even those men who worried about the prospects for the future were divided for a time by the Crusade. A thunderstorm that strikes down trees just outside one's windows distracts attention from an earthquake on the other side of the globe that kills thousands. To the Woman's Club, where earthquakes in economics and politics were not allowed mention, the thunderstorm of the Temperance Crusade had the proportions of a tornado.

After a statewide meeting in Columbus in February, churchwomen had returned to Waynesboro fired with enthusiasm to do there what had already been done in other towns in the state. Club meetings through February and March had continued to concern themselves, uncontroversially, with Contemporary Leaders of American Thought, but everyone was conscious of the flaming issue that divided the members. Mrs. Ballard and Mrs. McKinney had been in Columbus; they were two of the leaders who prepared the campaign. Eliza Ballard was eager to join the fray, perhaps largely because that was what she expected it to be. Eliza had not yet arrived at the utter cynicism of middle age, indifferent even to a good fight. But Thomasina had listened to her father when, temperance advocate though he was, he expressed himself as opposed to the crusaders' methods because of their doubtful legality. In the face of his wife's indignation and astonishment, he had seen fit to warn her: "Some day, some saloonkeeper will refuse to be swept off his feet, and will appeal to the court for protection."

"The owners of fugitive slaves used to appeal to the court, too, and you never paid any attention." Mrs. Ballard let it go at that; she had felt for some time that the Judge had let financial misfortune affect his initiative. Although surprised at this defection on the part of one who had stood with her for a generation on all questions of reform, she did not discuss it further. Thomasina, on the other hand, was glad to be fortified by her father's views in her desire to stand aloof. She hated above all else in the world to be conspicuous; and besides, her family never paid any attention to Samuel's music pupils, but she knew well enough that there were Germans among them whose fathers either sold beer or drank it. And Samuel had a profound distaste, too, for unladylike proceedings of any kind. Thomasina was not moved by her mother's assumptions that she was one of them, nor by her insistence that she should be. Douglas Gardiner, now reading law under the Judge's tutelage, also cautioned his aunts. Those two ladies, who might have joined in any undertaking that promised to forward his career, were relieved when he repeated Judge Ballard's views. They cared little for Waynesboro, where their only interests were church, Club, and their nephew's career; and they were too repelled by reform, in general and in particular, to be concerned about the town's morals. They even enjoyed Mr. Bonner's sardonic comments in the editorial columns of his paper.

Amanda, Mrs. Lowrey, and Mrs. Tyler believed fervently in the Cause, Kitty with less enthusiasm. There was no question of Amanda's leaving her public schoolroom to take part, and from the Female College only Mrs. Lowrey could get away. Mrs. Deming, intent on restoring her husband's good name, became one of the leaders. Mrs. McCune was excused from participation by her delicate condition after a miscarriage; Anne Gordon, remembering the brandy bottle in her sideboard, firmly but quietly said "No." As for Sally, there was no question as to where she stood: her father liked his wine, her husband liked his beer; she had never seen that either was the worse for his indulgence, and she was certainly not going to help persecute those who made their pleasure possible. Her "No" was emphatic, and she went about with her nose in the air and an invisible chip on her shoulder.

The Crusade began one April morning with a prayer meeting at the First Reformed Presbyterian Church. It was crowded to the doors, each congregation a flock shepherded by its own pastors. After prayers and a hymn, the meeting was turned over to Mrs. Ballard, the president of the local Temperance Union. She was never one to waste time in getting down to the business in hand. Describing the plan of operation, she said, "It has been decided, on the basis of experience in other communities, to attack first those dispensers of alcoholic beverages who are most easily moved, leaving the hardest-hearted to the last. The most easily moved are the pharmacists, who are dependent for the bulk of their trade on Christian good-will. I call now for volunteers to make the rounds of the pharmacies, while the rest of us remain here to pray."

With a promptness that suggested prearrangement, Mrs. McKinney rose; her example was followed by eighteen or twenty other women. They collected at the rear of the church, marched down the steps, right-turned on the brick sidewalk, and started downtown two by two, each with her hands primly gloved, each with a hymn book and a bundle of tracts under her arm. When the little parade came down Chillicothe Street to the Court House square, it attracted a sizable audience: in every shop door men stood to watch; knots of idlers gathered on the corners, some not above making ribald comment; a few ragged boys, who should have been in school, ran and leaped on the curbstones. Some of the women walked with flaming cheeks, their eyes on the ground; some held their heads high, eyes front, features frozen with self-consciousness. But a few, hardened by their experience as campaigners for abolition and woman's rights, were entirely at ease, and passed out their tracts to the scoffers. And ahead of them all tramped Mrs. McKinney, with a sturdy militant fling. Outside Mr. Thirkield's drugstore she halted her little band, turned to face them, and said, "Let us sing before entering, 'The Battle Hymn of the Republic.'"

Mr. Thirkield was one of Mr. McKinney's congregation, an honest and sincere Presbyterian. Perhaps there had been some prearrangement with him. When the hymn was finished he came to the door and invited the crusaders in.

"I believe that your cause is a good one, ladies. I have never been accustomed"—he cleared his throat deprecatingly—"to selling liquor over my counter, thus encouraging the evils of drunkenness. And I have been convinced that medical science no longer recommends the use of alcohol to be taken internally. But if the doctors insist on prescribing it—if they feel they must—let their patients go elsewhere! I have disposed of my small stock of wines and brandies, and I am ready to sign the pledge."

It was given him, and when he had solemnly written down his name, Mrs. McKinney prayed, the ladies sang again, and they proceeded on their way, looking, most of them, a little less like martyrs on the way to execution. They had been successful, and that was what counted, even though they had missed the excitement of smashing bottles and some of them may have wondered just how Mr. Thirkield had "disposed" of his stock.

By mid-afternoon—the ladies had not stopped for lunch, nor slackened in their endeavors—all the druggists had signed the pledge. The first low outwork of the foe had been scaled.

The next day the crusaders, some five hundred strong, met at the Presbyterian church, and the same program was followed, except that Mrs. Ballard turned the meeting over to the Methodist minister's wife and volunteered to lead a party to Tim O'Reilly's in the West End. If this seemed like rash foolhardiness, still, encouraged by their success, the response was vigorous; and at least fifty women marched behind Mrs. Ballard and Mrs. McKinney, who struck up a hymn as they passed the Court House, "God moves in a mysterious way."

Some at least of the marching band had never been in the "Goose Pasture" end of town before, at least on foot. But they sang "Ye fearful saints, fresh courage take" with shrill confident voices as they came beneath the sign that read "O'Reilly: Grocery and Provision Store." No one could have been in doubt as to what "Provision" included: the smell of cheap whiskey seeped around the door and hung thick in the air. If the women had qualms, none of them showed it. They stopped long enough on the sidewalk to finish their hymn, for the second time through, and then walked in. The room they entered was empty of persons, and almost empty altogether: there were counters, with shelves behind them, around three sides of the room, with so little on the shelves that "grocery" was an obvious misnomer, even to anyone who had not known O'Reilly's by reputation.

The door to an inner room was open; from thence issued not only the smell of whiskey, which brought many handkerchiefs from muffs to noses, but also the sound of a baby crying wearily and hopelessly and of subdued voices, male and female, in argument. With an expressionless face Mrs. Ballard turned to face the women who filled the space behind her, between the counters.

"Now, once more: 'God moves in a mysterious way.'"

The baby squalled louder, as if indignant at the noise, but the dispute ceased. As Mrs. McKinney lifted her voice in prayer, there came immediately the sound of a scuffle and slap from a back room, and a woman shot through the open door, as if she had been held so hard as to have lost her balance when released. She brought up against the counter, and clung to it for support, her tawny hair loose over one shoulder, her torn dress twisted and awry. She did not wait for the prayer to cease, but began to curse in a low voice, venomously.

"Oh, Lord," Mrs. McKinney lifted her voice. "We come not in our poor strength alone."

"Git out o' me shop, ev'ry damn' one o' yez, ye—"

"We beseech thee in Thy infinite mercy to save this family, to soften their hearts that they may see the evil of this unholy traffic."

"We've no need at all iv yer black heretic prayers! When we pray we pray in our own church. Holy Mither o' God! Bless this family, is it indade! This family don't want yer prayers."

"Thou, O God, wilt bring this woman to hear our words! Let them enter into her heart like arrows of conviction."

"Ye're naught but a set o' street-walkers!" The woman hiccuped suddenly, and drew herself up. "Oh, I know this kind o' thing! It's like the epi—epizootic. 'T goes all around 'n' then goes away agin."

Some in the rear of the close-packed band, unable to see the staggering woman for the bonnets between, said rashly, in a voice of shocked amazement, "Why, I believe the creature is drunk!"

"'Cray-thure,' is it? I'll 'cray-thure' yez!" She turned to the almost empty shelf behind her, seized a canister, and thumped it down on the counter before her. "I give yez fair warning: 'tis cayenne pepper, this is! Get out o' me shop immejitly, or yez get it in yer interferin' faces."

A brawny Irishman, young as the woman, with a pale, black-browed, grim face, came through the inner door and seized her hands from behind.

"Ye'd better go, ladies, me woife ain't hersilf."

The women began to edge out the door. Only Mrs. Ballard paused on the threshold. "We do not accept one rebuff as final, you understand. We'll be back tomorrow, and hope to find your wife in a more reasonable frame of mind."

Outside the door she and Mrs. McKinney marshaled their somewhat chastened crusaders, and led them on to the next Irish saloonkeeper. Here, and on their later visits that forenoon, they were content to remain on the outside, kneeling in the dirt paths for their prayers, holding their tracts and hymnbooks; the subdued prayer, the louder singing, drew groups of ragamuffins and tatterdemalion women in shawls, but no more saloon-keepers were encountered that day.

On the following morning, when the congregations had assembled at the Methodist church, Mrs. Ballard's report of their experience at the hands of the O'Reillys inspired an even larger number of volunteers. The procession that started for the West End was longer than it had been. They had chosen a psalm for their marching song:

> Are all the foes of Sion fools,
> Who thus destroy her saints?
> Do they not know her Saviour rules,
> And pities her complaints?
>
> They shall be seized with sad surprise,
> For God's avenging arm
> Shall crush the hand that dares arise
> To do his children harm.
>
> In vain the sons of Satan boast
> Of armies in array:
> When God on high dismays their host
> They fall an easy prey.

The sound of women's high voices lifted in song was an answer to the curious who had gathered on the corners asking, "Are they out today?" More citizens than usual were in the street that morning, having heard of the previous day's confrontation, and since it was market day, there were farmers in town: all were ready to fall in behind the marching women, or to stroll along the opposite side of the street, level with them, aloof, but in a position not to miss anything pleasurably exciting.

Tim O'Reilly was waiting for them in his door, an axe in his hand. The women came down upon him singing; at sight of the axe, one little elderly Methodist in the front rank, in an old-fashioned bonnet and shawl, knelt before him, with obvious pain in stiffened joints, and began to pray, mournfully, for the hard of heart. Until she had finished, every movement was suspended, but when she had been lifted to her feet by her friends, the young man called out, shifting the axe in his hand, "Yez see, Oi'm ready for yez this toime." Then he smiled wryly. "Don't never be thinkin Oi'm fer takin' the axe to yez, now!" Sad and hard as this young face looked, still he plainly relished the drama of the moment. "Oi know well it's roight yez are about the whiskey, bad cess to it! An' Oi've the axe ready for me own barrels!"

After an astonished pause and hesitation, cheers rang out. Mrs. Ballard sent a small boy from among the spectators to the Methodist church with a message. Presently while Tim was rolling a cask out of the empty grocery, church bells pealed out in a triumphant clangor. Although Tim's stock was not a large one, by the time he had carried out his few bottles to stand beside the cask, spectators were streaming toward the spot.

Tim held up two bottles. "It's me own home ye would destroy entoirely." He brought them crashing down on the edge of the cask. "But ye'll do no more divil's work be moy hand."

To the accompaniment of cheers from the spectators and the Doxology from the ladies, he broke every bottle and then with his axe smashed the cask, so that the gutter did, as Mr. Bonner said that evening in the *Torchlight*, "literally run with whiskey." The evil odor hung in the chilly April air. When all was done, amidst Methodist shouts of "Hallelujah," murmured words of prayer, and a repetition of the Doxology, Mrs. Ballard got the ladies into line and started them off emboldened by success for the dreaded and notorious "Shades of Death" and "The Mule's Ear," uptown, in the alley between Chillicothe and Spring streets. She herself stopped to speak to Tim, her conscience sore because she had judged him hopelessly and adamantinely wicked. Now she said, her own tongue twisted a little by the influence of his brogue, "It's a brave thing you've done, throwing away your bread and butter. Come to me next week, and I'll see if there isn't something even in these hard times that we can find for you to do."

After Tim O'Reilly's capitulation, the other Irishmen were easy. Swayed by their pure delight in melodrama, or a desire for cheers for themselves like those O'Reilly had had, or perhaps even honestly persuaded, for the time being at any rate, that they had been pursuing an evil course, one after another of them, as if possessed by a hysterical love of destruction, smashed bottles and casks in the gutter. The end of a day of such triumph sent the ladies home uplifted, assured of invincibility, emotionally exhausted but ecstatic.

Yet there was not one of them who did not know that the hardest part of their fight lay before them: that the citadel had yet to be taken, and that the Germans were not so volatile and easily moved as the Irish. The next morning's meeting began with prayerful sobriety. Some moments were devoted to a discussion of the best way to approach Mr. Hoffmann. They knew that he permitted no drunkenness in his beer parlor, which he regarded indeed as an extension of his home; there would be no consciousness in his mind of harm brought on women and children. He had boys and girls of his own, in addition to his sisters, now married; perhaps for their sakes he would want to earn the approval of Waynesboro? But Mrs. Ballard saw any such plea as useless: what he was doing was not disapproved of by any of his friends or associates. They would have to rely on "The Appeal to Dramsellers" and to prayer, singing, and exhortation, as they had so far done, so successfully.

The group that descended on Mr. Hoffmann was the largest that had been out, so that although it entered his doors with little hesitation, it found but scant room inside for kneeling, what with the benches along the wall, the square tables, the chairs, the wide bar. The smell of beer was as revolting to the ladies, and as sickening, as the smell of whiskey; but except for that reassuring proof of evil, the interior of Mr. Hoffmann's could not but be a shock to them, after what they had seen in the last few days: the spotless red-checked tablecloths, the shining pewter mugs and pottery steins on the polished bar, the gleaming mirror behind it above the beer kegs, the fireplace in the rear wall, with the rack of long-stemmed pipes on the mantel, and red-faced Mr. Hoffmann behind the counter, presenting to them a counterfeit of the geniality he felt for his customers.

The ladies knelt to pray beneath his amiable gaze. Not until they had struggled to their feet again did he speak, in this thick, good-natured guttural, from which, as he proceeded, the good nature and geniality oozed gradually away.

"I haf not ze custom, ladies, of turning decent respectable folk from my door. I make you velcome, until you haf said for vot you haf come. But I varn you, it iss useless." His s's hissed sharply. "I pay my license to ze guffernment und py ze law uff zat guffernment, not any vun uff you hass any right to pusy-pody into my pusiness."

Without answering him, the ladies conducted the meeting. His face grew more and more congested as he was compelled to listen to a reading of the "Appeal to Dramsellers," which accused him of wickedness he had never been, would never be, responsible for.

After the closing prayer Mrs. Ballard said, "I regret, Mr. Hoffmann, that you have chosen to meet us in this uncompromising spirit, defying any appeal to your conscience. But your heart may be moved overnight, like poor Tim O'Reilly's. You may expect us again in the morning."

The unfortunate choice of the word "defy," as though he were a prisoner before the bar, the comparison of him with that poor hopeless devil of an O'Reilly, Mrs. Ballard's tone of complacent superiority—all wrought upon him so mightily and so confusingly, pushed him so far toward incoherent wrath, that it was a wonder he could begin as quietly as he did.

"I vill vun fair varning giff you. *So.* Leaf my premises, und come no more, or it vill pe ze vorse." Then it was as if something exploded in his mind: the faces of Mrs. Ballard and Mrs. McKinney, closest to him, became blurred; he saw only, between him and the door, outlined against it, the aquiline features and the disdainful hauteur of Mrs. Deming. He brought his heavy fists down with a knuckle-bruising thump on the counter and leaned forward. "Hypocrites! Vited sepulchres!" He shot out a long arm and pointed to her with a finger shaking with rage. "Iss dot voman's money more honest yet zan mine? Vere iss it her furs und ear-rings und plumes—"

Mrs. McKinney interrupted, speaking to the ladies. "Let us go. The man seems quite unregenerate, but the ways of the Lord are beyond understanding, and He may yet move his heart."

The crusade moved on to other beer parlors in town, but there were no triumphant bells rung that morning. Instead, at the crowded lunch, served by the Methodist Ladies Aid in the church basement, it was decided to put into operation another device that had proved effective elsewhere. A crusader would be posted outside the door of each beer parlor, with notebook and pencil to record the names of customers. It was suspected that such customers of the beer parlors, and particularly of Mr. Hoffmann, might be known by name to the crusaders—as they never would have been in the Irish West End—and might not enjoy having their visits recorded. Other ladies went elsewhere, but it was Mrs. Deming who carried her camp chair to Mr. Hoffmann's door and sat there all afternoon, in the wind, her hands in her muff. There were few names to record. Mr. Hoffmann, who well knew why she was there, was restrained by his wife, who had wept all morning and was still now and then mopping her eyes, from going forth and attempting to dislodge her. But he slipped out the back door, leaving such business as there was in her hands, and uptown to consult his brother-in-law Herman Lichtenstein, as a lawyer.

Next morning he was ready for the return of the women. But instead of an axe he had a paper and pencil in his hand. He waited in the door for Mrs. McKinney to address him first; he had promised his wife not to lose his temper, but he would not let them pass.

"Will you join us in prayer this morning, Mr. Hoffmann?"

"My praying iss in my closet done, as ze Gut Buch says. But I vill so long listen."

He bowed his head. But when the prayer was over and the hymn started, he began to write on the paper, which he held against the door-jamb.

"*Nun*"—he waved the paper at them when they had finished singing and moved closer to him for the exhortation, "Varning vunce I gafe you. I haf here your names. Go already—zis minute—or I call on ze law. I am no t'ief, or a highvayman, zat you ziss nonsense at my door should make. You vill see vedder my pusiness iss to pe interfered vis." He called over his shoulder, inside the door, "Kommen Sie, Heinrich, stehen Sie hier," and then added in English, for the women to hear, "Vis politeness listen, aber say nussing, und keep zem outside. I haf pusiness, aber soon I vill pack return."

Nothing could have served so well as this vague threat to persuade the ladies to stay on, most of them. Perhaps two or three at the outskirts of the crowd slipped away home. The rest were determined to wear Mr. Hoffmann down. Lunch was being served that day in the fireman's hall, and they wanted a victory to proclaim.

No more than fifteen or twenty minutes later, Douglas Gardiner came limping down Chillicothe Street, and wormed his way through the small-boy-and-idler fringe that now surrounded the crusaders whenever they appeared. Mrs. Ballard saw him, and thinking perhaps he bore a message from the Judge, pushed through to meet him.

He took off his hat and smiled a little, the usual sardonic gleam in his eye.

"I thought I should warn you, Mrs. Ballard, Hoffmann and his lawyer are in the Common Pleas court, petitioning for an injunction."

"Injunction?"

"Yes. To stop your ruining his trade. He has all your names."

"So that's what he meant! But Judge White wouldn't grant any such injunction."

"He hasn't any choice. Surely Judge Ballard told you? He sent me with the message, after Judge White sent his clerk across to warn us. All this is clearly illegal, and if anyone complains—" He laughed at her surprise. "It's restraint of trade. It's a public nuisance. It's disorderly conduct."

Her first angry flush died away, her head lifted, and she exclaimed, "Martyrs!" She had no word of thanks for Douglas, but turned back to the singing women and raised her hand for silence.

"Ladies! Your attention, please! Mr. Hoffmann has gone to court for an injunction against us. If we remain here until his return, we may well be arrested. All those who feel unequal to suffering martyrdom"—she breathed like a war horse, her head back—"*martyrdom* for our Cause—had better disperse at once."

No one dispersed. She looked around at them approvingly. "Very well. Let us continue, until we see what happens, whether he is so unwise as to carry out this course."

He was so unwise. He returned, presently, and stood at the door, with lumbering old Bill Clayton, the police chief, beside him, looking very sheepish. The ladies fell silent when he held up his hand.

"Read it, Billy."

Billy read the injunction.

"Nun—zis nonsense stops, or off to chail you go for contempt of court. I took your names, und de chief ze varrants hass."

No one knew better than Mrs. Ballard the value of martyrdom.

"Let us sing, ladies: 'How firm a foundation.'"

The policeman, with Mr. Hoffmann at his elbow, could not avoid serving his warrants. The hymn singing never ceased.

And still singing, the arrested ladies lined up two by two and marched off to court, shepherded by the reluctant officer. The block of Chillicothe Street from Mr. Hoffmann's to the Court House square echoed to the fifth stanza of "How firm a foundation."

> When through fiery trials their pathway shall lie,
> My grace all-sufficient shall be thy supply,
> The flame shall not hurt thee; I only design
> Thy dross to consume, and thy gold to refine.

Along the Court House square they sang the hymn through again, skillfully timing it so as to enter the court on the triumphant last stanza:

> The soul that on Jesus had leaned for repose,
> *I will not, I will not,* desert to his foes;
> That soul, though all hell should endeavor to shake,
> *I'll never,* no *never,* no *never forsake*!

Forty-seven of Waynesboro's most respectable churchwomen were lined up in the Common Pleas court before the judge. He explained to them, as one would to children, or to saints unwitting of the world, why the law permitted them to be enjoined; he warned them rather less tenderly that if they repeated the offense, they would have to be punished. "I do not believe," he said, stifling his doubts as he watched Mrs. Ballard, "that any of you ladies would care for our jails. Or the workhouse."

The Crusade came to an abrupt end. But after a fashion, the ladies' work was done. It is true that the Irish, unable to find work to do, or perhaps not trying very hard, soon had their grogshops going again. The real harvest, ironically enough, was among the Germans. German wives and mothers, contented enough with the customs of the fatherland while their children were small, had been made aware for the first time that those children would never have an equal and accepted place in the town while their fathers carried on what was considered a disreputable business. Gradually they made an impression on their husbands, gradually the beer parlors were closed—not that year or the next, but within the next decade.

The first German to renounce the "devil's trade" was Mr. Hoffmann, after he had first exercised his rights by going to court. He and his wife agreed that although they could not have known ahead of time that their children would be handicapped in the new country by what had been respectable enough in the old, they did know now; and since they had two small children who were Americans—born in America—for whose sake it would be better if they were bakers, why, bakers they would be. There was of course no chopping up of beer kegs in the gutter; Mr. Hoffmann bided his time until his barman Heinrich could make arrangements to borrow money from the brewers, and then he sold out to him. The men of Waynesboro who wanted occasionally to sit down at a table with a red-checked cloth and drink a stein of lager could still do so.

The most immediate and most conspicuous success of the campaign was the salvation of the O'Reillys. Mrs. Ballard was determined to help him. After appealing to all the Methodists of her congregation in vain, she heard that Dr. Gordon had had to let his stablehand-and-coachman go; he was an elderly Negro who had grown too helplessly crippled with rheumatism to be able to care for the doctor's horses. It took courage to appeal to Dr. Gordon, who had certainly shown no sympathy with the Cause, and who was, probably, a "scoffer." But Mrs. Ballard did not lack courage, and besides she had known young Dock Gordon since he'd been a barefooted farm boy. She called on him in his office.

To her surprise, John listened to her story with sympathy. He explained: he had attended young Mrs. O'Reilly before her child was born, and had delivered her baby; she had not then been a drunkard. Nor at that time had Tim been laid off by the railroad, and of necessity taken to selling first groceries and then, in desperation, whiskey. Tim's loss of his job coming while his wife was still weak, unable to care for an ailing, always crying child—all those things taken with the sudden accessibility of an anaesthetic—had been her downfall. John had heard before the Temperance Crusade began that things were going pitifully wrong with the O'Reillys. But if Tim meant what he said, the doctor thought his wife could be saved; what she mostly needed was good food and self-respect. He would be glad to do something, if only because so often there was nothing he could do, and if Tim knew anything about horses, as most Irishmen did, he would take him on.

And so Tim was hired, "temporarily," he insisted, until the railroad would need him again. And when his wife "got the liquor out of her system," as John put it, assisting the process with an emetic for Tim to put in her glass, she could have the job of scrubbing up the offices and keeping them clean. And if the two were sometimes paid "in kind," why so was the doctor himself, and it was chiefly good food that they needed anyway. He paid enough cash to enable them to hire a decent room, and thought perhaps if Mary really straightened up, he might sometime let them have the rooms over the offices that had been Dr. Alexander's.

Not the least comic aspect of the Crusade, through those April days when it was at its height and afterward, was the sublime unawareness of any such commotion on the part of the ladies of the Club in meeting assembled. Nor was the continuing investigation by Congress of the Credit Mobilier affair alluded to. The standing of Mrs. Deming was in no way different from what it had always been. The first Club meeting after the appearance of various of its members in court was to have been devoted to a review of Mark Twain's *Gilded Age*, but no one was surprised that Thomasina, whose assigned topic it was, substituted a critique of the novels of Victor Hugo. The *Gilded Age* might have been embarrassing, and Victor Hugo was much more appealing to one of Thomasina's romantic disposition than Mark Twain would ever be. Moreover, as she read from a copy of *Harper's Weekly*, which she had brought along to bolster her own judgment, "Hugo was not only the grandest figure in French literature, but the compeer of Homer, Dante and Shakespeare." No one could conceivably make any such claims for Mark Twain, and Thomasina was not inclined, then or later, to concern herself overmuch with the pattern for the year's work that the Program Committee had designed. She cared nothing at all that Victor Hugo could scarcely be called a "Contemporary Leader of American Thought."

The '72–'73 Club year came to an end in May; summers in Waynesboro were altogether too hot for any intellectual activity. Sensible Waynesboro women spent the months at home: in the mornings canning, preserving, and pickling, in the afternoons relaxing in shuttered houses, only taking to their porches late in the day. But devoted newspaper readers as they were, they could not escape the deepening sense of gloom hanging over the country. The money market grew tighter as the summer passed, and one unfavorable bank statement followed another. Banks began to fail—the first on the eighth of September. And Jay Cooke and Company on the tenth. To men like Ludwig and Mr. Cochran, who thought they had steeled themselves to expect the worst, that news was like the end of the world. If the government had repudiated its debt, it could have been no more frightening. And the brief closing of the Stock Exchange was an anticlimax. But Mr. Cochran's bank held out, and the financial panic did not hurt Ludwig, who had held on to his government bonds. But General Deming did say, meeting him uptown one day, "I told you so," and Ludwig acknowledged, "Thanks for your warning, I'm not committed to something I might not be able to handle." The General clapped him on the shoulder and said, "You're all right, then? Congratulations," and passed on, feeling the warm glow of an acknowledged benefactor. And perhaps when it came time to choose a candidate in '74, young Rausch would think he owed him something.

Ludwig was not nearly so confident as he sounded to the General. True, there was no large debt to worry about. The panic, so far as Wall Street was concerned, blew over—slowly, it seemed, yet in comparatively brief time. Suspended banks reopened and carried on what business there was by means of clearing house certificates. But industry had come to a standstill. Few orders for rope came in to Rausch Cordage Company; when they had finished the work in hand, there would be little to do. As Ludwig expressed it to himself, "We must batten down and ride out the storm." He was determined to keep the mill running and his men at work through the winter. While good weather lasted, he need not worry about his Negro hands: they would rather fish than work any day, and they all had gardens. But if they were laid off when winter came, they would suffer. His solution was to cut the pay of all by cutting their hours of work, rather than lay off any. He bought coal by the carload, had it hauled to the mill, and sold it by the hundredweight for what it had cost him. He listened to every tale of hardship that came to him in the office or followed him home. He kept his handful of expert workmen together by making rope that piled up in the warehouse, turned his unskilled labor to making anything that might sell: bedrope, fenders for ships and boats, even oakum.

By October he was spending much of his time working for the Republican candidates for state office who would be up for election in that fall of '73. It was a rather listless campaign, what with the deepening depression and the scandals in Washington; Ludwig did what he could. He was glad to accept the offer of General Deming to speak whenever called upon; he had fooled himself into believing the Republicans could win: he might fool an audience. Ludwig wondered whether in spite of all that had been said the General wanted at heart to run again himself in '74; but he sent him out in the district to speak for the reelection of the Governor—a hopeless course, Ludwig was sure. 1873 was just not a Republican year—and he in the event was proved right.

Fortunately for Waynesboro, its favorite investment, made long before the war, was in the Whitewater-Waynesboro Railway—known familiarly as "the Dub-yuh-Dub-yuh"—a short line built in the first days of railroading, but since then leased at an annual rent by the P.C.C. & St.L., to make it a part of the road's main east and west line. W.W. directors paid dividends with the rent money. Long after, when the P.C.C. & St.L. became a part of the Pennsylvania System, the rent for the W.W. was still a first charge on that road, and W.W. stock was handed down from parent to child for generations, never sold and never to be bought. Dr. Alexander was one of those whose savings had been invested in the first building of the W.W. in the fifties, and Anne had held on to his stock. The Gordons now could count on its dividends, and there was, besides, the farm that Kate had left to their Johnny and which his father rented to a tenant on shares. As he told Anne, they could always eat, however bad things got. Afterward the chief memory the Gordons had of the great '73 depression was the nuisance of small paper money—shinplasters of every kind and denomination, whose value changed every day, so that one had to read the morning paper before knowing what a purse full of change was worth—that, and how doctor bills were paid with butter and eggs, chickens and sausage, maple syrup, and a thousand less welcome things that they didn't need.

The hardest hit of Waynesboro's more prominent citizens was Judge Ballard. After having been caught in the flurry that followed the Gould-Fiske attempt to corner gold, he had refrained from speculation. But he still longed for a fortune large enough to leave his family secure, and he had been tempted by the Jay Cooke offer of Northern Pacific bonds at a price that would ensure their paying eight percent. He had easily justified the "investment": twice the Northern Pacific was proposed and not built, but Jay Cooke was an honest man and a financial genius. Had he not managed the bond issues that financed the Civil War? The Judge sold what securities he had, including his W.W. shares, to buy N.P. bonds. The ruin of Jay Cooke was the ruin of the Judge. There was but one thing to comfort him: he had gone back to the practice of corporation law, which had once been so lucrative.

When he confessed to his family that his loss had left him without capital, his womenfolk did not again suggest leaving the home he had built, and they considerably spared him their sympathy. But the shock of their poverty enabled them to see him with the clear eyes of strangers, and they for the first time realized that he was an aging man. In the law office with him were his longtime partner, old Timothy Merrill, trying to hold on until his orphaned grandson, a boy of ten or twelve, could take over; Douglas Gardiner, just admitted to the bar; and a couple of clerks. The depression had no effect on the number of clients who came for legal advice, although it limited sadly their ability to pay for it. Eliza persuaded her father to discharge the clerks and take her into the office to do their work. At any other time Waynesboro might have been scandalized at the spectacle of a lady—even one of the "new women"—in an office. In the circumstances, however, it was accepted as right and proper, and Eliza was praised not so much for acting in accordance with her beliefs in independence for women as for the sacrifice she was making for her family.

With the coming of fall, the Woman's Club had resumed its meetings. Even when things were at their worst, "depression" was a word not mentioned by the ladies; discussion of one's own or another's financial difficulties would have been considered vulgar. Programs planned in the summer were faithfully carried out, all of them as always purely literary.

Anne Gordon presented her paper early in the fall, and shortly thereafter absented herself from the fortnightly meetings and withdrew altogether from public view before her welcome pregnancy became too obvious. (Mrs. McCune, too, soon found herself in no fit condition to go out; a delicate woman who was in the fall of '73 the mother of four children, she was rather an object of sympathy than of congratulations.) Anne, living a reclusive life, devoted most of her time to Johnny, teaching him his letters, reading to him, playing endless games. Johnny was four that fall, a lively boy, neat, compact, small-boned and dark like this father, with dimples and a flashing smile, whose curls his father thought should be cut, and whose petticoats gave way to pantaloons. Sally Rausch dropped in almost daily on her way to see her mother, sometimes accompanied by her two children, sometimes not. The Rausch children, Elsa and Ernest, were sturdy, blond, loving babies. Sally never forbore teasing Anne for getting herself in an interesting condition just when she was needed to help plan for the Club Christmas party, then always concluded by stating that she herself was ready for another child; she wanted a big family. Anne's baby, a girl, was born in the spring and named Belinda for her grandmother. Sally had protested, "An old-fashioned name like that! She will hate it!"

They went on to wondering what the McCunes would name their newborn boy. Since they already had a Matthew and a Mark, it seemed inevitable that the baby should be "Luke." Sally said that, considering what outlandish names you could find in the Bible, "Luke" was ordinary enough, "Not like 'Ruhamah,' for instance."

"The other girl's name sounds like something out of Shakespeare, not the Bible. Mrs. McCune must have a romantic streak her husband was willing to indulge in those days."

"He's wiped out any such nonsense, then. Just living with him would be enough."

Anne was just able to be up and about again when Sally stopped by to say triumphantly that now it was her turn; she would have another boy in the fall and sensibly name him "Charles" for her father.

Not everyone was so lighthearted in the spring, summer, and fall of 1874.

Congress adjourned, having done nothing much. President Grant had to a degree redeemed himself in the eyes of solid citizens by his veto of the inflationary bill Congress had passed in April. General Deming came home in not quite the low spirits of 1873, but he was intelligent enough to see what was coming: he was not afraid that the Seventh District would send a Democrat to the House, but he did not think the next several years could be happy ones for Republicans in Congress. Besides, he knew that Ludwig Rausch had decided it was time for him to retire. He wrote a dignified letter to the *Torchlight*, in which he announced his withdrawal from politics, and promised to support whatever candidate the General Committee chose to nominate. And if there were those who thought he was making a virtue of necessity, they did not say so.

For an off-year election, that of '74 roused a good deal of heat and clamor. Waynesboro and the Seventh District elected Mr. Liddell by a comfortable margin, although in the state the Democrats gained six congressmen. The trend was countrywide: the Forty-fifth Congress would be Democratic. As Ludwig said to the General, the Forty-fourth Congress in its lame duck session beginning in December would certainly have to save the country from inflation, because the Forty-fifth, elected on an easy money platform, would not dare do so.

And that was the business that immediately concerned Congress when it reassembled in December of '74. The bill for resumption of specie payments was reported to the Senate by Senator Sherman on the twenty-seventh of December, voted on and passed that day, turned over to, and passed by, the House on the seventh of January. The President signed it immediately. The Forty-fourth Congress had other pressing bills that kept it in session until midnight of 3 March 1875, when it adjourned; the Forty-fifth Congress was organized on the 6th of March with a Democratic speaker. By that time General Deming was home to stay, a private citizen for the first time in many years.

In that spring of '75, he came home in triumph. The conservative citizens of Waynesboro had been pleased by the eleventh-hour accomplishments of the Forty-fourth Congress. Mr. Cochran, Mr. Bonner, and other leading men of the business community congratulated him as if he had been the sole savior of his country. "Politics is a mighty damn funny business," he said to his wife. "If we'd only passed those bills last summer. But no—and now I'm out, there's never been anyone, to hear them tell it, that did better service in Congress."

But Ludwig said to his wife, "What's that quotation I want? I tried to think of it when I saw Deming this afternoon. 'Nothing in his political life became him like the leaving of it.'"

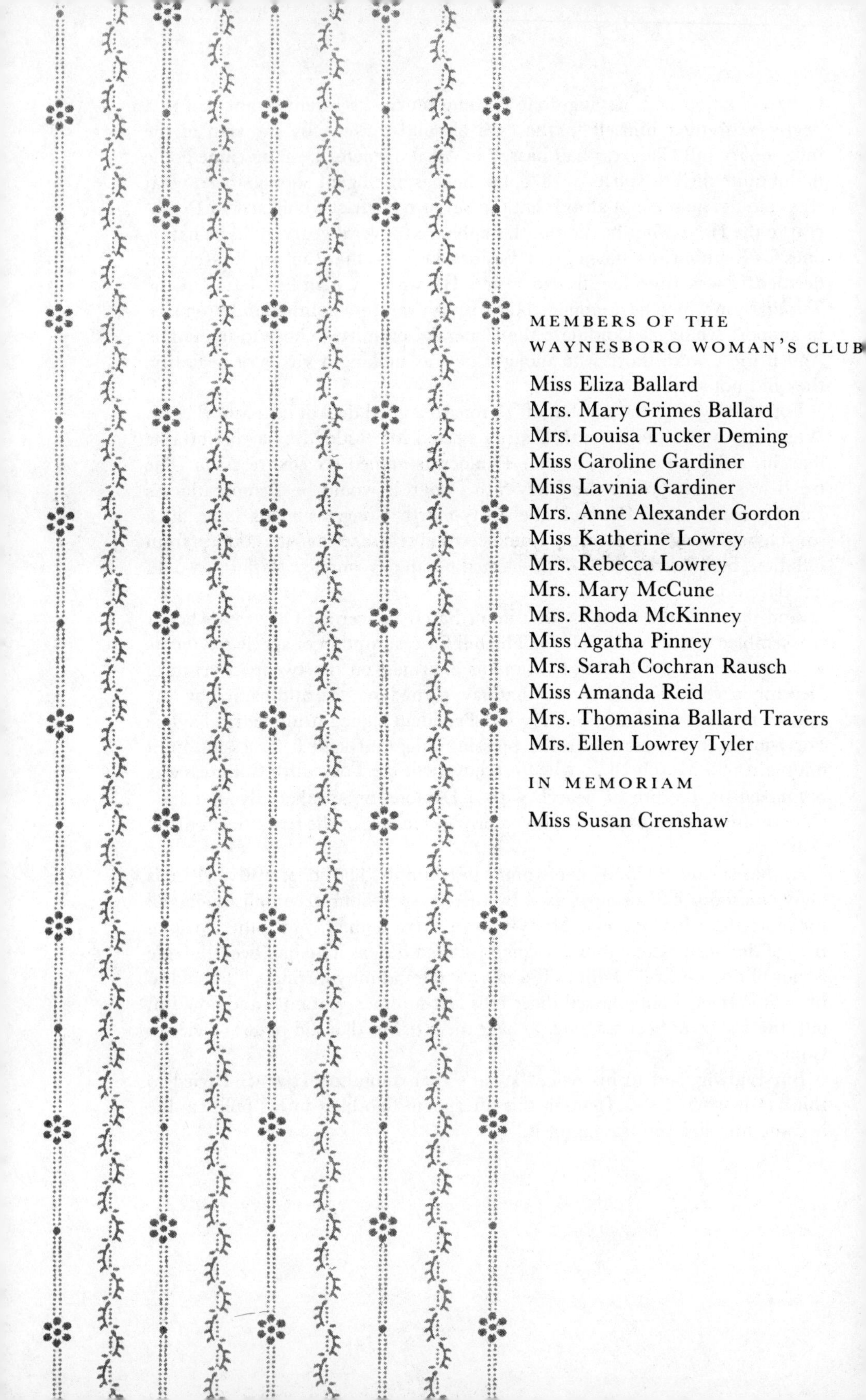

MEMBERS OF THE
WAYNESBORO WOMAN'S CLUB

Miss Eliza Ballard
Mrs. Mary Grimes Ballard
Mrs. Louisa Tucker Deming
Miss Caroline Gardiner
Miss Lavinia Gardiner
Mrs. Anne Alexander Gordon
Miss Katherine Lowrey
Mrs. Rebecca Lowrey
Mrs. Mary McCune
Mrs. Rhoda McKinney
Miss Agatha Pinney
Mrs. Sarah Cochran Rausch
Miss Amanda Reid
Mrs. Thomasina Ballard Travers
Mrs. Ellen Lowrey Tyler

IN MEMORIAM

Miss Susan Crenshaw

1875

"The organization of a subscription library . . ."

The program of the Waynesboro Woman's Club for the year 1875 was passed out to the members at the first meeting of the year. The subject was "Leading Novelists of the Nineteenth Century on the Continent of Europe." Anne Gordon was scheduled to deliver an essay on George Sand on the afternoon of May nineteenth; the program for that meeting included also "A Musical Interlude: Chopin," by Mrs. Thomasina Ballard Travers.

On a sunny morning in April, Anne proposed to set to work in earnest on her paper. She came out on the recessed side porch bringing the baby with her in the carriage that had been Johnny's once: a miniature buggy, with a collapsible hood and a long tongue to pull it by. She had her lap desk under one arm, but the well of the carriage was full of paper, some clean and some covered with notes, a book, and a handful of pencils. The energetic baby was bouncing on her cushions and kicking at them all. Anne gathered them up and went to sit down on the edge of the porch, her feet on the step below, the desk open on her lap.

But before she began to work, she gave herself over to rejoicing that spring had finally come. From somewhere far off came the low iterative note of the mourning dove. She wondered idly whether anyone had ever heard a dove in the spring without saying in his mind, "The voice of the turtle—" It is hard to realize that the country had at last got through a second bitter winter. After the first of the year, it had turned cold, gloomy, and wet. Many poor, still unemployed, had had to be taken care of by the churches; and there had been a bad outbreak first of diphtheria, then scarlet fever. Both had spread through the town; a number had died; one family among John's patients had lost all its children, four of them, one after another. The last few months had been the hardest for John since his marriage; he had despaired, partly because he was so convinced the epidemics had been unnecessary. If Lister could prevent the infection of surgical wounds by disinfection with carbolic acid, if, as Semmelweiss believed, childbed fever was carried from patient to patient by the doctor, then you could put two and two together, John said, coming up with his own answer: a liberal use of carbolic acid solution could prevent spread of even such contagious diseases as these were. He tried to persuade the mothers of sick children to hang a sheet kept damp with the solution in the door of the sickroom, and to wash themselves in it and change their clothes before entering another part of the house. He faithfully followed such a routine himself, taking with him on his calls an old linen coat to wear in the sickroom, washing it out every night in carbolic acid solution. But for most mothers, such a rigamarole was too time-consuming, especially since they thought it nonsense. The town, not encouraged by the older doctors, was full of jest about "Dock's newfangled notions."

Night after night, John had got out of bed when he thought Anne was asleep; sometimes she had heard him walking up and down the hall; sometimes he had gone downstairs to read. In the morning she would find a book left open on the bed in the room that had been her father's. In the course of the winter, he had got through most of the dark old books that Dr. Alexander had kept there in his bookcase, not the Dickens, but the Fielding, the Smollett, the Sterne—books that Anne had never looked into because she had been given to understand that they were not novels for formal consumption. Some nights John did not come home at all, or could not. Anne was never sure whether he was with a patient or walking off his misery in the streets. He was so strained, so uncommunicative, that she could not ask him, and was left to endure in silence the realization that she was being of no help to him.

He had, however, had at least one success to his credit. One mother had obeyed his orders, and only one of her children had had diphtheria. That child, however, had been almost mortally ill; he had been saved in the old-fashioned herioc way: John had thrust a tube in his throat and had sucked the strangling membrane loose. And the Jordans had embarrassed John by their gratitude. "I can't convince them I wasn't risking my own life," he complained, "like the hero of some melodramatic novel. They won't listen to me when I say I can't have diphtheria again, having had it once." But Anne had prevented his refusing the payment the Jordans offered. Like most of Waynesboro, where the depression seemed to dig in deeper as the years passed, they had no money for the doctor's bills; but Mr. Jordan, the town's "Tinner and Roofer," had had in his shop so long that he despaired of selling it one of the new hot-air furnaces; he offered to install it in the Gordon house, and thus pay John for having saved his boy's life. John himself was too Spartan ever to have thought of spending money for a furnace, but Anne persuaded him to accept the offer, at least to the extent of letting Mr. Jordan put the furnace in, and then squaring accounts with him when the work was done.

Now Anne, sitting on the step in the April sun, hugged her knees around the still unopened desk and thought how very pleasant it would be to have a warm house next winter, warm upstairs and downstairs, and even in the halls. Of course, they would be torn up most of the summer. John meant to have the house piped for gas at the same time, since Waynesboro had a new company making water-gas for illumination; and between gas pipes and furnace pipes, the whole place would have to be replastered at least in part and certainly repapered. But it would be worth it in the end; these modern innovations, as Anne knew from her familiarity with the Cochrans' house, certainly contributed to the comfort of living. In the meantime, she and Martha had given the house a cleaning that would do until after the workmen had been and gone, and she knew that inside the door all was fresh and shining and smelling of soap and furniture polish. The winter and its troubles had been scrubbed away. Even John must soon be John again, and not a remote and bleakly suffering stranger.

Anne opened her lap desk. She felt as if her mind had been scrubbed and furnished, too, and made ready for use. Not that she liked the subject on which she was to use it. The problem of what to say about George Sand dismayed her. What little she knew about "her" author, as the Club ladies had a way of putting it, was very little, and that little not suitable for presentation to a circle of females. "Drat that Eliza Ballard!" she thought in exasperation as she made aimless squiggles on one of her sheets of clean paper. Surely no one but Eliza would have dared provide for the same day's entertainment an essay on George Sand and the performance of a Chopin composition. Samuel Travers was probably even now helping Thomasina with the Chopin, but at least Thomasina wouldn't have to say anything.

Writing the paper would be easier if she could only get hold of more of George Sand's works to read and criticize. If she could discuss a number of the novels, she might manage a reasonably long paper, without going into the more unmentionable aspects of her subject's life. As it was, practically all that she knew was unmentionable. She looked with distaste at the book beside her. Although she really could afford to buy books this spring, she had sent to Stewart and Kidd's, in Cincinnati, for whatever they had by George Sand, and this was what she had got: *Mademoiselle Merquem*. She had read it, and had felt more baffled than before. Surely this was not the kind of book Eliza liked? But Anne would rather disappoint Eliza than go to her and ask for help or advice. Anne might ask Amanda. But what could she possibly know about George Sand—Amanda Reid, Reformed Presbyterian, B.A., spinster, and teacher of youth?

What she really needed, what Waynesboro needed, was a subscription library, such as other towns had.

Anne sighed, dumped the clean paper and her notes inside her desk, and set it on the porch floor beside her. Today was not, emphatically, a good day for concentrating on work that one did not want to do. The lilac bushes along the fence were heavy and sweet with bloom, the bleeding heart in the corner of the porch steps was nodding with flowers. It had been her mother's bleeding heart, and Anne loved it for her sake, as she loved the lilies of the valley in the shade of the lattice that concealed the outhouse, and the garden heliotrope along the brick path that led to it. The breeze that bent the bleeding heart was soft and sweet; the green of the new leaves everywhere was so gay and tender a color that it touched your heart. The light of the morning was vivid and intense.

In her carriage the baby bounced and gurgled and murmured to herself. Around the corner of the dining room, from the back yard, came the squeak of a wheelbarrow. Tim O'Reilly, loaned by the doctor for a day's work in the yard, was bringing a load of manure to dig into the flower bed that ran along the dining room walls, and young John, cavorting at his heels, was helping him. Johnny had progressed from kilts to pantaloons and a round little jacket, with the wide white collar of his blouse worn outside it. His curls had long since been shorn, but his hair was rather long that day, and the soft wind blew it across his forehead in a thick fringe. His black eyes shone, and the dimples in his round cheeks appeared and disappeared as he trotted along laughing beside Tim.

"There's Mamma," he said superfluously, as the wheelbarrow was set down at the angle where the brick path branched off to the steps where she was sitting. "I'm helping Tim. He wants me to."

Tim took off his hat, "Oi'm sorry, Miz Gordon, Oi didn't know you'd be wantin' to sit here this day. It's some other toime I'd better be choosin' for this load o' muck."

"Oh, no! Best get it in. I'll need to get my seeds planted soon. I don't mind: it's a good healthy smell. But I'd just as lief Johnny didn't get in it. Come up here beside me, son, and I'll tell you a story. Or get me a blade of grass and I'll show you something I learned to do when I was your age."

She closed her book on one blade of grass while she took another between her two thumbs and blew against its edge. She showed Johnny how to hold the grass in his pudgy fists; he screwed up his face and blew. She plucked some leaves from the honeysuckle on the post behind her, and popped them against her teeth. The little boy tried that too, but succeeded only in getting his mouth full of leaf. Anne laughed so merrily at his disgusted look that he too could only laugh, but he threw the torn leaf from him. Tim lifted the empty wheelbarrow with the spade in it, and went back to the stable yard for another load.

"The wheelbarrow squeaks," Johnny said, with the air of one making an interesting and hitherto unnoted discovery.

"The poor wheelbarrow is so old its bones ache. It says 'Oh, oh, oh! I'm not so spry as I used to be, Oh, oh, oh!' Then it goes along muttering to itself the way old people do, 'Time I was left to take my ease in the woodshed. I've done my share of work in this yard. That Mr. Grindstone, now, he has all the luck—he doesn't have to go trundling about the world this way!' And so on, grumble, grumble, whine, whine. Maybe if we asked Tim to give Mr. Wheelbarrow a good drink of oil, he would feel better."

Johnny laughed in delight and edged closer to her on the step. "What does Mr. Grindstone say? Tim let me turn for a while this morning when he was sharpening the sickle." His nose twitched. He loved the woodshed: its rotten-wood smell, the cobwebs, all the saws hanging on the wall, the little square window that wouldn't open because of the trumpet vine growing thickly over it, making a dim green light inside unless you left the door ajar.

"Well, what did he say, then? You heard him. Did he grumble?"

"He didn't like it very well, I guess, that he only gets drinks of water when Mr. Wheelbarrow gets oil. But I don't think he whined. Oh, I don't know, Mamma, what did he say?"

"He said 'Whats-s-s this-s-s? S-s-s-sickles for the grass-s-s I'd like to be the s-s-sickle, out in the s-s-sun. Here I s-s-sit in the woods-s-shed, doing my work in the dark. And Mr. Wheelbarrow has all the fun out in the world every day!" Anne added, "It's really very silly for them to call each other 'Mr.', they've been neighbors in the woodshed so long. But they had a falling out long ago when they were both in love with Miss Saw-Horse, and they've said 'Mr.' ever since, though once upon a time, when Mr. Wheelbarrow was young, they were friends."

"Wasn't Mr. Grindstone young, too?" The grubby fist was on her knee, the black eyes intent on her face, the dimple deep in one cheek.

"Oh, he's much, much older than Mr. Wheelbarrow, really, but he doesn't show his age. He's too old for Miss Saw-Horse, but he didn't think so himself, naturally, and he used to be quite angry when Mr. Wheelbarrow managed to get put on her side of the woodshed. Mr. Wheelbarrow would come in from the yard saying, 'Please put me in that corner! Please put me in that corner!' You see, he squeaked in those days, too, but he didn't grumble, and whoever had hold of him put him down quick to stop the squeaks, and would leave Mr. Wheelbarrow close to Miss Saw-Horse, and all night long they could look out the window and watch the stars between the leaves of the trumpet vine. But in the morning Mr. Wheelbarrow would be taken out again, mad as hops because Mr. Grindstone would be left all alone with Miss Saw-Horse, and he wouldn't be able to hear a word they said."

This fantasy could be strung out indefinitely. Tim, now spading along the house wall, listened too, and chuckled, and sometimes threw in a comment, "That Miss Saw-Horse, now, faith an' she sounds loike a fickle cray-thure."

When the doctor came across the back yard to lunch, his appearance put an end to the storytelling. The boy ran to meet him, and returned clinging to his hand and swinging around his knees.

"Mr. Wheelbarrow and Mr. Grindstone both wanted to marry Miss Saw-Horse once upon a time," he said.

"Indeed! And what has Mr. Saw to say to that?"

"You're confusing us, John. There isn't any Mr. Saw in our story." Anne rose from the step, the book she had hardly opened under he arm. Her husband tapped her affectionately on the top of her head, with bent finger snapping from his thumb, kissed her cheek, then crossed to the baby, who was struggling against the straps that held her, lifting her arms to her father. He took her up tenderly and held her face against his cheek.

"Bless the baby—be quiet—I've got you safe."

Anne stood behind and watched them, the baby's closely curling soft black hair just visible over her father's shoulder. She wondered sometimes whether John loved the child so much because he saw that she looked like Kate; she had never dared ask him because she hoped that if he had not seen the resemblance, he never would.

During lunch the doctor suggested that Anne and the boy might like to drive with him into the country after his office hours; he had a few calls to make, but only a few—no contagious cases, the epidemics had run their course.

"Unless it should blow up a rain by four o'clock. You never can tell about April. But the country is at its best—dogwood and red-bud. We can come back around by the farm. I want to see how the plowing's getting along, and there's a new colt and that beagle pup they promised Johnny. I tell you, Anne, we might even have a picnic. Martha can stay with Binny."

"Oh, Papa!" Johnny said.

"Of course we will," Anne said. "I was going to work this morning and didn't, so why should I work this afternoon? I was going to walk over to the school to ask Amanda for help, but tomorrow will do."

"You mean to say Club-paper season has rolled 'round again?" John and Ludwig both adopted a put-upon attitude when their wives were writing papers, pretending that meals were neglected, socks undarned, buttons left missing.

"Yes, but today's too nice a day."

Late that afternoon they drove into the farmyard, after all John's calls had been made. Anne went to the barn with her husband and son to admire the new colt and the beagle puppy; then she returned to the buggy and lifted down the picnic basket.

"The hill-pasture, John? It's sunny there, and maybe the ground is dry." They walked down the farm lane behind the barnyard, through the pasture gate, across a level stretch that gave damply beneath their feet and was starred with clumps of marsh marigolds, then up the long slow hill to its top. Anne spread out the robe, John put down the picnic basket, Johnny set about gathering a bouquet of spring-beauties for his mother that would close and droop before he could transfer them from his hot fist to her lap. Anne arranged her skirts as smoothly and as properly as she could. "You know," she said, "I believe I actually preferred hoops. At least they folded up."

John dropped to the robe beside her. Before them the country lay fair and open: the gentle curves of its hills dark against the western sky, its fields either black ploughed earth or young wheat so green, so bright it hurt, not the eye but the heart, as all evanescent beauty does. Below them spread the Gordon farm, fields, maple grove, woodlot, pastures full of sheep and their lambs, the barns and barnyard, the orchard white with bloom, and the back of the old house—the original log cabin still in use as a summer kitchen, then the stone walls rising from a series of rooftops to the ridge pole with the big double chimney at each end.

When the little boy with his handful of flowers came circling within his father's reach, John swept him onto his shoulder and pointed to the house.

"That is where I lived when I was a little boy. Did you know that? And the log cabin, that is where your great-grandfather lived when he first came here from Carolina, when all this was nothing but trees and trees and trees, and he cut down some to make his cabin, and cleared a field or two to start."

Anne got to her knees, opened the picnic basket and began taking out their supper. She remembered how her Grandfather Alexander had talked about his boyhood in the log cabin to Johnny when he was only a baby. But now the child might remember the stories his father told him, for there was the log cabin standing, plain to be seen.

"Why did he come, Papa, if there were only trees here?"

"Where he lived before, in North Carolina, the colored people were slaves. He didn't like that, and so he came away. That's what they always told us children. But they lived in western Carolina, and I think mountains were worse than trees. Anyway his brother left at the same time, only he didn't mind the colored people's being slaves, and so he went to Mississippi. I saw my cousins there when I was in the Army."

Anne called their attention to the meal. They turned about and took their places at the edge of the cloth. Johnny said, "Did you live in the log cabin when you were little?"

"No. The stone house was built before I was born." John went on talking while they ate. When they had finished, Johnny ran off down the hill again, to return to the barn for his puppy. Anne put the dishes and the cloth in the basket, and sat down to watch the sun set. John lay on his back on the robe. She stretched her feet out and made a lap for his head. He yawned, and smiled up at her.

"I feel like school's out for good."

She ran her fingers through his hair. "Just spring? Or no more scarlet fever?"

"No new cases for three weeks. I've got my fingers crossed. It was bad for a while."

"I know."

"Do you? I feel like I'd been away—far away for a long time. How could you know?"

"Do you think I don't miss you when you go away?"

His eyes widened oddly, or perhaps it only looked odd because she was seeing his face so obliquely from above. Did he think, perhaps, that because he did not mention his troubles, she was not aware of them? She sighed. "I don't see why you care so much, when you're doing all that anybody could."

"Not care? When the Raffertys lose every child? Oh, Anne!"

"But Mrs. Jordan did what you said, and only one child caught it. Doesn't that prove you're right?"

"To me, but not to others. It's a hard time to be practicing medicine. Maybe all times are. But so many discoveries are being made—Lister and Pasteur—and even most doctors won't believe. But some of us know now it isn't the hand of God that wipes out whole families, like the Raffertys, but pure simple human ignorance."

"But the Raffertys will go on thinking it's the hand of God, encouraged by the priest, and in another ten years they'll have another handful of children."

"Sometimes I think I would be more successful if I left the new ideas alone. The Jordan children's escape—it might be pure accident, after all. And I'm sure most of my patients would have more faith in me if I went along in the old way."

"But you wouldn't have faith in yourself."

"I don't anyway. But I pretend to seem confident, because confidence begets confidence, and a patient's faith is half the battle."

"I know. One's doctor must be only less than God." Anne, wondering as to whether she had been blasphemous, was quite sure when he answered, although she could not help laughing.

"Yes. I think I'll grow a full beard. Like His, to hide behind."

"John!"

"Surely if God has a beard, that is why? I can't believe, seeing the world is what it is, that He is as confident about it all as we like to think."

"John! You are really shocking. Anyway, I don't believe I'd like you with a beard. So ticklish. How did we get started on this, anyway?"

"I only started out to explain why I felt like a boy out of school." He sat up and smoothed his rumpled hair. "Now I must go back and see what the evening's office hours produce." He helped her to her feet, folded the robe, picked up the basket, and with a hand at her elbow went off down the hill at her side, Johnny and the puppy cavorting ahead of them.

The sun set clear: they had seen it go down in a haze of rose and amethyst before they left the farm. But the next afternoon it rained. At about the time for school to close, Anne put on her waterproof cloak and boots, took her umbrella, and set out to catch Amanda before she left the schoolhouse. It would be more conventional to call on her at home, of course, but that would mean a long walk, and the school was just a step, through on Linden Street to Chillicothe, and down Chillicothe a block. A newly instituted high school was being conducted, temporarily, in the brick house that had been Mr. Hugh McMillan's Academy for Boys. It was not far from Miss Crenshaw's house, where Fritz Klein and his family now lived. "Funny," Anne thought, "the Germans don't all live close together like the Irish. We'll have soon forgotten they ever were Germans, just as we forgot long since that the Harbaughs and the Baughmans and the other Pennsylvania Dutch were once German. And Ludwig!" Noting the neat prim freshness of the green shutters on the Klein house, her thoughts drifted idly from Fritz to Mr. Lichtenstein, and on to the bond issue for a new high school that the town was to vote on in the fall election. "More fuss over that, I'll be bound, than over whether or not Governor Hayes is reelected."

The renovated Boys' Academy was an old-fashioned, square, severe brick building, two stories high, with ill-lighted halls down its center and two rooms on each side on both floors. It had been replastered, repainted, revarnished by the public school board when they bought it; but already, Anne noticed as she stood in its door, the hall smelled like dust, chalk, and damp, long-worn woolens. She had not intended to go inside until school was dismissed, but she could not walk up and down outside in the hard rain without seeming eccentric, or in trouble—"Be taken for a parent, like as not," she told herself, "come to see what's wrong with her Mary." And so she peered inside, into the malodorous gloom, saw an empty bench along the wall, and slid into the corner of it just as a gong sounded clangorously at the end of the hall. After an instant the doors slammed open, and boys with a few girls among them filled the hall and the stairs from the second floor. She drew her booted feet and her dripping umbrella back against the bench, and waited until all the pupils had dispersed except for a stray boy or so. She asked one of them for Amanda's room.

There, Amanda had just thrown open the windows to their widest extent, in spite of the rain that splashed on the sills. She returned to her desk to collect what papers and books she must take home, started toward the closet for cloak, hat, and umbrella, looked up and saw Anne in the doorway.

"Good afternoon, Amanda. I hope you don't mind my pursuing you here. I wanted to see you, and I didn't know what time you got home afternoons. Besides, it's such a long walk."

"Good afternoon, Anne; you're very welcome, of course. I'm afraid there are no facilities for making you a cup of tea. However, make yourself at home." Amanda spoke in the defensively curt way she was still sometimes startled into taking with Anne or Sally.

Anne looked around the bare room as she came forward: the notched, scratched desks, the blackboards, the black stove in the corner. The fresh wind, heavy with rain, blew through the room, but the smell of damp wool was even thicker here than in the hall. There were no engravings on the schoolroom wall of the Acropolis or Coliseum, no busts of antique Romans, no bookcase full of ponderous volumes. Anne perched on the corner of a desk in the front row and studied Amanda a moment before she spoke. Amanda had on a drab merino frock. She looked tired, and the knot of hair at her neck hung loosely in the net that had slipped half off her head. But Amanda's hair always looked unkempt; she had a mind above such things.

"Do you like it here as well as at the College?" Anne asked her, curiously.

"I was just thinking before you came in." Amanda wrinkled her nose. "The atmosphere is certainly very different. But yes, I think I do. When I changed, it was for the sake of the salary: I never pretended otherwise. Mother wouldn't consider leaving Waynesboro, and this is the best I can do here. But I expected to loathe it." Amanda laughed briefly, in self-scorn. "I was grim about it, like a Christian martyr. I have always suspected that the martyrs were unpleasant to live with."

"Oh, damnably," Anne agreed, thinking of Mrs. Reid, and that Amanda had reason to know.

"You put it forcibly." Amanda lifted her eyebrows. "However, I don't feel that way now. One couldn't, working with Mr. Fletcher and Mr. Lichtenstein. They are true zealots."

"Mr. Lichtenstein?" It was Anne's turn to lift her eyebrows.

"Yes. Don't judge by externals. You're not that stupid. You know that every step taken for the school's improvement, from bringing Mr. Fletcher here to the bond issue next fall, has been due to him. Why should people lift their eyebrows just because he speaks broken English, and is fat? I know he likes his glass of beer," she hastened to add, apologetically, "but that was the way he was brought up. And outside of school one needn't—"

"I know." Anne cut her off to save her the unwisdom of saying that outside of school one need not know Mr. Lichtenstein, since John and Ludwig did, and liked him. There would be no point of going into that.

"What I was trying to explain," Amanda's brows cleared, "I have never exactly put it into words in my own mind. I suppose that I am just beginning to see it clearly, so perhaps I cannot explain it. I am a part now, not of something that is dying, but of something that is growing, that will become more and more important instead of less and less. Knowing that—having it in the air you breathe, along with the chalk—makes you enthusiastic. When I made the change, I made it so that I could give Mother a decent old age. But I thought that my own life would be wasted, meaningless to me and everyone else. Futile."

"Everyone feels that, Amanda, one time or another. After all, 'Man's days are as grass,' and women's more so." Anne was thinking that Amanda should have been a boy; then she could have escaped to become a scholar: a learned and distinguished scholar-gentleman in the society of other scholars. This was no place for one of Amanda's abilities, whatever she had persuaded herself to believe.

"I don't feel so now," Amanda continued. "It is different, somehow, with boys to teach. Of course, there are not yet many pupils in the high school, thirty-odd this year. And most of them are boys who are ambitious and are preparing themselves for college. They actually want to learn. The three in the Virgil class. Besides, boys are pleasanter to teach than girls: they don't dodge and squirm down devious paths in their minds. If you ask them questions they can't answer, they say they don't know." Then she added as if it were the most surprising thing in the world, and Anne, remembering the Female Academy, could understand: "They have intellectual curiosity: they want to find out. And girls after all, when and if you have taught them, what do they do? Get married!" Amanda's disgust was genuine. Anne did not laugh. "Out of a lifetime's teaching of boys, there will be a few who will become great and famous men, and one will have the satisfaction of having helped them at the start." Amanda ended her thoughts on that subject.

Amanda had set her desk to rights while she talked; now she went to close the windows.

"You don't care to stay here, do you? The janitor will be in presently to clean. You haven't told me yet what you wanted to see me about."

"I'll walk along with you if you are ready to go. Will you stop in at my house on your way? We could have tea there, if you like."

Amanda shook her head. "Mother will be looking for me."

They went out and up the street together, separated by their two umbrellas, talking less intimately than they had done in the empty schoolroom.

"What I wanted of you was help. On my Club paper. George Sand."

Amanda laughed shortly. "That is like Eliza, isn't it? She thinks she prefers novels about real life, when actually what she likes is melodrama, if only it is grim enough. I know nothing about George Sand, and don't know that I want to."

"I just thought maybe you could tell me where to find out something about her. The bookseller in Cincinnati had only one of her books, and it's certainly melodrama, but fantastically romantic. Eliza wouldn't like it. I could review that, but, remember what you thought of the first Club paper I ever wrote, on Browning? I know now what-all I should cover; life, education, character, relations with contemporary critics, what school of writing she belonged to, whom she influenced. But how? Where can I find out about all those things?"

"I should think you could tell whom she influenced, just by reading."

"If *Mademoiselle Marquem* influenced anything, it's the serials that run in *Harper's Weekly*. But she's written dozens of other things. I don't see why Waynesboro can't have a circulating library. Other towns do."

"I don't either. I suppose no one's ever thought of it."

They had come to the corner of Linden Street.

"It's stopped raining, Anne." Amanda put her umbrella down, and shook it free of water. Anne tipped hers back over her shoulder, lifted her face to the sky, swung the umbrella around, and put it down. Drops continued to spatter on them from the young green leaves of the curbside trees, but the flowing clouds were rent and torn, and there were blue depths between them. Suddenly the bright April sunshine poured down upon the two young women standing on the crooked granite curbstone, studying the muddy street they must cross, the almost submerged crossing stones.

"You go first." Anne picked up her full flowing skirt with a practiced gesture. As she stepped up on the opposite curb and once more took her place beside Amanda, she said, "Well, why don't we? A library, I mean."

"The Club could sponsor it."

"Mrs. Tyler hasn't had a new project to set her hand to for a long time."

"We could collect whatever books people were willing to contribute from their own libraries, to start with. We should have to raise a great deal of money, too." The thought of a great deal of money awed Amanda.

"Not so much from any one if lots of people subscribed. Club members could take charge in the library, by turns. There'd only be rent, and coal and light, and books. We should have to raise enough money to get started with. A benefit, or a carnival, like the ones in wartime that the Sanitary Commission had. Remember?

"We can bring it up at the next Club meeting. Shall you, or I?"

"Oh, you, Amanda. They'd never take me seriously. And maybe you'd better talk to Mrs. Ballard about it first. If she approved, she would have everything organized in her mind before we ever voted on it."

The next Club meeting was at the Demings'. The General's house since its reconstruction differed in plan from most Waynesboro dwellings. At one corner bulged a round tower, all curved glass windows. A wide veranda ended at the tower; here, close to the curved windows, the front door opened on a short hall. At a right angle to the length of the hall, on the tower side, rose the wide, shallow staircase. The tower room on the second floor was the stair-landing and on the third, the General's study, but on the ground floor it was a formal little reception hall, all palm trees and light gilt chairs, with a round mirror and a console table against the flat inner wall. The staircase banisters and newel post ended there, a little above the floor of the entrance hall; one wide step ran at right angle to the foot of the stairs and across an arc of the tower room. This elevation gave an advantage to a hostess receiving a caller; Mrs. Deming made the most of it on occasions. But the members of the Club were too many to be welcomed there; they were ushered by the maid to the living room at the end of the hall to leave their wraps, and then led back to the drawing room, across the entrance hall from the stairs. A long room ending in a deep bay with two windows and a fireplace in the center, it ran the length of the veranda, with more windows than wall. Guests who sat on the opposite side of the room could, when bored, watch the coming and going on lower Market Street. Although shadowed by the veranda, the sun slanted in the windows in the bay and lighted Mrs. Deming's New England mahogany and the flowered Brussels carpet. The ladies chose their chairs and settled down for a long afternoon. The business meeting had been postponed until after the reading of the day's essay, since Amanda would of necessity be late to meetings until school was out. After she came in the president asked if there were any new business. Amanda rose and read the resolution, which she and Mrs. Ballard had prepared: "Resolved, that the Waynesboro Woman's Club sponsor the formation of a Circulating Library, for the use and benefit of the citizens of Waynesboro."

Anne had previously discussed the idea with Sally. Sally was wholehearted in her approval, even though she bought whatever book she wanted, so that the tall walnut bookcases in her living room were stuffed to overflowing. She had even been able to lend Anne some George Sand, in French. Anne had protested. Sally had scolded: "You should keep up your French. After all we suffered learning it. I intend to, anyway. Especially with Ludwig speaking German to the children."

Anne had taken the books meekly, and had returned to the matter of the library. Would Sally help?

"I don't know why you think of these things at such inconvenient times. The baby is coming in August. One more Club meeting is about all I shall be able to go to. And I do love to have my finger in all the pies," she wailed. "But if I have any ideas, I can at least contribute them."

Anne left it at that. She knew that Sally would have ideas.

Amanda had already discussed the matter of a subscription library with Mrs. Ballard and Thomasina, and Mrs. Ballard had consulted Mrs. Deming and Mrs. McKinney, her two most indefatigable colleagues in the never-ending struggle against the saloons. Mrs. Deming had expressed an unqualified willingness to support the movement. "My husband has been handicapped sorely in his work by the inaccessibility of books here. He misses the Library of Congress, and continual trips to Columbus or Cincinnati become tiresome." (As all Waynesboro knew, the General in his retirement was writing a history of the brigade he had for a while commanded in the war.) Mrs. Deming had then suggested that she invite the ladies to remain for a social hour after the Club program was over, so that they might have a chance to discuss ways and means. And she sent the General's stableman around with little notes to all the members.

The resolution had been presented by Amanda, and voted on favorably; it had been voted, too, that Mrs. Ballard should appoint the chairmen of whatever committees she might think necessary, those chairmen to choose their own committees from the whole town of Waynesboro. (The ideas to the composition of the necessary committees had been Sally's—or Ludwig's—offered to Anne, and by Anne passed on to Amanda.) The meeting had then adjourned. But before the ladies could really get started talking, while Mrs. Deming's neat handed maid was passing the teacups and cakes, General Deming and little Julia, hand in hand, appeared in the door. Any other Waynesboro husband would have fled the scene, but the affable ways of the politician had become second nature to the General.

"Julia and I desired to make our bows, and express our gratification that such a learned circle should honor us with their presence." He bowed, and the elegant little girl took her ruffles in her hands, slid back one slippered foot, and dipped her knees. Then with unsmiling gravity she took her father's hand again. Julia was a fragile-looking child; her long, fine ash-blond hair was held back from her pale face with a round comb and fell in a smooth silken mass about her shoulders. Her white dress was spotless, not a ruffle was crumpled.

Miss Pinney, at the far end of the room, said in an awed voice, "Isn't she angelic! I always think of Little Eva. And such lovely manners." Her murmur was audible as far as the door. Julia let go her father's hand and sidled into the room as far as the brocaded sofa where Anne and Sally sat, and which the maid was approaching with a plate of cakes. After an appraising glance from one to the other, she said to Anne, turning her back to the sofa's edge, "Help me, please. So that I shan't muss my frock."

Anne lifted her, hands under the child's arms, and thumped her down, perhaps unnecessarily hard, on the corner of the sofa. Then she turned a mocking glance on Sally on her other hand.

Sally muttered, "Ought to be turned loose for an afternoon with ours! Muss her frock, indeed!"

This rather ill-mannered criticism of one of her hostess's belongings was fortunately lost in General Deming's powerful voice sounding again from the door.

"It is most commendable that this Club should so have the town's interests at heart," he boomed. "Be sure that you can count on me for support in any way. In *any* way," he added firmly. "This is an endeavor which must be crowned with success."

He bowed again, and withdrew. Julia remained beside Anne in the corner of the sofa, with the cake plate within reach on the piecrust table where the maid had placed it. Anne watched the child while she listened to the talk that seemed, amazingly, to be giving substance to her idea. No one else noticed, but Anne decided that Julia Deming was neither so fragile nor so *spirituelle* as she looked.

Some of the ladies were considering possible sites for the library; others racked their brains for the names of fellow townsfolk who could be called upon to raise money, or at least to become subscribers. Sally spoke in defense of the motion to choose only the chairmen of committees from the Club. "To make it a success we must interest all the groups in town. And if they work for it, they will be interested. There really oughtn't to be these water-tight groups in a town this size, anyway." Sally stopped short of "Ludwig says." This sentiment encouraged Mrs. Ballard to decide that Mrs. Rausch should be chairman of the membership committee. "You can manage that, my dear, without—er—going out much; your committee can come to you." Mrs. Tyler was appointed chairman of the committee to find a site and arrange about heat and light and all the etceteras. Amanda was to collect donated books, and, when there was money, choose other books to spend it on. And

Mrs. Gordon was handed the responsibility of thinking of possible donors and ways of raising money.

"Of course," Mrs. Ballard said, holding up her teacup to the maid who had returned for it, "at the next business meeting of the Club I shall name these committee chairmen in due form, so that they can be written in the minutes. But in the meantime, you can be thinking of good members for your committees."

Anne had listened while she watched Julia eat macaroons; she was more than a little frightened. She must do what she could with George Sand quickly. Mrs. Ballard had picked her to raise money because she had been so ready with her suggestions to Amanda. A carnival! What did she know about getting up a carnival? She had been a girl in school when Sanitary Commission carnivals were held for the soldiers during the war, and all she knew about them was that they had been more pure fun than anything else in her experience.

And so while Sally talked over with Ludwig possible leaders of various church groups, like Mr. Heitzel, the Lutheran minister, and while she made up her membership committee, including in it various ministers' wives, Douglas Gardiner, now practicing law, and Mrs. Bonner, who might persuade Mr. Bonner to say helpful things about the proposed library in the *Torchlight*, Anne went to Mrs. Cochran and Mrs. Edwards and Mrs. Harbaugh, whose husband had the grain-and-feed store, because they had been the organizers of the Sanitary Commission carnivals and to young women like Mrs. Fritz Klein and Kitty Lowrey, who would not shrink from actual toil. All committee chairmen set to with a will, appointed members from the churches and the women's auxiliaries of masculine lodges, and all rolled up their sleeves and went to work. They did not confine their efforts to the carnival, by any means; not a week that summer was without its lawn fete, sponsored by one church group or another: a strawberry festival, a raspberry festival, a watermelon festival, or when no fruit of the earth ripened at the appropriate time, an ice cream festival. Chinese lanterns hung glowing between the trees; trestle tables were set up and chairs borrowed from various Sunday school rooms; music was furnished free by the Veterans' Band. And all the men in town, from Judge Ballard to Herman Lichtenstein to the McCunes and the McKinneys, felt it an obligation to go and eat ice cream and pay for slices of cakes that their own wives had baked in their own kitchens. On Saturdays there were food sales (strudel and pumpernickel became known to Anglo-Saxon families that had never tasted them before) and rummage sales, which provided a good deal of rather limp finery to be picked up by women from the East End who had no white folks they worked for, and hence no way to acquire what they craved except by paying for it. In June, General Deming gave a lecture in the Opera House on "The Battle of Chickamauga," which was, as the *Torchlight* said, "well attended." A few weeks later, Professor Lowrey spoke on "Rome in the Days of Augustus" to an even larger house; his audience comprised members of the Methodist church and alumnae of the Female College, accompanied by their husbands, children, parents, and such friends as had been dragooned into buying tickets. These last, driven by their consciences to attend at least one lecture, chose the professor's. As they said, "Everybody knows all about the Battle of Chickamauga: after all, half the men in town fought there. But who knows anything about the Roman Empire?"

Most people, although the country was still in the depths of the depression, managed to find a quarter to spend here and there, now and again, and the library fund slowly increased. But the really Herculean efforts of the Finance Committee were being reserved for the carnival, to be held for three nights toward the end of August in the Armory. Through the heat of the summer, even while her house was torn up and full of tinners, plasterers and paperers, Anne worked on her plans. Convinced that her committee knew more than she did about how to plan it, she let them decide that it would be a "Carnival of Books." Each chosen author would be represented by a booth, to serve as a rallying point for those costumed as characters from his works. There, articles of food or dress, or useful hand-made objects, as appropriate as possible to the author, would be sold. "Like pumpkin pies," said Mrs. McKinney, with her choked humorless smile, "so suited to our New England poet." She and her Longfellow committee were meeting with Anne to be told what was expected of them. "And we can decorate the booth with corn shocks."

"Better make it Paul Revere's lanterns. Or, I tell you, the village smithy. The carnival is going to be in August." Anne had long since ceased to be surprised at the slight awareness of the realities of scene, season, and weather exhibited by lady reformers. But as she said to John that night, "You would think she would connect pumpkin pies with Thanksgiving."

"Has a mind above 'em, no doubt."

"And Amanda! She may be teaching boys, but she hasn't learned much about them. She's afraid we'll not be able to get the men into costumes."

"D'you think you will?"

"We couldn't stop them. Oh, I know there'll be a great fuss, and we'll be expected to use persuasion, but it will be pretense. Men love to get themselves up. Why else are they Knights of Pythias and Knights Templars and such?"

And John, who was a loyal Mason, had no convincing answer.

The authors to be represented at the carnival were the ones whose characters would presumably be recognized by the multitude: Tennyson and Longfellow, Sir Walter Scott and Dickens, Irving, Cooper, and Mrs. Stowe, Victor Hugo, Schiller, and Goethe. Anne, moved by Sally, could see the importance of winning support from the German group, and asked Mrs. Fritz Klein to take the Schiller booth, and Miss Riegel, the new teacher of German in the high school, the Goethe; but Miss Riegel demurred: too few people (she had her own judgment of Waynesboro) would recognize the characters of Goethe.

Hans Christian Andersen would be a better subject. Anne was grateful to her, for she was right; and the fairy-tale booth, with little blond boys and girls as the Tin Soldier, the Snow Queen, and all the others, made the most charming booth of the carnival.

The old Armory, where the Waynesboro Grays had drilled before the war but which had since been little used, was a great rattling, ramshackle barn of a place, and needed a housewife's thorough cleaning before it could be decorated. Anne and her committee, aproned and with their heads tied up, saw to it that the cleaning was done, and did a large part of it themselves; then the worst shortcomings of its stark and battered interior were concealed by bunting and colored paper, and the booths erected around the edge of its floor also were beflagged and festooned. The carnival was held in the last week of August, on the last three nights of the week: the enforced absence of those who worked in the various stores on Saturday night would be more than made up for by the attendance of farmers and their wives who would be in town.

When "The" Thursday night came, Anne was so tired and so weighed down by her sense of responsibility that she forgot she had thought it would be fun. She had succeeded in getting John there, having persuaded him that no one would think of choosing a carnival night for an office call, and that he could leave a note on the door, just in case. She had moreover got him, sheepish but not daring to remonstrate, into his costume as Barnaby Rudge. With a floppy hat and a raven for his shoulder made of black calico wired and stuffed, he was paired with Kitty Lowrey's Dolly Varden. Johnny was there as Tiny Tim. He had no sooner been turned over to Judge Ballard (Scrooge), however, before he slipped away and created such confusion—almost bedlam—by flourishing his crutch wildly that his mother had to pursue him and threaten to transform him into another character unless he left the crutch hanging around his neck unused.

Carnivals, Anne thought, were really for the children. Johnny and Elsa and their friends were transported: the crowds were mysterious and wonderful, known and familiar people new and different in their costumes; the triumphant music of the band, the babble of voices, the movement around the booths. Anne was right: they would remember it always; although the details might be forgotten, merged with recollections of later carnivals, the memory would survive of an untrammeled hour blazing with excitement. The children were even allowed to join in the Grand March, absorbed among the adults, most of them hand in hand with a parent; Miss Riegel's lot, from the Hans Christian Andersen booth, marched altogether, sedate and disciplined, having apparently been born with an aptitude for parading. The Grand March gave one part of Waynesboro a chance to see another part of the town in costume; in fact, the costumed part enjoyed the chance to see itself.

As the marchers began to line up, General Deming, who always acted as grand marshall of the Decoration Day and Fourth of July parades, stepped onto the floor at the sound of a drum roll from the band and gestured the onlookers to the edges of the floor. Dressed as a rather heavy-set but still recognizable George Washington (whatever the theme, there had to be a George Washington), he fell in at the head of the line to complete the first foursome, the other three characters from the Sir Walter Scott booth: Ludwig, in a kilt, as Rob Roy, and between them a most unlikely Madge Wildfire (Mrs. Cochran) and a convincingly sharp-featured Queen Elizabeth (Mrs. Deming); among those behind them were Ivanhoe, with his Rebecca and Rowena. The next group was made up of Mrs. Ballard's Dickens characters: the Judge as Scrooge, young Johnny Gordon, the crutch still swinging from the rope around his neck, hand-in-hand with Elsa, an exuberantly healthy Little Nell; also recognizable were Aunt Betsey Trotwood, Miss Havisham, in a torn and draggled café au lait-colored paper muslin wedding gown, Mr. Micawber, and Mrs. Jellyby, with her buttons all unbuttoned down her back. In the German contingent, next in line, could be recognized Wilhelm Tell and Maria Stuart, who were followed by the fairy-tale children, and, bringing up the end, the characters of Cooper and Longfellow. Anne had been asked by Mrs. McKinney to be Evangeline, and she found herself lined up with Amanda (as a rather grim Priscilla), the Reverend Mr. McKinney (Captain Miles Standish), and a student as John Alden.

The General put the marchers through their paces, barking his orders in a military voice that carried clearly over the full-volume military music of the band. As the marchers moved up the floor, skirts swirled, heavy boots tramped. They came down the middle, swung alternately left and right, went up each side of the room and at the top came together in a line of eight. In eights they tramped down again, heads up and arms swinging, the children scuttling to keep up once more, came together, and swept down the floor sixteen abreast. Then they began to reverse the formation, the lines of sixteen becoming eight abreast, four, then two. In twos they marched in diagonal lines from two corners of the room to the other two corners, turned and went back, making double diagonal lines. The band played steadily: "Tramp, Tramp, Tramp" and "Marching through Georgia" and "Tenting Tonight." The march grew faster and faster, and feet fairly twinkled. Laughter rose in a chorus from the marchers as well as from the watchers along the sidelines.

The General was getting short of breath and red in the face; he signaled the band, which began to play "Home, Sweet Home." The marchers came down the floor sixteen abreast one final time, and broke up, laughing, looking for families, going for one last ice or lemonade. And when they had dispersed, the band played "Hail, Columbia," and young Mrs. Lichtenstein, once one of the "Hoffmann girls" who now looked more nearly the cartoonists' Columbia than any native daughter of Waynesboro, tall, blond, deep-bosomed, posed on a table at the end of the hall in a white Grecian robe with a shield of stars and stripes and a piece of bunting crossed from shoulder to waist. The band swung into "The Star Spangled Banner"; everyone stood at attention until it was ended, and then started for the exit. Anne took the box of money from the ticket office and gave it to Mr. Cochran to put in the bank.

Thus the first night and the second. Saturday night was a little different, a little wilder and more unrestrained: citizens who had hitherto been content to stand on the sidelines and watch on the last evening came in costume and joined in the Grand March. There were not so many of them as to throw the whole event out of hand—out of General Deming's hand, at least—but the lively march took on something of the nature of a cakewalk, and the costumed groups lost their representative character, with pirates, witches, and clowns among them. The newcomers were unabashed in their noisy equipment, and, as Anne asked herself, why shouldn't they be? They had bought admission tickets, and the *Torchlight* had stated that all who attended in costume would take part in the Grand March.

But those who had represented literary figures might perhaps be embarrassed by the far from decorous addition to their numbers, as Anne knew that John undoubtedly was by the wild-looking gypsy who hung on his arm, her black braids swinging, her bracelets jangling, her wide scarlet skirt swirling about her light feet. John, taking her through the march, had a cold, unhappy, aloof air; but when, in crossing diagonal lines from corner to corner, Anne and her partner came face to face with the pair, John winked at her and rolled his eyes in mock despair, and Anne, grinning back at him, wrinkled her nose in a burlesque of disdain. She looked as gay as a child, John thought, and as mischievous. And she was feeling gay because the last evening was almost over, and they had made a lot of money for the library, and nothing had really gone wrong. There wasn't any way, so far as she could see, by which they could have had a carnival and invited the public and still excluded people like the Floods if they wanted to come. Anne had recognized the Flood girl in that instant of passing, transformed though she was by the gypsy costume from her usual slatternly appearance. Old Man Flood ran the hotel across the tracks from the railroad depot, if hotel it could be called; and going to or from the cars, one could see the Flood girls in one or another open window, leaning on the sill. John was probably the only person there outside her own acquaintances that the Flood girl would know; he had doctored her father. "Zeldorah. That's her name." Anne said it as though she had been groping about in her memory, said it to Sally the next afternoon, when the Gordons had gone to the Rausches' after their Sunday dinner, in order that Sally might have a full, feminine account of the goings-on. Sally was still inclined to be cross because she had missed the summer's activities and was especially snappish now that she was under the strain of expecting her baby any day; but at the end of Anne's description, she only lifted an eyebrow and said offhandedly "Doctors and politicians, they do know the oddest people."

John and Ludwig had gone out on the veranda with their pipes; the children were playing in the side yard with the beagle puppy, which Johnny had insisted on bringing along. Anne and Sally, in the living room with Belinda pulling herself up at her mother's knee and plumping herself down on the floor again, could hear the voices from outside: the mens' a low rumble from the porch, the children's shriller, louder: Johnny teasing Elsa: "Shaney, Shaney! Can't catch me!" The two young women could have been as confidential as they liked, but there was not, apparently, any withheld confidences still to be shared.

At any rate, Anne's chief effort in behalf of the library was now behind. She could return to the matters of everyday life, rejoice with Sally when her second son was born and duly named Charles, and steel herself to send Johnny off to school for the first time, when September came. He and Elsa, along with Charlotte Bonner, a young Evans, orphan nephew of the Reverend Mr. Evans, the Thirkield boy, and a half-dozen others were starting with Miss Pinney in the infant's school at the College. Whatever Ludwig might think, Sally had never considered sending Elsa to the public school; she had set herself to oppose her husband if necessary, but he had only laughed. "She won't learn anything, but that won't matter for a year or two. She already knows her letters." Ludwig suspected that the old institution on the hill would not long survive, and his daughter was still a baby. And so every schoolday morning Elsa rode as far as the Gordons' with her father, and then walked up Market Street hill with Johnny.

Club meetings began again in the middle of September, and the chat of the ladies, while they assembled and after adjournment, was all about the library committees and the progress that was being made. Amanda's Book Committee had solicited contributions, and when it had taken stock of what was offered made a list of such additional volumes as must be bought. That there was no George Sand on the list did not surprise Anne; that committee, like most of them, was made up of a representative from each of the churches, but she did say to Sally that it wasn't fair really, because they owed the library, didn't they, to the inaccessibility of George Sand's works.

Eliza, on Mrs. Tyler's committee, found a room that would serve their purpose: in the same building, across narrow Wood Street from the Court House, and on the same floor as the rooms of Ballard, Gardiner and Merrill, and of a couple of other offices. It was a big empty storeroom at the far end of the corridor, and Eliza persuaded Levi Baughman, who owned the building, to let them have it rent free if they paid for fixing it up. "Old Levi," a recluse, lived alone in the turreted brick mansion he had built for a wife who had died and a family that had never materialized; it stood dark and silent among its trees on its corner hardly impinging on the consciousness of any who passed it. No one ever saw the old man except when he went about town once a month collecting his rents; but the intrepid Eliza had gone there, rung his doorbell and been admitted, and had asked him for the use of the room, free. It was an act that seemed more courageous to Waynesboro than many other

Ballard ventures of earlier years in the cause of reform—"bearding the old hermit in his den," it was called, and was not esteemed the less lightly because everyone (unjustly) suspected that old Levi thought the Library would soon dissolve and fail and that he would be left with another rentable property on his hands.

Much work had to be done on the room before it could be taken over; but carpenters and plasterers in the fall of '75 were willing to work at anything for comparatively little, and soon walls and ceiling were plastered. A half-dozen slim iron columns with small but elaborate Corinthian capitals were set up, in two rows of three each, to support the ceiling; and gas chandeliers were put in, a modern innovation made possible by the new Waynesboro Illuminating Gas Company. When all that had been done, the whole room was painted: the floor, walls, and columns shoulder high, an economical public-institution brown, ceiling and the upper part of walls and columns a rather arsenical green. A semi-octagonal counter with shelves and desk space on the inside was placed in the middle of the room, back to the windows; behind it, close enough to keep the librarian's back warm, a big pot-bellied stove was put up, of the sort that warmed stores and depot waiting rooms, and the many feet of black pipe, from stove to chimney, were suspended from the ceiling in wire slings. When this work was finished, the bookcases were moved in and ranged around the walls. These, like so many of the books, were contributions out of attics, or over-crowded houses: some of them were very tall, so that books on the top shelves could not be seen without a ladder. Others were low and wasted a lot of wall space; some were of walnut, plain or with carved cornices, or even Corinthian columns at the corners, and some were varnished yellow pine; but they all had glass doors that would lock, and the various keys were tagged with numbers so that the librarian could pick out the right one quickly when a subscriber wanted a book. Some of the bookcases, the plainer ones, were those Judge Ballard had deemed unworthy of a place in his new home and had stored in his barn; the handsomer ones were given by the aged widow of Judge Robertson, who had been Common Pleas Judge long ago and had died before the war. Mrs. Robertson gave not only the bookcases but the books they held: such odd lots and broken sets as her son (or his wife) did not want, and so the Waynesboro Subscription Library began its first year of service with volumes three to seven of Hume's *History of England*, twelve to fifteen of Bisset's, and volumes two and ten alone of Smollett's. As the quavering old lady explained to Amanda, the Judge lent his books to anyone. "If he was alive mebbe he could tell you whose attic those missing volumes are in, but I misdoubt it, after all this time."

By the end of October, all the books, the donated and the purchased, had been delivered to the Library. There they were sorted by Amanda's committee into such categories as seemed to them logical: History, Biography, Travel, and so on. The books were numbered in white ink on their spines, and their titles, authors, and numbers set down in a ledger. The numbering and listing had begun before the books had all been collected, unfortunately for system and order. The first catalogue, a little pamphlet printed by Mr. Bonner in his odd-job shop, its cover ornamented free of charge with birds and books and scrolls, was copied from the ledger; one and two were Blake's *Pictorial History of the Great Rebellion*; number three Robertson's *History of the Middle Ages*, and four and five the two volumes of Whitelaw Reid's *Ohio in the War*. But the first catalogue was not so long, nor the shelves so many, that you could not find any book you wanted in fairly short order.

Mr. Bonner also printed slips to be pasted in each book: "Property of the Waynesboro Subscription Library," and "Gift of ______," with a space for the donor's name and another for the catalogue number, and made up the cards to be sold to Waynesboro citizens, each one of which would entitle its possessor to borrow one book at a time from the library.

For the first few years, funds would certainly be too limited to hire a librarian. The members of the Club agreed to take turns themselves behind the desk when the library was open on Tuesday, Thursday, and Saturday afternoons. The schoolteachers would share the Saturdays when they were free and housewives were their busiest. There would be no evening hours, since no lady would be permitted by her menfolk to be alone in that empty building after dark; no one even suggested it.

Since most of the subscribers would be members of the Waynesboro Woman's Club, it was agreed that the ladies could not take upon themselves the sole responsibility of financing and operating the new institution. A meeting open to all subscribers was decided upon. There would be a dedication ceremony and an election of officers, all this to be followed by a gala celebration. The date chosen was the last Friday in November. All the men in Waynesboro who were concentrating on getting Mr. Hayes elected governor of Ohio for the third time would have politics off their minds by then, and on the Friday after Thanksgiving, the Lowreys, Amanda, and any other schoolteachers who were interested in helping would be free to offer their time.

It only remained to move the books from the tables and boxes where they had been piled as they were catalogued to the shelves where they would be kept and to arrange them in proper order. Anne volunteered to spend an afternoon with Thomasina at that arduous task. When the time came, the day was an example of what mid-November could be like at its worst: rain, sleet, snow, rain again, and ice on everything. When John came in for lunch, he had a message for Anne: Thomasina was in bed with a cold; he had put her there himself, after having been sent out to the Ballard house for that purpose by the Judge.

John, when he entered by the kitchen door, was wearing the heavy army cape that he had never given up, that he always wore in winter because, he said, it was so much warmer and more comfortable than any overcoat. He had long ago ripped off the epaulettes and the gold cord from its collar, but the elaborately braided frogs by which it was fastened still gave it a military air. Now he took it off before the sitting room fire and shook it; water spattered and hissed on the grate.

"I wouldn't go either, if I were you. Not on a day like this."

"But I promised. And we'll never have those books ready by the twenty-sixth if everyone stays in on account of the weather."

"I'll take you up then before I go to the office. I told Tim not to unhitch Molly because I supposed you'd be stubborn about it."

When they stopped before the building housing the library, John scrambled out, tied Molly to the hitching rail, helped Anne to the curb, and followed at her heels up the boxed-in stairs and down the corridor to the end room.

"I'll make sure there's a fire before I leave you."

Anne unlocked the door with the key that had been entrusted to her and pushed it open. The smell of paint flooded out and washed over them, but there was no warmth with it. If the janitor of the building had been asked to build a fire, he had forgotten it.

John said, "You can't stay here. The place is freezing." Then as he saw her prepared to argue, he gave in. "Never mind. I'll build a fire. I see there's coal in the bucket. You go sit in Ballard's office with Eliza until I get it started."

Meekly she retraced her steps, slipped unobtrusively into the outer room where Eliza presided, explained her presence, and sat down in one of the chairs outside the railing that barred Eliza from the world. There were others waiting—a couple of men—so that she couldn't chat with Eliza, and at any rate, Eliza was very busy with a big ledger. Anne folded her hands in her lap and waited. Fifteen or twenty minutes later, John stuck his head around the edge of the door and summoned her. Outside in the hall, he swung the broadcloth cape from around his shoulders and put it on hers.

"Keep this on until it warms up in there. Don't poke that fire, but don't forget it, either. Just put a piece of coal on now and then, gently. And don't start out to walk home in this wet, either, even if it's only a little way. I'll come for you when I'm through at the office. I don't think I'll be late, but if I am, *wait*. And don't wear yourself out." He tipped her chin up with the hand that had held the cape around her neck, patted her cheek lightly, turned and ran away down the echoing bare floor and wooden stairs.

Inside the library, Anne wasted no time in inaction. She walked around the room once to measure what had been done already. Down the left side of the room she looked over the bookcases against that wall: History, Biography and Travel were in place on the shelves. Beyond, in the rear corner and between the windows that looked out upon the alley, some shed roofs, the sheriff's back yard, and the county jail, all obscured now by the sleet that flawed the glass, stood bookcases still empty, with the books intended for them piled in heaps on the floor. Anne read the cards tacked on the doors above the keyholes. One said "Religion and Theology," and one "Literature and Miscellany." She passed them, passed the stove, where now she could see the fire burning brightly behind the mica in the door, passed the librarian's counter, where she dropped the cumbersome cape John had wrapped her in, and went on to the bookcases in the other long wall. In these cases Juvenile and Adult Fiction were to be kept; Anne, who had had no part in deciding what new books had been bought, was more interested in getting her hands on these than on "Religion and Theology."

The novels had been given the highest numbers, and they had been arranged alphabetically by author instead of first-acquired, first-numbered. Authors in A began with 10001, because it seemed quite possible to the women, who were inventing their cataloguing system as they went along, that the library might some day have ten thousand books that were not fiction. The novels, duly labeled and numbered, had been piled in baskets and on the floor before the bookcases that were to receive them. Anne, kneeling on the floor, sorted them out: Alcott, Aldrich, Austen. She dragged the stepladder from the other side of the room and hoisted Alcott, Aldrich, and Austen to the top shelf. "Silly place for them," she thought. "Imagine Alcott on the top shelf." She moved them down one shelf. There weren't books enough to fill the cases, anyway; one might as well leave the top shelf entirely empty as to have all the shelves only partly full, which had been done in other cases. "Who's doing this, anyway?" she thought. On the floor again she came upon a couple of "Anons" and frowned at them: *Ought We to Visit Her* and *Cast Away in The Cold.* Those would certainly do very well on the top shelf, even though their numbers were higher than the Alcotts and the Aldriches. Her system might seem erratic to her sister club women, but surely—she would explain to them that she put all the "Anons" on the top shelf to make it easier for the acting librarians, because surely no one would ever want to read them. She went up the ladder again with the two books, but before she put them on the otherwise empty shelf, she looked inside the covers for a name. The flyleaves had been cut out of both. "Somebody like Mrs. McCune," she thought, uncharitably. "If she reads novels at all, that's just the kind." The fellowship of the Woman's Club had not increased her regard for Mrs. McCune.

She went on then, with Auerback and Bjornsen and Cherbuliez, sometimes and sometimes not resisting her desire to look into them, to read the first paragraph. These books were new, a part, along with Turgenev and others, of the "Leisure Hour Series"; Anne knew that they had been bought at the suggestion of Amanda Reid, and she had respect enough for Amanda's brains—more respect, she thought, passing on the ladder to contemplate what she did think—than she had for anyone else's brains—as *brains*, at least: intelligence, bookbrains, as distinct from good-commonsense brains, which no doubt men excelled in. And if Amanda thought the Leisure Hour Series should be in a library, then she, Anne, intended to read it.

Communing with herself in this disjointed fashion, dipping into book after book and then scurrying up and down the ladder to make up for wasted time, she filled one bookcase and then another while the afternoon wore away and she was oblivious to its passing. The day darkened, rain and sleet slashed at the windows, and the wind blew in around the ill-fitting sashes. There came a moment when Anne shivered as she knelt on the floor beside a pile of books; she pulled her dolman closer at her neck, then of a sudden became fully awake to the day and hour. The fire! She scrambled to her feet, crossed the room, and swung the stove door open: it was out, nearly, if not quite. Putting on coal and opening the draughts would never save it now. She picked up the poker, stirred among the ashes and slabs of black clinker. Red glowed, paled, went out, glowed, paled. There was coal in the box but no paper or kindling. John must have gotten what he had needed to start the fire from the janitor. She too could hunt him up but hadn't a notion where to look, and it didn't seem very ladylike to go prowling around alley doors in search of him. She could go to Eliza, down the hall in her father's office, but Eliza had more important things to do than look after her, and besides, she would be so scathing. No: if the fire was out, it was out. She put a couple of pieces of coal on and opened the draughts, but nothing happened. She thought with some exasperation of how John would laugh and say, "I told you so." And the room was very cold, suddenly, and dark. She looked at the watch hung on a chain around her neck and tucked in her belt. Four o'clock, very nearly. John's office hours were officially over; he was often kept there by a rush of patients, but surely not on a day like this; even if he had been called into the country, he ought to be back before long. He had told her to wait, and now balancing the cold inside against the cold and the ice outside, she decided to obey. She picked up the cape from the desk where she had laid it, put it around her, and huddled into it, crossing her arms under it around her ribs and catching it close with the tips of her fingers. It smelled faintly of stale tobacco; it must have been hanging all summer on the hatrack in the office hallway. The cape was warm, but heavy. Anne suddenly realized how tired she was and how stiff from the lifting and carrying, the stooping and climbing that she had done. She was not sure she could begin again, but if she could keep moving, she would not be so cold. She dropped the cape from her fingers, to let it hang loose; then as she turned to move back toward the piles of books, she thrust her hands, for a last bit of warmth, deep into its slit pockets. They were capacious, but full: her fingers identified gloves, and soiled handkerchiefs that she should have put in the wash six months ago if only John had brought the cape home to her, to be put up in camphor against the moths. What careless creatures men were! At the very bottom of the left hand pocket her fingers came upon what felt like a wad of paper. Idly she fished it up to view: a grubby square of paper, folded and refolded until it measured hardly more than an inch across. It had been folded so long that the edges were rubbed and it was grayish in color; bits of dust and crumbs of tobacco had collected in the creases. A written summons to John, she supposed, from one of his more illiterate patients. Without any particular curiosity, almost automatically, she unfolded and read it. The note had no salutation, no punctuation, and the writing in pencil on cheap paper was so bad as to be almost illegible, but it bore a date in the upper corner, March 1, and read "Of corse you can cum tonite if you give the ole man time to drink hisself stoopid an git to bed first." It was signed Z.F., and under the initials, in still wider handwriting, scrawled the length of the bit of paper were the words "Dont fergit the stockins."

Anne thought, "What a crazy thing! How careless of John to leave it in his pocket, anything so open to misinterpretation!"

Then it was as if a slowly moving fist had caught her hard in the midriff. Stiff with shock, the strength drained from her knees, she managed to reach the ladder and drop to the lowest step and sit there. It was only then that her heart began to pound, slow and hard at first, then fast and harder.

Nothing, of a sudden, seemed real. It was not in real life that wives found notes from other women in their husband's pockets. It was only in cliché-filled, banal novels. Dizzily she tipped her head back and looked up at the top shelf. Was it possible that such things were put into such novels—*Ought We to Visit Her* and *Cast Away in The Cold*—because they did happen in real life?

What she thought, the words coming into her mind without volition, was "Don't come, not now, not yet. Give me time."

Because if he came now, he would know that something had happened. And she hadn't decided whether she wanted him to know, whether she would accuse, demand, or like a sick animal conceal her hurt.

Feverishly she debated how to dispose of the note. Burn it? But the fire was out, and besides, if he ever remembered it had been in his pocket—But if she left it there, when he came upon it he would wonder all his life. Quickly she plucked a hairpin from her head, ripped an inch-long hole in the lining of the pocket, pushed the note through it, and shook it well down between the cape and its lining.

Z.F. was that Flood girl, of course. Rigidly Anne set her teeth, as a help in curbing her nausea and forcing pictures out of her mind. She began to shiver and could not stop. When the nausea was less violent, she lowered her hand from over her mouth and her rigid jaw. She rose slowly, knowing that she must compose herself. She went back to the desk with the cape, and laid it down. No matter how cold she got she could not wear it.

This was what her father's long-forgotten warning had meant: that now and then John must find escape from being himself—and find it in turning to anonymous, welcoming flesh. Her father, who loved John, too, would have forgiven him; he had long ago prepared her to forgive him. Forgive without ever letting him know that she knew, and she had promised; but was she equal to that? She must have time to think, but not now; now she must compose herself outwardly, so as to give herself a chance to find time later to think. Even weep, perhaps. Certainly now she must be her usual self. John would come at any moment. She returned to the stepladder hurriedly, clumsily, blinded. She would not weep; she held her head back and forced herself to return to her work; she even forced herself to pay attention to what she was doing, noticing titles and authors as she shelved the works of Charles Reade, Sir Walter Scott, Thackeray. She moved as rapidly as possible, stooping to pick up the books, stretching to lift them to the upper shelves, squatting to slip them onto the lower ones. But always, uncontrollably, she shivered, however tight her teeth were clenched. It grew darker and darker outside, and she could hardly see the titles on the books in her hand. She was cold, cold to the marrow of her bones, her hands were numb and stiff; there was no feeling in her feet. She hardly realized herself how her surface emotion was a rapidly accumulating irritation with the husband who was keeping her waiting here in the cold.

But when, just after the town clock struck five, she heard him coming from the far end of the corridor, she made a dash for the counter, seized the cape, and swung it around her. John would think she had lost her mind if she didn't have it on. She got back to the ladder, and was standing there when he opened the door. She held to the ladder with one hand because she trembled so. She made no step, no sound, so that he had to come all the way inside the door before he saw her standing there in the gloom.

He must have felt accusation in her silence. "I'm sorry, Anne. I never thought—"

She flared out at him. *"I should think you would be sorry."* Her tones were quiet enough, but furious. Never in her life had she spoken to him so. He had been coming rapidly toward her, but he stopped short, as if she had struck him in the face. And he looked completely bewildered. Anne's irritation drained away: whatever emotion she felt, it was no longer that. She might truly as well have struck him, she thought, as speak so, after all these years.

He said again, "I'm sorry. Office hours were over early—no one there on such a day, but I had to go to the country, and the roads are all mud and ice. I am sorry, Anne. Maybe you should have gone home."

"But you told me to wait. And I thought you'd never come. The fire went out."

"Good God, Anne, how'd you do it?" He saw that there were tears on her cheek and wisely did not laugh, but put his arms around her. Then he felt her shake. "Why, honey, you've caught a chill. Why didn't you go down the hall and sit with Eliza, or hunt the janitor?"

"I didn't notice the cold for a while. Then I thought I'd be warmer moving."

He held her for a moment in his arms to try to stop her trembling, then said, "Come on, let's get home. You're having a regular chill."

She was silent all the slow way home, while Molly walked the freezing ruts cautiously. But her teeth chattered spasmodically. Once inside the house,

John took the cape from around her, picked her up, and placed her in her rocker in the sitting room, in front of the fire. The house was warm: beautifully warm. John had started the new furnace. Nevertheless, her hands trembled as she held them to the blaze.

"Your throat is sore, isn't it? I'll get Martha." John went on toward the back of the house. Almost before Anne knew what had happened, she was in the downstairs bedroom that had been her father's; John was undressing her, slipping her nightrobe over her head, wrapping her in her peignoir. When she had taken her hairpins out and let her braids slide from their heavy coil on the back of her head down across her shoulders, Martha was ready for her, with a stone hot water bottle for her feet. John watched her pull them into the bed and sink back on the pillows; then he handed her the cup of steaming toddy.

"Sit up long enough to drink this." She took it obediently, and began to sip, staring out over the brim, not looking at him.

"You think I'm going to be sick?" It was the custom for any ill member of the family to be put in that bed because it saved so many trips up and down stairs.

John snorted. "Maybe just a cold. But even if you're all right tomorrow, you'll be better off down here tonight. Tim had a message for me from the Martins when I got in—but whether I'm home or not, you're likely to be disturbed upstairs: the night bell, even pebbles on the window."

"A baby?" For the first time since she had crossed the threshold, her voice had some animation. He would be gone all night, if that were it. She handed him her cup. "Take it, that's all I can get down."

He returned it. "Drink it all, Anne. There's hardly enough whiskey in it to warm you. Turn out the lamp and go to sleep as soon as you've done. I must get Martha to give me my supper, and get along. Tim can go with me and bring Molly back to the stable. It's such an awful night. In the morning Sam Martin can bring me home. When I've gone, Martha will feed the children and get them to bed. Ready, now?" He took the cup, bent to kiss her forehead, turned out the lamp on the candle stand beside the bed.

Warm and comfortable so long as she didn't try to swallow, drowsy and numb from the toddy, Anne lay in the dark, half-listening to the sounds of the house, half-drifting in surrender to the blessed drowsiness. She heard John come into the hall from the dining room, stop before her door, then go on: his steps were firm and quick, and audible even on the carpeted floor. After time enough to pick up his cape and bag, he went out the street door. She had heard it close with a thud behind him. Then after a long silence, Martha and the children passed on their way to the stairs. She heard the colored woman speak to Johnny: "No, now, not tonight. Yo' Maw come home with a bad col' and yo' Paw he done tell her to go to sleep." She could follow their way up the stairs and down the hall. She was not free yet, for Martha would return. She must have dozed off; she was not conscious of an interval's having passed when she heard the doorknob turn.

"Martha?"

"We' you' asleep? Ah neveh meant to wake yo'."

"No. fill the hot water bottle again, will you, Martha? Wait, I'll light the lamp."

"I'll light it."

The match flared. Anne noted with relief that there were others in the holder at the head of the bed. She might not want to watch the night out in darkness. Martha brought back the stone bottle and slipped it in at her feet.

"Anything else, Miz Anne? A musta'd plasteh?"

"No. I'll be all right, Martha. You go along, as soon as you've made sure the children are asleep and covered."

Martha turned the lamp out, closed the door behind her. Anne could hear her ponderous footsteps on the way to the kitchen.

Even while she was listening, she fell asleep again. When she awoke, the numbing effect of the whiskey had worn off, but not the stimulation. Her mind began to circle, to wheel, to seek the reason for the profound sense of woe with which she had wakened. Then memory, sweeping back, told her why. She had planned to think. But not like this, like whirling wheels. She had intended to be in control of whatever wheels went round. She sat up, slipped out of bed, and knelt on the floor. Her throat hurt, and her upper lip itched. She had actually caught a cold, then; but the room was warm, and anyway, if she caught more cold—pneumonia, even—wouldn't it give her time? Time to get used—to get adjusted—wasn't that the word? She reached for the peignoir hung over the post of the bed and pulled it around her shoulders.

What had she meant to pray for? "Dear Father in Heaven"—then what? "Unto thee will I cry, O Lord, my rock"—"When my father and my mother forsake me, then the Lord will take me up." They had sung that psalm in church only last Sunday: "Should friends and kindred, near and dear, leave me to want or die"—But this wasn't praying: this was only feeling sorry for herself, and she could do that presently, without prayer, when she had decided. She began again: "Our Father who art in Heaven—" But the words in her mind were more a kind of catechism than a prayer. "What would you, God, have me do?"—"Whatever is best."—"Best for whom?"—"For them. John. The children."—"Wouldn't it be best not to know?"—"Too late for that."—"For no one to know I know?"

There was no answer from God. She would have to decide for herself. She stayed on her knees.

Could she bear it? Sure that outsiders must know, that they must think her a complaisant fool?

"That hasn't anything to do with what's best. That is pride. Would you ruin three lives for selfish pride?"

No. She could bear it. But didn't she want to bear it, rather than accuse John? Was it cowardice? Was she looking not for the best, but the easiest? Because she loved him. Did she love him still?

And as if they were being read to her, she heard the words "Beareth all things, believeth all things, hopeth all things, endureth all things."

Without knowing that she had decided anything, she crawled back into bed, and as she laid her head on the pillow, shock and revulsion swept over her again. *John* had done this. She was not, she thought, grown up enough to face it. It was as if she had been masquerading in a woman's clothes, play-acting at housekeeping, taking the lead in a game of wife and mother—and she thought, "I know why I can't let him know. Things could never be the same again. The children would feel trouble in the air. *John, you fool! That I should have to protect your children from your wickedness!*"

She was crying now, against her will and intention, in slow almost noiseless sobs. Tears ran across her cheeks and wet the frill of her night gown around her neck.

And if she had decided to accuse him? There could only be reproaches. Or could she ask him for a promise against another time? His promise! Her heart stopped for a moment, as it had there at the very first. She had asked him for one promise, and he had granted it. She had told him—how sure she had been!—that she would never ask another. Did she wish now that she had waited? No! Better this, if there must be something. But suddenly she knew, far more certainly knew than if she had ever heard him plead it as an excuse—as he would not have done, never, never—that for him it had been escape from himself, to non-identity, only less desperate than the ultimate turning to the dark. If it must be this way or Kate's way, then let it be this way. He was alive, hers, and the father of her children, and he loved her when he—

If only she didn't have to see him for a day, a week, a month. Nor have to respond to his love-making. For it might be a long time before she could accept this betrayal and forget it.

Could anything ever be the same again?

To Anne, sobbing in the dark, feeling very sorry for herself, the commonplace words were heartbreaking. She thought, "You say them so often in a lifetime. When your first puppy dies, nothing will ever be the same. When you outgrow pantalettes, and let your frocks down to the ground, when your mother dies, when you pin your braids up, when your brother and all the boys go off to war, nothing will ever be the same. When your brother is killed. When you finish school. When you marry and have children, when you learn your husband has been unfaithful: there are only the same words, not ordinary ones for the important things, and portentous ones for such a time as this, when never again would everything be clear and shared and open. Lady Macbeth," she thought. "College, Mrs. Lowrey, Miss Tucker, 'Old Teapot.' And I didn't feel sorry for her, when he was disgraced."

She surrendered utterly then to her need for tears. She turned over on her face, put her hands above her head to grasp the spindles of the spool bed, her fingers circling them. Lying so, her face buried in the pillow, she wept like an abandoned child, her mind blank, her heart swollen with grief. Until her head was stuffed and her nose blocked and her throat swollen, she wept.

It was when she turned over again on her back, brushed her damp hair back from her nose, and lifted the pillow to feel for a clean handkerchief in place of her sodden one, that she heard the footsteps: young Johnny, in the room overhead, alighting from his high fourposter with a thump. But why? Then she remembered the new furnace, which she hadn't gotten used to, not enough to think about it ahead of time. The pipe went up in the corner of this room to the hot-air register in Johnny's room. He had heard her crying. With hardly a need to take thought, she struck a match, wincing from the flare of light against her eyes, tilted the chimney of the lamp, turned up the wick, lighted it, and replaced the chimney. She sat listening: he might go back to bed, he might come downstairs. It would depend on how much courage he had. But there would be a lamp in the upper hall, and once halfway down he could see the light from her transom. She listened with all her might. The padding footsteps crossed the room overhead to the door. With a single movement her covers were back, she was out of bed and over the floor to the secretary-bookcase. Thank heaven her father's old edition of Dickens was still where he had left it. She pulled *The Old Curiosity Shop* off the shelf and was back in bed, the covers up around her, before she heard—or felt, rather than heard—Johnny's steps on the carpeted stairs: he was dropping down slowly, one foot at a time. From the point where he could see the light from her room, he came more quickly, but he had given her time to find the chapter she wanted in the table of contents, and turn to the page. When she heard him breathing outside her door, she called out.

"Is that you, Son? Come in."

He opened the door and peered through the crack, then slipped in, shivering in his little boy's nightshirt.

"Now will you tell me why you're out of bed in the middle of the night, and why you're prowling around the house without a dressing gown?"

Her voice and words were severe, but she was smiling at him over a thick book open on her knee. He crossed to the bed and stood there.

"Mamma? I thought—Martha wouldn't let me come in and say good-night because you were sick, and I thought I heard you. Papa isn't in his room: I went in and felt the bed, so I thought I'd better see. Have you not got a pain?"

"Get up on the foot of the bed and wrap my peignoir around you before you catch your death. That's it. No, I haven't a pain, and I'm not sick, except I've caught a miserable cold. But if you thought you heard me crying, you did: I couldn't sleep, and I was reading, and it was about a little girl who died."

Johnny regarded her gravely, but he could not restrain the sigh of relief that escaped him.

"Mamma, it was only a story? I thought you must be terrible sick."

"'Only a story.' Let me read you a page." And to make her lie convincing, she began to read, "'For she was dead. There upon her little bed.'"

She kept on reading, although at the moment Little Nell's deathbed did not seem truly heartbreaking. She read through the paragraph that began "She was dead, and past all help, or need of it." Then she looked up for her son's comment.

"What was the matter with her that she died?"

"Matter! How like your father! As if storytellers had to think of things like that: in their books people die when they want them to, and no one asks what was the matter. It isn't so real as all that."

"It isn't true? It's just a made-up story? Then why do you cry?"

"That's one of the things no male, man or boy, will ever understand. I think it's because grown-up people get so used to not crying when they're hurt—you know how soon you have to begin to learn that? But women like to let go once in a while, and so they weep over imaginary death, in books." (And may God forgive me, she thought, looking up to meet the boy's grave regard.) "Tonight I had this awful cold, and my head was stopped up, and I couldn't breathe, and my throat was sore, too sore to swallow, and so it seemed being miserable over an imaginary trouble was just what I needed. But I'm sorry I wakened you: you must skip back to bed now." She stole a quick glance at her watch on the candle stand. One thirty! John might come in. "Dear me, Son, it's after midnight, you've never been up so late before. Skip along, and I'll make a bargain with you: I won't tell your father you came downstairs in the middle of the night, if you won't tell him I sat up and read when I was supposed to be asleep."

He slipped off the bed, discarded her peignoir; threw his arms around her neck in an impulsive gesture of affection, said, "I promise, Mamma," and went out, tiptoeing.

John, when he did come in not so very much later, peeked in on her, but she pretended to be asleep, so that it was not until after his breakfast, when he was ready to start on his morning calls, that he came to stand by her bed and found her awake.

"Anne? How do you feel?"

She blinked at him sleepily, ran her fingers around her chin and under her ears.

"Poorly. Don't scold me, John. My throat is sore. I think I'm going to have a quinsy."

"No doubt. Don't you always? Annie, love, I'm sorry."

And have quinsy she did. But however excruciating the pain, she welcomed the respite it gave her. Not that she had ever questioned her first decision: her impulsive play-acting for the boy had been instinctive. Yet she saw that for her, in this case, reason and will, instinct and compulsion, were one. By the time the quinsy had burst and she had recovered, she had determined to bury at the bottom of her mind anything "unpleasant" and never let it affect her children. She had worked and worried her mind around until she saw herself as the self-sacrificing mother. Then at noon, at lunch, the very first time she was up for a meal with her family, she was cross with Johnny. She should have realized that his high spirits were his natural reaction to the restoration of his normal world. But she was in no mood to make allowances. He sat on one side of the table; Belinda in her high chair was opposite, at Anne's right hand. The boy was playing peek-a-boo with the baby, bending to duck his head under the table. With his hands he clutched the table's edge; his fingers slipped; the cloth jerked, his plate, silverware, and a glass went over. His mother's hand came down flat, a sharp slap on the table beside her. "Johnny! No more of that! Leave the table at once."

He looked up at her, so suddenly woebegone that Anne's heart smote her. And the boy's father, at the end of the table, laughed.

"Forgive him, Anne: he's only too elated because you're up again. Run for a cloth, Son, to wipe up the water. Mamma didn't mean to sound so cross: she'll let you finish your meal if you sit up properly to the table. It's a sure sign, you know," and he winked at Johnny, "anyone as cross as that is pretty well recovered."

Anne said nothing. "But I feel cross," she thought, "just as cross as I sounded, and surely I have reason." She stopped short on that self-revelation. "I have been feeling so noble, and that's what comes of it, thinking I've a right to be as irritable as I please. What fun the saints and martyrs must have been to live with!" Amanda, she remembered, had once said something of the sort. Amanda had felt martyred, too, and had got over it. Anne managed a smile and an apologetic word for both male members of her family.

That night she returned to her own room for the first time. John went upstairs with her. There was no ringing of the night bell to save her; she would find out now whether she could conceal her knowledge, her pain, her bitterness. She lay in the dark, John's head on her shoulder, his hand on her breast, and tried to remember, to be the same as on other nights; she pretended. There was a strange shadowy impression in her mind of a third person mingling in their embrace. She exorcised the horrid ghost. If she shivered a little—

"You know," she said suddenly, "I think I wish you would grow a beard, after all. I've changed my mind."

John stiffened, then began to laugh, relaxed, and rolled over on his back, quaking with mirth.

"Dear Mrs. Shandy! Yes, I wound the clock."

"What are you talking about?"

"Nothing—never mind—but why, my darling, do you think of beards just now?"

"Why not? I was just wondering how it would feel." And in her own mind, "Everything would be so different, then—easier, maybe." But she began to laugh, too, and John teased her a little longer before he came back to her arms; and by then she was ready and did not have to pretend. And when he was lying asleep beside her, she was, as she thought, completely honest with herself at last. "Nothing will ever be quite the same as it was, but he'll never know because, God help me, I could not live if he were not to love me still." For she had never doubted that he loved her, and would, unless she made it impossible.

As for the library, the official opening was held on the appointed evening, after the subscribers met first in the Assembly Room in the Court House, and elected a board: Mrs. Ballard, Mrs. Ludwig Rausch, the Reverend Mr. Heitzel, Mr. Douglas Gardiner, and young Mr. Voorhees-in-the-bank. (Waynesboro always spoke of him so: he was not a native but "from away," and had so far not impinged strongly enough on the town's consciousness not to need identifying.) The reception in the library proper, where the books were not in order on their shelves, was a great success, with an overcoming of obstacles in the serving of tea and coffee that only women would understand, and a final charging-out of books on the new cards that left the shelves almost bare.

Anne bore home her copy of Turgenev with all the pride of accomplishment. Of course, as she told herself, if she hadn't thought of a library, someone else would have; but it was pleasant, and it helped her forget a little that incurable, aching bruise to think that she had seen her idea so successfully fulfilled.

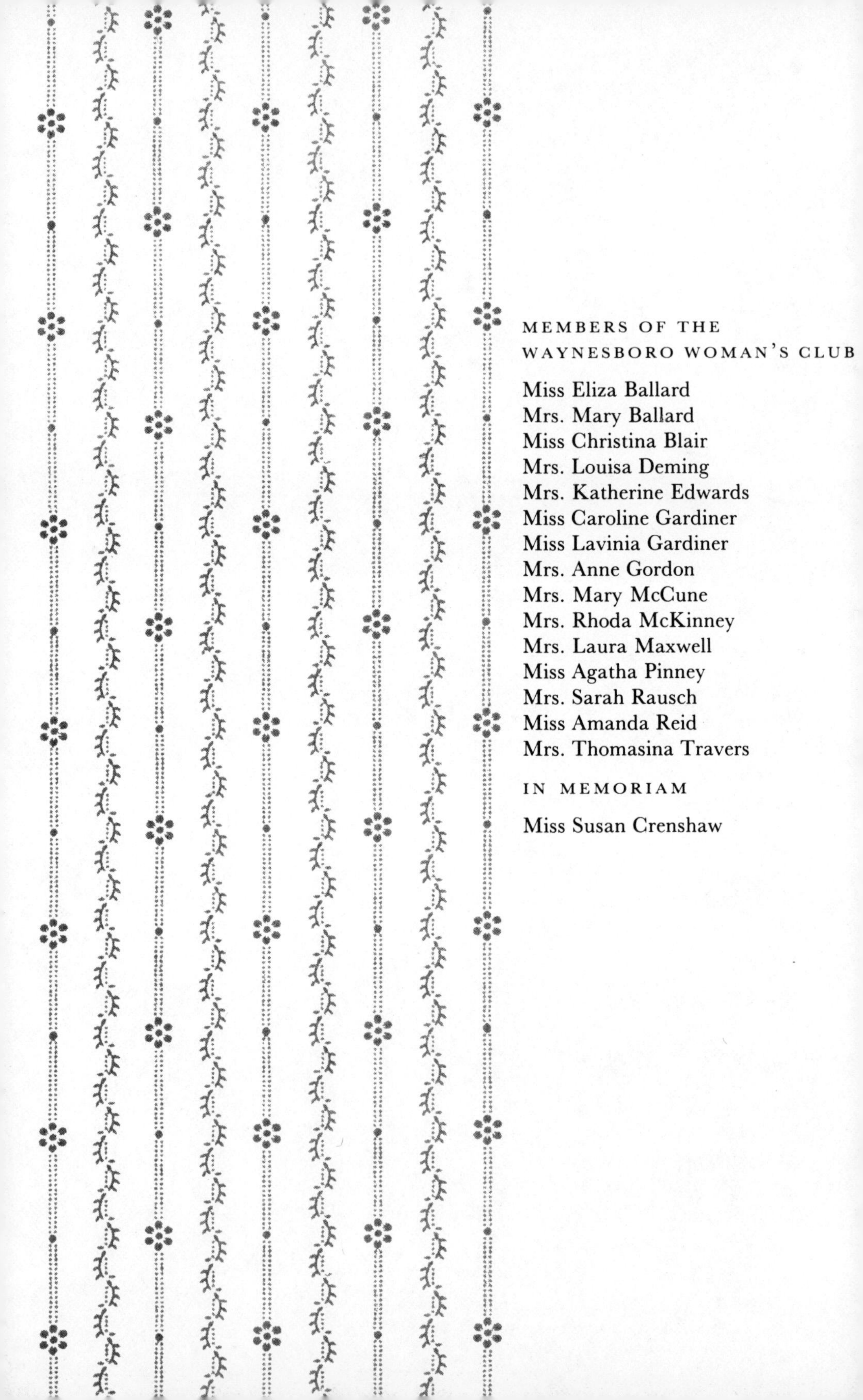

MEMBERS OF THE
WAYNESBORO WOMAN'S CLUB

Miss Eliza Ballard
Mrs. Mary Ballard
Miss Christina Blair
Mrs. Louisa Deming
Mrs. Katherine Edwards
Miss Caroline Gardiner
Miss Lavinia Gardiner
Mrs. Anne Gordon
Mrs. Mary McCune
Mrs. Rhoda McKinney
Mrs. Laura Maxwell
Miss Agatha Pinney
Mrs. Sarah Rausch
Miss Amanda Reid
Mrs. Thomasina Travers

IN MEMORIAM

Miss Susan Crenshaw

❋ 1875–1876 ❋

"A year of change for Waynesboro and the Woman's Club. . . ."

Change seems to come inevitably and naturally, as if man's finger need not be put to the wheel, and after any event there is a question as to whether the wheel would not have turned anyway, or was not turning already. But one whose finger has been lifted to pull against the dead weight of inertia feels responsible, rightly or wrongly, for what comes.

On an afternoon in early November in 1875, four of the younger members of the Woman's Club met at Sally Rausch's to work on costumes for the Christmas party. Sally had decided that this year they should present scenes from Shakespeare: the balcony scene from *Romeo and Juliet*, the court scene from *The Merchant of Venice*, and a couple of others equally familiar. This would be Sally's, and the Club's, first venture into actual dramatics. Those who knew her plans had not protested; since she would provide the party, she had a right to choose the form of entertainment to be offered the gentlemen. Or perhaps they agreed with her when she said, "Those scenes are positively banal. No one could think of them as theatre." They all knew that the strictest of the Reformed Presbyterians considered any celebration of Christmas to be popish. They would decline Sally's invitation to the Club's party and dinner at her house.

The four in Sally's sitting room that afternoon had known each other all their lives. It was a Wednesday, chosen so that Kitty Lowrey could come, and she and Sally sat close to the hearth with their feet on the fender, regardless of the possibility of scorching their soles. Thomasina Ballard Travers, more ladylike, sat beside them in an armless rocker, with yards of purple paper muslin billowing over her lap, her long, plain, gentle face blank with concentration as she labored awkwardly to attach skirt and bodice. Anne Gordon was behind them, at the sewing machine that Sally had dragged into the sitting room, its rollers squeaking under her vigorous handling.

The talk was comfortable, desultory, dying away under the clatter of the sewing machine, rising again to cover the small occasions of their Waynesboro days. Sometimes they were all silent, and then they could hear from upstairs the squeak of Cassie's rocking chair and the voices of the two babies, little Belinda Gordon—"Binney" as she had first pronounced her name—and Charles Rausch. The older children were out-of-doors. The choice of Wednesday for the women's afternoon together meant that the children would be underfoot; Miss Pinney's infant school, along with the college, had its half-holiday then. Fortunately a light snow had fallen, and Johnny Gordon and Elsa and even three-year-old Ernest Rausch, round as a butterball in his winter wraps, had been turned out to make the most of it. The number of voices audible to those in the house suggested that the children of the neighborhood had all gathered inside the Rausch fences. But the clamor was remote and happy, and the girls were not troubled by it as they skipped, a sentence here, a sentence there, from Club meetings and programs to the increasing patronage of the Subscription Library; from politics local and national back again to the library desk and whatever amusing encounter any one of them had had there with a subscriber. Anne had little to say. Sally thought she was not even listening, since the sewing machine had no regard for the conversation, but often drowned it out. Anne was sewing as if her life depended on it, something remote in her bent profile, her wide expressive mouth stretched into a line of effort. When she turned her head once, so that the light from the windows behind her fell across her cheek, the bone below her temple caught a highlight, leaving shadows in the hollows above and below. Anne's bones had never been visible before: that attack of quinsy, Sally concluded, had pulled her down more than it had seemed at the time. At that moment Anne's attention was caught by a remark as to the havoc created among the library cards by an afternoon of Mrs. McCune's presiding at the desk. "I'd rather take her place when she's sick," Kitty said, "than straighten up after her. And goodness knows, I have little enough free time, without giving it all to the library."

"Poor Mrs. McCune! I feel sorry for her."

"She's pathetic," Sally said briskly, "but useless. You weren't any more pleased than I was to have her in the Club."

"I know." Once, Anne thought, she had been young enough to be contemptuous of people like Mrs. McCune. Suddenly, it seemed, she had grown older than Sally: now she could be sorry for these fumblers. For of course, inside, to themselves, they were not inept, they were only unhappy, without knowing why, and mute endurers of daily life.

"It's because she's taken such a shine to you," Sally went on. "She rubs against you like a stray cat. You're too softhearted."

Sally might never be bruised enough by life to learn to feel sorry for the Mrs. McCunes of this world. "Maybe," Anne admitted. "But even so I feel responsible, somehow." She might never have noticed Mrs. McCune, or really been aware of her, had she not so often found her after or before Club meetings, drooping against the wall near a parlor door, waiting for someone to go through it with her. "But don't you see how sad it is—that she should have to look to me for what she wants? I don't really know her."

"What do you think she wants?"

"Reassurance, I should think, that she counts as a person. Oh, I know, she isn't equal to anything that is expected of her in a managing, practical sort of way as a minister's wife—even with her family, they say."

"Then let her husband's parishioners reassure her."

"But, Sally, she's an intelligent woman: her Club papers are good. And she hasn't a chance in the world to be a *person.* It must be awful: to have what you aren't equal to thrust upon you, and no chance at all to do what you are equal to. And to be married to the Reverend Mr. McCune—" Anne shuddered. "And all those children. Five, isn't it? It's queer about ministers: you wouldn't think they would be so—so—" She remembered the unmarried Kitty, and paused on a suspended breath.

"Uxorious is the word you want," Kitty said obligingly. Sally laughed, Thomasina blushed, and Anne turned the wheel of the sewing machine with the palm of her hand and began to pedal furiously.

Presently Sally remarked that Ludwig thought Governor Haynes might be nominated by the Republicans at their '76 convention, since his election for the third time as governor that fall on a hard-money platform and in a Democratic year had given him prestige in the East. Thomasina, glad to have the subject changed, more accustomed to talking politics than personalities, took up the subject. If Governor Hayes was nominated, her father would feel able to support the regular ticket: he was an old acquaintance of the Governor, and had faith in his integrity. She smiled placatingly at Sally: she longed to have her father restored to the esteem of Republican Waynesboro. And even her mother, she added as an afterthought, expected to attend the Temperance Party's convention, rejoicing that Mrs. Hayes's views on temperance were so well-known. "And of course Mama will attend the Woman's Suffrage Convention."

"Of course," Sally agreed politely. "How many parties does your mother belong to?"

They all laughed, even Thomasina. The sewing machine was stilled for a moment while Anne straightened and turned her material. In the silence the voices of the children outside became more distinctly audible. The lot of them, with Ernest on the sled, trailed around the side of the house, past the floor-length windows. Johnny Gordon was pulling.

"Get off the sled, Ernie," he ordered. "It's Shaney's turn."

"Who's 'Shaney'?" Kitty said.

"It's Elsa," Sally said. "Johnny calls her that. He picked it up from Ludwig: 'schöne Elsa.' 'Shaney' is as close as he can come. Awful, isn't it? Fortunately she won't let anyone else call her that, not even Ernest. Listen."

The young women cocked their heads. A piping voice shrilled, "Shaney!

Shaney!"—and the retort came at once: "Schrecklicher Knabe! Sei stille! Gebrauche nicht den Namen!"

Thomasina smiled. "What an advantage your children have, growing up bilingual. When I think how I struggled over German!"

"Elsa adores her father: she will learn anything from him. With anyone else she uses German for what wouldn't sound polite in English."

Kitty had risen with Romeo's cloak over her arm and gone to the window to watch the children. She still moved with the rangy free gracelessness of the tomboy she had been, but Sally, watching her, decided that she was looking older: thin and distinctly edgy. "Sizing up all your friends," Sally scolded herself, dropping her eyes to the sewing in her lap. "But just the same," she went on thinking, "it's a pity Kitty's engagement to Sheldon Edwards has gone on for almost three years."

When Kitty returned to her chair and resumed her sewing without a word, Sally asked, "Are you getting tired sitting still? We'll have coffee and cake presently, but Amanda promised to drop in and judge the costumes."

"It wasn't that. It's just that I'm afraid I was breaking the tenth commandment. Envying you and Anne your children." Her thin fair-skinned cheeks flushed quickly. Thomasina looked uncomfortable, and her face reddened slowly in sympathy or shock.

"Haven't you and Sheldon felt free to make any plans?" Sally had known Sheldon Edwards as long as she could remember: his mother was one of her mother's closest friends. His father and his father's brother-in-law, James Sheldon, owned the largest and most prosperous dry-goods store in town; he was a good match for Kitty. Sally had only a mild liking for one who seemed to her a milk-and-water youth. She could not understand his attachment to a blue stocking tomboy like Kitty, nor could she imagine wanting so much to be married to him that it gave her the fidgets. Sheldon was a tallish but very slender, narrow-faced young man with a good straight nose and rebelliously curly yellow hair. His air of neatness and precision made the dry-goods store seem a suitable place for him. The town had been surprised at his coming back after his graduation from Oberlin, instead of going on to larger fields to make his fortune. He seemed an odd match for a Lowrey, though: he was too much like his mother, who was what Sally called "nasty-nice." The Edwardses were well-to-do, of course, but a lifetime of poverty would never make wealth seem of first importance to a Lowrey. That was not what Kitty wanted.

"How can we make plans?" she said now. "I should give him up. But Sheldon is so patient, and—" Smiling crookedly at the needle in her hand, she looked for a moment the mischievous wretch she had been at sixteen. "I'll be doggoned if I'm going to be that noble."

"Kitty," Thomasina protested.

"Really, Thomasina, for one of a family of emancipated women, you are the most conventional—let her swear if she likes. Kitty, surely your father can get someone else to teach Latin in your place."

"He'd have to pay anyone else." She lifted her head from her hemming and looked at her friends. Anne, having finished her last seam, snapped the thread, bundled the full skirt into her lap, and turned her chair to face the others. "Do you mean to say," Kitty went on, "you really don't know how bad things are?" She paused a moment, thinking of some way to tell them, some little thing that would be proof. "Why, we've even had to stop taking the *Torchlight.* We are still feeding our student boarders, but the family lives mostly on bread and honey, or bread and sorghum. Mamma gives us our choice."

They all laughed: how could they not, knowing Mrs. Lowrey as they did? But their laughter was subdued. Kitty's friends understood only too well. "Depression" had become settled hard times, a condition to be accepted and adjusted to. Everyone was pinched; shortage of money was taken for granted, but they had not known the school had slipped downhill so far.

Anne said sadly, "It doesn't seem so long ago." They knew what she meant: not so long since they had been girls in school, and the Waynesboro Female College had been a flourishing and respected institution.

"It's too bad," Sally said, with the briskness that goes with concluding one aspect of a subject in order to turn to another. "It used to be such a good school. I can't think of anyone I'd rather rent this house to than you and Sheldon. Ludwig and I are moving in with Papa and Mamma after Christmas." Then, in answer to exclamation and question she explained. "Ludwig says it is the only thing to do: I hate it on his account and the children's: here they can make all the rumpus they like and not bother anyone. But Mamma's cataracts have got so bad she can barely see to get around. Her heart isn't good, either, so Papa isn't very comfortable about her being alone every day with just the servants. Then Ludwig has had to spend so much time traveling these last few years, looking for orders for the mill, and he says he'll be easier in his mind if we're up there at Papa's, instead of here, with no one but Cassie."

"You aren't going to sell?"

"No. Who has money to buy these days? Besides, we might want to come back sometime, who knows? When the children have grown up and married and we're all alone." She laughed, as if at the absurdity of believing that time could really play such a trick. "Ludwig is sentimental, anyway, and we started housekeeping here, and have been happy. It's a pleasant house, Kitty—big enough, and room for children upstairs. I thought you and Sheldon might not mind renting, just at first."

"I wouldn't. I'd rent a shack for a home with him. But it's hopeless. And the tantalizing thing is that Papa had a good offer from the Methodist Church this fall. They're starting a new Female Seminary in Kansas somewhere—Drury, Kansas. They wanted him to be principal, and offered to pay him a salary. But of course he couldn't take it."

"Why ever not?"

Kitty was silent a moment. She understood how her father had been reluctant to give up what he had created and become a sort of hired man, however superior. But it had not been that which had made the change impossible.

"The College buildings are mortgaged. Didn't you know? No, I suppose bankers don't tell whose mortgages they hold, or they'd never do any business. There's something so shameful about a mortgage."

"Kitty, that's nonsense. It's a sensible way to raise money." Sally rejected any notion that the bank conducted a shameful business.

"Maybe. But it gives one the same feeling as going in a pawnbroker's shop. Not that I ever have."

They laughed again. Anne said, "You've been reading too many novels. You know: 'Your fair daughter's hand, or I'll foreclose!'"

"The bank gets its interest, doesn't it? Look, Kitty, the depression will be over some day. Papa really thinks we're on the way out of it now. But lots of people have been in trouble since '73."

"It isn't so much the depression. The College is being pinched to death between the public high schools and the new women's colleges. No, Papa will never be able to pay off the loan, and he's too conscientious to walk off and leave the buildings for the bank to take over; what would it do with them? The Lowreys will go on, scraping and pinching to make the interest payments on the mortgage."

"Why doesn't he sell them?" This was Thomasina. Sally and Anne stared at her, taken aback by such innocence of the real world. Kitty replied bitterly, "To whom and for what? There'll never be another girls' school here."

"No. But Kitty, didn't you know the Reformed Presbyterian Theological Seminary in Aberdeen, Pennsylvania, is to be merged with this one? Here, in Waynesboro? I know it hasn't been in the paper, but you must have heard: the R.P.'s are not very pleased about it, some of them, because the Aberdeen Seminary is New Side, and the church here has always been Old Side. It was Amanda who told me: her mother is upset because she's afraid some other arrangement will be made for boarding the students. At any rate, they have to find larger buildings for the combined seminary. Ask Amanda when she comes."

Kitty sighed ruefully. "Amanda's given me up. She's disappointed in me because I'm not going to devote my life to learning and scholarship and teaching; she acts as if I had betrayed her and Oberlin both."

"I know. Amanda's funny," Thomasina said softly. "But she'll forgive you in time. She has me, almost." She joined the others in laughing at the absurdity of it, but added, "It's more comfortable to be forgiven, even if you haven't done anything wrong."

When Amanda came in after school, she confirmed what Thomasina had said. The Reformed Presbyterians, with one seminary in Pittsburgh, had decided they did not need a second one in Pennsylvania. Dr. MacKenzie, president of the Waynesboro Seminary, wanted to retire when the school year ended; the church would bring the Aberdeen seminary—president, faculty, and students—to Waynesboro. If they could find suitable buildings, the move would be made in the summer vacation; if they had to build, it would not be so soon. The present location of the Waynesboro Seminary was out of the question: the old house they used for a school building would be inadequate, and there was no dormitory: the boys roomed out among the members of the congregation. "And I hope," Amanda said, "that the new seminary will board the students, too. I am tired of falling over theologues in our house."

"Your mother would never be satisfied doing nothing," Thomasina protested.

"And so I must let her go on being happy in her own peculiar way? I suppose so." Amanda, who never spoke of her personal life, unless it was to Thomasina, immediately regretted her uncharacteristic outburst, and turned the company's attention to the costumes she was to criticize. Sally presently brought the coffee and cakes she had promised. Kitty, not knowing what she could do with the information she had acquired, elicited from her friends vows of silence in regard to the affairs of the Female College. "I'd be an old maid all my life," she said fiercely, "rather than hurt Papa, and he would be worse than hurt if he knew I'd told it around that the College is bankrupt."

They swore solemnly to hold their tongues, but Kitty, though still unmarried, suspected that most things got told, sooner or later, on the connubial pillow. If she were to use her knowledge, she must use it at once. She could tell her father, and he would go, hat in hand, to the Reformed Presbyterians. But it would be humiliating, an open admission of failure. If an offer were to come from the church, on the other hand, his pride might be saved. She spent most of a wakeful night trying to think how she might bring it about without her hand being seen in it. It had not occcurred to her to say anything to her mother or sister. Even if they did not almost automatically react with antagonism to anything she suggested, they would be sure to do so if it were a question of giving up the school. They did not want to do that, nor to leave Waynesboro; they were determined optimists: in another year, things would be better. And Kitty could understand their attitude: the Methodist Church had not offered them positions in the new school in Kansas, as teachers or housekeepers. They would have nothing there to manage, or mismanage. Kitty gritted her teeth in the dark, staring into it from her pillow. If she were to say anything to her father, he would consult his wife. It was hopeless, unless the Reformed Presbyterians—her circling thoughts came back to that—were to approach him with an offer. She did not know any R.P.'s well except those in the Club, and Amanda's mother. She could not think of anyone more unsuitable as an emissary than Mrs. Reid. The bank—Mr. Cochran—might make suggestions to her father, but she could not go to him: she imagined herself, with sinking heart, her knees shaking, outside the grilled teller's window, asking to see the bank president. But Judge Ballard—since Thomasina had thought the merger plans were common knowledge, her father must be aware of them. She could go to him: there would be no grilled window, only Eliza Ballard in the other office, and she was not afraid of Eliza Ballard; she knew her too well. That comforting thought was enough to allow her to relax and go to sleep: she would see him in the morning.

If Eliza, presiding behind the barrier in the anteroom of the Ballard, Gardiner, and Merrill offices, was surprised when Kitty came in and inquired for the Judge, in a business-like manner oddly at variance with her wind-blown shivery look, she gave no sign of it, but announced, "Miss Kitty Lowrey to see you," at the door of her father's office, and motioned Kitty into his private room.

The Judge seemed remote and surprisingly strange, sitting straight, with an air of interrogation, in his chair at the far side of a huge square table, felt-covered and paper-strewn, banked with drawers to the right of the kneehole on all four sides. Kitty stopped at the side opposite him and stood for a minute, not really looking at, but taking in, the room: table and glass-doored bookcases full of somber black-bound volumes; two windows overlooking the square, and between them an old velveteen-covered sofa, with springs bulging here and sagging there, and between the furniture so little floor space that a path was well-worn in the grosgrain carpet, around the table, to the windows, as if lawyers had need to keep their eyes on the Court House. She gave herself a moment longer by looking out those windows, a bleak view in the winter: leafless trees, dead grass, time-blackened bricks. Kitty turned to face Judge Ballard, her knees shaking after all: in his own office the Judge was more awe-inspiring than she had expected.

He had risen on her entrance. With a breath-taking lurch of her heart, she settled into the hard chair that he indicated, opposite him, across the vast expanse of desk.

"This is a consultation, is it? You have come for advice?" He smiled at her, a little as though she were still in pigtails.

"I don't really suppose it's a lawyer I need, but I didn't know where else to go." She smiled at the ineptitude of her opening, but continued with characteristic directness, "Are you complimented when people can't think of anyone else to go to in a quandary?"

He laughed briefly, and one of his heavy overhanging eyebrows climbed to a diabolical slant. "Little Kitty Lowrey! You're too young for quandaries."

"It's about Papa, and the school." She explained the situation to him: the financial state of the Female College, the Drury, Kansas, offer to her father, the possibility that the buildings might be what the Reformed Presbyterians were looking for. "If you could help, I might be able to pay you after—after—"

"I see. Your quandary is how to bring together the parties concerned. I understand. Never mind about paying after. If I can be of assistance to you, I shall be helping others at the same time. The Reformed Presbyterians, I believe, are most anxious not to have to build. I will broach the matter to Mr. Cochran and to Dr. MacKenzie. And if there should be a legal fee due, it would be due from one of them." His brows were straight now, bent frowningly upon a flushed and uneasy Kitty. Judge Ballard did look frighteningly severe, but if you weren't distracted by the eyebrows, you could see how kind his eyes were; and if he was pompous, that was just his way. Kitty blushed at finding the derogatory adjective in her mind.

"It is good of you to take the trouble." She thanked him, then, with dignity and without confusion. "But there's just one more thing: if anything comes of it, would Papa need to know I came to you? His pride would not be so hurt if he thought the offer, if there is an offer, came from the Reformed Presbyterians."

"No one need know you've been to me. I will drop in at the bank and see Mr. Cochran first; it will be through him that the Synod will learn that an offer for the Female College buildings might not be refused."

He came around his table to shake hands with her, and when she had gone returned to his chair and dropped into it so heavily it creaked. "These young people," he thought, "putting change in motion." They hadn't any conception, of course, of what it would mean to a man, growing old, to acknowledge his life work a failure—to start again in raw new country, among strangers, as if he were young and had energy to spare when really all the energy one had was just enough to go through the same old motions, almost automatically.

Neither banks nor church bodies move rapidly as a rule, but not long after the first of the year, Dr. MacKenzie, Mr. Cochran, and a stranger called at the Lowreys' one evening to see the professor on business. Mrs. Tyler had answered the door; while the four men were closeted in her father's study, she and Mrs. Lowrey, busy with the week's mending piled on the table between them, gave themselves over to conjecture. Kitty kept her head bent above the Virgil she was to teach the next day. She had heard of no consequences of her visit to Judge Ballard, and had been half-relieved, so uncertain was she that she had done right. Now she knew that something had come of it, after all these days. She made her breathing slow and steady, unexcited, but she dared not lift her eyes.

A long time passed before the three women heard voices in the hall, and the outer door closing. Professor Lowrey came to the sitting room threshold and stood there, one hand on the doorknob, his sparse hair tousled, a dazed look on his face. It was almost as though he were looking at a strange scene instead of a familiar one, Kitty thought, and suddenly he became strange to her, too: she saw not her father, but a small, shaken elderly man with a dazzled shifting glance and an unkempt ruffled beard.

"Well, Papa?" Mrs. Tyler, always impatient, was not one to feel the queerness of the atmosphere. She spoke sharply. "What did Mr. Cochran want at this time of night? Is he going to foreclose the mortgage and turn us out?"

"Melodrama!" He rolled the word out with a kind of indulgent contempt before he came close to stand beside the table and look at his womenfolk across it, over the lamp. "He cannot foreclose the mortgage before it is due, so long as the interest is paid. But he has been approached with an offer. The Reformed Presbyterians would like to buy our buildings for their consolidated seminary."

This announcement made little more impression on his wife and elder daughter than if he had said, "They would like to buy my right arm." It was only after he had continued silently to look at them that Ellen protested. "What is the matter, Papa? The bank can't force you to sell, can it? How could we get along without the buildings?"

"My dear girl!" The dazzled look was gone from his eyes: he surveyed Ellen with his bright bird-glance as if she were the only specimen in captivity of an incomprehensible species. He often looked at Ellen like that, and spoke to her in a way that made her younger than Kitty, in spite of her blowsy middle-age. "Have you no sense of reality at all? We have discussed our financial situation often enough, I should think."

"But I have always said you are unduly pessimistic. When times get better, the school will be successful again. And times will get better, when the specie resumption bill goes into effect."

Professor Lowrey picked up a book from a pile on the table and slapped it down again with a loud bang, one of his classroom tricks, used to recall wandering minds. Now, when they all looked at him in astonishment, he thrust his hands into his pockets, turned away from the table, revolved in a full circle until he stood once more looking down on them.

"I cannot understand why supposedly intelligent females should share in the assumption so unhappily prevalent that the resumption of specie payments—in another four years, mind you—will cure every citizen's ills. It will not cure ours, Ellen, you may be confident. Our day here is past. Another few years and all young ladies in this part of the country will be going to high school and college with their brothers. Only where there are as yet no public schools worthy the name is there a place for a Female College."

Mrs. Lowrey took off her spectacles that she might see her husband better. "Did you ever write a definite answer to the Methodist Board of Education, declining their offer of that school in Kansas?" Mrs. Lowrey might be erratic, but she was quick enough to understand her husband.

He answered her more gently than he had spoken before. "No, I haven't. I asked to be allowed to defer my decision until after the beginning of our winter term. In spite of your hopes and Ellen's, I feared that I might be forced to accept it. I do not know why they offered it to me, there must be younger men; but perhaps experience and the fact that there is no likelihood of any schoolgirl thinking of me foolishly—At any rate, I have been fortunate enough to be honored by the church."

The truth sank in. Ellen said, "You mean that you have agreed to sell the school? Actually sell?"

"I have agreed to sell the buildings for the mortgage and something above that. Mr. Cochran has persuaded the Reformed Presbyterians to make him an offer, provided the buildings are in good condition."

"But what is to become of us?"

"Your mother, who is no longer young but has spirit enough for two, will come with me to Kansas. I do not need to ask her. Kitty will at last be free to marry. As for you, you are free to make your own choice. Return to your husband, if he will have you for the children's sake, after all this time. Or find yourself some sort of occupation, if you cannot be satisfied as a housewife. Of course, as long as I have a roof to offer you—you and your children—I shall be glad."

"Oh, no Papa!" Kitty exclaimed. "Don't let her."

Ellen rose, dropping the sheet she had been patching from her lap to the floor, where it lay about her in a dramatic white heap. Over its folds she glared at Kitty. "What a noble expression of gratitude! I might have known. After giving the best years of my life to helping my parents and the school and the town, who cares? I can go or stay."

"You talk like a bad novel." And that was strange because Ellen didn't read bad novels. Was it possible the bad novelists knew that people like Ellen did talk that way? Kitty was exhilarated by the chance, now that she would no longer have to live with her, to give Ellen a piece of her mind. "Gratitude! Neither the town nor the school asked you to drop your own concerns and interfere with theirs, and Papa and Mamma never asked you to desert your husband and descend on them with a locust horde."

Mrs. Lowrey reached over and tapped Kitty sharply on the top of her head with a thimbled finger. And Kitty, startled, was carried back to her childhood so swiftly that she broke off a choked laugh.

"Hush, both of you! Your father has not even had a chance to tell us who was here, what they offered." Mrs. Lowrey turned to her husband. "Was it a fair offer?"

"The stranger was a Dr. Armstrong, chairman of the committee appointed by the General Assembly to make plans for the merger. He was empowered to make what Mr. Cochran considers a liberal offer." Professor Lowrey cleared his throat. "It will cover the mortgage, pay our debts, and leave us with a small sum for our old age. Surely you agree with me that it is better to sell on those terms than to struggle on to bankruptcy. I accepted the offer." He turned to the door. They heard him go down the hall to the study.

The women were silent for a moment after he had gone. Mrs. Tyler spoke first. "Are the boys in, Mamma, do you know? Will you check on them, Kitty? I think I shall retire if you will excuse me. This has been a blow to me. An hour of prayer over my own decision—"

Kitty uttered a rude wordless exclamation. "How do you know the girls are in?"

While Mrs. Tyler had been serving as matron of the dormitory, her girls had been growing up; they lived with her there in rooms in the half-empty building. When she spent an evening at her mother's or elsewhere, she depended on them not only to be within doors themselves at the prescribed time but to report any illegal goings and comings among the boarders. But the boys slept in third-floor bedrooms at the Lowreys'.

"I can trust the girls. But I can't take care of the dormitory and keep an eye on the boys."

"A dilemma," Kitty mocked. "To suggest that I check on them is to admit that you can't trust them."

"Kitty, that's enough. Remember that Ellen has been an unpaid teacher and matron for years now; we do owe her our gratitude."

Kitty wanted to remind her mother that food and clothing for six people over a period of years was no negligible payment, but that would be going too far: let Ellen not be given the chance to say, "So you begrudge us the food we eat." But she did protest when Mrs. Lowrey gathered up the sewing from her lap and laid it on the table with some remark about seeing whether the boys were in their beds.

"Oh, Mamma! Not up all those stairs tonight."

Mrs. Lowrey, paying no attention, turned to the door. Ellen, perhaps ashamed, rose and joined her, and the two women went out together. Kitty waited until she heard them overhead, then slipped down the hall to her father's study and opened the door a crack. Professor Lowrey was sitting low in his old leather-covered easy chair, slumped down, chin on chest, so that his beard was spread thinly over his string tie, and his untidy white hair lay like feathers against the cracked leather chairback.

"Papa, may I come in for a moment?"

She went to stand before him on the hearth. He did not lift his head, but looked up at her over his spectacles, through the tufts of his straggling eyebrows.

"Papa, I know it will be an awful wrench, leaving Waynesboro. Shall you mind dreadfully?"

"My dear child, the offer was a godsend. Providence intervened to save us. Or—you show all the symptoms of an uneasy conscience—did you give Providence a nudge?" He twinkled at her obliquely. "Somehow the idea seems to have got around to the proper places that we might be willing to sell. Do you feel the need to reassure yourself? Wish me to tell you that I am not inconsolable?" She said nothing, too taken aback. She had forgotten his years of experience at reading girls' minds. He smiled at her and continued. "Of course it is a wrench. I came here as a young man; I founded this school and built it up. I expected to leave it after me, a permanent institution. I should have known better: no one can foresee how long an institution will be of service in a changing world. I was wrong in my expectation, that is all. I can be philosophical about it; the school to which I devoted my life has become an obstacle."

"But, Papa—"

"Oh, I know. My lifework has been the teaching I have done; my memorial the minds I have formed." His tone was dry, almost ironic. "But it is a mortal weakness to desire to leave some tangible evidence of one's having lived. Besides one's womenfolk. However, you will be happy here, and Ellen will always be sure that she is useful and needed wherever she goes. It will be hard for your mother to go to a new place, at her age. But do not worry."

"About Mamma? Certainly not. She'll be in her element, once she's there. It's you." She wanted to say, "Don't be too lonely," but the words stuck in her throat. He wouldn't be lonely teaching, no more lonely than he had always been. But somehow, for some reason, although she had been so earnest to save his pride, she had not seen him until now as a small, pitiable old man.

"I only rejoice that the church thinks I am still able to undertake the establishing of a new school at my age. No, Kitty, you may marry your young man with a light heart." He looked away from her to the meager fire in the grate behind her. My one regret is that we shall be so far removed from you."

For a long moment they were silent. He stared into the fire; she looked down at him. She thought that now she knew when one was finally grown-up, nothing of the child remaining: it was when you felt sorry for your parents, who had once been as far beyond pity as God Himself. She wished for a moment she had never called on Judge Ballard. Then she moved to leave the room, and as she passed, laid her hand on the back of his chair.

"I'm sorry, Papa. I suppose these things have to happen to people's plans—their hopes."

"If life were not sometimes hard, we should have no muscles, mental or moral. I have lived long enough with the Greeks and the Bible to flatter myself that I make a fair Christian Stoic. 'Oh, wretched I, to whom this misfortune has happened! Nay, happy I, to whom, this being happened, I can continue without grief, neither wounded by that which is present, not in fear of that which is to come.'" He leaned forward and stretched a hand to the revolving bookcase beside his desk, pulled a book from its place and riffled its pages. "This is the passage: 'Upon all occasions of sorrow remember henceforth to make use of this dogma, that whatsoever it is that has happened unto thee, is in very deed no such thing of itself as a misfortune, but that to bear it generously, is certainly great happiness.'" He looked up at Kitty then, over his spectacles, beaming. There were tears on her cheeks. The light died from his eyes. "But what—?"

"Oh, Papa! Is life so hard, always, that we have to prepare ourselves to endure it by collecting these maxims, these—"

"'Maxims'! Marcus Aurelius? My dear Kitty! No, of course one doesn't 'collect maxims.' You've got hold of the wrong end of the stick. No. The Christian philosopher assimilates his Bible, his Plato, his Marcus Aurelius, and they make his character, as the food he eats makes his body. But that, too, is said here better than I can say it. Wait." He turned more pages. "'Such as thy thoughts and ordinary cogitations are, such will thy mind be in time. For the soul doth as it were receive its tincture from the imagination. Dye it therefore and thoroughly soak it with the assiduity of thy cogitations.'" When he looked up again, Kitty was smiling, after a fashion. "You don't know Marcus Aurelius? I have failed in my duty to you. Let me present you with this copy, duly inscribed."

He rose and went behind his desk. Kitty took up the lamp from the table by the door and carried it over to his side.

"But if it means so much to you, what will you do without it?"

"Read it in Greek, out of my other copy." He opened the worn book and wrote in it below his name on the flyleaf, "To Kitty Lowrey from her father, January 17, 1876." He peered over the desk for a blotter, and then took up the book to blow on the wet ink.

"Thank you, Papa. It will mean a lot to me because it means so much to you."

"Read it as you read your Bible, and then in time of trouble you won't have to go looking for maxims." But he chuckled as he handed it to her. "Not but what I comprehend the source of your error. The Christian philosopher who is also a teacher can, and does, draw on a formidable store of maxims to arm the young."

Several weeks passed before the sale of the school was completed, and news of the transaction was published in the *Torchlight*. After the last commencement of the Waynesboro Female College, in June, its campus and buildings would become the property of the Waynesboro-Aberdeen Reformed Presbyterian Theological Seminary. The Reverend Dr. Blair, president of the Aberdeen Seminary and president-to-be of the consolidated institution, would reside in the Lowrey house. The Seminary would convert to its own use both the College dormitory and classroom building, but, having no need for the one-room brick schoolhouse where for many years Miss Pinney had taught the primary day-school as an adjunct to the College, the Seminary officials agreed to rent it to her, so that she might continue, as an independent venture, her private school for girls and boys. The same edition of the *Torchlight* that carried the story of the sale contained Miss Pinney's modest advertisement announcing her intention and her terms. In the column of personal doings, comings and goings, and parties and meetings, was a paragraph on the welcome addition to Waynesboro church and social circles, not only of the Blairs, but of three professors, their wives, and children, who would come from Aberdeen to Waynesboro in the following autumn.

This last item meant that three men would soon be house-hunting. Little building had been done in Waynesboro during the hard times, and there were few houses for rent of respectable size and location. Sheldon Edwards went at once to call on Ludwig Rausch, and obtained the promise of the Linden Street cottage for Kitty and him on their return from their honeymoon. They would be married after Commencement, before the Lowreys went West.

The Rausches moved in with Sally's parents late in March, at housecleaning time, when everything was bound to be topsy-turvy anyway. Mr. Cochran had had his small study, behind the drawing room, turned into a bedroom for him and his wife, in spite of her voiced conviction that a bedchamber on the ground floor was out of the question: countrified, if not actually backwoodsy. The end of the butler's pantry, behind the new bedroom, was made into a bath and dressing room, with a tub the size of a sarcophagus, enclosed in mahogany, and a mahogany dressing table with a marble top and a mirror draped in dotted Swiss. The small side porch on which the study had opened was made into a conservatory, all glass, with ferns and vines and a tinkling wall fountain, so that when Mrs. Cochran could not go out, she would have at least the illusion of outdoors—light and fragrance. These arrangements made it possible to turn over to the Rausches the whole of the upstairs: a sitting room, where they could be alone together in the evenings, if they so desired, and bedrooms for them all. When they wanted to entertain houseguests, the children could be sent to the third floor, with Cassie to look after them. This contingency came naturally to mind, for Ludwig's family—mother, father, sister Minna, and Minna's rather new husband—had long since been invited to visit with Ludwig on their way to the Centennial Exposition in Philadelphia. Ludwig also wanted to see the Centennial, and proposed to join his family to his father's for a joint expedition, if his father would choose the right time for going: somewhere toward the end of the summer, if Sally could manage to get away.

Ludwig could not go earlier because he had been chosen to attend the Republican Convention in June as an alternate to Mr. Liddell, of Whitewater. This 1876 Convention would be his first, and he made no attempt to conceal his delight or to pretend to take his appointment as a matter of course. Sally lamented that she could not go with him, and he was torn between his conviction that a political convention was no place for a lady and his certainty that his wife would shine like a jewel among other wives of the Ohio delegation. Her going was out of the question: if she could leave her mother, there was still the year-old Charles, who could not be left at home or kept in a hotel room. (Sally was to say, long afterward, half with wry amusement, half with real regret, "For years after I was married, I missed everything. I always had a baby or had one coming.")

Like other Waynesboro Republicans, Ludwig believed that prosperity would return with the resumption of specie payment for greenbacks, but the Resumption Act passed by Congress was not to go into effect before January of 1879, so that the Treasury Department might have time to build up the gold reserve. But if the Democrats won the election in 1876, then the Resumption Act would be repealed. If the Republicans were successful in electing a president, thus making sure of the soundness of the country's finances, Ludwig intended to carry out his long-postponed plans to build a new mill on the river side of the yard; he could do it cheaply in these bad times, indeed, could use his own half-employed Negro hands as hod-carriers, perhaps even as bricklayers. He would then be ready for prosperity when it arrived in the wake of actual resumption. Politics had never been a mere game to Ludwig: now he was more seriously concerned than ever. Through all the horrors of the Whisky Ring exposure of the year before and the new scandals of this spring of 1876, he remained unshaken in his belief that for the country's good the Republicans must remain in power. He discussed the prospects with John Gordon one evening when he had dropped into the office on the chance of finding Dock free to play a game of chess.

Since the Hoffmanns had given up the beer parlor, Ludwig and Mr. Lichtenstein had fallen into the way of playing chess evenings in the middle of Dock's office suite. When he had no one waiting for him, Dock joined them: when he was busy, he conducted his patients to the consulting room by way of the hall, leaving the players undisturbed. On that particular evening there was no one there but Dock himself, sitting in his battered armchair with his feet on the fender of a burned-out-fire grate. He was a good person to talk politics with: Republican, of course, but disinterested enough to be cool as to the party's chances. And, as he told Ludwig, he didn't figure the chances were any too good. The Democrats had carried the off-year elections in '74; the House was Democratic and the Senate Republican, but by the narrowest margin. True, the Republicans had been helped some by the foolish belligerence of the "Confederate Brigadiers" sent back to Congress by the Democrats of reconstructed states, but hardly enough to outweigh Republican scandals. And the Republicans were torn by factionalism. The voters certainly wouldn't give Grant a third term; the Grant men—Conkling of New York, anyway—wouldn't have Blaine, Blaine wouldn't have Grant, and the Civil Service reformers wouldn't have anyone from either faction. They would probably want Bristow, the former Secretary of the Treasury, who had exposed the Whisky Ring. But neither Blaine nor Grant men would accept Bristow.

During this summary of what Ludwig knew better than John, Mr. Lichtenstein came in.

"Blaine," he grumbled at Ludwig. "You sons uff Forty-eighters, haf you forgotten your brinciples? Can you agcept Blaine wizout gagging?"

"No. But I'll accept him," Ludwig retorted, "rather than see the Democrats in power. But I don't think it will come to that. All these factions have nothing against Governor Hayes; he has a good chance of being nominated. Even Judge Ballard will come back into the party if he is. The Judge thinks there's a good chance, too—he isn't going off with Mrs. Ballard to the Prohibition party convention in May."

"Brohibition barty! Such foolishness. Ven zere are real issues for ze country to debate."

"You may get Hayes nominated," John contributed, "but elected? Who outside of Ohio has ever heard of him?"

"It will be a tough campaign. But he's a hard money man. That will help in the East."

So Ludwig went off to Cincinnati on the fourteenth of June, with Mr. Liddell, the district delegate, and with General Deming, Judge Ballard, and several other supporters of Governor Hayes who had tickets of admission to the hall.

While they were gone, Waynesboro had, to distract its attention from politics, the last Commencement at the Female College and Kitty Lowrey's wedding. For the Commencement everyone entitled to be present turned out, and many old students came back to hear Professor Lowrey for the last time, and to honor him and Mrs. Lowrey and bid them farewell. Like the Commencement of '68, this one was held on the campus under the trees, and after the al fresco luncheon, when students and Commencement guests had gone, the Lowreys' and Edwardses' friends gathered together under one of the maple trees, where Sheldon and the Methodist minister waited. Kitty and her father came to them down a path cleared before them by Miss Pinney's infant school, stretching ribbons and dropping out at intervals to hold them. Kitty and Sheldon were married standing side by side on the roots of the maple tree, with the minister backed against its trunk. It was an unconventional wedding, and not one that the Edwardses could really approve of. But as Kitty's friends knew, the whole weight of preparing for a formal wedding, either in the Lowreys' house or the church, would have fallen on her shoulders, and they applauded her good sense. Even Sally Rausch, who ordinarily preferred the formal, said to Anne when it was over and they had separated Johnny and Elsa from their ribbons and headed toward the receiving line, "After all, anything to get them married. Kitty was pining away before our eyes. She's been teaching for three years now. I was thinking a minute ago: remember how funny we thought it was, the year we graduated, for anyone as old as Miss Tucker to get married?"

"She was older than Kitty."

"Of course, years. But I suppose Kitty seems old to those children who were graduated this morning."

Kitty looked a mere girl, as she stood in line with her new husband and two sets of parents equally ill at ease, her thin face flushed and eager, her soft hair blowing loose from her veil in wisps across her forehead. Sheldon, beside her, was not only handsome, his blond hair irrepressibly curling, his narrow face fine almost to distinction, he was also unmistakably happy and proud. Sally was not sure that she had actually been a factor in the accomplishment of their marriage, simply through having a house to rent and saying so, but it was pleasant to think she had pulled a string, and by pulling it had set things in motion. Perhaps she was herself a little like the war-horse sniffing the battle from afar that she likened Ludwig to, on the evening the Gordons dined with the Rausches and the Cochrans a few days after the Convention had been adjourned.

They had duly congratulated Ludwig on the nomination of Governor Hayes.

"Now they've actually pulled it off," Sally said, "Ludwig is probably in politics for life."

"Be reasonable, can't you?" He grinned at his wife down the length of the table. "I had nothing to do with it. Not a single vote. Liddell was there for every session."

"There will be a next time."

"Perhaps in four years there won't be any important issue at stake. After all, it's only because I believe in certain things, for the good of the country, that I'm in politics, even ankle-deep."

John Gordon raised an eyebrow, opened his mouth to speak, then caught the eye of Mr. Cochran and closed it again. Mr. Cochran sat next to his wife so that he could help her, even if that help went only so far as serving her when the white-jacketed houseman brought the vegetable around, telling her what he was putting on her plate and unobtrusively cutting her meat. Now he smiled a little at John, shook his head, and said, "He believes it. Of course it is what all politicians say."

"But I'm not a politician."

Sally laughed and quoted the verse about the war-horse. "Ludwig, you know it was fun, and exciting—tell them."

"This time it was fun. Next time my man might not win. But what is there to tell? It was all in the papers."

"From the inside—let us have the true story." John had finished his meat course, having grown accustomed to cleaning a plate in a hurry. He leaned forward to listen.

" 'The inside'? Senator Sherman managed it for the Governor. Five ballots and nobody budged. Blaine's opponents were still opponents, even if his supporters did almost tear the place to pieces after Ingersoll's speech. He never could quite get a majority. But it's strange, the hold he has on his followers. They'd have gone down the aisle jumping through hoops if it would have helped."

"But wasn't it the same with Conkling and the other Grant men?" Anne smiled when they laughed at her. "Am I being naïve? I supposed it was a matter of personal loyalty. You chose the man you admired."

"And every delegate loved his candidate?" Ludwig chuckled. "Conkling told the New Yorkers what to do, and they did it, for fear of reprisals. Blaine's people do love him, but after five ballots his opponents were more stubborn and unbreakable than ever. The opposition couldn't see Blaine as a messiah, and the more they were told to love him, the less they felt like doing it and the more contemptuous they became of the poor fools who did, until finally they were willing to take anyone *but* him. And on each ballot the Governor picked up a few votes to add to Ohio's solid forty. Then there was a recess, and Senator Sherman moved around a bit."

" 'Skillful maneuvering', the papers called it," John interrupted. "What kind of bargains did he make?"

"I don't know. I know no principles were sacrificed: the Governor wouldn't have stood for it. I suppose the Senator saw all the Grant leaders and convinced them the General hadn't a chance against Blaine. It had to be someone the reform element would accept, too. Reformers and Grant men all thought better Hayes than Blaine!"

"Funny thing is, he'll do the Grant men more damage than Blaine would." John was amused by the obvious weaknesses of politicians.

"He's an honester man, you mean? Anyway, when the Convention reconvened and the sixth ballot was taken, they began the break to Hayes: Zack Chandler and Michigan first. The Blaine votes held, but when Conkling gave the nod and Arthur voted the New York delegation for Hayes, that was the end—the rest couldn't move fast enough, Morton and Indiana first."

"It must have been exciting," Anne said. "I wish I could have been there."

"It *was* exciting," Ludwig agreed. "You get carried away. But I'm not sure, actually, that Senator Sherman wouldn't make a better president than Hayes. He has a keener mind."

"My boy, haven't you learned yet?" His father-in-law was gently cynical. "When we get presidents with brains it's purely by accident. Who was ever selected for his brains? We choose them for other qualities, or because they can be elected."

"I know. It's a pity the Senator hasn't the General's magnetism and his gift for inspiring devotion. At any rate, after this election, you can count me a Sherman man. How about you, Dock?"

"Yes, I agree. I prefer brains, myself. Although sometimes the brainy man is too complex; he doesn't see things as clearly black and white as someone simpler may. He may hesitate, or seem to waver, when really he's thinking things through, studying all sides of a problem. But for General Sherman's sake, I'd like to see his brother president, even if he himself despises politics. The Senator's done more for the country, in his unspectacular way, more to get it back on an even keel, than anyone else since the war; he deserves to be president. However, Hayes wouldn't be bad; he's been a good governor. A little rigid, maybe. Narrow-minded."

"'Wouldn't'? Or 'won't'?"

"You still have to elect him."

"And that is not going to be easy." Mr. Cochran spoke dryly. "I can remember a time when you young men were boys, before the war, when no one took it for granted that the Democratic party could not win an election. In fact, they generally did. And don't forget, they took the House in '74. And I don't suppose Blaine's people are going to be very enthusiastic."

"Possibly not. But Blaine's a party man, first of all. He will campaign for Hayes."

"If times were not so hard." John sighed. "I see more of that than you do, I suppose. The farmers are in debt, and won't want to pay that debt in hard dollars. The working man isn't working. Tim O'Reilly has been with me how long now? And he besieges the railroad with his petitions to be taken back, but to no effect."

"We'll just have to work on it from now till November," Sally retorted. "Can't you see your answer in Ludwig's eye?"

But much happened that summer to keep the country's mind off the election: Indian wars and the massacre at Little Big Horn; the Centennial Exposition in Philadelphia; and on the Fourth, the whole country's celebration of its hundredth birthday, flag-bedraped and noisy with fireworks and oratory. Only toward the end of August did the noise of the campaign begin to sound over all and through all. Governor Hayes stayed close to home, but every other Republican, including the disappointed Blaine, traveled and made speeches for him. The campaign had begun with the moderates in control, Schurz at Hayes's elbow advising that it be fought out on the issues of reform and sound money. But the Democrats, gloating over Republican corruption, became so vindictive as to rouse in Republican bosoms a suspicion, which they still refused to acknowledge, that the war had settled nothing. By August the bloody shirt was waving: "A Democratic victory will bring the Rebellion into power," and, from the mouth of the Vice-Presidential candidate, "Let your ballots protect the work so effectually done by your bayonets at Gettysburg." A "United South victory" and Tilden's antiwar record became the campaign issues, and the mildest and most moderate citizens, remembering what the war had cost them, cheered on the fire-eaters.

In Waynesboro, in August and September, there were barbecues and picnics; jaunts in haywagons and carriages to all the villages in the county, and delegations came from nearby villages to march in the torchlight parade. No errant Republican was booed that night: Judge Ballard had not only returned to the ranks but was actually campaigning for Governor Hayes. The usual battle was fought in the West End when the parade tried to penetrate that Irish-Democratic territory, a "spontaneous" move not made without due precaution, which meant that every marcher carried a rock in his throwing hand, while his burning torch flared over his left shoulder. Later, when the Irish, or the Democrats (synonymous terms in Waynesboro), staged their parade, they climbed the hill to the East End, where their ranks were thrown into disorder and they were finally driven off by the Negroes. Heads were knocked and ribs bruised in both encounters, and two high tides of invasion were marked by a litter of broken top-hats, burned-out torches and torn transparencies. But it all came under the head of clean fun, and there were no hard feelings beyond the enduring antipathy that kept the two ends of town strangers and apart.

Early in September, Governor Hayes, on his way from Columbus to Cincinnati, stopped over between trains to spend a few hours with his old friend Judge Ballard. Fritz drove the Judge to the railroad station to meet the Governor and the two or three traveling with him; after Fritz had deposited the gentlemen at the steps beneath the Judge's porte-cochere, he drove off again to the ropewalk to leave a note the Governor had amiably agreed should be sent, inviting Ludwig Rausch to meet the guests. In 1876 no one (unless it were, still, Mrs. Ballard and Mrs. McKinney, behind closed doors) would have called Ludwig "ward heeler"; there was no question as to his ability to do more than any other man in the county for a Republican candidate. But Ludwig's talents were used mostly in caucus, in the choice of local candidates, for the county and district would go Republican as certainly as it had done in every election since 1856. The presidential nominee's visit to Waynesboro did not make history, not even a footnote to history. But for two children it became a memory of having been in the presence of greatness—greatness unrecognized of itself, but impressed upon them by their elders.

Ludwig, with other district leaders, had paid his respects to Governor Hayes in Columbus on the day he was formally notified of his nomination; there he had been one of hundreds. He appreciated the Judge's courtesy in offering to present him again as an individual, to be tied in the party leader's mind to a place and a district. He appreciated it so much that he wanted to extend the privilege to his family. It was impossible to take Sally, since she had not been invited, but he could take Elsa; she could sit in the carriage until and unless he called her. That would mean taking Reuben to drive. He went home in his buggy, left orders in the kitchen for the carriage, and hurried up the back stairs to clean off the tar and oil of his working day. He explained to Sally, who snatched Elsa when she came in from school. Johnny Gordon was with her; he almost always dallied in the Cochran yard on his way home. Elsa said "Johnny, too," not quite knowing what the excitement was about, but willing to submit if he were going with them. Sally said, "Why not?" and scrubbed him, too, and combed his hair.

"Your mother will worry," she said. "Tell your Uncle Ludwig to drive down that way and tell her where you are going."

They drove down Market Street in order to pass the Gordons', but there was no need to stop: Anne was weeding the asters at the end of the porch. They paused close to the curb, and Ludwig called to her that he was borrowing Johnny for a while; no sense in telling the neighborhood what for: neither the Governor nor the Judge would thank him if a crowd collected. As the carriage turned back to Main Street, he explained to the children that they were to stay with Reuben in the carriage unless he summoned them; they were to be on their best behavior, and they might have a chance to meet Governor Hayes. It was Reuben who explained to them, while they sat in the carriage beside Judge Ballard's Negro-boy hitching post, while the horses stamped the flies off and the harness jingled, just why they should sit in the carriage like a "little lady and gemmun" instead of coming up to sit with him and play at holding the reins.

"You see them gemmuns on the lawn?" Johnny and Elsa saw them, with less interest than they saw the gleaming rumps of Mr. Cochran's bays—a group of men in black frock coats in a circle of rocking chairs, in the shade of the Judge's maple trees. "One amongst um gwun be Pres'dent these hyah U-ninted States."

"President? General Grant is President. He was my Papa's general," Johnny informed Reuben.

"Ain' gwan be Pres'dent much longeh—he through."

Elsa and Johnny studied the group on the lawn with more interest, but it seemed a long time before Ludwig came and fetched them.

"Just long enough to you to make your manners," he told them. "I wanted you to have this to remember."

He had reckoned without Governor Hayes's affection for children. He presented Elsa, and she was taken up on a black broadcloth knee; Ludwig gave Johnny a special introduction: "The son of one of our Waynesboro doctors who served through the way as Assistant Surgeon of the Forty-sixth Ohio." Elsa was allowed to slip down, and the boy took her place, while she stood at the side of the chair within the embrace of a fatherly arm.

"Don't take them right away again. Can't they have some lemonade, too?" The gentlemen's tall empty glasses were standing in the grass, but there was lemonade in the pitcher and clean glasses on the tray that stood on the rustic table. Ludwig poured the lemonade; they drank it while over the rims of their glasses they studied the man who was "gwun be Pres'dent." Johnny was impressed by the beard, which was so much longer and more flowing than his father's, by the kindness of eye and voice, and more vaguely by the few minutes of rambling talk before Ludwig took them away, talk that circled away from him and Elsa, although he knew they had not been forgotten by the man who held them: it concerned itself with the Centennial Exposition, the Corliss engine, and Mr. Bell's talking telephone. Johnny, when he had been at the Exposition in the summer with his mother and father and Binny, had himself seen and marveled at the talking telephone. But he might not afterward have remembered anything about that afternoon on the Ballard lawn had he not announced that evening at his own dinner table that he had been to a party for Governor Hayes.

His mother was horrified at what she thought was a fib. "That's impossible, Johnny. Where did Uncle Ludwig take you?"

"Way out to the end of Main Street. And it was. Uncle Ludwig said it was."

"It's not impossible, Anne. Someone in my office this afternoon said that the Governor was at Judge Ballard's today."

"Oh, dear! With a dirty face and hands and your collar mussed."

"Aunt Sally took us in and washed us. And that's what they said, 'Governor Hayes.'" Johnny was taken aback, not only that the identity of his new acquaintance was questioned, but that the acquaintanceship itself should seem so preposterous. "Reuben said he's goin' to be President of the United States, but"—Johnny had the air of one granting that that would be too much to believe—"President Grant is President. I know that much."

"You know too much. President Grant has had his turn. What'd he look like, Son?"

"Beard down to here," Johnny said sulkily, indicating a spot in the neighborhood of his sash. "I sat on his lap. I could see plain."

"Of course it was Hayes. Who else? And he *is* going to be President, maybe, when President Grant steps down next year. It's something to remember all your life that you sat on his knee once."

And so, always when Johnny saw the name of President Hayes, he remembered a kind voice, a long beard, talk of Mr. Bell's telephone, all swimming together, rather, in the heat of a September afternoon, against a background of green and gold, dapples of sunshine falling between leaves, moving when the branches moved, and the clink of ice in lemonade glasses, under him the smoothness of broadcloth—but first and last and most clearly, the beard, the kindness.

In the meantime, not unnoticed or untalked of, in spite of the other preoccupations of the summer, the new president of the Theological Seminary brought his family (one daughter) and his books and furniture to town and set up housekeeping where the Lowreys had lived. There was not much food for talk. If Dr. Blair had hired local Negroes for servants, then the town would have been informed of his domestic affairs in short order, but he had brought a Pennsylvania Dutch couple with him. For a few days all the information circulated was what a few Reformed Presbyterians knew: he was a widower of sixty-odd, who had lost the two sons of his first wife in the war, and had now only the one daughter of his deceased second wife, a young lady of eighteen. She had been educated at his knee to such effect that she had been capable of teaching, and had actually taught, Hebrew to the theologues of the Aberdeen Seminary. Waynesboro in general heard that item with some dismay, even with mockery, but the ladies of the Woman's Club were delighted as well as curious. They would of course make formal calls upon her as soon as it could be assumed that the house was garnished for receiving them. She might be worthy of taking Mrs. Lowrey's place.

But it was Dr. Gordon, not one of the ladies, who first made the acquaintance of the Blairs. He told Anne at the noon meal that the manservant had that morning brought him a note from Dr. Blair, asking him to call at his earliest convenience. He would go there first thing after office hours.

"In your frock coat, please, John!" Anne was flattered for him, since there were two Reformed Presbyterian doctors in town. "Dr. Wright always wears one, and the other older men. You should look as important as they do."

"And my plug-hat, I suppose?" John grunted, but capitulated when she promised to have the hat brushed, the coat pressed, and both taken in an immaculate state to the office.

"And look around you," she commanded, "particularly at *her*."

Shortly after four that August afternoon, Dr. Gordon was admitted to the Blairs'; his hat was taken from him by the capped and aproned female servant, and laid respectfully, its silken surface unmarred, on the marble-topped table outside the parlor door.

"The doctor, sir? You are expected. This way, please." She led him down the hall to the door of the room that had been Professor Lowrey's study. John, following at her heels, had time to wonder at the amenities of Aberdeen, Pennsylvania, which town had apparently produced this paragon of a servant. He thought of the free-and-easy Negro housemen and hired girls and nursemaids he knew, and grinned to himself. The Blairs were going to be a new experience for Waynesboro.

The study door was opened for him, the announcement made: "The doctor, sir."

John, bag in hand, passed her and stepped beyond the threshold. He saw at a glance that even though the furniture was different, the general aspect of the room was what it had always been: full bookcases, lining the walls, topped with white plaster busts, books on the desk, over and among the papers that littered it, and on most of the chairs.

Dr. Blair was in an easy chair close to the far window, beyond the fireplace. John took him in at a glance: a burly man, with the barrel chest that came of a lifelong struggle to empty his lungs, smooth-shaven, nearly bald, sparse broad sandy brows above bright blue eyes, a massive jaw. At his shoulder, between his chair and the folded shutter, stood a slim round-faced girl with a smooth crown of braids. John had no need to be told why he had been called: the heavy man in the chair choked and coughed with the effort of every blocked breath.

"Dr. Gordon?" He managed to utter the words, his jowls scarlet with the effort of breathing and speaking all at once. "Come in, sir."

John came forward as far as the fireplace and bowed as gracefully as he knew how.

"Christina, my dear . . . may I present Dr. Gordon? Sir . . . my daughter."

"Miss Blair." John bowed again. The girl behind the chair inclined her head, paused for a few polite words, excused herself, and was gone. He fixed her picture in his mind as well as he could, for Anne's sake, but with hardly a pause turned back to his prospective patient.

"I hope you are not laboring under a misapprehension, Dr. Blair." If they were going to be so very formal, he would meet them on their ground. "Or that my Scottish name has misled you. I was raised a Presbyterian, but I am not a member of your congregation."

"Not Reformed, eh?" Dr. Blair, wheezing with every labored word, looked at him from lowered brows. John thought his eyes twinkled. "You are warning me?"

"Two of our Waynesboro physicians are Reformed Presbyterians."

"They will take it . . . amiss?" He puffed, gasped, underwent a paroxysm of coughing, and then went on. "Shouldn't wonder . . . But I'm not . . . in any way . . . beholden to the local congregation. No. I . . . made inquiries. Turn that chair around, Doctor, . . . sit down."

John took the straight chair from the desk, turned it to face Dr. Blair at close range, and sat down. "You are very kind, sir. I don't know what friends of mine you inquired of."

"Never mind . . . that. I was told . . . you are a capable physician . . . and a formidable chess player." He gestured toward a chess table beyond the desk, which was set with a few pieces for an end game.

"A new reason for choosing a physician. But I should be glad to try a game with you any time, without doctoring you for it. There are not so many chess players in Waynesboro."

"My only recreation . . . Can't even walk much, to speak of. And although my daughter is . . . able to learn . . . any text-book subject . . . even of teaching . . . Hebrew to . . . budding theologues . . . no need of that, here . . . Waynesboro Seminary has a good man . . . Professor Ramsey . . . teaching Hebrew . . . An uncommon intelligence, Christina's . . . but incapable of chess, like most females . . . But for the present . . . you would like to know . . . why I summoned you?"

"You hardly need to say." Indeed the room was noisy with the sound of Dr. Blair's struggle with his bronchial tubes. "You have had asthma all your life: the development of your chest suggests as much—but do you always suffer to such an extent?"

Dr. Blair shook his head. "It's the season . . . the climate. Usually . . . I go North for . . . August and early September . . . but with this move to be made . . ." He gestured to indicate what there was no need to explain. "Can you help me?"

"Some, perhaps. A little tincture of laudanum to relieve the paroxysms. An inhalant that may clear the bronchial tubes. But asthma is one of the many human ills that we can't do much for." John smiled. He was quite ready to be honest with this friendly, ugly, suffering scholar. "Do you know what brings it on?" He opened his bag and took out the stethoscope that much of Waynesboro still considered a newfangled toy, pushed back the black alpaca jacket, and examined Dr. Blair's heart; he asked other questions, gave some advice, and prepared to leave. "I'll send my man up with the medicines."

"That's all, then?" Dr. Blair demanded. "No calomel? . . . No jalap? . . . Young man . . . you're unique among doctors."

"They wouldn't help your asthma. Of course, it's always well to keep the bowels open."

"Oh, I know . . . I know. I have always thought the Forty-first Psalm . . . metrical version . . . the doctor's psalm. 'Blessed is the man whose bowels move.' "

John laughed in an explosive, startled fashion; then, abashed, choked off the noise. "You don't mean—it isn't—"

Dr. Blair struggled out of his chair, turned to the bookcase beyond the window, pulled a small brown leather book off an open shelf, found the place, and handed it to John.

Blessed is the man whose bowels move
And melt with pity toward the poor.

John struggled with his voice. "You don't mean—you don't *sing* this in church?"

"No, not really." Dr. Blair had dropped back into his chair. "If you will look at the title page . . . you will see . . . a German . . . Reformed psaltery. My mother . . . she was a Crumbaugh."

"One always thinks of you western Pennsylvanians as pure Ulster Irish. I don't know why. There are plenty of Pennsylvania Dutch around here."

"We're a . . . mixture. Irish, Scottish . . . Welsh . . . German. But Calvinists predominate. However . . . our Reformed Presbyterian psalter . . . is less . . . lively than that one. We . . . sing 'Blest is . . . the man whose . . . heart can move.' "

John laughed again and handed back the little book. "About the chess: I don't have much time for it. But drop in at my office almost any evening and you may find someone to play with you. I have a couple of friends who come in once or twice a week." He did not name his friends, but neither did he shrink from the idea of Dr. Blair across the table from Ludwig Rausch or Herman Lichtenstein. It might seem an odd juxtaposition, but whether or not it worked would depend on how much Dr. Blair wanted his chess. "Sometimes, when I haven't many patients, I can manage a game myself."

After a few more words of conversation, John took his departure. He reported to Anne at the dinner table. Mealtime and bedtime were almost the only hours of the day when the two of them had much chance to talk over their individual experiences, and even then he was liable to be called away, or to be late getting in. But on that evening, they had a good leisurely meal, interrupted in their conversation only now and then by the two children between them, one on each side of the table, Binny, graduated from the high chair now, lifted to the proper level by a pile of her grandfather's old medical books. When John sat down after carving and took up his napkin, he said, "Now, Anne. The Blairs?"

"Yes, please."

"To go no further, of course. When Sally Rausch hears I was there, and inquires, you may say that I found them very agreeable."

Anne laughed. "As if you needed to tell me. I don't gossip about your patients."

"I know. But I suppose Waynesboro's curiosity has reached the boiling point. However—" He described Dr. Blair. "A heavy-set, massive-jowled, bald-headed man, puffing like a grampus."

Johnny, who seldom gave his attention to dinner-table talk, having better things to think of, now wanted to know what a grampus was.

"Bedogged if I know, Johnny—some kind of whale, I guess." He went on, then, to Anne about the Forty-first Psalm.

"Did you laugh?" Johnny demanded.

"Of course. It's only polite to laugh at your patients' jokes. But I would have laughed anyway. I thought it was funny. All the more so because it came from a strict old theological geezer like that."

"That just shows how little you've ever had to do with ministers. They're always primed with biblical jokes, meant to show how human they are. Jokes laymen would never dare to make, for fear of being thought blasphemous. Terrible puns of Bible names, like those Mr. McKinney makes. By the way, have you heard anything about his mother?" John was not the McKinneys' doctor.

"That she can't last much longer."

"It will be a blessing, for her and them, too. All these years. What about Miss Blair? Did you see her?"

"Only just. She disappeared after we had been introduced. Fairly tall. Fairly slim. Pale. Greenish-pale, probably anemic."

"I should think so, if she's been teaching Hebrew to theologues. D'you suppose that's true?"

"Yes. Her father said so. She won't here, because the Waynesboro Seminary is providing Professor Ramsey. But she can't play chess."

"Chess?"

John explained. Anne said, "Maybe she is human, then. Go on, tell me what she looks like."

"Reddish blond hair—'sandy,' in my vocabulary. Twisted up in a coil of braids around the top of her head. No bangs, no curls, no water-falls, no ear-bobs. Heavy-lidded eyes, light-colored, bluish or greenish. A round face, smooth and bland as a kitten's, particularly when she smiles.

"You don't make her sound very companionable, somehow."

"Why? Does it matter?"

"She's sure to be taken into the Club in Mrs. Lowrey's place. And one of the new professors' wives in Mrs. Tyler's. Oh, dear, it does seem like we're getting more and more theological."

But Anne's prediction was not immediately fulfilled. The first meeting of the Club in the fall of 1876 was held at the Cochran house. Present were Mrs. Ballard and both daughters, for the Judge got along without Eliza in his office on Club afternoons; the Misses Gardiner; Miss Pinney, who followed the old schedule of the Female College that made Wednesday a half-holiday; Mrs. McKinney, just returned from the trip with her mother-in-law's body to the home town the old lady had been trying to reach for so many years; Kitty Lowrey Edwards; Mrs. McCune, self-effacing, yet ready to attach herself to Anne or anyone else who offered a crumb of attention; Mrs. Deming; Anne; Sally herself and her mother as an invited guest.

Once Mrs. Cochran had been supercilious about the ladies and patronizing to them; now there was so little left in her life of all the old social round that she did not disdain to sit in her parlor and listen to the voices of those she could so dimly see. Of all present, only Mrs. McCune, whose husband's church the Blairs attended, could have felt acquainted with Miss Blair, although most of the ladies had made the formal calls that decorum required of them. Amanda had been expected to present Christina Blair's name for membership, but Amanda was not there. The public high school made no arrangements for half-holidays to oblige members of the Woman's Club, but Amanda ordinarily arrived in time for part of the program. That day she did not appear.

Mrs. Ballard as President spoke of the great loss the Club had suffered in the removal of Mrs. Lowrey and Mrs. Tyler from its midst, but nothing was said of new members. The ladies proceeded with their program. They were beginning a year of work on history: "The Queens of England in Chronicle, Song, and Story." The Waynesboro Subscription Library had not yet built up much of a historical collection. But it did possess a complete set of Strickland's *Queens of England*; it was that, perhaps, which had suggested an easy solution to the Program Committee's problem. The more scholarly among the ladies might pursue their researches beyond the one source, but for Mrs. McCune, who had the first paper, "Matilda, Queen of William the Conqueror," Strickland sufficed: indeed, more than sufficed, since so many of the circumstances of her life could not conceivably be spoken aloud to such an audience. But Matilda was interesting, even in Mrs. McCune's expurgated version of the eleventh century, and the ladies who heard the paper felt that the year would be a rewarding one.

Kitty Edwards had invited the Club to her house for its second meeting, when Thomasina would present the day's essay on "Maud the Good, Queen of Henry I." Kitty went into a frenzy of preparation, as once Anne Gordon had done as a bride, cleaning a house that had been cleaned thoroughly when she and Sheldon moved into it. For Kitty it was a labor of love. She was almost devout about it, because she had achieved her heart's desire: along with Sheldon, the beau ideal whom she adored, a house of her own where dirt and disorder were never to be permitted, not in even the darkest and remotest corner. Once they crept in, she knew, they were bafflingly hard to get rid of. And she had not been trained to the standard she set herself. Once or twice since her marriage, things had been allowed to pile up. Sheldon was not used to untidiness. His mother was the best housekeeper in town, and his father's store, where he worked as bookkeeper, was a model of tidiness. Nothing would alienate Sheldon so quickly as disorder. She had never ceased to wonder that he had not foreseen the danger and refrained from falling in love with her.

When he came home to his dinner on Tuesday evening (the Lowreys had had supper in the evenings—often enough, had the town only known, a supper of bread and jelly and tea; but the Edwardses' evening meal was dinner), Kitty met him at the door. She forgot her fatigue and aching bones to greet him with a beaming smile and triumphantly sparkling eyes. He stooped to pick up the *Torchlight* from the step, took off his hat, kissed her as she stood on the threshold, tucked her arm under his, entwined his fingers in hers, and started down the hall.

"Don't you notice anything?"

"The familiar fragrance of beeswax and furniture polish. And since I was sent to Mother's for lunch because you wanted me out of the way while you prepared for the ladies, I assume you have cleaned the house. But nothing looks different to me. It looked first-rate before."

"Thank you, you are nice. I know I'm not a good housekeeper yet."

"Yet! Heaven preserve us!" He dropped her arm and advanced far enough into the sitting room to toss his hat and newspaper on the center table; the hard derby landed with a crack, and went on sliding until it fell to the floor on the other side. He let it lie there, and turned to face her, laughing. "Kitty, darling. I've had enough good housekeeping to last me a lifetime."

"Oh, Shelly!" Her cry was a cry of anguish.

"D'you mean to say you *mind*?" He took her into one arm, and with the other hand tucked her head between his cheek and his shoulder. "Why, Kit! If you've been straining to keep our house like Mother's, I should think you'd be relieved. It never occurred to me—"

"You never even saw I was *trying*?" She wailed again. "Oh, Shelly! I can't bear for your mother to have done anything better for you than I do it."

"For me!" he snorted, "or Papa, either. Look, honey, I am a filthy creature. I bring dirt into the house, and I drop ashes. I will not be banished, in my own house, to the cellar or the outhouse with my pipe. I reserve my right to let the tobacco fall where it may, and to scent up the drawing-room draperies. I like to drop things wherever it's handiest. And I hate the house being put before the people who live in it."

"Yes, of course; but I've lived in such a muddle all my life. I think one reason I fell in love with you is that you were brought up so nice and clean."

They drew apart a little and smiled at one another ruefully. "But what of the six children you say we're going to have?" He teased her: "Won't they make a muddle?"

"Not when we have our own house—the one on some hilltop with a big yard and lots of trees and a porch all the way round. They'll play on the porch. Sheldon, didn't you want a good housekeeper?"

"I didn't marry you because I thought you weren't one. I don't like muddles either. Let's just be medium, shall we? You be a medium-good housekeeper, and I'll be medium-careful about pipe ashes and tossing things wherever's handiest, and you can be just medium about nagging."

"Oh, I won't nag. I'll pick up after you, and if it's too bad, I'll look martyred." She lifted her hand to touch the crisp ends of his hair. "I do love the way your hair curls over your ears."

"Then I need a haircut." He kissed her lightly on the cheek, took his newspaper from the table, and went to a chair with it. Kitty picked up his hat and took it to the hall. A house "medium-well" kept! She would not let Sheldon see it, but she had suffered a blow. A minor blow—nothing that called for Marcus Aurelius—but nevertheless a blow. Keeping house for Sheldon in the style to which he was accustomed had been for so long her dream. She was foolish, and Sheldon was right: it was his comfort that must come first with her.

"You're right, of course, Sheldon. But just the same, would you mind being careful, just tonight and tomorrow morning, not to spill ashes around? I don't want the Club ladies going home saying 'Blood will tell. Her mother over again.'"

The ladies who met the next afternoon could have found nothing to criticize. Sally was naturally the most interested, but she found nothing to disapprove in what Kitty had done with the house. Instead she complimented the bride when they had a moment alone together in the parlor bedroom. She stood before the bureau to see that her elaborate shining coiffure was in order around the edges of the curled brim of her small mannish hat, and spoke as she looked into the mirror.

"All new furniture, Kitty! What fun it must have been, buying it!"

"Sheldon got it through the store, quite advantageously, though Sheldon and Edwards don't sell furniture. It *is* handsome, I think, but somewhat overpowering." She grinned suddenly, her odd boyish grin, and dropped her matronly air. "I hardly know how to behave in the midst of it."

The high carved head of the walnut bed towered to the ceiling, projecting itself more portentously over the pile of bolster and pillows under their stiff-starched shams. The bureau where Sally stood had a swinging oval glass and, between small drawers at each side, a marble top, with three big drawers below. The wardrobe against the inside wall was wide and deep and tall enough to contain all the garments the Lowreys had ever possessed.

"Furniture gets heavier every year," Sally agreed, "and harder to move around for cleaning. I'm glad we got married when we did, though not much of ours was new. Ludwig was just starting, so most of it was out of Mamma's attic. Now it's back there." Sally sighed, then smiled at Kitty's reflection in the mirror. "I hated to give this house up but I'd rather you had it than anyone."

They went out together and found chairs and prepared to be attentive Club members. When the Club's hostess had settled herself, Mrs. Ballard called the meeting to order, quickly got the preliminary matters taken care of, then proceeded to new business and announced that the name of a proposed new member had been submitted for consideration, to be voted on two weeks hence. She fumbled for her glasses among the books on the table before her, snapped the case open, unfolded a slip of paper, and read the name as though she had never heard it before. "Miss Christina Blair." Then she removed her glasses and laid them on the table. Her swollen-knuckled hands were clumsy in the gloves; she moved slowly, but not until she was ready did she call on the Secretary to read the program of the day. Mrs. Deming had followed Amanda in that position; now, her voice edged with impatience, she read what everyone knew: the title of the paper for the day and the name of its author. The author rose, and the program began. Amanda came in before it was over, a little disheveled and not very successfully rid of the schoolroom chalk dust. It was clear that she had come directly from school, instead of going home first to dress. She squeezed into the loveseat against the wall. Without more than glancing at them, she fixed her attention on Thomasina and "Maude the Good." It was not until the program had ended that Amanda caught the President's eye, and was given the floor. She asked if Miss Blair's name had been presented to the ladies.

"It was in the order of business." To Mrs. Ballard it was inconceivable that parliamentary routine should not be followed.

"I apologize to you, Madame President, and the ladies," Amanda obliquely acknowledged the rebuke, "that I should have to miss the business part of all our meetings. I just wanted to say I hoped all would give their thoughtful consideration to the question of Miss Blair as a member. I speak with confidence when I say that she will be an addition to our group. She is a true scholar, and will be able to contribute much."

Two weeks later Miss Christina Blair was unanimously elected to membership in the Waynesboro Woman's Club. The Corresponding Secretary at once apprised her of the fact by note; the invitation was accepted with equal promptness, also by note, and Miss Blair made her first appearance as a Club member at the Club's next meeting held at the home of Mrs. Deming on the eighth of November. She arrived under the shelter of Sally's wings, picked up along with Miss Pinney and the Misses Gardiner and delivered by Reuben and the Cochran carriage.

It was a strange meeting, that one held on the eighth of November, 1876, the day after the presidential election. No Republican had gone to bed happy the night before: returns coming by telegraph and pasted on the *Torchlight* window had been increasingly bad, so that those who lingered uptown longest in the hope of a "swing" finally went home completely disheartened. And the Wednesday morning papers confirmed their worst fears: Tilden had been elected. The ladies of the Club met in a gloom not dissimilar to that of the French aristocrats in the face of the Revolution. Before the meeting they made no allusion to the evil tidings, however heavy their spirits might be. Instead, they spoke words of welcome to their new member, and then took their places in Mrs. Deming's handsome drawing room to conduct their business and to listen to the paper on "Matilda, Daughter of Henry I." But if nothing was said, much was felt. Dismay was universal. For once the ladies all held the same view. Perhaps nothing could so have united them, at least temporarily, as that shared emotion, which was to be stretched out, increasingly tense, for another four months.

And Miss Blair could not more immediately have made herself one with them than she did that afternoon when she gave expression to the first shadow of hope that had been offered: hope that all might not yet be lost. The meeting had been adjourned, but the ladies had not yet dispersed. They were standing around rather like those left behind at a funeral, when hearse and carriages had departed for the cemetery. One said "Isn't it dreadful!" and another agreed "Shocking!" Then all sighed and were silent, and so heard

Miss Blair and saw the round young face, so innocently empty, come to life, break into a prim little smile that dimpled her smooth cheek. She was thanking her hostess for her hospitality.

"Not a very happy occasion, I fear, for your introduction into the Club." Mrs. Deming shook hands like a chief mourner.

"But my father says"—then the smile, the dimple—"not to give up hope too soon. He says we should have faith in the Great Jehovah and the Republican National Committee. Of course," she added hastily, "he was paraphrasing Ethan Allen, not breaking the Third Commandment. But he really believes it. He really thinks the election may not be lost."

The older ladies mentally blessed her heart, and went away feeling not quite so much as if the bottom had dropped out of their world. And indeed, before the evening papers went to press, other and more important Republicans had come to the same conclusion as Dr. Blair, and the *Torchlight* printed Zack Chandler's ringing pronouncement that Hayes had carried Louisiana, Florida, and South Carolina, and, with 185 electoral votes, was elected. But it was not to be that easy: in a few days it became clear that the election was so close that the result would have to be decided by the House of Representatives.

One evening early in the following week, Dr. Blair dropped in at John Gordon's office for a game of chess, and expressed to the men he found there his faith in the ultimate triumph of the right. He had turned up several times before, at first on the pretext that he needed more asthma medicine. Now, with colder weather and no pollen blowing around he was better, and lately he had been appearing without any excuse. Sometimes he had found no one there but the doctor, and if no patients appeared, the two of them had an uninterrupted game of chess. Sometimes Ludwig had come in, sometimes Lichtenstein, sometimes both; then, if Dock was not busy, there would be two games going at once. On that night soon after the election, all three young men were there when Dr. Blair turned up. Ludwig and Herman Lichtenstein were playing a halfhearted game against each other, while Dock perched on one corner of his long table, one leg swinging. They made the older man welcome, and in a word or two acquainted him with the subject under discussion. They had known his political affiliation since his first appearance among them, and had learned of one distinction between New Side and Old Side Covenanters: Dr. Blair did not consider the government of his country a matter with which he should not concern himself just because the Constitution made no reference to the Deity. Ordinarily they delighted in his political views, which were expressed with so much force and eloquence; on that night they were feeling distinctly glum, and what they wanted was one sound reason for hoping.

Dr. Blair dropped his bulk into the creaking swivel chair at Dock's desk, turning it to face them; he wheezed a moment, then said "Oh, ye of little faith!"

Ludwig was quick to ask for more. "You think, then, the Republicans can pull this out of the fire?"

"If the party in power can't do the counting of votes in the unreconstructed states, making sure the Negro votes are counted, then the party has lost its wits. But it had better move, if it hasn't already. You don't doubt, do you, that Democratic emissaries are already on the cars, headed south with bagsful of clinking gold pieces?"

"You sink, sir, ve should outbid ze Democrats?"

"I think we should fight the Devil with fire. Is your conscience troubled? Think, then: d'you doubt for a moment that if the freed Negroes in the reconstructed states have been allowed to cast the vote we guaranteed 'em, those States would have gone Republican? Then it is our responsibility to see that Negro votes are counted in the states where troops were at hand to see that they weren't kept from the polls. And if they are counted, the party is safe."

His sturdy declaration heartened the younger men, but after Dr. Blair had played a short victorious game with Ludwig, and had scolded him for letting his mind wander, he departed. The other three lingered a moment to chuckle over his character and personality.

"The Reformed Presbyterian," said John. "His Sabbath begins at sundown on Saturday. Cards, dancing, and the theatre are tools of the Devil. He will have no instrumental music in his church, and will sing only Psalms. He believes in foreordination, but that doesn't keep him from going into action."

"He agrees vit zat vun—who vass it?—who said he beliefed not all scamps are Democrats, but all Democrats are scamps."

"Yes." Ludwig laughed. "He has a point, though. Free and honest elections in the South, with the Negro voting, would assure a Republican victory. Let us see to it, then, that the results are the same as if the Ku Klux Klan had not interfered."

"The end justifies the means." John, who had moved from the table to his deep leather armchair by the fire, and had been sitting with his feet comfortably high on the fender, now rose, yawning as he spoke. "You don't believe that, Ludwig."

"As a principle, no. In this case—" Ludwig rose, too, gathered up the chessmen and put them in their box. "Mein Gott im Himmel! It's important."

"Of course it is. I used to think it would be best to forget the Rebs, and forget—but who wants them governing the country? This campaign, they've been sounding like abused innocents who'd never heard of rebellion, much less ever lost a war. Anyway, it looks like you boys've got a mighty powerful addition to your own company of Devil-fighters!"

As autumn turned to winter, the political deadlock continued. On the sixth of December certified electors met in the states and returned 185 votes for Hayes, 184 for Tilden. Democrats roared; the threat was made that Hayes would never be inaugurated. The Democratic House insisted upon exercising its privilege of deciding disputed elections; the Republican Senate stood upon its right to decide which were the truly chosen electors. Party leaders and partisan newspapers bellowed threats; Democrats who had seen the prize within their grasp promised bloodshed if deprived of it. President Grant called troops to Washington. Suspense hung over the country, a storm cloud giving forth lightning and thunder. Then in mid-December first the House and then the Senate voted to appoint committees to meet together and devise some peaceable means of settling the dilemma. Tension was relieved at least until such time as the committees would report back to Congress for action.

In the meantime life went on, daily routine uninterrupted. The women more easily than the men (perhaps because of a greater faith in Jehovah or a less cynical distrust of politicians) busied themselves about other things, as if no crisis thickened the air. Sally Rausch, particularly, was not one to sit with folded hands waiting for events on whose outcome she could have no influence. She roused herself to action after the Club meeting on November 22, when the name of the wife of the Seminary's professor of apologetics, Mrs. Maxwell, was presented for membership in the Club. As she said to Anne on the way home, it was just as she had feared: the theological party would soon take over the Club.

"I didn't lament over the loss of Ellen Tyler, and Miss Blair seems agreeable enough, but exchanging Mrs. Lowrey for an R.P. professor's wife is just too much." She laughed. "I never supposed I'd think of Mrs. Lowrey with fond regret."

"Mrs. Maxwell may be a good Club member. Remember, we thought once we could never endure Mrs. McKinney."

"I can't say my feeling for her is much warmer than that," Sally said tartly. "Is it true that she and Mr. McKinney have adopted that colored child they took from the County Home to do their work?"

"Not *adopted*. She told the Ladies' Aid about it. When they gave up hope of having children of their own, they decided to adopt one. Then old Mrs. McKinney got so bad, they knew they must wait. After she died, they started looking around, but they decided there couldn't be a child anywhere who could need what they might do for it more than the one in their kitchen. She's an orphan, with a lot of good-for-nothing older brothers, so Mr. McKinney went to court and had himself appointed her guardian. They plan to educate her. I think myself," Anne was pink-cheeked, "it is the act of true Christians. Better Christians than you and I."

"Oh, no doubt about it," Sally agreed cheerfully. "But odd, you must admit. Where will she go to school?"

"Until she's ready for high school, to the East End Lincoln School, where she's been going right along."

"Don't be huffy, Anne, just because I think your minister peculiar. You haven't any great feeling for the McKinneys."

"Respect, though."

"Well, I suppose. Though it's hard to respect fanaticism. Anyway, the ministerial atmosphere of the Club is getting too awful. You know what I'd like to do?" As she went on to explain, Anne saw that it was not a chance, flitting notion that Sally had just that moment lighted upon, but a thought-out plan. For her Christmas party, the Club would act a play. For this first time, it had better be Shakespeare: one of the inoffensive plays, or one with the offensive bits omitted. She would read plays for the next two weeks, and at the next Club meeting—she paused in her quick speech to look sidelong at Anne—she would ask Miss Blair to take the leading role.

"Miss Blair! You'll be doing well if she comes to see it."

"You haven't sized her up the way I have. I think she likes leading roles. And wouldn't that make the R.P.'s sit up and take notice!"

After the next meeting, on which occasion Mrs. Maxwell was duly and unanimously elected to membership, the hostess asked Miss Blair to stay a moment, with Anne, Thomasina and Eliza Ballard, Kitty Edwards, and Amanda. When she had shaken hands with the departing elders, and had her chosen group alone in the drawing room, she made a little speech about how, after all these years, she thought they might attempt a real play at the Christmas party. The single scenes had been very well received the year before; it was time they tried something more ambitious.

"What play?" Amanda looked rather grim. Miss Blair, who did not speak, looked blandly interested.

"Shakespeare, of course. Not one of the plays we did scenes from last year. I thought perhaps—*Cymbeline*." Sally tossed out the title offhandedly. Anne repressed a laugh; she doubted if Sally had ever read it before that week, she herself never had.

"Cymbeline?" Miss Blair began slowly. "But the—the central situation—"

"Exactly," Amanda snapped her off. "Don't you realize, Sally Rausch, that most of our church people, like my mother and the McCunes and the Maxwells, and Miss Blair, think that Shakespeare is an instrument of evil?"

"Oh, but surely—" Miss Blair sounded as if she wanted to argue this, but she was interrupted again, this time by Sally.

"I thought of *Cymbeline* with Miss Blair in mind. We have all taken turns at playing leading parts. Imogene must be played by someone young and you," she turned to the girl, "you're the one among us to do it."

Only now did Anne realize the whole of Sally's scheme. She held her breath; so did the others. But if they expected outraged indignation, they were in for a surprise. Miss Blair's heavy-lidded eyes opened wide, dimples showed briefly as she smiled.

"You want me to play Imogene? Oh, I should enjoy it, above all things. Of course, on condition Papa gives his consent. I always loved 'Hark, hark the lark' and 'Golden lads and girls.'" She rose and laid a light hand on Sally's shoulder; her smile died in wistfulness as she spoke:

"Nay, stay a little,
Were you but riding forth to air yourself
Such parting were too petty—"

Sally, somewhat taken aback, said, "You *know* the part?"

"Only a line, here and there. It would not take long to learn. But we do not have much time, do we? I shall let you know at once what Papa says."

Sally saw them all out but Anne, whom she found, when she returned to the drawing room, shaking with mirth.

"Sally—Oh, dear! You had her sized up, all right. But she's going to give you a run for your money!"

"What do you mean? That chit? She's made up her mind what she wants and is going after it. But what do you suppose it is?"

"What other women want, I suppose. House, husband, and children. And besides that, the top position, wherever she is."

"But for husband, not a theologian."

Anne considered it. "No, I shouldn't think so. Being a minister's wife would not put her where she wants to be. But it will be interesting to watch."

The time was so short between that Club meeting and the December night Sally had chosen for her party that afternoons thenceforth, and even some evenings, must of necessity be given over to preparation of it. The play was ruthlessly cut: they would perform only the opening scenes, the scenes between Iachimo and Imogene, the forest scenes with Imogene and her brothers, and the finale of the play, shortened to suit the cast. Sally would summarize the gaps in the story between the acts. But even so shortened, the play required more actors than there were young women in the Club. Amanda resolutely refused to take part. "I haven't time," she insisted, and when they reminded her that Eliza Ballard too had only her evenings for rehearsals, she said, "Eliza doesn't have papers to correct at night. Besides, I should never have a moment's peace at home if I took up play-acting." Her friends, knowing her mother, gave over trying to persuade her. And, as Sally said, Mrs. Deming would make a better queen, anyway. "'Old Teapot' was born to be a wicked stepmother." When Mrs. Deming had consented, the Ballard daughters were commissioned to beseech their mother to be Cymbeline. To their astonishment, Mrs. Ballard agreed without demur. It was Anne's contention, after they got used to the idea, that Mrs. Ballard had been play-acting after a fashion all her life: at least, the feel of the boards beneath her feet and the audience before her must be as natural as breathing. Sally, on the other hand, attributed the alacrity of her acceptance to the universal fascination of grease paint. "Before long, there won't be anyone who will refuse to be in a Club play. Don't say I'm not a broadening influence."

Unfortunately, Mrs. Ballard proved incapable of memorizing, and the first act threatened to lose its force, since the king's fiercest speeches had to be read through a lorgnette, from slips of paper clasped in hands so drawn and stiffened by rheumatism that the pages were fumbled, sometimes confused, and the place lost. But Mrs. Ballard was so amazingly humble in her desire not to ruin everything for "you young people" that they forgave her, with growing affection. Mrs. Deming, on the other hand, was coldly perfect in her part, but she too was plainly enjoying herself, and forebore to criticize, so that fun was not altogether subdued in her presence.

Sally brought down from the Cochran attic costumes that they had made the year before, to be worn now by Postumus and Iachimo and Imogene-disguised-as-a-boy. The queen and Imogene in the earlier scenes they draped classically in paper muslin, and from a sheet evolved a toga for Mrs. Ballard. A toga was really the costume she was born to wear. Less appropriate to her character was the tall pointed crown they made for her of gilt-paper, but they had to devise some means of concealing her gray hair. Then, as Sally said, since Shakespeare put the play back in Roman times (although Iachimo was a Renaissance character if she ever had met one, blood brother to the Borgias), it would be easy and appropriate to put the brothers and their tutor-kidnapper into classic costumes, too, only not quite so long or voluminous as togas, because who could imagine prowling around in the forest in togas?

From the first rehearsal they all knew that Miss Blair could carry the play. Hers was the rare, true gift; she became Imogene when she appeared. The others had only to play up to her. That she should have such a talent was more astonishing but not more pleasing than that she should also be discovered to have a beautiful singing voice: a soaring clear soprano without a single shrill note. Thomasina's Samuel had set "Hark, hark the lark" to a simple, singable tune ("Elizabethan," Sally had commanded). Whether Elizabethan or not, the tune was pretty and catching, and soon they were all going about humming it. One evening during a pause in a rehearsal, Christina Blair happened to sing aloud a few phrases of the song. Those who heard insisted that she should be one of those to sing it "on the night." Sally had planned to set tall screens, brought from elsewhere in the house, across the corner of the parlor-stage, in order to hide the piano. All the singers had parts in the play, of course, so they were to stand behind the screen while Sally, as Cloten, stood at its edge, in the hall door, to direct them. They were not actually "singers," except of hymns on Sunday; and but for Sally herself and Thomasina, there was no music in them. They were so timid about their ability to deal with "Hark, hark the lark" that they were happpy to be hidden behind the screen, and rejoiced when they heard Miss Blair sing. Christina could as well as not be with them; between the song and her entrance on the stage, there was a passage between Cloten, Cymbeline, and the queen; she could slip into the hall from behind the screen and make her entrance in front of it. Sally was an ingenious stage manager, and Miss Blair was pleasantly amenable to her suggestions.

Stage manager, but not director. She did not presume to tell the members of her cast how to act their parts. As she said, one thing about Shakespeare: if you just read his lines intelligently, it was almost enough, without any acting. The only one with whom she remonstrated was Kitty, who, as Iachimo, did not seem villainous enough.

Kitty protested, "You cut all his villainous speeches and it isn't my fault if Shakespeare gave him the most poetic bits in the play. I don't believe he is meant to be all villain: he repents in act five, doesn't he?" And she continued to put her heart into "The crickets sing, and man's o'er-labored sense Repairs itself by rest."

They all knew that as Shakespearean actors they were absurd. They expected their menfolk to laugh at them, but their main purpose, after all, was to have pleasure themselves, and to entertain the gentlemen. This year though they had two surprises, bound to please any male: the grace and charm of Miss Blair, and the spectacle of Mrs. Ballard making herself ridiculous, knowing it, and not minding, so that all the men who had wanted to for so long could laugh at her to her face, with no feelings hurt.

Invitations to the party were written, delivered, and replied to. Members of the Club accepted with pleasure for themselves and for husbands, fathers, nephews; there were no repercussions among the Reformed Presbyterians. To be sure, the kind of "Entertainment to be provided by Members of the Waynesboro Woman's Club" was not specified, nor was it mentioned at the regular meeting on the twentieth of December; all that was said was "We shall see you on Friday evening, then." The three young women who did not take Reformed Presbyterianism as seriously as its adherents wondered whether Mrs. Maxwell and Mrs. McCune did not know what was in preparation, or whether they knew and, with Amanda, were in a conspiracy of silence against their husbands and Mrs. Reid. Or perhaps the fact that Dr. Blair was permitting Christina to act in a Shakespeare play made Shakespeare acceptable to them all. Sally would have liked to know; it was disappointing to have lighted the fuse of a firecracker and hear no explosion.

On "the night" the Gordons were driven up the hill by Tim O'Reilly in the old family sleigh that had been Dr. Alexander's; John would not leave Molly standing all a long winter evening in the cold, when there was no necessity for it. The tired horse went slowly up the hill, sleighbells jangling *andante*: the sleigh was heavy and the snow wet and soft. Anne could see the Cochran house long before they reached it, the light streaming across the porch from the long parlor windows, and intermittently down over the steps from the briefly opened front door. She recognized Dr. Blair and Christina, halfway between gate and door, Christina carrying over her arm the costumes she was to wear. Anne had taken her party frock and her Arviragus costume to Sally's that afternoon, and was wearing, under her long cloak, the doublet and hose of Postumus; she had a moment's misgiving as she thought of her exposed legs, but she need see no one after she had taken her wraps off until she appeared in her part, when she would have a cape. The cast was to go directly to Sally's bedroom—the actors' dressing room—to leave their cloaks, and she had rebelled against putting on her best watered silk at home, taking it off, and finally putting it on again. She would dress for supper when the play was over, and in the meantime wrap her coat around her legs. Another couple approached the gate, downhill from College Street, as the Blairs neared the porch steps, and another sleigh was at the carriage block ahead of them, so that Tim had to draw to the curb behind it and wait. The sound of sleighbells died on the air; there was only an occasional muted clash as one horse or the other stamped a foot.

Sheldon Edwards came around his sleigh, through the snow, and helped Kitty down; she dropped light as a feather on the carriage block, then, looking up past the gate, saw the Blairs, as the door above them opened. In her clear carrying voice she called, "'All of her, that is out-of-doors, most rich,'" and when Christina turned to look around, continued,

> "If she be furnished with a mind so rare,
> She is alone the Arabian bird!"

Christina contented herself with an airy salute as she and her father went into the house. The Edwardses followed them up the walk. Their livery-stable sleigh was driven off, and Tim picked up his reins. The sleighbells rang; Molly stepped forward toward the carriage block. By that time the couple coming down the hill were within hearing distance. The sound of the bells died away, and on the still winter night the Reverend Mr. McCune's voice was thinly, clearly audible.

"—play-acting again. I told you before that it was unseemly; that I would lend my countenance to no more such occasions." He dropped her arm, and stood still.

Mrs. McCune took a step away from him. "But I thought when Dr. Blair permitted Christina—"

"So? Dr. Blair's daughter, play-acting? Well, Dr. Blair's principles and mine are not alike: I have known that for some time. Come, Mary: let us not be stumbling blocks in the way of the young."

"But we can't just not appear. We accepted the invitation in *writing*."

"The meat offered to idols!" In a dry, dreadful voice Mr. McCune pursued her with words as she resumed walking. "'For if any man hast see thee which knowledge sit at meat in the idol's temple, shall not the conscience of him which is weak be emboldened. . . . And through thy knowledge shall the weak brother perish. . . .?'"

Mrs. McCune had reached the gate. Neither had paid any attention to the sleigh at the curb, and the Gordons sat frozen, hoping to remain invisible. Mrs. McCune turned and backed against the gate in the position so familiar to Anne: her hands close to her side, fingers spread, palms flat on the iron.

"You go on home, if your conscience bids you. No one's soul is endangered by my being here. They won't even notice that I *am* here. But I cannot be so rude—"

Mr. McCune took a slow step toward her, and another. Tim O'Reilly grunted. Molly would stand without holding; he got out of the sleigh on his side and came around to the carriage block to help Anne. She kept one hand in her muff, with the other she threw back the carriage robe, and her cloak with it; as she stepped down, her legs were uncovered. At that moment the McCunes first became aware of them. If he had intended to seize his wife and carry her away, Mr. McCune was shocked out of his intention. He stopped in his tracks, stared at Anne in horror, and went off up the hill. Anne did not wait for John; she did not wait even to pull her cloak together around her. Mrs. McCune was watching, her gloved fingers clasped now around the ironwork. Anne went directly to her, but did not touch her; instead she reached for the handle of the gate, to open it. Mrs. McCune turned then and stepped inside with Anne. Anne held the gate for John, trying to speak easily as she did so. "Mr. McCune had to answer a pastoral call? We'll be glad to have you go in with us."

"You heard," Mrs. McCune said, in a half-whisper. "I don't know what came over me." Anne took her trembling arm. She was frightened to death, but still defiant. She said in a shaking voice, "I don't think it is wrong."

"Nor do I," Anne assured her. "And one doesn't always have to give in to a husband. It just spoils them." Why should his wife be so terrified of that pinch-faced, sandy-haired little man? "I wouldn't worry about it."

John, who had stopped for a few words with Tim to give the two women a confidential moment together, now came up to Anne's other side, and the three of them went up the sloping brick walk to the house. A white-aproned, white-capped, beaming colored girl stepped forward, behind the white-jacketed houseman (Reuben, doubling his parts) who admitted them and directed them on their way: "Gemmun rest they coats in the rea' bedroom, Doctah. Ladies go to the right hand bedroom. Miz Go'don, yo' knows yo' way."

John and Anne headed for the stairs, but Mrs. McCune, ignoring or ignorant of the social fiction that assumed them invisible until they had come down again, wraps removed and toilets repaired, to be announced by Reuben, went wide of the Gordons to where Sally was standing with Ludwig in the drawing room door.

"Mr. McCune is so sorry," she said in a thick, choked voice. "A sudden pastoral call prevents him—he sends his regrets."

Anne and John were by that time on the stairs. Anne thought, "Anyway, she caught the line I threw her." She said, "John, wait and take her down. She's scared to death. Be nice to her, will you?"

"Why on earth? Never interfere in family quarrels. Don't you know better?" He spoke with repressed but real anger.

"But John! What could I do? I feel—"

"I know. You feel so sorry for her. But it's a fine way to get yourself in trouble with everyone."

"Will you wait for her?"

"Yes. I'll wait for her."

He went off toward the room whose half-open door showed a bed covered with overcoats and gleaming silk hats. Anne stood until Mrs. McCune came up to her at the head of the stairs.

"John will wait for you here. He will be glad to have company, since I'll not be coming down before the play begins."

Mrs. McCune's hand closed convulsively around her arm. "But wasn't he angry?"

"With you? Why should he be? Let's see who's in here. Maybe someone else would like to go in on John's other arm."

She reached the door of Elsa's bedroom, where tonight the ladies were leaving their wraps. The Rausch children, with Cassie as warden, had been swept up another flight of stairs to the third floor. In the room were Mrs. Maxwell, still almost a stranger to Anne, the Misses Gardiner, who would have Douglas somewhere waiting for them, and Miss Pinney.

"Good evening, everyone," she greeted them from the threshold. "Here's Mrs. McCune, bereft of a husband for the night—some sudden call on him. Miss Pinney, take her under your wing, will you?" Miss Pinney was at the bureau mirror, fumbling with her strayed locks. Anne said, warmly, "How nice you look tonight. There's nothing really quite so stately, is there, as black silk?"

Miss Pinney caught her eye in the mirror and smiled. "Dear Anne—dear Mrs. McCune, I shall be delighted if you will keep me company. But how sad for Reverend McCune! Not a sickbed call, I hope."

Mrs. McCune passed Anne and went into the room, fumbling with the hook and eye at the neck of her worn black velvet dolman. "Oh, no—at least—"

Anne said briskly, "John will be waiting for you in the hall. He will be glad to offer you an arm, Miss Pinney."

And she was out of the room and off down the hall. Poor John! She hoped she hadn't ruined his evening, but it would serve him right for being so husbandish. And not even Sally, she told herself, could have carried off a difficult social *contretemps* with more aplomb. But somehow she did not believe Mrs. McCune would enjoy the evening much: she was too frightened, and she would be thinking of afterward, at home.

The play was acted with vigor and enthusiasm, and was received with the warmth always accorded parlor theatricals whose cast is made up of wives and daughters. Of all the ministers and theologians, only Mr. McCune was absent. The McKinneys, the Maxwells, and Dr. Blair sat in the front line of chairs. John deposited his two ladies on the love seat that finished out that row, and went himself to sit behind them with Sheldon, Ludwig, Douglas Gardiner, and the Misses Gardiner at the end of the row to subdue the gentlemen if they scoffed. But husbands were well-behaved, remembering that Judge Ballard was somewhere behind them, and their chairs (Mrs. Cochran's fragile reception chairs) did not shake too much at Mrs. Ballard's public-lecture-admonition gesture when she came to "Thou basest thing, avoid hence from my sight." Somehow, by the lift of an eyebrow, the curl of a lip, the cock of her gold-paper crown, early jolted askew by the vigor of her acting, she told the audience that she knew as well as they that she was making a fool of herself, but that she was enjoying it, and why should they not, too? Laughter increased from one of her scenes to another; the gentleman began to feel warmly toward Mrs. Ballard for the evening at least, and she bade fair to be the star of the play. She would have been, had not Christina's acting moved them from mirth to sympathy. She even carried off without losing her composure the one incident that could have sent laughter rocketing out of bounds. (Anne, in the hall, watching through the door until time for her scenes, could distinguish John's laugh among the others, and was glad he was enjoying himself, but hoped he would not be too unrestrained.) Iachimo could not manage the clasp of the bracelet he proposed to steal from the sleeping Imogene, and kept on saying, more and more desperately, "Come off, come off, come off," until Imogene, as it were in her sleep, dropped the arm from where it lay gracefully relaxed along the back of the sofa, and with the other hand obligingly unclasped the bracelet to the delight of the audience. Vociferous applause rewarded the unseen singers of "Hark, hark, the lark"; an encore was demanded, when the others all fell silent after the first lines and let Miss Blair finish it solo. At the end of the play the gentlemen's bravos were satisfactorily hearty, and compliments, begrudged by no Club member, since they now regarded Christina as their own prodigy, flew thick about her bright head.

Supper was served after the cast had reappeared in conventional evening dress. Sally had assigned Douglas Gardiner to Christina for a dinner partner, and put them at a small table for four, with Anne and Sheldon. Not all the ladies and the gentlemen attached to them could now sit at the Cochran dining table, even when it was drawn to full length, so several small tables had been set in the library. In the dining room were the Cochrans, the McKinneys, Judge and Mrs. Ballard, the Demings, the Maxwells, Dr. Blair, and Sally herself. Ludwig was at a small table with Miss Pinney, Mrs. Reid, and Samuel Travers. The other tables had only one man each. Sally whispered an apology to John when she showed him his place card. "I'm sorry, Dock. There are just too many extra females. And when Mr. McCune didn't show up, that made it worse." So John sat down with Kitty, Thomasina, and Mrs. McCune. Anne, glancing now and then at her husband, knew exactly when the fun went out of the party for him. He started to eat his way zestfully through one of Sally's best suppers, beginning with oysters, and far too rapidly, so that he had a long wait between each course, when he fell silent, making no small talk, his face darkened, a morose eye on the female with him, not even responding except with a word or two to Kitty's lighthearted chatter.

When, finally, the guests in the dining room pushed their chairs back, it was almost as if he had been released. And his abrupt rising was like a signal for the dispersal of the party, although he had not, like some of the more sedate elders who hurried upstairs for their wraps, a conscience-stricken air of having stayed out beyond a respectable hour. Anne saw his impatience, however; she did not try to keep him for a post-mortem of the evening with Sally and Ludwig. They were among the first to go.

They walked home. John had told Tim not to come back for them: the horse had had a long day, and it was not much of a walk. The night had turned colder, and the snow, crusted over, crunched under their feet. Anne put her hand under John's arm as they went down the steps, but neither spoke until they were outside the gate and had turned down the hill. Then Anne felt she had waited long enough.

"I'm sorry, John. I didn't intend to saddle you with Mrs. McCune all evening."

"You didn't. The supper table was Sally's doing."

"But what happened? First you were enjoying yourself, and then all of a sudden, you weren't."

"What do you mean? The play was funny in spots, and I laughed. Then it was over and I didn't laugh any more."

"It was more than that. At the supper table it was if the weight of the world suddenly descended on your shoulders."

"'Mortality weighs heavily on me tonight.' Where did I read that? Not long ago—a little leather-covered book on a candle-stand by someone's bed. M'hm—Thomasina's, when she had that touch of pleurisy, while I was taking her temperature."

Anne felt that he was talking to divert her attention. It was not John's way to think aloud. She fell silent, waiting for more. They came to the foot of the hill. Except for the wavering gas street lamps, and far across the square a light in Thirkield's drugstore, all was dark and quiet. Finally she said, "What do you mean?"

"'Mortality weighs heavily'? I enjoyed the play, but Shakespeare isn't exactly a cheerful fellow, would you say? 'Sceptre, learning, physic must all follow this and come to dust.'"

"But what made you so glum?"

"Skeletons beneath the flesh beginning to show." At Anne's exclamation he patted her hand, still on his arm. "Not, not that bad, Anne. People growing old, that's all. Mrs. Ballard worse crippled with rheumatism every year. The veins standing out on Judge Ballard's forehead like worms. Miss Pinney getting shaky."

"But you see those people all the time. I know it's sad, when it's someone you've known all your life, but it isn't like you to look around and see Death leering over everyone's shoulder, like a wood-block print out of the Middle Ages."

"Heaven forbid. No. It was Mrs. McCune. I didn't really got a good look at her until we sat down at the supper table. She's a sick woman. I suppose that was why she was so overwrought that she turned on him. I'm sorry I was cross, Anne. But mixing in family rows only means trouble."

"But I didn't! I only picked her up after he'd gone off. And of course she looked sick—she was sick with fright at what she was going home to."

John hesitated in his walk. "Who's taking her home? I was so anxious to get away I never thought to ask."

"Kitty and Sheldon. It's all right."

He wished he could say "It's all right." Mrs. McCune was almost certainly pregnant, and almost as certainly had pulmonary tuberculosis. But she was not his patient to worry about.

Anne put in words what he had left unspoken. "I suppose she's going to have another baby. She almost always is. But you don't have to fret about her."

"No. But I didn't feel very jolly, sitting across from her. On the other hand, what about Kitty?"

"Kitty? There's nothing the matter with her."

"You mean she hasn't whispered to you, in strictest confidence?"

"Oh, no! You mean she's going to have a baby, too? Oh, she'd say so, if she knew it. She's been shouting from the housetops that she aims to have at least six, because Sheldon did so hate being an only child."

"Kitty would surely have the wit to guess. Maybe she's been to Doc Edwards. After all, he is Sheldon's uncle."

"The Lowreys always had you."

"She's an Edwards now. Kitty's so narrow through the hips she won't have her babies easily. And she looks a bit puffy around the eyes."

"She's worked too hard, maybe, on the play. But she was good."

"Yes. So was Miss Blair. And as for Mrs. Ballard: I found myself actually feeling fond of her—anyone who minds so little making a guy of herself."

"It was a success, wasn't it?"

"Oh, howling. I wouldn't miss one of Sally's do's for the world, and this was the best, so far. Tell her so for me when you get together tomorrow to hash it over. And don't tell her I had an attack of the vapors." He laughed, then took off one glove, grasped Anne's hand, and slipped them together into her muff. Her fingers, warm and strong, took hold of his. "You had fun, too, didn't you? Doing it? But I'm glad it's over. I've scarcely seen you for weeks. I don't even think you realize how close Christmas is, and that the children are in a perfect fever."

"Now, John. You know the upstairs hall cupboard is full of their Christmas."

"I know." They had reached the gate. John had his hand on it, to open it, but suspended the action to finish what he was saying. "I know, but your mind's been off somewhere else a good part of the time. Don't you realize we want your undivided attention?"

And before he opened the gate, he leaned forward and kissed her cheek, pushing out of his way the white knit fascinator she wore. "Dear Anne! What a grumpy old man I'm getting to be. Not fit to be a husband."

"Well," she said, a little tartly, "I didn't see any husband tonight I'd trade you for." And they went on into the house, laughing.

MEMBERS OF THE
WAYNESBORO WOMAN'S CLUB

Miss Eliza Ballard
Mrs. Mary Ballard
Miss Christina Blair
Mrs. Louisa Deming
Mrs. Katherine Edwards
Miss Caroline Gardiner
Miss Lavinia Gardiner
Mrs. Anne Gordon
Mrs. Mary McCune
Mrs. Rhoda McKinney
Mrs. Laura Maxwell
Miss Agatha Pinney
Mrs. Sarah Rausch
Miss Amanda Reid
Mrs. Thomasina Travers

IN MEMORIAM

Miss Susan Crenshaw

* 1877 *

"The dark angel . . . the boatman pale . . ."

After the Christmas holiday citizens who had been able to forget for a while their country's plight were caught up again in the mounting tension over the still-undecided election. Daily routines were carried out almost absentmindedly; men went to their labor; the high points of the day were the arrival, morning and afternoon, of the newspapers. In Waynesboro the only obtainable morning paper, brought up from Cincinnati on the W. & W., was of a Democratic cast, and readers simmered all day after they had read that Grant was bringing soldiers into Washington to prevent, by force if necessary, the inauguration of the duly elected president, Samuel Tilden. In the evening temperatures were cooled by Mr. Bonner's declaration in the *Torchlight* that from election day it had been clear that the Republicans had carried the three states still occupied by federal troops, where no interference with the Negroes' voting had been allowed. The returns from those states had been certified by the commissioners sent to their capitals by the Republican National Committee. The commissioners were well-known as honorable men; they had carried out an honest investigation. That the Democratic commissioners, sent by their committee, did not agree and certified different sets of electors was to have been expected. Were they not, after all, *Democrats*—that is to say, Copperheads or Rebels too soon forgiven? Mr. Bonner's opinions made Waynesboro Republicans feel better, but gave them only a modicum of hope.

In January the committee appointed by Congress to find a way to end the deadlock made its report, which was acted upon at once. By joint resolution an Electoral Commission was provided for, which would pass upon the credentials of the electors from the states that had had two sets of men certified; on this Commission would be five Senators, five Representatives and five Supreme Court Justices. House and Senate would choose their men. Obviously three Representatives would be Democrats and two Republicans, three Senators would be Republican and two Democratic. Four of the Justices were named by the authors of the resolution, two who had once been Republicans, two who had once been Democrats. These four Justices were to choose a fifth from among the members of the court, and his would be the all-important tie-breaking vote. Democrats had supported the resolution because they felt certain that Associate Justice Davis would be appointed. Davis had been a staunch friend of Lincoln and at one time a Republican, but had turned Democratic before his elevation to the Supreme Court and was known to be a Tilden supporter. Republican hopes fell.

The joint resolution was passed on the twenty-fourth of January. On the twenty-fifth the legislature of Illinois elected Judge Davis a Senator. He resigned from the Court. The four already chosen Justices turned to Judge Bradley; he was appointed to be the fifth of their number on the Electoral Commission. Associate Justice Bradley had always been a Republican; there was no reason to suppose he had forgotten his earlier allegiance. Republicans drew a long breath of relief. The only question in their minds now was whether the Democrats were as dangerous as they were pretending to be: whether they would permit Hayes to be peacefully inaugurated. They still breathed fire, but Washington was heavily guarded and Grant in the White House in control.

All these events, rumors, threats, and counterthreats provided endless food for conversation in parlors, around dining tables, in drugstores, saloons, and the Court House. One of these discussions caught General Deming one evening in February when he had strolled uptown to pick up the latest reports. He almost always went out after dinner, to smoke the cigar he was not encouraged to smoke in the house unless he withdrew to his study in the tower. He preferred going uptown; he usually stopped in at Thirkield's drugstore, giving himself a few minutes of the masculine companionship he had missed since he had embarked upon so lonely an undertaking as writing a book. Most days he worked on the history of his brigade. He had thought of it in the beginning as a way to pass time. Louisa, however, had taken it seriously, and had let it be known to all her friends that since her husband had withdrawn from politics, he had turned author, and was writing his memoirs. For several years he had enjoyed himself, visiting a comrade here and a comrade there, taking notes on their recollections, borrowing diaries and letters, and afterward corresponding with them: "Dear Comrade Johnson," "Dear Comrade Jones." But once he settled down to the actual writing, hermit-like in his tower study, he somehow lost touch with everything that was going on. Now the book had been finished (*The Story of a Buckeye Brigade in the Great Rebellion*), printed, and sold, except for a few copies still piled in the study. He was at a loose end, and eager to take up again a man's life in the town. That particular night he found several friends at the cigar counter in Thirkield's drugstore, and joined their conversation: mostly gossip, some debate. He was with them until after ten, caught up in the political arguments. When he finally went home, he found his wife alone by the living room fire, embroidery in her hands, embroidery silks laid out, color after color, across the arm of the chair.

"Julia has gone to bed, of course." He had hung up his hat and overcoat and come to stand beside her, warming his hands at the grate.

"Long ago. She didn't want to go before you came in, but it got to be way past her bedtime."

"I know. I got interested, talking to Bonner and Judge Ballard and young Gardiner." One thing about Louisa, she never asked where he had been or reproached him. But something—the color of her aloofness—pushed him into explanation. "I don't like disappointing the child, I'll just slip upstairs and see if she's asleep."

"Don't waken her, George." She smiled a little; the disappointment was greater on his side than the child's. If she had not, as wife and mother, disciplined them both, Julia would be sadly spoiled.

Upstairs, General Deming opened as quietly as possible the door to his daughter's room, a room separated by double doors, now closed, from her parents' big front chamber. A night-light, a small oil lamp on the mantelpiece, showed the familiar dotted-Swiss bower to the General: a valance around the four-post bed, draperies from the top of the dressing-table mirror, tied back with bows, curtains at the windows, and in the midst of all that starched crispness, the child, a warm small curled-up knot in the middle of the big bed, her pale gold hair spread on the pillow. His heart yearning with tenderness and the wonder that he always felt when he saw her so, wonder that a being so delicate and so fair should have sprung from his loins, he stood watching her for a moment, then was about to withdraw as silently as was possible, when she opened her eyes.

"You were going away without kissing me good-night."

"I didn't mean to wake you. I just came up to make sure you were here."

"You didn't wake me. I've been waiting and waiting and waiting."

He knew that half a minute earlier she had been sound asleep, but he did not tease her. "I'm sorry, Julie." He sat down on the bed and with his thick-fingered red hand smoothed the hair from her cheeks. "I met some friends who wanted to talk to me. I couldn't get away from them. Now kiss me good-night, then go to sleep like a good girl."

He stooped to kiss her; she rolled over, straightened from her knot with a downward lunge of her feet, and put her hands on his arms.

"Do you love me most?"

"You and Mother." She was always trying him on that one. His answer was always the same, and she invariably accepted it with a smile, as though she knew better. Julia was keen as a whip: you couldn't fool her about some things, even if she was only six years old.

"I love you most," she said now.

"Mother and me."

"You." She sat up and leaned against him.

"Both." He kissed her. "Now get under the covers quick, and go back to sleep, or I'll be blamed for keeping you awake."

Downstairs again, he crossed the room behind Louisa and sat down in the chair on the other side of the hearth. She looked up briefly from her embroidery. "She woke up?"

"She said she hadn't been asleep—she'd been waiting for me. Julia's a great little girl."

"She thinks you're a great man." She smiled as she turned her embroidery hoops under the lamp.

Something—the smile, her tone—struck home to him like a physical pang. "She thinks—*she* thinks." A child's impossible faith. The room was silent except for the ticking of the mantelpiece clock and the hardly audible fluttering of the small flames around the coals. He spread his hands on his knees and looked at them: thick, red, awkward, with light hair furring his fingers between knuckles and first joint. How had they got like that? Middle-aged. Not old, but how did time do so to a man, slipping like sand through his fingers, marking them so? They didn't even look familiar, suddenly. He knew what his hands really looked like: *his* hands, in gloves, holding a horse's reins. In wind and sleet, marching on an icy road. How long ago? Nashville, and General Thomas: the last battle. He hadn't relived it writing his book as he did now in this brief instant, looking at his hands. And General Thomas was dead, and Brigadier-General Deming—

He clenched his fists, then moved them to the arms of the chair, out of his sight. "Well," he said heavily, "you and I know I'm not a great man. But, I served my country and I've written a book. Will that be enough for Julia to be proud of? I'd like her to be proud."

"She'll be proud."

"Bonner likes the book, by the way. And when Bonner says so, you know he means it."

"Everyone who has spoken to me about it has been most complimentary. You saw Mr. Bonner tonight? I would not have supposed he had thought for anything just now but whether we are to have an inauguration in March."

"We discussed that, too. One thing led to another. The book came up because I put it in the hands of disabled veterans to sell, and it put a little something in their pockets. Bonner is pushing for bigger pensions. The cripples and soldiers' widows and orphans are having a bad time this winter. They depend mostly on charity, and when times are so hard who can afford to be charitable?"

"I could name several. The Rausches. Mr. Cochran. Wasn't Ludwig Rausch there? I thought he never missed a drug-store convention."

"No. Judge Ballard, Bonner, and some others. Rausch is out of town. I understand he's so confident of good times coming, now Hayes is sure to be president, that he's planning to build a new mill."

"Aren't you confident?"

"Ye-es. Yes I am. It will help everyone to get a hundred cents' worth of groceries for a dollar instead of only half that. But it's going to be hard on the poor devils who borrowed the fifty-cent dollars. They'll have to pay back hundred-cent ones, with twice as much wheat or corn, or twice as many hours' work."

"I know. I do read the papers. They're full of the debtors' woes. The moral of that is, don't borrow. But I don't see why Ludwig Rausch should build a mill just now. Won't he have to borrow? Of course, it's convenient to have a banker for a father-in-law, but I can't imagine Mr. Cochran doing anything rash. And I understand Rausch Cordage has been barely making ends meet."

"That's all anyone's been doing since '73. But I don't think you need to worry over Rausch Cordage. Ludwig's got a nice little business there."

"I wasn't worrying." She laughed, and he looked at her doubtfully. It sounded almost malicious. "After all, why should we concern ourselves over what happens to Ludwig Rausch? He didn't concern himself over your misfortunes."

"Oh, Louisa! That's water under the bridge."

"You're too magnanimous. And let me say this, George, I wasn't the only one in Waynesboro to wonder why he went to live with the Cochrans if his business was doing so well."

"Her mother needed her there. I should hope my daughter would do as much."

"And if he hasn't been making money, how can he build a new mill without borrowing?"

"He won't do that. He might issue stock. All the stock now is in his hands and his family's. He didn't come here a beggar boy, to marry the richest girl in town. There's money back of him—his uncle has a wholesale hardware business in Cincinnati, and his father in Iowa is a meat-packer. I suppose they'll put money in his business if he wants them to. He won't need to go to the local bank. It would be a good thing for the town if he would sell stock to the public, but he won't; he'll want to keep control in his own hands."

"You mean you would *buy* Rausch Cordage stock?" For the first time Mrs. Deming put down her embroidery and looked at him.

"You don't like to believe it, I know, but that young man is a comer. Yes, I'd buy his stock."

"He's too involved in politics to run a business. I just don't believe he's sound."

"Sometimes being in politics is a help," her husband said wryly. "He's almost sure to be named State Committeeman from this district."

"But that will take still more of his time."

"And he'll know everyone of political importance in the state."

"State Committeeman!" Mrs. Deming drew a long breath as she realized what that would mean. "Then, more than ever, he'll have the say about who goes to Congress from here."

"No. The district convention."

"You know as well as I do—I see now why you think it would be a good idea to buy Rausch Cordage stock."

It took a moment for his slower mind to follow hers. Then he flushed, not in anger but in humiliation.

"My dear! Are you never going to let me forget?"

She stared at him in honest astonishment. "George, believe me, I had no thought of old sores. It was just that if you helped him out in a pinch, then he might do you a favor."

"Do you want to go back to Washington so much? There isn't a hair's breadth of difference between what you're suggesting and what happened before. Only this: it's so plain even I can see it would be crooked." He concluded on an accusatory note. Had she really, then, all along, thought him dishonest?

She heard the hurt in his voice and studied his face for a moment before replying.

"George, I swear I don't know what is honest in politics and what isn't. So much of it seems to me favors exchanged. Forgive me for being stupid." She put down her embroidery hoop, rose, went to where he was sitting, and put a hand on his shoulder, an undemonstrative woman's gesture. "It was just—I thought you wanted to go to Washington again. I am quite contented here. A big frog in a small puddle," she added, with an attempt at a light touch.

"All that matters to me is that you and Julie should be happy. Anyway, you're making a fuss about nothing. I'll never be chosen to run for Congress again. I've been shelved. I don't care about Washington. I admit I'd like to be nominated again for something, just so I'll know the party still had faith in me." On his coarse ruddy face an incongruously wistful expression showed for an instant. "Though I hear Liddell's health is precarious. They say Rausch wants young Gardiner to run for Prosecutor next election, so maybe he's grooming him for Congress."

"That whippersnapper!" Mrs. Deming went back to her chair, resumed her work. "Why, he couldn't get elected to anything; he's the most disagreeable young man in town. It's ridiculous."

"Well, it was just idle speculation on my part. But let's count on staying right here, Louisa, and not torment ourselves. Bonner wants me to write another book," he added, abruptly. "A history of the county. It seems there isn't any."

"Indians and pioneers? That would be the kind of historical research you enjoy and do so well, and you could be home with us. Write it in two volumes, then," she added dryly. "Volume two, 'Biographies of leading citizens' with photographs so the book will sell. And perhaps I can work on it with you."

"Of course. Didn't you put *Buckeye Brigade* into proper English for me? Bonner will help with material—seems he has collected a lot. But first he's got the disabled veterans on his mind, and I promised we'd help with whatever project his wife cooks up. Will you go see her?"

"Certainly." There was more than one way to cook a goose, if George wanted to go back into politics. "And if Ludwig Rausch is away from home, Sally will be at loose ends, more or less. There are servants enough to look after her mother, and her children don't hamper her if there's something she wants to do. She is a very capable organizer. I'll call on Mrs. Bonner first with suggestions, if she hasn't anything in mind."

General Deming's report that Ludwig Rausch was out of town was accurate. For four years now he had been hoping to build a new mill to add to what he had already built, with machines to form and lay rope. He had postponed taking even the first step toward it because of the general paralysis of industry. Now, although the depression seemed worse than ever in that winter of '76–'77, Ludwig was so sure of Hayes's election, and that as president Hayes would put the Specie Resumption Act into effect, that he set about planning the new mill. Before consulting an engineer or a contractor, he wanted to know more about successful cordage companies, how they were set up, the most efficient arrangement of buildings and machines in the buildings, and where to get the best machines. He expected that it would take a month to find out all he wanted to know.

His letters to Sally were so given over to accounts of what he had seen that she felt free to read parts of them at least to her father. Ludwig wrote that the presidents, or managers, of the eastern manufacturers were affable, a bit condescending, and perfectly willing to turn him over to mill superintendents for inspection tours. "None of them," Ludwig wrote, "expect competition from a small plant in the Middle West."

Mr. Cochran was disdainful. "Those fellows can't see over the Appalachians. They have looked toward the Atlantic too long."

"That's what Ludwig says." And she read, "Marine rope is what they have always made, and they think they always will. There are still enough sailing vessels of one sort or another to keep them busy turning out rigging. But they don't see, or won't admit, that the success of the steamship numbers the days of sail. Of course, any kind of boat will still need rope, if only to tie up to a wharf. But it is a declining market."

"He's right, of course." His father-in-law approved of this farsightedness. "The big market for rope will be around here, what with increased shipping on the lakes and the spread of farming across the plains."

In one of his letters Ludwig wrote that Rausch Cordage, in his person, had been invited to join the Cordage Institute, the industry's instrument for regulating the trade and preventing price-cutting. He was pleased and flattered; Sally knew that he was enjoying himself, and not missing his family too much. She, on the other hand, found daily life comparatively flat and stale without him, but she had not begun to be bored, in the company of parents, children, and books, before she had been drawn into the town project set in motion by Mrs. Bonner and Mrs. Deming.

One a rainy afternoon in February, she sat in her upstairs living room, keeping the little boys with her so that downstairs her mother might rest undisturbed. She often spent inclement afternoons in that manner, taking the boys when they woke from their naps so that Cassie might have the time for sewing, or to lend a hand with the laundry. That particular day was Cassie's afternoon off, and she had gone to her family in the East End, slipping away from the back door unheeding of the rain, a newspaper-covered market basket dragging on her arm.

Sally, beside the fireplace, her feet in soft house slippers cocked comfortably on the fender, was alone upstairs except for the boys. Elsa had not come home from school. No one had called, or was likely to, in such weather. Sally read, engrossed in her book but aware of the children's placid singsong. Charles, the baby, blond like the other two children and even more placid of disposition, was lying on his stomach, close to Ernest, his chin on his fists, his nose against the glass of the floor-length window, watching the rain hit the flat tin roof of the veranda, scarcely a foot below. The raindrops fell, bounced, danced away, fell, bounced. "Rain fairies," he said dreamily. Ernest, sitting cross-legged with a picture book on his knees, paid him no attention. The room was quiet except for the squeak of Sally's rocker.

Then Charles's attention was distracted from the veranda roof to what was for him the distant scene: the fence, the gate, the street beyond it, which could be seen now when there were no leaves on the trees. He nudged Ernest and said, "Somebody's coming, Mamma."

Sally got to her feet at once. "A caller? In this weather?" She learned nothing from her observation of the woman who let the gate swing shut behind her, while holding an umbrella over her head, and with the other hand gathering up her skirts, except that it was no one she knew well enough to recognize from her walk. "Someone to leave cards on your grandmother, I expect." She went back to her chair by the fire. But in a moment the Cochran housemaid appeared at the door with a card on a silver tray.

"To see you, Ma'am."

Sally took the card. "Mrs. Bonner. I must go down as soon as I've changed my slippers. Cassie isn't back yet, I suppose? Then I'm afraid I'll have to ask you to sit with the boys for a few minutes. Rose is looking out for Mamma?"

"Yes'm, an' Reuben, he down there. He sent me up."

"Just so there's someone to answer the door. I sha'n't be long, I'm sure. He showed her into the drawing room?" Only intimate friends were taken into the room across the hall, the family gathering place, with the double doors into the dining room, that was known in that house as "the library." Sally knew Mrs. Bonner only as one in a small town always knows other women of comparable standing but different age, and she was sure that something other than the ritual of afternoon calls had brought her to the house on such a day, and wondered how long it would take her to get around to it, even as they exchanged the commonplace polite phrases customary on such an occasion. Mrs. Bonner was a good fifteen years older than Sally. She and Mr. Bonner had been married for four or five years and had two children before the war began. After Mr. Bonner's release from his imprisonment, they had had two more, one of whom, Charlotte, was Elsa's age and one of her intimates at Miss Pinney's school. Perhaps something had come up concerning the school.

Mrs. Bonner was a tall dark woman who wore steel-rimmed spectacles that emphasized the wide black eyebrows, almost meeting over the bridge of her nose. The glasses and the heavy brows gave her an air of severity, even of temper. But she was not responsible for her eyebrows, and behind her glasses her eyes twinkled at Sally.

"I'm afraid I took advantage of the rainy weather," she said, immediately after they had seated themselves. "I was sure I would find you at home."

"How flattering! Just so you didn't catch your death," Sally smiled at her.

"Or bring puddles of water with me into your drawing room. Well, now you know: this isn't one of those polite calls one starts off on a round of, hoping everyone will be out so the whole list can be scratched off in an afternoon."

Sally laughed. She concluded that candor to the point of indiscretion must be a characteristic of all the Bonners. "Is there something I can do for you?"

"I hope so. That is, I know you can, and hope you will. The Ladies' Aid of our church" (Mrs. Bonner was a Methodist, whatever her husband might or might not be) "have found that there is a good deal of suffering this winter among the widows and orphans of the soldiers, and in families where the father is crippled. We can look after our own, after a fashion, but it doesn't seem as if it should be left to the churches. Everyone should be concerned. Oh, I know there are pensions, but they aren't enough to support whole families."

"Of course. The war that cost them so much was everyone's war. I'm sorry. I knew there was suffering this winter—my husband has felt compelled to let his hands take coal from the company bins, for instance—but I'm afraid I hadn't thought much about those who weren't working at all. Do you want a subscription?"

"I wouldn't refuse it." Mrs. Bonner returned the smile. "But that isn't all. We've been thinking there should be an organization of some kind. Perhaps an auxiliary to the G.A.R. But so many Waynesboro veterans haven't joined the G.A.R. Mr. Bonner himself—"

"I know. Ludwig joined; he thought it was a good idea to have such an organization, and besides—politics—you understand how that is. But Dock Gordon, for example, he says most of the membership is three-months' men and squirrel-hunters, and he'd rather belong to his regimental organization because he does like seeing those men occasionally."

"We could have regimental auxiliaries; two full regiments and a company of cavalry went from this county, but that wouldn't include the wives, like you and Anne Gordon, whose husbands happened to be in other regiments. The only thing to do is build up an organization of all the wives, daughters, and mothers too, maybe, of all the soldiers. But in the meantime children are going hungry. So we've decided to try to make the whole town aware of their trouble, and put as many people as possible to work to help them. It was Mrs. Deming's idea, in the first place. The General knows how much suffering there is. We thought of a carnival; there hasn't been one in Waynesboro since the one for the library. But then we decided on a play instead."

"A benefit performance at the Opera House? Good! We haven't had a play here since hard times began. But I should think it would cost so much to get a good company that there wouldn't be much left for charity."

"I guess I didn't make myself clear. I meant a home talent performance."

"Oh, put on a play ourselves? What fun!" Sally sat forward on her chair, glowing. "I always have wanted to. Only—do you think—with so many Reformed Presbyterians?"

"That's where you come in. We plan to engage one of those professional companies who will send someone to direct the cast and manage everything for a percentage of the receipts. But we must have a local person to head a committee, to persuade people to take part, arrange for the ticket sale, and so on. And there is a group here—your Woman's Club! If they push it, and your mother's friends help, it will go."

"But isn't Mrs. Ballard a member of your Ladies' Aid? Isn't she the one you want?"

"A member, yes, but she isn't as young as she once was. And not every element in town would take kindly to working under Mrs. Ballard. She has managed to antagonize a good many people. Mrs. Deming suggested we ask you."

"Mrs. Deming! But, why? I mean, wouldn't she like to do it herself?"

"She suggested you because of the play you produced for the Woman's Club before Christmas. She said Miss Blair was astoundingly good, and that if you could persuade her once, maybe you could again. Of course, how you ever did persuade the daughter of the president of a Reformed Presbyterian seminary to act in a play is a mystery to everyone."

Sally laughed. "She didn't take persuading, she jumped at the chance. She loved it. You know, I've often thought—" She smiled at Mrs. Bonner, tipping her head a little to one side, venturing a slight indiscretion herself. "It's the same urge—talent or whatever you call it—that sends some men onto the stage and some into the ministry, depending on their background. And I suppose she inherits her father's urge."

"But he doesn't preach, does he? I thought he just ran the Seminary."

"Not often, I guess. But he must have started out preaching. Of course he couldn't now, with that awful asthma. Ludwig always says he's glad their chess games are played at Dock's office, otherwise he wouldn't be able to put his mind on the board for fear of Dr. Blair's choking to death. But a play for the Club and a play for the public are two different things. Christina might not want to do that, or he might not want her to."

"In a good cause? Will you ask her?"

"I'll be glad to. One thing, the Blairs are very patriotic. You think if she's in it, the R.P.'s will be willing to go? They might, some of them. Who else would you need? There's Anne Gordon and Kitty Edwards—no, not Kitty—she's—you know—Dock has her on the sofa with her feet up."

Mrs. Bonner nodded.

"But Sheldon might." Sally continued. "Or, I tell you—Henry Voorhees, in the bank. He'd make a good hero. A bit namby-pamby, but noble looking. How many would you need of the people I know? What is the play, have you decided?"

"The professional decided for us. A smash-bang, spy-and-battle melodrama about the war, with a general and soldiers and a fife and drum corps and lots of gunpowder. A pair of lovers and considerable humor of the obvious sort."

"A general? Why not General Deming? He would be so flattered, and he wouldn't have to act: he could just be himself as he was on the battlefield."

Mrs. Bonner smiled a little sardonically. "From what I have heard, he would do better to act a little. But I agree, he would be a good one to have in it. He has his friends and admirers."

"Then you can tell me whom you want me to ask. And whatever else you want me to do. Ludwig is away, and time hangs on my hands. When do we start?"

They were deep in discussion when the front door opened and closed, and the muted sounds of whispers and giggles, scuffling, and the rattle of umbrellas dropping into the stand in the vestibule were audible in the drawing room. The noise, subdued as it was, was hushed by Elsa's voice.

"Be quiet, can't you? Gran'mother's prob'ly asleep. Wait here while I go ask."

Sally excused herself to Mrs. Bonner and opened the door into the hall.

"I am in here, Elsa, with a guest. Take off your wet wraps and come speak to Mrs. Bonner."

"I'm not wet." She came into the room and offered Mrs. Bonner a damp hand, at the same time making a little bob of a curtsey. "How do you do? Charlotte's here, too." Over her shoulder she called, "Come in, Char. It's only your mother."

Charlotte entered, and dipped in the same bob to Elsa's mother. The curtsey so scrupulously taught her young ladies by Miss Pinney was one of the things that led parents to say, "Well, at least she teaches them beautiful manners."

Elsa did not wait for Charlotte to finish being polite. She said, "Mamma, can we go down to Johnny's to play for a while?"

"Is Johnny out there, too? Tell him to come in."

Johnny slipped in, round cap in hand, and bowed first to one lady and then the other. But the swinging gesture, cap-to-heart, once and a second time, was somewhat exaggerated; he was grinning, and the dimple was deep in his cheeks.

"Please, Aunt Sally, can Elsa and Charlotte come down to our house? It's too wet to play outside, and Mamma won't mind."

"I'm sure she wouldn't. But today Elsa must go upstairs and stay with the boys. Cassie's out, and Tishy has work to do in the dining room. You two may go up with Elsa, if you like."

"If we play quietly, I suppose." Elsa was disposed to be sulky.

"Yes, if you play quietly. Grandmother is resting."

Johnny edged toward the door. "I guess I'd better go. Mamma won't know where I am."

"I'm sorry, Johnny. Some other time."

"Charlotte, you go up with Elsa. When I'm ready to go, I'll let you know."

When the front door had closed again and the sound of two pairs of light feet had died away at the head of the stairs, Sally turned back to Mrs. Bonner.

"It's too bad. I have to keep the children quiet for Mamma's sake, she is so nervous and easily upset. I hate not being where children can make all the noise they want to. Elsa's friends don't like to come here. On the other hand, Mamma could hardly get along without me, her eyes are so bad." Sally was not accustomed to explaining her situation to anyone with whom she was not on intimate terms, but she did not want Mrs. Bonner to think children were not welcome in her home.

Mrs. Bonner merely said, "I know. Yet children need grandparents, too." And they returned to their planning.

After dinner that night, when the young Rausches had been put to bed, Sally went out on the veranda to look at the weather; if it had stopped raining she would go down to the Gordons'. The old impulse was strong in her to share with Anne so exciting a piece of news as a prospective home talent play. But the rain had turned to wet, sticky snow, and she withdrew into the house shivering. On the next afternoon, when Cassie was once more on hand to entertain the little boys with "Possum up a gum tree" and other items of an almost unlimited number, she wrapped and booted herself, had the carriage brought round, and was driven by Reuben first to the Blairs' and then to Anne's. She had already sent a note to Henry Voorhees by her father's hand when he went to the bank.

By the time she reached the Gordons', late in the day, she had settled the future of her two principals, in her own mind at least. Of the play itself she made less to Anne than she would have done the night before; it was old news to her now, and probably to Anne also. But that Christina Blair and Henry Voorhees would play opposite each other as hero and heroine was still hers to tell, fresh and of interest. As she said to Anne, Henry Voorhees might be unexciting, but at least he wasn't a theologue.

"Henry Voorhees? I thought at Christmas you were handing Christina over to Doug Gardiner."

Sally grimaced. "Doug is so *soured,* for a young man. He'll never marry. Anyway, she needs a manageable husband."

"Is Henry manageable?" Anne suspected she saw through Sally's motives more clearly than Sally did herself. She would always be able to keep Henry

Voorhees in his place, a teller in her father's bank. Aloud she said, "I can hardly believe Christina Blair would be in a play and let herself be made love to in public."

"Are you so surprised? You saw her do Imogene. Why, when I asked her, her face lighted up as if I'd offered her the world on a platter. And no wonder. Imagine having spent your girlhood teaching Hebrew to theologues. And now she hasn't even that to occupy her. She's just keeping house—a more unsuitable occupation for her I can't imagine—and entertaining students for her father, I suppose, and church work, and the Club. It is not enough for anyone with her brains and energy. Besides, she has had a taste of acting. There's something about being in a play; it lets you drop your identity, you're set free, for an hour or so, anyway. But she didn't say she would be in it, she said she must consult her father. She's so grown-up, though, in her manner—not only grown-up but positively middle-aged—that I can't think he won't allow her to use her own judgment. She said he would consider it a worthy cause. His two sons, her half-brothers, were killed in the war."

"I know. But the Arps will have a conniption-fit." "Arps" was a disrespectful telescoping of the abbreviation "R.P.," used occasionally by the townsfolk of other denominations when they were feeling especially tired by the rigidity of the Reformed Presbyterians. The two young women were silent for a moment, relishing the prospect of the "conniption-fit." Then Anne said, "I suppose I'll not see much of you the rest of the winter if you are going to turn theatrical manager. What about the Club? And your library afternoon?"

"But I'm not going to manage it. There's to be a professional producer. And I won't be in it, only persuade others to be. Anyway, rehearsals will have to be at night; from what Mrs. Bonner said, the cast will be mostly men, soldiers and so on. Besides, if they need you, you'll be in it yourself."

"Oh, no, Sally. I neglected my family for *Cymbeline* before Christmas; I'm not going to do it again now. Why, John even pretended to think I'd forgotten to get the children's Christmas. No. If you need someone, get her somewhere else—out of the Goose Pasture, if need be. Didn't you say Mrs. Bonner wanted the whole town in it?"

Sally did not try very hard to persuade her; she believed that there would be very few women's parts in the play. When she left Anne, she went on to the Bonners' to report and to arrange for the next steps to be taken. By the time Ludwig came home from his eastern trip, with his valise full of sketch plans and his head full of ideas, she was knee-deep in work for the production of *Color Guard.*

Waynesboro found the play a welcome distraction as the end of February approached and the Electoral Commission dragged on at its work of accrediting electors and counting their ballots. Ludwig reported a good deal of threatening talk on the part of eastern Democrats, but he had also heard rumors of a conference called by Judge Stanley Matthews, representing

Hayes: a secret meeting between top Republicans, including Sherman and Garfield, and the leading Democrats from the South, at which a bargain had been struck; no further obstruction, and particularly no violent obstruction to the inauguration of Hayes on the part of southern Democrats, and, in return, the speedy withdrawal of all federal troops from the South.

"I don't know whether it's true," Ludwig said, "but it could be. Hayes has never liked the Radical Reconstruction policy."

"If there hadn't been troops in those states, he wouldn't have been elected."

"No. Ironical, eh? Well, we'll know how true it is by how things go."

The bargain was reputed to have been struck on the twenty-sixth of February. After that, the accrediting of electors was completed in a rush; their votes were counted on March second, and Hayes declared the President-elect. He was peacefully inaugurated on the fourth, and the country drew a long breath of relief. The total withdrawal of federal troops from the South in April did not seem very dangerous or dreadful to any except the vituperative Conkling, Ben Wade, and other Stalwarts, who were also enraged by Hayes's appointment of the quondam Liberal Republican Schurz to his Cabinet. And there were a few others, too, like Judge Ballard who felt that all hope of educating the Negro and giving him a voice in his own destiny had been surrendered. The country as a whole was sick of politics and willing to let Hayes carry on his struggle for honesty in government without their interest or support. Of course, as Ludwig said to Sally, the Democrats were bound to say the election was stolen, and would say so to the end of time, piously pretending that everything on their side had been open and aboveboard. "Tilden doesn't wear a halo, so far as I know—a Tammany peace Democrat. Personally, I don't believe the election was stolen, whatever hanky-panky there may have been in busting the stalemate, because I and everyone else knows that if the Negroes in the reconstructed states had been allowed to vote, most of them would have voted Republican. Now that we've let the Ku Klux get the upper hand, Bonner thinks none of them ever will again, not in our lifetime."

"Negroes vote, or the South go Republican?"

"Either."

"But I thought you didn't like having troops in the South any more than Hayes does."

"I don't. It's all been wrong. The South has been wrong, and so have we. And remember the South will have more representation in Congress after the next census, because each Negro will count as a citizen instead of just two-thirds of one. Ironical, again."

"Republicans will just have to carry elections without the South."

"And we can, so long as there's no split. But—"

"Oh, let it go, Ludwig. We had enough of politics with Papa at the dinner table. The fuss and worry is over for four years at least."

They had gone upstairs after dinner so that the children might have a romp with their father before they were sent to bed. Now Ludwig and Sally were in their bedroom, themselves preparing to retire as they talked. He had spent the day at the mill checking what had gone on in his absence. He had found, as he had expected, that nothing untoward had happened, but the "younger" Roseboom was getting impatient to retire. Ludwig had looked and found a possible superintendent for the new mill in his tour of eastern plants. All this, along with the political situation, had been discussed at the dinner table. Now Sally, having so summarily dismissed the one question, brought up the other.

"Tell me about your new man from Baltimore."

"I ran into him while I was going through the Arnold mill, and he came to see me at the hotel afterward. I didn't want to be put in the position of hiring Arnolds' man away from them, if he's good, and if he isn't, I don't want him. So next day I went back to Arnolds' and asked about him. Seems he's a good man—has learned ropemaking from A to Z since he went to work for them right after the war. They knew he wanted to get away from Baltimore—some family mix-up. So they won't hold it against me if I hire him. He'll be coming out before long to look us over and decide."

"But 'family mix-up'? That sounds dubious, somehow. Didn't they explain?"

"Some. Seems he'd married a girl while his artillery battery was on duty near Washington, and he could get to Baltimore occasionally—a girl his mother and sister disapproved of—wouldn't have anything to do with. Nothing wrong with her, except she was Irish. His brothers fought in the war, in both Armies, but the Reb brothers came home after Appomattox and they turned thumbs down, too. The Union brothers went West, so they were no help."

"What's his name?"

"Bodien. I said that didn't sound so high-and-mighty aristocratic to me. No 'de.'"

"Bodien." Sally tried the strange name on her tongue. "Is it, in Maryland?"

"About as aristocratic as 'Rausch' in Ohio." He grinned at her. "They explained—straight-faced, mind you—that his mother had made a 'mésalliance' too." Ludwig paused to chuckle. "But Papa Bodien, a French-German or German-Frenchman from Alsace, died young, after fathering half-a-dozen boys and a girl, so she took them home and ate humble pie. Now, I guess, she's worse than her folks were. She was a Maryland Archer, no less. Did you ever hear of a Maryland Archer?"

"I know nothing about Maryland families, except that a lot of the Germans in this country came here from around Hagerstown. And Papa's grandmother on his mother's side was a Maryland Forrester."

"Is that something special?"

"It is supposed to be. For all I know, she may have smoked a corncob pipe." Sally frowned a little. "Did you hire him?"

"I told him he could come and look the situation over. It's still in the air. Why?"

"Well, you know—the Irish. Waynesboro doesn't—he might not be helping matters much for his wife."

"Look, Sally, it's a disagreeable situation with his family that he wants to get away from. It's hard, having your brothers and sisters looking down on your wife, and your mother trying to pull your children away from their mother. Those are the circumstances as I understand them. I don't believe Captain Bodien would want, or expect, to be invited to your soirées. And I don't think his wife would give a damn for your Woman's Club," he concluded drily.

"That's all right, then. I just wanted to know what you expected of me," she said, with wifely humility. Ludwig laughed, and she hastened to add, "What's he like?"

"Like an Old Army man." Ludwig smiled as he remembered the short, square-set figure. "That is what he was, a gunner in the Regular Army before the war. U. S. Field Artillery."

"But, not an officer? If they were so aristocratic?"

"No. He ran away from home and enlisted when he was seventeen because, being the youngest son, they wanted to make him a priest."

"Oh dear, Catholics?"

"All the way down to him. Archers. Courseys. Bodiens. His wife. He isn't, most emphatically."

"He fought all through the war?"

"I believe so. Anyway, he was a captain when he was discharged, and in a Regular Army outfit that means something. I didn't ask him how he got to be captain, we had other things to discuss. But if he comes to Waynesboro, he will come as a mill superintendent, not as president of a bank."

"Did you hear of much hardship among veterans in the East?" Sally was endeavoring to lead up to the subject of the play that she had undertaken to promote, and that she had not mentioned in any of her letters. "There are soldiers' widows and orphans right here in Waynesboro that aren't getting enough to eat or wear."

"I didn't know, but I'm not surprised."

"I thought things were supposed to be getting better. Tim O'Reilly has finally got back on the railroad. Dock hired Martha's brother-in-law in his place—that Lonzo Mustard that used to work at the mill. D'you suppose Tim's wife will keep straight once she's out from under Dock's eye?"

"I don't see why not. They've got their pride back, if Tim's an engineer again. It's true that things are looking up some, but wages are low; the railroads have cut theirs, and I shouldn't be surprised if there was trouble. But what about the widows and orphans? They have it hard in the best of times. Who's stirred up about it? The G.A.R. might do something."

"Mrs. Bonner came to see me. The Ladies' Aid of their church is getting up a home talent play, a benefit."

Ludwig groaned. "She wanted you to be in it?"

"No—no she didn't."

"Not *me?* Oh, no! You made no promises for me?"

"Of course not. But they need all the men they can get, for soldiers. Wouldn't you, if it just meant walking on in your old uniform?"

"Not even that. I'm going to have no time for foolishness once Hayes is inaugurated. But Mrs. Bonner must have wanted something."

"Just to sort of ask my help. I'm looking out for costumes and properties, and seeing that all the parts are taken and that they get to rehearsals." She finished with mischief in her smile. "Making sure when a rehearsal is over that Henry Voorhees has a chance to beau Miss Blair home. They're the hero and heroine."

"Henry's a poor stick for an actor. Who else is in it? Anne?"

"No. Anne all of a sudden has begun talking about having neglected her family."

"Have you heard any gossip about Dock?"

"No, but I wouldn't be surprised if there were. Anne knows about his infidelities, of course, but she'd be burned at the stake before admitting it!"

"Yes," he said slowly, "not only out of pride but out of loyalty. The sad thing is I can't think he can help it. There's a darkness in him no one can reach, not even Anne. The war hurt him, inside, in a way those of us who fought and moved on never felt."

"Oh, pooh the war!" Sally said vigorously. "I've known Dock Gordon all my life. He was always like that: fits of moping."

"That kind of man must seek release somewhere—he has to—from himself. Some in liquor, some in petticoats, some in cards. It's as if the pressure of their own identity becomes unendurable. But you know you like Dock."

"Of course I like him. And trust him as a doctor, without reservation. But I wouldn't be his wife."

"That's good." He rose from his chair, crossed the room and bent above her, rubbing his cheek against her fair hair, crossing his arms around her neck. "Do you realize I'm a starved man home from a journey that has separated him for a month from his wife?"

But a few moments later, when he was sitting on the edge of the high-headboarded walnut bed, stooping over to unlace his shoes, and puffing a little as he spoke, he returned to the subject of the play.

"How do the Reformed Presbyterians and the Seminary folk like the idea of the sainted Miss Blair taking to the public stage?"

"I haven't heard. I hope I shall at the next Club meeting. But it's a chance for her to escape from the Seminary, if she wants to. In serving Henry Voorhees up to her this way, I feel as if I were snatching her from a fate worse than death."

Rehearsals for *Color Guard* continued for a couple of weeks after the inauguration, and everyone was so caught up in the excitement of it that the long, troubled winter was forgotten temporarily. Even the West End Irish who were among the cast (for had they not, too, been soldiers in Waynesboro regiments?) in the veterans' fife and drum corps and the low comedy parts were uplifted by their play-acting, and forgot their grievances as Democrats.

Color Guard was presented three times, and for three nights the Opera House was crowded. Even the second balcony was full to overflowing.

The play had not much plot, or perhaps too much; no one tried to follow it. There was instead marching and countermarching, unintelligible orders bellowed by General Deming in his uniform with the starred epaulettes, and an amount of small-arms fire and flag-waving that lifted little boys (and girls too, if they were like Elsa Rausch) into ecstasy. One line, intended seriously, brought gales of mirth from the house—a house that after all was composed mainly of veterans and their families. At the beginning of a skirmish with a handful of tattered Rebels, a soldier of "our side" called out to the hero "Bob Mason, a Scout" (Henry Voorhees) "Don't shoot, Bob! The cowards are afraid to fire!" This astonishing calumny was heard the first night in a silence that lasted several seconds before poor Bob was rocked back on his heels by a shout of masculine laughter. On the second and third nights, the moment was awaited with joyful anticipation, and when it came there was immediate counteradvice from the audience: "Don't you believe him, Bob!" "That's not the kind of Rebs I met!" "Shoot first or you'll never get a chance!"

In such a play, with its battle action, the stirring music of fife, drum, and bugle, and the pervasive odor of gunpowder permeating the air beyond the footlights, there was little place for scenes of young love. The very few minor women's parts were taken by representatives of various town groups. But Miss Christina Blair, who saw her lover off to the war and welcomed him home again, made the most of her role and won the hearts of her audience by the grace of her acting and particularly by the clear, easy sweetness of her voice when she sang to Bob on his return to her parlor "Juanita" and "Silver Threads Among the Gold" and "Believe Me If All Those Endearing Young Charms." If her audience could have had its way, it would have kept her singing to him all night, instead of allowing the curtain to come down.

On the third night Ludwig went to the play with the older children, and Sally sat with them instead of busying herself backstage. Once it was over and they were outside, he said, "It was worth sitting through all the foolishness just to hear that young woman sing. Mein Himmel! What a voice! And the pity of it! She'll be wasted, singing psalms all her life. And there are hundreds of girls with no voices trying to reach the concert stage."

"Of course she could never be a concert singer." Sally renounced a career for Miss Blair with no qualms. "She was funny at rehearsals. She kept saying, 'Never mind that part of it now. I'll sing when the time comes. I think the director began to believe she couldn't carry a tune, and was afraid she'd have to be thrown out of the part. So just once he insisted. He listened open-mouthed, and afterward I heard him ask her if he could help her get an audition with some great teacher. She just looked at him with that bland look of hers and said, 'Perhaps you don't understand my position here.'"

Ludwig laughed, but said, "She has great gifts."

"Oh, gifts! A brilliant mind, or she wouldn't have been teaching Hebrew at sixteen. A lovely voice. Acting ability. All for nothing because she was born a woman and a Blair."

"It's not the 'woman' so much as it is the 'Blair.'"

After the play the town rang for a few days with praises of Miss Blair. Its citizens forgot how very funny it had seemed, just a few months earlier, that a young girl, a pretty young girl, should be teaching Hebrew, and how that activity had set her off as something of a freak. Now they rejoiced that Miss Blair was settled in Waynesboro, to be called on for singing or acting when the need arose. But although some Reformed Presbyterians attended *Color Guard*, moved to forget for once the brimstone associations of The Stage both for the sake of war widows, orphans, and disabled and out of acceptance that whatever the Blairs did must be right in the sight of God, still there were others who held to their Covenanter tenets, who would hold to them though the skies fell. Amont them were the Reverend Mr. McCune and Mrs. Reid, who believed that President Blair and his daughter were making of themselves a stumbling block in the way of the righteous.

Amanda had been sure that her mother's rigidly adhered to rules of conduct would not permit her to countenance a stage performance before a public that had paid admission. Nevertheless, she sounded her out one evening when the theologues had eaten and gone, the dishes had been washed up after their dinner, and Mrs. Reid had joined her in the sitting room, where she had sat down at the round center table to work on the usual pile of Latin papers. Mrs. Reid dropped into her chair with a sigh that could hardly be ignored. It gave Amanda an opening.

"Mother, you work too hard. You need not continue to board the students; we can live on my salary. And now that there are twice as many of them, they overrun our capacity."

Since the two seminaries had been merged, the rather small rooms of the Reid house were crowded with the long tables used to seat the students. Both the parlor and the parlor bedroom had been turned into dining rooms, their original furniture stacked away in the barn. Downstairs only the sitting room was reserved for the Reids' personal use.

"I am managing quite well, with Mary Wilcox to help with the serving and the washing up."

"But you shouldn't work all the time. You could take an hour or two off now and then, just to enjoy yourself."

"Life wasn't meant to be *enjoyed!*" Mrs. Reid was tight-lipped. "And I prefer not to live on your salary, until I must. You will need all you can save before you are my age."

Her tone implied that her daughter could not, as an old woman, look out for herself. Amanda knew that her mother's motive in continuing to board the students was wholly righteous, and almost purely unselfish and sacrificial, but her martyrdom made the sacrifice hard to accept.

"I have plenty of time to save for my old age."

"You'd best be setting about it. You're past thirty."

"Yes. But can't we get a little harmless pleasure out of life as we go along?"

"Pleasure?"

"I know: enjoyment isn't what God put us on this earth for. I believe that too. But I like a little fun now and then, and I'd like you to have some, too. Will you go to *Color Guard* with me? I told Kurt Müller when he came to my desk with tickets that I would buy one, perhaps two."

"Then tell him tomorrow that you have changed your mind. Of course, I am not going to the theater, and neither are you. I have always been afraid of your associations with the women in that Club of yours. Oh, Amanda! Think what your father would say!"

"He died when I was so very small, I have no idea what he would say. Perhaps he would have changed with the times."

"You know that he lived and died an Old Light Covenanter. He would have forbidden you to go."

"You just got through reminding me that I am thirty-one years old. I intend to go. The only question is whether you will go with me."

"Amanda, what makes you so hard?" Then she answered her own question. "Schoolteachers all get like that. They are so in the habit of laying down the law. No. You remember that I went to the Christmas party at the Cochrans' with you, against my better judgment, and found that you had kept me in the dark. If I had known beforehand it was going to be a play, I wouldn't have gone. I should have suspected that was what the Cochran girl—what's her name—Rausch—had been working up to all these years, with her Christmas parties and heathenish trees and tableaux."

"But there wasn't anything in that Christmas play."

"I was never in my life so disgusted and mortified! With gentlemen present, the daughter of the president of the Reformed Presbyterian Theological Seminary acting a bedroom scene, actually lying down on what was supposed to be a *bed*, while that villain ogled her. I grant you, her limbs were covered, but what must any man have had in his mind?"

"He wasn't a man, he was Kitty Edwards."

"But the men in the audience? What could they have been thinking?"

"What the rest of us had in our minds, no doubt. That she looked very pretty lying there, but that the effect became merely humorous when they had all that trouble getting the bracelet off. Certainly her father laughed." Amanda wondered if all good women's minds turned nasty when they got old enough.

"I saw him laughing. It has always seemed strange to me how anyone who is so careless of what is right and seemly could have been given his position. *Now* I can't understand what the Synod was thinking of."

"*Color Guard* is being given for a cause he supports. This isn't play-acting just for a party. Though I have no doubt the cast enjoys it," Amanda added honestly.

"The government is paying pensions to widows and the disabled, is it not? I cannot see that they are our responsibility."

"If you could see Kurt Müller and one or two others whom I teach, you would not speak so without pity. They are in rags and undernourished. Besides—" She was going to say something about Christ's views on responsibility for those who starved, but decided it was wiser to let it go.

"What are they doing in high school, then? Let them quit and go to work."

"But Mother—" Amanda felt, as she often did, that she could not bear to argue with her mother another moment, but some driving necessity in her to explain pushed her on. "Don't you know anything about the world you are living in? These are hard times. Grown men cannot find work, let alone half-grown boys."

"No, Amanda; school teaching certainly does not agree with you. So overbearing. And you come home so cross. I suppose you hold it in all day, then let me have the full benefit at night."

"I'm sorry, Mother." Amanda gave it up, turned to work on her papers. There just might be something in what her mother had said; it was easy enough to cherish a completely false picture of oneself. She did not think she felt cross at school—not very often—she liked it too well; but she must try to control at home the irritation that mastered her there. "Mastered" was the right word, and it frightened her. Sometimes she could feel her skull red inside, inflamed not with fury, just irritability. She kept her eyes resolutely on the paper in front of her until she actually saw it, and began half-automatically to check the errors. She said no more about the play, that night or afterward, but her mother was unable to let a subject alone. She told Amanda so often in the next few days that she forbade her to put a foot inside the Opera House that she perhaps thought she would be obeyed. For when the night came, and the Ballard carriage stopped before their house and the Judge himself came to the door while Samuel Travers, who was driving, held the horses—when Amanda appeared on the staircase dressed to go out, Mrs. Reid, who had opened the door, stood like one stricken. She could hardly enunciate an audible good evening to the Judge.

He spoke of her to Amanda as they went down the path. "Your mother? Is she ill?"

"No. Shocked and hurt that I should act against her convictions and go to the Opera House."

"Then Dr. Blair's approval—or perhaps I should say his complaisance—doesn't move her?"

"No. But don't trouble yourself about it, Judge Ballard. I cannot let her make my life for me entirely, and she may in time come to accept the fact that I am grown up."

But if the day were to come when Mrs. Reid would admit that Amanda must live her life by her own conscience and not another's, there was no forgiving sign of such a change of heart in the days after the play. She had a grievance, and she nursed it. When she had worried herself long enough over her inability to waken her daughter's conscience, she decided to hand the problem over to the one person who might move Amanda: her pastor.

She did not start for the McCunes' empty-handed. Mrs. McCune, who was pregnant with what would be her sixth child, had been absent from Sabbath Day services and midweek prayer meetings for several weeks. Mrs. Reid assumed with an inward, fastidious shudder that she had grown suggestively unsightly and was hiding herself away from the congregation. But she might be feeling unwell enough to welcome invalid food, and in any case, with her big family, would welcome a contribution. When Mrs. Reid had washed the dishes after the students' noon dinner, she made a big bowl of floating island, and carrying it carefully between the palms of her hands started her long walk; in Linden Street, past the muddy vacant stretches where the high winds of March whipped her heavy skirts about her ankles and she was helpless to untwist them, or to cling to her bonnet. She half-hoped, all the way up the hill, that she would hear a carriage coming along behind her; surely any acquaintance, seeing her burden, would give her a lift. But no one in all the length of Linden Street was driving abroad. Her bowl was becoming very heavy by the time she crossed Market Street at the Alexanders' corner. "Alexander House" it had been, was, and always would be, to her. She had liked Mrs. Alexander, long ago when they had been young women, although the doctor's wife had been plain Presbyterian and not Reformed, but she could not approve of her daughter, who had married a godless man and in spite of that took life gaily, always quick to laugh. That disapproval did not prevent her pausing on the brick pavement when she saw Anne driving her phaeton-buggy down the alley between the house and the doctor's office, with Lonzo behind her shutting the stable-yard gate.

Anne pulled the old mare to a stop where the sidewalk passed the end of the alley. "Good afternoon, Mrs. Reid. Can I take you somewhere?"

"I wouldn't want to take you out of your way."

"I'm driving to the farm to pick up some eggs and butter. The doctor hasn't had time this week."

She leaned over and took the bowl of floating island as Mrs. Reid lifted it up.

"No, you needn't get down to help me, thank you. I'm still spry enough." She climbed in as Anne cramped the wheel for her. "I'm taking a bit of floating island to Mrs. McCune, same time's I consult him about a matter of conscience."

Anne thought, "Poor Amanda," and asked aloud if Mrs. McCune was ill. "'She hasn't been to Club for quite a while, but I thought it was just that she wasn't going out now."

"I don't know as she's sick. But she's bound to have more than she can do, in her condition, and I thought a dessert for the family wouldn't come amiss."

Anne's conscience smote her a little because she had not paid more attention to Mrs. McCune. The few times they had both been present at Club meetings since the New Year, the events of the Christmas party, the horrid scene at the gate, had lain between them, not spoken of, but not forgotten. Mrs. McCune, instead of waylaying, had seemed almost to be avoiding her, and Anne had cooperated; she admitted it now to herself. She had felt relieved. And during all these weeks that Mrs. McCune had missed the fortnightly Club meetings, her inquiries had been casual ones. John had been so sure that night of the Christmas party that the poor woman was really ill. She should have called to inquire, herself.

The Reformed Presbyterian church stood on the east side of College Street, between Chillicothe and Sycamore, its back turned toward the approaching tide of colored folk in the East End. It was the oldest church in town. Other denominations had rebuilt, in mid-century or later, brick Victorian Gothic edifices filling their lots from front pavement to rear alley, but the old Reformed Presbyterian church still served a congregation that had long outgrown it, still stood in the middle of the grove of oak trees that had, on bygone Sabbaths, sheltered the families who sat beneath them to eat cold lunches between morning and afternoon preaching. The dark little building was well proportioned, brick, with square pilasters, also brick at the corners and down the side walls between the small-paned windows. The double-doored entrance was square, unadorned except for an acanthus-and-cockle-shell motif carved of wood and attached to the center of the lintel. Door frame and the entrance molding were all painted white.

The manse, next door, was also odd, simple, plain. It stood farther back from the street and in summer was well concealed by shrubs and low-hanging trees. The bleakness of March exposed it to passersby, austere and a little gloomy at the far end of the root-broken brick path.

Anne said, "You sit still, Mrs. Reid, while I hitch Molly, then I can come around and help you. I think I'll go in with you and inquire."

She got Mrs. Reid and the bowl of floating island safely to the ground. In silence they passed through the picket gate and up the uneven walk, dodging puddles and a residue of mud in shallower hollows. Anne kept her eyes on the house, thinking how unlikely it was that five children could live anywhere and not mitigate in the slightest any original grimness. It was one of the five who opened the door for them, a girl of eight or nine, with pigtails and bangs and a thin triangular face, all eyes and ears. Anne had never known one of the McCune children from another, but Mrs. Reid knew this one and called her by name.

"Good afternoon, Ariana. Is your father at home?"

"Yes, ma'am." The child opened the door to them. Mrs. Reid let the bowl of floating island slip slowly through her fingers until it came to rest on the hall table.

"You know me, surely, Ariana? Can't you say 'Yes, Mrs. Reid!' Will you ask your father if he will see me?"

"Yes, Mrs. Reid." The child looked inquiringly at Anne.

"This is Mrs. Gordon. She came to inquire for your mother. They are members of the same club."

"Oh, I know." The thin face came to life. "Johnny's mother." And with an odd grown-up inflection, "Mamma has mentioned you, But—" She hesitated and her voice came out toneless and flat. "She's sick."

"Then will you tell her for me, please, that I asked for her?" Suddenly Anne wanted to get out of the house, without even appeasing her conscience. "Just tell her that we miss her at the Club."

Before Ariana could reply, Mr. McCune came down the hall and advanced to greet them. Mrs. Reid explained the bowl on the table, and Ariana was instructed to take it to the kitchen.

"Did I hear you asking for me? Or did you come like a kind parishioner, to call on my wife?" For a moment he ignored Anne. The Reverend Mr. McCune was sandy-haired and browed, with a pointed nose and a nutcracker mouth and chin, spare and not very tall, unimpressive looking, with his quick jerking motions, his rapid bobbing walk. Some not of his flock might call him "a little grasshopper of a man," but members of his congregation and his family knew him better. Here, in his own hall, Anne felt his coldness as he listened to Mrs. Reid explaining she had come to see him primarily, but also to ask after his wife. Mrs. Gordon had been kind enough to give her a lift when she saw her passing, and decided to come in also, to inquire as to the health of Mrs. McCune.

"But the little girl says she is sick." Anne would have expressed her regrets and gone had he not caught her up abruptly.

"Oh, not ill, Mrs. Gordon. Just—er—indisposed and keeping to her room for a few days. The children do not understand these situations." He laughed, after a fashion.

"You think she would like to see me, then? Could the little girl, Ariana, show me to her room? While you are talking with Mrs. Reid?"

He froze instantly. "Oh, I think not—not without my announcing you. I am not sure from hour to hour. Would you be kind enough to wait in the parlor until I have my little talk with Mrs. Reid? And then we can all go up together for a few moments."

Anne allowed him to usher her into the tomblike parlor. She understood that for some reason Mr. McCune wanted her to see his wife, or he would not have stopped her departure, but that he did not want her to go upstairs alone, or visit Mrs. McCune without him. She did not see why, and she did not like it, but she gathered her cloak about her and prepared to wait, since evidently spiritual fortification of a member of his congregation came before attention to his wife.

Mrs. Reid followed him into his study, a cold musty room smelling of books, tidy but deep in dust. His children, or Ariana, at any rate, was surely old enough to keep the house dusted. But maybe he didn't want Ariana in his study; with so many children in the house, it might be his only refuge. Sighing, Mrs. Reid took the straight chair he offered her, beside his desk, and let her dark skirt fall in a half-circle on the floor at one side. She did not untie the strings of her flat black bonnet with the faded cotton lilacs under its edge, nor did she take off her gloves. She folded her hands in her lap and began her lament over the forward and perverse generation, and particularly over her daughter as a member of it. He promised to call soon and exhort Amanda.

"The church sociables offer our young people an outlet for their high spirits. But I suppose she's a little old, she could hardly play 'Spin the Platter' with a group including students of hers. We must see if we can't find something that will feed the minds of those Amanda's age, without destroying their convictions." Then he shifted the subject sideways a little, and did what was most important for Mrs. Reid's peace of mind: he agreed with her about Dr. Blair. "I—um—comprehend the source of this idea now taking root among us that *pleasure* is a desirable end in itself. To you and me—this is confidential, of course—that and other aberrations might disqualify a man for leadership in the church, however sound a scholar he might be, or however able an administrator. I know this dramatic performance had a charitable end in view, but it is my belief that it was given because the performers enjoyed doing it and the audience enjoyed seeing it, with no thought of the danger inherent in the *theater*. And I fear politics entered into the calculations of those who permitted it."

Mrs. Reid was bewildered: to drag in politics seemed to her to be going far afield. But Mr. McCune was emphatic. "I know that most New Side Covenanters now vote, but to go so far as to attempt to manipulate the votes of others—however, it is not for me to criticize a man chosen for an important post by the General Synod. And there is some slight excuse. You knew, probably, that his sons by his first wife were killed in battle. You perhaps did not know that he served for a while as chaplain of one of the Pittsburgh regiments. He never mentions it, I believe. I am given to understand that he still feels humiliated because his asthma prevented his taking the field. He had to resign before his regiment ever went into battle. But his time in the army no doubt helped to break down his guard against what *some* of us still regard as evil. And no doubt his sympathy for the young soldiers, whatever their backgrounds, left him with an interest in the physical as well as the spiritual welfare of the veterans, and consequently, an interest in politics."

When he had promised again to speak to Amanda, Mrs. Reid rose to rejoin Anne. "You're sure it will be advisable for Mrs. McCune to receive callers? I did not realize she was sick."

Mr. McCune repeated what he had said before, "I feel confident she is not really *ill*. She has these—er—difficulties at such times; she has preferred to keep to her room for the last fortnight. I thought you knew," and he smiled pathetically, "that Ariana and I were 'making do' in the kitchen, since you so kindly brought us the pudding."

"No, I didn't know. The last Sabbath Mrs. McCune was in church I thought she was looking very unwell, but I brought the floating island because I hoped she would enjoy it, and would save her some trouble with supper. But if she is in bed, she might prefer not to be bothered with visitors."

"She is not right down in bed. She has been suffering some from nausea, and is weak. She refuses to let me call the doctor; says it is just like all the other times. And I fear she has taken an irrational dislike to our good Dr. Wright. If you and Mrs. Gordon would talk to her for a moment, it might rouse her interest in the world outside her sickroom. I feel that this is a passing phase," he added, evading Mrs. Reid's eyes. "We have been through it before, but it is most upsetting while it lasts."

They came into the hall and stopped at the parlor door for Anne. She rose stiffly, the cold of the unheated room in her bones and a colder apprehension in her mind. As Mr. McCune waited for her, and she passed him at the threshold, she shivered; there was the shadow of a look of fear somewhere at the back of his pale-lashed, pale-blue, hastily averted eyes.

He led them upstairs and to the bedroom door. He entered, closing the door behind him, then after a moment, opened it and waved them in. As Anne followed Mrs. Reid, she thought the way he looked at the older woman confirmed what she had seen in his eyes below the stairs; he was wordlessly beseeching Mrs. Reid for reassurance. But that look of appeal was not forewarning enough for Anne. The shock she felt at the sight of Mrs. McCune must have shown on her face. But Mrs. Reid was in front of her, and, scarcely within the room, stopped stock-still for a moment, so that Anne, behind her, could bring her face to some degree of composure. She was thinking, "The woman is desperately ill. We have no business to be here." But she did not turn and flee because Mrs. McCune's eyes were closed; instead she made the most of the moment's respite.

The sick woman was half-sitting, half-lying in a deep armchair with her head back against a crumpled pillow. Her skin was yellow, with a tallowy shine, and drawn tight; the flesh had been burnt away from under it, so that the knifelike ridge of her nose and her narrow jaw looked as if they might cut through it. Under the tallow on her cheekbones burnt an ugly dark flush of fever. Her hands, folded above the great lump of unborn child, were like claws. To Anne it was incredible; this could not have happened in the little while since she had seen Mrs. McCune. She closed her eyes for a moment, with a barely suggested shake of her head, then opened them again. The light in the room was clear and hard, with a sunny March day's brilliance; there were no shadows to create unreal horrors. Anne swallowed and stepped forward to speak. Although Mrs. McCune's eyes remained shut, it was clearly out of exhaustion, or indifference; she was not asleep, for her hands moved from her lap to the arms of her chair.

Mr. McCune spoke first, in a cheerful voice that was false as mockery in that room. "Company for you, Mary. Wouldn't you like to talk with these ladies for a little while?"

Mary opened her eyes. They had a shallow glazed look. She tried to smile.

"Mrs. Reid?" Her voice was a thin thread of sound. "Mrs. Gordon? Come in, won't you, and sit down?"

Anne drew a long breath. "I am afraid I can't stop. I just wanted to bring you the good wishes of the ladies of the Club, and my own."

Mrs. Reid was settling herself in a straight chair beside the window. Anne looked at her pleadingly. She was sure they ought not to stay and force that sick woman, by their presence, to make any effort at all. But what could she say? Not "You look so awful I know we ought not to be here."

Mrs. McCune tried again. "Please. Won't you sit down?"

"I am afraid I must not this afternoon. I am on my way out to the farm for eggs for my family. Some other time, when I hope you will be feeling better."

Mrs. McCune looked over Anne's shoulder at her husband. There was more life in her eyes now, but it was a queer look, half-defiant, half-triumphant. "I'm sorry," she whispered. Then she was brought upright by a fit of coughing, which she stifled with the towel lying on the arm of her chair. When she had subdued the paroxysm, she went on. "I wouldn't mind if you would ask—would ask—your husband to stop by."

"Now, Mary." Her husband's voice was soothing, as to an unreasonable child, but there was no warmth in it. "You know that Dr. Wright would come if you would permit me to send for him. He has helped you before."

Mrs. McCune dropped her head back on the pillow behind her. Anne said, "Goodbye. I hope you will be over this ordeal soon. We miss you at the Club."

Mr. McCune followed her out of the room and down the stairs, talking as soon as the door closed behind him. His words were conventional, but there was an inimical glitter in his eyes.

"Please do not misunderstand, Mrs. Gordon. I am in no doubt as to your husband's qualifications as a physician. But Dr. Wright has always been our doctor. You, of course, know that in this—er—situation, ailing women have their whims. I think that I must not indulge her further but send for Wright, whether she wants him or not."

Anne's answer was cold, trembling on the verge of anger. He should have called a doctor long before this. "I understand perfectly, Mr. McCune. You may rest assured that I shall not deliver her message to my husband."

"Yes. I'm sure you appreciate—two physicians would be just one too many, would it not?" He laughed his high, self-conscious ministerial laugh as he opened the door for her. "I regret that you cannot stay longer. But Mary will be in good hands while Mrs. Reid stays with her, and I can go back to my work with an easy mind." He closed the door behind her. Anne stood for a moment on the doorstone, listening vaguely to children's voices from somewhere behind the house; the small Ariana probably had to stay home from school to look after the younger ones. She started down the walk with a firm-enough step, thinking about the children, but her mind was not made for that kind of hide-and-seek with unpleasant truth. When she reached the hitching post, her hands were trembling so that she could not unfasten Molly's strap. She stopped trying, and stood looking beyond the angle of the picket fence at the blur that was the church. Presently the scene came into focus, the mist cleared. She saw the late afternoon sun falling across the long wall at such an angle that all the irregularities in the old hand-made bricks were plain to see, casting their own small gray shadows. The black lines that were the shade of oak tree boughs slanted down and across the rosy bricks. She did not consciously think "beautiful" or "old," but somehow from their age and beauty she drew heart. Her fingers were her own again; she unbuckled the hitching strap. For a premonitory instant, she knew that she would never forget that moment; she would always have for hers that wall, its sun and shadow. But after she had turned the buggy and was on her way, she thought how much had gone into the building long ago: love of the church, every brick made by the hands of the congregation; love of one member for another, else they could not have done it. And what now had become of all that love? Mr. McCune and a congregation suited to his bigotry. Mrs. Reid.

Back in the manse, from the bedroom window, Mrs. Reid had watched her drive away. She felt forsaken; she had not meant to be left like this, alone with—with—she did not put into words in her own mind the rest of the sentence, but turned back toward Mrs. McCune, her eyes on the floor. She said, "I brought you some floating island. Would you like some now? I could call Ariana, or find a dish and spoon myself."

The sick face was turned to the pillow, the tallowy skin damp, the mouth expressing repugnance, as if Mrs. Reid herself were offensive.

"I couldn't. Thank you—kindness. But I can't keep anything down."

"Not anything?" The two women looked at each other. Pretense was forgotten. Mrs. Reid stammered, "How long—since—?"

"I forgot. Ariana—worries—would know. I've lost count—days." Mrs. McCune was caught by another spasm of coughing. When it died away leaving her exhausted, Mrs. Reid brought a damp cloth from the rack by the wash stand and wiped her face. She went on then, as if she had not been interrupted. "It will—pass. It always has."

"But haven't you seen the doctor? He could help you, surely."

Mrs. McCune moved her head on the pillow. "Not Dr. Wright. Never has—helped. So—ladylike. You can't—can't—you can't *lean* on him." A grimace that might have been meant for a smile pulled at her colorless mouth.

Mrs. Reid rose in her agitation. "But you must! I know I may seem like an interfering old woman, but I don't believe your husband realizes how very wretched you are."

"No." For the first time the clouded eyes cleared a little. "Didn't want him to know. First duty—wife—bearing children—without fuss." Surprisingly then, tears filled her eyes—surprisingly because she had looked so beyond all emotion. "The poor children—"

"We'll get a doctor for you, so that you will soon feel better. Today anyone can see you don't feel like company."

"Can't talk." She was torn by another spell of coughing, or half-coughing, half-retching. Once more Mrs. Reid wiped her face when it was over, noting with horror as she did so that the towel Mrs. McCune had dropped back on the arm of the chair was spotted with blood. She pretended not to notice, but returned the washcloth to the rack, said good-bye, and started for the door. Behind her the sick woman said again, "Dr. Gordon—he is so—I think his wife is so—" Then she gave it up and leaned back once more against her pillow, her eyes closed.

Mrs. Reid shut the bedroom door softly behind her. She stood for a moment at the head of the stairs shaking out and smoothing her skirts, as if thus to compose herself, then tiptoed down and went back along the hall to the study door. She tapped and was told to enter.

"Mrs. Reid? Going so soon?" Mr. McCune rose from the chair behind his desk, but did not leave it. She stopped in the doorway for her second interview with him.

"She's too sick for company. Mr. McCune, has she ever been quite so bad as this, other times?"

He hesitated. "It has always seemed so, yes. I fear she is not very strong."

"She should see a doctor."

"She won't hear of it. She has no faith in Dr. Wright." A gesture indicated his helplessness.

"She wants Dr. Gordon."

"A sick woman's caprice, surely? He is not in my congregation." His lips set in their thin line. "Nor any, to my knowledge. I do not propose to introduce an unregenerate man of that sort into my home."

"But Dr. Blair—"

"I am aware that Dr. Gordon is his physician. But I do not follow Blair's lead, as you know. And I cannot afford—"

To pay doctors' bills, she thought he had started to say. She also knew shuffling old Dr. Wright: he did not like responsibility, sole responsibility, in serious cases. And when he had been called in so late—too late? For a moment her heart raced, and she leaned against the door frame. Jerkily she said, "Do have Dr. Wright, then, and if he thinks it would help, he will suggest consulting Dr. Gordon. You know John's folks were Presbyterian. I don't understand that young man's ways, but no one would think you were countenancing them if Dr. Wright asked for him. I don't mean to argue with you. It would be presumptuous. But I think someone coming in from outside can see more clearly than you how—how very ill she is. You know," she dropped her voice, "you wouldn't want to have anything to reproach yourself with. It isn't that I approve of John Gordon, either—I've known him from a boy—but if he can do her any good—"

Having said her say, she waited for no good-byes, but closed the study door behind her.

Anne in the meantime had been on her way to the Gordon farm. It was a short drive, ordinarily, even behind old Molly, but that day it seemed endless because she could not get the picture of Mrs. McCune out of her mind. She was remorseful; she should have known. Had it been anyone else—well, almost anyone else—in the Club, she would have known. She wanted to tell John, but she had no moment alone with him until after their evening dinner, when the children had been excused and Martha had cleared off the dessert dishes and left them with their coffee. Martha might hear—she might even tell—but what she told would never get back to a white ear, so it didn't matter.

"John, you remember that night coming home from Sally's Christmas party, what you said about Mrs. McCune's condition? Could she have been saved then by good doctoring?"

"I doubt it. Why? Is she—"

She told him what she had seen that afternoon. "And she wants you, John. She told me to tell you. And that makes it more dreadful. Because you can't go, can you?"

"Certainly not. Wright is their man."

"You know Dr. Wright never was very good. Any of his patients just medium sick he scares into thinking they're dying, then effects miraculous cures. But let anyone be *really* sick and he asks for a consultation. No more deathbeds in his practice than he can help."

"You never got that from me."

"No. From Papa." She spoke contemptuously.

"Of course he wouldn't charge his pastor's family, so there wouldn't be *that* reason for not giving up the case. But I'm not looking for deathbeds, myself." He pushed his coffee cup back and rose from his chair, thus indicating there was to be no further discussion of Dr. Wright or the McCunes.

But a few days later he did to a certain extent unburden himself to Anne, since she had been cognizant from the beginning of the case of Mary McCune. He had returned directly home from the manse. It was not quite noon, and Johnny had not come in from school. Binny was playing with her rag doll on the floor around Anne's skirts, but she was not old enough to count as audience. Anne was in her rocker at one side of the hearth, her lap full of darning basket and mended and unmended socks.

"Has something happened? You're home early."

"I've been up to McCune's." He crossed behind her to his chair at the other end of the fender. "Wright called me in as a consulting physician."

"He was bound to call in someone. I expect she asked for you."

"Maybe. As you said the other day, Wright always calls in someone if a case threatens to end fatally. He's going to enjoy turning this one over to me; she wanted me, she's got me, and she's going to die. In his eyes it'll even up a bit for the Blairs."

"Oh, John! Then you can't save her?"

"Not a chance. Didn't you know when you saw her the other day that she is a dying woman? Of course you did, though maybe you didn't admit it to yourself." He smiled at her wearily.

"But John?"

"As I told you at Christmas, advanced case of phthisis, complicated by pregnancy. Now, pernicious vomiting. I told the Reverend so in plain words. There was some biddy from the church helping in the sickroom, but when we came out of the Reverend's study, she was dusting in the hall. I suspect her of having had an ear at the keyhole, so everyone in town will soon know. But you don't—"

"Naturally not. Oh, dear, how awful! How sad for him and those poor children!"

"The children, yes. Him, no. He the same as murdered her."

"He, or Dr. Wright?"

"He admitted he knew she had a 'bit of lung trouble.' She's carrying his—what's the number?—sixth child."

"Did you call him a murderer? It would be just like you."

Anne straightened from her darning and looked at him, clear-eyed. Unexpectedly the thought flashed through her mind: "Funny the things husbands hate to see other husbands do to their wives."

"Not in so many words." John, glowering, gave her an expurgated account of the morning. Dr. Wright had stopped in his office to ask if he would be willing to go with him to the McCunes. "So I got my plug hat out of the cupboard, and my frock coat." He smiled at Anne. She had always wanted him to dress formally for all his calls, as her father had done; he would do so only when going out as consultant with one of the older physicians.

They had found Mrs. McCune in her chair by the window. The medical men had got rid of Mr. McCune as quickly as possible, and had gone to stand by her chair. She tried to smile at John as Dr. Wright said, "We've brought a younger man to see you, in the hope he knows some newfangled treatment that will help you." Dr. Wright was a round-faced little man with a benign countenance, an unctuous voice, and a way of gesturing airily with his soft white hands. Mrs. McCune looked from him to John, to John's hands, strong, firm, reddened by carbolic solution; she even tried to smile again as he took her wrist to feel her pulse. But when he reached into his bag for his stethoscope, she leaned her head back and closed her eyes.

Finally he too sank back into the chair he had pulled up; he sat looking at her, absently swinging the stethoscope. She opened her eyes then. The question in them he did not answer.

"Do you feel better sitting up? Breathe easier? Or is it just that you won't give up?"

"The children—so frightened—never seen me down—sick—"

"You will have to think of yourself now. We'll manage somehow about the children. You would be better off in bed." John picked up the bottle of medicine from the stand beside her and looked at it. Dr. Wright said, "To stop the vomiting."

"But it hasn't stopped?"

She moved her head sideways in negation.

"How long since you have retained any food?"

She moved her head again.

"We'll try to find something that will help. If you will excuse us, Dr. Wright and I will get in a corner somewhere and talk over what is best to do."

She besought him with her burned-out eyes. "You'll come again?"

He hesitated. Dr. Wright said, "Of course he will. I knew all along you would prefer a younger man than I am coming to visit you." The falsely jovial notes hung and died in the close air of the bedroom. "You will take over, won't you, Dr. Gordon? The patient's preference is everything in a case of this kind."

John almost cried out against this. As if it were not too late. He merely looked his protest, and after a long pause said, "Very well. If Mr. McCune desires it. I must see him," he said to Mrs. McCune. "Then I'll be back." The two doctors left the room. The upper hall was empty. At its far end, where the stairs went down, they stopped for their discussion. Dr. Wright explained again that he had been called in but a few days before. Too late, he feared, with a question mark in his voice. John agreed grimly. "The woman's starved to death. We can try rectal feeding. But even if that succeeds, with the help of opium—there's still the phthisis." And he bit off the words savagely: "Now for McCune."

They went downstairs. Dr. Wright knocked on the study door, led the way in, and would have introduced Dr. Gordon to the older man. He was cut short.

"I am acquainted with Dr. Gordon. Our wives are—er—friends." The memory of the Christmas party hung between them.

For a moment there was silence, then Mr. McCune said, "Well, gentlemen?" in a voice that showed he had courage for no more words.

John, at his dourest, kept silent and left it to Dr. Wright, who said softly, "We hope we can make her more comfortable."

"'More comfortable'? Doctor, what do you mean? The women who have been buzzing about my ears have led me to believe that Mary was worse than just 'uncomfortable.' So all this panic comes down to making her 'more comfortable'!"

"It is too late for anything more." The muscles worked along John's jawbones.

"'Too late'? You mean—too near her time?"

"Too near her time. Yes. But not exactly as you mean it."

"You are trying to tell me that my wife is—is not—is not going to get over this? That she will not recover because you were not called in sooner?" Mr.

McCune sat bolt upright behind his desk. There was outrage in his tone. He did not inspire pity.

"Having a doctor sooner wouldn't have helped, unless months ago you would have consented to an abortion."

"An—! No! That the child was conceived was the will of God, to have destroyed it would have been murder."

John restrained himself. "I supposed that would be your attitude. In that case, it was too late from the moment the child was conceived." He paused, hesitated, continued. "In fact, it's been too late for a long time. Didn't you know that your wife has consumption? That would have killed her, anyway—perhaps not so quickly, if she had not been subjected to the strain of child-bearing."

It was then that Mr. McCune admitted that he had known she had lung trouble. "But," he said, "she always seemed well except when—"

"She was nearing the end of a pregnancy?"

He nodded.

"You've been married how long?"

"Eleven years."

"How many children?"

"Five, not counting this one. One miscarriage."

"Then she's been pregnant most of her married life?"

"Yes. I suppose." Mr. McCune's face was rigid, his mouth drawn. "I hadn't thought of it like that. We considered that God had blessed us above most. What is His will we must accept." He bent his head for a moment; his lips moved in prayer.

John waited. When Mr. McCune looked up again he said, "Whether it was you or the Lord that was responsible, I wouldn't presume to say. But this last child was just one too many."

Later, when he was talking to Anne, John skipped over his examination of Mrs. McCune and the state he had found her in, but he reported what he had said to her husband. Anne groaned when he unburdened himself of this part of his story. "Didn't he call you blasphemous? You'll never have another R.P. patient."

"And do you think I care?"

"But John! Weren't you sorry for him? I mean, *couldn't* you be? Didn't he feel it, that his wife was going to die?"

"I don't know." There had been a moment at the end of their interview when Mr. McCune had said through that stiff mouth, "I cannot believe that it is the will of God that Mary should be lost to us, when we need her so."

John put his hands on the desk and leaned toward Mr. McCune, stiff-armed. "You mean you still think that she will recover? Then call in some other physician. I do not care to be responsible, if you expect miracles."

Dr. Wright twittered nervously, "Now, now, gentlemen! The Reverend

Mr. McCune expects no miracles. Reverend, you must believe us. Of course, while there is life there is hope, and prayer accomplishes much."

"Death is looking out of her eyes now," John cut him off. "I've seen it too often not to recognize it."

Then had come the moment when John had felt a twinge of pity, when Mr. McCune had said, in a lost, bleak voice, "But what am I to do?"

John, accustomed to dealing with troubles of this sort, said, "Is there anyone to nurse your wife?"

"Mrs. Milburn, in our church, does that kind of work."

"Then send one of the children to fetch her. Tell her to put Mrs. McCune to bed. Say that I'll be back to show her what to do. Is there anyone who could keep house for you for a few weeks, until you make permanent arrangements?"

"Permanent—I refuse—Mary has a cousin in Hanover, Indiana, who is unmarried and might be willing. I could telegraph her."

"Do. Someone will have to get the meals, keep the house going. Mrs. Milburn will need to spend all her time in the sickroom." John looked appraisingly at the man behind the desk. "I am sorry if I have seemed brutal to you. I hate to see anyone die so young. It makes a doctor feel so helpless." He had growled out the apology because the minister had for a moment looked so shrunken and pitiful. He regretted it when Mr. McCune drew himself up and murmured, "Who am I to question the Lord's will? The Lord giveth and the Lord taketh away."

With an angry snort, John had turned and walked out of the study, leaving Dr. Wright to follow when he pleased.

Later, when the news had spread, the Reformed Presbyterian congregation came to the help of their stricken minister and his family. Until Mrs. McCune's cousin arrived to keep house for him, the women of his church took turns every day, cooking and cleaning. If they also commented, among themselves, on the sad state in which they found the manse, it was only among themselves; Reformed Presbyterians did not criticize Reformed Presbyterians to outsiders. Without hesitation they farmed out the children among themselves, until the worst should be over; Matthew, Mark, and Luke (there would be no "John") and the younger girl, a plain, sandy-haired child of five, named Ruhamah. Ariana was invited as a guest not to the house of one of the congregation but to the Samuel Traverses'. The arrangement came about through Amanda Reid and in spite of Mr. McCune's opposition. He was reluctant to permit her to go to a non-Calvinist, and therefore presumably unsaved, family, however distinguished its members in the eyes of the world. Amanda had been horrified by her mother's first report of Mrs. McCune's condition, and had wanted to ask for Ariana herself when the children were parceled out; she was moved by pity, and feared that the sensitive little girl would be entrusted to awkward hands, however kind, and that her suffering would go unnoticed. The brothers and sisters she knew only through having observed the line of them in the ministerial pew at church services, but Ariana was in her Sabbath school class. And Amanda knew her as a child tense, like an arrow in a drawn bow, and quick as the arrow in flight; it was as if she had been shaped by the absurd name Mrs. McCune had been allowed to give her. She was unlike the McCunes in looks also; her eyes gray, dark-lashed, her nose straight, the lower part of her face narrow, perhaps a little too sharp. Against her thick plaits, her large, transparently thin ears stood out in an odd Puckish fashion. Amanda, not by nature a lover of children, wanted her spared as much grief as possible. But for the Reids to take her was out of the question; Amanda deplored the circumstances to Thomasina as they walked home together from a Club meeting a few days after Mrs. McCune's condition had become generally known.

Thomasina said, "Oh, let me, Amanda! I haven't half enough to do, even with my writing." Thomasina would never have so much as mentioned "my writing" to anyone except Amanda, who saw it as she did herself: a way to earn a few dollars—moral tales like her mother's for Sunday school papers, and rhymes for boys and girls. Now she was not even aware of having used the words that would once have made her self-conscious; she was remembering her father's account of his orphaned boyhood. "Separating brothers and sisters that way at a time when they might share their sorrow, even if it's only for a little while, is hard for them to bear. And Ariana could stay upstairs with Samuel and me. She wouldn't bother anyone, and maybe we could make it a little easier for her."

Thomasina had her way. That very evening she had Fritz drive her to the McCunes', overbore the minister's protests, and led the child out to the carriage, herself bearing the pitiful little bundle of clothes it had not been worth sending Fritz in for.

The Ballards did not insist that Thomasina keep the child upstairs in her apartment. They were charitable in practice as well as in principle; even Eliza would have called herself so. At first Ariana came downstairs only for meals, clinging to Thomasina's hand. But her awe of the magnificent house soon wore off; she knew before long that Judge Ballard was kind, although he was old, stiff, and remote, and talked like a book. In a little while the quiet child had won her way into their affections. One evening while they were all in the sitting room having tea after dinner, she went to stand by Eliza's chair.

"Mrs. Travers says I may call her Aunt Thomasina. Would you like me to call you Aunt Eliza?"

Eliza said, sharply as always, "I think I am not likely to have any real nieces." And, more kindly, "If I were to adopt one, I can't think of any I would rather adopt than you." They smiled at each other; Eliza had never been so appealed to before. The child took it for granted that in offering her affection, she was offering what was desirable, and in this she was quite right. While Eliza was no more demonstrative than before, she probably felt a deeper affection for the child than did Thomasina, who loved so much more easily. Ariana's sorrowful, subdued behavior touched them all, and they went out of their way to make her as happy as possible. Every afternoon when school was dismissed, Thomasina was waiting with the carriage at the schoolyard gate, and took her home to see her mother, at whose bedside she would stand wide-eyed and trembling, while her mother tried, and sometimes was able, to smooth her bangs or touch her cheek. Then she would visit her father in his study and endure hearing all the must-nots he impressed upon her. She did not tell him that she was having music lessons with "Uncle" Samuel Travers. She knew that he would not approve; the children who came for lessons were those like Johnny Gordon and Elsa Rausch and Charlotte Bonner and Sophie Klein, none of whom went to his church. She said "Yes, Papa" and "No, Papa," and every time she returned in the Ballard carriage to the Ballard house, she felt more as if she were going home. She might have pretended that it was home had it not been for her mother. After Mrs. McCune's death, when the cousin from Indiana had agreed to stay and keep house for Mr. McCune and the children were collected and taken back to the manse, Ariana was heartbroken, not only because her mother had died, but because she had not wanted to leave the Ballards. She would have cried herself to sleep every night had she not shared a bed with Ruhamah. Instead, she swallowed her grief, until it was transmuted into a wordless contempt for the rawboned, graceless cousin, and was revealed only by the expression in her gray eyes when the cousin's glance met them.

Mrs. McCune died in April, slipping indifferently out of a world in which she could no longer pretend to take an interest. What she thought of her life and the lives of others, she hinted at only once when, in one of her last clear moments, she whispered to John that she was glad she was taking the unborn child with her. "God is more merciful to it," she said, but what she meant by "more" was left to be guessed at.

The gap closed after her, unfelt except by her family. Yet Anne knew that John had suffered. "It's being called in after the fight is lost that makes a fellow feel so useless," he burst out once. "As if you hadn't adversary enough against you, starting even." Anne did not know, and would not, John hoped, since it would make her so angry, how his loyal patients were complaining to him that it was being said by certain Reformed Presbyterians that "young Dr. Gordon wasn't so successful, after all," and that he had insulted their minister in his own study.

Members of the Woman's Club attended the funeral, and afterward held a Memorial meeting. The program was short. There was little that any of them could say about Mrs. McCune; she had not been a member for long, and they felt that they had not known her well.

"I still think, even if it isn't decent to say so," Sally commented afterward to Anne, "there wasn't much to know."

But Anne had been wallowing (Sally's word) in remorse because she had not been kinder to the poor woman. Now she said indignantly, "How could there be? She never had a chance to be a *person.* I keep thinking what a bright pretty young girl she must have been, and then married to that—that fanatic—and never another chance to be anything more than a—a brood mare. I wish I had realized in time—"

"In time for what? There was nothing you could have done. How is Kitty Edwards?"

The transition was not so abrupt as it seemed, for Kitty had had a miscarriage earlier in the spring. She was John Gordon's patient, having gone to him soon after Christmas, as soon as she was sure that she was pregnant, although Dr. Edwards, another of the town's senior doctors, was Sheldon's uncle. She explained to John, "I just told Sheldon that Dr. Alexander had been the Lowrey doctor till he died, then we'd gone to you. And he said, 'Of course go to Dock. I know what an old fuddy-duddy Uncle Nate is as well as you!'"

From that first day John had been troubled about her. She was not strong, nor built for easy child-bearing, and already her kidneys were affected. He told her to spend as much time as she could resting, with her feet up, to do only light work, and never to exert herself. Perhaps she was not sufficiently impressed by him, or thought she knew better. Some of his orders she ignored; she must keep the house fit for Sheldon, oversee the girl in the kitchen and the old woman in the laundry. She lost the child.

John was stern with her, after she had recovered enough to stand up to it.

"Look, Kitty," he said, "you're a black mark against me. You would have paid more attention to your Uncle Nate. I hope you are properly repentant."

To his amazement her eyes filled with tears. "Oh, Dock, you don't realize—how humiliating. I simply couldn't believe that I wasn't equal to anything—that I wasn't as good as Anne or Sally Rausch. When I felt awful, I just told myself 'This is the way women feel, then,' and I quoted to myself 'unvariable steadfastness,'" and she picked up a little book from the candle stand beside her bed, ran her fingers tenderly across the calf binding before she opened it and read to him, "'unvariable steadfastness and not to regard anything at all, though never so little, but right and reason; and always, whether in the sharpest pains, or after the loss of a child, or in long diseases, to be still the same man.' Papa's Marcus Aurelius," she explained, as she closed and replaced the book. "He gave it to me to help me through things like this, I suppose." And she cried out, "I wanted that baby so! And Sheldon did, too. When can I try again?"

He was startled. "Not for a long while. I mean it, Kitty. When you are up and about, you will still have to come to the office until we get the kidney condition cleared up."

"I'll do whatever you say. But I mean to have children."

"When you are equal to it, not before." Beard and mustache did not hide the grimness of his mouth. "Shall I tell Sheldon, or will you?"

"Oh, don't frighten him, Dock. I'll tell him, I promise you."

Nevertheless, John did not think it amiss to warn Sheldon. "She's bent and determined to have children. All right, when she's able. Not before, do you understand?"

He was brusquer than he need have been, perhaps, but Sheldon took it gratefully. He had been frightened, and besides he felt sorry for Dock, who had regretted Kitty's miscarriage almost as much as they, and had that and the McCune affair on top of the usual spring epidemics, and the inevitable deaths of the old and the consumptive, and besides was having to endure the criticism of the followers of Dr. Wright and Uncle Nate Edwards. Sheldon was not surprised that Dock looked tired—drawn and hollow-cheeked.

The summer that followed was hard for everyone: for John, for Sheldon (and Sheldon and Edwards), for Ludwig Rausch, and for the women who loved them. Afterward, because '77 turned out to be the last of the depression years, it was difficult to remember how, at the time, it had seemed to be the worst of them all, with no immediate hope in sight. The inauguration of Hayes had wrought no miracle. The government bogged down in a struggle between the new President, who wanted Civil Service reform, and Conkling and the Stalwarts in Congress, who did not. Hope was deferred; John Sherman, the new Secretary of the Treasury, was quietly, even secretly, carrying out his refunding program in preparation for The Day, but the Resumption Act would not go into effect for another two and a half years.

Worst of all were the labor troubles that began with railroad strikes in July, developed into riots and, finally, in Baltimore and Pittsburgh, into what amounted almost to battle and siege, ending with the destruction by fire of the Pennsylvania Railroad's property in Pittsburgh. The violence was a breathtaking shock to newspaper readers, who could take calmly all accounts of revolutionary outbreaks on the other side of the Atlantic but found them incomprehensible when they carried a Pennsylvania or an Ohio dateline. "Abroad" was another world. There "lower classes" were plainly so-called, and one could easily believe that those people might be starved, abused, downtrodden. But in America working men should know that in a depression they were lucky to have jobs, without asking hard-pressed employers for more pay. When good times came again, they would get their share and could begin their climb. Joining a union seemed like saying you planned to stay where you were. Americans of the old stock were bewildered, for why, unless a man had aspirations to rise above his beginnings, should he come to America at all? And immigrants even in hard times crowded the steerage of every ship that crossed the Atlantic. America would give them their chance to earn their way once things took a turn for the better, but they, and emphatically the country, would be better off if they left their socialism and anarchism behind them.

So it was argued, in drugstores and on the Court House benches and around family dining tables; but those who voiced such theories, as if the strikers were an unknown mysterious race of men, were unconsciously concealing their chagrin and sense of betrayal, for they knew well enough that among union members were men they had considered friends, in a casual way: the engineers and firemen who waved so blithe a greeting when an engine passed a crossing, the roundhouse men and switchmen from the West End; Irishmen like Tim O'Reilly. There was something appalling in the thought of Tim O'Reilly, merry, kindhearted, well-intentioned, transformed into a murderous fiend like those who fought the railroad in Pittsburgh. Poor Tim, who had so recently achieved his never-forgotten dream and got back his engineer's job, was out on strike like all the others. He didn't like it, but he told John Gordon he'd "niver let it be said he betrayed his friends." John had offered to lend him money, pulling him out of the cigar store one day in order to do it privately. But Tim had a bit laid by, for an emergency. "Av cour-rse," he said, rolling his eyes and his R's toward John, "ye may hev to wait a wee bit to git paid for the new baby." But the other engineers were standing firm without help from the outside, and he would too. When John inquired for his wife, he declared she was "stiddy as a rock an' not a fear in her head. Ye put us on our feet once, Dock, we'll stand on 'em now an' take what comes. But the blessin's av the saints on ye for yer kindness."

MEMBERS OF THE WAYNESBORO WOMAN'S CLUB

Miss Eliza Ballard
Mrs. Mary Ballard
Mrs. Esther Beattie
Miss Christina Blair
Mrs. Louisa Deming
Mrs. Katherine Edwards
Miss Caroline Gardiner
Miss Lavinia Gardiner
Mrs. Anne Gordon
Mrs. Rhoda McKinney
Mrs. Laura Maxwell
Miss Agatha Pinney
Mrs. Sarah Rausch
Miss Amanda Reid
Mrs. Thomasina Travers

IN MEMORIAM

Miss Susan Crenshaw
Mrs. Mary McCune

* 1878 *

"A new Club bride was honored . . ."

The year 1877 had been such a troubling one that all were glad when it ended. But looking back from January of 1878, Waynesboro citizens could see, as they read Mr. Bonner's résumé of the events of 1877, that as long ago as the end of the summer there had been signs of a business recovery. Strike-produced riots had ended, and order had been restored. A bumper crop of wheat had coincided with a famine in Europe; American grain had to be moved to Atlantic ports by rail or water. Lake shipping had increased, and shipyards had begun to build new carriers. The railroads had recalled laid-off employees, and were moving long-unused boxcars out of their yards.

Ludwig Rausch had trusted those signs of returning prosperity; as early as the fall of '77, he had commenced what he had so long postponed: the building of an addition to his mill. He bought more of the land that lay behind his yard, and moved the fence back, not a very costly first step. But to build the addition, he must raise capital. The company's reserves had been depleted by his determination to hold on to his labor force, even though it meant selling below cost or storing the products. A larger demand than expected for binder twine for the not-yet-planted winter wheat crop had helped his financial condition, but a cordage manufacturer needed liquid capital: rope was sold on six months' credit, but hemp had to be contracted for when the price was low, even if it wouldn't be needed for some months. Ludwig preferred not to seek a bank loan, and was determined not to turn his close corporation into an open one, with stockbrokers selling to anyone. Mr. Cochran came to the rescue, buying enough shares in Sally's name to supply the necessary capital.

Ludwig had spent a large part of the preceding winter looking over mill layouts along the East Coast, and he had learned much. Company executives had been affable; they had arranged for him to be shown all he had wanted to see. They had been even supercilious, he thought, about a small plant in the

Midwest, and he considered them shortsighted. They were making beautiful marine rope for a declining market; steel was being used more and more for sea-going vessels, and steamboats were supplanting sail. They were not looking inland: when he mentioned binder twine to one superintendent, he was told that there would not be much demand for that product for years to come, if ever. Ludwig had not felt obliged to tell them what they should have known: that Appleby was working on a combined reaper and twine binder, and that soon all the fertile land in the Plains states would be under the plough. He could see that they still viewed that part of the country as it was named in the geographies of their youth: The Great American Desert. Nor did he tell them that shipping on the Great Lakes was increasing steadily; wheat was being moved by water from Chicago to Buffalo, and iron ore from Lake Superior to Cleveland.

Armed with the knowledge he had gained from his tour, and with the Cochran money in hand, Ludwig, in the fall of 1877, asked a Cincinnati contractor to come to Waynesboro to make an estimate based on Ludwig's plans. He agreed to come, and to bring with him a consulting engineer. It was obvious to Ludwig that he would do almost anything to get the contract, so worried was he over the difficulties of the building trade in such hard times.

The two men came, looked over the ground and buildings, studied the plans in Ludwig's office, and the contractor went away with the contract in his pocket. Before 1877 came to an end, and before winter made it impossible to work in the ground, the foundations were laid and the brick walls had begun to rise. By January of '78, from his office window, Ludwig could see his new mill going up: a long one, on the river side of the yard, at right angles to the older preparation mill: a new ropewalk to hold forming and laying machinery. At the street end there would be a small office for the new superintendent; on the newly acquired land a larger powerhouse must be built to accommodate the contracted-for Corliss engine that would run all the machinery. Of the mill that Ludwig had bought there would remain only the tarring shed, picturesque in a ramshackle way, standing free of the other buildings to avoid the danger of fire, and the original ropewalk, where twine and rope were still made by hand for out-of-the-ordinary specifications.

Ludwig kept his mill hands at work through the winter on the preparation of hemp, from rough fiber to smooth oiled-and-tarred silver, and those in the ropewalk worked at whatever orders came in. The Negroes and unskilled white labor put in their time squatting there, in the corners, pulling oakum and making fenders of raveled rope ends for ships on the Great Lakes. Ludwig had some success selling rope in Cleveland, a success that may have been helped by his acquaintance with Mark Hanna at Rhodes and Company. That developing friendship might or might not be profitable, but at any rate it gave him great pleasure. The two men had in common not only business interests but loyalty to the Republican party, their belief in a sound money policy, and their hope for the future development of Great Lakes shipping.

During the 1877 labor troubles in Pittsburgh, Ludwig had laughed at anyone who asked if his mill hands were being troublesome. The spinners hardly considered themselves "hands," and as for the unskilled laborers, they would not know the meaning of the word "union." Ludwig called his men, black or white, by their first names, and knew their family connections and responsibilities; he had always been on good terms with them, informal and unceremonious: he was "Cap'n" to them, or "Boss." Before the arrival of Captain Bodien, Ludwig was a little uneasy, wondering whether he could retain the hands' easy relationship with him when the new mill was finished, and a mill superintendent as well as their foremen stood between him and them.

Captain Bodien arrived in Waynesboro by the first of February. The construction work had been about half-completed. The Captain would not bring his family to Waynesboro until June, when his boy and girl would be out of school. In the meantime he would find a house they could move into.

The first day he came to the mill to take up his new position, Ludwig called the hands together at noon to introduce their new superintendent. The men gathered for a few moments in the cobbled yard, with the tar pan sputtering and smoking behind them. Ludwig told them that Captain Bodien, since his discharge from the Army in '65, had been employed by one of the biggest cordage companies in the country, and that Rausch Cordage Company was lucky to get him. "I think I have learned enough to be able to run the mill, but it does no one any good, you or me, to run the mill at a loss. So I must be free to travel to find customers for what we make. And while I am doing that, Captain Bodien will oversee the work here. He knows all there is to know about making most kinds of rope, and if I can land orders for other kinds, he'll learn to make those. We'll all learn together."

The workmen accepted Captain Bodien as their immediate boss more willingly, probably, than if one of their foremen had been promoted over the others. Captain Bodien was not in any way an alien figure. The white laborers, all except the youngest of them, had seen his like often enough in the army: a stocky, bow-legged artilleryman, with a wad of chewing tobacco lumped on one cheek, long black mustache, saber-scarred face, clear blue eyes, and a bald head. The Negroes, as Ludwig soon saw (and was a little hurt by seeing), stepped livelier for the new superintendent than they had done for him, and were more respectful. He spoke of it to Captain Bodien one afternoon when they were returning to the office from a tour of the mill.

"With me," Ludwig said, "they always act like they're trying to hoodwink me just to see how far they can go. Sometimes I wonder if I turned round quick enough I'd catch them grinning. But they get their work done, and I like them. And," he added defensively, "I think they like me."

"Reckon they do." Captain Bodien spat into the canal. The two men had stopped a moment to look down at the quiet water. Bodien studied Ludwig with a sidelong look. "You never had much to do with niggers, did you?"

"Never saw many until the war. Then they were just contraband. Useful as servants around the camp, but a nuisance in the mass."

"My father was a slaveholder. I grew up with them. They know it without being told."

"I suppose they haven't been free long enough for it to have sunk into their bones that they're working for themselves now. They're still trying to get the best of the overseer—me, that is."

"They'll never get it out of their bones, certainly not this generation. Anyway, however happy they are to be free, they're still more at home with southerners."

"Didn't you tell me your father died when you were a child?"

"Yes. I can just remember him. He made hats in Baltimore—the last of the tall beaver hats. His workmen were sold after he died, but we had a houseful of servants, more than we needed, and my mother wouldn't sell them. Instead she took us home to her folks', slaves and all— Don't worry about the niggers: I've played with 'em and worked with 'em, and they'll like me all the better for my seeing through 'em. Don't worry about the white men, either. Mostly veterans, aren't they?"

In June, just when the new mill was finished, Captain Bodien moved his family to Waynesboro, into the house in the West End that he had found for them. It antedated the Irish settlement of that part of town. The dwelling had once been the tanner's, and the tannery, now fallen to rack and ruin, was in a far corner of the property; and because no one had ever wanted to live within nose-reach of a tannery, the grounds around the house had not been cut into building lots until the tannery had fallen into disuse. Then the heirs to the property had sold a row of lots along the street on the north side of the property, and another row along the Cincinnati Pike on the west side. Small houses built on those lots hid the big house from passersby, and it had been almost forgotten. It was a dignified relic of the Greek Revival period that could easily be restored to its original beauty, and the land behind it could be planted to garden or orchard, but the neighborhood was not one that existed in the consciousness of Protestant Waynesboro. Captain Bodien had chosen it, he explained to Ludwig, because there his wife would feel at home, "with the church bells ding-dongin' in her ears all day long. She knows, and my children know, what I think of the Catholic church. I let her send the girl to convent school in Baltimore, but the boy will go to public school here. I know all about the Catholics," he said wryly. "I ought to. I was raised one. But my wife suits me as she is, and if she wants to live around the corner from the priest, I've got nothing against it—not so long as he stays away from me."

Ludwig had little interest in Captain Bodien's domestic or religious life. What he was interested in was his skill as a ropemaker. The Captain had learned what he knew in a Baltimore ropewalk. The industry in seaport towns was suffering not only from the general depression but from the decline in the building of sailing vessels, and in the supplanting, now begun, of hempen by wire-rope rigging. Other types of cordage were being made in small amounts by seaboard manufacturers, but it wasn't what they wanted to make—"fool with," as they put it. Companies with the smell of the sea coming in their windows did not like bothering with small orders of rope for the lumber industry, or for farms. Or, lately, for oil wells. Ludwig did; he had been selling bull line and cat line, derrick line, and torpedo line, as well as drilling cable in small amounts to independent oil well diggers: now the Standard Oil Company was expanding from a refining industry to the ownership and exploitation of oil wells to supply their own raw material. Ludwig had succeeded, the last time he had been in Cleveland, in obtaining an order from them for drilling cable. He wanted it to be right, since, as he explained to Bodien, it looked as though the Standard Oil Company would soon own all the oil in Ohio and in Pennsylvania, too.

Captain Bodien had never made drilling cable. Ludwig went to his office with him and together they studied the specifications for the rope ordered. Ludwig spread out on the superintendent's desk a fistful of pages of calculations to go over with him.

"Cable-laid to resist abrasion, and hard-laid, too," Ludwig explained, as he indicated the high ratio of twist in the strand. "It runs up and down through an iron cylinder. Soft-laid cable would fray out in no time."

"They'll soon be using wire rope there, too." The half-statement, half-question, was a little sour.

"They're beginning to," Ludwig admitted. "We'll not have many more orders for these long lines. But even with wire rope, they have to use two-hundred-fifty feet of hemp rope—a 'cracker'—on the end. Drilling cable has to be elastic, and wire rope end is fastened to the cutter and the cutter dropped through an iron cylinder on to the rock to be drilled. If the rope isn't elastic, the cutter sticks in the rock. Hemp cable will stretch, then rebound, and pull the cutter back with it."

"I see that," Bodien said. "But hard-laid cable isn't as strong as soft-laid."

"No, but for that kind of work it lasts longer. Two-hundred-and-fifty feet of cable on the wire rope will give elasticity enough: it has to be replaced every few weeks, but a two-hundred-fathom coil lasts a good while. The verdammte depression has slowed down drilling for new wells. I'm going to Cleveland soon, to Rhodes and Company and the ships' chandlers; even lake steamers will always need mooring lines, cargo nets, dragnets, towlines. Get me a piece of this drilling cable laid, and I'll take it along to the Standard Oil people to see if they are satisfied. If they are, it might mean a lot."

As the men talked, they heard through the open window, carried on the hot wind across the canal, the usual sounds of the mill: the clatter of machinery, the voices of men in the yard, and, in addition, the ringing sound of horses' hooves on the cobbles. A shipment of rope was going out of the mill by dray to the railroad freight depot. The noises were too familiar to both men to disturb them; undistracted, they went on with their discussion. But suddenly there was a crescendo of sound: a clang of hooves, in faster tempo, as if from startled horses, voices raised in shouts of warning, a heavy thud, and then a cry that rose to a scream of anguish. By that time Ludwig had begun running, Captain Bodien at his heels, but their view was cut off by a circle of workmen. The drayman had the horses' bridles, and was leading them forward. Ludwig came up behind the men; they moved to make way for him.

"Zack!"

A big Negro lay on the cobbles, his eyes rolled back in his head, still screaming in a muted fashion, as though through closed jaws. On his legs, tilted awkwardly, lay a burlaped coil of rope. Two or three men were hesitantly pulling at it.

"You men! Get in there and lift that coil. Don't haul at it. Easy now!"

Ludwig had never spoken to them in just that voice; it was an echo of Captain Rausch Sixth Iowa, on the battle line. They leaped to obey him. The big Negro rolled his eyes in Ludwig's direction. Ludwig saw the grotesque angling of the leg the coil had fallen on, and the blood soaking through Zack's canvas pants. Above the waist he was naked, shining like polished ebony. The smell of the sweat of agony was stronger in that close circle than the all-pervading scent of tar.

"Back, men. Give him room to breathe. All right, Zack. We'll look out for you now." Ludwig went down on one knee, a reassuring hand on Zack's shoulder. "You, Simmons, go hell-for-leather for Dr. Gordon."

Ludwig, with his penknife, began to hack through the stiff canvas overalls where the blood was spreading. A workman silently offered him a knife, one he had been using to open bales of hemp. Taking it, Ludwig grunted his thanks. He ripped the pants leg open, laid the stained canvas back. The men had been watching quietly; now there was only dead silence. It frightened Zack; he began moaning again.

"Now, Zack—hush—you've got a broken leg, I guess, but other men have had broken legs and lived through it. You know I'll look after you while you're laid off."

Even as he spoke, Ludwig pulled his handkerchief from his pocket, shook his head, tossed it aside. "Not big enough. Get me a rope-end, someone, and oakum to pad it with. I'll make a tourniquet."

They all stirred, moving back as if released from the ugly sight, yet hesitant to leave it. The edge of the coil had caught the thigh bone above the knee and broken it; one jagged bone end had pierced the flesh and protruded from Zack's black skin. Blood poured from the torn flesh.

Someone brought the rope and oakum; Ludwig looped the rope around the leg above the break, packed the oakum under it, and twisted it tight. There was nothing else he could do until Dock got there. His eyes on the slowing flow of blood, he held out one hand, groped for Zack's, took it in his. Strangely, for a moment, the scene faded out; he was conscious only of an old, old familiarity with the limp hand of a strong man—the aftermath of all the battles. Then his swimming head cleared; he saw the yard again, the cobbles, his cobbles, blood-spattered. He sat back on his haunches, still holding Zack's hand. "I'll stay right with you, Zack, until the doctor comes." Then he turned his clear blue eyes, a little hot now, on those workmen who still lingered. "How'd it happen?"

"Zack was loadin'. Simmons was in the dray. You know how strong Zack is: he rolled them coils up the ramp hisself. I guess the hosses was scared somehow—that driver couldn't 've been a holdin' the reins tight—the hosses jumped around enough to send that last coil rollin' back down the ramp—it caught Zack."

Ludwig was sure that was as much as anyone would ever be able to tell him. Pure accident. Someone careless maybe—the driver, or a workman too close to the horses. He stayed squatting in the sun and the heat, in the smell of sweat and blood, until he heard steps coming up behind him, through the yard gate. He rose then, stiffly.

"All right, Zack. The doctor's here."

John, with his bag, came to stand beside them. He waited for a long moment, it seemed to Ludwig, before he looked up to meet his eyes. "Compound fracture of the femur." Their eyes held. John had no need to say more: Ludwig knew as well as he how many legs and arms had been amputated because of compound fractures.

"Bring me water. Let's get him cleaned up, first." John loosened the tourniquet and after a moment retied it. "And something for packing the wound with carbolic solution. More oakum will do."

He took a glittering syringe from his bag, and a morphine tablet. Most of the men had never seen a hypodermic needle before; they watched in fascinated horror as he dissolved the tablet and filled the syringe.

Zack moaned, and put up a protesting hand. "Doc—" The word was a hoarse, terrified whisper. "Doan' cut it off—Lawdy—whut—"

"Hush, man. I'm not going to cut it off. This is to put you to sleep so it won't hurt you when you're moved."

He plunged the hypodermic into Zack's arm, and waited until the morphine had taken effect. Then he brought the ends of bone together as well as he could, saturated a handful of oakum with carbolic solution, laid it in the torn wound, and splinted the leg with pieces of board and rope silently offered him.

"Now we can get him home." He looked up at the bed of the dray. Ludwig interpreted his glance.

"You—Bill Emmons and Jake—get that rope out of the dray—careful, two men to a coil. You two"—he nodded to two shaking Negroes, watching from a safe distance—"bring the door of the tar-shed. It's never shut, anyway. You can pull it off its hinges with a good tug."

The drayman had been waiting all this time, sickened, but not too sickened to be curious—frightened too, perhaps, by a feeling of responsibility. He held the horses' heads while Zack was placed on the door and lifted up to the wagon bed. He drove them, then, Ludwig and John joggling beside Zack, trying to hold him steady, the long way up to the cabin in the East End.

Ludwig had sent someone ahead to warn his wife; she was collapsed in a rocking chair when the dray stopped. Ludwig had to call for neighbors, already gathered at the picket fence, to help them. Zack was too heavy for two of them to carry. They brought him into the two-room cabin and laid him, door and all, on the corn-shuck mattress of his bed in the dark inner room. Half-roused by the moving, he groaned, opened his eyes, whispered "Doctuh?"

"I'm here, Zack. You go back to sleep while I look after you properly."

John looked about him as Zack lay back on the board. The wife would be useless. He signaled to Ludwig to hold Zack's shoulders. The giant Negro rolled his head.

"Doctuh—Yo' di'n promise you woul'n' tek mah laig. What Zack do 'thout his laig?"

"I won't unless I must, to save your life. Listen, Zack: are you worth as much as the white men that fought to set you free? If you're not, the fighting was wasted. If you are, then you can stand to lose a leg as well as the crippled soldiers you see on the street every day of your life."

"Yassuh. But white men mo' use' to bein' brave. Yo' save mah laig, Doctuh, o' Ah die sho'."

"I'll save it if I can. That's a promise."

Later, a long while later, when they left the house both John and Ludwig were white-faced, exhausted by the ordeal of caring for the injured man and dealing with his wife, bringing her to some degree of sanity, so that they could give her directions for his care.

"She won't do what I say, poor ignorant soul. I wish we had a hospital."

"Will you have to amputate?"

"I suppose I will, in the end."

"Zack's always been so proud of his strength, poor devil. It's all he had."

"I'd like to try to save it. A compound fracture always has meant amputation, but I don't think it should. Lister has saved one or two—there've been papers of his printed. I'll try carbolic acid dressings as he suggests. I'll know in a day or two if there is blood poisoning. It's a risk, you understand: there will be those who will consider it almost malpractice."

Ludwig caught his breath. "If it will have to be done anyway to save him, go ahead and do it, Dock."

"It won't save him. Did you ever see a one-legged nigger? He will die of shock. But my reputation would be saved because I had done what had always been accepted as a necessity."

"Dock—"

"The only chance of saving the man's life, as I see it, is to save his leg. So we'll try it."

John was late home for lunch that day, but he did not have to explain. Johnny, in the way of small boys, had picked up the story of Zack's accident and passed it on to his mother. He was still hanging around when his father came in, and waited while his mother brought lunch from the oven. When John had begun to eat, the boy could contain himself no longer.

"Papa, will you have to cut his leg off?"

Anne rebuked him. "Not while your father's eating."

"Nor any other time." John was gruff. "I'll do the best I can for Zack. That's all you need to know."

"But Papa, if I'm going to be a doctor, I have to know."

"Not now, Johnny."

Johnny departed, crestfallen. His father finished eating and without more words went out through the kitchen and on through the back door and yard to the office. The next few days he spent largely in Zack's unpainted shack, fighting the big man's terrors, promising he would not amputate the leg unless he must.

"Dock, Zack a no-good niggah 'thout he laig."

"All right, Zack."

"Mought's well be daid."

"That's not so, Zack. Your boss will see you have a job, and you have a woman to take care of."

Fighting the heat that clogged the little room, the smell of carbolic, the smell of frightened people, calming Zack's wife: "You say not to take his leg off. Any other doctor would have taken it off at once. If he dies of blood-poisoning—"

"No, suh. Zack die ef'n he laig cut off."

John tried to explain the danger to her: "If it poisons his blood, then I'll have to take it off. Suppose I wait too long?"

"Cain' wait too long. Zack die then anyway, ef'n you do, ef'n you don't."

Then one morning when John went into the room, he smelled it. Gangrene. Blood poisoning he had feared, but gangrene—the never-forgotten—Through nausea held down, he gave his orders calmly. Neighbors to hold Zack while he chloroformed him, neighbors to carry him to the kitchen, where the door he had been carried home on was to be scrubbed with boiling water and laid on the kitchen table. More boiling water for the instruments: the knives, the saw he had hoped never to have to use again. He opened his battered instrument case.

He was late again that day for lunch, and again Johnny had picked up the news.

"Mamma, you know that Zack? Papa cut off his leg, and he died."

Anne's heart sank. "Who told you?"

"Bob Wright. He went home at recess for sump'n. His gran'pa said *he* would have cut the leg off right away before something—something green got a start."

"Not gangrene?"

"What is gangrene?"

"Not at the table, Johnny."

Little Binny, a silent listener, ate her lunch, finished, and was dismissed to the kitchen and Martha. The others waited. When John came in, he sat down at the table with no more than a grunt by way of salutation. After his plate had been put before him, he picked up his knife and fork, held them a moment, put them down, pushed the plate from him. Without a word he rose and left the house by way of the door to the side porch. Anne tinkled the bell for Martha to come clear the table, told Johnny to go out to play, and went herself to the sitting room, where she sat down in her rocker in front of the covered grate. She was frightened. Too frightened to read, or even knit. "All that," she thought, "all that to go through again?" Zack, or any patient, black or white, would have been no threat to her father's peace of mind, once he had done all he could. But John—And the other doctors would be on him like hound dogs on a hurt rabbit; they had been hoping—perhaps not *hoping* but watching—for some mischance like this.

It was four o'clock before John came in and sought her, found her still in the rocker, her knitting in her hands, a kind of everydayness that she was offering him. He came to stand before her, one foot on the fender, his left arm extended along the mantel's edge.

"I'm sorry, Anne, for rushing out like that at noon."

"Johnny told me about Zack." Anne, studying his face, spoke quietly. "But you couldn't have done anything else, could you?"

"No."

"Would it have made any difference if you had amputated at once?"

"One can never be positive, but, no, I don't think so. Zack died of fear—shock—something—not the amputation. But I failed." With his fist he struck the under side of the mantel two or three times, gently. "I failed in what I was trying to do, and to prove. I'll be criticized for trying, I suppose. I can stand that. I would do it again. It ought not to be necessary; all this whacking off of arms and legs. But going into that room this morning, and knowing with the first breath I drew: that foul thickness in the air. Gangrene. I'll never get it out of my nostrils. It will haunt me all my life."

While Anne was wondering, with relief, at his having, uncharacteristically, said so much, he turned from the fireplace and laid his hand on her shoulder for a minute as he passed behind her chair, but his face did not lighten; it was bleak, white and drawn, as if he had grown thin in a morning.

Anne stopped him. "Before you start on your afternoon calls, let me make you some tea, bring you a slice of roast beef. You haven't had a bite since breakfast."

He had scarcely drunk a cup of tea and gone before Sally Rausch came in. She had come, she said, that she and Anne might console each other for having husbands so easily upset. Ludwig, too, was taking Zack's death hard.

"Though why he should think it his fault—or Dock's either—I can't imagine. One of those accidents no one was to blame for. I know if anyone could have saved him, it's Dock. Ludwig thinks so, too. Anyway, he's soon going on another trip, so it will slip out of his mind, I hope."

Ludwig made provision for Zack's widow: an annuity to keep her going until her children were old enough to work, and then he pushed the accident to the back of his mind. It was easier for him than it was for John. Ludwig was planning another trip to Cleveland, where he might secure more orders from the Standard Oil Company, and might further his acquaintance with Mark Hanna. Rhodes and Company, among their other enterprises, owned their own vessels for transporting ore from Lake Superior. Rope was used on ore carriers as well as on the boats that carried grain from Chicago.

He came back from Cleveland with orders enough to keep the mill going at a profit for several months. But he was not satisfied. He said so to Sally one night after they had gone to bed and were lying side by side, engaged in one of those companionable end-of-the-day discussions, in which she recounted the small events of domestic life and he talked about the mill and his business, and each half-listened to the other and half-concentrated on remembering what else there was to be told.

"There must be more business to be found somewhere. I've about decided to try New Orleans. Ought to be able to beat the eastern fellows. We're closer, and so we'll have lower transportation costs, especially if we ship by river-boat."

Sally was astonished. "Did you say *New Orleans*?"

"Yes. Why not? Reconstruction's over. They're back in the Union."

"I know. But it's hard to get used to the idea. Surely they wouldn't buy from us?"

"Why not? There's no cordage made in the South. And there's all that shipping trade. I think it might be interesting. I'd like to see Vicksburg again. Even Duckport Landing."

"Where you were in the hospital? Where Dock was?"

"Poor Dock! Left on his own in charge of that place, with no help but a few convalescent soldiers for orderlies. Right in the midst of the unhealthiest swamps in Louisiana, a boy of twenty-two or three. He might easily have died of despair. I wonder what it all looks like now—I can't imagine it without the Army. Would you like to go, Sally? It's time you and I had a trip together."

"Would I like to go? Yes, I would like to go!" Sally sat up in bed, indignantly. "And you ask me on the very day when I had decided I must go to see Dock tomorrow. I think I am going to have another baby. I wasn't going to tell you until I was sure."

"Sally! Little Ludwig on the way!" He sat up too, took her in his arms, and kissed away her indignation. "You don't mind, do you, Liebchen?"

"No. Of course not. I want to have my family and get it over with. But someday," she threatened him, "I'm going to be sorry for all I missed while I was young. Ludwig," she said, with a change of intonation, forgetting her pretense of a grievance as she moved from his arms and dropped back on her pillows. "Why don't you get Dock to go with you? He needs it—he's had an awful year. Mrs. McCune and Dr. Wright talked scandalously when Kitty Edwards went to Dock instead of to him."

"Yes. After all, he's Lowrey's uncle."

"You don't think it will hurt John?"

"No, but it will worry him. He's got that look again. Morose. Restive."

"Restive?"

"Call it that."

"You think he'd be less 'restive' in New Orleans?"

"It might get some of the poison out of his system, if he went with you and looked at Vicksburg and Duckport again. You think it was the nightmare of the War that made him—"

"That made him a man who is driven to any length sometimes to get away from himself. You think if he looked in broad daylight at the places he sees in his nightmares they wouldn't haunt him any more? Maybe. But he won't go."

However, John did go. He accepted Ludwig's invitation gratefully. He might have gone anywhere just then, to get away from his own bed, and Anne, whose nights he troubled by his groaning in his sleep and by the hours he spent smoking the night away. Besides, strangely enough, not long before Ludwig spoke to him about the trip, he had had a disquieting letter from his father's cousin, whose plantation was not far from Memphis. John had been welcomed at the Gordon place in '62, after Shiloh, when the Fifteenth Corps was stationed in comparative idleness in the neighborhood. The old man had been a stubborn Unionist, and so the plantation had not only been spared, it had been protected by Federal orders after the Army had got that far South. Before that it had been protected because his sons had been Confederate soldiers. They had been killed at Shiloh. In '62 the widow of one, with her little girl, lived with her father-in-law. She had not appeared at any time while John was there. Cousin Robert had apologized for her bitterness; after Shiloh and the death of her husband, she had planned to take the child home to New Orleans; then word came of the fall of that city, and she was caught: nowhere to turn to escape from her enemies. The little girl, who would not be shut in a bedroom when John was there, was hostile and impudent. She was a peaked little yellow thing, shaking with ague, which John had treated with the quinine he should have been taking himself. At least that, he had thought, was not stealing from the store of drugs entrusted to him by his government. He had excused her hostility, since it had been taught her, and her bad temper, since she was ill. He pitied woman and child and forgave them their enmity, even after the night he was ambushed on his way back to camp, and knew that someone in the house had sent word of his whereabouts to the bushwhackers lurking in the neighborhood. He had got away unscathed, thanks to his horse, or he might have felt differently.

Since the war he had heard a few times from his Cousin Robert. He knew that the widow had taken the child to New Orleans, and that not long afterward she had died there in a yellow fever epidemic; that Cousin Robert had gone after the little girl, his sole surviving descendant, and had taken her back to the plantation to bring up as best he could. The letter that came in August was the first in several years. John felt it as a reproach, since he had forgotten the southern Gordons, and had been unconcerned as to their welfare. "The only blood-kin I have left, so far as I know," he told Anne.

Cousin Robert had written about the difficulty of carrying on with the plantation since Reconstruction had ended. Animosity—of the state, as well as of people in general and the Ku Klux Klan in particular—against those natives who had been Unionists, as well as against Scalawags and Carpetbaggers, had been malignant and purposeful. No hands dared work on the plantation. He had been driven to hiring a Confederate veteran as overseer—"one of the bottom rails now on top"—and, he suspected, a member of the Klan. That had helped for a while. But now he was in arrears with his taxes, his creditors in New Orleans were clamoring, and the only way he could see to save the plantation was for his granddaughter to marry the overseer and give her the land. A Confederate veteran could get credit when he himself couldn't.

"It sounds like stock melodrama, doesn't it? The mortgaged estate, the villain prepared to buy the heroine's hand, and all the rest of it." Anne handed him back the letter, which he had given her to read. "Do you suppose that's all true? Or is he a little cracked?"

"It could be true, judging by the newspaper stories. Or he could, by now, be cracked. He wasn't, when I knew him. Or he could be prejudiced against the overseer: Cousin Robert kind of set himself up as an aristocrat." John laughed. "A delusion the Ohio Gordons never suffered from."

"But what does he expect you to do?"

"Nothing, I hope. He must know I can't go around squaring up other people's debts. He had to get it all off his chest, I suppose, and no one near would sympathize. But I wish I knew. Hang it! I do owe him something."

He wished so much to know that when Ludwig suggested that he accompany him to New Orleans and have a look at their old battlefields on the way, he wavered and was half inclined to accept, so that it took little urging on Anne's part to persuade him. It was arranged that he would leave the boat in Memphis for his visit to his cousin, rejoining Ludwig in New Orleans. They would then stop at Vicksburg and perhaps at Shiloh on the way back. So far as Vicksburg was concerned, John's attitude was that of one humoring a harmless bit of childishness. As to Duckport, he said he hoped never to see the place again this side of Hell. And Shiloh. He gave a gruff negative to Johnny's plea that he be taken along and shown the battlefields: there was nothing that he wanted to show the child and say, "I was there."

While the two men were away, Anne invited the Woman's Club to come to her house for the first meeting of the fall. She had been quick to invite them so as to give herself something to do and think about. She had been living under a strain almost equal to John's. He had rejected the comfort of her love, her passion, and she had been half sick with apprehension, fearing, but not putting her thoughts into words in her mind lest she make them come true. He must find release—escape—somewhere, and she offered him no escape, only an intensification of his identity, because they were one. He was her husband and her lover—and John Gordon. A pair of hose? A ten-dollar bill? She had persuaded him to go with Ludwig. Then, at least, it would not happen in Waynesboro; she need not know. But she felt again the desolate ache, the revulsion. To banish it, she threw herself into her housecleaning for the Club.

On the afternoon of that meeting, the ladies voted to ask Mrs. Professor Beattie to become a member, filling the vacancy caused by the death of "our dear Mrs. McCune." That death had taken all the fight out of Anne and Sally, for the time at least; they did not protest even to each other the inclusion in the Club of another Seminary wife.

What Sally did not know was that Amanda had seen the injustice of inviting two theological newcomers to join the Club while continuing to ignore the wife of the professor who had been at the Seminary for so many years, since long before the merger. Mrs. Beattie, whom all the Club members knew at least casually, was a short plump homebody with two adolescent boys who were being taught their Latin by Amanda. Their presence before her reminded her of their mother's existence. She took the necessary step to remedy what she felt had been wrong, preparing a slip of paper for Madame President signed by herself, and Christina Blair and Laura Maxwell as second, presenting the name of Mrs. Esther Beattie as a candidate for membership; the vote would be taken at the next meeting. Amanda knew that in this case there was no necessity for any preliminary "sounding out" as to her willingness to join, nor any question as to the Club's vote. Never yet had anyone been blackballed.

Anne, who was in a captious mood that fall, thought, "Another body to act as librarian-for-a-day!" Mrs. Beattie had never volunteered for that chore, but now it would be a responsibility. Anne was thoroughly tired of giving so much of her time to the library. Now she rebelled, saying in her mind "No more!" Before the Club adjourned, she put her intention into spoken words: she had served long enough. She supposed that her Waynesboro contemporaries who had given afternoons to that chore would also be ready to make way for the next generation. The older members of the Club who had acted as librarians with her for so long agreed with her enthusiastically, and the younger ones accepted what they recognized as a duty, but with a provision: someone, possibly a high school student, should be hired to shelve returned books, and generally keep the room in order.

The library trustees were faced with the necessity of raising money, since the funds from membership subscriptions must be used to buy books. They foresaw the day, not too far ahead, when the volunteer librarian system would have to be given up. The next generation of Waynesboro ladies might not be willing to offer free services. To the trustees it seemed only sensible to campaign for enough money to meet both needs, the immediate one and the slightly more distant one.

In 1878 the accepted and customary way to raise money was by sponsoring a series of lectures. For that contribution to Waynesboro culture, the library trustees could turn to the Seminary, where there were professors so fascinated by the subjects in which they specialized that they would welcome the opportunity to speak about them to an audience of adults without expecting to be paid for doing so.

When asked, Professor Maxwell, a distinguished archeologist, professed himself delighted to be given the opportunity to help such a worthy cause. He would deliver a series on "The History of Jerusalem." Most of Waynesboro's more intellectual citizens bought tickets. Among them were Sally and Anne: two tickets each, although they well knew they would never get their husbands to the Opera House to listen to any such subject.

Other Waynesboro citizens felt more enthusiasm than they over Jerusalem. The Reverend Mr. McCune had not neglected his pastoral duties after the death of his wife. He had long since made the call on Amanda that he had promised her mother he would make, and had continued to call on occasional evenings, as a minister responsible for one of his flock. He was not a man to recognize any woman as formidable, and respect for his calling was too deeply ingrained in Amanda to permit her to be so with him. She had agreed meekly that worldliness must be kept out of the church: that "our young people" were all too easily influenced; that it was becoming difficult to discipline them into observance of the Saturday-at-sundown to Monday-morning Sabbath, since so many parents were required to work in the stores on Saturday evenings. Mr. McCune had play-acting obsessively on his mind: especially pernicious was the permitting of young people to attend—much less to take part in—theatrical performances. One evening when Amanda still had Latin papers to correct, and was impatient for his departure, she took issue with him, speaking in the tone of voice in which she would have uttered a dismissing sentence to a pupil.

"I am sure you understand that I should never think of attending a commercial theatrical performance. In the case of *Color Guard* I felt that I was justified by its purpose."

"A very charitable purpose. But surely the same end could have been attained by a special collection in the churches?"

"Then each congregation would have wanted its money spent on its own widows and orphans. Some widows and children would have been left out. *Color Guard* brought the whole town together as it has not been since the soldiers were mustered out. And surely it is good that the town as a whole should feel responsible for its regiments' widows and cripples?"

"You think so?" His mouth was drawn into an implacable line. "I personally do not desire to feel one with the Papists, and I should not like to think that any member of my congregation did. I can see, if you cannot, what harm has been done by that play. There is something about the atmosphere of the stage, behind the scenes as well as before the footlights, that seems to loosen moral fiber—that leads young inexperienced girls, particularly, to forget their calling and predestinate election."

She resisted the impulse to say, "Since they are predestinate, can they help themselves?" She was shocked at the impulse: predestination was a dogma not to be questioned. She knew what he was thinking of: everyone who had seen the stage love-making of Christina Blair and Henry Voorhees was on the alert, and Amanda was as aware as anyone that he was being "attentive" to her. Of course it would be a shocking thing if Christina married out of her church, but would not that too have been foreordained? Amanda preferred not to be drawn into any further discussion with Mr. McCune, and was silent until he rose to go.

Months had passed since the presentation of *Color Guard*, but the relationship between Henry and Christina seemed not to have advanced or changed. Henry perhaps spent more evenings in the Blair parlor, but it ended there. Various conjectures were made: the R.P.'s said that of course Christina would not marry anyone who was not a professed Christian (that is, not a Reformed Presbyterian). Other acquaintances believed that of course Christina could not leave her father; most of Waynesboro found it hard to imagine Henry as an ardent suitor. But just when it had been settled that the situation was static and would remain so, various changes occurred.

Henry Voorhees began to attend the Reformed Presbyterian church. He was promoted to assistant cashier in the bank, thus becoming, in a worldly sense, a suitable mate for Miss Blair. And finally he went to Mr. McCune and asked to be allowed to become a member of his church: his interrogation by the Elders was satisfactory, and he was duly received into the Fellowship of Communion with the Reformed Presbyterians. Soon after the religious barrier had been removed, the engagement of Henry and Christina was announced, and the wedding followed almost immediately. It was a quiet affair: the ceremony was held in the Blair parlor, with only Seminary professors and their wives present to witness it. It was over in a few minutes. Henry then shifted from his rooming house to the Blairs': it was true enough that Christina felt she could not leave her father.

The marriage took place in September. By that time there was no question as to Sally's pregnancy. At Club meetings, which she was still attending, she met questioning or critical glances with her usual aplomb. She was determined not to withdraw from public view until she had honored the new Club bride with a Club tea; after all, there was now a rather tenuous connection between her and Christina: Henry Voorhees was one of the top executives in her father's bank. The Seminary wives had already entertained for the bride at an afternoon reception: a gathering at which Reformed Presbyterian ladies paused at the receiving line long enough to wish her well, proceeded to drink a cup of tea, and departed. That and Sally's tea were the only social occasions that honored Christina, who accepted all good wishes with her familiar bland smile.

For Sally it was her last appearance in public for the time being. She lamented particularly the necessity of foregoing the Club Christmas party, but even she was not ready to fly in the face of such fixed convention. She disappeared from public view.

The Reverend Mr. McCune continued to call on Amanda. On his first visit after the wedding, she came as near teasing as it was possible for her to come. "You see, the influence for good was greater than that for evil. Mr. Voorhees was predestinate to election also."

"Amanda—er—Miss Reid!" He eyed her severely. "No man can know that. It is not a subject for jesting."

He gave her his hat and followed her into the sitting room, where Mrs. Reid huddled close to the lamp, darning linen napkins. Amanda's books and papers were scattered over the center table. She had not asked herself why Mr. McCune kept making these evening visits: pastoral calls were one of his obligations, and she was not at home afternoons. It was inconceivable that their minister should not be made welcome at any time and as often as he wished to come. If she had thought about it, she would have supposed that his home might seem dreary to him with that rawboned cousin of Mrs. McCune's there in his wife's place.

Now she said, "Do please have this chair, won't you? And talk with Mother while I finish the last of these papers. It won't take but a moment."

"Ah, but before you become engrossed, I have a request. Will you consent to accompany me to Dr. Maxwell's lectures on Jerusalem? I feel that hearing those lectures together would be a most rewarding experience."

Amanda was astounded. She glanced up at him briefly, but did not look at her mother, who she knew would be eyeing her over her spectacles.

"But, your cousin?"

"My wife's cousin will attend with the older children. This is an educational opportunity they must not miss."

"But I bought two tickets for Mother and me."

"Your mother can no doubt find someone who would be delighted to go as her guest. Please do not say 'no.' I look forward to hearing Professor Maxwell in your company as an intellectual treat."

Mrs. Reid cleared her throat. "Now, Amanda, do not deny yourself on my account." Her tone was almost sprightly. "I can ask Mrs. Forbes to go with me. It would be such a pleasure to be able to do something for someone, for a change."

Amanda had run out of "buts." "Very well, then. And thank you very much. The first lecture is Friday evening, I believe?"

He in his turn thanked her, then pulled a chair close to Mrs. Reid and entered upon an ostentatiously low-voiced conversation with her. Amanda could no longer pretend to be busy with her papers. She turned away from the table and joined them. But she had so little to say and was so unwilling to say it that he took his departure before many minutes had passed.

When she returned to the sitting room after showing him out, her mother said, without looking up from her darning, "I know it must be intolerable to you to have no room in which you can entertain callers without the presence of a third person. I couldn't go to bed without darning those napkins. But I do wish you would put yourself out a little, even if you do feel spied upon."

"What do you mean, Mother? Mr. McCune wasn't calling on me alone."

"Don't be coy, Amanda. You're no schoolgirl. It's quite obvious he's begun to look about."

"Coy!" Amanda was horrified. "Mother, how *can* you! Mary McCune hasn't been dead six months."

"Six months can be a long time to a man with five motherless children."

"His children are being cared for." Amanda stood stiffly, frowning, beside the table. She laid one hand on her books. "If I thought you were right, I would not attend the lectures with him."

"Oh, well," her mother said hastily, "I may be imagining it. You go to the lectures with him and enjoy yourself."

"Enjoy!" Amanda was shocked by the sudden realization that if you thought of Mr. McCune as your minister, that was one thing; if you considered him as a man, it was very different. "He is without a doubt the dullest person I ever spent an evening with." She turned and went out, up to her low-ceiled bedroom, unheeding her mother's protest. She crossed to the hassock by her slit of a window under the sloping ceiling, whence she could look out at the stars. They were still there. Her consternation quieted; she laughed at herself for having been shaken by her mother's imaginings. "I was determined never to marry a theologue, and give up my books. How much less, then, a minister with five children!" But it was all nonsense—her mother's wish being father to a fantastic thought. The stars in the night sky were close and brilliant, and Mr. McCune was nothing. The light on the treetops meant that the moon was coming up behind the house: a late gibbous moon shining on autumn-thinned boughs. "Traditur dies die novaeque pergunt interire lunae." The lines came unexpectedly into her mind; she did not ask herself why: "Day upon day passes and new moons continue to perish." So many moons in Horace: "errantem lunem" and "Nox erat et caelo fulgebat luna sereno." She preferred her books to any marriage possible to her; thinking of the poetry of Horace, she thought too, "My books! What does that mean in practice! Caesar and Cicero and Virgil." And she found for herself one more quotation for the occasion as she pulled herself from the hassock to start getting ready for bed: "Amphora coepit Institui: currente rota cur urceus exit?" She was able to laugh at herself wryly: what kind of wine-jar would she have made? The running wheel, or the Potter, meant her to be a good serviceable pitcher: Caesar, Cicero, Virgil. No one, certainly not Mr. McCune, could see her as anything else.

But after the first lecture, she was not so sure; and on the way home from the second, she learned that her mother had been right. It was an inclement night; the first cold rain of the autumn was falling unremittingly; leaves were dropping from the trees by the hundreds and plastering themselves on the path. Mr. McCune took her arm protectively—almost, Amanda thought with revulsion, tenderly—as he held his wide umbrella overhead and guided her down the uneven bricks on the dark slope of Linden Street hill. She had never felt so helplessly locked up with anyone as she did with him under that umbrella. Nor was he adept at gallantry; often, as he stepped over a puddle, he knocked her bonnet awry and sent the rain in showers down her neck.

She cast about desperately for something to say: something that would put a space between them. "Are your children appreciating the lectures? I thought perhaps last time the subject matter was over their heads. Ariana, particularly, seemed a little restless."

"Oh, Ariana! A difficult child at a difficult age. She misses her mother very much."

"Of course, she must. Though I thought she seemed, except for her grief, quite contented at the Ballards'. I mean, I believed and felt that they have not found her 'difficult.'"

"I should never have let her go there. That is part of the trouble. She would have been happy to come home, had her mother recovered. I find it hard to gain her confidence, or to persuade her to accept her loss as God's will."

"It is sad if she is grieving alone and secretly. I shouldn't have supposed it, the few times I have seen her. But then: I don't pretend to understand children."

"Not understand children! How can you say that, Amanda, when you teach them?"

"Not children. Not for a moment would I consider teaching children. They do not like me, and I do not care for them."

"Amanda, that cannot be true. You belittle yourself." His voice was as tender as his hand under her arm.

"It is quite true."

"Then you would not consider becoming the mother of a family of five? Even if I were thrown in, as a husband?" The unction of his voice betrayed his certainty that she would admit that with him thrown in—

She stopped for a moment, stock-still. The umbrella tipped forward away from her. Rain soaked her bonnet, her shoulders. She thought how typical—how like her—to have to listen to that kind of proposal on such a night.

"Please—please—" she pleaded with him, her voice dry and choked. "Do not say any more. I meant what I said. Children are stranger to me than all the beasts of the field, and I cannot imagine—"

"You are serious? You mean what you are implying?" Mr. McCune was astounded, indignant. "Are you quite sure you wouldn't like to talk it over with your mother?" He had got the umbrella back over her head, and was leaning forward to peer at her face in the dark. She pulled back, then started off again down the hill. Once more, caught by surprise, he failed her with the umbrella. Rain splashed in her face. She was angry and sick at heart.

"I will talk it over with her." Her voice was sharp, a little bitter. How could she escape that ordeal? She knew for a certainty that he had already spoken to her mother, and that he had been given firm assurances. There would of necessity be another of those distressing arguments over her right to choose her own life. "But I am quite, quite sure. I prefer teaching." They had reached the Reid gate at last, the Reid footpath, the Reid doorstep. She held out her hand to him. She was unwilling to ask him in. "I am sorry if you are disappointed in me. And of course," she added hastily, minding her manners, "I am grateful for your high opinion of me, and honored. But I should not be at all successful in taking Mary's place, and should end by making all of you very unhappy. It is impossible. But I do thank you for the pleasure of attending the lectures in your company. You will want to take someone else to the rest of them."

"Oh, ho, there's no reason—"

"In the circumstances I couldn't think of continuing."

She turned and went into the house, her cheeks burning in her sudden awakening to the public commitment she had in a sense made by accompanying him to the lectures. All Waynesboro saying, like her mother, "Reverend McCune already looking around," and "Amanda Reid: so suitable, just the right age and born to be a minister's wife."

She went directly into the sitting room without taking off her cloak and bonnet. Her mother, brought home in the Ballard carriage, was there before her, dry and neat, waiting.

"Amanda, you're soaking wet."

"Mr. McCune is not very practiced in gallantry with an umbrella." Amanda's tone was dry.

"Why didn't you ask him in?"

"I had had quite enough of Mr. McCune for one night."

"What do you mean, Amanda?" Mrs. Reid's hair was tight in its bun, but she made the familiar gesture, a habit acquired in the kitchen, of pushing stray locks from her forehead with the back of her hand.

"You were quite right about what he had in mind." Amanda was abrupt, unconciliatory. "If I had only believed you, I could have avoided a preposterous interview."

"You mean that you would have refused to listen to an honorable proposal of marriage by the minister of your church, and that you think that proposal preposterous?"

"It wasn't exactly a proposal. Just hints. But it sufficed."

"You are behaving like a girl of seventeen. Why must you be so standoffish? You will discourage him before he comes to the point."

"That was my intention. Mother, you cannot be serious. You know how awkward I am with children. And I do not care for Mr. McCune."

"At your age you cannot afford to be romantic. What is the matter with Mr. McCune?"

"Everything. At any rate, you should know by this time that I have no desire to be married. Particularly not to a man who finds himself with five children on his hands, and does not know what to do with them. Can't you see that the situation is revolting?"

"Have you no womanly feelings at all?" Mrs. Reid had risen and was standing close to Amanda. Her chin was trembling with her futile petulance. "Some day, when you're an old woman, you'll be boasting that you're an old maid from choice and not necessity. But when you are all alone, you'll be sorry, in your heart."

"I may be sorry to be alone, but I'll never regret Mr. McCune." In a softer voice she added, "Mother, did you think at all about what you would do? You wouldn't like being here alone, nor living with the McCunes, either."

"I could manage. I always have. And I should be proud to be the minister's mother-in-law."

Amanda went upstairs seething with anger. At least, she told herself, she had been able to keep her temper, although she felt, fairly or not, that the responsibility for the humiliation of having been caught in such a ridiculous predicament was her mother's. She even said "Ridiculous!" aloud and angrily when she reached the top of the stairs, and cringed at the thought of how her friends would smile if they knew—even Thomasina, who might go so far as to think she should have married Mr. McCune for Ariana's sake. But they would never know. She must bind her mother to secrecy—for Mr. McCune's sake; on that ground her mother would hold her tongue, for the man was clearly going to marry someone, and soon. As for her, she had chosen her life; it might be meager (pitcher, not wine-jar), but it was not without its rewards; and at least it had dignity, and a place in the community was hers by right of her own achievement.

Mr. McCune returned no more to the Reids'. He was soon married to the first Mrs. McCune's Indiana cousin. His congregation may have thought he could have waited a little while longer, but they forgave him the brevity of his mourning because they were sure he had married "for the sake of the children." The children themselves, except for Ariana, accepted the change calmly; they had grown used to Cousin Belle, and the only alteration in the household was her moving into their father's bedroom. Ariana would not adjust to the change; she kept her lips right-shut in her stepmother's presence, and spent all the time she could at the Ballards', running there from school, seldom coming home before suppertime and often not before bedtime. To Thomasina she never complained. She would slip upstairs to the Traverses' sitting room, where she would sit quietly listening to the music lessons in the "studio" beyond. Thomasina, too shy to make much over her, was nevertheless delighted and flattered to have her company; she would welcome Ariana gently and make her feel at home by offering her a book to read from her collection of childhood favorites, and would then continue with her own reading or writing. When five o'clock came, the child would put her book down, put on her wraps, and say good-bye, sometimes kissing Thomasina in a sudden affectionate lunge, sometimes saying, "I'll just see if Aunt Eliza's home before I go." And if Eliza had come in from her father's office, she would take the child into her bedroom and let her talk. Ariana was astute enough to know that she could say things to Eliza that she could not, without a reproof, say to Thomasina. She was not, however, vehement or fierce. She would sit on Eliza's straight desk chair, hands clasped between her knees, feet dangling. And sometimes there would be tears on her cheeks.

"I am going to run away. I can't bear her to be *there*."

"So long as when you run, you run here. What does she do that is so awful?"

"She doesn't do anything. But she's there—where my mother—"

"She doesn't beat you?"

On the evening that Eliza asked her that, Ariana was for a moment struck dumb. "Of course not. I dare her to. No, she just tells Papa, and he whips us. But then," she admitted, "it was always like that. Papa was always the one who whipped us. But the awful thing," and she whispered it, the tears brimming over, "she wants us to call her 'Mamma.' And Ruhamah and the boys *do* it. Ruie is so little, and Luke—maybe they've forgotten already. But Matt and Mark—*I* call her Cousin Belle," Ariana added proudly.

That was one of the evenings when Eliza kept her for dinner to spare her any comment the swollen eyes might have caused at home, sending Johann to the manse with a note for the new Mrs. McCune. And whether her father approved or disapproved, he gave no sign. Whatever misgiving he may have felt as to the safety of her soul, it would be difficult, in Waynesboro, to find an acceptable reason for forbidding her to go to the Ballards'. Besides, supper at the McCune table was certainly an easier meal when that white-faced, silent little image was absent.

Amanda had been right in supposing that her attendance with Mr. McCune at two of the Maxwell lectures would not go unnoticed. Eyebrows had been lifted; there had been a few smiles, a few conjectures. John Gordon and Ludwig Rausch had by that time returned from the South, but as their wives had foreseen, they had refused to be edified by Professor Maxwell. By the date of the first lecture, Sally was not going out; she gave her series tickets to Miss Pinney, apologizing to Anne afterward: "She's too poor to buy even one; she will enjoy being there, especially if she has a guest. As for me, I'm glad to be spared."

Anne of course reported to her the presence of Amanda and Mr. McCune together at the first two lectures, and they enjoyed speculating. But after the third lecture, when Amanda had appeared in the company of her mother, Sally said, "She had better sense. I always thought so."

Anne retorted, "She's got better sense than to marry anybody."

Sally was startled by the sharpness of the tone, but asked no questions, although she had wondered. Ludwig had written her from New Orleans after Dock had rejoined him. She remembered the phrases of his letter: something about Dock's turning up in New Orleans looking like the cat who'd been in the cream jug. Something too about his being in a "strange state," "excited," but "He's forgotten his troubles." The two of them had gone to Vicksburg, Ludwig had reported in another letter. They had climbed all over the fortifications, trying to find the trenches where their regiments had been during the siege. "You would be surprised how much a place can change in fifteen years—landmarks get lost in underbrush. I do think it was a good idea for Dock to look at it by the light of day. He suggested himself that we stop at Shiloh on our way back."

Ludwig reported on the Shiloh expedition after he got home. It had been a queer one, he admitted. "After we left the river bluff, there was nothing familiar. This road, that road, this gully, that gully, these trees, those bushes—nothing to say I'd ever seen them before. Of course we all fought in a nightmare at Shiloh—lost babes in the wood. Dock was lucky that time: the wounded—the ones that could be got away before the Rebs trampled over them—were carried back to the river bluff. For the surgeons there was none of that fight-and-run, stand-fight-and-run, this way, that way."

"I suppose the doctors had a peaceful day, cutting off arms and legs."

Ludwig laughed ruefully. "Couldn't have been much fun." If Sally thought it was all just arms and legs, let her think so. "I don't believe going back bothered him more than it did me. It's something none of us, long as we live, will ever get straight in our minds. Such a queer lost corner of woods, just the way we left it, seems like. You can't walk through the brush yet without kicking up canteens and broken guns and swords and shell fragments. Both of us brought some home, souvenirs for the boys. Anyway, Dock's all right, no problem there."

Anne would not have called her husband a "problem." She had lived for a long while now with that darkness in John, and she had accepted it, however much his cure for it might hurt. Someday he might be different, when they were so old it no longer mattered, or when he had got used to not being able to save all his patients. Now he was what he was; there were times when he could not bear being himself, and sought—what? Oblivion? She loved him and always would, in part just because he did care so much and took things so hard. And if he had to find his own way out of the depths where he sometimes fell, she could only stand by and wait. For she remembered the promise she had exacted of him—how long ago that seemed now!—and that he would keep: he would never in his desire to escape his imprisoning identity take Kate's way out. She could ask no more. She must hold her tongue and never show even by a quiver how angry she was, how hurt to sickness. The sharp remark to Sally about the unwisdom of marrying was a spark thrown off unexpectedly from a fire banked down to smother out.

But she had never told herself that she would cease to feel John's derelictions, and she had been both angry and hurt when she had first seen him on his return from New Orleans.

When the two men were due home, she had taken the children and gone to meet the Cincinnati train. It was a rainy day, and she had had the curtains put on the buggy; driving it, she felt a little like a farm woman in town for Saturday, particularly since Sally showed up in full panoply: barouche, top up, Reuben driving, and a boy to leap down and hold the horses' heads if the trains frightened them. The Rausches waited in the barouche, but Johnny escaped from the buggy while Anne was tying Molly to the hitching rack: the Indianapolis train was waiting at the platform, and Johnny wanted to see whether Tim O'Reilly was the engineer. Anne was so concerned with catching him before he came to harm that she almost missed the arrival of the Cincinnati train on the other side of the depot. She had to run back and snatch Binny from the buggy; she reached the car steps breathless, rain-spattered, and wind-blown, a child clutched in each hand, in time to see Ludwig leap down and sweep his three children to one side while he embraced Sally in an unrestrained bear hug, shouting one of his unintelligible German endearments.

John followed him down the car steps. When Anne saw him, she knew. She could not have told how, or why, except that he seemed a bit reluctant to greet her. Afraid of the first few moments. He picked Binny up and swung her to his level to be kissed, and shook hands with Johnny before he said, "Well, Anne?" and kissed her cheek. When he did that, she felt again, for a blind moment, a sick lost dizziness. In the buggy, the four of them crowded behind the curtains, she was given a moment's respite by the excited chatter of the children. Then, in their own hall, when she was thinking that she could not bear to feel in him again, of all things, reluctance, he dropped his wide-brimmed military-looking hat, unfastened and hung up his cape, and said, "God, Anne, I'm glad to be home."

"You didn't enjoy yourself, then?" The sickness at her heart diminished; she still felt lightheaded.

"With Ludwig, yes. We played old soldier to a fare-ye-well." They went into the sitting room, Johnny hanging on his arm with both hands; Binny, her short black curls flying, leaped about him in squealing abandon.

"Sit down on that hassock, Binny. You're making me dizzy. You'll be sick, getting so overwrought. I believe you run wild when I'm not at home."

Subdued at once, the child sat down, stiffly, with her hands clenched on her knees. Her eyes brimmed with tears.

"Now, honey," John said to her as he dropped into his leather chair and pulled Anne down on its arm, "I didn't mean to scold, but you do get too excited."

"You've never been away before," Anne reminded him. "They've been counting the days."

Johnny hung on the other arm of the chair. "Papa! Papa!"

"And I'm not going again, not without you. Johnny, can you drag my grip in here?"

The little boy scampered off and brought the valise in, holding it before him with both hands so that it swung heavily from one knee to the other. He plunked it down on the floor at his father's feet.

"Papa, what'd you bring us?"

"For shame, Johnny," his mother reproved him. "Don't let him have it, John—he knows better than to ask."

"What'd he want the old grip in here for, then?"

"Binny can have her present anyway." John smiled at her, still sitting upright on the hassock, but bouncing a little, the tears on her cheeks forgotten, her black eyes alight.

"Oh, Papa!" Johnny, squatting by the valise, sank back on his heels and studied his father's face. He was so solemn that for a moment the dimple was smoothed out of his cheek.

"No, of course your mother didn't mean it. I brought you so much I almost had to carry my shirts home over my arm." He spread the valise open. "First, here's a doll for Binny. A real French doll from Paris." He opened the box and took from it a wax doll dressed in the latest mode, beruffled and bustled.

"John, what a beauty! But she's too little. She'll spoil it."

"Of course. But she'll have other dolls, and she'll never love this one as much as she does this minute." He gave it to Binny. She took it in her arms without a smile, but with an excited little bounce, a caught breath, and a light transforming her face. She pushed herself back on the hassock until her feet stuck out in front of her, nursing the doll in one arm, touching it gingerly with a finger of the other hand: its cheek, its bonnet, its hands; she was lost in ecstatic contemplation.

Next came a coil of rope. Johnny looked a little dashed.

"It's a lariat, Son. Your uncle Ludwig got some for his boys, too. Seems New Orleans is the jumping-off place for Texas nowadays. These are what the cowboys use to lasso cattle on the range. You know: Chisholm Trail. West of the Pecos." He smiled a little, fingering the stiff cream-colored rope. "Ludwig got interested," he went on to Anne. "Some agent down there he went to see about selling rope for him asked him why he didn't make lariat rope. So he brought some to see how it's made, and some for the boys, too."

"A little young?"

"They'll grow up to them. He thought maybe Captain Bodien might know how to use them. He was in the Army out West, you know, before the War."

"Thank you, Papa." Johnny took the coil of hard rope a little doubtfully.

"Here's a box of pralines, for everybody. Put it away for now. And here's something else for you. If you can read. Have you learned to read at that dame's school you go to?"

"John!" Anne protested. "He's eight years old!"

"You know I can read." The boy was reproachful.

"I was teasing," John admitted. "This is about a boy who lived in a town on the Mississippi River. I don't believe our ladies' library will get it, so I bought you a copy."

Anne said again, "He's too little."

"Maybe you're too little for what I got you. What do you think, Johnny? Shall we let her have it?" He opened a white box and lifted up from the cotton that lined it what seemed like an endless string of beads, round amethyst beads separated by a series of crystal disks, graduated in size from small at each end to large in the middle.

"John! How lovely! But you shouldn't have. Where did you find it?"

"In a little old shop in Royal Street. Probably belonged to some proud Creole beauty. Poor devils! Mighty few of them know how to go about *working*. Never had to, of course, and now they live from month to month by selling what they own."

"I'd be heartbroken if I had to sell these. I won't feel right about wearing them." Anne was letting the beads slip from one hand to the other.

"Why not? Somebody was probably mighty glad to get what I paid for 'em. The War wasn't your fault, was it? Put them on, and wear 'em." Once more he dipped into his valise. "And a souvenir for Johnny. A canteen I stumbled over walking across Shiloh battlefield."

Johnny dropped rope and book and took the corroded and dented canteen reverently in both hands.

"You mean it was some soldier's?" He ran a stubby finger over the letters U.S.A. "Was he killed?"

"Maybe. Or maybe he just dropped his canteen and skedaddled."

"There's a hole in it." Johnny put his finger in the triangular tear in the metal. "Did a bullet make it?"

"Probably or a minny ball. Anyway, a canteen with a hole in it isn't much good for holding water. Probably why it was thrown away."

"Thank you, Papa. I like this best of all." Johnny smiled, one of his mischievous dimpling smiles.

"I suspected you would. Boys your age are sure to be bloodthirsty."

"Were you at Shiloh, your own self?"

"Yes, I was there. Two days and a night between, trying to pick up the wounded and put them together again. We'll talk about it some other time." He got to his feet. "Come upstairs with me, Anne, while I clean up. The train was filthy."

Anne, the beads dangling from her fingers as she followed him, thought that the trip had done him good, whatever had happened. She had never known him of his own accord to mention the war to Johnny, and he had always evaded brusquely any questions—the kind of questions a small boy was bound to ask a father about his battles.

Alone in the bedroom, the door closed behind them, John took his wife into his arms; she put a hand on each of his shoulders, and tucked her cheek under his jawbone. She said, "Your beard prickles, cut short that way," but she did not move, and he tightened his arms about her.

"I'm glad to be back."

"I missed you."

But they did not look at each other when they drew apart. Anne thought, "I do not want to know. I'll listen to his words and not beyond them. I cannot suffer—not like the first time—not again." She denied the heart-sickness that had shaken her a little earlier.

She said, going away from him a little distance to lean against the tall bedpost, "Tell me about your cousins. Was it bad? You never wrote me a word about them."

He followed her, used the step to the high bed, and sat there, leaning back sideways against her embroidered pillow shams.

"Like something out of Poe. Decadent. Rotting away. Rotten door sills. Leaky roof. Rain, mildew. Neglect for fifteen years in that climate was bound to do it, but it was horrible to see. All the lovely old things in that house still there, but moldy. The mirrors clouded, the furniture falling to pieces. Money could fix it up again, I suppose. But the rot goes deeper. In '62 Cousin Robert was what the South likes to boast about: the perfect flower of civilization. Urbane and courtly as all get-out. One of the great planters: thousands of acres of cotton land. Now he's a shambling old man, sitting at his desk turning over papers, too sodden with whiskey to know what they mean. Because he fought Secession he hadn't a friend left when his side won. A defeated people can be mighty vindictive. His sons had not survived, so their having been Rebs didn't help any. The Ku Klux Klan frightened Cousin Robert's niggers away; he couldn't plant or get credit. So he found this overseer, a Klansman himself probably, because after that the Klan left them alone, and the niggers drifted back. But there's no money for house-servants, beyond a cook."

Anne thought, "But I've heard all this before. And I never heard him use so many words to say so little. To avoid mentioning what? Whom? His cousin Jessamine?" She said, "What's he like, this Stevens? Did your young cousin marry him?"

John slipped down from the bed, crossed to the washstand, poured water from the pitcher into the bowl.

"A long, lank, sallow poor-white. Not very young. I had supposed, because he had fought, that he would be in his thirties, like most of us. Unreasonable to me, of course. He must be forty-five, maybe fifty." He had taken off his coat, unfastened his cuff links, rolled up his shirt sleeves.

"She married him?"

"Yes. I wish I'd known more about the situation sooner. But I don't see how I could have done any more if I'd tried. It was a way to save the land, you see." He stopped splashing for a moment and stared at his hands in the water. There had been a dry, wrenched pain in his voice, as if his throat had tightened.

Anne watched him, miserable in her certainty. It might be better if she were not so almost clairvoyant with John: better if he could still deceive her. She said, "What is she like, the granddaughter?"

"Young! She couldn't have been more than four or five when I first saw her, so, nineteen or twenty. And married to that mudsill, and Cousin Robert in a haze of alcohol or he would never have permitted it."

"Pretty?"

"No. But would be, if she lived in a decent climate and were properly fed. Black hair, hungry eyes, fine bones. Thin and yellow. Malaria, of course."

Still the doctor, she thought, even while she wanted to ask him, with the same bitter grief in her voice as was in her mind: "*John, how did it happen*?" Instead she forced her voice to a flat thinness, trying to keep her mind on surface matters. "Why did she marry him?"

"She had little choice. Not many beaux in Mississippi these days, and no one went near the place, anyway. The hope is, I suppose, he'll make a good crop of cotton next year, and then at least there'll be money."

John went on talking. "She hates the plantation, and no wonder, the way it is now. She remembers New Orleans as a paradise—even the first post-war years, when she was just getting old enough to remember. She couldn't have held out against the two men; no one could who was so young and anemic and sick with malaria. So what could I have done if I'd known about it in time? Nothing but fill her full of iron and quinine."

His tone was so disgusted that Anne smiled a little. "Carried her off, like some knight out of a romance."

"Good Lord, no! I felt like I was leaving a nightmare behind when I left that house. But I am sorry for her." There was something inimical in Anne's face; her lids were dropped so that he could not see her eyes. "Look," he argued with her, "a minute ago you were feeling sorry for some perfectly imaginary Creole, selling her necklace. Can't you feel sorry for a girl like Jessamine? I spent a couple of nights there, and it was enough."

He wiped his face and hands, and crossing the room, began to unpack his valise, throwing soiled clothes in a heap on the floor, moving to the chest of drawers with his brushes, box of collar buttons, cravats, and case of razors. "If you'd seen her that first night, so young and so humiliated—"

Anne, watching him, burned with hatred suddenly, unexpectedly. She was horrified; she had never supposed she could feel like that. The taste of her jealousy was sour in her mouth. She said, meekly, "If you want me to be sorry for her, I will."

"You would be, if you knew—moldy old house and two rotted men."

Anne said, "Maybe she'll have children, then she won't mind so much."

John blurted out, "She can't. The man's impotent." He looked then so suddenly blank about the eyes, his jaw clenched and mouth tight-lipped, that Anne knew, in a clear-eyed moment of shock, that he would have taken the words back if he could. She stared at him. "But John! You mean to say she *told* you that?"

He came back to where she was still leaning against the bedpost, and pushed himself up to where he had been lying before.

"Look, Anne: she hasn't a soul to unburden herself to. And to her, I am a middle-aged doctor. I treated her for malaria when she wasn't much older than Binny. Who would she tell, if not a doctor? It was after dinner, that first night I was there, when both men had drunk themselves into a stupor. Cousin Robert with his head down on his arms. Stevens lolling back in his chair, leering at us. In the drawing room, on a mildewed horsehair sofa, she burst into tears, and to comfort her, I said what you said, just now, about children. And she told me. She said then that Cousin Robert would kill Stevens if he ever found it out. And I suppose he would, because what Cousin Robert wanted was to keep the land to be handed down to great-grandsons."

"She would like children?"

"I suppose so," John said shortly.

Anne was thrown off balance: could she have been wrong? Such a cold-blooded approach. She shuddered.

"I know," John was watching her. "It has *East Lynne* beat a mile."

"Mightn't he get over it?"

"I don't know. Depends on what caused it. A wound, no. Undernourishment, chills and fever, nerves: he might."

"Good gracious," Anne murmured weakly.

"A nightmare." Anne was staring at him, a question in her eyes; he smiled, but he was thankful for his beard and mustache: a twist of the mouth was sometimes too revealing.

He was saved the necessity of sitting longer under those probing eyes by a crash downstairs. A crash of broken glass and then a long frightening silence.

Anne said, "That rope—the lamp—" and was whirling out the door almost before he slid off the bed. He followed her headlong flight down the stairs, her skirts snatched up in both hands. In the parlor he found her face to face with Johnny, who stood with lowered head, eyes down, hands behind him, the lariat trailing over the carpet. A conch shell and the bottle of Jordan water from the what-not were broken on the floor. His father sympathized with Johnny: to be made to feel guilty by a woman who was in the right was one of life's severer afflictions. Moreover, he did not consider Anne's loss a serious one. But this was her case to handle, and she was in a flaming temper.

"In the parlor, of all things!" Johnny muttered something about "more room." "That's no plaything for the house! Your father should have had better sense, I must say."

She was not only angry, she did not care who knew it. John marveled at the sixth sense of women: guilt and shame were in the air, and she blamed them both, but him primarily. He stepped into the room and, standing behind her, put his arms around her waist. He spoke to Johnny over her shoulder.

"A lariat is to be used outdoors, and only outdoors. Coil it up, then bring a broom and dustpan and clean up that mess."

" 'Mess'! That's all a man cares. Those were my mother's and now they're gone. The Jordan water!"

"Pshaw, Anne—Fill a bottle with well water and label it, and who will know the difference?"

"I will. Mamma was so proud of it. Old Mr. Ely—he'd married her and Papa—brought it to her from the Holy Land—got it himself from the River Jordan." There were tears in her voice.

"Women take the cake," he thought. Anne's unfailing sense of humor, where is it now? Tears over nothing! "Do as I say, Johnny. Clean it up. Where's Binny?"

"Gone to show Martha her doll."

"Bring her back with you when you fetch the broom. I've hardly seen the child."

When Johnny had gone out, he turned Anne about in his arms and held her once more cheek to cheek.

"I'm sorry, honey. I suppose it was a silly present for a little boy."

She drew away from him and blew her nose. "*I'm* sorry. But I was frightened—that awful crash, then nothing. I was afraid Binny was hurt, or a lamp knocked over and coal oil all over the carpet."

"Binny will let you know when she's hurt; she has a good yelling apparatus. Come sit down and tell me what you've been doing. What's the news in Waynesboro? How many of my patients am I going to have left? I must go see Edwards presently and find out if there are calls I should make."

That evening he kept his regular office hours. Life in the Gordon house slipped back into normal routine. Except for what lay buried in mind and heart, it was as if John had never been away.

The trip made a little more difference, outwardly and immediately, to the Rausches—or to the Rausch Cordage Company. Ludwig and Captain Bodien took the lariat to pieces to study, and decided that they could make it. But lariat rope could never be more than another sideline. More important was the connection Ludwig had made with young Mr. Thibaudeau. He was an energetic and determined young Creole, not afraid of work, who had started a brokerage and ship-chandler concern when he had come of age. He promised to try to sell Ludwig's rope exclusively even with business in the doldrums, and when things improved, they would see what he could do. Other firms sold the rope of eastern manufacturers, but Thibaudeau and Ludwig would have the advantage of lower shipping costs, and besides he should be able to build a good business with the Cajun fishermen, whose country he knew and whose language he could speak. For the first time, Ludwig would have an agent who would sell no other rope than Rausch cordage.

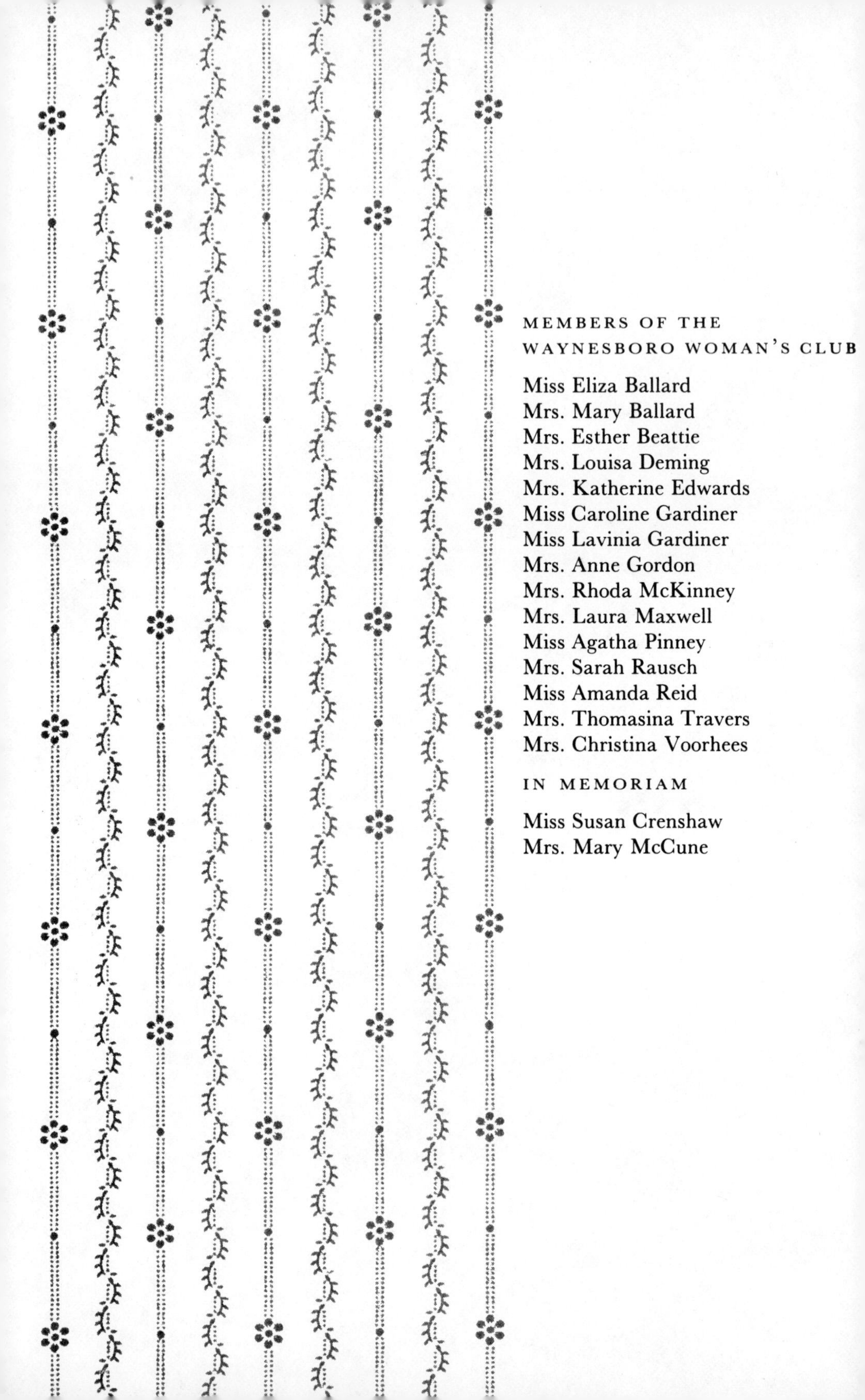

MEMBERS OF THE
WAYNESBORO WOMAN'S CLUB

Miss Eliza Ballard
Mrs. Mary Ballard
Mrs. Esther Beattie
Mrs. Louisa Deming
Mrs. Katherine Edwards
Miss Caroline Gardiner
Miss Lavinia Gardiner
Mrs. Anne Gordon
Mrs. Rhoda McKinney
Mrs. Laura Maxwell
Miss Agatha Pinney
Mrs. Sarah Rausch
Miss Amanda Reid
Mrs. Thomasina Travers
Mrs. Christina Voorhees

IN MEMORIAM

Miss Susan Crenshaw
Mrs. Mary McCune

1879

"The Club members are concerned about the education of their children."

The winter of 1879 found Ludwig Rausch a happy and satisfied man. He sat in his office on a morning in February, idle for once, reflecting on the past, the immediate past, and the present. His and Sally's fourth child and third son, Ludwig Junior, was almost a month old, a thriving baby; the other children were healthy, reasonably intelligent, and growing fast. The new brick mill, comparatively fireproof, was finished. Now every step in the manufacture of rope was carried on in the two big buildings with the most modern machinery. In the original ropewalk nothing was made but oakum and lath yarn. The tarring shed still stood in the cobbled yard: if it caught on fire and burned down, no great harm would be done; and since lath yarn had to be tarred, it was economical to do it in the old shed, close to the old ropewalk. Spinning yarn from hemp was still partly a hand process. Inexperienced spinners could learn their trade making lath yarn, which was not a finished product or intended to be: beginners under skilled foremen walked the length of the weather-beaten shed on the canal bank, while boys with their first working papers turned the wheels for them.

From the raw but, to Ludwig, beautifully clean-cut brick buildings with their evenly spaced windows, there came a heartening roar of machinery. Business had improved; the mill was running ten hours a day six days a week. The steam siren that called the hands to work and released them from it blew at six-thirty, eleven-thirty, twelve-thirty, and five-thirty. The piercing rise and fall of the factory whistle was audible everywhere, and already others than mill hands had come to rely on it and find it a convenience: "Hurry with your lunch, children, you'll be late to school: there goes the half-past-twelve whistle"; or "Yes, you can go play with him after school, but don't stay a minute after the whistle blows at suppertime."

Ludwig had gradually turned over the actual oversight of the manufacturing process, the management of the mill itself, to Captain Bodien. Except for occasional forays to see that some particular rope was being laid to specifications, Ludwig worked in his office, or went on the road in his insatiable search for orders, or devoted a part of his time and energy to politics.

The year 1878 had been a bad one for Republicans. As in many off-year elections, the trend had been against the party in power. President Hayes was not a popularity-seeker; even before his election as president he had announced his intention to serve only one term, and as a consequence had had little influence on divergent elements in the party. Civil Service reform, which had been one of his campaign pledges, had made small headway against its opponents in Congress, and the quondam Liberals, who had returned to the party to vote for him, were disappointed and aggrieved. John Sherman, the Secretary of the Treasury, had carried through a harsh policy of deflation, in preparation for the resumption of specie payments. The Greenback party, made up of those who had suffered from this policy, had helped defeat the Republicans in the fall, when, for the first time since the war, Democratic majorities had been returned in both houses of Congress. Sherman, however, had stuck to his guns, even though in December, in his own state, he had been jeered at and hissed when he attempted to make a speech. He had persisted in refunding the debt, and confidence in the dollar had been restored; when the day came for the Resumption Act to go into effect, Sherman was ready with the gold needed to redeem any paper bills presented. Since paper bills were easier to handle than gold coins, they continued to circulate at par. Whatever a Democratic Congress might propose, that good could not be undone: the country was back on the gold standard, its finances were secure, and John Sherman deserved to be the next President. Ludwig at least had done his part; the Seventh District, with his perhaps unnecessary assistance, had remained true to its allegiance and returned Mr. Liddell to the House for another term.

The summer and fall of '78, for the second year in succession, had seen the reaping of bumper crops at a time when the harvest abroad had been a failure, so that wheat flowed overseas and gold flowed back. Had not the election been held before the farmers felt the consequences, the Greenback party might have died a-borning. Ludwig felt sure it would dissolve and disappear before 1880. He was not even much troubled by the election results: there were fairly good men in all the county offices, good Party men, at any rate, and one of them was Douglas Gardiner, whom he had persuaded to run for prosecuting attorney. Ludwig had for some time believed that the young man could make a name for himself, and had been more than ready to give him a push along the road. Gardiner might even, in time, make a good politician, if he would interest himself—if he would learn to curb his sarcastic tongue and modify his rather contemptuous manner. He saw the prosecutor's office as a step toward a judgeship. He and Ludwig had had a long talk one evening late in October, when Ludwig had been in the Merrill, Ballard, Gardiner office, about the inadequacy of the state's judicial system: no Appellate Court between the Courts of Common Pleas and the State

Supreme Court. Since the founding of the state, the Supreme Court had been forced to ride circuit in pairs, in order to hear the cases piled up in county court houses, and had been able to sit in Columbus as a court of the whole for only a small part of the year.

By the late '70s the Supreme Court was four years in arrears, with its docket continuing to pile up. The convention for the revision of the state constitution had proposed the establishment of circuit courts, with separate judges, to stand between the already existing courts. But the proposed alterations to the constitution were voted on as a whole, not article by article, and had been rejected by the electorate.

"Inevitably, the Supreme Court is behind," Douglas had said. "So far behind they'll never catch up, with literally thousands of cases waiting. Imagine the pressure on a man's mind. It made Judge Ballard old before his time, and would have killed him if he had not resigned. I couldn't understand why the proposed revisions of the constitution were rejected by the voters."

"Too many special interests against one or another of its provisions. The temperance people opposed a license law for saloon-keepers, since that would make the liquor trade legal; the 'wets' voted with them because they did not want the restrictions a license law would impose. Corporations were opposed to any reforms in corporate laws that would restrain them."

On an earlier occasion, when Ludwig had suggested to Douglas that he might move up from a county office to Congress, Douglas had said, "I really think I would prefer the state legislature. I might do some good there." On the evening when they had discussed the state judicial system, Ludwig had come to understand the previously incomprehensible remark. At any rate, Douglas had consented to run for prosecutor because he could fill that office and at the same time continue his practice of law. In the partnership he now carried most of the burden: old Jake Merrill had retired; his grandson was a boy; and Judge Ballard took only a few cases, for the railroad or other corporations.

All these things passed through Ludwig's mind in untroubled revery as he sat smoking at his desk. When he heard the sleighbells outside, he rose to put on hat, overcoat, and gloves. In cold weather Ludwig never left his horse hitched at the office hitching rack: Reuben drove him down in the morning, brought the horse for him at noon, and spent the hour between the 11:30 and 12:30 whistles with his Negro friends who ate their lunches and kept warm around the tar shed. When Ludwig returned for the afternoon, Reuben took the horse home, and came back again at five-thirty.

Still in a meditative mood, Ludwig drove up Chillicothe Street at a sedate pace, holding hard on the reins to restrain his big bay gelding, to whom the light sleigh was hardly more of drag than a baby carriage would have been. But on the long slope toward town, he recognized Dock Gordon ahead of him in his cutter, plug hat and all; Dock must have been in consultation with old Edwards or Wright. John was poking along behind staid old reliable Molly.

Ludwig chuckled, loosed his reins, and slapped them on Tecumseh's back. The rhythmical slow jingle of the sleigh bells broke into a helter-skelter clash and clang as "Cump" snorted, shook his head, and settled into a fast trot. They passed Dock at the next corner—Molly might have been standing still. At the end of the block, Ludwig turned Cump left on Linden Street and so on around the block, and passed Dock a second time just as he reached the office hitching post. There Ludwig pulled Cump around and went back to greet John with a grin and a salute with his whip.

"Nice bit o' horseflesh, eh, Dock?"

"What d'you mean, shaming poor old Molly that way?" John threw back his robe, descended, came around to smooth Molly's nose before he snapped on the hitching strap. "You wouldn't have done that if I'd had Becky out this morning."

"I've heard a lot about that sorrel mare. Want to race?"

"You bet." The mare had been born and raised on the Gordon farm, and trained there by an old darky who was not much good at anything else, but excellent with horses. John was very proud of Becky. Now he settled quickly the terms of the race, and when Ludwig had driven on, went into his office, dropped his bag on his desk, unfastened his cape and swung it over his arm, picked up his mail, and went out the side door. In the stable yard he called "Lonzo" to no effect; he went on and entered the house by way of the kitchen.

"Hey, Martha! That good-for-nothing Lonzo warming himself in here?"

Martha was in the rocking chair close to the stove; Lonzo was tipped back on the hind legs of a straight chair, his stocking feet curled over the nickel trimming that ran around the base of the big coal range. The front legs of the chair thumped to the floor. Lonzo rose.

"Yes-sah. Mahty col' mawnin' in the stable, Docteh." He grinned, unabashed. With one prehensile foot he groped under the stove for his boots.

"Go fetch Molly in—unhitch and look after her, and when you've done that, hitch Becky to the cutter. At least—Lunch ready, Martha?"

"Yes-sah. Ah jes' taken yo' pie outen the oven."

"I'll want Becky by one o'clock. Going to race her this afternoon."

Johnny, at the sound of his father's voice, had left his mother and Binny by the sitting room fire and gone to meet him. He reached the dining room door in time to hear.

"Oh, Papa!" All the ecstasy of hope was in his voice. "Can I go? Can I ride with you? Who you racing?"

"But school? Ah, no, it's Wednesday. Well, I don't see why not, if you think you can hold on. If Mamma thinks it's all right. I'm racing your Uncle Ludwig and his General William Tecumseh Sherman."

"Oh, Papa! D'you think Becky can beat *Cump*?"

They had reached the sitting room door.

"What's all this?"

"Mamma! Please! Our Becky against Cump Rausch and Papa says he'll take me."

Binny slipped out of her child's rocker, her curling short hair electric, her eyes wide and sparkling.

"Me too, Papa!"

John thrust his letters in his pocket, tossed his cape on the sofa, and picked her up.

"Little Me-Too! Not this time, Binny: young ladies don't ride in races. Can we have lunch, Anne? I'm meeting Ludwig at the Sycamore Street railroad crossing at one. We'll race up Sycamore Street from there, three heats."

Sycamore was the wide quiet residential street beyond Chillicothe toward the railroad station; it was the accepted street for winter races because there was so little traffic on it.

"That's such a rough street—full of holes—are you sure you won't be overturned, or Johnny thrown out?" Then having put herself on record as wife and mother, just in case there was some mishap, Anne rose to lead them to the dining room.

Binny had sat silent but disconsolate on John's knee, her eyes cast down and all the light dimmed from her face.

"Never mind, Baby." Her father put a finger under her chin and lifted her face, so that she must look at him. "If you like, I'll take you sleigh-riding in the country this afternoon—you and Mamma, after office hours."

She threw her arms around his neck.

To Anne he said, "I tell you: you and Johnny come with me and Binny late this afternoon. I'll have Lonzo hitch Molly to the big sleigh. I've only two country calls to make after office hours; old Phillips is down with lumbago and Mrs. Irvine—nothing contagious, nothing that will keep me long." He saw how dubious Johnny looked, and added to him, "Or have you some important engagement?"

"Well—I—uh—have a kind of engagement. I promised Shaney, while her gran'ma was taking her nap, we were going to work on our entrenchments—a lot of us—in their front yard."

"Oh, Johnny! Poor Mrs. Cochran!" his mother remonstrated. "Why not make your fort in our front yard, where no one will mind your noise?"

"Because the Enemy doesn't come this way."

"Enemy! Who's the enemy?" His father frowned, fork suspended, thinking of the colored children who lived in the East End, up beyond the Cochrans.

But Johnny had nothing on his conscience. He wriggled a little, then grinned at his father. "The students."

"Dear me!" Anne kept her face straight. "You mean you snowball the *theologues*?"

"Well, they snowball back. And there's more of them, even when Char Bonner's with us, and Sophie Klein an' Bill Thirkield."

"I guess the students can look after themselves, Anne. They're not preachers yet."

"Then," Johnny continued, "when Mr. Cochran comes home from the bank an' takes Shaney's gran'ma for a sleigh ride, we all go inside to get warm an' slide down the laundry chute."

"Slide down—" At this his father would have remonstrated.

"Sally and I used to slide down the laundry chute," Anne interposed. "It's made for it. It isn't a straight drop; it slants back past the vegetable cellar to the laundry. They won't kill themselves, but they may drive Mrs. Cochran crazy."

"But—" Johnny said, again ignoring the interruptions. "Shaney has an ol' music lesson at four, an' has to go all the way out to ol' Travers's. She'll haf to start early. I expect I'll be home by ha' past three."

"Very well. If you're here we'll take you, otherwise not. And you, Anne?"

She shook her head. "Club meeting."

"Can't you skip it for once?"

"No. To say that I would rather go sleigh-riding would be a poor excuse. It's at the Gardiners', too."

"Can I take you up? It's cold for walking, and I'll have time to do that between our race and my office hours."

Lonzo had brought Becky and the cutter around to the hitching post in front, but he had not fastened the mare: he held her until Johnny and his father came out. The boy was so excited his mother had hardly been able to get his coat and mittens on, and his round fur cap. John had taken up his cape from the sitting room sofa, and in the hall, from the hatrack, a cap like Johnny's, gone rather moth-eaten and mangy looking, that he wore for country calls in the winter. They climbed into the sleigh, and Lonzo let go of Becky's bridle.

On Sycamore Street there were two or three drivers trying out their horses. The air, so cold and dry even at midday that it glued their nostrils together, rang with the clear bells and the thud of horses' hooves on the packed snow. At the railroad crossing Ludwig waited, hanging to the reins while his impatient gelding tossed his head, pranced, curvetted, swished his tail, stamped, backed, and kept the bells on his harness jangling in a harsh unrhythmic clangor. When John drew up beside him, he called to a man turning a sleigh fifty or sixty feet up Sycamore Street. "Clear the street will you, Coppard? It's a wager. We want a clear track."

The man saluted with his whip, then cracked it above his horse's back and went careening up the street, shouting, "A match! Clear the way! A trotting crack! Clear the way! The bay gelding against the sorrel mare!"

While they waited, Johnny sat beside his father, quivering with excitement. Ludwig raised his hand to his cap in a broad parody of a salute. "Cap'n Gordon, sir! Glad to see you've sportsmanship enough to handicap yourself with a little extra weight."

The few passersby who had stopped to watch laughed sympathetically: the bay gelding was big and powerful, and Ludwig so broad-shouldered that alone he almost filled the cutter; on the other hand, the mare was fine and small-boned, Dock Gordon was slight and trim, the boy built like him. It looked a preposterous match. The mare stood quietly in contrast to the restless bay, only her flickering nostrils and alert head showing any awareness of the other horse and the onlookers.

"Papa, do you think we have a chance?" Johnny whispered. He was frightened for Becky, now, and would almost rather not be there than see her humiliated, and his father.

"I think so: Becky's better trained. But that's a powerful horse. If we lose, no wails out of you!"

"Oh, no, Papa."

Ludwig, who had been watching their forerunner out of sight up Sycamore Street, said, "Let's go." He leaned over and flipped a coin to a boy at the side of the street. "Give us the count, will you, Bub? Up to four—"

"Bub" obliged. "*One* for the money, *two* for the show —"

Reins were tightened in strong hands. Johnny clutched the side of the sleigh.

"*Three* to make ready, four to *go*!"

Sleigh bells clashed. Horses' heads tossed as the reins were loosened. Chunks of frozen snow and gravel were thrown high by pounding hooves. Becky got off to a quicker start, her high head swinging with her swift trot. Johnny bounced in his seat: they were flying; they might have been in the air, so smooth beneath the runners was the hard snow. Sleigh bells behind them stayed behind, and were only a spur to the eager little mare. They swept up Sycamore Street; everyone cleared out of their way, leaving the slow uphill slope empty except for the onlookers at the curb. At the Main Street corner Becky was still ahead. The horses could not be stopped there; self-appointed guardians of the commonweal stood in the center of Main Street to halt the usual sporadic traffic of delivery wagons, hacks, drays, and sleighs. There were by now groups of onlookers on all the corners. Johnny distinguished no faces as they swept past, but when Becky had been slowed, stopped, and turned, and was on her way back to the starting point, he identified a group of friends. He swept off his cap to wave it, and uttered a triumphant "Ya-ay!"

"You'll frighten Becky if you're not careful." But his father was smiling, too, all over his usually unrevealing serious face. He saw the group that Johnny was greeting: one a girl in a plaid frock and a short jacket, a Scottish bonnet with streamers cocked over one ear and her honey-colored hair tumbled thickly on her shoulders: Elsa Rausch, Johnny's "Shaney." But the boy's eyes, sidelong, enraptured, backward turned while there was a chance of seeing, had not been on Elsa but on one of the girls with her: the slimmer, smaller one in a red pelisse or whatever name the fool women were calling a cloak this winter—the one with the silvery hair flowing smooth as silk from below a round flat little fur hat with a feather rising from it just at the middle of her forehead. She carried a round muff that matched the hat, and her hands had stayed in it while Elsa was waving.

As they loped past and on down Sycamore Street toward the railroad crossing, John said, "Who are the young ladies with Elsa?"

"Char Bonner."

"In the fur hat?"

"Oh, no. That was Julia Deming." He sighed almost reverently.

"Ah—and does she help build entrenchments? And slide down laundry chutes?"

"No." Johnny eyed his father warily, sidelong, uncertain whether or not he was being teased. "She doesn't like our games much. She thinks boys are too rough. But," and again the heartfelt sigh, "she's pretty, isn't she?"

"Has pretty hair, at least—that was about all I could see."

In the second heat Ludwig had the gelding under better control at the start; the power of the big bay carried him up the hill ahead of Becky, and across Main Street well in the lead. When the cutters were turned back once more, it was Elsa's turn to say "Ya-ay," and wave the Highland bonnet. Johnny waved back, and grinned at her. She was too far away to see that, in the anguish of disappointment, the grin was closer to a grimace. But perhaps Ludwig saw it. For in the third, Cump again took the lead, then broke, halfway along the course, when the mare was edging up on him. Before Ludwig could control the gelding and bring him back to a trot, Becky had swept past and could not be overtaken. The little mare was greeted by the augmented crowd on the corner of Main Street, and there were shouts of "Good for you, Dock!" But Johnny uttered no final triumphant "Ya-ay" because his father muttered to him, "Don't crow, now."

When they had stopped the cutters, well above Main Street, John put the reins for a moment into his son's proud hands, and went over to shake hands with Ludwig, who had also got down from his sleigh and gone to his horse's head.

"D'you do that on purpose?"

"Do what?" Ludwig asked in seemingly genuine astonishment. "Break his gait? Lose a race on purpose? A horse with that name? Besides, there might have been some bets in that crowd."

"Of course you wouldn't. I just thought maybe, on the boy's account."

"Donnerwetter! Dock, you know better. I'm fond of Johnny, but not to the point of betraying Cump. That gelding is the apple of my eye. I'm just not as good a driver as you are. If you'd been driving him, you would've won. Maybe. The mare's a beauty, and well-trained. Lose on purpose! Not by a blame sight."

John took his word for it, but he was glad that there had at least been no bets between the two of them. When he had driven Becky back to the stable, he sent Johnny to tell Anne he would be at the door at ten-to-two to take her to her Club; when the message had been delivered, Johnny could go on to the Rausches' for his afternoon program.

"But no gloating," he said. "It was a near thing, and I doubt if we proved Becky's better than Cump."

"But she's *good?*" Johnny asked anxiously.

"She's very, very good, and that's all that's important." He went into the stable with Lonzo to see that Becky was properly cared for, while Johnny went prancing into the house with the tale of their triumph trembling on his lips. He paused in the pantry to snatch an apple from the barrel, and went on to the sitting room. When Anne heard him in the dining room, she looked up expectantly. He appeared in the door expressing his jubilance with his own habitual gesture: arms high above head, he was tossing the apple from one hand to the other, the whole upper part of his body swinging a little. Anne smiled as she took it all in: the glowing boy, the grace of his body, the red apple flying.

"You won, I see."

"We won. Two heats out of three." He took an enormous crunching bite out of the apple. "Papa says tell you he'll be here at ten-to-two. Can I go now?"

At a few minutes before two, John drove staid old brown Molly out of the alley and around to the hitching post. Anne came out and John helped her into the sleigh.

"You won your race, Johnny said. He was quite transported."

"Yes. Becky is our darling, Johnny's and mine. But I'd feel better about it if I thought Ludwig had got the best out of that gelding of his."

On Main Street, in the Court House block, they saw Kitty Edwards come out of Sheldon and Edwards' Dry Goods Emporium, just as they approached.

"There's Kitty, on her way to Club. Pick her up, John—save her the walk."

"Glad to, if two fashionable young ladies can squeeze into this seat without crushing their folderols beyond repair."

They drew up to Kitty and stopped in the gutter. When Anne spoke to her, she started as if recalled from a dream; a faint mischievous smile curved her mouth, made her thin cheeks look fuller.

"I was just wondering," she said almost absent-mindedly, as she stopped on the curb. "Anne—Dock—how nice of you!"

John twisted the reins around the whip, when Anne indicated by her uplifted white-gloved hands her reluctance to take them, alighted, and went around to lift Kitty into the sleigh.

"How are you, Kitty?" he asked her, hand under her elbow. "I haven't seen you for a long while."

"There's been no need." She laughed at him as she pulled the buffalo robe up over her "folderols." "Doesn't that prove I've been good?"

Kitty had had a second miscarriage the year before and had been very ill. John had been compassionate and kind until she had recovered, then he had scolded, threatened, and talked seriously to Sheldon again. Now, as he returned to his place on the other side of Anne and untwisted the reins, he said, "I don't know. You look awfully complacent about something—a cat-in-the-cream look."

She laughed. "If I do, it's really nothing to do with me. Just something—Sheldon and Edwards' business is about to boom: did you know the prettiest girl in town is clerking there now—Captain Bodien's daughter? I wonder why? He must make enough. But that's none of my concern," she added hastily. "Dock, don't you think that soon now I can try again?"

"Not until you've had a thorough going over, my girl."

"Here, here," Anne protested. Kitty's candor was embarrassing. "This isn't the office."

"Doesn't Dock tell you about your friends' troubles? I've always wondered. No? But it doesn't matter in my case. I don't mind your knowing."

Anne changed the subject. But after they had been delivered at the Gardiner gate, and were standing while Anne worked gingerly at its icy latch, Kitty returned to it.

"You know, whatever Dock says—" From under her stylish little rolled-brim hat, her unstylish wispy light brown hair was as usual blowing across her forehead. But there was color in her thin face, and her blue eyes shone with merriment and some deeper fire.

"I don't care what Dock says," she repeated, "I'm going to have children if it kills me."

Anne put up a hand and brushed the blown hair out of Kitty's eyes as if she had been a child. "Kitty, do mind what he says." She spoke lightly, but she caught her breath. This was one of those moments, she knew; she recognized them, and they were usually foreboding moments, somehow—an instant she would never forget: the wintry afternoon, the icy gate, the packed dirty snow, and Kitty's slight figure drawn up so gallantly to utter those words of dedication.

She got the gate open and they went through. They were halfway up the walk before Kitty returned to an awareness of just where they were, whose steps they were about to climb.

"Oh, Anne! I meant to tell you as soon as Dock had gone, and there's no time, now—but it's going to stun all Waynesboro when it bursts."

Anne laughed as she rang the Gardiners' doorbell. This was more like Kitty's usual extravagancies: she had an unquenchable thirst for drama. "You can tell me after the meeting."

"Not here, I can't. Not another word. Another time, maybe."

But during the Club meeting, as Kitty studied with unconscious absorption the two Misses Gardiner, she decided that she had far better not tell it at all, even to Anne, who was not a gossip. Miss Lavinia and Miss Caroline Gardiner: two very cold women, she thought, whose central core of being was pride, the deadliest of the seven deadly sins. Two women withdrawn from the world into an anemic hauteur that was authoritative enough to establish in the minds of others their own estimate of themselves. Authoritative enough to carry off without any evidence of self-consciousness Miss Lavinia's crinolines: not made over-pre-war gowns, in these days of their nephew's success, but new billowy hoop skirts of heavy corded sild or *moire antique* created for her by the town's leading dressmaker. She had never explained why she was still wearing such outmoded styles in the late '70s, but Kitty had supposed she simply preferred them, as she obviously preferred everything antebellum to the contemporary world; now, with sudden insight, Kitty saw that the eccentricity was another manifestation of pride—Pride with a capital P. If Miss Lavinia, to the day of her death, never gave up wearing hoop skirts, no one would remember that there had been a time when she had been so poor she had had no choice: she had had to wear her old gowns when fashionable women were giving up hoops—at least, circular hoops—and were for the first time appearing in skirts that were straight and close down the front. Miss Lavinia was capable of persuading herself that the new style was indecent. Kitty smiled to herself as she looked at her now, planted ramrod straight in a gilt chair, her heavy black silk skirt sweeping a wide space around her. On the other side of the door, Miss Caroline sat equally straight on another of those uncomfortable French gilt chairs; she at least was modish enough in a tight bodice, draped overskirt, and bustle. They had stood just inside that door to receive their guests, and then taken the chairs on either side, as if to guard it.

"Guardians of the house! That is how they would see themselves," Kitty thought, "ready to repel any outsiders. If they only knew!" Certainly she, Kitty, must never be responsible for their knowing, and what had seemed to her an hour ago amusing, even pleasing, suddenly ceased to be a matter to take lightly.

Kitty had left home early that afternoon in order that she might stop at the store for a pair of white gloves. Sheldon and Edwards' was a constant delight to her, with its dusky interior smelling faintly of the woolens heaped in bolts on the shelves and on the dark scissors-scarred counters, with their laces and embroideries in glass cases, their silks, satins, and brocades. The clerks were all elderly maidens of either sex, or hungry widows proud to work, for however meager a livelihood, in so respectable an establishment. Year in and year out they remained at their posts: Miss Allie, Miss Amanda, Mr. Arthur, and so on, under the eyes of Mr. Sheldon, tall, slender, with a small head, baby-blue eyes, aquiline nose, and a yellowish-white beard that fell to his top vest-button, and Mr. Edwards, shorter, squarer of shoulder and face, with sideburns that exaggerated the squareness. Like the clerks, they had been the same since Kitty's first memory of them. Sheldon Edwards, who had grown up from child to man under the clerks' eyes, was new in the store: he had been there for five years, a mere no-time-at-all to those who had been crossing the threshold for a generation. After his apprenticeship as clerk, Sheldon had been promoted to bookkeeper; now he had an office on the second floor at the back of the store, behind the wrought-iron grille where he made change for the clerks from the drawer of the till and kept the books at a high desk to one side. Kitty thought it must all be very dull for him, but he never complained; and it would have been foolish for him to have shrugged off the store and looked for something else to do: Mr. Sheldon and Mr. Edwards were brothers-in-law, and the Sheldons' only son—only child—had been killed in the war. Sheldon, if he was bored, never said so: he just preferred not to talk about the store when he came home in the evening.

Whenever Kitty entered and appeared in the yard-goods aisle or the fancy-goods-and-notions aisle, Mr. Sheldon and Mr. Edwards dropped whatever they were doing, unless dancing attendance to one of Waynesboro's more important dowagers, and came to welcome her in their most courtly manner. They invariably assured her that the store was hers, and she knew that in a sense it was; she would have enjoyed a bout of extravagance, just because she had never in her life been free to be extravagant, but she had better judgment. She had been married to Sheldon for almost three years, but she suspected that some of those Waynesboro dowagers, who had perhaps sent their daughters to her father to be educated, felt superior enough in their financial security to be still expecting a jumped-up Lowrey to lose her head. It amused her secretly to disappoint them, since she was quite happy to live by the scale of values inculcated in her by her father. She would thank the two older men, then go down the aisle and up the stairs to Sheldon's grille and stand there until he turned from his books and put his hand on his change drawer, accepting as a clerk the unseen figure that he had been aware of even before he looked up. She would laugh; he would see her, and laugh, too, and manipulate the lock in the inside of the door, open it, and usher her in with "And what can I do for Mrs. Edwards today?"

On that afternoon she had gone down the right-hand aisle, past the notions counter, with the intention of following the established routine, but on the way she had almost tripped over her own feet, so startled was she by the new face behind the glove counter. A new face, and a young and very pretty face. She recovered herself and went on, but she had taken in a vivid impression of white skin, rose-tinted cheeks, dark curling hair, black brows and lashes, violet eyes, and a heart-shaped contour of forehead, cheekbones, and chin. An Irish face, surely?

She did not wait for Sheldon to look up from the ledgers before which he stood. She said, "Psst! Let me in!"

He turned, smiled, said, "Bless you! Why the conspiratorial tone?" He opened the door for her. "And what can I do for Madame?"

"A pair of white gloves, remember? But first, tell me, who is the dazzling beauty? And why—didn't—I know?" On the last words she dropped her voice to a sepulchral whisper. Sheldon put his arm around her and swung her close to face him.

"Goose! Dear goose!"

"No, but tell me."

"I don't know why I haven't before, but when I'm here, I live with the store, and when I'm home, I like to forget it."

"Isn't she Irish? Why on earth?"

"Muterspaugh hired one to draw the West End trade." Muterspaugh was "The Store's" competitor, across Chillicothe Street from the Court House. "It worked so well that we had to find one, too, to draw 'em back. And we found a prettier one." Sheldon looked so smug that Kitty laughed.

"I should think so." She knew by sight buxom red-headed Norah McDonnell, who clerked at Muterspaugh's. "What's her name?"

"Barbara Bodien."

"Bodien? Isn't he the superintendent at the ropewalk? Does she need to work?"

He shrugged. "I shouldn't think so. Maybe she was bored. Maybe she wanted to get out of the West End."

"Why do they live down there? He isn't a Catholic, is he?"

"I believe not. But his wife is—very devout, I'm told. Maybe he lives there for her sake, or just because it's closer to the mill. He's fixed up one of the nicest old houses in town: you know, the old Inskip place once out in the country; now it's surrounded by the West End. I don't know how devout the girl is, but I have my doubts. Listen, Kitty, you mustn't breathe a word of this—"

She was about to cross her heart, child-fashion, when the street door crashed shut with such a bang that they could hear it at the far end of the store. Sheldon peered through the grille.

"Keep out of sight behind this post here. I won't have to tell you—you can see for yourself."

Kitty stood behind him instead of the post, and peered around him. The twilight of the store was deepened by the brilliance of sun on snow beyond the distant front windows, but there was no need for light: she identified the man who had entered by his limp. No one else in town walked quite like that.

"Doug Gardiner? But why not? I know men don't come here much except on errands for their womenfolk, but—or do you mean—?"

"He's been in before this week. Bought a pair of gloves for one of his aunts. Probably brought them in to change today."

Douglas stopped at the glove counter, took a parcel from his overcoat pocket, and handed it to the girl. Their heads bent together in consultation.

"But he's as old as we are," Kitty murmured in protest. "She's a mere child."

"Eighteen. D'you think it is our duty to protect her?"

Kitty giggled into his shoulder blade. "From Doug? Do you think he's really enamored?"

"I'm sure I don't know. But I know him. After all, we went through Mr. McMillan's school together. If he is, he'll marry her."

"Oh, he couldn't! Not *marry* her."

"Why not? Nothing wrong with her, and her face would be preferable to his aunts' at the breakfast table. Of course, she might say no."

"But, Sheldon—" Kitty stepped backward from her husband, keeping behind him until she was out of sight from the glove counter. In a loud voice she said, "Sheldon, I must be going, if I'm to get my gloves and not be late for Club."

He turned toward her, finger on his lips. She shook her head and would have passed him, but he laid a hand on her arm.

"You'll embarrass them."

"I never embarrassed anyone in my life." She smiled at him twinkling.

"I guess you never did." He stooped quickly and kissed her cheek, murmured, "Not a word about this to anyone, mind? Don't spoil it."

"D'you think for a minute," and she dropped her voice again, "those old ladies out there don't pass on everything they see in the store?"

"I suppose they do. But they're only bystanders, Kit, and so's their audience." Both thought fleetingly of aged parents, ailing spouses, waiting at home for evening and the day's news from The Store. "But the people you know are too close: they might think they should interfere. Let's let them play it out. Doug deserves that much."

Kitty in her turn kissed him on the cheek and said, "Very well," meekly enough. She made a mental reservation in favor of Anne Gordon, who never told anything she heard except to Sally Rausch, and not even to her if she was asked not to. But after Kitty had let slip her chance to gossip with Anne before they reached the Gardiner gate and was sitting in the Gardiner parlor, thinking of the couple as she had seen them at the glove counter, she let the Club meeting drone on without her attention while she studied the Misses Gardiner in their chairs at either side of the door. She decided Sheldon was right: there were things better not touched with words, spoiled with handling.

She had emerged from Sheldon's office and gone directly down the aisle to the glove counter. The man and the girl on its opposite side had forgotten the parcel that lay between them, but they were not engaged in any romantic interchange. Doug was talking about some trotting race on Sycamore Street that day.

Kitty said, "Good afternoon, Doug. And Miss Bodien, isn't it? My husband—they call him 'young Edwards' in the store—has told me about you. Do you suppose you can fit me with a pair of white gloves, so that I shall not be ashamed to go to my Club meeting? It's at your house this afternoon, Doug."

"I know." He smiled wryly. "One might suppose my aunts have the dirtiest house in town. It is scrubbed from garret to cellar for a Woman's Club meeting." He picked up his gloves and derby hat from the swinging stool beside him. "I must go along. I think these gloves will be a better size for Aunt Caroline."

"If they're not, I'll be glad to change them again." Miss Bodien looked bewildered. Kitty was sure the gloves had not been changed at all. She suppressed a smile, but perhaps Miss Bodien saw the twitch of her lips, for the rose in her young cheeks grew deeper. But she was flustered: she held herself with dignity.

"Don't go, Doug." Kitty took the stool where his hat had been, put her elbow on the counter, held her hand in the air to be fitted. "A size four, I think. I always suspected you lawyers wandered around town between cases, enjoying yourselves and seeing what you could see. Go ahead with what you were talking about: who raced whom, and who won?"

Douglas described the three-heat trotting race that Dock Gordon had won with his young mare. Barbara Bodien's violet eyes were on his face even as she pulled a tight white glove on Kitty's thin hand, smoothed it, and tugged at its buttons. Kitty watched her: the rapt beautiful eyes, and her smiling mouth, open a little as if she were slightly breathless. When Douglas had finished, she suspended for a moment her work on the glove, and said in her low voice, "I wish I had seen it. Was my father there? He does love a good horse. But he would have been sorry Mr. Rausch lost. He would have bet on him, I guess."

"I would have bet on that bay gelding myself." Douglas, laughing now, the sardonic cast of his face relaxed, whistled through his teeth, "You bet on the bob-tail nag."

With the aid of a button hook, the glove was finally fastened. Kitty said, "That will do, I think. Would you mind putting the other one on for me?" She changed her position, put the other elbow on the velvet-padded counter. "The best horse doesn't always win. Sometimes it's the driver. After all, Dock spends a good part of every day behind a horse."

Later, in the Gardiner parlor, she asked herself why she had been so pleased. Surely not just because she liked other people to be in love. She turned her eyes to let them sweep over Mrs. Henry Voorhees. Christina's sleepy-looking, heavy eyelids were lowered, she was smiling a little to herself, as complacent—She was growing plumper, surely? Probably is doing her duty by her husband, bearing his child. She imagined, in a momentary flash of insight, Christina and that stick Henry Voorhees in joyous abandon, begetting a child. She could feel herself flushing at the indecency of her thoughts. It wouldn't be like that; it would be a duty with Christina. And here she was. A pang caught Kitty in the chest, a real physical sensation; she fought it off and dragged her mind back to what she had been thinking about. She had not been moved by the Blair-Voorhees match because it had been so eminently suitable: no obstacle whatever. But Douglas Gardiner, whom she liked, soured and spoiled though his youth had been—Doug and the daughter of an ex-artilleryman turned mill superintendent and his Irish Catholic wife: there would not only be obstacles, there would be fireworks. Kitty drew a deep breath, and reproached herself: she was a grown married woman, and she still loved excitement like a child. But she was making far too much of what was a small incident, just seeing the man and the girl together. Sheldon was right: she mustn't talk to anyone. She sighed and turned her attention to the essayist.

Anne, too, was having trouble keeping her mind on the meeting. "All these old ladies," she thought resentfully, and was surprised at herself. She had never felt like this before: as if it were all a waste of time. She sat where she could see through the front windows the bright sun on piled snow and the bluish shadows of tree trunks. She wanted to be not here but riding in the country with John and the children, jogging along behind Molly, with the sleigh bells making their pace seem faster than it was. The air would be fresh and cold: her nostrils dilated at the thought. The air of the white-and-gold drawing room was dry and dead. She wrinkled her nose a little, disliking it. It was not that it smelled: the Misses Gardiner were far too perfect housekeepers for that. But it was so lifeless that a good honest smell would have been better. To fight off stifled sensation, Anne turned her mind to her sisters of the Club. Mrs. McKinney was delivering in her phlegmatic manner a dull "Tribute to Bayard Taylor." Mr. Taylor had just died when the Program Committee had been at work the previous spring, and a "tribute" was considered his due. Mrs. Ballard was slowly being crippled by rheumatism: her hands were already disfigured, the joints swollen, red, and stiff, and sometimes at the end of a long meeting she had to be helped to rise from her chair. But though she moved with some difficulty, she could hold papers, or the gavel, and she conducted a meeting with as certain a grasp of parliamentary procedure as she had ever shown. Most of the ladies were present, but Amanda had not come in from school yet, and Miss Pinney was absent. Anne thought that perhaps a part of her heaviness of spirit was bad conscience: she had not known that Miss Pinney was suffering from sciatica until Mrs. Deming had presented regrets in her name to the other ladies when the roll was called. "She begged to be excused this afternoon, her sciatica is troubling her again. I have thought she would not be able to walk even so short a distance, but when I sent a note to school this morning with Julia, saying that General Deming would stop for her with the carriage, she declined: she did not feel equal to the effort."

Anne and Sally had looked at each other guiltily as the cool voice came to a period. As mothers with children in Miss Pinney's school, they should have known, and as two who had once been her pupils themselves, they should have offered to bring her; she should not have been left to the intimidating joviality of General Deming. Poor Miss Pinney! She led so dull a life that the Club meant more to her than to most of them. Anne looked them over again—the ones she knew intimately, the ones she was coming to know rather well, the ones she scarcely knew at all—and tried to decide what the Waynesboro Woman's Club meant to them. She and Sally and Kitty Edwards at least had better things to do with their time. But Sally enjoyed having the Club on which to exercise her bent for managing people and events.

It was not until the paper had been read and its author thanked by the

President and a desultory discussion of the merits of Bayard Taylor had flagged that anything out of routine occurred. Amanda Reid, who had slipped in while Mrs. McKinney was still reading, waited until all was said that anyone could dredge up for saying, and then attracted Mrs. Ballard's attention and was given the floor.

"Madame President and Ladies. As you know, I was asked to serve as chairman of the Program Committee for next year. We are already at work. It has never been the custom of the Committee to consult the Club as a whole; it has been assumed that those entrusted with the task could be depended upon to produce acceptable results. But we think you should be asked about a suggestion for one of our fall meetings. The proposal is that we give an afternoon to the children of our Club members: persuade them to perform for us. I felt that those of you who have children should be consulted as to whether you would be willing to help with such a program."

Mrs. Maxwell, who was childless, considered it a delightful idea. Mrs. Beattie, mother of two half-grown sons, thought that perhaps there were not enough children in the Club old enough for such an undertaking.

Anne, in a contradictory mood all of a sudden, said, "Madame President. Ladies. If it is to be done at all, it had better be done this next year. The little boys will soon be too old to be willing to speak pieces at such a gathering." Then, ashamed, she smiled placatingly at Mrs. Beattie.

Thomasina broke in, much too eager to bother with parliamentary form. Her mother rapped the gavel in vain to bring her to order. "We counted them up." For Thomasina to be so unselfconscious was rare indeed: Anne decided the idea must have been hers in the first place: she was on the Committee with Amanda and Christina Voorhees. "Two Gordons, three Rausches old enough," Thomasina hurried on, "one Deming, two Beatties, Mrs. McKinney's little girl"—she gave no time for gasps at the idea of a Negro child—"and the McCunes, five of them." Thomasina's voice trailed away. No one responded, and Thomasina murmured hesitantly, "Surely dear Mrs. McCune's children are Club children?" Without further discussion the ladies ungrudgingly agreed to give an afternoon to the children if Thomasina would prepare them.

Only the Ballards knew of the battle Ariana had fought, after her mother's death, for her father's permission to continue the music lessons Samuel Travers had begun out of love for the child. But most of them could guess that it was on her account that Thomasina had set her heart on a "children's afternoon." Sally said, "My children would love to perform: they like to 'be in' things." Anne said, "I can still speak for Belinda, and I'll do my best with Johnny." Mrs. Deming said, "Julia will do whatever is expected of her."

That seemed to settle it; without a formal vote the members signified their willingness to include such an afternoon on the next year's program. When a move to adjourn had been made and the ladies rose, Sally and Anne bore down on Mrs. Deming.

"We're so sorry about Miss Pinney. We didn't know."

"Julia says she brings a hot-water bottle to school and holds it in her lap all morning. Surely your children noticed it?" Mrs. Deming looked mildly amused, as if it were slightly funny that the two young mothers should consider themselves grown up enough to shoulder the responsibilities of parenthood. They bristled a little.

"They could hardly not notice it," Sally said. "They are not blind."

"Johnny never tells us what goes on in school. It's all a deep, dark secret."

"Julia has always confided in her parents, I am glad to say: there is little we do not hear about, sooner or later. But as you know, she attends Miss Pinney's school only in the mornings: we feel she needs the companionship of children her own age at least to that extent. She learns more rapidly at home with me in the afternoons."

"I am sure Julia is very bright." Sally was offhandedly complimentary. "But she would get more companionship if she stayed home mornings and went to school afternoons. It is after school the children have their fun."

"Sliding down the laundry chute, for instance." Anne kept her face solemn.

Mrs. Deming made it plain that she was trying not to look shocked. "Julia is too delicate for such rough games, I fear. But about Miss Pinney: I stopped to see her on the way here, and found her very miserable indeed. She had a brief spell of sciatica last winter, you remember, but she says this is more severe. However, she has great courage. The state of her house shows how limited her strength is, but she insists that she is perfectly able to carry on her little school—that sciatica has has no effect on the mind, and that Dr. Wright has prescribed medicine which relieves the pain."

"Poor soul," Anne murmured. "Of course she can't give up until she absolutely has to. I don't suppose she has been able to save anything: what would she live on?"

That was the last word on the subject, all that anyone could say. Anne and Sally bade good-bye to Mrs. Deming, congratulated Mrs. McKinney on her "tribute," thanked the Misses Gardiner for their hospitality, and went across the hall for their wraps. There Anne looked for Kitty Edwards; she had gone, apparently, while they were talking to Mrs. Deming. "There was something she couldn't wait to tell me," Anne explained. "But you know Kitty: it was probably something unimportant that had struck her funny."

No mother was so unwise as to mention in January a program her children would be expected to take part in the following October: there would be no point in risking rebellion so far ahead of time, nor in rousing enthusiasm that would go stale. But Thomasina told her husband about it when they were alone after dinner. Samuel had exchanged his black jacket and waistcoat for the gray flannel smoking jacket that he donned for such hours of comfortable privacy, non-smoker though he was.

"You must teach Ariana something for her to play for the ladies. It will be a great opportunity for her."

Samuel smoothed his thinning hair, a gesture of his indecisive moments.

"What would her father say? You know how hard it was to convince him that playing the piano was merely an accomplishment every young lady should have, and not a surrender to the world and the devil. Would he allow her to play in public?"

"It wouldn't be 'in public.' Only the members of the Club her mother belonged to. I do so want the ladies to realize what a gifted child she is." Thomasina studied her husband with the wistful expression that sat so incongruously on her long, heavy-boned face. Samuel was stouter than he had been; he parted his mousy hair far on the side, just above his ear, so as to have enough to comb up and over his bald spot. Thomasina had come to realize that he would never after all be the American Schubert, but was convinced that he was as fine a teacher as any in the conservatories, and that the town gave him less respect than was his due. He would one day be famous through one of his pupils. That dream, which was almost a purpose in Thomasina's purposeless life, had had its part in the plans she was making for Ariana. Ariana would turn out to be a genius. What would become of the child should that happen to be true did not trouble her. Geniuses were not to be held down by stern Calvinist fathers, and she, Thomasina, would help her to get free. "She is talented, Samuel," she repeated.

"In some ways she is. She is very quick; she is imaginative and sensitive and has a creative mind, perhaps." But Samuel was reluctant to bolster his wife's dream. "But that doesn't make her a musician. She hasn't the patience or the firmness—the strength, physical and nervous—or whatever you want to call it—to make her a true musician. There is something elusive, quick-silver, about her: here one minute—her attention, I mean—and gone the next. She isn't half the musician Elsa Rausch is, and she's a year older."

"Elsa!" Thomasina thought of the bright-cheeked, wind-blown child who scurried up the stairs to her music lesson, always breathless, always as if it were something to be got through quickly. "I can't imagine her taking anything seriously."

"At her age? No. She's a tomboy, all helter-skelter. She comes up here thinking only of the fun she's missing, and how to get away as quickly as possible. But she loves music, and once she's at the piano she is carried away. There's music in her blood—the German in her, I suppose. She plays with a kind of power, with authority and feeling. And just because music is as natural to her as breathing, she enjoys trying something difficult, something that is a challenge. She has patience, too, German patience and thoroughness. She practices."

"I don't know when. She seems always to be romping about with other children. Amanda says the theologues complain about how the boys and girls on Market Street torment them."

"Those young gentlemen take themselves too seriously."

"It seems so unfair. Elsa has—can have—everything. And Ariana—"

"I will find something for Ariana to play—something showy—and teach her to play it. But I can give Elsa something more difficult the week before your program, and she will play it better."

"Oh, Samuel! And I had so hoped—"

"Hoped what, my dear?"

"That Ariana would convince the Club of her talent, so that maybe all together we could do something for her. Help with her education. Eliza and I would be glad to do that, if we could afford it. We can't, and her father can't even if he would."

"It doesn't cost much to educate a minister's daughter at a church college. At any rate, she's just a little girl. When the time comes and she knows what kind of education she wants, maybe we can help. In the meantime, we can afford to give her music lessons."

"Yes. I had so hoped she would be famous some day. Then you would be famous too, because you had taught her."

"I have been a disappointment to you, Thomasina, turning out to be only a plodding music teacher."

"Oh, no. I wouldn't want you to be any different. It is only for your sake. Vague, bright dreams, as usual. You know I'm used to passing from dream to dream: when one fades, there's another. It makes life less humdrum. But truly: I wouldn't want you different. And fame might spoil you completely." She smiled at him in a watery-eyed fashion.

"It's a great pity—" Samuel flushed over his round comfortable face, to the edge of his sparse hair. "It's a great affliction that we have not been blessed."

"It is the Lord's will: I accepted that long ago. It was one reason why I thought it was meant I should do something for Ariana."

"Don't let go of that dream, my dear. It may come true. You yourself could teach her something about writing: it may be that her talent lies in that direction. And, after all, is there anyone in your Club who could afford to educate her? Those who have any means have children of their own."

"I thought maybe all of us together. I know: most of the ladies have children, and Mrs. McKinney is already educating one child. It's an odd thing, Samuel, did you ever notice? Ordinarily, people like ministers, or people who work for causes or in public speak from platforms seldom see an individual near at hand that they could do something for. I don't think Mamma is uncharitable; it's just that she believes, I suppose, that doing good person by person is too slow, and doesn't solve any problem, actually. But I do admire people who *act* in the unassuming way the McKinneys have acted. They could so easily have adopted a white child after old Mrs. McKinney died—it would surely have meant more to them—but instead they got themselves appointed guardians of that little Negro waif from the County Home who worked for them, and are educating her."

"But she's only going to the free colored school in the East End."

"I know. They didn't want to cut her off from her own people. And she is allowed to have her friends there when she likes: it's her home. And they've promised to send her to college if she does well in school."

"It seems better to me to make no promises. But Ariana has a long way to go before she's ready for college. And in the meantime, music lessons."

At the moment what Ariana's music lessons did for her was to bring her into contact with Elsa Rausch. The two children had not been thrown together before: their families were not of the same Protestant denomination; they attended different schools. Ariana was a little the elder, but Elsa had a vitality and quality of leadership entirely lacking in the other, and after they had become acquainted through their meetings on the Ballard stairs and in Mr. Travers's studio, Elsa attached Ariana to herself and to the group of children who plotted and played and fought together. And the tricks suggested by Ariana's inventiveness that were played on the theological students in the spring of 1879 were new, effective, and, to the perpetrators, mirth-provoking.

That particular group of children had also been enlarged by the addition of Sophie Klein and such other younger Kleins as were permitted to "tag along." The Kleins had climbed steadily from huckster wagon through the one-room grocery store to their present beautiful mouth-watering establishment on the corner of Sycamore Street and Main, with its big gold-lettered signboard, FANCY GROCERIES, and from the apartment over the first store where Fritz Klein had taken his bride a decade before, to Miss Crenshaw's cottage, and then to the new brick house that they had built in place of an old frame one in the big yard across the street from the Rausches. Whatever misgivings Sally Rausch might have felt as to the Klein children's forebears—one uncle a saloon-keeper-turned-baker, the grandfather a market gardener, whose son and their father was the grocer from whom she bought her provisions—she placed no interdiction on the Klein house, whose children were as well-drilled as her own in manners and deportment. On more afternoons than not there appeared sooner or later in the Klein kitchen Elsa and her brother Ernest, Johnny Gordon and the Thirkield boy, Charlotte Bonner and her younger brother and, as the spring advanced, Ariana McCune. Mrs. Fritz Klein, born Hoffmann, who had once pulled beerhandles in her brother's saloon, had been trained to hospitality, and her Sophie's friends were not only welcome in her house so long as they stayed out of the parlor, but were plied with cookies, pretzels, and the very special crackers that Mr. Hoffmann made in his bakery: round, hard crackers eaten as butter sandwiches, with fresh country butter curling over the edge as they were bitten into. Most Waynesboro housewives bought them from Mr. Hoffmann when he stopped his horse and his high narrow baker's cart at their gates, but at the Kleins' they were in inexhaustible supply. They were especially satisfying to after-school appetites, when Mrs. Klein spread them with the butter in the yellow crock that Sophie brought up from the pie-safe in the cellar. And Mrs. Klein, whose own children were round and rosy, tried hard to cover Ariana's bones. "Let's fat you up a little," she would say, tucking just one more cookie or one more pair of buttered crackers into her hand before they all went outside to play. Ariana was not always with them in the afternoon: too often she would be wanted at home for housework or to mind the other children; but after the spring had advanced to the point where the twilights were long enough to permit playing out after supper, she could always join them, since once the dishes were done there were no more chores for her at home.

That spring the students who passed to and fro on the Klein side of the street on their way to supper at Mrs. Reid's and back again, for the first time encountered snakes slithering across their pathway in the dusk, and were fooled by the key trick. These were games for the twilight when the world could be but half-seen. A key was suspended by a long string over a bough above the path; the string was taken over the bough of another tree in the Klein yard, close to the fence, and the end clutched tight in the grubby fist of one of the children concealed in the fence-corner of the lilacs and syringas. When the last pair of strolling students had passed, in the dusk, in the shadows of the leafing trees, then the string was allowed to run out through loosened fingers until the key had dropped with a metallic clang on the brick sidewalk, close on their heels. Before the victims could turn it was jerked up again out of sight; a hapless theologue, thinking that something valuable had fallen from a pocket, would search and search in vain; perhaps would get down on his hands and knees and pat the bricks or run his fingers through the grass at the pavement's edge. So long as no one of those hidden among the bushes broke down and giggled, the key trick always worked, for no poor theological student could afford to lose a coin, whatever its denomination.

Most of the students—undernourished, narrow-chested, pimply, solemn youths—were poor game, but several were foemen worthy of the most ingenious forms of attack, notable among them a Canadian Scot known to the children as "Red" McCallum. He was a tall, gangling, loose-jointed young man, with a spirit that matched his hair, who enjoyed as much as they did his forays among them, when he would vault the Klein fence to pursue and scatter them. On an evening in early May, the children prepared a new trap for "Red." They had learned from Ariana that he was courting one of the R.P. maidens who had grown to marriageable age. They saw that he was not among those returning, crocodile fashion, from Mrs. Reid's; Johnny Gordon and Billy Thirkield, sent on a scouting expedition, saw him in the parlor where Ariana had said he would be. They had no idea how long he might stay; it might, they thought, be as late as nine or nine-thirty; but he might possibly return before they had to go home, and so they prepared for him. One of the boys shinnied up the curbside tree to its first branch, and hauled up after him by a cord a lard pail full of water; this was balanced in the fork of a bough that overhung the pavement. The string was then taken once around the trunk of that tree, carried across to a tree in the Klein yard and tied to it at what they considered to be the height of their victim's Adam's apple. The pail was so precariously balanced that the question was not whether it would be dislodged by a jerk on the string but whether it would stay in place long enough. When all adjustments had been made with breathless care, those present sought their hiding places under the bushes and settled down for a long wait. They lay on their stomachs or sat cross-legged, and talked idly, as children do, only hushing and holding their breaths when some passerby approached. They had an exaggerated idea of "Red" McCallum's height: not one of the three or four passersby was tall enough to walk into the string: they all went under it without seeing it. Time passed; it grew dark, deep dark, under the trees. The town clock struck nine, and Ariana began to fidget: none of them was allowed out after nine, but only Ariana would be punished by worse than a scolding for disobedience; she was trying to decide whether the severity of the whipping she was sure to receive would depend on how long she overstayed her time, when another pair of footsteps was heard approaching from down the hill.

"Quiet!" Johnny Gordon was in the fence corner under a shield of trumpet vine, whence he could look down the street as far as the feeble gas light on the corner. "Here he comes!" A masculine figure crossed the street under the light. "No, it isn't," he added. "Keep still! It's only ol' Dr. Blair." Then the enormity of what was about to happen struck him; in an ecstasy of mingled horror and delight he began to quiver, but suppressed his mirth to whisper "*He's got a plug hat on!*" and buried his face in his arms. Ariana rose to her feet, but Elsa pulled her down again. It was too late to do anything.

The ponderous footsteps came on like the tread of doom. Dr. Blair wheezed with every step, occasionally groaned. Behind the fence hands were clapped over mouths or handkerchiefs stuffed into them. Fortunately, Dr. Blair's high hat sat lightly on his massive head. As he passed under the string, the hat was knocked off; it rolled, spilling papers in every direction. But Dr. Blair's momentum carried him forward a step or two, and the small pail of water, jerked over, spilled its contents behind him.

He stopped with a polysyllabic exclamation that the children took to be some kind of theological oath; then, with his hands on his hips, he surveyed as well as he could in the dark the black blot that was his hat, the papers scattered where water was now running between the bricks, the empty pail swinging against the tree trunk, catching and reflecting some fugitive gleam of light. As he stood there, he heard the light scuffling and exploding breaths from inside the fence.

Inhaling with a gasp, he let go in a thunder: "The Lord will smite thee with the botch of Egypt"—wheeze—"and with the emrods"—wheeze—"and with the scab and with the itch." Then, after a prolonged struggle of choking and coughing, "Come out of there, ye generation of vipers!"

There had been some subdued, hysterical tittering; now all laughter ceased.

"Come out, I say!"

Ariana whispered, "I better go. I'll be whipped anyway, it's so late." She scrambled to her hands and knees, crawled out from under the syringa, and started toward the gate. The others watched her, appalled. By the time her dragging footsteps had taken her back down the path to the irate old man, he had a match box out of his pocket. He struck a match on the fence and in its sulphurous glare frowned upon her.

"Bless my soul! Aren't you the Reverend Mr. McCune's—?"

She was past speech. In the instant's light her eyes were wild; her ears, with hair and hair-ribbon tucked behind them, more flaring and elfin than usual. Johnny knew that if her father got wind of what happened she would not only be whipped, she would be prayed over, a fate worse than death. He could not stand it. With one lunge he was on the fence, threw his legs over, and dropped on the other side.

"Please, sir! She didn't do it. She can't shinny up a tree. Please don't tell on her, sir! She'd catch it like sixty at home."

"And you won't? For assaulting a harmless old man with buckets of water? Who is your father?"

"Dr. Gordon. Yes, sir: I expect I will."

There was another explosion from tortured bronchial tubes. When the spasm of coughing was over, Dr. Blair said, "Gordon! The Gordons were ever a wild lot, since Edom o' that ilk. A good strapping, my boy. But if you will pick up my hat and my papers, we'll say no more about it."

Johnny bent hurriedly to gather the scattered envelopes and documents. "It wasn't meant for you, sir. If you hadn't been wearing a plug hat—"

"It would have missed me? Ha-r-rumph! I can see that."

Johnny handed him the papers and a somewhat dented and damp silk hat.

"For whom was this lethal trap planned?"

Johnny fidgeted, shook his head, locked his hands behind him, said finally, in confusion, "One of the—one of the—students."

"My students? But none of them is six feet tall—ha, yes—Donald McCallum? Ha-r-rumph! No doubt McCallum can look after himself, and McCallums and Gordons have ever been on opposite sides of a feud. But hereafter be sure ye catch no innocent bystander in your toils, hear?"

Dr. Blair restored his papers to their receptacle, clapped his hat on his head, and turned away. Ariana had long since run off home; now the other children dispersed.

Probably no parent would ever have learned of the incident if Johnny had not been curious about the strange oath he had heard, or thought he had heard. For several days he mulled it over in his mind, and in private tried it on his tongue, but one evening at dinner it came out, the question he had been wanting to ask—came out spontaneously, without conscious volition—indeed, with immediate regret for his rashness. If it turned out to be a swear word, he would be sent from the table.

"Papa, what's an athema mare?"

Silence followed, but it was a puzzled rather than a shocked silence.

"What's what?"

"An athema mare, an athema—"

"I don't believe you heard it right. You did hear it?"

"I thought it was a cuss word. I just wondered, that's all." He returned to his dish of strawberries, as if he had dismissed the whole matter from his mind.

But his mother had got her teeth in it, now. "Johnny, you are *not* to hang around men who use rough language. I have told you often enough. Was it Mr. Bodien?"

"Oh, no, it wasn't, Mamma." Johnny regarded his mother solemnly, the dimples in abeyance. "Cap'n" Bodien had become, since the days of the first lariat, a Pied Piper to Waynesboro boys because of his stories about the Old Army, Indian fighting, the Civil War. To be forbidden his company was unthinkable. "Cap'n Bodien never swears at us."

His father, having finished his strawberries, rolled up his napkin, thrust it into his napkin ring, and pushed his chair back. "Out with it, Johnny. What you mean is that someone *was* swearing at you. What was that word again?"

"I *wasn't* hanging around men that use rough language," he insisted virtuously. "An' I thought it was 'an athema mare, an'athema—' "

Anne suddenly lifted her napkin to her face. She could perhaps keep her eyes expressionless, but not her mouth. Presently, from behind the napkin, she said, "I know, John. 'Anathema maranatha.' One of the students, I suppose. What were you doing?"

"It wasn't one of the students. What does it mean?"

"I don't know, exactly. It is a curse in the Bible."

His father was not to be distracted. "It wasn't Mr. McCune, I hope? Or Mr. McKinney?"

"No, Papa."

By cross-questioning, they got the story out of him. By the time he was banished from the table, he had managed to finish his strawberries. Binny was slower; she lingered until she had pursued the last drop of cream around her dish and back again. When she finally asked to be excused and slipped down from her chair, she went into the sitting room where Johnny had been told to wait.

She stood beside his chair, where he sat sprawled out, chin on chest, and touched his arm. "You won't get a whipping, I don't guess," she whispered. "They laughed an' laughed an' laughed." Johnny turned; the two pairs of brown eyes, so alike, looked into each other, asking for and being given comfort. "They weren't *awful* mad."

But when his parents came in a few minutes later, they were forbiddingly solemn. Johnny, they had decided, must apologize to Dr. Blair. He must, moreover, cease and desist from playing practical jokes. They were dangerous. "Moreover" was a heavy word on his father's tongue. Johnny shied away from the thought of an apology: another fate worse than death.

"It wasn't dangerous. It was only a little ol' lard bucket. Tin."

"How would you like to be cracked on the head with a bucket full of water?"

"He wasn't, I told you. And besides, he said, 'We'll say no more about it.'"

"No argument, Johnny. An apology is in order. Mind what I say."

"You mean I got to go up to his house in broad daylight, an' ring his doorbell?"

"Well, no. You might bother him when he didn't want to be bothered. Come to the office tonight: he may drop in for a game of chess. If not tonight, tomorrow night, every night until he does come in."

That prospect was hardly more pleasing than the picture of himself on Dr. Blair's doorstep. But he had perforce to obey. He spent that evening on a stiff chair in the hall outside his father's offices, outwardly resigned, inwardly trembling. From the waiting room he could hear the shuffling of feet, and in the inner consulting room, his father's voice. The center room, where the chess board was always set up, was empty for an hour that to Johnny was interminably long. He was glad that his father was engaged with a patient when Dr. Blair did finally come in by the hall door, and pass by, inches from him, without so much as a glance. Johnny followed him into the center room, to stand, breath-caught, until he was bidden to speak.

The apology was quickly spoken and quickly acknowledged and Johnny, mind relieved, made his escape. But the affair of Dr. Blair's silk hat cast a damper, at least for the remainder of that term, on the juvenile war with the students. It was also not without other consequences. After Dr. Blair had dismissed Johnny with a not unkind "Ha-r-rumph! Apology accepted. Unnecessary, I told you, say no more about it," he sat hunched bear-like over the chess table, frowning, wheezing, picking up one piece after another to scan it, carefully, before setting it in place again.

John took his patient out by way of the hall, in the door of the waiting room said, "Just a moment," and came in to where Dr. Blair was sitting.

"That boy of mine apologize?"

Dr. Blair looked up through his grizzled heavy brows, his head still sunk so far forward that his jowls were heavy over his collar.

"Yes. Unnecessary."

"I don't believe the children meant to annoy you."

"No, no. Certainly not. And that boy of yours need not have owned up, you know. He came over the fence—" Dr. Blair laughed; his laughter caught in his throat; he coughed and could not stop. Ludwig came in just then, hung his hat on the rack and waited while John brought a glass of water or medicine. Dr. Blair took it, waved a heavy hand to bid them have patience, got his bronchial tubes open, and said, "Came over the fence to save the little McCune from my wrath. I suppose he thought I would devour her. Or tell her father. No doubt I made noises like a flesh-eating ogre. I was startled. Now he has apologized, and I have accepted his apology."

John went out to summon the next patient into the consulting room.

Ludwig took the chair across the chess table from Dr. Blair, who greeted him gruffly.

"What's this all about?"

"You didn't hear about how the children dumped a pail of water on my hat?"

Ludwig's lips twitched as his eyes rested on that battered article, turned upside down on the floor beside Dr. Blair's chair, its crown still full of water-stained papers.

"No, I didn't. Children don't tell their parents such things. D'you mean to say Johnny Gordon told his father?"

"Must have. Apologized—here, tonight—certainly not voluntarily."

"Were my children involved?"

"I don't know. Don't want to know. Want it clearly understood that the perpetrators have been forgiven, and the perpetration has nothing to do with what I am about to say."

"And that is?" Ludwig was stiffened by the immediate if controlled hostility with which a parent prepares to hear criticism of his offspring.

"Don't bristle, man! I wouldn't know your children if I saw them. Didn't know Dock Gordon's boy until he told me who he was that night. But they do attend that dame's school in the Seminary, do they not?"

Ludwig nodded. "Their mother's idea. But I didn't figure it would hurt them, young as they are. At least they wouldn't learn any wildness there."

Dr. Blair wheezed and rolled his heavy body around in his chair impatiently. "Tut, man! They've no need to learn it. Did ye never hear of Original Sin? But that has nothing to do with what I am saying. I should have spoken long ago, perhaps. But you know what the agreement was: so long as she was able to keep school, the little lady—what's her name—Pinney—was to have the use of that room. I did not wish to be accused of using underhand methods to get her out, but now that we do need the space—"

"What's the matter with her school?" Ludwig was impatient.

"They may not be learning wickedness from Miss Pinney, but they are not learning anything else, either. Can't be. She hasn't the least control over them. They are out on the campus playing their games most of the day. I assumed if you knew they were wasting years of their lives and a deal of your money, you would want to investigate."

Ludwig was in part dismayed, in part amused. "I'll look into it. Of course the children would never put an end to such a blissful state of affairs by mentioning it. It could have gone on indefinitely. I'm obliged to you, sir."

Ludwig waited no longer than the next noon to make his inquisition. Noon was the only hour he was sure of having, in any intimate sort of way, all his family at the table together. Breakfast was hurried and piecemeal. In the evening before dinner and again after dinner, there was too much coming and going, too much wandering in and out, and off-to-bed-with-you-promptly. Mr. and Mrs. Cochran dined with the Rausches, taking their proper places at head and foot of the table; for the children that meal was a long hour of disciplined good behavior, of speaking when spoken to, of trying not to see their grandmother fumble blindly with her food. Conversation was restrained and trivial unless the men talked business or politics. But at noon Mr. Cochran took his lunch on a table in his wife's room; she stayed in bed and ate from a tray. For the Rausches the noon meal was a time when they could be together and at ease, when the children could have guests, when they could eat robustly and chatter as they ate.

On that particular day Elsa asked Johnny to eat with them. After the previous evening's embarrassment, Johnny was glad enough to be away from home. He ate at Elsa's house once a week or so, anyway, sending word home by any friend who would pass by the Gordon house. He sat down in the place quickly laid for him. It was bad luck for Johnny, trying to escape his parents' disapproval, to run into Ludwig's day for getting-to-the-bottom-of-this. And it was he who gave Ludwig just the cue he needed. Under cover, as he thought, of the babble of conversation, he said to Elsa, between him and her father, "Tomorrow's arithmetic problems are in my jacket pocket. Bill Thirkield took them down for us."

Ludwig interrupted what he was saying to Sally and turned a thunderous brow on the two who sat on his right hand. "Why didn't you copy down your own arithmetic problems?"

Elsa looked blank and astonished, but she dared not keep silent. As she so often did with her father, she spoke now in German, laying a claim to his special favor, emphasizing the bond between them. "Wir waren nicht da. Wir waren nur für ein Augenblick ausgegangen."

"Was it recess time?" Sally suggested helpfully. "Did Billy stay in to copy the problems?" But she broke off: two guilty faces stopped her.

Elsa said, "Oh, Papa! There's only one more week of school. It's too nice to stay in."

"Nevertheless, you are supposed to be in school. Can't Miss Pinney keep you there? What do you do? Just get up and walk out?" His penetrating glance shifted to Johnny.

Johnny laughed. His dimple showed fleetingly. This was Uncle Ludwig, not his father. "No, sir. Not exactly." Then perceiving from the sternness of the adult eyes boring into his that the question was not to be evaded, he said, "We slide out of our seats down on our hands and knees and back up the aisle and out of the door. But we don't all go at once," he added virtuously. "We kind of take turns."

"Only those times," contributed Elsa, hardily brave now that the ice had been broken, "when she goes to sleep."

"Miss Pinney? Goes to sleep?"

"Yes. Her head nods until her hair all comes down. Then we most always all go except Julia Deming."

"Julia was out this morning," Johnny was defensive.

"Just because you promised her a daisy crown. Of all the silly—"

Some unresolved argument seemed about to boil up again. Ludwig interrupted it.

"*What do you mean*? Can't Miss Pinney keep awake to teach her school?"

Johnny and Elsa, even Ernest, who was in his second year at school, looked at him in astonishment. It had never occurred to them that their parents, who knew everything except what their children succeeded in keeping from them, had been ignorant of Miss Pinney's weakness. Ernest, so far a silent, wide-eyed listener, surprised at finding out that school was not supposed to be what it always had been in his experience, held his forkful of potatoes and gravy suspended in the air. "She's a dope-fiend," he said explanatorily to his father.

Ludwig tossed down his napkin and pushed back his chair. Sally, after her angry "*What*!" said, "Ernest, you must not say such things. You don't know the meaning of the words."

Elsa protested. "But Mamma, everybody says so. Didn't you know? She's half asleep all the time, and sometimes—"

"You see," the doctor's son explained, "she's got sciatica. She told us so herself when she came to school with a hot-water bottle the first time. 'N' it's painful, I guess, an' she takes—at least we thought—"

"Is your father her doctor?"

"I don't think so. I've never been there with him, when I've gone along on his rounds."

"Of course not, Ludwig. You don't think Dock would have let this go on? If there is anything in the ridiculous story. A lot of children making up tales. Why, she comes to Club meetings and doesn't fall asleep." But Sally's voice remained suspended doubtfully. Miss Pinney had been absent from Club meetings rather consistently. "Poor old soul!" she concluded, finally.

"'Poor old soul' she may be," Ludwig retorted. "But how about our children? Come here, Elsa." He turned his chair around and stood Elsa between his knees. "Let's see what you have learned. Give me the sum of 47 and 39."

"Oh, Papa! Not in my head."

"Teufel! Is it so hard, then? What is the sum of 7 and 9?"

Elsa's hands were behind her back. Johnny could see her fingers moving. So could her mother, from the foot of the table, but she said nothing. Elsa got it finally.

"Sixteen."

"Nine and five?"

That was quicker. "Fourteen."

Sally laughed. She could not contain it longer. Ludwig looked at her questioningly; she shook her head. But he guessed, and brought Elsa's hands around and held them. "Eight and seven?"

The child's fingers wriggled in vain in his firm grasp. She shook her head.

"Gott im Himmel! Well, then, where is the island of Madagascar?"

Johnny, who loved maps, knew that one. He whispered, "Southeast of Africa."

Ludwig leaned over to look around Elsa's shoulder. "No help, young man. Now Elsa: Where is Nova Zembla?"

"Oh, Ludwig, be reasonable," Sally pleaded with him. "Who does know where Nova Zembla is?"

"I do. I did, when I was no older than Elsa. Try history, then. When was the battle of Saratoga, and who was in command?"

But Elsa liked history. After she had answered a few more questions he let her go.

"Off with you, now. Back to school. And stay there. And no more of this talk of 'dope-fiends.' You understand, Elsa? Ernest? Johnny?"

They nodded vigorously and made their escape. After Cassie had been summoned to take Charles and the baby for their naps, husband and wife faced each other across the length of the dining table.

"Who told you, Ludwig? Someone must have."

"Yes, I was laying for them. Dr. Blair told me they spend their days playing in the Seminary grounds. He thought we should know. I would have said something to you last night, only—"

"Only, you wanted to get it out of them without my—"

"Did you have no suspicion, Sally?"

"You certainly can't think—of course I didn't. I knew that Miss Pinney had sciatica in the winter. Mrs. Deming reported that at a Club meeting when Miss Pinney was absent—said she brought her hot-water bottle to school. Julia had told her. Yes, that was the day she said Julia told her *everything!* Ha! I wonder if she tells her she backs up a schoolroom aisle on her hands and knees so that Johnny Gordon can make her a daisy crown?" Then the absurdity of the picture struck her and she began to laugh. "Oh, Ludwig! And you were so hard on Elsa."

"Hard on her! The child can't *add!* And 'dope'! D'you suppose the old lady's taking laudanum or something? Or does she lie awake with her sciatica at night and sleep by day?"

"I'll see what I can find out. Talk to Anne, though she wouldn't know anything. Dock isn't Miss Pinney's doctor. But Anne and I could call on her."

"Whatever the case, it is plain enough that the children are learning nothing. They must transfer to the public school in the fall."

"Oh, dear, Ludwig! The public school? Their manners! And who knows what they might pick up—the itch."

"They will go to the public school in the fall. Manners are learned at home. And I do not believe the schools are overrun with verminous children. Ask your friend, Miss Reid."

"But what about poor old Pinney?"

"I regret being the cause of misfortune to anyone. But plainly she's been taking our money under false pretenses."

"Oh, no! She wouldn't. I mean: of course she thinks she's been teaching them. Well, I'll go talk to Anne this afternoon."

She rang the bell on the table as she rose, so that the impatient Tishy could clear the table; Ludwig stopped for a word or two with his mother-in-law; Mr. Cochran went out with him to ride as far as the bank. When the men had gone, Sally saw her mother comfortably settled for her afternoon nap, with the little colored maid within call, and went upstairs to dress. The baby was already asleep, but Charles was in the sitting room with Cassie; he followed his mother into the bedroom and played about her feet with his horse and wagon while she was changing. Cassie came to help with petticoats and bustle and all the dress fastenings. Sally got out hat and gloves. Charles did not care for the signs of imminent desertion. She hushed his clamor.

"By the time you've had your nap I'll be home again. You'll never miss me."

"Are you going to Binny's house?"

"No." She had remembered that it was Anne's afternoon at the library. "Be a good boy, Charles, and I'll take you to play with Binny another day."

Dressed for the street, her stiff, crisp little straw hat set severely straight over her brow, in front of her coiled braids, her long skirt with its deep ruffles at the hem and its superabundance of puffs and flounces behing gathered up cautiously in a gloved hand, she went downstairs. She peeked in on her mother and saw her already asleep. So was Rosie, the young "upstairs girl" who doubled as her mother's attendant in the absence of her family; she looked uncomfortable, slumped in a Boston rocker in the corner of the room, but Sally did not disturb her; she would hear when Mrs. Cochran roused. Instead, she tiptoed out and started for the library.

In the library she found Anne on a stepladder, shifting books along a shelf.

"Madam, may I have a book?"

"Sally! You made me jump." Anne sat down gingerly on the top of the stepladder, and folded her hands in her lap. "My, how I do admire you!" She took in the stylish figure, from feet to head and back again. "Going calling? Or is all this just for the library? You always look like Godey's. '*Soigńee*' I believe is the word."

"It is a woman's duty to look her best always," Sally said primly. Then she added, half-laughing, half-grim, "But I assure you this afternoon I gave my appearance little thought; I am all mother, with a palpitating bosom. Do come down from that ridiculous perch so I can talk to you. What on earth are you doing up there, anyway?" On Sally's afternoons at the library, she sat behind the desk and read when she was not being interrupted by patrons.

Anne stood up, book in hand, and with some awkward manipulation of skirt and petticoats managed to turn around and back down the ladder.

"It was the Misses Gardiners' turn here last. You know they both come on their afternoons, and one sits at the desk and the other dusts the books. Finicky, those women. Haven't you ever noticed how clean the books are kept? You never have to blow the dust off them, the way you sometimes have to at my house. But when the dusting is done, it doesn't matter where the books go. I was just putting them where they belong."

The library was less bleak than it had been in the first years of its existence. At the far end of the room, close to the windows, a long table stood crosswise, with chairs beside it and piles of magazines on it; another, that looked as if it had come from someone's dining room and had had its legs shortened, stood between the stove and the wall; on it were a stereopticon and piles of photographs: an amusement for children on rainy afternoons. All the windows were open, and battered magazines fluttered in a strong breeze.

"Better shut the window, hadn't you? Those magazines will be torn to pieces."

"I need open windows after the Gardiners have been here. Haven't you ever noticed how they take all the air out of a room, all the life? And they do not understand the purpose of a library. They leave little notes for the President of the Association, saying that such and such a child left fingermarks on a book. Now me, I am always delighted to find a book that looks as if it had been read. The longer I know those two women, the more I wonder that Douglas turned out even halfway human."

Anne pulled a chair from the magazine table and carried it inside the U-shaped desk, so that Sally could sit beside her.

"You really enjoy doing this, don't you?"

Anne stiffened, turned to look at Sally, a queer strained expression for a moment putting lines in her face, around her mouth. Then she smiled, and the stiffness was gone; she said, "Yes. Yes, I do. I've gotten to feel at home here. But I can't really afford the time. I ought to be at home right now, putting up strawberries. How is the library fund coming along?"

"Slowly, but it's growing." The banker's daughter was in a position to know. "In a few more years we should have enough to hire a librarian. And it is a help to have the pages to shelve the books. When we've got them taught what they should know, we can turn it all over to the younger women to operate."

"What were you palpitating about? You'd better tell me before someone comes in. Has Johnny done something he shouldn't?"

"Not only Johnny. All of them." Sally had turned so sober that Anne was surprised; she had not expected anything really serious. "You know that Miss Pinney has been having sciatica."

"Yes, I knew it. So did you. Mrs. Deming told us, don't you remember?"

"Yes, I remember. I meant to call on the poor old soul, but just never got around to it. Time slips away so fast."

"I went up there a while back—oh, in the middle of May, I guess, after she had missed Club so much."

"Why didn't you tell me?"

"I suppose I just didn't want to put it into words. It was kind of pitiful."

"She is peculiar, then?"

"'Peculiar'? She's sick. I went in one afternoon after school. She'd been lying down, her hair was all frowzy and her clothes mussed, and she looked half asleep. She apologized for her house." Anne swallowed, remembering the fetid odor of the tight-shut little cottage. "She said maybe I didn't realize what a strain teaching little folks can be: she had to rest when she got home. She took me into her parlor. I don't think anyone had been in there for months. I suppose she eats in her kitchen and sits and sleeps in her bedroom. The dust was thick. And the *spiders*!"

"Spiders?"

"Inside—all over the windows, the window sills, in the corners—thick cobwebs and huge, fat, revolting spiders. All the furniture was in the center of the room, pulled away from the walls. She said she was afraid of them."

"And that didn't seem peculiar to you?" Sally asked dryly.

"No, I didn't think of it like that." Anne frowned, spoke slowly. "I could imagine its happening to me, and anything you can imagine happening to yourself doesn't seem too queer, does it? First, just one spider, and if you were in great pain when you walked, you might not take the trouble—you would think 'it will die soon, anyway.' Then another and another and another. And you would feel they were closing in on you. First, you would pull all the furniture out from the walls and the corners and sit in the middle of the room. Then, as they came closer and closer, you would walk out of the room and shut the door behind you."

"What did you do?"

"Made a proper afternoon call. Twenty minutes."

"All in the midst of the spiders?"

"I thought of asking her for a broom and going after them, but it seemed to me that would be an insulting way for a caller to behave. So the next day I baked a cake and sent Lonzo up with it, and told him to somehow get the conversation around to spiders, and offer to get rid of them for her; then put the furniture back where it belongs, and go outside and cut back the bushes outside her windows. That's why the spiders come in: all those overgrown bushes beating against the windows; the room is a green twilight, like being way under water. And he came back and said he'd done it all. I haven't been back since, to see."

"What did you and she talk about, all among the spiders?"

"The children, mostly—she's so proud of them."

"And she knew what she was talking about?"

"Certainly. Sally, are you suggesting that she isn't right in her mind? Of course she is. She's old and sick and pathetic—and all alone. I could have wept when I closed her gate behind me. But she's perfectly sane. What's all this about?"

"What a blind, sentimental goose you are. Of course old age is pitiful. I see it at home every day, and it makes me feel sad that it must be. But it must: it comes to all of us unless we die before we reach it. Wouldn't you rather grow old, even if you were pathetic, than die young?"

"I'm not sure," Anne said slowly. "I suppose I wouldn't seem pathetic to myself. But to be alone. It's a blessing Miss Pinney has her school."

"But it *isn't*, Anne. That's what I'm trying to tell you, and you're just being willfully obtuse. She isn't able, nor fit, to keep school."

"You mean her sciatica interferes with her teaching?"

"Interferes!" Sally repeated to her then what Dr. Blair had told Ludwig, and went on to recount the luncheon-time revelations.

"Oh, the scamps!" Anne breathed, her eyes horrified. "The wretches."

They eyed each other ruefully, then laughed a little, amused against their will.

"What are we to do, Sally?"

"I know what I am going to do. Ludwig told me. When he speaks in a certain tone of voice—we shall send Elsa and Ernest to public school in the fall."

"That's all we can do, I suppose. Oh, dear! I have promised Binny she could start next year at Miss Pinney's. But she'll just be five; maybe I can keep her home another year. But we can't let it go at that, can we? What about the Bonners? And the Thirkields? And Julia Deming?"

They smiled at each other. There was at least that small pleasure to be found in the exposure.

"Julia tells her mother everything," Sally said sweetly, "so the Demings must not mind."

"Of course, Julia goes to school just for companionship; she is taught at home. Just the same, you know nothing has been said to Old Teapot about dope fiends, and daisy crowns, and so on. I am glad of it. I thought Julia sounded a most unnatural child."

"Skip the Demings, then. But what about the others?"

"Oh, Sally, school will be out in a little while, and then there will be July and August—"

"And you think she might die and solve the problem?"

"If you tell everyone, and she doesn't have any pupils, what would happen to Miss Pinney? We couldn't do it."

"We can't let matters drift, for her sake, as well as our childrens'. I was thinking on the way down here—" Sally spoke in a brisker tone, and Anne knew that already she had evolved a plan and was about to take action. "First, we must find out whether she is really taking drugs."

"How?"

"Couldn't Dock?"

"Ask questions? About someone else's patient? No." Anne had been touched on an old sore; the image of Mrs. McCune would come to her mind if she let it.

"I doubt if it's true," Sally said, soothingly. "How would those babies know? She's probably sleepy from long nights lying awake."

"It could be true. The older doctors are pretty free with laudanum. John—" She broke off, realizing her indiscretion.

"We'll just have to find out who her doctor is: there should be some way. But at any rate, she isn't teaching. Do you suppose if what we did about our children forced her to close the school, she would have anything to live on?"

"Of course she wouldn't. I doubt she's ever been paid more than enough to just scrape by."

"Then we'll have to see she doesn't starve. Take up a collection from her old friends and pupils—give her enough each month."

"Who's to tell her? That she's through, forever? That we can't trust our children to her any longer? That she's reached the end? How awful!"

"Maybe it could be worked out. Dr. Blair said to Ludwig the reason he's kept quiet so long is that he didn't want to be suspected of trying to get that room away from her in violation of the agreement with the Lowreys. But the seminary needs the room."

"She could rent another room, somewhere else."

"Oh, Anne! You don't honestly think she has energy enough left for that? And if we had a purse for her, an annuity, she might be glad to be able to give up."

"You work it out. I'm not going to interfere in anyone's life."

"You would take Johnny out of her school, and not say why to anyone? But you were the one who brought up the Bonners and the others. Besides, you know it would leak out: why you did it, I mean. Everyone always knows, sooner or later, things like that, and exaggerates. She would be destroyed."

"Sound out someone else, Sally. I'll help as much as I can, with money. Don't say anything more now."

Footsteps outside had given warning. Sally rose, dragged her chair back from the desk, and came back outside to look at the booklist.

"It's Mrs. Sheldon and Mrs. Edwards. Oh, Lud! I'm going. But you'll talk to John tonight?"

Anne nodded. Sally spoke for a moment to the older women, and then went out without waiting to hunt for a book. Thereafter Anne's time at the library was taken up by its subscribers: Waynesboro ladies out in the afternoon in what John would call "full fig," on their way to leave cards or visit formally with their acquaintances, or at the library to exchange their or their husbands' books. When school was out, children drifted in by twos and threes, or alone. Anne had learned to know them by their parents' cards, the public school children who might or might not be Johnny's friends: Sophie Klein, who was gulping down the Katy books at the rate of one every two or three days; one little Lichtenstein, who seemed hardly old enough to read, but obviously was; Ariana McCune, who liked fairy tales. And there were a few high school boys, like Kurt Mueller, for they read only serious books: history, mostly, and Roman history at that.

When five o'clock came, Anne was not sorry; she urged them out, closed the windows, straightened the room, put on her hat and gloves, and went out, locking the door behind her. She went along the corridor quickly: the key was kept in the Ballard, Gardiner, and Merrill office; sometimes, if you were delayed, those premises were closed. Then there was nothing to do but hang it on the hook by the library door, not a really safe place for it. Anne was glad to see the door to the outer office open.

Because it was open, her entrance went unnoticed. No one was there except Eliza Ballard. She was not as usual bent over the ledgers on her desk but standing at the window, to one side, stooped a little as if peering out.

"Here's the library key." Anne tossed it jingling against the paper knife on the desk beyond the barrier. Eliza jumped and turned, her hand at her throat.

"You startled me."

"I'm sorry. I thought you must have heard me coming." Anne knew her heels had clicked coming down the corridor. What had Eliza been looking at? "Has something happened in the street?" That window commanded a comprehensive view.

Eliza had turned her back to look out again. "No. I happened to see Douglas Gardiner close the window of his office in the Court House, and wondered whether he would come back here. If not, I can lock up and go home. My father is defending a railroad case in Columbus; he won't be back tonight."

There was something queerly avid in the way Eliza stood in the window, her head cocked, watching. Like a buzzard. Anne, from where she stood outside the railing, was cut off from any view of the street below, or the near side of the Court House square, but she could see the portico and the steps and the wide brick plaza that sloped down to Chillicothe Street. Douglas Gardiner came out of the Court House door and down the steps. Eliza stiffened, withdrew a little further to one side, but continued to watch. He turned right on Chillicothe Street. Both women saw him reach the corner, cross Main Street and enter one of the big double doors of Sheldon and Edwards.

Eliza straightened and turned from the window, a derisive half-smile at the corners of her mouth; she looked at the same time pleased and contemptuous. Anne thought, mildly interested in Eliza's curiosity, it wasn't just that she wanted to know whether Douglas would return to the office. "You can put your books away," she said. "Surely he won't be back here, if he has to do some shopping for his aunts. Come along and walk part of the way with me."

"His aunts?" Eliza smiled as if to indicate that she was repressing volumes, but all she said was "Just lock the door and walk away, leaving all that?" With a proprietary air she indicated the ledgers, the letter books, the piles of briefs. "Much of it is extremely confidential. It wouldn't have been left lying about all day if Papa had been here. But Douglas is in and out, and he always wants to find things where he left them."

"She dislikes him," Anne thought, "two sharp-tongued people in one office."

Eliza went on, "I dread for Papa to have to go out of town, not only—"

Eliza was frowning now. If she had wanted Anne to tease her with questions, she had forgotten it; when she spoke of her father, she was serious. "It throws too much responsibility on me. Douglas's time is mostly spent in the Court House now he's prosecutor. But it's not that so much as that I don't think Papa is equal to it. He is too old to act as a trial lawyer. I worry about it, but I don't say anything at home: Mamma and Thomasina don't notice, so why upset them? But I wish I could get him to the doctor. He hasn't been, has he?"

"Not that I know of, but John doesn't name over his patients to me."

With each word the emphasis with which Eliza had begun to speak had weakened. Anne realized she had been trying to divert her attention. "She knows that I caught her watching, and is embarrassed; she wants me to forget it. But forget what, I wonder?" She said, "I'll go along, then. The library key's on the desk there."

She paused outside the door long enough to see Eliza turn back to the window; then she went on out and down the steps. Eliza was odd; she'd always been odd, with never a good word for anyone. But who wouldn't be at least a little peculiar, brought up as Eliza had been, in the midst of causes, of Reforms, never allowed to forget the Rights of Women, serious-minded and never to have any fun? It was a wonder that Thomasina was as nearly like other people as she was. Anne dismissed Eliza from her mind as she crossed the square and followed where Douglas Gardiner had passed a few minutes before. But instead of turning onto Main Street she walked on down Chillicothe: she hoped to find John alone in his office, so that she could tell him about Miss Pinney and hear his judgment where there were no small pitchers about. But he was not there. She took the shortcut home, through the yards by way of the alley, and went to the side-porch door.

The children were in the kitchen with Martha; that meant that their father was not in the house either. They heard her come in and followed her into the sitting room. She dropped the library book she had brought onto the oval table with its long maroon cover that stood in the center of the room and served as a catch-all for newspapers, schoolbooks, Johnny's round cap, and Johnny's dog-eared copy of the Westminster Catechism, which he was reluctantly learning, question and answer by question and answer.

"Hang up your cap, Johnny. There's enough on that table without it." Her own hat and gloves she laid on the sloping arm of the sofa—she would take them upstairs when she went. With a two-handed gesture she lifted her braids from where they had been flattened to her head, then sat down in her rocker and let Binny climb on her lap. Johnny came back from the hall and stood close at her side—stood uneasily, first one foot and then the other on her rocker. She put an arm around his waist to draw him close, but when he stiffened, she let him go and lifted her hand to brush a tossed lock back from his forehead.

"Mamma." He was anxious. "Did you see Aunt Sally?"

"Yes, I saw her. Do you think you have done well to plague a sick old lady who has always been kind to you?"

"Who is sick?" That was Binny.

"Miss Pinney."

"She doesn't mind, Mamma. She doesn't even notice. She takes drugs. Everybody says so."

"And just who is 'everybody'?"

"Oh, you know. Bill Thirkield. He sees her in the drugstore. And she sleeps all the time. She doesn't even wash any more." He laughed, a little horrified crow of laughter. "Mamma, she *smells!*"

"*Johnny!*" Anne was profoundly shocked. "How can you be so *vulgar!* No. I don't want you to say anything more. I want you to go sit on the sofa and try to think, if you can, what it would be like to be old and sick and poor and all alone. First, hand me Binny's book—*Little Ladders to Learning*—there on table. I'll hear her read."

When John came in, Anne indicated to Johnny by a look that his term of ostracism was over. But he sat on where he was, a gravely troubled look on his face.

"Papa, what's sciatica?"

John told him as well as he could in terms the child could understand.

"What kind of medicine do you give for it?"

"Depends on what causes it. Sometimes it's a symptom rather than a disease. Why? Who has sciatica?"

"Miss Pinney. I thought maybe you gave opium for it."

"I don't give Miss Pinney anything. She isn't my patient. But why opium?"

"It makes you sleepy, don't it?"

"Yes. But so does lying awake all night with the pain of sciatica."

John had brought the paper in with him. He sat down and flipped it open. From behind it he looked at Anne, the question in his eyes, "What is all this about?"

She shook her head, meaning "later." She said, "Run out, Johnny, and tell Martha your father's home. She can serve dinner when she's ready." Then, because Binny had pushed back the book her mother had been holding for her, and was obviously about to report on Johnny's disgrace to her father, Anne said, "Never mind, Binny," and began talking herself to forestall the child. The first subject that came to mind was Eliza Ballard in the law office window. It spun easily off some top level of her awareness of her day: she could tell it without thinking. It could be of no interest to John, but it served to make him laugh.

"I wonder," he said, "how many people realize Eliza's gimlet eye is upon them."

"Not 'them'—at least not this afternoon. Just Doug Gardiner. I can't think why. He was going on some perfectly innocent errand for his aunts."

Johnny returned to summon them to dinner. At the table they spoke of other things. But Anne's bit of idle observation was passed on as a warning: the next time John encountered Douglas Gardiner at the tobacconist's, in the shade of the wooden Indian outside its threshold, he said, "By the way, Gardiner, I understand from my wife that Eliza Ballard keeps a keen eye from the office window on the shopping habits of her gentlemen acquaintances. Anne couldn't understand her interest, and I don't either, but I thought I might mention it to you." He touched a finger to his hat in a sketch of a military salute, and eyes still twinkling, went on about his business. Douglas let himself down heavily on his crippled foot in its built-up shoe, bit down hard on his pipe stem, and muttered an epithet under his breath. A couple of weeks later, Sheldon Edwards said to Kitty, when she stopped in the store one afternoon, "Doug hasn't been in for quite a while. I guess that's blown over." Kitty looked disappointed, but said only, "Then it's a good thing I didn't tell anyone, isn't it?"

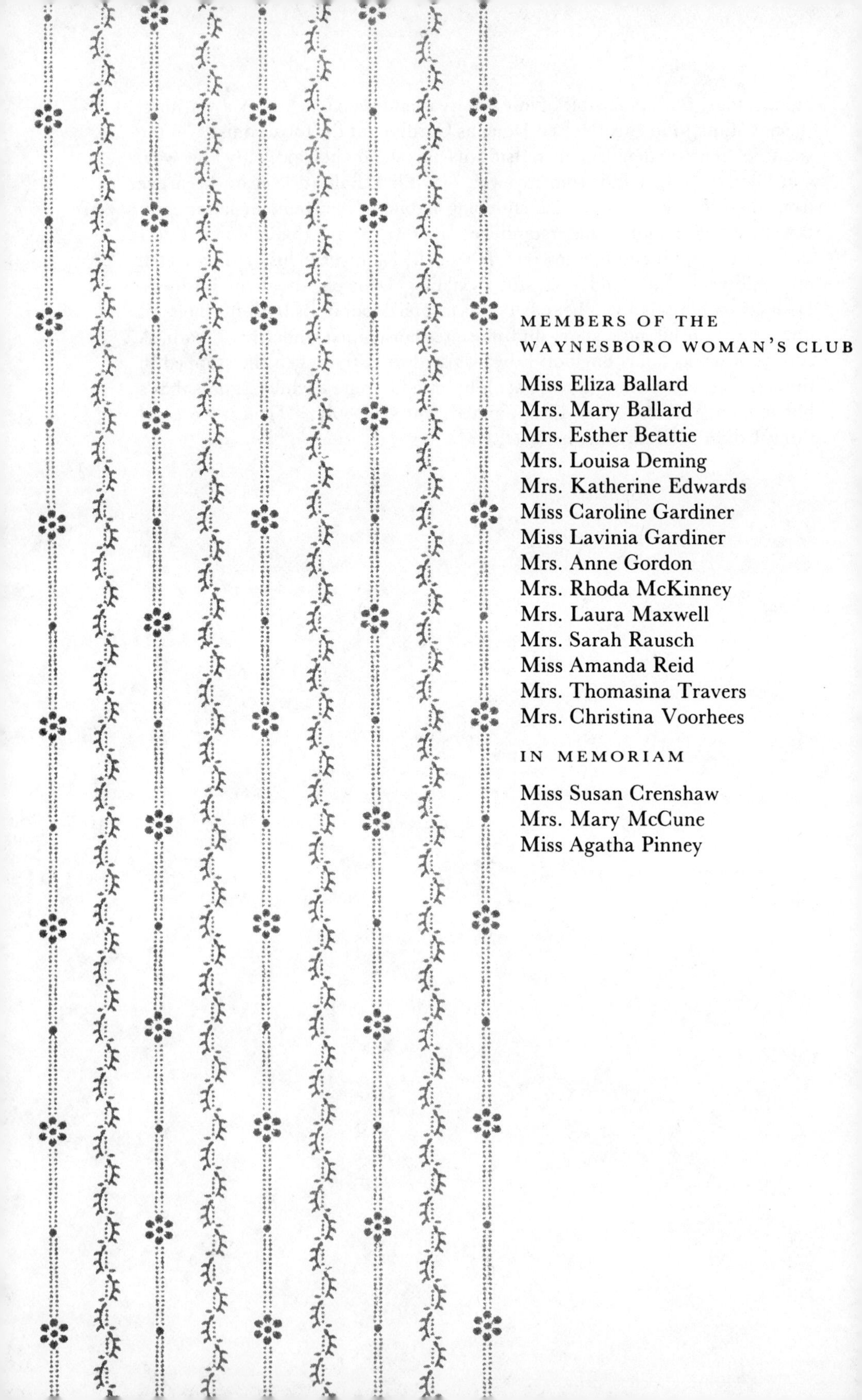

MEMBERS OF THE
WAYNESBORO WOMAN'S CLUB

Miss Eliza Ballard
Mrs. Mary Ballard
Mrs. Esther Beattie
Mrs. Louisa Deming
Mrs. Katherine Edwards
Miss Caroline Gardiner
Miss Lavinia Gardiner
Mrs. Anne Gordon
Mrs. Rhoda McKinney
Mrs. Laura Maxwell
Mrs. Sarah Rausch
Miss Amanda Reid
Mrs. Thomasina Travers
Mrs. Christina Voorhees

IN MEMORIAM

Miss Susan Crenshaw
Mrs. Mary McCune
Miss Agatha Pinney

1879

"The Club lost a devoted and loyal member . . ."

In the meantime, the affairs of Miss Pinney had been taken in hand. Dr. Blair, on being consulted, confirmed that indeed the Seminary could use the room if released from its obligation to Miss Pinney: the Seminary library was overflowing its present quarters in a room upstairs. If the good people of the town would not resent it as a cruelty, he would broach the subject to Miss Pinney whenever the committee of ladies signified their readiness to take over the responsibility of providing for her.

Anne was not one of the committee: she felt an invincible repugnance to taking any active part in the arrangements for what was left of Miss Pinney's life. She contributed to the fund being collected, but beyond that she would not go; she left the soliciting of other Waynesboro mothers, teachers, church-women, and clubwomen to Sally, Mrs. Deming, and Mrs. Bonner. These three, who had constituted themselves a Committee for the Pinney Annuity Fund, hoped to collect money enough to last her the rest of her life, but if they failed in that, they professed themselves willing to solicit again, another year.

When the time came to inform Miss Pinney that her teaching days were over, they were not quite so eager. But it had to be done. Sally and Mrs. Bonner agreed that they would accompany her, but Mrs. Deming was the one to do it; after all, in the days of the Lowreys, she and Miss Pinney had been colleagues. Coolly contemptuous of the two cowards trailing in her wake, Mrs. Deming led them up Miss Pinney's walk one afternoon shortly before the end of the school year. They were admitted by a bewildered old lady and ushered into her parlor. (The spiders, Sally noticed, were being kept at bay: the furniture was ranged primly against the walls. But the house smelled, even in June, with the windows open.)

When the amenities had been observed, Miss Pinney weakly gave them an opening. "This looks like a delegation," she ventured tremulously. "Is there something I can do for you ladies?"

"In a sense, dear Miss Pinney, it is a delegation. We have been asked by a group of mothers and friends of yours to tell you how very courageous we think you have been to continue your teaching this year, so much of the time in great pain. We fear that if you attempt to carry on the school for another year it will be at too great a risk to your health."

Miss Pinney's face—her vague blue eyes—expressed only bewilderment. "But in another year, surely, my sciatica will have improved. Dr. Wright says—" Her voice trailed off.

Mrs. Deming began again, in a more business-like tone. "Perhaps you do not know that the Seminary would like very much to have the use of that room."

"But they agreed to allow me the use of it, so long as I need it."

"Oh, yes, we realize that. And they are quite ready to abide by the terms of the agreement. But we thought you might like to know that they are willing to take it off your hands; in the circumstances, you might be glad not to have that rent to pay."

"I do pay them rent. It has always been paid." Then her pride betrayed her into a misunderstanding of their purpose. "If my little school is in the way, of course I shall surrender the room to the Seminary." From that moment, while the ladies were there and afterward, her poor scuttling brain was going over the town, street by street, looking for a room she could move her school into. But Mrs. Deming was quite sure that she had accomplished her mission, and had persuaded Miss Pinney that her teaching days were over. It had been agreed beforehand that nothing would be said about the pension: that was to be reserved for a great surprise at the conclusion of the exercises on the last day of school.

Only Sally was a little dubious. As they filed out through the gate, she asked, "Do you think she understood what we were driving at?"

"She seemed to me to be in full possession of her faculties. I do not see how she could have possibly misunderstood." But Sally did not quite share Mrs. Deming's opinion, and she passed on her misgivings to Anne, who found herself climbing the hill to the old school on Closing Day with trembling knees. Johnny had a piece to speak or she would not have gone. Afterward she thought it had been the most dismal occasion she had ever sat through.

The schoolroom was pleasantly cool to those just come in from the June sun. But after you had sat there for a while on one of the straight hard chairs borrowed from Seminary classrooms for the occasion, your bones stiffened and the atmosphere struck damp and dank at the soles of your feet and the nape of your neck. The light was dim. Miss Pinney, fidgeting at her desk, was ruffled and beaded, but her hair was untidy, her features blurred, without line. Whatever the old lady's habit, she had taken no laudanum that day: she was awake in every nerve, twitching her hands, jerking when she brought them into view. The scrubbed little boys, the starched little girls, got through their songs and "pieces" with not more than the normal amount of stammering and flat notes. When the last child had spoken, Miss Pinney pulled herself to her feet and stood clutching her desk, while she uttered the conventional words of praise to her pupils, of gratitude to their parents. Then she explained briefly that since the Seminary desired the use of the room where they were now gathered together, she must find another location for her school. Before fall she would find a place and let them know.

Sally and Anne exchanged horrified glances; everyone else looked bewildered. But while Miss Pinney stood, waiting for them all, parents and children, to rise for the singing of "America," Mrs. Deming got to her feet, swept down the aisle, and asked Miss Pinney to be seated while she, deputed by the parents, expressed their appreciation for all that had been done for their children. The words were warm, but the tone was cool, concealing (or failing to conceal, Anne thought) her contempt for the piece of human wreckage beside her. She always looked a little—something about the curve of her nostrils—as if she smelled something offensive; now the expression was intensified and expressed undisguised distaste. And she was ineffably condescending. Anne squirmed: anyone could have done this better, more graciously, but who else would have been willing to do it at all? Not she. It little behooved her to be critical.

"As I believe you all know," Mrs. Deming said from the platform, "Miss Pinney has carried on her school this year in very difficult circumstances. In spite of ill health and much pain, she has continued day after day to teach our children, with a fortitude that has seemed to us nothing less than heroic. Now, added to her burdens, is this necessity, willingly undertaken by her to oblige the Seminary, of finding another adequate and wholesome location for her school. We cannot believe that she would ever come to feel at home elsewhere than in these old familiar surroundings, dear to all of us because of long years of association with her and her school. We have decided that we cannot ask this sacrifice of one who has served so long and so nobly; nor suffer her to start anew, ill as she is, in some strange place."

Miss Pinney looked frightened and twitched all over when Mrs. Deming let the echoes of that sentiment die away in the heavy air. Anne thought, "Come to the point, you fool—don't you see you're frightening her, and she still doesn't understand." Anne was holding her breath; perhaps most of the audience was. Mrs. Deming herself may have been doubtful. After a moment, with an even more pronounced look of distaste, she stooped over Miss Pinney and said plainly that all parents whose children had been in her charge felt that they must not demand of her that she teach them another year. Then she straightened and continued her speech, half to Miss Pinney and half to those in front of her, saying that because they owed her a debt of gratitude beyond payment for her having taught their children not only the three R's but the meaning and the habit of good manners and good conduct, they were delighted to be able to present her with this purse and its contents. The contents were merely an earnest of what was to come. Every month of her life a like amount would be paid to her by the bank. There the bulk of this farewell gift, this token of appreciation not only from parents but from former pupils, from other teachers, from the members of her club and her church, had been deposited. Mr. Cochran and Mr. Voorhees had very kindly consented to act as trustees. If any question occurred to Miss Pinney at a later time, she could apply to them, and they would explain.

Befuddled little Miss Pinney had not tried to get to her feet. She held out her hand for the purse. Her mouth trembled; tears wet the pouches under her eyes. The children sat dazed, their known world breaking up around them. The audience of mothers and a few fathers applauded politely. Miss Pinney struggled for words, bit her lip, held her hand to her chin for a moment, and finally succeeded in saying, "Mrs. Deming and friends—I cannot speak—allow me—thank you."

After a moment's silence, the audience clapped again, in response to Mrs. Deming's gesture with the hand Miss Pinney could not see. Anne thought desperately, "Why don't people go home, leave her—" and herself rose and broke the spell. Mothers started up the aisle to the door. Their children, hearing the clatter, turned to look back over their shoulders, then rose to scramble after their elders, without waiting for any singing of "America." Johnny caught up with his mother on the steps, elbowing his way through clusters of children and adults.

"Why didn't you wait for the closing exercises? We weren't through."

"I thought Miss Pinney had had enough."

"Oh." Then, because plainly he was not on his mother's mind, "Did I do all right?"

"What? Oh, yes, very well, Johnny. I could hear every word, and you didn't forget."

They walked silently as far as the gate. Johnny held it open for his mother, then as he rejoined her, said, "That about the money—Julia's mother—does that mean Miss Pinney won't be having school any more? Where'll we go?"

"To the Public School."

"The school down on Chillicothe Street? Where Sophie and the McCunes go? All of us? Shaney? Julia?"

"Yes, all of you. Elsa, the Bonners, Bill Thirkield. I don't know about Julia. Do you mind?"

"Mind? No. I think it will be better, don't you?" His manner was gravely judicious. He drew a long sigh, then the exuberance natural to the day broke surface: "But that won't be for a *long* time. Not till September. *School's out!*"

School was out. The Seminary closed for the summer, and the theologues scattered. The top of Market Street hill, and its slope down past the Kleins' on one side and the Cochrans' house on the other, were suddenly deserted, quiet through long summer afternoons and evenings. Boys were off and away, following their own devices. Girls practiced and went to their music lessons, or played tame housekeeping games under the shrubbery. Elsa Rausch was also studying arithmetic with one of the public school teachers, and because she could not bear her father's disapprobation, she applied herself and learned her combinations so that she no longer needed to count on her fingers.

Johnny Gordon was responsible for the new diversion that came to occupy many of the children's idle evening hours. Sent to Thirkield's one evening on an errand for his father, his attention was caught by a word overheard by chance: Mr. Bonner and Captain Bodien, lingering at the cigar counter, were engaged in an amiable argument as to whether the Army of the Potomac or the Western armies had won the war. Johnny was all ears. In those days most veterans were too busy earning their livings, too glad to relax with a newspaper in the evenings, to talk much about the war, and John Gordon never mentioned it. But what with Fourth of July and political speeches, and military funerals conducted by the G.A.R., echoes of battles lingered in the air, and the children were tantalized.

On that particular evening, Captain Bodien's eye caught Johnny's just as he said "Gettysburg."

Johnny ventured breathlessly, "Were you at Gettysburg, Captain?"

Mr. Thirkield leaned over the counter, "Doesn't Dock want that medicine, Johnny?"

Captain Bodien said, "Better cut along, boy. If you want to hear about Gettysburg, you go to the Saturday night band concerts. Look for me on the bench by the cannon and I'll tell you about it."

The Court House square was the scene of Waynesboro's weekly band concerts. By '79 the old iron fence had been taken down: the county commissioners had come to consider its upkeep an unnecessary expense. At once the local G.A.R., in a misguided display of patriotism, mounted a Civil War cannon in the corner, pointed at the intersection of Wood and Market streets, and put an iron bench behind it, under a big sycamore tree.

The band (veterans and sons of veterans) was popular, and Saturday night was a time given over to recreation, except among the Reformed Presbyterians, whose Sabbath still began at sundown. The audience assembled in family groups, which soon disintegrated: children were reluctant to spend long evenings on the hard camp chairs placed in rows close to the bandstand, and soon escaped to follow their own devices with only the parental admonition "Don't leave the square. Meet us here at the end."

On the evening when Johnny had been promised the story of Gettysburg, Captain Bodien found awaiting him beside the cannon a small group of children, both boys and girls, some of whom he did not even know. He did not object to an audience. That night was the first of many like it. He would sit on the bench and draw maps of his battles in the dust and gravel: to Johnny and various others, those particular battles would always be wavering lines of thousands of nameless soldiers pressing forward or drawing back, with Battery B of the Fourth U.S. Artillery in the center, large as a brigade or a division, standing firm however great the slaughter, in a farmyard at Antietam, sweeping the railroad cut the first day at Gettysburg.

From the Civil War the Captain's reminiscences reached back to antebellum days when the battery was in Utah serving as cavalry where the mountains made artillery useless, fighting Indians. The children were so enchanted by stories of Indians, Mormons, and the Pony Express that the Captain invited them to his house to see his mementoes: Indian blankets, tomahawks, pipes, along with Civil War weapons: his carbine, his own saber, the saber he had captured from a too brash young Confederate cavalryman. After that exciting evening, several times a week a varying group of children collected at Captain Bodien's, on the back porch or in his study.

The only parent to protest was Elsa Rausch's mother. The children were being kept out of mischief, and were safely home before dark. But one evening when Elsa was unduly late, she was sent immediately to bed, and Sally followed shortly to have "a little talk" with her daughter.

"What is the great fascination that Captain Bodien has for all you children?"

"Oh, Mamma! He's done *everything.* He was in the army before the war, and fought Indians and Mormons. Once he was tomahawked and they put a silver plate in his head where the bone was smashed." Seeing her mother's look of incredulity, she added, "You can see the scar. Cap'n Bodien's been bald ever since."

"I can see he would be."

"His battery was in Utah when the war began. They hadn't gotten any supplies for a long time, because the ol' Secretary was an ol' Rebel, only he hadn't told anybody yet—just stopped their food supplies. And their tongues swelled up and got black, and their teeth fell out. That ol' Secretary quit and went South after Lincoln was elected. They were ordered back to Washington, an' it took so long to march all the way from Utah back to St. Joe, Missouri, with their guns, that the Battle of Bull Run was fought while they were on the way and they didn't even know it."

Sally laughed. "You've got it all down pat, haven't you? I can see that Captain Bodien would be good company, like Baron Munchausen."

The allusion was lost on Elsa. "An' he fought all through the war with his battery, an' once he was sabered by enemy cavalry, trying to take his cannon." Seeing his mother's doubtful expression, she insisted: "He's got a scar from it, round his cheek—anybody can see that scar, even when he's got a hat on."

"It's as good as reading history, isn't it? But you mustn't go running after him with the boys."

In their own room Sally reported to her husband. "Tomahawked! Tongues swollen black."

"It could be true, you know. Scurvy. Floyd did what he could to ruin the Regular Army while he was still in Buchanan's cabinet."

"Well, your captain has certainly bewitched the children. But Elsa mustn't run after him. I refuse to let her be bewitched, except at secondhand."

One night Johnny turned up at home earlier than usual, and with little to say. His mother, who was sitting on the side porch while Binny darted about the yard catching fireflies, thought he seemed crestfallen.

"What's the matter, Johnny? Captain Bodien run out of stories?"

"No. How could he? The war lasted four whole years, besides the Indians. But there was going to be other company tonight. He said we'd have to be pretty quiet in his library. An' we thought mebbe we'd better come home."

His mother leaned forward, to lay a hand on his shoulder as he dropped to the porch step. "Oh, dear, Johnny. Have you been making a nuisance of yourself?" The rocker squeaked as she moved. "Maybe that was just a polite way of saying he doesn't want little boys around all the time."

"Oh, no. It was a special visitor, he said. Someone coming to call on his daughter."

"The very pretty girl who clerks in Sheldon and Edwards? I'm not surprised."

"I know who it is, too." Johnny's voice became more cheerful; like any human, he relished having a bit of news to tell. "Doug Gardiner."

"*Mister* Gardiner to you, jackanapes," Anne said automatically, before absorbing the meaning of his statement. Then: "Oh, no, Johnny! That's impossible."

"He was coming down the other side of the street when we came away. We saw him: you can always tell *Mr.* Gardiner by the way he limps. Besides, everyone knows he's sweet on her."

"Johnny, what has come over you? Such a common way of talking! And how would you little boys know about things like that?"

"Well, we've seen him around. I bet Papa has, too—you ask him, if you don't believe me."

"Oh, I believe you." Anne remembered suddenly the afternoon she had seen Eliza watching from her office window. She was startled, in a pleasant sort of way, just because all Waynesboro would be shocked. "All Waynesboro"—that was what Kitty Edwards had said, as far back as last winter, so she knew, too. Anne without further thought dealt with the problem at hand. "But it may not be serious, you know, Johnny. Gentlemen may pay attention to a number of young ladies before choosing a wife. So you must not repeat this. Do you understand? It might do a great deal of harm. Particularly to Miss Bodien. Promise?"

"All right, Mamma. Cross my heart. I like Barb'ra." After a moment's silence he said tentatively, "Miss Bodien."

"That's better."

"Now I guess I'll go over to the office an' see if I can help Papa get things ready for tomorrow."

Johnny scrambled to his feet and with something of a strut went down off the steps and across the yard to the back gate. It was just beginning to get really dark, dark enough to see the fireflies easily, but Anne called Binney to her. She laughed at herself, but she had felt a real pang at seeing Johnny go off through that gate: boys, it seemed, did not have to be very old before they asserted their independence, and found better things to do than sit with the womenfolk. She drew Binny to her in a sudden warm embrace. "Not much company for us, is he? Never mind: you tell me a story about the fireflies."

But she only half-listened to the child on her lap. She was thinking of Johnny's helping his father. It was not a mere idle boast: some boys were early at making up their minds what they wanted to do and be. Johnny would not be ten until fall, but he was going to be a doctor. He spent a good deal of time in the office, boiling instruments and making bandages and piling them ready in a glass-doored bookcase they had carried down from her father's old room upstairs. And John encouraged him, and so Anne knew that her husband was not so unhappy in his profession as she had feared he might be, in spite of the dark times when he felt futile and helpless.

Most Waynesboro boys, after a few weeks of freedom, of fishing and swimming in river or canal, found jobs of one sort or another for the summer months, and there was no distinction between those who attended public school and those who had gone to Miss Pinney. They passed the Waynesboro *Torchlight* late in the sleepy afternoons, or they worked for their fathers in their shops, like Billy Thirkield in the drugstore, or they went into the ropewalk as wheel boys. There was always a shortage of labor at the mill in the summer: many Negro hands "laid off" because they could manage comfortably enough by fishing, raising a few chickens and a few rows of vegetables, and mowing a lawn now and then. Captain Bodien shifted the larger, stronger boys to the absentees' places, and hired children to turn the wheels for the spinners in the ropewalk. It was hard work and exacting, for the wheels had to be turned at an unvarying rate of speed as it twisted the fibers in the hands of the spinners backing down the walk; but perhaps for that very reason, it was considered the most desirable of all summer jobs.

Miss Pinney's former pupils, along with other Waynesboro boys, were thus happily occupied in one way or another; the summer lay ahead of them, a golden, sunlit endless stretch of time. They forgot the school year past, seldom looked forward to the one to come. Nor did their elders give thought to Miss Pinney: she was a problem solved. The Demings had gone to Massachusetts for the summer. Mrs. Ballard, defying her rheumatism, went with the Judge to a Woman's Suffrage Convention. Housewives who stayed at home were making jam and jelly, putting up peas and beans for the winter. Miss Pinney was left alone in her decaying, unpainted, shrubs-and-peony-buried cottage. Anne and Sally had walked up there one afternoon to make the call their consciences demanded, but there had been no answer to their knock. Their eyes questioned each other as they slipped their cards under the door: should they be concerned or relieved? Relieved at their escape, or concerned lest Miss Pinney might be inside in a drugged stupor? Relief proved stronger: if she were ill, she could contrive to let someone know, surely, and they need not worry about her starving. Since she owned her house and the taxes on it must be infinitesimal, she could live without trouble on the twenty-five a month that her trustees would pay her. The two young women went down the overgrown brick path slowly at first, then with increased rapidity: with a question in their minds as they turned from the door, with eagerness to get away as they approached the gate, and with what amounted to a washing-of-the-hands as they closed it behind them. Neither of them really wanted to suffer vicariously, to try to put herself in Miss Pinney's place, to imagine what it would be like to live in her fogged world.

In the ordinary course of a day, no white person passed that way: the location of her cottage made it easy to forget Miss Pinney. The street beyond the top of the hill was an old part of the town: the first Covenanter settlers had lived there. Miss Pinney's mother had found the vacant cottage surrounded by the homes of Negroes so that its price was one she could pay, bought it, and worked her fingers to the bone, dressmaking for Waynesboro ladies, so that she and the child might be secure. The Reverend Mr. Pinney had been a circuit-riding Methodist preacher in the early days of the century; he had died young of the consumption consequent upon exposure to all kinds of weather. Once for a brief while he had been in Waynesboro with his wife, staying with various Methodists while he preached for them; Mrs. Pinney chose it for her widowhood: she had kept in touch with the friends she had made in the town; she settled down to sew for her living, and herself taught the young Agatha until she was prepared to attend one of the Methodist Female Seminaries where the way was made easy for the daughters of preachers, and she could earn her board and tuition by teaching classes of small children. Agatha had begun as pedagogue at the age of fifteen or sixteen; when the Lowreys had started the school in Waynesboro, they had given her the chance to teach the infant classes at their Female Seminary. That had all been a long, long while ago. Even before the Lowreys had gone, the cottage, so old that there was perhaps a log cabin under the clapboards, had become almost an outpost of the white town. Now, Miss Pinney had none but colored neighbors. It did not bother her: they were friendly; they might be curious about her behind their inscrutability, but she preferred being surrounded by people she did not know to being overlooked and spied upon by acquaintances. She never did discover how much those around her knew: how accurately they had placed her as to standing in the white community, nor did she learn how kind they were, how compassionate and ready to help if she needed help. She kept her iron gate closed and her front door locked.

Those first weeks after her school had been put to an end, Miss Pinney stayed home; she did not bother to answer her door when a rare visitor pulled the knob that set the bell inside to jangling: she gritted her teeth until it was silent again. She bought her few groceries from a tumble-down Negro store on a nearby corner, and occasionally got bread or crackers from Mr. Hoffmann when he came past with his cart. She could not have told anyone what it was like, living as she did, in a twilight world. From the moment when her schoolroom emptied for the last time, when she knew that in any real sense life for her was over, she had not tried very hard to brush the mists away, to see clearly the Waynesboro that had now done with her.

On that last afternoon of school when everyone else had gone, Mrs. Deming had waited to help her.

"Can I be of any further assistance, Miss Pinney? The General and I should be pleased to drive you home."

The old lady had turned to face her, brushing vaguely at her forehead as though she had walked through cobwebs.

"Dear Louisa! Mrs. Deming! I can't thank you adequately for what you have done. I understand—all the ladies—but your idea, I am sure. But no, if you will allow me, I shall sit here quietly till I have collected myself a little, and then I must pack up." She indicated the pictures about the wall, the globe, the books and papers on the window sills.

"Dear Miss Pinney, I know that this has been a very tiring day. Let me send our stable boy up in the morning to move all this for you."

"So kind," Miss Pinney murmured, shifting in agony on her hard chair. "So very thoughtful. I'll just get them together before I go, so that he can pick them up. I'll leave the key with the Seminary janitor and your boy can get it from him. He is honest? And careful?"

Mrs. Deming reassured her and took her leave. Miss Pinney, alone at the end of an infinitely long afternoon, pulled a gray-grimed handkerchief from her reticule, dabbed at her eyes once more threatening to overflow. Then she took from her desk drawer a tall bottle and a spoon. It was only after the pain began to ease and her drawn nerves to relax that she touched the purse on the table before her. "So kind of the ladies," she murmured to herself. "What was it Louisa had said? A similar sum every month as long as you live." A pension, like the soldiers and the superannuated preachers. She could pay her bills: pay Mr. Thirkield, who had begun to be reluctant to fill her medicine bottle. She forgot that a moment before she had felt herself facing a death-in-life because her work was ended and she would have nothing to keep her going. Now she thought: never to have to teach again or to handle unruly children, never again to be forced to struggle out of her bed in the morning, beaten down by pain, never to need to hide to keep her world from knowing how she could not endure to go from hour to hour without something to relieve her agony.

She opened the purse. In it, wrapped in tissue, were five five-dollar gold pieces. Gold pieces! She had not seen any since before the war. She laid them in a row on the desk and touched them, one after another, with a trembling forefinger. But five gold pieces was only twenty-five dollars. A cold air touched the back of her neck, slipped down her spine. On twenty-five dollars how often could she have the comforting medicine bottle refilled? Of course the ladies did not realize: such a very expensive medicine, but beyond price. Beyond price because the pain went and old age was forgotten and the drowsy peace that lasted for a timeless while was as blessed as any of childhood's bright-colored dreams.

Before the month was out, in spite of the little she spent for food, Miss Pinney had used the gold pieces. When the laudanum bottle was empty, she had nothing left with which to pay for having it refilled. There was but one thing to do: ask Mr. Thirkield to oblige her again as he had done before. Or she could hand him the bottle, and when it had been filled, just say, "Put it on my account, please"; she knew the ritual: she had heard other ladies use it many times. She tidied herself, after a fashion, combed her hair, put on her most presentable summer frock and her bonnet, and took her father's cane, with its curved handle, from the umbrella rack by the door. So fortunate it had been left there all these years: she could not have walked downtown without it, now that her limb was likely to give way beneath her.

In Thirkield's drugstore she put on as assured a manner as she could assume. She brushed away the clerks and asked for Mr. Thirkield. To him she said, "I assume that my credit is good, since I am no longer in arrears. Could you let me—" She held the empty bottle in front of him.

He began shaking his head before she had finished. Her voice faltered; she let the question hang incompleted between them.

"'Fraid not, Miss Pinney." His manner was respectful, grave. He had suffered on Miss Pinney's account: Waynesboro ladies—his wife, even—could not see why he had not known, especially since Billy had been in her school. "No more credit to anyone. Cash business only. It's a new rule. I was getting in too deep." He hoped she would never learn it was a rule for her only. "Besides, the doctors have been after me to sell laudanum on prescription only, and I have agreed."

"But I did have a prescription once. Isn't it in your book?"

He shook his head. "Outdated. You must get a new one, or ask your doctor to give you a bottle himself. He most likely keeps some on hand. That, or come back with a new prescription and the money."

Miss Pinney staggered a little before she got a firm grasp on her cane. She stared at Mr. Thirkield. She had never been so humiliated in public before. But there was no one to hear her shame except a cluster of young people in the front of the store, and they were too fascinated by Mr. Thirkield's new soda fountain to be paying any attention to her. She crept past them, out the door, and down the street the few yards to the bank on the corner. There she asked to see Mr. Cochran. In his office, sitting in the chair beside his desk, she felt a little better. She had known Charles Cochran all his life. Although considerably younger than she, still he must be feeling age creeping up on him; he should understand her need better than had the younger Mr. Thirkield. She asked him if he would advance her a small amount of the principal from which she was being paid, a pension each month.

"You see," she explained, "I had some accumulated bills to pay. I couldn't make the twenty-five dollars last for the month. But next month—"

Like Mr. Thirkield, he began to shake his head before she had finished, but she persisted. "I am confident that I shall never live to use it all. I am getting on, you know."

He was kind to her, reassuring, almost jovial, insofar as such a precise sort of man could be jovial. That he made the attempt was perhaps the measure of his embarrassment.

"You may outlive us all, Miss Pinney. You know you little hardworking women have wonderful staying power. I am very sorry, but I am sure you will understand: Mr. Voorhees and I are only trustees of the fund placed in our hands to see that it isn't lost or stolen. We can only follow instructions as to how it is used. If we betrayed out trust, Mr. Gardiner might hail us into court." Struck by her crushed look, he added, "It isn't long, you know, until the first of the month. I am sure your grocer would give you credit. Shall I speak to Mr. Klein on your behalf?"

She shook her head. She was all at sea. Who was Mr. Klein? So many new people. "Thank you for your kindness. I misunderstood, I fear. I thought the money was mine."

"And so it is. But in trust, so that no one can take advantage—get it away. And Mr. Voorhees and I must abide by the terms of the trust."

Miss Pinney managed to rise, her hands climbing the cane, which was taller than she was sitting down. Mr. Cochran bowed her out of his office, the queer, limping, shabby, unclean little woman. He went himself to the other door of his office and through it, to stand behind the teller at his grille, to see that she got out of the heavy door safely.

"Sam!" He leaned over the teller's shoulder to call to the colored man sweeping in a hit-or-miss fashion around the entrance. "Open the door for Miss Pinney!" Then he said, almost as loudly, to Henry Voorhees at the cashier's window on his right, "Pour soul! They're keeping her short purposely, hoping to get her off the opium."

Miss Pinney was not deaf, and when her nerves were screwed as tight as they were that afternoon, her hearing was abnormally acute. She caught the word "opium," it echoed and reechoed through her head, like a ball bounding back and forth in an empty room. *Opium!* So that was what they thought! And it was only laudanum, prescribed by her doctor. Maybe if she told them that? But it might be she took too much—some people did—hadn't they said Dr. Alexander?—But it was a perfectly *respectable* medicine, and what else was there to stop the pain? She had heard "keeping her short," too. How could they be so cruel? She would go see Douglas Gardiner. She had somehow got the impression that he was ultimately responsible. She had taught Douglas not so very long ago before he and Sheldon Edwards had exchanged petticoats for pantaloons, at her infant school for the Reverend Mr. McMillan's Select Establishment for the Sons of Gentlemen. What, she wondered, had become of Mr. McMillan, long since departed from Waynesboro? He would be old, too, or dead—safely dead. She would go see Douglas Gardiner. If she could only talk as well as she could think: words came to her easily when she was thinking, like "petticoats for pantaloons." She stumbled from the curb to the dust of Chillicothe Street without noticing the big horses thundering down upon her in front of the Court House, hauling the tank wagon of coal oil from which house-to-house sales were still made, for lighting the houses of Waynesboro. She had to wait in the middle of the street for them to pass, in the dust, beside horse droppings that sparrows were pecking at. She noticed as the wagon went jolting by that the spigot was not turned tight, and coal oil dripped, making black curled-up circles in the dust and assailing the nostrils with its sharp smell. Coal oil, she remembered, was something else she needed, but to a lesser degree: after all, it was light until her bedtime. She got over the street, finally, and up on the Court House curb. The bricks of the path were uneven, and she had trouble with her cane and her stumbling feet, but her mind went back to "petticoats and pantaloons." "'You minded what I said when you were in petticoats,'" I shall tell him.

She reached Wood Street, crossed, found the narrow stairs that led to library and offices, including that of Ballard, Gardiner, and Merrill, and pulled herself up them, her cane hooked over her shoulder, using both hands on the firm rails bracketed to the walls, laboriously lifting her good leg and dragging the bad one up after it. The pain was very bad now after all the walking she had done; her heart thumped, her knees threatened to give way, she trembled all over, and a nerve over her cheekbone twitched as rapidly as her heart beat beneath her ribs. And nothing would ease the pain but her medicine.

In the lawyers' office she grasped the rail and leaned against it to stop her shaking. She was surprised when a woman rose from behind a desk and came toward her. A lawyer's office—no place for a woman.

"Good morning, Miss Pinney. Would you like to see Papa about something?"

"Oh, Eliza! Good morning. I had forgotten you would be here. No, it is Douglas I came to see. If you would be kind enough to tell him."

"Douglas is in his office in the Court House today. He's prosecuting attorney, you know."

"Prosecuting—no, I didn't know. Or I'd forgotten."

"You could try over there. He might be free."

"Oh, no. No. I don't want the prosecuting attorney. It was just about my money. I thought maybe I could get a little in advance, out of the principal. I seem to be running a little short this month." She attempted a rueful laugh, the sort of laugh that would be natural to a person who had been just a bit careless with a large allowance.

"But Mr. Gardiner has nothing to do with that. Mr. Cochran and Mr. Voorhees are the trustees, I believe. I suggest that you see one of them."

Miss Pinney fumbled for her grimy handkerchief and wiped her damp nose, her twitching face. "Yes—well—Eliza—thank you."

She got outside the door, but could go no farther. She leaned against the wall, one bony hand clinging to the door frame: she would rest for a moment, just long enough to get down those stairs. And standing so, for the second time that morning she overheard words not intended for her ears. From an inner office there was the rumble of a masculine voice: Judge Ballard, presumably, speaking to Eliza. Eliza said, "Miss Pinney. She wants an advance on her monthly pension. For some reason she had the idea that Douglas could arrange it for her. She seems to think there is a vast principal lying in the bank in her name."

The remote voice spoke again, and Eliza replied. "But you know they collected just enough to keep her going for a year. If she lives that long, they will have to take up another collection. Silly. I said so at the time, and I say it again. Silly, and cruel, too. I knew how it would be. They're not letting her have enough to buy the laudanum that might keep her comfortable until it kills her, and without it she's falling to pieces."

When Miss Pinney once more became aware of her surroundings, she found herself climbing Market Street hill, without the least idea how she had got there. And when she looked up the street, the Cochrans' iron fence at her hand, the new brick house opposite, it was all as strange to her, as alien, as if distorted in a nightmare. "What am I doing here?" she thought. "This is not where I belong. How did I come to be here, now, like this?" Even when she came to the Seminary and out of long habit put her hand on the gate, it did not look to her like anywhere she had ever been. Past the Seminary, almost home, all thoughts went whirling away; she could only concentrate on putting one foot in front of the other foot without falling. Not far from her home she was spoken to by a little colored boy. Unseeing, she had almost walked into him where he was spinning a top on the hard-packed clay of the path.

"Pleas'm, a' yo' all right? Want me to he'p yo' home?"

She looked at him, blear-eyed, bewildered. "Thank you. I fear I wasn't watching where I was going. I am quite all right—just a trifle lame."

The little boy stared. "Yes'm. Ah thought yo's blind."

She staggered on from that encounter, walking as straight and as firmly as she could, trying not to waver from side to side of the path. She knew the child was watching her retreating back. Did he think she was falling to pieces? Collect the pieces—collection—another collection another year—Like mite boxes for the missionaries. Drop a penny in the box for poor old Agatha Pinney. The ladies had been so careful of her feelings, making her believe a pension was no more than her due. But Eliza—Her nose was running again, and tears streamed down her cheeks, but she had reached her own fence corner and was groping her way along the pickets toward her gate. She had always been ready to believe people, even Louisa Tucker, when she told her how much they had appreciated her. And they were all sneering behind her back, like Eliza: "Thinks she has a vast principal, when really we're passing the collection box." If only the Lowreys hadn't gone—Gone? Gone somewhere? Dead? At the gate she said, quite loud, "Mrs. Lowrey! Mrs. Lowrey!" as if she were calling someone.

The little colored boy, who had followed her, his bare feet padding silently on the path, looked toward the cottage. But whoever she was calling never came. The lame old lady got the gate open, and staggered up the walk to the door between the piney-bushes. He watched until she was safe inside, then he went back to his top.

He was the last person to see Miss Pinney alive. He was one of the cluster of Negroes gathered at her gate the next morning when the coroner and the prosecutor and the doctor came: his elders pushed him forward to tell his story. The doctor gave him a penny, but no one said anything but "All right, Sonny, you clear off now."

That was in the middle of the morning. A few minutes earlier, Johnny Gordon, white-faced and keyed-up, had dashed into the house calling his mother.

"Mom! Oh, Mamma!" He found her in the kitchen, stared at her a second, gasping, then blurted out, "Miss Pinney's dead!"

"Miss Pinney! Oh, Johnny! How could she be?"

"They came for Papa. That's what they said. I was there."

Anne backed to the rocker by the window, dropped into it, fingers over her mouth. Binny, who had been playing with her dolls outside the kitchen porch, came to the door to see what had happened. Anne said, "You play outside, Binny. It isn't dinnertime yet." She drew Johnny to her. She could feel his trembling; for his sake she must not appear as sick at heart as she felt.

"What was it, Johnny? Heart attack? After all, she was an old lady. But why did they come for Papa? He wasn't her doctor."

"Mr. Crawford came." Mr. Crawford was the coroner and undertaker. "They couldn't find her own doctor. All Mr. Crawford knew was that some colored woman found her. Do you s'pose she took too much?"

"'Took too much'?"

"Too much dope. Drug fiends do sometimes, don't they?"

"Johnny!" She held him off from her to look at him. Perhaps he was not shocked or frightened, but just excited at having a tale of calamity to tell. As the best of us almost always are, she thought, unless the calamity is ours. "Don't talk so. You don't know what you are talking about."

"But they do, don't they?"

"Don't be so ghoulish." There was no doubt about it. Johnny was actually finding a kind of relish in this, and not less because of the horror he had at first felt.

"But, Mamma, I've got to know about things like that if I'm going to be a doctor."

"That's a long way off. Now you're just—Johnny, you must never, never say things like that, or think them, about anyone. Even if they should be true. Doctors don't."

Johnny dropped his air of reasonableness and looked crestfallen. When his mother said nothing more, he turned, slipped out through the screen door, and went back toward his father's office.

Martha, from the stove where she was cooking the cherries for the winter's pies, said, "He's too little. He di'n ought to know 'bout that po' soul."

"How much do you know, Martha? Do you know her neighbors?"

"Yes'm. They be good to he' ef'n she let 'um. But she keep to he'se'f. Sometimes they leave a bakin' on he' steps. Light bread o' biscuits o' a piece a cake. They know how much she don' eat, 'cause she trade fo' he' groceries at Elmo's the' on the co'ne'. They do the' bes' to keep he' f'om sta'vin."

"I'm sure they do—did. They've been better than those of us who have been her friends. But somehow, you don't realize—"

"No'm. Gotta live next do' to see what gwun on."

Anne rose. "If we're late, keep lunch hot, will you? I expect the doctor will be held up." She followed Johnny out the porch door. "And keep an eye on Binny, will you? No, Binny, you stay with Martha. I'm just going over to Papa's office."

With any luck she would find the office empty: a patient who had come in would not wait when he found the doctor called out on an emergency. She found Johnny folding bandages and piling them up. No one else came in before his father appeared. The boy kept his head bent over his work and let his mother ask the questions.

"Is it true, John? Miss Pinney is dead?"

"Yes, it's true. Johnny, haven't you finished those bandages?"

"Tell us," Anne insisted. "Johnny must hear. I'm sure he has the wrong idea."

"Her next door neighbor went in to see if she was all right. Seems she always kept an eye out for Miss Pinney's morning walk out-back; if she saw her, she knew she was still on her feet. But this morning she didn't see her."

"Was it laudanum?" Anne held her breath.

"No. Positively not. Johnny, you can tell all your beastly chums who have been calling her 'dope fiend' that she did not die of an overdose of laudanum. It was easy to tell: you know opium leaves its mark."

"What mark?"

"Look it up." He nodded toward the bookcase crammed with heavy volumes.

"What did she die of, then?"

"Heart failure. She had gone into a closet for something, and the door jammed shut behind her. I suppose she was frightened when she couldn't get out, and if she couldn't get her breath—she was old and sick; her heart failed. I don't think any of us ought to wish that she had gone on living, when she suffered so much. Let's leave it at that, and say no more about it."

Anne stared at him blindly, through eyes blurred with tears, then turned and went out, across the alley between the two back gates and up the path to the house. John, in the office, said, "I'm going along home with your mother now. She's known Miss Pinney all her life, and she feels bad about this. I want you to stay here and finish those bandages. We'll wait dinner for you."

He followed Anne into the sitting room. Binny was still with Martha.

"That isn't all, is it?"

"M'ph," he hesitated. "No, edited for children. But that's the story we'll stick to, if possible. The darky next door knew. When she didn't see Miss Pinney go to the outhouse, she pulled some vegetables for an excuse, and went to see if she was sick. She couldn't find Miss Pinney, but the closet door was fast shut. Then she sent a boy for Doug Gardiner."

"But why?"

"She works at the Gardiners' sometimes when they need extra help, knew Doug was connected with the law somehow or other, and preferred him to the police, I suppose. She sent word she was sure Miss Pinney was dead, so Doug got hold of Crawford, and Crawford got hold of me."

"But why the closet? I mean, if Miss Pinney was in there, she mightn't be dead."

"Miss Pinney had gone into that closet with a lighted candle, locked herself in, and tried to burn the house and do away with herself by setting fire to the clothes hanging there. It was the stink of burned wool and wood that led the darky to the closet. The edges of the door were charred, but it wouldn't open. We had to chop the lock free."

Anne looked at him, white-faced. She said nothing.

"Don't look like that, Anne. Of course no one in her right mind would try such a thing. But the fire hadn't burned very much, or very long—just smothered out, no air—nothing very inflammable in there. Fortunately there wasn't a drop of coal oil in the house. We looked, to explain the candle. She was hardly burned at all, only her clothes, a little. She died of heart failure—probably unconscious before the fire went out."

"You mean she did it on purpose? Suicide?" Anne whispered the word, her eyes blank with horror. "But couldn't it have been an accident?"

"They key was on the inside of the closet door."

"But John—to deliberately light a fire—Oh, no, I don't believe it. Surely she would just have taken an overdose of laudanum. Why—"

"Two whys. There wasn't any laudanum in the house. We checked with Thirkield. He said she was in for some yesterday and he wouldn't let her have it. And if the house had caught on fire, it would have been an accident—no one would have known. Some last remnant of pride."

"But why? Why at all, I mean? Wasn't she making out with what we collected for her?"

"The laudanum, Anne. She had none, and she couldn't go on without it. She'd even tried to get an advance from Cochran the day before. Doug knew about that. The money she was getting just wasn't enough to keep her supplied."

"I know—that was Mrs. Deming's idea: break her of the habit. I wouldn't have. It was cruel." She dropped her voice to a whisper. "I remember Papa too well. I know how it is."

John did not like the stricken look on her face. He drew her to him and sat down with her on the couch by the window; with his arm around her, he brought her head to his shoulder and laid his cheek on her bright brown hair.

"Believe me, Anne, it is better so."

"No," she said, rebelliously. "She could have come to any of us."

"After what you had already done for her, come and admit her desperate necessity? Look, Anne: respect and admire her a little, can't you? Poor, old, sick, half-crazed, degraded by drug-taking—yet there was a point beyond which life could not beat her down. She had pride and courage."

Anne was trembling in his arms. He was sure that she was not listening: she was intent on her own line of thought. "It isn't always the deaths people die that are heartbreaking. It's the lives they have lived," she said.

"Their deaths are often not heartbreaking at all. The longer I live, the more I respect that poor devil, man. Life—just the day-by-day living of it, I mean—has cost him everything, you think: everything of character he ever had in him; then at the end you see it hasn't, after all. He still has courage left to face death—even welcome it—to stand up to the dark."

"John—"

"Yes, I know. You think it isn't to be the dark, at the end. Well, if there is a heaven, Miss Pinney will be there. She earned it."

"But she was so good a Christian, such a Methodist. She couldn't have thought that was the way to Heaven."

"She was past being able to think. One of the things that life had cost her. I suppose she acted on impulse: confused but resolute." He kept one arm around her, but with his other hand took both hers and held them in her lap. "Listen, Anne. I am a better Presbyterian than you, backslider that I am. The measure of a man's life is not the happiness he has known; at the end there should not be a balancing of happiness and sorrow, but an estimate of how well one's life has been used. Miss Pinney used her small powers to the fullest."

"And she will be judged accordingly? I suppose so, but do you think that when she—when anyone—faces the end, he remembers how useful he has been?"

"Most often he is not thinking back over his life at all. He is concentrated on drawing his next breath. But even if you were right, who can measure the happiness in a man's life? Everyone is born to sorrow as the sparks fly upward: isn't that in the Bible somewhere? Grief, pain, sorrow, those are big things—the world can see them, weigh them. Shame, even, since we are all human, but that the world does not always see." John sighed. "Happiness is small things. Love, of course, is not a small thing—but it is the small ways in which love expresses itself that make in the end for happiness, not the overwhelming passion. And some go through life happily without love—our kind of love. I mean happiness can be just sunlight on a treetop, a field of green wheat in the spring, a look in someone's eyes, a smile—even so slight a thing as a blue sky and a spring wind. Who can add up such moments in a man's lifetime? Not even the dying man himself; he will have forgotten most of them."

Anne sat without moving in the circle of John's arms, only turning her hands to grasp his. It was unlike the naturally inarticulate John to speak as he had done: he had never revealed so fully his innermost thoughts before, and probably would never do so again. She did not want to spoil the moment. But he had not touched, really, the cause of her grief.

"It was all our fault," she said finally. "If we hadn't interfered."

"But you just said you weren't on the committee."

"I wasn't, no. But I helped—gave some money."

John freed his hand from her clasp, touched her cheek, felt the tears.

"Don't, Anne. You are not to blame yourself. Or the others, for that matter. What did you do that you wish undone? Would you have let the children go on as they had been doing in her school? Or other people's children? Could you have taken them out without thinking of what was to become of her? We went over all this, more than once."

"I know. We acted for the best. People almost always do, and so often it turns out all wrong. Will it be in the paper? Must the children know?"

"Doug and I went to see Bonner. His boy and girl were in her school, too, so for once he agreed to soft-pedal the thing. The coroner will say 'death by misadventure' and so will the *Torchlight*. But I expect the children will hear: that neighbor woman had a pretty good idea. But it won't seem important to them for long: Miss Pinney was so old, in their eyes, and what happens to the old just isn't important to children."

He shifted her head and wiped her eyes. She went to wash her face, and then they met again in the dining room; Martha called the children in from the back porch, and put lunch on the table.

Johnny eyed them carefully as he slipped into his chair and took his napkin from its ring.

"Martha says she don't believe it, but Lonzo told me Miss Pinney killed herself."

"How could Lonzo know? He hasn't been out of the stable yard all morning."

"Is it true?"

"Johnny, no one can possibly know why Miss Pinney went into that closet with a lighted candle in her hand. Except that she had no coal oil, so she couldn't have carried a lamp."

"And don't," his mother broke in, a catch in her voice, "don't ever believe anyone has killed himself intentionally, not if it could possibly have been an accident."

"But Mamma, people do, don't they, if they're sick or crazy or something?"

"At least give them the benefit of the doubt. Don't just jump to the conclusion that they have been so cowardly."

"Cowardly?" Johnny shivered exaggeratedly. "I'd be scared."

"Cowardly because we should live out our lives, as God intended, and take what comes." Maybe not exactly 'cowardly'; it would take courage of a sort. But it cancels everything out, it is a denial of life—of all a lifetime held that was good: all the faith, all the love, every happy moment." Anne might almost have been talking to herself: her family and her servant listened in dumb astonishment to the usually self-contained woman. "It's as if there weren't memories enough—as if nothing in life had been enough—to balance a bad moment. But surely, if you trust God, you can believe the bad moments pass, and the good memories are worth enough."

Johnny, who had never heard his mother talk so—almost like a preacher—hung his head in embarrassment. His father looked at her steadily, and was surprised, when he caught her eye, to see in it, besides rejection of his judgment, a quick and quickly veiled look of fear. Her fingers were white, so hard did they grip the table edge, wrinkling the tablecloth. "That old terror," he thought, "for me. But that was years ago."

"Tell your friends," he said to Johnny, with all his authority as parent and physician, "that I was called in to give the medical opinion. Miss Pinney died of heart failure, induced by an accident. Now let's hear no more about it, at the dinner table, especially. And you quit suffering," he said to his wife, "over other people's lives. Some live to be old and alone and sick, and they do the best they can. That's all anyone can do."

Miss Pinney was buried two days later, from the Methodist church. The congregation was there in mass; the ladies of the Club who were at home dutifully attended. A cluster of colored women slipped into the back pews. Some mothers of Miss Pinney's pupils brought them to the funeral, but most, like Anne, left them at home, preferring that they forget the manner of their teacher's going.

Forgetting came easily to them all. The high point of the summer, the Fourth of July, was upon them; boys and girls were very patriotic and very military, drilling in the home streets: artillery drill, taught them by Captain Bodien, when they were not making mischief with torpedoes and cannon crackers.

The Fourth past, the summer quietened, became even more somnolent. Nothing much happened in the way of births, deaths, and marriages, except that Christina Voorhees bore a son, named Blair for her father. In August, when the summer was hottest, there were Sunday school picnics, between thunderstorms and lawn fetes and the County Fair. The vacation that had seemed so endless at its beginning slipped away through the children's fingers; the public school opened the first week of September. Miss Pinney's pupils were examined and sorted out—even Julia Deming, who had somehow prevailed upon her parents to permit her to attend. Johnny, Elsa, and Billy Thirkield, and Julia, who was a year younger, went into the fifth grade. That was not so great a humiliation to the others as having Charlotte Bonner put into the sixth grade with Ariana McCune, Sophie Klein, and Rudy Lichtenstein.

The public school teachers congratulated themselves that Miss Pinney's pupils were scattered among them; they were at first a disruptive influence. But under firm hands, they settled down, as did other new pupils: children of a few recent German immigrants, and the previously tamed returning students. Peace was established and maintained in the classroom. Those few children whose mothers were members of the Woman's Club had troubles of their own on their minds. The day of the "Children's Hour" on the Club program was beginning to loom close; they had been warned and were being driven to prepare.

The first Club meeting of the fall was a Memorial meeting for Miss Pinney. Mrs. Deming read an obituary; Mrs. Sheldon Edwards read a brief tribute to Miss Pinney as a teacher, written by Professor Lowrey for the occasion and sent to Kitty; Mrs. Ballard spoke briefly of her as a lifelong friend and fellow church member. Some of the ladies felt sad; some assumed sadness, and would not have admitted that the occasion was in fact perfunctory rather than mournful. And Sally Rausch, on the way home, said to Anne that she supposed it wasn't decent, but for once she was not going to let the R.P. women get ahead of her: if they wanted theological women in the Club, very well, but this time it was going to be a Baptist for a change: she had slipped Mrs. Ballard a name to be proposed for membership in Miss Pinney's place. "If they like ministers' wives so very much, they can take in Mrs. Evans."

"What's she like, Sally? The boys have been around the house a few times. Butter wouldn't melt in their mouths. But I believe one of them—Gilbert, the nephew?—had a fight with Johnny first-off. He came home with a bloody shirt one day."

"Gilbert had a black eye. It seems he called Elsa 'Shaney,' and she was going to let him. Elsa rather adopted them at first—there are so few Baptists. But I believe Gilbert calls her 'Elsa' now. Surely you wouldn't hold a bloody shirt against Mrs. Evans?"

"Take up a children's squabble? Of course not. Ministers' children are proverbial, anyway. What's she like?"

"Oh, rather like a chickadee—very Welsh, small and quick and dark. Black hair slicked straight back, a widow's peak. Tilts her head to one side when she talks. Quakerish in dress. But under that meek air, there's lots of fire. She's intelligent; I think well-educated. Her two boys look like her, but Gilbert—Mr. Evans' dead brother's boy—is different: bigger, slower, blonder, and I should think milder-tempered, in spite of the fight. I wonder if we can't get them in the Children's Hour? We had better be preparing for that."

"Aren't you going a bit fast? She isn't a member yet."

"But you know she will be. Why not?"

Why not, indeed? Mrs. Ballard presented her name at the next meeting, and two weeks from that date it was voted on, a unanimously favorable vote. But there was not time for the Evans boys to learn "pieces" for the Children's Hour: the mid-November meeting was the dedicated day, and it was upon them.

Proud and occasionally stern mothers and a scrupulous music teacher worked hard for the occasion, although even for them there were surprises in store. The meeting was at the Cochran house because of the double drawing room, which could so easily be divided into stage and auditorium by the use of screens. Thomasina, as nervous as any of the children, was in charge; she was no disciplinarian, but the small children, who were to begin the program, and the older ones who were to come in after school, were all equally impressed with the importance of the occasion. Even those who had been in the schoolhouse all afternoon were moderately clean and moderately tidy. No one would ever have guessed that there had been trouble with Binny Gordon: When Anne had first told her what was expected of her, her response had been a flat "no," followed by weeping; John unfortunately had been home that evening, and had called her "Little Rain-in-the-Face," as he sometimes did when he was disturbed by her exaggerated emotional responses. Anne had looked him silent, then set about persuading the child. "You can learn 'The Children's Hour' for the Club, Binny. You wouldn't want me to be the only mother to have to say, 'My little girl couldn't do it.' "

"I can. I just don't want to."

"Oh, Binny! Johnny doesn't mind."

"The heck I don't. Oh, well," in response to his mother's pleading look, "I already know 'Sheridan's Ride,' and it doesn't take a minute to say it."

"Not 'The Children's Hour.' It's too long. And anyway, it's silly." Binny said this with a resentful look at her father, through the tears still on her lashes. "Could I say the one about the traveler who never came back?"

This stated preference left them all blank until Johnny remembered: he had read it to her out of his reader and she had wanted to know what had happened to the traveler. He found his book and skimmed through it until he found the page. "It's called 'The Tide Rises, the Tide Falls.' "

"But why, Binny?"

"It's such a sad poem, and so *mysterious*."

Such a word coming from a five-year-old was determinant: Anne let her have her way.

Now she was to be first on the program. "Best let her get it over with," Anne had said to Thomasina, "before the older children come in."

With her short dark curls, her wild black eyes—wild at least in such a situation—small for her age, she was a child adults were fond of calling "so original." Now, having located her mother, she smiled suddenly, and then bowed, tossing her curls. Her voice was grave and soft; she did not hurry through the sad, "mysterious" poem, "The tide rises, the tide falls. The twilight darkens, the curlew calls." She lost herself in it: in the music and the sorrow, and her eyes widened and darkened as she came to the melancholy close, "but nevermore returns the traveler to the shore. The tide rises, the tide falls." When she fell silent, she stood a minute, then the spatter of applause came, she smiled as one recalled to herself, curtsied, and ignoring the beckoning finger of Cassie, waiting in the hall, went to sit squeezed in the chair with her mother because, as she said quite audibly, she wanted to hear the program.

Charles and Ernest Rausch, looking like scrubbed blond cherubs, stood by the piano, hands clasped behind their backs, and sang *Der Erlkönig* to Elsa's accompaniment. The little boys' voices were sweet and true; like all the Rausches music came to them as naturally as breathing. They sang an encore, beamed at their audience, and disappeared into the hall where Cassie was waiting for them.

When they had gone, Elsa began to play. Thomasina had been prepared to keep her at the piano until the other children came in. The reluctant ones had been bribed by the promise of refreshments, and they were all, actually, willing enough to show off, even though their knees might quake. Even Rachel Tobias, the McKinneys' little colored girl, showed up promptly. Mrs. McKinney had taken the precaution of asking Thomasina if Rachel were supposed to take part; Thomasina had said "Yes, certainly," with emphasis but some hidden misgivings. If anyone objected to hearing Rachel sing, or to seeing her with the other children on terms of equality, they could stay home. No one did, not even the Gardiners. The children knew Rachel and accepted her without a second thought; if anyone was scandalized, it was Cassie.

The boys and girls came in a solid group, Rachel, whose school was closer than the white school, waited at the gate for the others. They erupted all together into the front hall, and were brought to a stop and a silence by a sound of the piano. No one except Thomasina even noticed the disturbance. When Elsa played the piano, people listened: she performed with strength, control, authority and feeling the piano selection Mr. Travers had suggested and had helped her with. She displayed a mastery, Thomasina thought half regretfully, half with ungrudging admiration, that none of Samuel's other pupils could equal: he was right, she thought, as he always was about music and musicians. She played better than Ariana, who was a year older; but then, Elsa had a musical background, and perhaps the ladies would be deceived: Ariana's playing was more tempestuous, more spectacular. Thomasina did not risk letting her play directly after Elsa. Johnny followed, instead: as unselfconscious as a bird in a tree: he came to the middle of the stage, grinning, and launched forthwith into "Sheridan's Ride" with a good deal of free play of hands and dramatic thundering, "And Sheridan fifteen miles away." He did not linger when he bowed but escaped to the hall, scuffling a little with Julia Deming as she tried to pass him, then slipped out of sight with a crow of laughter, and into Cassie's capable hands, Anne hoped.

Julia, fair-skinned and delicate, her ash-gold hair on her shoulders, in a full skirted white frock with blue ribbons, recited "The Lady of Shalott," the whole of it, without hesitation, in a voice clear, cool, and sweet. After her, a contrast that could not have been stronger, came Rachel Tobias, black like ebony, visibly frightened, showing the whites of her eyes like a skittery horse, but ready to lift her voice, warm and husky, and sing without so much as a tuning fork to help, "Go Down, Moses" and "Swing Low, Sweet Chariot." The ladies applauded until she had to sing again: Thomasina summoned her back from the safety of the hall. Mrs. McKinney, smiling her double-chinned smile, said, "'Old Black Joe,' Rachel," and the child might have had to go all through Stephen Foster had not Thomasina intervened. "You are asking too much of her," she said, "and there are others to be heard from." Rachel smiled at her gratefully, and slipped out.

The Beattie boys followed her on the "stage": they had prepared a dramatic scene for the ladies. At a loss themselves, they had asked their mother for suggestions, and she had said, "Why not part of 'Julius Caesar'? You've been studying it, haven't you?" Like most active church women, she had little time for extras at home, and she had left them to their own devices. What they had chosen to do was as surprising and as funny to her as to the other ladies. The two boys, togaed in sheets that she hoped were not her best ones, helmeted in stewpans whose handles angled out and down between their shoulder blades, burlesqued the quarrel scene between Brutus and Cassius on the eve of Philippi to such effect that most of their audience had recourse to handkerchiefs to wipe away the tears of laughter.

The startling performance of the afternoon was another dramatic exercise, planned by Ariana and participated in by all the McCune children. Ariana had begged Thomasina to allow them to do it. "Something from the Bible," she had said. "Papa will like that, and maybe he won't think about my playing the piano." Not even Thomasina knew what they were going to do. "It will be all right on the day," Ariana had said. "I'm helping them. It's a surprise."

Her father would have been as surprised as Thomasina was to be. Ariana had avoided future trouble by asking his permission to teach them Bible verses to say for the ladies of her mother's Club. He did not like to be reminded of the Club; he always felt Ariana's antagonism. She was as alien to him as a stranger, but he was pleased at any hint of religiosity from that quarter, and gave a willing permission, saying only, "One of the Psalms, I suppose? The little ones have many of them by heart." What she had in mind was not a Psalm. The story in the Bible that she most relished was the story of Jezebel and the dogs, and Ahab and the king—but she saw it would be impossible to dramatize: no wall, no dogs. She chose instead those chapters of Judges that told of the prophetess Deborah: as dramatized by her and enacted by the McCunes, they were broken up into a first scene, Deborah with Barak the son of Abinoam (Ruhamah and her oldest brother Matthew, costumed in what looked suspiciously like bedspreads, with a tea towel for Barak's headdress); a second scene, the tent of Heber the Kenite, and Jael his wife, and Sisera, coming to hide with them: Matthew as Sisera, and Mark as the husband Heber, hovering on the outskirts, and Ariana as Jael, welcoming Sisera, offering him "butter in a lordly dish," putting him to bed on the floor, and then bringing from behind the screen a croquet stake and mallet, flourishing them to make clear her intention, placing herself between the audience and Sisera on his pallet, and bringing down the mallet on the stake with such resounding thwacks that Sally wondered if her mother's carpet would be holed by Ariana's vigor. The ladies were stunned into motionless silence by the gleaming wild ferocity in her eye and the evident relish with which she wielded the mallet; for a moment they did not even applaud the conclusion of scene two. Scene three was the Song of Deborah, spoken by Ruhamah and Matthew in concert. Ariana had not been able to instill into Ruhamah any real dramatic feeling, althought the child had obediently memorized the thirty-one verses; Ariana would have liked to be Deborah as well as Jael; having to choose, she chose Jael, however much she would have enjoyed saying "the stars in their courses fought against Sisera." She was quite taken aback at the praise afterward lavished on Ruhamah just for having learned the verses; memorizing was nothing: they had been getting by heart chapters of the Bible since they could talk. But if the ladies had little to say of her acting of Jael, they lavished on her their praise of her musical number. Ariana's piano selection was the concluding number; she played with such verve that, as Thomasina had hoped, the fireworks concealed the imperfections. After she had finished, played an encore, and the applause had died away, it was quite clear that no more was to follow, and the formal meeting of the Woman's Club was adjourned. But the ladies stayed on for Sally's "social hour." The children, except for the Beattie boys, who had escaped, were collected and seated around the dining room table under supervision of Cassie. Rose passed tea and cakes to the ladies in the drawing room, where they buzzed and chattered; they called Ruhamah McCune a "phenomenon," and then turned to Ariana at last, and Thomasina could rejoice: Jael had made her uncomfortable, but they were not talking of that. "A musical prodigy." "If only her mother could have heard her." "She is a credit to you, Thomasina, and to Mr. Travers; we know how much trouble you have taken to develop her talent." Eliza Ballard, the only one of them all who felt any sympathy for the Jael-Ariana, and thought she understood her, listened sourly while Thomasina, flushed with pleasure, her kind blue eyes shining, beamed more happily over the praise than if Ariana had been her own. "All the children covered themselves with glory," she said, "but we do think Ariana extraordinarily gifted. And so little chance to make anything of her gift. But perhaps a way can be found."

Anne lingered, as she almost always did when the Club met with Sally, until all had gone, and the two of them could talk over the afternoon. Sally's comments were vigorous as always: "Ariana McCune! Thomasina, poor besotted creature, thinks she is both genius and angel. More like a faery changeling, not quite human. Imagine her putting that infant Ruhamah through her paces the way she did. And as for her 'gift'—she has a gift for the stage certainly. Did you see her face when she was putting the tent pin into Sisera?"

"I saw Christina's face: she was shocked white. Do you think she is going to see herself as a stumbling block, all that acting?"

Sally laughed. "Oh, Christina! I suppose she could. Anne, Elsa was good, wasn't she? Her father thinks she can be a real musician. But what difference does it make, beyond the fact that it gives us all pleasure? She wouldn't ever go on the concert stage, and will never need to teach, I hope. No, I was just wishing the Ballards had clearer insight so far as Ariana is concerned. They've set their hearts on her turning out to be a genius, but they are sure to be disappointed. That child has something bewitching about her and imagination enough for six, but it might be heartbreaking to let yourself become attached to her."

"I know. She's like quicksilver: no one will ever be able to put a finger on her. There won't be much comfort in doting on her. But she isn't the Ballards', after all. And her father won't let her escape him and his church." Then she broke off at a tangent. "The children did well, but you know, Sally, this afternoon left me feeling sad. How quickly the waters close over you when you've gone down! Most of those children—some of them anyway—were taught by Miss Pinney, and I listened specially and not one person spoke her name all afternoon."

"Are you still lamenting because no one grieves for that poor soul? One of your and two of my children, and Julia Deming, went to school to her. And for this program, you taught yours, and Teapot taught Julia, and Samuel Travers taught mine. Why should anyone have thought of Miss Pinney?"

"But she taught them to be teachable, at least. And they have some idea of manners. And she would so have loved to see them perform."

"Ten years ago she would have. Or five, maybe. But if she'd been here today, she'd have slept through it. I don't wish her alive again. That's always a mistake, Anne: life and the world move on."

"Perhaps." Then Anne smiled. "I must try to remember that I am a matron of thirty, too old to be sentimental. But just the same, I can't help being sorry that no one even thought of poor old Miss Pinney."

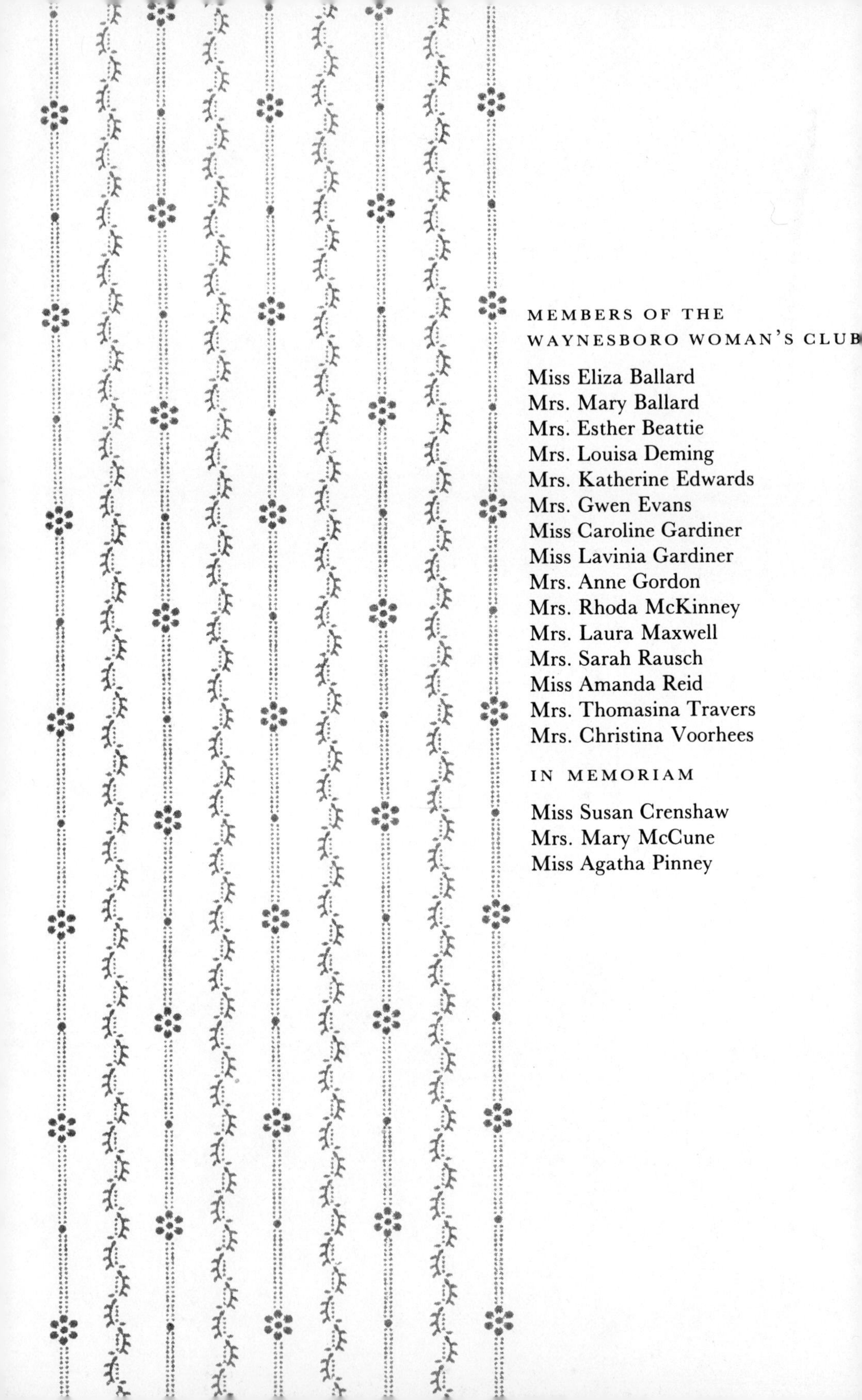

MEMBERS OF THE
WAYNESBORO WOMAN'S CLUB

Miss Eliza Ballard
Mrs. Mary Ballard
Mrs. Esther Beattie
Mrs. Louisa Deming
Mrs. Katherine Edwards
Mrs. Gwen Evans
Miss Caroline Gardiner
Miss Lavinia Gardiner
Mrs. Anne Gordon
Mrs. Rhoda McKinney
Mrs. Laura Maxwell
Mrs. Sarah Rausch
Miss Amanda Reid
Mrs. Thomasina Travers
Mrs. Christina Voorhees

IN MEMORIAM

Miss Susan Crenshaw
Mrs. Mary McCune
Miss Agatha Pinney

1880

"A wedding of interest to the ladies . . ."

On a Wednesday morning in January of 1880, Eliza Ballard and her father, on their way to the office, arrived rather earlier than usual at the Court House corner. It was an inclement day; sleet mixed with rain had filled the streets with icy puddles, and for once Judge Ballard had asked Johann to drive them uptown. Ordinarily they walked, Judge Ballard claiming that the exercise was beneficial, but on that morning he had a will case coming up, and he did not wish to be hurried. Eliza had been glad enough to get away from the house. The Club was to meet there that afternoon, and she had spent the previous evening helping to open up the drawing room. She would trust no other member of her family nor the family retainers, aging as they were, to climb a stepladder tall enough to untie and remove the bag that wrapped the chandelier. She had got that done, and had helped remove dust-sheets from sofas and chairs; the cleaning could be done this morning without her assistance. Since they never used the drawing room, nor opened it up except for meetings of various organizations, getting it swept, dusted, aired, and warmed was a real undertaking, one that she was pleased to be justified in leaving to Thomasina and Johann's wife, under her mother's rather casual supervision. She was cheerful enough as the old phaeton turned the corner of Wood Street and stopped to wait for a break between the knots of children crossing that street on their way down Market to the schoolhouse. And then, among them, she saw Ariana McCune.

Ariana, tall for her thirteen years and too thin, all hands and feet, so that her ankle bones seemed to knock each other at every step, was skipping along, heedless of the puddles and the ice, looking up at a boy striding beside her, a big boy, a hobbledehoy, who was talking fiercely, with wild gestures, and Ariana's face was lit up as from a light within. Eliza felt a sudden pang. Since the death of Mrs. McCune, Ariana was at the Ballards' weekly for her piano lessons, and intermittently, whenever she could escape her home chores, for practice on Samuel's piano. Quite often she stayed for a meal or at least a visit, and she was happy and contented there, or so at least Eliza had thought. Since Eliza was home so little in the daytime, she saw less of Ariana than did Thomasina, but felt, unconsciously perhaps, that she had a special claim on the child simply because, wordlessly and without any outward sign except the warmth of her welcome, she cared so much and, like Thomasina, had dreamed of a better future for her than an attachment to some ordinary male. With all her talents a career of some kind did not seem too much to hope for. The pang that had struck Eliza at the sight of Ariana's glowing face, a kind of jealousy that the child could be happy elsewhere than with them, deepened almost to horror when the boy turned his head and she saw that he was that bastard of Abby Mercer's. She allowed herself to use the word, fiercely, in her mind, and felt sicker for it. Ariana was too fine, too rare, to glow in that fashion at any boy, let alone the Mercer boy. And she was only thirteen. The Ballards had given a birthday party for her not too long ago, with cake and candles, and all her brothers and her sister Ruhamah there to help her celebrate.

Had Eliza but known it, Ariana was at the moment entranced less by Ben Mercer himself than by his declared intention of running away. In the spring or the summer, whenever the circus came to town, he was going with it; no more Waynesboro or strict, old-fashioned grandparents for him. He did not explain the circumstances of his life to Ariana: that his mother, having disgraced her parents, had run away; there were rumors that she had been seen in some city where no one knew her. His grandparents had accepted him as their responsibility, a burden taken on, he had been made to feel, because it was their duty, not because they felt any affection for him. They seemed only to care that he did not, like his mother, disgrace them; they were bringing him up as rigorously and as strictly as they had been indulgent with Abby. He did not know why they were so ironhard with him, but he did know that he was going to run away. This was the first time he had revealed this firm intention to anyone: he was showing off to Ariana his dauntless courage; he did not suspect that she would have liked to run with him, and that was why she listened with held breath and glowing face.

Eliza, seeing her so afire in that boy's company, was outraged and hurt that Ariana could come alive like that for anyone other than the Ballards. Her mind was in a turmoil as she followed her father up the stairs to the office; she stood in silence while he found the office key in his pocket and used it, followed him inside, took the mail from the basket under the slot in the door, and with it in her hand stood watching him collect the papers he wanted from his desk and thrust them into his briefcase. When he had gone, she sorted the mail, deposited it on the addressees' desks, and sat down at her own, all without a thought as to what she was doing. Eliza had once known Abby Mercer: the Mercers, like the Ballards, were Methodists, and Abby had been in the class with Thomasina at the Female College; now she tried to remember what she had heard at the time of Abby's disgrace. It was not much: even the most radical reforming mothers who were quite capable of discussing on a public platform The Evils of Prostitution shielded their young from any knowledge of a particular instance of feminine weakness, especially when someone known was involved.

Eliza, thinking back, remembered how scornful she had been of the flirtatious female students, making the most in the spring of '61, of the little time left them before all the boys went off to war: of smuggled notes, of girls slipping out of windows. But Abby's fall occurred much later, after the war and after the Ballard girls had finished their schooling. They did not see much of their Waynesboro schoolmates, but Eliza remembered the attack of asthma her sister had had when she first heard about Abby Mercer's disgrace: she had been literally sickened by it. Eliza had felt only contempt for Abby. Such a fool! But she had been present, she now remembered, at the church the morning the baby was baptized. By that time Abby had disappeared, leaving her son with his grandparents. There had been talk: like the dying Rachel, Abby had called him "Benoni"—"child of sorrow"—but at the baptismal font, his grandparents, like Jacob of old, had changed his name to a happier one: "Benjamin"—"fortunate." As it turned out, either would have served: he was never called anything but "Ben." That had been the year all the soldiers came home—'65? Then the boy must be fifteen: too old for Ariana to be listening to. Now, for the first time, Eliza wondered about the father's identity. There had been an arrangement of some kind: bastardy proceedings, settled out of court. Eliza lifted her head, her nostrils dilating as she drew a quick breath. Old Mr. Merrill had been the Mercers' lawyer in the paternity suit, she remembered that much. Merrill was dead now, but he had been a partner of her father's; the files containing his records had been kept in the office.

She rose, unlocked the safe, and took out her notebooks; on the desk she opened them, ready for the day's work, along with yesterday's mail, and the drafts of answers she was to put into shape and copy. If Doug Gardiner should come in before going to his office in the Court House, he would find her bent over them. Once they were arranged, she could hunt out the Mercer papers. She would not have admitted why she wanted to know who had fathered the boy: that she was curious or that it might give her a weapon. When her day's work was laid out on her desk, she rose and stood for a moment listening. Doug usually spent his mornings in the prosecutor's office or the courtroom; if he did come here she would hear his limping step in time. And at any rate, as secretary she had a perfect right.

She went quickly to the big cupboard on whose shelves were piled the dusty steel deed boxes of years gone by. It took her a while, and a deal of wearisome shifting, piling, and repiling, to find the one labeled MERCER. She put things to rights on the shelves before she took it out, emerging from behind the cupboard doors with grimy hands and disheveled hair. The box was locked, but that presented no problem; she had been sent to that cupboard too often not to know where her father kept the keys to the boxes. In a moment she had the contents on the desk.

Everything was there in the records: names, the sum paid. But she had never heard of the man: he had been a clerk in the Grand Hotel, and had left town before the birth of the child. She was so disappointed that she could hardly accept the flat truth. She was still turning over the papers in absorbed concentration when she heard Doug approaching the office door. It was too late to put them away, but if she acted unconcerned he might not pay attention to what she was doing; he often did not even glance in her direction, unless he had given her work to do for him.

His work! She was aghast at her forgetfulness: he had handed her a list of references to look up—precedents—yesterday afternoon. She sat still, her fingers quiet over the papers as he came to stand behind her.

"Well, Eliza, doing a little historical research? Planning to give the Mercers a chapter in your 'Secret History of Waynesboro'?"

Her sallow face lost what little color it had. "I just wanted to know. I was interested."

"So I see. But it might be wiser if you confined your interest to contemporary affairs. Do you have that material ready for me?"

"No." Eliza made no attempt to excuse herself.

"Would you mind getting at it, then? I must check all those precedents before the State vs. Bromley comes up in the Common Pleas Court tomorrow. These fraud cases can be difficult when land and family relationships are involved. I can't stay to help you: my desk in the Court House is piled high."

"I have all these letters to write for Ballard, Gardiner, and Merrill. I fear I shall not be able to get it done." Her tone was cold and dry as his. "You have no doubt forgotten that the Woman's Club meets at our house this afternoon, and that I do not work on Club afternoons."

"Eliza, if you had not wasted the morning on what does not concern you, you might be halfway through your work by this time. Put that file away where it belongs and we will say no more about your investigations. But Club or no Club, my work must be finished today. You do understand, do you not, the functions of a confidential clerk in a law office?"

Eliza, seething with rage, the blood back in her cheeks in two angry spots, put the Mercer papers in their box, locked it, and returned it to the cupboard, took down from the bookcase the reference works on Douglas's list and laid it on her desk. "Clerk," indeed!

Doug in the inner office ripped open his mail. She could hear the papers rattling. More letters for her to answer, no doubt. But when he came out, he said no more, but simply departed in silence.

Eliza marked the entry he wanted, laid the book aside, and went for the next one. "We'll say no more about it" sounded a little like a withheld threat. But with what, after all, could he charge her? Fortunately, marking references in law books required no mental effort. By the time she had them all in a pile, with slips in them to mark the pages wanted, she had calmed down to the point where she could begin on the letters. But she had not nearly finished when her father came in at noon to take her home. She explained that she must sacrifice her lunch hour in order to get home for the Club meeting: if they would put a plate in the oven for her, she would be along as soon as she could get there. She knew that actually there was nothing very urgent about any of the letters still to be answered, but her mood had changed to one of martyrdom. It was after two when she reached home, her sense of grievance not abated by her long walk through sleet and slush. She slipped quietly in the side door. The meeting had begun: she could hear her mother's executive-officer voice in the drawing room. She went into the kitchen and found the plate of beef and potatoes that had been left for her, still hot in the oven of the kitchen range, but dried beyond palatability. She unbuttoned her wet boots, slipped them off, and ate in her stocking feet at the kitchen table, left her plate in the sink, under the dripping spout of the pump, took up her shoes, and reached her room by way of the service stairs from the kitchen. She was now in no hurry to join the Club ladies; it was the principle of the thing that had made her angry, rather than any great desire to hear Miss Caroline Gardiner's paper. Refusing to think further of her humiliation at Doug Gardiner's hands, she removed her office frock and climbed into the new gown she had had made for the Club meetings: an iron-gray faille whose skirt had a deep box-plaited flounce, an overskirt of lilac foulard caught up in a curved fold across the front and draped across the back into a waterfall of puffs. It was a far more elaborate costume than any Ballard was accustomed to wear; Eliza had perhaps allowed a recent small increase in her pay to go to her head, but she had planned to appear at her best this afternoon, a living denial of what she knew was a general impression of the Ballard financial status. Thomasina and her mother might not be aware of or resent it, but she was, and did. Even now, with her day ruined, she felt better when she had finished with her hair, had whipped the protective towel from her shoulders, and looked herself over in her glass.

She took up her handkerchief and left the room. At the top of the stairs she paused long enough to hear the steady flow of Miss Gardiner's words, and knew that the essayist was in the middle of her paper: the voice had not taken on the quickened tempo that indicated an approaching conclusion. She sighed, adjusted her overskirt one last time, and tiptoed down the side stairs to the drawing room door. Sally Rausch was seated at the end of the sofa, just inside; she moved closer to Kitty Edwards to make room, and smiled at Eliza in the friendliest fashion, but her eyebrows had gone up; and Eliza, who had wanted to impress the ladies with her elegance, resented what she took to be evidence of astonishment. She was not soothed when, after Miss Gardiner had finished, Sally leaned over and whispered, "How nice you look, Eliza! But how worldly!"

Finally, the program for the next meeting was read, and the Club stood adjourned; Eliza rose and began to pass from one to another of the members, speaking the words of welcome she should have been there to speak at the side of her mother and sister. By the time she reached the fireplace, her mother had moved away from the presidential table to the door, to bid farewell to any lady who might be taking her departure at once. Thomasina was close on her heels. But the Misses Gardiner still stood beside the hearth while Miss Caroline responded to commendatory comments on her paper. Miss Lavinia was free to greet Eliza.

"Miss Ballard, delightful to see you. Such a pity you had to miss the first part of the essay. But"—and she glanced quickly over Eliza's costume, from hem to collar, while her gloved hands caressed briefly the front breadth of her billowing crinoline—"we should no doubt rejoice that Ballard, Gardiner, and Merrill are so very busy. It must be a privilege to work with your father: such a distinguished man! And of course we think Douglas is a pleasant person to be associated with."

"Very pleasant!" Eliza said through gritted teeth. It was just the drop too much. "We have been busy, indeed. I see very little of Mr. Gardiner: he spends most of his days in the Prosecutor's office. But it must be a relief to you to know that he has no time now to indulge his interest in a certain young person."

The words were spoken in a low voice, but there was a sharpness in the tone that was unmistakable. Only Miss Caroline turned to listen, while the women near at hand stiffened and fell silent: Sally, Anne, and Kitty, who had come together in the center of the room, and Amanda and Mrs. McKinney on the other side of the fireplace.

Miss Caroline, although overshadowed by her sister, was in some respects the sharper of the two: she felt the acid in Eliza's voice and would have concealed their ignorance of "any young person." "Young men are expected to be a little foolish now and then. It would be a pity—"

But Miss Lavinia cut in. "There is no young woman on his mind, Miss Ballard, if that is what you mean. Other men may be foolish, as my sister suggests, but Douglas has never done anything he has been ashamed to tell us."

"Oh? Then since you know nothing about it, I must have been mistaken." Eliza was tasting the pleasure of retaliation. "When he was making those daily trips to Sheldon and Edwards, all last summer, he really was running your errands. I thought he was going to see that pretty little Bodien girl. Like so many spinsters, I was seeing romance where there wasn't any."

Eliza laughed, an artificial, social laugh so unnatural to her that Kitty stared, and forgot to pretend that she was listening to Sally Rausch. Eliza turned under the fixity of her gaze, and said to her, "Tell me, Kitty, now that errands no longer take Douglas there, isn't he missed in Sheldon and Edwards?"

Kitty, so suddenly caught, could not deceive Eliza into thinking she had not been listening; spontaneously she said the wrong thing. "Miss Bodien is no longer with Sheldon and Edwards." She used her most quenching voice, a voice unheard since her schoolteaching days. But Eliza was not to be quenched by Kitty Edwards.

"Oh?" She could make the monosyllable very expressive. "No doubt it became intolerable, having her carry on her social life in the store. But she must miss it, unless—"

The "unless" said everything. The Misses Gardiner were frozen in white-faced dismay. Eliza continued, "But I should think the store would miss her: she attracted so many customers. Or did she attract too many?"

"Certainly not. Whoever heard of too many customers? The store does miss her, but she could not be prevailed upon to stay. She didn't really need to work. I suspect she started out of boredom, but she is so young no doubt she got tired of the confinement and the long hours. Papa Edwards hired Miss Tiernan to take her place, to hold the West End trade."

"Oh, yes, Miss Rose Tiernan? So comfortably middle-aged, isn't she?" And Eliza moved away to the other side of the fireplace to speak to Amanda and Mrs. McKinney.

Sally stepped into her place beside the Misses Gardiner. "I hope you ladies will drive home with me? I had Reuben get the barouche out today, the weather is so very inclement. I have Anne and Kitty with me, but we can all squeeze in."

"Thank you very much. We had a hack from the livery stable bring us out, but we did not like to keep it waiting."

The five of them made their escape as quickly as possible; the coachman's boy in the stable door saw them on the porte cochere and gave Reuben the word, then ran to help the ladies in, bundling the Misses Gardiner and Kitty into the forward-looking seat, while Anne and Sally climbed into the other facing them.

"Tell Reuben," Sally told the boy as he prepared to close the door, "the Misses Gardiner first, then Mrs. Edwards." She knew that Reuben, who thought he owned the horses, would be indignant to have to go all the way up to the top of Sycamore, then back to the Edwardses', down the Linden Street hill and up again to the Gordons', and on up the Market Street hill, through all the ice and slush, when he could have dropped Kitty and then Anne without retracing a step.

Ordinarily Sally was considerate of both servants and horses, but today was different. Others might have ignored the recent scene in the Ballard drawing room: there had been bustle enough in getting the five of them into the barouche to have made a new topic of conversation seem quite natural, but that was not Sally's way. As they started out the Ballard gate, she said, easily and naturally as always, "What was all that nonsense about? Eliza's, I mean."

"Was it nonsense, Mrs. Rausch?" Miss Lavinia was still white about the lips. "I failed to understand."

"So did everyone else, you may be sure. I suppose Douglas annoyed her by keeping her late at the office. Eliza is always a little—temperish."

Anne took it up. "It's a pity she doesn't have more interests of her own, to keep her mind off other people's."

The remark fell like a stone: the Misses Gardiner did not relax or smile. No one tried again. Kitty began instead to talk about Miss Caroline's essay. They were all relieved when Reuben stopped at the Gardiner gate, and the boy climbed down, umbrella in hand, to assist the ladies to alight. When he had opened the gate without getting the umbrella in anyone's eye, and was escorting them up the walk, Anne sighed with relief.

"Sally, will you please tell me *why* you didn't let the matter drop?"

"Why?" she asked with surprise. "I was trying to help Doug, of course. His aunts will lay into him properly when he gets home. But I didn't convince them, and I must say neither of you helped much. Eliza throws out these outrageous hints, and everybody believes them." Sally was stopped by the guilt on the faces opposite her: both Kitty and Anne looked like children caught in the jampot. "You don't mean to say you believe—?"

The boy returned, scrambled to his seat up front with Reuben, and the barouche turned to go back to Linden Street.

"Oh, Sally," Anne moaned, "you're going to be so put out with me."

"What are you talking about?"

"I knew about it last year."

"What! That Doug Gardiner was interested in the Bodien girl? Nonsense. I don't believe it. Why didn't you tell me whatever it was you heard? I could have put you straight. Look: the girl's a *Catholic*. At least her mother is, and Irish to boot. She's a shopgirl, and her father works at the mill."

"What difference does that make?" Kitty's eyes were snapping. "Sheldon's a shopboy, as far as that goes."

"It's hardly the same thing. I mean Doug Gardiner wouldn't marry a girl like that, and I can't conceive of his pursuing anyone for any other purpose—not that decent young man. Oh, he may have come into the store to talk to her a time or two."

"Sally, listen, it wasn't just a time or two."

"I should have told you," said Anne, "then you'd have gotten over being shocked. But I didn't know you felt so superior to the Bodiens, as if they were outside the pale or something. And besides, something else put it out of my mind. Miss Pinney, last summer. And anyway, she'd quit working at Sheldon and Edwards, and so— But you know how the boys trail after Captain Bodien, hanging on his every word."

"Girls, too," Sally admitted, "when given a chance. I cannot see the attraction. He's such a common little man—and he *chews*."

"He invited the boys to his house to see his trophies—sabers, that sort of thing. They went, evenings, all last summer, to listen to his stories. Then they quit going, all of a sudden. Johnny told me why: the parlor was being used by Doug and the girl, and a lot of noisy boys weren't welcome, even in the Captain's study. And I know why they started using the parlor instead of Sheldon and Edwards' glove counter. I never told you this, either, Kitty."

And she went on with the story of the afternoon when she had stopped in the Ballard office with the library key, and had seen Eliza watching Doug from the window. "It was the same afternoon, I think, Sally, that you came to the library to tell me about Miss Pinney and the children. You can see why my mind got switched off. But I did think Eliza's behavior was odd enough to remark on, to John. I didn't know why she was watching, but I supposed John did, and knew what was going on. Men always do, somehow."

"Sheldon did, of course, and so did I after a while, but he made me swear not to tell."

"How men do hang together! I suppose John must have warned Doug that Eliza was watching him, and Doug just quit going there."

"And I honestly thought it was over," Kitty said, "when he stopped coming in the store."

"When did she quit her job?"

"Sometime in the fall. And I for one am glad he's going to her home to see her—it's the only proper way—and why shouldn't he marry her, I should like to know?" Kitty was on the defensive: she had not forgotten how insignificant she had felt when Sheldon married her.

Sally went into her reasons. The subject lasted until she had dropped Kitty and then Anne. She continued to think about it after she was alone, and was determined to take it up with Ludwig when she had a chance.

As the Misses Gardiner planned to discuss it with Douglas. They had few words for each other, except that after they had been deposited at their door by the Rausches' colored boy, Miss Caroline said, "I think that Douglas should be warned that he is being gossiped about."

"Yes. After dinner."

In the meantime, Anne had sped into her house, bursting to tell John of the Gardiner-Bodien affair, but was given no chance to begin. John was waiting for her with a letter from his cousin Jessamine.

She stiffened at his first words, but did not turn her eyes from his face.

"Cousin Robert is dead. And Jessamine has a baby, four weeks old, so Stevens must have recovered. Less alcohol, maybe, and better food. A good cotton crop seemingly has put them on their feet. Cousin Robert had a stroke in the fall, but he was so happy that she was pregnant at last that he *simply would not let go* until after the baby was born. She would have let me know sooner, except that she was so busy with the baby and Cousin Robert. It's a very southern-young-ladyish letter, all underscoring." He handed the letter to Anne, realizing of a sudden his great relief, as from a weight he had not realized he was carrying.

Anne, letter in hand, read bits of it aloud: "'You will be sorry to hear that Grandfather *passed away* two weeks ago. It was a blessed release for him, as he had been *completely helpless* following a stroke in November. He hung on to life *desperately*. He was so *happy* that at last I was going to have a baby, and was *determined* to see it—an heir to the plantation. That is my *second piece* of news. I have a son, named Rodney for his father.'"

"She doesn't seem to be much upset about her grandfather." Anne's voice was cool, a little contemptuous.

"How could she be? An old man helplessly paralyzed."

"It is odd she didn't let you know. You haven't heard from her, have you?" The question came out flatly, but with indifference, as though it was a matter of slight importance. "Not since you were down there?"

"Not a word. Cousin Robert wrote once to answer my note thanking them for their hospitality. Nothing since. I liked the emphasis on how different things are now." He laughed. Exuberance welled up in him. *No consequences.* Wasn't that what little Jessamine was saying? "I suppose all it takes to dissipate a House-of-Usher atmosphere is money enough to put on a new roof and scrape away the mildew. Maybe it can even make a sober gentleman out of a drunken mudsill."

"Did Mr. Stevens see what you thought of him? Maybe that is why she didn't let you know in time to get to her grandfather's funeral."

"Maybe. I wouldn't have gone. What does it matter anyway?" It wasn't like Anne to harp on a subject. "Let's wish 'em luck and forget 'em." He was thinking, "Why didn't she ask me for help if she needed it? Probably never wanted to see me again. The whole episode—just because she wanted a child!"

"You will have to write her."

"I suppose so. Condolences and congratulations. And that will be that. Probably never hear from her again. What was it you were bursting to tell me when you came in? Something—"

At that moment the street door slammed. Anne said, "Johnny, home from whatever he's been doing since school let out. It's five o'clock. I suppose Binny's in the kitchen with Martha?"

"I came in the side door."

"It was just a bit of gossip. Not important, really. It can wait until the children are in bed." And she went to the kitchen to collect Binny and get her washed and combed for dinner.

Dinner at the Gardiners' was a formal hour. It had been so even in the penny-pinching days, when one slipshod servant had been cook, waitress, and housemaid. Now there was a young colored waitress in uniform to stand next to the sideboard when she was not serving. Dinner-table conversation was confined to innocuous topics of the day. Douglas asked how his aunt's paper had been received, and teased her about having stage fright. They asked about his day in the Court House, and were totally uninterested in the replies. There were occasional silences, but Douglas did not appear to notice his aunts' stiff self-consciousness. When the dessert plates had been removed, the waitress poured Douglas a glass of port and put the decanter on the table beside him. He rose and opened the door for his aunts' departure. They had never forgotten, nor allowed him to forget, their father's old Virginia ways.

The sisters went into the living room and took their chairs on either side of the fire burning in the grate; they did not pick up books or embroidery hoops, but sat with hands folded, waiting. Usually, Douglas joined them there for a half-hour before he went into his study for the evening. At least, they had supposed him to be in the study. But that room, on the other side of the house, behind the drawing room, had an outside door. And they had never dreamed of intruding on him when the hall door was closed. The maid came in after they had been sitting in solemn silence for a few minutes, to put coal on the fire. Miss Lavinia took a fan from the table beside her and held it to keep the heat from her face.

"Lutie, please ask Mr. Gardiner to stop in here for a moment when he leaves the dining room."

In a little while, Douglas came stumping in, a question on his thin, sardonic face. His Aunt Lavinia indicated the low-armed velveteen-upholstered chair between the two of them, directly facing the hearth. She swallowed and cleared her throat: this was not going to be easy.

"Douglas, we have had very little complaint to make of your conduct since you were left in our charge. But I suppose we shall never feel we have fully discharged our responsibility."

Douglas raised an eyebrow. "I am grown up. What is it, Aunt Lavinia?"

"It has come to our ears that there is—that you have—that your conduct has given rise to gossip." She pronounced the word with thin distaste.

Douglas's mouth stiffened. "Eliza Ballard? I made her very angry this morning, when I found her snooping into matters that were none of her concern." He knew what was coming: after all, Dock Gordon had warned him. He had planned to tell his aunts about Barbara when she was a little older—had had more time to make sure. He was not now prepared to sustain the argument he knew was coming, but he would do his best. He assumed his courtroom expression—redoubtable, he hoped—and waited.

Aunt Caroline sounded doubtful. "You mean it was deliberate falsification? Young Mrs. Rausch attempted to persuade us so, but—"

"Sally Rausch? Did your whole precious Club hear this gossip?"

"No—no, Douglas. Only a few. But, is there any truth in it?"

"Whatever Eliza Ballard may be, Aunt Caroline, I don't believe she is a downright liar. What is it exactly that I am being accused of?"

His Aunt Lavinia took over again. "You are supposed to have been pursuing some young shopgirl in the Sheldon and Edwards store. With the further hint that since she has left their employ there may be a reason for it."

"It may be," his Aunt Caroline intervened, "that you did stop to pass the time of day with her occasionally? That would be enough—"

Douglas may or may not have heard her. Nostrils flaring, but with his voice under control, he said to his Aunt Lavinia, "I am supposed to have pursued to her ruin a young and innocent girl? Do you believe it?"

They were silent for a moment. Douglas thought, "This is not happening. Do they think an *East Lynne* world is *real*? Are they acting out a prescribed scene?"

His Aunt Caroline could not let the silence continue. She said, "We were startled, Douglas. We know young men do these things. But you have never been like that."

Douglas stretched his misshapen foot before him and displayed it scornfully. "No. For that reason if no other, I have not been like that and am not now. I have never had the slightest intention of seducing Barbara Bodien."

Both aunts caught their breath at the word, perhaps for the first time spoken in their presence. Miss Lavinia again lifted her fan before her face. "These legal terms are too blunt to be used in the home."

"Then: I have not gotten her into trouble. I believe that is the phrase commonly used in a domestic conversation."

There was an implication in his words. His Aunt Caroline stirred uneasily in her chair. "You did know her, then? But you are not responsible—"

"I am responsible for her leaving the store. There was no need for her to go to work there, but I am glad she did, or I should never have seen her."

"That was why she did go to work, no doubt, to catch some—"

Douglas continued, unheeding the interruption. "I am responsible for her leaving the store. I persuaded her to give it up because I knew Waynesboro gossip. And because I knew that when I came to tell you, you would use the word you did use: 'shopgirl.'"

Both ladies stiffened. Miss Lavinia leaned forward in the armless chair that allowed her skirts to billow about her. "Tell us what?"

"Aunt Lavinia, you are unbelievable. This is America and the nineteenth century."

"Lavinia, he is trying to tell us"—Miss Caroline watched his face—"that he is planning to marry this—this—young person."

"Marry? *Marry?* But he can't do that. Why, Douglas?"

"Because I am in love with her."

"In love with an ignorant mill hand's ignorant daughter? When the town is full of suitable girls? This is just an infatuation with a pretty face. Give yourself time."

Douglas smiled thinly. To his mind there was a paucity of "suitable" girls in Waynesboro. "In the first place, neither Barbara nor her father is ignorant. They are civilized, educated people. As to why: she is beautiful, certainly, or I might never have noticed her. But that is not important. What is important is that she is the only girl I have ever met who never looked at me with pity."

"Pity!" Both outraged ladies echoed his word.

"Do you think many girls can look at me and forget that?" He indicated his thick-booted foot with a wave of his hand. "Barbara never thinks of it. She looks at me."

"Then you are still seeing her? Miss Ballard implied that it had blown over."

"Haven't you been listening? Of course I have been seeing her, quite properly, in her mother's parlor. I hope to marry her."

"Douglas, you cannot marry her. A Gardiner and a mill hand's daughter.

It is unthinkable. We have preserved through a good many thin years our proper station in life. To marry out of one's class—"

"You used the word 'hope,'" his Aunt Caroline cut in. "Does that mean you have not yet asked her? You must have had some misgivings yourself. It is not too late—"

He looked at them sternly, trying to keep contempt and anger from his face and voice. "It was too late, so far as I was concerned, the first day I saw her. Either I marry her and have a happy family life, or I live alone, growing more and more bitter and resentful of my lameness."

If he was appealing to their sympathy, he failed. Miss Caroline clung to the point she had made. "But if you have been hanging back all this time, there must have been some reason, some wisdom you are not conscious of, trying to save you from such a mistake."

"There are reasons. She is very young. I doubt if she has known many men outside her family; she should have some choice, and I shall be offering her damaged goods, after all. She will not be eighteen until spring: she was born when her father was in camp near Washington, with his battery, in the spring of '62."

Miss Lavinia had retreated into frigid silence, but Miss Caroline persisted. "Have I not heard that the Bodiens are Catholics?"

"Make no mistake, Aunt Caroline: Roman Catholic, Irish, mill hand's daughter, I shall ask her to marry me. But because I should like to make this as easy for you as possible, let me go over just this once, since Barbara needs no defense, what I know about her family. Her mother is a Catholic, and Irish to boot. Her father's family are and always have been Catholics; they are an old Baltimore family who objected to his marrying an Irish girl. The Captain is not a Catholic." Douglas smiled as he thought of the vitriolic quality of the Captain's attacks on the church. "Captain Bodien's mother is first cousin to an archbishop, no less. After her husband died and she had returned to her parents' home with her children, she planned for her youngest son to enter the priesthood. He did not care for the prospect. At seventeen he ran away and enlisted in the army. He has never stopped hating the church for its influence over his mother. And I suspect, his wife. His two children are technically Catholic: they were baptized; of course their mother saw to that. The boy may still be a believer. Barbara is not. She goes to church with her mother occasionally, I guess, but not to mass or confession. I doubt whether she believes in a single dogma of the church: their father has worked hard on that."

"Why are you telling us all this? Why did Captain Bodien confide in you? So that you could defend him?"

"From what? He knows I hope to be his son-in-law. Why shouldn't he tell me about his life, his background?" Certainly Douglas would not tell his aunts why Captain Bodien had talked to him so freely: it had been a warning, for Barbara's sake and his, of what lay ahead of those who married against stubborn family opposition. Douglas could hear him now: "Tess—Theresa

MacDonald, she was—was one of the reasons I didn't want to go into the priesthood, young as I was—sixteen, seventeen—but old enough to know my mind. And when the Battery got back from the West, summer of '61, first leave I had, I married her. I thought in wartime my mother would forgive it—she forgave everything else: my being in what she thought was the wrong army, even my having left the church, though of course she never gave up on that. Nor has Tess, I may say. She's still wasting her time and money praying for me. But Mother never forgave my marriage. To be Irish was to be lower class. I warn you, my boy, women can be damn hard and unrelenting."

After Douglas's last defiant question, hurled at his aunts, there was a long silence. Then his Aunt Lavinia said, not looking at him, "Of course a—seduction—would have been reprehensible. But marriage! Marriage is for a man's whole life."

"I intend it to be."

"Lavinia, he says he has not proposed to the girl, that she is too young. Perhaps it would be better to drop the matter for the present."

Douglas retorted bitterly. "I had not intended to 'propose' immediately, although I have expressed my intentions to her father. But if there is gossip about us, then the sooner the better. I will ask her tonight."

"Oh Douglas! You won't go out on a night like this? All this ice—"

He laughed a little at his Aunt Caroline's anticlimactic protest, but there was nothing to laugh at in his Aunt Lavinia's response.

"Then," she said, her lip curling scornfully, "it will be said that you had to."

"Time, Aunt Lavinia, will disprove that calumny."

"Do you mean to say that you intend to bring her *here*, to our home?"

"It is my house."

"You can't put us out; by your father's will we are to be here while we live." His Aunt Caroline's voice trembled.

"Don't be absurd, Aunt Carrie. I don't want to put you out. I only want you to take Barbara in. But if you cannot recognize her as my wife and the mistress of my house, perhaps I had better let Ludwig Rausch send me to Congress, if he can. He has been after me to let my name be put before the District Convention ever since Liddell announced his retirement. I have refused because I did not want you to have to live on a reduced income again. But I will not ask my wife to submit to hostility or condescension. If we spent most of two years in Washington, you would have time to get used to the idea." And Barbara, he thought, would acquire the poise and the confidence necessary to deal with them. "You might even be willing to welcome us home."

He studied them, not really hopefully. They said nothing, only looked back at him with cold eyes in rigid faces. He struggled to his feet, shrugged as he looked from one to the other, then turned and left the room. He felt his limping exit as a humiliation: one should be able to stride away from such a scene. But with Barbara he forgot his deformity and was like other people. He put on his overcoat and hat, and took a cane from the umbrella rack. He seldom carried one, but after the day's sleet, the brick paths might be icy. He closed the front door firmly but quietly behind him.

The next day, in the middle of the morning, Captain Bodien crossed the cobblestoned mill yard and banged his way through the door into Ludwig's presence. There he laid on Ludwig's desk a two-foot-long sample of rope.

"The new lay for Burns-Hadley Company." A coil of defective rope had been sent back from Cleveland by the Great Lakes Navigation Company. Ludwig and Captain Bodien had been outraged that the mill of which they were so proud should have turned out slipshod work. Now the new rope was a good excuse for Captain Bodien's appearance in the office.

Ludwig twisted it in his hands. "That's better. Firm enough, I think, for their derrick line. What caused the trouble before?"

"One strand not formed with the correct tension, so the rope came apart. Pure carelessness. It won't happen again. Jim Stowe is out as foreman." He picked up the sample. "All right to go ahead and lay the rope?"

"Go ahead."

Captain Bodien nodded. "I'll tell 'em. Then I'd like to have a word with you if you've got the time." He went to the back window and signaled to someone in the mill door. Ludwig pulled a Windsor chair up close to his own, behind the desk, and gestured toward it.

"I'd like some advice. About my daughter."

Ludwig leaned back in his swivel chair, laughing. It squeaked in protest; Ludwig was growing heavier with the years. He opened a desk drawer and took out a square of black plug tobacco, which he offered to the Captain. This had become a ritual between the two men: Captain Bodien always got rid of his chew before he entered the office, but if he sat down to talk, Ludwig gave him another. Ludwig himself filled his pipe.

"Considering my own daughter's a child still, I've no experience to base advice on. But fire away."

"Young Gardiner wants to marry Barbara. He spoke to me a good while back, but said he'd wait to ask her until she was older—wanted to give her time to look around, I reckon. Took me all of a heap; she's hardly more'n a baby, seems to me. Born in June of '62, when our brigade was outside Washington. We were ordered out to be part of Johnny Pope's army, and that jackass marched us to hell an' gone all over northern Virginia, and wound up with Second Bull Run. And damn it, man, that's only yesterday. Reason I remember it so well, I never even had a chance to get to Baltimore to see the baby until after Antietam, in September. After Douglas spoke to me, I kept my mouth shut and watched her, and soon enough saw she was thinkin' of nothin' but him. So that part of it's all right. But—"

"Yes?"

"Douglas was down last night. Told me there was gossip. Took Barbie into the parlor and proposed. Good old-fashioned do. Wouldn't be surprised but that he got down on his knees. Came out, both of 'em, all starry-eyed. Question is, should I let 'em?"

"The question is a little late, isn't it, if you didn't choke Doug off in the beginning? Besides, why not? Nothing wrong with Doug, except that club foot, and if she doesn't mind that—"

Captain Bodien looked at his employer steady-eyed. "You know damn well why not. Because I don't want her to be unhappy. I've heard about those cold-blooded aunts of his. If they turn thumbs down, will the whole town be with them?"

Ludwig was silent for a moment. He had argued a long while with Sally the night before, protesting that Bodiens were good enough for Gardiners. Fragments of their dialogue flitted through his mind: "Shanty Irish! His aunts will never accept her." "Bodien isn't Irish. I don't know what his father was, he doesn't. Alsatian, probably—lots of them in Maryland. His mother's name was Archer, a good name there, I understand." "Nothing will persuade me that that bow-legged, tobacco-chewing little man has any blue blood in him." "Gunners with artillery ammunition in their caissons learned to chew because they dared not smoke." He had tried to draw her away from her subject, but Sally, unmoved, had come back with "Anyway, he married an Irish Catholic."

Now Ludwig swung his chair around to look out the window while he relighted his pipe.

"I suppose by 'whole town' you mean Doug's friends and their wives. They're not exactly the whole town. But no, they won't, as you say, turn thumbs down, not all of them, certainly. I won't. The Gordons won't, nor the Sheldon Edwardses. Soon no one will."

"I've been a damn fool," the Captain said, bluntly. "I came here to escape exactly the same fix. I wanted my wife to be happy, away from my folks. Queer, isn't it? Time takes us around in circles—more like an eddy than a current. When we got here, I could have settled in any part of town, but for her sake I bought that old Inskip place, there among the West End Irish, where she would make friends, even if it did mean those God-damned church bells dinging in my ears morning, noon, and night. And I never gave a thought to the children—never gave them a chance."

"Looks to me like the girl's made her own chance."

"But if she's miserable—"

"She won't be miserable if she's in love with Doug. I bet it has been worth it to your wife."

"I reckon I can't stop them. They want to be married in the spring. Should they just go to the preacher, or should I give her a bang-up wedding?"

"No priest?"

"No priest, dammit. That would mean the whole rigmarole—promising to bring up their children in the church—no, sir. She'll be married by Douglas's minister. I told him that I doubted he could make a real Presbyterian out of her, I had done too good a job of making her a skeptic. But he's welcome to try."

"Then I'd say a bang-up wedding. Get all the self-styled social leaders there and show 'em."

"I don't know any social leaders." His tone was ironic. "Mother's cousin the archbishop wouldn't countenance my heretical ideas, and my sisters have never forgiven me for being in the Union Army. I had a brother in the Rebel Army killed at Gettysburg, you see, and maybe I killed him. Nor for marrying Tess. Two other Rebel brothers survived, but they've never forgiven me, either. Two brothers were in the Union Army, out West now—too far away. The Old Man might come if I asked him, but he isn't exactly High Society."

Ludwig knew from many a reference that the Old Man was one-time Major Stewart, living in Cincinnati, Orderly Sergeant of the battery before the war when Augustus Bodien had been Sergeant. Then, in '61, when Captain Gibbon, the battery's Commanding Officer, was made Brigadier General, Stewart had been promoted to Lieutenant, and Bodien to Orderly Sergeant. After many battles and many casualties, Stewart advanced to Captain, commanding the battery, and Bodien to Lieutenant. In the long stalemate before Petersburg, Stewart had given in to the effects of many wounds, had resigned, had been breveted Major, and had gone, leaving Bodien as Captain in command of the battery. Major Stewart came back to the battery just once: to lead it in the final Grand Review in Washington.

"I'd ask him," Ludwig grinned. If the two veterans got to reminiscing in the hearing of some of Waynesboro's cynical doubters (including Sally), their doubts might be resolved. "Where is General Gibbon? Why don't you ask him, too?"

"That'd be flying pretty high, wouldn't it? He's out West, fighting Indians. But as it happens, Stewart wrote me not long ago the General had to go to Washington for some reason, and he was going to stop off and see Stewart on his way back West. If I can find out from the Old Man when that will be, and persuade Barbie to set the wedding date then. By God, he just might come." An oddly wistful look touched the square solid face for a moment. "When Barbie was born, spring of '62, he didn't command just the battery, he commanded the whole brigade. But I know he would remember me: you don't forget the non-coms who fought Indians under you, or marched alongside of you for twelve hundred miles. If he and the Major got to talking, it might prove that I haven't stretched the truth telling stories to the boys as much as some folks seem to think, not more'n any soldier, half an hour after a battle, when he tries to remember just what did happen. General Gibbon would be a help."

"I know what you mean. I never have been able to match my Shiloh with anyone else's, or with the maps. Or, for that matter, with the field itself. I went back once, and saw a place I might never have seen before."

"Another reason," Captain Bodien chuckled, the memory of an eighteen-year-old spring in his mind still, "they called her the Battery Baby on account of her name. Her mother had said way back in the spring that, boy or girl, it had to have a saint's name. So I told her a girl should be named Barbara for the gunner's saint. You know, Saint Barbara looking down from her battlement with her arms full of cannon and cannon balls, one of the fairy tales women and priests can persuade themselves to believe. Anyway, I told Tess that if any of the saints could protect me it was Barbara."

"And it worked?"

"She thought it did. There was just this saber cut I got in a hand-to-hand tussle over the guns at Cedar Creek." He touched the ridge of flesh that ran in a curve from cheek-bone to jaw line. "That was on detached service, with Sheridan in the Valley. The Rebels never got that close to Battery B's guns. Stewart's guns were virgin at Appomattox."

He was swinging the piece of rope between his knees, staring at it blankly—or at the past.

"You ought to write it all down."

The words recalled the mill superintendent to his present duties. "I'm no hand with a pen. Besides," he grinned, "I'm no gentleman of leisure, like General Deming. Still, he did put together a pretty good book." He stood up. "I'm sorry I took up so much of your time. But I wanted to know how you thought it would work out. You know all these people who can make it pleasant for Barbara, or not."

"My acquaintance with the Misses Gardiner is very limited. I cannot even guess about them. The rest of Waynesboro—it'll work out. You'll see."

When he had gone, Ludwig sat for a moment before he returned to his correspondence. He must see Doug Gardiner again about running for Congress: this matter of marrying a girl his aunts wouldn't approve of might be just the added nudge that would make him consent. Ludwig wished impatiently that the Waynesboro Telephone Company, recently organized, would soon get the lines put in: it would be unbelievably convenient to have a telephone. As it was, he must wait until afternoon and hope to catch Doug in the Court House. He had no intention of appearing in the law office on so private a matter.

As it turned out, his talk with Douglas was more than satisfactory. He had caught him just before the Court House closed, and waited until the prosecutor had disposed of his last problem and had got rid of the last pestering lawyer before he tackled him. Then, when they were alone, he sat down in the visitor's chair, across the desk from Doug, offered him a cigar, and lighted one himself. He preferred his pipe, but for some reason cigars were recognized as a part of political palavering.

"I just dropped by," he said, "in the hope that I could persuade you to change your mind about running in Liddell's place. The District Convention isn't far off, now."

"Liddell's really in bad health? I wouldn't be causing trouble in the party?"

"He's got heart trouble. He won't run again, regardless."

"Boone County is a stronghold of the Stalwarts, isn't it? Grant men?"

"So-so. But Republican, whoever runs."

"Wouldn't General Deming like to go back?"

Ludwig stared at him. "Of course he would. So would his wife. He's been mending his fences. Have you seen his book?"

"*The Buckeye Brigade*? Privately printed, wasn't it? Must have cost him a pretty penny."

"He had enough subscribers promised beforehand, I would suppose, to pay for the printing. Then he got out-of-work veterans, one-legged, one-armed veterans, to sell it, house-to-house. Helped them and him too. Who could refuse to buy it?"

"It isn't a bad book, as a matter of fact."

"No. Best part of it, though, are the anecdotes contributed by his 'dear comrades.' I'll wager he wrote every living man who served in that brigade for his recollections, and then sold him a copy."

"Naturally. But some of the reminiscences were vivid enough to make you see it all—old soldiers remembering, not thinking of any personal gain. But the point is, will he oppose me at the Convention if I decide to let my name be proposed?"

"He's an organization man: he won't make trouble. I hear some of the Boone County Stalwarts would like to run him. But what he still wants after all these years, and his wife, too, is vindication—the restoration of his reputation. To be put back in Congress by the Stalwarts, as one of the Conkling-Platt-Cameron combination, would do nothing to that end. I think I can make him see that. Another thing. Your expenses. You would draw your share from the law partnership even if you weren't here?"

"I could, but I wouldn't. If Judge Ballard does all the work—and all the big cases still go to him, you know—he must have all the income. Of course, I could be here part of the time."

"Yes. Congress is not always in session, Gott sei dank!"

Both men laughed. Ludwig, as he sat chatting with so much ease, was studying the younger man: the smooth-shaven, thin, sardonic face, so familiar for the last dozen years and now so subtly changed: the tension gone, the brows less severely drawn, the mouth less contemptuous. And Ludwig, who would have called Douglas "tight-lipped," noticed for the first time the full lower lip. There was a passionate nature there, usually hidden behind sarcasm, but plain to be apprehended now that the man was relaxed and happy.

Douglas shifted under the acute gaze. "Why do you want me to run?"

"I told you before: Republican principles, honesty, and brains."

"I know. Say it again and make it convincing."

"And availability."

"If I consent to run."

"Do you think I have some ulterior motive? That I think I can make you dance to my whistle? But I'm not whistling, and I'm not going to. All the party expects of any Republican representative is that he vote according to party principles, and that he do what he can for his district, if it isn't against the interests of the country."

"In the matter of tariffs, for instance?"

"Yes, for instance."

"Party principles change from time to time, and from faction to faction."

"The faction I'm speaking for wants peace with the South, which we have, thanks to Hayes. Honesty in government, which we have, as far as Hayes has been able to manage it with a hostile Congress and the Stalwarts opposing Civil Service reform. All right?"

"All right so far."

"Beyond that the fundamental principles that all Republican factions agree on: sound money, a protective tariff. All right?"

"All right."

"Well, then?"

Douglas smiled wryly. "I told you I couldn't afford it, when you asked me before. I can afford it even less now, since I am about to be married. You knew that?"

Ludwig nodded. "Cap'n Bodien said something. I didn't know it was to be immediately."

"This spring. Afford it or not, I am going to say 'yes' to you now, unless it would mean trouble in the party. Don't push it against opposition."

"There'll be no need to push it. I'll propose your name to the District Convention, that's all. If the delegates should happen to prefer someone else, that is their privilege."

His tone said he believed the delegates would be waiting for him to propose a name. Douglas thought, "So far, in so short a time. State Committeeman and biggest power in the Seventh District—all he need do is propose a name!" He himself did not hanker for that kind of power; he thought that perhaps Ludwig had not, either, in the beginning; he believed the big one-time soldier candid to the point of simplicity: he had gone into politics from patriotic motives, and if he was inclined to think of the interest of the country and the interest of the manufacturer as inseparable, who was to say that he was wrong? But now, Douglas thought, the patriotic motive had been somewhat overlaid with a love of the game for the game's sake. He said again, "If it doesn't make trouble in the District, then, yes, you may propose my name." He stood up and reached across the desk. The two men shook hands; then, as Douglas came around the desk to escort his caller to the door, he said abruptly, "My getting married won't make any difference?"

"Since young ladies who might prefer young bachelors to represent them," Ludwig's eyes twinkled, "do not have the vote, no, I can't see it would make any difference. It helps a man in Washington to have a wife to act as hostess for him. But perhaps I should say—" Ludwig paused at the door, frowning a little, wary of any assumption with this rather stiff young man that they were on confidential terms, but Bodien might say something—"your prospective father-in-law consulted me this morning—wanted to know if I thought his girl would be happy with you, or looked down on. You mustn't blame him—he has suffered, you know, and his wife." Smiling again, Ludwig touched the younger man on the shoulder. "Gott im Himmel! That kind of foolishness is bad enough in Baltimore. Here it is impossible, I give my word."

The two men shook hands again, and Ludwig went out. Douglas remained staring at the closed door, standing on his good foot, letting the other drag, his mind a confusion of mixed emotions: resentment of any discussion of his affairs, any assumption that the town might even think— He appreciated at the same time Ludwig's keenness. "He knew I would change my mind, and why." Underlying the words in his mind was a realization that Ludwig was more astute than he had given him credit for. The ability to read men's motives might be the secret of his increasing power. Consciously he went on thinking: "So he gave his word that Barbie would be accepted!" For a moment he was stirred to anger and contempt. Barbara needed no defense. He amended it, "should need no defense." He recognized the difference, and that Rausch would be no mean ally. But did he understand women as well as men, and could he manage them? Then Douglas smiled mockingly at his own question. "If he can't, should I be surprised, or critical, I who cannot manage two old-maid aunts?"

On the next evening the *Torchlight* carried on its society page (known in the town as "the gossip page") the paragraph that had been sent in: "Captain and Mrs. Augustus P. Bodien announce the engagement of their daughter Barbara to Mr. Douglas Gardiner, son of the late Mr. and Mrs. Ralph Gardiner," followed by half-a-column on the history of the Gardiner family in Waynesboro, and the army career of Captain Bodien, who "recently removed from Baltimore to our fair city, to become the General Manager and Mill Superintendent of the Rausch Cordage Company."

Many in Waynesboro read the item with astonishment, and a few with a sense of outrage: the Misses Gardiner, Eliza Ballard, and Sally Rausch.

Sally brandished the paper at her husband when he came up to their sitting room before dinner and stooped to kiss her.

"Ludwig Rausch! He's going to marry her! And will you please tell me by what right Mr. Bodien calls himself 'Captain' and 'General Manager'? He's no more a captain than you, or Dock Gordon."

"He was Regular Army, Sally. That makes a difference. Dock and I don't want any military titles. Though the hands call me Captain, most of them. Or 'Cap.'" Ludwig laughed. "And as for 'General Manager,' that's what he is—he manages the mill."

"I hate to see people like that getting notions. I suppose this will put an end to your hopes for a political career for Doug?"

"What has got into you, my girl? Of course it hasn't. Why should it? On the contrary, he'll make a better candidate. I never thought he'd make a good campaigner—too dry and sarcastic. You'd be surprised how he's loosened up. And he can take her around with him: she's a pretty girl, and a touch of romance never did a man any harm."

"Ludwig, you're hopeless! Do you approve of this?"

"Doug is old enough to know his own mind, and she is a good, well-brought-up girl."

"Just so he realizes she will never be received."

"Sally—from you—what a word! 'Received'? As a guest? As a friend? The Misses Gardiner may hold aloof, but they have almost ceased to count: they do not entertain much any more. But you and I and our friends— Do not get yourself laughed at, Sally, or make enemies. Of course we'll 'receive' her. You will have a dinner party for them."

"A—dinner?"

"Of course. If all goes well, Douglas will be the new Seventh District Representative. We entertained for Liddell and his wife, didn't we? Who was she before she married? Do you know?"

"That was different. That was an obligation."

"And so would this be, and a much greater one." Ludwig had been standing behind her chair all this time; now he moved around to face her and saw to his astonishment that there were tears in her eyes. He pulled his leather armchair close and sat down bending toward her, hands between knees. "Liebchen, it doesn't matter all that much to you, and you would not take it so, were you not already so upset. You've been so worried about your mother you're half-sick and ready to fly off the handle at any little thing. After she has seen the specialist in Cincinnati tomorrow you may feel better." He laid one hand on hers; she grasped it gratefully, and held on. There was no need to say more: it had all been said so many times. Mrs. Cochran was now so blinded by cataracts that she could hardly find her way across a room, and she had so often bumped into chairs and occasional tables that she had grown reluctant to leave her quarters. She took all her meals there; she lay on her bed for hours at a time, refusing even to be read to; it was difficult to persuade her to go on her daily drive with her husband. Dock Gordon was afraid that she was slipping into melancholia; he had been trying for a long while to convince her that she should have the cataracts removed. But she was adamant: not while she could tell light from dark: too many cataract operations—at any rate the ones she knew about—had been catastrophic failures. Then one night when Ludwig had come into Dock's office for a chess game, John had shown him an article in a medical journal about a certain Dr. Julius Jacobson of Königsberg, who for the last dozen years had been operating for cataract: "the best eye man in the world," John had called him. If Mrs. Cochran's family wanted to save her reason, her husband had better take her to Jacobson. She could stand the trip: her heart was not good, but digitalis in small amounts would take care of that, long enough, anyway. The heart was more easily doctored than the mind. The advice had shaken Mrs. Cochran's family: it was one thing to go abroad for pleasure when you were young enough to enjoy it, quite another to go thousands of miles for an operation when you were ill and aging. But Mrs. Cochran, when the possibility was suggested to her, welcomed it. However, she would not stir without the word of someone more experienced than "young Dock." John had therefore written the man who had taught him ophthalmology twenty years before, and made an appointment for him to see Mrs. Cochran. Mr. Cochran made his plans to be away as long as need be: Ludwig was added to the bank's Board of Directors, to keep his father-in-law in touch and speak for him at meetings; letters had been written, one to Dr. Jacobson and an answer received, and another to Ludwig's aunts, uncles, and cousins in Saxony, who although a long way from Königsberg, would be pleased to have them stop for a visit on the way, coming and going, and so break their journey.

Happily for all concerned, the Cincinnati specialist agreed with John, confirming his faith in Dr. Jacobson, and advising the trip. Passage was engaged for the Cochrans and for Mrs. Cochran's maid, Rose, and the three were put on the train for New York. After it had pulled out, Sally stood looking after it, tears in her eyes. Ludwig took her hand in both of his. "They will be all right, Liebchen."

"I hope so. It's only that all of a sudden, standing on that platform, they looked so tiny and so old. I should have gone to New York with them."

"And come home alone on the train? Only if I could have gone with you."

Sally went home feeling sad and regretful, but in the house she found that pent-up childish spirits had been released completely. When she entered the hall, alone and without warning, Ludwig having gone back to his office, she came upon the children sliding down the banisters, Elsa landing against the newel post with a resounding thump just as her mother opened the door from the vestibule.

"Elsa!" Sally went to stand beside her just as Charles thrust his fat leg over the banister at the beginning of its curve. "Charles! Get down off there this instant! You'll fall and kill yourself!"

"Oh, Mamma! He's been down a dozen times."

Sally ran her finger along a deep fresh scratch in the banister, the mark of the buttons down the front of Elsa's frock.

"How could you! Your grandmother and grandfather scarcely out of the house! If Grandmother comes back with her sight restored and sees the banister scratched like this, what will she say? Really, it's too bad of you children—as if you rejoiced at their being gone." Then suddenly she too felt as if a burden had rolled off her back, as if time, careless and easy, stretched out before her. "Pshaw!" she said. "What does it matter? Go ahead, just so you don't kill yourselves, but Elsa: cover those buttons with a pinafore."

For that winter at least, the Cochran house became the gathering place of the children who were Elsa's friends; Charles and Ernest and sometimes Binny Gordon "tagged along," more or less tolerated, and were given all the parts in any game that no one else wanted to play. Sally and Ludwig, too, took advantage of their elders' absence: they invited their friends to dinner parties and evenings of whist. But Sally postponed thinking of entertaining in honor of the newly betrothed couple, although she was sure in her heart that Ludwig would insist upon it, whenever he thought the time was ripe.

After Captain Bodien had learned from his friend Major Stewart when General Gibbon was to be in Cincinnati, the wedding was set for late April. One morning he went to Ludwig's office to show him a note he had just received from the General: "Major Stewart has forwarded to me your invitation to your daughter's wedding, and has informed me that it is the 'Battery Baby' who is to be married. I expect to be in Cincinnati for a few days on my way back to my post from Washington. I shall be delighted to accompany Major Stewart to Waynesboro for the happy occasion. It may be that we shall have an opportunity to match our memories of past days." Captain Bodien made no pretense of concealing his surprised gratification.

"I didn't think he could have forgotten," he said, with glowing face, "but I didn't really think he'd take the trouble to come up here. Let's not tell anyone, eh? Let 'em be surprised when they see him."

Once the wedding date had been set, Douglas insisted that Barbara should accompany him on a tour of the Gardiner house: it needed redecorating, and she should have it done as she liked. She had remonstrated. "It's your aunts' house. I don't want to change anything."

"It's your house. Their home is there, of course: I could not turn them out if I wanted to, and of course I don't. They're all the family I have, and they sacrificed everything—even their comfort, I fear—to put me through college and law school."

Barbara said no more. She was very much in love with Douglas, and trusted him to make her way smooth. She would suggest no changes in the house as it stood. Then the aunts might not mind so much her coming into it. But the afternoon spent going over the house was a painful experience in spite of her conciliatory intentions. She and Douglas had found the Misses Gardiner awaiting them in the drawing room; their reception was as formal as if they had both been strangers.

The affianced couple were offered two of the small gold chairs; the maid appeared with small glasses of sherry and a plate of biscuits on a tray.

Miss Lavinia said, "Douglas tells us he wants you to see the house. We realize that you would like to become accustomed to it, such a large house. This is the drawing room. It has not been changed in any way since our parents, Douglas's grandparents, furnished it with their treasures from Virginia."

Barbara could feel the angry color warming her cheeks. Doug leaned across the space between them and took her hand.

"The idea is, Aunt Lavinia, that now it is to be Barbara's house and there might be some things she would like changed. It is high time: look at the draperies, cracked along all the folds. And the wallpaper—"

"If it wouldn't cost too much," Barbara said, trying to please everyone, "maybe it could be done over with the same paper and the same curtains."

Miss Caroline smiled, a polite fixed smile. "We hoped that you would see that the style of decoration suits the house. Modern furniture is so very massive and ornate. But of course you would like a room where you could have your own things and feel at home with them. We believe that the room above this, the guest-room, would make a very pleasant sitting room for you."

Now Douglas too was angry. He saw no reason to conceal it. He rose and put down his sherry glass on the nearest table.

"No, Aunt Caroline. It isn't going to be like that at all. This will be my wife's drawing room. She will entertain her guests here, or in the sitting room or library, as she prefers. We will use the dining room when we entertain. You will always be welcome to join us, but if you prefer to live apart, you may arrange a sitting room upstairs. And what is more, my wife will order the house, manage the servants, plan the meals."

Miss Lavinia kept an implacable silence. Miss Caroline said, "Oh? She seems a little young and inexperienced." And to Barbara, "Do you think you can manage Negro servants? Or would you prefer Irish servants from the West End?"

The color deepened in Barbara's cheeks, but she kept any sign of anger out of her voice. "I was brought up in Baltimore. With nigra servants. Grandmother Bodien's servants stayed on with her after they were freed. They helped raise me. I can manage the nigras."

"Come along then, Barbara, and I'll introduce them: there are only two, after all: the cook and the housemaid-waitress. You will excuse us, Aunt Lavinia? Aunt Caroline?"

They did not return to the drawing room from the kitchen. Douglas took her everywhere, upstairs and down, except into his aunts' bedrooms. She said very little, except to repeat that she had no desire to change anything. He was troubled by her silence. When they had closed the heavy front door behind them, he said, "Is it too much to ask, Barbie? We don't have to live here."

"Of course we do, for a while anyway. Till you go to Congress. Do you want to knuckle under?"

"I don't want you to be unhappy."

"I'll manage," she said shortly.

When they reached the gate, and he would have turned her down the hill with him, she drew away.

"You go on back to your office, Doug. I'll go this way."

"But—"

"Let me walk it off." She turned abruptly and left him standing there, looking after her. She did not want him to see that her mouth was unsteady, her chin trembling. She had felt so gay, so youthfully proud, walking up Sycamore Street with him. She was not going to crawl down it, tears in her eyes.

Doug always knew what was in her mind, whatever the words she used.

He went off down the hill as she started in the other direction. Perhaps he should have gone with her, but she obviously wanted to be alone, and it was no day for a lame man to do unnecessary walking. Barbara might find her anger evaporating quickly in the miserable weather. The calendar might say March, but it was wintry still: clouds were low and heavy and the wind damp and cutting; the deep snow on the ground was turning soft, and sinking away from the tree trunks, hardly thawing, but not hard-frozen, either. On the path it was packed, bumpy but hard and slick, black with soot and grime. Barbara trudged carefully up the slope to the corner, turned to her left along College Street, where it was level and easier walking. At Market she turned left again, down the hill toward the Cochran house.

The Cochran place (house, stable, and yard) filled half the block, separated from its neighbor on the west by an alley as wide as some West End streets. The yard was fenced: iron across the front and halfway down the sides, then high boards beyond the stable entrance. The iron fence had elaborate gates, double where the drive ran back to the end of the front porch, single for the brick pavement that ascended across the center of the front yard to the porch steps and the door. As Barbara approached, she heard children, somewhere back behind the high board fence, invisible. As she drew near the voices came more clearly: first the thin sound of a tin trumpet, its notes approximating the artillery call to attention, then the orders in a boyish voice: "Drivers, mount! Cannoneers, mount! Attention! Forward, march!" A string of children came into view beyond the far front corner of the house: one, ahead, swinging a wooden sword, shouting commands, several pulling on the shafts and wheels detached from some old buggy, with a big wooden box (a croquet-mallet box, perhaps?) tied to the axle and two boys sitting on it, perched precariously, swaying as the ropes slipped, but with their arms precisely folded, as cannoneers' should be, the other children running alongside. As the wheels began to move easily, the boy in front—Johnny Gordon, Barbara saw now—swung his sword, yelled "Trot! Gallop!" and they all went thundering along across the front yard to the far front corner.

"Trot! Walk!"

The wheels slowed. The shafts were swung around and dropped, the box untied and pulled to the ground. Already within a snow-built fortification, a drain-pipe cannon bore on the street. The boys who had been sitting on the box opened its lid and began to pile its load of snowballs on the ground.

"Forward into battery! Action front!"

Barbara had seen her father putting these boys through artillery drill the previous summer, for their amusement and his. They had learned their lesson well, and had taught a number of girls, seemingly. Barbara did not know the girls, but they were helping to man the gun: gunner with ramrod, cannoneers with ammunition, one standing at the side of the wheel ready to pull the lanyard. The only lack—she looked up and down the empty street—

was an enemy. She knew that any living figure would serve the purpose, and hesitated, about to turn back. It was too late: Johnny had seen her.

"Hi!" he called. Then to the girl beside him, "Enemy in sight! Blow the bugle!"

The tin trumpet shrilled again. Johnny gave his orders. "Load—cannister—double! Cut fuses one second!"

Two soft snowballs came spatting at her feet. At least, they were playing fair: one gun, one snowball, or "double cannister," two at most. Those not throwing were going through the proper motions: gunner with ramrod, ammunition passing from hand to hand, one boy with a piece of string, pulling the lanyard from within the shelter of the fort.

"Ready! By the piece! Fire at will!"

Barbara ducked behind the nearest tree, stepping through the deepest snow to the bare circle around its base. She ripped off her spotless white gloves, thrust them into the muff now dangling from her wrist, made two good-sized, medium-hard snowballs. In less than no time she, Barbara Bodien, about to become Mrs. Douglas Gardiner, was involved in a snowball fight with a lot of children. Her aim was not very good, but she got one good hit and called out, "Number one cannoneer down, mortally wounded." There was a brief argument, but one boy went back a little, withdrawn from the fight. She threw her balls while the cannon was being loaded, and stepped behind the tree when the cannon fired back. She calculated that she had time between shots to reach the next tree downhill, but was so impeded by the snow and her skirts that a snowball hit somewhere in the thickness of her ruffles in the rear. She was beginning to feel more than slightly disheveled, but was still popping out from behind her tree to fire, when she saw Mrs. Sheldon Edwards coming up the hill in such dignity of muff, pelisse, flounce, and pleat, that she could only be out on a round of afternoon calls. Barbara wanted to sink through the ground: she knew young Mrs. Edwards only slightly as the wife of her former employer. What she would think was past imagining. But to slide around the tree trunk would be to expose herself to the relentless gunners. She stood her ground and waited.

Kitty, coming up the hill from a succession of calls, hoping to conclude her afternoon with a sociable chat at Sally's, saw first the children in the yard and then the figure behind the tree. Barbara Bodien, throwing snowballs like a child, just when all Doug's friends had been persuaded to approve of her. Across the street a lace curtain moved. Mrs. Klein was watching, but Mrs. Klein didn't matter. Sally might be watching, too, and that did matter.

When she reached the tree just downhill from the one that sheltered Barbara, she slipped behind it.

"Reinforcements!" she called. "I haven't been in a snowball fight for years. What fun!" She in turn stripped off her white gloves, stuffed them in her muff, and hung it by its cord on a projection from the tree trunk.

"But you're so—you'll ruin your clothes."

"I've made my formal calls. I'm on my way to drop in here." She nodded her head toward the Cochran house.

Barbara smiled gratefully. "Just because I've disgraced myself, need you?"

Kitty thought she had never seen her look so pretty: violet eyes flashing, cheeks glowing, hat askew, snow-bespattered.

"You see," the girl went on, all out of breath, "it's my father's battery; he taught them all this drill and they're practicing on me. But you—"

"I'll show them," Kitty promised. She threw a truer ball than Barbara; her first one caught Elsa on the shoulder.

"Bugler wounded," Barbara called, and Elsa withdrew.

"You're not so bad wounded you can't bring up ammunition," they heard Johnny say, and Elsa set about making snowballs. There were further shots from both sides. Kitty grew as breathless and bespattered as Barbara. She made one last straight hard throw that caught Johnny full in the chest.

"Commanding officer mortally wounded."

Kitty reached up for her muff and drew out a handkerchief, which she waved up and down beside the tree. "Flag of truce," she called. "Let's have a cease fire. We're badly outnumbered, but you have wounded to look after. Agreed?"

"Agreed." Johnny sat up from his supine position in the snow, and brushed the evidence of his mortal wound from his jacket. "You all right?" He was apprehensive now, and regretful that he had been carried away. Boys were not expected to snowball young ladies.

"We're all right. I haven't had so much fun since—well, since I was your age, I guess." Kitty had come out from behind her tree and met Barbara on the path. She straightened the girl's hat, brushed her off, was brushed off in turn. Barbara explained how she happened to be in the neighborhood, and they parted, Kitty moving on to the gate and Barbara turning downhill. She was still exhilarated, her heart still beating fast, her breath short. She had had her ill humor knocked out of her—she felt equal to anything, even aunts. She would stop at Doug's office and tell him she was sorry she had been cross. She had never been in either of his offices: the Ballard, Gardiner, Merrill one, or the Prosecutor's, in the Court House. She knew that ladies did not ordinarily set foot inside the Court House except of legal necessity, or on Decoration Day, when they took over the halls for the assembling of bouquets for soldiers' graves, but surely it would be all right. She glanced down to see that her skirts were in order, and for the first time realized the enormity of her conduct. The soft snow had soaked her pleats and flounces to her knees. Instead of going to the Court House, she must take a back way home. She turned left at the lower corner of the Cochran place and slipped along the alley, past Chillicothe, past Sycamore, to the obscure street that ran along the railroad yard, in the shadow of the trestle that carried the tracks from one hill, over intervening streets, to the other, where the depot was. She could slip down that street to the West End and home, unseen. But seen or not, she was terribly aware that hers had not been the kind of behavior suited to Mrs. Douglas Gardiner. She must subdue herself to ladylikeness, or not marry Doug, which was unthinkable.

Kitty Edwards had paused just long enough to wipe her hands on her handkerchief and pull her gloves on, and then opened the Cochran gate and trudged up the brick path to the house. The children had ceased all activity to watch her. In spite of the reassuring wave of her hand, they began to drift away, back toward the stables. Elsa blew her trumpet half-heartedly; two cannoneers picked up the shafts of the caisson and slowly drew it off.

Kitty smiled as she rang the doorbell. It might have been kinder of her to forget her intended call, but Sally might well have seen the whole thing from a window. The maid answered the bell, offered a tray for her card, and ushered her into the empty drawing room. She took a stiff rosewood chair close to the window, back to the light, but she had to rise when Sally came into the room, and her bedraggled skirts were in plain sight.

"Kitty! How nice of you! On such a dull afternoon. Come into the library where there's a fire and we can be comfortable."

Kitty had to pass in front of her through one door, across the hall, through another door; the evidence was incontrovertible.

"Kitty! You're soaking! Do you mean to say those wretched children—I heard their racket outside the drawing room windows, but couldn't see them from in here. It's such a relief that they *can* be noisy while Mamma and Papa are away. And I was taking notes for my club paper."

"It wasn't their fault. An artillery battery has to have an enemy, and Barbara Bodien and I just happened along. It was as much fun for us as it was for them."

"Come close to the fire and dry your skirts and boots. You'll catch your death. I'll have Tishy bring tea." She pulled two rocking chairs close to the fire, took Kitty's muff and gloves and cloak and put them on the arm of the sofa by the window, went out for a word to the maid, returned and pulled a chair close to the hearth for Kitty.

"Now explain. What were you doing with Miss Bodien? She wasn't coming to call?"

"Oh, no. She was involved in battle when I came on the scene. I helped her out." Kitty held her hands to the fire. They were cold, red, and stiff. "I haven't had so much fun since— I just pitched in and forgot everything."

"How tactful of you!" Sally laughed. "Did you think I might be watching and turn thumbs down?"

Kitty evaded the question. "I was thinking, coming up the walk, she's really closer to the age of those children than she is to Doug's. So if she relapses into childishness once in a while— They say every boy in town knows Captain Bodien, so I suppose they know her, too."

"Of course. As an equal, a playmate. What Doug Gardiner is thinking of I can't imagine. It is most unsuitable, in age and in every other way."

"Doug had taken her to call on his aunts, I gathered. A painful experience, doubtless. She was letting off steam."

"Did she tell you that?"

"Of course not. Only that that was where she had been. I wonder she has the courage to marry him."

"Pshaw! She's marrying him for position, of course."

"She's in love with him. I've seen her look at him, when she didn't know anyone was watching. D'you suppose anyone has ever loved Doug Gardiner before? But think what her devotion will have to endure at the hands of the Gardiner aunts, if it is to survive. 'Suffer long' and all the rest of it."

Tishy brought the tea tray and put it on the marble-topped table at one side of the fireplace; in a moment she returned with the big silver urn. Sally moved her chair closer, set a cup and saucer under the spigot.

"Ludwig thinks I should entertain for them."

"D'you mind? I thought you liked giving parties. Sheldon wants me to have one, too—he and Doug have been friends so long—but for me it's a real undertaking. Terrifies me."

Sally went off at a tangent. "Must she be taken into the Woman's Club?"

Kitty laughed. "I can't think of anything she would care less about. Forget it: the aunts would probably blackball her anyway."

"Are you getting dry, Kitty? Truly, the children must be dealt with, they've gotten sadly out of hand. They've lived for so long in such a repressive atmosphere. Charles and Ernest have never really known anything else, and they're far too good. Stodgy, I think sometimes. Mind you: they're ours, and I love them dearly, but I don't want them to be *dull*. But Ludwig, Junior, and he's only two—Cassie has him upstairs now—he has already thought up more devilment than the other two boys put together."

"And Elsa?"

"Oh, Elsa. She adores her father and he thinks she can do no wrong. She hates being a girl. I suspect she has the best brain of our lot, but she may as well be reconciled. I shall have to take her in hand soon."

"I envy you. I'd take any kind of child, stodgy or not, good, bad, indifferent. I'm—Dock has given me a very grudging permission to try again, now."

The talk grew more hushed over the teacups, here touching upon, there dealing in detail, with the more ghoulish aspects of the feminine physique and its aberrations. The daylight waned, gathering dusk darkened the room. The noisy shouting of the children, parting at the front gate, came remotely to the library. Kitty rose and put her empty teacup on the table just as Elsa and her two brothers came into the house and paused in the hall to take their wraps off.

"Come here and let me see how wet you are."

Elsa hesitated at the threshold when she saw the guest still there. Kitty, as she turned to pick up her muff and gloves from the sofa, smiled over her shoulder. Elsa came in, followed by the boys. "We're not wet, Mamma.

We've been to the Kleins'; we're dried off." Elsa's darkening golden hair was tumbled over her shoulders, her eyes and cheeks were bright. "Mamma, could I have a bugle? Please? A real one?"

"Whatever for?"

"To play. I could. Listen." She had brought in with her the tin trumpet; she lifted it to her lips and blew recognizably the notes of reveille.

"Mercy, Elsa! What a racket!"

"Nobody else can play this, so they have to let me be bugler. But I'd like a real bugle. Johnny always wants to command; he knows the drill, but they say I can't throw good enough to be a cannoneer."

"*Well* enough," her mother corrected automatically. "You don't need to be anything but a well-behaved little girl. But if you must play with the boys, just be glad they let you, and don't think you can order them around. And of course you cannot have a bugle. Who ever heard of such a thing? Your neck muscles would puff out like a balloon. Must you go, Kitty? Ludwig will be home presently, and can drive you home. It's such a long walk, and it's nearly dark."

"There's no need. I'm to meet Sheldon at the store at closing time. We're having dinner at his folks'. He wants to get a horse," she added, quickly on the defensive, "but I should be afraid to drive it. I've never driven a horse in my life."

Kitty went out the front door just as Ludwig came in from the back hall. "Caller?" he said to Sally as she turned back from closing the door.

"Just Kitty Edwards."

He went to the library with her and beamed happily at his assembled children. "Everybody here, eh? How gemütlich."

Elsa began chattering to him in rapid German as he took his chair by the fire and snapped his evening paper open.

"Schöne Elsa, how often must I say it? Speak English in your mother's presence. And no, you may not have a bugle. What a notion! Has your mother not already said 'no'? A bugle is not for young ladies."

"I have already said 'no.' You children go wash up for dinner. And Elsa, comb your hair. Tell Cassie to bring the baby down." When they had gone, she murmured, "The influence of Captain Bodien."

Her husband smiled at her over the top of his paper. "More likely the wish to be unique among maidens."

"I don't know. Kitty came in looking like a wild woman." She told him about the snowball fight. "Kitty says," she concluded, "that Sheldon wants her to entertain for Barbara Bodien. She isn't any more eager than I am."

"We must do what is right."

"I'll have a dinner for them after they are married, after Doug has been chosen to be the candidate for Congress—in his honor."

Ludwig did not press her; he recognized with amusement the reason for this long postponement: before her marriage Miss Bodien could not be asked to dinner without her parents.

Mrs. Kitty Edwards solved her problem not long after that wintry day by inviting her friends and her mother-in-law's to an afternoon reception to meet Miss Bodien. Barbara's mother was there, in the receiving line next to Barbara, where there was no chance of getting much out of her beyond a "How d'you do" and "So pleased." The senior Mrs. Edwards, who had little faith in Kitty's *savoir faire* as hostess at a formal reception, took over and managed the affair with a capable and experienced hand, and Kitty was relieved, not only because she had in truth been frightened by the prospect of staging a large affair, but because to Sheldon's mother the pleasure of giving a party at someone else's expense (Mrs. Edwards was the least bit "near") prevented any objections or questions beyond a few murmurs: "All these new people. I don't quite like—just who *are* they, dear?" On the afternoon she was graciousness itself, and everyone followed her example—everyone but the Misses Gardiner, who endured the affair briefly, with no display of false cordiality, but were coldly correct.

After that one party, the Gardiner-Bodien match slipped into the background. Waynesboro's attention was fixed on politics. At the District Convention in early spring, Douglas Gardiner was duly chosen as the party's candidate for the Seventh's Representative in Congress. General Deming refused to allow his name to be proposed by the Boone County Stalwarts. He might be an old windbag, but he could be counted on to support the party candidate's platform, whatever that might turn out to be.

Mrs. Deming had understood and supported the General in his decision, although the Stalwarts just might have succeeded in sending him back to Congress; she did not demur when he explained to her. "I don't care," he had said, haughtily, "to be tagged again as a cat's paw for Conkling and Company. For General Grant I feel only pity: they are supporting him for a third term only to keep Blaine out, and because they think they can control him. Grant is an ingenuous man, ruined by his so-called friends."

"You are quite right in your decision," she reassured him. "It would be too bad if you had to pick up and go to Washington now, when you are making such good progress with your history of the county."

He could amuse himself with his book, she thought, for quite a long while, although "amuse" was perhaps not a fair word; he had done very well with *The Buckeye Brigade:* had made an amount of money that had surprised her, and in doing so, had helped unemployed or crippled comrades in arms.

Ludwig would attend the State Convention of the Republican Party in April as a State Committeeman; he was almost certain to be chosen as one of the delegates to the National Convention. He was already preparing, by an unending series of letters, to fight for a united delegation in support of John Sherman at Chicago. Even for those who were not actively involved in politics, the quadrennial excitement was beginning to mount. No Ohioan questioned the desirability of choosing another citizen of the state to replace Hayes. The President had by this last year of his term succeeded in alienating many former supporters; indifferent to his political future, since, as he had said from the beginning, he would not serve again, he had demanded with a stubbornness irritating to Congress that his promised Civil Service measures be enacted, with the result that the deadlock between executive and legislative branches prevented the passage of any bill of importance. More cynical citizens thought that no bad thing: too many laws were passed anyway; what the country needed, now that the Resumption Act had gone safely into effect, was to be let alone. But government could not be indefinitely deadlocked: a President must be chosen who could act with Congress. The gray, austere man with the long beard must be superseded by a better politician. So far as Waynesboro and its county were concerned, they held the President in as high esteem as ever, and were confident that his support would, like theirs, go to John Sherman as the man to succeed him: had not President Hayes stood by his Secretary of the Treasury through thick and thin? Knots of citizens in the cigar store, in the drugstore, in the Court House, and in John Gordon's office argued with some vehemence, and ladies, less ready than men to compromise, less hesitant to call opponents enemies, reacted with righteous wrath to newspaper cartoons and editorials. Most Republicans, like the men who played chess in John's office, were agreed: the Stalwarts, with Conkling leading them and Grant as a figurehead, would be locked in combat with the Blaine men, and a compromise candidate would finally be chosen. They were hopeful that John Sherman would be that man, and some of them—Ludwig certainly—were developing the warm loyalty that often follows the espousing of a cause originally adopted for purely logical reasons.

"It's a pity," Ludwig said one evening in John's office, when he, Lichtenstein, and Dr. Blair were all present, "that he's a man people don't warm up to. He's not a man without feeling, just reserved, like Hayes."

"Everyone knows Hayes is a warmhearted man." Dr. Blair's admiration for the President and of his wife, the teetotaling Lucy, had suffered no diminution.

"Yes. But did they, before he was elected? Sherman will make a better President." Ludwig was emphatic. "More experience in Congress, and these years as Secretary of the Treasury. He knows finances: he went ahead with his sound money policy in spite of opposition, even threats. I like a man who dares to be unpopular."

John, who had come to stand in the door to the inner office just as the chess players finished their game, said, "Men who dare to be unpopular don't often get elected."

"But time has proved that he was right about the Resumption Act. That's all water under the bridge."

Dr. Blair grunted. "No need to get heated with us, Rausch. We all agree. But I regret the choice of Garfield to lead the delegation. At heart, he's Blaine's man."

This conversation took place after the State Convention, where Ludwig had been troubled by the difficulty of winning over Blaine's supporters. Now he nodded a vigorous assent. "I wouldn't have chosen him. Garfield is indebted to Blaine for various favors. But Sherman wanted him. The Ohio delegation will include one or two Blaine men, but I don't think Garfield would dare—"

"He hass a flexible conscience, I sink." Mr. Lichtenstein had not forgotten the past.

"He and Blaine are the same cut of cloth," John agreed. "I hope Sherman knows what he is doing."

"There's been some whispering about Garfield himself, if a dark horse has to be chosen." That was Dr. Blair. "He's a good, God-fearing man, but sometimes politicians can do wicked things and still persuade themselves they are acting in all righteousness."

"I don't think he'd dare," Ludwig said again.

So the men talked, the days passed, life went on; but even really important occurrences—births, deaths, marriages—did not entirely obliterate from the collective consciousness an underlying awareness of the approaching party conventions. Not even the prospect of the Bodien-Gardiner wedding entirely superseded politics as a subject of conjecture and surmise, although it was a more than usually interesting event to much of Waynesboro. However, the actual occasion, on the last of April, wiped out of the minds of those present every other preoccupation—for several hours at least.

All of Douglas's friends and associates had been invited to the wedding, including the Rausches, the Edwardses, the Gordons, the Ballards. He had surveyed with a somewhat jaundiced eye the handsomely engraved silver epergne sent his bride-elect by the Ballards but had said nothing to spoil Barbara's pleasure in it. He was not surprised by the flood of presents—Waynesboro would conform to the conventions—nor by the acceptance of invitations to wedding and wedding reception; his friends were curious enough to be willing to pay the price of admission: recognition of his wife. Barbara's father, on the other hand, was naïvely delighted. "It's going to be all right for Barbara," he said to his wife, "you'll see. The boss told me so, and I believe him. The old aunts may be slow to come around, but everyone else will be good to her."

"And why not, I should like to know?" Mrs. Bodien, though liking Doug, still in her heart disapproved of the match. If only Barbara was marrying in the church. "Anyway, it don't matter what the town thinks. You worry too much, Gus. They're in love with each other. Shouldn't that be enough?"

"Is it? Has it always been, to you?"

"It has been worth everything, an' well you know it. If only—" But she knew better than to voice her concern over their souls' salvation: her husband's and Barbara's (Stewart she still kept in line), and anyway, please God, there was still time. "If only," she said again, tranquilly, "we weren't losing her."

"We'll not lose her. Your family didn't lose you."

She thought, "This may be different," but she said only, "And a grand comfort they'll be to me at the wedding, Jim and Dan an' theirs. Else the bride's family would have few guests on their side of the aisle—only your army mates."

Captain Bodien chuckled. General Gibbon would hardly relish being called his "mate." But he would be there: he had promised, and that was an unshadowed pleasure to the one-time artillery captain's one-time sergeant.

The groom's friends and family were prepared for the MacDonald brothers, their wives and children—Barbara's uncles, aunts, and cousins; they were not disappointed: the big, jovial, coarse-grained Irishmen, their buxom wives, and hearty children were just what had been expected. Some were surprised that the Bodien parlor was not filled with West End Irish, not realizing in their ignorance that few devout Catholics would countenance so heretical a proceeding as the marriage of one nominally theirs to a Protestant by a Presbyterian minister. They were still more surprised by the Bodien house, which none of them had entered before. If the children had not been with them, to ease them over their astonishment, they might even have been uncomfortable. But since the invitations had read "and family," the three older Rausches and the two Gordons were there, among others, and helped their parents by being not at all taken aback by the Bodien hall and parlor.

When Captain Bodien had bought the derelict Inskip house, he had done so not only for his wife's sake, but also because, in spite of its run-down condition, it reminded him of the houses he had known in his boyhood: houses of his grandparents, his uncles and cousins in the Maryland countryside. With good reason: it resembled them. Built by a Marylander in the twenties, it was a square two-story central block, with a one-story wing on each side. Its ornaments and trimmings, cornice, door, corner pilasters, were in the then fashionable Federalist manner. Captain Bodien had contented himself with repairs and fresh paint. The brick house with its white trim, green shutters, and wide tall chimneys looked more like a southern plantation house than, some of the wedding guests thought resentfully, it had any right to look. Indoors the tables held bowls of lilacs, and lilacs were banked in all the corners, but the flowers did not conceal the beauty of the curving stairs, nor of the low-ceiled rooms with their classic doors and mantels, nor of the old mahogany furniture pushed back against the parlor walls. There the guests were ushered by young Stewart Bodien—another surprise—at fifteen a trim, handsome boy, gray-eyed and black-haired like Barbara, but more aquiline in feature, with high cheekbones and a clean jawline. Waynesboro guests were led to one side of the ribboned aisle that led from the hall to the lilac-filled fireplace; on the other side were the MacDonalds and Captain Bodien's army friends, all brass buttons and gold braid: the slightly built officer whose close-cropped hair and mustache added to his look of distinction, and the stocky, red-faced one, whose uniform had a Decoration-Day-only look. Johnny Gordon at sight of them gripped his mother's hand convulsively. "It's General Gibbon," he whispered. The whisper carried; everyone stared harder. His mother shushed him. The piano in the sitting room was being played; the Reverend Mr. McKinney came to stand before the fireplace: in his Sabbath frock-coat, his finger in place in his book, he looked quite composed, overdoing it a little to the point of smugness. Douglas Gardiner limped in from the hall, his best man Sheldon Edwards beside him, to take his place in front of the minister; he stood so that he could watch the hall door and the foot of the staircase, his jaw so clenched that his face muscles were rigid. But no one noticed him. Barbara, long train sweeping down the stairs behind her, came to the newel post where her father waited, and into the parlor on his arm. She came smiling, and when Douglas stepped to her side, he returned that loving, confident smile, and relaxed. The ceremony was over in a moment. As Johnny complained later, "It didn't last long enough." His father asked, "Long enough for what? To justify our getting all togged out? I agree. But I guess it will take."

The bride and groom went out between the ribbons to form a receiving line with the senior Bodiens at the foot of the staircase. Barbara's brother came along and removed the ribbons; the ranks of guests broke, mingled, endured the receiving line, and passed on to the dining room. Anne could feel the excitement in her children, one on each hand. "Their first wedding," she thought. With Binny it could have been that, but with Johnny she knew it was the awe-inspiring realization that he was under the same roof with Captain Bodien's General Gibbon and his "Old Man," the Major Stewart whose part Johnny was taking when he ordered "Drivers mount!" In his eagerness he lost his mother in the throng, came up with the Rausches, and took his place in line next to Elsa; General Gibbon was just ahead of them, shaking hands with Barbara. He stooped over her. "An old soldier's privilege, my dear." He kissed her cheek. "After all, you were the Battery Baby, and named Barbara so that your saint would protect us gunners."

Barbara, beautiful beyond everyday in her veil and white dress, her eyes dark with emotion, her cheeks blazing, her heart-shaped face still tilted as she had turned it for his kiss, said, "It was good of you to come; it means so much to Papa, and to me. It almost seems as if I were remembering, too. I've heard all about you since I was a child. May I present my husband, Mr. Gardiner? He is going to be our next Congressman."

A stiffening about the General's mouth suggested that perhaps he was not an enthusiastic admirer of Congressmen, but he shook hands and spoke pleasantly with Doug, and moved on, until he stopped before Captain Bodien.

"Well, Sergeant, it's been a long time."

Captain Bodien took a firm grip of the proffered hand. "Nigh fifteen years since you used to come to our part of the Petersburg line and give us battery drill, just to keep your hand in."

"To keep you up to snuff, you mean—a jumped-up Captain like you. You might have forgotten all you ever knew about light artillery, dug in those lines."

"I don't blame you, sir. After the Old Man was invalided out," Captain

Bodien gave his hand to Major Stewart, "the battery wasn't the same. I couldn't take his place. Wait around, will you? I'll be out of this in a minute."

Presently the receiving line broke up; the bride and groom and the Sheldon Edwardses took their places at the bride's table, along with her brother Stewart and a cousin or two. Other guests were served standing, wherever they might be. Johnny and Elsa, by this time pushed back against the wall, doggedly worked their way through the crowd to the Captain's study, in the other wing of the house: they were following the uniforms, elbowing here and ducking there. Behind them Captain Bodien herded the Rausches and Gordons, who were trying to catch up with their children, toward the same refuge, leaving to his wife and her caterer all further responsibility for their other guests.

"Sorry I can't offer you a man's drink instead of the lemonade they're passing around, but I'll see we have some food in here." He leaned into the hall, spoke a word to someone, came in, and closed the door behind him. "We've got some teetotalers out there, and I can't risk getting Barbara off on the wrong foot. Later, when everyone's gone— In the meantime, I wanted you to meet these friends: Mrs. Rausch and Captain Rausch, late of the Sixth Iowa. Mrs. Gordon and Captain Gordon, Assistant Surgeon of the Forty-sixth Ohio."

Johnny, who had never heard his father called "Captain" before, listened open-mouthed while the appropriate things were said, until Captain Bodien, a hand on the backbone of each of them, gently propelled Johnny and Elsa into a position directly before the officers.

"Here are two gunners for you, sir. Young Lieutenant Gordon in command of a battery section; Bugler Rausch, sounding all the bugle calls. They know the drill, General; the boys spent all last summer on it. And Major Stewart, two friends of mine: Lieutenant Gordon and Bugler Rausch."

Elsa looked a little confused, but stood her ground firmly, shaking the hands offered her. Johnny dared not look over his shoulder—he could almost feel parental hands reaching out to snatch him back from the limelight. He was scared, but knew that if he did not speak out he would regret it all his life; this was his one chance.

"General Gibbon, sir: do you remember South Mountain? Do you remember Antietam?"

"Johnny—" His father cut him short.

"Let him ask his questions, Captain. I'm getting old, you know, which means that I like an audience for tales of my younger days. Yes, I remember our Brigade taking Turner's Gap, if that is what you mean: Stewart taking his section of the battery right up the turnpike, with the infantry in the fields, two regiments on each side. As pretty a sight as you ever saw, a dress parade into battle, in full sight of General McClellan and most of the Army on the higher slopes. Right up the turnpike into the Gap. And Antietam—no one who was there could forget it, the fighting my Brigade did, and the punishment they took, eh, Stewart? The battery in the barnyard among the haystacks, and across in the cornfield what seemed like the whole Rebel Army behind a rail fence."

"And you fired one of the guns when there weren't men enough left to man it?"

"The gun I'd put in the road to keep it clear. Yes, I remember. The ground sloped down and behind them, and the cannoneers left were too excited to see that every time she recoiled, her elevation increased, and she was shooting over the heads of the Rebs. I changed the elevation screw and pulled the lanyard once or twice myself. But the guns by the haystacks had it hotter, shot and shell and every kind of ball, over the heads of our men coming back out of the cornfield, and the Rebs leaping up with a yell to come after the battery. But Lieutenant Stewart foiled 'em."

The eager children looked to the "Old Man." His blue eyes twinkled in his ruddy face, his curled mustache bristled. "Double canister fast as we could ram it home and pull the lanyard. That sent 'em back and gave us time to limber, with what few horses we had left. It was time to git, an' we got."

"You took the guns out?" Johnny knew, but wanted the whole story from the man responsible.

"You're doggone right we took 'em out, under orders from the General here."

"Too few men left to handle them, anyway."

"In a hurry, before the Rebs came back. The battery had lost forty men and thirty horses in a few minutes. A little longer an' we'd not've had horses enough. And the whole brigade had lost—how many, sir?"

"So many it was never quite the same again. It was still the Iron Brigade, and we made soldiers of the new regiment we got. They proved it at Gettysburg, but too many of the best were gone. The young volunteers, the boys like your fathers. Of course the Old Regulars, like Stewart and Bodien, they knew all the tricks—they survived."

"But Major Stewart was wounded."

"Yes. Bodien, you were one of the wounded at Antietam, too, weren't you? I'd forgotten. You know, since I've been back at western posts, fighting campaigns against Indians again, the War of the Rebellion seems longer ago than the year at Camp Floyd, and the Mormons and the Utes. If anyone had asked me about Bodien's wound, I'd have said 'Yes, an Indian tomahawk that didn't go deep enough to kill him, so the Army surgeons just took out the bone splinters and put in a silver plate.' That's why he's bald as a billiard ball, the back of his head. Still work all right, Bodien?"

"Good as my own skull, I reckon."

"D'you remember '61, and the march back to Missouri? Twelve hundred miles, guns, cannon, horses—at least you gunners could ride. Poor devils of infantrymen: they had to walk. And we weren't sure we wouldn't be attacked on the way. And the news we got when we reached St. Joe: first that Bull Run had been won, and we were afraid the war would be over before we got there?

H'mph! Then that the battle had been lost and the Army dispersed, and we were afraid we were too late to save the country. We missed Bull Run. But maybe you were there?" he asked John and Ludwig.

Ludwig shook his head. John said, "I was. First Ohio. And I was dispersed all right. I spent the night under a bridge."

They all laughed. General Gibbon said, "Then it was after that you were a surgeon?"

"Yes. I hadn't quite finished at the medical college in April of '61. I reenlisted in the Second Ohio after Bull Run. I chose the Second because my best Waynesboro friends were in it, but in the spring they furloughed me to go back home and finish my studies and get my M.D. They needed surgeons. Then I was sent to the Forty-sixth Ohio."

"That was in the Western Army, of course. No more of the Army of the Potomac for you? Talking about it all makes it seem like yesterday, but it's getting to be a long while ago."

"You've seen a lot of fighting since, sir, haven't you?" Captain Bodien was as interested as the children. "What's it been like?"

"Indian fighting. You know what it is like. Slippery devils—you never know where they are. My command had to go in after the Custer massacre, and clean up." He paused, perhaps out of regard for the children. Just then they heard the commotion in the hall that signaled the bride's approach to the staircase, the throwing of her bouquet. Those in Captain Bodien's library left that comfortable masculine room, with its dark furniture, leather chairs, and full bookcases, its old-soldier decoration of saber and carbine hung above the mantel, and returned to the lilac-scented hall. In another short while, the bride and groom departed in a shower of rice, and the Waynesboro guests made their farewells one by one, leaving the two old soldiers to linger as they chose.

As a social event the wedding had been at least a surface success: two worlds or three, or fragments thereof, had met and mingled amiably; only the faces of the Misses Gardiner had shown aloofness; no one had even seemed to look curiously at anyone else, except for those few who were not accustomed to Miss Lavinia's wide-spreading crinolines. But with the possible exception of the bride and groom and certainly that of the bride's father, those who had enjoyed the occasion most wholeheartedly were the children.

The Gordons drove away in the surrey that served them as a family conveyance, Johnny and his father on the front seat, Anne and Binny in the back. They were behind old Molly, and other carriages pressed to pass them. While her father was slapping the reins to induce Molly to move over, Binny, who had been silent through the long scene in the parlor, and had stood close to her mother where the men with the booming voices would not notice her, said in a small voice to Anne, "Was Papa a soldier, too?"

Anne said, "Yes, of course he was." Johnny said, "Well, aren't you a mug, not to know that," and John said, "No."

"Don't confuse her, John. Yes, he was, Binny."

"Not a fighting soldier. I just picked up the pieces after a battle and patched them together again as best I could."

"The war was awful, and Papa doesn't like to talk about it. But sometimes your country has to be fought for, and you have to do it."

Binny's voice was still smaller. "Was it a *big* war?"

"Well, you *are* a—"

"Don't say that again, Johnny."

"It was just about the biggest war in the whole history of the world, wasn't it, Papa?"

"The most men fighting, maybe."

"That general, Papa, was he your general?" Binny persisted. "Was he as big as your general?"

John smiled, staring straight over Molly's ears. "No, not as big. My general was the best of the lot: General Sherman. Remember his name. Maybe you'll get to see him, one of these days. He's in command of all the Army, now."

"But there isn't a war now?"

"No. Only with the Indians out west."

"Will he remember you if we ever see him?"

"No. I was just one of thousands; I don't suppose he ever heard my name. Unless he should remember how I pestered the higher command about closing that hospital in Duckport. It took an order from him, finally, to do it."

"That's enough, Binny," her mother said. "Does gold braid have all that effect on you? Didn't you like the bride?" She smoothed the little girl's tossed hair, quieted her with a touch. Binny was six, a little older than Charles Rausch, who was learning to bugle on the tin trumpet scorned by Elsa. Binny would be wanting to join the other children any day now: she would start to school in the fall, and that always made children independent. Anne remembered her own childhood, her devoted tagging after her brother Rob, and the snubbings she had endured. She didn't want Binny to suffer that unwanted feeling, but she would, of course. Any small girl with older brothers was sure to.

It was after they had reached home and were in the sitting room at loose ends, that Johnny sighed and said, "There's only one thing more I'd've liked. I wish we could have had some battery drill for Major Stewart and the General."

"But this wasn't a G.A.R. reunion you've been to. This was a *wedding*!"

The Rausches, coachman-driven, were home before the Gordons. Not until they had reached their bedroom, and the children had been sent to change from their wedding garments, did their parents exchange more than the most superficial comments.

But, before Ludwig and Sally could really begin to deal with the wedding from their different points of view, Elsa, clad in chemise and petticoats, came to stand in the door.

"Will there be another war, Papa?"

"Goodness gracious alive, child!" Her mother's response was vigorous. "I should hope not!"

"I wish there would."

"You don't know what you're talking about. War is horrible."

"But General Gibbon and Major Stewart and Captain Bodien, they liked it. They were heroes. It must have been exciting, and adventurous."

"It wouldn't be adventurous for you, my girl. You'd be left sitting at home, waiting and waiting. You don't think young ladies share in the heroics, do you?"

Elsa fell silent, standing there leaning against the door jamb. She never thought of herself as a young lady in any possible war. She would disguise herself, cut off her hair.

Her father spoke then, for the first time, with so intense an effort to express himself and make the impression he wanted to make that he sounded almost ponderous. The effect was so unlike him that Elsa cast him a startled sidelong look.

"Old soldiers! Elsa, General Gibbon and the others—they did not *enjoy* the war. I did not enjoy it, not for one minute. Your Uncle Dock is fairly sick when he thinks of it. Those men today: what they like is *remembering* it. They look back from the middle age and think, 'The biggest thing that ever happened in this country, and we had a part in it. Life meant something then.' Now life is pretty humdrum: even for General Gibbon out on the plains, maybe. Now, it hasn't so much flavor, because they know it will go on, not be cut off and ended any moment. They see that what they're doing isn't really so very important by comparison, and so they remember and say, 'I was there.' But none of them would want a son to have to go through what they went through."

"Do you like to remember, Papa?"

His intent face was smoothed blank by astonishment. "But I am not—Gott in Himmel!" He sighed, and then chuckled. "I suppose I am middle-aged! It's crept up on me. But my life has plenty of flavor." He reached across the space between the chairs to take Sally's hand. "Besides, I'm too busy to spend time remembering, yet awhile."

"Go get some clothes on, Elsa. You're indecent."

When they were alone Sally said, "Your Captain Bodien is very clever. But the little scene with General Gibbon and Major what's-his-name didn't fool me a little bit—you know it was a put-up job."

"But why?"

"To prove we were all wrong about him and his family."

"And it didn't?"

"It proved he wasn't such a liar as we thought. If General Gibbon says all those things happened, like being tomahawked, then of course they did. And I suppose that house was like what he knew as a boy, and the furniture, or he wouldn't be so unaware of it—so at home. But after all, Ludwig, he did enlist as a private in the Regular Army before the war, and then the privates were mostly scamps, weren't they? Then when he married out of his class—"

"Tchut, Sally! Class! Who knows the background of any stranger who comes to town? In this place, at this time, it's a word without meaning. We judge a man for himself."

"Nonsense. You know well enough one can always recognize one's own kind of people."

"So—? Captain Bodien married 'beneath him,' yes? Then he must not hope for his children to do better?"

"He should have thought of his children beforehand. The boy is a handsome youngster, but he's even more Irish in coloring than his sister."

"I can't see that Stewart looks anything like the MacDonalds."

"Let's hope Doug's children aren't throwbacks to *them.*"

Ludwig chuckled. "I admit I wouldn't trust one of the MacDonalds alone with a ballot box, but they're likable fellows. And Gardiner blood won't be any the worse for a little red in it, a little warmth and gaiety."

"Poor Miss Lavinia! Poor Miss Caroline!"

"Poor First Witch! Poor Second Witch! They looked like something out of Macbeth, even in their silks and satins. You know you don't really like them, Sally."

"They aren't so bad when you get to know them. In the Club—"

"Anyway, after the election they won't be annoyed for a while. Maybe all the little Gardiners will be born in Washington."

"It was you who told me I must learn to like all the members of the Club, remember? Mrs. McKinney looked as if she had bitten into an unripe persimmon while the Reverend was reading the marriage ceremony!"

"I know. Catholics in the same room with her. She'll get over it when young Mrs. Gardiner joins her church. A brand from the burning."

"Is she going to—"

"Her father advised her to. That's all I know."

"But doesn't she believe *anything*? Doesn't it matter to her?"

Ludwig looked at her quizzically. "Isn't it a wife's duty to join her husband's church? I seem to remember—but no, I doubt whether she believes much. Her father's a freethinker, to put it mildly, and he said he'd kept her head free of nonsense."

"You like Captain Bodien, don't you?"

"I like him. I don't expect him to become a part of our social life, if that's what is on your mind. His importance to me lies in his work at the mill. He knows rope and how to make it; he has the mill organized—every hand does twice the work he used to—and I'm free to put in my time looking for business. You know how much money we've been making."

"I thought that was better times."

"It's partly that. Partly it has been the bumper crops of these last few years. We never used to sell much twine for harvesting, because only old-fashioned farmers hand-tied their sheaves, and the reapers and binders used wire. Now Deere has a twine binder on the market, and we have a warehouse full of binder twine waiting. I had that much foresight. But mostly the mill runs smoothly because Bodien is there to see that it does. And I hope his family will be happy in Waynesboro, because then he'll stay."

"I see. Well, we'll have the Gardiners to dinner after the Conventions."

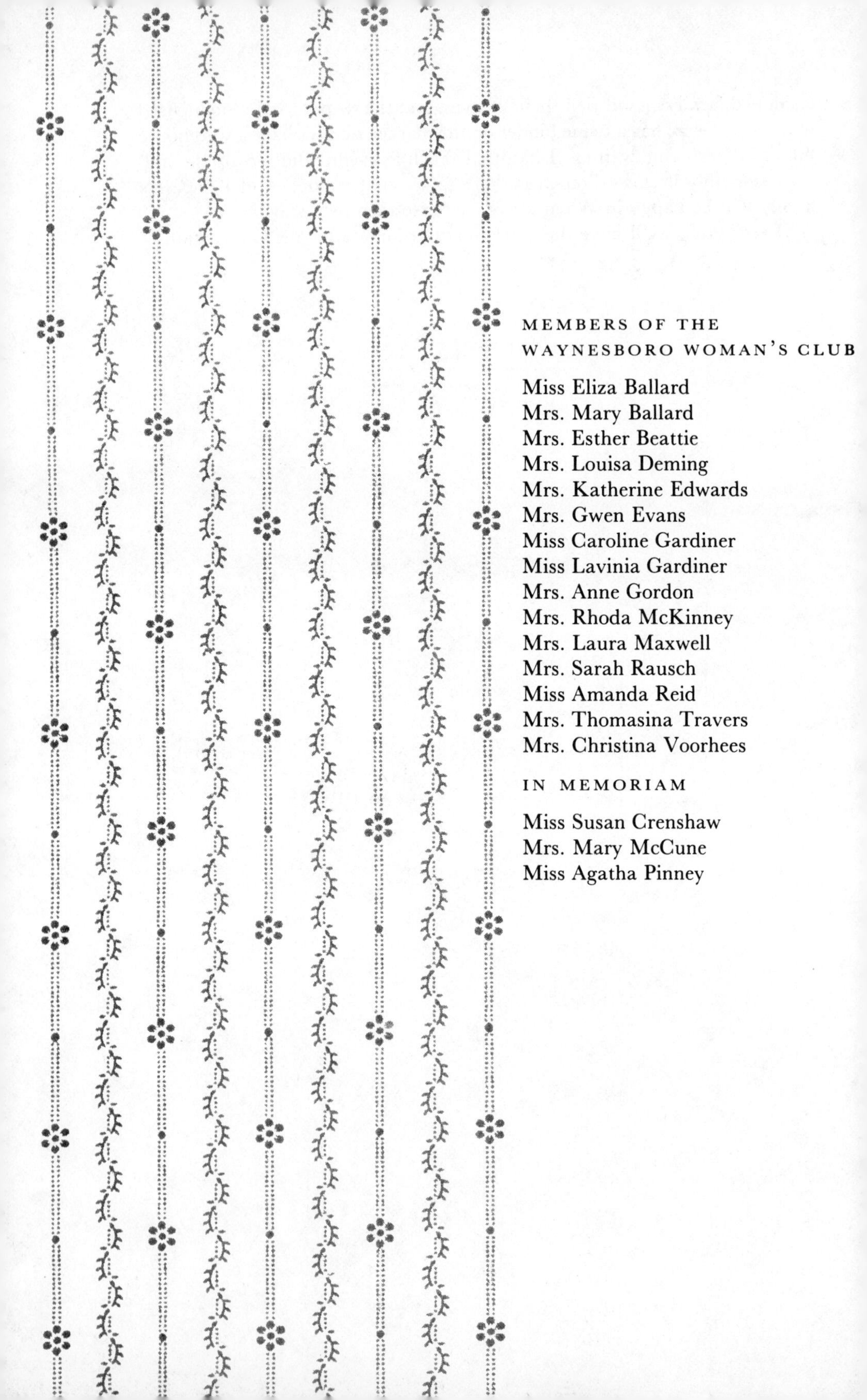

MEMBERS OF THE
WAYNESBORO WOMAN'S CLUB

Miss Eliza Ballard
Mrs. Mary Ballard
Mrs. Esther Beattie
Mrs. Louisa Deming
Mrs. Katherine Edwards
Mrs. Gwen Evans
Miss Caroline Gardiner
Miss Lavinia Gardiner
Mrs. Anne Gordon
Mrs. Rhoda McKinney
Mrs. Laura Maxwell
Mrs. Sarah Rausch
Miss Amanda Reid
Mrs. Thomasina Travers
Mrs. Christina Voorhees

IN MEMORIAM

Miss Susan Crenshaw
Mrs. Mary McCune
Miss Agatha Pinney

* 1880–1881 *

"We take our politics seriously . . ."

Once the Gardiner wedding was over, Waynesboro turned to a new conversation: politics, and discussion of National Convention prospects and possibilities. Mr. and Mrs. Bonner intended to go to Chicago so that Mr. Bonner could send his own dispatches to the *Torchlight;* they were taking the two younger children and leaving the oldest son, a youth of twenty-two or three, to run the paper in their absence. General Deming had obtained a spectator's gallery ticket; but he would not think of exposing his wife to the coarse masculinity of a political convention. The Rausches were the first away. They were taking the children to Burlington to stay with their Rausch grandparents and their Aunt Minna and her family; Sally would not leave them in the big house with only servants to look after them. Parents, four children, and Cassie were borne away to Iowa long enough before the Convention for Sally and Ludwig to visit briefly with his family. Elsa was stubbornly rebellious at being treated like a child: Charlotte Bonner was going to the Convention, why couldn't she? Well, anyway, Charlotte was going to Chicago to stay in a hotel, why couldn't she? She was not convinced by the distinction explained by her parents: her father was a delegate, her mother would be expected to act as one of the Ohio delegation hostesses, and would have no time. Besides, Sally (with no fear of coarse masculinity) expected to go to every session of the Convention; she wasn't going to miss a word. Elsa protested in vain that she, too, wanted to hear the Convention. She went to Burlington.

Waynesboro seemed strangely empty when the politicians had gone, considering how few they were, actually. Time hung on one's hands: there seemed to be nothing to do but wait for the evening paper. Mr. Bonner's pre-Convention stories were full of color and prejudice, satire and sarcasm, but all that his readers learned from the *Torchlight* (or from the Cincinnati papers, for that matter) was that the two bitterly feuding Republican factions—the

Stalwarts for Grant, bossed by Conkling and his fellows on the one hand, and on the other, the "Blaine of Maine" men—had dug their heels in and would not budge. The Ohio delegation, instructed by the State Convention to vote for Sherman, held the balance of power and might cast the deciding vote. It was being wooed by Blaine supporters. The Convention opened on Tuesday, June 2; but as early as the Saturday before, rumors began to circulate that Conkling and Simon Cameron were scheming to put through a resolution to adopt the unit rule; Mr. Bonner had the whole story in the Monday evening *Torchlight*. Waynesboro therefore was prepared for the time-wasting, nerve-wracking, but triumphant contest that followed, when Garfield persuaded the Ohio delegation to vote with the Blaine men to defeat Conkling's resolution. Mr. Bonner was pleased; his more astute readers realized that so far as the Ohio delegation was concerned, the unit rule might help Sherman more than it would hurt him, but understood too that its adoption must be prevented, lest the Stalwarts stampede the Convention for Grant.

Mr. Lichtenstein, Dr. Blair, and John Gordon had an earnest session in the doctor's office Tuesday night, with the *Cincinnati Enquirer* and the *Torchlight* on the table before them.

"McLean is a Democrat, zo vot ze *Enquirer* says macht nichts. But I like it not." The heavy-jowled, drooping-mustached German scowled at the headlines. "Blaine vill get some votes from ze Ohio delegation, it iss expected, no? And Garfield iss allzu admiring of Blaine, nicht wahr?"

"But Sherman is not. So long as he controls the delegation, Ohio won't go to Blaine." Dr. Blair was offering such hope as he reasonably could. "Oh, a few votes, perhaps."

"I haf seen Mr. Secretary of ze Treasury, John Sherman. A fine eager head, like a hawk. Aber it iss—vot iss ze word—mental? Nein—*intellectual*. Eagerness. No heart. Kein Gemütlichkeit."

"A cold man," John agreed, "but only outwardly, I think. He is devoted to his brother, and the General is anything but cold. Anyway, I'm for him, for the General's sake."

With none of the leading candidates present at the Convention, it soon became as evident to all newspaper readers as to the delegates themselves that Garfield, representing the Sherman forces on the floor, was the only rival, in impressiveness, of Senator Conkling. Two handsome men, giants in size, formidable in their oratorical prowess, they confronted each other, one holding his followers by his vituperative powers, the other winning men to him by his moderation and reasonableness. Candidates were put in nomination at the fourth session, on Saturday evening, to the traditional accompaniment of roaring enthusiasm. Voting began on Monday, and ballot after ballot followed for two wearing days. The Conkling men, the Stalwart three hundred, gave their vote to ex-President Grant over and over again, but the scattered vote for favorite sons began to go to Sherman, and for a short while, his followers were hopeful. But after three more ballots with no change, Wisconsin shifted to Garfield; on the next, Indiana followed suit: and on the thirty-sixth, when the news came that Sherman had released his delegates, the stampede began. The bandwagon rolled, and the state flags were borne triumphantly to Garfield's seat.

The nomination of a vice-president came quickly, and the Convention ended on a cynical note, not without an ironic touch of humor. To conciliate the Stalwarts, one of their number was chosen: Chester Arthur, the same man whom President Hayes, in his fight for Civil Service reform, had so long opposed, and had eventually succeeded in removing as Collector of the Port of New York. Conkling ordered the nominee to refuse to accept the honor, but for the first time in his political life Arthur refused to obey a command from that source. The Stalwarts seemed to be falling apart in their defeat, in spite of the stubborn Three Hundred.

That at least was the hope offered by Mr. Bonner, the first to return home from Chicago. Always an anti rather than a pro, it was of less importance to him that Garfield had been nominated than it was that Grant had not been, and that Conkling had been defeated. Although he referred in his *Torchlight* editorial to the cloud that had touched Garfield in the Credit Mobilier scandal, he emphasized rather the General's war record, and credited him with great courage, reminding his readers how the General had tried to stop the soldiers fleeing from Chickamauga.

General Deming came back inflated with triumph, uttering paeans of praise: Garfield had no equal in nobility of mind, in magnanimity, in personal charm; with him as standard-bearer, the party could not fail to sweep the country. "Even President Hayes," he told his avid listeners in the cigar store, "said Garfield would be easier to elect than Sherman: he had fewer enemies." And he understood that Sherman and Garfield had come to an understanding before the Convention: Garfield would fight for Sherman as long as Sherman had a chance, then Sherman's delegates would go to Garfield.

General Deming, in spite of his loud confidence, seemed to Ludwig's friends and Sherman's supporters to be on the defensive; it occurred to some that he might be rejoicing vicariously in this triumph of one who had been smudged, however lightly, by the scandal that had ruined his own political career. When John Gordon reported the General's attitude to Anne, she said, "He was probably one of the gallery claque that shouted for Garfield every time he took the floor. Do you think it could be true that Garfield planned all that applause ahead of time?" Such flagrant disloyalty was beyond Anne's comprehension.

"There's no more honor among politicians than among thieves. But we'll know when Ludwig gets home, if he's in a humor to talk about it."

The Rausches were the last to return, having gone first to Burlington to retrieve their children. Sally had arranged before leaving Waynesboro to have her dinner party for the Gardiners as soon after the Convention as possible. She wasted no time in sending Reuben around with formal invitations—"To honor Mr. and Mrs. Douglas Gardiner"—to the Gordons, the

Sheldon Edwardses, to the Voorheeses and Dr. Blair, to Judge and Mrs. Ballard, and to General and Mrs. Deming, the last four for Douglas's sake rather than for the pleasure of their company. Judge Ballard was Doug's senior partner, and General Deming had been magnanimous about the choice of Doug for candidate to Congress. To Anne, Sally included an informal note: "Come early so we can say the things to you and John that we can't say publicly."

As a consequence of the note, the Gordons were admitted to the Rausches' drawing room before Ludwig came down. Sally was there to greet them. She was what John called "all gussied up," her hair in an elaborate high chignon, held by jeweled combs, her gown an olive-green brocade with a tight low-cut bodice and a skirt tight before and full behind, a bustle exaggerating gathered flounces and a train, jewels in her ears and bracelets on her wrists. She had about her still something of the air of a *grande dame*, one who is not only at home in the larger world but accustomed also to put others at ease in its rarefied air.

She and Anne kissed delicately, rice-powdered cheek to rice-powdered cheek. Sally said, "Ludwig is having shirt-stud trouble. He'll be down directly."

"It's nice to have you home," Anne smiled at her, "but after all that excitement you are going to find Waynesboro mighty pokey."

"It *was* exciting—the most exciting week of my life." Her eyes sparkled, the reflection still in them, Anne thought, of the flaring gaslights in the convention hall. "I loved it all—acting as one of the hostesses of the Ohio delegation, having a chance to meet the wives of men Ludwig knows, like Mrs. Foraker and Mrs. Hanna. And to tell you the truth, it was a little hard for me to remember that Garfield wasn't my candidate. He is so noble looking, so big and vital and so graceful in all his gestures: a man to have the heart out of you with a smile and a word."

"That is what General Deming says," John teased her.

"Don't tell Ludwig I said it, then. Anyway, I didn't say he *was* my man."

Just then they heard Ludwig on the stairs. John moved to the door to meet him.

"Welcome home, Mr. President-Maker!"

"Beim Himmel, Dock! Mockery on top of all else! That I cannot take."

"Sorry, Ludwig." The two men shook hands. "Tell us, Ludwig, before the others come. How did it happen?"

"Blendwerk der Hölle! Der pfiffig—"

"Ludwig's lucky," Sally laughed. "He can always swear in German."

"I can say it in English. Fiendish deceit."

"You do think, then, that from the first Garfield meant to have it?"

Ludwig groaned, thrust his crossed feet in front of him, slid down in the rosewood chair that was too small for his bulk.

"I don't know. Let's say he was ready to take advantage of any opening. We'll never be sure. But who was responsible for that claque in the gallery that shouted 'Garfield!' at every excuse? I'm sure he didn't hire them himself, but whether he knew—"

"Let me tell the beginning, Ludwig. You're leaving out all of the atmosphere." Sally's description was so vivid it re-created for Anne and John that Saturday night when the nominating speeches were made: the bannered hall, its flaring lights, its crowded floor and packed gallery, the excited delirious delegates who had risen to cheer for Blaine and those who had shouted for Grant. And the audience in the gallery: "Fifteen thousand people," she said, awe in her voice. "You never heard anything like it. And those who had been to conventions before said the same thing. Yelling and stamping. Then finally, it was Garfield's turn to nominate Sherman. You tell them, Ludwig."

"You read his speech? You know then how persuasive and reasonable it sounded. He had a magnificent voice, and he knows how to use it. He began by referring to 'a human ocean in a tempest.' Then he went on to say that there is something in the raging billows to rouse the dullest man, but it is only when the tempest is over that the astronomer takes the 'level from which he measures all terrestrial heights and depths.' It was a good analogy, and he went on to make the moral plain: it wasn't in this hour of enthusiasm, by seven hundred and fifty-six delegates, that the destiny of the Republican party would be decided, but by four million Republican firesides, where the voters with their wives and children, et cetera, et cetera. Then he worked up to God preparing the verdict on 'what we decide here tonight,' and finished that period and began a new one. It was a real oration, the kind we used to know in Rhetoric. His next sentence was 'But now, gentlemen, what do we want?' And he paused, and there was a shout from the gallery, 'Garfield!' That pause made it seem as if he was waiting for it. Of course, he went on with his speech, and the Ohio delegation held its ovation for Sherman. But I tell you, John, I felt sick all over. Everything he had said but the biographical bits fit him as well as Sherman, and there we were, in his hands." Ludwig broke off and mangled his sprucely combed mustache with a broad hand. "I felt exactly the same as I felt at Shiloh that first morning. Remember, Dock? After the first attack, when our left had given way, Sherman got the rest of us back to a new line; the dead and wounded were hauled away in wagons. You were somewhere waiting for the wagons, I suppose? Well, we managed to place the new line—all green troops, no training—trying our best, and the Rebs were coming screaming at us through the woods and across the gullies. A battery was sent to the center of our line to help us hold—its commander was killed, and those gunners limbered up and skedaddled out of there, leaving us."

"You held, though. We got our wounded off, back to the river."

"We held an hour and a half, and that was the end of two regiments for the day. I've never been clear what happened afterward."

Sally put out a beseeching hand. "Ludwig, this is 1880. What has Shiloh to do with it?"

"Nothing, except that I'll never forget what I felt when I saw those guns run off. And I felt exactly the same when I listened to Garfield's speech: there go the big guns."

The doorbell rang, and Reuben announced Mr. and Mrs. Voorhees. All rose for greetings. With her bland smile Christina Voorhees looked Ludwig up and down. "You've been talking politics. I can tell by looking at you." Indeed, Ludwig had lost, in the fervor of his speaking, the crisp, well-groomed appearance of his first entrance. His face was flushed, his hair rumpled, his mustache askew, his tucked shirt front bulging. "You should have waited. Papa will want me to report every word you said."

Sally cut in. "We regret so very much that Dr. Blair felt unable to come." Actually, an extra man would have made awkward seating arrangements at her dinner table. Ludwig more sincerely echoed her regrets, then added, "When General Deming comes, he will tell you how right the Convention was in its choice."

"But there must have been treachery somewhere, Papa says."

"Didn't he also say," and the solemnity of John's voice matched hers, "that politics is a dirty game?"

Ludwig grunted. "Accusations! Nothing can be proved. Best forget it and not cause dissension in the party."

Other guests came close upon one another, then. Dinner was announced; they went into the dining room, young Mrs. Gardiner on Ludwig's arm, Sally bringing up the rear with Douglas. For a while after they were seated, talk was general and politics in abeyance, but the subject was brought up again by General Deming. The company had for a moment broken up into couples, and Judge Ballard was saying to Barbara that he was glad the new Congress would not be elected until fall, and would not convene until after the inauguration in March. "I shall be losing my right hand, you know, when Douglas goes to Washington. Young Merrill takes his bar examination this summer, and will come into the office as a partner: we have held his grandfather's place open for him. I am glad that Douglas will be here for a while to guide him. I am getting too old, and am far too busy, to take on a fledgling partner and teach him courtroom procedure."

He was overheard by General Deming, a little further down the table on the other side. "You are satisfied, then, that the Republican ticket will be elected?"

The Judge raised his eyebrows. "As to the national ticket, I have no idea. This district, however, is most assuredly a safe one."

"Good many Grant men over in Boone County. They might be vindictive enough to vote Democratic. But yes, I should think the Seventh District will surely go Republican." And the General continued pontifically, "I personally have every confidence that we will carry the country without difficulty. The South will go against us, of course, since the Rebels have been allowed to slip back into control down there, but General Garfield has the personality to reconcile feuding elements in the rest of the country."

"Even the Grant men? You seem to think they may be a problem in Boone

County." Kitty, next to him, was being mischievous. "What we're waiting to hear, General," she continued, "is how he got the nomination. Was he working for it all along?"

"Certainly not. He did his best for Sherman, but it was a losing cause. When the stampede began, he was stunned. He rose to make a point of order, and was almost incoherent. Fortunately, the chairman overruled him, or the delegates might still be there casting their ballots."

Everyone at the table had read of that incident in the *Torchlight,* but now they all looked to Ludwig for confirmation.

"It is true that he tried to speak. General Garfield has a conscience. Of course he wanted the nomination, what politician wouldn't? But how much he knew of what was going on I think is the question. Sherman trusted the Ohio delegation leader, but Governor Foster was for Garfield from the first. I understand that leaders of other state delegations told him they had votes for Sherman; that when he thought the psychological moment had come, he was to let them know. But he never called for them. There was a time when Sherman's votes got up to one hundred and twenty; a few more scattered votes from other states might have started a bandwagon."

"But why, Ludwig?" Anne was horrified: betrayal of a trust seemed to her an even blacker sin than disloyalty. "Why would Foster and Garfield lead the delegation for Sherman if they didn't really want him?"

"They were chosen by the State Convention because Sherman wanted them. And they did stand by him through thirty-odd ballots. But Governor Foster's a politician too. Now Garfield will have to resign as Senator, just after the legislature elected him. What Garfield wants will have weight with the legislature. They say the Governor would like to be chosen when it meets to elect someone in Garfield's stead."

"A bargain, then?" Judge Ballard was contemptuous.

"We may know, when and if it happens. I think myself Sherman should go back to the Senate. He is at home there, and a real power."

"You think he won't stay on as Secretary of the Treasury under Garfield?" Christina was shocked. As a young banker's wife, she had had a wholesome respect for John Sherman instilled in her.

Ludwig smiled at her innocence. "No. I don't. Garfield would not be comfortable in such close association with Sherman."

"Yes," Judge Ballard agreed. "We are never so uncomfortable as in association with someone we have wronged. And whatever you say of the chairman's cutting Garfield off, he could have managed to decline the nomination. But I have always suspected Garfield to be a man weak in character, in spite of his impressive personality and physique. Ever since the Credit Mobilier business."

Mrs. Deming, on the Judge's left, looked down and across the table to her husband, a warning glance at the flushed man, who was about to speak; she said cooly what he would have said hotly.

"It doesn't seem to have occurred to any of you gentlemen—you politicians become so cynical—that perhaps General Garfield accepted the nomination in the interests of the party and the country, even at some risk to his reputation for honorable dealing, knowing his motive would be questioned. Perhaps the chairman was right in not letting him speak. If Sherman's cause was hopeless, and Garfield's nomination would make it possible for Blaine men and Stalwarts to be reconciled—?"

Ludwig sent her a grateful smile, however doubtful he was that the Stalwarts would remain reconciled beyond the point where they ceased to rule; he thought that although now they might prefer Garfield to Blaine, they would in the end make as much trouble for him as they had for Hayes. But he said, "I think you are right, Mrs. Deming. We will all support General Garfield, since he has been nominated, and it ill behooves us now to question his motives."

Judge Ballard looked stubborn, and opened his mouth to speak, perhaps to protest that "we"; but Ludwig went on smoothly, "And all that General Deming has said, and many others have said, about Garfield is true: he is a man of very great personal magnetism; it will be hard for anyone to resist him. I doubt that the Stalwarts can do so."

Mrs. Ballard, who had been silent since the talk had turned to politics, now lifted her head like a war horse, and breathed fire. "Politicians! Forgiving for expediency's sake dubious activities of some very dubious gentlemen, all ready now to support a dubious candidate in the interests of the party. As for the party leaders responsible, you don't like them, and yet you deny women the right to vote, knowing that when they do, they will tolerate no such hole-in-the-corner proceedings. I defy any of you to give me a sound reason for refusing women the vote. The real reason you will never admit: you fear you would not be able to manipulate your parties as you do now, since women, you think, are incalculable."

Ludwig laughed. "The day will certainly come, Mrs. Ballard, when women will vote. I admit I am not looking forward to it: political matters would be too complicated—but I doubt whether their vote would have the effect you believe it would. Women will think as they have been brought up to think, and vote accordingly, as we men do, mostly." He looked around the table, a teasing light in his eyes. "Tell me, ladies, whatever you may think of the recent proceedings in Chicago, would any of you, with the possible exception of Mrs. Ballard herself, vote for a *Democrat*?"

Mrs. Ballard joined in the general laugh. "You turn the tables on me neatly. And I deserve it. A dinner table—and such a very pleasant one—is no place to mount a hobby horse." She nodded her head at Ludwig in friendly fashion, and they all laughed again in relief, remembering a time when Mrs. Ballard, younger and less mellow, would not have dismounted a hobby horse for anyone.

When their guests had gone, the Rausches did not turn again to the subject of politics. Ludwig congratulated Sally on the success of her dinner, and she admitted that it had gone well, all things considered.

"And I must say," she conceded, "the Gardiners seem happy. Doug isn't used to being adored. It agrees with him: he isn't so sarcastic."

"She holds her own in society?"

"Conversationally? She has little to say. Perhaps she is shy. But you must admit the women weren't given much chance, were they?"

"She found her way through the silverware without fumbling, and, *meine Liebe*, anyone who can do that at your dinner table—forks for this, forks for that, soup spoons, dessert spoons, coffee spoons, fish knives, meat knives—Gott im Himmel! Anyone who can do that is an initiate."

"You know that you like a properly appointed table. I wonder how Doug's aunts have been since the bridal couple got home. I can't help feeling it would have been better to wait till they get to Washington to start a baby. Think of going through a pregnancy shut up in that house!"

"You females! How long have they been married?"

"It doesn't take long, as you should remember. Oh, I know it doesn't show. But I'll be surprised if I'm wrong. And she won't have a bit of trouble, but poor Kitty Edwards—"

"Kitty, too?"

"Yes. And she looks awful. She told me that Dock had said that after tonight she was to go to bed and stay there, if she hoped to carry this one."

Sally was no more mistaken about Barbara Gardiner than she was about Kitty Edwards. Both young women shortly disappeared from public view: Kitty to spend her days in or on the bed, with John Gordon keeping a concerned eye on her; Barbara to devote her time, healthy young person that she was, to sewing many fine seams in long baby dresses, or hemming diapers. Douglas was much away, campaigning on his own and the party's account; and when he was at home, the pressure of his neglected law practice meant that he must spend his evenings preparing briefs or helping young Merrill. Barbara was not having an easy time. Happy as she was in her love for Doug, and his for her, and in the thought of the baby coming, she dreamed of the day when they could get away from Waynesboro. She crossed her fingers sometimes, however certain everyone was that Doug would be elected. The days were not so hard; she had been quite right about the servants: she knew how to handle them, and they were devoted to her; and whenever it was not raining or too hot, she was outdoors with old grizzled Tobe, the newly hired yard man, trying to persuade the neglected borders to bloom again. But the evenings were an endurance test. She had been sure, in her youthful confidence, that she could win the aunts to friendliness, but by midsummer she was reduced to a dumb acceptance. When Doug was not in the house, Barbara sat in the sitting room with his aunts, the sewing in her lap an excuse for keeping her head bent while they talked across her from their chairs at either side of the fireplace. She had quickly learned not to attempt to enter the conversation: any remark she made they ignored; for them, she was simply not there. And they always chose a subject of which she knew nothing: their childhood in Virginia, their ancestors, Doug's long-dead father and mother. She could have gone directly upstairs from the dinner table, but she was determined not to give in; and to make it seem to Doug that all was well, she continued to go to the sitting room with the older women, evening after evening.

One night Doug finished his work early and went to join the ladies; on the thick carpet even his halting step was silent, and he approached the sitting room door unnoticed. Not hearing Barbara's voice, he supposed she had gone up to their bedroom; he would say good-night to his aunts, and join her. Then he caught through the half-open door an oblique glimpse of her, in her usual chair, her head bent over her sewing. He stood still, even as his heart stopped for an instant: he loved her so dearly and she looked so young, so exposed and vulnerable, like a child playing grown-up, her hair on top of her head in the latest top-heavy mode, her neck so long and so slender. His whole being filled with tenderness; he stayed for a moment where he was, just to watch her. And so he overheard a bit of the dialogue being carried on by his aunts.

Aunt Lavinia was saying, "Do you remember the visit Cousin Willie Sue made at our house when we were small? All the young gentlemen calling on her? And the time the rope swing broke when one of them pushed her too high?"

"I remember. She always defied the proprieties, but she would not have liked seeing herself then: hoops flopping up, skirts flying, pantalettes exposed."

"And she went down right over the well-curb into the well, and had to be fished out looking like a drowned rat."

"She brought it on herself, permitting such liberties. She was fortunate not to have broken her back on the well-curb."

"Yes," Aunt Caroline laughed, "I remember Cousin Willie Sue very well. Sometimes young Mrs. Edwards reminds me of her, something about her, though she hasn't her flirtatious ways."

"Speaking of Mrs. Edwards, I wonder if it is true that she is *enceinte* again?" Aunt Lavinia uttered the French word with a kind of fastidious distaste. "If so, she will be absent from the Club meetings this next season."

"And if it is true that Professor Beattie plans to leave the Seminary, there will be a vacancy to be filled."

"That is the drawback to inviting so many theologians' wives to become members: they are likely to be with us too short a time to contribute very much."

"But Lavinia, who else is there of sufficient intellectual background and capacity to make good Club members?"

Doug had had enough. He stepped into the room. "Ah, you are there, Barbie. I didn't hear your voice and thought you must have gone up. I am afraid my aunts must believe you are deaf and dumb, or that it is your astral body sitting with them."

The words were light enough in tone, but Barbara was frightened—Doug was so whitely, coldly angry. Even his aunts looked startled.

Miss Lavinia said, "There are very few of our experiences that your wife could have an interest in. Naturally."

"And naturally there are no other subjects for an evening's conversation."

"We discuss what interests us."

"It is most unnatural for my wife to sit silent all evening, like a little ghost."

"Your wife is at liberty to retire when she is bored by our company."

"No, Aunt Lavinia." He limped into the room as far as the round center table and leaned over it, his clenched fists knuckle down on its surface. He had never believed his aunts capable of deliberate rudeness; they had always seemed to him *Godey's Ladies Book* personified, so far as manners were concerned. "No," he said again, "if you must spend your evenings recalling the days of your youth, *you* may retire and converse in the privacy of your sitting-room upstairs. This is Barbara's place, and there is no reason why she should not have guests here who can interest her, if you can't. Her father and mother, for example."

His Aunt Lavinia rose, said, "Come, Caroline," and swept from the room. When they had gone up the stairs and out of hearing, Doug crossed to Barbara's chair and leaned over it, his arms about her shoulders, his cheek on her hair.

"My darling, I love you with all my heart, but you are so young. I have done wrong, subjecting you to this sort of thing."

"Doug—" her voice shook. "I love you, too. But just now you frightened me. If you were ever to speak to me like that, I would shrivel up inside."

"But I never would or could."

"I could make you angry, not meaning to. Or our children could: I think that would shrivel me just as much. You should feel sorry for your aunts, Doug. I have you and you have me and soon we'll have the baby. But they have nothing: they had you but now they have lost you."

"They never had me—not if you mean that once I cared for them as you care for your family. Gratitude, yes. Respect, even affection. But now—"

"I wish you wouldn't, Doug." She loosened his arm and pulled him around to face her. "Interfere, I mean. Let me keep on trying. It is a kind of challenge. To persuade them to accept me, at least. They will never like me, of course. Why should they? I am not good enough or wise enough for you, but once they recognize that what is done is done—"

"It is I who am not good enough. Fifteen years older and soured on life."

"What nonsense!"

"Perhaps they will at least be more courteous to you now."

"I'd rather they'd be courteous because I've proved I deserve it than because you scolded them."

"But the arrogance of them! I wouldn't have believed it: sitting there with you and saying there's no one in Waynesboro worthy to be in their Club!"

She opened her eyes in astonishment, and then began to laugh, a genuine laugh, surprised out of her.

"The Woman's Club of Waynesboro? Oh, Doug. I wouldn't dream of such a thing! Then I *would* be bored—if I weren't scared to death first. Heaven help us! I'm not only not suited to the Club, it isn't suited to me. I can go through life quite happily without trying to be intellectual."

"You've a better brain than any of them," he protested.

"There's nothing wrong with my brain, I hope. But that's different from being intellectual. I didn't mind at all their talking about possible Club members. All I mind is the coldness—but Doug: if I can't melt them, I must learn not to feel it. Let it alone, and it will work out. I have more spunk than you think."

He took her sewing from her lap, laid it on the table, drew her to her feet, and took her up to bed. After that night, when he was home, he made a point of going with her from dinner to the sitting room, and starting a general conversation before he left them for the library. He supposed it was allowed to die when he withdrew, but there was no help for it: to act as county prosecutor, a practicing lawyer, a tutor for Tim Merrill, and a candidate for Congress was almost more than he could manage, even working nights; he had perforce to leave Barbara to meet her challenge.

The campaign quickened as August passed. Ludwig gave less and less time to his business (there were orders enough in hand to keep the mill going full time, and all seemed to run smoothly under Captain Bodien's management) and more and more of his attention to politics. The Rausches entertained the Honorable John Sherman when he stopped between trains in Waynesboro on his way to Cincinnati to make his first speech for Garfield. Ludwig accompanied him to the city, had the pleasure of meeting again with Mr. Foraker and other Cincinnati Republicans, heard the speech, and returned to report on it, not only to Sally at home but to his acquaintances in the drugstore and his friends in Dock's office.

"The Democrats are assailing your friend Sherman, I see," Dr. Blair gave him his opening. "Call his speech 'openly partisan.'"

"Yes. Of course it was partisan. What do they expect? But they fasten on the last paragraph and conveniently forget the rest of it: the difference in aims, principles, and achievements between the parties. They should remember all that the present administration has accomplished: the financial measures, the resumption of specie payments, refunding and reduction of the public debt, getting the country back on a sound financial footing. Sherman went over the measures proposed by the Democrats and what their enactment would mean to the country. At the end he got round to the Ku Klux Klan outrages and the treatment of the Negroes in the South, and the Democrats fasten on that, shout 'partisan,' and forget all the rest. Trouble is, they haven't any other issue—the country is prosperous and Hayes's administration has put an end to the 'corruption' outcry. So they reopen old wounds, and try to win sympathy for the South, while Garfield sits up in Mentor and tells his campaigners to fight on the issue of sound money and the tariff. I wish we could, but it won't work: the ex-Rebs in Congress have been making too much noise. We'll be hearing more and more about Hampton and the Ku Klux Klan."

"Ze wrong vay to put in ze right man, if he iss ze right man." Mr. Lichtenstein was not a great admirer of Garfield.

"Yes. We would have saved the country a lot of future trouble," Dr. Blair spoke slowly, consideringly, "if Reconstruction could have lasted long enough to have secured the rights of the Negro."

Ludwig sighed. "True. But how? Without the compromise on Reconstruction, Hayes could hardly have been inaugurated peacefully. And Tilden as President wouldn't have helped, not the Negro or anyone else, unless it was those same ex-Rebs. All the Republicans can do now is to make sure the country doesn't forget the Negro is being brutally mistreated. Public opinion—"

"Northern public opinion will never force the South to give the Negro the vote." John was blunt. "I'm not even sure he should have it what with the appalling ignorance, even here."

"I know." Ludwig rose to go. "There are more important issues before the country, but you'll see: we'll be fighting the War of the Rebellion over again. With General Hancock—'Hancock the Superb'—the Democratic candidate. There's irony for you."

Ludwig was quite right. Before long even the children had picked up the torchlight-parade song and were singing it ad nauseam:

> Treason makes its boast, my boys,
> And seeks to rule again.
> Our Jim shall meet its host, my boys,
> And strike with might and main!
> Once more he'll crush the foe, my boys,
> With arm and bosom bare;
> And this shall be his field, my boys,
> The Presidential Chair!

Brigadier-General of Volunteers James A. Garfield was running on his war record. And Major-General Hancock, who had done incomparably more to "crush the foe" than his opponent, could not make the same use of his renown because so many of his possible supporters had once been Rebel soldiers. Why remind them of Gettysburg? Still, there were many veterans of the Army of the Potomac who loved and revered General Hancock; no Republican was altogether easy in his mind until after the state elections in Ohio and other "October states," which went Republican in their choice of state officials, and almost ensured the party's triumph in November. Even so, it was a near thing: Garfield won fifty-nine more electoral votes than Hancock, but only seven thousand or so more popular votes. The result was enough to make Republican politicians view the future with misgivings.

The ladies of the Waynesboro Woman's Club were not so concerned about the results of the election as they were about Kitty Edwards's pregnancy and its approaching outcome. In the middle of November she gave birth, successfully at last, to a son, named Lowrey for her family. The announcement in the *Torchlight* was a simple statement of fact. Only Anne, among the members of the Club, knew how great the danger had been, and how immeasurable John's anxiety, which had not been entirely dispelled by the event itself, and how exalted Kitty was, even in her illness, and how great Sheldon's relief and pleasure.

To all who were friends of the two young women, the birth of Barbara Gardiner's child was an anticlimax: no one had felt any reason to worry about her, except perhaps her husband. To Douglas it was the most momentous event of his life by far, more important than his recent election as Representative from the Seventh District to the Forty-seventh Congress of the United States. Barbara's daughter was born late in December, in the middle of the night, and so Miss Lavinia and Miss Caroline, though roused from sleep by the inevitable commotion, could ignore it. They made their appearance at the breakfast table at the usual time. Douglas, a little wan, joined them belatedly, and demanded a cup of coffee.

Aunt Lavinia, temporarily restored to her old position behind the coffee urn, obliged him, but said nothing. He took the cup in an unsteady hand.

"Aunt Lavinia? Aunt Caroline? You couldn't have slept through that hubbub last night. Are you not even going to inquire?"

"We naturally suppose you will inform us in your own good time."

Aunt Caroline was a little more interested. "We hope you got the doctor in time?"

"Yes. My wife was delivered of a daughter. Both are doing well."

"A daughter? I trust you are not disappointed?"

"No. I am pleased. And relieved that Barbara—"

"As Nurse Watkins says, it is a natural process. And, by the way, how long may we expect to have Nurse Watkins with us?"

Douglas laughed; he could not help it: he did not himself suffer Nurse Watkins gladly. "Ten days at least, Dock says. Till Barbara is up and about and able to take care of the baby. The baby is to be called 'Lavinia,'" he added, offhandedly.

"Ah! Your idea or hers? A hopeful gesture?"

Once again Douglas felt the cold anger that hardened him against them. Barbara had tried so long, had been so wise—beyond her years, it seemed to him—yet still she was rejected.

"I see no need for gestures. If you deny yourselves the pleasure of being one family with us, the loss is yours. As for the name, I prefer 'Theresa' myself—a far prettier name, and Mother Bodien's, as no doubt you know.

Barbara, however, insists that the first child should have a name from the father's side of the family. And 'Lavinia' was my grandmother's name. You, Aunt Lavinia, were named for her."

"At any rate, it is not, so far as I know," Aunt Caroline hesitated, "a saint's name. As Theresa—your wife's family will want the baby baptized in their church?"

Doug without another word rose from his place and returned upstairs. "So much hate," he thought, "and no reason for it. Except it gives them a purpose in life. I would never have believed it. I may have to spend the rest of my life in Washington."

A little while later, having once more admired the baby that he secretly hoped would soon look more human, and then taken his place by Barbara's bed, he said, "Look, Barbara, is your mother going to be very unhappy about this baby?"

She knew what he meant. "I don't know, Doug. The more she loves it, the more unhappy she will be. You see, she isn't too unhappy about the rest of us. Stewart is still a pretty good practicing Catholic. Papa and I were baptized in the church: all we have to do is come back and confess our sins. She is serenely hopeful—goes on saying masses every day for the salvation of our souls. But the baby—if anything should happen to her, and she had never been baptized— Oh, Doug: isn't it silly? Here we all are, trying to get to Heaven, if there is a Heaven, and what does it matter, whether we take a train or—or go on horseback? It's so foolish and makes so much sadness." She wound up more than a little breathless, so that Nurse Watkins came hurrying to the foot of the bed. Barbara waved her away. "I'm all right. Tired and sleepy, but glad it's over, and the baby is all right. The baby *is* all right?"

They reassured her. Doug said, "You're talking too much. Try to go to sleep. I can stay a little while. Nurse, why don't you go down and get Lutie to fix your breakfast? I told her about the baby, but she would love to have all the details from you." Nurse Watkins tiptoed out. "Now, Barbie." He took her hand. "Try to go to sleep."

She shook her head on the pillow, further tangling the matted black hair. "Not while you're here."

"And don't worry about your mother. I want you to be as happy as I am."

"You are happy?"

He smiled at her, kissed her forehead. "Yes. I am. That's why I want everyone to be. Your mother is a good, warmhearted, loving woman."

"Yes. I am glad you feel that." Then she smiled at him, a little doubtfully. "But I know what Mamma would do if we ever left the baby with her. We could do that some day if you really don't mind. Some day when you and I have to go somewhere—and it wouldn't count against us because it would have been done without our knowledge or consent."

And so one day in mid-January they carried a bundled and shawled baby down to the Bodiens, and themselves took a train for Columbus. The legislature was meeting to elect a Senator in Garfield's place, and it was natural that Douglas should want to be there.

Mrs. Bodien hardly waited for them to get out of the house; she had made up her mind beforehand what she must do, she would act at once and get it over with. She put on her cloak and bonnet, rewrapped the baby, and went with it to the priest's house. In less time than it had taken to get the infant's cloak and bonnet off, she was safely baptized Lavinia Anne, and her grandmother was teary with joy, relief, and sheer nervousness. When Barbara and her husband returned and she confessed what she had done, they were not so shocked as she had feared, and were not at all put out with her. "Lavinia Anne is a nice name," Doug said, and Barbara's only admonition was just "If you have to talk about this, please make it clear that it was your doing, not mine."

Mrs. Bodien felt no need to talk about it at all. She could say prayers for the baby as well as for the rest of her family, and if anything should happen to it while it was still an infant, which the saints forbid, it was safe.

Doug and Barbara on their day in Columbus had watched the legislature again elect John Sherman to the Senate. The Rausches were also there, and the four of them went home on the train together, Doug and Ludwig discussing the election they had just seen, agreeing that Foster's withdrawal of his candidacy in favor of Sherman threw some doubt on the rumored bargain between the Governor and Garfield. They went on to discuss the probable cabinet appointments to be made by the new President, and agreed that Blaine would undoubtedly be Secretary of State. They agreed, too, that it was absolutely right that John Sherman should go back to the Senate.

The two women were mostly silent, letting the men's talk wash over them; Barbara, a little smile playing about her mouth, was thinking about her mother and the baby, and Doug's amused understanding of the situation. Sally, watching her, thought how pretty the young girl was, and how poised, though she never had much to say for herself. They might be thrown together quite a lot by the chances of politics; already the two men were talking of going to the inauguration together, and she, Sally, had no intention of missing that occasion; and of course, Mrs. Douglas Gardiner would not, since her husband would be there as a member of the new Congress summoned by outgoing President Hayes to meet on March 4, Inauguration Day, in special session.

The inauguration, attended by the Rausches and the Gardiners, was exciting only for what it was, not for anything that happened. There was not even a "what now?" in the air, or in the press, since Hayes was handing over the executive office to a friend and fellow Republican: nothing was in question but what the Stalwarts would do about Civil Service reform and presidential appointments. It was something, perhaps, to have attended an Inaugural Ball, but that was about all it amounted to in Sally's eyes.

Congress adjourned on the twentieth of May having done little but talk. But Conkling and Platt had resigned their seats as Senators angry at having been thwarted by Garfield over the question of New York patronage. With them safely at home in New York and new men chosen, the country breathed a sigh of relief. Garfield would now have clear sailing.

With Congress in adjournment the Gardiners came home to Waynesboro. Barbara, her pregnancy over and fit again to appear in public, acted on her father's advice, and began attending her husband's church. Doug had not up to this time felt any necessity to own a horse and carriage, nor did he now since he expected to be in Waynesboro only part of each year. But for some time he had hired a carriage and a driver from the livery stable for this weekly occasion. At the Presbyterian hitching rail, he would climb out while the livery-stable man held the horses, and would help the ladies to alight. Presbyterian children had got in the habit of collecting in the vestibule in the interval between Sunday school and the church service, to observe this endlessly interesting ceremony. It was the elder Miss Gardiner in particular who fascinated them: the great bell-shaped hoop skirt, the shawl, the bonnet, the mitts, all in the mode of fifteen or twenty years past, before they were born. She was a true eccentric in their eyes.

The hoop skirts crowded the carriage a little when Barbara joined them, but no one commented on it. When they reached the church and Doug climbed out first, as usual, the children were peering around the doors. There was a sprinkling of other arriving worshipers, but it was the children who first reached their family pews with word of the newcomer. Some did not know her, some knew only who she was, and some like Johnny Gordon knew her well. He slipped into his mother's pew and squeezed into the space she had left for him at the end. Binny, on her other side, was trying to read her Sunday School paper, paying no attention.

"Mamma!" he whispered. "Guess who's here. Barbara!"

She bent a stern look upon him. "SH-SH! The organist's ready to begin. This is *church*. Turn around and sit properly. And I have told you before *not* to call Mrs. Douglas Gardiner 'Barbara'!" She knew well enough whom he had meant.

When the service was over, she made haste to get up the aisle to the vestibule: she was not sure how many of her Presbyterian fellows would welcome a baptized Catholic. She made her own greeting to Barbara almost artificially hearty before she passed her on to Mr. McKinney, shaking congregational hands at the outer door, and turned to speak to Douglas and his aunts.

On the way home from church, Johnny, prancing along with Binny ahead of his mother, turned to ask over his shoulder, "Don't those old ladies *like* Barbara?"

"Johnny! I have told you enough times—"

"Mrs. Gardiner, then. But I always did call her Barbara and she didn't mind. Well, don't they?"

"I don't know any reason why they wouldn't like her, do you?"

"No. But they don't look like they liked her." Johnny felt obscurely that his mother wasn't answering his question but that he had better not persist. He was fond of Barbara, who had always, at her father's house, treated him as an equal. His heart filled with sympathy for her, having to live with those old—those old— He longed to do something to show her how he felt, something spectacular, in the knight-errantry line, to *show* the old ladies. He dreamed impossible dreams all the way home.

He was not the only one who would have liked "to show the old ladies." As Anne told her husband, while they were waiting for dinner and the children had gone to the kitchen to oversee its serving, the Misses Gardiner had almost frightened her, their expressions were so icy. "I had meant to say something pleasant about how good it was to see them all there together, but the best I could manage was 'Good morning.' It was just as if they resented her being there."

"Of course they resented it."

"But, *church*!"

"It removes one of their grounds of complaint against her. They prefer to regard her as one of that lowly breed, The Irish Catholic. I'll wager that poor girl is having no easy time with those two old harpies."

Johnny did not forget his hope of doing something spectacular to "show those old ladies." But any of his preposterous dreams, such as rescuing Barbara from a burning house and leaving the aunts to their fate, were not dreams for sober daylight; they were reserved for the brief interval between the moment his head hit his pillow and his drifting off to sleep. But his determination to do something for Barbara persisted: just what he wanted to "show the old ladies" was not clear enough for him to have put it into words, but he felt his meaning, his intention, and one day in June he was provided with an opportunity to make a gesture, at least.

It was one of those midsummer days so rare in southern Ohio, when the sun shone from an unflawed sky and yet it was not hot; a fresh breeze blew through the trees, and there was a scent of green leaves fluttering and a fainter fragrance of blooming clover fields not too far distant. Roses were in bloom on all the old-fashioned bushes; peonies, the last of the season, were dropping their big pink petals to be carried over the lawn by the breeze. And cherries were ripe. Johnny was set to picking those still on the Gordon trees. His mother had canned all the cherries she could bear to, and they had eaten all they could eat uncanned, in cobblers and pies, and even uncooked but well-sugared and served for dinner from her mother's big compote. Now Johnny was picking cherries to give to such of Anne's friends as could use them; there were not many, since back yards held one cherry tree at least, but she made a list, while he was climbing in and out through the branches, and she could hear the occasional snap of a twig and scramble of a foot. Binny was out there somewhere, too, perhaps sulking still because she had been forbidden to climb the trees with Johnny. She had been given an old paring knife, instead, and told that if she wanted to make herself useful, she could weed the brick path down the length of the back yard, and dig the moss out from the cracks where it turned the corner under the grape arbor that screened the outhouse. Anne promised her a penny for every yard of path she got clean, but did not really expect her to stick to such an irksome chore.

In the beginning, Binny had rather liked digging out the moss in the damp cool corner back behind the arbor: there was a certain satisfaction in seeing the clean deep black cracks. But her knees hurt before she had covered a yard; she tried squatting, then lay down on her stomach and wormed herself backward, pushing with knees and elbows, staining her pinafore from top to hem with the damp earth and moss; she smeared her face with dirt as she brushed her short curls out of her eyes. The thought of the number of pennies it was possible for her to earn ceased to lure her: she looked back over what she had done and calculated that she must have earned at least three, which would buy three licorice shoestrings at Mrs. Feeley's little grocery. That was enough. She sighed and stood up, peering through the grape vines for Johnny's figure looming among the leaves of the cherry tree. She would have liked to be up there, where the wind was. Nothing had been said about the grape arbor. By standing in the curve of one sturdy vine, a foot or so above the ground, she could just pull herself up to sit on the first two-by-four that ran the length of the arbor; using the vine again, she could get to the second, the third. Then her heart failed her: she could climb no higher, and she was afraid she could not get down. She would ask Johnny to help her when he had finished. In the meantime she liked it where she was.

Unhappily for her, just as Johnny came swinging down, having filled what he thought of as the millionth bucket, her father came home for lunch through the gate from the stable yard. If he was startled when he saw her, so little and so high and so precariously perched, his exclamation sounded like anger.

"Binny! What are you doing up there? Get down at once."

"I can't."

He came to stand beneath her, caught her under the arms, let her down to the ground with a thump, and looked her up and down with grim displeasure.

"I must say I never saw a dirtier little girl. What on earth have you been doing?"

"Weeding the path. Mamma wanted me to."

"From up in the grape arbor?"

"I got tired."

"Come in the house at once and get washed up. You're a disgrace." And with a none too gentle hand he propelled her up the unweeded path. Inside he left her washing at the kitchen pump, under Martha's supervision, and drew Anne after him into the living room.

"That child will kill herself. Up in the grape arbor—"

"I set her to weeding the path, but I didn't suppose she would stick to it. The grape arbor? But John, you can't keep the children out of the grape arbor. We used to be all over it when I was little."

"I'll wager you never looked as filthy as Binny looked."

At that moment Johnny came in, Martha said lunch was ready, and the three of them went to sit at the table with a scrubbed and sullen Binny, already put in her chair by Martha. As they ate, Anne told Johnny what she wanted him to do with the cherries that now filled every bucket and dishpan; he was to fill a couple of lard buckets, deliver cherries, return, refill the buckets, deliver more cherries. "And here is the list of houses where you are to go."

Johnny glanced at it rebelliously. "How do I know where all these people live?"

"You know where the McKinneys live, and Dr. Blair. Look over the list. Any you don't know you can ask me."

Scowling, Johnny took the paper, but his brow cleared and his heart leaped when he saw the name Deming.

"I'll guess I'll go to the Demings' last," he said, in what he hoped was an unrevealing voice. "They don't live so very far." Then the thought struck him. "Could I have one bucket for a friend of mine? I picked 'em, Mamma."

"What friend? Never mind, I don't need to know. You've earned one pailful. But not Elsa. The Rausches have more cherry trees than we have."

"Transparent little boy," Anne thought when he had gone. He was willing to deliver all those cherries all over town, on the chance at the end of seeing Julia Deming, who, as nearly as she could read him, figured as the bright-haired princess of his dreams. She wondered idly who the "friend" was, thought of Ariana McCune as a possibility, and dismissed the matter from her mind. Johnny spent the warm early afternoon trudging back and forth with the pails of cherries, and was free at last to go to the Demings'—and the Gardiners'. It was mid-afternoon when he rang the Gardiners' doorbell; there was no one in sight, no one in the yard, and the front door was closed, contrary to Waynesboro custom, where in the summertime the big doors stood open behind hooked screens. His heart began to thump; he wondered if he had done wrong. What if one of the old ladies came? But the bell was answered by a neatly aproned colored maid.

"Is—is Barbara here?" he stammered, in his trepidation forgetting the "Mrs. Gardiner." "I'm—I'm bringing her some cherries."

"Delivery boys go round to the back." She closed the door in his face. It was a moment of awful humiliation for Johnny; he wished he could sink through the step, but there was nothing for it but to "go round back," and go he did, his head hanging so low he did not even see the Gardiner cherry trees, full of fruit.

Orillia had not meant to humiliate him. Like all servants everywhere, and colored servants particularly, she was quite aware of the tensions in the Gardiner house, and was passionately on the side of her young mistress. Her only thought had been to get him out of sight as quickly as possible—a little boy with, of all things, a pail of cherries—a boy who called Miz Douglas "Barbara"—best to get him out of sight before Miss Lavinia or Miss Caroline should see him, or ask questions. At the kitchen door she opened the screen and let him in.

"We di'n o'de' no cherries, boy."

Lutie, now the cook, enjoying a between-meals cup of coffee at the kitchen table, looked Johnny over.

"You send that boy to the back do', Rilly? Ain' no call to do that, that Dock Go'don's boy."

Johnny might not know Lutie, but she knew him: she was a friend of Martha's. "Come on in, chile, now you' hyah, an' tell us whuffo' the cherries."

"I know you didn't order them. They're a present. We had so many—I thought maybe Mrs. Gardiner would like these. They're just picked fresh, an' no wormy ones."

"We got trees full of cherries—but nemmind. Ah reckon Miz Douglas sho' to 'preciate the kind thought."

"Isn't she here?"

"Yas, she here. Yo' Rilly—yo' tell he' she got a calle'—in the kitchen cause yo' so stupid. An' yo'—whut yo' name? Johnny? Res' yo'se'f on yonde' chair."

Presently Barbara came in, trailed by the sheepish Orillia. "Why, Johnny! I'm glad to see you. It's been a long time. But what—why?"

"That mah fault," Orillia admitted. "Ah thought he bin a delivery boy."

"I was bringing the cherries for you. I wanted to do something, now you're married, an' a baby an' all. I mean," he gulped, "to show I hadn't forgotten what fun we used to have when you were still home. But she says," and he tipped his head toward Lutie, "you got all the cherries you need."

"Our cherries are still on the trees. And no one to pick them. Tobe's too rheumatic. Did she tell you that? So we'll use these for a pie for dinner, Lutie."

"Yas'm."

Johnny's face lighted for a moment. "I'll pick your trees for you. I'd like to." And then he remembered. "Only, next week I'm going out to the farm to help with cutting the wheat." Doleful as he managed to look, he could not quite keep the pride out of his voice. "Harvest's early this year, we had such a warm spring." He managed to sound knowledgeable.

Barbara smiled at him. "I know harvesting the wheat is more important than cherries. We'll get them picked somehow. If you know any boys—"

"I'll see what I can do," he assured her gravely, his humiliation forgotten. He took the empty lard bucket home, filled it, and turned up with a full pail at the Demings' at three-thirty or so, and had an idyllic if unexciting afternoon playing checkers with Julia, letting her win one or two games, boasting of his coming week on the farm as a harvest hand. Julia did not seem to see that helping pile the tied wheat in shocks would be a privilege, but at least she did not ask to be taken along, as Shaney had done. He had had an awful argument with Shaney: girls didn't help in the fields at harvest time. It was his farm and he wasn't going to let her. But she had overborne him—the usual end of their arguments—and had dragged him along with her to ask her mother. Thank goodness, Aunt Sally had some sense.

"You want to help Johnny with the harvesting? Yes, I know it's his farm, but he doesn't hire the hands, not until he's of age. And yes, I know they're going to use our twine in the new binder, but that doesn't entitle you to be there. Do you know what girls do on a farm at harvest time? They peel potatoes and clean chickens, and cook, and cook some more, and then they wash the dishes. If you care to spend a week doing that kind of work—"

Imagine Shaney wanting to cook and wash dishes in a hot farmhouse kitchen! Johnny went off alone, triumphantly, for his week with the harvest hands, following the reaper and binder, learning, under instruction, to pile the sheaves so that they would shed water and dry out for the threshing later on. He went to bed in the farmhouse bedroom too tired at night to shake the seeds and the chaff out of his clothes.

Her rejection had rankled with Elsa. It seemed to her that every day she lived she hated more the prospect before her: the compulsion to grow up to be a lady. If Johnny had a farm, didn't she have, so to speak, a rope mill? She had a good notion to cut her hair, borrow some trousers—Johnny's, maybe, although she was bigger than he was—and go to work at the mill. But not alone, he must come with her.

When Johnny came home, she had surprisingly little difficulty in persuading him to join her in what she planned as a day's prank, but what he secretly hoped might lead to a steady job. He had earned a little money for his work on the farm, a new experience. His father never paid him for all he did in the office; apprentice doctors, he said, were not paid: they worked for the experience. So having money in his pocket was a pleasant novelty to Johnny, and if he could get taken on as a wheel boy—

He rose at dawn one morning, and waited for Elsa in the stable, in hand a shirt and a pair of overalls he had worn on the farm. She appeared promptly, and climbed into the loft to change her clothes and stuff her hair into a visored cap (she had not quite dared, after all, to cut it off). Johnny had already bargained with two wheel boys (brothers, whom they knew in school) to let them take their places for just that one day: they could have their fifty cents apiece for the day's work just as if they had been there. Not unwilling to take a holiday, knowing that Elsa was the big boss's daughter, the two boys had agreed willingly enough. When the six-thirty whistle blew, two capped and overalled newcomers joined the other hands at the mill gate.

When Ludwig went into his office at eight, after the mill had been running for an hour and a half, Captain Bodien, who had been waiting for him, followed him in.

"Boss, I wish you would do something for me. Go look in the old ropewalk—cast your eyes on the wheel boys."

"The wheel boys? What—?"

"No." Captain Bodien tried to conceal the mirth that twinkled in his eyes. "I'm not going to tell you. You go see for yourself."

Ludwig went, looked, and for a moment saw nothing out of the way. The row of wheel boys at the near end of the walk stood with their backs to the spinners moving away from them as the boys heaved the wheels over. Then—because the two farthest figures were so much smaller than the others, or because the wheels were not turning as smoothly as they should—his eye fixed on them. Johnny he recognized at once, Elsa not until after a second, harder look: the overalls, the cap half over her face and bulging oddly above, changed her appearance so completely; and besides, her being there was so stunning a surprise that he choked back the bellow that was his first reaction, and without distracting their attention, absorbed as it was in their effort, he returned to his office.

Captain Bodien was waiting for him, grinning. Ludwig stared at him. "I'll be damned," he said. "Did you take them on?"

"No. They came in with the others. Hoped the foreman wouldn't spot 'em, I reckon. When he did, they told him the Bradley boys couldn't come today, an' they were taking their place. Shall I send them packing?"

Ludwig blew out his cheeks, his mustache. "The Bradleys have probably gone fishing. We'd be short two wheel boys. Won't hurt 'em to do a day's work, I guess—teach 'em something, maybe. Only, it's pretty hot in there: if they look like keeling over, tell the foreman to take 'em off. Otherwise, send 'em to me when the last whistle blows."

"That I'll do. But remember, they're friends of mine. I didn't tell you a thing."

"That's right. You didn't." Ludwig grinned back at the Captain.

At five-thirty, two exhausted children, their faces white beneath the smudges of sweat and oil, presented themselves at Ludwig's door. He took one look at them and motioned them in. "Sit down and explain yourselves."

"Papa, how did you know?" It was almost a wail from Elsa—Elsa, who might grumble but never whined. "Did Captain Bodien tell you?"

"I saw you. Don't you suppose I keep an eye on my mill? Now, why?

"I wanted to show him," Elsa put a little more spirit in her voice. "Girls are good as boys. Him and his farm."

He looked her over. She was tall for her age, taller than Johnny, and in the tight overalls she looked sturdier.

"Where'd you get that rig?"

"It's Johnny's. I changed into it in their stable loft. Except the cap. I bought that at the Cheap Store."

"A daughter of mine in that get-up! Ach, Himmel! Well, Johnny?"

"Yes sir." Johnny gulped. "I thought if I proved I could do it, maybe I could get a job for the summer."

"I see. And do you still think you want it?"

Johnny's dimple showed briefly. "No, sir. I guess not. All day—every day—up and over, down and around, and *heave* and nothing to look at but the wheel and the rope that turns the things the threads are fastened to."

"Whirls," Ludwig supplied automatically. "Fibers. In a day of work you grasped the principle of spinning yarn?"

"Yes, sir. I think so. The ends of the threads—fibers—are fastened to the, uh—whirls, and the wheel revolves the whirls, and that twists the fiber."

"Yarn, as soon as it is twisted."

"Yes, sir. Yarn. And the spinner backs down the ropewalk, and the yarn keeps twisting, and whenever a—fiber ends, he starts a new one."

"Well, he keeps the yarn even, anyway. Expert job, spinning."

"Yes, sir."

"You may have learned something about making rope. Something you don't really need to know. I let you finish out the day, both of you, hoping you would learn something. Just how lucky you are, maybe, that you don't have to do a day laborer's work, Johnny. Even if you still wanted it, I wouldn't give you a job. First, because you don't need it, and there are those who do. The Bradley boys, for instance; the six dollars they earn in a week between 'em is the difference between having enough to eat and going hungry. They will be on the job tomorrow, I suppose?

"The second reason: you mean to be a doctor, don't you? Don't you know you could ruin your hands, doing a wheel boy's work? Injure them, or make them big and stiff. A doctor has to take care of his hands."

"Yes, sir."

"Elsa, you were looking for a summer job, too?"

"No. I didn't know Johnny was. It was just for today."

"Where do your mothers think you are?"

"We told them we were going on a picnic. And we did, Papa. We brought our lunches and ate under the willows on the towpath. So it wasn't a lie."

"Just a prevarication. Shall we go home now? If you were really wheel boys, you would walk home, but you don't look as if you could, either of you."

"But I have to stop at Johnny's and change."

"You will go home as you are. Did you think you could hide this escapade from your mother? You can fetch your petticoats some other time."

At home Ludwig took Elsa in with him by the side door; he changed his shoes in the back hall, as was his custom when he had been on the tarry floors of the mill; he indicated to Elsa that she was to put her boots on the closet floor with his, and wordlessly pushed her, stocking-footed, into the sitting room.

Sally looked up from her book as they entered. After a second's disbelief, she recognized, with astonishment and horror, her daughter.

"Elsa! What—? A picnic?"

"She has spent the day working in the mill. As a wheel boy. Have Cassie put her to bed, and take her up a tray. She's too tired to take in anything you may want to say to her. Leave it till morning, Liebchen."

When Elsa, without a murmur, had dragged herself upstairs, Ludwig told his story.

"They won't try that again," he concluded. "It hurt to see them, they were so dead beat. Like two waifs out of Dickens."

"You're far too indulgent with that child." Sally's mouth was a hard line. "A daughter of ours, spending the day in *trousers* among common laborers, in the *mill*! And I suppose you think she should not even be scolded?"

"I didn't say that. Of course she must be scolded. In the morning, after a good night's sleep. As for the overalls, I doubt if anybody but Cap'n Bodien and I knew she was a girl. After all, she's a child, no curves yet. And the 'common laborers' would have been too busy to notice. The foreman shouldn't have allowed it, of course: they are too little for the work. I won't have children that age in the mill. At least," he hesitated, "there aren't any that small. Maybe I should fix an age limit."

In the morning Sally was in her daughter's room before the child was fairly awake, and Elsa learned the extent of her naughtiness: how costume, occupation, and association could affect her reputation as a young lady; what an enormity she had committed in deceiving her mother; how wrong she was in preferring to associate with the boys.

"It was Johnny's idea, I suppose. I think you had better not see so much of him hereafter."

"No, Mamma." Elsa had let the scolding roll over her, unprotesting; she had heard most of it before and had expected it now, though it was rather more severe than any scolding she had hitherto experienced. But the last threat roused her to protest. "It was my idea. I had to *beg* him. I just wanted to show him girls are as good as boys. They are, too. He was tireder than I was."

"But Elsa, they're not. They're not 'as good.' At least in the same way. Girls—women—are not meant for the same—" Sally was melted to tenderness by the thought of the woman's life that Elsa had to look forward to. She stepped from the foot of the bed where she had been standing like an accusing angel to the side where she could sit down by Elsa. Thinking "She's not old enough for this, but she must be restrained somehow"; thinking too "Perhaps it's as well this happened this summer, it's just a childish escapade, and anyone who knows about it will laugh." Thinking these things with half her mind, she explained to a stricken Elsa in plain terms and explicitly the peculiar functions and disabilities of the female body.

"So you see," she concluded, "you have to be careful not to overstrain yourself."

Elsa was revolted by the thought of what lay ahead of her as a woman. She was not sure that she ever wanted to see a boy again, not even Johnny. For the rest of the summer she was, if not subdued, at least very careful not to offend again: she did not want to be reminded of the horrors her mother had prepared her for. She saw little of Johnny except when all the children played together, in the evenings, their old games of Run, Sheep, Run and Hide and Seek, or went down to the Bodiens' to spend time listening to the Captain.

On that same morning when Elsa was being told the unpleasant facts of life, Ludwig summoned the ropewalk foreman into his office, along with Captain Bodien.

"I'm not going to call you on the carpet," he said to the foreman. "I know you didn't recognize those children yesterday. But that isn't the point. The point is, they were too little for the job. There are too many boys, particularly if their fathers are in the mill, who work here summers, when they really aren't big enough. There has never been a rule about it, but let's make one now. Don't hire a wheel boy, even in the summer, unless he's old enough to get his working papers. And even then, not if he isn't tall enough to turn the wheel easily."

"Yes, sir. And those already working?"

"Let them finish out the summer. I know their families need their wages."

Captain Bodien had been a silent audience at the interview. When the foreman had been dismissed, he said, "You know, Cap'n, I've got a son who'd like to be working here."

"But I thought you wanted him to go to West Point? There shouldn't be any trouble over the appointment, you know."

"That's what *I* want. What *he* wants is to be an engineer. I tell him he can learn engineering at West Point, but he'd have to stay in the army three years. If he came into the mill for a summer, he might change his mind, or he might not; he thinks he would learn something about machinery here, and I think he might decide he preferred the army. Anyway, I haven't taken him on because I didn't know whether you would think it right."

"Nonsense, man. Because he's your son, you mean? We have to give our boys a good start, and teach them, or who will take over when we're done? I intend to put my boys in the mill when they're old enough to turn a wheel. Stewart is—what—fifteen?"

"Sixteen. And strong. It would only be for the rest of the summer. He has another year in high school."

"The way wheel boys come and go, there'll be a place for him before long. It wouldn't do to fire a boy to make way for him."

So presently, Stewart Bodien became a wheel boy for Rausch Cordage Company, and if anyone in Waynesboro outside the mill folk knew anything about it, it was accepted as the natural thing: summer jobs for boys were usually in their father's businesses; and besides, if you were a mill hand, so would your sons be: once a mill hand, always a mill hand, and that was what Captain Bodien really was, when you came right down to it, whatever his titles, pay, and pretensions.

June came to an end, in heat and somnolence. Sally Rausch kept an eye on her daughter, but saw nothing amiss beyond an unusual quietness and the reserve that had come between them. All the Waynesboro children had begun to concentrate on their preparations for the Fourth, saving pennies for firecrackers and torpedoes and "bombs," making great plans for the day that marked for them the high peak of the summer. Mr. and Mrs. Cochran returned from their long stay in Europe, and the Rausch children ceased to be so constantly underfoot. Mrs. Cochran, though forced to wear thick disfiguring glasses, was at least able to see again: she could take care of herself, move about, and eat without embarrassment. She even talked hopefully with Mrs. Sheldon and Mrs. Edwards, when they called, about resuming her social life. She was full of grateful praise for her surgeon, yet to Sally her mother seemed very frail; she grieved silently, and at the same time regretted having to banish the children, when they were indoors, to their rooms upstairs. Because she sympathized with them, she let Elsa and the two older boys go often to the Gordons to play.

One afternoon shortly after lunch, Sally put some fancy work in her sewing bag and went down herself to the Gordons'. She had hardly seen Anne all summer, and they could have a good visit while Mrs. Cochran napped under the eyes of Rose. A noisy game was going on in the Gordon side yard: not only were there two Gordons there and three Rausches, there were also the Bonners, Charlotte and brother, Sophie Klein, Billy Thirkield, Ariana McCune, the Evans boy (the minister's orphan nephew), and Rudy Lichtenstein. Sally identified them all at a glance before she sat down on the sofa and spread out her sewing around her.

"Elsa troubles me," she said. "Here she is, growing up, and after that day at the mill, I felt I had to tell her why she mustn't strain herself, how girls are made."

"You didn't! That baby! Mercy! How fast they grow up! I can't believe it."

"Better too early than too late: I'll never forget the shock I had—but now there's a wall between us. If she's afraid I am going to talk again about what horrors await her, she needn't worry: I've said my say."

"The trouble is, you're exactly alike, the two of you, you're bound to strike sparks."

"Elsa like me? Oh, no! I was never such a rough and tumble—"

"Have you forgotten when we were small and used to traipse after my brother Rob and his friends? But that wasn't what I meant. You are so alike in disposition."

"She strikes sparks out of me, I admit." Sally laughed. "Maybe I was rough and tumble, once—but I never minded being a girl, and I never thought of any conceivable future but marrying and bringing up a family. Elsa wants to be a boy and go marching off to war. Trouble is, her father spoils Elsa and she goes to him; she doesn't come to me."

"She's too like you. Just as Binny is too like her father—or his sister. I have to stand between them. I must get her in soon, washed up, quieted down, before he gets home. She's the apple of his eye, but how can she know that, when, just because she is, she must be perfect, not in the least like his sister Kate."

Sally understood all that was implied in those few quick words: Dock would not want his child to grow up to be like his unhappy sister.

"I've always known she took after Kate," Anne continued, "but I don't think he ever saw it until a few weeks ago." She told Sally about the morning when he had dragged Binny out of the grape arbor and into the house. "I could tell then, by the way he looked at her, what he was thinking. "Men!" she said scornfully. "The child won't be seven until fall: a little early to be worrying. And the best way to make her odd is to make her unhappy. Since then it's been nothing but manners—table manners—and clean hands and face—and I know he doesn't realize he's nagging. I'm sorry, Sally, to blow off steam to you, but you do know what I'm talking about."

"And maybe I needed to hear it—maybe I've been nagging, too, without realizing it." They changed the subject, chatted for a while until Sally said, "I must go: Mother will be awake after her nap, and I promised to take her for a drive. I'll call the children and take them along with me."

The two of them went out to the side porch just as John came through the alley gate and started up the walk. He did not so much as glance at the children. Anne saw his face and said, "Something's happened. He doesn't leave the office this early."

Sally, standing beside her, saw how white he was, shocked and horrified. "Bad news." John, approaching, looked up and saw the wondering faces of the two women watching him.

"Haven't you heard?" He did not wait to get within low-voiced range. "Didn't you hear the newsboys calling? Bonner's got an extra out already. Garfield's been shot!"

The children stopped as suddenly stock-still as if they had been playing "Still waters, no more moving." The two women heard him and were transfixed, disbelief fighting with consternation.

"Tell us—"

"Don't ask me questions, because I don't know any more. Only that there has been an attempted assassination. Johnny"—he flipped him a penny—"go get one of those extras."

"He isn't dead, then?" Sally was first in command of herself.

"I guess not. They say not."

"I must go. Ludwig will have news as soon as anyone." She called her children and departed with them. The others dispersed, quickly and quietly, a subdued lot. Suddenly it seemed that home was the place to be.

That second day of July marked the end of summer-as-usual. The next two months were quiet. All the preparations that had been made for a noisy Fourth were canceled: no one had the heart to celebrate; there would be no firecrackers and rockets while the President lay fighting for his life. Every hot day began with the question "Is he still alive?" and dragged its slow length along till time for the evening paper. Even those who had not been moved by Garfield's eloquence and were dubious as to the strength of his character felt the weight of calamity, and an unsettling bewilderment: why—how—could it have happened? The shooting of Lincoln had left a heavier burden of grief on the people, but that had been comprehensible: the Rebels had hated him, and some had hated him to madness. But Garfield could hardly be called "enemy" by any man, and the whole idea of political assassination was an importation from Europe: anarchism as a belief had been brought in by immigrants. Somehow it seemed to mean that henceforth America would be different, its people less confident of the safety of their government: a disquieting thought.

The nation held its breath while the strong man lay dying, holding death at arm's length for the rest of the summer. And when the end came, and the lying-in-state was over, when the President's body had been taken back to Ohio for burial, then Republicans looked at each other a little sheepishly and murmured "Chet Arthur." The man whom Hayes had removed as Collector of the Port of New York because he had permitted "irregularities" among his underlings—he was now President.

Garfield died on the eighteenth of September. Arthur was sworn in immediately and at once set a date for a special session of Congress. The Douglas Gardiners packed their trunks for their return to Washington, and the Misses Gardiner prepared the house for entertaining the Woman's Club.

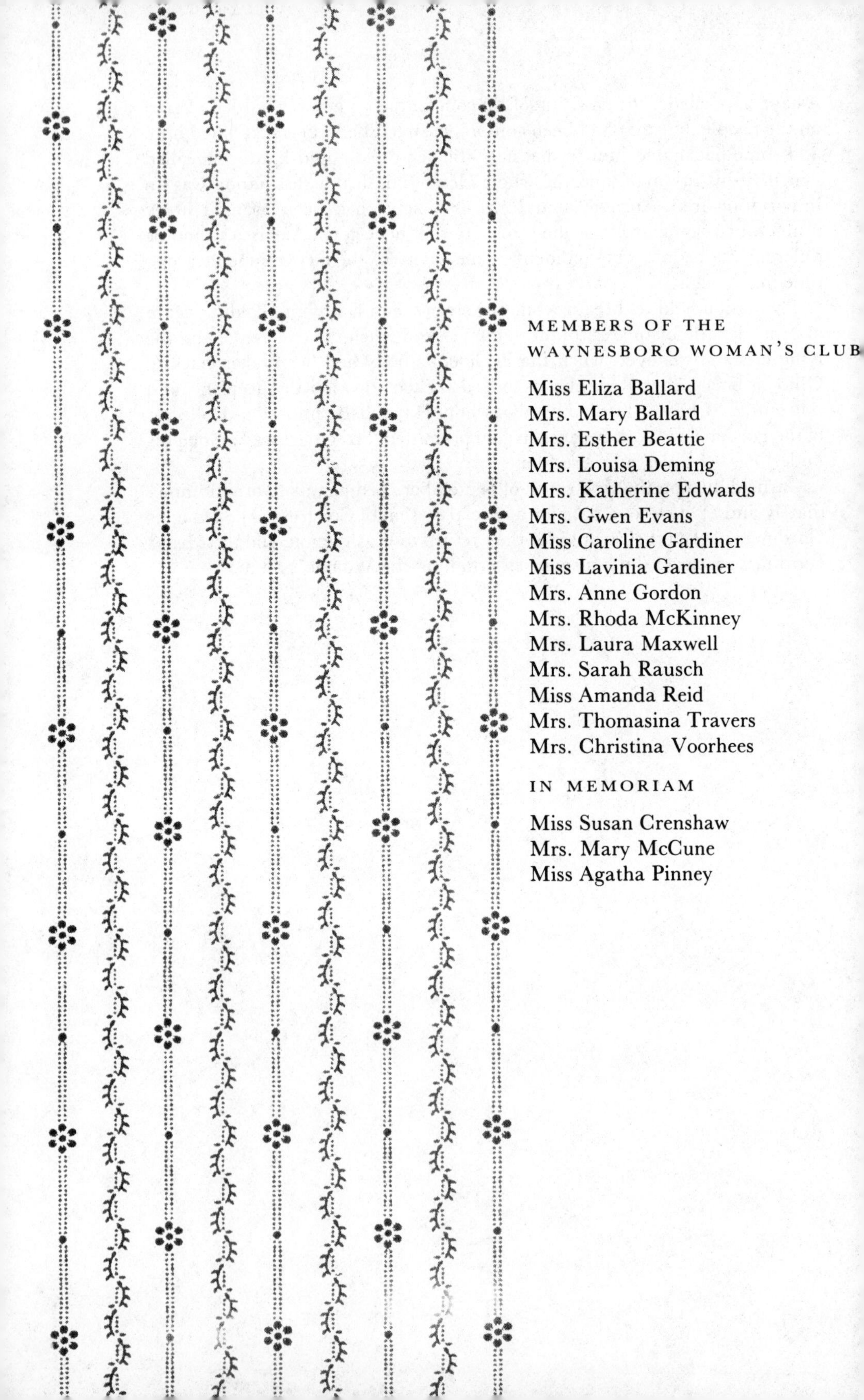

MEMBERS OF THE
WAYNESBORO WOMAN'S CLUB

Miss Eliza Ballard
Mrs. Mary Ballard
Mrs. Esther Beattie
Mrs. Louisa Deming
Mrs. Katherine Edwards
Mrs. Gwen Evans
Miss Caroline Gardiner
Miss Lavinia Gardiner
Mrs. Anne Gordon
Mrs. Rhoda McKinney
Mrs. Laura Maxwell
Mrs. Sarah Rausch
Miss Amanda Reid
Mrs. Thomasina Travers
Mrs. Christina Voorhees

IN MEMORIAM

Miss Susan Crenshaw
Mrs. Mary McCune
Miss Agatha Pinney

1884–1885

"Waynesboro was shocked by the loss of its most distinguished citizen . . ."

On a rainy afternoon in November—the twelfth, to be exact, just a week and a day after the 1884 election—the Waynesboro Woman's Club met with Mrs. Deming. At the hour when the ladies were assembling, Amanda Reid sat at her desk in the Latin classroom of the high school, supervising a test. Her second-year Latin students were struggling to put English sentences into Caesarian Latin, and to explain the grammatical rules involved. Her expression was so forbidding as her eyes went from one to another of them that her pupils would have been surprised could they have known how little her thoughts were centered on them. True, she let her mind wander down any vagrant way suggested by a face or an attitude that struck her eyes, but more insistently in her thoughts was the appalling realization that she had that morning committed herself to a course she might regret.

Elizabeth Talmadge was coming to live with her. A new young teacher of English, she had appealed to Amanda a few weeks earlier to suggest a place for her to live: the house where she had taken a room was uncomfortable and cramped, and the other boarders, with whom she had her meals, were dull defeated widows and old maids. Amanda, who knew all too much about boarders, said, without a moment's hesitation, surprising herself, since she was little inclined to be impulsive, "Come live with me."

Now she stirred at her desk, and repressed a sigh. The class before her seemed, most of them, concentrated on their task, but the atmosphere of the room was not conducive to alertness: it was the last hour of the day; the air was stuffy, laden with chalk dust and smelling of wet woolens. Had she opened a window there would have been protests about the draught, probably from Julia Deming. Amanda's glance rested on Julia briefly: she was growing tall, but was still slender, still pale, her corn-silk hair still worn flowing down her back, confined only by a ribbon above her forehead and behind her ears. She was working away serenely if slowly: her mother saw to it that she learned her lessons. But Julia, who was not yet fourteen, should not have been in this class with the fifteen-year-olds. Her air of fragility had persuaded all the boys, however uncouth, to treat her as if she were breakable. And Julia, though she might pretend to be unaware, made the most of their attitude: she was the fairy-tale princess, gracious and friendly, somehow misplaced in their midst. Amanda for one did not take Julia's presumed picture of herself very seriously.

The boys had not had much time that fall to think about girls: not until this last week, after the election. During the closing weeks of the campaign they had thought, dreamed, and talked of nothing else. Blaine was trying again, this time against a clever and experienced man. Amanda was glad that the season's insanity was over, even if it had left her pupils sleepy, indifferent, and apathetic in the shock of their disappointment and the reaction from all the excitement. The boys had worked hard and confidently, collecting all the loose pieces of lumber they could find—particularly staves from the tar barrels at the rope walk—for their post-election-night bonfire; then after all their efforts it had been the privilege of the sons of Democrats, from the West End, to light the bonfire and celebrate a victory. Amanda, who had not really believed it would make much difference whether Blaine or Cleveland was inaugurated in March, felt only relief when the air of tension had gone from her classroom, along with the campaign buttons. She could understand why these particular boys had been so keyed up: after all, presidential elections came only once in four years, and you caught only one of them at the right age, for first you were too young to be more than an onlooker at the center-of-town bonfire, and then you were forever too old to ransack the town for combustibles. She suspected that the boys, being at the age for it, had thrown themselves into wholehearted acceptance of the "plumed knight" epithet, and had been more enthusiastic about Blaine than were their fathers. She might be wrong; she might be attributing to male adults her own feeling about Blaine. His orations, which she conscientiously read when they appeared in print, had failed to inspire her, however eloquent he might seem to an audience. Waynesboro, staunchly Republican as always, had produced only one outspoken Mugwump: Mr. Lichtenstein. He was still, however unorthodox his politics, president of the school board, and she hoped that his Republican friends would not turn against him the next time he must run for reelection. He had been on the board for years now, and had improved the school beyond measure, but what did party loyalty mean in a school board member? She wondered whether men like Doug Gardiner, who had campaigned hard not only for himself but for the whole ticket, or like Ludwig Rausch, who had held the local voters in line and had probably pulled strings reaching far beyond the county line, would feel vindictive about the Mugwumps. After all, both of them, along with other county and district leaders, had supported Sherman and not Blaine at the June convention.

The boys had been so shocked and confounded by the election results that they were only now beginning to recover, and to take a normal interest in girls. Amanda watched Johnny Gordon for a moment: he was as untroubled as Julia by the task set him, but worked far more rapidly; he would finish the test, and there would be few errors in his paper. He liked Latin; he had solemnly explained to her that a knowledge of Latin was necessary to a doctor. Elsa Rausch was writing as rapidly as Johnny, but she would make more mistakes; she was a little slapdash in her ways still, except about her music. At present, Amanda thought, there were but two things that really engaged her attention: Johnny Gordon, whom she ordered around as if she owned him (and Johnny, smiling, obeyed or not, as he chose), and her music lessons in Cincinnati: a new adventure for Elsa. That fall Samuel Travers had told the Rausch parents that he had taught Elsa all that he could, and recommended a more advanced teacher; as a result, she went to Cincinnati on Saturdays, chaperoned on the train by Rose, who had been Mrs. Cochran's maid and nurse until she had died last spring. Amanda sighed as she watched Elsa ruffle her long bang with an impatient hand. These young ladies and their bangs! There were but two girls in her classes who had not chopped off half their hair to the length of a few inches and trained it down over their foreheads to their very eyebrows: Julia Deming, who would not have been permitted to sacrifice all that gold, and Ariana McCune, who was restrained from such worldliness and wore her hair in plaits pinned tight around her head. At least to start with in the morning they were tight; now the slipping braids and loose hair ends made a fuzz about the crown of her head. There was something "farouche"—Amanda thought that was the word—about Ariana. Although she was older than her classmates, "*Nondum subacta ferre iugum cervice:* Not yet was she fit to be broken to the yoke." Amanda watched the girl as she scrawled a few words and then thrust her pen savagely into the inkwell embedded in a corner of her desk. Amanda felt compassion for her: she looked half-sick, her eyes hollow and shadowed. But Ariana had been the cause of a rupture between her and the Ballards, Eliza and even Thomasina, who had been a lifelong and steadfast friend.

She knew what Ariana's paper would be like: illegible and spattered with blots. Miss Pinney's pupils had at least been taught penmanship: Johnny, Elsa, Julia, Bill Thirkield, they all wrote a beautiful flowing script, distinguishable at a glance from that of the products of Waynesboro's public school. Johnny particularly wrote in a neat minute hand almost like engraving; he was altogether a neat boy, neat-minded and neat-fingered—at least to start with, Amanda amended, taking in his rumpled shirt and wet trouser cuffs. But there was nothing of the hobbledehoy about him at fifteen, and nothing of the reputed Gordon waywardness. She had never really known his father when she was a girl, nor did she now, beyond casual encounters at Club Christmas parties. The Reids had always been Dr. Wright's patients: even when her mother lay dying, those awful days last summer, she would not let Amanda call another doctor. Amanda shied away from the recollection; she studied Johnny and wondered what kind of physician he would make. She remembered the first time she had ever seen him to know him, at the Club's Children's Hour Program. How many years ago? She remembered Ariana, too, as Jael acting the murder of Sisera. She turned her eyes from Johnny back to Ariana; their glances crossed, and for a moment the child looked almost murderous. Like Jael indeed. Amanda smiled to herself, a little thin-lipped: Ariana no doubt thought her teacher "picked on her." So, alas, did Eliza and Thomasina, although they would not have used the school-girl phrases. And all because Amanda had refused last spring to promote Ariana to third-year Latin. Even now, obviously, Ariana was in trouble with a simple exercise in Latin prose, in spite of the fact that she was ploughing her way through Caesar for the second time. When the report cards had been passed out the previous June, Ariana had been outraged. As Amanda had expected, the girl had fled to the Ballards for comfort before going home to certain condemnation and punishment.

What Amanda had not foreseen was that the Ballard sisters would take up her cause. They had presented themselves at the Reid door, marched into the parlor, and demanded (Eliza) and begged (Thomasina) that she alter the failing mark in Latin II. Amanda had been so astonished and so shocked that she had been perhaps too curt. "But once report cards are out they cannot be changed," she said tartly.

"Exceptions can be made to every rule. Or you could pretend to have made a mistake in copying the grades."

"Eliza! What are you asking?"

"Surely," Thomasina intervened, "when everything is taken into consideration—"

"What should I take into consideration, beyond the fact that she does not know enough Latin to go on with a class that will be reading Cicero next year?"

"Not even if I tutor her this summer?"

"Possibly." Amanda wondered how much of her Latin Thomasina remembered, but wisely did not say so. "I cannot change her mark. But if she can pass an examination in the fall, she might be permitted to go ahead."

"But it's the *failure*, Amanda. She feels disgraced."

"She isn't the only one. Would it be just to change her mark and not the others? Or would you have me change them all?"

"The others don't have Ariana's father. He's a scholar, and your minister, Amanda."

"What does that have to do with it?" Amanda was tight-lipped. "She has not done the work, and I gave her a failing mark. I don't think she minds, except that her pride is hurt. And I suppose it will be made difficult for her at home. But really she will be happier in the next class: most of her friends are in it, and they are not all brilliant students. In the class she has been in she has had to compete with Charlotte Bonner and Sophie Klein and Rudy Lichtenstein. That was so impossible she didn't even try. Going over the work again with Elsa Rausch and Johnny Gordon and Julia Deming and others of Miss Pinney's children, she may care enough to try. But I doubt it," she had concluded flatly.

"You are prejudiced against her. She isn't stupid. Why isn't she interested enough to learn? Aren't you a teacher? Why can't you teach Ariana?"

This from Eliza hurt, particularly since it was a question Amanda had asked herself. She had searched her conscience as to whether the antagonism between Ariana and her had carried over from the days when Mr. McCune—but Ariana had known nothing about that; it was nonsense to think—

"I can't teach her because she doesn't care to learn. That is why I hope, in a class with her friends—"

"But she is such an ardent soul! I can't imagine her not throwing herself headlong into any undertaking."

"She has not been ardent about Caesar's *Gallic Wars*, believe me."

"What, then?" Eliza pounced. "Boys?"

"Boys—as boys? No, I don't think so. I never see her alone with one—at least not since the Mercer boy ran away with the circus. They had their heads together on occasion last year, but I'm sure that was just the attraction of one free spirit for another."

"What do you mean, 'free spirit'?" Eliza was so fierce that Amanda was taken aback.

"A rebel, I suppose. A kicker-against-the-pricks. A dreamer-of-escape. It's a pity she's a girl. Boys can escape if they want to: if they are trapped, it is their own fault."

"Like the Mercer boy? What an escape: the circus! But I am glad he is gone: perhaps next year she will apply herself. Thomasina and I have planned an 'escape' for her, when the time comes: an education."

That was Eliza; Thomasina broke in:

"What are you talking about, Amanda: 'trapped'? I know her home life isn't very happy, but 'trapped'? Why is she trapped, more than any other?"

"We're all trapped, Thomasina, we females—in one way or another. It has been Ariana's misfortune to find it out while she is young."

"But that's nonsense," Thomasina protested. "I am not trapped. I had my choice."

"Perhaps Amanda hopes Ariana will run away." Eliza was cold now, her face pinched. "Then her presence won't be a reminder every day that once she hoped Mr. McCune would release her from *her* trap."

Amanda could feel her face grow rigid; her knees shook; she told herself "Don't say it, don't say it." Thomasina saved her: she turned on her sister.

"That is indecent, Eliza! You've let yourself get carried away. You can't possibly believe that Amanda wanted that dreadful little man. You must apologize to her."

"I apologize. I should not have said that." Eliza did not look particularly regretful, but Thomasina covered for her.

"We only came to ask you, Amanda: just *please* don't fail her. It will make her more unhappy, more of a rebel."

"I cannot make exceptions for *any* reason, Thomasina. When my pupils finish their second year of Latin, they are supposed to have finished with Caesar and to know their Latin grammar: know it well enough to be able to read Cicero. And Ariana—" Amanda tried to smile, "ask her about the second periphrastic conjugation: she won't know what you are talking about, much less how it is used."

Thomasina, who had long since forgotten the second periphrastic, said, "You drag that in to prove that we can't help her. But I can review my Latin grammar."

"And you can try to teach her. I wish you joy."

"I never knew you to be so hard. Can't you find it in your heart to sympathize with the child?"

"I sympathize with any motherless child. But Ariana is not the only one I teach. The others do not use it to excuse neglect of their studies."

"Does she neglect them all?" Eliza was quick to seize the point. "You were the only teacher who failed her."

"That may be. Whether she does her work in other subjects, whether other teachers are honest in their appraisal or not, is none of my concern. But I do have some regard for my own integrity: the marks I give mean what they say. I am surprised that you do not understand that: I always thought the Ballards had a high regard for integrity."

"Oh Amanda, what a big word for such a small thing!"

"Small? Perhaps. But teaching with integrity is my work. The work I expect to be doing all my life."

"Then you won't do this for us? Let Ariana pass?"

"No. Not even for you. You have no right to ask it."

That had been Amanda's last word. The disagreeable scene had made such an impression on her that she had come to wonder how she had been able to withstand them without showing her anger. Then her mother had fallen fatally ill, and in the strain of that time, the quarrel with the Ballards had slipped into the background of her mind. She had not seen them again until her mother's death. Then, as a family, the Ballards had done all the proper, helpful things. But Thomasina had not been in and out of the house during her mother's illness, inquiring, helping, sitting with Amanda, as once upon a time she would have been. This estrangement was far deeper than that which had followed Thomasina's marriage. She did not even know now whether Thomasina had made any attempt to teach Ariana her Latin: at any rate, there had been no request in September for a make-up examination.

Now, awaiting the end of the afternoon in her classroom, she lived again the scene with the Ballards; it was not Eliza's almost unbearable insult that echoed in her mind, but Thomasina's word "small." She thought, "It is how I have spent my life—on small things, making the trivial important so as not to feel trapped." For how many years? Now she was free. Her mother no longer needed her. She refused to allow herself to relive those dreadful hours when the old woman had fought so bitterly against dying, but now, as so many times since returning from the cemetery to an empty house, she wondered at how much she missed her mother after all: an old woman to whom she had been a dutiful daughter but whom she had found it difficult to love. Still, after all these months she dreaded going home to a dark house. She missed even the querulousness and the reproaches; she missed the voice of another human to whom she had been attached by indissoluble ties. She had looked forward to being free—now she was free—and where was she to go? She was forty. She did not know enough, she had forgotten too much, to be able to teach in a college, even though there were now colleges for women in the East, taught by women. She would need a graduate degree, and not only did she shrink from the thought of matching her mind with the minds of younger students, there was not enough money. She had never been able to save, having for so long carried the responsibility for taxes, repairs, and all the thousand things. Her mother had left her a little: a surprisingly large amount, if you considered how it had been earned, but for the purchase of Amanda's freedom too little. "At least," she thought, "the Seminary students are out from under foot." They were being fed by another Reformed Presbyterian widow. She had the house to herself: it was all hers, and there was pleasure in that thought. But after she got home in the afternoons, and through the long evenings, no other voice.

Now she had blurted out that invitation to Elizabeth Talmadge to come share the house with her. She had realized the moment she spoke that she was acknowledging to herself (probably no one else had ever doubted it) that she would be spending the rest of her life in Waynesboro. In defense, she had taken pains at once to ward Elizabeth off: "As I said, you could have your own bedroom and share the downstairs rooms with me. But there are only stoves and fireplaces for heat. It's a long walk to school on a rainy day, or in the snow."

And Elizabeth had said, startling Amanda, "But I could use the kitchen? Get my own meals?"

Amanda had marveled. "You mean you like to cook? Yes, you could get your own meals, or we could eat together and take turns cooking." Then, hastily, "But do think it over—look around some more—you might not like it at all."

And Elizabeth had thought, and looked, and told her that morning that she would like to move in with her.

So much for freedom, Amanda thought now. "If I am trapped again, it is by my own act. Of course, if it doesn't work out—but—trapped." And astonished at herself even as she moved, she brought her clenched fist down on her desk.

Her class looked up, startled. Amanda recovered herself, looked at the clock on the wall above the blackboard. "Ten more minutes only. If you have finished, look over your work carefully and correct any errors you find. If you have not finished, do your best to do so in the time remaining. I want the papers passed up promptly when the bell rings."

All those papers! She would have to take them with her to the Club meeting. At the Demings'. That was why Julia was so dressed up: she would pass the tea. The children of other Club members were expected to, and did gladly, make themselves scarce when the meetings were at their mothers'. But at the Demings' tea was always served, even though there was an unwritten rule against serving refreshments at a Club meeting. ("We do not want to be seduced," Mrs. Ballard had once said, "into seeing who can bake the richest cake.") This ritual helped to emphasize Mrs. Deming's Boston origin.

The bell rang. Amanda waited for the papers to be brought to her desk, then dismissed her class and went to the closet for her wraps, stopping only a moment to look in the mirror hung on the inside of the door. She could see the short hairs loose around her ears and neck. While she was trying to pin them back and get her hat on properly, Julia came to stand beside her, booted and cloaked, her little round hat flat on the top of her head, and her pale hair smooth as glass on her shoulders.

"Miss Reid, I didn't have a chance to speak to you before. Papa said the weather is so bad he would come for us to take us to the Club. He's outside, with the buggy. Will you ride with us?"

Amanda was grateful, in spite of the fact that she could never find much to say to General Deming. Now, as she climbed into the curtained buggy ahead of Julia, she thanked him for his consideration.

"Couldn't let two ladies come to my house all wet and muddy. Pull the robe over your knees—that's right."

Amanda had not been so close to the General for a long while; she thought he was looking older: the once ruddy cheeks were a fine network of blood vessels, and his mustache was white. He must be—the war had been over for almost twenty years—and he had certainly been close to forty then. He must be nearing sixty now, and well-embarked on his third career. Soldier, politician, and now historian, of a sort.

"I understand from Mrs. Deming," she said, "that your history of this county was so successful as to induce you to move on to Boone County."

"That is correct. I derive great pleasure from such work: the research, the writing. But unlike my last book, this one takes me from home a great deal. I miss being with Louisa and Julia every day."

"We miss you, Papa." Julia responded to her cue, but then added what she should not have done, dimming her father's picture of himself as scholar and author. "But maybe you will make a *great deal* of money."

"A great deal of money is not ordinarily the reward of an historian, Pet. Of course I hope to be recompensed for the time spent and the work involved. But that is on the knees of the gods."

Depending, Amanda thought, on how many of Boone County's leading citizens "subscribe" in order to have their pictures and biographies included in their county's history. Of course, in time, someone might want to know who had been its leading citizens. She wondered what it would be like to have to live with this kind, bumbling, pompous, affectionate, egotistical man, and so wondering, went into the Club meeting in somewhat better spirits: there were worse fates than being alone, worse ways of being trapped. Whose life—what woman's life, she amended—was not dull, once you were middle-aged?

She slipped into the Deming parlor as quietly as possible, having left books and papers on the turret window seat, her cloak on the rack, and her umbrella in the stand. Mrs. Beattie was reading a paper on "The Creole Novels of George Washington Cable." The subject of the year's program was "The Renaissance of Southern Literature"; privately, Amanda considered that what had never been born could hardly be reborn, and the Club was wasting its time. She thought, "What simpletons women are! That way of life was abominable. We were all opposed to slavery and fought to end it. Now these new authors make it seem like Arcadia, and we are beguiled and enchanted." She glanced at Mrs. Ballard, rigid in her stiff chair behind the occasional table that held her gavel, papers, program, and spectacles: Mrs. Ballard had been an abolitionist since Amanda could remember. Now her face was expressionless, but she was at least attentive. Amanda set herself to listen, too: she might learn something, since she never read fiction at all. But in spite of herself, her mind wandered. Elizabeth Talmadge. Elizabeth was young, attractive, and would be getting married one of these days; on the other hand, she was an excellent teacher, well-educated (Oberlin, 1880), and knew classic literature as well as English (Amanda knew that, since her brighter students were always coming out with "But Miss Talmadge says—"). She was pleasant in manner, easily agreeable, and she would be company. Two people going into an empty house at the day's end would be better than going in alone and facing the empty chair beside the parlor table. But why had she let herself slip into that trapped feeling? Amanda had little sympathy for self-pity in anyone, least of all herself. Her lot was no worse than the common lot, no worse than— She let herself look around the group: that of the Misses Gardiner, who she was sure made themselves miserable and would have done so in any circumstances. Or of Eliza Ballard, so soured on life; or even Thomasina, who still seemed to believe her Samuel all she had thought him to be when they were married, but who must, if she were honest with herself, admit in the secret places of her mind that he would never set the world on fire, that he was indeed a laughable figure, a little dapper-dandy of a man, going bald. Mrs. Ballard, who could have been happy fighting in any worthy cause, now so crippled and so wracked with pain as to be out of any new or continuing crusade. Sally Rausch: Sally looked prosperous, healthy, and content, and her days could hardly be dull, with four children, but her life would bore to death anyone whose interests were intellectual. Mrs. Christina Blair Voorhees, too, looked well satisfied with herself and her world: she was still the youngest member of the Club, although now the possessor of a successful husband, two healthy children, and a secure place in the life of

Waynesboro, but self-satisfaction was making her blander. Of what use was her truly scholarly mind? Anne Gordon probably would not have traded places with anyone. Kitty Edwards had changed in the last few years: she had lost her springing Lowrey vitality; her face was a little puffy and pasty-white. Her boy was four years old or thereabouts: was she trying again? Amanda thought that probably everyone looked at Kitty with that surmise, as if she were simply a not very successful breeding animal. In revulsion Amanda looked away. Amanda had no very high opinion of most of her fellow Club members; she remembered now with some sadness, as for any lost illusion, how eager she had been for its organization, so that there might be some mental stimulus in the town where she must live. But whatever its shortcomings, the Club was all there was, its members the best-educated, the most intelligent: she must make the most of it. Nevertheless, she wouldn't for anything in the world have been any one of the others. To *have* what some of them had, yes, of course, but to *be* one of them, no! And not one of them would have been Amanda Reid, or anyone but herself. Queer: no one ever wanted to be someone else. It was a matter of identity: you simply could not imagine wanting to *be* someone else, even if you would like to lead someone else's life. And if you were still yourself, your life would be what you were suited to. I can dream of a life away from Waynesboro, a scholarly life, with other scholars, but I should still be Amanda Reid. So I might as well resign myself to leading the life foreordained for Amanda Reid: smelly classrooms, papers, stupid pupils, but once in a while a rewarding one. For Amanda Reid it is better than the lives that any of these others are leading. The housewives particularly. If there was one thing she thoroughly detested, it was housekeeping. She should be glad that Elizabeth would share that burden with her. At that point Amanda was smiling—inwardly, laughing—at herself; she caught the eye of Anne Gordon across the room, and sobered instantly. "Probably wonders what there is to smile at: certainly nothing in Mrs. Beattie's paper. An hour ago I should have wondered too. Now I sit here feeling superior, because I cannot imagine what it would be like living in some of these small minds. But of course you wouldn't know it was dull: you would be quite satisfied."

When the meeting had adjourned, and the ladies were moving about in a moment's brief respite from hard chairs, before the tea was brought in, Amanda made a point of moving to Anne's side, to say something that would explain the smile Anne had caught.

"I've been wanting to say how much I enjoy having your son in my Caesar class."

"Johnny likes Latin. He doesn't do so well in everything. But he has never been a worry to us."

Anne suspected that she must have sounded ungracious. She put a hand on Amanda's arm before they moved apart. "I'm sorry to have been so abrupt. I should have said 'Thank you.' Any mother loves to hear her child praised. Binny *does* worry us. She's in bed with another of those awful throats, possibly tonsillitis. She's better, but I must get home: Martha is good with her, but she may not be able to keep her down."

Anne had been afraid that Binny's sore throat might develop into the always dreaded diphtheria. If that new young Dr. Warren had not painted the gagging child's throat with that horrible silver nitrate, it would have been easier to see whether or not it was going to be diphtheria—but perhaps the silver nitrate had saved Binny from tonsillitis. Anne privately believed John's refusal to treat his own family a medical superstition, but she was glad that Dr. Warren had come to Waynesboro to practice: she no longer had to entrust Binny to one of the old fuddy-duddies. Fortunately, Binny liked Dr. Warren, a gawky country boy married to a country girl: tall, bony, sandy-haired, not impressive to look at but a strong man, capable and infinitely kind. She moved to the door, explaining to Mrs. Deming that she had a sick child at home and could not stop for tea, said pleasantly to the Misses Gardiner, as she edged around Miss Lavinia's absurd hoop skirt, that she supposed they would be very lonely when Douglas and his family returned to Washington, but congratulated them on the fact that he had been reelected, waved a farewell greeting to Sally across the room, and made her escape. Kitty Edwards followed her into the hall.

"Anne, I saw your horse at the hitching post. Have you time to take me home? I suppose Dock wants the horse and buggy when his office hours are over."

"He can have the mare hitched up if he needs her. He would certainly not like it if I let you walk home on a miserable day like this."

"Sheldon wanted me to engage a hack, but I knew I could beg a ride home."

"You should have waited until the meeting was over, then you could have gone in style. Sally and the Ballards will have their carriages coming."

"No. I've had enough. I'm tired."

Anne looked at her sharply, but said no more until she had helped Kitty into the buggy, unhitched Molly, and climbed in herself under the oilcloth curtains. Then she ventured to remonstrate, rather tentatively. "Hasn't John told you to stay in bed, or at least flat on your back, again?"

"In another couple of weeks. I guess he's right put out with me."

"With both of you, goose. After all—"

"No. I cajoled Sheldon. And I felt fine, and Dock said if I was determined—so why not?"

Anne doubted whether John had given his approval. She said, "And now?"

"Oh now. I'm sick every morning, of course. I'll be all right after I go to bed to stay. In a way I dread it—such a waste of time. In another, selfish way I'm glad: I sha'n't have to go in the store and be cheerful for Sheldon's uncle's sake. I was in there yesterday, and Uncle John—he has been so good to me, and I love him for it—but to see that beard, and his shirt front all spotted with blood, and to pretend not to see it. It makes me sick for him."

"I know." Everyone in Waynesboro knew. Mr. Sheldon had a throat cancer, or cancer of the thyroid. Anne wasn't sure which, but to him it could matter very little: he was doomed, and he knew it. But he insisted on going to the store, and his old friends and customers had to stay away, or ignore the bloodstained beard.

"And Aunt Mattie Sheldon is so fastidious. Almost worse than Mother Edwards. It must give her the horrors. But she is very good: she never shows any revulsion, not so much as a quiver. Queer, isn't it? People always have to face up to what they're by nature least well equipped to face."

"It is in our weaknesses, or in a virtue carried to excess, I suppose, that we are tested. It seems as if it were on purpose. I thought of it all those years when Sally was so patient with her mother. Sally isn't by nature patient."

"No. Anne, can nothing be done?"

"For Mr. Sheldon? John isn't his doctor, but I suppose not. But don't you get all worked up about it, Kitty. You're going to have troubles enough of your own."

"I won't. But wouldn't it be wonderful if we could all die quietly when our time comes. Like my mother and father. One after the other. I think he just quit after Mamma died. Forgive me, Anne."

"Why shouldn't you tell me your troubles?" The buggy was by now at the Edwardses' gate; Sheldon and Kitty and little Lowrey still lived in the house rented from the Rausches, out on Linden Street; there had never been a time, somehow, when they had felt like building the house they had planned, a big house on the edge of town with wide porches and acres of yard for a big family of children.

"Don't get too blue thinking about these things, Kitty, while you're in bed. You've got little Lowrey to amuse you, and Sheldon, and I'll drop in with all the gossip."

Back at the Demings', Eliza Ballard, who knew that the Douglas Gardiners had already returned to Washington, had stood close enough to overhear Anne's farewell speech to the Misses Gardiner, and dismissed the pretty bit of social pretense as so much hypocrisy: Anne's pretending to take it for granted that all the Gardiners were one happy family, when she must know better. The Douglas Gardiners had not waited for Congress to reconvene on the first of December before they went back; Douglas would probably not have come home at all had he not had to campaign for reelection. And he probably wanted to look over what was happening in the law office. Tim Merrill, whose grandfather's partnership had been held for him, had gone in with Judge Ballard and Doug as soon as he had passed his bar examination, and now was beginning to take hold: he was all right when it came to deeds, trusts, title-searching, wills, all that sort of thing, and was even becoming an effective trial lawyer, in the minor criminal and civil cases that came to them, in spite of his appearance. Tim was younger looking than his age: round-faced, curly-haired, almost cherubic: it might be that his courtroom antagonists expected him to be kind, easy-going, even stupid. Stupid he was not, but he was still more or less at a loss in the intricacies of corporation law, and it was as a corporation lawyer that Judge Ballard excelled, and earned most of the money that was made by the firm. It was strange that it should be so, since once upon a time he had mistrusted corporations, and had been sickened by the corruption the railroad companies had been responsible for. Perhaps the Pennsylvania was not corrupt, or the cases it brought to its lawyer were righteous ones. So far as Eliza could tell, they were, and she made a point of studying them in the office. But what corporations paid their lawyers wasn't a drop in the bucket compared with what they paid their officers. And now, she thought bitterly, taking in Sally's expensive elegance, Ballard, Gardiner, and Merrill were working on a franchise application for Ludwig Rausch and his associates for the Columbus and Southwestern Ohio Electrical Railroad Company. If Judge Ballard succeeded in obtaining it, he would be paid a lawyer's fee, and Ludwig Rausch and his out-of-town friends, as officers and stockholders, would pick up their thousands, perhaps even their tens of thousands. Of course, the promoters might fail to raise the capital they needed. Eliza thought it was really preposterous to believe that because Mr. Hanna was planning to start an electric street railway in Cleveland, a cross-country one would also be profitable, even if it did take in all the little towns not on the railroad. True, Ludwig had so far been successful, and her father had faith in the plan. But it seemed to her a wild dream; she would not have invested a penny in such an enterprise, and she hoped her father would be equally sensible. She admitted that the telephone seemed to be successful, and the electric street lights.

Eliza went to get her cup of tea from Mrs. Deming, who was pouring, and returned to sit beside Sally Rausch on the end of the sofa, next to the small straight chair Miss Gardiner had chosen because it gave her room for her billowing skirts.

"We are seeing a good deal of your husband these days in our office. I hope he is satisfied with the progress Papa is making."

"Ludwig never discusses business with me."(And that, thought Eliza, was probably a whopper. Sally was no fool, and her father having been a banker all her life, she had probably heard, first and last, a great deal about finance.) "But there have been no complaints about Ballard, Gardiner, and Merrill. At any rate, everything in the business world is more or less in a state of suspense now, waiting for Cleveland to show his hand. You know: tariffs and that sort of thing." Then Sally leaned forward across Eliza to address Miss Gardiner. "And speaking of tariffs, when does Douglas go back to Washington?"

Miss Lavinia could not avoid Sally's direct question, as she had evaded replying to Anne's congratulations. "They have already gone. Mrs. Gardiner is expecting a child, you know." Sally did know, as did Eliza: everyone always knew that sort of thing in Waynesboro. This one would be the Gardiners' third child: one every two years.

"Douglas, his wife and children, their nursemaid," Miss Lavinia continued. "Quite an entourage. They traveled in a drawing room, of course, but it seemed not quite nice for her to be seen in public, on a *train*—she is so very conspicuously *enceinte*. No doubt Caroline and I are old-fashioned. But Douglas was afraid to wait until the first of December, when Congress reconvenes: the baby might have been born here, and then he would have been unable to get away, or would have had to leave his wife and children. In spite of her unsightliness, we were glad to have them return to their small house in Georgetown. Their first child was born in our house, you will remember. Caroline and I were sadly discommoded by the commotion, and the disruption of the household: the monthly nurse even shared our meals. Now we are quite quiet and peaceful once more."

This was a long speech for Miss Lavinia. She missed no opportunity, Sally thought, to let anyone and everyone know how she and her sister felt about Mrs. Douglas Gardiner. Sally, now that she had been relieved of any fear of being expected to launch the Bodien girl into Waynesboro society, had almost forgiven Doug for having married her: Barbara was making him a good wife, bearing his children, and by her devotion mellowing his gritty nature. Sally took a cookie from the plate that Julia was passing and settled back for a chat with Amanda, in the chair to her right, realizing as she did so that living alone had made Amanda more talkative. Once in two weeks Amanda had a chance to visit with her friends. Otherwise, only schoolchildren, other teachers, and once or twice a week, the congregation of the Reformed Presbyterian church. Sally hardly considered people in these classifications conversible, and she set herself to be agreeable.

And, indeed, since Amanda had fought her way out of her earlier moroseness, she was enjoying the afternoon. She was pleased, too, when the meeting broke up and the Ballards' Johann rang the doorbell to announce the carriage, that Mrs. Ballard asked her to ride home with them. She would have been happier had it been Thomasina's invitation, but—

As they drove away, Mrs. Ballard asked her how school was going. She replied briefly, avoiding any mention of her pupils. She told them that Elizabeth Talmadge was coming to share her house with her. "I think we shall get along. She is a very intelligent, well-read girl, and I think a good teacher."

When Johann had stopped the carriage at the Reid gate and was escorting Amanda up the path, holding the umbrella over her head, Eliza said, "How unlike Amanda all that sounded."

"You mean asking a friend to live with her? It seems to me very natural: she could not enjoy living all alone."

"But, Mamma: a young girl half her age whom she first met just a few weeks ago? All Amanda knows about her is that she is well-read and intelligent. That may not be enough to ensure her amiability. But what I really meant was all that talk: Amanda is turning into a chatterbox."

"Don't be unkind, Eliza. Remember that Amanda has no one to talk to from one week's end to the next."

"Just the whole high school. I should think she would be so tired at the end of the day that she would enjoy her solitude."

"And grow to be more and more like poor Miss Pinney? No, Eliza. One of the things the Bible tells us is that God saw that it was not good for man to be alone."

Eliza could have made any one of several retorts that bubbled in her mind: that God had been mistaken; that Adam would have been better off alone; that since her mother had read and accepted Darwin, to say nothing of Huxley and Spencer, surely she did not take the first chapters of Genesis seriously. But she restrained herself, replying only that she hoped Amanda knew what she was doing, and to Johann, taking up the reins again, that he had better hurry a little, so that he could get up to the office in time to pick up the Judge, or "he will start to walk home, and he shouldn't, in this weather. He is always so tired at the end of the day."

So far as Eliza could see, she was the only one of the three of them who worried about her father. Where the law firm was concerned, things were going well: they did not have to pinch pennies so hard as they had for a while; Johann and his wife had been given their arrears of pay, and now were paid their wages each week. That seemed to be all that Thomasina and her mother noticed; they seemed to assume that now things would go on in this tranquil way indefinitely. Eliza was of another mind: she had seen how shaky her father had grown, how fumbling, how very forgetful—or seeming forgetful because he had not been concentrating on the problems or papers before him; it was as if he were listening to something far away and more important—at least that was how he sometimes impressed her, and she had not the courage to ask anyone, "Haven't you noticed?" She did not blame her sister and mother: somehow the Judge had the reserve of strength needed to pull himself together when he reached home and to be himself throughout dinner and the evening. Just as, Eliza admitted, he always pulled himself together for an interview with a client, and was able to be clear, firm, and decisive.

But even Eliza was not worrying about him the next morning: he had gone into his inner office and set to work on the franchise papers for Ludwig Rausch. She could not see him from her outer desk, although the door was ajar, but she could hear the rapid turning of pages, the scratch of his pen. The two of them were alone: Tim Merrill was in court, and Doug of course had returned to Washington; therefore, the rattling of papers could have come only from her father. Eliza, at work on the account books spread open before her on her desk, was comfortably aware of the sounds of normal activity from the other office, just barely aware, so that when they ceased suddenly it was a second before her attention was caught. She waited, suspended pen in hand, to hear the crackle of another paper. Instead, after what seemed to her an eternity of silence, what she heard was a choked, cut-off outcry, a creak of the swivel chair, the crash of a book knocked to the floor. For an instant she was incapable of movement; she was not even thinking, actually, but there were words in her mind: "This is it. You always wondered how you would measure up in an emergency." So actually did she feel her heart in her throat that she put her hand up to her tight collar. But she fought down her blind terror and forced herself into the other room.

Her father's head and shoulders were on his desk, his arms swinging. His breathing was slow, spasmodic, noisy. Acting without volition, instinctively, she braced herself against the back of his chair so that it could not roll, and with tremendous but controlled effort, pulled his shoulders back. His head lolled helplessly. Holding him up with an arm over his shoulder and under his chin, she succeeded in pushing the chair over to the old leather couch, with the faded afghan folded at its foot. She was desperately frightened, but in spite of her sick feeling and the strengthlessness of her knees, she somehow managed to move him—"*dump* him," she thought wildly—onto the couch. She turned him on his back, untied his cravat, unfastened his collar, pulled him up until his head was on the curved end of the couch, pulled the afghan out from under his feet, and spread it over him. Then for the first time, she began to shake; her knees gave way: she dropped into the chair. His face was flushed, his eyes half-closed, showing the whites, his mouth hung open; he still breathed snoringly, and saliva ran down from his open mouth. She took her handkerchief and wiped his face. He must have a doctor at once. She rose and started for the door—someone along the hall—but no one: job printers, insurance agents, notaries—would have a horse at hand. Walking would be too slow. She turned back and went to the window: someone surely would be driving past. She wrested the window open. When she first looked out, her palms on the window sill, the street was empty. But as she was about to withdraw, she heard the tinkling of a familiar bell: Mr. Hoffmann's baker's cart turning the corner from Chillicothe Street. Mr. Hoffmann himself was nearly hidden on his perch inside, but she could see his hands holding the reins that rose steeply from his horse's back to the little window at the front of the cart. He would help if she could catch him—no matter that the Ballard women had crusaded against his beer-parlor. Now the baker's cart was moving at an easy trot; she would never catch him if she went all the way down the stairs. She would have to call from the window. The curious would come running, but there was no other way. Casting all decorum to the winds, she thrust head and shoulders out of the window, still bracing herself on the sill, and called. Mr. Hoffmann was on the other side of the cart, but he heard. Eliza thanked God when she saw him lean over to the little window on his right and look up.

"Mr. Hoffmann"—Eliza's throat closed on the word "Papa." She choked it back, she must not shout it to the winds; anyone might hear and carry the word, even home before she could warn them. "I need help. Could you please come up here?"

At his nodded agreement, his hand lifted to show that he understood, she drew back from the window, looked at her father in passing, went through the outer office and along the passage. When she saw the round little German start up the stairs, she was so relieved that she leaned weakly against the wall, clinging to the handrail.

"My father has been taken very ill. There's no one in the office but me. Could you go for Dr. Gordon for me?"

"Of course. At vunce. Zere iss nossing I could do for you first? You haf not ze telephone?"

"No, no telephone. Please hurry." For a blurred moment Eliza's mind went back to the installation of Waynesboro's telephone system: the two younger members of the firm had wanted to subscribe, but Judge Ballard had overruled them: it would be an unnecessary expense: "No one wants a lawyer in all that hurry," he had said. Eliza, without consciously having walked the corridor, found herself back in the office. Her father remained as he had been: it was a relief to hear his rough breathing again. She had left the window open so that the air might make it easier for him, but she stood to one side of it, out of sight from the street. Mr. Hoffmann had already got his horse turned around, and with whip waving above it and the reins slapping its back, it was careening around the corner into Chillicothe Street. "Oh, charioteer!" Eliza laughed, so near hysteria that she clapped her hand over her mouth. Since Mr. Hoffmann had never been know to whip his horse, the few passersby, the idlers on the Court House plaza, stood staring. Curious faces appeared at the Court House windows. Someone would surely come. Hating the human race for its ghoulish curiosity, she went back to the outer office and locked the door into the corridor. If she waited at the window, she could see the doctor coming, or Tim Merrill, if anyone ventured to call him from the courtroom. She turned back to her father. He was still alive, his chest heaving, his face congested. She turned her eyes from him, trying to pray. She found that she was looking at the cracked leather of the sofa beyond his head, at the framed photograph on the wall above him, faded and spotted; the Supreme Court of the State of Ohio, taken long ago when her father had been one of its judges. "Not here, not like this," she thought, aware of the dust-covered file boxes piled in the cupboard, the musty books in the bookcases, his scratched and battered desk. She began to walk, forcing her shaking knees to hold her, couch to window, window to door, looking down on the street, listening for steps on the stairs, in her mind still rebelling: "He was a great man, and now, this shabby office, these trivial affairs." She was afraid to stop moving, lest her legs refuse to act once stopped. Terror and a profound hopelessness made her weak, shaken by an apprehension like lead. Her father's breath still came in the horribly jerky way. She felt under the afghan for his hand. He was not aware of her, his hand limp in hers; no use even to try to give him that comfort: a hand to hold. She went to the window again, in time to see the doctor's horse and buggy moving rapidly up Chillicothe Street. Only then did she think that he might have been out of his office. Mr. Hoffmann might not have found him. She moved slowly now, hanging on to desks and chairs, the railing of the outer office, and unlocked the corridor door. Somehow, in the interval while she had been away from the window, Tim Merrill had managed to cross the Court House lawn and climb the stairs; he was at the doctor's shoulder as she let them in.

"It's Papa." She paused to lock the door again. Behind her they had stopped stock-still, hearing that breathing that for such an eternity had shut out every other sound.

Then even as the doctor strode to the connecting door, with one brief wordless compassionate glance at her, the sound ceased. All paused, stood, listened—and there was nothing. Eliza seized the railing, hung on it. "What—?" John Gordon went into the inner room, closing the door quietly behind him. Tim Merrill took her arm, supported her while he pulled the chair back from her desk, and pressed her into it. She was hardly seated, in rigid outward control of herself, however much she might be trembling inwardly, when John came back, closing the door behind him, and with his hand still on the knob, shook his head.

"You mean," young Tim asked helplessly, "the Judge—? That quick?"

"Mercifully quick. Probably he never knew."

"He cried out—"

"An instant only, then. Remember, Eliza: he might have lived on, paralyzed, unconscious. You wouldn't have wanted that for him."

"No." She shuddered. "But it shouldn't have been like this. His life shouldn't have ended in a shabby office in a mean little town. He was a great man."

"You will find that everyone agrees to that. Waynesboro knows it, as do his friends all over the country." Tim touched her shoulder gently. He might not have described the offices of Ballard, Gardiner, and Merrill in her terms, but he was young, with a career ahead of him. He could get away.

"Everything he gave up, he gave up for us." If Eliza wanted to talk, John thought, watching her, let her talk for a few minutes—let her recover that way from the shock. "He was a poor boy," she went on. "Did you know that? His father died when he was little, and he and the other children were farmed out to uncles and aunts. He didn't want that for us. He wanted to have money enough to take care of Mamma and us. So he gave up being a judge and came back here to this—"

"Eliza, you must not torment yourself. He resigned from the Supreme Court and came back because there was something he wanted more than the prestige of being a judge. He wanted you, all of you, to be happy and comfortable."

Tim was rising to the occasion well for such a young man, John thought. But he took over: there was no time to be lost.

"Eliza, your father was not an unhappy man here in Waynesboro. I knew him, like everyone else: he was not an unhappy man. If you must feel sorry for him, save it until tonight; when you are alone in your bed, weep for him then. But not now. We need your help."

"I know." But she swayed in her chair.

John crossed to her; Tim moved back as John put his hands on her shoulder and pushed her forward. "Get your head down. You will be all right in a minute."

Head on her knees, she heard herself thinking, "Doctors! Everything will be all right in a minute."

The two men were in low-voiced conversation behind her. John was saying, "We must get the body out of here quickly, before the curious gather. Which undertaker?"

"Crawford, I suppose. He belongs to their church. Eliza?"

"Yes." She lifted her head. "But Mamma?"

"I know. She must be told at once, before she learns of it some other way. Shall I go?"

"I must go. She mustn't hear of it from some outsider. Of course you aren't an outsider, Tim, or John either. But—"

"Good, Eliza." John came to stand in front of her, look down at her. "It will take all your strength, and you have had a great shock, but you are right. Your mother and sister will both lean on you."

("And so much for Samuel Travers," Eliza thought. "He doesn't come to mind as a tower of strength." She had not herself remembered him until that moment.) "But I've no way—Johann won't come for us before noon."

"Of course I'll drive you out." John was his brusque self once more. "They may need me. Tim, give us a good start, then go round to Crawford and have him take the Judge out of here. The family can let him know later where they want him taken: home or the church."

"Oh—home, please."

John put a firm hand under Eliza's elbow, and helped her to her feet. As she stood up, she caught a glimpse of her father's afghan-covered figure and of his desk. She went into the inner office. She did not lift the afghan to look at his face again, nor even look in that direction. She went to his desk, opened a drawer and swept the scattered papers into it, and locked it. After that she put on hat and cloak, accepted John's hand under her arm, and let him help her downstairs into his buggy. All the long way out Main Street she was silent, until she could no longer refrain from asking the question that was echoing wildly in her mind.

"Tell me, John. If I had been quicker—if we had a telephone—would it have made any difference?"

"Not the slightest. Never think that, Eliza. Once it happened, no one could have done anything. It was a massive cerebral hemorrhage. Apoplexy. Or a stroke, if you like a less medical word."

"If we had guessed—been forewarned—could you have forestalled it?"

He stole a sidelong glance at Eliza. She looked old and drawn, her face white. "She isn't a young woman any more," he thought, "yet she is younger than I, a few years. In her forties." For the first time in his life, he saw himself as a middle-aged man. They were all, his contemporaries, middle-aged.

Mature men and women, they should be able to stand up to life. As Eliza was doing.

"I don't know of anything," he replied to her question. "With what we call the 'apoplectic subject'—the man who eats too much, drinks too much, grows too heavy and red in the face—yes, we can tell him to stop living so hard, and if he obeys he may put off the end. But your father did none of those things. He did not live too hard. I suspect he worked too hard—drove himself too far. There is too much we don't know about strokes—about a lot of things. I suspect that your father would have chosen to go like this, at his desk, rather than to become a useless old man. He was how old—seventy-one or two? And he had had a good life, Eliza. He was fortunate to die quickly, with no diminution of his powers. Only a doctor can know just how blessed he was. Believe me."

Eliza, who had known John Gordon all her life, after a fashion, had never heard him make so long a speech. She had always respected his ability but had doubted his strength of character. And Ballards, she thought wryly, laid great emphasis on strength of character. Being a doctor, she thought, had made him a sadder man than he had been boy, but it had made him—the biblical phrase came to her mind—"the shadow of a rock in the desert."

As they turned in at the Ballard gate and approached the porte cochere John said, "Can you go through this, Eliza?"

She drew a long breath. "I can because I must. I just learned that about myself this morning. I always wondered how I would behave in an emergency."

"You behaved very well, Eliza. Comfort yourself with that knowledge." John stopped the buggy, helped her down, and left Molly standing with just the weight he attached to her hitching rope to hold her. He went with Eliza into the house.

"Mamma will be at her desk in the sitting room," Eliza whispered. "In spite of her hands, she manages to do some writing."

When they stood in the living room door, Mrs. Ballard looked up from the litter of papers on her desk. She started to rise, frightened by their sudden appearance. Eliza so white, the doctor so grave.

"Eliza! What is it? You are ill?"

"Not I, Mamma."

Mrs. Ballard sank back into her chair. "Your father?"

Eliza nodded; she was incapable of words.

"Where is he? Did you bring him home? Shall I call Johann to help?"

"No need, Mamma. He won't be coming home." "Alive" she could not bring herself to say.

Mrs. Ballard did not need the word. She took it silently, only staring at them. John once more took Eliza by the elbow—she was trembling again; he led her to a chair and lowered her into it.

"He died quickly, without suffering, Mrs. Ballard. Eliza sent for me immediately. She did what she could, but there was nothing— It was a mercifully fatal stroke: had he survived, he would have been paralyzed, unable to move or speak." (Might as well say so, although there were no certainties in medicine, God knew.) "You wouldn't have wanted that for him."

Mrs. Ballard stared, from Eliza to John to her crippled fingers, which she could no longer open, which must until she died remained curled like claws into her palms. As if bemused she said finally, "I always thought I should go first. I worried. He would have been so lost. Now it is I—" She hesitated, then went on staunchly, a little more as if she were speaking to them as well as to herself, "I am the one who will go to him. Heaven will be a—a homier place, with Thomas already there."

John's quick ears caught the sound of steps on the stairs; Thomasina and her husband. They stopped halfway from the bottom when John came to stand at the newel post. Thomasina took her hand away from her mouth, clung to the banister.

"What is it?" she whispered. "Is it Papa?"

"Yes."

"Dead?"

"Yes."

"But he was all right at breakfast." Thomasina's chin quivered, her pale blue eyes overflowed.

"A stroke. He went quickly and without pain." This was the third time he had had to give that assurance. But Thomasina, with her annual hay fever and perennial asthma, had been his patient for years; he not only felt free to speak firmly, but knew that he must. "Whatever you feel, Thomasina, you must keep yourself fit to help your mother. She will need you when the first shock wears off. And Eliza: this has been very hard for her. She was there, you know." In spite of his firmness, he half expected her to turn and fling herself into her Samuel's arms. But whatever her inclination, Samuel had his hands on her shoulders, and so took her on down to the hall.

"We must go to her, my dear. It is hardest for her, you know."

They went across the hall and into the living room. John was hesitating as to whether he should wait or slip out when Samuel returned, having closed the door behind them.

"They are weeping together. It will do them no harm?" Samuel's hands were shaking and he was pale, but he spoke composedly.

"Don't let it get out of hand, that's all. And remember that Eliza has borne the brunt of this. She was alone with him. If she shows any sign of delayed shock, send for me. Or I can give her a bromide before I go."

"They would rather face it, I think."

"Eliza would be better for a sleep, if you can persuade her. There is a bottle in my bag. I can leave a dose or two. Is there anything else I can do? I left Merrill to see the undertaker and have the body brought home."

"Nothing, Doctor. Unless, as you say, one of them gives way. But I have known the Ballard women for a good while now: it would not be like them to collapse. When the first shock has worn off, I can keep their minds occupied, making funeral arrangements. Mr. Bonner will want an obituary for the *Torchlight:* I can help prepare that, but they will have to supply me with the data. There will be many friends to notify: I can send the telegrams, but they will have to list names and addresses for me. Mrs. Ballard will want to see the minister, and the parlor must be made ready for the coffin: I will see Johann about that; he and his wife must be told at once, anyway. There must be visitation hours, I suppose. And Mrs. Ballard will want a church funeral."

John listened with some astonishment. Sam Travers was not so useless, after all. He kept his head.

"That's right; keep them busy. But I warn you: it will not be until after all the strain and excitement of the funeral has worn off that they will really feel their loss. When the funeral is over and they go back to ordinary living, it will be hard for them to remember that the Judge is no longer here, and every time they wake up to it, every time they unconsciously listen for his step on the stairs, and don't hear it—it will hit them all over again."

"You know that, too? How you store up things to tell someone, and the someone isn't there when you get home? I remember when my mother— Is it a universal experience? I used to blame myself for forgetting even for a moment. But the Ballards have had little experience with death. Mother Ballard's parents died so long ago, I doubt if she remembers, and the girls never—"

"You may need me. Send Johann if you do. Now, I'll go get the bromide." John went thoughtfully back to his buggy and returned carrying his bag. As he poured out several doses of bromide from a large bottle to the small one Samuel had brought, his hand steady and not a drop spilled, he was silent; but when he had finished he said, "Three teaspoons is a hypnotic dose; it wouldn't hurt any of them, but Eliza particularly." Then he dropped his bedside manner and said with characteristic bluntness, as he studied the balding middle-aged man beside him, "Tell me, Travers, were you in the war?"

Sam's fair skin flushed unbecomingly. "In a manner of speaking. I was a noncombatant, a bandsman. I don't talk about it: I don't think it anything to boast about. Why?"

"I understand: I was a noncombatant myself, and *I* don't talk about it. But if you were in some regimental band, you were a stretcher-bearer when your regiment got into a fight. Under fire. I have seen—well, I don't think it a thing you need hide. As to why, I just wondered where you learned to think so clearly and act so decisively in an emergency."

Sam smiled back. "Not to be expected in a small-town music teacher?"

The two men shook hands—two men who had met frequently and indifferently and now suddenly were friends. John picked up his bag and let himself out while Samuel went to the kitchen to see whether Johann's wife was there, or Johann himself.

Judge Ballard's funeral was the most awesome that the town had ever seen. Its citizens respected the man dead more than they had the man living, since the proof of his greatness was visible: Waynesboro was for a few days host to a greater number of distinguished men and women than the townspeople had ever seen at one time. Such old leaders of the abolition movement as still survived came to do him honor, along with friends of Mrs. Ballard and the Judge who had been and were leaders in such other reform movements as woman's suffrage and the Prohibition party, and one-time Liberal Republicans whom he had supported, like Carl Schurz and Godkin and Justice of the Supreme Court Stanley Matthews, come all the way from Washington to pay his respects to his old friend, and ex-President and Mrs. Hayes, down from Fremont. All these, mingled with Waynesboro men, women, and children, filed past the coffin where it lay in state below the pulpit of the Methodist church. On the afternoon of the funeral, Court House offices and most business houses were closed; the church was packed to overflowing. The State Supreme Court justices were honorary pallbearers, the coffin being carried actually by younger, stronger men. The funeral cortege was watched with interest from windows along the route: that was President Hayes and his wife, and Judge Matthews in the carriage behind the family's, that was Mr. Schurz and Mr. Godkin with the Ludwig Rausches. (An odd combination, that: there was some surprised "h'mphing" from onlookers who recognized them. The truth was that Sally Rausch had sent a note to the Ballards the day after the Judge's death: she and Ludwig would be glad to extend their hospitality to any funeral guests the Ballards could not accommodate.)

After the burial the distinguished guests lingered, chatting in the bleak autumnal graveyard. They were old friends who did not, nowadays, see each other often: as the minutes ticked away, they became less mindful of the raw hole in the ground behind them, and their voices rose as they became more cheerful. (Eliza, as their carriage waited, watched them and hoped her mother didn't notice. "This is the most awful part of a funeral," she thought. "Once the coffin is lowered, they are cheerful as if they were having a reunion picnic. They *enjoy* themselves.")

Ludwig Rausch and his wife, with their two guests in tow, stopped to speak to the Hayeses. "This is a loss to us, sir."

"A loss, yes. It puts a period—a full stop—to a certain era in the country's history. There are few now left to fight for the principles and causes that Judge Ballard felt so deeply. With the exception of such as my two friends here." He indicated the Rausches. "I am afraid," and he smiled ruefully, "power—political power—has passed from men of Judge Ballard's caliber into the hands of those backed by money. Every death among our old leaders brings that fact more clearly home: an era has ended." He laid a hand on Ludwig's arm. "You young men must see that love of money does not corrupt the state completely." He shook hands with Ludwig and Sally, with Mr. Schurz and Mr. Godkin, and when he turned away apologized to his wife and Judge Matthews for having kept them waiting in the cold. "I felt that I must have a word with Ludwig Rausch."

"Politics, even on such an occasion?"

"Most of all on such an occasion. We have lost a leader of courage and principle. I wanted to make clear to young Rausch that I do not care for the way the world is wagging. He is not without power in this district. One era has ended; now it is up to men of his age and stamp."

No more was said: they entered their carriage, and they and the Ballards drove off, back to the house on Main Street. There condolences were once more spoken, and farewells; the Ballard ladies were excused to retire to their rooms, and the guests were given a high tea, supervised by Samuel Travers, and seen into the carriage again for their departure to the railroad station. The ladies might have hoped they would stay, postponing the hour when their aloneness must be faced, and the house's stillness. Samuel knew they were exhausted; he hoped they would sleep. Up to that point he had kept his word: he had given them no time to think, to regret, to wish. When the afternoon had worn on to dusk, he sent Mrs. Johann upstairs to ask whether they would like supper trays sent up, or would rather come down. They rejected the notion that anyone should have to carry trays to three able-bodied women; they trailed down to the dining room. Eliza and Thomasina made a pretense of eating some of the food brought to the house by their Waynesboro friends and that had now been piled on their plates. Mrs. Ballard only stared at hers, napkin lifted to her mouth.

"Mamma, you must eat something to keep up your strength. Do try the ham—Anne Gordon sent it from their farm. It is very good." But Thomasina pleaded with her in vain.

"Tonight I can't. Tomorrow it may be easier. If you will excuse me, I think I shall retire now."

"Would you like me to come up with you?"

"Eat your supper, Thomasina. I am quite capable of putting myself to bed. If Samuel wouldn't mind going up the stairs with me."

The sisters, left alone, stared at each other dismayed: their mother had never before admitted to having any difficulty with the stairs.

"This has been too much for her; it will break her."

"She has been breaking for some time. Have you no eyes, Thomasina? You know how much she suffers from her rheumatism. Constant pain, at her age, is enough to break anyone, without this blow added. But I hope she will get a good sleep and feel better tomorrow. There are things that must be seen to."

Thomasina stared at her. "By 'things' I suppose you mean Papa's affairs: his will, his estate? Eliza, how can you? He is only just in his grave!"

"I can because I must. We cannot know where we stand without Douglas Gardiner: he even had Papa's will in his strong box. He came home just for the funeral. With his wife in her condition, he wants to get back to Washington as soon as possible. He has promised us tomorrow."

"You don't like Douglas Gardiner, do you?" Thomasina was responding to tone rather than to words. "Papa trusted him, and thought him brilliant."

"My liking or not liking him does not matter. He is our lawyer, bequeathed to us by Papa."

"Will you keep on at the office?"

"Who knows, at this point, whether there will even be an office?"

Douglas Gardiner spent that same evening at the Rausches', discussing the same question with Ludwig in his study.

"I am sorry, Ludwig, but you must see I shall have to resign from the House."

"But you have just been reelected."

"I know. But the law practice here must be carried on. It can't be handled by Tim Merrill alone, with me in Washington a good part of the time. I won't say that it is more important to me than being in Congress, or that I haven't liked representing the district, but—"

"Merrill's young. And hasn't learned much about corporation law. You know, of course, that the Judge was working for me and my associates on an application to the state for a franchise for our proposed electric railway; I agree with you: Tim couldn't handle that. But you are just at the beginning of a promising political career. You resign and there will have to be a special election for your successor—next fall, I suppose—and whoever is elected will feel entitled to more than one term."

"I realize all that. If I come home and take up the law in earnest, it will be for the rest of my life. But it is a question of money, purely and simply. Our law practice has supported one single man, Tim; one family, the Ballards; and partly supported another family, mine. Of course I have had my salary as Representative, but even if we could live on that, there are my aunts, and what of the Ballards? No, the law practice must be carried on aggressively, and it is corporation law that brings us the big fees."

"Can you buy the Ballard share of the partnership? Or must you continue to divide any profits into three parts?"

"That depends on the Ballards. I have no idea what they will want to do. Of course, the partnership articles give them the option of selling to us or holding on as silent partners."

"I suppose Eliza has never been paid much. There wouldn't be much saving there."

"If we let her go? No. She was hired because what little she was paid could be kept in the family. But Eliza, even with Sam Travers's help—and I suppose he does help—couldn't support her family and that house."

"They won't sell the house?"

"Filial piety would forbid it, even if they were willing to consider such a thing. The Judge was prouder of having built that house for his womenfolk probably than of anything else in his career. No, that burden is on their backs forever. There is no way out but for me to resign and come home and take up where the Judge left off. But there will be no room for Eliza and me both in those offices. That is another of my problems. It isn't just the antipathy between us; in that office, with all those confidential papers at her elbow, she is a menace."

"Menace?" Ludwig was amused. He knew that Eliza was considered a somewhat embittered and gossipy spinster, but he could not believe her to be untrustworthy. "You don't mean she would talk about confidential matters?" Ludwig was taking Douglas with a grain of salt: he knew he could be a rather difficult young man.

"Talk? I don't know. I should hate to risk it—who knows what she might come out with in some moment of provocation? Whether she delves simply out of curiosity—to store away nuggets of information in order to gloat over what she *could* say—or whether for some end of her own, she might use them, I haven't an idea. I do know she delves."

"Oh, come. I can hardly believe that of a Ballard." Ludwig's voice trailed away, and then he resumed on a brisker note. "Is she capable?"

"Oh, extremely. Keeps the books meticulously, takes care of our correspondence, copies our briefs. It will be hard to find anyone to take her place. And I don't know how to go about telling her—"

"Maybe I can help you. I've been thinking for a long while that we need a secretary at the mill to take care of the correspondence. The bookkeeper hasn't time for it. I have to answer every letter myself. It would save my time. And she could make up the payroll, lots of odds and ends. At the mill she would be out of mischief; we have no local dealings, no personal correspondence, no material for a gossip."

"She could do the work. But could you stand having her there, day after day?"

Ludwig laughed. "She would have a desk outside, in the bookkeeper's office. D'you suppose she'd be willing to learn to use one of these newfangled typewriters? Most letters that come to us now are typewritten."

"I don't know. It would take manual dexterity, I suppose. At any rate, we shall need her in our office at least until I get home from Washington to stay. That may be the first of January, or not until March."

"I hate to see a promising political career interrupted. But the time may come when you can pick it up again."

"Not very soon, if ever. Tim and I shall be hard put to earn what will be needed."

From this concluding remark, Ludwig guessed that the two partners would, if given their choice, buy out the Ballard interest. And so indeed it proved.

The next morning Douglas went out to the Ballards' with a briefcase full of papers. He read them the will: Mrs. Ballard was to have all personal property, and a life interest in the house. At her death Eliza was to have the house except for the Travers's apartment on the second floor, which was to be Thomasina's absolutely. Expenses—repairs and taxes—would be paid jointly. The sisters listened to this provision, Eliza with a rigid face, Thomasina with her handkerchief at her eyes. Douglas had no way of knowing what they were thinking, although he could be fairly sure their father had guaranteed them a troubled future. But each sister could pretty well guess what was in the other's mind: Eliza that Thomasina was congratulating herself that no matter what happened she and Samuel could not be turned out, nor Samuel, if he should outlive her: Thomasina's will would take care of that; Eliza was as tied to that man as if she had married him herself. And Thomasina, for her part, was sure that Eliza resented that "absolutely." Eliza had done so much for her father—for them all—that she deserved to have the house, but Thomasina wondered whether her father had realized that she would not even be able to use the drawing room without Eliza's permission. Not that the drawing room was ever used, except for Club meetings or funerals. And of course as long as her mother lived—

Douglas, having allowed time for the terms of the will to be absorbed by the still-dazed women, proceeded with the schedule of the personal property, which was to be Mrs. Ballard's: all except a couple of thousand dollars "to my faithful Johann Kleinschmidt and his wife Herta."

"There is a five thousand dollar life insurance policy. There is also almost fifteen thousand in government bonds which the Judge bought over the last few years. No stocks of any kind."

Mrs. Ballard sighed. "Then he kept his promise." At Douglas's inquiring glance she explained briefly. "He gambled, although I believe he did not consider it gambling. He was badlly hurt in a financial way by stocks that suddenly lost their value. I am glad there are none, now: I do not believe in speculation of that kind."

Douglas wondered: it could be that if the Judge had kept his stocks, his bequest to his wife might have been larger.

"And besides these sums, there is his partnership in the law firm."

He was astonished at their astonishment. "Didn't you know that is inheritable? When the articles of agreement were drawn up, it was provided that on the death of a partner, his heirs could retain his share of the partnership or could sell it to the other partners. When old Mr. Merrill died, his share of the partnership was held in trust for Tim and the income used for his education, until he came of age and could either sell or become an active partner. Now it is your turn to choose between selling your third of the partnership to us, or continuing to receive one-third of the income."

"We trust you implicitly, Douglas. Which do you advise?"

"Thank you." He did not look at Eliza. "There are advantages and disadvantages either way. The income of the firm might increase, and your third of it grow larger with the years. On the other hand, it may very well decrease, without Judge Ballard—Eliza will agree with that, I am sure. It is speculative, too, as you see. If you decided to sell, it would be for a sum fixed now, to be paid in installments biennially for the next six years. That provision—spreading out the payments—is also in the partnership articles."

"We could not ask for the whole amount?" Eliza asked sharply. She did indeed believe that without her father the law firm would founder, perhaps within the six years.

"You cannot, Eliza. And you must surely know that Tim and I could not raise the whole amount immediately."

"I suspect," Mrs. Ballard smiled fleetingly, "that Eliza wants me to have everything now in case I do not live another six years. That is nonsense, Eliza. I have never cared greatly for money. It would be pleasant to have—one could do a great deal of good—but it seems to me of relative unimportance. And we can manage very well with the life insurance and the bonds until the three payments are made. Twenty-thousand dollars seems to me a great deal of money: much more than I ever thought I should have."

Doug looked at her as he might have looked at the babes in the wood, "You understand, Mrs. Ballard: that twenty thousand dollars, plus whatever you get from the partnership, is your *capital*. It is all you will ever have. If possible you should live on the income from it."

"It still seems to me like a lot of money." Mrs. Ballard was bewildered. "You mean if the insurance money were also invested in bonds, we should be able to live on the interest from those bonds?"

"Government bonds do not pay a very high interest." Douglas hedged.

Eliza broke in, with an insect-be-gone sort of gesture toward her mother, as if to hush her display of innocence. "If we sell Papa's share of the partnership, who would tell us how much it is worth? You and Tim?"

"You yourself must have an idea how much it is worth. You kept the books. You know how much we made in a year. Take, say, the average of the last five years' income, call that interest, figure the capital, and divide it by three. But no, of course we wouldn't ask you to take our word. And leave ourselves open to accusations of having robbed the widow and orphans? We would get someone from outside to examine the books. Henry Voorhees, say, or Mr. Cochran."

"Mr. Cochran, please. Thomas always trusted him as an honorable man. Not that I doubt your integrity for a moment, Douglas. But I understand why you would not want to take the responsibility." Then Mrs. Ballard wavered. "But you think we might fare better if we continued as—'sleeping partners' is the term, is it not?—and shared the annual income?"

"You might be better off. You might be worse."

"I'm only thinking about the girls."

"Now, Mamma. You would be gambling, just as Papa did with the stocks."

"I hoped that you would not have to continue working, Eliza. With that much money—"

Eliza had a sudden bleak vision of doing nothing day after day. "Of course I shall have to keep on working. I must see the books are in order for auditing, for one thing. When shall you want them?"

"I must go back to Washington this afternoon. Have Tim make the arrangements with Mr. Cochran, get the books to him, and when I come home again we can talk terms."

Eliza was glad that she had kept the books herself. She knew that everything was entered; that no fee, however small, had been forgotten. She went up to the office the next day. Tim's court case had not been concluded; there would be no one in the office if she were to stay home. She steeled herself to unlock the door. All was exactly as it had been left when they had carried her father out. The papers she had thrust so hastily in his desk drawer were still there. With a kind of blank disbelief, she smoothed out the creases. That he would never touch them again, that he would not at any moment enter the door, returned from some errand to the Court House—she looked over her shoulder at the cracked leather sofa and shuddered. She could never look at it again without seeing her father there, without hearing his breathing echo in the room. Eliza had not yet learned how quickly time can break the association between the inanimate, unchanging object (like a piece of furniture—a bed, a chair, a couch) and a moment of sorrow. Hastily she scooped the papers out of the drawer, closed the door to the inner office behind her, and carried them to her desk. She was trying to get them in some kind of order, forcing herself to concentrate, when Ludwig Rausch came in.

"Good morning, Eliza. I had scarcely dared hope I'd find you here, but since you are, I'd like to talk to you. Tim is in court?"

She nodded as she looked at him inquiringly.

"Those are the papers your father was working on? The franchise for the Columbus and Southwestern Ohio Electric Railway?"

"Yes. I was getting them in order to put them away till—"

"That's right. They'll have to wait until Douglas gets home. And they are more or less confidential, so put them in your safe. That was not what I wanted to talk to you about."

"Something I can do for you?"

"I am not sure." He brought a chair and put it beside her at the desk, thinking as he did so how astonished and dismayed Sally had been when he had told her he proposed to hire Eliza as a secretary.

"She's malicious," Sally had flared, "a mischief-maker. And such a bitter tongue."

"You may be right," he had conceded, "but if she's capable—and Doug says she is—then those things won't matter in our office. We'd put her out with the bookkeeper, and there wouldn't be anything for her to gossip about. Letters from customers, from hemp dealers. The payroll. And if I hire her, I'll be helping three people. Myself, because the business has grown to the place where I can't manage the correspondence and do anything else. Eliza, because I can pay her more than she's been getting. And Doug—"

Sally had pounced. "Doug wants to get rid of her?"

"Yes. For some reason the two of them have got in each other's bad books."

"Two sharp tongues."

Now Ludwig, sitting down and crossing his legs, looked at Eliza. A homely woman, certainly—enough to make any female sharp-tongued—but her blue eyes were clear and steady.

"Tell me, do you expect to continue in your present capacity in this office?"

"I must be here until Mr. Gardiner returns." And why should it be Ludwig Rausch's affair? "The office door can't just be locked when Tim is out. After that, I don't know. Nothing has been said."

"I am in need of a secretary. I know of no other woman in Waynesboro who has had office experience. Would your two lawyers consider me a robber if I asked you to come to Rausch Cordage Company?"

Eliza was so astounded that for a moment she was speechless, biting her tongue to keep from blurting out that Douglas at least would be glad to be rid of her. Finally she said, "I had been thinking: if Ballard, Gardiner, and Merrill had no further need of my services, I might find a position with the telephone company. I understand that they employ ladies at their exchange. But a factory—I don't know what Mamma would say."

"But your mother believes in the emancipation of women, doesn't she?" Ludwig almost laughed, thinking how he would tell Sally what Waynesboro had been spared: if Eliza was the gossip Sally thought her, then the telephone exchange was the last place. He had been one of the first to have telephones installed, both at home and in his office, but he was extremely careful what he said over the wire. He controlled his face and said, "I think I can pay you more than the telephone company."

"But law, legal terms, are all I know. I should be all at sea with business correspondence."

"Business terms are not so difficult as law terms; it wouldn't take you long. What I need is someone who can open and sort the mail for me, write my letters, make up the payroll when Captain Bodien brings in the time sheets. None of it is complicated, just time-consuming. It would help, of course, if a secretary could take dictation in shorthand and use the typewriter. Have you ever seen a typewriter?"

Eliza shook her head. "I took dictation from Papa sometimes, but not in shorthand. And as you see, we do not have a typewriter." This suggestion that she master a machine she considered the most preposterous bit of the whole preposterous offer.

"You could learn to use one, I am sure. If you decide to accept my offer, I could buy one and have it put here, temporarily, for you to practice on in your odd moments. As to remuneration: of course I have no idea what your salary is here. I'd be willing to pay you fifteen dollars a week to start."

Eliza blinked. The offer suddenly seemed less preposterous. Twenty-five a month she had been getting from the lawyers; of course she had been willing to work for that to put more money in her father's pocket, saving him the expense of a law clerk. But sixty dollars a month!

"And of course," Ludwig grinned at her, "every other Wednesday afternoon off. I know how much you ladies enjoy your Club."

"Thank you very much," Eliza managed finally. "It is a generous expression of confidence. Naturally, I shall have to consult my mother. You don't demand an immediate answer?"

"No. Take your time. And of course talk it over at home. But please ask them to keep the matter confidential." This, he thought, could be a test of Eliza's trustworthiness. But he had to scramble around in his mind to find a reason for its being kept a secret. "I don't want to be bothered with every young woman in Waynesboro besieging me for a position." He would ask Sally to keep her ears peeled: if the news leaked out, it would get back to her.

"Certainly. I understand. And I will let you know shortly."

Eliza stared blankly at the door after Ludwig had closed it behind him. Of course the whole idea was ridiculous; it was out of the question. The Rausch mill, at the other end of nowhere. And she would have to walk. Johann would soon retire, he and his wife, with their two thousand, and the horse would have to be sold: that had been settled already. She thought of the winters, the snow, and the summers, even worse. No. She could not do it, but she would "consult" her mother and Thomasina, if for no other reason than to let them know that her services were valued.

But her sister's reaction put her back up immediately. Thomasina laughed, actually laughed, for the first time since her father's death.

"Oh, Eliza! Those rough mill hands! A *factory*! You couldn't! Tell her, Mamma, she mustn't. Think of Papa's good name, Eliza, don't be tempted by the money."

There were a thousand things Eliza could have said: she could have reminded her sister that she had not objected to standing on woman's rights platforms with mill girls—that they all believed there was no place a woman could not fill. She held her tongue.

Her mother said, "This is for Eliza to decide. She's a grown woman." She looked at Eliza as if for the first time realizing the fact. (And I am over forty, Eliza thought.)

Thomasina had not done. "You know that Papa would forbid it. Have you forgotten how he disliked Ludwig Rausch's politics? And his anti-prohibition stand? And that time the Republicans *booed* Papa?"

"That's all water under the bridge, long ago. These last years Mamma and Papa have never hesitated to accept the Rausches' hospitality—nor you and I, for that matter. And when Papa died, he was working on a corporation matter for Ludwig Rausch. If he was not ashamed to take Rausch money, why should I be?"

"But just fancy, Eliza: going and coming in the West End with all those mill hands, smelling so of tar! To have to associate with rough men like Captain Bodien! How can you?"

"I have never heard that Captain Bodien is an undesirable character. He is Douglas Gardiner's father-in-law."

"You had enough to say at the time of that marriage."

Eliza went on, ignoring the last remark. "The only man I shall be asked to associate with—share an office with—is little Mr. Wilbur Ashton, the bookkeeper. You may remember that Mr. Ashton is a member of our church."

"Of course I know Mr. Ashton." The argument was suspended for a moment, that they might look at a mind's-eye picture of mousy Mr. Ashton, in the pew with his equally mouse-like wife and their row of children.

"And I doubt very much," Eliza went back to the first point in Thomasina's last speech, "whether Mr. Rausch or Mr. Ashton go to work with the mill hands at six-thirty." Somehow, in the course of the argument, Eliza had made up her mind to accept Ludwig's offer. "I will of course pay Mamma for my room and board."

"Don't be ridiculous, Eliza," her mother was roused to respond, somewhat tartly. "We shall let you pay your share of the grocery and other housekeeping bills, but 'room'—no. If you are determined to do this. It is, I am afraid, allying yourself with everything a liberal and reforming mind finds objectionable: underpaid, overworked labor, and child labor. Not that I think Ludwig Rausch any worse than any other employer. He is a kind man, personally, I think."

"At any rate, neither of you is to say a word about this to anyone. Mr. Rausch agreed that I must consult you, but until I have Papa's books ready for the auditors and can move to Rausch Cordage Company, it is to be confidential. He particularly requested it, Thomasina, not a word to anyone."

"You know very well I shall tell Samuel." While they paused to give the matter due thought, they heard the tinkling notes of his last music lesson of the day come to their ears from overhead.

"Samuel is no babbler. But please don't go running to Amanda, or anyone else," Eliza added, remembering how little they had seen of Amanda lately, "blurting out your disapproval."

"However much I may disapprove—and I do—you know that I shall say nothing if you ask me not to." Thomasina rose with some dignity and went upstairs. In a few moments Eliza and her mother heard a child clattering down the stairs and out the side door. Samuel would be free to dry his wife's tears.

"She feels her father's death very keenly, Eliza. Be forbearing."

"No one has to be forbearing with you, and the loss weighs most heavily on you."

Her mother considered for a moment. "I shall never cease to miss him, although I suppose I shall get over this numbed, half-alive feeling. But my time alone cannot be long. And to Thomasina her father was like the rock of ages."

Eliza knew that this was true; she also knew that she had been closer to her father these last years than Thomasina, simply because she had worked with and for him. She said no more. But on the following morning she wrote to

Ludwig a formal note of acceptance of his offer. She preferred not to resign, she told him, until Mr. Gardiner had returned, and he might want her to remain with Gardiner and Merrill until she could be replaced. Would Mr. Rausch therefore please continue to keep the matter confidential?

Ludwig showed the note to Sally. "Wants to tell Doug to his face, I suppose. Thinks it will be a blow to him, maybe. I wonder whatever happened in that office to put the two of them at sword's point."

"It wasn't at the office, it was at a Club meeting. That busybody of an Eliza mentioning—oh, so casually, as if of course Doug's aunts knew all about it—something about his interest in the pretty litlle Bodien girl. They went home with fire in their eyes and, I suppose, tackled Doug about it. He announced his intentions right after that, and it might have all blown over if it hadn't been interfered with."

"But Liebchen, that was years ago, even if you are right."

"It was the winter before the 1880 convention. Remember? Four years ago—four and a half. Oh, I suppose there has been fuel added to the fire since then, in the office."

"But why would she—?"

"Pure malicious mischief. I told you."

"At least she hasn't talked about my offer."

"Apparently not. For her own reasons. I must call on the Ballards soon." Sally changed the subject abruptly, aware that she had been as horrid about Eliza as Eliza ever was about anyone. "Mrs. Ballard and Thomasina will be at home even if Eliza is working. I do hate making condolence calls."

"No Club Christmas party this year?"

"No. It would seem indecent, wouldn't it, so soon? And with three Ballard women in mourning, it would not be a very happy occasion. Christina will be pleased, at any rate: she thinks the celebration of Christmas a pagan practice."

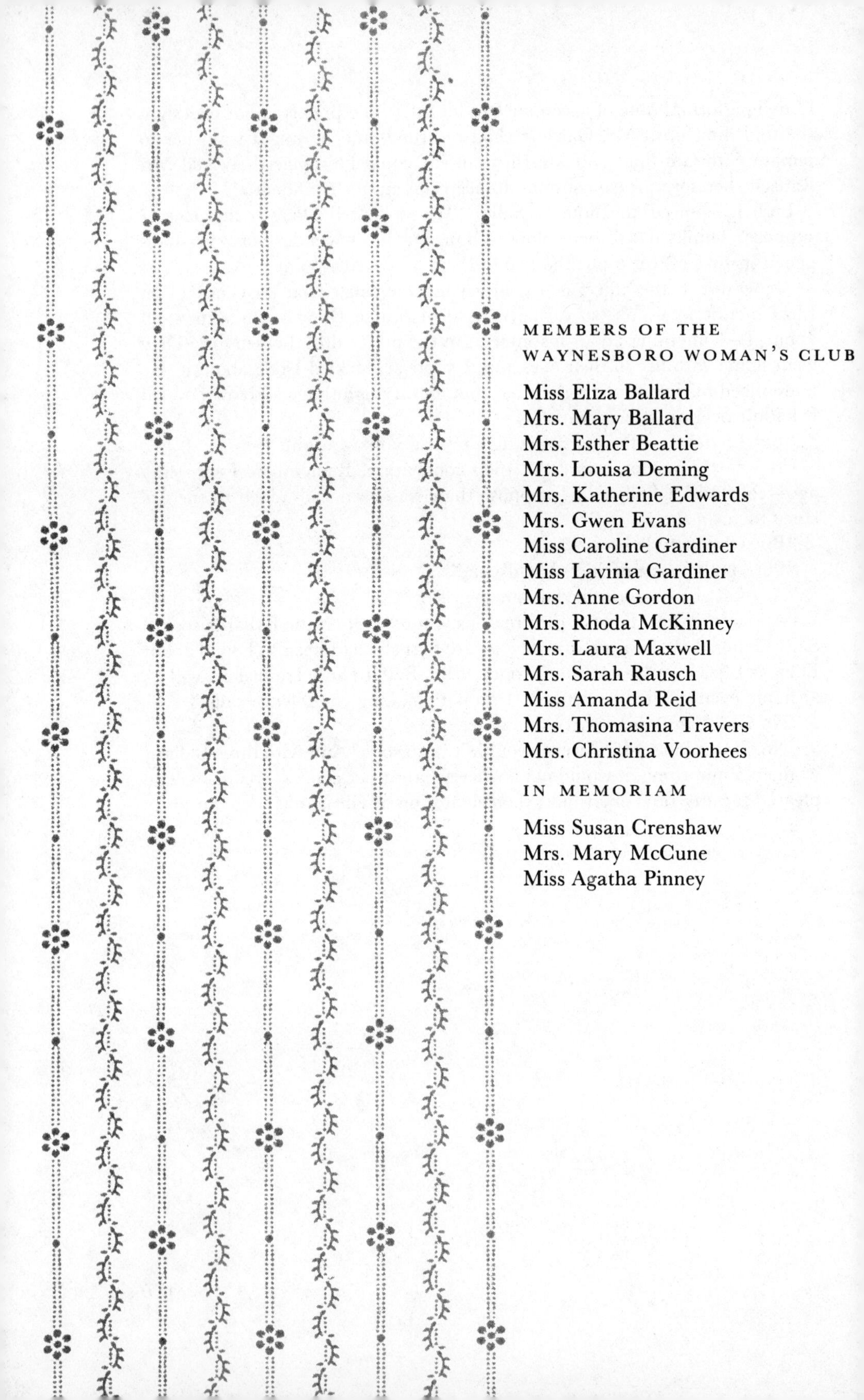

MEMBERS OF THE WAYNESBORO WOMAN'S CLUB

Miss Eliza Ballard
Mrs. Mary Ballard
Mrs. Esther Beattie
Mrs. Louisa Deming
Mrs. Katherine Edwards
Mrs. Gwen Evans
Miss Caroline Gardiner
Miss Lavinia Gardiner
Mrs. Anne Gordon
Mrs. Rhoda McKinney
Mrs. Laura Maxwell
Mrs. Sarah Rausch
Miss Amanda Reid
Mrs. Thomasina Travers
Mrs. Christina Voorhees

IN MEMORIAM

Miss Susan Crenshaw
Mrs. Mary McCune
Miss Agatha Pinney

* 1885–1886 *

"The Club accepts with regret the resignation of its first President."

After the proper interval of leaving the Ballards alone to mourn the dead, their friends and acquaintances came, dropping their engraved cards in the salver on the stand in the hall, uttering a few words of condolence, squeezing Thomasina's limp hand, shaking Mrs. Ballard's gently. The calls were a nightmare to Thomasina: these were her best and oldest friends who behaved so unnaturally, sitting bolt upright in the cold drawing room, which seemed so dark and unused, speaking so few and such formal words that there could be no real communication with them. Methodist ladies came, Mrs. Bonner came, and Mrs. Dry-Goods Edwards, Mrs. Doctor Edwards, and Mrs. Sheldon; the Cochrans, the members of the W.C.T.U.; and members of the Club: Amanda, Anne and Sally together; the Seminary wives, the ministers' wives, and Christina Voorhees, who came on a Sabbath afternoon when Henry was at home with the children. Mrs. Ballard, Thomasina, and Eliza were all there, Eliza practically silent, annoyed at the invasion of her one day at home, and Thomasina speaking only when surprised into it. The burden of the conversation rested on Christina and Mrs. Ballard.

It was Christina's parting speech that precipitated the matter of the presidency of the Woman's Club. She had stayed the correct ten minutes and was about to rise when she said, "I am sure, dear Mrs. Ballard, that with the consolation of your religion to uphold you, you will be able to sustain this great sorrow, and can soon pick up your active life again. We miss you greatly at the Club."

Mrs. Ballard looked at her misshapen hands, lying in her lap. "I feel no worse, physically, than usual. But my disability increases with age. I have decided that I can no longer serve as the President of the Club."

"Oh, but my *dear* Mrs. Ballard!" Christina was dismayed. The previous January, Sally Rausch had been elected Vice-President, with the offhanded casualness usually given the selection of that officer, and without a thought that she would ever actually step into the chair except on such occasions as the President happened to be absent. "No one, I am sure," she said, "can conceive of the Club without you." Her sleepy kitten eyes widened. "Nor of having a new President."

"I am not proposing to resign from the Club. It is even somewhat reluctantly that I conform to the conventions and public opinion and absent myself for a few months from the meetings. Visible proof of mourning seems to me unnecessary: why should I have to demonstrate to the public what I feel? It is no one else's concern. However, as to a new President: I am sure Mrs. Rausch will preside capably at the few meetings between now and the first January meeting. Then, at the time for electing new officers, I will make my intentions known, and the Club can elect a new President."

"Do you not suppose that out of indifference, or lethargy, Mrs. Rausch will be elected?"

"Indeed, it is possible. But why not?" Mrs. Ballard's eyebrows had risen; she could be definitely quelling when she chose. "She is a very able young woman, and she has done a great deal for the Club."

"Her Christmas parties, you mean? I was glad she had the wisdom to not have one this year; I hope not only for your sakes. Such a celebration of a heathen holiday seems to me most unfitting for a group of Christians."

"But Christina," Thomasina blurted out, unexpectedly even to herself, "you have always enjoyed them, and loved taking part in plays, and singing."

"I have come to see, now that I have two children whose moral natures are in my charge, that I was in error. Serious error. However, I recognize that Mrs. Rausch manages social affairs with beautiful ease and grace. I do beg your pardon: I should not have indicated my reluctance to see her in your place. You have filled it so perfectly that it seemed someone older, wiser, perhaps a firmer Christian—"

"She is a faithful member of the Baptist church, I believe."

"Oh, I am sure. But isn't she perhaps a little looser in her interpretation of the Baptist faith than other Baptists can approve of? I know she cannot be rebuked by the church officers: her father must be almost the sole support—"

"My dear Christina, please take the advice of an old woman: let your opinion of Mrs. Rausch be confined to this room. The Woman's Club is not, after all, a missionary society; there must be room in it for a diversity of views. If you prefer someone else for the Presidency, you may so vote when the day for elections comes. But let me beg you: do not do any electioneering; nothing could more certainly destroy the Club than its division into factions."

"I beg your pardon. I spoke thoughtlessly in my surprise." Christina had flushed a little under Mrs. Ballard's severe gaze. "I came meaning only to endeavor to hearten you in your sorrow, and I have distressed you instead. I should not dream of taking any action, or speaking any words that could damage the Club."

When she had been shown out, the three Ballards moved to the sitting room, where it was less chilly. It was not until they had seated themselves comfortably in the warm room with cushioned rockers that one of them ventured to speak. That one was Thomasina: she had been shocked by her mother's declaration of intent, and attempted to dissuade her. But Eliza took her mother's side: "Mamma is being very sensible. She has been President of the Club since its founding, and it is high time she turned the responsibility over to someone else. The time to do it is, as she says, before election of officers in January." Eliza became suddenly less formal, more vigorous in her speaking: "If she waits until the obligations of mourning permit her to attend meetings again, Christina Voorhees may have had time to cook something up."

This brought two responses, her mother's first and most emphatic: "You know very well, Eliza, that I care nothing for what is called 'mourning etiquette.' I do not believe in the sequestering of one's self for a specified number of months and then appearing in public veiled in black: I do not see what it proves, except that one is acquainted with the dictates of society. It seems to me almost a denial of one's belief that a loved one has exchanged the trials of this life for the peace of another happier one. It is only because your father was highly regarded in this community, and I prefer not to seem wanting in respect to his memory, that I conform. But I shall resume attendance at Club meetings after the first of the year."

Thomasina had closed her mouth to await her mother's conclusion, then she said to Eliza, sharply for her, "You think Sally Rausch would make a good President?"

"I don't see why not. She enjoys holding the reins, and she does it very well."

"The Rausches have *bought* you."

"Thomasina, that was uncalled for." Mrs. Ballard's reproof was made in so severe a tone that both her daughters stared at her. "This bickering, over trivial matters, so soon. I should like you to examine your impulses before you speak. You have always liked Sally Rausch. She and her husband have done many things for us. They have sent their children to Samuel for music lessons: Elsa till this year, the boys still. Can you think of any reason why you have turned against her, except that you dislike the idea of Eliza's going to work at the Rausch mill?"

"I suppose you are right." Thomasina wiped her streaming eyes and nose; she had not been so rebuked since she had been a child. "I am sorry."

"And do not make any effort to elect anyone President of the Club: leave it to the ladies. Please. I know we are all still overwrought, but do stop weeping, Thomasina. Say nothing of what Christina burst out with, here or anywhere. Just don't mention it at all."

But Eliza did mention it the next time Ludwig stopped in the law office, to see how she was making out with the typewriter he had had delivered there. (A great monstrous noisy machine Eliza was half afraid of. But by persistent pecking away and much concentration on the instruction book, she was making progress.) Ludwig approved her diligence and nodded his head over a letter she showed him, errorless and perfect.

"But I could have written it by hand more quickly," she admitted.

"Speed will come with practice. And anyway, a typewritten letter looks better. You are taking care of your mother's business correspondence by way of practice?" The letter he had seen had been an answer to a letter of condolence from some official or other of the woman's suffrage movement.

"She can hardly hold a pen now, her hands are so locked into their position. She has been dictating her letters to me at night, and I bring them here to copy. I assumed it did not matter what I practiced on, and the office isn't very busy."

"Of course it doesn't matter. How is your mother otherwise?"

"She is cheerful. In a way she seems not to feel her loss as much as Thomasina and I. Thomasina dissolves into tears at the slightest provocation. But Mamma cannot bring herself to take any interest in everyday things, somehow. She is getting old; she thinks Papa is standing on some golden shore waiting for her and the wait will not be a long one."

"Your mother is by nature an energetic woman, concerned over many problems. This phase will pass. Her natural vigor will soon be restored."

"Perhaps. But in the meantime she intends to resign as President of the Woman's Club."

Ludwig laughed. "Is that important?"

"Not really. Not to her, anyway, but it means she is letting go. It may seem so to some Club members. Sally—she is Vice-President, you know. But I believe I am supposed not to mention Mamma's intention." Eliza clamped her lips shut, having said as much as she had meant to say. Ludwig departed, wondering.

He repeated the odd conversation to Sally. "She wasn't supposed to mention it, however, so better not pass it on."

"Ludwig, you are gullible!"

"Why? You think she wanted you to know? What does it matter to you who is President? I thought she had just let it slip."

"Eliza doesn't let things slip. It isn't important to me, but I'm sure she thought it would be. She loves mischief, you know. I warned you."

Ludwig shook his head over the suspicious nature of even the kindest-hearted of women. But when Sally had seen him off for the afternoon, she put on her wraps and walked the few blocks to the Gordons'. She and Anne were becoming used to the telephone, and often called one another in the morning, just to keep in touch. But you didn't gossip over the telephone: you had to remember the probably listening ear of the girl in the exchange.

"I've a bit of news," she announced, once seated by the Gordon hearth. "It reached me by way of Ludwig who got it from Eliza Ballard. Anne, don't put any more coal on that fire, you'll put it out. Here, give me the bellows."

"John says I have a genius for extinguishing a fire." She watched Sally, whose cheeks were still flushed with the cold, her lips parted as she exerted herself with the bellows. "What news? Where did Ludwig run into Eliza, for goodness' sake? Do put that bellows down. Let the fire go out if it wants to. It's warm enough in here."

Sally had not told Anne of the proposed removal of Eliza to Ludwig's office; she did not intend to now. It was not only that Ludwig's test of Eliza's trustworthiness would be worthless if his wife talked about what was supposed to be confidential (she thought the test a poor one, anyway: of course Eliza could be trusted with a secret in which she had a monetary interest; it was about other people's affairs that she talked); it was also and rather that she could not bear Ludwig to seem foolish to anyone, not even Anne. And so she said, "He was in the law office this morning. You know Eliza is still there, until the Judge's estate is settled. Eliza told him that her mother is going to resign as Club President. For some reason her mother doesn't want the word spread around, so it is obvious Eliza wanted me to know. But why? I suppose Mrs. Ballard won't let her name be put up again, when we elect officers. But why should she want it to be kept secret? Why should Eliza care whether I know? I don't blame Mrs. Ballard: she's so crippled and suffers so much, she should have done it long ago. But does Eliza think because I am Vice-President—?"

Anne looked at her questioningly. "Does she think you want it? But you don't surely? Or," more slowly, "do you?"

"Ten years ago, I should have jeered at the idea. Now, here I am, middle-aged, busy as I can be, with four active children, a big house, and a lot of entertaining for Ludwig's friends from out of town; but silly as it may seem, I would like it. I have come to care a good deal about that Club, just because it is something apart from domesticity, I suppose: you do have to use your mind at least once a year."

Anne withheld any comment on Sally's odd desire: no doubt about it, she did enjoy managing people and events. "But should Eliza care whether you want it?"

"Oh, you know Eliza," Sally said carelessly. "She thrives on dissension, especially if she has started it. It's the only excitement in a dull life. And I suppose she thinks someone else wants it."

"Who would? Mrs. Deming?"

"Or Christina Voorhees. I don't know why I think so, except that I should hate her to have it. If no one knows beforehand of Mrs. Ballard's intention, out of sheer lethargy the ladies might move me from Vice-President to President. But if Christina knows, maybe Eliza isn't just muddying the waters, maybe she's warning me. Maybe she'd rather have me than Christina."

"But still, why? Christina's much more the Ballard sort than you are. And why do you dislike her so much? I didn't know you did."

"Oh, I like her well enough. But not for Club President. She's so bigoted. Don't look so surprised, Anne. I know she used to love play-acting, but now she sees it as a snare for the unwary, and refuses to countenance it. She warned me, no more Christmas plays. And in other ways. Haven't you ever noticed how she stays away from the Club if someone is to review a book that has love affairs in it, particularly illicit ones? Oh, she may be broad for an R.P. seminary president's daughter, but did she ever come in the library on your afternoon there? She came not long ago when I was at the desk, and there was a copy of *Tom Sawyer* lying there and she looked at it as if it were a—a puff adder. Did you ever read *Tom Sawyer*?"

"No. I thought it was a children's book. Johnny loves it, or did when he was a little boy."

"Christina reads every juvenile book before it reaches the shelves. For the sake of other people's children, no doubt; hers are surely too small to read."

"Blair must be five or six. Binny could read before she started to school. The little girl—Jane?—must be two or three. I am sure Christina means her children to be prodigies."

"Do read *Tom Sawyer* yourself sometime; some children's books one is never too old for. See how wicked you think it is. If you don't know the book, I don't suppose I can make you understand. It probably seems sacrilegious to a Christian of her stamp: it is very funny about backwoods church and Sunday School. Anyway, I asked Christina what was the matter with the book—I thought perhaps someone had torn some pages out—and she said—violently for her—she's so contained always—'*All* the pages should be torn out. This book is evil. No child should be allowed to read it. If I had not been trained to respect the property rights of others, I should have destroyed it the first time I looked through it!"

"Good gracious, Sally, is it that bad?"

"It isn't bad at all. That's what I'm telling you. I said to her there were worse things in Holy Writ than there were in *Tom Sawyer,* that the Bible is full of stories we should think indecent if we found them anywhere else."

"Sally, you didn't!"

"Indeed I did. I got quite hot under the collar."

"And she didn't, of course."

"No. Just looked bland and superior. I can imagine what she thinks of me, and I don't care. Neither of us said anything more, and it wasn't important, really. It is hard enough to keep the library going, without squabbling among ourselves. But I am thankful she isn't on the Board of Managers or the Book Committee. She would guard the morals of the public as she does those of the Club. I was on the Club Program Committee with her last year. I wanted to spend a year on the Russian novelists: you know, Tolstoi, Dostoevski, Gogol. We don't know anything about them, and they're *important*, at least if you care about the novel as a serious work of art. But Christina was scandalized, and the other Committee members went along with her, and that is why we are spending a year on the Southern Renaissance."

At that point Binny came dancing in, bringing a blast of cold air with her.

"Mamma! Oh, I didn't see you, Aunt Sally."

"I wish you would learn to say 'good afternoon' properly, Binny. Did you want something?"

"Where's Johnny?"

"He hasn't come in yet. Take your wraps off and hang them up. Then wash your hands and face. Truly, I don't see how you can get so grimy at school. After that sit down here with us and apply yourself to your Catechism. You haven't learned even one question and answer this week."

The glow faded from Binny's face, to be replaced by a mutinous scowl. "Oh, Mamma, I haven't *got* the Catechism. It's such a little book it just seems to disappear. I haven't seen it anywhere. Besides, my legs ache."

"You can sit down and rest them, then. You always seem to have growing pains when you're told to do something you don't want to do. If you can't find your Catechism, then bring your hemstitching and come sit with us like a lady. But first, wash your hands and tidy your hair."

Binny went out; they could hear her slowly climbing the stairs.

"Aren't you a little hard on her, Anne?" Sally wouldn't say so, but she thought Binny was so exactly like John's long-dead sister that there was little hope of changing her. "Imagine spending the afternoons after school learning the Presbyterian Catechism!"

"If I'm not hard on her, John will be when he comes home."

"I can't imagine Dock caring a button about the Catechism."

"He doesn't. But he expects to come in and find her neat, clean, and quietly occupied."

"Oh, men and their ideas of what their womenfolk should be!"

"It's more than that. There's a kind of antagonism." Anne paused. "John almost sneers when he scolds. I know he doesn't realize how he sounds, but she withdraws into sullenness. It makes both of them cross and unhappy."

"Didn't you tell me once that Elsa and I are too much alike not to rub each other the wrong way? Same with Binny and her father."

"I know. I shouldn't have said anything. It will pass."

"Ludwig Junior is the one who troubles me. You can always make a girl behave, but a headstrong boy— Oh, well, no use borrowing trouble. I must go: my children will be home from school, too."

Binny returned, tidy herself, but with a disordered, overflowing sewing basket and a grimy, half-hemstitched handkerchief.

"You can just bet," she protested sulkily, "Johnny's looking for persimmons."

"And if he is, I wouldn't let you go: it is too cold and damp. Here, pull your rocker up by the fire and let me see you get to work on that handkerchief. Isn't it to be a Christmas present?"

"Yes. For Martha."

Sally rose. Belinda, now the model female child, put sewing and sewing basket down and curtsied.

"Good-bye, Aunt Sally."

"Good-bye, Belinda." Sally kept her face straight. "Good-bye, Anne."

"But wait. You haven't told me what to do about the Club Presidency."

"Do!" Sally looked at her in astonishment. "Nothing. Oh dear, did you think I wanted you to go out and electioneer? That's exactly what Eliza wants."

"I could speak to a few members. Kitty—she's in bed now, but she could send her vote. Amanda, maybe."

"I can just hear you," Sally laughed. "About as subtle as a sledge hammer. 'Sally Rausch would like to be President of the Woman's Club: will you vote for her?' "

"How else?"

"How indeed! No. It simply can't be done, that way or any way at all, without creating factions in the Club. No." Sally smiled at her old friend. "Don't do anything. I was just blowing off steam."

"Let it go?" Anne said doubtfully. "I never knew you not to go after what you want."

"In this case I wouldn't demean myself. Just forget it."

Anne did indeed forget all about Sally, the Club Presidency, the Club itself, during the next several weeks. In December, a few days after Sally's call, Binny fell ill: suddenly and shockingly ill.

Anne was wakened in the night by a wail that was almost a scream; the cry "Papa" was hardly distinguishable in the anguished voice. Anne came awake at once, and out of her bed. Binny, sick: the cry was one of pain and not nightmare terror. John, humped under the covers beside her, had not been roused. He could sleep through any noise but his night bell: she had always been the one to answer a child's cry in the night. She would go see, before she roused him. Barefoot and in her nightgown she crossed the hall, not stopping to pick up the night lamp from its stand at the head of the stairs. Binny's room was never deep dark because of the street light on the corner, and now that all the leaves were down, Anne could see the child motionless in the big bed, knees drawn up, eyes wide open and glittering, her mouth open to scream again.

"Binny, I'm here. What is it?" Anne stooped to put her arm under the child, to lift her head to her shoulder, a mother's immemorial gesture. But Binny fended off the reaching hands.

"No—no!" She was screaming again. "Papa? I want Papa!" And suddenly the tears were flowing down her cheeks. "Isn't he here?"

"He's here. I'll wake him. Don't cry."

Anne returned to the hall, picked up the night light, called peremptorily "John! It's Binny!" From the door she could see Binny's contorted position, every muscle rigid.

"Binny! What *is* it? Don't cry, Papa's coming."

John came to the door behind her and took the lamp from her hand. He had jumped from the bed when Anne called and had struggled into his robe as he crossed the hall. "I'm here, Binny. What is it? Go put something on over that gown, Anne; you'll catch your death." Then he held the lamp up and saw the child's twisted body.

Anne waited while he took Binny's reaching hands in one of his, and with the other brushed the damp tangled hair back from her forehead. He looked for one instant at her flushed face, and still holding her hands, tossed back the covers and touched gently one of the bent knees. She screamed again.

"Oh, John! What is it?"

"Acute inflammatory rheumatism. No doubt about it. Rheumatic fever." He drew the covers over her again. "Hold on now, Binny, just a minute longer. I'll get something that will stop that pain. Anne, don't sit on the bed—don't joggle it. Just stand here and let her hold your hands. I'll be right back." He left the room quietly, not closing the door behind him. Anne, holding Binny's hands, heard him racing down the stairs for the bag always left ready for him in the front hall. He was back in an unbelievably short time. "Get a better lamp, Anne, so that I can see what I am doing. And bring me the glass from that washstand there." He had the bag open and was feeling among the clinking bottles.

"Oh, John, not laudanum?"

"The pain must be relieved. Morphia would be quicker, but—fetch the lamp from our room, then go downstairs and put the kettle on to boil. Hot fomentations may help."

Anne brought the lamp from their bedroom and lighted it, then fled to the stairs, still barefooted, robe trailing from her arms as she tried to pull it on. She gave one fleeting thought to Johnny, in his room down the hall: boys his age could sleep through anything. The house was dark; fortunately her feet knew every step of the way. In the kitchen she lighted the bracket lamp over the range, shook down the banked fire, opened the drafts, removed the stove lid, and put the full teakettle over the flame. The watched water did not boil, would not boil; she paced the floor, her feet icy on the cold boards. She dared not leave to go upstairs for slippers: the water might be ready before she got back. Finally it did boil; she snatched up the kettle and, holding it well away from her, returned the long distance through the hall and up the stairs.

"In the wash bowl, Anne. Soak a towel in it, wring it out—let me have it. Those knees must be agonizing."

Binny had not moved; only her eyes were never still. Anne could see that she was drenched in sweat; even the bed was soaked. John was still holding her hands. "It will be better in a little while. Believe me, Binny, it will be better." He spoke soothingly as he let go her hands, took the first towel from Anne, waited for her to turn the covers back, and laid it gently across Binny's knees and around them. He kept up his quiet murmur. "Only a little while, now."

"Papa—" The word came on a long sigh.

"I'm here. I won't go away: I'm right here." He pulled the covers up and took her hands again. Slowly, gradually she relaxed, except for the clinging fingers.

"Bring some dry towels. Her gown is soaked—I'll try to get it off. She can lie until morning wrapped in towels. The sheets should be changed—can you put dry ones on that side of the bed? I'll move her over there when I get her gown off, and you can fix them on this side."

Between them they got the wet nightgown off the child, and the sheet changed.

"Now go back to bed, Anne: you must get some rest; tomorrow will be a hard day, and there will be a good many tomorrows. You will need all your strength. I'll spend the night here beside her. She'll be asleep in a minute."

"I know it's you she wants. But I don't think I can sleep. And you will have patients to see tomorrow."

"I've spent many a night like this: don't worry about me. If you can't sleep, I'll give you a bromide. But first put more water on the stove. And pull that chair over here."

"You can't sit all night in Binny's little rocker. Wait a minute." She flew across the hall and dragged the big rocking chair out of their bedroom. As she yanked it over the sill of Binny's door, the child jerked and moaned in her half sleep.

"I'll take it, Anne." He lifted the chair and let it down lightly beside the bed. "My poor love, you have never seen rheumatic fever, have you? I have known children to scream when the bed was jostled, the pain was so excruciating. What I don't see—" and he looked again at the comatose child. "Wasn't there any warning? I haven't heard her complain of aching legs."

"I have," Anne whispered. "Oh, John, I laughed at her growing pains. I thought she was just making excuses for not doing what I wanted her to do."

"And she wouldn't say anything to me because she was afraid."

"Afraid you would laugh at her, too, poor baby."

"It wouldn't have made any difference, except we might have been forewarned. There's no way I know of to forestall rheumatic fever: we don't even know, really, what causes it. We'll have Dr. Warren in, come morning."

Life for the Gordons after that was a nightmare of pain and the fight against it. Anne was reluctant for John to call Dr. Warren, but she knew that he could not and must not bear the responsibility for his own child. If anything happened—she would not put it into words, even in her own mind, more starkly than that: if anything happened to Binny and her father had been her doctor, it would be an unbearable blow to him. And Binny did not want anyone but John to come near her. When Anne said as much to him, he overruled her. "Anne, we must. Warren is good with children: she liked him the last time she had tonsillitis: she may come to welcome him. I know that he will prescribe exactly what I would prescribe: in the morning, calomel, then rhubarb and soda. You and Martha will have your hands full getting a screaming child on and off a bedpan. After that, salicylic acid, hot fomentations."

"How long?"

"I don't know. Several weeks, maybe, before the pain is all gone. Then a long time in bed—possibly all winter—as long as she runs a fever. It will be hard for you, Anne. Shall I try to get a practical nurse?"

"Hard for me? I was thinking of Binny. No, Martha will help, if the child will let either of us touch her."

"She will when there is less pain. She must be bathed whenever she sweats her bedclothes wet; she must have hot fomentations on her knees, constantly renewed. I'll bring some oiled silk from the office to put over the towels."

"We can manage, John. We'll have to have Pearl oftener than once a week to do the laundry. Otherwise—"

But it soon became clear that they could not do it—not alone: baths, bedpans, hot fomentations, and meals to be cooked and the doorbell answered. John came in one morning while the child's pain was still at its worst to find both Binny and Anne, standing near her, in tears.

"What is it, Anne?" He stood at the bed, looking from one to the other.

"She screams when I come into the room, even when I wear house slippers. That is what—wrenched me so. Martha can come in, you and Dr. Warren, even Johnny—he's much better at moving her than I am."

Binny's tears ran back over her temples into her hair. "You bounce," she whispered.

"Martha shuffles, Anne. You *step* firmly. But we can splint Binny's knees the next time Dr. Warren comes. Immobilize them and she won't feel it so much when the bed shakes. All right, Binny? We'll make you as comfortable as we can. It isn't that you don't want Mamma with you, is it?"

Binny looked frightened. "Oh, no. I want her. If she won't comb my hair."

John looked at the tangled mat of black curls. "Tell you what, we'll just whack all that off. Then it won't have to be combed. Get me a pair of scissors, Anne."

She obeyed docilely, but fled the room when she had put the shears in John's hands.

"Turn your head, Binny. You didn't know I could barber, did you? Or that doctors—surgeons, anyway—started out by being barbers, hundreds of years ago? First they were called barbers, then barber-chirurgeons, then finally, barbers were one thing and surgeons another. But a doctor is still a handy man with the scissors."

Talking to her as he clipped, he soon had all her hair off, cut close to her head. He scooped the curls up in his hands. "Now, let's see Mamma try to comb that."

The shorn, woebegone Binny managed a smile. "Can I see?"

"When you're better—when you can sit up and hold a mirror. I'll be right back."

Hands still full, he went across to the bedroom, where there was a wastebasket. There he found Anne lying face down on a crumpled pillow, crying quietly.

"Oh, John!" She lifted her head as she saw what he carried. "Let me keep a lock of it!"

"My dear, foolish wife! Her hair will be long again in no time." He disposed of the clinging strands in the waste basket, then returned to sit beside her on the bed.

"Anne, you are exhausted, or you would not break down like this." His tone was half tender, half exasperated. "You must have help—if not a nurse, then someone to help Martha with the housework. There is a time coming when you will need all your strength: when Binny is better, she won't want you out of her sight; you will have to play with her, read to her—anything to keep her in bed. And she will be cross and irritable. It will be harder for you than all the baths and bedpans. I have seen it happen: mothers who have been frightened turn cross out of exhaustion, just when their children are turning cross, too, because they have got back the strength for it. What about that niece of Martha's? What's her name? Lou something. One of those nieces and nephews she supports, mostly from our kitchen."

"Louline," Anne said. "She's awfully young, but I'll ask Martha. Is that someone at the door?"

"Lie still. It's Dr. Warren. I'll go. At least, Louline could answer the doorbell."

Having to answer the doorbell was one of Martha's complaints. People were kind: they came to inquire, and to leave delicacies; everyone, from Anne's friends of the Woman's Club and the Presbyterian church to farmwife patients of John's, the neighbors, and Binny's school friends. Mr. Klein came one morning, himself bringing a basket of fruit instead of sending his delivery boy. Anne, who had for once answered the bell herself, was moved almost to tears.

"Mr. Klein! How very kind of you!"

"Not zo, surely. Ve haf been friends for many years, ze Frau Doktorin and ze fruit peddler? Since I began in Vaynesboro, vis a cart, and you and Meine Berta vere bos—vot you say?—eggspecting. Und now, your Johnny and meine Sophie zey are friends. Vy not a little fruit for ze sick Mädchen?"

Anne took the fruit, thanked him, and when he had gone, carried it to the kitchen to add to the custards, the jellies, the puddings already there.

Martha surveyed it gloomily. "Johnny got to eat some o' dis trash. White folks think ah can't cook for mah baby?"

"They think nothing of the kind, and you know it. They are trying to help by saving your time, so you can be with Binny. She'd rather have you than me."

"Now, no, Miz Anne: it's jes' yo' so brisk."

Anne took an orange from Mr. Klein's basket and held it to her nose.

"Christmas oranges! How good they smell. Martha, Christmas is right on us. What can we do for Johnny?"

"Same lak always. Turkey fo' dinner, an' all the fixin's."

"It won't be the same. If Binny were better—a little tree in her room—but she wouldn't take any interest. Poor Johnny!"

Johnny was indeed suffering. When all the little he had learned from his father about doctoring had been put to use—lifting and turning the child, helping with the fomentations—he would back off to the door and stand leaning against it, looking so forlorn that Anne would take pity and send him away.

"Thank you for all your help, Johnny. We don't need anything more now. When Binny is better, we'll need your help most of the time to keep her quiet and entertained. Amuse yourself while you can—go up to Elsa's if you've nothing better to do: you know Aunt Sally said you should come there when you liked and stay as long as you liked."

And Johnny, even though he might mutter something about "bossy ole Shaney," would disappear and not return until dinnertime. Christmas at home seemed so little like Christmas, in spite of his presents and Martha's turkey, he spent the afternoon partly at the Rausches', where the day was as riotous as always, and partly in his father's office. There in the middle room he slumped in the deep leather chair by the grate where no fire burned, and read the medical books from the glass-doored bookcase: his Grandfather Alexander's and his father's, and more recently purchased volumes. And after that day, he returned there often, searching for what he could find out about rheumatic fever. It was not very comfortable reading. Once when his father had got rid of his last patient and came out to stand by the fire a minute before setting out on house calls, Johnny looked up from the heavy book in his lap to say, "Papa, it says here that the sequel to rheumatic fever may be 'a malignant endocarditis.' I know what 'malignant' means. 'Endocarditis' is a kind of heart trouble?"

"Yes. But don't worry. So far Binny's heart is all right."

"How can you be sure?"

"Let us say I am as sure as a fair-to-middling doctor can be. Dr. Warren and I both go over her with the stethoscope every morning. Medical books are never happy reading: they prepare a student for the worst. I would say stay away from them, only you have been very good with Binny. I think you will be a better doctor someday than I have ever been."

Johnny protested, although his face lightened. "No, I can only—well, anyway: Binny is getting better?"

"I think so. Don't you? Less fever, less pain. Don't pass on to your mother what you have just been reading: she is worried enough as it is."

But Anne was not a doctor's daughter and a doctor's wife for nothing. She had stopped herself from asking about Binny's heart only because she had been afraid of the answer. And she did not ask until the pain had subsided and the child was definitely better: there was no more screaming when the bed was jostled, or when the hot fomentations were changed. John lost something of his strained look. His wife knew that the weeks had been even harder for him than for her, since he had necessarily taken care of his practice, and might be out at all hours and then up early the next morning. When one day she asked at breakfast about such patients as were her friends or acquaintances, he was brusque with her in the normal fashion.

"Dr. Blair? His asthma has gone on too long. He has emphysema. If you don't know what that is, Johnny will look it up for you." He grinned at his son. "As for Kitty—doing as might have been expected."

Anne did not probe. Soon, with Louline helping downstairs and Martha in the sickroom, she would be able to get out to see Kitty. Now, she thought, she could ask about Binny.

"John, I know Binny is better. I am not so worried as I was. But there are things I remember having heard about rheumatic fever. Tell me the truth: is it likely to recur? And does it always leave a damaged heart?

"Recurrence is always possible. Even likely. No one knows what causes rheumatic fever, but there are a few precautions we can take. Never let her get overtired or overexposed to cold or damp."

"Is she going to be left with a bad heart?"

"There is no sign of it, so far as Warren and I can tell. Now that Binny is better and can stand a thorough examination, I'll write to Cincinnati and ask Dr. Krebs if he will come up for a consultation. He's the best heart specialist in these parts. I should like to be quite sure myself."

On the day he wrote the specialist, John received, and forgot, until bedtime, a note from his cousin Jessamine. He reported to Anne then, as he took the missive out of his pocket and dropped it in the waste basket. The news, compared with all he was going through right then, was of little concern. Jessamine had written to announce the death of her husband. "Just that," he said to Anne. "Not a word about what killed him. She can't think it much of a loss, even if he has made the plantation profitable."

"That's no way to talk. She may be lonesome now, both men gone."

Dr. Krebs came, examined Binny, and confirmed the younger doctors' findings: no discernible heart damage. The days passed; Binny continued to improve, although a lingering fever kept her in bed. To make life easier for everyone, the downstairs bedroom was turned into a daytime sickroom: Binny was carried down every morning and put in bed there by her father; Anne and Martha no longer had to climb the stairs innumerable times. Every night her father carried her back to her bedroom, so that Anne would not have to sleep on a cot at her side, alone downstairs. Having her in the first-floor bedroom made it easier for her friends to drift in for a few minutes now and then on their way home from school. As John had foreseen, Binny became very difficult: she tyrannized over her mother, Martha was her slave, and Louline, Martha's pretty young niece, proud to be part of the doctor's household, ran unnecessary errands uncomplainingly. Johnny, now no longer needed as a 'prentice doctor, played endless games of checkers with the child. But he was cock-a-hoop in his relief: he blocked those fearful words "malignant endocarditis" out of his mind, and when he was not being quiet in Binny's room he was outdoors playing shinny or some other noisy game. One day after school he brought Elsa and Julia Deming to see Binny.

"Mamma, I thought maybe Binny would like to see Julia and Shaney. And besides, I wanted to ask—"

The girls spoke to Anne. Elsa went to the bed and said, "Hello, Binny. I'm so glad you're better. Is there anything I can get you? Or do? Anything at all?"

But Julia stepped close to the head of the bed and laid a slim white hand on Binny's short curls. "How sweet you look with your short hair. Such pretty hair, too. Would you like me to brush it for you?" Without awaiting an answer (or, thought Anne, without so much as a "by your leave" to her), Julia brought a hairbrush from the chest of drawers and began gently to brush the crisp locks back from Binny's forehead. Anne, watching, was provoked: she didn't know why she had never been able to warm up to Julia Deming, but now she resented her cool taking over; and the adoring light in Binny's eyes as they rested on that pretty face aroused her to un-Christian judgments. "Ministering angel," she thought, "that's her own picture of herself. Play-acting, and not for Binny, or me, either. For the other two, and particularly Johnny." She said aloud, "You wanted to ask me something, Johnny?"

"Yes. There's going to be a bobsled ride, with an oyster stew supper afterward. Billy Thirkield's father will let us keep the stew hot on top of the drugstore stove, an' Mrs. Bonner will make it. Miss Talmadge is going to be the chaperon, and Shaney's and Julia's mothers say they can go." He stopped breathless, and his mother laughed.

"I'm only too glad to see you want to do something besides clump around the house. Of course you can go, if you are sure Miss Talmadge is going."

Binny said in a loud voice, "No." Julia in astonishment held the hairbrush suspended. "*I've* never been on a bobsled ride. Johnny can just wait till I am well."

"Don't be foolish, Binny," her mother said. "Even if you were well, you could not go on Johnny's parties. You are not old enough for bobsled rides."

But Julia, who had returned the hairbrush to the chest of drawers, said, "Never mind, Binny. Next year we'll take you on bob-rides and maple sugar parties. It's a promise."

"It would be wiser, Julia, not to make promises you can't keep. Binny's a little girl: even next year she won't be old enough for maple-sugar frolics. Get along now, all of you. Binny's had enough. And Elsa, tell your mother I thank her for adopting Johnny."

Johnny after that afternoon spent less of his time at home and more of it with his friends. Most of Anne's days and evenings were given over to reading to Binny. They worked their way through all the old favorites: *Lady Jane, Black Beauty,* all the *Five Little Peppers, What Katy Did,* and the Alcotts, which Binny knew by heart. When they had exhausted the books for little girls, she began on those written for boys: Johnny's and the library's.

John by then had returned to his regular office hour schedule, and was not home in the evenings. One night, for the first time in a long while, Ludwig and Mr. Lichtenstein dropped in for a game of chess. Ludwig's vitality was like a tonic to John.

"How is Binny, Dock? You can leave her now?"

"She's better, but bored. Look, would you run over and visit with her for a little while? It would do her good. We'll set up the chess game while you're gone; by the time you're back there'll be someone wanting to see me, and you can take my place."

When the doorbell rang, Anne moved from the downstairs bedroom to the hall to see who it was. Martha opened the door to Ludwig and would have taken him into the parlor, but he caught sight of Anne. He gave his coat and hat to Martha and went on down the hall.

"Evening, Anne. Dock wanted me to come see Binny. Thought she needed a change, I guess—said she was strong enough now for rough company like me." He took Anne's hand for a moment. "This has been tough on you, Anne."

"Binny will be glad to see you."

Binny's face lighted when she saw him. "Oh, Uncle Ludwig! Will you tell me about the war? Papa won't. He says you fought and he only mended."

"She's obsessed," Anne said, "ever since I brought her *Boys of '61* from the library. I didn't think it very suitable, but—"

"It's *good,*" Binny said. "I don't see why it's only the boys who hear about the war."

"I don't know either, if you're interested." Ludwig sat down in the rocker by the bed. It creaked a little under his weight. "What do you want me to tell you? Anne, do go somewhere and rest for a while. Binny and I will be all right. We're going to talk about the war."

Anne smoothed the bedclothes and plumped Binny's pillows, then left them together.

"Now, where shall I begin?"

"I want to hear about General Grant and General Sherman. Did you know them? Do you think I'll ever see them?"

Ludwig thought of General Grant, fighting off death at that hour. He answered the first part of her question.

"Well, you couldn't exactly say I knew them. They were top generals, you know, and top generals don't know captains. But we used to see General Grant sometimes at the siege of Vicksburg, He would go round our lines. But he commanded the whole army. We saw General Sherman oftener because he just commanded our corps. And he kept a pretty close watch over us."

"Tell me about the time you saw him that you remember the best."

Ludwig considered. "I suppose just before the Battle of Chattanooga. Do you know about that battle?"

"I know that there was the Battle Above the Clouds first, and then everybody in the army fought the Battle of Chattanooga, and they drove the Rebels off the mountains and they *ran.*"

"Well, yes. But first the whole army had to get in line for the battle. The river loops like this, see, with the mountains all around." Ludwig was making a relief map of sorts with the bedclothes. "There's this S curve and Chattanooga is in this loop. We held the town but not the mountains. General Sherman's corps was to make the main attack, way over on this side of Chattanooga, where Missionary Ridge comes down to the river. And it had to move there without the Rebs knowing it, from way on this other side. So we crossed the river here, and marched past the town on the other side of the river, and got here, where we had to cross back over to get at Missionary Ridge. And we had to do it at night, so the Rebs wouldn't know we were there. It was midnight before we were ready to get on the boats—a hundred or so small boats—and as we moved down to them, in the dark, giving our orders to our men, not knowing what we'd run into on the other side, there was this officer in a cape going from one boat to the next, saying, "Quiet, boys, quiet." And after he'd spoken you couldn't hear anything but the river lapping against the boats. I knew then it was General Sherman. When he came to my boat, sure enough, it was the General himself, right there to see that all went well. And I think I said so to the boys—something like 'The General's here. It's all right. Just go quiet.' And we weren't scared any more."

The two of them were silent for a moment, then Binny said, "And was it all right?"

"Oh, we had a he—heck of a battle next day, and didn't get anywhere, and it was Thomas's army that took Missionary Ridge. But yes, we always knew everything would be all right if Sherman was there." He looked at the child thoughtfully. "You know, Binny, I just might manage someday, at a reunion or something, to show you General Sherman. Mind you, it's not a promise."

"I—I know." Binny breathed through parted lips. "But if you can?"

"If I can."

After that Ludwig dropped in once a week or so to tell Binny about his battles. And Sally came one afternoon for the "good gossip" Anne had demanded. Binny scowled at the visitor.

"Mamma's reading to me. Don't stop, Mamma."

"You are growing to be an impossibly rude little girl. Speak to Aunt Sally properly. Then she and I are going into the sitting room for a visit. I haven't seen her in days, and besides, my voice is gone." She held up the book she had been reading to show Sally. *Tom Sawyer*. "I've read everything suitable for a little girl. Now I'm reading this."

Sally laughed. "You know you were curious. Do you find it so scandalous?"

"It's a wonderful book. But it just might give children ideas. About Sunday school, for instance. Now, Binny: I am going in the other room with Aunt Sally. You play with your paper dolls for a while."

"Paper dolls! Give me the book."

Anne propped Binny up with another pillow, handed *Tom Sawyer* over to her, and went with Sally into the living room.

"It's always a relief, isn't it, when they reach the irritable stage. I can see she's better. But you look like a ghost, Anne. You should try to get out more."

"Pretty soon I can. In the meantime, tell me what's been happening. I've neglected so many obligations, like my turn at the library."

"Oh, that's been taken care of: we've taken turns; it hasn't been too bad. Though I really think the time's come when we should pay someone—one of the high school girls, maybe—to come late in the afternoon and help shelve the books. Our fund to hire a librarian is not growing very fast. As for news, I suppose you have already heard from Dock everything I know. I find that very little happens in this town the men don't know about, traipsing the way they do from cigar store to barber shop to drugstore. You knew about the Doug Gardiners' baby, and that they're home?"

Anne nodded. Young Mrs. Gardiner had given birth in Georgetown to a third daughter; Doug had resigned his seat in the House, and a special election would be held to replace him. "They probably wished for a boy."

"Probably. As for Kitty, you must know more about her than I do. Poor old Mr. Sheldon is still going to the store. Customers dodge him, of course. Who wants to look death in the face? But Sheldon won't tell him not to come."

"I know. It can't be much longer. And Dr. Blair—"

"What about Dr. Blair?" Sally asked sharply.

"I didn't mean that the way it sounded, naming him in the same breath with Mr. Sheldon. But he does have asthma, and he isn't getting any younger."

Sally studied her thoughtfully, but did not press the question. "Christina said something of the sort yesterday. Anne, you haven't asked me a word about the Club meeting."

"Of course! Yesterday! Election of officers! What happened?"

"Election of officers," Sally teased her. "Mrs. Ballard sent a note asking that she not be reelected. The secretary read it. Then Christina made a speech, a very pretty gracious little speech, telling the ladies how much I had done for the Club, and moved that they make me President by acclamation."

"But, Sally! Then she didn't have her heart set—how nice for you, if you really want it."

"Maybe she just didn't want to be defeated. Because she would have been. Don't ask me how, or why. Anyway, Mrs. Deming seconded Christina's motion, and she wouldn't have, if it hadn't been prearranged. I don't pretend to understand it. I didn't do any maneuvering. I think it was Eliza. How or why, I don't know."

"Eliza? I never thought she was a particularly devoted friend of yours. Or any of the Ballards."

"I know. What you may not have heard—it hasn't been announced—is that Eliza has given up her position in her father's law office. She is going to be Ludwig's secretary."

"*Eliza?* What on earth—"

"Possessed him? I don't know. He only says he needs someone, and Eliza has brains. She has already learned to use a typewriter, I believe. I told him he would rue the day, but he wouldn't listen."

"So now you are President of the Club?"

"Yes. And Mrs. Deming is Vice-President, Mrs. Evans one secretary and Mrs. Maxwell the other, and Eliza the Treasurer." Then Sally began to laugh. "This I am almost ashamed to tell you. If I hadn't been conscienceless, I would have stood up and stopped them yesterday. After all these years, and me middle-aged—if thirty-five is middle-aged—I don't feel middle-aged, do you?"

"Right now I feel eighty. But I'll get over it. Go on."

"At thirty-five I'm going to have a baby. A baby, with a daughter almost fifteen. I blush for myself. I haven't had the courage to go see Dock."

"Oh, Sally! Ashamed? And there's poor Kitty!"

"I know. Just the way things always go, by contraries. Tell me about Kitty. What does Dock think? I thought she looked bad the last time I saw her."

"He says she's as well as can be expected, but he put her to bed. I'll try to get out to see her before the week's over."

On the following afternoon, in spite of Binny's protests, Anne left her in Martha's charge and walked the long way out to the Edwards house, taking pleasure in the brisk movement and the air that almost had a breath of spring in it, chill as it was. At the Edwardses' she was ushered into the parlor bedroom by the colored nursemaid, who said, between front door and bedroom door, "It a long time sence we seed yo', Mis Gordon. How yo' li'l gi'l? Mis' Edwards gwun be pleased. Ah taken the boy in he' room a while ago. Ah'll fetch him out so's yo'all kin visit."

"No, leave him, a little while, anyway. I'd like to see him."

In the bedroom, so stuffy-seeming after her dose of the outdoors, Anne found mother and child contentedly pursuing their different diversions in silence. Five-year-old Lowrey, a blond, blue-eyed, narrow-headed child like his father, was building a wall on the floor with a battered set of dominoes. Kitty, propped high on pillows, a bit waxy in color and puffy about the eyes, had a book open on her chest. Her soft hair was thrust behind her ears, but the shorter locks straggled across her forehead and cheeks. When she looked up and saw Anne, she closed her book and spoke gently to the child. He rose, scattering the dominoes, and offered a small soft-boned hand to his mother's guest.

"I am glad to see you, Lowrey," Anne said gravely. "You are helping take care of your mother?"

"Mamma isn't *sick*," he protested, a flick of terror in his eyes. "She's just resting."

"I know. Isn't it nice that she can rest, and you can keep her company?"

"He has kept me company long enough. Netty," to the girl who had lingered on the doorsill, "take him now—get him outdoors—it's a fine day. There's spring in the air, isn't there, Anne?"

"Well, yes, but you know we'll have more bad weather—it's too early. Good-bye, Lowrey. I'm so glad to have seen you." And then, to Kitty, "What a solemn, old-fashioned child you have produced! And how much he looks like Sheldon!"

"Looks and *is*. It is very gratifying. Pull up a chair, Anne."

"I suppose you are quite happy lying here if someone provides you with books. What is it now?" She indicated the face-down, open volume.

"The poems of Sidney Lanier. I've been trying to keep up with the Club. It gives me something to think about. I don't even see much of Lowrey: you think he's solemn, but you know what a five-year-old boy is like. Active. I just hope he isn't being spoiled to death between Netty and his father and grandparents."

"Very few small boys of my acquaintance are so obedient or have such nice manners."

"The Edwards inheritance. I'm so glad to see you. Tell me about poor little Binny and how she is."

"Right now, an imp of Satan. Which means that she is recovering, thank God. She will be up and about again before long. I feel as though I were walking on air—unsure of solid ground beneath my feet. She was so ill for so long."

"You look tired."

"I'm getting rested, slowly. John feels it more than I do, now. Reaction, I suppose. And of course he kept up with his practice, right through the worst of it."

"I know. He takes it so hard when he runs up against something he can't do anything to help. In spite of his bright, beautiful bedside manner, there were times when I knew he was in the depths. And so I read to him out of

Papa's Marcus Aurelius—that's my own resource in moments of gloom. I've done it before. This time I had been looking through it for passages to help me brace myself with. Like this—" Kitty sat up and pushed books to one side and rummaged on the bedside candle stand until she found the one she wanted, and opened it at a marker. "'Let not things future trouble thee. For if necessity so require that they come to pass, thou shalt be provided for them with the same reason, by which whatsoever is now present is made both tolerable and acceptable unto thee.' Of course Dock denied that the present was either tolerable or acceptable. So I gave him 'Remember withal through how many things thou hast already passed, and how much thou hast been able to endure.' And 'Nothing can happen to thee, which is not incidental to thee, since thou art a man.'"

Anne was laughing at her earnestness. "I can't believe a Roman philosopher's precepts would appeal much to John. He's not a patient man. He's thinking of Binny and you and—others."

Kitty studied her a moment. "No, he isn't a patient man. But he has been patient with me. It would all be easier for him, as a doctor, I mean, if he didn't care so much—let his emotions get involved. But I want him to be involved with me and of course his other patients do, too. This isn't the first time I have discussed philosophy with him, though I suppose he wouldn't call it that. He believes that man's life should be useful; that he should use his powers, whatever they are, to the utmost. And so do I. And the only power I have is to serve my family by having children. I told Dock that, and he said if that was the way I felt, go ahead and try again, though it might kill me. I don't think he really believes it will, and certainly I don't. And look at Lowrey: it was worth it, wasn't it?"

Anne, who privately thought John had been depending on Sheldon to deny Kitty the child she wanted, laid her hand on Kitty's, on the book now closed on her knee. "Lowrey is a lovely child, and I feel sure this one will be. And that's enough philosophy for today. I came for something less high-flown: a good gossip. You know I have seen almost no one for more than a minute at a time, and everyone comes to see you. So tell me: how did it happen Sally was elected President of the Club, and by acclamation, at that?"

"I heard that story from Amanda." Kitty laughed, sighed, laid Marcus Aurelius back on the stand. "Mrs. Deming—Old Teapot herself—went to Amanda to speak for Sally. Told her Eliza Ballard had written her a note, suggesting Sally was the member best qualified in every way: most experienced, most willing to go to all kinds of trouble, most naturally a leader. Anyway—this is my guess—Teapot knew that if she didn't do what Eliza suggested, Eliza would take care that Sally found it out. And whatever the Demings' and the Rausches' feelings for each other, the General does owe Ludwig a good deal. Amanda was willing to go along, and to come to me for my support. Maybe she would have been willing anyway, but I think she's looking for a tit for her tat. She wants that friend who has gone to live with her—Talmadge, is it?—to be taken into the Club."

"And Amanda lined up the R.P.'s, including Christina herself?"

"I shouldn't be surprised. Dear me, Anne: why should women be given the vote? They operate in exactly the same way as men, politically. The stage where they can act is so small it doesn't matter, but can't you imagine them at political conventions?"

"But this is so unexpected. I simply cannot imagine Amanda stooping to ask that kind of favor."

"It wasn't stooping, was it? To want me to vote for Sally? I should have done anyway. Oh, I know what you mean—acting under pressure: I admit that doesn't seem like Amanda. But there it is."

"The Beatties are really leaving town, then?"

"I believe so. He feels that he must be more active, must preach: he's accepted a charge, and will go when the Seminary term has ended."

The two young women might conjecture all they liked: there was one factor in Amanda's willingness to do as Eliza asked of which they could know nothing. She had been hurt by Eliza's indirect approach, using Mrs. Deming. She and Eliza were better and older friends than she and Mrs. Deming. But their quarrel, if you could call it that, over Ariana, had never been fully made up. Now, if Eliza was willing to ask a favor of her, even by means of a go-between, then surely she must want to let bygones be bygones. And Amanda thought it a favor easily granted, since Sally seemed to her the logical member to become President of the Club. She had no great respect for Sally's intellectual capacities, but she recognized in her a competence in practical matters that she herself lacked. The only practical thing she had ever done, perhaps, was to persuade Elizabeth Talmadge to come and live with her. For after a while of tentative approaches to friendship, they had found they liked being together. Elizabeth enjoyed having the run of the house, instead of being confined to one room; she liked to cook, and really enjoyed her alternate week in the kitchen, whereas Amanda went about her task of getting dinners, in her turn, with the grim resignation of a Christian martyr. If Elizabeth often felt inclined to take over from her and do all the cooking, she restrained herself: it would never do, she realized, to suggest to Amanda that there were areas in which she was inferior; it was rather that than any fear of slipping into the position of servant to the older woman that kept her silent over the scorched fried potatoes and the dried-out meat she was so often and so apologetically served.

In spite of the difference in their ages and the disparity of their backgrounds (Elizabeth had grown up in Cleveland in an altogether more sophisticated atmosphere than Amanda had known), they not only got on amiably together; they enjoyed each other's company. Evenings they spent on either side of the round table in the sitting room where Mrs. Reid had used to sit with her darning, Elizabeth reading English papers, Amanda correcting

Latin exercises; each of them reading to the other egregious errors and exclaiming over them.

One evening shortly after Elizabeth had moved in with Amanda, she had looked up from a paper to say, "This Ariana McCune: do you know her, her background? She's the most fanciful young 'un."

"That is the right word for Ariana. I wish she fancied doing her Latin exercises." Amanda explained Ariana as best she could, and concluded, "It would be a great blessing if she could do really well in something."

"She could write well: she's careless, sloppy, all over the place, but she has real imagination. A little high-flown, perhaps. She isn't so strong on the dreary elements of English grammar. Why particularly do you want her to do well? Because you feel sorry for her?"

"Partly, I suppose. But one always hopes one's students will do well in some field. However, yes, especially Ariana, because there are friends of mine who take a great interest in the girl. Her mother belonged to the Woman's Club, and various members helped for a while with the children, and Ariana came to be almost like a—well, niece—to the Ballards."

"I see." Privately Elizabeth considered Amanda's earnestness about her Club a small-town eccentricity; she had never seen the ladies assembled, indeed, had met but a few of them; but she supposed, offhandedly, that they would seem to her funny, taken together if not separately. Now she said, "I suppose they hadn't much else to think of, elderly and most of them spinsters."

Amanda, her hands quiet on her papers, looked at her new friend in astonishment before she smiled, "You are so young! I suppose they would seem elderly to you. But—" and she ran over the members rapidly in her mind, "only three or four can be over fifty, some are about my age, and at least four are younger. And the Misses Gardiner and Eliza Ballard are the only spinsters."

"They are no doubt all very agreeable ladies, taken singly. But together, at meetings, don't they bore you?"

"Sometimes," Amanda admitted honestly. "There aren't many intellectual giants among them. You would be a great addition to the Club, Elizabeth."

"I?" The girl was astonished. "Isn't your membership full?"

"At this moment. But Professor Beattie is leaving the Seminary in June to accept a charge in Indiana. There will be a vacancy when his wife resigns."

"Do you always think of filling vacancies so far ahead?"

"If we know they are coming. It pays to get a proposed name in early, with two to second."

"Who would second my name? I don't know any of those people."

"Mrs. Rausch and Mrs. Gordon know you as their children's English teacher. But the Ballards would second your name if I asked them, I think."

"The 'Misses Gardiner,' are they related to the Gardiner who has just resigned from Congress and come home to Waynesboro to live? Won't his wife become a member?"

"I doubt it. The Misses Gardiner are his aunts, but, for one thing, she has a new baby and two other small children."

"There's no hurry about it, is there? I'd like to think it over. And to be sure they want me." There was something forbidding about the way in which Amanda had said "The Misses Gardiner." She wouldn't want to be blackballed, even by the Waynesboro Woman's Club.

"There are only two qualifications: intelligence and education. They would vote you in. And you might enjoy knowing them—some of them, anyway. Waynesboro is a town that isn't too easy for a stranger. It's an old town, and families have lived here since its beginning and are quite content to go on seeing only the people they have always seen."

"Yes, I know." Elizabeth's social life in Waynesboro had been limited to school functions. Church she had attended with Amanda, but the Reformed Presbyterian ladies apparently eschewed everything in the nature of frivolity. "I might enjoy making their acquaintance. All right, Amanda. If you think it is a good idea."

"I should take pleasure in your being a member, at any rate. But I had to sound you out first. It wouldn't do," and Amanda smiled thinly, "to invite someone to join and have her refuse. Not the Waynesboro Woman's Club. Silly, isn't it?"

"And having sounded me out, you now go and sound out the members?"

"That's about it," Amanda admitted. "If there are objections from any quarter, the name is quietly dropped. No one is ever blackballed. Of course I wouldn't be telling you all this if I didn't know that in your case it would be all right."

Elizabeth thought, "So you've already sounded out the members." Aloud she said again, "All right."

In due course the secretary received Amanda's note, proposing for membership in the Waynesboro Woman's Club, whenever a vacancy might occur, Miss Elizabeth Talmadge; the seconds were Mrs. Samuel Travers and Mrs. Voorhees.

Mrs. Beattie resigned from the Club at the first meeting in May "to allow the ladies time to replace me before the summer holiday." By that time Sally had withdrawn from public view, and Mrs. Deming was presiding. The ladies regretfully accepted Mrs. Beattie's resignation; Mrs. Deming asked the secretary to read the name of the proposed new member (a name that was no surprise to anyone present), and Amanda expounded briefly the qualifications of Miss Talmadge. A fortnight later the matter came before the Club for a vote, and the new member was unanimously elected.

By that time the Ballards, though still not ready to accept invitations to social occasions, had resumed attendance at Club meetings. Kitty Edwards had borne her second son, not without great danger and damage to herself:

John Gordon had for almost a week spent the nights on a couch outside Kitty's room, in case there were signs of an emergency. But in due time she was delivered of a healthy son, and if her doctor and her husband were sick with fear throughout the ordeal and with exhaustion when it was over, she in contrast was transported with happiness.

Binny Gordon by late spring had resumed a normal life; her mother even had the heart to scold her the day she found all the "lost" copies of the Catechism. There had been a great upheaval in the house since Binny's recovery; her illness had proved the necessity of an inside bathroom. And it would be sensible to put in pipes for illuminating gas at the same time, with lamps in every room. If they had one bathroom, they might as well have two. And so carpenters, bricklayers, and plumbers had made the house a shambles and life intolerable for everyone in it for several weeks; when they had done, there was a beautiful bathroom at the end of the hall upstairs where there had been a never-used maid's or sewing room: in it were a walnut-covered tub big as a sarcophagus, a wash basin, and a flush toilet with a tank overhead and a long chain hanging down. On the first floor a closet off the bedroom had been turned into a smaller bathroom: wash basin and toilet but no tub. Then, the aftermath of the construction had to be dealt with: plaster dust, sawdust, brick dust, splinters, and nails had somehow penetrated to every corner of the house and a really thorough house-cleaning had been necessary. For another couple of weeks Anne's family was made miserable by her activities. All the carpets were taken up and hung over the clothesline to be beaten. When Anne and Martha and Louline, who was still at the Gordons' and beginning to look like a permanency, were on their hands and knees with tack-pullers, working on the parlor carpet, Martha, crouched in the corner under the piano, incautiously breaking into exclamations, gave Binny away.

"What happen hyuh, Mis Anne? Dese tacks all loose." She pulled back the carpet from the angle of the baseboard. "Whut Ah fin'?"

"I don't know. What?"

"Ah decla'!" Martha was not slow. "Nothin' but ol' paper, Ah reckon."

"Let me see!" Anne turned from where she was kneeling to peer across the room.

If the carpet was coming up, there in the presence of her mother, there was no hope of protecting Binny. Martha sighed. "All them Chu'ch books that lil gal fo'eve' losin'. How you suppose they got the'?"

Anne scrambled to her feet and went to kneel by Martha. There under the loose carpet lay in a dusty row half a dozen copies of the *Westminster Shorter Catechism.*

"How do I suppose they got there? I suppose Binny hid them there. The deceitful little monkey! How many times has she told me she—" she hesitated over the word "lost." She couldn't remember, but thought that it had usually been "My Catechism's gone." And "gone" it most certainly had been. But if there had been no actual verbal lying, the intent to deceive was unmistakable.

"Now, don' yo spank he', Mis Anne. She mahty sick chile."

"Not now she isn't. She's too big to spank, but willing or not she is going to learn her Catechism. The little heathen!"

With the evidence in hand, Anne lay in wait for Binny to return from school; she had been allowed to resume attendance only on the condition that she come home immediately and rest. When she came banging in, Anne mutely held before her the several copies of the Catechism.

"Oh. You found them."

"Certainly I found them. We're taking the parlor carpet up. What possessed you to deceive me in such a way?"

"I never had a chance to take them out," Binny wailed. "There was always someone around."

"You don't sound very repentant."

"Mamma, I can't learn all that stuff!"

"Stuff!" Anne flushed with anger. "Your ancestors fought and died so that they might have the right to profess the beliefs that you call 'stuff.' And if you avoided any downright lies, you certainly worked to deceive me. Now you are going to learn every word of this."

"Mamma—"

"At least one question and answer every day. Go up to your room, get in bed, and learn the first question and answer before I bring your supper up to you."

If Binny had been spoiled by her long illness, she was due to become unspoiled very quickly. When John came home to his dinner and asked for her, her sin was reported. Unfortunately he thought it was funny.

"I wonder why she didn't burn them and be done with it?"

"I suppose," Anne was forced to smile, "she thought that would be sacrilegious and didn't quite dare. John, I know you don't take the Catechism seriously, but you cannot approve of her deceit. Don't you dare go up there and let her know you think it is funny."

"Very well. I'll go up and lecture her on the evils of fibbing to her parents."

"No, not that either. I have scolded her enough." Anne had been so happy at the dissolution of the antagonism between John and Binny that she wanted nothing to rouse it again. She was even willing to be in Binny's eyes the stern disciplinarian, the tormentor-over-trifles like uncombed hair, dirty hands, and unseemly table manners.

So Binny learned the Catechism. The weeks passed, school came to an end, summer began, little different from other summers, except that everyone was a little older, and somehow a little quieter. For in the background of every adult mind was the knowledge that General Grant was dying even as he pushed his memoirs to conclusion. When the end came, in July, there was not a veteran of his armies who did not suddenly feel himself older.

"A piece of us is gone. A piece of our lives," Ludwig said to John one evening in the doctor's office.

"Yes. It's been twenty years. Time passes without your being aware— then, suddenly, you realize— I'm tired of hearing people quote that nothing in his life became him like his leaving of it. The years between have made them forget what he did once. I don't mean he didn't meet his end heroically: no one knows better than I that he was a hero. But so is poor old Mr. Sheldon, in the same boat exactly. A good death is not so important as a fruitful life. Has everyone forgotten Vicksburg and Appomattox?"

"I thought perhaps you had. That is quite a speech for you."

"Of course I haven't forgotten. Certain memories will be with us on our deathbeds."

"Do you know that there is to be a reunion, an encampment of the Sherman Brigade at Odell's Lake the last week in August? The General will be there. He never misses a reunion."

"You are going? You want to see him again before it is too late?"

"I want us all to go. Not to the encampment, but for a day, to see the General. You, Anne, your children, and all the Rausches. Even Sally, if she feels equal to it. The new baby should be a month old by that time. We could go to Mansfield, stay at the hotel overnight, go to Odell's Lake, hear the General, return to Mansfield and home the next day."

"You have it all planned. But drag six children along?"

"If you and Anne will go, we can manage. If I have to go by myself, I can only take one child, and that would have to be Binny because I promised her she should see General Sherman someday."

"You promised Binny?"

"If you don't think it would be too much for her?"

"And the others would have to stay at home?"

"Together we could manage. After all Johnny and Elsa are very grown-up now."

John snorted. "Not so grown-up as they think. But four Rausches must not be disappointed for one Gordon. I'll talk to Anne."

Tentative plans were made for the expedition, once it was known that General Sherman would indeed go from a family reunion at his brother's in Mansfield to speak to the encamped veterans. Nothing was said to Binny or any of the children, lest they be disappointed. They would have to wait until Sally had had her baby and John and Ludwig knew that she would be able to go if she could tear herself away. At the moment there was no thought in Sally's mind except for the new son she had been so reluctant to bear. When she was first shown the squalling mite, she exclaimed, "Why, he looks like Papa!" This Ludwig thought very funny, but Sally insisted, quite seriously: "I have borne you four blond Rausches. This one is a Cochran."

"But you're blond yourself. And Elsa is—"

"Don't say Elsa is like me. If she were, I could manage her better."

"Has Elsa been giving you trouble? I thought she was behaving quite grown-up."

"Oh, no, no trouble. She just wants to do the opposite of whatever I want her to do. I don't want her, now she's halfway through high school and a young lady, running after Johnny Gordon as if she were still a tomboy in short skirts. Oh, it's nothing, Ludwig, really. But this baby I'm sure I'll understand."

Late that afternoon, when the doctor came to see Sally, Ludwig intercepted him as he was about to depart. He told him Sally had agreed somewhat reluctantly to their plans. "Just now the baby seems to satisfy her. She wants to call him Paul. I just hope she doesn't spoil him. I need sensible sons to take over from me."

"Your interests are so diverse you can use 'em all."

Ludwig was doing that summer enough to keep any other three men busy: running the mill, or at least seeing that it did run; getting the Columbus and Southwestern Ohio Electric Railroad under way, now that Doug Gardiner had taken care of the franchise business: buying land for a right-of-way, having it surveyed for the shortest and most profitable route, investigating every town and village for possible station sites; all in addition to working with his political friends on the problem of electing Joseph Foraker, who had been beaten in '83, governor of Ohio. And never losing sight of the fact that he was also still hoping to see John Sherman chosen as the Republicans' candidate for President in 1888.

It was Ludwig's involvement in state politics rather than the fact that he and John Gordon had both been in the Sherman Brigade that procured for him and his party favored treatment at the reunion. John Sherman and his relatives went from their family reunion in Mansfield to Odell's Lake by train, the same train that carried the Waynesboro contingent. Senator Sherman recognized Ludwig on the platform and left his family long enough to shake hands, utter a few words of greeting, and invite him to share the speaker's stand later. The conductor's "All aboard" rang out before Ludwig could protest, or introduce his party. Binny, whose rapture had been wordless but infinite since she had first heard of the proposed excursion, now clung to her mother's arm and peered around her.

"Mamma, that isn't the General?"

"Oh, no, the tall man in uniform."

But Binny was being hustled on the train before she had a chance to really look. Once they were seated, John put a restraining hand on her knee.

"Binny, you must not get so excited. If you can't control yourself, you will be very tired afterward. And maybe sick. You don't want another winter in bed, do you?"

She closed her mouth hard, shook her head.

"Then sit quietly and look out the window. Keep your hands off that sooty window sill: do try to get there still looking like a lady."

Binny could not care about being tired *afterward;* it was *now*. But she kept her eyes obediently on the passing landscape, the flashing telegraph poles, the wires that dipped and rose again so dizzily, but inwardly her being was ecstatic with anticipation. She turned only once to look questioningly at Ludwig when he rose; he winked at her, then went swaying along the car's length, out through the door and into the next car. When he finally returned he leaned over her shoulder to say: "All right, Binny, you'll have a chance to meet the General when we get off the train. He promised."

Binny could only smile. She wanted to say something but could not; she hoped Uncle Ludwig would not think she did not care; she did not know how her face was transfigured with joy.

When the train reached the lake and stopped, she would have fallen all over herself and her mother had it not been for her father's restraining hand on her shoulder.

"There's no hurry."

How could her father be sure? The General might forget his promise when he saw the crowd awaiting him, half or more of them in uniform. But he did not forget. When Ludwig had got the young people lined up, he led them to the end of the next car, where all the Shermans were disembarking. When the General saw them coming, he stepped aside and waited. Binny saw a tall man in a rumpled uniform, hat in hand, a lined face, and thinning hair that stirred in the breeze.

Ludwig saluted. "Captain Rausch of the Sixth Iowa, sir."

"Corse's regiment." The lined face broke into a grin. "Remember Allatoona?"

"Yes, sir. 'Hold the fort.' This is Capain Gordon, Assistant Surgeon, Forty-sixth Ohio."

General Sherman studied John for a moment. "I am familiar with the name, young man. I am not sure that I ever saw you, but I have not forgotten your communications: you pestered every medical officer up to Corps level about that Duckport hospital."

"Yes, sir." John looked uncomfortable. "It was a pest-hole, and it took an order from you to get it closed. I have the paper still: your aide sent me a duplicate. You said, 'Hasn't anything been done yet about the Duckport hospital? See that it is closed and the sick and wounded moved.' That order was a godsend to me, but I wouldn't have supposed you would remember." The two men shook hands. Johnny stood very straight at his father's side, and Binny, holding her mother's hand, was jigging on her toes. John presented Anne. General Sherman bowed, looked from her to the children. "And these are yours?" He bent to take Binny's hand; when she was a little shy about giving it, he put both hands on her shoulders and stooped and kissed her cheek. "Didn't they tell you? I always kiss the pretty girls." He shook hands with Johnny, and then turned to the Rausches, ranged in line next to Ludwig. "And these tow-heads are yours, Captain Rausch?" He kissed Elsa, too, and Elsa, who had put up her back hair in a chignon and wore a pert hat tilted over one eye, thinking she looked very grown up, blushed to the edge of her bangs. The General shook hands with the boys, and then excused himself, waving a hand toward the crowd that was threatening to engulf the group on the platform.

"I must go with our escort to the speaker's stand, however much I might prefer seeking out my comrades. Perhaps I may see you later, when the speeches are over?"

Binny, letting go her mother's hand, would have followed him blindly, a kite tail to the escort that had formed, had her mother not stopped her. "Here—here—you stay with us. Ludwig, what next?"

"We'll find a place near the speaker's stand where we can listen. Have to sit on the grass, I'm afraid. There will be all kinds of preliminaries before the General has his turn. Dock, would you like to circulate through the crowd, after our families are settled? Lots of our old friends here."

John laughed. "I'd better stay with the children. We might get separated in this jam."

Ludwig found a place for them under a tree, where they could see and hear unless the press became too great. "I'll be back before the General speaks," he said, and left them. The speeches began: General Finley introduced the Senator, who in turn introduced his brother. Both were brief: Ludwig just got back in time to drop on the grass beside his party before the General began to speak. John had been leaning against the trunk of a tree, obviously not listening to the speakers. "He's as enraptured as Binny," Anne thought, "just because his name meant something to General Sherman." She looked from Johnny to Binny: they were listening to the General with all the intentness possible as he came to 'very old comrades of the War' through 'as long as we live let us come together whenever we can, and if we can bring back the memories of those glorious days it will do us good, and still more, good to the children who will look up to us as examples'—and on for fifteen or twenty minutes more. Finally he came to an end; the crowd surged toward the platform to shake his hand.

"Let's go too, Mamma. Papa?"

"Binny, you would be smothered in that crowd. No. It is time for us to be getting back to the railroad station." And with Binny's hand firmly in his, John resolutely led the way against the stream of men, in uniform and out. "We had our moment. You have not only seen General Sherman, he *kissed* you."

"I know. And he remembered you, Papa. Aren't you glad? This is the happiest day of my life. I must tell Uncle Ludwig."

"Yes, you must—he arranged it. And, yes, I am glad."

But after they were safely back in the Mansfield Hotel and the exhausted Anne, Sally, and all the children had been sent up to bed, John and Ludwig went into the bar for a drink. John was very silent.

"You aren't sorry you came, Dock?"

"Sorry? Oh, no. It is something the children will always remember. I'm grateful to you for arranging it. And it was flattering to have my name recognized, unless you mentioned it when you were talking to the Shermans earlier?" Ludwig denied it, as John had thought he would. But the General must at least have remembered about the Duckport hospital, if only as a nuisance. After a pause he added, "But I'm not sure I wanted to see him again, Ludwig. He's getting to be an old man; talks like one. 'Memories of those glorious days.' That's not the General Sherman who fought the war."

"No. Age makes us all sentimental."

The two men finished their drinks and went upstairs to their rooms. John stood for a moment before he turned off the gas-light, to look at Binny, smiling in her sleep. For her at least the day had been pure, unadulterated delight.

That reunion of the Sherman Brigade was nonpolitical, yet somehow it seemed to usher in the beginning of a new political campaign: Governor Hoadley and the man he had defeated in '83 were battling it out again for the governorship of Ohio. Mr. Foraker came to Waynesboro to make a speech; when the bands had seen him off at the railroad station and most of the town had gone home to bed, Ludwig climbed on the train to accompany him to Cleveland. The item figured in the *Torchlight* account of the occasion: "On his departure from Waynesboro, Mr. Foraker was accompanied by Mr. Ludwig Rausch, who will also be a guest at the home of Mr. Marcus Hanna of Cleveland, where further campaign strategy will be discussed."

Amanda Reid, once more sitting at a desk before a test-taking Latin class, smiled a little as she thought of the impression that paragraph had made the previous evening on her friend Elizabeth. They had been sharing the *Torchlight*, half and half, at the sitting room table, before they went to work on their papers, and Elizabeth could not resist reading aloud the articles that interested her, before Amanda had a chance to read them herself. After reading that paragraph, Elizabeth said, "That is the Club President's husband, I suppose? Does he know Mr. Hanna?"

"Has known him for years, I should suppose. Don't politicians always know each other?"

"But Mr. Hanna! I could live in Cleveland all my life, as my family has, and never even see Mr. Hanna."

"You are impressed?"

"Yes, in a way I suppose I am. Naïve of me, you think? There is more to Waynesboro than meets the eye."

Amanda had laughed then at her candor, her impressionability; she smiled now, at her desk, remembering. Elizabeth's weaknesses were very human, very young, and very easy to put up with. They had been together almost a year now. A year ago Amanda had been doubtful of her wisdom, had almost regretted becoming involved in close friendship with another person: she had too often found friendship a betrayal. But there had been nothing at all to be afraid of. Their being together had worked out perfectly. Elizabeth was a fine teacher; she had a good mind; she was enjoying the Club (she and Sally were already preparing for the Christmas play: Olivia and Viola and the necessary others in scenes from *Twelfth Night)*, and she and Elizabeth Talmadge were firm friends.

And yet, she had been glad to have the summer alone, with Elizabeth home for the vacation: not to have to be sociable was a relief. At any rate, she was sure that after this year Elizabeth would not be with her. Tim Merrill was spending too many evenings in the parlor, and acting as her escort too many times not to be serious in his intentions. Elizabeth would be another friend lost to matrimony.

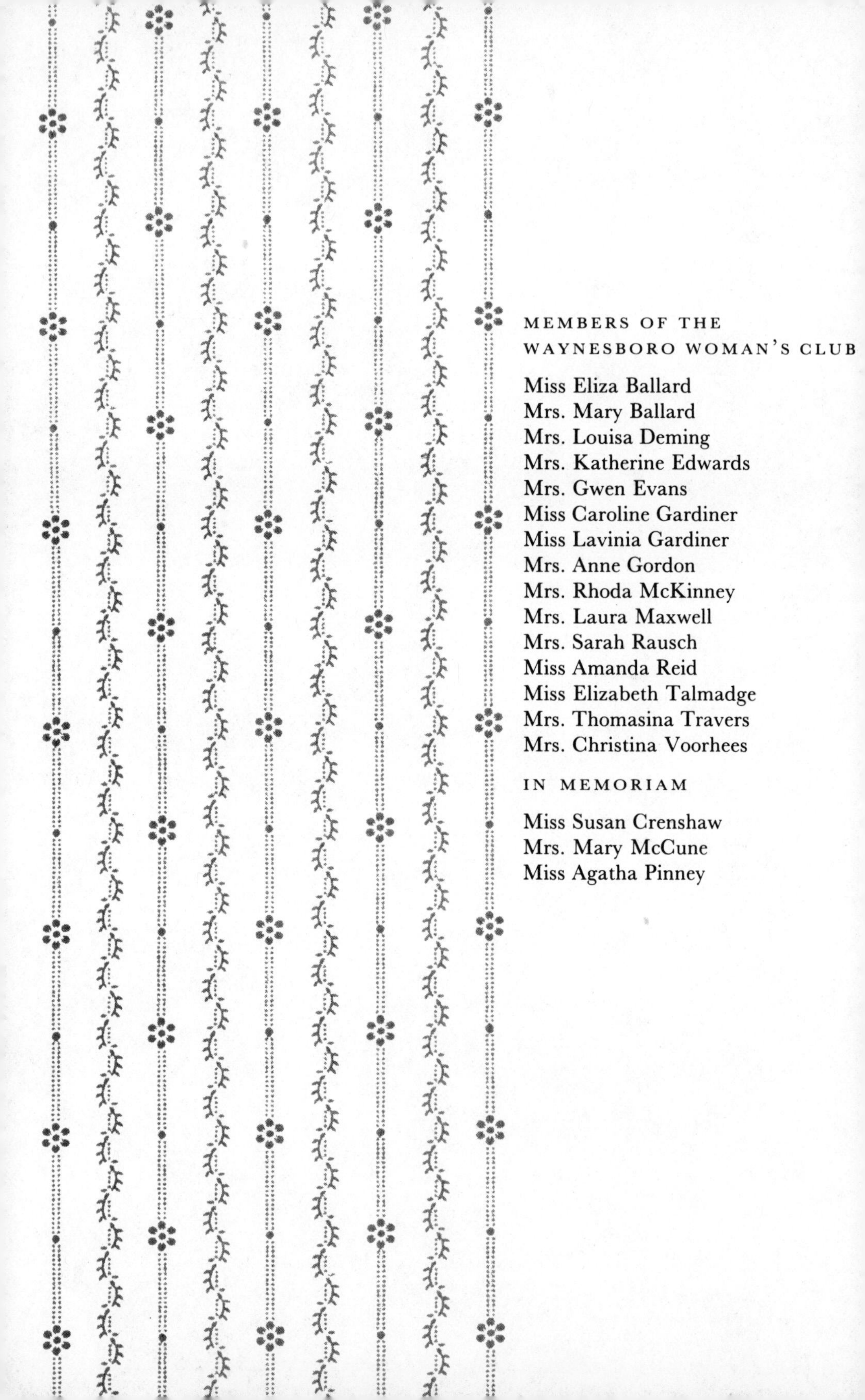

MEMBERS OF THE
WAYNESBORO WOMAN'S CLUB

Miss Eliza Ballard
Mrs. Mary Ballard
Mrs. Louisa Deming
Mrs. Katherine Edwards
Mrs. Gwen Evans
Miss Caroline Gardiner
Miss Lavinia Gardiner
Mrs. Anne Gordon
Mrs. Rhoda McKinney
Mrs. Laura Maxwell
Mrs. Sarah Rausch
Miss Amanda Reid
Miss Elizabeth Talmadge
Mrs. Thomasina Travers
Mrs. Christina Voorhees

IN MEMORIAM

Miss Susan Crenshaw
Mrs. Mary McCune
Miss Agatha Pinney

* 1886 *

"Again the fatal asterisk of death . . ."

The Program Committee for 1886–87 was chaired by a reluctant Eliza Ballard, with Elizabeth Talmadge and Mrs. McKinney as the other members. Eliza (having given the matter considerable thought) decided it was time for the Club to deal with contemporary literature however unladylike or un-Christian its content. Before her two assistants came to spend an evening with her, she made out a list of possible subjects. Some she knew would not be acceptable, but she felt sure that if she gave way amiably on those, others less certainly offensive might slip by. When she read her list of authors and their most recent works, she had the pleasure of seeing Mrs. McKinney's eyebrows rise at the inclusion of Zola's *Nana* and Maupassant's *Une Vie*. With seeming reluctance she then agreed to substitute for the former Wallace's *Ben Hur*, for the latter Olive Schreiner's *Story of an African Farm*, thereby managing to retain Hardy's *The Return of the Native*, Meredith's *Diana of the Crossways*, and Henry James's *Portrait of a Lady*. Mrs. McKinney read so little fiction that she knew only what books were notorious and the subject of sermons. She did say that "it was a pity that such frivolous writers seemed unable to find some subject other than marital infidelity. And, so many poets, like Matthew Arnold, seemed to have been shaken in their faith by modern scientific dogma. But whoever might write on Matthew Arnold would be free, of course, to criticize his weakness." She was pleased at the inclusion of Alfred Lord Tennyson.

"Thomasina," Eliza said, "would love to do an essay on the Poet Laureate."

Elizabeth waited for Eliza to finish before making her one objection: "Why Tourgée? All the others on your list are great writers."

"I put him in for my mother. She thinks he has done such fine work against the Klan and for the cause of the Negro."

When Mrs. McKinney emphatically agreed, Elizabeth withdrew her demurrer. "I hope," Eliza said to Elizabeth, "that you will consent to be chairman of the Christmas entertainment. I thought perhaps some songs from Gilbert and Sullivan? That meeting will be on December fifteenth. Christina might help."

Elizabeth objected only feebly, but said she was sure Christina would not take part. "Since her father's condition has deteriorated so, she spends a great deal of her time with him. And besides, now that she has children whose moral principles she is responsible for, she has developed religious scruples. She believes that her youth was misspent: that theatricals are not only a waste of time but positively wicked. I am sure the Christmas entertainment will have to do without her."

"You are in a position to know, going to the same church with Amanda," Eliza said. "But I don't believe her father is that narrow. Well, at any rate, see what you can do."

The Committee then agreed it would not be necessary to meet again, that the topics could be assigned to the ladies in the alphabetical order of their names.

When the printed programs were mailed to club members in midsummer, there were some groans of dismay, but no great scramble to exchange one author for another: it was too soon, except for those who must be ready for September, to worry about Club papers; programs were tucked away in desk drawers to be thought about when it became necessary.

The first Club meeting was all business: officers' reports, an introduction to the program by Eliza (who thus avoided having to write a paper), and a piano solo, politely encored, by Thomasina. The second meeting, on September 22, was held at Anne Gordon's. All were in a relaxed mood, ready to be entertained rather than enlightened: Tourgée as an author required little thought, however seriously regarded by Mrs. Ballard. For only a moment were their faces grave: when the roll was called, there was no response to "Mrs. Katherine Edwards." Kitty had developed Bright's disease after the birth of her second son. The secretary hurried to the next name on the roll: the program for the day was read. Mrs. Ballard, unable to rise from the chair she had been helped to, remained seated to read the essay she had dictated to the always willing Thomasina. Her crippled hands could no longer hold a pencil.

After she had done and been thanked, the meeting adjourned, and the ladies dispersed. Sally Rausch lingered in the Gordon parlor just long enough to exchange a few remarks concerning Mrs. Ballard's paper and her crippled condition, passed on two expressions of regret for those more gravely ill, Dr. Blair and Kitty, and rejoiced that it had been a quiet summer: no great upheavals in the world or in Waynesboro.

It was right after that that Ariana McCune ran away from home.

For several days her disappearance went unnoted except by members of her family. At school on Friday (Ariana had not been graduated with her class in the spring of 1886: she had still a year of Latin to make up, and at her own suggestion was doing some writing for Miss Talmadge), her absence was assumed to be due to illness, and neither her brothers nor Ruhamah told anyone otherwise.

Ariana was the subject of casual mention at the Gordons' on Saturday morning, but she was not uppermost in anyone's mind. It was a beautiful warm September day, and there might not be many more Saturdays like it. Johnny and a few of his friends had decided to have a spur-of-the-moment picnic: they would drive out to the Gordon farm in the Rausch and Deming buggies, and spend the day nutting in the woods nearby; they would take a picnic lunch, prepared by Mrs. Rausch and Mrs. Deming, or their cooks. Julia Deming came with Johnny to plead for permission to take Binny along. Binny, who had been prepared beforehand, was present at the conference; she awaited the verdict wordlessly, but the ecstasy of her expectation was written on her face.

"But you are all too old for Binny: you will wear her out. And why should you want her tagging along? She has friends her own age."

"We want her," Julia said, "because we like having her. And *I* won't wear her out, I promise you: I do not expect to scramble through the underbrush, catching my skirts on the briars. Binny and I can find a nice sunny spot and spread Papa's buffalo robe on the ground and enjoy the lovely day."

It was in fact so summery a day as to be no threat to Binny, who promised happily to sit with Julia, although her mother knew that ordinarily she was one who loved to scramble through woods, briars or not.

"Very well," Anne said finally, "if you, Johnny, promise to see she doesn't get overtired. Who is going on this picnic, anyway?"

"Julia an' Binny an' me in Julia's buggy. I can drive their horse, General Deming says. Elsa in their buggy, with Bill Thirkield and Gib Evans. I bet she won't let them drive."

"You need another girl. Whatever's happened to Ariana McCune? She always used to be with you."

"Well, I dunno. Her father never let her do anything we asked her to do, like bobsledding, or coasting on Friday nights on South Hill, or maple-sugar-camp parties—so we kinda got out o' the way of asking her. Besides, Ariana's funny: she never used to be such a scaredy cat, but now she just writes poetry for Miss Talmadge. It's like she's sort of—I dunno—got curled in on herself, her back to everybody. Anyway, she must be sick—she wasn't at school yesterday."

Anne thought little of this: girls Ariana's age were likely to miss a day of school now and then. She saw the three young people into the buggy, with a parting encouragement: "Enjoy yourselves," and a last admonition: "Don't let Binny wear herself out, and if you want Martha to make pies and dumplings next week, be sure to bring back apples from the farm." Then without further thought of Ariana, she returned to the house and her Saturday morning housekeeping chores.

That Sabbath morning the Reformed Presbyterian congregation was startled by the icy bitter wrath of the Reverend Mr. McCune's sermon. Ordinarily his preaching was so dull as to permit relaxation, dozing, or even sound naps in the pews before him. But that morning no one slept. A recognition of the unusual came first with the minister's choice of a Scripture reading from the first chapter of the Epistle of Paul to the Romans, verses 18 to 32:

> For the wrath of God is revealed from heaven against all ungodliness of men, who hold the truth in unrighteousness. . . . Professing themselves to be wise, they became fools, and changed the glory of the incorruptible God into an image made like to corruptible man, and to birds, and to four-footed beasts, and creeping things. Wherefore God also gave them up to an uncleanness through the lusts of their own hearts, to dishonor their own bodies between themselves: Who changed the truth of God into a lie, and worshiped and served the creature more than the Creator, who is blessed forever. Amen. For their women did change their natural use into that which is against nature: And likewise also the men, leaving the natural use of the woman, burned in their lust one toward one another, men with men working that which is unseemly, and receiving in themselves that recompense of their error which was meet.

After the first stiffening shock at hearing read aloud from the pulpit the comparatively unfamiliar, outspoken diatribe by Paul the Apostle, most members of the congregation sat with lowered eyes: however much they might wonder which of their fellows was suspected of sinning in these particular ways, they dared not risk even so much as a sidelong glance at their neighbors. But Amanda, in her pew on the middle aisle, with Elizabeth Talmadge beside her, felt in her minister's icy voice a restrained fire, a burn like that which one feels on taking hold of an iron gate on a zero morning. Something had happened. She looked from him to the pew, far front and to her left, where the McCunes were ranged: the second Mrs. McCune on the aisle; Matt, the oldest, now a theologue, on the far end, and between them the younger children: Mark, Ruhamah, and Luke. But Ariana was not there. Was she in disgrace rather than ill? But what could the child have done to deserve Saint Paul at his most furious? With an increasing nausea, Amanda listened to the sermon. With Paul as his authority, Mr. McCune declared that all other sins grew out of "vile affections"—misuse of the body which was the temple of God. And as Paul had written to the members of the church in Rome and not to heathen idolators, so their minister felt compelled to speak to his flock, lest there be among them also "covenant-breakers." Let them search out the ways of their children lest among the daughters of Zion and the sons of the Covenant there were unnatural desires, satisfaction of lusts that would condemn them utterly, "worthy of death."

Amanda sat like a stone through the final psalm-singing and the benediction; even when the congregation began to stream out and Elizabeth, beside her, rose and looked at her questioningly, she could not for a moment move.

Then she whispered fiercely. "The side door," and motioned Elizabeth along the pew in the other direction. When they were outside on the step, in the fresh cool air, Elizabeth looked at her again: Amanda had never before failed to go as convention required to the front door, taking her place in the hand-shaking line filing past Mr. McCune.

"I couldn't *shake hands*—not this morning."

"It was pretty awful. I always suspected Saint Paul of being obsessed by the flesh. The idea of— Has your minister the same phobia?"

"Paul was dealing with the Romans—a different matter." Amanda could not let the implied criticism of the apostle go unrebuked. "You know about Roman life in his time: all kinds of horrid immoral practices were everyday matters. I suppose they were not even recognized as immoral by the first Christians. And as Paul said, in their minds the conception of an incorruptible God was changed to God made in their image; Paul had to lead them beyond their limitations. But the first chapter of Romans cannot possibly be applicable to our church members: they may be all kind of sinners, but they were born into the Covenant of Grace, they grew up with the idea of an incorruptible God."

"What do you suppose set him off?"

"I don't know," Amanda was abrupt. "I don't want to know. We should have got rid of Mr. McCune long ago: as a minister he is almost useless, and as a preacher worse."

They said no more. Amanda, in spite of "not wanting to know," intended to ask one of the Mccunes the next day whether Ariana was ill. Mark was in her third-year Latin class, Ruhamah in the second; she could catch one of them coming or going from her room.

Because Amanda, surrounded as she would have been by other church members, had not been able to bring herself to face Mr. McCune and inquire about Ariana, the news of her disappearance was first made known outside her family to Dr. Blair. Although Dr. Blair had resigned as president of the Seminary, he and the Voorhees family still lived in the president's house: Dr. Maxwell had been appointed acting president but stayed on where he had lived since coming to Waynesboro, across the street from the Gardiners'; there was no reason for anyone to move until a permanent appointment had been made. Dr. Maxwell did not seem to young Matthew McCune a person to go to in trouble: Dr. Blair, however incapacitated, might understand how he felt. After a stiff and silent cold Sabbath lunch at the manse, Matt went back to the Seminary; and instead of going to his room in the dormitory, he went on to the president's house, up the brick path and up the steps, slowly but resolutely. To the housekeeper who opened the door he said, "Dr. Blair? Could I see him?"

"You are one of the students, yes? Then you know yet: the Doctor ain't able for it."

"Then Mrs. Voorhees, please. It is urgent."

She ushered him into the shuttered parlor. Christina came in a moment.

He rose from the chair he had taken; one trouser leg, caught by the top of his boot, hung in wrinkles about his calf. He was turning his hat round and round in his big-boned hands. A hobbledehoy, Christina thought, like most of the students: a country boy who must somehow be brought to ministerial ease and dignity. Matt resembled his father in his sandy coloring, but he did not have Mr. McCune's mean, pinched features; his blue eyes were wide, candid, and, at the moment, beseeching.

"Is there something I can do for you?"

"I hoped I could see your father. I need his help."

Christina shook her head slowly. "You know that it is very difficult for him to breathe even without talking. You couldn't tell me?"

"You couldn't help."

"Could you tell him about it and let him write his answer?"

Matt's face brightened. "If I could just tell him, he might know what to do."

She led the boy into her father's cluttered study. The room was hot; the air smelled of medicine and was full of the sound of the old man's heavy breathing. He was propped by cushions into an upright position in an old leather armchair; a heavy leather-bound volume lay open on the lapboard across his knees. As the two came to the door, he pushed his glasses to the top of his head and closed the book on a finger. Christina took the book from him and laid it open on his desk; she picked up a pencil and pad and put them on the lapboard.

"Matthew McCune, Papa. He wants your help. I told him he could tell you his troubles, and if you had a word of advice you could write it. You are not to get upset and start talking." She started away from his side, but he stopped her with a gesture. "You want me to stay? But this may be something Matthew will not want me to hear." By this time Christina too had come to the conclusion that the morning's sermon, which she had thought horrid, had been inspired by some impelling personal reason. Was it possible that Matt—?

He relieved her mind by saying, "It doesn't matter. It will be all over Waynesboro by night. Ariana's run away from home."

Both his hearers exclaimed. Christina said, "With somebody? She has eloped?"

"I don't think so. I don't know. But who would she elope with? She didn't care a straw about boys. Did you know Ariana, sir?"

Dr. Blair nodded and scrawled a few words on his pad. "Once. Little girl. Mischief."

Matt, even in his trouble, was able to smile. "She was a tomboy once. But growing up, something took all the heart out of her. She was always antagonistic."

Dr. Blair nodded; he need write no answer to that. He did write: "How old? Could this be a prank?"

"No, sir. She's eighteen now."

The old man stared at him unbelievingly. So short a time ago! How few years it took for a child to grow up. He saw again in his memory the skinny frightened little girl, his plug hat in a puddle of water, Johnny Gordon coming over the fence. "Of age, then," he wrote on his tablet.

Matt nodded miserably. "She couldn't be forced back, and anyway Papa says she may not come back: his door is closed to her forever." He saw the grim look on Dr. Blair's face. "That is what his God has told him he must do: he spent all day Saturday in his study praying, 'wrestling in prayer,' he said. When he came out he told us that we must forget Ariana, and quoted Leviticus: 'And the daughter of any priest, if she profane herself by playing the whore she profaneth her father: she shall be burnt by fire.'"

Dr. Blair inhaled sharply, strangled over his breath, and began coughing. Christina snatched a bottle of medicine from the table beside him and poured a tablespoonful.

"I'm sorry, sir. I promised not to upset you. But she *wasn't*—she *didn't*—how could she? She was home all the time, helping with the work: washing and ironing and cooking. When she wasn't at school or at the Ballards'."

"But," Christina hesitated, "this judgment of your father's—is it just because she ran away, or did she do something before?"

"I don't know. There must have been something, but what Mamma won't say: she just clamps her lips tight shut. Papa says not to discuss it. The children don't know. Ariana went to bed early that night, Ruie says. You know she had a room of her own after I came to the Seminary to live. And Ruie came upstairs—we all have to do our lessons downstairs in the study, on account of no lamps upstairs. When Ruie went up, Mamma was going into Ariana's room with a lamp, and sounded awful, Ruie said, and began scolding."

"Perhaps," Christina offered, "she was reading some forbidden book in bed."

"She hasn't a lamp to read by. Didn't I say we had to use the study lamp? Anyway, in the morning she was gone. I guess Papa and Mamma thought she had gone out to walk—she did sometimes. Anyway it was that night, Friday night, that they knew she had really gone. And Saturday Papa spent praying and writing his sermon. And now Ariana has been gone three days and—*where is she?* I'd like to know she's safe, even if we couldn't bring her home. Ariana and I are the only ones who remember our own mother, and she was so different."

"That is why she was antagonistic to her stepmother?"

"She and Papa both thought Ariana was flighty, worldly. They were always after her—and all those music lessons: I think they resented them."

Dr. Blair wrote a question for Christina: "Could she have gone to the Ballards'?"

Christina shook her head. "They might have taken her in if she was very unhappy, but they would have lost no time in informing her father. Papa, how can anyone know what she picked up in the public schools? Or what associations she formed? I am more than ever determined: my children shall be taught at home."

Her father wrote in capitals on his pad, "JUDGE NOT."

Matthew broke into speech again, almost incoherent, having come to the heart of his trouble. "Judge me, not Ariana. I should have looked out for her: stayed at home this year, even if I was studying at the Seminary. But—" and like any youth he launched into self-justification, however much his conscience hurt. "It is so crowded in that house—so hard to work, all of us in the study—and I earned the money last summer—and Ariana said 'Get out, now you can,' and I thought she wanted my room all for herself. There's only four bedrooms, you see, for seven of us, and she's always been in with Ruhamah. Now all I can think is 'Take heed lest by any means this liberty of yours become a stumbling block to them that are weak.'" The boy dropped his head into his hands.

Dr. Blair looked at him compassionately. He took up his pencil, wrote for several minutes, nudged Matt with the corner of the pad and indicated that he was to read: "Do not blame yourself. What happened was bound to happen. Remember Paul also wrote that we are 'predestined according to the purpose of Him who worketh all things after the counsel of His own will'"; then, below two heavy black lines: "What do you think I could do?"

"I'm not asking you to appeal to Papa. He wouldn't listen. But if I knew where to look for her, just to make sure she is all right. She has always dreamed of going on the stage, but how?"

Christina exclaimed. Dr. Blair shook his head, and wrote: "Money?"

"Has she any, you mean? I don't think so. I don't even know how she could get away."

Dr. Blair tapped his pad with his pencil, thoughtfully; then he wrote: "I can do nothing on the Sabbath. Tomorrow I will consult friends who know more of the world. They may give us advice on how to trace her. Say nothing about this to anyone until you hear from me."

Matthew said, "Yes, sir," and "Thank you for listening to me," and went out with Christina.

But he had no opportunity before the next morning to tell the younger children to "Say nothing," and they were not deft at evading questions. Mark, indeed, answered flatly when Amanda stopped him after class to ask him if Ariana was ill.

"No. She's run away."

"*Run away!* But Mark—why? Where?"

"Don't know where. Don't know why, either. Not really. Except she got an awful lambasting from Mamma the other night. That was Thursday. In the morning she was gone. That was Friday, and we didn't know she'd really gone till that night. She didn't come home, and Papa looked in the hall closet for his valise. It wasn't there."

Amanda caught her breath. "But that's three days ago. She could be anywhere, now. Well, don't talk about it, Mark. People are bound to make it out worse than it is: she probably told someone where she was going."

When she had let the boy go, Amanda found herself trembling in an absurd fashion; she leaned against the door frame momentarily, thinking, "Why should this affect me so? What is Ariana McCune to me? One weak student the fewer." But she knew why she trembled: Mr. McCune's sermon, his Scripture reading "For even the women—" and, less sickening but more to be dreaded, the certainty that Eliza and Thomasina would hold her to blame: had Ariana only passed that year of Latin, and so been graduated with her class—perhaps she, Amanda Reid, *was* responsible. She would have to go to the Ballards' at once, after school: they might know where or to whom or with whom Ariana had fled.

But when, standing on the Travers threshold, at the foot of the stairs the music pupils used, she said bluntly to Thomasina, answering the door, "Do you know where Ariana McCune's run off to?" she saw by Thomasina's bewildered face that she had not heard the news.

"Come in, Amanda. Come upstairs. No. Ariana usually runs to us if she is unhappy. She missed her music lesson Friday. We thought she was sick. What has happened?"

Thomasina led her upstairs to the Travers sitting room; not until she was there, safely in a chair, did Amanda come out with, "She's run away. Clear away from Waynesboro, last Friday. I thought you might know—"

"*Ariana?* But why? She knew that we planned a course at the conservatory for her."

Amanda had no intention of saying more than she must. "I think her stepmother scolded her once too often. At any rate, Mark said she was scolded Thursday evening, and on Friday morning she was gone."

"Without a word!" Thomasina's eyes filled. "And after all we have tried to do! Run off with some boy, I suppose. Samuel always feared that she lacked steadiness of purpose."

"That is all you—listen, Thomasina: the point is Ariana's safety. You know no one she could go to out of town?"

"She had no relatives. We were all she had, she always said. She must after all have kept secrets from us."

"Any child keeps secrets from any adult. Surely you remember that from your own childhood. You think it isn't for us to bother, then, trying to find her?"

"She's eighteen, and if she's eloped, what can we do? I thought she cared more for us—all of us—than to go without a word."

"She went suddenly, on an impulse, I suppose: there would be no time for a word. You may hear from her: if you do, let me know. I am concerned about what may happen to her, if you are not. Tell Eliza; she may have some idea."

Amanda went home, astonished at Thomasina's reaction, relieved that the blame for Ariana's defection had not been laid on her shoulders, but still not quite easy in her conscience.

At about the same time that Amanda entered her own front door, Anne Gordon, spending her afternoon in charge of the library, watched Ruhamah McCune moving listlessly from one bookcase to another with an armful of books to be shelved. Ruhamah had been engaged by the Library Board of Trustees to work there afternoons after school; there was more to do now than shelving returned books and otherwise tidying up. The high school girls first hired had done little but giggle and "carry on." Ruhamah had a conscience; she worked. The other girls were dismissed and she was given a steady job.

Ordinarily she was a good worker. Perhaps whatever illness had kept Ariana out of school was something catching. At a moment when the big room was free of borrowers and readers, Anne had an opportunity to question her: she asked, "Don't you feel well, child? Or is something the matter? You look so—"

"Oh, yes, ma'am. I feel all right." Ruhamah turned troubled eyes on her interrogator.

"I thought you might have caught whatever illness kept Ariana from school last week." Ruhamah's stricken look alerted her. "Or wasn't she sick? Was she just playing hookey?"

As Mark had done with Amanda, Ruhamah blurted out, "Ariana's run away." And to Anne's dismay, she burst into tears.

"Look here, my dear. If it will make you feel better, you must tell me about it. Take this." Anne rummaged in the desk drawer for the clean handkerchief she knew was there, handed it to the child, then looked over her shoulder at the clock on the back wall. "Better wait though till five, then we can lock the door, and no one can interrupt us."

Ruhamah, still sniffling, returned to her shelving while Anne sorted cards, filed them, and cleared the desk. At five she rose, locked the door, and went to one of the tables, motioning to Ruhamah to join her: sitting around the corner from her at the table would be less intimidating than facing her across the high desk.

"Now, if Ariana is in trouble—if there is anything I can do to help, tell me. You know Ariana has been a friend of Johnny's for years, and I used to see quite a lot of her."

"Papa said not to discuss it. But someone ought to know who doesn't just think it is God's will."

Before Anne had time to consider whether she was doing right in encouraging Mr. McCune's daughter to disobey him, the story came pouring out. Ruhamah had evidently in the moments of waiting got it in some kind of order in her mind.

"It all started Thursday night. Ariana went to bed early. I don't know why, it was hardly dark—you know she has Matt's room all to herself, now he's in the Seminary. I did my lessons in the study. When I was starting up to bed, I saw Mamma go in Ariana's room. She had a lamp in her hand and held it up high to see, and she said 'Ariana!' in an awful voice, and went on in and shut the door. I went up to my room. I didn't want to hear, but I couldn't help, some of it." Ruhamah began to shiver. She put her elbows on the table and bent her head to rest it on her clenched fists. "What could Ariana do that was so wicked all alone in the dark? I don't understand."

Anne began to wish she had never started her questioning.

"I heard," Ruhamah continued, on a gasping breath, "something about 'vile' and 'nasty,' and Ariana yelled at her 'You're the nasty one,' then Mamma said 'Don't you know you're taking the sure road not only to damnation but to madness?'" Sobs shook the thin bent shoulders again. "I heard all that and I know that's what she said. Do you think Ariana's going crazy?"

"No." Anne closed her eyes for a moment, crossed her arms at her waist as if she had a pain there. "The poor child," she thought, "no mother to tell her—without words like 'vile' and 'nasty'—but just 'Keep your nightdress down around your feet, like a lady.'" "No," she said again, fighting down the nausea, "I think Mrs. McCune was so angry she didn't know what she was saying. Couldn't Ariana have been reading something she wasn't permitted to read?"

Ruhamah shook her head. "We don't have any lamps in our rooms. Only candles to go to bed by. And her room was dark until Mamma went in."

"Maybe you just thought so. Maybe Ariana knows Johnny's trick: making a tent of the bedclothes over a chair and getting under it with a book and candle. If it was that, I don't wonder your mother was angry: it is a terribly dangerous thing to do. Johnny's father paddled him once when he was little."

Ruhamah looked doubtful. "I don't think Papa would have preached the way he did—"

Anne, who had heard no reports of Mr. McCune's sermon, said, "Maybe he was preaching about children running away. And that is the important thing, isn't it? You want her found and brought back."

"Papa says 'No'—we are to forget her. He thinks she has eloped. Maybe he hopes she will be so unhappy she will beg to come back, like the Prodigal Son. But I know that she hasn't eloped. Who would there be, that she knew? I don't want her to be unhappy. And I'm scared."

"Do you know where she might go?"

Ruhamah shook her head. "Papa thinks she couldn't go far. I heard him say that to Mamma: that she hadn't any money. I knew better. She left me a note; I found it Friday morning on my pillow. I didn't tell anyone, so no one else knew she'd gone till that night. I wanted her to have a head start. I suppose I was very wicked, and I don't care. But suppose something awful has happened to her?"

"I don't suppose anything of the kind. Lots of young women of eighteen are making their way in the world and are perfectly capable of looking out for themselves." And if she thought it unlikely that Ariana would be one of them, she was not going to say so. "What about the money? You were going to tell me—"

Ruhamah unbuttoned a section of her tight high-bosomed frock and pulled out a crumpled bit of paper. "The note—"

Anne took it. "Dear Ruie" (it was such a scrawl that it might well have been written in the dark). "I have to get away. I'm sorry I couldn't wait to say good-bye. I'm borrowing your money. I owe you 28 dollars and 50 cents. I'll send it to you as soon as I can. I hate to do this to you, but it won't be for long. Good-bye—Your loving sister Ariana McCune."

Anne handed the paper back. "But what a shame! All you've saved."

"The money, you mean? Oh, no. She knew I would have let her have it if she could have asked. Ariana never could earn money or save it, here. But she could get almost anywhere on twenty-eight fifty, couldn't she?"

"She could get pretty far." But she couldn't live on it for long. "She could be traced, I should think."

"She always wanted to go on the stage."

"That mightn't be so easy to do, right off. Look, Ruhamah, don't say anything more to anyone, especially about the scolding—just let people think she has eloped if they must think anything. I'll tell my husband that she's run away and see if he has any ideas about how to find her. Wasn't there anyone outside Waynesboro she might go to?"

Ruhamah hesitated. "She used to talk to me—that was when we still slept together—about how she and Ben Mercer were going to run away together. But that was before he ran away by himself. He didn't wait for her."

"Could they have been writing to each other all this time?"

Ruhamah shook her head. "Papa goes for the mail himself. Unless Ben sent letters for her to someone else."

"You don't know who his friends were?"

"I didn't even know him by sight."

"Well, run along home and say nothing, and try not to worry. I'll see what I can find out."

Ruhamah looked her gratitude, nodded her head, and went for her cloak and hat. Anne waited for her to go before she locked the door and took the key down the hall to leave in the Gardiner and Merrill office. On the way home she tried to sort out her thoughts and subdue her grief at the sure knowledge that here was a young life ruined. She must decide just how much she could tell John to persuade him to take some action: he was sure to consider it none of his business. But at home she found only the children in the living room.

Johnny looked up from the paper he was reading. "Pop had to go into the country on a confinement case. He said not to wait dinner, he'd probably be out there most of the night."

So all her rehearsed speeches would have to wait. As it turned out, wait for another twenty-four hours. At whatever time John got home, he went to bed downstairs rather than disturb her, and neither the breakfast nor the luncheon table, with the children there and Louline coming and going, offered any opportunity for confidences. But when he came in that afternoon after making his house calls, the children were out, busy about their own affairs, and the two parents had the sitting room to themselves. Together they asked each other, "Have you heard—Ariana?"

"Ruhamah told me yesterday at the library. But how did you—?"

"First, yesterday morning, Dr. Blair, when I stopped in there. Seems Matt McCune had appealed to him, and he appealed to me. I didn't like to say anything before the children, at least till I knew a little more. Then this afternoon Ludwig stopped in."

"Ludwig? How did he get involved in this?"

"Eliza Ballard."

"Oh, Eliza. I'd forgotten. Of course. It still seems funny, for her to be working for Ludwig."

"She's a very competent woman, according to him. And he doesn't like for her to be upset."

Eliza had told him the story when she was in that Tuesday morning. He had seen at once that she was ill, or that something had happened: she was white-faced and hollow-eyed, and her hands shook as she laid the mail on his desk.

"What is it, Eliza? Are you ill? Or your mother?"

"No. We are in our usual health. Here is that letter you have been looking for from the hemp dealer."

"Just put it down. You look like you'd been dragged through a knothole. Can't I help?"

She looked at him consideringly, her expression bleak.

"I don't see how. Ariana McCune's run away from home."

"Ariana? Oh, yes, your little protégée—yours and your sister's and Travers's. Where did she run to? With somebody? She must be as old as Elsa, about. Did she elope?"

Eliza shook her head. "Not with anyone in Waynesboro. There wasn't anyone. No: she had one scolding too many and went off alone in the middle of the night without any money. Why couldn't she have come to us?"

"Because you would have been duty-bound to send her home. Do you want her brought back?"

Eliza shook her head. "No one wants her back—but me. Her brother told Amanda Reid their father said she was never to darken his door again. Sounds like a melodrama, doesn't it?"

(And Ludwig, reporting to John, had said, "Can you imagine that hard-hearted, sanctimonious old bastard? One of my children could always come *home* no matter what he had done!")

"And," Eliza had continued, "Thomasina feels betrayed. She can't go beyond what *she* feels. She had made plans, she and Samuel. They were going to make a concert pianist out of Ariana. It wouldn't occur to them that she just might not care for their plans. You know," she said thoughtfully, "I don't believe they ever really looked at Ariana to see what she was like. Thomasina, anyway. Ariana was such a delightful child: it was easy, I suppose, to make her over, in your mind, into what you would have liked your child to be. Now Thomasina sees the difference between the real Ariana and her imagined Ariana. She expected gratitude—from a young, thoughtless, unhappy girl. Thomasina is a fool."

"And your mother?"

"Oh, Mamma! When she isn't in too much pain to think at all, she's thinking of woman suffrage and the Woman's Christian Temperance Union. She's got past thinking of any personal sorrows. Heaven is so near. Haven't you noticed old people are like that—just waiting, not wanting to be disturbed by any emotion?"

Ludwig nodded, thinking of his father-in-law, who was also sitting out his days in his study, waiting, his only link with the world his interest in the day's financial news and how the bank would be affected. He said, "How about you?"

"I am not in the habit of seeing people as better than they are," Eliza said drily. "It is the real Ariana I was fond of. Am fond of. I didn't expect much of her. I know better than to expect people to do what I want them to do, out of gratitude. But I'm fond of the silly child, and I'd like to know she's all right."

"It shouldn't be hard to find out. Where would she be likely to go?"

"She dreamed of being an actress. Even Samuel never thought she loved her music as she should have. But if you're eighteen, alone, know no one and have no money, how do you go about getting on the stage?"

"Sounds hopeless, doesn't it?" Ludwig groaned inwardly: Heaven knew what the girl might get into. "Isn't there some relative? Someone she might go to?"

"No relative that she knew of." Then Eliza drew a long breath. "There was a boy, the Mercer boy. Amanda said all they had in common was that they were both rebels. But I saw her with him once, and the way she looked at him. But he ran off to the circus three or four years ago."

"And in spite of all common sense, you think she may have joined him?"

Eliza nodded. "It could have been a complete surprise to him. On the other hand, they might have been corresponding. Or I could be completely wrong. She could be alone somewhere: it's that that worries me. Anything could happen to her."

And so Ludwig repeated Eliza's story to John, who said, "It is an appalling thought, you know. An innocent girl—too innocent—alone in some city, tackling theatrical agents. I promised to try to trace her. Do you think we should go to Doug Gardiner? I don't believe Eliza would like that."

"Let's keep the law out of it for a while, anyway."

When John had his chance to talk to Anne, he said, "So you see, we're both involved, Ludwig and I. But it ought not be be too hard to trace her: there's only the railroad out of town. Eliza said something to Ludwig about the Mercer boy and Ariana, and we remembered after we had scratched our heads a bit, the summer when the circus was here and the Mercer boy ran off with it: our family and Ludwig's went together, remember? It was Robinson's Circus, and Robinson's winter headquarters are in Cincinnati. I suppose they would be in winter quarters by now. There's a four-thirty-in-the-morning train to Cincinnati. It leaves New York some time the day before and arrives in Cincinnati early enough for businessmen to do a day's work. I telephoned the depot: the conductor is back in New York today. But Tim O'Reilly is the engineer: he takes over the train here for the run to Cincinnati and makes the return trip this far. He should be home tonight. I'll send Johnny with a note, asking him to come to the office. He just might have seen her. There wouldn't be many people on the platform that early. If he didn't see her, he can ask the conductor."

A somewhat bewildered Tim O'Reilly, dressed in his best blue serge, derby hat cocked over one eye, turned up at the doctor's office that evening: a Tim O'Reilly grown burly with the years, so that his vest buttons looked ready to pop, red-faced from the sun and wind endured as he peered from his engine-cab window day after day.

He nodded to Ludwig, also there, and turned to John. "You said I could do you a favor, Doctor. You know you've only got to ask."

"I know, Tim. How are you? I don't see much of you these days."

"We're the fine and healthy lot, praise be to the saints."

John introduced him to Ludwig: the two men shook hands. Ludwig said, "We know each other well enough to wave when I'm taking his train. And his oldest boy is working in the mill."

"Only till he's the age for the railroad."

"That's understood." Ludwig twinkled. "A railroader's family sticks with the railroad."

"What we wanted to ask you, Tim: did a young girl get on your train last Friday morning, all alone? I know that's several days ago, but—"

"'Dade an' she did, Doctor. I seen her, all wrapped up in a shawl, with a valise. I wouldn't forget because it ain't a likely sight: you could tell she was young, spite of the shawl, and it ain't every day of the week we pick up someone like that at that hour of the morning. Sure an' it wouldn't be one of yours, runnin' away?"

"Not one of ours, no. The Reverend Mr. McCune's oldest. We promised we'd try to find her. She was alone? Did anyone meet her?"

"Alone, in the depot here. I never looked to see in the Cincinnati depot: I just turned the engine over to the yard engineer and went in the depot for a cup o' tay. Do you know who would be after meetin' her?"

They explained the possible connection with the Mercer boy. Ludwig and John looked at each other. John said: "Someone should hunt him up and ask. I can't get away just now: there are patients I can't leave."

"I know." Both men thought of Kitty Edwards, of Dr. Blair. "It's up to me, I reckon."

"Look, sir: them circus folk are clannish and they ain't used to the likes of you. They might just button their lips. Better let me. I have time to kill in Cincinnati, anyway, between trains. You'll be wantin' to know if she's with this boy name o' Mercer, an' her plans if any?"

"That's it, Tim. If you find her, tell her I'll repay the money she borrowed from her sister: no use getting that child in trouble. Her father would see any mail that came—probably open it. Ariana can repay me when she's able. Are you sure you don't mind giving up your time to this?"

"'Tain't nothin', Doctor, to what I'd do for you if you asked."

Tim reported back the next morning at John's office. "I seen him—the boy. 'Twasn't no job findin' the circus' winter quarters. He was there, helpin' feed the animals. He was right sassy at first: asked what business I'd be havin', askin' questions. I thought for a minute he was goin' to let out with a 'Hey, Rube!' an' there'd be trouble, but I said no one was goin' to drag her home case he did know—her friends just wanted to be sure she was safe. So he said, 'She's safe enough. I took her over the river an' married her.'"

"So it *was* an elopement."

Tim grinned. "Maybe, after a manner o' speakin'. I think he was surprised as you, when she turned up. He said it was the only way he could keep her with him an' tell the roughnecks 'hands off.' 'She's a baby,' he said, 'she don't know nothin'. No, no one need worry about her: she won't let me even so much as touch her.' 'Give her time,' says I, 'she'll get over that.' But I wanted to know if he could keep her in clothes an' victuals, an' he said again it wasn't no business o' mine, but he could an' all—an' anyway she was already workin', helpin' the wardrobe mistress, sewin' on next spring's costumes."

"Then she did learn something useful from her stepmother."

"She likes it, he says; it's different from any sewin' she ever done before. So I told him what you said about the twenty-eight dollars and fifty cents." Tim pulled out his wallet and extracted two ten dollar bills. "He said all she'd spent was for her ticket an' a couple o' meals before she found him. You're to take this for her sister, an' he'll send the eight-fifty when they next get paid."

"Proud, eh? Maybe they'll get along. The boy's grandparents were too strict with him—never let him forget—but at least they taught him right from wrong. Did he say anything about her going on the stage? She won't be content sewing forever."

"He said the sewin's just to give him time. 'There's circus people know stage people. We'll make connections all right. First thing Waynesboro knows she'll be back there, playin' in *Uncle Tom's Cabin*. We mean to show 'em', says he."

"Good God! I hope not—that would set the old man off."

John thanked Tim and sent him on his way. When he was alone again, he telephoned Ludwig: the two men agreed that all had been done that they could do. John would report to Matt McCune by way of Dr. Blair; to Ruhamah by way of Anne, turning over to her the twenty dollars; Ludwig could tell Eliza. That done, they could wash their hands of the affair.

The *Torchlight* carried an item the next evening that set to rest conjecture if not gossip: headed "Wedding in Kentucky," it said, "Miss Ariana McCune of this city and Mr. Ben Mercer, late of this city and now with the John Robinson Circus, have been united in marriage in Covington, Kentucky. The friends of Miss McCune, who rumor says have recently been troubled by her mysterious disappearance, will no doubt be pleased to hear of this romantic elopement, news of which has been reported to *The Torchlight* by unimpeachable sources." Mr. McCune cancelled his subscription.

The verdict of Ariana's one-time playmates was expressed for all by John Gordon: "Ariana married! Well, isn't she a juggins! She hasn't had any fun yet!" The Waynesboro High School seniors, who were taking melancholy pleasure in the thought that whatever they did together was for the last time, were crowding as much fun as possible into that fall and winter.

Amanda Reid felt, against all reason, somehow to blame for Ariana's fate, but she was at least relieved of the struggle to keep her up to the mark in Latin. Elizabeth Talmadge in a mild sort of way regretted the loss: with the optimism and ardor of a young teacher, she had convinced herself that she had had in her hands for instruction a young poet, or at least a young writer; now of course that opportunity was lost.

Christina Voorhees was shocked and stricken with a sense of guilt. She had scarcely known the child, but she had seen her in the ministerial pew on Sabbath mornings. Now it was being whispered in the congregation that Ariana had run away with the intention of going on the stage. What had put such an idea in her head, unless it was the knowledge that she, Christina Voorhees, had been play-acting for years, for the Club—and for the *public*, in *Color Guard?* She had, of course, given up such wickedness after her children were born. She could only be glad that she had renounced such sinful frivolity, too late in Ariana's case, but not—surely?—too late for her Blair and Janey. Then, after the first shock, she remembered how long ago Ariana had, as Jael, murdered Sisera, and now she assuaged her guilt by deciding that Ariana's fate, for some mysterious purpose, had been predestined.

Whatever Thomasina suffered from Ariana's defection, only she and her husband knew: she seemed as happy as was normal for her, although her asthma troubled her more than usual all that fall. Only Eliza set herself stubbornly against this wiping out of Ariana's name. For one thing, she felt herself justified of her most pessimistic fears for the child; for another, she could not be thrown off balance by the shattering of illusions. She had seen Ariana as she was, and had loved her. She wrote a note to Mrs. Ben Mercer, care of the John Robinson Circus: she penned no reproaches, expressed no disappointment, said merely that Ariana was not to forget that if she was ever in difficulty, or needed a home, she must feel free to turn to her; the latchstring would always be out. To this rather curt note she expected no reply, and received none. She buried deep in her mind the belief, if not the hope, that Ariana would some day need her. She mentioned her name no more after Ludwig reported what Tim O'Reilly had learned. She recovered her rather sour composure, and went about her business. John and Ludwig, who had for more than an hour or two given Ariana first place in their thoughts, returned to their personal preoccupations: with John that meant his patients, with Ludwig, business. Politics was in abeyance, insofar as that was ever true in Ohio; Foraker was proving to be an able administrator in spite of his more flamboyant qualities (the qualities that made him popular with the voters), and his term had another year to run. Nor was there a Senate seat at stake. But for Ludwig there was a dark cloud on the business horizon: there were rumors afloat that a cordage trust was being organized; such an assocation would endeavor to bring into their combination every cordage mill in the country or to force it out of business. Like Standard Oil: Ohio Republicans were still bitter over the almost open purchase by Standard Oil of a U.S. Senatorship for the old-time but not very-much-respected Democrat, Henry Payne. Ludwig was resolute in his determination to hang on to the business he had created, but he foresaw troubled times.

At the Club meeting on the sixth of October, Mrs. Deming read an intelligent paper on "Thomas Hardy's *Return of the Native*": she would have preferred, really, to deal critically with Howells' *Rise of Silas Lapham;* she did not believe that a middle-western novelist could really know Boston well enough to write about it. But since the Howells paper was scheduled for the spring, she had not asked Mrs. Maxwell to trade subjects with her: true, she had plenty on her mind now, but she could not be sure that she would not have even more in the spring.

What she had on her mind was Julia. Julia, with her ash-blonde hair, clear-cut features, and a certain grace, could do better than take for a husband someone who would be tied to a stuffy small town like Waynesboro. But what chance had she to meet the distinguished young man she should marry? Julia had always been a model of deportment and devoted to her parents, but she was stubborn in pursuit of what she wanted, and her father would always support her wishes. Her mother wished they could afford to send her East to a really fine school for this last year, instead of to the town high school. For it was apparently the custom for high school seniors to pair off and stay paired, and Julia, who was only sixteen, was seeing altogether too much of Johnny Gordon.

Mrs. Deming expressed something of her misgivings to the General and was pooh-poohed for her pains. "What's the matter with Johnny Gordon?" he wanted to know. He folded his paper and put it aside; they were alone in the sitting room that evening; Julia had gone out. "Going in for doctoring, isn't he?" He folded his hands across his well-developed paunch and gave her his full attention. He was always ready to listen to anything that had to do with Julia.

"So far as I know, there is nothing wrong with the boy. But I don't care for this pairing off while they are still in school. And all that business about Ariana McCune may give them ideas."

"Oh, nonsense, my dear Louisa! Julia's a child still. And as to 'pairing off,' seems to me they're always going off together in crowds to parties, picnics, or nutting. Johnny doesn't come alone and spend the evening in the parlor, does he?"

Mrs. Deming could not help laughing. "No. He comes in on a Saturday afternoon sometimes for a game of checkers. No, it's just that I should like Julia to see something of the world—have opportunities to meet distinguished young men with broader backgrounds: I don't want her to be satisfied to settle down here in this backwater, contented with a boy who isn't good enough for her."

"There's plenty of time; we'll see she gets her opportunities. I didn't realize you considered Waynesboro a 'backwater.'"

"It isn't for me, George," his wife said quickly. "I have been very happy here. But for Julia, I'd like wider horizons."

"Maybe she'd be as happy here as you've been," he said, grateful for her reassurance. Personally he hoped that Julia would marry a Waynesboro boy and live in the town, where he could see her every day.

"At any rate," Mrs. Deming had gone on, "the season for running wild in the woods is about over." The last nutting expedition had made her uneasy. She could not be as warmly grateful for the walnuts as she should have been: they had been dried on the Gordon back porch roof and gallantly hulled by Johnny, lest Julia stain her hands; Julia's mother saw that Johnny imagined Julia a being altogether superior; he wouldn't have dreamed of hulling any other girl's walnuts.

"I should have worried even more," Mrs. Deming had continued, "if she weren't always so determined to take the little Gordon girl with them."

"Why? It does seem odd, somehow."

"Oh, it's natural enough." Mrs. Deming sometimes understood her daughter very well. "She secures Johnny's devotion by her tenderness for his delicate little sister, and at the same time keeps him at arm's length."

"Then what is there to worry about?" The General's interest and curiosity had been aroused. "Shouldn't we have them here some evening? All the crowd, I mean? A party?" But he saw at once by her horrified face that it had not been a happy suggestion.

"As you know, George, I enjoy entertaining, when it can be done properly: the ladies of the Club, the Ladies' Aid Society, the Missionary Society. But you can have no idea how disruptive a high school party can be: the noise, the chasing all over the house—and the *food.* It is all very well for Mrs. Ludwig Rausch, who has servants at her beck and call. As for Anne Gordon, she doesn't seem to mind having her house wrecked. That is where tonight's party is: a taffy pull, of all things!"

"You make it sound as if Julia's classmates are very ill-bred."

"I don't mean to. I think the ill-bred children have dropped out of school before this. It's just that they're young and high-spirited, and I don't want them to be high-spirited pulling taffy in my house."

Anne Gordon was a far less scrupulous housekeeper than Mrs. Deming;

nevertheless, she had felt some reluctance to permit Johnny to have the party he had begged for: a previous taffy pull had left candy all over the kitchen, from stove to table to walls to doorknobs, and had induced in Martha a "mis'ry" in her back that had made her grumpy all week. But this was the last year at home for Johnny and his friends; they were entitled to their fun. She gave her consent on condition that she cook the candy, thus making sure that it would be pullable and not remain a semi-liquid mass, and that they stay in the kitchen until they had finished pulling it. She even gave Binny permission to stay up for a while, although she did warn her, "First thing you know, they'll be calling you 'Little Me-Too' again." Binny did not care what they called her, so long as she could anticipate Julia's smile, her light touch on her hair or on her shoulder now and then as she passed by.

The Gordon kitchen was full of boys and girls—and noises—while Anne boiled the taffy in a big kettle on the coal range. She watched them without seeming to as she stirred the candy. Some familiar faces were missing: Sophie Klein, Charlotte Bonner, Rudy Lichtenstein, all graduates of the previous June, had gone off to college. Most of the girls were pretty only because they were young, but Julia and Elsa stood out: delicate-boned Julia, with her silvery hair, and the more robust Elsa, her once fair hair beginning to darken, but holding still a rich deep gold where the light struck it. Elsa—Anne sighed: Elsa was flirting outrageously with Bill Thirkield, who obviously was taking it as a lighthearted game, and with Gilbert Evans, who clearly was not. But Elsa's eyes wandered too often from her victims to Johnny. And Johnny—and Binny, too, for that matter—had eyes only for Julia. How perverse the young could be!

When the candy was ready for pulling, Anne turned it over to them, hoping that she would not find it on the ceiling in the morning, and went into the sitting room to look for John: it was after nine, and his office hours should be over.

She found him in her low rocker by the fire, leaning back, his feet on the fender, his hands folded at his waist, the unfolded newspaper over his face. But he was not asleep: as she came in, he removed the paper, took his feet from the fender, and pushed himself up in the chair.

"Noisy, ain't they?"

"Well, yes. But they're having fun. Did you have a hard day?" She thought he was looking very tired, drained of vitality.

"I did, rather. Didn't have a chance to tell you at dinnertime, there was such a buzz over this party. I had to tap Kitty again today. I don't believe it will be much longer."

After a moment's silence Anne said, "Do you think she realizes? Was she conscious?"

"More or less. Yes, she realizes. Gave me her Marcus Aurelius today that had been her father's. Said something about my needing it more than Sheldon. I wonder why?"

"Because you're such a heathen." Anne was a little tart. "Sheldon is a good Christian; his faith—"

"Will sustain him? I hope so: he's taking it hard—blames himself—can't bear to look at the baby."

Then, cutting through the noises of laughter from the kitchen came the sound of the telephone bell. John rose, said, "Sometimes I think that is the greatest invention of the century, sometimes I think it is a curse."

After a moment he returned to the sitting room door, hat and bag in hand, coat over his arm.

"Sheldon. Kitty has gone into convulsions. Uremic poisoning. I'll saddle the mare and ride out. Quicker than hitching up."

"John, I'd like to be there. With Sheldon. He will need someone—a woman—especially after. He knows how I feel about Kitty."

"I am sure he will, in spite of his faith. But you can't leave these young people. Perhaps when they are gone." He crossed the sitting room and went out the side porch door on his way to the stable, not running but moving with a controlled swiftness that showed how his vitality had come surging back.

Anne was of no mind to await the end of Johnny's party: she had named midnight as the hour when it must end, and she had no desire to stop their fun early, whatever she might be feeling. She went to the telephone in the hall, took down the receiver, cranked the handle vigorously, and gave the operator the Rausch number. The girl was quick, Anne thought: she had been listening to John's call, and knew. And Ludwig was almost as quick in answering his ring.

"Ludwig, is Sally there? Is she doing anything special? Could she come down here?"

"What is it, Anne? Something happen at your party? Can I help?"

"The party? Oh, no. But I need a chaperone in a hurry. Kitty—John's gone to her—she's in convulsions; he thinks it's the end. I'd like to be there to help—to make it as easy for Sheldon as possible."

"Catch your breath, Anne. I'll call Sally, and while you're explaining to her, I'll go rouse Reuben to help me hitch the buggy. Of course she'll come."

"Wouldn't it be quicker for her to walk?"

"To your house, yes. But how do you propose to get out to the Edwardses'?"

While she waited for Sally to come to the phone, Anne applauded Ludwig's quick grasp of a situation and the speed with which he could act. Like John, a man for a crisis. When she had explained her need more coherently to Sally and secured a ready acquiescence, she went through the back hall to the kitchen door; she paused before entering. How happy they sounded! Only the young—but "happy" was not the word. One could be happy at any age. "Lighthearted"—only the young could be so lighthearted. She called Johnny into the dining room.

"As soon as your Aunt Sally comes to take over as chaperone here, I am going out. Kitty Edwards. But don't let it spoil your fun. Supper is all set out for you on the table. I meant to make Welsh rarebit, but I guess there's enough without it, sandwiches and so on."

She collected hat and cloak and was ready when the Rausches stopped at the hitching post; she was out the door, down the path, and out the gate by the time Sally had alighted from the buggy.

"I'm sorry to drag you out, but I'm grateful. I couldn't leave them. Don't let them misbehave, send them home at twelve, and don't wait for me. My children are grown enough to be left, thank goodness. The front door's unlocked. Don't lock it—I don't have my key, and I may not come in with John."

She whisked herself into the buggy. Ludwig said again, "Catch your breath, Anne," as he turned the buggy into Linden Street.

"Little Kitty Edwards," he said sadly. "She's too young to die. She'll be missed."

"We 'shall not look upon her like again.' That's a quotation from something—what?" Anne said numbly. "I should know—Kitty was one of the world's rarest: generous and loving; her friends, her babies, her husband, her God. And you know, I don't believe she ever got over feeling that she wasn't quite worthy of Sheldon."

"He will take this hard, even though he must have known it was coming."

"That's why I want to be there. His mother—well, you know his mother—and anyway, she is keeping the little boys."

At the Edwards hitching post, they found not only John's saddled mare but another horse and carriage. Anne peered at it. "Doug Gardiner's. That's a relief: Sheldon isn't alone, then."

Ludwig climbed down and helped her to alight.

"Thanks, Ludwig. And don't worry about my getting home; if we're not here all night, Doug will take me."

She hesitated at the front door, turned the knob, and slipped in quietly and stood for a minute when she had shut it, listening. The closed door to the parlor bedroom, where Kitty had been ill so often and now so long, did not quite block the sounds from within: sounds as of a struggle, a threshing about, and John's quiet voice.

A glance through the open door on the left showed her an empty drawing room; she tiptoed down the hall to the sitting room, out of range of the heartbreaking sounds. There she found not only Doug Gardiner but his wife and old Mr. Edwards. Doug rose when she came in and spoke to her in a subdued voice, but the old man did not even look up: he was staring into the fireplace, and the tears on his cheeks shone in the light from the flames.

"I'm glad you're here, Doug. How did you know?"

"Sheldon telephoned me. But he hasn't been outside that door since we came."

"He will need you when it's over."

The sound of voices roused Mr. Edwards; he turned to look over his shoulder at them. "So good of you to come," he murmured. "She had so many friends, our little Kitty." He groped for a handkerchief, and wiped his face. "And so much to live for. I feel like Job, crying out to my God as to an adversary. 'For the arrows of the Almighty are within me, the poison whereof drinketh up my spirit: the terrors of God do set themselves in array against me.' I pray, and my prayer is not answered: she is not spared, and my useless life—"

Anne went to stand beside him; she said, her low voice clear and sweet: "Job said, 'Man that is born of a woman is of few days, and full of trouble. He cometh forth like a flower and is cut down—' but he said too, 'The Lord gave, and the Lord hath taken away; blessed be the name of the Lord.' And the Psalmist, he said, 'As for man, his days are as grass; as a flower of the field so he flourisheth. For the wind passeth over it and it is gone; and the place thereof shall know it no more.' Those are the saddest words in the world, I think. But you know how it goes on: 'But the mercy of the Lord is from everlasting to everlasting upon them that fear him, and his righteousness unto children's children;' and 'Precious in the sight of the Lord is the death of his saints.'"

Anne's heart was wrung as she looked down at the old man. The last time she had seen Mr. Edwards in the store, as always he had been brisk, alert, dapper. Now he was broken. But he smiled at her as best he could, and sighed like a child who has been long weeping. "She had a merry heart," he said, and then, after a moment, "She will add to the joy of the saints."

He turned back to contemplation of the fire, and Anne moved over to the Gardiners, taking a light rocking chair and pulling it close to the sofa where they sat.

"It was good of you to come with Doug," she said to Barbara. Barbara was pregnant again, and would bear her fourth child before Christmas.

"Kitty has been very good to me from the beginning. She never seemed to think it odd that Doug wanted to marry me."

"My dear—"

"I don't mean that Doug's friends haven't all been kind to me. They have—you have—but I am sure everyone but Kitty was startled by his choice. And there was once, before we were married, when everyone's eyebrows might have gone up if she had not come to the rescue of my reputation." She told Anne about the afternoon when Kitty had joined her in the snowball fight with the children. "So many years ago, but it seems like yesterday."

Anne smiled at her. "It seems impossible to me, too. Those children, Johnny, Elsa, are as old now as you were then." But the years had counted for Barbara, she thought; she was pretty as ever, but the vulnerable look of the very young was gone: she was indeed a "matron." Now the heart-shaped face was fuller, she was plumper than she had been, heavy with the unborn child, and her manner was more confident.

None of the four in the room felt any necessity to make further conversation; they sat and waited. At the sound of the bedroom door being opened, they all stiffened. Anne, who could see from her chair into the hall, said, "It's John," and rose and went to meet him.

He had his handkerchief in his hand, and he was wiping his forehead and sweaty cheekbones. "She has slipped into a coma. The worst is over. But there's no knowing how long; are you sure you want to stay? You may be up all night."

"When it is over, there will be things to do that Sheldon would rather have me do, and Barbara, than old Mrs. Stroud. Things you don't want strangers to do."

John could have protested that Mrs. Stroud, the practical nurse who was the best that Waynesboro offered—a widowed farm woman, kind, obedient, but trained only by experience—had been taking care of Kitty too long to be a stranger, but he said nothing. He knew what Anne meant: Sheldon would prefer having Kitty made ready for the undertaker by truly loving hands. He went back into the bedroom; Anne returned to the other watchers.

"There has been a change?" Barbara whispered.

"Yes. She's gone into a coma."

"I think I'll go make sure there's a fire in the range and hot water in the reservoir."

"Hot water?" Doug was bewildered.

"She will have to be bathed."

"You're too young for such an ordeal," Anne protested. "I can do it."

"We'll both do it." Barbara smiled briefly. "Don't forget I was raised among the Irish."

After another long, long wait, there came to strained ears the sound of the bedroom doorknob turning, the click of the latch. Mr. Edwards, who had seemed to be in a daze, struggled to his feet and was in the hall in time to meet Sheldon, hold out his arms to his son. Wordlessly the two embraced, Sheldon's head for a moment on the old man's shoulder. Behind them John too came into the hall and closed the bedroom door; he nodded to the women, his hand still on the doorknob. Anne, with Barbara at her heels, went by way of the other sitting room door into the back hall, and thence to the bedroom. Mrs. Stroud was pulling the bedclothes back, to sling them over the foot of the bed.

"We'll do that, if you will bring us hot water, cloths, and towels. And aprons and clean sheets." Anne was looking at the tumbled bed rather than at Kitty's still face, after one glance had told her the eyes were closed: John would have done that, his last gesture.

"Yes, of course," Mrs. Stroud said, "and a napkin to tie around her face just until—you will find a clean nightdress in the second drawer. It will be a comfort to her poor husband to know that her friends did the last thing for her that could be done on this earth."

When the three of them had finished their ministrations and Kitty lay straight and still, the sheet drawn up over her face, Anne and Barbara returned to the sitting room. Sheldon was in a chair close to the fire, shivering; Mr. Edwards and Doug were where they had been; and John was standing with an elbow on the mantelpiece, watching Sheldon. While Barbara hesitated in the doorway and then went to sit again by her husband, Anne crossed the room to Sheldon and put her hand on his shoulder. He lifted his head to look at her, his face ravaged.

"She is—? You have—? Anne, as long as I live I shall never forget what you have done, you and Barbara. I can go back to her?"

"Yes. Sheldon, Kitty was too young to die, I know. But don't grieve too much: she had everything she wanted of life. What do years matter, if they are all empty? Hers were so full: she had you and the boys, and love and happiness enough for a long lifetime."

"And I should rejoice that her suffering is ended? When it was I—" Sheldon spoke bitterly.

"I didn't say that. Only that you must weigh in the balance against your grief the great happiness she found in your life together. But yes, I think you should rejoice that her suffering is ended. It doesn't mean that she has ended, she has simply—gone on." Anne stumbled over the words she had so often heard her minister use.

Sheldon, staring up at her, lost a little of his frozen look, even managed, briefly, the shadow of a smile. "Anne, I am going to hear all that from Mr. McKinney. All I feel now is that she is gone—and I am left without her, for forever and ever."

"Not 'forever and ever,'" Anne said stubbornly. "Just till—"

"I know." He looked at her more gently. "Till I join her. I do believe that. But the years will be very long."

"You will have the two boys to raise, and children grow up so quickly, in the blink of an eye. You will be surprised some day to find how fast the years have gone."

Sheldon rose, straightened his tie, and pulled down his rumpled jacket. "I'm going back to her. John, will you take Papa home with you and Anne? No, Papa, there's no use your spending the rest of the night in that chair. And John, will you notify the undertaker? Crawford, I suppose."

"Certainly. But I came on horseback. Doug, will you—?"

Doug said, "Of course. And come back and spend the night with Sheldon. How about Mrs. Stroud? I suppose she's gone to bed here? She's been staying?"

"Yes," Barbara said quietly. "Directly we'd finished she went upstairs. Let's go."

John had a moment with Anne in the hall, helping her with her cloak. He had been shaken by the ease and assurance of communication between her and Sheldon. He had always known that one part of Anne's mind had been untouched by him, her faith rejecting his unbelief; now he had seen how she had met Sheldon on a ground where he and she, husband and wife, could never meet. He bit back the scornful words on his tongue—"Do you really believe all that nonsense?"—and feeling her trembling as he put his hands on her shoulders with her cloak, said instead, "This has been a strain on you. I'll give you a bromide when I get home."

And Anne thought, sadly, "A doctor's medicine for grief: 'a bromide.'" And, having gone tearless through the night, she began to weep soundlessly; words ran through her mind, "'Not poppy, nor mandragora, nor all the drowsy syrups of the East—'"

John turned her to face him, wiped her cheeks with his carbolic-scented handkerchief, held her tenderly for a moment, and then helped her to the door and out into the Gardiner carriage.

She reached home ahead of him: he would have stopped at the undertaker's, of course. The front door was unlocked, the gas turned low, still burning in the hall chandelier, although outside the day had begun to break. There was a note from Sally in the card tray: "Party over, children in bed, kitchen cleaned and dishes washed. Go right to bed, sleep as long as you can, and telephone me when you wake tomorrow."

When Anne talked to Sally on the telephone the next morning, she was as brief as possible in telling of the night before; she did not want to talk about it. Sally did not press her; instead she suggested that they attend the funeral together, and then went on to speak of the following week's Club meeting: it would of course be a Memorial meeting for Kitty. She would ask Amanda, who had at one time been so close to the Lowreys, to write of Kitty as a schoolgirl. Of Kitty as a wife and mother would she?

Anne broke in on her. "Don't ask me. I should break down. Do it yourself."

"Then who would pay the last tribute, Kitty as a Club member?"

"Mrs. Ballard. Who else?"

The Memorial meeting was held: tears were shed. Young Kitty Edwards was more sincerely mourned than other lost members: her going left a felt absence that made it hard to choose a successor, as though the place should be held for her return.

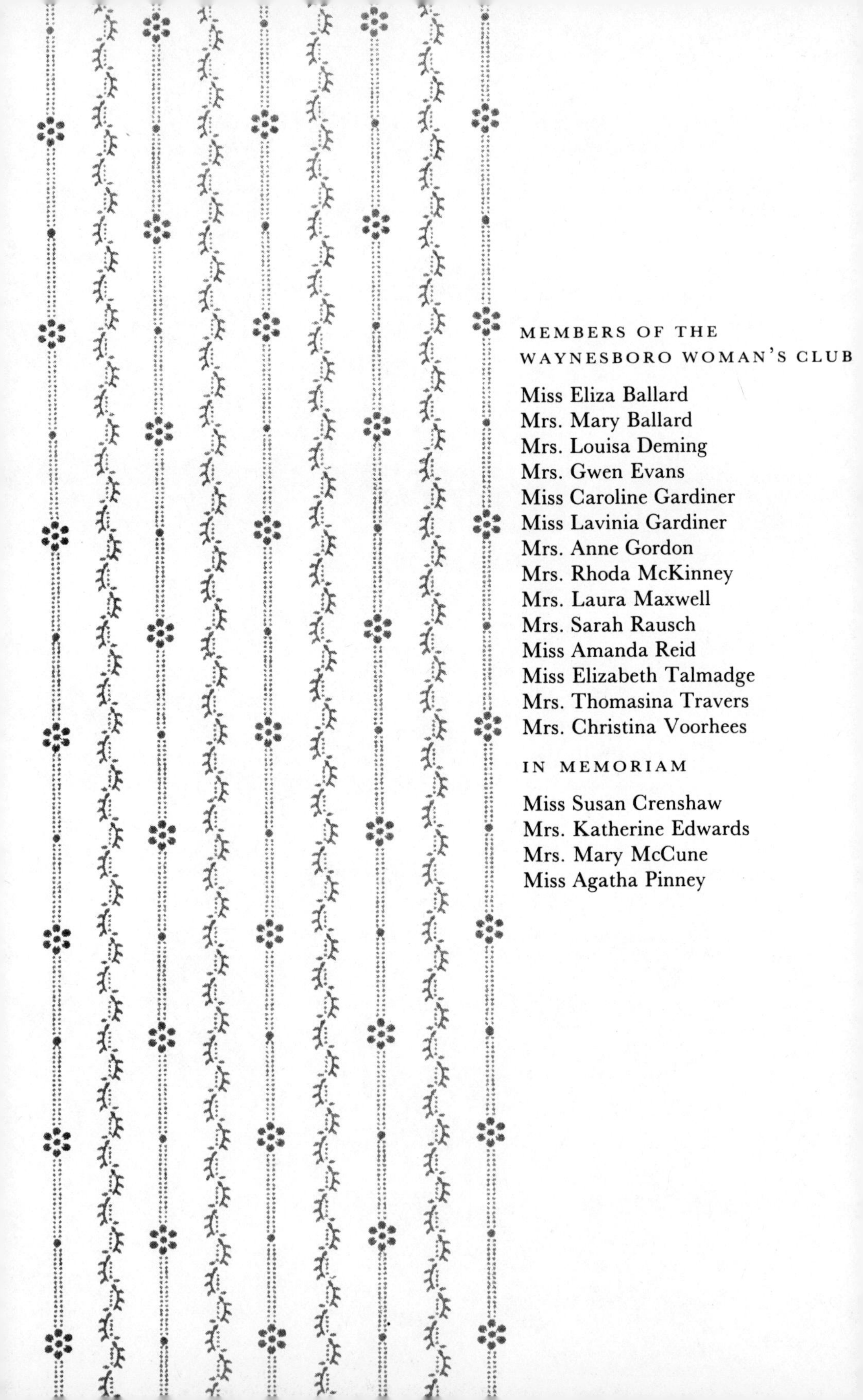

MEMBERS OF THE
WAYNESBORO WOMAN'S CLUB

Miss Eliza Ballard
Mrs. Mary Ballard
Mrs. Louisa Deming
Mrs. Gwen Evans
Miss Caroline Gardiner
Miss Lavinia Gardiner
Mrs. Anne Gordon
Mrs. Rhoda McKinney
Mrs. Laura Maxwell
Mrs. Sarah Rausch
Miss Amanda Reid
Miss Elizabeth Talmadge
Mrs. Thomasina Travers
Mrs. Christina Voorhees

IN MEMORIAM

Miss Susan Crenshaw
Mrs. Katherine Edwards
Mrs. Mary McCune
Miss Agatha Pinney

1886–1887

"Waynesboro suffers the loss of Dr. Blair, its greatest man and scholar; we sympathize with his daughter."

The presentation of Mrs. Deming's paper had been postponed for the Memorial meeting. Since it had been finished for the due date, she was left with time on her hands. She became preoccupied again with thoughts of Julia's future. She had always hoped to send her East for a year: the Demings were now in less-straitened circumstances than they had been; it was still a surprise that the General's books brought in so much money. She welcomed it, since by a little pinching they could manage a year in boarding school for Julia, but Julia had been firmly against it. Her mother had never supposed she could get her into college. The child did well enough at her books, with a little tutoring, but she had no interest in them. She was, however, worthy of a place in the highest society, and one would have thought she would jump at a chance to meet girls with background. Instead, she had set her heart on, of all things, art school! Julia, who had never had a paint brush in her hand! Her mother knew very well *why:* Johnny would be in medical school in Cincinnati next year, and Elsa Rausch was going to the conservatory of music. Julia would not want to lose Johnny to Elsa. Mrs. Deming understood her daughter: Elsa had everything money could buy and talent besides (or so everyone said) while Julia had what Elsa so obviously wanted. But these silly childish jealousies! Julia would forgo all her chances to find a more suitable husband just to play dog in the manger. And she had had the wit (no one could accuse Julia of being stupid when it came to getting what she wanted) to approach her doting father first, and he could see nothing wrong with the idea: a little accomplishment in the artistic way was just what a lady needed. She would be close to home and could spend her Saturdays and Sundays in Waynesboro, and as to her living in a boardinghouse, unchaperoned, they would be mighty particular about that. The Rausches were letting their girl go to the conservatory, weren't they? He didn't see why his wife was so determined to have Julia marry some rich eastern fellow—live in New York, probably, where they would never see her or her children.

Mrs. Deming sighed. The General could be swayed in his decisions about most things; indeed, he often asked for advice; but about Julia he could be pigheaded, and he had so spoiled the girl that she was pigheaded too about having her own way. The only thing on Mrs. Deming's side was time: next September was a long way off, and much could happen; she must endeavor to make the East seem more alluring. She regretted bitterly the newly instituted dancing class. In Waynesboro of all places! A teacher of the dance came up from Cincinnati once a week (induced to come to so unlikely a spot by the Rausches, one suspected: a guarantee or something of the sort). Class was held in the Odd Fellows Hall, a great barnlike room over Fritz Klein's grocery, and was attended by such Waynesboro young people as had not been taught that dancing was one of the Evils of the Day, a Devil's Snare. Julia was of course permitted to join, along with Elsa and Johnny Gordon. Mrs. Deming had been reluctant to part with the fee that might have paid for extras at a boarding school, but to be able to dance easily and gracefully was essential to a young lady in society. More deeply she regretted the introduction into Waynesboro of any new diversion that might help induce the young to stay there.

The dancing class was also on Mrs. Evans's mind on the afternoon she had set aside for making a start on her Club paper. It was a problem, even if an unimportant one. Mrs. Evans still dressed like a Quaker: dark plain silk in a day of ruffles and furbelows: black hair drawn straight into a knot at the back of neck. She was such an eagerly responsive little birdlike woman, with a mind swooping and darting at its objective, the way a chickadee flies, that the other members had grown fond of her, although only the Baptist Sally Rausch ever saw her except at meetings. They were always aware, of course, that she was a Baptist minister's wife, though she herself never seemed conscious of it, as Mrs. McKinney and Mrs. Maxwell continuously and obviously were, and they would have been astonished (even Sally) had they realized that Mrs. Evans refrained from any participation in the simple events and receptions, afternoon teas, dinners of what might be called Waynesboro society because she considered that aspect of the town's life worldly and worse than valueless. Now her husband's orphaned nephew, Gilbert, whom she had welcomed as a son, was taking dancing lessons!

On an afternoon in November, she had gone upstairs with *The Portrait of a Lady*, bristling with torn-paper markers, a pad of paper, pencils, and her lap desk and settled down in the front bedroom where she could work without being interrupted by three males coming and going. It was cold; it even looked like snow, and the unheated room was icy. Huddled in a shawl, she sat down on the hard bench that stood at the foot of the big double bed, and tried to concoct an opening sentence, as she watched through the front windows how fast the maple leaves were falling. That meant the front walk would have to be swept, and the back yard raked. Soon there would be snow to be shoveled. The Baptist parsonage was an old, old house, built so close to the brick sidewalk that the steps actually encroached; that meant less path to keep clear than many families had, but there was a big yard behind the house, and the leaves were a problem in the autumn. It was more than David should do, though he would never admit it. He had gone out that afternoon to make congregational calls; she hoped that one of the boys, Gilbert from high school or Owen from the Seminary, would come home first and get the sweeping and raking done.

She turned back to her book, but before she could even begin to concentrate, she heard the front door open and close. That would be Owen; she knew all their footsteps. Quickly she went out to the head of the stairs, before he could get his wraps off, and called down to him to please sweep the walk and rake the yard before it rained or snowed. He looked up, smiled, saluted, and went on through the house to the back porch where garden tools were kept. Owen was a very satisfactory son, like his older brother who was now a minister with his own congregation, down among the Welsh in the coal-mining section of the state. It did not seem odd to any member of the Evans family that the boys should attend a Reformed Presbyterian seminary. Greek and Hebrew were the same wherever they were taught, and as for the systematic theology, both denominations were Calvinist, and on such matters as infant baptism, the Evans boys could make their own reservations. The plain truth was that there was not enough money to send them away to school: not when they could live at home and be well-educated for so little.

Owen had no more use for a social life than his parents and would be happy as a minister. She was not so sure about Gilbert. Just where would Gilbert find himself? He was a sweet-natured boy, without either ambition or great capability. He did have the rather negative quality of persistence: whatever he drifted into he would stay with, perhaps achieving simply by the passage of time what he would never accomplish by daring or imagination. He might even drift into the ministry. She suspected that there were many churches with parsons of that sort, and she did not like it. The Baptist church needed none who had not felt irresistibly the call of the Lord and were ready to dedicate their lives to His service.

When finally she heard Gilbert come in, she hurried into the hall and called to him over the banister. He came bounding up the stairs, having dropped his books on the lowest step, and followed her into the bedroom.

"Goodness gracious, Aunt Gwen. What are you doing up here in the cold? Hiding away?"

Head on one side, she smiled up at him. "What niminy-piminy oaths from a great fellow like you!"

"You wouldn't like it if I used anything stronger."

"No, I wouldn't. And in case you suspect I came up here to waylay you for a private talk, you are mistaken. I came up to make a start on my Club paper. Such a long book to read and criticize! And such characters!"

There had been enough talk at the dinner table about Henry James for him to know what his aunt was talking about. "Do get it done quickly, so that we sha'n't be eating cold meals for weeks while you are being owlish over your paper."

"Don't exaggerate, Gilbert. You know I've always managed to keep my family fed. No, I came up to work, but you kept coming between me and the book. I worry about you."

"The dancing lessons? But Aunt Gwen, we talked it over and you said to follow the dictates of my conscience. And I'm using my own money that I earned this summer."

"I know. You have never asked us for anything you knew we couldn't afford, or would think wasteful."

"Aunt Gwen, the Rausches are giving a New Year's Eve dance at the Odd Fellows Hall. Elsa told me today. There will be written invitations soon. Would you rather I didn't go?"

So that was why he was so airily lighthearted. She must not spoil it for him by saying, "It's not the money. I'm worried for fear you are being drawn into a world that can never be yours."

Instead she said, "No. You must do as you think right for you."

"It won't be a real, grown-up ball. All the dancing class will be invited, even Ludwig Rausch Junior. And their parents, I guess."

And probably some boys, she thought, who weren't in the dancing class, to even up the sexes. An unattached male was so often included in party arrangements just because he was that; he need be nothing more. She felt a little bitter on Gilbert's account: he was on the fringe of a world that would surely, sooner or later, wall him out. But she had thought better of warning him: he would have to bear the hurt when it was inflicted. Instead she said, "Are you going to be satisfied to go to the Seminary with Owen next year?"

"Yes. Why not? It is an education. I have told you and Uncle David: I do not feel called to the ministry. Not yet, at any rate. But I don't know what I would like to do, so the call may come. If it does, then surely I won't mind giving up the friends you disapprove of."

She shook her head at him. "I don't disapprove of them. They are nice enough young people. But you won't see much of them, once you are graduated."

"Maybe not. They'll be going away to school, most of them. But they'll be home summers." On that cold afternoon in November he was already looking forward to summer evenings on the Rausches' tennis court or their front porch. "Even if I am working, I'll have some time."

He had spent the last summer in the want-ad department of the *Torchlight*, and expected to do the same another year, and have the same kind of fun with the same friends. His Aunt Gwen loved him rather sadly, hoping that his confidence in himself would never be destroyed. She dismissed him, with a word about getting to work on Henry James, and put him out of her mind. When, shortly afterward, his invitation to the dance was delivered at the front door, with a card enclosed bearing the name "Miss Elsa Rausch," she decided that she had worried unnecessarily about his future. She was sure that Sally Rausch, in spite of her easy manners, did nothing without due consideration and foresight: she was asking Gib to be Elsa's escort to the dance either because she felt him to be so inconsequential as not to be taken seriously when Elsa was just at the age to take someone seriously, or she considered him an acceptable—was "suitor" too strong a word?—for Elsa. If that were the case, anyone who knew Mrs. Rausch would know that the impossible might just become the possible.

The Club met at the Gardiners' for the last programmed meeting of the year. Anne, since the night Kitty died, had not seen Barbara except for friendly nods across the church auditorium on Sunday mornings. (It was odd how close you could come to someone, then not see them again for weeks.) She hoped for at least a moment with her at her aunts' (the house would always be the aunts' house to Club members). Not that Barbara ever appeared at the Club meetings held there; as usual there was only the colored maid in the hall, capped and white-aproned, and the Misses Lavinia and Caroline in the parlor doorway.

"Is Mrs. Gardiner at home, Lutie?" Anne asked the maid.

"No'm. She taken the children out to the Edwards'."

Miss Caroline, at the parlor door, overheard. When Anne, having "rested" her cloak in the library, approached the sisters on her return, Miss Caroline said, "You were asking for Mrs. Gardiner? Her home sees little of her these days. Even in her condition, when it is most improper for her to be out, she is managing a double nursery: spends most days at the Edwardses'. Of course we could not have so many children underfoot here. There, there is no one to be disturbed unless Mr. Edwards is at home."

Anne ignored the tail end of the curt little speech, and only thought, how like Barbara: Kitty's other friends might be feeling sorry for her motherless boys, but Barbara, no matter what her condition, was doing what she could. With a few politely false words of pleasure at being entertained in their delightful home, she slipped in past the Misses Gardiner, took one of the uncomfortable gilt chairs, beside Mrs. McKinney, and prepared to listen with at least half an ear to Mrs. Evans, happily aware that two meetings and the Christmas party would intervene before her essay was due.

She was unpleasantly surprised. After Sally, presiding, had worked the Club through old business, of which there was none, and the secretary had read a note received from Sheldon Edwards expressing his appreciation of the Club's condolences on the death of his wife, she had gone on to new business and her invitation to the Club to meet at her house on the afternoon of December 15 for a Christmas party and program, presently being prepared by Miss Talmadge and her committee. There was not the slightest obligation on Sally's part to apologize for not having the Club for an evening affair, with husbands and various unattached males included in the invitation, but she felt that an explanation was needed. She said, "The ladies will, I am sure, be delighted with the program being rehearsed, and I hope will not find an afternoon affair too dull. To tell the truth," she added bluntly, "I hadn't the heart for it, so soon after the loss of Mrs. Edwards. We would only be reminded of the many parts she acted for us." She was about to call for the reading of the program of the day, and only asked for "any other new business" as a matter of routine, when she was interrupted by an insistent "Madame President" from Miss Lavinia Gardiner. Recognized by Sally, that lady rose, adjusted her skirt to her satisfaction, and addressed the chair.

"Madame President, and Ladies of the Club: my sister and I find ourselves in a dilemma. We have hitherto endeavored to fulfill our obligations to the Woman's Club to the very best of our ability. But we are quite unequal to this year's assigned subjects. Having spent some time reading Mr. Meredith's *Diana of the Crossways* and the works of Pierre Loti, we find the one morally reprehensible, and the other too exotic for comprehension. We therefore beg your indulgence. At the beginning of the year's program, we were told that we might feel free to trade assignments; we would now like to suggest that my sister exchange topics with Mrs. Gordon, who is next on the list after us, and that I take Mrs. Rausch's subject, 'Trollope.' Our learned President reads French so very easily that I am sure she can deal intelligently with Monsieur Pierre Loti. Or we might substitute essays, reminiscent of course, on 'Childhood Days in Antebellum Virginia.' It would be much more convenient for us, however, if we could do our studying and writing when the commotion attendant upon the birth of a child in the house is over and done with."

Whether Club members were embarrassed by this speech was uncertain, but it was clear that the two chosen victims were angry: Anne Gordon, who had looked forward to Christina Rosetti, read at leisure after the holidays, and who did not much like Meredith; and Sally Rausch, who shrank inwardly at the thought of "Childhood Days in Antebellum Virginia," but was more annoyed by the assumption that she would be pleased to take Pierre Loti instead of, late in the spring, a comparatively simple subject like Trollope. But Sally was equal to the emergency: with a composed presidential face she said, "I feel sure the Program Committee will agree to these exchanges if those involved are willing. We cannot ask you, on such short notice, to prepare chapters of reminiscences, delightful as that would be. No doubt Mrs. Gordon can produce an essay on Mr. Meredith for the next meeting?" For the first time she looked at Anne, who nodded briefly, and without a smile. "The first after Christmas."

"Those arrogant old so-and-so's," Anne was thinking, "and the vulgarity of speaking so about the ordeal ahead of Barbara—let alone being expected to deal with Meredith early in January—"

Anne returned home still in a rebellious mood, but the Club and its affairs were at once wiped from her mind: she found John waiting for her, in a very glum humor, with a letter from his cousin Jessamine Gordon Stevens. Anne took it as he handed it to her, standing stock still for a moment, still hatted, gloved, and cloaked, the letter still in its envelope.

"You haven't heard from her in ages, have you? Not since she let you know her husband had died. What now?"

John grunted. "Read it. You'll see."

Anne stripped off her gloves, dropped her cloak on the back of a chair, and, unfolding the letter, read it aloud:

Dear Cousin John:

As my *only living kin*, I hope I can turn to you for help, or at least for *advice*. I have been told that I *must get* my son Rodney out of *this climate*. He is a delicate child and has not been able to *shake off the attack of malaria* he had last summer. The doctor is *so accustomed to everyone* having malaria that he takes it for granted. He stuffed Rodney so full of quinine the poor little boy could *hardly stand*. But the minister of the church which we attend came to call this week and was *quite shocked*. He told me that children could DIE of malaria: that I must take the boy away. Is this *true?* I did not know that *anyone died* of malaria. If it is true, we must move from here. But where? I have a few friends in New Orleans, but *yellow fever* frightens me even more than malaria. Could we move to Waynesboro? Do you advise it? Do you have malaria there? If I sell the plantation, there will be *money* enough to *live on*. I have consulted Grandfather's lawyer in Memphis, and he says there will be no trouble in *selling* it: If none of my neighbors wants to add our *thousands of acres* to what they have, it will be snatched up by the syndicate of Yankees who are buying so much cotton land. After the *sacrifices* made by *all* to keep the land in the family, it *breaks my heart* to sell it when it should be kept for Rodney's *inheritance*. But I could not manage it from a distance; I have a good overseer, but I don't know how good he would be if I were not here to keep an eye on him.

I hope you will be willing to *advise* me. Would Waynesboro, Ohio, be a good place for a little boy? If you think we should *move away* from this climate up north, would you be willing to help us find a place to live? *Anxiously* awaiting your reply,

Your cousin Jessamine Gordon Stevens.

Thoughts, half-thoughts, chased through Anne's mind as she handed the letter back to John. "Quite an—emphatic—missive, isn't it? The poor little boy! You don't want her in Waynesboro, do you? Why not? Is it true a child can die of malaria?"

"Anyone can die of malaria, given certain conditions. A child, yes, certainly, if he has a bad case. But God damn it, why here?"

"Because you're her only kin. She wants a man to lean on. A lawyer is hardly enough."

"I don't want any God-damned relatives hanging round my neck."

"Where are the children, that you feel so free to swear?"

"Sorry, dear. Johnny's in the office, tidying up after the patients I saw this afternoon. I'm to take him with me shortly. I've a few house calls to make before dinner. Binny I haven't seen."

"It's all right. I told her she could go play with the Rausch boys after school, if they played inside and not in the snow. So if you must swear—"

"By God! I feel like it. Here we are going along smooth and easy, a peaceful sort of life. I don't *want* any complications."

Anne thought, blindly, "What kind of complications?" She said, "You can't tell her to stay away from Waynesboro. What reason could you give? And with a child's life in the balance— But would she really move up here, expecting you to have found a house for her? I think she means to be asked for a visit."

"A *visit?* Here in our house?"

"Why not?" Anne said drily. "Other people have their relatives visit." It was eight or nine years since John had made that trip to Mississippi, and she had almost forgotten; but now she was shaken by the same certainty she had felt on his return, on first seeing him. Why else his peculiar reluctance? Her mouth was full of bitterness, like a surge of gall, but she went on, "You may answer her letter as you please. I shall write and invite her to spend Christmas with us, and bring Rodney. That she mustn't *think* of *moving* in the dead of winter—I can underscore too—but that we should be *delighted* to have them visit us for the *holidays* and she can see for herself what she thinks of Waynesboro."

"But Christmas!"

"There'll be lots going on in the party line. It won't be so hard to entertain her. And if she isn't used to snow, she may decide it is no place to live."

"And after all," she thought, turning to pick up her cloak, preparatory to changing out of her best afternoon costume, "there was never any evidence that John—only that certainty—" a certainty that she now discovered had grown no weaker with the years. What was she bringing upon herself?

The prospect of what lay ahead of her had to be dismissed from her mind while she concentrated on *Diana of the Crossways*. At least she had read it, and she had no hesitation about speaking her mind. She must get it written before guests arrived.

In the meantime, Anne had written to Cousin Jessamine. Before her letter could be answered, Mrs. Douglas Gardiner gave birth to her fourth child. As soon as Anne thought Barbara would feel equal to a visitor, she went to call. To her amazement, Miss Lavinia Gardiner answered her ring.

"Mrs. Gordon! How do you do? Come in, please. As you see we are for the time being deprived of the services of a maid: Lutie has taken the children down to their grandparents', and everything here is at sixes and sevens. And all for one more little girl: four, now."

Without giving Anne a chance to ask for Barbara, Miss Lavinia conducted her to the parlor.

"Do please take a chair. If you will excuse me, I will go summon my sister."

"But I really came—"

Before she had a chance to finish, Miss Lavinia was gone; Anne resigned herself to the fifteen minutes of a correct afternoon call. The sisters remarked on the weather, inquired as to the Gordons' health, and then dwelt largely on their disappointment (a failure on Barbara's part, was the implication) that Douglas's fourth child was another girl.

"And of course it must have been a *bitter* disappointment to him. I am sure he kept hoping for a son to carry on our name to another generation."

Anne said, "It is not too late."

"*Five* children? Oh, surely not. Even one who has been brought up a Catholic must draw the line somewhere."

"Then you must console yourselves with the thought that little boys are very much noisier in the house than little girls."

Anne stayed with them the requisite fifteen minutes, then asked if she might see Barbara and was sent unescorted upstairs. In Barbara's room the baby was lifted from its crib to be admired, and then the monthly nurse disappeared with it. Anne stayed but a few minutes; nothing much was said, although Anne was reassured as to Doug's disappointment.

"I'm sure he hoped for a boy," Barbara said. She was leaning against her pillow, touseled as to hair, but radiant with happiness and good health. "He won't admit it now. He says he is proud of what he calls his 'bevy of girls.'"

Anne thought of what Douglas Gardiner had been like as a youth: bitter, sarcastic; that this should be the same man who was now the proud father of four daughters struck her as fantastic. The things life did to people. "Of course he's proud," she said. "I never saw so many pretty little girls in one family." The oldest, she thought, Lavinia, was a beautiful child: violet-eyed, dark-haired; Caroline was like her; Veronica, who was not yet two, was fairer, light-haired, blue-eyed, perhaps not beautiful, but very pretty.

"They are good children, too. But Doug says this is enough. Four children are as many as anyone can afford to have. I think he was frightened, a little—you know, Kitty—"

"I know. And I agree with him, even though you are the picture of happy well-being. But four should be enough. Just think what it will cost you for weddings alone."

They both laughed: it was utterly preposterous on that afternoon to think of marrying off four little girls, the oldest of whom could be no more than six. As Anne left Barbara, she was quite sure that its father and mother were completely satisfied with the mite in the crib.

A short time later, Anne's invitation to Cousin Jessamine and her Rodney was accepted. With *great* pleasure. However, Jessamine professed herself to be so *terrified* of changing from one railroad depot to another in a *strange place* like Cincinnati that John, still grumpy about the whole thing, felt compelled to go to the city to meet her. Anne encouraged him: let them get their meeting over, whatever was involved, without her. But she had Lonzo hitch the mare to the carriage and drive her to the depot on the day of arrival: the carriage was seldom out of the Gordons' stable, but she would do this in style if it killed her.

Then, when they got off the train, John and the pretty dark woman, so young looking, and the sallow, scrawny little old man of a boy, tall for seven years, her heart beat wildly against the tight band constricting it. But she went steadily forward. It was nothing in the adults' attitude toward each other that had so stricken her: it was the child, with Johnny's and Johnny's father's eyes, his carriage, and when he pulled off his cap to speak to her and offer his hand, even the way his hair grew. It was everything—and nothing you could put your finger on: John's son. The dates, the years of his age, a whole year wrong. It didn't matter: his mother was making him a year younger, so that no one—not even John—would know. Then as she took his hand, Rodney smiled at her shyly, trustingly, and her heart turned over; whatever the truth might be, she would have to put the matter right out of her mind, for no one could dislike or be indifferent to this child. Like Johnny, he too was a boy to love.

She forced herself to be cordial to Jessamine, to accept her cousinly kiss, and then led them to the carriage. She had brought this on herself: she would have to accept not only Rodney but his mother, too, and make what she could of it.

The visit went surprisingly well. Jessamine, with her soft accent, her ceaseless chatter, her gaiety and her anecdotes, made it easy for them. And she was so pretty: oval-faced, olive skinned, with flyaway brows, eyes set in her head in the Gordon way but light in color, hazel or amber, with her soft straight black hair curled in a fringe above her brows and the mass of it in piled braids on the crown of her head: she was so pretty that the children were drawn to her irresistibly. And they were tolerant (Johnny) and kind (Binny) to the listless little boy. As for John, when he was forced to make his appearance, he was friendly in an offhand casual sort of way. Anne contrived to act the older sister, full of wisdom and good advice. She took Cousin Jessamine to Sally's Christmas tea for the Club, to see Elizabeth Talmadge and her cast act and sing a few songs from *Pinafore*. All the ladies were charmed by "your delightful cousin"—"these irresistible southern girls"—"we understand Mrs. Stevens is thinking of moving to Waynesboro. What a delightful addition to our society!"

Christmas itself was a family affair: stockings, a tree, presents all around, and a turkey dinner. After dinner Rodney, who was a rather silent little boy, all eyes, demanded his firecrackers.

"Firecrackers?" The Gordons were astonished.

"We have firecrackers on Christmas at home. Y'all don't up here? Because of the snow?"

"Fourth of July," Binny explained.

Rodney looked bewildered. His mother laughed. "No July Fo'th celebrations in Mississippi since the war. Never mind, Rodney, you can have your fireworks when we get home. You just settle down with your cousins. Play some quiet games inside. Parcheesi, maybe?"

Rodney, who had attached himself like a barnacle to Johnny and been tolerated beyond what might have been expected of a high school senior, was in no mood for Parcheesi.

"Maman, s'il vous plait—"

"Don't be rude, Rodney. Whatever it is, say it in English."

"Please. I want to play in the snow."

His mother looked at John, who said, "Wrap him up well and let Johnny pull him on Binny's sled. It won't do him any harm."

Rodney had had one attack of chills and fever since he had been at the Gordons'. Once had been enough for Anne, who quite understood Jessamine's concern, but John said that it was all right for the boys to go out, and Johnny was quite willing: anything was better than Parcheesi. There were feeble pleas from Binny, who knew very well that playing in the snow was forbidden her. She returned to the books she had received that morning, and the two boys went for the sled.

"I declare your Johnny is the *nicest* thing. You say he graduates from school this comin' June?"

"Yes. He'll be in medical school next year. Binny will be starting high school. And Rodney, if you move to Waynesboro?"

"I can't exactly tell you. He's been sharing a tutor with neighbor plantation boys. He can read, I do know. Reckon they'll just have to find out where he belongs. He's had mighty little schoolin', but he's only seven goin' on eight."

"But he speaks French?"

"New O'lins French." Jessamine laughed. "I grew up speakin' it—Maman was Creole, you know. I have used it with Rodney: it's such an easy way for children—"

"I know. Only in Waynesboro it's apt to be German, if a child is bilingual."

The conversation threatened to die, but Jessamine revived it: no long silence was a comfortable silence in her view. Cousin Anne's delightful friend Mrs Rausch, she was German? Oh, it was only Mr. Rausch. And what a charming daughter they had, did they not? Quite a fine musician, judging from her piano playing for the ladies at the tea. Of course one expected Germans to be musical—and on and on. John, who had not contributed so much as an encouraging "Yes" or "No" to the conversation, threatened to doze off; he was relieved when the telephone rang and he could excuse himself.

Between Christmas and New Year's, the two women looked for a house that Jessamine might consider as a possible home. The Sheldon house, where the late Mr. Sheldon of Sheldon and Edwards had lived, was the only good solid brick house in town that was unoccupied; Mrs. Sheldon had finally gone to live with the senior Edwardses, unequal longer to the daily ordeal of loneliness. The house stood halfway up the Linden Street hill, with a good yard, lots of trees, and a sizable brick barn and carriage house. If Jessamine bought it, she would want the upstairs of the carriage house made into quarters for her servants: Rodney's nursemaid, the cook, the groom.

"Shall I bring my saddle horse?"

"To Waynesboro? You can ride if you want to, but you will ride alone. No one here rides horseback." Anne refrained from saying that for night calls John often rode: saddling and bridling were so much quicker than hitching up. "But you will want a carriage, and a carriage horse or pair." Anne was quite willing to go along with Jessamine's desire to cut a dashing figure.

The Gordons took her, along with Binny, to the Rausches' dance on New Year's Eve. (Johnny had been as usual assigned to Julia Deming as an escort.) The dance was an informal affair with just three out-of-town musicians to play for the assembled company: the members of the dancing class, the dancing instructor himself (a little baldheaded bearded man, spry for his years), and some others who knew how to dance, like Charlotte Bonner and Sophie Klein, home from their eastern college for the holidays, and Elizabeth Talmadge and Tim Merrill, who had been asked to escort her. The various parents, invited as probable on-lookers, lined up in the chairs against the wall, but Sally and Ludwig danced, as did Elizabeth and Tim, and Jessamine, who thoroughly enjoyed herself.

That was on a Saturday night. The Stevenses started off on Monday morning on their return trip to Memphis. Jessamine had been convinced that she and Rodney could cross Cincinnati in a cab without danger; John and Anne put them on the train in the Waynesboro depot, and went home afterward wordless and exhausted. Once in the sitting room, which was still in holiday disorder, they pulled rockers to the fireplace and sank into them. The children were not there, not even Binny with one of her new books.

"Probably with Martha," Anne thought. She was too tired to investigate.

John said, "Well, do you want them in Waynesboro?"

"We're committed. And I certainly don't want Rodney to die."

"Funny, he doesn't look a bit like his mother. Or his father, fortunately. A throwback to the Gordons, I reckon."

Anne's hands, lying in her lap, came together in a convulsive grip. He *didn't* know. Had he even suspected, he would have been morosely silent on the subject of Rodney's looks. What blind owls men were! Apparently Jessamine had never told him; and if she hadn't told him, she would never tell anybody. Why should she? An illegitimate child. It would remain a secret known to one woman, believed by another, both of whom would do their best to forget it. And Anne would try to convince herself that she was wrong.

She said, "Was she always like this? Such a chatterbox, I mean?"

"The only other time I saw her—in the summer of '77, wasn't it?—she was a damsel in distress, living in a rundown plantation house with two drunkards. Since then—once the cotton money began to come in, I suppose—the house has been restored to all its former grandeur, galleries and columns, and no leaks in the roof. The two men have died and she has a son on whom she dotes, so I suppose it was all worth it to her, in the end. Of course she isn't the same woman. I suppose she leads a lonely life, even if her neighbors have forgiven her her grandfather: the plantation is remote—she probably has no one to talk to most of the time, except the boy and the servants. I have seen enough of loneliness. I know you laugh because my calls on what you call my old women, the widows and spinsters living alone, take so much of my time. But their need for an ear to listen to them is as great as their need for medicine. Jessamine will always be afraid of silence, I guess, but once she has neighbors she will get talked out."

"Maybe, but it's hard to believe. Who would have thought that just listening could be so taxing?" Of course it wasn't the listening for words that had worn her out, it was another sort of listening altogether. But somehow the feeling of revulsion, the irrepressible shudder of spirit that she had felt when Jessamine had at first come close, those had gone. She was tired, tired to death, but that was all.

Anne was glad, when the holidays were past and Club meetings had begun again, that her paper was over and done with. It was going to be a busy spring, with the Stevenses' move to Waynesboro and Johnny's graduation from high school. The purchase of the Sheldon house was being taken care of by Jessamine's Memphis lawyer and Tim Merrill; once the title was clear, it could be seen what needed to be done to make it comfortable. For a Mississippian a new furnace, probably, better plumbing and a new bathroom installed, piping for gaslights, and the making over of the upper floor of the carriage house to accommodate Jessamine's servants: an apartment where haylofts had been. (Martha had a word to say on the subject of those servants: "Maybe that lady gwun be su'prised. Maybe they won't want to live in no ba'n. They still slaves in Mizsippi, but not hyeh—no, Ma'am, not hyeh they ain't, an' they soon gwun fin' it out!") Anne did not mind the prospect of taking the responsibility for all that needed to be done: having fairly recently been through it all in their own house, she knew the plumbers, the carpenters, the other workmen who would be involved. It would be far better to see to it herself than to have Jessamine staying with them all those weeks while the work went on; and besides, no matter for whom she would be doing it, there would be pleasure no woman could resist in making over an old house.

As the winter passed, the work was begun: the new and larger furnace installed so that the house could be heated and the plumbers and gas-fitters could go to work. Anne carried on a busy correspondence with Cousin Jessamine. There were bills to be sent, and samples of wallpaper; questions to be answered about a kitchen stove and bathroom fittings: the house was to be all ready by the time it was warm enough to move. Sally Rausch complained that she never saw Anne except at Club.

"I hope you are not so enchanted by young Mrs. Stevens that you won't have time for your old friends."

Anne regarded her in amazement. "I am not in the least enchanted. I don't really know her, and I find that constant sweet palaver very tiresome. But she is John's cousin—she has no one else to turn to, and she has a sick child. I feel responsible."

"I'll be glad when you get back in circulation. Not that I am going to have much leisure myself the next couple of weeks. It is time for me to tackle 'Monsieur Pierre Loti.'"

By that time, the second of March, the Gardiner sisters had read their papers on their chosen subjects; and Mrs. McKinney had said what she had wanted to say about *Ben Hur*. Mrs. McKinney was a happy and somewhat smug woman, contented with her own small world: church, church organizations, the Club, her husband and her sort-of-adopted child. Rachel, whom they had sent to Tuskegee, was now teaching in the South, and her progress filled her foster-parents with pride and the deep satisfaction of a good deed done. And Mrs. McKinney had enjoyed the Lea Wallace paper as much as if she had invented him.

Mrs. Maxwell's mind was not so completely at peace. Even at her age, when her husband should perhaps be thinking of retirement, she continued to be ambitious for him: she hoped that he could finish his days as president of the Theological Seminary. He was still acting president: no appointment could be made until the General Synod met in its annual session. Dr. Blair, in a dying condition, could hardly be asked to move from the president's house, but Mrs. Maxwell occasionally caught herself thinking what changes she would like to make in it should they ever move over there. Then she would feel guilty knowing how deeply shocked her husband would be. She was glad to have William Dean Howells to put her mind on, however hard it was to keep it there.

Mrs. Maxwell's essay on *The Rise of Silas Lapham* was duly presented. Christina Voorhees was absent from the meeting. Mrs. Maxwell did not esteem herself the more highly because she could not help wondering— As the ladies sat on after the meeting to enjoy Mrs. Deming's usual tea and cookies and an exchange of mild gossip, several, after complimenting the day's essayist, asked her about Dr. Blair; she could tell them nothing beyond what they already knew: that he was a hair's-breadth away from death. "He may have taken a sudden turn for the worse. Knowing his condition, his daughter may have been reluctant to leave him for any length of time."

Anne and Sally walked home from that meeting. March had come in like the proverbial lamb: a warm clear wind was blowing, tumbling piled clouds against a high blue sky. The brick path was damp with the last of the melting snow, and the ladies had to gather up their skirts in gloved hands and step warily. Said Sally, struggling with her ruffles, "Today, in books and out, if you want to damn someone, you only need to call him 'rich.' It always suggests ill-gotten gains, as if it were impossible to make money honestly."

"Johnny's father set him straight on that very subject the other evening: Johnny'd come out with some socialistic notions he had picked up somewhere. His father told him any man who made two blades of grass grow where one had grown before had served his country: had provided the public with something needed, given employment to workers, and earned profits to be reinvested for further production. He said, 'Your Uncle Ludwig is a good example.'"

Sally laughed. "I'll tell Ludwig: he'll be pleased. But I didn't mean *he* was rich. Far from it: he's worried this spring because he thinks small family concerns like his are in danger. Business hasn't been too good—so many of the big rope companies have left the Cordage Association he thinks it will be dissolved."

"Cordage Association?"

"An association of cordage companies, with gentlemen's agreements on price-cutting and other things. If the big companies get out and start cutting prices—sell below cost—they can stand the loss for a while. The small companies can't. They just could be forced out of business, especially if the big companies organize a trust, as they seem to be doing. You know, like Standard Oil."

"I can see it would be worrisome. But Ludwig will manage. I have every faith in him."

"Oh, so do I." But Sally sighed. "It may be a tight pinch for a while. I tell him not to worry, the important things are all right: five healthy, fairly well-behaved children. Even Papa's pretty good, though he's getting a bit cantankerous. Ludwig Junior nearly drives him out of his mind, practicing the violin or being noisy in less forgivable ways. But Papa idolizes little Paul: spoils him frightfully."

Anne laughed. "You all spoil him. Fortunately he's a happy natured child." The youngest Rausch, now a year and a half old, was totally unlike the other boys in appearance: a throwback to some Cochran, possibly, he was dark-haired, violet-eyed, an impish mite with an irresistible charm.

"I don't believe Paul will be as unmanageable as Ludwig Junior," said his mother. "Ludwig's only eight, but unless he's practicing his violin, he is off and away, Heaven knows where."

The two women parted at the Gordon gate. Sally went on home, intending to tackle Pierre Loti in the morning, having read what she could get hold of, and taken notes. Before she had closed the front door behind her, however, she learned that she could not spend the next day as she had planned.

Elsa, who had been watching for her with the normal youthful, or human, pleasure in having a piece of bad news to report, went to the door to meet her with, "Mamma, Dr. Blair is dead."

"Are you sure? Where did you hear it?"

"I stopped at Uncle Dock's office with Johnny: he had some bones he's been putting together he wanted me to see. His father came in and told us. I guess Uncle Dock knew Dr. Blair, sort of—played chess with him or something."

"We were all friends of Dr. Blair," Sally said. "It is a loss to the town: he was such a learned scholar that he gave Waynesboro a sort of prestige. But it is a release for him, and nothing to grieve over. Tell your father, will you, when he comes in? I must go change out of this uncomfortable gown."

"And that means another funeral," she thought, climbing the stairs slowly and sadly. "One after another, these last few years. First thing we know, *we'll* be the old folks." Then she laughed at herself. Old age was not quite that close: she had a baby only a couple of years old. She changed into a looser and less easily ruined garment and went into the nursery to take little Paul from Cassie and help him downstairs for a before-dinner romp.

The funeral services for Dr. Blair crowded the small Reformed Presbyterian church to its utmost limits. There were not many there from out of town: the stated clerk and the moderator of the General Assembly, and a few fellow theologians, friends and relatives from Pennsylvania; but most of Waynesboro went, feeling truly that the town had lost a leading citizen. The students attended en masse, in the front pews, with the strongest of them acting as pallbearers. Honorary pallbearers were the Seminary professors, Dr. Gordon, Ludwig Rausch, and Mr. Lichtenstein, to the bewilderment of those who had not known of the chess games in John's office. Mr. McCune, sitting undistinguished in a pew with his wife and children, was particularly affronted: he had not been asked to preach the funeral sermon for a member of his own congregation. That duty, perhaps understandably, was performed by Dr. Maxwell; but those three men so noticeably honored, no doubt at Dr. Blair's request, were two of them atheists and one of them almost certainly a Jew. ("Thumbing his nose at the fanatics," John had said.) Mr. McCune had begun to feel that he had outlasted his usefulness in Waynesboro: his congregation, whose members would never criticize their minister to outsiders, had nevertheless made him feel these last few months something distinctly like disapprobation. Because of Ariana? His thoughts shied away from that question and returned to the puzzling attitude of those who were still his flock, who should be not only reverent but generous. There had been a noticeable falling off in the number of farmers who left contributions of food on his doorstep, and of those merchants and professional men who had hitherto tithed for the church. If he could catch the stated clerk while he was in Waynesboro, he would ask if there was a vacant pulpit in some other presbytery.

An appointment to fill Dr. Blair's position could not be made for another few months. In the interim Dr. Maxwell continued to act as president. Christina, when Mrs. Maxwell made her condolence call, brought up the subject of vacating the house. "I thought," she said, with her usual serene composure, "perhaps you would like to trade houses with us."

"My dear Christina! What an untimely thought!" Mrs. Maxwell was rather severe with her because she was being severe with herself, forbearing to look around the room she was in. "There is no reason to feel sure that my husband will be given your father's place; there may be many scholars in the church more distinguished than he. No, let us remain as we are until the General Assembly meets." And so the Maxwells stayed in the house across the street from the Gardiners, and the Voorhees family lived on in the president's house, with one difference: Dr. Blair's Pennsylvania Dutch couple, who had been so faithful for so many years, went home to their own people. Christina was hurt by their defection, although she accepted their decision calmly. She did not know how she could manage without them: two children, a husband, the house, and no cook. She considered her education ruefully: she could teach Hebrew, but she could not feed her family. There were colored women who could cook, but she shrank from the thought, having never in her life had any contact with Negroes. She decided that what other women could do, she could do. And she should have a Club meeting while the house was still moderately clean after its polishing for the funeral. She would invite them at the next meeting. She thumbed through a calendar: that would be the thirtieth. Would the ladies think it too soon after her father's death? Waynesboro was very conventional. But surely they would understand: though she grieved that the past, when her father was in his prime, was over and done with, except in her memory, she could not grieve over his death—not after having heard the struggle for his every breath so many weary years. The death and suffering had been ordained, the latter endured with Christian resignation, even writing on his pad one day, holding the pencil in his trembling fingers: "Do not grieve for me. Like Job I am being tested and like Job my faith survives. 'He knoweth the way that I take; when he hath tried me I shall come forth like gold.' Put the Bible up now and pull the chess table over, with the problem Dock left this morning." That was after he had spent days and nights in his chair, unable to lie down to sleep; he knew his end was near. She must have looked disapproving, for he had added in a shaky scrawl on the paper, "Don't worry about my soul. I am either 'elect according to the foreknowledge of God the Father' or I am not, and precious little I can do about it."

"Of course you are," she said when she had deciphered the writing, " 'to an inheritance incorruptible and undefiled, that fadeth not away, reserved in heaven for you.' "

He took paper and pencil again. "If you believe that, then you are not to mourn for me. No black. No trappings of woe."

Christina went to the Club meeting at the Ballards', defiantly wearing the frock in which she was accustomed to appear, and invited the ladies to meet with her on March 30. At the Ballards' Sally read her paper on Pierre Loti:

however easily she read French, her inaptitude for the exotic and sensuous made her treatment somewhat confusing to her audience. She had only just managed to get it written in the intervals of her family concerns and her social life. The house was overrun with young people that spring: Elsa and her classmates coming and going, playing the piano and singing, until Sally thought that if she heard "In the Evening by the Moonlight" one more time she would have to leave home. But Ludwig enjoyed having them gather there, and only her father was seriously bothered by the noise and confusion.

Anne had not been at the Club meeting on the day when Sally was the essayist. She sent her regrets: she was busy helping Jessamine get moved into the Sheldon house. Sally resented her absence, though glad Anne had the sense not to bring a stranger to the meeting as a guest. Sally was not proud of her effort to explain and defend Pierre Loti, and besides, Cousin Jessamine would be sure to believe that she might become a member. Sally wanted more of a chance to look her over before any such irremediable step was taken.

At that moment, actually, the moving had been done, and the house almost completely ordered. There were only knick-knacks and bric-a-brac to dispose of. Jessamine got up from where she had been kneeling by a half-empty box and went to Anne with a daguerreotype in her hand.

"D'you reckon I can put this on my mantelpiece in this Yankee town?"

Anne opened the case and held it so that she could see the picture. She caught her breath. "It's your father? It could almost be John if the uniform were different—only John was younger then, when he went off to the war. Of course, put it up. The war is over for years. Believe me, there are no hard feelings any more, except maybe at election time. We Yankees have been too enchanted by Uncle Remus and others." By all means, Anne thought: "Put it where everyone can see it, so they'll know who it is Rodney looks like."

"It's a funny thing," Jessamine took the daguerreotype and stood looking at it sadly. "I neve' even saw him, to remember. He went off to the wa' when I was a baby, and he never came back home again: fi'st, because Grandfathe' was a Union man, and then because the plantation was in the part of Mississippi the Yankees held. I was only fou' when he was killed. An' now I have a boy who's the spittin' image of him—skipped a whole generation: Rodney doesn't look like me or his fathe', but like my Papa." She set the daguerreotype on the mantel. "I just hope when he's raised, he takes afte' him."

The two women went on with their work, chatting inconsequentially until Jessamine said, "You and Cousin John go to the Presbyterian chu'ch, I reckon? All the Go'dons do. Are the' nice folks in the congregation? I just wonde' how I'm goin' to get acquainted up No'th."

"The congregation's all right. You'll get acquainted."

"What about the Club you' missin' this evenin' on my account?"

Anne laughed. "Its members are my friends but I wouldn't call them social leaders, exactly. It is presumably an intellectual group, meeting to improve the minds of the members. But no one lets it be known she would like to be a member: it just isn't done. Anyone who isn't a member pretends it doesn't exist, or that she never heard of it."

"What does it do, then, that it amounts to so much?"

"I'm not sure it does amount to much. Only—" Anne thought, "Funny. I hadn't realized I felt like this. It's just we've all been members so long and know each other so well, we're comfortable together—" She said, "We read essays and criticize each other's. And take care of the library desk by turns, because we started it. I'm afraid you'd find it very dull. Parties, like the one at Sally's that I took you to, come only once or twice a year."

Jessamine had privately thought the ladies at Mrs. Rausch's Christmas tea and theatricals a very dowdy lot, but she wanted to be a part of Waynesboro life not only for Rodney's sake but for her own: she was not so old—not yet thirty—as to have done with a personal life. The Woman's Club might be a start, even if most of its members seemed to be old women.

"If you want to join the Woman's Club," Anne went on, amused in spite of herself at the thought, "don't push it: let on you never heard of it, don't mention it, but cultivate one of its members. If I proposed your name you would probably be voted in, but it might be grudgingly because everyone would think I'd done it for a relative."

Jessamine put her head on one side. "Yes," she said slowly, "I can see it might be so. Who'd you suggest?"

Anne, still smiling, thought, "She's really serious!" said, "Now, let me think—" running over the members in her mind, rejecting names, hesitating. Elizabeth Talmadge was closest to Jessamine in age, probably, but she was too new. Not Sally, certainly. "The only one I can think it would seem natural for you to be bosom friends with is Christina Voorhees. Her father was mighty strong against the Rebels: his sons were killed in the war. But now he's dead, I don't believe Christina would feel the same way. Her husband's cashier of the bank: you've probably met him in your business dealings." Anne went on with a brief description of Christina, her background, her personality.

"She's a Refo'med Presbyterian? Then I reckon I'd better go to that church. Would you mind?"

"I? Not at all. Why should I? If you can stand it. They're awfully strict. No cards, no dancing, no hot meals on the Sabbath. Not all their members observe the rules, but Christina does."

Mrs. Stevens very shortly thereafter transferred her membership from her Mississippi church to the Reformed Presbyterian church of Waynesboro. She was just in time for the resignation of the Reverend Mr. McCune, who had found in a small town in western Pennsylvania a church with a vacant pulpit and a congregation willing to call him to fill it. Until it chose another minister, the Waynesboro congregation would rely on substitutes, mostly theologues from the Seminary. Oddly, church members thought, the only student who declined the opportunity to practice sermonizing was Matthew McCune. Mark, who had one more year in high school, and Luke, still a child, made no objection to the move. Ruhamah, quiet, obedient Ruhamah, on the other hand, said obstinately she was not going. She was earning enough money at the library to live on, barely; she could find a room in Waynesboro and finish high school. "I know I am not of age. You can *force* me to go. But I would come back when I had the chance."

The girl of fifteen said no more, but her father quailed at the threat of another runaway. Moreover, her cold, inimical expression told her father all she might have said. Since Ariana's flight, he had been aware of Ruhamah's antagonism; it was not comfortable to live with.

He made one protest: "I don't know who would willingly be responsible for a fifteen-year-old girl."

"Mrs. Dunbar. As you know, she has a houseful of country girls who come into high school and stay with her and eat with her five days a week. I am sure she would take me for seven. I asked her how much it would cost and I can just do it."

Mrs. Dunbar was a member of the Reformed Presbyterian church: he knew her well, and that what Ruhamah had said was true. He gave in more easily than Ruhamah had expected; she had not the experience to perceive that a man like her father found it difficult to live with mute but obvious and unrelenting disapproval that he could not overcome or deal with in any way. And so all the McCunes except Ruhamah and Matt, at the Seminary, departed from Waynesboro, Ruhamah having been consigned to the oversight of her brother.

Amanda Reid and Elizabeth Talmadge were at this time working together on their Club papers; they had been assigned such similar subjects that they could almost collaborate: Amanda, who would rather have enjoyed writing a criticism of *Ben Hur*, instead working on Howe's *Story of a Country Town*; Elizabeth on Eggleston's *Hoosier Schoolmaster*—Realism in American Literature, I and II. Amanda was particularly contented through those March weeks: she was far from sorry to see the last of Mr. McCune, since it was important to her to be in accord with her minister. She was still comfortable and happy with Elizabeth, although she had no illusions as to the permanence of the arrangement. Young Mr. Merrill had been all too attentive since the Rausches' holiday dance: many an evening the young couple spent in Amanda's parlor, while she worked alone at the center table in her sitting room, correcting Latin papers. She suspected that the collaboration on realistic middle-western fiction would be her last chance to work in pleasant companionship with Elizabeth.

By the time Amanda had her paper ready, she thought ruefully that rarely in her life had she wasted so much time on anything so trivial, however much she had enjoyed doing it.

By that tag-end of March, spring was well on the way: crocuses, snowdrops, and even some audacious jonquils were in bloom in every front yard. Pupils were always restless in the spring, and Amanda would be glad when school was out, although Elizabeth would be going home to Cleveland for the summer. And she might not come back, at least to teach and live with her. Amanda had never got over her revulsion against marriage: there was about it a kind of license to indecency. She understood Saint Paul's point of view, but she suspected there was something queer about her, since most females thought of nothing but how to accomplish it. There was really only one possible unattached male, so far as she knew, in Waynesboro: young Tim Merrill, and Elizabeth seemed to have snared him. There was of course Sheldon Edwards. He would probably some day want a mother for his two boys, however monastic a life he was presently leading: store and home and the long walk between, church on Sabbath, with the older boy Lowrey. Amanda sometimes saw them on their way as she walked up Linden Street hill.

Amanda was fond enough of Elizabeth to hope that she would be successful, if acquisition of a husband was what she considered success, and was glad she had got in ahead of Mrs. Stevens, who also was obviously (at least to Amanda) "looking about," as the phrase went. Amanda did not warm up much to Mrs. Stevens, and could not feel it natural that she should join their church, as she had done, by letter. She suspected Jessamine of some ulterior motive, although she could not conceive what it might be: there were no eligible single men in that congregation, only farmers and theologues. It was odd how Christina Voorhees had taken her up. Amanda reproached herself for making these uncharitable judgments, even in her mind.

Unlike Eliza Ballard, she did not give them substance by voicing them. Eliza, as might have been expected, had kept a jaundiced eye on Mrs. Jessamine Stevens since her advent: she was altogether too charming to be true. Eliza had met her only a few times, but she could foresee what the developing intimacy between her and Christina Voorhees would lead to: in the fall, when the Club had recovered from the loss of Kitty Edwards, and had come to realize the need for a new active member. She wondered how Anne Gordon would like that; she considered Anne a fool, whether she was in actuality a too-trusting wife, or was just pretending to be. Eliza hinted as much to Sally Rausch the afternoon of April eleventh, after the Club meeting at which Miss Elizabeth Talmadge read "Realism in Indiana: 'A Hoosier Schoolmaster,' by Edward Eggleston."

The ladies of the Club, after adjournment, congratulated Elizabeth, and some of them sympathized with her for having had to spend time on such "a dull, dreary book"; she had made the most of it, "although such drab realism could hardly be to her taste." As the members prepared to depart, there were some murmurs among them as to the possibility of inviting that "delightful Mrs. Stevens" to become a member of the Club. Eliza said to Sally when they were next to each other for a moment, awaiting their chance to speak to the author of the day, that if the little Stevens boy was as ill as he seemed to be, she wouldn't think Mrs. Stevens would feel she could take the time to be a very active member of the Club.

"Little Rodney? He has malaria, a hangover from last summer, with rather bad attacks only occasionally. He'll outgrow it in time."

"Oh? I thought it must be something really serious, the doctor's buggy is so often at their gate when I go to work in the mornings."

"It's plain you've never raised any children, or you would know they always choose the deadliest hour of the night to be ill. A widow with only one child is bound to be apprehensive, and Dock's her only relative: no doubt he is a great comfort to her."

"Oh, no doubt." Eliza twisted her mouth in an imitation smile, skeptical and scornful, and moved away.

"And also no doubt," Sally thought, "you walk in Linden Street instead of Main just to see." Eliza had to be at the Rausch Cordage Company office at nine in the morning: rather early for Dock to be out making calls, but on the other hand, rather late to be leaving. Sally did not really take Eliza's innuendo very seriously, angry as it had made her: it was another "truth universally acknowledged" that a young widow with a child would like a husband, a good respectable marriage. Certainly any prudent woman (and Sally was sure that beneath the soft-soap manners, Jessamine Stevens was sufficiently prudent) would not venture into any forbidden territory in Waynesboro.

The next Club meeting was a musical afternoon at the Rausches, with Thomasina playing for the ladies, and Elsa and Ludwig Junior dropping in after school to perform together on piano and violin. At the last meeting of the year, May thirteenth at Mrs. McKinney's, Christina favored the members with a dissertation on "Contemporary American Historians." It was far shorter (to the relief of some) than the Club was accustomed to hearing from its author. Christina, still servantless, had found her hands full that spring: in addition to striving—in vain, as she was well aware—to keep the house reasonably clean, to serve up to her family meals she knew were unappetizing, to give her children the attention they should have (she was not one to turn them over to servants, like some she could name), she had begun to go through her father's books and papers, putting aside most of the theologies to present to the Seminary library, sorting out papers that could be destroyed: old family letters, bills, receipts, sermons, correspondence with other ministers and professors. For no matter who was chosen by the General Assembly to take her father's place, the Voorhees family would certainly have to move before long. She had not had much time for the historians.

Sally Rausch, rising from her stiff parlor chair in Mrs. McKinney's stiff parlor, thought that Anne, who had been absent, had not missed much. She thanked Mrs. McKinney for her hospitality, shepherded her two passengers, the Gardiner sisters, out the door to her carriage, even as she complimented the author of the day.

She caught herself sighing as she listened to the Misses Gardiners' polite murmurings: Poor Anne! What should have been gala days ahead, with their young people graduating, was going to be another difficult season for the Gordons: Binny was ill again and in bed, and her mother in the depths of despair. Sally had not heard the words "rheumatic fever," but had no doubt that was what it would prove to be. "The wretched child!" Sally thought, "it is her own fault." For Anne had told her how Binny had gone out at dawn for violets on May Day morning, for Julia Deming. "I can't understand it," Anne had said, "that both my children should be so bewitched by that girl. I only hope that when Johnny gets away to medical school he'll come to his senses." What Anne had not reported to Sally was the set-to between John and his daughter in the kitchen that morning. On the first of May all the children went to the woods for flowers for their May baskets, but not, most of them, at the break of day. John had come into the kitchen from a call into the country that had kept him until dawn, and had found Binny in the kitchen standing over a great heap of violets, a handful of watercress, and some marsh marigolds.

"What got you up at this ungodly hour? D'you mean to say you've been *out* already?"

"I went out early to be sure to find enough violets before they were all picked. For a May basket."

"*A* May basket? There's enough violets there for all your friends. Is there something so special about one May basket?"

"It's for Julia," Binny had said proudly but anxiously. "She's so *nice* to me, Papa."

"But you know you've no business to be doing this sort of thing, for Julia or anyone else. D'you want to be sick again? And you look like a tramp: your hair blown into a regular thistle, your hands blue with cold. And your feet: you can't pick flowers at this hour this time of year without getting your feet soaking wet."

Her high-buttoned boots were in fact sodden to their tops. Binny thrust them out, obediently if resentfully, for her father to see.

"Good God! Even your petticoats! Go get your clothes off and go straight to bed until breakfast time. Have you other boots you can wear to school?"

"This is Saturday."

"So it is. So much the better. Go to bed and stay there. I'll ask Martha to take you up some breakfast."

"But Papa! The violets!"

"They'll keep. Where does Martha keep her dishpan? Oh, here—"

He pumped water in the pan and swept the whole unsorted mass of flowers and greens into it. "And don't let me ever hear of your doing such a damn fool trick again."

A tearful Binny crept upstairs. Her father shook down the stove, opened the drafts, put kindling and coal on the glowing embers and set about making himself a pot of coffee. Before it had time to boil, Anne came in, fully dressed in her crisp morning calico, to find a morose husband staring unseeingly at the stove.

"What's the matter? I heard you and Binny—"

"This infernal stove! Is it always so slow to catch?" Then he indicated the dishpan full of flowers in the sink. "Your daughter's been out already and brought in all those, so she must have been traipsing around in the wet for hours. For a May basket for Julia Deming. I swear she grows more like my sister Kate every day. What's so special about Julia Deming, for God's sake?"

"Oh, John! It's just a schoolgirl crush. Julia was nice to her when she was sick, and Julia doesn't do anything to discourage devotion from anyone. Binny will outgrow it. Where is she?"

"She was sopping wet to her waist, very nearly. I sent her to bed—said Martha would take up her breakfast—in the hope she wouldn't take cold. She mustn't run that risk."

"I know. I'm sorry I didn't hear her get up." Anne set about rescuing the flowers and putting them in vases. Binny, comfortably curled up in her bed, put her father's scolding out of her mind: all it really had room for these days was her joyous adoration of Julia. Now she was emotionally exalted and triumphant at the thought of all those violets, enough to make such a May basket as had never been seen. She was so deeply in love that nothing else mattered to her, certainly nothing so mundane as home, family, even scoldings. And she could, today, wait patiently for evening. Most Saturdays, when her family thought she was at the library, she would walk around blocks in the hope of meeting Julia, or go past the Deming house. And sometimes Julia was there, on the porch with friends; sometimes she would be encountered walking with them uptown. Then she would award Binny her most dazzling smile, or, if she was alone, she might even touch Binny, one of these spine-tingling touches, on the arm or shoulder, or she might stop for a moment or two and talk to her, or brush Binny's hair out of her eyes with a lingering gentle movement.

On that Saturday, Binny was allowed to get up for lunch, and spent the afternoon filling her May basket, a concoction of fringed and curled lavender tissue paper glued round and round a wide-mouthed cornucopia with a braided tissue paper handle. In the evening, in the dusk, the first stars just coming out, a market basket on her arm carried most carefully so as not to displace the violets so reverently arranged, Binny set out down the street to the Demings'. She was walking on air, in rapture wishing on the first star she saw, that Julia would—well, would at least like the May basket. She had never known quite such an exultation before; it swept over her, crown to toe. At the Demings' she crept up on the porch, hung the basket carefully on the doorknob, rang the bell, and scurried away, as May basket convention required. She did not however run very far: just to the shelter of the big curbside maple tree. Julia answered the door: she would be expecting May baskets, although the boys and girls her own age would not be out until it was real nighttime and deep dark—those of them who had not given up May baskets as altogether too childish. Binny could see her by the light from the hall: she lifted the May basket off the doorknob; Binny could hear her exclaim with delight as she took it inside. Binny would have asked no other reward—not just then, at any rate: she expected to hear Julia in a day or two saying, "The most beautiful May basket! *Who* do you suppose could have—?" But Julia had paused behind the still half-open front door just long enough to put the flowers down; she came back and called "Binny! Binny Gordon! No, don't run away. It's no use. I know it's you. No one else in the world—"

Binny, who had ducked back behind the tree trunk, came out sheepishly, suddenly overcome with shyness. Julia tripped across the porch, down to the gate, put one hand on Binny's shoulder to draw her closer, and with the other brushed the curls back from her forehead.

"Darling Binny! Of course I knew it was you: no one else would have picked those *millions* of violets just for me. It's the most beautiful May basket I ever saw, and I do thank you, darling Binny!" She leaned over the gate, tilted the child's head back, and kissed her full on the mouth. Binny, paralyzed with astonishment, flooded with an ecstasy that shook her physically, could only stare, starry-eyed. "Don't look so surprised, honey! Didn't you know I'd be thrilled to death? The beautiful basket and all the trouble you took to make it—and all those violets: I didn't know there were so many in the world. Where did you find them?"

A bemused Binny thought she really wanted to know. "Along the edge of the cemetery, by the railroad. That's where they're biggest. I'm glad you like them—it wasn't anything, really."

She walked home without really knowing that she was walking home, aware only of the shiver down her backbone and the strange yearning that swept her body, roused by the feel of Julia's lips on hers. At home she slipped upstairs without joining her mother in the sitting room: she wanted to be alone so that she could relive the evening over and over again. She only said "Yes" when her mother called to know if it was she, and "Good-night, Mamma. I'm going to bed now."

"A good thing. You were out so early this morning." Anne was too wise to go into the hall to watch her climb the stairs, or to ask whether Julia had been pleased; that the child was uplifted by joy she could tell well enough from the exalted note in her voice.

A week passed, ten days, and Binny showed no signs of a cold; her parents relaxed their watchfulness. Then one afternoon when she came in from school, she surprised her mother by saying she did not want an apple—no, nor a piece of gingerbread, either, and accompanied the shake of her head with what was clearly a painful attempt to swallow.

"Binny! Do you have a sore throat?"

Binny hesitated. She had concealed her condition as best she could, afraid to admit it, and afraid too of what it might mean; she had kept silent, hoping it would go away. But it would be a relief to confide her fears, and let someone else share them. "Yes," she said, "kind of."

"And rheumatic pains?"

Tall as she was growing to be—too tall to cast herself on her mother's lap—she dropped to the floor by her mother's rocker, laid her head on her mother's breast, her arms dangling, and after one long gulping breath began to weep silently, the tears running down her cheeks.

"Mamma, I don't want to be sick again. And Papa will scold."

"Did your father ever scold you when you were sick?" Her mother took a handkerchief from her belt to wipe the streaming eyes.

"No. But—"

"The pain can't be as bad as the other time. Remember how you screamed?" Anne felt sick at heart, almost faint with dread. But she set herself to comfort her child.

"It isn't bad—only my legs ache."

"Come, we'll get you to bed. Maybe it's just a bad cold."

When John came in and Anne had told him, he too was dismayed.

"Don't scold her, John."

"Scold her? Poor baby, am I such an ogre? Anyway, her frolic on May Day morning probably had nothing to do with this—too long ago. But a second bout of rheumatic fever— Did you take her temperature?"

"She has a fever. But the pains aren't anything like before. Won't it make a difference that we're catching it earlier? And a cold can make your bones ache. Couldn't it be just that?"

"How long has she had the sore throat?"

Anne could only shake her head.

"Well, we'll see what we can do. I have salicylic acid in my bag in the hall."

They went upstairs together to find Binny, feverish and her eyes glittering, watching the door for them. Her father brought pills and a glass of water.

"Here—take these—maybe we can stop the pain before it gets bad. And don't worry about any scolding: I don't think you picked this up gathering your violets, unless you've had a sore throat longer than I believe you could keep quiet about it. But you must make up your mind to stay in bed a bit—a week or so after the fever's gone, and all the pain."

"Oh, Papa! Two weeks? Three weeks?"

"Or maybe a month."

Tears welled in her eyes. "Then I won't see Commencement? Johnny and Elsa and Julia?"

"It's possible, so don't get your hopes up. On the other hand, you may get over this quickly. Dr. Warren and I will do our best."

She smiled at him. "I'd rather you than Dr. Warren."

"Two minds are better than one, you know."

The Gordons faced and endured another ordeal of sickness-in-the-house. It was easier to cope with because of the new gaslights and the new bathrooms, and Binny was not suffering the agonies she had suffered previously. But the fever lingered, and she grew listless and indifferent. John warned Anne: "To go through one bout of rheumatic fever and escape without endocarditis is none too common. A second bout is likely to do real damage: leave her with a rheumatic heart for the rest of her life."

He and Dr. Warren used their stethoscopes every morning and looked so solemn that Anne was frightened. She said one morning, "The Cincinnati doctor, won't he come examine her?"

"Of course he would. We can ask him a little later. It's too early to tell yet."

And Anne was more frightened. She was sure that John and Dr. Warren felt no need to call in a specialist: their own stethoscopes told them. She had little enthusiasm for Johnny's Commencement. And that was sad for him: Binny's sickness and his parents' concern shadowed those days that he might, and should, have felt were the most important of his life.

On Commencement morning Julia and Elsa came to the Gordons' to show Binny their graduation finery: ruffled and flounced white dresses; hats, white straw, wide over their foreheads, narrow in back above their great knots of hair; long white kid gloves above their elbows and in their arms great sheaves of roses. And Binny did not really care: not as she would have cared a few months earlier.

The Gordon parents attended the Commencement exercises, hard as it always was for John to leave his office in mid-morning. Anne was tired, how tired she had not realized until, once seated in the Opera House, she folded her hands in her lap and tried to give her attention to the proceedings. It was a hot June morning, the Opera House seat was hard. She tried to restrain her restlessness as the endless number of addresses by the graduates followed one another; actually she heard very little: Johnny's Latin Salutatory, of which she understood scarcely a word (Where had her Latin gone? She had known it once!) but which pleased her both for Johnny's sake and for Amanda's; his address, "Nineteenth Century Advances in Medicine," which she hoped John was proud of; Elsa's uncharacteristically moral and serious "Effort the Price of Success," and Julia's flowing "Childhood in Literature," which Anne thought omitted more than it contained; and Billy Thirkield's Valedictory. One could not be actually bored by the program: the eager young faces were so pleasant to watch. It had not occurred to one of them yet, she thought sadly, that he just might not in the years ahead have all he wanted, and counted on, from life; or that those years could be darkened by sorrows, many and inevitable. She could have wept for them, taking their diplomas from Mr. Lichtenstein, smiling their thanks, so happily sure of the future.

As for the young graduates themselves, their adulthood, if you could call it that, was being ushered in joyously enough: the Rausches were having a Commencement Ball that night after the Class Supper for such of the graduates and other high school students as were permitted and knew how to dance. After that, they would begin to scatter: some would go to work at once, some after a long idle summer would be going away to school, and after a year or two they would wonder why they had thought they cared so much for each other on this last day together.

MEMBERS OF THE
WAYNESBORO WOMAN'S CLUB

Miss Eliza Ballard
Mrs. Louisa Deming
Mrs. Gwen Evans
Miss Caroline Gardiner
Miss Lavinia Gardiner
Mrs. Anne Gordon
Mrs. Rhoda McKinney
Mrs. Laura Maxwell
Mrs. Elizabeth Merrill
Mrs. Sara Rausch
Miss Amanda Reid
Mrs. Jessamine Stevens
Mrs. Thomasina Travers
Mrs. Christina Voorhees

IN MEMORIAM

Mrs. Mary Ballard
Miss Susan Crenshaw
Mrs. Katherine Edwards
Mrs. Mary McCune
Miss Agatha Pinney

* 1887–1888 *

"The children we call 'ours' are beginning their careers in the adult world."

In Waynesboro, on the surface at least, one summer was very like another: to the casual eye the children playing their games in the big yards behind the iron fences were eternally the same as the girls and boys of the year before and the year before that. But the games of one season were played by another generation than those who had played them three or four years earlier, so quickly does childhood pass into adolescence, adolescence into adulthood. The young girls who had romped through the summer days so recently now played sedate tennis matches on the Rausches' court, sat on front porches in chattering groups in the afternoons, with palm-leaf fans and pitchers of iced lemonade. They spent their evenings on the same porches with young gentlemen strumming banjoes and guitars, or went for long slow buggy rides in the country. They all, June graduates from the high school as well as Sophie Klein and Charlotte Bonner, home for vacation from their eastern colleges, considered themselves grown-up, prepared for adult life. And so did the boys, with more justification. Those who had finished school in the spring were soberly at work: some in jobs they hoped would be permanent; some learning from their fathers, in humble positions, what they would go on to college to learn about from books; Rudy Lichtenstein, after his first year at the university, was in his father's office; Billy Thirkield in the fall would go to the college of pharmacy in the city, but was in the meantime clerk, janitor, and general factotum in his father's drugstore, doing anything and everything but fill prescriptions; Johnny Gordon, accepted as a doctor's assistant by most patients, acted under his father's watchful eye as a very tentative diagnostician, and was learning how to bandage wounds and splint broken limbs; he drove the mare for his father on his daily rounds through the countryside and carried the battered old bag, having already replaced, under supervision, the drugs that had been used the day before. Even Ernest

Rausch, fifteen that summer, had been put to work as a wheel boy in the mill. Naturally if he were ever to inherit his father's place in the business, he had need to know it firsthand from the ground up. Ludwig could have let him off: in another year or so there would be little use for the old ropewalk. Already yarn was handspun for only the most exacting specifications of valued customers; soon there would be no further need of wheel boys. But Ludwig thought the hand-spinning process a part of his son's education, and Ernest was a husky, well-grown boy: a summer's hard work would do him no harm.

Ernest's next brother, Charles, was free as air still: old enough not to be nursemaided, not old enough to be put to work. Ludwig Junior, at nine, was not permitted so much independence, but he did not always heed the matutinal injunction of every Waynesboro mother whose children had gone to school for several years unattended, and could no longer be kept within the home fences, but could be told, "Don't go where you can't hear me call you," or "Don't go away without asking first," commands so habitually heard as to be in fact unheard. And luckily (or perhaps unluckily for him) the child was born with charm, and his smile was irresistible. The group of children Ludwig Junior's age included Lowrey Edwards, Lavinia Gardiner (sometimes with five-year-old Caroline tagging along), a Klein, a Lichtenstein, and various others, depending on the neighborhood they had chosen for their gathering: out Linden Street at the Edwardses', up Chillicothe Street at the Gardiners', up Market at the Kleins' or the Rausches'. The long summer evenings were most of them spent at the Gardiners', on the chance that Captain Bodien might come to see his daughter and granddaughters, and could be induced to tell them tales of the Old West, Indians, Mormons, the Pony Express. Young Ludwig, as entranced by Captain Bodien's stories as his sister and older brother had been, always appeared on those evenings, however far afield he might have gone for his day's exploits. He was more than a handful for his mother and the faithful Cassie, who had but one child now to fuss over, scold, and care for: little Paul.

Later in the summer Rodney Stevens became one of the group: he had won complete acceptance on the evening when he had stood up to them in the presence of Captain Bodien. He was, they considered, unfit for the Captain's stories; they taunted him: "Your father was a Rebel! Your Grandpa was a Rebel! Johnny Reb!" He, at eight or nine, knowing little of what it was all about, had retorted, "They weren't Rebels! They were good soldiers. And my Grandpa was killed. And all your grandfathers were damned Yankees!" To the other children's astonishment and chagrin, Captain Bodien had come to his support. "Now you just forget that 'Rebel' business. I know that's what we called them, but they were mighty good soldiers, and we ran from them often enough. I'm proud of Rodney, not being afraid to face you all." They decided they had best be proud of Rodney, too, if Captain Bodien felt that way about him.

The Voorhees children never won acceptance as friends and equals. Their parents had traded houses with the Maxwells when the Professor had finally been named president of the Seminary. The Voorheeses' new home, across from the Gardiners', seemed more a part of the town than the old one on the Seminary campus. However much Christina held herself and her children aloof, the Voorheeses had become more visible. Waynesboro's verdict was that Blair and Jane Voorhees were bound to grow up mighty queer: they were not permitted to go to school, but were taught at home by their mother; they never actually "played" with their contemporaries; they were occasionally allowed to go across the street to the Gardiners', late in the day, when all small fry had been "cleaned up for the afternoon," and the most riotous game was a decorous "Drop the Handkerchief."

Rodney Stevens' very first afternoon "out to play" had been at the Voorheeses'. Although he still had bouts of malaria, he was a much healthier child than when his mother had first brought him to Waynesboro. When he was sent, on Christina Voorhees' express invitation, to visit her children, Jessamine put him in the charge of her colored maid-and-nursemaid, and saw them off together. In the late afternoon she went herself to call on Christina and to collect him. By that time he was not at the Voorheeses', but across the street at the Gardiners', one of a noisy group in a circle on the Gardiner side lawn. Miss Lavinia and Miss Caroline had long since come to realize that Barbara was not always going to take, or send, her children somewhere else to play; the sisters Gardiner believed their place was the most popular playground in town. They could not fault Barbara on her little girls' manners: the older ones—old enough to be teachable—were respectful to their elders, curtsied nicely when introduced, and spoke when spoken to. But with other children they were as noisy and obstreperous as any; even Veronica, two years old, could yell with the best of them toppling head over heels in her effort to keep up, picking herself up again, sometimes with a laugh, sometimes with a wail. The aunts looked forward shudderingly to the time when baby Mary would have graduated from her carriage. They could only rejoice that their suite of upstairs rooms was on the side of the house away from the big spread of yard, and that they could shut their windows against the noise.

On the afternoon that Rodney had been bold enough to join them instead of staying at the Voorheeses', where he was supposed to be, Christina was offhand about it when Jessamine came for him: the children, hers and Rodney, had got to quarreling, and when she called them in to put a stop to it, Rodney had simply walked out the gate and across the street. She did not know what had started the quarrel, but thought it possible that he was a little spoiled, having been ill so much. No more annoying comment on her child can be made to a mother, but Jessamine suppressed any show of emotion: she had worked too hard for her friendship with Christina to endanger it; she said in her sweetest voice and broadest Mississippi accent, "He has been too much alone. He needs the company of other children. We we' so isolated on the plantation. No school—just tutoring with other plantation boys. It was kind of you to invite him, an' mighty rude of him not to come when you called. You must let your children visit him some day: I'll see that he behaves mo' like a gentleman." She drank a cup of tea with Christina, sent for the nursemaid Cally from the kitchen where she had quite evidently spent the afternoon with the Voorhees cook-and-maid-of-all-work, crossed the street to call Rodney; then, trailing the two of them behind her, having made it clear that they were in disfavor, walked home without a spoken reproach until she got them into the living room.

"Cally, I sent you with Rodney to see that he behaved himself."

"Ah was ast into the kitchen whalst they played. Chillun hyah ain' watched so much."

"You were supposed to keep an eye on him."

"Yas'm. Ah knowed they was fussin', but Ah di'n know Rodney taken off like that. Ah thought he come when Miz Voo'hees call."

"Mamma, I don't need—"

"You're too little to know what you need. Evidently: since you left your host an' went somewheah else. When you're invited to someone's house to play with the children theah, that is what you're supposed to do. How did it happen I found you across the street?"

"They were having more fun."

"But you don't know those chil'ren. You know Blaih and Jane from Sabbath school."

"That Blair, he plays too rough. And I do too know them: Lowrey Edwards lives out on this street." He dropped his voice. "He—did you know, Mamma—*he hasn't got any mother?* And I know Vinny Gardiner."

"Neveh mind. They may be nice children, but you we'n't invited to thei' house and you we' invited to Blai's."

"Mamma, can I go to school in the fall? Blair says he's *never* goin' to school—his mother knows more than any old school teacher."

"I'm su' she does. But I don't, so of cou'se you will go to school if you are well enough. But remembe' afte' this: Miz Voo'hees is my friend, whom I esteem highly; Mr. Voo'hees is my banke'. And any way: you must neveh be rude to anyone in any ci'cumstances."

She sent him off to his playroom suitably chastened and turned to the young Negress who had been standing waiting, hands clasped before her.

"Cally, you must know what happened?"

"Yes'm. Rodney too nice to tell yo'. That Blai' hit him with a brick when Rodney jus' hit him with a little ol' switch off the apple-tree. That Blai'! He dunno how to play. He think that fun, hittin' somun with a brick. Ah di'n know Rodney taken off lak that, but Ah don' blame him. An' those a' nice chillun: that li'l Lowrey and the li'l Gya'dne' gi'ls. Lutie tell me they play nice, an' Rubina done say—"

"Who's Lutie? Who's Rubina?"

"Lutie's the Gya'dne's housemaid; Rubina's Miz Voo'hees'."

"My goodness, Cally, do you know all the se'vants in this town?"

"Mos' of 'um. They Zion Baptis', lak me. That Rubina, you know what Ah think? I think Mis Voo'hees not use' to hi'ed gi'ls. Else Rubina woul'n' talk so disrespectful."

"Nonsense. Mrs. Voo'hees is used to white se'vants, not to good-fo'-nothin' niggehs. And you know bette' than to let any se'vant talk disrespectfully about a friend of mine."

"Yes'm. But yo' ask me. Rubina say she on'y wuk fo' 'em a little while, since they move. They use' to live in that da'k ol' house unde' the trees, up whe' all the students at. No one fo' them chillun to play with—that's how come that Blai' think it playin' to hit somun with a brick. Rubina say the' mothe' done dete'mine to keep them unspotted from the wo'ld. Ah tell you', Miz Jessamine, yo' try to keep Rodney unspotted, you gwun have all the boys an gi'ls makin' fun of him. They think they done outgrown nussmaids."

"That's enough, Cally. I don't ca' what Rubina said. And I don't want you to pick up the ways of these triflin' No'th'n niggehs. If you do, I'll send you back to Mississippi."

"Yas'm." Cally rolled her eyes away from her mistress. She had no desire to return to Mississippi; she was enjoying the freer air of Waynesboro. She had not realized quite yet that her mistress' threat was an empty one: that she would not have to go to Mississippi just because she was "sent."

After that day Rodney was allowed to play with the children who gathered in one yard or another, sometimes in his. And he was allowed to go unaccompanied by Cally, though his mother would never have admitted that she had taken advice from her maid. Occasionally the two small Voorhees children were permitted to cross the street and join those in the Gardiner yard; when this occurred the others in a short while drifted away: "I gotta go now." It was not Jane they objected to: she was only five, and harmless, a pale, blonde, silent little girl (whom the colored maids and nursemaids called a "meachin' li'l ol' thing" and suspected of tale-bearing); it was Blair the others could not play with peaceably for more than a few minutes: he liked to tell them what to do, and when they did otherwise, he would grow angry and start throwing rocks or whatever came to hand. "He hasn't got any *sense*" they would say to protesting adults. Christina was as well pleased, really, that her children did not care for playing with the others, particularly with that "rough little Rausch boy," a year older than Blair, and capable of handling him and any two others at the same time.

Young Ludwig's mother worried about him. She was sure he would rebel against going into the mill. Not that she wanted that for him: she saw him in her mind's eye as, in time, a famous concert violinist. One thing about the boy: if you could pin him down before he escaped, and set him to practicing, he would be carried away, forget himself, and keep playing until he was called to a meal. But there were other times when he needed a strong hand on the rein. Sally was not ready to admit yet that hers was not strong enough; she was unwilling to trouble his father with disciplinary problems at home: he had enough on his mind that summer. At least, Ludwig Junior was obstreperously healthy; one thing that made him a difficult child was his superabundance of energy and high spirits. She thought of all the mothers who had anemic, listless children, or really ill ones, like Binny Gordon, and rejoiced in her own good fortune.

Ludwig Senior, too, in spite of the financial problems on his mind, had time that summer for thought of Binny, still in bed at the end of June. He stopped in John's office on his way home late one afternoon to ask whether he might visit her, as he had done before. It was after office hours, and all the patients who had come in had been taken care of and dismissed. He found the two Gordons in the middle office, where the chess table had been pushed aside, talking gravely together. Johnny looked suspiciously teary and ashamed of it; he turned away at Ludwig's entrance and began to pack up the disordered chessmen.

Ludwig greeted them, and said, "You are worried about Binny? But I thought this was a lighter case than the last."

"She is not suffering so acutely. The pain is not so bad."

"But?"

"There is a heart involvement. No doubt about it."

"Serious?" Ludwig was shocked. That a child—

"It can be very serious. We had Krebs up from Cincinnati: he confirmed our diagnosis and agreed that Warren is doing what can be done."

"You think Warren is a good man?"

"Very good. He may look like an overgrown country boy, but he knows medicine."

Ludwig had never thought of the tall Dr. Warren, rawboned and thin, as "overgrown." But that was what he would look like to Dock, who was so slight and neat and compact. "I'm glad you think he's good. The town could use more doctors. I really stopped in to ask whether I might spend an evening with Binny now and then. She must get mighty bored, lying there in bed."

"Of course. Thanks. Just don't excite her." John sighed. "You won't find her as responsive as before, or as interested in your old soldier's tales. She isn't much interested in anything, not even in getting out of bed. I suspect she's uneasy all the time: a heart irregularity can be terrifying even though it may not be serious."

"As she improves she will get over that. Tell her I'll stop in some evening when I'm free. Right now I'm all tied up, I'm on the way to Doug Gardiner; we have an appointment to discuss a patent matter. Stewart Bodien's out in the buggy waiting for me. That boy is going to be worth his weight in gold to me, one of these days."

Stewart Bodien had gone back to Rausch Cordage Company on his graduation from Sheffield in preference to West Point, to his father's disappointment. He stayed only long enough to gain experience in industrial engineering, but expected to move on at the first good opportunity. Now it looked as if he would be staying at the rope mill indefinitely. He had been put in charge of the maintenance of all the mill machinery, even of the Corliss steam engine that provided the power to run the mill and was Ludwig's pride and joy. Stewart had been given a machine shop: an extemporized, roughly built extension of the power house. Manufacturing processes had become more and more complex. Fewer laborers were needed as new labor-saving machines were invented. They were temperamental and needed babying. However, Stewart had time in his little shop to use his mind, and he had no misgivings at all (as his father had) about the increasing use of machinery. Looking about to see what could be done as well or better by machine as by hand, he had lighted upon the tarring process, still carried on as it had always been by two laborers pulling the spun yarns through the tar tank while two others shoveled coal into the red-hot firebox underneath to keep the tar fluid. He had spent the winter first thinking, then drawing, then finally constructing a model. He hoped it would be possible to tar yarn by his machine. If so, the primitive tarring shed could be done away with. When his model was finished, he went one day to the office to tell Ludwig he had something to show him if he would come to the machine shop.

Stewart looked a good deal like his father: the same hawk nose, although his face was not so broad in structure, in forehead, cheek, or jaw. Black-browed, black-haired, he had usually an impassive Red Indian sort of look, but Ludwig, walking beside him to the machine shop, could feel the suppressed excitement in the young man. Inside his makeshift quarters, Stewart whipped the tarpaulin cover off the model on his workbench.

"My first invention," he said, with an attempt to be casual. "I don't know if you'll think it useful."

Ludwig studied it a moment: the rectangular tank, perhaps eighteen inches long and a third as wide, copper-lined, with coils of copper wire ranged along the bottom; a wide-mouthed tube at one end, at the other, one smaller in circumference, with a double-geared wheel attached, and at intervals along the sides a row of hooks, obviously movable. Ludwig was puzzled.

"It's a tarring machine." Stewart was a little dashed: his boss should have seen at a glance what it was. "It isn't a real working model. Let me show you." He took a handful of pieces of yarn from his pocket, inserted them in the wider tube, pulled them the length of the tank, and thrust them through.

"Of course. Wie dumm! One man could do it all: feed the yarns in here and the hauling apparatus would pull it through. The coils of wire in the tank represent steam coils, I suppose? That isn't new: most companies, I believe, heat tar that way."

"Yes, sir, I know. It's an economical method. An underground pipe carries steam from the boiler, with risk of fire removed. But some of it is new. The gears are placed to keep the yarn moving at the correct speed to give it the right amount of tar. And the small tube at the far end will squeeze out the surplus, and drop the yarn into canisters."

"Yes, the steam would be no problem. And one difficulty would be solved: the problem of excess tar. The pulling end would have to be fairly strong. Tarred yarn is heavy."

"That's why the wheel here is double-geared." Stewart revealed his eagerness and his pleasure at Ludwig's ready comprehension.

"Where would you put it?" Ludwig glanced out the window to the far end of the cobbled yard where in the dilapidated old open-sided tarring shed two Negroes were feeding yarn in and pulling yarn out of the tank above the red-hot firebox while two others were shoveling coal on the fire.

"It wouldn't have to be so far away as that. There'd be no danger of fire. Say between the spinning mill and the forming yard. Yarn could be brought from the spinners to be tarred, and when it had dried, taken to be formed into strands. The canisters could be moved by boys."

"Yes. But we don't tar all of our rope, by any means."

"I know. Just marine ropes, binder twine, or other kinds that will be exposed to the weather."

"Does Captain Bodien think this would be practical?"

"I haven't said anything to him about it, for fear he would think the old way of tarring was good enough and I was just wasting my time."

Ludwig laughed. "You mustn't be too hard on us two old fogies. You probably had your doubts about me, too."

"No sir, you've bought too much modern machinery for me to question your readiness."

"See if you can find your father, will you? I'd like to ask him what he thinks of it."

Captain Bodien was too proud of his son to say he considered a tarring machine unnecessary, though he must have thought there would be many days when it would not be used. But then the steam could be cut off and turned on again when it was needed it: it would not take so long as building up a coal fire that could heat the tar to the necessary 220 degrees.

"I can see," he said, "that if it worked it would save us money both in labor and in fuel."

Ernest was probably the only one of his sons, Ludwig thought, who would ever work as a wheel boy. The others could start by hauling canisters of yarn first to the tarring machine, and then back to the forming mill. In his mind's eye he saw it already in operation. "Could you make that machine in your shop here?"

"Well, no, sir. It's hardly got the facilities. I'd have to take the drawings to the city."

"And watch over its construction yourself, I hope. Bodien, ever see a tarring machine before?"

"Not like this. Tarring is just one of those dirty jobs that has to be done."

"And sometimes it gets done in a slipshod way, so that the tar is thick here and thin there, and the yarn has to be thrown away, or used for oakum or ships' fenders. Come on back to the office with me, both of you, and we'll talk terms."

By the time they had got seated, Stewart had recovered somewhat from his astonishment. "I don't understand, Mr. Rausch. I made this for the company, on company time."

"I know. And the first machine: the company will pay the cost of making it, and it will be ours. But" (Ludwig's mind was bolder than Stewart's dared to be) "there's no reason, given a proper machine shop and a few machinists, why we shouldn't make more and sell them. If it works, of course. So there are things to consider. First, you must patent this at once. If someone is ahead of you, Washington will let us know, but do it before you take the model and drawings to anyone. You have drawings?"

"I can copy the working drawings I made." Stewart grinned. "They're kind of dog-eared now."

"We'll patent it and have one machine made. If it works, there's only one reason why we couldn't build a machine shop and make more: shortage of capital. As your father knows, I have tied up all the company's reserve capital I dare use for the purchase of hemp. There's more coming: the warehouse is so full now I may have to rent storage space. I have reason to believe the rumor going around that the biggest York State cordage companies are going to join in a trust. If they do, they will set out to buy up or ruin small companies like this. You know how trusts operate?"

"You lower prices below cost, and small companies can't do that. When they fail, you raise your prices as high as you like."

"Yes. And in this case I look for the first step toward getting rid of competition to be an attempt to corner the raw material. That might be possible now that American hemp isn't raised any more and it all has to be imported. So I have bought all the hemp, hard and soft fiber both, that we could afford to buy. If I guessed wrong and the cost of hemp should go down, we could be hurt bad: we'd have to sell rope below cost to keep our market. So, at this moment, a new machine shop is out of the question."

"Yes, sir."

Captain Bodien said, "I have some savings I could invest. Could the machine shop be incorporated separately from the rope company?"

"Rausch and Bodien? I don't see why not. But that will have to wait. First, the patent, then the machine and a building to put it in. By that time we should know something more about the mill's chances of surviving. However, if it works, Stewart has at least earned an increase in pay. And an understanding about his inventions. So long as you stick to rope machinery, Stewart, and work out your problems on company time, all results will be the property of the company. But if it should be salable to other companies, you will be entitled to a royalty on every machine sold. That will never make you rich: there aren't that many cordage companies left."

"And most of them import machinery, Glasgow-made," Captain Bodien said. "I'd like to see more machine tool companies in this country making cordage machinery. The British have the wrong idea, making machines so heavy and indestructible that they will last forever. And so expensive they almost have to. Machinery should not cost so much that it cannot be discarded when a better and more efficient machine is invented. I know you bought the very best machinery to be had when you bought from Combe, Barker, and Combe in Glasgow, but how long will it be before you can afford to replace it?"

Ludwig said, "It will last my lifetime. But I had to get the best I could. I saw this fight shaping up."

"I know, sir, I didn't mean to be critical. There just isn't much American machinery now, and I suppose a trust could corner that, too. But when more is made, I think it will be on a fundamentally different notion of what machinery should be."

"That day will doubtless come. In the meantime, Stewart, back to your possible inventions. Anything you cook up on your own time with materials that you have purchased and that has nothing to do with rope will be yours, absolutely, to do what you like with: sell or manufacture. However, if I let you use the company machine shop, will you as a courtesy, not an obligation, let me have first refusal on anything you come up with? There may come a day when I'll have surplus capital again."

"How about that Columbus and Southwestern Interurban Line, Cap'n Rausch?"

Ludwig grimaced. "I can't get out of that now. The surveying has all been done for the right-of-way, and the land bought. They'll start leveling off the ground and laying track any day now. But it will take a while before we have a return on our investment. And I can't sell out: too many other people have put their money in it on the strength of my recommendation. Why, Bodien? Did you buy some stock in that?"

"A little. I'm under no obligation to hold it, I suppose, if I want to use the money to help Stewart."

"None at all. But don't do it. You wouldn't get any kind of price on it now, and once that road is running, it's going to be a gold mine."

"Pity the other threat had to come up just now."

"Or at all, Lord knows, but it can't be helped. We'll have to weather the storm as best we can. I have no intention of selling the mill to any trust, and I'll fight any attempt to put us out of business. At any rate, the first thing now is the patent."

Something of all this Ludwig explained to the two Gordons the afternoon he stopped in their office: long enough to ask about Binny and to express his pleasure over Stewart Bodien and make clear the reason for the appointment with Doug Gardiner. When he had gone, John stood looking after him, smiling. "There's a man who has everything he wants of life: a delightful wife and a healthy family, a successful business; he'll wind up a millionaire before he's done. Johnny, for the last time let me ask you: are you sure you want to be a doctor? It isn't too late."

"But you know I have wanted it ever since I can remember. I'd rather be a doctor than a millionaire."

"Well, I doubt whether you'd be a millionaire in any case: Gordons don't have the knack. But if you are going into medicine with the romantic notion of easing suffering, of saving lives, of grateful patients—do forget all that and look at the other side."

John paced his office a moment while Johnny watched him, wondering: his father did not often talk about his profession in a general way.

"Sit down, Johnny, and listen: I am serious." John went to his desk, swung his swivel chair around and dropped into it. "Have you thought of the suffering you will have to watch and can't relieve? Of the lives you might save—good, useful lives—if only you knew more? We all are so ignorant still."

"Like Binny, you mean?" The words came harshly from Johnny's tight throat.

"Like Binny," his father said sadly. "If she gets better, it won't be because Dr. Warren or I know anything that will cure endocarditis. Nor any other doctor, so far as I can discover." With a gesture over his shoulder, he indicated the books and magazines piled on the desk behind him. "That is one thing you will have to face: the frustration, the helplessness, a doctor feels when he is presented with a hopeless case that he believes he could cure if only he knew more. But that is not the worst. The worst is when a case becomes hopeless because he guessed wrong in the first place."

Johnny looked his astonishment. "But you have never lost a case because you were wrong!"

John smiled grimly. "I think you really believe that. I'm grateful. But yes: I have guessed wrong, or gambled on taking a chance with some new treatment." He thought of the Negro whose leg he had tried to save so long ago, of Kitty Edwards, who, if he had just put his foot down— "And I have lost patients I shouldn't have lost. That's a hard thing to live with. And you have to live with it, get used to it, not let it affect you, because if you do you're no use to anyone. The next time you see Death come out of the corner of a room to stand by the bedside, you have to be bold enough to gamble again, if need be."

"I suppose," Johnny said slowly, a little white around the mouth, "that—Death"—he stumbled over the word—"is never farther away than the corner of the room. And always wins in the end."

"Yes. The inevitably triumphant adversary. But one other thing you do learn, after a while: a doctor fights Death to the end, but he comes to know that his adversary is not always something to be frightened of. Death can even be a friend."

"But look, Papa." Johnny pulled himself together and spoke more firmly. "There's been a lot learned in the last few years. Doctors know more than they used to. About microbes, I mean. Won't it be easier to cure diseases when we know what causes them?"

"We've known how to prevent smallpox since the eighteenth century without knowing what caused it. Now we know what causes typhoid and diphtheria and tuberculosis, and we can do something to prevent their spreading, but we still don't know any more about curing them. Tuberculosis is still our number one killer. However, I grant you, surgery is less dangerous than it used to be, now we know that wounds must be kept sterile. And it may be that in your days as a physician all these problems will be solved. I don't want to discourage you; I just want to be sure you realize what you are up against."

"I do, Papa. But I'm not discouraged." "Who knows," he did not say, "but I may be another Lister, another Virchow."

John was still thinking of all the young people who had not been brought to him until their tuberculosis was well advanced, just because their frightened parents could not admit to their minds the dread word "consumption."

"You've got two patients now, haven't you, where Death is creeping out of the corner of the room?"

"More than that." John was brooding over the doomed boys and girls. He could recommend a change of climate or that new sanitarium of Dr. Trudeau's at Lake Placid, and if there was money enough, the patient might be taken to one place or the other, but to no good end, usually, the disease being too far advanced before a doctor ever saw it. "What two were you thinking of?"

"Mr. Cochran. Mrs. Ballard."

"Those are cases where Death is as much friend as foe. They have lived full lives, usefully and happily, and the skeleton in the corner can't be stood off forever. They both know very well the end cannot be far away, though we don't admit it to each other. They are ready and cheerful enough, just waiting. Mr. Cochran's senile myocarditis is distressing but not painful; he can be kept fairly comfortable. Mrs. Ballard, on the other hand, suffers very much, yet refuses to let me give her analgesic drugs: I believe she thinks pain is meant to be endured—a sort of test. She's a fighter, that old lady. She has Mrs. Johann, as she calls her, who is surely as old as she, to get her up into a wheel chair every morning early: she prefers not to let the girls ("Girls!" Johnny though in astonishment) see what it costs her in pain. The day will come soon when she can't get out of bed, but she may lie there helpless for quite a while. I don't know why she fights so, except that it is her nature." John suspected that he knew one possible reason, a reason not to be put in words by him to Johnny, or by Mrs. Ballard herself to anyone: when she died, how would her daughters behave, tied to each other and to that house as they were by their father's will? John had broached the subject to Sam Travers one day when he had caught him alone, and Sam had asked him for the truth "confidentially."

"Sam, she is hanging on by strength of will, no matter what the cost in suffering. Why? Life holds nothing for her now but pain and more pain. She is not afraid of death: what is she afraid of?"

"Don't say any of that to Thomasina, will you? Every day her mother is able to get out of bed is a day won, in her eyes. And of course it's her daughters that Mother Ballard's worrying about. How they will behave in a divided house. Eliza has always been openly contemptuous of me, and of Thomasina for marrying me. I can see why she feels that way, but Thomasina and I have been happy together."

John said, "I know you have, and I know why. You are exactly the sort of person she needs. She idolized her father, but she was dragged around to too many platforms when she was young, asthma and all. She didn't need a Reformer for a husband: she had enough of that. As to Eliza, does her mother think there may be trouble when she's gone?"

"I suspect so. Eliza has grown quite away from her old relationship with Thomasina—especially since Ariana McCune ran away, though Thomasina had nothing to do with it."

John made an impatient sound. "How women— Look, Travers: can't you work something out and put on an act for Mrs. Ballard? Give her some peace of mind. I don't suppose they actually quarrel in her presence."

"They don't quarrel at all. They simply don't communicate."

"Doesn't she ever see the girls together?"

Samuel was not startled by the word "girls"; he too thought of them so. "Rarely, if ever. Eliza goes to speak to her mother before she leaves for work. Thomasina spends the day with her and Eliza the evening."

"If they care about her, and I know they do, get them in there hand in hand. You put it to Thomasina, and let her put it to Eliza."

Sam laughed at the absurd picture, but promised; and under his urging, the sisters took to spending their evenings together in their mother's room, with a show of amity: if they found it hard to put up with each other, neither let it show. One thing they had in common, and could discuss: the Waynesboro Woman's Club; should the long unfilled vacancy caused by the death of Kitty Edwards be given to that Mrs. Stevens everyone thought so charming?

Eliza could not resist a sharp comment. "I don't believe Mrs. Stevens has a thought in her head, nor what we should consider an education. 'Charming' she may be to some, but there are—"

"Eliza, please," Thomasina begged her wordlessly to desist. "We have until fall to think about it."

"And by fall there will be two vacancies," their mother interrupted them. "I want you, Thomasina, to write a letter of resignation for me to Mrs. Rausch. Tomorrow morning. So long as I could read, and dictate an essay to you, I felt that I was doing my share for the Club. But now it would be unfair for me to retain my membership. No, don't protest. It has meant something to me in the past, sometimes a great deal. Astonishing how attached one can become to a group of essentially incompatible women. But it means little to me now. If I occasionally relive the past, it is a past longer ago and far more meaningful. Please let the Program Committee know that my name is not be included as an essayist."

Vice-President Sally Rausch replaced Mrs. Ballard as President for the rest of the Club year. One of her first responsibilities was the appointment of a Program Committee. She chose Mrs. Maxwell chairman; she could be as intellectual as she liked. Mrs. Evans and Amanda would be the other members of the committee. It was a serious group with varied backgrounds, but all agreed that they must choose a subject that the ladies would find rewarding; not fiction, which they thought hardly worth spending time on. Beyond that no one offered an idea until Mrs. Maxwell, feeling she had allowed the others ample time, made her own suggestion: "We have learned a great deal in the Club about many aspects of literature, but we have never, I believe, dealt with the great historians."

Amanda thought, "She has probably soaked up history from her husband until she's full and running over." Aloud she said, "A good idea: there are historians enough and to spare: the Greeks, the Romans, Gibbon."

The subject closed, the committee had little trouble in assigning every lady a subject: historians were pretty much of a muchness, with the exception of Gibbon. And of Froissart: Mrs. Maxwell spent some time in deliberating on whether to include so light-minded an author as Froissart, but by midsummer it was fairly certain that Mrs. Jessamine Stevens would be elected to Club membership in the fall; Froissart would be a suitable subject for her: a frivolous historian and a frivolous woman; besides, hadn't southerners always been fascinated by the days of chivalry? But since Mrs. Stevens could hardly be asked to do a paper almost immediately after becoming a Club member, Froissart must be taken out of chronological order. She could put him with Green and *The Short History of the English People*, even if Green did say (she found the reference) that Froissart was too inaccurate for use as an authority. She would leave blank the name of the essayist; in fact, there would be two blanks, since someone must be chosen to take Mrs. Ballard's place.

When she had completed her program, the committee met once more, and accepted what she had done with only slight demur: she had assigned Anne the very first paper of the fall: the Greek historians Herodotus and Thucydides. Amanda reminded the other committee members that Anne had a sick child.

"That is one reason I assigned her an early paper. Little Belinda is still in bed, is she not, and her mother pretty well confined to the house? She may have more time now than later, and the boy is still at home: he can bring her the books she needs. But someone can consult her. We must show the program to the President first thing." They knew that Sally, having appointed a committee, would accept its work, but it would be proper to submit it to her for her approval. Mrs. Evans was deputed to call on Mrs. Rausch.

Mrs. Evans duly appeared at Sally's with the program in her purse. It was a hot afternoon, and Sally seated her guest on the front porch and had Rose bring a pitcher of iced lemonade, glasses, and cookies. When Rose had filled the glasses and withdrawn, the two women exchanged the usual amenities before settling down to business. A polite inquiry as to Mr. Cochran's health was answered as politely. That taken care of, Mrs. Evans asked about the "the little Gordon girl."

"She is still running a fever, and is still in bed."

"I asked because our committee has assigned Mrs. Gordon the very first essay." Mrs. Evans fumbled in her purse and brought out the crumpled sheet of paper. "We decided on 'Great Historians,' and naturally the program begins with the Greeks. An interesting subject, but it will take work, and I personally thought it would be expecting a great deal of Mrs. Gordon."

"I'll ask her before you send the program to be printed. It would be good for her to have something to think of besides Binny, even if she had to spend an afternoon or two at the library using the encyclopedia. She has two colored women who can sit with Binny, if need be."

Mrs. Evans handed the program to Sally.

"We think it will make an informative year. More profitable than spending time on fiction. The blanks are for the new members we elect. Their names will have to be written in."

When Mrs. Evans had gone, Sally went into the house for hat and gloves; she would consult Anne at once. In the Gordon sitting room, Anne inquired about Mr. Cochran. Sally's reply was a little different from, and more troubled than, the one she had made to Mrs. Evans.

"He's sitting in his room, waiting. You know he's downstairs now, in the room we fixed for Mamma. He won't stay in bed: Ludwig helps him get up and dressed, then he sits the day through until dinnertime. So far, with Ludwig's help, he manages to get to the dinner table. Then he goes back to bed. The only surviving interest he has is in his meals. It's awful to see someone outlive—wanting to use his mind. But there's nothing anyone can do, except hope that when the end comes, it will be quick and easy. How is Binny?"

"She's better, Dr. Warren and John both say. She has very little fever now. But after her temperature is normal, she will have to be another two weeks in bed at least, before she can even try sitting up in an armchair. The doctors claim that children sometimes get over a rheumatic heart, or learn to live with it. But I—"

Sally thought Anne looked very tired and strained: haggard, really. "But of course you worry."

Anne echoed in her mind, "Of course I worry." Sally had no idea what it was like, living your days in dread, waking in the morning heavy-hearted, thinking, Why? What?"—then having it all sweep over you.

"Yes, I worry," she said. "But I think Dr. Warren is a good man—as good as we could have, if there must be someone besides John. Binny likes him, fortunately. Odd: he looks so sort of raw, even at his age—clumsy and awkward. Those big unpadded bones, I suppose. But he's very gentle with her, and kind, and so strong he can move her without hurting her."

"Binny's fallen in love with her doctor, like most females? That seems normal."

"Well, hardly that. She would rather have her father. But I think John's a little jealous: last time she was sick she would hardly let anyone but him touch her. She accepted Dr. Warren hardly realizing that he was there. Now she listens for the doorbell. You and Ludwig have been her only visitors: I keep Mr. McKinney down here when he calls, and I haven't let the young people come in. Your Charles stopped by one afternoon to inquire. Did he tell you? So nice of him: that's ordinarily such a thoughtless age. Of course Johnny has been busy every day with his father, so he hasn't brought Julia or Elsa in."

"Wait, Anne," Sally thought. "She wouldn't run on like that if she weren't starved for someone to talk to: it isn't like Anne to chatter." She said, "I came to show you the new Club program. The ladies put you down for the first paper, but they weren't sure you would be able to do it."

Anne glanced at the sheet Sally had given her. "The Greek historians! Sally, I don't know *anything* about the Greek historians. Except Xenophon. Remember translating so many parasangs a day?"

"It is hardly worth while to write on something you already know about. I mean, what does it profit you? Besides, no one else—unless it's Amanda, and she's to do the Romans—knows the first thing about the Greek historians. You will have to look them up, I suppose. If you feel you can't do it now, it can be switched to a later date. Anne, for your own sake do it; you need something else to think about beside Binny, and you need to get out, if it's only to the library."

"I suppose so. I might as well get my essay off my mind early. It won't be much of a paper, not by Amanda's standards, anyway." Anne thought, "I know what this summer is like, with Binny sick, but the fall and winter?" She could not rid herself of the foreboding that weakened her knees, sometimes. "Tell the committee I'll do it. If anything should happen, you will have to take over."

"Nothing's going to happen, Anne. You'll see."

The program for the next Club year was sent to the printer, and would be ready for distribution at the first meeting in the fall. One name needed to be changed: Elizabeth Talmadge was to marry Tim Merrill that summer. (There were those who said, "At last," or "At least they surely know each other." Quite unfairly. They had been pairing off for not more than two or three years.) It was a wrench for Elizabeth to give up teaching, which she loved. Tim—cheerful, easy-going Tim—had not pressed her, or hurried her decision; he was sure that her intellect was superior to his, and that she would be making a sacrifice. But the day had come when Elizabeth had decided there would be no sacrifice: she no longer wanted to go on without him. The wedding was in Cleveland, at her home, with no Waynesboro friends present. Tim had no family, Doug Gardiner could not get away, and Amanda declined her invitation.

Summer passed, slowly for some, all too rapidly for others. Mr. Cochran died peacefully in his sleep and was buried from the Baptist church, with the whole business community and all of Sally's and Ludwig's friends in attendance at the funeral.

It had been an uneasy season for Ludwig, with the threat of an eastern monopoly hanging in the air. The blow fell in August when four of the largest New York rope manufacturers announced the formation of the National Cordage Company. However disquieting this news was, it had been expected, and Ludwig left justified in his gamble with hemp when the price of fiber began to go up. Later, when the trust attempted to corner the hemp production of the world and other rope companies could obtain raw material only through a London broker, the price rose from the seven and one-half cents Ludwig had paid, to nine cents in September, then to twelve. But that did not happen at once. By the first of August, Ludwig knew although he had hemp enough to keep the mill running for a while, he was going to have a fight on his hands.

Sally said to her husband a few days after her father's funeral that now her father's estate would be hers, Ludwig would have that capital to draw on.

"That is your money, Liebchen. I will not touch it."

"Don't be so noble. What's mine is yours, and I will not stand by and let you lose the mill."

"I am not going to lose the mill. We can see it through without your money." Ludwig was resolved: yet it was something of a comfort to know that his father-in-law's not inconsiderable fortune, mostly in bank and railroad stock, was there to be used as collateral in case of necessity.

But the mill was not Ludwig's only problem: there was another state election coming in October. Foraker was to run for a second term as governor; he had been an excellent administrator and had succeeded in getting some needed laws passed by the legislature, but his tactics as a politician disturbed less flamboyant Republicans. To President Cleveland's suggestion that captured Confederate battle flags be returned to the southern states. Foraker responded with a sort of "over-my-dead-body" defiance: no "Rebel flags" would be returned from Ohio while he was governor. This statement was so applauded by the populace (as Foraker said, "They lapped it up") that he waved the bloody flag in the campaign of '87 as vigorously as it had ever been waved, and deservedly won the nickname "Fire-Alarm Foraker." His reelection was so certain that Ludwig exerted himself only to the extent required by his position as county central committee chairman, but he looked forward with some misgivings to the presidential campaign of the next year. Cleveland had been so conservative in his fiscal policies and his handling of labor problems that it might be difficult for the Republicans to find an issue on which to oppose him, and it might be that they would have to resort to "the bloody flag" again in 1888.

As summer day followed summer day, Mrs. Ballard seemed unchanged. Binny slowly grew better: she was able to sit in the easy chair that had been put close to her bedroom window, and then to be downstairs for part of the day. Her father carried her down when he came in the morning and laid her on the sitting room sofa, and Dr. Warren carried her up again when he came in the afternoon. John was inclined, however, to be morose and silent, and Binny seemed indifferent about getting out of bed. Anne felt no lessening of her apprehension. She remembered from her childhood the sudden exuberance that came with the knowledge that the illness endured was now over, however long it took to convince one's elders. She had seen nothing of that in Binny, who was too listless to be anything but patient and submissive. John, when pinned down, said only, "No one can tell yet. But she'll probably always have some valvular trouble." Anne did not find Herodotus and Thucydides altogether distracting: at best they could be called a counter-irritant, since her search at the library was frustrating. True, there was some material in the encyclopedia, but she wanted the histories themselves. Finally she sent Johnny to borrow anything Dr. Maxwell might have bearing on the subject, and thereafter tried to lose herself in Thucydides and the *Peloponnesian War*, a cataclysm she remembered vaguely from Professor Lowrey's ancient history class.

In September, Waynesboro children went back to school, all but Binny, who was still walking no farther than from bed to chair or, downstairs, once in a while to the dining room for lunch with the family. Some of the older boys and girls who had been graduated in June kept their summer jobs and began their lives' work, or, if a girl, settled down as daughter-of-the-house until such time as a suitor might offer. The more fortunate ones went off to school and college: among others Johnny, Elsa, and Julia. None of the girls ventured to follow Charlotte Bonner and Sophie Klein to a real college. Julia, as her mother had foreseen, easily persuaded her father to allow her to go to art school in Cincinnati: General Deming again said, "Why not?" She could be home most Saturdays and Sundays: that was surely better than having her far away. Painting in watercolor was an excellent lady-like accomplishment, and if she roomed with Elsa Rausch, what could happen to her? Elsa had flatly refused to go live with her father's cousins: she intended to enjoy her freedom. No more of that nonsense about no-young-lady-walks-alone-in-the-city, and if the penalty she had to pay was rooming with Julia Deming, then so be it. They would at any rate be going to different schools, and whatever Julia might make of her art classes, Elsa intended to work hard at the conservatory, and to see Johnny occasionally (as often as possible, she admitted to herself), although he would certainly be grinding away at his books at the medical school, as would Billy Thirkield at the college of pharmacy.

Their parents, listening weekends to lively reports of their days, may have wondered whether any of them were doing any work at all: there were new and unfamiliar names on their lips every time they came home. The young suburbanite Cincinnatians who joined them on the "accommodation" train on Monday mornings, or hailed them from a station platform to beg them to alight and go home with them for breakfast, saying, "What does it matter if you miss a class just this once?" The Gordons knew, however, that Johnny actually was at medical school: he always talked about it at the dinner table, when almost any other topic would have been preferred.

"I saw my first operation this week: an abdominal, and the fellow sitting next to me in the theater was so sick I thought he was going to faint. He stuck it out, but kept saying, 'If I had my money out of this, I'd go into law!' "

They laughed at that, but not at the story of how the third-year students, working at dissecting cadavers, sliced off the ears and at the first opportunity nailed them to telephone poles. Anne expressed her irrepressible horror then and there; later, when Johnny had gone out, his father showed more understanding. "Medical students' pranks are apt to be gruesome," he assured her. "It's a kind of reaction. They are seeing so much that is horrible for the first time. It's part of the hardening process."

"Do they have to be hard?"

"They better be, to a certain extent, or they'll never be able to go through what's ahead of them."

"John, have you ever been sorry? You aren't hard, at all."

"Just a thin-skinned old woman? If I am, you're the only one who knows it," he said, confident of his bedside manner. "But if you mean, am I sorry that I went back to doctoring, no. It is what I was meant to be. I wouldn't have been worth a plugged nickel at anything else. I only hope that Johnny will feel the same at my age; he's thin-skinned too, you know."

It was perhaps that quality of compassion in Johnny, or his capacity for friendship, that led him to make with Elsa the excursion into what her mother considered, in spite of Elsa's vigorous denial, the slums of Cincinnati. Sally did not hear of the exploit until the October twelfth meeting of the Club at Mrs. Deming's. Jessamine Stevens had been voted in as a member, and was being welcomed at one of Mrs. Deming's teas. By that time Anne had dealt, quite adequately in the judgment of her peers, with the Greek historians; and Amanda had discussed the Romans exhaustively and exhaustingly. That day Christina read her essay on Josephus. Afterward, as the ladies were drinking their tea, Jessamine whispered to Anne, who was introducing her as their new member, "My goodness! I'm scared to death of you ladies! Y'all know so much!"

"You should have heard Amanda's paper last time; it was truly scholarly, at length. But remember: I warned you you might be bored."

"You su'ly did. I'm not bo'ed, just impressed and frightened." Anne thought, "She in Kitty's place! She can't fill it, not if she lives to be a hundred. It will always be Kitty's." "I think it was tremendously interestin'."

And Anne thought, "How exaggerated 'Mizsippi' becomes when an impression is to be made," and turned Cousin Jessamine over to Christina, now relieved of the burden of her essay to be delivered. Anne made her way to Sally's side in time to hear their hostess say, "I understand that Elsa has been taking a look at parts of Cincinnati not generally considered suitable for young ladies."

"What do you mean?" Sally was blunt.

"Oh, I supposed you had given your permission. It was that week the young people did not come home; we have told Julia not to come unless the others do: we do not want her on the cars alone. The next week, of course, I asked her why they had stayed. She reported that Elsa said she was going on a slumming expedition that Saturday with Johnny, and that she changed into her oldest clothes in preparation."

"Oh, Mrs. Deming!" Anne laughed. "I am afraid she was teasing Julia." ("And I know why," she thought; "for once she was going to have an afternoon with Johnny without Julia trailing along.") "She and Johnny, as soon as the circus went into winter quarters, hunted up the boardinghouse where the Mercers stayed before, to see if Ariana McCune and her husband were there."

"But—where?"

"They had got the address from someone: John or Ludwig, or maybe Eliza."

"Elsa's idea," her mother said tartly. "She always could twist Johnny around her little finger."

"I don't know," his mother said, "Johnny always liked Ariana: he might have looked for her of his own accord. But I don't believe he would have taken Elsa to a circus boardinghouse if she hadn't insisted. At any rate, the trip was all for nothing: the Mercers weren't there. Someone—an animal trainer, I believe, who knew the Mercer boy—told them Ariana had got herself a place with a touring theatrical company as seamstress and, as I understand it, a kind of understudy for all the female parts. Her husband went with her, of course, I believe as scene shifter and a kind of general roustabout."

"How very sad," Mrs. Deming murmured. "*Ariana McCune*, of all people!"

"She is probably quite happy," Anne retorted. "I believe she has always wanted to go on the stage. I'm sorry I didn't tell you, Sally—I supposed Elsa had reported. I told Eliza and Ruhamah. I thought they had a right to know. They'd completely lost touch with her after the circus went on the road last spring. I couldn't give them the name of the stock company: Johnny didn't get it. Either the animal man didn't know, or wouldn't tell. Circus people are pretty wary of outsiders."

"At least I can be glad they didn't take Julia," Mrs. Deming said.

"I'm sure they came to no harm," Sally replied smoothly. But she had a scolding in store for Elsa when she came home again.

That weekend gave her an opportunity. Elsa protested: "It wasn't a slum, Mamma. It was a perfectly clean boardinghouse."

"But *circus* people! Hobnobbing with them in what must at least be an undesirable part of town."

Unfortunately for the effectiveness of Sally's scolding, Ludwig came in at that moment, home early from the mill on a Saturday afternoon.

"Are you scolding Elsa for trying to find an old friend just to ask how she is faring?"

"I was. There are places that are most unsuitable for a daughter of ours to go poking her nose in. But it's never any use trying to scold Elsa when you're around."

"Oh, Mamma! I'm grown up. And Johnny was with me."

"And," said Ludwig, "Mr. John Robinson is a highly respected citizen of Cincinnati."

"That doesn't mean his hired hands are necessarily respectable."

"All this fuss over me," Elsa said. "No one knows where Ariana has gone, and no one seems to care."

Elsa was right: few did care. Ariana had been with a circus last year, this year she was with a theatrical company, and what was the difference, really? In either case she was of no further concern to Waynesboro. But Eliza Ballard was troubled, and in her trouble lay awake nights; Ruhamah wept her young heart out in the room she had been living in at Mrs. Duncan's, since she had clung to the hope that Ariana would some day come home, and she was determined to have a place for her, paid for out of her library money. Now Ariana was gone beyond reach.

That Club meeting at the Demings' was Anne's last for a while. A few days after that, when Binny had been carried upstairs by Dr. Warren and comfortably tucked in her bed, Anne, sitting beside her in the easy chair, thinking she had dropped off to sleep, was reading with her usual absorption, when a smothered gasp startled her. She looked up: Binny, white as the sheets and wild-eyed, was sitting bold upright in bed, gasping for breath. In an instant Anne was beside her, holding her hand.

"What is it, Binny? No, don't try to tell me. Just lie down again." Anne let go her hand, took her wrist. In spite of all too much experience, she was not expert at pulse-taking, but the irregularity of the beat was terrifyingly evident. The child began to cough: quick, dry coughs. Anne moved to the bed-table, took up the old brass bell that had been put there by Binny to ring in case she wanted something in the rare intervals when she was left alone, then quickly went with it to the stair rail and rang it hard. Back in the bedroom she piled the pillows at Binny's head and propped her up on them.

"Mamma—" The coughing had stopped, but Binny's breathing was quick and shallow.

"No, don't talk, Binny. Just lie quiet and get your breath. I'll send Louline for your father. You're going to be all right: don't be frightened."

Anne heard Louline's hurrying footsteps in the hall, and went to hang over the rail.

"Louline: run over to the doctor's office and tell him we need him."

"Yes'm." Louline looked frightened, but she turned and ran. It might have been quicker, Anne thought, if she had telephoned, but she couldn't have gone downstairs and left Binny alone. If only Martha or Louline would get over their terror of the magic contraption of the wall in the passageway!

Before thought of the telephone had run through her mind, she was back beside the bed. "Binny, can you breathe slower than that and deeper? I think your heart would quiet down." She took the thin wrist in hers again. "If I say the Twenty-Third Psalm for you as if it were poetry, would you try to breathe in time with it?"

Wide-eyed, the terror fading a little, Binny nodded.

"'The *Lord* is my *shepherd*, I *shall* not *want'* —" Anne repeated the Psalm slowly. When she had finished, Binny said, "The chapter about 'Remember now thy Creator,' Mamma. I like it better."

And so when John came running up the stairs, he heard Anne saying in a soothing sing-song, "'Or *ever* the *golden bowl* be *broken* or the *pitcher*—'"

He thought, "How dismal! Why choose those passages?"—and was in the room looking at Binny with Anne beside her, finger on her pulse.

"Is she better?"

"I think so. Quieter, anyway."

"What was it, Binny?" From the opposite side of the bed, he took her other wrist.

"Everything—just *stopped*—inside me. And the bed and the floor and the house fell out from under me. And then I couldn't breathe."

"Nothing *really* stopped, you know. It just felt like it for an instant. Now it feels as if your heart were skipping a beat, doesn't it? But it really isn't—it's just that once in a while a beat is so weak you can't feel it. And I brought the medicine for that." He took a bottle of pills from his pocket—explained to Anne "digitalis,"—shook a couple of the tiny pills into her hand, reached for the glass of water on the table, and held it while Binny got the pills down. "Not bad, were they? You know, Binny, I think you will have to wait until you are stronger before you come to the dining room to eat. Anyway, you had better stay in bed."

Binny clung to his hand. "I don't mind, Papa. But I was in bed."

"I know. But you had been downstairs." He laid her hand gently on the quilt. "You'll feel all right now. Just don't get scared. Mamma will stay with you, and maybe she can think of some more cheerful poetry to say."

A glimmer of mischief shone in Binny's eyes. "Oh, Papa! The *Bible*, not poetry." She intoned solemnly, "While the *sun* or the *light* or the *moon* or the *stars* be not *darkened*—"

"Whatever you like, but lie quietly till I get back or Dr. Warren comes."

"Oh, John! Must you go out?"

"'Fraid so, if only to get rid of an office full of patients. I'll rush them through and I'll call Warren. She'll be all right now, Anne. If Warren comes before I get back, tell him I gave her digitalis."

By the time Dr. Warren came and John returned, Binny was asleep. She even had a little color in her face. Anne stayed in the room: she wanted to hear what they said. But they waited until they had got down to the front door. When John came upstairs again, she went into the hall to meet him.

"What did he say?"

"That she had better have a sedative when she wakens, so that she will have a quiet night. A small dose of chloral hydrate will be better for her than bromide. I'll pour a dose when I go down. She won't like it—it's nasty stuff—but it will keep her safe asleep through the night. The poor baby was frightened. That 'falling away' sensation—what the bigwigs call a 'sense of imminent dissolution'—is not uncommon in heart cases."

"You are going out *again?*"

"I have to. The Taylor girl has had a hemorrhage: I promised to get there as soon as I could. And I don't know how long I'll be. Give Binny very little dinner—custard or something like that—then the chloral. You go to bed yourself when it has taken effect. I'll be no longer than I can help. And the Taylors have a telephone—put in when Lily got so bad. It's one of those country lines with a dozen farms on it, but I think the operator could get me if you need me. Or you can get Warren, unless he is out too."

Anne ate a solitary dinner—ate it really to please old Martha, who had taken to grumbling and scolding as if Anne were still the child she had first known. Louline sat with Binny and coaxed the bowl of custard down, spoonful by spoonful. When Anne had finished her meal, she took Louline's place, gave Binny the sedative, and sat down in the easy chair to wait for her to fall asleep, which she did, suddenly and completely. Anne stayed until she caught herself nodding; it was still early, but she was so tired that she rose and prepared for bed. The act of undressing, washing, combing her hair, roused her from her drowsiness; she lay in her bed hopelessly wakeful, straining her ears for any sound from the room across the hall. When John came in, he looked in on Binny first, and then, in the bedroom, found Anne lying motionless on her back in the bed, her eyes closed. Because the light from the night lamp was so dim, it was not until he was lying beside her that he knew she was awake and that her cheeks were wet with tears.

"Anne—"

"She isn't going to get well, is she?"

He did not answer, even when he had put an arm under her and drawn her close, so that her wet cheek was on her shoulder.

"John?"

"No. Today we knew for certain. Don't think we were keeping anything from you. We didn't know. But, yes: there's a failure of compensation. What do names matter? Don't cry, Anne. We did everything we could."

"Oh, John! I'm not blaming anyone. But—" The tears were soaking John's nightshirt; he wiped her face with a handkerchief as best he could. "She is so young. It breaks my heart to see her frightened the way she was this afternoon. Must it happen again?"

"It is a symptom, what is called 'cardiac anxiety.' A patient knows somehow that something is very wrong. The digitalis may help, sedatives help."

"How long?"

He was silent; he could not answer.

"Not long, then?"

He tightened the arm under her, and with the other hand turned her on her side, so that she was resting against him; he took her hand in his and held it against his cheek.

"John?"

"I think—not long. We can't know exactly, of course."

After that night Anne stayed with Binny: she would not go out, she could hardly be persuaded to go downstairs to eat; many a night when John was heavily asleep beside her she crept out of bed and went to sit the hours through in the easy chair at Binny's side. Daytimes, when Binny was awake, she was calm and cheerful; nighttimes she wept. John expostulated to no avail; finally he sent word to Sally to come and drag Anne out. But Sally's pleas had no effect.

"Do come to Club meeting this week, Anne. You really owe it to yourself and your family. I know Binny's very sick, but—"

"She's dying, Sally. How can I spare any time away from her? How would I feel afterward, thinking, 'There was that afternoon' or even 'that hour' when I could have been with her."

Johnny still came home for weekends when he could afford to leave his books: desolate weekends, when he tried to subdue his own sorrow and help his mother; she would not listen to him either. And so when the end came, in the middle of the night, it was Anne who was with Binny. She was half-asleep in the big chair, the night-light behind her, when she was roused by the sound of movement. Binny was propped high on pillows; she had been unable for some days to sleep lying down; her hands, when Anne looked at her, were moving restlessly over the quilt. Then, suddenly she sat up straighter, threw her head back for one last gasping breath, and crumpled forward and sideways on the bed.

"Binny! Oh, no!" Anne had her in her arms in an instant, lifting her to the support of her shoulder even as she called John. He came at once, took Binny from Anne's arms, laid her down, head on the pillows, and felt for a pulse.

"She's gone, isn't she? And I wasn't even holding her hand."

"Anne." John, haggard and old-looking as he suddenly was, spoke with a firm and unshaken voice. "She was asleep, wasn't she? She didn't even have time to be frightened. It is the best way to go." He saw her sway on her feet. "Go. Leave everything to me now. Go back to bed and sleep if you can. There's nothing now for you to be listening for."

"But there are things—"

"I'll take care of everything. Here." He poured a dose of chloral hydrate into Binny's glass, added some water, and handed it to Anne; she drank it dully, wondering at his calm acceptance, as if Binny had been just another patient.

She dragged herself, John holding her elbow, back to her bed, dropped into it, and almost at once fell into a heavy, drugged sleep. She slept halfway through the next morning, woke bewildered, until she remembered. When she looked into Binny's room and saw the bed empty and made up, she dressed and went downstairs to find John.

He said, "I have done everything there is to do. Everything except call Mr. McKinney." His jaw tightened for a moment; he was white around the mouth.

"I'll do that. Not on the telephone. I couldn't. I'll send a note around by hand."

"First, though, you must eat your breakfast. Martha has it ready for you. You know, Anne: she loved Binny, too, and the only way she has of showing it now is by doing things for you. Don't disappoint her."

A moment later he heard her talking to Martha in the dining room, even condoling with her. "She would have been an invalid all her life. Maybe it is better."

"She's too young."

"She has escaped the sorrow and trouble that come to us all, man and woman alike. She is in Heaven, Martha, forever young. You believe that?"

"Yas'm."

John, listening, knew that she would not speak so to him, an unbeliever. How could she? But she would be in control of herself now, accepting the loss of Binny as an edict of Heaven. A wave of desolation swept over him. He went through the dining room to the kitchen door, saying to Anne as he passed her, "I can't bear to see anyone. I'll be in the office."

The two distressed women looked after him.

"He feel it bad."

"Yes. He couldn't save her. He'll blame himself."

"No call fo' that."

"No." Anne thought, "All the more reason why I must pull myself together."

Martha had no need to answer the doorbell. Both Sally Rausch and Jessamine Stevens came in to be there, to greet any callers, while upstairs Anne received Mr. McKinney, who would be in charge of the funeral services, and who prayed with her and offered his Christian condolences. In the afternoon she was in her bedroom alone when the undertaker's men brought the casket, set it up in the parlor, opened the lid, and departed, leaving the front door hung with crepe. Johnny got home (bringing Elsa and Julia with him, for the funeral), spent a while in the parlor, and came up to his mother with red-rimmed eyes. Anne was glad John had escaped to his office, but wished he were not alone; she was relieved when Johnny went to sit with him. Downstairs there was a regular bustle: neighbors and friends left cakes and pies with Martha, going around to the kitchen door rather than trouble the family; callers came to the front door and were greeted quietly, by whom Anne did not care. At dinnertime an exhausted family sat down to eat what they could of their neighbors' offerings; Anne went to bed immediately, and the two men came upstairs shortly after; John crawled in beside her as numb as she, Anne thought. When she woke in the middle of the night and he was not there, she was startled: surely he had not, on this night, gone out on a call? Then she saw by the light from the corner street lamp that his clothes were still on the chair where he had dropped them. She rose, found slippers and robe, and went silently downstairs to the parlor.

Here a night-lamp was burning. John was there: he had pulled a stiff parlor chair close to the coffin; his head was down, leaning on his crossed arms.

Anne might have turned and gone upstairs, leaving him alone with his grief, but he heard her slight movement and looked up. His face was lined with anguish, the lines furrow-deep, shadowed as they were in the dim light.

"John."

"Anne, I disturbed you?"

His face was so stricken that she went to him at once and touched his shoulder.

"There is no consolation for me," he said, bitterly. "Don't quote Scripture."

"Oh, John!"

He rose almost violently, tipping the light chair so that Anne had to catch it, took her in his arms, and held her closely, his one hand pressing her head to his shoulder.

"Forgive me, my dearest love. Help me to forgive myself: Binny is gone. It's too late. If I had only known—"

"That's what one always thinks," she murmured: "If only I could go back and do it over." She hardly knew what she was saying, she only knew the depths of his sorrow. "You mustn't blame yourself. You promised you wouldn't."

"Not for her death. For the griefs of her short life. If I could have foreseen—" He let his hands slip from around her and went back to stand looking down at the child's peaceful face. "I wanted her to grow up to be a happy woman. If I had known childhood was all she was to have—it breaks my heart now to think of all the tears she shed because it was always 'Go wash your hands' or 'Go comb your hair.'" His hand reached a little way toward the short dark curls, for once so neatly disposed.

Anne saw that he could not bear to touch them. She thought, "You wanted her to be perfect"; she did not say it: it would be confirmation of all he was blaming himself for now. He had been sitting here with all these things in his mind, and they had tumbled out. He had not intended to say them, and if she had not come down—

"She had a happy childhood. If you had asked her forgiveness, she wouldn't have known what you were talking about. A few tears, dried at once and forgotten. What are scoldings to a child? And I scolded her too. Remember the Catechisms? She went her way regardless of scoldings. And she showed her feeling for you when she was sick and turned from everyone else:

it had to be you, no one else would do. She clung to you with the complete abandon that goes with utter faith and love." She put her hand on one of his. "She was a happy child; don't remember the occasional tears: remember how transparently joyous she could be for some small reason. Oh, John! She was my baby and I loved her with all my heart. I can't bear to think what our life will be without her. But she might not have grown up to be a happy woman."

"You think she will eternally be thirteen, running in the meadows of Heaven, the wind in her hair, gathering—"

"Amaranth and asphodel?" "So you too," she thought, "remember Kate."

"Violets," he corrected her. "What would Heaven be without violets?" Then he broke down and began to weep, the strangled rough sobs of a man who had not shed tears for many years. Anne waited. He brought himself under control. "Go back to bed, Anne, please. Let me spend the night beside her this one more time."

She sighed. "I'm sorry I cannot help."

"You have helped. Go to bed, dear Anne, just let me sit with her, to promise her I'll not fail others as I failed her."

"You did not fail her," Anne insisted stubbornly.

"Nor you, I suppose? Nor my sister Kate? How can one love and be so without comprehension? Now there are only you and Johnny. I promise I will not fail *you* in any way I can help."

Once more he took her in his arms and kissed her. She turned to the door and the staircase. She knew what he meant, was promising, and believed him. She felt in the midst of her grief a certain peace. "But," she thought, "I would not have bought peace at such a price. To have Binny here well and whole, I would have endured to the end of time."

The next day dragged out interminably. John went to sit alone in his closed office. Anne spent it conventionally in her bedroom. Cousin Jessamine came early in the afternoon, to represent the family when callers began to come.

"I'll be he' the rest of the day. You just rest."

Anne did not sleep: there was too much bustle downstairs. All those people expressing their sympathy in the only way they knew. And strangely, exhausted though she was, she found a certain comfort. People were kind.

Downstairs, Sally Rausch joined Jessamine; together they marshalled the callers past the coffin: Fritz Klein and his wife, Mr. Lichtenstein and his wife, all saying what needed to be said in their heavily accented gutteral English; Tim O'Reilly and his wife, Ludwig and Elsa, the Demings, the General bluff in his manners but kind: "Let me express my sympathy. Julia was so fond of little Belinda." Julia let her father speak for her, and averted her eyes from the casket. Sheldon Edwards came: "Tell Anne if there is anything in the world I can do—" And the Douglas Gardiners: "Let us help, if there is anything." Club members, Presbyterians, John's patients, some of them unknown to Sally or Jessamine. Finally, the long day came to an end, and the Gordons were left alone.

The funeral service was held the next afternoon in the parlor. The three Gordons stayed upstairs, tight-lipped and alone. It was a bright day for December, but there was a cold wind blowing. No one was tempted to stand and visit in the cemetery; people dispersed quickly. The Gordons were driven home to a house whose emptiness they must learn to get used to.

There were a number of families in Waynesboro that night who looked at their healthy offspring around the dinner table, rejoiced and were ashamed of rejoicing. Sheldon Edwards watched his two, the little one still in high chair, thoughtfully and sadly. His housekeeper, a farmer's widow John had found for him, understood at once.

"You don't need to do no worryin' about them," she assured him. "They're real healthy little boys."

"I guess they are," he smiled at her. "But if one of them ever has a sore throat—"

"I'll take care of it—don't worry—goose grease and camphor my mother always used."

"Call the doctor, too, please," Sheldon said. "The old-fashioned remedies might work, but I wouldn't want to wait and see." He wondered whether anyone could tell that he felt a barrier—his guilt—between him and Richie.

At the Gardiners', Douglas and Barbara looked with satisfaction at their four: two on each side, the baby tied into her high chair, at her mother's side; Veronica on a dictionary at her father's end of the table. The aunts dined in their upstairs sitting room most evenings, although that involved the carrying of trays up and down. Four children meant a certain amount of *messiness*, they explained to Douglas, and were too often heard as well as seen. Barbara suggested rather tentatively that perhaps she should give the children their dinner early; Douglas vetoed the idea firmly and without hesitation: how would they ever learn table manners, or how to converse sensibly if they did not dine formally with their parents? "Formally" was not the word to describe precisely the Gardiner dinner hour. The smaller girls were undeniably "messy," and the older ones all too eager to recount everything that had happened to them on that day. Sometimes they descended to squabbling and were either hushed immediately or sent from the table. Douglas was ordinarily quick to say "You must learn to control yourselves," but on that evening after the funeral, he let them run on, growing louder and louder until Barbara intervened: "Quiet, children! You know better than to shout at the dinner table!"

Douglas smiled at her. "I thought just this once it was good to hear them, after this afternoon."

"Yes, but they don't know why, and they do know better."

The Rausch dinner table was quieter; Sally always let Cassie give little Paul his supper, and she could and sometimes did send Ludwig Junior to join them, if he misbehaved. But that night they were all subdued: Binny Gordon they had known well, and she had been Charles's favorite playmate. Their parents' eyes met over the table, having taken in their healthy if unhappy looks.

Ludwig said, "Wie beglückt, dass unsere Kinder solch Apfelgesichte sind—"

Sally said, piously, "Gott sei dank." If Elsa objected, at eighteen, to being called "applecheeked," she said nothing, but toyed dismally with her dinner. Binny had been so young and so *alive*. You could die young: it was a shock to Elsa. At any rate, she had had the courage to do what Julia evaded: look at Binny in her coffin. At the cemetery Johnny had called her "Shaney" for the first time in a long while. He had understood how she felt.

At dinner that evening Ludwig was too preoccupied to pay any more than usual attention to his children, filling and refilling their plates as Rose brought them to him. "I have't had a chance to tell you," he said to Sally. "Representatives of the National Cordage Company are coming to see me tomorrow."

"With an offer to buy?"

"So I assume. It is what they have been doing everywhere else. If so, I'll let them look over the mill, just to show them what kind of competition we can give them, and then say 'No' politely and firmly. They may be surprised by the mill. Stewart Bodien's tarring machine is in operation, and he is on the road, selling orders for it to our competitors."

"If it gives us an edge, I should think you would keep it a secret." That was Ernest's contribution: he might be a wheel boy in the mill; at home he was a rope manufacturer.

"No. If you have something good, patent it and put it on the market at once. Keep it secret and someone else will come up with another machine for the same purpose. And the tarring machine is going well. The only thing on my mind, really, is the need for fluid capital. No National Cordage people are going to see my books."

"There's Papa's bank stock. Surely you could borrow on it."

"From the bank here? No. It is a sound, conservative bank, and most of the county uses it. I wouldn't abuse my position as president if I could. Besides, it is a small bank, really. If I have to borrow, I'll go to Cincinnati and borrow on the mill's assets. The debt could be funded and paid off over the years. I shan't need your father's stock—not yet, certainly. This may be a long-drawn-out fight."

The deputation from the National Cordage Company appeared at Ludwig's office the next morning: one a Mr. Simpson, an officer of a company newly absorbed by the trust whom Ludwig had met occasionally at Cordage Association meetings; the other two were, Ludwig suspected, financial experts. All three were arrayed like bankers: broadcloth frock coats and silk hats. Ludwig smiled inwardly: if they expected to overawe the small back-country manufacturer, he would surprise them; it was not without reason that he had come to the mill that morning in his roughest work clothes, even his heavy, thick-soled, tarry boots. Eliza was a little ashamed for him. He had insisted on her leaving her door into his office open; why she couldn't imagine.

When they came, Ludwig rose and greeted them cordially and shook hands. He took the silk hats, put them on the rack with his battered derby, and invited them to take the chairs he had placed for them.

"I am honored by your call, gentlemen, but I am afraid you have come on a fruitless errand."

"Perhaps not." Mr. Simpson opened the interview. "I know you wrote us that Rausch Cordage Company is not for sale, but we hope to persuade you to change your mind. We are prepared to offer you a fair figure—a very fair figure. But confidentially—very confidentially, you understand." He indicated the open door beyond which stood Eliza's desk, with Eliza pretending to be busy with the letters on it.

"Ah? Oh, my secretary, you mean? I assure you, the affairs of this company are safe with her: she is in my confidence. She knows as much about the finances of Rausch Cordage as I do."

"We are familiar with your reputation, your very good reputation, and have studied the figures of the old Cordage Association pool. You consistently sold above your quota and paid your two cents a pound into the pool."

"I have always tried to satisfy my customers without regard to the pool. I know that some companies preferred to under-produce, taking their two cents a pound recompense, rather than work a little harder."

"And now that the Cordage Association has collapsed, you are in an excellent position, as of today. You have kept your customers?"

"My profit and loss figures have never been made public. Rausch Cordage Company is a closed corporation: all the stock is in the hands of members of my family, the majority in mine. Do you mean to say you are prepared to make me an offer on the basis of the pool reports?"

"Hardly that." One of the financial experts took over. "We shall need to go into some detail with you as to the value of your plant, your output, your outstanding orders, your debts."

"Naturally. Our greatest asset is the mill. A conducted tour is in order, I think."

Mr. Simpson, who was curious and capable of understanding what he was about to see, rose with alacrity; the others with more reluctance. Ludwig marshalled his guests toward the door giving onto the cobbled yard. Eliza was startled: could he be thinking of selling, after all? But behind his back he twiddled his fingers at her and the bookkeeper, who had come to stand by her desk in order to see.

"He's making fools out of them," Eliza gloated: "That's why he dressed like that."

Outside, Ludwig showed them no mercy: he began by indicating the canal on whose bank the old ropewalk stood, explaining that in the beginning it was built there because of the cheapness of water transportation. "Now of course the canal is disused, but it gives us an ample water supply. The main line of the railroad is on the other side of the canal; there is a trestle crossing the canal and a siding to our warehouse."

"Very convenient. However, is there not danger of being flooded out, between canal and river?"

"Perhaps. So far it has never happened. Now, the preparation room: first the softening machines." The air around the fiber machines, where the hemp was oiled, was heavy with the revolting smell of degras. Ludwig forbore smiling at the expression of repugnance on the two strangers' faces, and merely cautioned them to be careful not to let the oil splatter over them. From there Ludwig showed them the spinning machines, where the manila hemp came down from overhead in a great honey-colored waterfall to the whirling bobbins, and the tarring machine, whose invention and operation Ludwig explained, emphasizing its economy and usefulness. "One of our boys, the mill superintendent's son, came up with this. We have made a few tarring machines like this for sale. It is patented, naturally," Ludwig added, twinkling. He led them on to the two-hundred-foot-long rope mill proper, and introduced Captain Bodien as "mill superintendent and expert rope man." Last of all he showed them, in the power house, the Allis-Corliss tandem horizontal steam engine that supplied the horsepower to keep the machinery moving.

When, a long time after they had left it, they returned to the office, Ludwig threw a couple of pieces of sacking on the floor for them to wipe their once immaculate boots on. "I am sorry, gentlemen: a rope mill is not the place for formal clothes. But I feel that there is nothing so convincing as seeing with one's own eyes. What did you think of our layout, Mr. Simpson?"

"Quite up-to-date and efficient. But the actual manufacture of rope is really of less importance than the profits. The size of our offer would naturally depend on that."

"The truth of the matter is," Ludwig's cordial manner was cooling with every word, "the National Cordage Company is not trying to buy this mill in order to use it, whatever the profits, but in order to close it down. Remove the good machinery that would be useful elsewhere and stop production here."

There was a silence. Finally one of the background figures spoke. "Small mills like this are uneconomical. The country can be supplied with sufficient rope without them. By the National Cordage Company. Already we control twenty-eight hundred spindles and about thirty percent of the country's output."

"Do you think you can take over the mills that supply the other seventy percent?"

"We have no such ambitious plans at present."

"If you do, you might as well forget them. Some of us intend to stay in business independently. I showed you the mill in order to convince you that is not an inefficient, outdated concern that I would be glad to unload. Can you tell me why I should sell a mill as well-equipped as the one you have seen and as profitable as it has been, and throw two hundred or so people out of work? No, gentlemen, I made this business and I intend to keep it."

"You may find it difficult to compete with us."

"I may. But the National Cordage Company may find that it is embarking on a dangerous course. I happen to know that Senator Sherman proposes to introduce an antitrust bill in the next session of Congress, to prevent restraint of trade. Ohio has been unhappily aware of the power a trust can bring to bear, since the Standard Oil Company bought a senatorship for the Honorable Henry B. Payne." Ludwig could not help hoping that they had noticed the framed photograph of John Sherman that hung on the wall behind his desk, and was inscribed "To a faithful friend, with gratitude, John Sherman."

One of the financiers spoke. "Senator Sherman is a great man and deserves well of his country. But on this issue I do not believe he will carry Congress with him. We are to accept, then, that Rausch Cordage Company is not for sale whatever the price?"

"That is my firm decision."

"Then, when, or if, you change your mind, do inform us, so that we may enter into negotiations."

They rose, shook hands again, and departed. Ludwig went to speak to Eliza. "For once, Eliza, you may broadcast company affairs, and the tenor of this interview: I should like the town to be reassured that it is not about to have two-hundred-odd unemployed workers thrust upon it to be taken care of. It is possible that your account of this interview may be more convincing than any statement I could make."

"I don't understand why you were so polite to them. In your place I think I would have turned them out before they ever got started."

Ludwig looked at her in astonishment. "I thought I rather showed there toward the end that I was getting hot under the collar, and that would have been a mistake. Nothing is ever gained by making enemies gratuitously. They are going to fight me and all the other rope companies they can't buy up. And I am going to fight them, tooth and nail. But that doesn't mean that we'll always be opposed to each other. Some day we may be fighting on the same side."

"It hardly seems likely." Eliza sniffed to show how she felt about the National Cordage Company, and Ludwig thought, "How like a woman: an opponent is necessarily an enemy."

He was so late for lunch that noon that Sally, who usually waited for him, had eaten and gone to spend the afternoon with "po' Miz Go'don," Rose explained, as she served him. The older boys had returned to school, and Cassie had taken Paul upstairs for his nap. So Ludwig ate alone, hurriedly, and it was not until he came home that evening that he had a chance to report to Sally. The hour the two of them customarily spent together in the library before dinner, alone or with the boys coming and going, was one of the pleasantest of the day for both of them. On that late afternoon there was a brisk fire in the coal grate; Sally sat to one side of it, a new French novel open on her lap; Paul was sitting on the hearthrug with a pile of blocks. Ludwig came in, picked him up, gave him a smacking kiss and a bear hug, put him down again, picked up the *Torchlight* from the table where Sally had put it, and sat down in the "gentlemen's chair" across from her rocker.

"Your expected callers showed up, I suppose?"

He laughed and gave her a full account of the morning, concluding with his words to Eliza. "The emissaries from the National Cordage Company would have liked me to close the door to her office. I told them she was my confidential secretary." Ludwig chuckled. "But I don't want anyone in Waynesboro to be in any doubt as to my intentions—and believe me, all Waynesboro must be wondering: those three gentlemen spent last night at the Ewing House. I could say until I was blue in the face that I had no intention of selling, and some would still wonder. But when Eliza gives everyone—your Club members, Miss Allison in the Post Office, the Methodist church—her full account of what happened this morning, they will be convinced."

"It is none of Waynesboro's business what you do. Why do you—"

"Yes, it is. I have a certain responsibility to the town, now that the mill supports so many families. Besides, some of my laborers might drift off to the cities if they thought they were going to lose their jobs. Eliza will make a good story of it: she couldn't see why I treated them so cordially—thought they should have been shown the door once they had made their proposition. Women can't see, even the best of them, that it doesn't pay to be rude to an opponent."

"I can't see much point in pretending to be friendly. Of course sometimes you have to, but it can be difficult."

Sally's frown was so portentous as she spoke that Ludwig laughed again. "Who is it you dislike so much now?"

Her brow cleared; she smiled at him. "That sounds as if I made a habit of disliking people. I don't really, but—I know, she's a member of the Club now, and I must like *all* Club members, especially now I'm President. And," she added slowly, "it's a funny thing: I do like them all, in a way; there is a kind of bond; we have something in common. But Mrs. Jessamine Gordon Stevens can be very irritating. The way she has taken over at the Gordons'."

Ludwig's gaze rested on her fondly: "She's jealous," he thought, "and hasn't looked at herself squarely enough to see it." Aloud he said, "You have to remember: southerners set great store on blood kinship, and she hasn't any relatives, at least on her father's side. And neither Dock nor Anne have so much as a cousin, except her, have they? She has a look of the family, and that boy of hers is the spittin' image of Johnny at his age."

"He's a solemn child. Because he's been sick so much, I suppose. Johnny wasn't like that, he was a gay little boy. Rodney's the 'spittin' image' of Jessamine's father: she has a daguerreotype of him on her parlor mantle, in a Confederate uniform, of course."

"That's what I said. I'd know a Gordon if I met him in Timbuctoo: it's those round, full dark eyes. I don't mean pop-eyed, but not set deep beneath their eyebrows either. What was it upset you so today?"

"I went to see Anne, and was told by Mrs. Stevens—and you wouldn't think she'd answer the door with Martha and Louline there—that Anne was resting; she would inquire as to whether she felt like receiving callers. And old Martha, bless her, she'd come into the hall to answer the bell, and she said, 'Miss Sally, you just run right upstairs like always. Course she wants to see you.' And so I did. I found her in Binny's room, sorting and bundling up the child's clothes: some for Martha and Louline to take to the East End, some for Mrs. McKinney to give the church missionary society. 'Cousin Jessamine' may have believed she was resting. I remonstrated with her: said all that clearing out could wait. She said it was better to do it right away or she could never make herself do it at all: it would bring it all back to mind. And she's right, of course. She was all strung up. She kept rubbing the back of one hand with the palm of the other when I had persuaded her to sit down. But when I said she and Dock had better go away somewhere and get rested, she looked at me as if she thought I had lost my mind. She said, 'And come back to this empty house? No, we have to get used to it sometime, and it had better be now.' "

"Johnny went back to the city with the girls this morning?"

"Yes. Anne said he wanted to stay but they thought he'd better go—he would miss too many lectures. But the real reason, she said, was that if he'd stayed home, he'd be bearing the burden of their grief as well as his own, and he was too young for that—she and John were grown-up, and what they had to bear they could bear."

"There's the Presbyterian speaking."

"Yes. But she went on to say—she was saying things to me she can't say to Dock—she said she believed Binny was happier in Heaven than she could have been on earth. You know: the orthodox speech, only she believes it. She went on: Binny was so young, and life at that age is good; she couldn't help grieving that the child couldn't have had more of it; after all, Heaven is for eternity; it could have waited. And she said that of course she hadn't said anything like that to John: she just kept telling him that Binny was free of pain, saved from grief, happy, forever young."

"I doubt if Dock goes further than agreeing that the child is free from pain and saved from grief."

"Oh, she knows that. She says he's been reading Marcus Aurelius. It seems Kitty Edwards before she died gave him her father's copy. But Anne doesn't think he's found much consolation there. And she said she was so glad I had come: she could say things like that to me, 'Imagine saying them to Cousin Jessamine,' she said. I asked her if Jessamine hadn't kind of taken over. She smiled at that, first time I had seen her smile: it made her look more natural. You know: Anne was never a beauty, exactly, but she had a beautiful mouth: wide, but so defined, like sculpture. And she has been through these last months with her teeth clenched, I suppose: it has thinned her mouth until it's hardly more than a line."

"Anne is still a young woman: her teeth will come unclenched. What about Cousin Jessamine?"

"She said Cousin Jessamine thought she ought to go into seclusion for a while: that's the proper thing if you're in mourning, and Cousin Jessamine is nothing if not proper. But—and I could have shaken her—she was glad Cousin Jessamine was downstairs to greet callers: she didn't want to see anyone and submit to condolences. And whenever she heard Jessamine start upstairs, she went into her room, closed the door, and pretended to be asleep, so she wouldn't have to talk to her."

"But that's the worst possible way—"

"I know. It is so easy to be sensible for other people, isn't it? I've been racking my brains since I got home trying to think of a way to get Jessamine out of there, and I think I have a glimmering of an idea. I had thought I wouldn't give the Club a Christmas party this year, what with Papa's death and now Binny's, and Mrs. Ballard almost any time. But I think we could have an afternoon tea, as we did last year, without any acting, just music. I understand from Christina that Jessamine has a very pleasing contralto voice. We could make up a quartet: those two and Mrs. Evans, who sings like a bird, and Elizabeth Merrill, who can at least carry a tune. An afternoon of carols, maybe even using the children, in costume. Something Dickensy." Sally was elaborating on her idea even as she gave it voice. "Christina doesn't believe in Christmas, but surely she couldn't refuse to sing carols. There would have to be rehearsals day and night from now till Christmas, since it's so close. It would keep Jessamine occupied. The Club meets tomorrow: I'll suggest it."

"That would be good." Ludwig gave an absent-minded approval as he shook open the *Torchlight*. "The President's message to Congress should be in the paper tonight." Congress had convened a couple of days earlier.

"It is. You won't like it. Mr. Bonner didn't."

"Oh, naturally." Ludwig settled down to read. Sally picked Paul up from the hearthrug. "It's your supper time, Sweety: let's go find Cassie."

When she returned, she found Ludwig beaming, a picture of delight.

"What—"

"That Democrat's hanged himself. He proposes to cut the tariff because in the past three years a dangerous surplus, one hundred and twenty-two million dollars, has accumulated in the Treasury, a surplus over government expenses. And the only way we can rid ourselves of the menace is by cutting the tariff. The man has handed us a campaign issue on a silver platter, and no pun intended."

"You mean there weren't any issues before?" It was issue enough to Sally that Cleveland was a Democrat.

"Not really. President Cleveland hasn't been so very different from Garfield and Arthur: conservative in fiscal matters, and keeping order in the country. With men like Governor Foraker and, say, Bonner making the campaign speeches and writing the editorials, we would have fallen back on the 'bloody shirt' again."

"It served the Governor in his fall campaign. And I do agree with Mr. Bonner that the disenfranchisement of the Negro in the South is a disgrace."

"I suppose if you'd spent a year in Andersonville you would wave the bloody shirt the rest of your life. But I did not realize that enfranchisement of the Negro was one of your heart's causes."

"It never was," Sally admitted. "I've never been much of a one for 'causes.' But I called on Mrs. McKinney the other afternoon. She had just had a letter from Rachel Tobias. You remember the little colored girl they raised? She's teaching Negro children in what passes for a school in Alabama somewhere. Such a despairing letter; Mrs. McKinney read parts of it to me: she was all worked up. The school is run on contributions; there is little or nothing with which to pay the teachers, and no compulsion on the children to attend. The Negroes, according to Rachel, have been effectively disenfranchised over the last ten years, and if they can't vote, what hope is there of getting decent schools for them? Or of getting away from what amounts to bondage to the land: they're all sharecroppers and never get out of debt to the landowners. I could see she was right: what was the point of all that fighting, if the Negro isn't any better off than he was before?"

"You forget: 'all that fighting' kept us one united country. Oh, in a way, I can see myself that the Radical Republicans were right, though I didn't think so at the time: we should have seen the thing through in Reconstruction days and not cleared the troops out of the South until Negro rights would be protected. But then: we would have had Tilden for President instead of Hayes. And now, it would be impossible to enforce those rights without sending troops in again: and who wants that?"

"Mrs. McKinney didn't go that far: she just hoped the Republicans could do some vague something if they win the '88 election. But Mrs. Ballard—I called on her the same day; I was making the rounds—I brought the subject up because I wanted to talk about something besides how she felt. She was quite fierce about it. She had been dictating a letter to some Indiana congressman because he's made speeches about the abuses the Negro has been suffering."

"Mrs. Ballard! There's a change for you! There wasn't anyone hotter to put an end to Reconstruction and the Radicals than the Liberal Republicans. Has she forgotten the Judge bolted the Republican party in '72 because he didn't like the Radicals? And was a Mugwump in '84?"

"Be honest, Ludwig: all that was because of Republican corruption, not because of Negro rights."

"True enough. Nevertheless, it is odd to have Mrs. Ballard lined up with the bloody-shirt boys. Personally, I'm glad the President has given us a real issue: the Negro problem is insoluble, far as I can see. I can't imagine Mrs. Ballard caring about protective tariffs on imported goods: like most so-called liberals, she no doubt thinks of protection as a way by which employers make themselves rich, not as a means by which they can afford to pay the working man more than he is paid anywhere else in the world. As for the 'menace' of that one hundred and twenty-two million: I look forward to hearing Senator Sherman on the subject. Doesn't it occur to that idiot in the White House that it could be applied on the public debt: interest payments reduced, bonds retired?"

"You aren't afraid of a tariff reduction?"

"Of course I'm afraid of a tariff reduction. But I'm not very much afraid that a bill reducing tariffs could be passed in Congress. If it is, it will get in its deadly work between now and next November, and there's the election won."

Ludwig turned the paper back to reread the President's message as it had been delivered to Congress and printed in full by the *Torchlight;* Sally went back to her novel. The boys came in together, Ernest now released from the mill by school, but still full of the dignity of what he considered his adulthood, with Charles and Ludwig trailing behind him, sparring at each other as they came.

"Dinner ready?" they demanded as with one voice.

"Quiet, boys, for goodness's sake. If you're that hungry, go upstairs and eat with Cassie and Paul."

They were not very responsive to that suggestion, but if they had to await dinner, they would be conversational while they waited, and their parents had perforce to listen.

At the meeting of the Woman's Club on the next afternoon, Sally propounded her idea for a Christmas tea at her home on the twenty-first: an afternoon of Christmas music, with Elizabeth Merrill again acting as chairman of a committee to plan the program. Since that was but a few days away, there would be little time for preparation, but she was quite sure that "our musicians" were capable of providing the Club with an enjoyable afternoon. After the meeting, Sally cornered Elizabeth and made more definite suggestions: she understood that Mrs. Stevens had a delightful voice, she knew that Mrs. Evans could sing, Christina might be willing and she, Elizabeth, would make a fourth? Thomasina would play for them, and surely they knew enough carols?

For the next week those members of the Woman's Club who were musical (with the exception of Christina, who firmly declined to take part) were busy afternoon and evenings. Mrs. Stevens had no more free days to spend at the Gordons' protecting Anne, and Anne forced herself to return to a more or less normal life, although she had little heart for it, even suffering once or twice the strange foreignness in a queer world that children sometimes feel: "What am I doing here? Why am I Anne Gordon? How odd that I should be Anne Gordon." But however determinedly she climbed toward the normal, she stayed away from Sally's Christmas party, not because she cared about the convention for mourners, but because she could not face having to watch all those children, Binny's friends, healthy and happy and enjoying their worlds.

The afternoon turned out to be an enjoyable one: the carolers came stamping in, three adults in high silk hats, broadcloth coats, woolen scarves, and flowing capes; the children in caps and scarves and pantalettes. The voices of the three women blended well; they sang alone the more difficult carols like "Adeste, fideles" in Latin and the medieval "The first Nowell the angel did say," and "When Christ was born of Marie free," then turned to the easier familiar tunes to which the children added their piping voices. When the program had ended, with a few encores thrown in, the boys and girls were taken off by Cassie for a treat around the dining room table, and the ladies were served a sumptuous tea in the Rausch drawing room.

After that the Club would meet no more until January fourth, when Sally would enlighten the ladies with her essay on Macaulay. In between came Christmas, jubilant as always in most Waynesboro homes, subdued at the Gordons' and at the Ballards', where Mrs. Ballard lay mortally ill; and New Year's, when the young men, instead of going one by one to make their calls, hired a dray, placed their mothers' kitchen chairs in rows on its bed, and made the rounds together from house to house where the ladies were "at home." Johnny went with them: his parents had insisted. What with beer at the Bonners' and Kleins', where Sophie was home for the holidays, and wine at the Rausches' and even the Demings', where for once the General had overridden his wife (it was customary, wasn't it?), the boys were all slightly overtaken, and their driver, when the afternoon ended, unloaded them each at his own door, and made sure that every mother got her own kitchen chair back. Johnny, who foolishly hoped that his condition would pass unnoticed, was saved a scolding by his father's thinking the whole thing funny. After he had gone upstairs for the nap he sorely needed, he could still hear his father's voice down in the sitting room. He would have been surprised could he have heard the words: "It's a good thing for him, Anne. He's been sad too long; he was bound to break out somewhere, sometime, and this is a good place and time: right here at home."

"But *drunk*! How *could* they?"

"His hosts, you mean? I don't suppose for a minute they realized; it probably didn't hit those silly young idiots until they got out in the cold after their last call. And anyway, if Johnny never gets any drunker than he was when he came in just now, you've nothing to worry about."

But that New Year's escapade became one of Waynesboro's favorite stories, to be told with glee or with horror, depending on one's point of view; and General Deming's standing in the community was raised or lowered, again according to how you looked at it. (Of course everyone knew what to expect at those other houses, but the *Demings*!) General Deming, who wanted very much to be one of his district's representatives at the Republican National Convention in June, lost nothing among politicians by having shown himself "a good fellow." Temperance, or prohibition, had been a hot issue in the state for the last decade, and General Deming had gone along with his party and Governor Foraker in favor of the amendment to the state constitution that would permit the legislature to pass laws taxing the liquor trade: an amendment that had been voted down before by the odd combination of the Prohibitionists, who considered that such a law condoned the sale of liquor, and the "liquor interests," who did not want either taxation or licensing. General Deming's stand had disappointed some of his old friends, but had helped him with party regulars.

As 1888 dragged to its end, politics began once more to be an overriding concern, first with those engaged in it and then with the general electorate; and as Ludwig had foreseen, the tariff was going to be the chief issue. Parties agreed that taxes should be reduced, but Senator Sherman, in a speech in the Senate in response to the President's message, had made clear the Republican position: protect industry by the tariff on imports; reduce internal taxes. The tariff bill introduced in the House came up for consideration on the twenty-first of April. A few days earlier the Ohio Republicans, in convention at Dayton, had voted unanimously to support Senator Sherman as their presidental candidate. Since Blaine had declared himself out of the race, there would be no Blaine supporters to disrupt the delegation; in the beginning at any rate, though Hanna, who was Sherman's manager, may have felt uneasy about the loyalty of Governor Foraker, who was of course a delegate at large, as was William McKinley, the well-known expert on the tariff and a friend of Mark Hanna. Whatever questions there may have been about the Governor, on the surface the delegation was united and would go to the National Convention in June to nominate Sherman if possible. Ludwig kept to himself his doubts as to whether it could be done, although he thought Sherman should be the candidate, and would fight for him to the end, as he had fought so many times before. He was less than wholehearted that spring in his political commitment in general because he was deeply involved in his fight with the National Cordage Company, whose control was spreading and whose prices were undercutting independent manufacturers. But its attempt to corner the hemp supply failed: that spring the price of manila began to fall; it became evident that the National Cordage Company had overextended itself and been forced to withdraw its support of the hemp market. Ludwig, having borrowed money for the purpose on a short-term-loan basis in Cincinnati, was able to fill his warehouse again with fiber at a price of six and a half cents, less than he had paid the year before. At the time the bill to reduce the tariff was still being debated in the House; even if it should pass there, Ludwig saw little likelihood of its passing in the Senate. He went off to the Convention in June in the company of General Deming, his mind easier than it had been for several months, but without the expectation of victory that had made him so eager in '80 and only less so in '84. He discouraged Sally from accompanying him, and she was willing to stay home: the boys were too much of a handful to be taken to Aunt Minna in Burlington or left at home with Cassie.

Once at the Convention, the quadrennial excitement caught Ludwig in its tide, rising as it did through all the days of addresses and nominating speeches, to the point of actual balloting. At least, he thought, this year Ohio was sticking together. Foraker and McKinley might be and probably were jealous of each other, and when after several indecisive ballots it was rumored that Blaine would after all consent to run, Foraker, who was quick to suspect that the delegation would go to McKinley once Sherman's cause was recognized as hopeless, let it be known he would support "the plumed knight"; but when another firm refusal came from Blaine, Foraker quickly returned to his sworn allegiance with the pretense of having never left it. McKinley, on the other hand, when he continued to receive a few votes on every ballot, interrupted the roll call to speak to the Convention: his loyalty to Sherman and his own integrity demanded that he ask that no more votes be cast for him. He had stood on a chair to speak, and no one who heard him or noted his pallor, his agitation, could question his sincerity, and the hardened politicians and the cynical newspaper reporters were genuinely moved. Seven ballots were cast before Saturday night's adjournment, with Sherman getting a plurality of the votes, but nothing like a majority. Perhaps if Sunday had not intervened—but according to a rumor everywhere accepted, a bargain was made on that day between Tom Flatt, still in control of the New York delegation, and the Indiana manager for Benjamin Harrison. At any rate, Harrison was nominated. And Ludwig, who had promised himself that this time he would not be disappointed, was left again with the bitter taste of defeat in his mouth. On that last day he exchanged a few words with Mr. Hanna before the delegation split up and went their ways. They agreed that it had been the last chance for the Senator: if Harrison was elected, he would want a second term, and by 1896 Sherman would be an old man. "He deserved better of his country," Mark Hanna said. "But," and his face cleared, "what do you think of Major McKinley? He too is a man of integrity and sound principle and policy, and he is a man with more warmth than the Senator. He too deserves our loyalty and best services. In the meantime we shall have our work cut out for us if we are to elect General Harrison."

"If it weren't for the tariff—" Ludwig was going to say that if it weren't for the tariff question, he wouldn't much care, but Mr. Hanna cut in.

"Yes, the tariff—that is the issue that will elect him."

Ludwig had not let Sally know when to expect him, and so there was no one in the Waynesboro depot to meet him; he had not wanted to be commiserated with in public. At home he was greeted with the unfailing warmth and delight of a family that had missed him, and there were the anticipated cries of "Too bad, Ludwig!" and "What a shame, Papa!" Then Sally said, "This Harrison: what is he like? Oh, I know that he's been in Congress and made speeches on the tariff and on the Negro question in the South. But what's he like?"

Ludwig shivered, and chattered his teeth in a mock chill.

"What does that mean, for goodness' sake?"

"Just that when General Harrison comes into a room, the temperature drops twenty degrees."

"Won't it be hard to elect a man like that?"

"We'll elect him: we must, or see things go to pot. We won't be electing 'a man like that,' but a Republican. The damnable irony of politics: the objection to Senator Sherman has always been that he is cold, without appeal to the ordinary voter. Then we turn around and nominate a man like Harrison." He shivered again. "But he is a man of integrity: I don't know what Tom Platt expects to get out of his bargain."

And so the Republicans campaigned on the tariff issue, and for the first time since the Civil War, the emotional bloody shirt appeal was not heard. Campaign speeches were not so rousing as in other years, and Congress was continued in session until October, most leading Republicans forced of necessity to remain in Washington to debate the tariff bill that had been introduced in the House in April. But the year was the hundredth anniversary of the Marietta settlement, and the celebrations throughout the state were made the occasion of a great deal of "nonpolitical" oratory. In August the national encampment of the Grand Army of the Republic was held in Columbus. That, too, was presumably "nonpolitical," although the G.A.R. had been since its organization a principal support of the Republican party (Union soldiers, all of them, after all). On the day of the parade, to the great indignation of any Democrats present, seventy thousand over-heated marchers had been provided with fans bearing Harrison's picture. Ludwig was one of those marchers; he had for many years been nominally a member of the G.A.R. for reasons of policy, but had seldom attended any meetings larger than those of his own country. But that August, when the encampment was to be so close to Waynesboro, he decided to go. He had tried to persuade John Gordon to go with him. One of his points was that General Sherman was to be on the reviewing stand: he was getting old, and they might not have another chance to see him. But John said, "I don't want to see the General an old man. I'd rather remember the last time." Ludwig understood but still tried to argue: never again would there be so many veterans marching; from then on there would be fewer every year. John remained adamant. But on Ludwig's return he was not spared a glowing account of the event: most particularly that of his visit to the reviewing stand, introduced there before the parade by Governor Foraker.

"The General is looking older—you were right about that. But his memory is good as ever. He remembered—" Ludwig hesitated, stopped a moment by John's clenched jaw—"He asked about you, and where the 'little girls' were. I told him about Binny. He asked me to remind you that he knew what it was to lose a child."

"So he does. Remember Willy Sherman dying of typhoid at Memphis in the middle of the Vicksburg campaign? That was hard. How could he go on, I wonder?"

"He wanted to be remembered to you, with his sympathy."

John's eyes misted over. He could not bring himself to say anything beyond a murmured "Thank you."

The election in November was in one sense scarcely a "sweeping" victory for the Republicans: Harrison had the greatest number of electoral votes, but Cleveland the majority of popular votes. On the other hand, for the first time in sixteen years the Republicans had won not only the executive branch of the government but the legislative as well: there would be a Republican majority in both houses of Congress, and no more nonsense, it was to be hoped, about reduction of the tariff.

Mrs. McKinney was happier over the decision of Harrison than many a good stalwart Republican. "He is a good man," she wrote Rachel, "and he will do something to alleviate the sufferings of your people."

And Mrs. Ballard died, happy in the same illusion. To the bitter end she had retained perfect clarity of mind; even when she was helpless physically and required attention day and night, she clung to her sustaining interest in the affairs of mankind. She had Thomasina read the newspaper to her inch by inch, and when some new atrocity had been committed against a Negro in the South, or some helpless woman had met with injustice in the courts, she was roused to letters, dictating to Thomasina by day what Eliza would type at the office: letters to the editor, whether it was Mr. Bonner of the *Torchlight*, or Mr. McLean of the *Cincinnati Enquirer*, of Whitelaw Reid of the *New York Tribune;* and letters to politicians, some of whom she rebuked, some of whom she praised.

John was dubious as to the effect on her of her fevered mental activity. He spoke of his doubts to Eliza one evening when he was late with his call and she had come home from work.

"She's wearing herself out, fretting over these things, and so uselessly. And wearing you out too."

"I know: for all the good her letters do, I might as well drop them down the cistern. But I can't tell her that. What does it matter? At this point?"

He could only say that doctors tried to keep their patients alive as long as possible; he knew it could not be long at best. He was surprised that she had clung to life as long as she had, and not at all surprised when Sam came for him one evening not long after the election.

"She is gone," Sam told him as he climbed into John's buggy with him, "but I know you must come and tell us so. Funny thing, once the election returns were in and Harrison's election certain, she just let go. Sort of a 'Nunc dimittis.' She was so sure that he was on the side of the angels—her angels—and could accomplish wonders."

"He's a cold-blooded cuss. Honest enough, I guess, but not really moved by the Negroes' plight, nor on anyone's side but Benjamin Harrison's."

"However much we are horrified by every lynching, there's nothing can be done about it now: it's too late. And as for Woman Suffrage, we'll not see it in our lifetime. Mother Ballard and all the old friends she corresponded with, like Mrs. Stanton, outlived the age of reform."

Mrs. Ballard's funeral was a purely local affair: the women still alive who had shared so many platforms with her were too old to travel so far. The church was crowded, but with Waynesboro Methodists, members of the W.C.T.U., the Woman's Club. It seemed strange to those who remembered Judge Ballard's funeral: in her heyday, Mrs. Ballard had been as well-known a platform personality as he.

The Waynesboro Woman's Club paid Mrs. Ballard due honor as a charter member and its first President, interrupting the 1888–89 program, "New Books by Old Friends," to do so. Sally, who perhaps felt guilty because she had not loved Mrs. Ballard as much as she might, planned carefully a meeting that would touch on all aspects of her life: Amanda, a paper on the Abolition Movement and Mrs. Ballard; Mrs. Deming, the Woman Suffrage Cause and Mrs. Ballard; Mrs. McKinney, the Temperance Movement and Mrs. Ballard; she herself spoke on Mrs. Ballard as Club member and Club President, and Anne Gordon spoke on "Informal Recollections of Mrs. Ballard," the tributes being interspersed with appropriate music by what everyone had come to recognize as "The Club Trio." It had been so long since Mrs. Ballard had been an active member the Club that newer members had not known her at all, and even some older ones had never seen her in her prime. And after all, Sally had said when she was trying to induce Anne to speak, Mrs. Ballard was by far the most distinguished member the Club had ever had or was likely to have. "She used to rile me, I admit: she was so anxious to improve the whole world, including me. But thinking back, I do believe the Club might never have survived the first years if she hadn't kept us up to the mark: with her there we would have been ashamed not to have done our best."

"I always felt sorry for the girls. But they never seemed to mind being dragged around to meetings and conventions. And I think she was kind, when she could turn her mind to it. I mean, I don't think she was ever deliberately unkind. Pity Eliza isn't more like her."

"Ludwig thinks the world of Eliza as a secretary. Funny, isn't it? But there's more that can be said for Mrs. Ballard than just that she was kind in an absent-minded sort of way, and I intend to say it."

The *In Memoriam* meeting was the longest and most formal the Club had ever held for a deceased member; and what with the music and speeches, some of the ladies were moved to tears, most to moist eyes (and the younger ones, who had not known her, to wonder why), and Thomasina, pathetically grateful for the appreciation of her mother, wept openly.

"Altogether," Anne said to John at the dinner table that night, "it was a 'dem'd moist disagreeable' occasion. She would have hated it herself."

"I'm not sure," he replied, slowly. "Everyone in the world likes praise. It's only human, and most of us don't hear much of it in our lifetimes. I got to know Mrs. Ballard pretty well. A fierce old woman in many ways, but she fought off death as long as she could just because she was worried about the girls not getting along together without her. She exacted a promise from

Eliza before the end—Eliza told me—that she would look out for Thomasina. Mrs. Ballard never thought of turning it around."

"You mean, asking Thomasina to watch over Eliza?" Anne was astonished.

"I know Eliza seems self-sufficient. Perhaps she is. But I think she is lonely."

"*Eliza?* She's the busiest busybody in town. There isn't room in her mind for loneliness. And just a year ago— John." She looked at him sadly. "It doesn't seem like a year, does it?"

"No," John crumpled his napkin, tossed it on the table, and pushed his chair back. "As long as we live, it will never seem longer ago than yesterday."

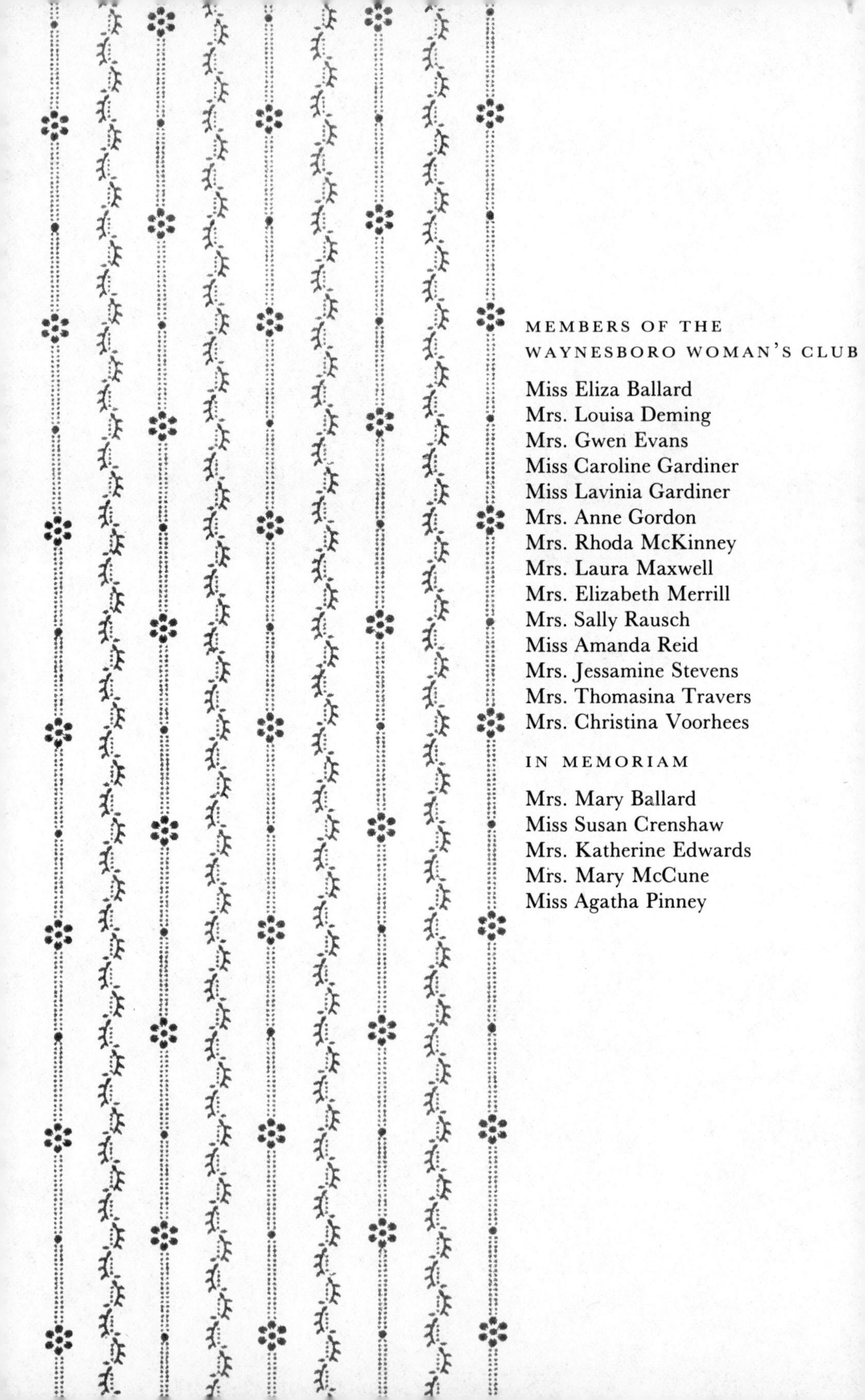

MEMBERS OF THE
WAYNESBORO WOMAN'S CLUB

Miss Eliza Ballard
Mrs. Louisa Deming
Mrs. Gwen Evans
Miss Caroline Gardiner
Miss Lavinia Gardiner
Mrs. Anne Gordon
Mrs. Rhoda McKinney
Mrs. Laura Maxwell
Mrs. Elizabeth Merrill
Mrs. Sally Rausch
Miss Amanda Reid
Mrs. Jessamine Stevens
Mrs. Thomasina Travers
Mrs. Christina Voorhees

IN MEMORIAM

Mrs. Mary Ballard
Miss Susan Crenshaw
Mrs. Katherine Edwards
Mrs. Mary McCune
Miss Agatha Pinney

* 1892 *

"One of our daughters returned to her home . . ."

On a cold blustery February evening, Ludwig Rausch dropped in at the doctors' office for a chat with John Gordon. The waiting room was empty of patients, although it was only eight o'clock: John was alone in the middle room, staring moodily at a chess problem set out on the board. The doctor was surprised to see Ludwig; had any of his family been ill, he would have telephoned.

"What brings you out in this weather?"

"It is an anniversary I thought I would like to spend with you. You haven't forgotten?"

John nodded toward the big calendar that hung on the office wall. "If I had, that would have reminded me." He swept the few chessmen off the board. "Pull up a chair and we'll have a game. No, I hadn't forgotten. That day was a kind of milestone for me, and for you too, I guess." He filled his empty pipe and lighted it. "All of a sudden, the last of our youth gone."

John and Ludwig at fifty no longer looked like young men: Ludwig's gray hairs scarcely showed on his blond head, but he had a middle-aged figure: he was heavier than he had ever been, and visibly thicker around the middle. John had not put on much weight, only enough to be described as stocky rather than slender; but his face was deeper-lined than Ludwig's, and his beard and hair were beginning to have a grizzled look. But looking young and not feeling young are two different things; each man had unconsciously felt himself the same as the boy who had gone off to war in '61, until the winter a year ago, the winter of 1891.

On that fourth of February whose anniversary the calendar marked, General Sherman had died in New York. By his own wish the funeral train that carried his body home to St. Louis had not stopped on the way for any last honors or ceremonial rites. But wherever old soldiers who had fought in his armies could manage to reach the tracks, they gathered to watch—just to watch the train go past. And to say good-bye not only to the General but to something that had been a part of themselves. Two or three, met at a crossing where the signal tinkled as they stood at salute, a handful, perhaps with a flag, perhaps with a bugle, in every village; and in the towns, platforms crowded with middle-aged men, some of them in ill-fitting uniforms, all standing at ramrod attention, saluting as the train drew slowly through and around a curve and out of sight. John and Ludwig had come unexpectedly together outside the Waynesboro depot; neither of them had spoken of his intention to go; both had acted on impulse, half reluctantly, a little shamefaced. They stood together wordlessly, along with other veterans, watching up the track for the engine's smoke. When it came in sight, they stiffened to attention and lifted their arms in salute, their faces rigid, but when the last car had pulled out of sight neither was dry-eyed. As the silent crowd began to drift away, Ludwig said, "Reuben's here with the buggy. Let me drop you off at the office."

"I'd rather walk, I think, thanks just the same. Do you feel, all of a sudden, the sum of the years that have passed? That is an old man they are taking home to bury, not the General."

"Yes. And we are not boys, Dock. Something has gone out of our lives forever with that train."

They had said no more; there was no need: there were enough shared memories to evoke shared emotion, not only memories of marches, fights, and sieges, but of a picnic day when the General had been kind to an enchanted Binny. It was of that John spoke on the evening a year later, when they were setting out the chessmen.

"You remember that day at Odell's Grove? All the children: in a way it seems as long ago as Vicksburg. In another way it seems like yesterday. How have we come so quickly to be fathers of grown men and women? Here's Johnny an M.D. and practicing."

"Where is your young man? Out on a case?"

"He's where he is mostly, of an evening, since the Demings got home. In their parlor. Sparking."

"Hasn't that affair been hanging fire a long time? What's the matter with Johnny? He's a very enterprising boy, most ways."

"It's the young lady who's reluctant. And the Demings. They took that long trip abroad last summer hoping to separate the two, I suspect. Looking for a duke for her, maybe."

Ludwig snorted, and John laughed. "That's the way I feel," he said. "It would have been no loss to Waynesboro if they could have brought it off. Johnny's heart would have been broken, but it would have mended. 'Men have died and worms have eaten them—' "

" 'But not for love.' Lord, how that takes me back; remember Kitty Edwards playing Rosalind in one of those Club Christmas plays? And that was a long, long while ago, too. Poor Kitty—so young—but she knew what love meant. You and I, Dock, have been lucky. More fortunate than our children."

John, a much more reticent man than Ludwig, made no reference to his own good fortune. Instead he said, "These long, unacknowledged engagements are the devil. I suspect the girl's shying away from marriage in maidenly distaste. I admit I am troubled about the prospect. But you: you are worried about Elsa? Surely not about your boys—not yet."

"No. Hardly." Beyond that Ludwig did not answer for a long minute; he was studying the chessboard. Then he sighed and said, "Yes, Elsa. She'll be coming home soon. She's been gone for two years now, far too long. I never could see why, anyway."

Elsa had been studying piano in Dresden, living with one of Ludwig's cousins and devoting herself to music with all the concentration she could muster. No one—not Ludwig, not her mother—no one but Elsa herself knew why she had suddenly decided that the Cincinnati Conservatory had nothing more to offer her, that she must advance her studies in Germany. The decision had been made on the night in their boardinghouse when Julia had come in late, starry-eyed, and had confided that Johnny had proposed to her. Elsa, hating herself, sick with despair, had said, "And of course you accepted."

"Of course *not*, you silly. Why, he isn't through medical school yet. I can't think what Papa would say. I told him to wait until he was established as a physician to ask me again. I wish he would consider practicing here in Cincinnati. I do like living in a city."

"He won't. He's going to be his father's partner."

"I know. And of course that will make it easier for him to get started. But I do think Waynesboro's poky."

"Well, I'll save my good wishes until you have said 'yes.'" Then Elsa had been sharper with Julia than she had ever permitted herself to be. "But I do think it is cruel of you to keep poor Johnny dangling."

"He's been dangling a long while, and hasn't seemed to mind."

And that was true—so true that Elsa had to fight back the tears. She would go far, far away, to Germany, and so not have to be a witness.

If her mother did not know of the particular incident that had precipitated Elsa's desire to go abroad, Sally had a fair idea. When Elsa had suggested to her father that he send her to Germany to advance her music, he was taken aback and on the point of refusing: how could he get along without her? And anyway, he couldn't afford it: he was having to lay off spinner girls, the rope business was so bad. Her mother had come to her rescue. "You won't use my money in your mill, so I'll use it to give Elsa her trip abroad."

"She can't make a trip like that alone, and I can't get away."

"Oh Papa! Lots of girls— Anyway, Sophie Klein and I can travel together. She's going to Berlin to study at the University." Sophie, two years out of college, had been teaching German in the high school, and saving her money by living at home. If Elsa had expected her mother to consider Fritz Klein's daughter an unsuitable traveling companion, she was mistaken. Sally had said, "I think it would be wise to let her go, Ludwig."

And Ludwig, wondering what his womenfolk were up to, had dropped the subject. But it had been but a few weeks since Sally had suggested giving Gib Evans a position as salesman at Rausch Cordage Company. Gib, once out of the Seminary, had gone to work at the *Torchlight* as advertising manager. The paper, since the death of Mr. Bonner, had been in the hands of his two older sons, and Charlotte, once she was at home with her B.A., had gone to work there, ostensibly as society editor, actually as general dogsbody, writing anything from editorials to the court news. The position of advertising manager was a new one: in his day the senior Mr. Bonner had himself procured what advertising the *Torchlight* carried. Gilbert Evans, in his beginner's zeal, had sought high and low for possible new advertisers, and had gone among other places to Rausch Cordage, to see whether some product of theirs could be advertised in the *Torchlight*. Ludwig had been amused: they made no retail sales, of course, but he had confided to Sally that Gib, who had haunted their house for years whenever Elsa was home, had more get-up-and-go than he had suspected. It was then that his wife had made her surprising suggestion: after all, she had said reasonably, Ludwig could not keep on forever the two roles of traveling salesman and manufacturer. And besides it would give Ludwig a chance to take Gib's measure.

"Why should I? The boy's nothing to me."

"Surely you have seen—he's been in love with Elsa for years."

"I could hardly have missed it. Every time I opened the parlor door, I stumbled over him. But they were children, then, in high school. I don't know how he feels now. I'm sure Elsa doesn't care a rap for him."

"He feels the same as ever, I am sure. And Elsa may come, in time—there isn't anyone else, not here."

Ludwig had said no more. Having concluded that Sally had picked Gib as a suitable husband for Elsa, he had given him a position as salesman for the mill products. And now, only a few weeks later, here was his wife wanting Elsa to go away for all of two years. He believed Elsa deserved a better husband than Gib Evans, and so perhaps it would be a good idea to get her away.

Once his consent had been given, Sally lost no time in tackling Elsa, pursuing her into her bedroom that same night.

"You're being sensible not to stay around here and suffer the humiliation of seeing Julia Deming snatch Johnny Gordon from under your nose."

"Mamma!" Elsa, taking down her heavy molasses-colored hair, leaned forward to catch her mother's eye in the mirror. "What do you mean?"

"Don't be a goose. You know what I mean. Why shouldn't I be outspoken? I'm your mother, after all."

"Is it so obvious?"

"Only to me, I hope. Possibly to Anne. I have never discussed it with her. Your father is blind as a bat."

"How does it happen you haven't discussed it with Aunt Anne?" Elsa said it bitterly, since she had believed she had hidden from the eyes of the world her hopeless love. "I thought you two discussed everything."

"I haven't discussed it because I shouldn't care to have Anne, of all people, know that I consider her son a poor prospect as a husband."

"*Johnny?* Why ever not?" Elsa had turned on her chair to stare at her mother.

"There's a queer streak in the Gordons. They just don't make good husbands."

"Uncle Dock? But I thought—"

In the face of Elsa's innocent astonishment, Sally backtracked hastily. "He's your father's best friend and one of mine. He is a very good doctor. But doctors don't make good husbands: out at all hours, never home on time for meals. And Dock is temperamental besides. Moody. Melancholy even. No one knows what an effort Anne has had to make to keep him shored up."

"If no one knows, maybe she hasn't. And Johnny isn't moody or temperamental. Maybe he takes after his mother."

"It's beside the point, anyway. Johnny Gordon has been in love with Julia Deming all his life. This is the point—and I want you to listen to me: I said I thought you were right in getting out now, and studying piano in Dresden is a good excuse. But what then? You can't turn concert pianist, no matter how good you are. That is out of the question. You could give piano lessons, but you would not like that kind of drudgery. What then?"

Elsa was silent, brushing her hair with a concentration that did not deceive her mother.

"Shall I tell you? In a couple of years you will get over this; you will come home and marry and settle down."

"You have a husband picked out for me, I suppose?"

"There is one at hand. Gib Evans. He has been in love with you since you were in high school."

"Gib! Oh, Mamma! He's a nothing. Why, I'd die first!"

"He's a better man than you know. Your father says—"

"So that's why this place for him at Rausch Cordage Company. Does Papa share this hope of yours?"

"He knows nothing about it. And it is hardly a hope, even. I just think that by the time you come home, unless you find a fairy prince in Germany, Gib will look very different to you."

Elsa made no further protestations: once she got away, her mother could scheme for all she cared. And Sally was well satisfied; she knew Gib would write to Elsa—bombard her with letters, probably—and she would never hear a word from Johnny. Time and absence would have their way with Elsa.

It had been after a Club meeting at the Evanses' that Mrs. Evans had asked Sally to stay when the other ladies were taking their leave. "I do want to talk to you," she said.

Sally looked out the parlor window to see Reuben and the carriage at the curb. The front wall of the Baptist parsonage was at the edge of the sidewalk (a situation that tempted some ladies who were not too interested in the essay being read to find distraction in the passersby). Sally could speak to Reuben from the door.

"Just a minute," she said to Mrs. Evans. "I brought Thomasina and the Gardiners. I'll ask Reuben to take them home and then come back for me."

She returned in a second, seated herself on Mrs. Evans's slippery horsehair sofa, and said, "Did you have something—?"

"On my mind? Yes, I did." Mrs. Evans sat down beside her, tilting her head to look up at the taller woman, her bright black eyes intent. "What are you planning for Gilbert?"

"Planning?"

"I have known you for a number of years, Sally Rausch. You don't do things purposelessly."

"The position with Rausch Cordage Company, you mean? They needed a salesman."

"But why Gilbert? There are better salesmen to be found, I am sure, and Gilbert knows nothing about rope. I used to fret when Gilbert was in high school: you made him so much at home at a—a level so much above his situation in life and so impossible for him to reach on his own. He was happy, but I worried because I thought that when the young people were out of school, he would be dropped and forgotten—that it was convenient at the time to have an escort for Elsa."

Sally was genuinely hurt. "That is most unfair. Gilbert was a nice boy, with a good background. We don't care how much our friends may have in their pockets, nor drop them just because—"

"No," Mrs. Evans hastened to say, "I know you don't. And we have lived in Waynesboro long enough to know that the young people who go through school together as intimate friends keep close—for a while. It was just that Gilbert couldn't keep up that kind of life, not unless he was boosted into a chance to make money. Now I have begun to wonder. Is it possible that you would be willing—would accept Gilbert as a son-in-law? I am sorry if I am presumptuous, but—"

"Does it seem so preposterous to you?" Sally smiled faintly. "This is a preposterous conversation, but I trust a confidential one?"

"Certainly. I don't tell my husband everything, and men don't understand the workings of the feminine mind, anyway. I know I am stepping in where the angels wouldn't dare, but I want Gilbert to have a happy life. And I don't think the way to a happy life is to be a rich woman's husband and a rich man's—" She hesitated. "Lackey" was too strong a word to use to Sally, although it was what she meant.

Sally broke in. "Don't say it, Gwen Evans. You and I have been friends for a number of years. You should not have so low an opinion of us. Ludwig's using any man as a 'lackey'—that was the word you gagged over, wasn't it?—is so out of character it is funny. Is all this because you think of us as 'rich'? When it is actually touch and go whether Ludwig can hang on to the mill, with the Cordage Trust fighting him? I tell you he *needed* a salesman."

Mrs. Evans thought how relative a matter wealth was. By Evans standards the Rausches were unquestionably rich. "If Gilbert had stayed with the *Torchlight*, he would have been there the rest of his life, probably, an ordinary everyday citizen, going to work in the morning, coming home in the evening. Is that what you were thinking? And that with Rausch Cordage he has a chance to get somewhere? But he might have been happier not getting anywhere. And you still haven't answered my question."

"About Gib as a son-in-law? The idea hasn't entered Ludwig's mind." Sally did not say she had attempted to plant it there. "As to Elsa, at the moment she is suffering the pangs of unrequited love. But we are sending her to Germany for two years: she wants to carry on her music. And two years abroad, if she stays that long, will cure her. As to whether Gib makes any impression on her as time passes, who can predict? But, knowing as you must that he has loved her for a long time, you surely believe he would be happy to marry her?"

"To marry her, yes. But to be married to her, I don't know. He has a sweet nature, but he's pliable. And Elsa—"

"Is the stronger? Perhaps. But I know Elsa well enough to know that if she were ever to marry him, she would make him a good and faithful wife and be a good mother to his children."

In the two years that had passed since that day, the subject had not been touched upon again by either of the two women. And there had been no further discussion between Sally and Ludwig of what seemed to him so impossible a conclusion for Elsa: all her talent, her character and mind, her striking good looks, wasted on a nonentity like Gilbert Evans.

Now, sitting in John Gordon's office, hunched over the chessboard, he knew better: he had Elsa's newly received letter in his pocket. He moved a rook, sat back, and said, "You know that Elsa saw the Demings in Dresden? Seeing them may have made her homesick. We had a letter from her this morning: she is coming home as soon as I send her the passage money."

"That's good news. We've missed Elsa." John's mind was now really on the game; he spoke absentmindedly. "What are her plans? Is she coming home to stay?"

"She has plans. And I don't like 'em." Ludwig's tone made John sit up, take his hand from the piece he was about to move. "She's coming home to marry Gib Evans."

"Gib!"

"You can't be more surprised than I am. He asked me when he first came to work for us whether he might pay his addresses to Elsa. Actually used those words, as I remember. I said, 'Go ahead.' Why not? Never dreaming—

I don't think then she cared whether she ever saw him again or not. He must be a very persuasive letter-writer. She says she has quite made up her mind: we are to announce her engagement in the *Torchlight* and say that the wedding is to be in April, the first week. They've even set the date. And I don't like it."

"Any reason, except a fond father's dislike of losing a daughter? He's a good young man."

"Eminently worthy," Ludwig said drily. "An enthusiastic salesman, and a good one, because he's pleasant and easy in his manner and knows what he is selling: I saw to that before I sent him on the road. But no imagination, no ideas of his own, and dull. Mein Gott! How Elsa— Of course I'm glad her home will be here. It was a queer letter altogether: I couldn't help feeling she was talking over my head to her mother; first of all she said her mother had been right: her study of music was a dead end; she had made up her mind to come home. Then she spoke about having seen the Demings on their way from Vienna to Hamburg to sail for home, and said Julia had taken it for granted she would be her bridesmaid when she was married. And her parents hadn't even announced her engagement yet. And she, Elsa, hadn't any intention of playing the part of confidante in white linen. I asked Sally what she meant by that, and Sally reminded me of the winter a few years ago when the Woman's Club had acted Sheridan's *The Critic* for the benefit of the library fund. I hadn't remembered much about it except that at the time it had seemed very funny—the ladies' attempts to look decent and still wear breeches—and their acting. Anyway, Elsa went on to say that she wasn't going to keep Gib in suspense any longer: she had written to tell him she was coming home to marry him, she hoped with our blessing. And then all about the announcement, and the date. And if it wouldn't upset Sheldon Edwards too much, to get him out of the Linden Street house—the house Sally and I lived in when we were first married, and Elsa was born in—so she and Gib could have it. That's nonsense, of course: there's plenty of room in our house, and Gib is out of town so much."

"She's got better sense, Ludwig. Far better to start out just the two of them. And it will be good for Sheldon to get out of that house. Too many sad memories overlaying the happy ones."

"Odd he's never married again. Most men whose marriages have been happy can't bear not to try it again."

"Anne says he never will, or not until the boys are grown and gone and he is lonely enough to want company. How women can be so sure of these things beats me."

"At any rate, there won't be any trouble over the house. Last time he sent me the rent check he said he didn't know how much longer he could stay. His mother and father are getting pretty feeble, and although they have servants to look after them, by day at least, Sheldon thinks he should be there at nights. But what do you suppose is Elsa's great rush, after all this time?"

John laughed. "Sounds to me as if seeing the Demings had made her think of home, and she hasn't any intention of letting Julia be the first bride."

"But she wouldn't marry a man she didn't care for just to spite Julia Deming. Not Elsa."

"Of course not. It's a matter of timing. I reckon she made up her mind a long while ago to marry Gilbert, after she'd had her fling. There's no accounting for the people that people fall in love with, and there's nothing wrong with Gilbert Evans." "Except," John thought, "he needs someone to prod him: he would be content to be a salesman all his life. And Elsa can do it without his ever knowing." "I don't think you've got anything to worry about," he went on. "Better Gilbert Evans than—" If he had meant to say "Julia Deming," and had checked himself out of loyalty to Johnny, his pause and the silence that fell between them allowed the sound of the outer office door to be heard even more clearly than usual.

"A patient this late on such a night? I must go see."

He opened the door between the office and the waiting room. Just inside the outer threshold a stocky young man, hat in hand, had paused, hesitating.

"I seen your light burning. I hoped you were still here. I just stopped on the way back to the depot."

"I'm still here." John interrupted the nervous flow of speech. "Is there anything I can do for you?" The young man seemed vaguely familiar; he must have known him some time, but not in this context: he had never been in the office, never been a patient.

"Not for me. For my wife."

"Do I know your wife?"

"You used to. She was Ariana McCune."

"Ariana! I'll be dogged! She is here?"

"She's sick, and I couldn't take care of her." The gruff young man seemed close to tears. "I always thought I'd manage to. Look after her, I mean. But when she couldn't act any more, the road company fired me too. I was a scene-shifter."

"You're young Mercer, of course. Ben, is it?"

"Yes. I mean to go back to the circus. I'm handy enough with animals so they'll be glad to have me. But it's no way for Ariana to live. Not now, the shape she's in. I can earn enough to pay to have her looked after till she's well again."

"Never mind about that, now. Where did you take her? To Ruhamah?"

"No. I didn't even know Ruhamah was here, or where she'd got to. I took her to the Ballards'. One of 'em wrote her, when we were first married, she could always come there, if she wanted to. She'd be welcome."

"You dumped her on Eliza Ballard, without so much as warning her?"

"Yes, sir." An ugly flush crept into the young man's cheeks. "I was afraid if I wrote, she might have changed her mind about the welcome. And I was kinda desperate. Ariana wouldn't hear of a hospital. An' Miss Ballard, she seemed real glad to take her in. They wouldn't want me there, I know, even if I didn't have to get back on the job. So I left her there and said I'd send a doctor. She was near faintin' by that time. I got a hack outside—you take that. I'll walk to the depot."

"Let me have your address, so I can let you know."

"John Robinson's Circus will reach me. I haven't found a room yet, for just one person. Do your best for her, won't you, doctor? We were gettin' along fine till she got sick. I'll manage to pay you."

"Don't worry about that. I always liked Ariana, and she was a friend of my son's. I'll see what's wrong, and let you know. I'll do my best for her." On an impulse he held out his hand. Ben Mercer shook it briefly and was gone. John caught the outside door before it closed, called to the hack driver, "Wait for me—" and went back to the inner office, where Ludwig was still staring at the chessmen.

"Ben Mercer," John said, and when he saw Ludwig's blank countenance, added, "Ariana McCune's husband. Surely you remember?"

"You mean they're back in Waynesboro?"

"She is. She's sick. He brought her and dumped her on Eliza Ballard."

"Eliza will be delighted to have her back. She's always believed and hoped."

"Sorry to run off like this. But first I must call Anne." He went to the wall telephone, ground the handle, gave his house number, and explained briefly to Anne, cutting short her exclamations. "I'll tell you about it when I've seen her. Just now I have a hack waiting. Tell Lafe to hitch the buggy and bring it out to the Ballards' so I can get back." He hung up the receiver, grumbling. "I don't know why I even mentioned Ariana's name. That was Lou Green at the telephone exchange; the news will be all over Waynesboro by morning." He picked up his hat and bag and waited for Ludwig to go out ahead of him so that he could turn out the light and lock the door.

On the way out Linden Street, with the livery horse clop-clopping along, shut in the damp straw-scented interior of the cab, John adjusted himself to the situation as best he could and achieved a measure of acceptance. He had a fair idea of what he would find: with her heritage Ariana could not have been expected to have the stamina for trouping with a road company. What a waste of a potentially happy life!

When the hack drew up under the Ballard porte cochere, Eliza opened the door; silhouetted against the light as she was, John could not see her expression. He was curt with the driver: "Stop in the office for your fare tomorrow. I'm in a hurry now." He turned to the door. Eliza was waiting for him. "It's Ariana." She drew a long breath, let it out in a sigh. "Perhaps it was foolish to send for you tonight: she's much better, now she knows she's welcome and has had a little rest. She was close to collapse when he brought her: limp and white as a sheet."

"Now I'm here, let me have a look at her."

Eliza took him upstairs and down the hall to her own bedroom. "I had him bring her in here for tonight. None of the other bedrooms was warm, or a bed made up."

The door was open. John followed Eliza in, to find Ariana propped up on pillows, looking half-mutinous, half-pleading. She was pale almost to transparency, except for the coin-sized feverish spots on her cheekbones. She was clearly exhausted. Her hair was in two neat braids over her shoulders; except that her face was so thin, she looked about sixteen—some other girl's sixteen, not Ariana McCune's. She had changed, all the elfish mischief gone. He turned a straight chair around to her side and put his bag on the floor.

"Well, Prodigal?"

"Don't call me that." She frowned. "I didn't want to come back, but I couldn't get rid of this cold. I never meant to see Waynesboro again."

"Don't say that, when Eliza has kept hoping you'd be back. How long have you had this 'cold'?"

"All winter, off and on. I couldn't get rid of it; rickety old opera houses, cold hotel rooms, railway platforms." As if to demonstrate, she began to cough, a dry, retching sound. She put both hands over her mouth; Eliza gave her a handkerchief from a pile on the candlestand by the bed; John took her wrist in his fingers and brought her arm down to lie on the bed while he took her pulse. When she had stopped coughing, he shook down a thermometer and popped it in her mouth.

"There, don't you dare cough. Just don't try to talk—it's that that starts one of those spells. Let me do the talking, you nod your head, or shake it. Do you have any pain?"

She nodded and put one hand to her side high up on the rib cage.

"Some pleurisy there, I suspect." John took his stethoscope from his bag and applied it to her side for a moment, then removed the thermometer and glanced at it. "What you need isn't so much medicine as absolute rest in bed, for a long while."

"But—"

"No 'buts.' Eliza can manage, can't you, Eliza?"

"Yes, of course."

"Or there's Ruhamah."

"Ruhamah? Didn't she go with Papa and the others?" But she seemed almost indifferent, unable to care, as if caring in itself might be taxing. "Ben wrote a friend to ask if Papa was still here; he said he was gone. I wouldn't have come otherwise."

"Eliza hasn't had time to tell you, I guess. Ruhamah wouldn't go. She was working at the library, you remember? Well, the ladies got tired of giving up their afternoons, so they put on a regular crusade a year or so back to raise money—lawn fetes, plays, lectures, spelling matches—so they could hire a librarian. Naturally they hired Ruhamah—she was through school just about then. But her salary is small. She lives in one room. You're better off here. But would you like to see her?"

"Little Ruhamah, grown up? Yes, I would."

"Eliza will get word to her. Anyone else? Johnny?"

She nodded, smiling. "Yes."

"He's a full-fledged M.D., you know. Maybe you'd like him to take over?"

She looked astonished, doubtful, and amused; she shook her head.

"Very well. I'll be in again in the morning to give you a real thorough going over. It's too late tonight; you need to sleep. I'll give Eliza something for you."

He rose, propped her up on a couple of pillows so that she could breathe, tucked her arms under the covers, which he pulled up to her ears; he picked up his bag, said "Good-night," and followed Eliza out of the room. When she would have stopped on the threshold, he nodded his head toward the stairs.

"I must talk to you, Eliza," and as they moved along the hall he added, "out of earshot."

She whirled to look at him. "But—"

"Downstairs. If Lafe is waiting outside with the buggy, may I ask him into the kitchen? The horse will stand, and it is very cold."

Lafe once settled, they returned to the dining room and sat down side by side in two of the chairs against the wall.

"It doesn't look good, Eliza."

"But pleurisy? That isn't really dangerous, is it?"

"She'll get over that, yes. But that dry pleurisy often accompanies tuberculosis."

The slight color faded from Eliza's face, leaving it sallow. "Consumption! But you hardly looked at her."

"I know. She was too exhausted. But the fever, the increased heart rate, the cough. When you've seen as many cases as I have, and with her heredity—"

"But her father's tough as a hickory stick. And her mother died in childbirth. And Ariana wouldn't— I asked the Mercer boy if she'd ever had children and he said the very idea terrified her because of her mother."

"Mrs. McCune died in childbirth because she had tuberculosis in an advanced stage. This will be a problem for you, Eliza. You must think it out. Keep her here, take care of her, or send her to Dr. Trudeau? Here, you'd have to have help, and take every precaution, you and Thomasina, not to contract the disease. Where is Thomasina? I should have expected—"

"Dying of curiosity, no doubt, wondering what is going on. But she doesn't come into my side of the house, unless I ask her."

"Then you'd better begin asking her." He thought, "The damn fool women—all because Eliza doesn't think well of Sam Travers. And Sam is a better man than she thinks."

"Thomasina has always been very delicate."

"She is subject to attacks of asthma, comparatively mild attacks. And for some reason, asthmatics are less liable to tuberculosis than you would be. I mean what I say about precautions, Eliza. Get her into another room, but let her keep the pillows she's sleeping on tonight." He went on to give her minute directions as to the safeguards to be taken, and the care Ariana must have: the food, the complete rest, the wide-open windows. "That's all for tonight," he concluded abruptly. He rummaged in his bag, brought out the inevitable bottle of bromide. "Get me a glass of water and a teaspoon." He measured three teaspoonfuls of the liquid into the glass. "Get it down her. This is just for tonight, you understand. She is in an overwrought state—probably was afraid to come back, in case you had changed your mind. Anyway, she must sleep tonight. I'll be back in the morning."

He went to the swing door to the kitchen, summoned Lafe, and said good-night to Eliza, who was holding the glass in an unsteady hand as she stood at the foot of the stairs. "We'll let ourselves out. Just give her that, see that the windows are open, screen off any draft, and save talking till tomorrow."

Eliza went upstairs, administered the draught to a restless patient, opened one window wide, hung a petticoat over the chair that was still beside the bed, to guard against drafts, took a bulky outing-flannel nightgown out of a drawer, and said, "Let me put this on you: you won't be warm enough in that." And when the exchange had been made she said, "Now go to sleep, Ariana. Don't worry about anything: just get rested. We'll talk in the morning." She turned down the wick in the lamp on the candlestand, blew the light out. She hesitated for a moment, wondering whether to stay, thought better of it, and left the room. She went to the door at the end of the hall that separated her half of the house from Thomasina's, unlocked and opened it. She was taken aback to find Thomasina, in nightgown and peignoir, lamp in hand, hesitating just beyond the threshold.

"Eliza, what is it? I saw the doctor's buggy going down the drive, and thought you must be ill."

"Not I. Ariana."

"*Ariana McCune?*"

"Mercer."

"But why? Why here?"

"Why not? I gave her to understand when she first married that she would always be welcome with me. Come in, Thomasina; don't stand there in the cold. We'll go downstairs where we won't disturb her."

"Can't I see her?"

"Not tonight. The doctor gave her a sleeping draught. Thought she was overexcited." Eliza led the way downstairs, where there were still lights: a gaslight in the hall chandelier, a kerosene lamp in the dining room. Halfway down the staircase, Eliza said over her shoulder, "Do you want to see her?"

"Oh, Eliza! Of course I do. I know: when she ran away I thought she had treated us abominably, Samuel particularly, he had done so much for her. But if she's sick and has nowhere to turn— Her marriage turned out badly, then?"

"Put that lamp out and set it down. You don't need it in here." She waited until Thomasina had rid herself of the lamp and pulled up a chair to the dining room table; she studied her sister abstractedly—the worn plain face, the hanging braids of graying hair that Thomasina's restless hands were pulling at. "As a matter of fact, I don't think it did turn out badly—at least he seems to have been good to her. Of course the life they led has ruined her health, but he's done his best to take care of her, I am sure, after getting her a chance to do what she most wanted to do in the world: act, on a real stage. But when she fell ill, it was too much for him: he couldn't support the two of them and nurse her too. So he's going back to work at the circus, expecting to be able to pay her expenses while she's here."

"That's no more than he should do, and it would be a help, until she can go back to him." She broke off, staring at Eliza. "What's the matter? What is it?"

"John Gordon thinks it is consumption."

"*Consumption!* Then she'll be here—"

"Shall we say 'indefinitely'? You may as well get used to the idea. You know very well we haven't the money to send her to Dr. Trudeau's sanitorium, which John suggested as a possibility."

"How can he be so sure? Just one visit?"

"He is coming back in the morning for a thorough examination. But make no mistake about it: he is sure. He gave me explicit instructions on how to avoid infection."

"Then—" Thomasina drew herself up on a long breath. "You must let me help."

"John says I must get someone to stay with her. If we could find someone for the nights, and to spell you while I am working, could you get her breakfast and lunch? I could manage dinner."

Thomasina flushed. "I'm not so helpless as you think. I've been feeding Samuel for a long while. But to go through all that again. Remember how it was with Mama."

"I know. It is easier to go out and earn the money than to stay home and do the nursing."

"But Ariana's young. She may get over it, if she has a good rest. It won't be just waiting. And John may be wrong. Consumption is the first thing a doctor thinks of when a young person is ill; and they aren't right always."

Eliza thought, "Let her be hopeful if she can." She waited while Thomasina relighted her lamp and went back upstairs, then turned out the gas chandelier with the gas-lighter that stood in the corner behind the staircase, picked up her own lamp, and followed her sister. She was exhausted emotionally, all the more so because she had kept such a tight rein on herself; she would have to sleep in the cold guest room, after she had dug out a pair of sheets and pillow cases and made up the bed, but she was more than ready to drop into it, cold or not.

John had left the horse and buggy for Lafe to unhitch, and went into the house. He found Anne alone, her feet on the fender before a dismal fire, a book on her lap that she had clearly just that instant put down. She held out her hands to the grate as she looked up at him, as if she had only then realized that she was cold.

"What about Ariana, John?"

"That will be a real bombshell for Waynesboro, won't it? Anne, if you wouldn't read so hard, you wouldn't forget the fire; you need to put a little coal on now and then."

"I didn't really need it: it isn't cold in here." But she waited while he picked up the tongs and replenished the fire.

"Now, if you just won't poke at it—" he said, replacing the tongs with a clatter. "Well, Ariana's husband brought her back to Eliza Ballard, who it seems had offered her a refuge if she ever needed one. He brought her back because she is ill and he cannot take care of her and earn a living, too."

"But how did Eliza—I hope she welcomed her, poor child. Will she be ill long?"

"Ludwig says Eliza has always hoped she would come back: wanted to say 'I told you so' to the prodigal, I suppose. Ludwig was in the office playing chess when young Mercer came in."

"Poor Eliza! She isn't that mean, John. She hasn't anyone who really wants or needs her affection. And she has always cared for Ariana. But Ariana is rather like a fairy changeling, incapable of love—after her mother died, anyway. I hope she can feel some warmth for Eliza. How long must she be there? I suppose her husband will want her back when she is all right again."

"Oh, unquestionably. There was no doubting his distress. But it will be a long while—"

"If ever, you were going to say? John, is she going the way her mother went?"

"She is not pregnant. I don't know why I say that so certainly: I haven't really examined her. But from what he said, I am sure."

"Don't dodge, please. You know I never say a word about your patients and I won't now. Is she consumptive?"

"I said I haven't examined her. But there's every sign of it."

"How awful!—for Eliza, too, but for her—a life wasted; she had real talent, you know. I have never forgotten the year she played Jael for the Club. If only she had been born in another place, to another family, but the 'stars in their courses—' Does Ruhamah know? She's a faithful little soul: she has stayed here in Waynesboro so that Ariana would have a place to come to. But they have been out of touch for a long time."

"Yes. Ariana didn't even know Ruhamah was here. Of course the Ballards were a fixture in her mind. But Ruhamah can't take care of her. The less she sees of her, the better. And if she doesn't know Ariana's here, she soon will: I was sorry afterward that I mentioned the name to you over the telephone."

"She ought to be told, before she hears it in some cruel fashion. Wait: there's Johnny coming in."

They listened to the clang of the gate, the steps on the porch, the hand on the doorknob. Then Johnny came rushing in, not stopping to take off his coat, carrying his derby in his hand. He looked as if he had been out not only in the high wind of a February night but in the higher wind of ecstasy. His face was radiant, his eyes rapt.

"At last!" he said. "Our engagement is to be announced soon. Julie will wear my ring when I find one for her; we'll be married in June."

"Congratulations, son." Anne got it out. She rose and with a hand on each shoulder reached up to kiss him. "I only hope you will be as happy as you deserve. You've been patient as Jacob: I only hope you have found a Rachel."

Johnny looked a little dashed. "Papa? You take it coolly, it seems to me."

"Of course I congratulate you, too. But it isn't exactly a surprise, you know. And you can't expect us to be uplifted to your blissful state."

"No. But you aren't either of you ordinarily so—what has happened? Something has."

"Yes. Ariana McCune is back." John told him about the evening.

Johnny was quick to realize what his father was not saying. "You think it is tuberculosis? No wonder. She must have had a rackety kind of life, traveling with a third-rate road company."

"We can't be sure until I have given her a more thorough examination."

"If it had been anyone but Ariana, you would have diagnosed it on sight. You are just trying to hope. The poor girl—so young. The rest of us are just getting started. I'd like to see her."

"She wants to see you. But not as a doctor."

Johnny smiled; traces of his dimples showed as lines in the man's cheeks. "Of course not. I'm a schoolboy to Ariana. Has anyone let her sister know?"

"That worries me, too," his mother said. "It will be all over town by morning. I'll try to get up to her boardinghouse before she leaves."

"Don't you think Eliza—"

"It would come better from me. She talked to me once about Ariana. And I can tell her she mustn't think of moving her into the boardinghouse. You said a minute ago Ruhamah mustn't see much of her. Because of the danger of her catching it?"

"Yes. She will have inherited the same tendency."

"I doubt it. She's a wiry little body, like her father. But of course she'll have to be careful."

Johnny had taken off his coat; he dropped it and his hat on the sofa and sat down there himself. Already he had turned from Ariana in his thoughts. Now he rose and said, "I think I'll go up. It's been a long day."

"Wait a minute," his father said. "I've another bombshell for you. At least I don't think you've heard." To his wife: "You haven't talked to Sally today?" Anne shook her head. "The Ariana business put it right out of my mind. Ludwig said they'd had a letter from Elsa today. She's coming home."

"That's no bombshell. She was bound to, some day, and Julia said when she saw her in Munich—"

"Wait, I'll tell you. She wants her father and mother to announce her engagement at once, in the *Torchlight:* she's coming home to marry Gilbert Evans. In April."

"Shaney! Gib Evans! That milksop!" Johnny sat down again. "Her mother managed that, I bet."

"Elsa's been in Germany for two years. How could her mother manage anything at that distance? And what's the matter with Gib Evans?"

"Nothing, really. Only Shaney could have married anyone—someone more of a person than Gib, anyway. But it'll work out, I guess: she can boss him to her heart's content and he won't mind. April, you said? That's rushing things."

Anne didn't say a word, but to herself she said, "How infinitely sad. All these misguided young people, spoiling their lives." She knew why Elsa wanted to be married so soon: she would not like all Waynesboro to think of her as eating her heart out for Johnny Gordon. If only the child had not always been so open, so forthright, so easily read.

"Well, Mamma?" Johnny grinned at her. "Are you stunned?"

"No. I think it is a very suitable match: they have gone together long enough to know each other well. And why not April? Why wait?"

"No reason, I guess. Only Julie's going to think she's doing it on purpose, just to be the first. She wanted Shaney for her maid of honor." He picked up his derby, and slung his coat over his shoulder. "Good-night, Pop. Good-night, Mom." He stopped to kiss his mother on the cheek. "You are happy for me, aren't you?"

"Johnny, I want you to have whatever you need to make you happy, and I have known for a long time that it was Julia. Yes, I am happy for you."

But when he had gone beyond hearing, his father said, with attempted lightness, "What a liar you are!"

"I do want him to be happy."

"We've talked about it often enough: you don't think Julia Deming is the one to do that."

"I'm sure she thinks she loves Johnny, but—"

"Speaking as a doctor, I should say she is a frigid woman."

"And all Johnny's warm heart gone to waste. We'll just have to make the best of it."

"The inevitable choice of parents of wrongheaded children: object and spoil relations with your child, or accept and put up with it."

"I wonder how the Rausches feel about Elsa and Gib Evans."

"About Sally I can only guess. Ludwig is suffering from mixed emotions: he doesn't think Gib is good enough for her, but there is no one else in Waynesboro, and he is delighted that she will be living here."

In the morning Anne rose early, breakfasted alone, and went out in the cold to walk to Mrs. Duncan's boardinghouse. She found Ruhamah at the breakfast table, beckoned to her, and led her to the parlor, empty at that hour, and dark, the curtains still drawn. Ruhamah was frightened.

"What has happened? Something has."

"Yes. I thought you should know before the news gets all over town. Ariana has come back. She is at the Ballards'."

After a sudden frozen stillness, Ruhamah was able to speak. "But why? All this time I've waited for her. Is she all right?"

"Be fair, Ruhamah. It seems when she first went away, Eliza Ballard wrote her and promised there would always be a welcome for her there. Did she know you were waiting?"

"No. Of course not," Ruhamah said slowly. "I couldn't write her any such letter then. Papa—and I was still in school. Afterward I couldn't get in touch with her; I hadn't any address. But why did she come back? Was her husband—" Ruhamah choked on the question; Anne put a hand on her arm.

"He did the best he could. He brought her back last night because she is ill and he had no way of taking care of her. He stopped on his way to the train to ask the doctor to see her."

"Oh, that's how you know. I must go to her—tell her I am working now."

"The library is not open this morning? If it is, I could substitute for you. But don't hurry out there: the doctor plans to examine her, and I am sure he wouldn't want her all excited. Give him time."

"Then she's really ill? What does he think?"

"He hasn't examined her, really. You can ask him after he has. He won't have gone yet. Come home with me and you can ride out with him. Then when he's through, you can talk to him."

When John and Johnny started for the Ballard house, a bundled-up Ruhamah was squeezed between them on the buggy seat. Eliza let them in, said "Good morning" rather stiffly to Ruhamah, and to the two doctors: "She's much better this morning, now she's had a good rest. You both want to see her?" She led them upstairs and into the bedroom, while Ruhamah sat down on one of the stiff hall chairs. Ariana was sitting propped up on pillows piled against the towering carved headboard of the walnut bed. Her hair was in neat braids, her eyes bright, and the tell-tale flush high on her cheekbones.

"Johnny! I'm so glad! And you really are grown up, aren't you, and doctoring? But I told your father—"

"I know what you told me. But Johnny is much more up-to-date than I am: I brought him along to help me with a diagnosis." John put his thermometer in her mouth, took her eggshell-frail wrist in his fingers; the three waited in silence until he laid her hand down, took the thermometer, and looked at it. "Better than last night, at any rate. Now, if you'll sit up. Eliza, can you pull that nightgown up so we can use our stethoscopes?" The bulkiness of the heavy nightgown on so wasted a body defeated her. "No, I see you can't."

"I put her in one of mine." Eliza flushed a little. "Hers were so flimsy, and with that cough—"

"Very sensible of you. But now get it off—just let her hold it up in front." The two men turned their backs: John closed the still-wide-open window.

"All right; she's ready."

The two doctors examined her thoroughly. Ariana was hunched miserably over her lifted knees, her face hidden, the discarded nightgown clutched to her breasts and shoulders. Her backbone was a mountain range, her ribs a series of lesser ridges with valleys between. Johnny just managed not to catch his breath at the sight; he leaned over with his stethoscope and followed his father's, pausing where his father had paused, sometimes even longer; he returned, when Eliza thought they must surely have finished, to a spot on her side. Finally John said, "That's it. Get the gown on again, and lie down. Don't button it: we must go over your chest front as well as back."

"Please, not Johnny."

"Ariana, you're a married woman and Johnny is a doctor, but all right."

Alone he went over her chest, scarcely needing to lift her childish flat breasts. When he had finished, he drew up the covers and tucked them in. She began to cough, struggled to sit up; he put an arm under her to help.

"Johnny, the codeine. Eliza, a teaspoon."

John waited for a pause in the paroxysm, administered the dose, and said, "That's a good girl. Just lie there quickly while Johnny and I withdraw to talk about you. I respect his opinion even if you don't. You stay with her, Eliza."

In the hall the two men had only to look at each other.

"There's no doubt, is there?" Johnny said finally.

"Not the slightest. Complicated by pleurisy. We can tell her she has pleurisy. That may be a help: it won't frighten her. Well, let's say it." They returned to the bedroom.

Ariana did not speak, nor did Eliza; they just looked at John with anxious eyes. Johnny thought, "A doctor's worst moment: when he knows there's nothing he can do, yet has to say something reassuring."

What John did say was, "Just as I thought: you have some pleurisy in the right lung. Not excessively painful, is it? But you've been coughing for a long time? What you need is rest in bed, flat on your back. Plenty of wholesome food, fresh air, and cod liver oil to put some flesh on your bones. Most important: fresh air. Open windows twenty-four hours a day, winter or not."

"Doctor: how long? Ben will be anxious. I must write him."

"Let Eliza write him. And I don't know how long. Until you are better."

"I'm better already. I'll even take the cod liver oil."

"H'mph! If I know Eliza, you'll take it. Now are you recovered enough from that ordeal to hear some good news?"

"'Good news'?" She repeated it as if the words had no meaning.

"I hope it's good. Ruhamah is waiting downstairs to see you."

"Oh, Ruhamah—I'd forgotten. I can't believe she's here and not with Papa. Yes: that's good news."

"We'll send her up."

In the hall Eliza said, "Well?" John said aloud, "Pleurisy" and under his breath, "Wait."

On the stairs, removed from the bedroom door, she said "Well?" again.

"The pleurisy is there, all right. So is the tuberculosis."

"Oh, no! I can't believe it: she seemed so much better this morning. Poor Ariana! Then all that about being in the fresh air all the time, that's the latest treatment for consumption?"

"It's the best we've come up with so far, for the pleurisy and the tuberculosis. Fresh air, absolute rest, and nourishing food."

"And how much good do they really do, any of them?" Eliza sounded bitter and sad, and John did not answer.

Ruhamah, who had shed her coat and hat, stood waiting for them at the newel post as they came down the stairs, an already round-shouldered little figure, her plain spectacled face turned up to them.

"What is it?" she quavered. "Can I see her now?"

"Certainly: she is very anxious to see you. As to what it is: we think it is chronic pleurisy. You must take every precaution not to catch it from her. Do not kiss her; do not even sit close. If you touch anything she has touched, wash your hands thoroughly. We can't have you down sick, too. I'm sure Eliza will be glad of your help if you have any time to spare."

"Of course. I have lots of time: library hours aren't very long: three afternoons and three mornings and Saturday evening. There's always plenty to do when it isn't open, but I can manage. I know I mustn't get sick—how could I work, then? I may go up now?"

"Yes. But Ruhamah, one more word: you will be shocked at her appearance. She is very thin. Don't let her see your reaction. We must keep her cheerful. Don't let her talk much: it makes her cough. Eliza, don't you go: there are instructions I want to give you. *Be careful:* give her old rags to use for handkerchiefs—have her drop them in a paper bag, then you burn the whole thing, bag and all." He continued with explicit directions as to other precautions to be taken.

Upstairs, Ruhamah ignored her thumping heart and marched steadily along the hall to the door she had heard the others come out of; she rapped lightly, opened it, and went in.

"Ruie! Stand there and let me look at you." Ariana was flat on the pillows, but she turned her eyes to follow her sister to the foot of the bed. "You're grown up! Everybody's grown up. Johnny, doctoring. And you look just the way I always knew you would look, like a little old maid. It's the glasses and your hair, done up in a bun like that. And you're just a young girl!"

Ariana did not look as sick as Ruhamah had expected: thin, yes, but she had a good color and her eyes were bright. And she was still a tease: calling her an old maid was just like the Ariana she had known as a child.

"Dr. Gordon said you weren't to talk: that it makes you cough. He said you didn't know I had stayed here so that you would have a place—"

Ariana shook her head. "How did Papa come to let you?"

"I just said I wasn't going. I had work: I could keep myself. Papa could have gone to court, maybe: I was a minor. But he knew I would run away, and runaway children are no help to a minister's reputation, are they? I was sure he'd think of that, so I stayed, no matter what." Ruhamah set her jaws, her chin showed stubborn. "And I've saved some money for you to use. But while you're sick you can hardly live in a boardinghouse."

"Is it a nice place for you? I've seen some boardinghouses—"

"You must have seen lots of things, been lots of places. When you're better, when you can talk, you can tell me your adventures."

"No adventures, Ruie. Just hard work. But acting—I love that. I could forget the hardships, everything."

"Your husband was good to you?"

"Yes. He did everything he could. Till I got to be too much of a problem for him. But you've no idea! This room seems like heaven to me." She embraced in a gesture the tall wardrobe, the bureau with its three large drawers below, its swinging mirror and two small drawers above, a marble top between them. "And a comfortable bed, all to myself! I'm to be moved to the spare room, but it's nice, too, I expect." She began to cough, struggled to control it, raised herself to one elbow to take a handkerchief from the table beside her.

"Ariana, you've been talking too much. The doctor said I wasn't to let you. Can I get you anything?"

Ariana shook her head, caught her breath, lay down again on the pillow.

"Please, Ariana, let me do the talking. You want to know about the boys? Matt has a charge in Pennsylvania. Mark wouldn't go to the Seminary: he's farming in Indiana; he'll buy land when he has enough money saved. Luke's still home, still in school. Matt is married: a lovely girl, he says, and such a help with the church work. I've never seen her. Mark isn't."

"You write them?"

"I try to keep in touch. We were so close once. But I only hear about Luke from the other boys. Papa won't let him write."

"So you're disowned too? Of course I knew I would be, but I didn't mean—"

"*Please* don't talk, Ariana. Just let me sit here a minute and then I must go; I have to get the library ready to open at one."

Downstairs the Traverses had been waiting their turn to see Ariana, Sam calm, Thomasina apprehensive, twisting her handkerchief around her fingers until it was limp.

Sam smiled at her. "Thomasina, how much help are you going to be if you go on like that?"

"I'm not 'going on.' I admit I'm a little nervous, but I'll be all right when I've seen her."

Eliza interrupted them. "Thomasina, will you come help me get the spare room ready? I've warmed the sheets, now I'll need to get out the blankets and air them. The windows must be open day and night."

By the time Ruhamah tore herself away, the spare room was ready: not only the bed made, but the furniture dusted and the windows open. The wind came through in a freezing blast. Thomasina protested. "It will kill her to be in such a cold room."

"Not if she's wrapped warm enough. Not with comforts under the bottom sheet, and blankets on top of her. Doctor's orders. There's Ruhamah." She went to the door. "Did you have a good visit?"

Ruhamah nodded. "I'm sorry, but I have to go now. But I can come three mornings a week: Monday, Wednesday, Friday, and evenings."

"Mornings will be a great help. I have to work every day, and Thomasina can't do it all. Evenings I'll be here, and will find someone to come nights."

"Then she mustn't be left alone at all?"

"No one can sit with her for long in that freezing room. But there should be someone within call, in case she wants something, or gets to coughing. And to see that she eats properly and takes her medicine."

Ruhamah said no more: how could she when she did not know what the doctors had told the Ballards? But the wide-open windows had settled all questions in her mind. She, who read everything that came into the library, knew about Dr. Trudeau and his theories. Dr. Gordon thought Ariana had consumption. She controlled her face until she got out of the house, then let the tears roll down her cheeks, regardless of the stinging cold.

Inside the house Sam Travers took his wife's arm, said, "Now, Thomasina—" and brought her down the hall to the bedroom door. Ariana turned her head on the pillow and stared at them, thinking how old everyone looks. She closed her eyes and said, "Don't come in unless you have forgiven me."

"Ariana, don't say that," Sam's voice was tranquil. "What is there to forgive?"

"Of course we forgive you," Thomasina spoke at almost the same instant. "Just at first I thought you had treated us—my husband particularly—ungratefully: he had worked so hard and we had such high hopes for you. But—"

"I know. I owe you so much, and I don't think I ever said, 'thank you.' But it was having your hopes disappointed that was worst, wasn't it?" Ariana spoke slowly, carefully: she wanted to get it all said without being interrupted by a coughing spell. "But you would have been disappointed whatever I had done. I never had it in me to be a real musician. And your sister: it was *me* she was fond of—*me*, not someone who might be a credit to her teacher some day."

"Don't be so hard on us." Thomasina was close to tears. "We were all fond of you."

"Oh, I know: 'poor, motherless child—' "

"Ariana, you are being unfair. If you had known how we loved you. Why, even the sound of your feet tearing up the stairs—"

"But it was Eliza who wrote me and said I could always have a home with her. So I knew you hadn't forgiven me."

"We long since forgave whatever there was to forgive."

Sam was firmer. "Ariana, we are glad you have come back. We may have failed to pass the test that Eliza passed. But we both love you dearly. That is true. It will be better if we all forget the past, except that you did come to us 'a poor motherless child' and we made you welcome. Now we make you welcome again, not asking for anything except that you try to feel for us what you once felt."

"Then you do forgive me?"

"If there was anything to forgive, I have forgotten it."

Ariana through lowered lashes looked at Thomasina, who was wiping her eyes. "You, too?" she asked inexorably.

"Oh, Ariana! Yes. I always thought of you as if you were my own child." She would have rushed to embrace her, but Ariana stopped that.

"Keep your distance, the doctor said. I didn't know pleurisy was catching, but he says it is." She closed her eyes and turned her head away.

Samuel said, "We must help Eliza move her into the other room, and then let her rest. She has had a hard morning." He went into the hall to summon Eliza, who was waiting with nightcap and flannel robe. She got Ariana up and robed, picked up the pillows she had been lying on, said, "Just down the hall," and led the way. The shift was made, Ariana on her feet disdaining help, trailing the oversized nightclothes along the hall floor.

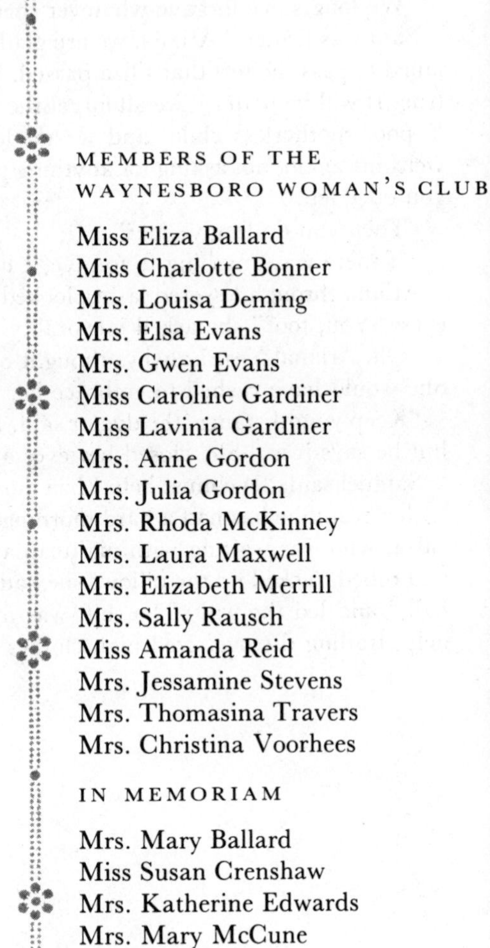

MEMBERS OF THE
WAYNESBORO WOMAN'S CLUB

Miss Eliza Ballard
Miss Charlotte Bonner
Mrs. Louisa Deming
Mrs. Elsa Evans
Mrs. Gwen Evans
Miss Caroline Gardiner
Miss Lavinia Gardiner
Mrs. Anne Gordon
Mrs. Julia Gordon
Mrs. Rhoda McKinney
Mrs. Laura Maxwell
Mrs. Elizabeth Merrill
Mrs. Sally Rausch
Miss Amanda Reid
Mrs. Jessamine Stevens
Mrs. Thomasina Travers
Mrs. Christina Voorhees

IN MEMORIAM

Mrs. Mary Ballard
Miss Susan Crenshaw
Mrs. Katherine Edwards
Mrs. Mary McCune
Miss Agatha Pinney

* 1892–1893 *

"The twenty-fifth anniversary year of our Club was highlighted by the weddings of two of our daughters."

One evening shortly after Ariana returned to Waynesboro, there were three items topping off Charlotte Bonner's "Social Notes" in the *Torchlight* that were of interest to a large part of the town:

> *Mrs. Ben Mercer Returns for Visit.* Her old friends will be delighted to learn that Mrs. Ariana McCune Mercer has returned to Waynesboro for a visit with Miss Eliza Ballard, but distressed, on the other hand, to hear that she has come for rest and recuperation after a long illness, and is not at present receiving visitors.
>
> *Betrothals:* Captain and Mrs. Ludwig Rausch announce the engagement and approaching marriage of their daughter Elsa to Mr. Gilbert Evans of this city. Captain Rausch is a well-known entrepreneur, promoter of a very successful Columbus and Cincinnati Interurban Electric Railway, and manufacturer and industrialist, president of Rausch Cordage Company, makers of rope and twine, and a member of the Republican State Committee; Mrs. Rausch is the daughter of the late Mr. Charles Cochran, president of the Waynesboro National Bank, and the late Mrs. Cochran. Mr. Evans, nephew of the Rev. Mr. David Evans, pastor of the Baptist Church, and Mrs. Evans, is employed in an executive capacity by Rausch Cordage Company. The wedding will be an event of early April.
>
> General and Mrs. George Deming announce the engagement and approaching marriage of their daughter Julia to Dr. John Alexander Gordon of this city. General Deming is one of our most distinguished citizens, who rose to the rank of Brevet-Brigadier General in the late War, and was afterward the Representative of the Seventh District in the House of Representatives in Washington, and since his retirement from politics has further distinguished himself as historian of his brigade and of several Ohio counties. Dr. Gordon, having recently earned his M.D. at the Medical College of Ohio, has recently joined his father, Dr. John Gordon, in his medical practice in this city. The happy couple will be united in matrimony in June.

When Johnny went to the Demings' to spend the evening with Julia, she met him at the door with the evening paper in her hand; before he could get his coat off, she was almost brandishing it in his face.

"Why didn't you tell me?"

"Tell you what, honey? I haven't had time today to tell anyone anything, starting with Ariana McCune. Is it that what has upset you? I didn't know she was back until I got home last night."

"Ariana McCune? No. Why should it? No, I mean Elsa Rausch. And don't tell me you didn't know that either: you have always been thick as thieves."

"Julie, darling, let's go into the parlor. Think I want your mother and father to hear you scolding me already?"

"I didn't mean to scold," she said in a softer voice, going before him to the parlor door. "And I must say Papa is tickled by the recognition he got in the *Torchlight* notice: there was much more about him than about Mr. Rausch." She took her accustomed place on the brocaded Empire sofa, and pulled her skirt close to indicate that he was to sit beside her. "It is just that Elsa is so *provoking*. She didn't say a word about being engaged when we saw her in Munich."

"It was as much a surprise to me as it was to you, believe me." He put his arm around her shoulders and drew her close, heedlessly crushing her ballooning sleeves, until her head was on his shoulder. "I haven't heard from Sh—from Elsa, only indirectly from her folks. We have never corresponded. Why should we? And to tell you the truth, I think it was a surprise to them: once she made up her mind, she wouldn't *ask* them—not Elsa—she would *inform* them."

"Gib is working for her father, isn't he? They must have had an inkling."

"Maybe. What difference to us?"

"Oh, none, of course. Only it is provoking. I wanted her to be my maid of honor, and I suppose it is childish of me, but I did want to be the first."

Johnny laughed. "You're a dear little goose! Whose fault is it you won't be first? Not mine, certainly." He tightened his arm around her, turned until he could lay his cheek against hers for a moment, then kissed her gently and sat back. "I brought you something. Aren't you interested?" He reached into his pocket for a jeweler's box. If she was disappointed to see on it the name of a local jeweler, she let no sign appear.

"Oh, my ring! I didn't think you would have it so soon."

"It's Mr. Weller's prettiest, I thought. Would you rather I'd let you choose your own? We can change it. It isn't much of a diamond, as diamonds go, but you know—"

"Dear Johnny! Of course I know. And I know it was chosen with love." She held her left hand across to him, and he slipped the ring on her finger.

To Johnny it was a thoroughly satisfactory evening, even their parting at the front door after he had gone to the living room to speak to her parents. To kiss her good-night, he first put his hands around her tiny waist, then took her into his arms. Overwhelmed by an irresistible yearning, he put one hand on her breast, and with the other arm held her tighter, his cheek bent to hers. She pulled away, not hastily but firmly.

"*Don't*, Johnny, I don't like such—liberties—not here, not now." If she sounded a little frightened, even a little repelled, he put it down to maidenly modesty and the proximity of her parents, down the hall beyond the open sitting room door; he withdrew his arms, kissed her lightly, and bade her good-night in gentlemanly fashion.

Once the door had closed behind him, she went in to show her mother and father her ring. When they had admired it with as much enthusiasm as they could muster, Mrs. Deming said, "If you are going up now, I will come with you. I want to talk with you."

In Julia's pink beruffled bedroom, she sat down on the edge of the bed, a practice ordinarily disapproved of, and pulled Julia down beside her. Seated side by side, they looked unmistakably mother and daughter. Julia seemed to have inherited nothing from her father; she was even a refined edition of her mother: her height less, and her weight, her features more delicate, her hair fairer. Now she waited, her eyes fixed on her mother's face, with a slight air of apprehension.

"Julia, I heard you in the hall. Johnny isn't repulsive to you, is he?"

"Johnny? Of course not. Papa didn't hear, did he? He would dislike it so: the idea of anyone *embracing*—"

Mrs. Deming laughed a little. "Once he would have. He wanted you kept a little girl. But now you are officially betrothed. Your father has very definite ideas about the rights of husbands." She rose, walked restlessly to Julia's dressing table, picked up her silver hairbrush, laid it down again. Some things were more easily said with your back turned. "Julia, you must be prepared for the physical side of marriage."

"Mamma, must you?" Julia flushed. "I didn't go to art school for nothing: I know how men and women are made."

"Yes, I think I must. Do you realize that marriage gives a husband by law certain rights? And that when men are—roused—there is something of the animal in even the best of them? Their exercise of their rights is bound to be repugnant to any well-brought-up young woman."

Julia had turned her eyes to her hands clasped in her lap. "Oh, Mamma, *must* you?" she said again.

"Julia, this is as painful to me as it is to you. But it is wrong to let any young girl go into marriage unprepared."

"Mamma?"

"I wasn't a young girl when I married. I knew what I was doing, and I have always been a dutiful wife. I just want to say this to you: from my experience, if you want a happy marriage, submit without complaint to any *legitimate* demand. If you find the physical side of marriage repulsive, don't let Johnny know it. Indulge him."

"Mamma, will it hurt?"

Mrs. Deming turned from the dressing table, came back to stand before her daughter, for the first time the light of compassion in her face. "Probably. At first. But remember: the reward of submitting is the child that may be conceived."

She turned away again. The interview that had been so painful to both of them was over; Julia had been instructed in the full duty of a wife. Mrs. Deming changed the subject briskly. "The Gordons' man brought a note around this evening: we are invited to dine with them next Tuesday."

"That is the proper thing, isn't it? It will be awful, though: being shown off for approval."

"Nonsense. The Gordons have known you all your life."

Julia, successfully diverted for a moment at least from the previous painful subject, said, "Johnny thinks I am a goose to mind about Elsa."

"So you are. You have Johnny, haven't you? I suppose Elsa didn't want to be pitied; didn't want her friends thinking she was hanging around hoping your marriage would fall through at the last minute. I wouldn't say so to him. It doesn't do to let men get ideas."

Julia laughed. "Johnny isn't the sort to believe it if I told him. He would never imagine girls—any girl—waiting round hoping to fall into his arms. And however Elsa may feel, Johnny sees her as a kind of bossy sister."

The dinner party, at which three Gordons entertained three Demings, was as stiff as such affairs must inevitably be; Mrs. Deming was at her most mannered, airing her social graces, making small talk with Anne and the young people, while the General talked politics with John. But one revelation toward the close of the ordeal threatened to blow the trivialities out of the window and disrupt the evening. The General, over his charlotte russe, said, with a fond glance at his daughter, "Julia is mighty put out that Elsa Rausch is beating her to the altar. No, now, admit it, honey: you naturally expected to be the first. But it will take us until June to get the house remodeled so that your apartment will be ready for you."

This piece of news was met by stunned silence on the part of the Gordon parents. Johnny did his awkward best to bridge the gap. "I'm afraid you will be involved in a lot of expense, sir. Quite unnecessarily. We could—"

"Nonsense, my boy. The expense will soon be recovered if you insist on paying rent. And it will mean everything to Mrs. Deming and me to keep Julia under our roof. Not—" and he winked, with an outrageous grimace, at the uncomfortable Johnny, "not that we expect to interfere with you love birds. No, no. Except for the entrance and the stairs, you will be quite private. The plans have all been drawn up."

When the Demings had departed, the Gordons moved from the parlor into the comfortable living room, and Johnny found himself confronted, as he had known he would be, by a horrified mother. His father removed himself from the storm center, picking up the paper from the table and taking it to the fire; he would glance at it and then go across to the office, where he had posted a "Will be late" notice in the glass of the door. Yet he was the first to speak.

"Bedogged if I ain't glad that's over. Those two are the most consummate bores in Waynesboro—she's so refined and he's so pompous."

Anne cut in, addressing her son. "Whatever induced you to agree to live under the same roof? I thought you had set your heart on fixing up the Gordon farmhouse?"

Johnny waved that cherished dream away as trivial and preposterous. "It wouldn't have done, Mamma. I was foolish to think of it. In the first place, I'd have had to rebuild the old tenant house for the Browns, after all these years." The farm, held in trust for Johnny during the years of his minority, had been turned over to him on his twenty-first birthday; fortunately for him the tenancy had been passed from aging father to capable middle-aged son. "And I wasn't even considering how hard it would be for Julia. You can see: she would be alone out there, 'way in the country, not only evenings but all night sometimes."

"A woman takes that into consideration when she makes up her mind to marry a doctor. I never minded. And then you children came along to keep me company."

"You didn't live in the country. Julia admits that she would be afraid, and I know she would be. She is not very—self-reliant, I guess, is the word."

"She never will be, if she lives in the same house as her parents. She could live in town in some other house. You wouldn't have to live with the Demings."

"We'll have our own house, is what it amounts to. And when I have to go out on night calls, she'll know her father and mother are just downstairs."

"Who suggested it, they or Julia?"

"She wants it and they want it. I don't know whose idea it was in the beginning."

"You didn't tell us because you knew we would think a young couple should have their own home."

"And because I knew you didn't feel very enthusiastic about General and Mrs. Deming. They're not really so bad, Mamma."

His father put the paper down. "You are grown up, Johnny. You must go your own way. Whether we think you're wise or not doesn't matter any more."

"Pappa, surely—" Johnny looked taken aback, hurt and very young as he stood there. "You don't disapprove of *Julia?*"

His mother was quick to go to him. "We would accept your choice, son, no matter who. No, of course we don't disapprove of Julia: you would not have been happy—you could never care for anyone else as you care for her. We know that, and we are happy for you. She is a very beautiful girl."

Johnny's face cleared, softened. "Julia is lovely, Mamma, and so generous about so much. You mustn't mind her wanting to live where she's always lived. Remember how fond she was of Binny, and how good about always wanting to take her along with us, even when I thought poor Binny was just a nuisance? I was so glad, afterward."

"Of course we remember. Binny adored her." Anne's eyes misted. "She would have been so happy for you now. You had better go back to check the office for your father first, if you are going to the Demings'."

When he had gone, John said, lowering his paper and studying the fire contemplatively, "You know that girl did go to all kinds of trouble to make Binny happy, giving her pleasure. Why?"

"I don't know. Perhaps she saw herself as Ministering Angel." For the first time Anne came to her own rocker at the other side of the hearth. "I think 'egoist' is the word. To me, at least, 'egotist' just means conceited. 'Egoist' is something more: a person who always sees himself as in the center; nothing, nobody, has any meaning to him except in relation to himself. Naturally an egoist wants everyone around to see him in the center too, and so he takes the trouble to work a little for their liking. And the trouble to act to perfection whatever part he's playing. I think that is why Julia was fond of Binny—and I think she was fond in her way, and did take trouble, because Binny plainly adored her. And it had an effect on Johnny: it bound him to her. Does any of this make sense to you? I'm not very good at explaining myself. And I may be all wrong."

"It makes this much sense: Johnny isn't—"

"Don't say it, please. As long as he keeps her in the center of his universe, he'll have no reason to read her as I do."

"A man whose whole life has to revolve around his wife if he's going to keep her happy is not going to be very good at his profession. Johnny's a good doctor, up to this point: he gives his whole mind to it."

"If he leaves it behind at the front door when he comes home, she'll never realize he hasn't been thinking of her all day. I don't really think Julia is very perceptive."

It was not long after that evening that the Rausches went to the depot to meet Elsa, her mother and father and the boys, except for Ernest, who was now in college in the East. She had been away for two whole years, but Ludwig, who would have liked to meet her in New York, had reluctantly, at Sally's urging, given way to Gib Evans, who had been on the road anyway, and could easily get to New York to meet the ship. In Waynesboro the two of them got off the train together and started hand in hand to greet her family. Gib was radiant; he could hardly let slip his grasp of her fingers when she moved to throw her arms around her father.

"Dear Papa! How well you look!" Her embrace was fervent; she stayed in his arms a long moment, head on his shoulder. "How I have missed you!"

"And whose fault?" Ludwig had been taken aback at her appearance: slim, stylish, tiny waist, puffed sleeves, wide-brimmed beribboned hat, and when you looked beyond the clothes, her face so fine-drawn, the bones plain: his girl grown older, a woman for sure. But her unrestrained demonstrativeness reassured him: she had not greatly changed. He disengaged her arms, turned her over to her mother for more kisses and embraces while he shook hands with Gib, and went to take her suitcase from the sleeping car porter and turn it and her baggage checks over to Reuben. By that time Elsa had come to Paul in her round of hugs and kisses; her astonishment at his size was only half pretended: when she had left him, he was a chubby five-year-old; now, almost seven, he was definitely a schoolboy; he had lost his baby look. Like all the Rausches, she adored him, and she might not even have known him had he not been with the family. She felt with a sudden pang that she had been away too long. She even said so, as she turned away from kissing him. "But I am back for good."

She moved toward the carriage, Gib at her side, her hand on his arm. "Thank you for taking such good care of me. I'll see you tonight?"

"Tonight. You'll want to visit with your family now." She shook hands with Reuben, who was waiting to help her into the carriage, almost as glad to see him as to see her family. He let Gib help her, stepping back himself to give a hand to Mrs. Rausch. Her father and the boys piled in helter-skelter after the ladies. Gib waved good-bye. "I'll see to your trunks."

An exhausting day followed, unpacking the gifts for the boys, going over with her father all the messages his cousins had sent, discussing with her mother, in brief snatches, the gossip of Waynesboro, the affairs of the Woman's Club and the present status of its members, and with her father, conditions in Germany: "The only thing I didn't like about it is the arrogance of the University students, and the military caste; even a woman has to get off the sidewalk if she meets two or three officers walking abreast," and listening to his mutters about Prussians and militarism, hearing at the same time her mother, going on about the Club.

"If only the Revolution of '48 had succeeded," her father said.

"If it had, you wouldn't be here, nor would any of the rest of us."And so they moved from criticizing Germany to a statement from Ludwig on the state of the union, politics, and business. "Gib says that Rausch Cordage Company is keeping its head above water." Then a noisy dinner and afterward, Gib with the family circle in the living room, discussing their plans for an April wedding. It was only after he had gone and Elsa said, "Good-night. It's been a long day," to her family and started up the stairs that her mother followed her, with the firm intention of saying what she felt must be said. Sally closed the bedroom door and leaned against it as Elsa moved to the dressing table to remove necklace and ear-rings.

"Elsa, are you sure you know what you're doing?"

"This is what you wanted, isn't it? Are you at this late date feeling qualms?"

"Why should I? I have brought no pressure to bear." Sally crossed the room to the low slipper chair by the grate, where a small pleasant coal fire was burning. "It has been your decision. But you seem so frozen, with just a hint of the rigid self-control of a martyr on the way to the stake."

"Oh, Mamma! You're being ridiculous. I am not borne up on the wings of ecstasy, if that is what you mean. But I don't feel the least martyred. You were right, of course: the life of a wife and a mother is the only one possible for me. And I know Gib well enough to know that we get along together. He will be a good husband, and I intend to make him a good wife: darn his socks and cook his meals and bear his children."

"Marriage is more than that."

"I know, I know. What you and Papa had. Have, for all I know."

Sally flushed. How old did she seem to this young daughter, for all her airs? "Leave your father and me out of it. We have been extraordinarily fortunate. But many a girl has got married, as you are doing, just for the sake of being married, without knowing what it involves."

"Believe me, Mamma: I know what it involves. I intend not to shrink from Gib's embraces, and if I cannot respond, I can pretend to. Does that satisfy you?"

Her mother sighed. "What plain speaking! You should not have said that."

"Because now you will always wonder? You needn't. I can and I will make Gib happy. And that way find a kind of—"

"Of happiness yourself? Oh, Elsa. I have wished something much better than that for you." Sally rose. Elsa went to her and, surprisingly, embraced her.

"It's all right, Mamma."

Sally said in a more normal tone, patting Elsa on the back, "I really think it will be, in time. There are more lasting things than— There is kindness, understanding, a home, a family. I am glad you don't want to live here. It is better to be on your own."

"It is all right about the Linden Street house?" The emotional moment had passed.

"Yes. Sheldon's mother and father are failing; they must both be well over eighty. He knows he should be in the house with them. And the boys aren't babies any more: Lowrey must be ten or eleven."

"It will be hard on them."

"You survived living with your grandparents. Do get to bed now, Elsa; you must be tired, and you must attend the Club meeting tomorrow as a guest: Jessamine Stevens is serving tea in your and Julia's honor."

At the previous Club meeting, immediately after the two engagements had been announced, Mrs. Evans had submitted, in writing as required by the constitution, a proposal for an amendment to that document: that the Club membership be increased to twenty. The amendment was sure to be adopted *nem. con.*: it was inconceivable that the daughters of two charter members should not be asked to join the Club. When the President had announced the result of that vote, the secretary would be asked to read the names of three new members: Julia, Elsa, and Charlotte Bonner, who had proved by acquiring her B.A. at a leading eastern woman's college that she was worthy of association with a group of intellectual women. There was nothing in the amendment to say that there must be twenty members: there was no hurry about filling the other two places. Julia and Elsa, present as guests, might be embarrassed by hearing their names read out, but it could not be helped: Mrs. Stevens was determined to be the first to honor the brides.

Had it not been for the tact of two women, the tea might in truth have been painful, for Julia if not for Elsa. First Anne Gordon had walked up to the Rausches' in the morning in order that she might greet Elsa with all the warmth and affection and desire for her happiness that she might have felt constrained to subdue in Julia's presence. And second, after the meeting, while the ladies were making much of Elsa, whom they had not seen for so long, Jessamine gave her attention to Julia, exclaiming in her soft voice that she would soon be calling her "cousin," admiring her ring, making much of her in every way.

Anne Gordon was both amused by the performance Jessamine had put on, and surprised by her perceptiveness. She had long since come to accept Jessamine as a relative and kind of friend, as one did accept relatives, in spite of their shortcomings; and besides, whatever the questions in her own mind, to make an intimate of her would quiet any surmises in the minds of others. She was genuinely fond of Rodney, who at thirteen was enough like what Johnny had once been to have found a place in her affections: he had not Johnny's light heart and merry ways—he was all too solemn a child—but in other traits, and particularly in his constant attendance at the doctors' office when he was not in school, rolling bandages, sterilizing instruments, reading the medical journals—all the things Johnny had once done. He had his heart set on becoming a doctor and a partner of the Gordons. But he had something of his mother in him, too: he was not vulnerable as Johnny and his father were vulnerable; he would have more detachment from the troubles of others, and he was more perceptive about people. That too had he got from his mother? Watching Jessamine with Julia, Anne realized that however little opportunity the woman had had to know the girl, she was catering to her egoism. Once, she turned to look over her shoulder at Anne with what could only be described as a conspiratorial look. And suddenly Anne found herself unwilling to conspire with Jessamine in an attempt to "handle," however tactfully, her soon-to-be daughter-in-law. After all, Anne had never seen Julia when she was not well-mannered and agreeable. Both women, Julia and Jessamine, were forever acting, at least in company, whatever character they wanted to be accepted as being. Twenty-four hours a day? Or did they sometimes forget the mirror, let slip the image? Or was it possible to act a part so long and so faithfully that that was what you became in the end? At any rate, she must not assume, but develop, a fondness for Julia. And why not? She had managed it with Jessamine.

When the program had come to an end and the social hour was about to begin, Anne made her way past small clusters of women to Julia's side, dismissing, when she reached the two Demings, Julia's mother.

"Do let me see that Julia gets her tea, Mrs. Deming. You are with her every day, and I have so few chances to see her." When Mrs. Deming, smiling graciously, had moved away, Anne said to Julia, "I truly would like to see more of you: I have scarcely heard a word about your European tour."

Julia laughed. "That's what it was: a tour. By the time we had done the galleries in Italy and Germany and the Louvre in Paris, it was such a jumble in my head that now I can scarcely remember which picture was where. Mamma was determined to educate me. One thing I did learn: I'll never be a painter. I was ashamed that I had ever spoiled a canvas. If Johnny ever had a notion I might like to set up an easel and get out my paints, he can forget it."

At that point Anne, all tender solicitude, guided her across the hall to the dining room, where Christina Voorhees was dispensing tea from Jessamine's silver service, and Jessamine was pressing on the ladies a choice assortment of southern sweetmeats and cookies, the salted pecans and bonbons that she and Cally had spent the previous day making and assembling. Moving around the table and away from it, groups broke up, separated, formed again with different members; everyone tried to reach the two girls being honored; voices rose; laughter came easily. At one point Anne found herself in a corner with Eliza Ballard, a safe spot, she had thought, for juggling plate and teacup.

"I suppose," she said, "that what is a happy occasion for the rest of us is a sad one for you. How is Ariana?"

"You mean because she isn't able to be here? But that does not prevent my pleasure in the good fortune of others." Eliza did not look particularly pleased, but then, she never did. "As to how she is: she has put on a little weight; she looks better. She thinks she will be up and about next week. But she coughs as hard as ever."

"Is she happy to be here? Or does she miss her husband?"

"Contented enough in a way. She considers herself to be living in the lap of luxury." Eliza breathed a scornful "H'mnph." "She was so near collapse when she came that she just let herself go—slept and slept. But now she is talking about when she can get back. She writes him every day, a line or two, and he sends her money, all he can spare, I've no doubt. He is coming up to see her Sunday: the trains are so he can make it up and back, with a few hours visit with her. I don't think she cares for him in the way you would expect a wife to care, but that may be because she is so ill. What she does feel is gratitude and a sense of obligation."

"And you," thought Anne, "would like if it he dropped right out of the picture, money or no money." She told Eliza that she knew John would want to talk to Ben, and hoped that he could manage it. She finished her tea and moved away to put her cup down.

The Club meetings Elsa attended after that through late winter and early spring were merely suspensions of her other activities: Sheldon moved himself, his boys, and his nursemaid to his mother's and left the Linden Street house empty. He admitted that his furniture would have to be stored in his mother's attic, with the exception of the great walnut bed that had been his and Kitty's: that he could use. The other pieces had been Kitty's too, and it just might happen that one of the boys might want them some day; at any rate he could not bring himself to part with them. Elsa thought it sad, rather morbid: a middle-aged man like Sheldon Edwards keeping the bed Kitty had died in, and everything she had touched. She had said to him one day before his move, when she had gone to the house to measure the windows, "You don't really want to go, do you, Mr. Edwards? Perhaps we could find another house."

"I should have had to move soon anyway. I cannot leave my mother and father in the care of hired help at their age." He smiled at her. "But I might have postponed it, so it is a good thing you have given me this nudge. I only hope you will be as happy here as we were, and your mother and father before us."

"I was born in this house, you know."

"And it doesn't seem so long ago, either." He looked at her with a kind of surprise, as if to say, "How did it happen?"

When the house was empty, Elsa and her mother went over it to see what renovations were needed, and soon had paper-hangers, painters, and plumbers busy, the last tearing up the second floor to put a bathroom in: "You will need it when you have children," Sally said. "I remember what a chore it was." They busied themselves over carpets, drapes (new), and furniture (mostly old). "Gib can't afford to buy new furniture for a whole house all at once, and I know how much is in our attic. I'd rather have Grandmother's old four-poster bed any day than one of those modish brass ones. I think they are hideous."

Gib dined with the Rausches when he was in town, but there was less said on those occasions about wedding preparations than about the state of the rope business in general and about Rausch Cordage Company in particular. ("You might as well get used to it," Sally said. "If it isn't business it will be politics." And Elsa had protested quite truthfully that she was interested in both.)

By early 1892 the National Cordage Company had something like ninety percent of the rope and cordage output of the country under its control, had become a great industrial giant, and was bent on ridding itself of all competition. Having failed to corner raw material, it had turned its attention to cordage machinery; by contracts with American and British machine-tool makers, it subsidized them in return for their refusal to sell machinery to other existing rope manufacturers. Ludwig had cause to bless the day he had built a machine shop for Stewart Bodien: not only was Rausch Cordage Company's machinery kept in perfect order, repaired and improved upon, even new machines made, but the shop was kept busy on orders from other rope companies that still defied the trust. By threats, by bluster, by promises to stockholders, by warning laborers that they would soon be out of jobs when their bosses failed, and even by erecting rival mills in rope-making towns, the National Cordage Company continued to absorb small independent manufacturers. The threats and intimidation did not much frighten Ludwig: control of the stock was in his own hands, and he had even persuaded his Cincinnati cousins to entrust their shares to him with their authority to protect the company any way he saw fit. Even warnings that they were working for a failing company, in the shape of handbills distributed to his laborers, he felt that he could handle. He called his men together one noon in the cobbled yard, and holding up one of the printed sheets Captain Bodien had picked up for him, he explained the situation. He pointed out that if the National Cordage Company put Rausch Cordage out of business, it would have no further use for them. He said he hoped they trusted him after all these years, and that he believed the company could weather the storm if they stuck by it. If they left, the plant might have to be closed. Then what? They knew rope and only rope; to find other jobs they would have to move from Waynesboro. The talk was aimed at the ordinary unskilled mill hands, Negro and white, even at the spinner girls who were standing around the fringe of the group, all ears. Ludwig knew that what he was saying did not apply to his expert ropemakers: they would not only be welcomed, they would be retained by the National Cordage Company; he was justifiably sure, and for good reason, that Bodien could deal with the skilled workmen: only three or four of them were tempted away by the National Cordage Company.

What did hurt, might hurt mortally, was the trust's price-cutting policy. To meet competition Ludwig had to sell below cost, and for three years Rausch Cordage, though holding on to most of its customers because of the quality of its rope, had operated at a loss. The time would come soon when Ludwig would have to borrow money from the Cincinnati banks, and the only collateral he had left, in addition to his cordage stock, was his holdings in the Columbus and Cincinnati Interurban Electric Company; these he was reluctant to offer as collateral since he hoped to retain control. The only ray of hope was the overblown financing of the National Cordage Company, which just might lead it into trouble. Its juggling with finances was writ large for anyone to read. The increase in capitalization from a million to fifteen million dollars of preferred stock, which was to pay eight percent, would be sold to the public. In 1891 ten million common shares had been placed in the hands of a New York financier, under whose expert manipulation the stock rose in price from seventy-three to over a hundred dollars, paying a ten percent dividend in 1891. Ludwig had gained information by way of his political friends with pipelines to Wall Street that convinced him it must be unsound. The subject was discussed at the dinner table one night when not only Gib but Stewart Bodien and the Douglas Gardiners were there.

The subject had come up as a digression from the inevitable discussion of politics. The country would elect a President in the fall; by March the prospects were the subject of debate at many Waynesboro dinner tables. Harrison would run again: he would control the Convention and could not be stopped, even were there a better candidate to present. Some of Harrison's foes, or of McKinley's friends, were suggesting his name, but Governor McKinley was a loyal man, as had been proved in the days of John Sherman's candidacy; besides, McKinley's friend Mark Hanna had better political sense: let the Governor wait until Harrison was out of the way. With both Sherman and Hanna at odds with Foraker, a good many Ohio Republicans, tired of the dissension, were willing to accept Harrison, whatever the consequences. Harrison was honest and a good administrator; he would not make a bad President, but he was not popular. He lacked magnetism—had in fact a very quenching sort of personality; he was hardly the sort to raise the hero-shout, although he had fought through the war, rising from second lieutenant of an Indiana regiment to brevet brigadier general, as opposed to Cleveland's having hired a substitute when drafted. But a war record almost thirty years after Appomattox meant less than it once had.

Cleveland, on the other hand, sure to be nominated again by the Democrats, had an undeniable hold on the country's affections. He had not been a bad President, either, and was a sound money man, but should his election sweep in a Democratic Congress, then tariffs would be lowered, there would be a tremendous and perhaps irresistible demand for the free coinage of silver, and the country's prosperity would be endangered.

"But," said Ludwig, when all these points had been canvassed, "a Democratic Congress just might give us a stronger anti-trust law than the Sherman Act has turned out to be, mangled as it was before being finally passed by a Congress determined to weaken it."

"Even as it is," Doug Gardiner volunteered, "I don't believe the Supreme Court would uphold it. It is Federal Government interfering with state business."

"Maybe that could be the reason there has been so little attempt to enforce it," Ludwig admitted. "Though most trusts are interstate. Certainly National Cordage is. But as the law is written it doesn't apply to National Cordage, because it calls itself a company rather than a trust. That's why I hoped the law might be strengthened."

As Rausch Cordage's attorney as well as Ludwig's, Doug was fairly familiar with Ludwig's troubles. "Is National Cordage really a threat?"

Sally cut in. "He's forgotten what a real threat is. Remember the seventies, Ludwig? You were making anything and everything at the mill just to keep going. Bed-rope, imagine! Ship fenders, oakum, box handles. And supplying your workmen with coal, besides."

Ludwig laughed. "Bed-rope and box handles—no use for them these days. But anything we can make cheaply and afford to sell cheaply, we are making. Quality rope we make at a greater loss, but we must hold our customers; oil-field ropes, marine ropes, transmission ropes. Even lariats. We can't keep it up forever, but the National Cordage Company is doing some pretty wild financing."

"So let us cross our fingers," Sally said, "and hope that they go bankrupt before we do. How I ever permitted you gentlemen to get started on such a subject I do not know. Elsa and I are accustomed to it, but poor Mrs. Gardiner must have been dreadfully bored."

"Bored?" Barbara was surprised. "No. I've learned a lot, just listening, about high finance. At our table it is seldom anything but 'Mind your manners.'"

"At any rate the gentlemen can carry on without us. I believe they are planning to have a business conference in the library after dinner. Coffee in the drawing room, Rose, for the three of us; let the gentlemen have theirs here." She rose, as did the two other women. "Perhaps Elsa will play for us while the men talk."

Sally had never become well acquainted with Barbara Gardiner; she looked forward to being able to resort to Elsa and the piano for after-dinner entertainment. She had forgotten that when Elsa was a child, she and Mrs. Gardiner had been friends. As Sally took her place behind the table where Rose put down the tray with the coffee pot and demitasse cups, Barbara and Elsa settled themselves side by side on two of the brocaded parlor chairs. Barbara had had plenty of time to study Elsa in her new dignity: high-piled hair and Paris gown of honey-colored satin, with its square decolletage and bouffant sleeves. She said, smiling at Elsa, "And to think that you were once the bugler for Battery B! I can hardly believe it."

"It is all this," Elsa indicated by a gesture the length of her gown, "that I can't believe. Sometimes I think I am play-acting in Mamma's finery: that it can't be real."

"You are to be married soon: you will find that real enough."

"I hope matrimony agrees with me as well as it does with you. You are still a beautiful girl."

"What nonsense! I am the matronly mother of four girls: Lavinia is eleven now; the others stairsteps."

"And they are all pretty too. I have seen you all driving around town with the surrey so full they looked like tumbling out. And it was only yesterday you were married. I remember it so well, and how much more interested Johnny Gordon and I were in your father's soldier friends than in the wedding itself." Remembering their grim faces at the wedding, she asked, "How are Mr. Gardiner's aunts?"

"They don't change much, except that they are getting to be very old ladies. I expect they seem so to you at Club meetings?"

"Yes. But they always did, I'm afraid." She did not say "And now not very clean old ladies, either," since she could hardly believe her own suspicions: it was inconceivable that the fastidious Gardiner sisters could slip into the negligence of old age.

Barbara continued, "We don't see much of them, really, these days: our chaotic meals were too much for them; now they have trays upstairs. They keep to their own apartment. Doug thinks we must get another maid to look after them: they don't like Lutie—will hardly let her in to clean their rooms. Old age is very sad."

"Your mother is well? I know your father is: his name is constantly on Papa's tongue."

Barbara brightened. "They are both well, thank you. And much the same as ever. Papa is living the war all over again with my children. They don't grow old."

Elsa said, "They won't let him grow old."

Barbara thought, half-amused and half-annoyed, "I should hope not. Papa can't be much older than Mrs. Rausch!" She said, "Doug and I are, I suppose, middle-aged."

Sally, who was all of forty-two, did not care for the idea, although, as she consoled herself, one could be middle-aged for a long, long while. She broke off her mulling over the idea and interrupted the conversation across the room from her. "Ring for Rose, will you, Elsa; she can take the coffee tray now. Then I hope you will play for us. There's no knowing how long the men will be in the library."

Ludwig had been very anxious to get the three men together with him: Douglas, who was his lawyer, Stewart Bodien, and Gib Evans. Stewart, who might have been supposed too busy with the rope machinery to have had any spare time, had been working nights on a model of a paper-making machine: one that would coat two sides of a roll of paper in one operation instead of two. Ludwig had studied it, and had seen the possibilities at once: paper could be made in half the time required by the old method, with half the machines and half the labor, and could be sold well under the going price and still be profitable. But pinched as he was, how could he finance it?

In the library he explained the situation to the other two men: young Bodien's invention would be a big thing, once a factory was built, machines installed, and workmen hired. Under the agreement they had made half-a-dozen years before, Stewart was free to do what he pleased with his invention; he was waiting, having patented it, to see whether Ludwig, with what help he could get, would be able to get a new corporation started. "He could sell the invention to any company that makes coated paper—he's perfectly free to do so—and very profitably, either paid outright or in royalties. But the profit would be much greater if we could set up our own factory, if he is willing to wait. I don't see how we could do it now, without new capital."

"I would be willing to wait," Stewart said slowly, "if I could be president of the new company."

"That would be fair enough," Ludwig conceded. "I could never give it the time it would take. There would have to be a board of directors, but if you and I were in control, we could manage it. I should like to be chairman of the board. But all that is for the future. The question is, how do we raise the money and should we apply for a corporation charter."

Gib, so much the youngest of the four men, shuffled his feet awkwardly.

"Excuse me, sir, but do you really want me here? I don't know anything about finance, or corporation law."

"You can't learn too soon: you are going to be my son-in-law; you may have to represent my interests sometime before my own sons are old enough."

Gib subsided, giving up any idea of joining Elsa in the parlor. Doug shoved his spectacles up over the bridge of his nose. "You think it will be a big thing? Is there much coated paper used?"

Ludwig looked at him in surprise. "You shouldn't have to look up any figures to know that. See here." He rose and pulled a heavy calf-bound book off the shelf behind him. "*Battles and Leaders of the Civil War*. Volume one of a four-volume set, all on coated paper, just as it was first printed in *Century Magazine*. How many sets of that do you suppose have been sold over the country? And how many copies of the *Century*? All the big magazines are printed on coated paper."

"I'm convinced," Douglas smiled at the ruffled Ludwig. "Just the same, we will need some figures before we're through. But if it will be such a big thing, how can you and Stewart capitalize it?"

Stewart laughed; Ludwig said, "Right now I couldn't capitalize a blacksmith shop. The question is, shall we make a stab at it? It would have to be an open corporation, with stock offered to the public. And I don't like to put time, thought, and hard work into a corporation I can't control, or Stewart and I between us."

"Thirty percent of the stock held by you and Bodien should give you control, if outsiders invest. Where were you thinking of putting this factory? There's no labor supply here."

"None to speak of, so long as the cordage company is operating, and Hoffmann's Bakery and the foundry." Ludwig snorted. "No, but labor would come here, if there were jobs. And once the movement started, Waynesboro might become another Madison City. Only it would smell worse. Would you like that, for yourself and your children? It would mean more money in a lot of pockets, including yours."

Doug shook his head. "No. That is money Waynesboro can do without. All those immigrants from East Europe. And if there were to be another depression, think— No."

"We have our eyes on a good flat piece of land on the outskirts of Madison City, close to the railroad. I agree that it would be better to go where the labor is, and is coming, fast. Stewart and I can manage the purchase price of the land. And if you think we are right to go ahead, there will be fees to the state for the corporation papers. Point is, Doug, if they're drawn up now, and a charter granted, we would be ready. Will you do that, and show them to us? By the time all the preliminaries are taken care of, I may see my way clear. But there are other questions, too. Should we issue only common stock, with a vote a share? Or some preferred stock, non-voting but with fixed dividends that would be cumulative until they could be paid?"

The conversation continued for a while, with both young men trying to understand the issues involved; finally Ludwig said, "Draw up the papers, Doug. Stewart and I will look them over when they are ready. And not a word of this outside, not for a while—it's too chancy still."

The gentlemen then joined the ladies, Gib going straight to the piano, where he sat down on the bench beside Elsa; Stewart drawing a chair close to his sister, to have a visit with her; Doug and Ludwig joining Sally. Business was forgotten for the evening, and indeed was not brought up again at the family dinner table afterward, whatever worried talks there might have been between Ludwig and Sally in the privacy of their bedroom.

If in the next few weeks Ludwig had his own preoccupations (business and politics), the minds of the women, not only the Rausch women but a large part of the female portion of Waynesboro society, were concentrated on the subject of all subjects best guaranteed to interest them: weddings. There were nuptial affairs of every sort, honoring both brides; in addition there were family dinners. Mrs. Voorhees gave a tea, Mrs. Gordon an afternoon reception, followed by a dinner for the two couples; the Rausches gave a ball at the Odd Fellows' Hall, to which everyone they knew of Waynesboro's young and moderately young was invited, and which all except the Reformed Presbyterians and the stricter Methodists attended.

Elsa would have preferred a small wedding, but her mother would have none of it. "Let's not make a hole-and-corner affair of this," she said. "The older Evans boy will be Gib's best man, I suppose, so you won't be obliged to ask Julia to be maid-of-honor. Bridesmaid, yes. But ask one of the Rausch cousins to be maid of honor: Ottilie in Cincinnati, or Aunt Minna's Greta: the Burlington Rausches plan to come for the wedding."

"What a hurly-burly, Mamma. Must we? Where will you put them all? Ernest will be home for his spring vacation."

"The boys can double up. And Anne has offered the use of her spare bedrooms if we need them. There's nothing for you to worry about. All you need have on your mind is choosing what colors you want your bridesmaids to wear. Shillito's will send samples. And Mrs. Woodman has promised to make their gowns, now that yours is almost finished."

And so Elsa and Gilbert Evans were married one April evening in a lilac-bedecked Baptist church; Elsa and her father were preceded down the aisle by a maid-of-honor, a double row of bridesmaids, and the youngest Gardiner as flower girl. Elsa was a stately bride, composed of demeanor, if a little pale; the ceremony was soon over, and relatives and close friends moved on to the wedding reception at the Rausches'. Johnny Gordon, who had been an usher, went down the receiving line behind Julia, who was looking her blonde best in her bridesmaid's pale green gown. He paused so long with Elsa's hand in his that he held up the line behind him, staring at her a long moment. Then he leaned to kiss her gently on the cheek, said abruptly, "Bless you, Shaney, be happy!"—wrung Gib's hand, and followed Julia through the thronged drawing room to the hall.

"Elsa looked tired to death," Julia said, as they reached a comparatively secluded corner under the stairs. "Was that what stopped you for so long? The doctor's eye?"

Johnny laughed. "No. Of course she's tired, but she's strong as a horse. No. What stopped me was her expression. She looked so—so *sweet*. That's a woman's word and not one to apply to Elsa ordinarily, but I don't know another to describe it. I think she really does love Gib."

"I hope so," Julia said virtuously. "She didn't have to marry him: it was her choice. But I wouldn't have said *sweet*—beautiful, maybe, but kind of stiff."

Johnny did not argue with her. Perhaps because he and Elsa knew each other so well, only he had noted the sweetness of her soft mouth, of her blue eyes. He said only, "We're to be at the bride's table, I believe. We might as well work our way toward it."

Eventually they found themselves with the other members of the bridal party drifting through the dining room door, all laughing and in high spirits, particularly the two oldest Rausch brothers, who had been ushers and were now paired off with cousins somewhere near their ages. When finally Gib and Elsa joined them and they took their places around the table, the hilarity increased still more. Johnny, a little slow in pushing Julia's chair under her, found his own place barred from him by the huge leg-of-mutton sleeves of Julia and Cousin Ottilie meeting each other over his chair.

"Sorry, ladies," he said, "but I intend to sit here, even if I do crush your sleeves."

Elsa, at the head of the table, flushed and excited, said, "Aren't fashions absurd? Mamma says the skirt of her wedding dress was fifteen yards around at the bottom, and her sleeves and her bodice were skin tight, but her waistband let her breathe. Mine doesn't."

"Nowadays you all have to hold your breaths," Johnny said, "so that you can get into your gowns at all. My two hands will very nearly go round Julia's waist. Seventeen inches isn't it, Julia? How you think your insides can work properly—"

"Listen to the doctor!" someone said. "Going in for dress reform, Johnny?"

"I just might."

With such nonsensical banter they toasted the bride and groom in Ludwig's champagne, ate their suppers, and dutifully applauded Elsa as she rose to cut the cake. After that it was soon over: Gib slipped up the back stairs to get out of his dress suit while Elsa made more of an exit up the front stairs, tossing her bouquet to Julia, and gathering up her train for the ascent. Presently the two reappeared in traveling costumes, and were pelted with the conventional shower of rice. As they made their farewell embraces, Elsa clung to her father for a moment, then went out to the night and the carriage, old Reuben still driving.

The senior Gordons walked home. They did not hurry: it would be a while before the cousins they were sheltering tore themselves away. Johnny had the

Gordons' horse and carriage for Julia: when they had climbed in and Johnny had picked up the reins, Julia sighed and dropped her head on his shoulder.

"Do you think we'll have to go through all this?"

"Well, I was more or less resigned to it. Won't your father and mother want it? Don't you want it?"

"I don't want to be as tired as Elsa looked."

Johnny who had not thought her looking particularly tired, went along with Julia in her judgment.

"I don't want you to be tired, sweetheart. But we've two more months before our wedding, and after this there won't be so many parties."

She lifted her head abruptly. "What do you mean?"

He had said the wrong thing, obviously. "Dear goose! Can't you see that everyone in town who would entertain for you and Elsa did it up all at once, economically, one party instead of two?"

"But I do have a few friends of my own, you know. And of course Mamma and Papa intend to give a ball."

Johnny groaned. "Do discourage them, Julie. There's the Republican Convention ahead for your father—enough to kill a man half his age, just in itself."

"Johnny!" Her voice was sharper. "Is there anything the matter with Papa?"

"No, no. Nothing in the world." Then, remembering the flushed face of the General, he qualified his statement with a doctor's caution. "Not so far as I know. He's just not as young as he once was."

"I'll try to persuade him to forget the ball, I guess." A safe guess since she had just invented it, knowing that if she wanted one she could have it. "But he will want a big church wedding. You know how he is: nothing too good, no expense too great."

"I not only know, I applaud. I reckon we can stand one big blow-out like this."

Julia had been right about one thing: there were still a few friends of her mother, members of the Methodist church for the most part, who did not know Elsa Rausch but wanted to honor Julia Deming, and so there were more teas and receptions to be got through. Then Elsa and Gib returned from their wedding trip, and Elsa gave a luncheon (her first attempt to entertain in her own home) for Julia, inviting a few of Julia's art school friends from Cincinnati, who would be her bridesmaids, as well as the members of the Woman's Club. Elsa took no credit for the success of her party—and it was a success in spite of the oil-and-water mixture of guests—since she had borrowed cook and waitress from her mother. (She was determined not to hire her own servants until she was sure they could afford it, and Gib when he was at home was suffering cheerfully some very odd meals.)

Johnny and Julia's wedding was set for the first of June, so that they could have a brief honeymoon in New England ("We can look up all the Boston cousins," a prospect that did not exactly elate Johnny). General and Mrs.

Deming would be in Minneapolis for the Convention week beginning the seventh, and then would make a leisurely return on the Great Lakes, sailing from Duluth on one of the Hanna Company's ships. For their first couple of weeks at home, the young Gordons would have the house to themselves: "If you want to dance fandangoes in your parlor, you needn't worry about disturbing anyone. Just so you don't knock the plaster down." The General's humor was a little ponderous.

The wedding of Deming to Gordon was almost exactly like the wedding of Rausch to Evans (indeed, was like any big fashionable church wedding) except that the Methodist church being larger, there were more guests invited to the wedding and fewer to the reception, since the Deming house was smaller than the Rausches'. Johnny and his Julia had their wedding trip, returned, and set up housekeeping. The Demings came home and reported on the Convention, which had been a dull one. Harrison had been renominated as expected. There had been a moment when Governor McKinley just might have swept in (there were 162 votes for him), but, as in 1888, he had disavowed his supporters, and his name had been dropped. General Deming went back to the county history he was working on, with his wife assisting; Johnny plunged into his practice; Julia amused herself as she had done before, as all girls did: she played ladylike tennis on the Rausch court, went bicycling on the country roads, spent the long afternoons on one porch or another. Before the summer was over Johnny had put a stop to the tennis and bicycling; Julia was pregnant. Her mother was astonished when Julia confessed to being "in the family way." "Already?" she said disapprovingly. But Julia insisted, "I wanted it. Won't you like a grandchild?" What she did not say (nor had said to Johnny when she had explained her wish, even on her honeymoon: "Let's start a baby right away") was that for almost a year she would be spared what she called in her own mind "all that." The discomforts of pregnancy could be more easily endured, she thought, than Johnny's ardors (although she was soon to change her mind), and for once she would come in ahead of Elsa Rausch Evans. But when Julia had confided her secret to Elsa, saying primly, "I shan't be going out much this fall," Elsa had been almost pitying; "Oh dear! So soon! No more fun, after the babies come. Mamma warned me: every time she wanted to go some place with Papa in those early years she was in the family way or had a baby and had to stay home. But then, five children: imagine! I don't intend that to happen."

"I can understand that with Gib away so much, you wouldn't want to be in a delicate condition. Aren't you afraid, alone at nights?"

"Afraid? No, of course not. It's rather a relief to be away from all that caterwauling at home: Ludwig not only tries to play the violin himself, he is teaching Paul. Paul wants to do everything Ludwig does, and Ludwig is amazingly patient with him. He isn't patient with anyone else. They come out here often so I can play accompaniments for them. Papa gave me the grand piano for a wedding present."

One way in which Elsa spent time was in short but frequent visits to

Ariana McCune Mercer, who was still an invalid at the Ballards'. (Johnny forbade Julia such visits.) Sometimes Ariana would seem much better: she would be up in a rocker, an afghan over her knees, a shawl over her shoulders. She would be gay and excited and full of plans: she would be back on the stage in no time; she would be back with Ben, who had always been so good to her. Other times she would be in bed in a melancholy humor: "Those silly doctors think I don't know what's the matter with me, when every time I cough, I cough blood. My time is so short, and I haven't done any of the things I wanted to do."

Everyone close to her knew which mood was the realistic one, although they could not help being relieved of their forebodings when they found her in one of the feverish, excited times. Ruhamah spent most mornings with her, following without protest the doctor's instructions as to precautions to be taken, and his insistence that she come to the office every little while for an examination.

"If we had caught Ariana's infection in an early stage, we might have been able to do something about it," John Gordon had said to her one day.

"You don't expect her to get well, do you?"

"You know that, surely?" John was gruff. "Can't you see how she is slipping? Ben saw it the last time he was here. It was the first time he had been able to come since the circus left winter quarters."

"I know. Poor Ben, he feels so responsible. He shouldn't. It was Ariana's doing."

"He's a good boy. He's done his best for her. She should have seen a doctor sooner."

Eliza said the same thing to Ludwig one afternoon in the mill office. He had been away so much that summer on politics and business, and had been so preoccupied when he was at his desk that he had hardly given a thought to Eliza. But on that particular afternoon when she brought him his letters to be signed, she actually swayed on her feet, clutching at his desk for support. He said, "Hold on, Eliza," as he got up and pushed the visitor's chair around the desk for her. "Sit still until you feel better." As she dropped into the chair, he took note not only of the gray in her nondescript-colored hair and the lines in her face, but of the slight shabbiness of her severe costume: long undraped skirt worn shiny, and bedraggled at the hem where it swept the floor; the fitted bodice with its high collar and row of buttons from top to bottom, and sleeves tight from shoulder to wrist. She must have been wearing that frock for years: it had been a long while since he had seen his womenfolk in anything but those absurd sleeves that ballooned between shoulder and elbow. He thought Eliza's style looked better, really, but he supposed that even she might like a new frock once in a while. "Are you ill?" he asked, as he watched a little color return to her cheeks.

She shook her head, her mouth hard shut; she had held it compressed for so many years that her lip had thinned to a line.

"Just tired. It's nothing."

"I thought you had help. Someone to stay at night, so that you could sleep."

"Yes. But last night was a bad night. Ariana had a hemorrhage. Mrs. Hopkins called me, but we couldn't stop it. I had to send Samuel for the doctor. We were up most of the night."

"Hemorrhage! Then she isn't getting better. I thought—"

Eliza shook her head. "She coughs up blood—oh, just a little—all the time. She tries to hide it, but we know. John Gordon knew from the first, I think. That boy she married just didn't get her to a doctor in time."

"It has been too much of a strain for you."

Eliza shook her head again. "I wouldn't have had it any other way. She came home, even if it was only to die. She trusted me that much." Her face softened. "I was so fond of her."

"And that has meant a lot to you."

"Everything." She was blinking back tears. "I hadn't any—"

"Of course." Ludwig cut her short, he wanted no weeping in his office; to see Eliza Ballard so uncharacteristically emotional was unnerving. "But you mustn't wear yourself out completely. Go home now and get some sleep. And the next time you are up all night, take the morning off. We can manage somehow."

When she had gone, he wondered about Eliza's expenses and who would pay for the funeral. That evening he drifted into John's office, found Mr. Lichtenstein at the chess table, and sat down to play a game with him while he waited for John to be free. Mr. Lichtenstein did not appear there as often as he had once; Ludwig was glad to see him. The two men began at once to talk of the state of the country and the coming election; Mr. Lichtenstein, still president of the school board, had practically given up a nonexistent legal practice, and was an insurance agent and a notary public, by which means he earned a sufficient living for his family, if not quite a comfortable one. Rudy Lichtenstein was through college and in law school. Max was in Ludwig Junior's class in school, and Ludwig Senior had been drawn at home into a debate against some Lichtenstein ideas. Ludwig tackled Mr. Lichtenstein at once, half annoyed, half in fun.

"It's a long time since we've met here, but I haven't lost track of you and your notions. My boy comes home with some half-cocked ideas he has picked up from your boy, and I have to knock them out of his head. Populism. Free silver. A graduated income tax. And to think you were once a Republican!"

Mr. Lichtenstein removed his meerschaum to smile at Ludwig. "And you were vunce a Revolutionary, *nicht wahr?* Or your vater, in 1848?"

"My father, yes. I was six years old in '48. But that was the old country, where there is no chance for the people to speak."

"Ze people here suffer, too—ze poor, ze vorkmen, ze farmers. And ze rich haf ze power. If a laboring man vorks up his courage to strike, he is shot down."

"Not often. You're thinking of the Homestead strike? That was a disquieting affair, I agree. Americans rioting, shooting and being shot at. And Frick himself shot by foreign anarchists."

"Eight guards killed and elefen striking laborers. Does that seem right to you?"

"No. Americans should not be killing each other, even if the strikers are very new Americans like those Slavs in the steel mills. But the Democratic program doesn't offer the answer. Low tariffs would mean competition with foreign wages. And free silver would not make the poor richer and the rich poorer. We'd have unlimited inflation, and that never helped a poor man. Look at the harm the Sherman Act has already done: the price of silver has gone down instead of up, and because the Treasury by law is required to buy fifty-four million ounces of it every year at a set price, the government is losing ten million annually and the value of the dollar continues to decline. Republicans will demand repeal of that bill."

"But you haf alvays beliefed Senator Sherman could do no wrong."

"The unfortunate Senator had his name tacked to that bill because he was chairman of the committee to work out a compromise between House and Senate versions, and the bill finally voted on was the best to be had, with the Senate in favor of free silver. It was a triumph of sorts to limit the amount the Treasury has to buy. No, the Populist demand for free silver and low tariffs is pure demagoguery: free silver will only make the mineowners richer, and low tariffs will mean lower wages or failing industries and fewer jobs."

"You are perhaps right. Und zo." Mr. Lichtenstein looked at Ludwig through the cloud of smoke from his big pipe. "Ze answer iss gofernment ownership of industry; gofernment management of ze money supply."

"Good God, man! You're an out-and-out Socialist."

"I zink zo, ya."

"Then there's no use arguing, is there? Let's get to our game." But Ludwig could not quite leave it at that. "And you are bringing up a brood of young Socialists?"

"Trying to. But Rudy, in law school—I sink he vill stick vit ze Democrats. And Max, in school vit your Ludwig: he listens to your boy, and I haf to deal vit his notions." They both laughed. "It iss gut, *nicht wahr*, zat ve can argue zese sings vitout anger?"

"Sehr gut," Ludwig agreed amiably. Shocked as he was to find that among his friends was one who actually called himself a Socialist, he was not really much afraid of Socialism gaining a hold in America. A convert to it meant one less Democrat. "But most of Waynesboro doesn't distinguish between Socialist and Anarchism. If I were you and wanted to stay on the school board, I'd pipe down about it until after the election."

They dropped their argument then and got on with their chess. When John's last patient had left, he joined the two men in the middle office. They had come to the end game, which Ludwig lost. Mr. Lichtenstein rose to his feet and made his farewells. "So you see, politics und chess do not mix. I should startle you zo efery time ve play. You haf not been of your game sinking."

When he was gone, John said, "Of what were you 'sinking'?"

"He just admitted to being a Socialist. Good God!"

"Mugwump to Socialist in ten years or so. Does it matter? He is a dreamer. If he had been a man to make money, he wouldn't be so ready to deal it out to others."

"And so far as the schools are concerned, he had dreamt to good purpose. I forgive him. I want to talk to you about Ariana McCune. Eliza was near collapse today."

"She had a rough night. She'll be all right."

"Ariana is dying?"

"Slowly. But inexorably."

"How about finances? This must be costing something."

"Ben Mercer sends what he can spare toward her doctor's bills. And you know that I'll never dun him. Lots of my patients can't pay. I take it out of the hides of you rich fellows. But how Eliza makes out I don't know. There's Mrs. Hopkins to be paid, and all the extra food."

"And soon, funeral expenses?"

"Yes. Ruhamah will want to use her savings, I reckon."

"I guess the thing to do is raise Eliza's pay. That means the bookkeeper, too." Of all the office help, only the bookkeeper had been there as long as Eliza. "It's a bad time for me, but they have earned it, and I have been too busy and too worried to give their worries a thought, I'm afraid."

"I am glad Eliza has been satisfactory. The women are so afraid of her tongue. I suppose you know all the Waynesboro scandals?"

"I could. Tongues go clackety-clack in the office most of the day, but I never listen. Sometimes the bookkeeper passes some particular titillating item on to me. Eliza wouldn't dream of gossiping to me. Nor about me, or business matters: who would be interested?"

Eliza's only mention of Ludwig that summer was made at home on the evening of the day when he had told her that he was increasing her salary. She met Thomasina and Sam on their way to spend a few minutes with Ariana. "I have had an increase in pay," she announced abruptly. "It will help. Samuel has been doing more than his share."

"Trouble with you is you want to do it all. You deserve the raise after all these years, but I do give piano lessons, you know: I shall continue to do my share." Sam was for him almost sarcastic.

"Mr. Rausch is being generous: he can't really afford to increase salaries just now, when he has this fight with the National Cordage Company on his hands." But Sam and Thomasina were not acquainted with the situation at the mill, and Eliza was quick to blunt the impression she might have made by changing the subject. "If the Democrats win the election on a low tariff platform, there may be trouble."

"Papa believed in free trade."

"Papa knew very little about business."

"But surely," Thomasina protested, "President Harrison will win. He is a good man. And Cleveland! we all know what he is."

"Oh, Thomasina! If you are hinting at that old scandal about his illegitimate child, that is all water under the bridge. It didn't keep him from being elected before, and it won't now. I am sure Mr. Rausch thinks Harrison will be beaten, though he is doing his share of work in the campaign."

"Working in that office with all those men is making you very coarse, Eliza. Papa and his political friends were never like that, and Mamma would think you most unladylike."

"You are turning our parents into something they never were. Mamma was a lady, but she would not have cared about seeming 'ladylike.' She would not have blanched at my saying 'illegitimate child,' if that is what upset you: you forget her campaign against prostitution. And she believed women should be free to work, to vote, to have lives of their own, to be emancipated. She believed in emancipation, first for the slaves, then for women. Papa believed in justice, which is not quite the same thing; still I do not think he would have disapproved of my working and being independent."

"While Papa lived," Thomasina said, ignoring Eliza's remarks, "we really had a window on the world. It still seems strange not to be in touch with national affairs."

They went into Ariana's room, and the subject was dropped. The Traverses exchanged a few words with Ariana and took their leave; Eliza settled down beside her for the evening.

Eliza had been right as to Ludwig's forecast of the election; he was not very hopeful. He did all that was expected of him as a State Committeeman, but his heart was not in it. He felt some relief when Congress adjourned on the fifth of August: they were plainly not going to repeal the Silver Act, but if they continued the session, they might do something to make the situation worse instead of leaving it as it was. It made him no happier to see the price of National Cordage shares increase until the stock stood at over a hundred; he kept telling himself that someone must be rigging the market, that it was a bubble so overblown that it must burst, but he was not sure his wish had not fathered the thought. His greatest pleasure those days, when he was in Waynesboro, was in Elsa's company and all the talk of her years in Germany and of the cousins whom he hardly remembered. Elsa often ate dinner with her family when Gib was away on business, and it warmed Ludwig's heart to have all his children at the table. Ernest, home from college, was again spending his summer vacation working in the mill; so was Charles, at fifteen, although not as wheel boy. Wheel boys were a thing of the past; youngsters now were "bobbin boys," carrying the heavy bobbins of yarn from the spinning jennys to the forming machine or the tar kettle. A bobbin boy was no less tired at the end of the day than the wheel boy had been. Charles, though robust, came home exhausted. He envied the superior status of Ernest, who now in his progress from beginning to end of ropemaking, could sit at a spinning jenny along with the girls, watching the yarn going into the machine, and splicing the sliver as necessary. Ernest loathed the spinning jennys because they were operated by girls, and he looked forward to his promotion to the forming machines. He would be glad, indeed, when his education in mill operations would be complete; Ernest could imagine himself selling rope, like Gib. In the meantime he loathed it all, and hoped his college friends would never hear how he spent his summers. But he knew better than to murmur at his fate, and his father was blissfully unaware of his feeling. Ludwig could look around the table at dinnertime, when Elsa was there, and think, "Just like old times," and laugh at himself, since "old times" were but a few years back, after all. How deplorably fast children grew up!

The summer passed. The Rausch boys were relieved from their drudgery and returned to their books, Charles to the high school, Ernest to his college in the East. They were among the few who found the fall pleasanter than the summer had been. The Rausch family were less high-spirited than usual. Ludwig was worried; consequently, when he was home, he tended to be withdrawn and abstracted and to interrupt the rapid cross fire of dinner table banter by suddenly coming alive with a "What's all that?" that cast a damper over the others. The matter of the new paper company was in abeyance; the papers had been drawn up by Gardiner and Merrill, and a charter of incorporation applied for, but capitalization at that moment was impossible. Gardiner and Merrill, in the persons of Doug Gardiner and Tim Merrill, were not particularly upset by the trouble of their client: Doug was happy with his family, and Tim and his wife, the former Elizabeth Talmadge, were living in a state of bliss in the old Merrill house in the south end of town, marveling daily at the perfection of their two-year-old daughter. Elizabeth was not yet ready to admit that a life of baby-tending and diaper-changing was somewhat lacking in intellectual stimulus; she was only slightly resentful that on the baby's account she had been forbidden by her usually easy-going husband to visit at the bedside of her one-time favorite pupil.

She tried to explain her dereliction to Amanda Reid one afternoon after the September Club meeting, but Amanda cut her short. By chance they had come together alone in the Voorheeses' hall, while the other ladies were still thanking Christina for her hospitality and making their polite farewells.

"I haven't seen her either. Eliza and Thomasina still hold me responsible for the unfortunate chain of circumstances: if only Ariana had passed her Latin and been graduated with her class, she would not have run away. It is quite irrational," Amanda said crossly, "too many ifs involved. At any rate, I doubt whether Ariana would care to see me. Not that I do not feel sorry for her, but I do not feel to blame."

Elizabeth had wondered a little whether Amanda had not by now eased somewhat the demands she made of her Latin students; and whether her conscience in regard to Ariana might not have troubled her a little. She should have known better: Amanda was growing more inflexible rather than less. On Elizabeth's defection (the marriage of any of her friends was still "defection" in Amanda's eyes), she had been surprised to find what a relief it was, in a way, to have her house to herself again, even at the cost of having to be her own housekeeper and cook: to have silence after so many voices all day long, to be able to concentrate uninterruptedly on her teaching was pure pleasure. Amanda loved to teach, not because she cared particularly for young people in the mass, but because she was so thoroughly imbued with, and convinced of, the importance of her subject matter; there was a unique reward in awakening a response in someone (almost every class had at least one pupil whose eyes would light up over a passage even in Caesar's *Gallic Wars*). That particular September she numbered among her pupils only one of the children of her fellow Club members: Charles Rausch, who was in her eyes a dull but conscientious plodder, absorbing sooner or later what he was supposed to know. Blair Voorhees, surely of high school age, was still being taught by his mother. The pupils in whom Amanda delighted were the young German-Americans: Kleins, Hoffmanns, Lichtensteins, and the sons and daughters of various butchers, bakers, and grocers. No doubt about it: in their case, the second-generation Americans would achieve professional standing, and some of them very high professional stature. Amanda was neither happy nor unhappy that fall. She accepted the present and found some pleasure in it; with equanimity she anticipated the future as it would undoubtedly be: exactly like the present and the past.

At the first Club meeting in September, the younger Mrs. John Gordon was conspicuous by her absence. Though no one would have guessed her condition from her appearance, she was making heavy weather of her pregnancy: sick every morning, petulant with Johnny because he was unable to help her to feel better, and because he had insisted on her seeing Dr. Warren. Over her protests as to how much she trusted him and his father, he had been firm: doctors never attended members of their own families.

"But I don't know Dr. Warren," she wailed.

"You will in time. He's a nice fellow and very competent."

"I don't care for his wife at all. She's so—so *pushy*."

Dr. Warren had made the great mistake of marrying a girl from his home town instead of choosing one from among the Waynesboro eligibles. Mrs. Warren was still "from away" after all their years of marriage, and she always would be, although accepted in her church and various other groups. The Warrens had several children; the senior Dr. Gordon had delivered the first, a boy somewhere near Rodney's age, Johnny the others, his father having turned over to him when he began to practice all the obstetrical work possible. Johnny did not improve matters when he said to Julia, "I found Mrs. Warren agreeable, and a model of what a wife should be in the eyes of a physician: one who takes her pregnancies in stride and has her babies without fuss. Now, Julie, don't look at me like that. I know the whole process is hell for some women; they can't help it: it's just the way they're made; and you mustn't think I am belittling your suffering."

Indeed, Johnny was worried about Julia, though both his father and Dr. Warren insisted she was perfectly healthy, or would be when she got over this morning sickness. "They don't know," Johnny thought, "how tiny her bones are. She may have trouble." Dread lay at the back of his mind all that fall. Naturally Julia's father and mother fretted, too, and Julia continued to be miserable.

Johnny's father was troubled over Ariana McCune, as were others that fall: Ruhamah and her school friends, to whom the approaching death of one of their own was a frightening hand clutching at the heart; the Traverses; and Eliza, although in an odd way she found herself comforted at fleeting moments by Ariana's being there; her distress was mitigated by the happy thought that it had been she to whom Ariana had turned and would not leave again. She had come home.

Anne Gordon could grieve for Ariana—so young to die—but in her private and personal life, she was content enough: Johnny was happy with his wife in spite of all his present worry, and Julia seemed to return his love, hanging on him as she did. There would soon be a grandchild. Anne was actually becoming fond of her daughter-in-law, or at least sympathetic. She knew too that Julia in spite of her obvious fear had no real idea of the ordeal ahead of her: Anne could pity her, which contributed to the affection she felt. Most of all, John, in spite of the frustration she knew he felt in the case of Ariana, was not running away from his suffering, growing remote and unreachable: he was accepting the inevitable defeat with a measure of equanimity, something he had been unable to do before except for old people who had had full lives; at fifty he had finally achieved the detachment so necessary to a physician.

Autumn was slipping away almost without notice. Through October, usually the finest month of the year, it rained ceaselessly, a slow steady rain. Leaves dropped from the trees never having had a scarlet season. They lay on the brick sidewalks, glued together by standing water. There was little excitement over the election, but its outcome weighed down the mood of Waynesboro. It had been the least suspenseful one since Grant's in '68. President Harrison carried Ohio, but not the country. Ludwig was shocked by the completeness of the Democratic victory: Cleveland had defeated Blaine in '84 by something like sixty thousand popular votes and one hundred and thirty-two in the electoral college. It was small comfort to know that Cleveland was a sound money man, conservative in all financial matters: who could tell what a Democratic Congress might do? Once Cleveland was inaugurated, he was sure to ask for the repeal of the Sherman Silver Act, which was proving so costly for the country, but would Congress respond? In addition to the troublesome matter of silver, the new Congress was sure to lower tariffs and would probably enact a graduated income tax.

At dinner one evening shortly after the election, Ludwig expounded to the boys the iniquity of the Silver Act. The boys felt they were already familiar with how he felt, but this did not stop Ludwig from painting the picture once again. The act, he explained, required the Secretary of the Treasury to coin two million ounces of silver bullion into standard dollars every month, so many ounces to the dollar. The senators from the silver states had expected this to prop up the price of silver; had it done so there would have been no trouble. But the price of silver declined, and the government still had to accept bullion at the price fixed by Congress: one dollar for every 412½ grains. The result was an excess of money in circulation, which in turn led to inflation: the more money there was in proportion to goods for sale, the higher the price of those goods.

"But why should anyone want that?" Charles puckered his brow in an attempt to follow these elementary lessons in economics according to his father.

"Debtors want it. They borrowed money when it had a certain value; they can repay it with money worth only half as much. They, and the senators from the silver-producing states, wanted free and unlimited coinage of silver—all the silver that was presented at the mint. Senator Sherman's compromise saved us from that, or the country's finances would have been in a chaotic state."

"And you will have to wait to build Rausch and Bodien Coated Papers? I should think you would have twice as much money, too."

"With costs twice as high? No one can expand or begin new industries while the financial situation is so uncertain."

Uncertain it remained. The lame duck Congress convened for the last time the first week in December; it did nothing much before it ceased to exist on the fourth of March. In January, Senator Sherman would present favorably from the Finance Committee a bill to repeal the Silver Act; the motion to take it up would be defeated, and there would be no further action or debate on that question. The affairs of the country in the last months of the year were in a state of suspended animation. Daily life went on as usual. Families went to church, men went to work and children to school, women kept house, ladies of leisure went to card parties, teas, and receptions, and those who were members of the Woman's Club prepared to stage a play.

Elizabeth Merrill was named chairman of the committee appointed to select it, and to assign parts and oversee the rehearsals. Jessamine Stevens and Anne Gordon were the other members. Meetings were at the Gordons' house, halfway between the other two. After some discussion as to its suitability for presentation to ladies, they settled on scenes from *Much Ado About Nothing*, and then spent the rest of the evening assigning parts. There would need to be some doubling up; there were many parts and few actors, since some members would necessarily be omitted: the Misses Gardiner, who could not be imagined on a stage; Julia Gordon because of her "condition"; Christina because of her adamant refusal to have anything to do with theatricals, or to recognize Christmas. The eagle-eyed ladies had some question about including Elsa in the cast, but agreed that at this point "nothing showed," and the full skirted Elizabethan costume would conceal her figure anyway. She should be put down as Beatrice, and Elizabeth (after some protest) as Benedict. Jessamine could do Hero, and Mrs. Deming was persuaded to play Claudio.

"Charlotte Bonner is a generation younger than Mrs. Deming," Elizabeth conceded, "but I can't see Charlotte doing a romantic part." They laughed: Charlotte was a tall ungainly girl, all bony ankles and elbows, with a sense of humor that would lead her to prefer Dogberry to Claudio. "And if Mrs. Evans can be persuaded to do Verges, she would be perfect. I know she's a minister's wife, but—"

"I am troubled about Christina," Jessamine said. "We were friends once, but she disapproves of me now, and I scarcely see her. I hate to see her draw apart." Jessamine, having in her first year in Waynesboro used Christina, was not of a mind to be ungrateful, or ready to let go of her now.

Elizabeth said, "Maybe we could get her to help with cutting the play. There are words in it that I don't know. If they are indecent, the men would be sure to laugh."

"What makes you think Christina would know?"

"I'm sure she does, the way she goes over the new library books to see that they are fit for reading." Anne laughed. "Not that many modern books contain objectionable Elizabethan words. But Christina had a scholar's education, and reads everything. She could do it. But I cannot understand her. She is much more bigoted than her father ever was."

"She feels responsible, in part at least, for Ariana McCune. If she had not countenanced play-acting, Ariana might not have gone on the stage."

"What nonsense!" Anne spoke vigorously. "Ariana made up her mind to go on the stage as soon as she knew the meaning of the word. You two weren't here the year we had a 'Children's Hour' and Ariana and one of her brothers acted Jael and Sisera. It sent chills down our spines to see a child that age portray hatred and venom as that child did."

Elizabeth said, "We'll depute Jessamine to ask her, and we'll meet again. Just those in the first act. We can't read it all at one sitting."

They settled on a date in the following week at the Gordons'. They broke up then, having spent an entire afternoon on what could have been done in an hour or so had there been fewer digressions.

The first gathering of those dragooned into being a part of the cast for *Much Ado* and who would make their appearance in the first act met at Anne Gordon's on the appointed evening in November. They would have the house to themselves at least until nine o'clock, and probably later, as John's office hours did not often end exactly on the hour. Each lady had brought her copy of Shakespeare's Collected Plays, or an individual copy of *Much Ado*. Christina had come as censor; Sally Rausch to play Leonate; Anne, who was doubling in all the small parts; Elsa to read Beatrice; Elizabeth, Benedict; Mrs. Deming as Claudine; and Jessamine as Hero. Thomasina had been persuaded to take the part of Don Pedro by the plea that she was needed, but actually because Eliza had said to Elizabeth that she did hope they could use Thomasina in the play: "She gets out only on Club meeting afternoons and to church, and she is so very nervous she can't be expected to stand this constant strain of attendance on Ariana. She has to be there day-times: there isn't any other way we can arrange it. We can't have her breaking down. I thought, if she could rehearse evenings, it would give her something to think about."

"How about yourself?" Elizabeth had asked.

"I can manage. I am away all day and only with Ariana in the evenings. Besides, I haven't Thomasina's sensitive nature." There had been a hint of contempt in Eliza's voice.

"Ariana is slipping?"

"It is hard to see how anyone so wasted away can hang on to life. But the doctor says it is surprising how strong that last unbroken thread can be. But yes, Ruhamah has written to Matt and Mark. Not much use in writing to her father, and Luke is still at home."

Christina, standing close by, had broken into the dialogue. "The boys are coming? Do not try to take them in, too, Eliza. You're worn out now. Let them stay with us. After all, I knew those boys well when their father was our minister, and Matt was a favorite of Papa's at the Seminary."

Eliza was genuinely grateful, if surprised. The Voorheeses never entertained guests. Christina was so notoriously a negligent housekeeper (more important things on her mind, her friends said) that it was suspected that she found it too much trouble to dust the house for company.

Before the three women drifted apart, they had agreed that Thomasina would be induced to take a part in the play, that rehearsals would be in the evening, and that the McCune boys, if and when they came, would stay at the Voorheeses'.

On the night of their first meeting, Sam Travers escorted his wife (Don Pedro) to the Gordons', and proposed to leave her on the doorstep. Anne would have none of it.

"Come in, do, it's raining hard again. Did you ever see such a dismal fall? You won't want to walk all the way home and back again."

Sam, who had hoped to get away uptown to the drugstore for an evening of masculine gossip, surrendered easily. After all, the men he might run into would not really welcome him: he knew that he was considered mighty ladylike by most Waynesboro males.

"Come into the sitting room by the fire," Anne led him to the door, looked at the fire doubtfully, "if you can keep it going. Find something to read. John will be in sometime. No one else will know you are here."

Sam picked up the morning *Enquirer* from the sitting room table and settled down for what he expected would be a thoroughly dull evening; instead, he found himself listening with growing amusement as the other ladies arrived, were taken to the parlor, and settled down to the evening's business.

Christina wasted no time: both scenes two and three of act one could be omitted; they were in the play solely to advance the plot, and their matter could be summarized by a narrator. Scene one would have to be acted, but as they read it, they must note what should be omitted; of course all the blasphemy, as well as the indecencies, must be struck out: they would not take the name of the Lord in vain, whatever Shakespeare might have seen fit to do. When they finally began the reading, the first exchange between Leonato, the messenger, and Beatrice went rapidly, Elsa reading Beatrice's part with spirit, until she stumbled over "God help the noble Claudio." "What am I to say? 'Heaven help'?"

"That would be very nearly as irreverent. Just skip the whole sentence."

As the reading progressed, it became quite clear to the now chuckling Sam that the ladies were running into some difficulty with their bowdlerizing because, for one thing, they had different editions of the play and, for another, they did not always understand the lines. When Anne had finished reading the messenger's speech, she slipped out to join her guest in the sitting room. She had hardly sat down before they heard Thomasina begin, as Don Pedro: "'I think this is your daughter,'" and Sally come back promptly: "'Her mother hath many times told me so.'" The next line would have been Elsa's: "'Were you in doubt, sir—'" Christina stopped her promptly: "Oh, ladies, please! Let us skip this speech that passes for wit! Cross out from Don Pedro's 'I think this is your daughter' down to 'Be happy, lady, for you are like an honorable father' and go on, with the passage as far as 'God Keep' and make that 'May your ladyship keep in that mind.'"

The cast got through the "Exeunt" of all except Benedict and Claudio, but the ladies remained in their chairs: no use exiting before they knew what and how much they were to say. Before Benedict and Claudio had launched into their exchange, Anne heard John at the dining room door. She went to meet him.

"You're home early."

"Beastly night—no one in to speak of. Johnny's gone home, too. If anyone wants me, he can find me here."

"The ladies are in the parlor reading *Much Ado*. You can come and listen with Sam Travers and me, if you will be quiet, to 'Shakespeare Made Decent.'"

John smiled, put a finger on his lips, tossed his derby and damp cape on the sofa, and pulled up a chair to join them. They could hear Elizabeth's voice distinctly, saying "'Look! Don Pedro is returned to seek you.'" Then Christina again, before Don Pedro could speak: "Ladies, do leave out the blasphemy when you come to it. Perhaps it would be better to just leave out all speeches with the 'God forbids.' Claudio says, 'If this were so, so were it utter'd,' and Don Pedro, 'Amen, if thou love her, for the lady is well worthy.'"

"All this skipping—" Thomasina was a little plaintive: "I find it difficult to keep the place. Oh, I see, but hadn't I better leave out the 'Amen' too? Just 'Very well, if you love her' and so on."

The reading resumed, Shakespeare as written, except for the omission of all blasphemy, until Benedict came to the speech beginning " 'That a woman conceived me, I thank her. That she brought me up, I likewise give her most humble thanks—' " Elizabeth was peremptorily stopped by Christina. "Just skip down to Don Pedro—'I shall see thee ere I die, look pale with love.' "

A long pause followed; Christina said "Don Pedro" again in a faintly chiding voice. Thomasina sounded completely confused.

"But I don't know where you are! I don't see anything about refusing to marry him, and there's all that about having a 'Recheat winded in my forehead.' What in the world is a 'recheat'?"

In the sitting room Sam Travers, shaking with laughter, said, "Listen to my innocent wife! She hasn't an idea what any of it means."

Anne laughed too, but said, "Neither have I. It seems to me quite unintelligible."

She would be spared having to understand: "Just skip all that," came Christina's firm voice. "Pick it up with 'I shall see thee, ere I die, look quite pale with love.' Just watch it, Thomasina: we'll omit Benedict's objectionable passages. In the next speech there is only one line of his fit to be spoken: 'With anger, with sickness, or with hunger, my lord: not with love.' "

A silence ensued: perhaps Thomasina was reading the omitted speech. Christina prompted her again: "Your turn, Don Pedro."

"Yes, I see. 'Well if ever thou dost fall from that faith, thou wilt prove a notable argument.' "

Jessamine read Benedict's harmless retort, and Thomasina, with more confidence in her voice, replied, "Well, as time shall try, in time the savage bull doth bear the yoke.' "

Then Jessamine: " 'The savage bull may, but if ever the sensible Benedict bear it—' "

Christina stopped her. "That is enough. Omit down to Don Pedro's next." There was the sound of turning pages. Thomasina said, "But the next speech is Claudio's."

"*Skip* it."

"Very well." Thomasina was growing resentful. "If 'horn-mad' means anything to you: 'Nay if Cupid have not spent all his quiver in Venice, thou wilt quake for this shortly.' "

"That's it. The rest of the scene is clear sailing. I hope you have marked the words and passages to be omitted. Thomasina—"

Anne rose from her fireside rocker. "They're almost through. I must get back."

The two men smiled at each other behind her back. Sam rose too. "Thomasina will be ready to go. You know those passages Mrs. Voorhees cut were completely obscure to her."

John laughed. "To most of the ladies, I reckon. But Mrs. Voorhees had to know, so that she can shield the others. She can come to no harm, of course: she is one of the elect. Poor mangled Shakespeare!"

After that evening the members of the Woman's Club gave themselves over to rehearsals, the making of costumes, and various other preparations for the presentation of "Scenes from *Much Ado About Nothing*" at the Rausches' home on Saturday evening the nineteenth of December, before an audience that would be composed of non-acting members, all attached gentlemen, and such other guests as might be invited. Constant evening rehearsals meant the disruption of various Waynesboro households and the discomfort of various family men. Husbands of longtime Club members were accustomed to these flurries of activity; most of them shrugged their shoulders and let the ladies have their fun. Younger, newer ones murmured, more in amazement than in exasperation, as when Gib said to his father-in-law, "You'd think this was the most important event of the year: Elsa can hardly think of anything else."

"You'll get used to it, my boy. And I wouldn't say it wasn't worth it. Wait till you see."

"And there's poor Ariana—"

"You were in school with Ariana, weren't you? You know, I wouldn't say this to Sally or Elsa, but I wouldn't be surprised if the ladies weren't keeping their fingers crossed. If Ariana were to die now, their fun would be spoiled."

This had some truth in it. Except for Thomasina, Club members were not sparing much thought for Ariana: they were concentrating on learning lines, entrances and exits, and other stage business. Poor Mrs. McKinney, who had been pressed into service to act Borachio along with Mrs. Maxwell's Conrade, proved to be as incapable as Mrs. Ballard had ever been of memorizing: whatever part she played, she would need the book in her hand. She asked to be allowed to change parts with Amanda (Borachio had more lines, and many of the scenes with Don John could be cut or eliminated entirely). Elizabeth, who had looked forward to seeing Amanda as prime villain, must perforce be content to see the part in the hands of the stolid Mrs. McKinney. Elizabeth managed the rehearsals, but not as efficiently as she might have liked: the ladies talked so much and laughed so hard, accomplished so little, seemingly, yet were advanced in intimacy by shared labors and shared laughter, so that there would always be that bond. Charlotte Bonner, for instance, who had been a member for so short a time and had not before been well known to many, doubled them up with her portrayal of Dogberry; and with little Mrs. Evans as Verges, the spectacle was enough to delight the most critical. No one had ever doubted that Charlotte had a fine mind, but that there was so much humor in her, that she could be so unselfconscious in playing the fool, came as something of a surprise. In an earlier day she would have been called a bluestocking; now in the minds of fellow Club members, she was a "scholar," and who could expect a scholar to be funny? And so Charlotte was taken to their hearts as she might not have been for years.

It was Charlotte, too, who never failed to inquire of Thomasina as to

Ariana's condition, and it was through her (after all, she worked for the newspaper) rather than through Thomasina that the ladies learned that two of Ariana's brothers had come to see her.

Shocked dumb at the sight of her, there had been little they could say and nothing they could do except sit beside her for a few minutes at a time. Matt, who remembered Ariana better that Mark could and whose heart bled for her, was the one who had the courage to speak to Mark and Ruhamah about what they all knew was coming.

"Ariana should be buried beside Mamma. Poor Ariana! Mamma loved her best, and none of this would have happened if she had lived."

"Papa would never permit it."

"Ruhamah, he isn't here. He doesn't care that she is dying. I told him she was. By what right—? He won't want to be buried here. He has another wife to be buried beside."

"He bought the lot. He has the deed. He would have to give his permission."

Matt clenched his teeth until the muscles around his jaws were stiff. "He will give his permission, then. I'll see to it, if I have to blackmail him with the threat of spreading the story around his presbytery. No man of God dare be so unforgiving." He relaxed a little. "Don't worry, Ruhamah. I'll see him on my way back to Sweetwater."

For Matt could not stay in Waynesboro: he had a congregation to minister to. Mark the farmer, who had little to do in the winter so long as someone tended his livestock, stayed on, still at the Voorheeses'. Having the boys there revived Ariana for a brief while. Before Matt left, Dr. Gordon assured him that there was time still: he could go back to his charge; he could be sent for. Ben could only come up from Cincinnati on Sundays. Mark gave way to him, somewhat grudgingly, since he had never understood why Ariana had run away, unless she had been enticed into an elopement. One Sunday afternoon when John came into Ariana's room, he found Ben still there, holding Ariana's hand; he looked surly and ill-tempered, an expression that John was sure was assumed to hide any other emotion. When he looked up and saw John, his brow cleared..

"Shouldn't I stay, Doctor? I want to be here if she needs me."

John shook his head. It was quite clear that Ben, who had clung to hope beyond all reason, had at last admitted to himself the truth. "Not now," John said softly. "She's a little better miraculously. I won't disturb her—she's asleep. I'll let you know. And don't worry about a place to stay overnight if you want to; we have a spare bedroom on the first floor, bathroom and all. You'll be welcome to use it."

Ariana hung on through the early weeks of December. The Woman's Club of Waynesboro presented "Scenes from *Much Ado About Nothing*" in the Rausch parlor, to the great delight of a predominantly masculine audience, whose mirth, exhibited in shouts of laughter, not always at the most appropriate moment, seemed to some of the cast rather excessive. Others of the actors, who appreciated the absurdity of the performance, let themselves go and threw themselves into their parts with real abandon: the Dogberry-Verges scenes brought down the house. By the time the play was ended, the actors divested of their costumes and properly dressed once more, and prepared to sit down to one of Sally's feasts, a great deal of laughter had cleared the air; discontent with the present and disquiet as to the future had been wiped from any mind harboring them, and the pleasure of laughing together had brought all—husbands, guests, cast—into at least temporary communion with one another. Over the years the ladies of the Club had grown confident enough of their power to entertain that they did not hesitate to invite guests as well as husbands to their plays: Mrs. Bonner and Charlotte's brothers were there, the Douglas Gardiners, invited by Mrs. Tim Merrill, Sheldon Edwards, invited by Jessamine Stevens, and Dr. and Mrs. Warren as Anne's guests. They were seated for dinner as they had been since the Club had been enlarged: as many as possible at Sally's table, drawn out to its greatest length; the rest at card tables set up in the back parlor and the library. Club members and their guests were put together, and single females scattered among them: Amanda Reid with the Bonners, Eliza with the two senior Evanses and their son Owen, home for Christmas. At Ludwig's insistence, Sally had put Elsa and Gib at the dining room table: he had seen nothing of Elsa for weeks, he had complained. It was because she was sitting at his right hand that she heard a piece of news there would have been no other chance to hear, perhaps on that particular evening.

Elsa had looked her father over as he took his place at the head of the table: she thought him still the most impressive looking man she knew, in spite of the thickening of his waistline and the scattering of gray in his blonde hair.

"You look happier than I've seen you looking in a long while," she said in an undertone as she leaned toward him. "It isn't just that you laughed so hard at us, is it?"

"Schöne Elsa, warum nicht? Es ist ein fröhlicher Abend gewesen—"

"Papa, don't be provoking."

"Rausch Cordage Company ends the year in the black. Does that satisfy you?"

"For the moment. I knew you had been worried." Elsa looked down the table to her mother's right: Gib had been of some use, then—he must have been. Papa hadn't made a place for him just— She broke off her thought and turned to Douglas Gardiner, sitting on her other side.

The Christmas play once off their minds, the members were able to pay more attention to what was going on around them, to think of their family Christmases, and after the twenty-fifth was past, of the usual round of church, afternoon calls, good works—and of Ariana McCune. The year was not out before Dr. Gordon told Ruhamah that she had better send for Matt again; he himself sent a telegram to Ben in Cincinnati. When he came directly from the train to the office, John took him home and turned him over to Anne, who made him welcome and showed him the downstairs bedroom.

"Being downstairs, you won't disturb us coming and going. I'll give you a front door key; then if you want to sit with Ariana through the night, or half of it, you can."

He was not in Waynesboro long. Ariana died quietly one night, too spent for any final struggle; he was with her, and so was Eliza, but there were no last words, no conscious glances even. Both felt lost, as if there should have been something, some word, some recognition.

Ben and Ariana's brothers stayed until after the funeral. Eliza and Thomasina would have had her buried on their family lot, near the imposing monument to Judge Ballard, but they could not dispute the right of the McCunes and Ben to make their own decision. Matt had came back to Waynesboro with the deed to the McCune lot; Ruhamah would have questioned him, but that he looked so grim when she opened her mouth to ask.

"It's a big lot," he said, when he handed her the paper. "I suppose Papa thought we'd all be buried there. Now I think he blames Mamma, in his twisted mind, for Ariana's being Ariana. He doesn't want to be buried there himself. So there'll be room for you, Ruhamah and for Ben, if he wants it. He has most of his life ahead of him, and who knows—?"

After the funeral was over, and the black-draped hearse and the few carriages had driven away in the sleet, slush, and mud of the miserable year-end weather, Matt and Ben encountered each other in the doctor's office. They had come with the same question: How much was owed to him still? John denied any debt. "Ben's been sending me money right along. You don't either of you owe me a thing. The undertaker, of course—"

"I've taken care of that," Ben said harshly, "I'll pay him off: we've agreed on terms."

"You should let Eliza help. I know she wants to," John argued.

"No, she has done enough. Ariana was my wife."

"It was good of you," Matt said, eyeing Ben uncertainly, "to agree to having her buried beside Mamma. Will you let me buy the headstone?"

"You know," Ben said slowly, "Ariana and I got along fine; we had fun together until she got sick. But I always knew. She was a little girl when her mother died, but she couldn't let her die: she cared more for her memory even when she was a woman grown than she ever did for me. Yes, I don't mind if you put up the headstone, one like her mother's." They all thought of the plain worn sandstone slab that marked the grave of the first Mrs. McCune.

Matt, flushed and angry, burst out, "I could buy a better one than that. Papa could have—"

Ben shook his head. "I like it. Just her name and the dates. And maybe if I don't live so long that I forget her— Of course I'll never forget her, I don't mean that. Someday—"

Matt said, "You would like to lie beside her on the other side? You have earned the right, if you still want it when the time comes. You've been better to Ariana than her own family."

"I was her family."

"I know. I didn't mean it that way. Papa is a cruel man. He killed two good women as surely as if he had shot them."

"Now, Matt," John said, to quiet him, "you know you don't mean that. Don't you believe their deaths were foreordained?"

Matt was silenced. Ben said, "Well, I don't."

"They were, you know. Whether you call it foreordained or heredity, their deaths were predestined: they were born with that susceptibility. There are always ifs, of course. If their lives had been different—but I think they would not have escaped. And you boys must watch for infection you may have picked up; go to a doctor and have an examination in a few weeks. And Matt, if you have children, watch them."

Ben Mercer and the McCune brothers left Waynesboro; Ariana soon would have been forgotten in her native town had it not been for Ruhamah and Eliza, who returned to work after the funeral still looking wan, haggard, and old. When she appeared in Ludwig's office to announce her presence, he eyed her sympathetically.

"You have been through a dreadful ordeal, Eliza. You should have stayed home until you were rested."

"I'm better off working. No time to think."

"She was fortunate in having you to come to."

"I was the fortunate one. For once in my life, helping someone—I was fond of."

"Now you're being foolish. You were the right hand of your father and mother."

"I was fond of them, of course. But if I hadn't been, it would still have been my duty. This was different."

"Pure altruism, you mean?"

"I said 'someone I was fond of.' It wasn't altruism at all. I was happy doing what I could for Ariana. And she did turn to me."

Eliza could not bring herself to say that there had been love given and love returned; "love" was not a word frequently on her tongue. But Ludwig understood what she felt and would not say.

"I still think you need rest, but if you would rather work, here are these letters to be answered."

Ludwig was not as hopeful in January as he had been before Christmas; true, Rausch Cordage Company surprisingly had made money in a year that had been very difficult; he could take care of the company's notes as they fell due, but he could not restore the company's reserve capital as well. The usual dividends must be paid to the Cincinnati cousins who had inherited their father's Rausch Company stock; his own dividends must be held for "cash assets," to pay debts, purchase raw material, carry the insurance on a warehouse full of unsold rope and binder twine—a thousand things.

And the National Cordage Company, the value of whose stock had risen to 142 on the market in December, had now in January paid a one hundred percent stock dividend. Ludwig's first thought when he read the brief notice on the *Enquirer*'s financial page, was the well-worn platitude "Whom the Gods would destroy." For a moment he was fired with the idea of taking a gamble: if he were to sell National Cordage Company stock short at its present inflated value, he might make a lot of money; on the other hand, if its price was pushed up even for a short time, he might be called on to cover. Ludwig was not by nature a gambler; he took no chance except where he himself by hard work and good judgment could control the outcome: Rausch Cordage Company; the Columbus and Cincinnati Electric Interurban Line. He couldn't really know that the National Cordage Company was not making enough money to justify their high-flying financing. He smiled to himself as he thought of what his father-in-law would have said to selling any stock short: Charles Cochran's investments had been in bank stock, the W. W. Railroad, and government bonds; he would never have thought of gambling on the Stock Exchange. No, the National Cordage Company could head for disaster without help from Ludwig Rausch: he would hold on to Rausch Cordage Company, a going concern.

He turned his thoughts to the future management of the company. Bodien and he were growing no younger. There might be someone in the mill who could follow Bodien as superintendent; he was more doubtful as to his own successor. Gib Evans was by this time knowledgeable enough about rope and about his customers to be fairly successful in selling it, considering the competition he had to meet: that contract he had obtained with the biggest wholesale house in Chicago had been a godsend. But whether Gib had the strength and decisiveness to manage the mill he questioned. His own two older sons obviously had not been gifted with the acumen for business or finance, and they had little interest in the manufacture of rope. This lack confounded Ludwig, who never went into the mill without feeling horizons opened, his imagination fired. Cables and hawsers; lake ships, river barges, seagoing vessels even; lariat rope: cowboys under the bluest of western skies; binder twine: his mind's eye saw the great grain fields of the prairie states, the ripe grain billowing for miles in the summer breeze; transmission ropes for the country's drive wheels; and for the swiftly developing oil wells. But the boys were simply not interested. As to Ludwig Junior: he might grow up to be more responsible than seemed likely at the present time; now he cared for nothing but his frolics and his music. It was a pity that of them all only Elsa had the right and proper qualities for running a business; it might be that her son (Ludwig was sure that the child she was carrying would be a son) would take after her rather than Gib, but to wait for a grandson to grow up would mean many years of keeping his own shoulder to the wheel. At any rate, he thought, for the time being he was in excellent health—the prime of life, really—and quite able to fight the National Cordage Company: it would be in his day, not his son's or his grandson's, that that battle must be won.

He did nevertheless let slip to Elsa one night when she was dining at home a brief expression of what had been on his mind. He had been talking of business in general: the growing financial stringency, the difficulties of raising money. He said, "Too bad you weren't a boy, Elsa. You could have taken over."

Elsa thought with sick disappointment, "Then he doesn't believe Gib—" She said reproachfully, "You know you don't mean that, just when I'm about to present you with a grandchild. Ludwig the third."

"Schöne Elsa, of course I don't mean it. Es freut mich sehr solch eine Tochter zu haben."

"Danke schön—aber—"

"Tut," Sally said, out of habit, from the other end of the table. "In English, please."

"I was going to say, Papa doesn't need to think of a successor for a long while yet. And he has four sons. He doesn't need to wish that I were one. I am quite satisfied with my sex."

"I am glad to hear it," her mother said drily. "There was a time when you weren't, I seem to remember."

It was quite true that Elsa was "satisfied"—more than that, she was happy in a quiet sort of way: she hoped and believed that Gib had felt no lack in his life with her; she was confident that with his child in her arms, there would be no lack.

But when she had first suspected that she was pregnant, she had gone to senior Dr. Gordon rather than to Johnny. As he ushered her into his office, she said, "I know you don't like to take obstetrical cases now Johnny's with you, but—"

He grinned at her, standing above her in the examining chair. "You think you are pregnant? What do you expect when you begin fooling around with the boys?"

"Uncle Dock! Here I come to you all starry-eyed and sort of uplifted—"

"And you want me to deliver your baby? What Johnny lacks in experience he makes up for in modern techniques."

"Please, Uncle Dock! I have known Johnny all my life. It would embarrass me to have him know me that way."

"I see." But he looked bewildered. Elsa thought Aunt Anne would understand, as he plainly did not. However, he agreed to take her case, and sent her away with sensible advice. "Don't take to your bed or sofa just because six months from now you are going to have a baby. You're a perfectly healthy young animal: live your normal life; don't get all skittish and vaporish and make Gib miserable because he thinks he's responsible. You're as responsible as he is."

"Of course. And we're both tickled to death to *be* responsible." But as she left his office, she wondered whether most of the pregnant women he encountered were "skittish" or whether he was thinking of Johnny and his Julia; she was happy enough in her own situation to hope that Johnny was not miserable, being made to feel "responsible."

It was true that Julia, nearing her time late in February or early in March, was making everyone around her suffer. But only her father was properly sympathetic, babying her in spite of his revulsion at the sight of her swollen body. To her mother, who had warned her of the unpleasant side of married life, she wailed, "Why didn't you tell me? This—this bloat—this awkwardness—I wish it were over." And her mother would reply, "Don't be silly, Julia. Other women before you have had babies: it is hardly an extraordinary condition." To Johnny, even when she was in his arms, Julia would make the same complaint: "Oh, how I wish this were over! I loathe myself every time I look in a mirror," and there would come the reply, "Then don't look in a mirror. To me you have never been more beautiful, but don't worry: you will soon be my slender Julia again, wasp waist and all." Johnny did not mean to be unfeeling: he considered that he must keep her in good heart, therefore he made little of her fears, light of her discomfort. But he himself was apprehensive almost beyond endurance: she was so small-boned, so delicate of frame, and women did die in childbirth. When her hour came and he turned her over to her doctor, he would have left the room: he did not think he could bear to see her suffer. She would not let him go. "No—no, Johnny! Hold my hand. If anything goes wrong, I want you here."

"Nothing is going wrong, Julia. Hold my hand if you like, the tighter the better. I'll be right here. It will be over soon now."

It was not over for long hours, agonizing hours, in spite of the chloroform she had been given; when the child was finally delivered, Julia was completely limp, a beaten animal, all her fair hair in a tangled mass from grinding it into the pillows. Johnny was hardly better: his face was wet with sweat; he felt racked and spent. Only Dr. Warren and the midwife were normal, pursuing their routines to completion. When the midwife laid the squirming mite in Johnny's arms, he drew a long breath and checked this baby, his son, as he had many another: ten fingers, ten toes, no defects, not even any birthmarks. He returned the baby to the midwife, who had in the interval tended Julia: washed her, straightened the bedclothes. "Just let her sleep now. When she wakes up rested, I'll get her fixed up."

But Julia made one last effort before she slipped off into into a drugged sleep: she reached for Johnny's hand; he leaned over and kissed her.

"It's all right, Julia. It's all over and we have a nice baby, perfectly whole and normal. A son."

"Oh? I had hoped for a girl." But Julia was not yet very much interested in the baby. "Johnny, if I'd known! Promise me—not any more."

Johnny caught his breath. "I wouldn't have you go through this again. I promise: not any more."

"Now that's rubbish," the midwife said, cheerful and bustling. "You know in a couple of years you'll be ready for another. You'll have forgotten all about this."

Julia opened her eyes, dull with drugs and exhaustion, and stared at her. "I won't forget. Neither will Johnny."

Dr. Warren, who had been standing looking down at the baby where the midwife had laid it in the crib, turned and said, "She'll be all right when she's had some rest. And the baby's fine. Hadn't we better tell her folks?"

"Of course. And I must call Mom, too."

When they went out, the sound of the bedroom door closing reached the sitting room downstairs; General and Mrs. Deming came into the hall. The General was half staggering, a man who had been sitting for hours with every muscle tense; he gripped the newel post and looked up at them.

"Is it—? Is she—? I never heard such screaming."

"She's perfectly all right. The baby is born, a healthy boy. She had had enough chloroform not to know she was screaming."

"She wasn't suffering, then?"

"Of course she was suffering. Ask your wife. But not nearly so much as you probably thought. Let her sleep for a while: Mrs. Milburn will call you when she is ready for you, then you can go up to see her and her son."

"A grandson!" The General's cramps had let go; he stood back from the newel post. "Is he all right?"

"He's fine. I have seen a number of newborn babies, you know. There isn't anything missing: he has all his fingers and toes, sound lungs—didn't you hear him?" Johnny, who had at that moment been thinking only of Julia, remembered now that first thin wail. "It won't be long before you can go up and see him. I must go call my mother: she will be anxious."

The General said, "What, no cigars? Come in, Doc Warren, and let me give you one." He had recovered his jauntiness.

Mrs. Deming, leading the way into the sitting room, thought, "Men! All alike. Once it is over they think it hasn't amounted to much: all that fuss over nothing. But Julia won't forget: not Julia, whatever they say about nature blotting the pain out of a woman's memory, to ensure her willingness." She was right: Julia did not forget. Neither, however, did Johnny.

The baby was duly baptized, in the Presbyterian church: Julia had followed her husband into his denomination, even though he was not much of a church-goer. Alexander Tucker Gordon. Julia, who had counted on a girl, had determined to name her for her two grandmothers: Anne Louise. The best she could do with a boy was to give him his grandmothers' family names. Johnny had not argued about the name: another John would be altogether too confusing. He hoped that his mother would not be hurt because Julia was already calling him "Tuck," although "Alex" would have done, however much of a mouthful "Alexander" would have been. Anne, like most grandmothers, fell in love with the baby, and spent a good deal of her time in Johnny's apartment while Julia was still in bed. Julia was nursing the baby: Anne thought with some amusement that she was now the Loving Mother rather than the Dutiful Wife. She had recovered her slim figure, her beauty, and her normal good health by the time she was out and about again. The midwife would stay with them until they found a colored nursemaid who could be trusted with the baby; in the meantime Julia took the child with her where she could. She and Johnny brought him along one afternoon when they had been asked to the older Gordons' for the afternoon and the evening meal.

"Isn't he a love?" Julia demanded, indicating the baby in Johnny's arms, so bundled up in long flannel cloak, tight bonnet, and all-enveloping blanket that it was impossible to see whether he was or not, unless one could judge by a vaguely waving hand that had worked loose.

Anne took him from her son. "Let me, Johnny. I'll take his cloak and bonnet off."

"I know you didn't especially ask us to bring him: but he has to be fed presently."

John had come in by the time the baby began to fret about his supper. Anne might be amused by Julia's latest picture of herself; John was disgusted when without so much as turning her chair, much less retiring to another room, Julia took the baby in her arms, unbuttoned her bodice, and bared her breast for the baby to suck. Her father-in-law picked up the evening paper and ostentatiously held it between himself and the revolting spectacle. Anne dared not smile: she thought Julia and the baby gurgling at her breast made a beautiful picture, and was well aware that Julia thought so too. She wished that John would behave himself, and not flap the paper around as he was doing to call attention to his disapproval: he must long since have read everything in those two pages of the *Torchlight*. But he did not lower it by an inch until after Julia had turned the baby over to Anne with a "There you are, Tuckems—go with grandmamma. He'll go to sleep now if you put him down on the spare room bed. Leave the door open so we can hear him, just in case. Now, in just a second," the sweet voice was soft and complacent, "I'll be all properly buttoned up again."

John looked over his paper cautiously, found that she had made herself decent, folded the paper and laid it aside. "What was that you called him? 'Tuckems'?"

"It is just a baby-talk name. Of course we'll call him Tucker. It will be a distinctive name."

Anne, returning from putting the baby down and covering him, picked up the discarded newspaper, laid it down on the center table on top of the clutter that had collected there in the course of the day, and said, "Louline's getting dinner on the table. We might as well go on out."

After dinner John left them to keep his office hours; Johnny would join him after he had taken his wife and baby home. It was late that night before John and Anne had any chance to talk over the evening: he came in to find her already in bed, lying straight on her back, propped up on pillows, Bible in hand, thick neat plaits over her shoulders, and looking far too young to be a grandmother. John undressed in a grumpy silence quickly, leaving everything where he could put his hand on it easily if he was called out. It was only when he lay down beside her that he said, "What did you think of that disgusting spectacle?" Anne did not answer for a moment; he could feel her shaking with laughter. "Did you think it was *funny*?"

"Oh, John! I think *you* are funny! You have looked at hundreds of women's breasts without a quiver."

"The breast of a patient is a piece of her anatomy, diseased or whole. But to see a woman nurse her baby in public, like a savage— And Julia has always been so prim and proper!"

"You could hardly call just in the family 'in public.' They made a lovely picture, and Johnny was so proud and tender."

"I hope I made it clear it was a picture I didn't care for?"

"Perfectly clear."

"She could very well have gone in the bedroom to nurse that baby. It was posed for our benefit. It was disgusting. Doesn't she know we're not *all* in love with her?"

"It wasn't for our benefit. She was being the perfect mother she sees herself as. And, no: I don't think she realizes we are not all in love with her. She has always been the center of her world: she can't see herself otherwise." Then Anne changed the subject. "Sally dropped in after lunch. She says Elsa is sure her baby will be a boy. Sally hopes she's right: the two boys would grow up together, then, and be friends, the third generation."

It was true that Sally Rausch hoped that her first grandchild would be a boy, but not exactly for the reason she had given; she had kept the more important reason to herself, and the burden of it was "Not again a Gordon in love with a Rausch, or a Rausch (Evans) in love with a Gordon, requited or unrequited."

Elsa's child was born late in the spring without fuss or undue suffering, though Gib, home for the ordeal, took it hard. That baby, too, was a boy, to everyone's delight and Sally's relief: Ludwig Evans. "Ludwig" was a name so familiar to the tongue of all concerned that it occurred to no one that it went oddly with "Evans."

In the meantime, in the winter and early spring, momentous events, to Ludwig at least, had taken place in the nation and on Wall Street. The President, duly inaugurated on the fourth of March, called in his inaugural address for repeal of the Sherman Act; he also spoke of the need to reduce the tariff, but in terms so vague that it was impossible to know what he would ask of Congress when it met. The address left an already shaken Wall Street shakier still. There was no doubt but that the compulsory coinage of silver under the Sherman Act was undermining government finances: treasury notes and silver dollars issued every month according to the law were being promptly turned in and exchanged for gold. The Treasury was being drained at an alarming rate. Panic was in the air. The National Cordage Company, which had always paid the necessary eight percent on its preferred stock, and as high as ten on the common, in the spring of 1893 found itself in great difficulty, even as Ludwig had foreseen. Its enormous debts to the banks, in the shape of demand loans and short-term paper borrowed on its immense inventory of rope, binder twine, and raw material, fell due, and two million five hundred dollars in new preferred stock was offered to the public, so that the notes could be paid. But the directors had misjudged the temper of the market. The shares moved slowly, and the price of both preferred and common stock dropped heavily to almost nothing. The company's paper borrowed on its inventory was dishonored: that meant bankruptcy. On the fourth of May a receiver was appointed.

Ludwig had expected it, had even wanted it, he admitted to himself. Nevertheless, he was glad he had not taken part in its downfall by short-selling its stock. But after a moment's thought, apprehension returned.

Sally was surprised by his solemn demeanor when he came home from the mill that Thursday afternoon. He saluted her with the newspaper before he came into the room to give her the conjugal evening kiss.

"You saw the news?" he asked her. "The National Cordage Company has failed."

"I saw it. I thought you'd be dancing the street. What—? I thought your troubles would be over."

"Sally, to rejoice in anyone's failure is not good. Think of all the stockholders and the laborers. Some of the individual companies in the association may be able to survive as independents, though I doubt it. It is true that we can breathe a little more easily: Rausch Cordage Company won't be harassed further by attempts to put us out of business." Ludwig sat down heavily in his big armchair, the paper on his knee. "But our troubles are far from over. The National Cordage Association has been overproducing for years—had to, to keep all its member companies at work. It was their enormous inventory of stored rope and binder twine that destroyed them in the end: they couldn't sell it; it was the collateral they had borrowed on, and they couldn't pay the notes when they fell due. What do you suppose will happen to all that rope?"

"It will be the property of their creditors, I suppose. I saw a receiver had been appointed. It will be sold."

"As rapidly as possible, for whatever it will bring. It will be thrown on the market and sold for a fraction of its value. National Cordage was one of the biggest trusts in the country; its failure is bound to set off a panic."

"Oh, Ludwig: not like the panic of the seventies?"

They both remembered all too vividly those difficult times. Ludwig said, "I hope not. I really don't think so: this will be a money panic. If we can get the Silver Act off the books, it may be over soon."

His hopes were not fulfilled. President Cleveland called an extra session of Congress in August of 1893, and the Sherman Act was repealed. But the economic condition of the country did not improve; the financial panic caused the failure of many industries, the closing of banks, and an increase in unemployment. To Ludwig the cause of the prolongation of hard times was crystal clear: Congress brought under debate an act to lower tariffs; while it was in the air, any importer would hold his hand in the hope of lowering his costs, and in the meantime, since the country depended on the tariff for revenue, it could not meet its budget; it was running into debt; every citizen who questioned its solvency demanded gold for his silver and for his paper money.

That the panic was fundamentally financial did not lessen its impact. Men were out of work; they saw no one to blame but their employers; they went on strike against large industries and small; there were criminal acts and even riots. Financiers and industrialists were shaken by labor's new truculence; they saw in it a dreadful portent of things to come: all those foreigners, those Hunkies and Polacks, were accustomed to violence in their home countries. Ludwig had reason to rejoice that his labor force was made up of the least volatile of men: except for the expert ropemakers and the mechanics of Rausch and Bodien, they were mostly Negroes, thankful to have jobs so long as bad weather lasted. Rausch Cordage continued to make rope and sell it for what they could get: they hung on and even managed to make a little money. But plans for a Rausch and Bodien Coated Paper Company were in abeyance for the time being; even Stewart Bodien, who being young was in a hurry, knew that it was no time to launch a new enterprise.

The wives of bankers and industrialists, businessmen, professional men, shop-keepers, read the newspapers, and they too, especially those old enough to remember the seventies, felt the cold finger of fear at the back of their necks. But they had after all other things to think of, and life went on through the summer of 1893 much as it had always done in spite of hard times.

Sally Rausch, President of the Waynesboro Woman's Club, appointed a committee to prepare a Club program for the year 1893–94, reminding them that the first meeting in September would be the twenty-fifth anniversary of the Club's first meeting. The important event was duly honored by the committee: the meeting on Wednesday the sixth of September would be given over to two papers: one by Miss Amanda Reid: "Reminiscences of Twenty-Five Years"; one by Mrs. Anne Gordon: "Recollections of Our Departed Members." During the rest of the year, the program would deal with American poetry of the last twenty-five years. One day was set aside for a Christmas Program, and one, the last, for an anniversary dinner at the home of its President. When copies of the program were delivered at the homes of the ladies, they either sighed with regret because they must go to work at once, or with relief because their assignments were for the post-Christmas months, and they would not have to think of them for a long while, thank goodness. All the ladies agreed when they chanced to meet each other on Waynesboro's summer occasions, that it was an interesting program, and would be very rewarding: it was so important to keep abreast of contemporary literature. Only Sally Rausch and Eliza Ballard, aware of conditions throughout the country through their closeness to Rausch Cordage Company, wondered, Sally tolerantly and Eliza contemptuously, whether their friends read the newspapers or were able to understand them.

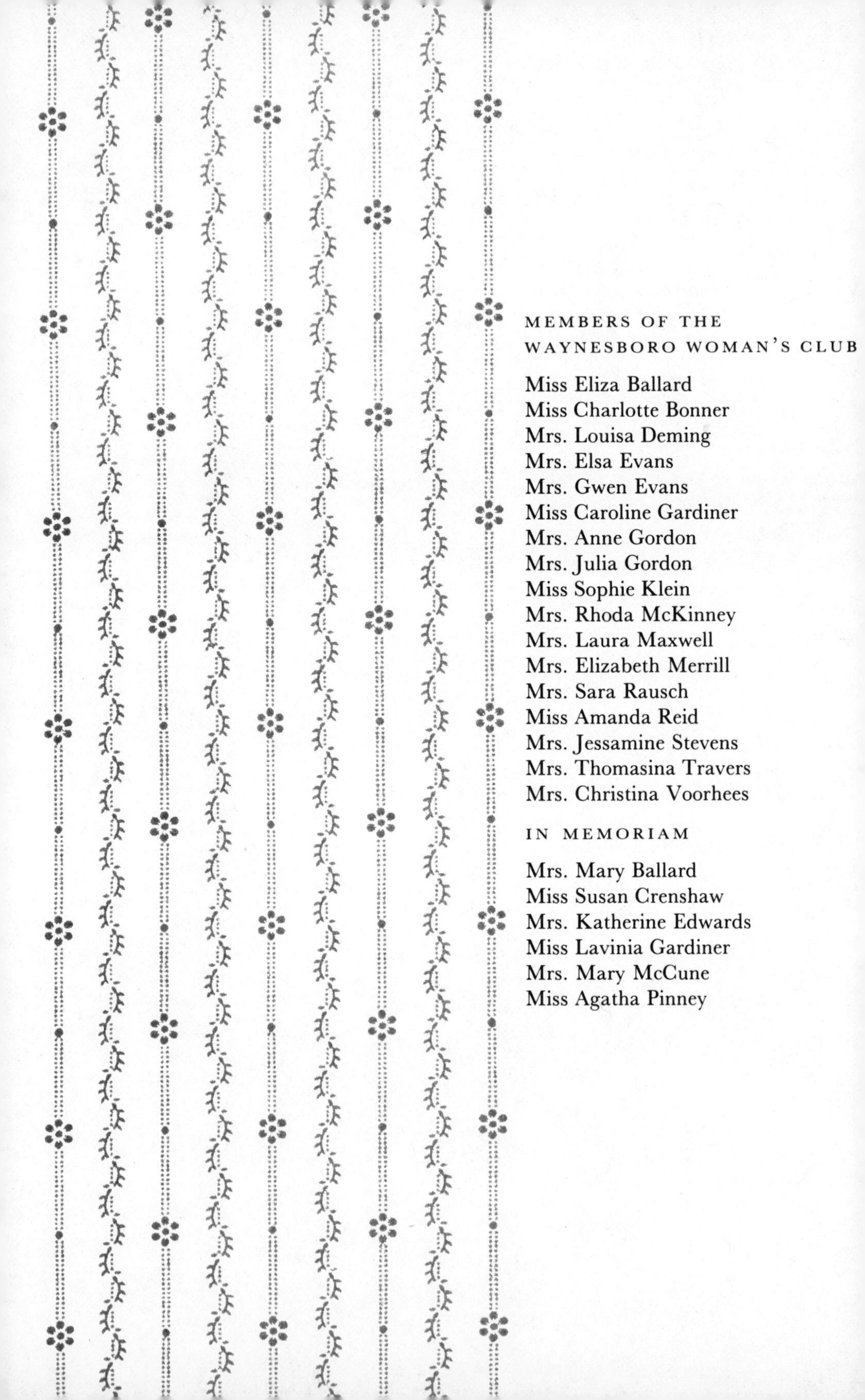

MEMBERS OF THE
WAYNESBORO WOMAN'S CLUB

Miss Eliza Ballard
Miss Charlotte Bonner
Mrs. Louisa Deming
Mrs. Elsa Evans
Mrs. Gwen Evans
Miss Caroline Gardiner
Mrs. Anne Gordon
Mrs. Julia Gordon
Miss Sophie Klein
Mrs. Rhoda McKinney
Mrs. Laura Maxwell
Mrs. Elizabeth Merrill
Mrs. Sara Rausch
Miss Amanda Reid
Mrs. Jessamine Stevens
Mrs. Thomasina Travers
Mrs. Christina Voorhees

IN MEMORIAM

Mrs. Mary Ballard
Miss Susan Crenshaw
Mrs. Katherine Edwards
Miss Lavinia Gardiner
Mrs. Mary McCune
Miss Agatha Pinney

* 1894–1895 *

"The Club extends sympathy . . . and offers congratulations . . ."

In early summer of 1894, Miss Lavinia Gardiner tripped over a rug in her upstairs sitting room, fell over a footstool, broke a rib, and developed pneumonia. For a time she was desperately ill; Dr. Gordon was in constant attendance, and when he saw the crisis approaching, arranged with Barbara to spend his nights until it was over, one way or the other, on the leather couch in the upstairs hall, snatching sleep when he could. The children were sent to the Bodiens', even quiet fourteen-year-old Lavinia, lest the sound of their feet on the stairs disturb the patient. Barbara's hands were full, even though the Misses Gardiner had their own maid and the doctor brought in one of the farm women who occasionally nursed his serious cases. John pulled Miss Lavinia through the crisis, or she pulled herself through. He never ceased to wonder at the stubbornness of poor, beaten human beings who held so determined a clutch on life, when one would have supposed that death would be welcome. Miss Lavinia would never completely recover. However, she did improve, and John went home to sleep nights. A great relief for him: in that upstairs apartment he had kept his eyes on his patient, his ears for her only; and his nose had grown accustomed to the revolting smell of unwashed old age living in unclean surroundings. He had many times found suddenly stricken patients who were filthy, but for the once fastidious Misses Gardiner to have sunk to such a state was proof of their deterioration. They couldn't be older than seventy-six or seventy-seven, but senility strikes at varying ages. While Miss Lavinia was helpless, the nurse could keep her bathed, in clean night clothes, and between clean sheets. John wished he could turn Mrs. Wilkins loose on Miss Caroline, who kept herself removed as far as possible from the sick bed. He warned the nurse to hold her tongue about the conditions she had found, and knew that she would, for, if she proved untrustworthy, he would not ask for her again. And if either he or Mrs. Wilkins had at first been inclined to blame Barbara, or even to wonder at her seeming neglect, they very soon learned that she was not responsible. Not even Douglas, let alone Barbara or any of the children, was permitted to enter the upstairs apartment, so far had the unhappy women carried their feud. If Douglas and Barbara suspected the state of affairs behind those locked doors, they were helpless to remedy them. Lutie, the housemaid and waitress, had been instructed to put the aunts' trays on the table outside their door. Fortunately for Barbara and the cook, they had always shared the family meals, their plates served by Doug at the dining room table. Not until Miss Lavinia's illness did there have to be special dishes prepared. One of the responsibilities of the aunts' maid was to take the trays in to them when Lutie tapped on their door, and when they had eaten, carry the dishes down to the kitchen. Her other duties were to keep the apartment clean and to see to their clothes. Since the aunts were indifferent about both matters, and resented being bothered, these duties were pretty well ignored.

John had never heard any talk about the Gardiner sisters: Doug's children must be very obedient or Doug a severe father (not impossible, John thought). Or they perhaps believed theirs a normal household. If they told things to their grandparents, the Bodiens were discreet. But John marveled: Waynesboro generally knew all there was to know, and more too. Before Miss Lavinia's accident the sisters had continued to make public appearances, at church and at the Woman's Club. Their doctor wondered how anyone could sit close to them: Anne had never peeped, but loyalty carried to an extreme was one of her virtues, and the Misses Gardiner were not only fellow Club members but fellow Presbyterians. Perhaps, however, the sisters washed their faces and necks for those public occasions. Strange, John thought one evening as he prepared to rise from his chair by the sick bed, how many forms the degenerative process could take: the Gardiner sisters had always been what Waynesboro called "nasty-nice," and now they could not be called "nice" at all. At the present moment he looked down at Miss Lavinia, drifting off to sleep; she was so clean as to look almost washed away: her pallor, her lank gray hair (what the fever had left of it), her blue-veined, paper-thin eyelids. It had been a triumph of sorts, he supposed, to have saved her. Mrs. Wilkins called it "God's will"; he thought a really merciful God would have snatched her out of his hands. When he had given the nurse instructions for the night, Miss Caroline ushered him out the door into the hall, and locked and bolted it behind him.

From the stairs, through the open front door, he could hear voices from the lawn: the children had been brought home, then. He stopped at the sitting room door to speak to their parents: he found Barbara alone; Doug had gone out somewhere. He paused only for a few words: "She'll do now, with good nursing. But this has put a great strain on her heart. She mustn't be allowed to exert herself. No, thanks: I can't stop: I must go help Johnny with office hours—no, don't get up: I can let myself out, and I know you're tired."

John went out into the dusk of a midsummer evening. The voices he had heard were coming from a group under the trees: Captain Bodien on a camp chair, children sprawled on the ground around him. Only little Mary was moving about, in pursuit of fireflies, so easily caught, so easily crushed in a small hot hand. The others were listening to Captain Bodien. John smiled: battle stories, no doubt; the same stories Johnny had listened to once, now undoubtedly grown even more dramatic with the passage of time. The size of the group indicated that not only the four Gardiners were there but also various friends, whatever boys and girls happened to be at loose ends on a summer evening too fine to be spent at home, indoors: Rodney Stevens he recognized, and Lowrey and Richard Edwards. Richy must be eight or nine. John felt sorry both for the boy and for his father; doctoring the brothers through their childhood diseases, he had seen that however conscientiously Sheldon endeavored to be the same to them both, one he loved, one he could hardly look at without a sense of guilt.

At the moment John need not have worried about Richy: the small boy was completely happy; his mind was full only of what he would do when he was grown up. Sheldon had taken both boys (never one without the other, anywhere, regardless of age) to hear the Reverend Dr. Maxwell lecture (for the Library Fund) on excavations in the Holy Land. Richy paid closer attention than did Lowrey: he was in fact enthralled. To dig and dig and find forgotten buried cities, to find the tools and things that showed how people had lived so many, many years ago: that was what he was going to do when he grew up. To Richy, at eight, fifty years and two or three thousand were indifferently "long ago." That evening in the Gardiner yard, he insisted on hearing about the Indians Captain Bodien had seen and fought against, and could not be quite convinced that the Captain had never seen a pueblo, where the cliff-dwellers had spent their lives. Captain Bodien knew nothing about Indians, except as fighting men. But Rodney Stevens (who also liked the Captain's stories of the Old West better than those of the Civil War) saved Richy from complete disappointment. "The cliff-dwellers were far away from here," he whispered, "but the mound-builders were all around, right here. There may even be a mound on the Gordon farm. Maybe we could dig into it, someday." All this low-voiced, so as not to interrupt the Captain. Richy, wide-eyed, whispered, "Will you wait for me? Just till I'm big enough to use a spade?" And Rodney whispered back, "I'll wait, I promise."

From his chair on the lawn, Captain Bodien had watched the doctor's departure. He finished the anecdote he had embarked upon and said, "That's all for tonight. It's Mary's bedtime. Come along, Snooks." He scooped her up, put her on his shoulder, and carried her to the steps, where he let her slide down. Hand in hand they mounted to the front door, opening the screen just in time to hear a sullen voice call from the top of the front staircase.

"Miz' Gya'dneh, yo' kin come git the trays now."

Captain Bodien was at the foot of the stairs before Barbara could get out of the living room. His face was scarlet, he was trembling with anger, his voice ominously level. To the little girl he said, "Go in with Mamma, honey," then to the Negress at the head of the stairs, "Were you speaking to my daughter?" She stared down at him in silence; he responded with a parade ground bark: "Answer me: were you speaking to my daughter?"

"Yes. Ah don' carry no trays."

"Yes, *sir*," he corrected her. She did not speak and he repeated himself. "Yes, *sir*."

"Yes, suh."

"Now, you pick those trays up, and take them down the back stairs to the kitchen."

"Ain' my job."

Barbara, in the doorway, said, "Papa, please."

He paid no attention, except to wave her back. "It is what you were hired for, to take care of those two ladies. What is your name?"

"Ef'n it's any yo' business: Abby Washin'ton."

"It is my business. It would be Mr. Gardiner's business if he were here, but he isn't. You Charley Washington's wife?"

"Yes—suh."

"You know that times are hard? That we have laid off hands this summer? Not Charley, yet. But if I were you, I'd try to hold on to my job. Now, go carry those trays down the back stairs."

"Papa—"

"You stay out of this. If you can't handle that triflin' impudent nigger, I can." He waited while Abby carried the trays along the upstairs hall toward the back stairs. Then he turned to Barbara. "Does Doug know this kind of thing goes on, you takin' orders from a maid?"

"Of course not. When he's home she's respectful enough, when she has occasion to come outside that locked door. And I don't tell him. It is too hard to get anyone."

"In times like these? Nonsense!"

"You don't know what the aunts are like to work for. And of course they put her up to this sort of thing, by example if not precept."

"If she quits, I'll find someone for you. She won't, believe me. Now go back to the sitting room: I want to talk to her."

Abby came flouncing back from the kitchen, then paused at the sight of him still standing by the newel post.

"I want a word with you, Abby Washington. Hereafter you are to treat Mrs. Gardiner with respect, or out you go."

"She don't hieh me, she cain' fieh me."

"Her husband can, and will, if I tell him what has been going on here. You are maid to the Misses Gardiner?"

"Yas, suh."

"You are expected to keep their apartment clean, take care of their clothes, look after them?"

"Yas, suh."

"You don't earn a nickel of your money. Every time their door is opened, the whole house stinks."

Abby rolled her eyes. "They don' lak me to clean. They cain' be bothered to clean theyselves."

"Then you bother. You take care of those two old ladies: do the work you're paid for. Now, you get back up there, and hereafter, you carry the trays down—down the back stairs. And if you don't turn over a new leaf, out you go."

Abby scuttled past him and slipped up the stairs. Captain Bodien went into the living room. Barbara was alone, slumped in a rocker; he thought she was weeping, but pretended not to notice.

"Where's Mary?"

"Lutie's putting her to bed tonight. It's just that all of a sudden everything seems too much."

"Barbie, I know you have to put up with the aunts, but with insolent servants, no."

"Don't say anything to Doug, will you, Papa? He has enough without—"

"I gave that nigger a dressing down she'll remember, I hope. At least she'll remember she'd better keep her job in case her husband doesn't."

"That sounds almost like blackmail. You wouldn't—?"

"We're laying off men because we have to, not because we want to. Charley's a good workman: we'll keep him as long as we can. But you don't need to tell her so. It's a pity Dock pulled Miss Lavinia through."

"Oh, Papa! Don't say that! He spent nights on that lumpy old couch."

"Barby, you haven't had an easy time, I know. If you could have foreseen this—have you ever been sorry?"

"Sorry?"

"You married Doug?"

"Doug? Oh, Papa! Of course not." She was round-eyed with astonishment. "I never expected married life would be all sugarplums. Doug and I have been happy together for all these years. And the girls are our joy and delight. The only thing is, sometimes I wish he weren't so bent on making little old ladies of them."

"Otherwise, he's perfect?" Captain Bodien laughed, his ruffled temper finally soothed. "Don't worry about the girls. They may be little ladies in the company of adults, but believe me, when they are with the other children they are exactly like them—as noisy as the Edwards boys."

"You are a comfort to me, Papa. I don't know that I exactly want them to be noisy. Sheldon does: if the boys aren't making a racket, he thinks there's something wrong."

"Odd he never married again, all these years."

"Sheldon? Oh, no. He has Kitty's sons. Maybe when they're grown up and gone, for company."

Her father dismissed the subject. "Where is Doug this evening?"

"Some conference with Mr. Rausch. About the paper mill." Her mind went to her brother. "How's Stewart? When does he get home with his bride?"

"Next week, I believe." The Captain spoke a little sharply. Proud as he was of Stewart, and pleased that the boy was devoted to his mother, he could not understand how anyone so intelligent could have remained a devout Catholic, even as a grown man. Now he had married an Irish Catholic girl who had grown up in Waynesboro's West End. Captain Bodien changed the subject again. Their conversation became desultory until the Captain rose to go. Barbara went with him to the gate, where she bade him good-night, noting as she returned that some of the children, three boys and three girls, were still sitting cross-legged in the grass. It was early: she needn't call her daughters in quite yet, since they seemed not to be bothered by the mosquitoes. She slapped at one herself, and hurried into the hall, closing the screen door firmly behind her. By the time Douglas got home, she had decided to say nothing of her father's dressing down of Abby; she made it a habit to spare him domestic difficulties whenever possible. Instead of talking about her evening, she spoke about her brother.

"Papa says Stewart will be back in another week. He and his Kathleen will stay at home with Papa and Mamma until they go to Madison City to start the Rausch and Bodien Paper Company. I'll be glad when they can move away. Kathy is as nice a girl as she is pretty, and Mamma is happy at last, with Stewart married to a good Catholic, certain to produce good Catholic grandchildren. But her father is just a foreman in the machine shop." Barbara trembled on the verge of saying, "And in Waynesboro she'll always be just a laborer's daughter." She bit it back, lest Douglas wonder whether she thought herself dismissed as "just a mill superintendent's daughter." She continued: "The trouble is, she has a passel of cousins that are pure shanty Irish. You can't even call the Hallorans 'lace curtain Irish.' And they'll be on Stewart's neck as long as he's here. Is Mr. Rausch hopeful of getting that paper mill started? Is that what you were conferring about tonight? I know that times are still so bad they're laying off hands at the ropewalk."

"Ludwig intends shortening their hours and cutting their pay instead of laying off more men: eight hours instead of ten for all of them, and five days a week instead of six. As for the paper mill, I don't know. Ludwig is itching to get started: blueprints have been drawn up, and Stewart has made some of the machinery in the shop here. But the country's finances are going from bad to worse. Gold is still draining from the Treasury in spite of the repeal of the Silver Act. The last government bonds issued had to be paid for with gold, but men who were willing to buy the bonds simply exchanged paper for gold at the banks, so that almost as much left the country's gold reserve as went in. When the gold is gone and there is only silver to back the paper money, the dollar won't be worth fifty cents. And labor grows more and more truculent. Look at the Pullman strike: begun in May and still going on, in spite of the President's troops."

"But you thought the President was right."

"Of course I did. The mails must go through, and a strike that disrupts railroad service can't be tolerated. But I also think George Pullman is a fool: putting his labor in company houses, cutting their pay without reducing their rent, and then refusing to meet with their leaders for a discussion of their grievances. It's the same all over the country. Ohio's been lucky so far: Governor McKinley is known to be a friend of labor. The only trouble here has been with the Stark County miners, and the Governor got National Guard companies there so fast that the violence was stopped without bloodshed. And the legislature has been cooperative: there's been that act fining employers for not permitting their laborers to join unions, and the industrial arbitration act. But our cities are filling up with Hungarians, Poles, Slavs, who are not averse to violence."

"But do you think Rausch Cordage will pull through?"

"Yes. Ludwig is a reasonable man who treats his men fairly. And he is lucky: the majority of them are unskilled, and Negroes to boot: the most docile, the least volatile. I doubt if they even mind being laid off in the summer. They garden, they catch fish, their wives work: it's a pleasant holiday for them. His trouble isn't with labor. It's a matter of sales and prices. The National Cordage Company almost ruined him. That failure triggered the panic."

"I know. Papa is eloquent on that subject. There isn't any money, then, for a new industry?"

"Ludwig won't take any profit that he makes selling rope for anything but restoring Rausch Cordage's cash reserves. But he must have made a lot out of the Columbus and Cincinnati Interurban. Ironic, isn't it? It seemed such a foolhardy enterprise in the beginning. There were those who thought it might cost him the ropewalk."

Waynesboro had grown accustomed to the interurban cars that had at first seemed so mammoth on quiet Chillicothe Street, and so noisy as they ground their way through town once every hour, bell clanging, wheels squealing, sparks flying from the trolley overhead. Citizens had also grown accustomed to using them. They might, and usually did, take the train to Columbus or to Cincinnati, although it cost more; but for shorter trips to towns or the hamlets that the trains bypassed or went through without stopping, the Interurban had become not only a convenience but a necessity. And a very profitable investment for its owners.

"I doubt," Douglas continued, "that he can bring himself to sell his C. & C. shares for capital for the paper company, but he can always borrow on them as collateral. Yes, to go back to your first question: he is going ahead with the construction of that mill."

"You think it will be all right? I'll be so glad for Stewart."

"I believe so," Doug answered slowly. "Ludwig counts on having capital enough to build the mill before the stock is issued and offered to the public. He hopes that by the time the building is ready the public will have money and be willing to invest it. Of course—I suppose I am too cautious: Ludwig would have got nowhere had he been unwilling to take a chance. A big mill building just might be an encumbrance on his hands: taxes can eat up a lot of money. But he reasons that in a depression the construction industry is hardest hit, since no one is willing to risk building a new factory or enlarging an old one, or even building a house. He figures he can get out-of-work builders, carpenters, hod carriers, bricklayers aplenty in Madison City. Stewart, as I said, has been making some of the machinery while things are slow in the rope business. With Ludwig backing him, he could build up a good machine tool business right here, without— However, there will be a paper mill, but not tomorrow. Conditions won't improve while Congress is still in session debating the tariff bill. When that matter is settled so American products are protected against cheap imports, the plant will be built. Ludwig asked me to join them tonight, not to advise him, but to explain to those he had assembled the course to be taken in the issuing of stock, and so on."

"Who else was there? I thought all this was to be kept so very quiet."

"Not at this point. We need publicity now, to prepare men's minds. Voorhees was there; I don't know why exactly, since Ludwig refuses to borrow money from the bank he's president of, and he won't touch his wife's bank stock, even as collateral. Voorhees may have money of his own to invest. Sheldon Edwards certainly does. Dock Gordon came in before we left. I don't know anything about his finances, or General Deming's."

"He was there? I never thought he was such a friend of Mr. Rausch. Of course they're in politics together. What was Mr. Rausch doing? Lining up prospective investors?"

"You don't have to like a prospective investor. However, Ludwig honestly thinks he is letting his friends in on the ground floor of something very good."

"And you?"

"I'll take a few shares. For Stewart's sake, and your father's. I daren't risk much. Somehow, General Deming didn't strike me as a very good prospect: tonight he was red in the face and thick around the ankles, and huffing and puffing like a man who's just run a race. And I saw Dock looking at him with what can only be described as a physician's eye. But he put himself down for some shares."

It was quite true that John was concerned about the General. He said so to Johnny one day in the office.

"I have noticed it too, Pop. He's an apoplectic subject if I ever saw one: arteriosclerosis, of course. He could have a coronary attack or a cerebral hemorrhage any day. I have done my best to persuade him to come in for an examination, which he pooh-poohs, or at least to cut down on his meals."

"How about his womenfolk? Haven't they any influence?"

"He worships the ground they walk on, but when it comes to good roast beef, no. Julia might persuade him, but the only time I tried to warn her, she refused to believe me. She just said, 'Oh, Johnny: Papa's always been like that—don't be doctoring all the time.' I believe she thinks he'll live forever."

Shortly after that, the blow fell. Johnny called one evening to say that the General had had a stroke: would his father come as soon as he could? Dr. Warren was there, but Julia had no faith in him.

John thumbtacked a note on the office door: "Called out. No office hours tonight," and set out for the Demings' on foot; those few blocks could be walked in less time than it would take to hitch up the horse."

The Deming front door was unlocked. He walked in to find Julia huddled close to the newel post, her fingers in her ears. From the bedroom down the hall came the sound of the General's breathing, dreadfully audible. When Julia heard the front door close announcing the doctor's presence, she looked up, took her fingers from her ears, listened wild-eyed, and said in a strained whisper, "That's Papa! Can you hear him?"

"Yes, I hear him. Is your mother in there?"

"Yes." Julia rose, clinging to the newel post; he could see how she trembled, and took her elbow in a steadying hand. "I ought to be in there, too. I ought to go—maybe Papa wants me. He would, at the end. But I am afraid. He wouldn't breathe that way, would he, if it weren't the end?"

"He might. Wait a minute till I look in. Tell me, first: you came down when you heard him fall?"

"He was on the floor. He had fallen forward, on his cheek, and he was *drooling*. It was horrible." She quivered like a tight-strung wire: "And Johnny was determined to call Dr. Warren. I didn't want him to. I wanted him to take care of Papa. If Papa dies, I'll never forgive him."

"Tut! You mustn't say things like that; you know you don't mean it. Just wait here a minute till I see."

He went to the bedroom door. Mrs. Deming, standing at the window staring out into the night, turned when she heard him. She was strained and white but by no means distraught. "Where is Julia?"

"Waiting outside. Before I bring her in, I want to see." What he saw was two doctors: Johnny at the foot of the bed, Dr. Warren at one side, both of them looking helplessly at the General, who in the last hour had become an old man. He lay unconscious, motionless except for the sudden lift of his chest as he fought for air. It was a spectacle John had witnessed many times: to him it was pitiful, not revolting or fearful. "I'll bring her in," he said abruptly. Julia, in the hall, was still leaning on the newel post.

"Your father is unconscious," he said. "I don't believe he will know you are there. But for your mother's sake and your own, too, you must screw up your courage. If you don't, you will remember all your life that you failed your father at the end."

She nodded. "Help me."

He supported her to the door; she trembled so that she could hardly walk. At the threshold she put her hands up, the tips of her fingers on her mouth in a gesture of horror; but she did go to the bedside, where she fell to her knees.

"Papa! Papa! Don't you hear me? Papa, it's me calling you: Julia. I never thought you would ever, ever not hear me if I called." Tears streamed down her cheeks; she gave a hiccupping sob.

Dr. Warren said gently, "He can't hear you. He is quite unconscious," wondering as he said it how she was able to believe that a loved voice could work miracles.

Her eyes swept the room. "Why don't you do something? Three of you doctors, and you stand there and do nothing." Her husband looked at her with loving, pitying eyes. Her mother came to stand beside Dr. Warren at the other side of the bed.

"Julia, control yourself. That is no way to help your father."

"Nor hurt him, either," Johnny said. He turned to his father. "She ought not to be here. She's too sensitive. Can't you get her away?"

She too turned to her father-in-law. "Can't you help him, either? He's going to die? You can save other people, like useless old Miss Gardiner, but Papa, you just stand there, and let him die."

"Julia, that's enough. Don't you see there's nothing can be done, except wait and hope?" Mrs. Deming turned to John. "I thought she should be here at this time. I was wrong. Can you get her upstairs to bed?"

John spoke peremptorily, all the authority of his long experience in his voice. "Get up from there at once. You can do nothing more. Come along with me now, out of the way."

Obediently she struggled to her feet, stumbling against the bed as she stepped on her long skirt.

"Come along with me," John said again, leading her into the hall. "Let the doctors see what they can do. We'll go upstairs. Where's the baby?"

She pushed her silky fair hair back from her face; it had escaped from its high twisted knot and was straggling like a child's. "He's asleep. The girl's up there with him: Johnny asked her to stay all night."

Johnny had followed them into the hall; he said to his father, "Get her to sleep, if you have to give her something. This has been an awful shock, and she is so sensitive and highstrung."

"She'll be all right. I'll put her to sleep." He turned back to Julia. "Let's go see whether the baby's all right."

Halfway up the long flight of stairs, her hysterical reproaches commenced again. "If only Johnny—if Papa dies, I'll never forgive him. Making Mamma call Dr. Warren."

He let her murmur until he got her to her bedroom. Then he plumped her down in her sewing rocker.

"Listen to me, my girl. If you go off into hysterics, I'll have to slap your face. *So listen.* You say Johnny didn't do anything. Didn't he turn your father over, loosen his collar, unfasten his clothes, get him to bed? Of course he did."

"Dr. Warren got here in time to help get him in the bed."

"A good thing. Your father is a big man."

"He should have done it himself."

"Done what?"

"Saved Papa's life. Dr. Warren's no good. Look at the trouble I had when Tucker was born. Look at poor little Binny."

"Dr. Warren's as good as Johnny or I, maybe better. And doctors simply do not take on members of their own families as patients. And there's been altogether too much of this 'never forgive' nonsense. Don't say it again. Everything is being done that can be done."

"How do you know? You didn't even look at him."

He decided to let her have it straight. "I have seen enough men in your father's condition. He has had a cerebral hemorrhage, a stroke."

Julia turned white, her eyes widened, went blank; it was as if up to that point, however genuine her terror, she had been half-dramatizing the crisis. "Then he *is* going to die?" And she began to moan.

John clapped his hand over her mouth. "Stop that at once!"

She struggled against his strength, then subsided completely and once more burst into tears. "But *Papa*! I can't get along— No one ever cared as much as he did what happened to me. What shall I do?"

"What everyone else does when the time comes. You are a grown woman, with a husband and baby. Yet you carry on like this."

"Then Papa is dying?"

"I don't know. Death can be a fortunate thing. If he lives, he might be paralyzed. Would you want that for him?"

"He would want to be alive, even in a wheel chair. I want him to be alive. Anything's better than being dead." She had begun to shake again; her chin trembled, and she was hardly intelligible.

"He might lie like a log in that bed, never conscious again."

"It's better than being underground. He might come to."

"Cling to that hope, then. The night will tell. Now, get ready for bed while I speak to your girl. If she'll pack some duds for Tuck, I'll take him home with me for a few days. Then you won't have him to worry about, and the girl can look after you."

"But I can't just go to bed, as if—"

"Then get that frock off. Put on something loose and lie down on the sofa there; if there's a change in your father's condition someone will call you." He intended her to be too deeply asleep to be roused by any call. The doctors downstairs must not have her on their hands again. He went through the apartment to the kitchen, found a frightened colored girl sitting, elbows on the table, her face in her hands. He told her to get Tuck ready to go with him, then to fetch the baby carriage from wherever it was kept; he would bring the baby down in a minute, when he had got Mrs. Gordon to bed. Then he returned to Julia. She had not moved; she still sat in the rocker, staring glassy-eyed.

"Stand up, Julia." He spoke more gently than before. "I'll unfasten your frock." When it had fallen to the floor he found a dressing gown in the wardrobe and put it around her shoulders.

"Julia, are you listening to me?"

"Yes. I'm to lie down. You'll take Tuck home with you. I'll be called."

"No more hysterics?"

She caught her breath: a long weary sigh. "No. I'll be all right."

She lay down on the couch; he pulled the afghan over her feet, then went to prepare his hypodermic. When he returned with it, he said, "This won't hurt more than a pinprick, and it will quiet your nerves."

"I want to wake up if they call."

Without reply he slipped the hypodermic into her arm, then pulled up the afghan and stood watching her for a moment. When he saw that she was going to be quiet, he went downstairs. Johnny met him at the sick room door.

"She is settled down?"

"Yes. She may remember in the morning that I was pretty rough with her. Try to convince her that it was the only way to treat her hysteria."

"What did you give her?"

"A small injection of morphine. She'll go to sleep. I'm taking the baby home with me."

"If her father dies in the night and she is asleep, she'll never forgive me."

John thought, "How easily some can say 'never forgive.'" He said, "You didn't do it. I did. If there is to be any unforgiveness, you can't have her on your hands in a state of shock. Not tonight. Your mother will be glad to have Tuck for a few days, and he'll be all right with her. If there's nothing I can do here, I'll go get him."

Mrs. Deming at the sound of their voices had come into the hall. Johnny returned to his post in the bedroom. She said to the older man, "Is there any chance?"

"I don't know. I haven't been close enough."

"Don't hedge. You have seen this sort of thing before."

"Yes. Sometimes people recover almost completely. Sometimes they partially recover and are more or less paralyzed, sometimes totally. Sometimes they die. Those are the possibilities. He did not die at once. The hemorrhage might clot and the clot be absorbed. I don't know."

"What did you do to quiet Julia? I never knew her to lose her self-control so completely before. But she has always been very close to her father."

"I give her a little morphine. She ought to sleep through the night. Should her father die, Johnny thinks she would hold it against him—would never forgive what was done for her good and yours."

"She would persuade herself that was not true," Mrs. Deming said drily. "She would never admit to herself her relief at not having to witness the end. You saw how terrified she was: she has never seen anyone die. In a little while she will have forgotten her revulsion and only remember that a good daughter—and she has been a good daughter—should have been at her father's deathbed, holding his hand."

"She'll blame me that she wasn't. And Johnny and Dr. Warren for letting him die. But you realize that with a cerebral hemorrhage—"

"I know. They have done all they could."

He said good-night, explained once more that he was taking the baby with him for a few days, and started for the stairs. The girl was about to come down again with Tuck in her arms. John stopped her.

"Wait, he's too heavy for you. I'll take him." He went up two steps at a time, and took the child from her. Tucker at eighteen months old was a solid chunk of a boy, and as active as a March wind when awake and afoot. Now, asleep, he had reverted to babyhood. He half roused when his grandfather took him, but slipped back into sleep at once; he snuggled into John's arm, dropped his head on his shoulder, and lifted one hand to his grandfather's cheek. The confiding gesture was oddly touching.

With his bag, the valise, and the baby John's hands were full, but he could manage so short a distance; the baby carriage would be a nuisance. Suddenly, John did not want to relinquish the child. Tucker (ridiculous name!) had always seemed to him Julia's child, and perhaps because he could not care greatly for her, he had not felt particularly drawn to her baby; and Tucker, held off by his grandfather's brusque straight-faced teasing, had never shown any great fondness for him, although he was a loving little boy with Anne. Now, walking with that trusting warm hand on his cheek, John realized, truly realized for the first time, that this was Johnny's son and his own flesh and blood, however unlike the Gordons he might be: he was big-boned, like the General, fair-haired like Julia, but he did, to his Grandmother Gordon's delight have the Gordon eyes. He was a strongly built boy, and handsome; he sturdily resisted babying and was as independent as a youngster that age could be. In fact, a thoroughly satisfactory child. That at least Johnny had, to make him happy. As he turned to close the gate, he saw that Mrs. Deming had come to the front door, which he had thoughtlessly left open. His mind reverted to the unhappy scene in which he had had a part. Poor Johnny!—who wouldn't believe it if told that anyone could be sorry for him. John made an effort to banish his disquiet from his mind. The beauty of the night, an August night, refreshingly cool after a hot day, made it easier. Moonlight drifted in patches through the trees; insects and tree toads chirped a loud chorus that fell silent progressively and momentarily as his footsteps echoed beneath the low-hanging maple boughs. How many August nights like this did a man have in his lifetime? Surely not many, by actual count, yet no man lived who had not known them as if from the beginning of the world.

When he reached home, no explanation was necessary. Anne said, "I'll put Tuck in the downstairs bedroom; if he should waken before we go to bed, we'll hear him. Perhaps I had better sleep with him: he might be frightened if he woke up in a strange place. When I've got him to bed, you can tell me what happened."

"Not much to tell. The General had a stroke. Doubt if he lasts the night. Julia was in a taking, but I got her off to bed with a dose of morphine."

His prognosis of the case was quite correct; General Deming died in the night. Julia woke in mid-morning to find Johnny, bleary-eyed and unshaven, sitting on the side of the bed. She had seen him like that often enough, when he had been out on all-night vigils; it took a moment for the fog to clear from her mind. Then she sat bolt upright in the bed.

"How's Papa?" Johnny did not answer. "He—he died? Oh, Johnny! And no one called me! Papa Dock promised!"

"Julie, he was in a coma. There wasn't a thing you could have said or done that would have got through to him. Don't cry, darling." He took her in his arms and let her weep on his shoulder.

"But—but what am I to do? I can't spare him—he was always there. Oh, Papa—"

"Darling," he said again, "it is sad, but it is natural: the older generation dies and leaves the younger, and they must learn to get along; and first thing you know, *they're* the old folks. When an old man dies as he did, quickly, without suffering, without even knowing, he is truly blessed. You must think of it that way. Please, Julia, try to pull yourself together. Your mother needs you."

"Can I see him?"

"Not now. The undertaker has been here. Your father will be brought back here, though your mother thinks there should be a church funeral. Right now, the dressmaker is here, for your mourning clothes."

"So many things to see to, aren't there? He must have a proper funeral: he was an important man."

"All that will be taken care of by the undertaker. He already has crepe on the door."

"They don't waste any time, do they? Into the ground in a hurry."

"Now, Julia." He held her close until she herself drew away.

"Tell Mamma I'll be right down."

Johnny, who had never seen any justification for the elaborate funeral rites that were the custom, realized now a very good reason for them: they distracted the minds of the bereaved from their sorrow. He almost smiled as he helped Julia into her clothes. "Let them have their show," he thought, and then rebuked himself; there was no question of the genuineness of the grief of wife and daughter.

Waynesboro made an event of the funeral of General Deming. Thirty years after the war not many towns still had generals to bury. The *Torchlight* printed several columns of biography and eulogy, the article being generally attributed to Charlotte Bonner, who was acknowledged to be the only real writer on the paper's staff. There were of course some cynics who remembered the caustic treatment General Deming had received in his political days at the hands of Mr. Bonner, and who muttered, "You've only got to live long enough," or "The *Torchlight* has gone soft—afraid of losing a subscriber." But on the whole the article was accepted as a fitting tribute to one of Waynesboro's leading citizens.

The funeral itself was in the hands of the undertaker and the local chapter of the G.A.R. The General was buried with full military honors, even to the salute of guns at the graveside and the sounding of taps by a bugler. Captain Bodien had seen to it that announcements of the occasion were sent to the newspapers of the state, inviting the veterans of General Deming's brigade to join the Waynesboro members in the funeral cortege. Old uniforms were taken out of mothballs and seams let out; a surprisingly long line of men in blue drew up in front of the hearse; men who had marched so far and for so long in their youth that in their middle age they could still hold a straight line and step in time to the Sons of Veterans' funeral march. The only thing missing was a gun carriage. The coffin was borne to the cemetery in the undertaker's hearse drawn by a pair of black horses, and was followed by the carriages of black-clad mourners. The whole town turned out to watch what seemed more like a parade than a funeral, and enjoyed it thoroughly. (The death and the funeral of Miss Lavinia Gardiner, which followed a few days later, were so anticlimactic as to go largely unnoticed by the public, except by her fellow members of the Woman's Club.)

A few days after the Deming funeral, Tim Merrill went one afternoon to read the General's will to his wife and daughter. General Deming had died in possession of a modest competence, earned by his books. He had left the house and one-third of his estate to his widow, the other two-thirds to Julia. Mrs. Deming would get not only her one-third of the personal property but also her pension as a general's widow, and the rent paid for the apartment where Johnny and Julia lived. She had long known his intentions: they were satisfactory to her. But she did hold Tim with one final question.

"A few weeks before George passed away, he told me he had agreed to invest in some new business Ludwig Rausch is planning to set up. Like most of Waynesboro, he thought Mr. Rausch infallible, and he hoped for our sakes, Julia's and mine, to be richer than he was. For many years he has bought nothing but government bonds—that kind of thing—and the return on them is small. I hated to see him go into something speculative—burnt fingers, you know. And I shall have too little to dare gamble with it. Do you think I shall be expected to honor my husband's commitment?"

"If he signed an agreement to purchase, you might be legally bound, but I cannot see Mr. Rausch holding you to it. At any rate, it will be months before that paper mill is in production and the shares are on the market. Why don't you talk to him? Or to Doug? He would know. He does the corporation law side of our partnership."

"From what George said, I suspected Mr. Rausch was turning first to his friends to raise the necessary capital, knowing they couldn't refuse him."

Tim Merrill was astonished. "Oh, no! It wasn't like that at all. You have no idea how absolutely Rausch believes in this new process of young Bodien's. He thinks he is doing his friends a favor, letting them in on the ground floor."

"Are you buying?"

"I asked Doug to put my name down for a few shares. I cannot spare much. Doug is subscribing."

"Your situation is not like mine: you can earn money to replace what you lose, if you lose it. I can't."

The next day she walked uptown to talk to Douglas Gardiner. In her heavy mourning, veiled, lifting her crepe skirts in both hands, Mrs. Deming climbed the dusty steps, and went down the corridor to the Gardiner-Merrill office. There she was reassured by Doug: there would be no demands on her for money. Ludwig, indeed, thought it would be unwise for her to risk any capital.

"He does think it is risky, then?"

"There is always a certain amount of risk in starting a new business, particularly in times as hard as these. He believes the industry will be profitable, but maybe not at first; he cannot make promises. He will certainly not expect you to buy stock, now that the General is gone."

"Thank him for me, will you? The money can stay where it is in government bonds. And I suppose," Mrs. Deming smiled a little, not really believing what she was saying, "I shall be very sorry. But there is nothing of the gambler in me; and besides, the General was badly hurt once, and I was surprised, really—"

"That he proposed to buy any of Ludwig's stock? I think he felt that he could not in the nature of things have much more time to earn money."

"You mean"—Mrs. Deming was startled—"that he had a premonition? That he knew his health was precarious?"

"No, no, no. I simply meant that he must be getting on—the paper didn't tell his age, but he must have been well over seventy. He was a general, which means he wasn't a boy when he went into the war thirty-odd years ago."

Mrs. Deming agreed, smiling politely: she would hate to believe George had known what was coming and concealed his knowledge, though he had never been good at concealing anything from her. "He felt young, I am sure," she said. "You know he was working on another county history. I intend looking over his notes and manuscript to see if I can't finish it."

Douglas realized that she didn't know the town gave her credit for having been the actual author—or at least, editor—of all the General's books. And she went away a little annoyed: after all, her husband shouldn't have seemed all that old to Douglas Gardiner, who must at the least be pushing forty. She was put out on George's account, and not a little on her own: of course she was not nearly so old as George. About Dock Gordon's age, she supposed. She wondered whether, like his father, Johnny was planning to put money in the Rausch paper company: she must speak to Julia about the disposal of her inheritance.

Julia, the dutiful wife, having been advised by her mother, turned to her husband for guidance. But Johnny refused to give it.

"Honey, what you inherit from your father will be yours absolutely. I am not going to tell you what to do with it. There are two alternatives: you must choose between them. Leave it where it is, and know that it is absolutely safe, but will never increase in value. Or sell the bonds, invest the money in stocks—Uncle Ludwig's or some other company's—and take the chance of losing it, or of becoming a rich woman."

Julia sighed. "I would dearly love to be a rich woman. When is Mr. Rausch going to get started on the new business? What will its shares cost?"

"No one can know that until the underwriters offer it on the market. Certainly it won't be right away; the way things are, he can't start tomorrow. The country's going to pot, looks like."

Julia sighed again. "Then I guess I had better hold on to the bonds."

The country was not in quite so fearsome a state as Johnny had indicated. Late in August the Pullman strike ended, and the laborers went back to work defeated; the country breathed a little easier, hoping that there would be no more violence. On the other hand, Congress had passed the Wilson-Gorman Tariff Act early in July, so monstrous and inconsistent a compromise between House and Senate that President Cleveland refused to sign it; he left it on his desk, and in ten days it became the law without his signature. The House had written a tariff-for-revenue-only bill; the Senate demanded protection for certain raw materials; for sugar, for instance, to placate the sugar trust, but not for wool, a concession to the woolen manufacturers but a provision that might well ruin American sheep farmers. The bill as passed would not provide enough revenue to carry on the government, although it included an income tax provision: two percent on incomes over four thousand a year, not a drop in the bucket so far as necessary revenue was concerned, and sure to be declared unconstitutional by the Supreme Court as being confiscatory. The wool provision and the revocation of reciprocal agreements angered the farmer; the removal of tariffs on some raw materials and not on others raised the hackles of manufacturers not favored. In sum, the depression would not be eased by such an act, but the Republicans might gain by it. If the party could carry the fall election, control the new Congress, the tariff act would most assuredly be replaced by one that would restore the country's prosperity. Ludwig, balancing pros and cons as best he could, had decided that he would go ahead with his plans for Rausch and Bodien Coated Paper, Inc. By the end of August his intentions were common knowledge in Waynesboro.

One afternoon in early September, Sheldon Lowrey called Ludwig at the office to ask whether he would receive a deputation of Waynesboro citizens to discuss the location of the proposed plant.

"Being a merchant myself, and a friend of yours, I have been dragooned into this, and as spokesman, at that. If you don't want to talk to us, say so."

"Of course I'll talk to you. At the house this evening. I'm tied here this afternoon. Say eight o'clock. Who and how many?"

"Our good solid burghers: Hoffmann, Klein, Thirkield. And I believe Voorhees. Why?"

Ludwig chuckled. "Just wanted to know how much beer to have sent in."

That evening Ludwig took his guests into his study, poured beer for all except Mr. Voorhees, who declined it, and sat down beside his desk, turned halfway from it, but with his beer stein close at hand.

"Well, gentlemen? You wanted to talk to me?"

"Yes," Sheldon said. "We are all merchants of one sort or another, even Voorhees here, who deals in money. Waynesboro's growth and prosperity would be promoted by a new industry. We should like to ask if it is too late to bring a new paper company here instead of its going to Madison City?"

Ludwig smiled: Sheldon, who had agreed to buy stock in the new company when it was issued, knew very well that it was too late: construction was already under way in Madison City. Sheldon was saying what he had been asked to say by others.

"Even if it was not too late, I would not change my mind. Believe me: young Bodien and I went into this very thoroughly, and decided against setting up a plant here. For one thing, there isn't a large enough labor force."

"But surely, Rausch—" Mr. Thirkield, now that the ice was broken, plunged in. "Labor would come here if it was needed. Waynesboro would grow."

"And trade would increase? That's your idea? Have you thought what kind of labor? Not the kind who came when the railroads were building, the Irish, the Germans. Have you been to Madison City lately? Eastern Europeans: Slovaks, Hungarians, Poles. Waynesboro as it is is a good town, a nice place to live, to raise children. Madison City is already spoiled: dirty, smoky, full of swarthy foreigners all too used to violence in their home countries. And paper-making—have you ever been in a town where there was a paper mill? The acids that have to be used: the smell is foul and permeating, believe me. No, if you want to make money on Rausch and Bodien Paper, buy stock when it comes on the market."

"You get used to smells and never notice them." Mr. Thirkield felt he was not presenting the strongest of arguments, but you had to answer your opponent's last point, not next to the last or the one before that.

"In Madison City, where there are already smells enough—soap, steel—that might be true. It wouldn't be true here. In Waynesboro you can still smell the lilacs when they bloom. Not in Madison City. And as you very well know: times are hard. There is enough unemployed labor in Madison City right now to supply us with workmen. In the meantime, they have to be taken care of by the county, or by charity. That's a problem I'd not like to see Waynesboro faced with."

Mr. Hoffmann, slow-spoken and perhaps slow-thinking, said, "You're laying off hands at ze rope mill now, yes? Zose colored folk can get along through ze summer. But come vinter, isn't zere going to be a problem here? And not all your labor is colored."

"The unskilled labor is, mostly. The skilled hands, spinner girls and such, are white, and of course the foremen. But the town won't have to keep my hands from starving: we'll take care of them through the winter. We've done it before and we can do it again, if need be."

"I see more of zis town zan any of you do. I drive my bakery cart up von street and down another." Mr. Hoffmann was frowning thoughtfully. "There are a good many white men loafing in ze West End, laid off by the railroad, who can't find work. You don't know, either, how many loaves of yesterday's bread I sell for a penny a loaf."

Ludwig thought, "Still driving that bakery cart, when he makes the best hard crackers to go with beer and cheese I've ever eaten." He said slowly, "We think when this mill gets going it will be a really big thing. The process is protected by patents. There'll be no competition for a while. We're starting small, times being what they are, but the number of Waynesboro's unemployed, even if they didn't go back to the railroad when they can, would never fill the need we foresee."

"It iss not good." Mr. Hoffmann was stubborn; he was not thinking only of how an increase in population would add to his income. "It iss not goodt zat a town should be a von-industry town. Here zere iss only your ropewalk and machine shop, beside ze railroad shops and yards and ze small foundry."

"You are right," Ludwig said. "It isn't good. The town would have been hurt if the National Cordage Company had succeeded in forcing us into bankruptcy. But think, man! You've the making of an industry yourself, in your bakery. If you started small, and were successful, you could enlarge. Patent your crackers and sell them wholesale. You say the labor is here. He's a good customer of the bank, eh, Voorhees? Or set up a corporation, let your friends invest."

Mr. Hoffmann gaped at him. "A—a biscuit factory! Vy not? Shust a little vun." Mr. Hoffmann, after all his years in Waynesboro, was still inclined to lapse into heavily accented English when excited. "It vould not hurt ze town—nein, nein—it could not. Ze smells vould be good smells, ze labor for zat kind of work is here: ze young Irish girls. But I vouldn't know—you vould help me?"

"With money? I can't, not now. With advice, with my experience, for what it is worth, certainly. Come see me any evening and we'll talk it over. It should help all of you: Voorhees could take care of your payroll, Fritz here can sell you apples for apple strudel, Sheldon can sell your workers their finery and Thirkield their medicine." They all laughed, a little ruefully. "Otherwise—I'm sorry to disappoint you. Rausch and Bodien is going up in Madison City. And if you still don't know why, you go look at the city sometime."

Ludwig did not really believe that when it came to the point, Mr. Hoffmann would risk his bakeshop, which was a sure provider of a small but apparently adequate income, on a chancy thing like a biscuit factory. He was wrong: Mr. Hoffmann dropped in one evening after dinner to ask his help. Rose answered the doorbell, and came to the library where Ludwig had settled down with Sally and the paper.

"Mr. Hoffmann to see you, sir."

"Hoffmann?" Sally looked up from her book. "How odd! What on earth—?"

"I know. He wants to see me on business. I won't be long."

"He wouldn't be very happy in the parlor. Do you want me to move? Paul—" Paul was lying on his stomach on the sofa, reading. "Your business friends should make appointments. We might have had dinner guests."

Ludwig laughed. "I'll take him into the study. Bring in some beer, will you, Rose? As for an appointment: Hoffmann's a simple man, it would never occur to him. If I hadn't been free, he'd just have come another time."

In the study the two men had their discussion. Mr. Hoffmann explained that he could raise the money necessary for a start: Fritz Klein, who was after all his brother-in-law, would come in, and various butchers and grocers, all of the same German-American group.

"Lichtenstein?" Ludwig asked, chuckling.

"You know he hasn't money to spare. Why?"

"He doesn't believe in capitalism, you know. I'd enjoy seeing him become a capitalist himself." At Mr. Hoffmann's reproachful look, he continued, "I didn't mean to joke about this. I know it is a serious step for you: no one knows it better. I remember how I felt when I bought the ropewalk in '68. Scared to death. Are you thinking of a closed corporation or an open one? All the stock in your hands and the hands of your friends? Or sold to the public?"

"I know ze difference." Mr. Hoffmann was reproachful. "A closed corporation, in ze beginning, anyway. A little more zan half in my hands and Fritz's—say 30 percent in mine and 25 in Fritz's—and ze rest spread around. What I don't know is how to go about it."

"Go to a lawyer. Gardiner and Merrill are best for corporation law. It will cost you, but you can hardly do without. Patent your recipe, or your process, invent a trademark and register it. Your lawyer will draw up articles of incorporation, and the state will give you a charter. Then you can go ahead. But if you want to end the depression, vote Republican in the fall."

While the men of Waynesboro were thus concentrated on business and politics, the women, except for the need to stretch every nickel in their purses, were as always more concerned with what seemed to them fundamental matters: births, marriages, deaths, the current scandals. And Anne Gordon, for the first time in her life, could hardly think of anything but the state of her body and mind. One evening, coming into the sitting room from an after-dinner session with Martha over the possible uses of the day's leftovers, she had been caught unexpectedly by a dizziness and sudden blindness that made her clutch the mantel for support. She must have made some sound, for John, who had not yet left for his office, looked up from his paper, then dropped it and went to her side.

"What is it, Anne?"

She shook her head, waited a moment for the enveloping blackness to disperse. "I don't know. I felt so dizzy—"

He led her to her rocker, got her seated, took her wrist to feel her pulse.

"How awful of me," she breathed. "I'm never sick. What—"

"I don't think it's anything, really. Your pulse is a little fast, but perfectly normal. But I want you to go to Warren for an examination, tomorrow. Just to be sure. Don't put it off."

"I'm all right now. A touch of indigestion, I suppose."

But she felt so miserable on the ensuing days, and John was so adamant, that she paid a visit to Dr. Warren. He found nothing wrong, to John's relief and her own annoyance. Doctors were all alike, she thought: "Where does it hurt?" and if it doesn't actually hurt, then it's all in your mind. She was not being quite fair to Dr. Warren, who had assured her that she was simply going through what women her age had to put up with, admitting, however, that it could affect one physically and nervously. Anne resolved to conceal what she felt—from John, from everyone. The dizzy spells, the hot flashes, came and went, and she sat them out most times in the rocking chair in her bedroom window, finding what distraction she could in the mild beauties of the street: the play of sun and shadow on the tall curbside maples, and the erratic diagonals of flying blackbirds against the late afternoon sky.

She made herself go to church with Johnny and Julia because going to church was her habit. One morning Mr. McKinney, in the course of a series of sermons on the seven deadly sins, preached against spiritual death in the living body: the sin that the Middle Ages called "Accidie," he explained. "Sloth is not a strong enough word, since it has come to mean mere laziness."

And Anne for one terrible instant had an almost irresistible impulse to rise and cry out, "Guilty." For "Accidie" was the word for her state of mind, unless "despair" came closer to what she felt. Her life was dust and ashes in her mouth: half-gone and she had done nothing, nothing at all in the years she had let slip through her fingers. She awoke sometimes in the early morning in her familiar bed, John sleeping beside her, and looked at the room suddenly grown fantastically alien, and could only ask, "What am I doing here? *I*, by name Anne Gordon. The name means nothing, and this isn't where I belong." And when the world righted itself and she had fought her way back, she would think, "I surely am losing my mind."

Strangest of all, she could not pray. She had not lost her faith: she believed in God and salvation. But suddenly God was not apart, to be addressed as a separate Being: He was involved in her alienation from her own name. God was one with her, with all the world. How could one expect Him to divide Himself and stand off and answer the prayers of so infinitesimal a fraction of his creation? No. There must be a Heaven, there was a God, but he was the sum of all: the circling spheres, infinity, eternity, and the souls of men.

Summer ended. In September, Club meetings began. In that year the ladies would take "A Look at German Literature." Anne attended the early fall meetings. But she trembled at the thought of having to write a paper on Heine by October twenty-ninth, and the idea of having to stand up and read it was a terrifying one.

Sally Rausch, Anne hoped, was the only one besides John who had an inkling of how she felt; when Sally came up to her bedroom one afternoon to visit, Anne said that rather than write a paper and read it to the Club, she would resign.

Sally took her threat calmly. "You can't do it. Think how much you would miss it, once you felt like yourself again." Sally, who was breezing through the middle forties with the minimum of trouble, was scarcely more sympathetic than John. She was hardhearted enough to laugh. "It's what comes of your sitting up here and brooding."

Then she was contrite. "I'm sorry, but it is such *nonsense*. You won't feel this way forever. Don't give way to it. The day when a woman knows she is through with that messy business forever should be the happiest day of her life. And all that old granny talk about becoming a dried-up stick is so much nonsense. I don't feel any more dried-up than I ever did. I don't feel any older, inside."

"I know. I don't feel old, particularly. But somehow I see everything on the bias, at a queer insane angle. But John says I'm all right."

"Oh, men! They don't know and can't imagine, not even doctors. Just hold on for a few months. Write your Club paper and prove to yourself that your mind still works. And no more nonsense about resigning." Sally stirred in her chair and leaned forward, elbows on her knees. "It's a funny thing—do you remember how we felt when the Club was organized? It would be something to do and it might be funny—all those old ladies. Now we're middle-aged, and the Club is a little more than just something to do. Somehow, there's a bond—something between us—between women who'd never see each other if it weren't for the Club. I even enjoy meeting with, let's say, Mrs. McKinney—once in two weeks. And you should admire all those older women: they went through what you're going through without so much as a whimper, so far as anyone ever knew. Surely you've pride enough to do what Amanda and the Ballards managed? And Mrs. Deming, come to that."

Anne said, rebelliously, "Maybe they didn't feel so awful." But she did manage a smile. "It's just that I always thought life was good, Heaven's greatest gift, meant to be lived with enjoyment. Worth the day-by-day dullness just for the small pleasures—like seeing the lilacs bloom in the spring. And now there seems to be nothing."

"What silliness you do talk! I suppose you aren't even interested in the prospective change in Club membership. But do pretend to be. Miss Lavinia Gardiner's death last week leaves a vacancy. But Miss Caroline will still be with us, I suppose. There will be just one place to fill. The young women—Elsa, Charlotte Bonner, Elizabeth Merrill—plan to propose the name of Sophie Klein."

"She is home, then?"

"Expected soon, I believe. With a doctor of philosophy degree from the University of Berlin."

"Will she stay in Waynesboro? She could teach almost anywhere, I should think."

"She has promised her family a year at home, Elsa says."

"Then there's no reason why she shouldn't be a member of the Club, is there?"

"Fritz Klein's daughter? You and I can remember when he was a huckster."

"He's a good citizen and a very kind man, goodhearted and generous. And Sophie is a brilliant girl, a *real* scholar. The Club is supposed to be an intellectual group."

"I know. I have no intention of opposing her membership. Elsa would never forgive me: she and Sophie have been friends all their lives, especially since they went to Germany together. But it shows how Waynesboro is changing."

"For the better. A member like Sophie might make our meetings more interesting."

"You do expect to attend them, then, in spite of your megrims. I'll bring you what books you need, if they aren't in our library. There isn't money enough to buy books that most of our subscribers would not read. If only we didn't have to depend on subscribers. Lots of towns have public libraries, tax-supported. I don't see why we shouldn't."

"With the men we have on City Council?"

"They're do-nothings, granted, and they do hate to spend the taxpayers' money except for what *they* consider absolute necessities, especially in an election year. But if enough pressure was brought to bear— And we have had that library on our hands far too long. I am sick to death of trying to pay Ruhamah's salary and buy books by getting up lecture courses, band concerts, and lawn fetes. It is high time the younger people were taking over. I said as much to Charlotte Bonner the other day. She's the one who said it was ridiculous Waynesboro shouldn't have a real tax-supported library. So I'm leaving it up to them: Elsa, Charlotte, Elizabeth Merrill, and, I suppose Julia, if she can forget her mourning."

"There are advantages in not being in the younger generation."

"Along with the disadvantages. Do take heart, Anne: if you just pretend to feel all right, you'll feel some better, at least. Dock must be leading a dog's life, coming home to such gloom every evening."

Sally's hearty common sense roused Anne's determination not to seem queer, no matter how out-of-balance she felt. And pride was a spur, as Sally had suggested: could she admit to herself that she had less strength of character than those members of the Club who never shirked an obligation however dull the resulting essay. She would write her paper. Reading with concentration, and taking notes, would give her something to distract her mind. When the sun shone, she went out in the yard; with Lafe doing most of the actual work, the leaves were raked and burned, the weeds pulled, the flower beds prepared for winter.

But even in the yard she could be swept by unreasoning panic: the fear of dying that most people endure sooner or later. Being dead might be a desirable state, but to die, to catch one's breath in vain— She admitted her cowardice: millions and millions had died before her, quietly, with no to-do, cowards as well as brave men; it could not be so dreadful, since so many had accomplished it. Then she would remember Binny, and the wild terror in her eyes. And she would weep silently: for Binny, for herself, for the flowers of the field that the wind passed over and they were gone.

When the Club assembled for the last meeting in October, Anne was there to read her paper, determined that no one would ever know what it had cost her. If her knees shook, her long skirts concealed the fact; she held her notebook so that no one could see how wet her palms were. At first her voice was not steady: that weakness she could not hide. But once absorbed in her reading, it turned out not to be the ordeal she had envisioned.

A good many Waynesboro women spent much of that fall in their rocking chairs: there was very little going on in the town to excite their interest. The men were again struck by the coming elections, when a new House of Representatives would be chosen. Nationally the makeup of the new Congress was of crucial importance: Democrats must be replaced by Republicans, and the menace of wild Democratic notions removed. But it was taken for granted that however close the fight might be elsewhere, the "Old Seventh" would reelect its present representative: the district had been Republican since the founding of the party and would presumably continue to be so. And it seemed to readers of newspapers that it would surely end in the return of the Republicans to power, so far as the legislative branch was concerned. The Democrats were badly split: on the one hand, Cleveland and supporters of the gold standard, on the other the Silverites and Populists. And the Republicans had a campaign issue: the enormities of the Democratic tariff act. However complacent the ladies of the Waynesboro Woman's Club and their husbands were, politicians were not taking chances. Ludwig Rausch did not neglect his duties as State Committeeman: and he let it be known in the mill that he believed prosperity would return to the country when a sound monetary policy was firmly established, and when the tariff on manufactured products was restored. Or, more simply, when the Democrats were out of Congress. Dodgers were posted in the mill, with figures showing that under the present law European countries and the British could sell rope and binder twine in New Orleans cheaper than Rausch Cordage Company could.

Once campaign plans were well in hand, Ludwig ceased to worry much about the election—to him, too, the result seemed certain. Republicans by and large were making their points effectively, in spite of the free silver clamor and the Populist threat. Senator John Sherman campaigned actively in Ohio; more important for the future, there were unlimited demands from all over the country for the services of Governor McKinley, a protective tariff advocate. He made speeches in sixteen states, many of them to supposedly hostile audiences, and was received with so much enthusiasm that '94 not only seemed certain to be a Republican year but McKinley began to appear to the country as well as to Ohio a probable presidential candidate in 1896.

For once Republican certainty was justified: the representation of the two parties in the House of Representatives was overwhelmingly reversed, and since the Republicans carried nearly every state legislature in the North, the Democratic majority in the Senate would be drastically reduced when terms expired and state legislatures chose replacements. A Republican triumph in 1896 began to look like a sure thing. Mark Hanna said as much to Ludwig when they encountered each other at a State Central Committee meeting. "'96 will be our year, and the Governor our man." Ludwig agreed, but with reservations as to what could happen before the new Congress would first meet in 1895. But stunned by their defeat, the lame duck Congress did nothing the rest of its term, while the country drifted. The depression continued, and the gold drain became an out-flowing tide. In January of 1895 the President called on Congress for remedial action, but met with no response. The President and his Secretary of the Treasury were forced into an alliance with Wall Street; after many emergency consultations, Morgan and Belmont in New York, along with Morgan and Rothschild in London, agreed to get the needed gold from abroad and replenish the country's bullion reserve; the loan would be repaid by a government bond issue to be sold abroad. Like a run on a country bank stopped by the arrival of a bag of money, the run on the country's Treasury ceased once the news became public; the President and the bankers between them had saved the country from bankruptcy. Merchants, bankers, industrialists could breathe again. But the unfortunate President, having put the safety of the country ahead of his own interests, found himself the object of a torrent of abuse from other Democrats—Silverites, Populists, farmers, debtors—to whom Wall Street was anathema and considered the source of all their troubles. President Cleveland and those officeholders who agreed with him were ruined politically, but the end of the run on the Treasury marked the beginning of an upswing, hesitating to be sure; confidence returned, and confidence was what was needed to set the business and industrial wheels to turning again.

During all this the construction of a mill for Rausch and Bodien Coated Paper, Inc., was completed. It was a much larger building than would be needed at once: at first the paper to be coated would be bought from established paper manufacturers; in time, it was hoped, the company could purchase machinery and make its own paper. Ludwig took upon himself the choice of an underwriter and the settling of terms for the sale of forty-nine percent of the proposed capitalization, all common stock. The rest he and Stewart must hold to keep control in their own hands. They would have to raise the money, one way or another, to pay for it. The matter of beginning manufacture was Stewart's responsibility; he would hire competent paper men to oversee production once he had the machinery set up, the machinery made in the Rausch and Bodien machine shop and stored ready in a Rausch Cordage warehouse. But actual production would have to wait on the provision of capital; it might take a while to sell the stock, though Ludwig and the underwriter had put out a promising prospectus.

As for Rausch Cordage Company, that business was still being hampered by the unsold stockpile built up by the defunct National Cordage Company; Ludwig's mill was not making much, but it could pay its bills, meet its payroll, and pay dividends to the cousins who still held stock. Ludwig rejoiced that some of that stock had in better days been sold back to him. The dividends due him he put back into the business, building up its reserve, using for himself and his family only the salary he drew as president.

However great his business concerns, Ludwig was a family man, and when he opened his back door, shucked off his oily tarred boots, and put on his slippers (a habit he still kept up), he shucked his preoccupations, too, and turned his attention to his family. Ernest was still at home, although he had about served his time in the mill; having gone the route, he was now working as shipping clerk. He was engaged to a girl he had met in the East, a finishing-school and New York suburb product, who had made her debut that winter. The wedding was planned for the spring. Ernest had been able to get away only for her coming-out ball, but his absence from all the other diversions offered that season's debutantes had not weakened his fiancée's attachment to Ernest (perhaps to Ludwig's disappointment). Ludwig had come to the hard decision that Ernest could never run the cordage company, even had his bride been willing to live in Waynesboro. But as Gib had once suggested, there was a need of a warehouse and a shipping office in Kansas City, from which binder twine could be moved quickly to the wheat fields. Binder twine was a seasonal product; until the yield could be calculated, no one could estimate how much would be needed, but once the crop was nearly ready to harvest the wholesale dealers would be needing the twine to fill the orders from local hardware stores, and those demands must be able to bypass the wholesalers. Ernest at once made it clear that he was not going to be that man, competent or not. Ludwig had suggested it casually, before the whole family assembled in the library awaiting dinner; Ernest's response had been a horrified exclamation: "Kansas City! Emily wouldn't want to live in *Kansas City*! Isn't there anything in the East?"

"You have been shipping clerk long enough to know that our customers are not in the East."

"Couldn't you send Gib to Kansas City and let me—? A salesman could live most anywhere."

"No, I couldn't. Gib is a good salesman, and has to live close enough to home to know what is going on in the mill."

Ludwig realized with a rueful pang that he could much more easily face the departure of Ernest from Waynesboro than that of Elsa: she would go with Gib if he went to Kansas City. Conscience hurting, and prompted somewhat by the thought that Emily's father, a stockbroker, could very easily find something for Ernest in New York that would tempt him and satisfy his bride, Ludwig, to forestall that eventuality, said, "How does New Orleans strike you as a possibility? We have a very good agent there, but he handles other products in addition to ours. I cannot take our business away from Toussaint; he has been a good man for us for many years. But he might consent to partnership if offered enough, and you could concentrate on rope."

Sally intervened. "Why haven't the two of you settled Ernest's future before this? It isn't like you."

"This is a family matter. I put it off, hoping Ernest would stay here and some day take my place. But he isn't interested. He can think about going in with Toussaint."

There was a certain glamor in the name "New Orleans" in those days when George Washington Cable was still writing. After due consideration Ernest agreed that it might suit his Emily; they could try it at any rate.

"If I buy you a partnership, and you decide you don't want it after all, you will be on your own. So make up your mind."

After consultation by mail, Ernest announced that Emily had consented to go with him to New Orleans. He would therefore accept his father's offer.

Ludwig, wondering how he had ever begotten such pomposity, made the necessary arrangements with Mr. Toussaint. The bride and groom would go directly from their wedding trip to Bermuda (Emily's father's wedding present) to New Orleans; they would make the trip there by boat instead of returning to New York. With this Ludwig had to be satisfied; the Kansas City warehouse could wait until Charles had finished college and learned something about the selling end of the rope business. But Ludwig said to himself that Charles had better by God marry a midwestern girl who would not think Kansas City an outpost of Purgatory. As for Ludwig Junior, he was a problem. There was no hope of making a businessman out of him; he was not so docile as the older boys: when put in the mill in the summer to learn the manufacturing side of the business, he did his work so badly that the foreman had to complain and he was let go. He was continually in and out of hot water in school; his intimates were what Sally considered undesirable. He seemed to care for nothing but his music; it was therefore decided by his parents in that spring of 1895 that in the fall he must go to a boarding school in New York, and study violin under a real master.

Ernest's wedding in May of that same year was attended by all of the Rausch family except Elsa, who was not able to go. She had just given birth to her second child, a girl to be called Jennifer, over Sally's protests: "An old-fashioned name like that! How peculiar! She will hate it when she grows up." Elsa simply said, "It doesn't seem peculiar to us. It was Gib's mother's name, and he likes it." Elsa had to await her mother's report of the wedding until the Rausches returned home. A very splendid affair, Sally called it; she hoped Emily's father would continue to prosper. "Your father thinks a stockbroker is the lowest form of male animal," she said. "I don't know why; he couldn't get along without one now. Of course, a stockbroker isn't *producing* anything. But still there was something lacking that our Waynesboro weddings have: some warmth that comes, I suppose, from our knowing each other so well. It wasn't that we felt like ducks out of water, we didn't—we received every proper attention. But you sensed that however intimate all those people seemed to be, they really hadn't known each other long."

"You mean that nobody's grandparents had known anyone else's grandparents?" Elsa, who could not imagine her mother feeling like a duck out of water in any circumstances, laughed at her now.

"Exactly. They were all *new* people, and somehow they seemed on guard. They were perfectly nice, well-mannered, refined, and undoubtedly rich, but—"

"But where did they come from?"

Sally could still laugh at herself. "It doesn't matter a bit, does it? We'll never see any of them again, except, I hope, Ernest's Emily. She's very pretty in an Amazonian sort of way: a big, strong-looking girl, I am glad to say. One always thinks of eastern society girls as pale and puny."

"Perfectly able, no doubt, to give you more grandchildren." Elsa's mother, as Elsa knew, had been upset by her decision to have but two children; now she had them, and she was through.

"I hope she will. Though small families seem to be the fashion nowadays. However—I suppose you attended the Club meeting that I missed?"

"Yes. The last meeting of the year. The ladies expressed regret at your absence. Mrs. Voorhees presided and enjoyed it very much."

"Don't be sarcastic. You know very well that at every election of officers I try to withdraw my name and am prevented."

"The ladies believe no one else would take the trouble you do. There was one piece of news at the meeting that you won't like very much. Sophie is going to marry Rudy Lichtenstein. She was telling people: no formal announcement for Sophie."

"*Lichtenstein! Marry!*" Sally could not have said whether she was more surprised that Sophie, whom she looked upon as another Amanda Reid, old maid and scholar born, was going to marry at all, or at her choice of a husband.

"I knew you wouldn't like it. You always thought Sophie would only be in Waynesboro a year or two."

"Sophie has been a very valuable Club member. I don't know why you say that in that tone: I have grown quite fond of Sophie."

("Funny," Elsa thought: "once anyone is *in* the Club, Mamma finds herself growing fond of her. A good thing, of course; otherwise she wouldn't make a very good President.")

"But a Lichtenstein!" Sally went on. "Their father is an out-and-out *Socialist*! But maybe— They say Rudy is a brilliant boy. Surely there won't be any future for him in Waynesboro?"

"Why not? He *is* brilliant. He has passed his bar exam—you missed that, in the *Torchlight* while you were gone. He intends to practice here." Better to be discreet, Elsa thought, and not say that he hoped in time to go into politics. "I don't think Rudy is a Socialist. A Democrat, yes. Maybe a Populist. A Silverite. He wants to get the feet of the rich off the necks of the poor."

"What nonsense!"

"Oh, Mamma, he'll get over it. Believe me, the Kleins are not radical."

"Mr. Lichtenstein, everyone thinks, is at least partly Jewish."

"And what of it? The nicest people I knew in Germany were Jews. I don't believe that would bother a German like Mr. Klein. Mr. Lichtenstein is more German by far than he is Jewish."

"I admit, the Germans do stick together." Her tone said that after all, it was only Fritz Klein's daughter who was marrying a Lichtenstein.

"They're no more German than Papa. He just got a head start. I knew you would be scandalized. But just remember, Mamma: Sophie is a friend of mine. I don't intend to give her up just because you don't like her married name."

"You must do as you think best. I have never invited a Lichtenstein into my house." She stopped: how could she say "and never will" when Sophie was a member of the Club? Instead she asked sharply, "How long have you known this?"

"Mamma! Sophie and Rudy were friends in school, and have been ever since. It wasn't until this spring that they got themselves engaged. I know what you are thinking: if I had known at the time, I ought not to have proposed her name for the Club. I declare: you're getting more snobbish every day!"

The two women had been talking in Sally's upstairs sitting room, the baby sleeping in the cradle brought down from the attic.

"There's your father coming in, and Charles. It's almost dinner time. You will have to wake the baby: her grandfather hasn't seen her since we got back."

"He can't see her more than a minute now. I must get home and cook Gib's dinner for him."

"What nonsense. Telephone him to come here."

"No, Mamma. I'm not going to start that. Besides, little Ludwig's there with only Cassie."

"It's lucky for you that Cassie is still able and willing, now that we don't need her."

"She isn't as spry as she used to be, but she loves the babies. I must run now. You and the Grossvater plan to come to dinner with us."

Elsa scooped up the baby, who woke whimpering, and the two women started down the stairs, Elsa preceded by her mother, carrying the baby over her shoulder and holding up her long skirt with the other hand.

At the foot of the stairs, his mother said to Charles, "Go stop the boy from putting up the horse: he can drive Elsa and the baby home."

"Never mind, Charles. I have the baby carriage here, and it won't go in the buggy." Elsa handed the baby to her father and stood on tiptoe to kiss him. "Admire your granddaughter for just one moment, then we must run. You tell him, Mamma, about Sophie. I can't stop now to hear him explode."

She let Charles lower the baby carriage down the porch steps, and laid the baby, now wrapped in a blanket and adorned with a deeply ruffled cap, on the cushions, waved good-bye, and took her departure.

Once inside, Ludwig said, "What am I expected to explode about?" When told, he took the news indifferently, since he considered it irrelevant to their lives. "Why should I explode? His father is a friend of mine, and the boys are bright. I hope Rudy will be a better provider than his father, though. I don't believe Lichtenstein has one nickel to rub against another, except what he makes in notary fees. He's never been interested in making money, as a man with his brains could easily do."

They went together into the library, took their usual chairs, and Ludwig opened his newspaper. Sally, however, had not finished what she wanted to say.

"Elsa doesn't *think* Rudy's a Socialist, but he believes the rich oppress the poor."

"He's not the only one who thinks that. With such notions he won't get far in Waynesboro—not in our day, anyhow."

Republicans in Ohio that spring and summer of '95 were less worried about Populists and Silverites than about a split in their own ranks. Mark Hanna, sure of McKinley's strength at home, had spent the winter in the South, working to secure McKinley delegates to the '96 Convention. Republican organizations there could not deliver votes in an election, but in nominating conventions they had a voice. The control of the Ohio Republican Convention in June was seized by Foraker and Foraker men: they chose the ticket and wrote the platform. Foraker's friend Bushnell was picked to run for Governor, at the close of McKinley's term. McKinley men therefore enthusiastically endorsed Foraker to be chosen Senator in 1896 and, as a matter of course but with little enthusiasm, announced their support of McKinley as the presidential candidate. This rather halfhearted gesture left open the possibility of a divided Ohio delegation at the '96 Republican Convention. McKinley men led by Hanna went into action, leaving to the Governor himself the task of making his great popularity with the people so evident that Ohio delegates would not dare desert him the following June. That summer McKinley spoke in many of the towns and cities of the state before many kinds of audiences, including coal miners and laborers, and always in favor of Foraker's hand-picked candidate for Governor. Everywhere he received a hearty and unqualified welcome; he was a man hard not to love in the way men do sometimes love a leader. The point was emphatically made: his popularity was so evident that it would be impossible for an Ohio delegation to the '96 Convention not to stand united behind his candidacy.

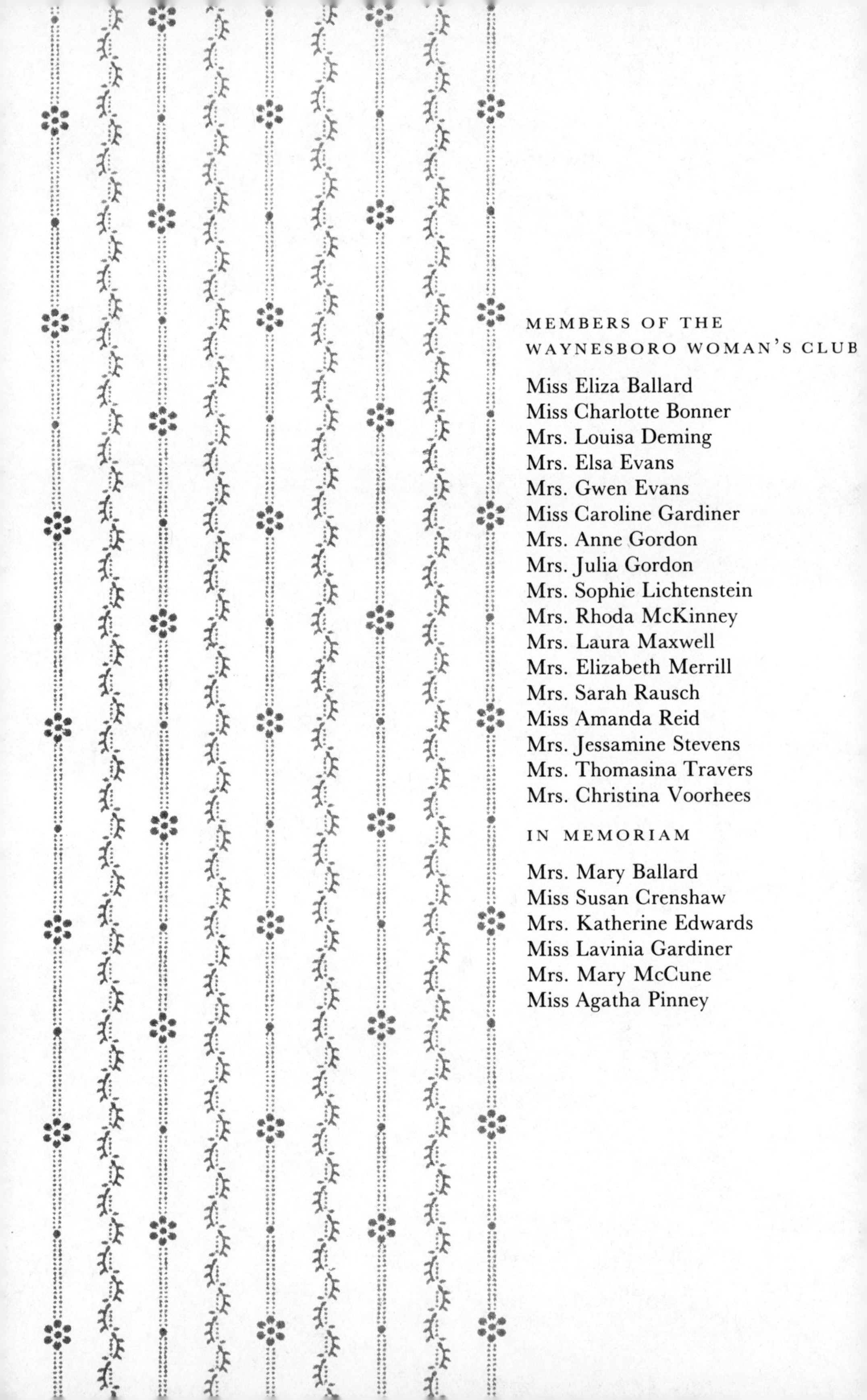

MEMBERS OF THE
WAYNESBORO WOMAN'S CLUB

Miss Eliza Ballard
Miss Charlotte Bonner
Mrs. Louisa Deming
Mrs. Elsa Evans
Mrs. Gwen Evans
Miss Caroline Gardiner
Mrs. Anne Gordon
Mrs. Julia Gordon
Mrs. Sophie Lichtenstein
Mrs. Rhoda McKinney
Mrs. Laura Maxwell
Mrs. Elizabeth Merrill
Mrs. Sarah Rausch
Miss Amanda Reid
Mrs. Jessamine Stevens
Mrs. Thomasina Travers
Mrs. Christina Voorhees

IN MEMORIAM

Mrs. Mary Ballard
Miss Susan Crenshaw
Mrs. Katherine Edwards
Miss Lavinia Gardiner
Mrs. Mary McCune
Miss Agatha Pinney

* 1895–1896 *

"The Club is determined that Waynesboro shall have a free public library."

While men of political bent were concentrating on these important contests, a group of the younger members of the Woman's Club were waging their own campaign. Elsa Evans, Charlotte Bonner, Elizabeth Merrill, and Sophie Klein (newly married and now Mrs. Lichtenstein) intended by hook or crook to wrest from the City Council sufficient tax support for a public library. On Ludwig's amused advice (as Elsa said, he knew all about campaigning), they had attempted during the late winter of '95 to prepare people's minds: as Ludwig had told Elsa, "Editorials in the *Torchlight*, petitions, that sort of thing." Elsa did not report to her friends that he had also said that he doubted whether they would get anywhere in an election year: spending the taxpayer's money was the last thing a councilman would want to do. "Maybe," Elsa had retorted, "we can scare them to death with petitions."

The self-appointed committee had first approached the Board of Trustees of the Waynesboro Subscription Library; it would be impossible to go over their heads since the proposal was that the new hoped-for public library should take over the existing subscription one. The Board at that time was composed of Amanda Reid, representing the Woman's Club, Sheldon Edwards, President Maxwell of the Theological Seminary, the Methodist minister, and another clergyman: Mr. Craig of the Reformed Presbyterian church. After the departure of Mr. McCune, that church had been ministered to by a succession of newly graduated youths from the Seminary who had stayed, it seemed to the R.P.'s, just long enough to win their brides from among their congregation and had then answered other calls, mostly to the Foreign Field. Wearying of constant change, the church had eventually located an oldish retired missionary, the Reverend Mr. Craig, who was glad enough to find a pulpit where he could end his days. Unfortunately, in the eyes of townspeople who were not members of his church, he bade fair to be as great a bigot as

Mr. McCune had been. There was also a remarkable similarity between his views and those of Christina Voorhees.

When one evening in early summer the four young women attended a Board meeting at the library, having asked for and been given permission to attend, Mr. Craig was braced and ready for them. They had expected no opposition to their proposal to turn the library over to the town: running it had been a thankless task, unpaid but not uncriticized. Moreover, they knew they would have the support of Amanda and Sheldon, who had been informed of their plans. They were startled to find that all the clergymen were against them, Mr. Craig the most vigorous in his opposition. As things stood, he explained to them kindly, the Board was in a position to decide what books Waynesboro could safely be allowed to read without contamination of its morals. With a public library, under the control of board members appointed by the City Council, who could know what inflammatory or subversive books might find their way to the shelves, to be read by irresponsible citizens. Of course, Mr. Craig assured them with some condescension, the young ladies could not be prevented from seeking funds for a public library. But personally he doubted whether the city fathers would be interested in the purveying of literature to the public, and he for one would use his influence against such foolishness. At any rate, the Subscription Library would continue as presently constituted, to be used by those who preferred books that were clean in every sense of the word.

Since Mr. Craig was supported in his opinion by the other reverend gentlemen, there was no point in even asking for a vote. But Elsa did not leave the meeting without speaking her mind. "We had hoped that with your acquiescence, a public library could begin in this same room, with an already fair-sized collection of books. If not, then I suppose it must start from scratch. But you surely realize that it has been the members of the Woman's Club who have raised the money for the support of this library, beyond what small amounts the subscriptions have brought in. Our mothers feel that they have done their share; they are ready to turn the responsibility over to us. It is a responsibility we do not intend to assume—not when it is the town's legal right to have a library supported by taxes."

As they gathered their long skirts in their hands and started down the dusty stairs, no one spoke except Elsa, who kept muttering in astonishment, "Did you ever! Did you *ever!*" When they came out onto the sidewalk, it was to an evening still not dark: their meeting had not taken long. Before parting they stopped a moment for a few unhappy comments. It was Charlotte who said, "A little man enjoying his mite of power. He isn't going to give it up without a struggle."

"But the others? Are they all so bigoted? Dr. Maxwell must know how hard his wife has worked all these years."

Charlotte said, "I simply cannot go one more time to hear Dr. Maxwell on digging up the Holy Land."

"Oh, well—" Sophie was not so fierce. "I expect he has liked giving all those lectures. Ministers do enjoy hearing their own voices."

Elsa ignored the frivolous comment. "If we get tax funds to start a public library, they'll give in. They can't keep the Subscription Library going without our help. They won't exert themselves to raise the necessary money, and with a free library in town, present subscribers will drop away like flies when a screen door is opened."

"Agreed. But what do we do next?"

"More editorials in the paper. That's your department, Charlotte. And petitions to the Mayor and City Council. Let's each draw one up, then get together and see what we have."

The editorials appeared; petitions were distributed to various stores, where it was hoped the attention of customers would be drawn to them and signatures obtained. They were also carried from house to house in the more respectable parts of town: a wearing business in warm weather, but a number of signatures were collected.

When it was felt that public opinion must surely be prepared, there was a meeting at Elsa's one summer afternoon for a discussion of the next step; the rather daunting prospect of bearding City Hall. Elsa included Julia Gordon in her summons: Julia after all had been one of their group.

Johnny drove his wife out Linden Street one afternoon early, before his office hours. Julia, still a mournful figure in her black gown, black gloves, and black hat, was a little resentful of Elsa's assumption that she would appear at her call, but too curious to stay away. She said, complacently, "She's been telling me what to do since I was a child, but I seldom pay any attention."

"I hope whatever she has in mind to undertake you'll agree to take part in. I hate your having been shut up at home. Aren't you kind of running this mourning business into the ground?"

"Papa hasn't been dead a year, I'd ask you to remember."

Because of Johnny's unkind remark, Julia, when he helped her out of the buggy, already had a chip on her shoulder: was prepared to object to whatever Elsa had in mind for her. She was the last to arrive; the others had walked out Linden Street to the Evanses'.

With Julia's arrival Elsa was ready to start the meeting. Elizabeth would direct the discussion; there was still between her and the others, although she was but five or six years older, something of the teacher-pupil relationship.

"Do let's be informal about it," she protested. "You all know what we're here for: to make plans for getting tax support for a public library."

"A public library? For everyone?" Julia said. "Do you mean to say you have been responsible for all those articles in the paper?"

"Primarily. We've had some help. Look, Julia: you know that our Subscription Library never has enough money. That funds must be raised every year?" Elizabeth slipped easily into a pedagoguish tone with Julia.

"And," said Elsa, "our mothers are tired of wearing themselves out.

They've done it so many years. I can even remember when they took turns at acting as librarian. Now they have turned it over to us. Do you want to spend your life getting up lawn fetes and band concerts?"

"No, I can't say that I do." Julia smiled. "It sounds horrid. And I know very well how hard Mamma has worked to secure funds to keep it open. But surely if we get a lot of new subscribers, that would do."

"No," Charlotte said shortly, "it wouldn't." She had come to the meeting from the *Torchlight* office; she had ink on her hands that she had been unable to wash off, and wore the dark skirt and jacket over a white shirtwaist that was her work-a-day uniform; she sat leaning back on Elsa's sofa, her long legs stretched in front of her, her bony face alight with enthusiasm. "Don't throw cold water. We're going to do it. There's no reason why Waynesboro shouldn't have a free library supported by taxes. A real public library."

"But," Julia was bewildered, "you mean *free*—that everyone in town could use?"

"Haven't you been reading our editorials? Of course, if it were tax-supported, it would have to be free. And why not? Everyone should have access to books."

"Every Tom, Dick, and Harry? Even the colored? Think how many books would have to be bought! And how *filthy* they would get! The childrens', anyway. I wouldn't want them brought into my home."

Elsa laughed. "You could do what Christina Voorhees does: buy your own children's books, and sew the pages together if there are things you don't want Tuck to read, or blot out the offending passages."

"What!" Charlotte sat up in astonishment.

"Didn't you know? I happen to because she gives the books to the library when her children have finished with them, and Ruhamah turns them over to Mamma to unsew: she doesn't dare do it herself. The books can't be refused—can't afford to be; they are accepted gratefully, even if some passages are crossed out with heavy black crayon."

"Isn't she—" They laughed; they had grown up in bookish households, and read without restriction whatever on the parental shelves had taken their fancy. But after a moment Elizabeth brought them back to the business in hand. "You all know that tax money can only be appropriated by the City Council and the Mayor. How do we go about persuading them?"

"Beard them in their dens." Julia was aghast. "You mean go to City Hall? *Talk* to them?" The expression on her face might have led one to believe she smelled something offensive—spittoons, say, and tobacco juice, or unwashed humanity.

"For goodness' sake, why not?" This was Charlotte again. Elsa was perfectly willing to let her do the arguing, and Charlotte was genuinely astonished at Julia's attitude. "I go to talk to them all the time, for the 'What's New at City Hall' column when our court reporter is somewhere else. They don't bite. Indeed, they've always been very pleasant, not only to voters but to women. Besides, Julia, most of those men were cronies of your father."

Julia flushed angrily. "'Cronies' they were not; they were men he needed to know for political reasons. He was always very careful to protect Mamma and me from what he called 'rough politicians.' And besides, what need is there for us—Elsa's father has only to say the word."

It was Elsa's turn to be angry. "Leave Papa out of this. He does not—he never has—concerned himself with town politics. He can't see that it is going to affect the country one way or another if Waynesboro citizens want an Irish Catholic West End Democrat for mayor."

"How did Dan Ryan ever get elected in the first place: a Democrat, in this town?" It was Sophie who wondered, Charlotte who told her.

"He's well-liked. Even by Republicans. He's been an all-right Mayor, so they keep reelecting him. Waynesboro could do a lot worse."

"You may not mind numbering him among your acquaintances," Julia said. "I do. And I am not sure that I like the idea of a *public* library. Certainly I am not going to involve myself in anything so—so *lowering* as campaigning."

"So unwomanly?" Charlotte said with something of menace in her tone.

"What's the matter with being womanly? I suppose you even believe in woman suffrage."

"Of course we do," Elsa said shortly. "And when we get it, I intend to vote."

"But your mother—"

"Oh, I know, she used to think old Mrs. Ballard was kind of funny. But she'll vote if she is given a chance—don't think she won't."

Elizabeth Merrill cut in. "All this is beside the point. I'm sorry, Julia, that you don't feel like helping us. Your name—your father's name—would mean so much to the men we have to persuade. And think of the appeal you would make in all that black: Dan Ryan's heart would bleed. But if you don't want to join us, we'll excuse you, and no hard feelings."

"Thank you," Julia said. "After all, you're my closest friends—I should hate for you to hold it against me—but I just can't agree with you about this. If you'll let me use your telephone, Elsa, I'll call Johnny: when he has a minute free, he will come for me."

In a short time Johnny drove up to the Evans gate. Elsa started down the path with Julia, said good-bye to her and waved to Johnny as he jumped from the buggy to help his wife in; then she returned to her meeting. She said as she rejoined the others, "I was afraid that would be her attitude, but I felt we had to ask her; no one likes to be overlooked. Besides, she's so pretty and delicate looking, she would bowl the men over. Julia would be much better at this sort of thing than I shall be: she would coax and be irresistible. I'm afraid I'll just up and tell them what they ought to do, and that will raise their hackles."

"You've changed, Elsa," Sophie said, consideringly. "You aren't so managing as you used to be when you were a young girl."

"No? The softening influence of having two children, no doubt."

Sophie thought, "The softening influence of loyally making the most of second-best." She knew very well that it was second-best; she had known Elsa too long not to have realized that. But Elsa was putting heart and mind into the successful effort to make Gib happy and be happy herself; and it had made a difference, somehow. "If you were just beginning to know her," Sophie said in her mind, "you might call her 'a sweet woman'—and what a word that would be for Elsa Rausch!"

And Elsa herself belied its fitness by saying shortly, "Let's get on with it. Where were we?"

When Johnny had waved to Elsa from the curbstone, he said to Julia, "Anyone else like a lift home? We could squeeze in one more."

Julia, stepping up to the buggy from the stone carriage step, Johnny's hand under her arm, said, "They aren't ready to go yet."

"What is it they are planning? Something you don't like?"

"They are going to campaign for tax support for a public library—actually go and ask the Mayor and the City Council for an appropriation. No. I don't think it nice." Then, since Johnny did not reply, she added, "Surely, you wouldn't like *me* to?"

"Not if you don't feel you can." Johnny was unsmiling, his face rather sad.

"They asked me just so they could use Papa's name. He would not have cared for that at all. Anyway, if I could bring myself to go to City Hall and talk to men like Dan Ryan, I still wouldn't do it. I think a public library, free to everyone, black and white, clean and dirty, is a horrible idea. Think of how filthy the books would be."

"I think you would find Dan Ryan a perfect gentleman. No matter what his opinion, he would treat you all like ladies. And the members of the Council are perfectly respectable citizens."

"Johnny! You think I did wrong?"

"I think you may have made a mistake. You have cut yourself off from all your friends' activities because you've been in mourning. Now that's about over—"

"I'll mourn for Papa as long as I live."

"Of course you will. But you don't need to wear black to remind you. And he wouldn't have liked you to be unhappy. I've worried about you because you haven't done anything for almost a year, outside of church and your Club, except at home. You take care of the baby and me, and crochet, crochet, crochet. That's no kind of life. And do you think you can keep your friends, if you never see them? They'll get used to doing things without you; and darling, you are so young—you should be enjoying yourself."

"If my friends forget me, I can manage without them, thank you. They don't matter a pin to me in comparison with my home and family." And she added rather spitefully, "If you must worry, worry about your mother. She has been most peculiar for a long time. She's shut herself up without any reason, not going out, not seeing people, not talking when she does see them."

A cold hand clutched Johnny's heart, but he said evenly, "She is going through a very trying period, physically and mentally. She will pull out of it. I have never known anyone who loves life—relishes it—as much as she does. Even the little things, like the first violets." He had happened upon her one afternoon in early spring, bending over the violets that grew along the side fence under the lilacs, turning back last autumn's leaves to show him and inviting him to share her pleasure. The violets, he thought, reminded her of Binny. "She will be all right," he said firmly.

"I am sure I hope so. She did not seem to be in love with life the last time I saw her."

"Why? What did she say?"

"Oh, nothing, really. Only that there comes a time in everyone's life when one wonders what it was all for."

"And so it does," Johnny said, more cheerfully. "That doesn't seem to me such an out-of-the-way remark from someone who isn't feeling up to snuff."

But just the same, when Johnny was ready to make his late afternoon calls, he tied his horse to the Gordon hitching post and went in to see his mother. He found her in her bedroom, in her rocker by the window.

"Mamma, it's a beautiful day. I thought you might like to ride in the country with me."

"I don't think so. Thank you, Johnny. I'd have to change. Why don't you take Julia?"

"She's been out once this afternoon. I'll tell you about it when I get you in the buggy. It's nonsense about your changing. Who's going to see you? Just get your bonnet on."

"'Bonnet,' indeed. Trimmed with black yet, I suppose? Men are really—Don't you know that only old ladies wear bonnets these days? Hand me my hat from the closet shelf."

Once in the buggy, spanking along with Johnny behind his young, over-eager horse, Anne, thinking only of getting safely home again, still roused herself for Johnny's sake. "What have Julia and her friends been up to?"

"Julia's friends, according to her, are up to no good: she will have none of it. They are planning to lay siege to Dan Ryan and the City Council in order to get tax money for a public library."

"Tax support? I remember Sally said something of the sort quite a while back. So they are the ones who have been writing all those pieces in the paper and carrying petitions around. Is it possible, I wonder? Think of the years we have struggled along, doing it all ourselves. Would it be legal?"

"One of them is Mrs. Tim Merrill. Tim must surely know whether it can be done or not."

"And Julia doesn't want to help? Why ever not? If she'd managed as many lawn fetes and lecture courses as her mother and I have—"

"She thinks they want to trade on her father's name. Nonsense, of course: he can't help or harm anyone now. And she hasn't a very high opinion of

City Hall. Her father's doing: he kept his womenfolk sheltered from politicians as if they were lepers."

"I don't know anyone who knew them better," Anne said drily. "Maybe he had reason."

"And she doesn't cotton much to the idea of a public library that all our citizens could use. I expect the books *would* get dirty—be regular germ carriers."

"You and your father are mad on the subject of germs. Surely a book couldn't carry them?"

"Surely it could. But there are germs everywhere: in the air we breathe, and the water we drink. Of course, we might have to buy Tuck's books."

"You read many a library book when you were a child."

"Their circulation was confined to the clean-handed section of town. But don't misunderstand me. I think it would be a very good thing. And I wish Julia did, and would help. She's been shut off too long from her friends. I can't persuade her to go out with them, even to play croquet. Every time someone laughs, she thinks her father's memory has been slighted. Lord, I'll be glad when she sheds that black. I suppose her mother will wear it another year, and Julia white or lavender or something. I don't know the rules, but whatever, she'll keep 'em. And before long her friends will be so used to her saying 'no' they'll quit asking her. She's young, Mamma. She should be getting some fun out of life. Can't you help me?"

"How? A middle-aged woman who doesn't go out herself?"

"Dammit, Mom!"

"Johnny!"

"I apologize. I'm sorry. But it's enough to make a saint swear. You must stop being a 'middle-aged woman who doesn't go out.' I know you don't feel well, and are sorry for yourself, but you should make an effort. No one can cure nerves but oneself."

"I see," Anne laughed and relaxed a little. "Dr. Johnny Gordon, curing two birds with one dose. Your father and you."

"It's been a year now. Pop's upset."

She caught her breath. "Johnny, not that long. I did get out all last winter. To Club meeting and church." She had resumed attendance at church because she found Mr. McKinney's sermons less upsetting than his pastoral visits, which he always concluded by praying for her.

"Seems to me I always find you upstairs in your rocker."

She did not reply. She was thinking, "I have wasted almost a year of my life, and spoiled a year of John's." She rode in silence the rest of the way, even when Johnny turned into a farmer's lane and stopped by the white picket fence that separated yard from fields. He said, "I have a call to make here. I won't be long." When he had lifted his bag down, opened the gate, and gone up the path, then, except for the grass-chomping horse, she was alone, sitting high and dizzy on the buggy seat. She curled her fingers around its edge, clutching it desperately, eyes closed, fearing to fall. She waited out the dizzy spell until it had passed. When she no longer felt the buggy swaying beneath her, she opened them to see not a revolving earth but stubble fields where grain had been harvested, and green fields of tall corn; on a far sloping pasture, grazing cattle; and ringing the horizon, dark in the summer sun, the trees—trees everywhere.

When Johnny came out, she straightened her shoulders and drew a long breath. As he climbed into the buggy beside her, she said, "I've been thinking. I must do better. As for Julia, remember the family picnics we used to have at the farm when you children were little? Would she enjoy something like that?"

"She might. I'll ask her. Thank you. I know it takes an effort for you even to make the suggestion. But it would be a start, for both of you."

"Let's plan it. How about asking Cousin Jessamine and Rodney? That would keep it in the family, and she's always good company. And," she hesitated, "Mrs. Deming?"

"We'll have to ask her, of course, but she won't go. And Rodney may have something better to do than go on a family picnic."

They were silent then until he stopped at the Gordon hitching post and got down to help her alight. Then she said, "Thank you for making me go with you. Some cobwebs have been brushed from my brain. They'll be back, I suppose: I doubt if I have got rid of all the spiders. But next time it may be easier. Let me know about the picnic."

If she had wondered whether John would declare himself too old for picnics, she need not have worried. He was so relieved to have her take the initiative for even the smallest end that he agreed without demur. On a warm golden summer day, they all drove out to the Gordon farm: the senior Gordons first, in the family surrey, John and Anne on the front seat, Jessamine and Rodney in back. Jessamine was suitably clad in white shirtwaist and dark skirt, a stiff straw sailor hat high and flat on her head; Rodney was resplendent in white duck trousers, a loud striped blazer, and a hat very like his mother's. Rodney at sixteen was very much the dude, and he didn't, Anne thought, look so much like Johnny as he once had: already he was taller, small-boned like all the Gordons, but so thin that he seemed all knobs, knees, and elbows, his face thin, too, all the Gordon look gone except for his eyes. Johnny and Julia, Tuck on the buggy seat between them, were close enough behind them to catch all their dust, a contingency Julia had surely not thought of when she dressed. Out of black at last, she had on a white barred dimity, with leg-of-mutton sleeves and a long flaring skirt, and wore a wide-brimmed white straw hat, trimmed with a bunch of flowers on each side and wide loops of wired ribbon towering above. The other women could not forbear exchanging a look; but after all, Anne thought, the girl had to wear her finery somewhere, and she did look enchantingly pretty, even though her "rig," as John would call it, was hardly the attire of a picnic.

At the farm they stopped to explain to the tenants why they were there, hitched the horses to the fence and let the men collect the baskets, and the carriage robes to sit on, and started for the hill, Rodney carrying Tuck, in his little white sailor suit, piggy-back style. Together they trudged up the long slope to the hilltop the Gordons had long ago chosen as a picnic site.

For the women it was more a pretense of enjoyment than the real thing: Anne endured, knowing that she would soon be home again; Julia, caring nothing for the country, was not an enthusiastic picnicker, disliking ants, crickets, and all other crawling, jumping, or flying insects; even when there were robes to sit on, Jessamine feared the evening damp for Rodney, who once in a while still had an occasional bout of malaria. The men were happier; they sprawled relaxed on the grass while the women set out the food. Happiest of all were the two boys: Rodney loved the country and eating with equal fervor; as far as food was concerned, he was a bottomless pit. When he saw the fried chicken coming out of the baskets, he knew there would be all a fellow could eat. And Tucker, who had grown to be two and a half without having seen the farm, or having been allowed to run at will, chased grasshoppers, or picked flowers of Queen Anne's lace for his mother and his grandmother; all this was unalloyed bliss.

After supper Rodney took Tucker to the pasture fence at the foot of the hill, where a curious plow horse had hung his nose over. Rodney had pilfered lumps of sugar from the picnic supply; the horse nibbled eagerly at his palm. He lifted the little boy to the top rail of the fence: from that perch Tuck, greatly daring, could pat the horse's nose and neck and mane, and when Rodney produced another lump of sugar, could, after several false starts, let the horse take it from his palm. Familiar as the child was with the hind end, the swishing tail, of his father's horse, he had never been so close to one before; this adventure, with Rodney holding him safe, was the climax to a perfect occasion. But if he was not afraid, his mother was. On the robe with the other adults, she protested: "Johnny, are you sure that horse won't bite?" Johnny laughed. "That's a farm horse, not the least bit dangerous," and Jessamine said, "He'll be all right with Rodney, he's very good with children." And John, between whom and the small boy had grown a close friendship in the last year, said, "He must have a pony when he's a little older."

"Rodney still wants to be a doctor?" Julia asked, idly. "If he's so good with children—"

"A surgeon, I believe, is his idea now. Isn't that so, Cousin Dock?"

"That would be better," Julia sighed. "He wouldn't be called out at all hours of the night for the most trivial reasons."

Johnny laughed at her. "It isn't that bad."

After that connubial exchange, they fell silent, watching dusk deepen on the grainfields and the corn, speaking only a desultory word now and then, until the lights of the town, a few miles away, began to shine at scattered points along the horizon. Then Julia rose, shook out her skirts, and said, "The mosquitoes are biting me: I'll go back to the buggy, I think. Call Rodney, will you, Johnny? Tell him it's past Tuck's bedtime."

"I'll go fetch them. Can you two carry the robes?" Julia was already halfway down the hill. "We'll bring the baskets."

And so in the twilight they drove home. And whatever reservations the two Gordon wives may have had, at least they knew the satisfaction of having pleased their husbands; and the men were happy because the shadow over their lives seemed to have lifted.

To a degree it was true. The Woman's Club programs for 1895–96 were distributed: "Poets of Greece and Rome." There were still mornings when Anne had to force herself to sit at her desk, to read and take notes on Theocritus; but she found that once there, her mind worked quite freely, and that the Idylls were a delight to read: she could take her time and enjoy them. Despair was at last only a memory. This time she found pleasure in writing her paper.

Julia, her year of mourning at an end, did not so often remind Johnny of her belief that her father's death was Dr. Warren's fault (and, by implication, Johnny's). She was bored, ready to think of other things; she was quite ready to join in games of croquet or take bicycle rides into the country with other young ladies. Unfortunately her closest friends were involved now in the campaign for a library.

They carried their petitions to City Hall and left them to be scrutinized; they interrupted the councilmen at their businesses to beg for their acquiescence. Sophie Klein, small and dun-colored as she was, could take fire; her brown eyes could snap, her temper flare as she harangued her father's German friends. Elsa would sometimes lay a restraining hand on her wrist: she would say, "Don't mind Sophie: she gets so stirred up, remembering how much better Germany is about spreading education and culture." And pleased to hear praise of the country they had left in disgust or despair, they agreed to sign petitions, or, if need be or the opportunity rose, to vote for the library.

Elizabeth Merrill, less sanguine than the younger women, expressed her discouragement to her husband one evening after dinner. Tired to death from tramping the streets all afternoon, then walking all the way home to cook dinner for her family, she had finally got her small children off to bed—three now, a girl and two boys—but she could hear them romping in the bedrooms, and would have to go up soon to settle them down, hear their prayers, and be a proper mother. She regarded with some exasperation her relaxed husband, in smoking jacket and slippers, pipe in mouth, slouched comfortably in his morris chair with the *Torchlight* in hand.

"Tim, do you suppose we can accomplish anything for the town by all this hard work? Why should those men in City Hall pay any attention to us? They know we can't vote."

"You had voters' signatures on your petitions, didn't you?" Tim looked at her over the edge of his paper.

"Yes. But we both know, and City Hall knows, that the library isn't important enough to those signers to influence their vote. In spite of the *Torchlight*'s editorials."

"If you don't get anywhere with Dan Ryan and his boys, there is another way you can go at it. Try the school board."

"The *school board*?"

"School boards are empowered by law to establish school district libraries."

"Oh—for the children."

"No. Public libraries, for the use of everyone."

"Tim Merrill! I could choke you! All that hard work when all we had to do—"

"Do you think the school board will be easier? No one should know better than you how cramped for funds the school board is."

"To all intents and purposes, the school board is Mr. Lichtenstein. Of course it would be easier. He *believes* in books."

"Try Dan Ryan first. It wouldn't be fair to go to the school board until you have been turned down by the city."

"And there's Sophie, married to Mr. Lichtenstein's son."

"Don't send Sophie. He wouldn't want to say 'no' to her, and he might have to. It would mean an increased school budget just when they're talking about a new school building for this part of town, and God knows we need it. The little brick four-room building is where I started in the first grade."

"But a new school building would mean an bond issue, wouldn't it? Or a special tax levy, to be voted on?"

"Certainly. So try Dan Ryan first."

The next afternoon Elizabeth gathered her hard-working committee together, and reported to them what her husband had so belatedly told her. "And Tim says keep Sophie out of it: it would go hard with Mr. Lichtenstein to have to say 'no' to her. And he says to pin Dan Ryan first to yes or no: it's hard enough for the school board to get money to run the schools."

The other three considered the prospect in silence for a moment, then Sophie said, "Thank you for not sending me to Papa Lichtenstein; even in this cause I should hate to beg a favor of him, especially one he wouldn't want to say 'no' to. I'll go with Charlotte to talk to Mayor Ryan, and then, depending on what he says, we can decide on the next step. You wouldn't mind talking to Papa Lichtenstein, would you, Elsa?"

"No. He's always been a friend of Papa's, even if they have gone different ways in politics. And Elizabeth can go with me. You wouldn't mind, Lib?"

"No. I always found Mr. Lichtenstein most cooperative when I was teaching school. Of course, I only asked for textbooks for poor students. I know he seems rather rough sometimes, but he doesn't mean it, really. He's very kind."

On the following day Sophie and Charlotte went early to City Hall, so early that Mayor Ryan was still hearing police court cases, and they had to wait. At last he burst into his office, borne as if on a high wind of wrath, swearing as he came: "That"—expletive, expletive—"Chief Burns! 'Chief' indeed! Of all the numbskulls—" When he saw the young women waiting for him on the bench outside the railing that enclosed the sacred space for his desk, he laughed ruefully. "I beg your pardon. But I must admit it comes as something of a surprise to find two lovely ladies waiting for me so early in the mornin'. And our Chief of Police is so exasperatin'. Do come inside me little fence here and we'll go in me private office. Private cupboard, more like it, but there's room for three chairs."

He seated them with a gallant gesture, retreated to his own swivel chair behind the desk, and continued. "You're back on the same errand, is it? Still badgerin' me? I admire the persistence of the female sex." He was middle-aged, exaggeratedly Irish, white-haired and ruddy, not handsome, but pleasant looking.

"We haven't had an answer from you yet, in spite of all the petitions we have turned over to you. Are we to have the library we are entitled to, or not?"

"You ladies use mighty strong words. The law *enables* us—it doesn't *entitle* you. And you just naturally wouldn't realize how hard times are—you haven't been touched, I don't suppose. But the town of Waynesboro may be settin' up soup kitchens this winter. How can we spend money for luxuries?"

Charlotte, although she had definitely been "touched" by the depression (the *Torchlight*'s subscriptions and advertising were both way down), still did not argue with him about family finances. She said, "We do not consider a library for the use of everyone a luxury. It is a necessity, if we are to have educated citizens. Don't you care whether your children have books?"

"My children are through school. I can't say they're great readers. But yes, I care that children have the right books in their schools. The Sisters have a library for the youngsters at St. Anne's."

"Times aren't as hard as you are making out," Sophie said, cutting. "Mr. Rausch is building a new factory in Madison City; he must believe—"

"And a hell of a lot of good that is going to do Waynesboro, beggin' your pardon."

"And Mr. Hoffmann is putting up a biscuit factory here."

"Hoffmann? Ain't he your uncle? Ain't you Fritz Klein's girl?"

"Yes. They both think things are going to get better. Depending on the election, of course."

"The election, of course," Mayor Ryan said, airily. "And they're prayin' for a good solid Republican victory to keep 'em safe, with their money bags. I hear Rausch's girl has been busy with these petitions: why doesn't she come to see me? There's questions I could ask her."

"Ask them of Mr. Rausch, why don't you?" Sophie was warming up. "He doesn't bite. And I can tell you why his daughter hasn't been to see you: She says her father has never taken a hand in town politics, and swears he never will, but if she came to see you, you might interpret it as a—a—"

"Threat? So I might. And true enough it is, for sure: he has never stooped to use his influence to affect the choice of any official below the county level. And I'm sorry I riled you—didn't mean to. So far as I know, Rausch is a good fellow and an honest man in politics, which is more than you can say for some. And I'm glad he don't want to tell me and the Council how to run the town. Because you ladies ain't going to get your library. Not this year. When things are better—if we get a Democrat for Governor this fall—come see me again, and maybe you'll find me more generous."

"To hear you talk," Charlotte said, rising and drawing herself to her ungraceful height, "anyone would think it was your money, not the town's. That what the town wants—"

"I'm trusted with the spendin' of it, me an' the Council. An' if the town wants something that simply ain't possible, then it's up to us to decide for them." He had risen as Charlotte did.

"In your greater wisdom?" Sophie could not resist it. She too got to her feet.

"You mean that sarcastic-like, but yes, in our greater wisdom: we know what the town needs and how much money we've got to pay for it. I'm sorry I can't give every citizen what he asks for. It's impossible. I hope you won't hold this refusal too much against us. Miss Bonner's always given us fair treatment in the *Torchlight*, for a Republican paper. I hope you will try to see our side of this question, Miss Bonner."

He got them out of his office with what Charlotte, on the way down the steps, called a lot of blarney. He was delighted to have met them, to have had a chance to talk to them, he was trying to do what was best for the town. He hoped they would come see him again at a more auspicious time.

"And that time will never come," Charlotte concluded. "The town isn't so poverty-stricken as he made out. Pity the poor taxpayer, yes, but all the taxpayers aren't so poor: the railroads pay taxes, and so does Rausch Cordage and all the others. The school board is probably more put to it for funds. If only he weren't a Catholic; Catholics are afraid of free and unrestricted reading."

Sophie sighed. "I'm sorry I didn't get anywhere. Because I'm going to have to give up all these public appearances."

Charlotte looked her over, smiling. "I have wondered a little how long you could keep this up. It does show, but how ridiculous it is to have to withdraw behind closed shutters! How long?"

"November, I think and hope. I'll be glad when it is over."

(Her wish was granted. Sophie gave birth to a boy early in that November and artfully gave him a German name: Friedrich, soon and for his lifetime to be shortened to Fritz.)

The next day, it was the turn of Elsa and Elizabeth Merrill to approach Mr. Lichtenstein; together they climbed the scuffed wooden staircase to the corridor from which his office opened. There he acted as notary public, sold a little insurance, ran the Waynesboro schools, and got a lot of reading done.

Rudy's new law office was across the hall; he had not come into his father's office, preferring independence.

Mr. Lichtenstein rose ponderously as they entered, peering at them through the thick-lensed glasses he had taken to wearing. His greeting was spoken on a rising inflection. "Goot morning, ladies? Vot—?" Then as they came closer he said, "Ach, now I know you zis vun," pointing at Elizabeth. "You vunce taught English in ze high school. Talmadge? Mrs. Timothy Merrill?"

Elizabeth shook hands with him. "It is flattering to be remembered after all these years."

"And zis lady? You vill introduce us?"

"I'm sorry—I supposed of course—Elsa, may I introduce Mr. Lichtenstein? Mrs. Gilbert Evans."

He smote his perspiring forehead with a fat palm. "Dummkopf! Allerdings! Mein oldt friend Ludvig's Tochter. But you I haf not seen since you vere in school noch. Your Vater I do not see often zese days."

"I know. He regrets it. Just because of politics—"

"Bitte, setzen Sie sich." He got them seated and eased himself back into his chair. "You mean"—his eyes twinkled behind the spectacles—"he vould like to see me? But I haf put myself beyont ze pale. It vas badt enough to be vot zey calledt a 'Mugvump,' but to be a Socialist, zat iss too far to go."

"Papa doesn't base his friendships on politics. He and Uncle Dock miss you at the chess table."

"Ach—vell, vell—I must drop in ze Doctor's office und haf a game. Now, ladies." He beamed at them. "Vill you permit zat I guess vot brings you here? I haf been expecting someone."

"You know what we are after?"

"Ya. From ze kleine Sophie, from ze petitions, from ze *Torchlight*, I know vot you are trying to do. Und from vot I know of ze Mayor, I know you vill not get it from him."

"You knew all along that we were bound to come to you? That the law permits—?"

He linked his thick hands together over his expansive abdomen, leaned back, and sighed, "Ya, I know ze law. I know all ze school laws und ze tax laws. I chust hoped you vouldn't find it out."

"My husband is a lawyer."

"Vell I know it. Und I know zis town needs a free library. But ze schools: zey need much, too."

"But you will help us?" Elsa had caught the rueful note in his guttural tones, which said that now that they had come to him, he must respond.

"I vill help you. You shall haf your library. If ze ozzer members of ze school board agree. Ve shall haf to see how much it costs."

The two young women were so astonished at the ease with which they had finally won that they could have wept to think of the time and strength wasted; still he would not have agreed had they not tried the Mayor first. They caught their breath and proceeded to enlighten him with the figures they knew so well by this time: the room, rent-free (if they could just bring about the turn-over of the Subscription Library). Mr. McKay the printer, who now owned the building where the library had been established, promised not to charge for it, however the library was supported: the room had not paid rent for so many years that he hardly considered it an asset. It would have to be heated in the winter, of course: that would mean buying coal for the stove; and Ruhamah McCune would have to be paid her twenty-five dollars a month.

"Zat iss not enough, iss it? How many hours iss she there?"

"The library is open three afternoons a week and Saturday evening. But as to how many hours she is there: I expect it is most of every day. She hasn't any other interest, as far as I know, and there's always work to be done, like cataloguing books and making out bills and cards. I know Mamma used to spend more time there than just her afternoon at the desk. I must say," Elsa added, "I never thought of it, but I don't see how Ruhamah manages. Of course she wears the same clothes year in and year out."

"Und maybe vould like somesing new vunce in a vile? She must haf more, so she can get some fun out of life, und safe for her old age."

"Then," said Elizabeth, "there are the books. That has been the real trouble. Many have been read to pieces, and we haven't money for replacements, let alone new ones. We should have a lot more money for books than we have had. Most of what is added to the library comes from family attics."

"I know. Ze sings my boys bring home! New books zere must be. I vill call a special meeting of ze school board. Zere vill be opposition, you know. Zose who subscribe to ze library may see ze need. Ze ozzers: zey don't read, so vy vould zey care?"

"But you think it will be all right?"

"It vill be all right, or I vill make ze t'reat to resign. I so do, vunce in a vile. Zen zey draw in zeir horns, zey don't vant to be bothered; chust to come to a meeting vunce a monse; zat iss enough." He laughed until he shook; the young women laughed with him, and rose to take their departure, thanking him with all their hearts. On the stairs outside they leaned one against each of the dusty walls, and looked across at each other. All that work, and at the end—so easy! But when they had recovered a little from the shock, Elsa said, "Maybe Papa was right: maybe all the groundwork he insisted on had more to do with it than we realize now. Well, next time we'll know how to campaign for what we want."

As autumn advanced, the Waynesboro Public Library became a certainty: money for its operation was appropriated by the school board, and a Board of Trustees appointed, one of whom, Mrs. Timothy Merrill, was chosen as a gesture toward the Woman's Club. The Trustees of the Subscription Library finally gave way: both Amanda and Sheldon Edwards resigned, saying there was no longer a need for their services; the three ministers were frightened at the thought of the efforts that would be required to continue raising the necessary funds, especially since so many subscriptions were being canceled. The two boards met together, and after a rather stiff discussion all possessions of the Subscription Library (catalogues, card files, books, desk, and other furniture) were turned over to the new board, along with the keys. A Waynesboro Public Library was a reality at last.

The Club had begun its fortnightly meetings in September; Anne was there in October to read her paper on Theocritus. John was working himself to exhaustion that fall combating cases of diphtheria among the school children and trying to prevent its becoming a real epidemic. He let Johnny take his other cases, knowing how Julia would feel were her husband to come into contact with the disease and perhaps carry it home to Tucker. She did not much like the idea of such a possibility herself. John was perfectly safe: he had had diphtheria as a boy.

If men like John Gordon, busy with their own affairs, were not much excited about the coming gubernatorial election, it was not surprising. However strenuous the campaigning, the results were not, in the minds of the Republicans, in any doubt. Waynesboro turned out in force only once to listen to an orator: Governor McKinley came to stay overnight at the Rausches', and spoke in the afternoon from the Court House steps to the citizens assembled there, and the next morning to the Rausch Cordage Company workmen gathered in the cobbled yard to hear him. The Governor won the same tumultuous response as he traveled from one end of the state to the other, even from miners and other laborers, as well as from farmers and businessmen. When the third of November had come and gone, the tabulated results of the voting were almost anticlimactic: the Republican Bushnell, Foraker's man, had been elected Governor by an even larger majority than McKinley's in '93; the new legislature, to meet in January, was so overwhelmingly Republican as to make certain the choice of Foraker as Senator on the expiration of the Democrat Brice's term.

In the relaxed days after the election, when it seemed that the winter would come and go without disturbing incident, Paul Rausch came down with diphtheria. Sally, at first admitting only a slight misgiving (children were always having sore throats), kept a rebellious boy home from school, put him to bed, and called the doctor. John was busy in the West End; it was the junior Dr. Gordon who came.

Johnny hardly needed to examine Paul; his breath was enough. But he swabbed his throat out, took his temperature, and said, "There's no doubt about it, Aunt Sally, he's picked up diphtheria somewhere."

"Diphtheria!" Sally's hand went to her throat. "I knew there were cases in town, but I thought it was the parochial school children."

"There are a few cases in the public schools. Don't be frightened: diphtheria isn't the dangerous disease it was before we had antitoxin. Fortunately, we have a supply, to combat what is beginning to look like an epidemic. Just let me call the office: Rod Stevens is there—he'll bring up a phial."

When Johnny returned from calling Rodney, he reported that his father had answered the phone and had offered to take over. "Would you feel safer with Paul in his hands? His diphtheria cases are all coming along in good shape."

While Sally hesitated, Paul, who had not to this point spoken, uttered a croaking "Johnny."

"But Paul! You like Uncle Dock."

"Johnny better."

Sally eyed the child doubtfully. "What has got into him? Your father is caring for the diphtheria cases? On account of little Tucker? Maybe we'd better have him."

Paul, who looked amazingly long stretched out under his covers, began lifting his knees and kicking out at the foot of the bed. "No, no. I want Johnny."

"Stop that, Paul. You're no baby. You're twelve years old. You'll just make yourself sick."

"I'll begin screaming."

"You'd better not, young man. You'll send your temperature soaring." Johnny placed a restraining hand on the lifting knees. "If it is so important to you, I'll be your doctor. Very flattering, you are. Believe me, most of our patients prefer the old doctor to the young one. There isn't really any danger of taking it home, Aunt Sally, if I'm careful. And Tucker has been inoculated. Paul may change his mind when I say that we'll begin medication with a dose of calomel to clean him out. And he must gargle every hour and a half—he won't like that either. First hydrogen peroxide and then chlorate of potash. I'll call Thirkield before I go and have them sent up. How about a nurse?"

"I'll take care of him."

"Bathe him, feed him, see that he gargles?"

"Yes. But what about the quarantine?"

"Of course. Get the draperies down off the windows. Have Rose boil them. Give him plenty of air, and keep him wrapped up warm. There must be strict isolation from the rest of the household." He ticked off the precautions that must be taken. "You're lucky Paul's the only one home. But what about Uncle Ludwig? You can't very well send him to Shaney, with those two babies."

"He's had diphtheria, I think."

"Then he'll be all right. Just don't let him inside the door, so he can't carry it. Let nothing go out of the room except the trays. Can you depend on your cook to boil them? Sometimes they can't see the necessity."

"I can depend on the cook and Rose."

The front doorbell rang: Rodney with the antitoxin. Sally called to Rose to answer the door and bring the phial up. Johnny, who had already scrubbed his hands in the bathroom and swabbed the child's buttock with alcohol, took the phial, punctured the seal with the hypodermic needle, and filled the syringe. Sally eyed the proceedings doubtfully. "Johnny, are you sure? It's so new—couldn't something go wrong?"

"No, I'm sure. It's what Pop would do, first thing. It's a godsend, this antitoxin. Before many years, diphtheria will be eradicated." He thrust the needle home, let the antitoxin flow slowly until the syringe was empty, withdrew the needle, slapped an alcohol-soaked piece of cotton over the puncture, and fastened it down with sticking plaster.

"There, that wasn't bad, was it?" The physician's inevitable question.

"It hurt, but I didn't yell. Will it be sore?"

"It could be, for a day or so. You may want to lie on your tummy."

He pulled the covers up, told Sally what the boy should and shouldn't have to eat, and took his departure.

Paul was at no time seriously ill; the quarantine period seemed to his parents and to Elsa interminably long; he himself was contented enough with books to read (and fumigated after); he spent his days waiting for Johnny to appear. This apparently sudden and, to his mother, inexplicable devotion to Johnny continued and was indeed the only lasting effect of his illness. He even said to his mother one day that he thought he would be a doctor when he grew up. "Maybe Uncle Dock will let me help in the office when I'm well, like Rodney."

"What nonsense! You haven't the slightest bent in that direction. What of your violin?"

He regarded her gravely from his pillow. "Don't you think saving people's lives is more important than playing the violin?"

"Doctors don't always save people's lives. And I think in a way music is just as important. Any art is, if it is real art."

Paul said no more. He did love his violin. The boys he went to school with thought it was a sissy thing to do, play the violin. He would not complain to his mother: she would say that if they had ever called his brother Ludwig a sissy, he hadn't minded, when Paul knew that Ludwig had been able to put a stop to it just by being so big and strong that he could lick any boy who dared try it. He wished Ludwig Junior were at home, instead of away at school.

Paul, on the doctor's orders, was to be kept home until the first of the year, when he would presumably have recovered from the possible effects, as Johnny warned them, of even a mild case of diphtheria: anemia, a functionally disturbed heart. While housebound, he spent his hours with his violin; and his teacher, who came up from the city once a week, encouraged Sally to believe that this last of her children might be the musical genius she had hoped for: Paul hadn't yet the emotional reach of Ludwig Junior; technically he was excellent, and could look forward to a brilliant career. But when Paul was given his freedom and was out and about, he began to haunt the doctors' office, offering to roll bandages, to help Rodney sterilize instruments and deliver medicine, and to ride with one or other of the doctors on afternoon calls. This phase lasted only briefly, but Paul never outgrew his conviction that Johnny could do no wrong.

Sally resumed her duties as President of the Waynesboro Woman's Club. She was in time to plan the usual Christmas party, and she appointed the committee. It was at one of those meetings that Julia Gordon said something about Paul's sudden interest in medicine. "I thought he was going to be a musician."

"It's just a passing notion. He was so interested in being doctored himself."

"I can't understand the fascination," Julia went on. "First there was Johnny himself, then Rodney Stevens, now Paul."

"Rodney is old enough now to know what he wants. Paul will get over it."

"I should think you would keep him away. He might pick up anything there."

"Oh, you can't forbid a boy his age from pursuing his interests, whether it's butterfly collecting or doctoring. It would just make him more stubborn."

Julia smiled. "I guess Paul generally manages to get his own way."

"What do you mean?" To suggest to a mother that her child is spoiled is to ask for instant dudgeon.

"Oh, nothing. Just that Johnny told me, when he was first sick, that you both wanted to call Papa Dock and he would have none of it."

"That's true. But you can't cross a child with a fever. You were afraid Johnny would bring diphtheria home? You've no idea how he scrubbed before he left."

"I'm always afraid to some extent." Julia shrugged. "It goes with being a doctor's wife, I guess. I know Mamma Gordon thinks I am foolishly nervous, but then she was a doctor's daughter, too: she's always been used to it."

"You'll have a hard time when Tucker wants to haunt his father's office."

"Heaven forbid!" Julia shuddered. "I should hate for him to take up medicine. Law or business."

"Tucker isn't quite three, is he? You won't have to worry for a while."

"I don't worry. I intend to see to it."

Sally laughed and changed the subject. Julia had a lot to learn about "seeing to it" that boys went the way you hoped and planned. There was Ludwig, counting on at least one of four boys to follow him at Rausch Cordage and so far disappointed: the older boys hadn't the brains—they would never set the world on fire, agreeable young men though they might be—and Ludwig Junior hadn't the stamina, his father thought, ever to amount to anything. Sally still had hopes for young Ludwig: she might spoil Paul, but Ludwig was the only one with fire in him, a spirit that made him the apple of her eye, however well she might try to conceal it. Ludwig Senior's hopes were now centered in Paul. And Paul had brains, but strength of character enough? She wondered. She thought again of how Ludwig had fretted and worried through those days when he could only stand in the door of Paul's bedroom and come no further; he had grown quite haggard before it was all safely over and the quarantine lifted.

The spring of '96 was an active one, and Ludwig had many things on his mind. Rausch Cordage could safely be left with Bodien in charge, but he had to see to it that through Gib what was made was also sold, even though the depression lingered. He was also concerned with making plans for Charles, who had still one more year at the state university: having spent his summers in the Waynesboro mill, he would be put in charge of the warehouse in Kansas City. Gib would be made sales manager with an office in Waynesboro, and the first branch agency would go to Charles. "I know Charles isn't the smartest young man in the world," Ludwig admitted to his wife, "but shipping orders out of a warehouse should be well within his capacity."

Ludwig was also busy with Rausch and Bodien Coated Paper, Inc. Common shares had been floated with fair success on a sluggish market, and there was enough capital in hand to start production; machinery had been installed, and capable men experienced in paper-making had been found and hired by Stewart. There was no dearth of labor. Production had been started, and the new company had obtained some orders. Stewart was managing the business, but Ludwig went down to Madison City by Interurban once a week to see that operations were proceeding smoothly and that nothing had gone wrong.

He had come home from one of those trips to say to Sally, laughing—she somehow felt that he had been laughing to himself all the way home—"Guess what? Stewart has got himself one of those newfangled horseless carriages."

"He has! Isn't he a little visionary and impractical?" Then her curiosity got the better of her. "What is it like? I've never ever seen one. Is it so funny?"

"It's mighty funny to see a carriage go down the street without horses. But I was laughing because he wanted to take me for what he called "a spin." I was willing enough, though it seemed to me a pretty rackety contraption, and sure enough, we hadn't gone a block before something went wrong and we were stuck in the middle of the street. I told him I thought I would stick to horses for a while."

"I hope his feelings weren't hurt."

"Not his. He didn't even know I was laughing at him. He honestly believes the internal combustion engine is the greatest invention of the century, and that we'll all be driving motor cars in no time. And he may be right. The horse may be on the way out."

Most of all, that late winter and spring of 1896, Ludwig, still a member of the Republican State Committee, was working with Mr. Hanna and other of McKinley's friends to make sure that right-thinking delegates were chosen to go to the National Convention; plans were being made, forehandedly, for the election itself. Ludwig had always felt that the country's well-being depended on the presidential elections, but he had never been so convinced of it as this year. There were all kinds of radical notions in the air: free silver, and free trade, and other Populist notions that could ruin not only him, his mills, and his workmen but all the industry and all the labor in the country. And the farmers, too, as they would learn when they sold their corn for basketfuls of money worth nothing.

His wife saw little of Ludwig as the spring wore on, or she saw him in the company of men he had asked to Waynesboro for councils of war—Hanna's lieutenants, McKinley's friends: Charles Dick, who one day would be senator; William Day, who would go in the end to the Supreme Court; Myron Herrick, the future governor and ambassador who in those early years became a fast friend of Ludwig's. Sally entertained them all, as well as Mark Hanna himself; she went with Ludwig to visit the Hannas in Cleveland, as she had done before; the air of victory foreordained, in which these men moved, determined her: she had been to National Conventions whose outcomes had been to say the least disappointing; she would go to this one and for once see Ludwig and his friends triumphant.

The Ohio Convention in March was a rousing success for the McKinley men; the delegates to the National Convention chosen by the State Convention were divided two and two between the Hanna and Foraker men; Foraker himself, chosen leader of Ohio's National delegates, made every effort to reassure the Hanna men of his good faith and firm intentions. Endorsements of McKinley from other states soon followed. By June only one possible rival remained in the field: Tom Reed of Maine, who would have the support of the New England delegations, and of two formidable bosses, Quay of Pennsylvania and Platt of New York, who had been McKinley's implacable enemies since he had said "that he would take the place, if it came to him, unmortgaged," and refused to promise cabinet posts to men of their choosing in return for their support. The obvious advantage held by McKinley in the early spring had set the yellow press of New York yapping at his heels; since Mark Hanna was a more vulnerable target than his candidate, he was made to seem the most infamous figure in political history by scurrilous articles and caricatures; the Hearst *Journal* cartoonist Davenport made of Mark Hanna the familiar bloated figure seated on money bags, the picture of greed, the enemy of the working man, who pulled the strings that made McKinley dance. These misrepresentations of a likable man who happened to have a genius for organization, and who had always been one of the state's most enlightened and liberal employers, hurt Hanna to the quick; outraged, he even threatened a libel suit against the *Journal*. Ludwig was almost as deeply incensed: "This picture of McKinley as a puppet is the most blatant falsehood. Mark Hanna respects and loves him, and knows better than to argue with him when he says 'no'—and he does say it and mean it."

All the Platt-inspired vituperation had little effect; McKinley's nomination had become almost certainty by the time the Convention met. The Rausches went off to St. Louis together in June. Sally was once again to be one of the hostesses of the Ohio delegation; she went with a light heart, since Ludwig was so certain of the outcome. She returned to Waynesboro in triumph, full of her experiences, and eager to talk to someone about them. She summoned Anne Gordon and Elsa Evans to tea on the afternoon after she reached home. She was alone; Ludwig had gone to Canton with innumerable others to "notify" and congratulate the nominee.

"The drama really began," Sally reported, "with the Resolution Committee's platform: the gold standard plank. When it was voted on affirmatively, the silver men got up and walked out. That was a sad thing to see, somehow; some of them were old men who had been Republicans all their lives. But everyone knew the Far Westerners wanted Free Silver, and we can better afford to lose them than the industrial East."

"To say nothing of the principle of the thing," Elsa interrupted. "I don't believe Papa would support anyone on the ground of expediency, just to win the election."

"Of course not. I didn't mean it that way. We've got to maintain the gold standard or we'll have more inflation and the country will go to pot. Well, on Thursday, came the nominating speeches. You read Senator Foraker's speech in the paper? He's a real old-time silver tongue: he managed to sustain suspense even when everyone there knew what he was warming up to, and when he came to McKinley's name the Convention went stark staring mad. It was bedlam. When he could finally make himself heard, he said, 'You seem to have heard my candidate's name before' and that set them off again. You could tell there and then what the vote would be. Just the same, the most thrilling part of any Convention comes with the roll call of the states: 'Alabama, 18 votes'—'Alabama casts 18 votes for McKinley,' Of course everyone knew Mr. Hanna had the southern delegates lined up, but just the same, to hear it. And after that the votes kept mounting up so fast that anyone who could add could figure that Ohio's vote would clinch the nomination. Of course it did, and that set off pandemonium again. But they finally were able to get on with the roll call; in the end McKinley tallied 660 plus, and Mr. Reed just 84."

"And Ludwig is overjoyed?"

"Of course, it's the first time in all his years of politicking that his man has been nominated. And he thinks the platform will mean the end of hard times."

"They're ending already," Elsa said, "maybe just in anticipation; but McKinley still has to be elected."

"Oh, he'll be elected all right. The Democrats are badly split, and the depression is about over. If McKinley should lose, and surely everyone knows it but the Populists and those wild men out West, the improvement in industry and banking and everything would come to a sudden end."

Republicans retained their serene certainty in the outcome of the election for exactly a month. They awaited with patronizing curiosity the doings of the Democratic Convention in Chicago in July: the party was torn with dissension; Cleveland and his solid money supporters were anathema to the free-silver men; and there were enough Populists from the farm states to hold the balance of power and control the Convention. But they had few prominent leaders, and none known to the country as a whole; the recognized leaders were all Cleveland supporters.

The platform proved to be even more radical than had been feared; a Resolution Committee selected one William Jennings Bryan from Nebraska (a young ex-Congressman who recently had been lecturing in the prairie country) to address the convention. The party then declared that he spoke for the masses; demanded first of all the free and unlimited coinage of both gold and silver at the ratio of sixteen to one; denounced the protective tariff, asking for stronger federal control of railroads, and trusts, censured government interference with strikes (a look back at Cleveland's use of troops in the Pullman strike) and the use of injunctions in labor disputes; and recommended an income tax in the face of the recent Supreme Court decision that such a tax would be unconstitutional. It was a platform to make conservatives shake in their shoes, and worse was to follow. After the report was read, Bryan spoke to the Convention. He had nothing new to say, nothing he had not said before in his speeches around the country, but now the whole nation was listening. Even the concluding metaphor that electrified the delegates had been used before: "You shall not press down upon the brow of labor this crown of thorns; you shall not crucify mankind upon a cross of gold." But if not new, it was new to many who then heard it for the first time; it stampeded the Convention, made Bryan the presidential candidate, and became the Democrats' rallying cry in the campaign.

To Republicans and conservative Democrats alike, all this was the most incredible folly. Many believed it to be a Red Revolution, threatening the country with disaster as it had not been threatened since 1860. Only McKinley remained serene, confident that when they hysteria was over, the people would make the right decision once they understood the underlying principles. He remained at Canton, receiving delegations on his front porch, while Hanna set about organizing a systematic collection of money from bankers, financiers, and industrialists—additional money that Bryan's nomination made necessary. The problem of instructing the electorate in the "underlying principles" could not be left entirely to McKinley on his front porch. There must be a larger than usual outlay for buttons, posters, parades, and rallies; there must be expense money for speakers, who were to go even to rural schoolhouses to talk to farmers; and the country must be flooded with tons of literature and every doorbell rung. Inflation was explained in words of one syllable to everyone who owned even a small piece of property or a little money in a savings bank. William Allen White wrote an anti-Populist tract, "What's the Matter with Kansas?" and a million copies of it were printed and distributed by the Republican Committee.

McKinley's campaign proved surprisingly effective; he was a simple and informal speaker and could make his points on free silver and the tariff quite clear to the many thousands who came in delegations to Canton to hear him. Republicans breathed a little easier as autumn advanced; nevertheless, they recognized that Bryan would inevitably carry the South and the Far West, and they continued unremittingly their campaign in the Middle West and the industrial East. The nation's excitement over the election increased in a steady crescendo.

At the height of the campaign, Rudy Lichtenstein, who was working for Bryan, showed that he was willing to jeopardize a budding law practice. He went into the Rausch Cordage Company office one morning to ask Ludwig Rausch's permission to address the mill hands—"bearding the lion in his den," as he said, unoriginally.

"I have no objection to your speaking to them in the yard during their noon hour. I'll tell Bodien to announce it. But I warn you: you won't get anywhere with them. They know that this mill and their wages depend on the election of McKinley."

"They've been told so, no doubt."

"Of course they have, and why not? I am not trying to hoodwink them: I believe it myself. A few more years of free trade and we'd go under. You don't believe that? Well, I've argued with your father many a time and gotten nowhere; I am not going to argue with you. You don't see Bryan as a dangerous man?"

"No."

"All right, go ahead and make your speech and see what response you get."

And as Rudy told Sophie afterward, it had been hopeless. The men scarcely listened to him. They were, he said, ignorant and stupid, and naturally believed what their employer told them. "And that's the way it is all over the country: labor is being coerced by employers."

"Are you sure that they would not suffer if Bryan is elected?" Sophie had, after all, been raised in a Republican household.

"What does a protective tariff do for them? It puts money in the pockets of their bosses. The gold standard helps the rich and hurts the poor: those who find themselves in debt, those—"

"But if their employers failed because of foreign competition, or their wages had to be cut— Oh, I know what you think, and outside this house I don't question your wisdom, believe me, Rudy. Just don't get into an argument with Papa."

"The Republicans are going to win this election. Because they have the money, not because they are right."

Many things besides Hanna's organization were working for McKinley that fall: things as fortuitous as the soaring price of wheat, as natural as the small businessman's awakening to the fact that he as well as the banker was a capitalist who would be badly hurt by free silver. Inevitably the reaction to the increasing radicalism of Bryan's speeches turned voters against him, and the Democrats knew that the silver magnates backing him were not exactly poor men. Still many Republicans went to the polls on that November morning in fear and trembling, and waited for the count in almost unendurable suspense.

The results were not slow in being reported: late on election day bulletins were pasted up in the *Torchlight* window. By midnight it was known that McKinley had a safe majority in the electoral college and a larger one in the popular vote than any candidate since Grant. All Republicans went to bed in exhausted relief: a threat to the country had been averted by the good sense of the people; the "free silver" nonsense had been put to an end for good and all; the recovery from the long depression would continue unchecked now that businessmen and industrialists knew they would be protected from foreign competition.

Ludwig was completely happy over the results of the election until, in January, John Sherman resigned his seat in the Senate to accept the proffered post of Secretary of State in the new administration, the resignation to take effect after the inauguration.

"So, the kingmaker wants to be king," Ludwig in a kind of sick anger exclaimed to Sally. He would not permit his anger to be seen outside his house, but he had to express himself somewhere. "After all these years of supporting Sherman—Hanna wants his Senate seat, and Sherman has been sacrificed to make room for him."

"But to be Secretary of State—isn't that an honor? A promotion?"

"I wonder whether he thinks so. He's an old man who has had no experience in foreign affairs. He won't hold that office a month: he isn't fitted for it. He knew the Senate like the back of his hand: he would have been safe there the rest of his life."

"Do you mean you think McKinley would appoint an unfit man to please Hanna?"

"I don't suppose McKinley realizes he is an unfit man. But with all this trouble over Cuba boiling up—I suppose Hanna has persuaded him that it is an honor to Sherman. McKinley has been loyal to Sherman all his political life, and would like to do something to honor him."

"But McKinley can't make Mr. Hanna Senator."

"No. And there may be trouble over it. Governor Bushnell is a Foraker man, and he and Foraker between them can pretty well tell the legislature what to do."

And in fact the Ohio legislature fought off making the appointment for a good six weeks, until the President-elect himself requested it. In the meantime, Hanna had been infuriated by the reluctance to appoint him, and Foraker and his friends were outraged at having to "take care" of a man they regarded as an enemy; their revenge came in the widespread rumors of Sherman's senility, and suggestions of a political intrigue. Ludwig was so sickened and disillusioned by the whole course of events (he had always taken Mark Hanna's disinterestedness for granted) that he vowed that he was done with politics forever, and resigned as State Central Committeeman. Nevertheless he accepted for himself and Sally an invitation to the inauguration and the inauguration ball, an occasion which Sally reported as having been an awful crush, but enjoyable if you liked that sort of thing.

Ludwig, who would gladly have omitted the ball, rejoiced to have heard the inaugural address in which McKinley said his administration would follow Washington's policy of non-involvement in the affairs of foreign nations. "War should never be entered upon until every agency of peace has failed." Which meant that unless the President were pushed into it by events and the men who wanted it, there would be no war with Spain over Cuba, although both parties in their platforms had expressed sympathy for Cuban independence, Congress had passed resolutions in favor of recognizing the insurgents as belligerents, and Cleveland in his final message to Congress had warned of the limits of American patience: "The United States is not a country to which peace is necessary." Ludwig was firmly convinced, in spite of the report of the abuses and cruelties of the Spaniards in Cuba, that Spain could be ousted from there without a war. War with Spain would be ridiculous, absurd, at any time, but especially just when the country was getting on its feet again.

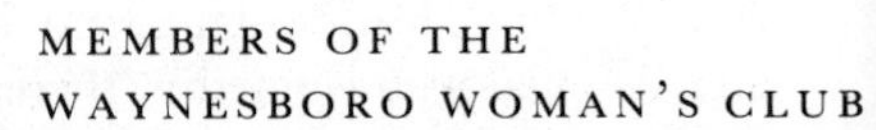

MEMBERS OF THE
WAYNESBORO WOMAN'S CLUB

Miss Eliza Ballard
Miss Charlotte Bonner
Mrs. Louisa Deming
Mrs. Elsa Evans
Mrs. Gwen Evans
Mrs. Anne Gordon
Mrs. Julia Gordon
Mrs. Sophie Lichtenstein
Mrs. Rhoda McKinney
Mrs. Laura Maxwell
Mrs. Elizabeth Merrill
Mrs. Sarah Rausch
Miss Amanda Reid
Mrs. Jessamine Stevens
Mrs. Thomasina Travers
Mrs. Christina Voorhees

IN MEMORIAM

Mrs. Mary Ballard
Miss Susan Crenshaw
Mrs. Katherine Edwards
Miss Caroline Gardiner
Miss Lavinia Gardiner
Mrs. Mary McCune
Miss Agatha Pinney

✻ 1898 ✻

"On Independence Day we celebrate a Club anniversary, a house-warming, and a great victory."

By late spring of 1898, Ludwig Rausch's country home, begun the year before, was finished and furnished, except for a few final touches like rugs and draperies. When all was done, the family, including Elsa, Gib, and their children, would transfer themselves to Hillcrest for the summer. The house stood at the top of a hill a few miles from Waynesboro on the old Madison City pike; it was not distinguished in architecture: just a square white frame house that looked from the road below less huge than it was because of the surrounding grassy lawns and the towering oak trees that had been left standing. It overlooked the long slope with its terraced stone path, the dusty country road the path led to, and beyond the road, the interurban traction line, the canal, and its towpath, lined with sycamore trees. The slow-moving river lay behind the house at a greater distance; barns and stables were off to the right, so that from the back porch there was a wide view: river, willow trees, fields, pastures, and wooded hills. A place intended for outdoor living, it had a twenty-foot-wide porch on all four sides, its roof supported by slender posts with railings between them except where interrupted by steps: to the front path, to the kitchen path, to the driveway on the right leading to the stables, and to the lawn and grove of oak trees on the fourth side. A hall wide as most rooms stretched from front door to back door, and separated the high-ceilinged rooms; an curving staircase led to an upstairs hall and the bedrooms on second and third floors—bedrooms enough for all the guests they could want: Ernest and his family, Charles and his family, Elsa and hers, Ludwig's sister Minna, including her children, their spouses, and her grandchildren.

Ludwig planned a housewarming for the Fourth of July, when they hoped to be in residence. On an afternoon in mid-June Sally went to the desk in the town house with the list of names Ludwig had given her, intending to write a number of informal invitations, her brisk air a rejection of her disinclination to do so. A large part of Waynesboro was to be asked to spend an afternoon and evening at Hillcrest: a combination housewarming, Fourth of July celebration, and thirtieth-anniversary dinner for the Woman's Club. Sally at forty-eight was the perfect picture of the stately dowager, above being troubled by any social occasion. Her hair, twisted into a figure-of-eight knot and anchored by a tortoise shell pin on the crown of her head, was darker than when she had been a girl, but there was no gray in it, and her face was unwrinkled. She had put on weight with the years, and her sternly corseted body was undeniably matronly; she had become what her masculine acquaintances might well call "a fine figure of a woman." She sat at her desk now, incongruously nibbling at her pen like a troubled schoolgirl, a lapse from her usual air of masterful capability. The truth was that she felt unsure of being able to manage the coming celebration.

The idea of a country house had seemed when Ludwig first proposed it something of an absurdity. Waynesboro itself was country enough: you could stand on any corner in the town in haying season and smell sweet clover, or when grain was being harvested suffer the annoyance of wheat-bugs blown in from surrounding fields to nip arms and face with pain out of all proportion to their size. But Sally had fallen in with his plans, wondering whether in the back of his mind all these years Ludwig had felt, perhaps unconsciously, an uneasiness at having lived most of his married life in what was in fact (and on the tongues of most townspeople) the Cochran house, and her property.

So far as expense was concerned, there had been no reason to demur: prosperity had returned with a rush after McKinley's inauguration two years before, what with the new protective tariff, the end at least for the time being of the free silver heresy, and bumper crops that had quieted Populist demands. And with the country's prosperity, Ludwig had advanced from being in the colloquial phrase "well-fixed" to undeniably wealthy. Rausch and Bodien Coated Paper Company had succeeded beyond the expectations of everyone except its founders, and had indeed already become a "big thing"; the C. & C. Interurban carried more passengers every year; Rausch Cordage Company, along with its subsidiary machine shop, was a small gold mine: small compared to the paper company but grown from what it had been a few years before. A new mill had been added to the plant, equipped with the latest machinery for the laying of the special kinds of rope the mill now made. Gib was not only sales manager now but had three traveling salesmen under him, so he spent little time on the road. The other office was full of desks: the bookkeeper had been made "auditor"; and other duties once the responsibility of Captain Bodien or Ludwig were now divided between a paymaster-timekeeper, a traffic manager, and a purchasing agent. Eliza was Ludwig's private secretary, and a new young woman took care of the other stenographic work. But Rausch Cordage Company was still a closed corporation, and profits were divided among a very few. In the spring of 1898 carloads of binder twine had already been consigned to the warehouse in

Kansas City, and with the country at war, government orders for big rope—hawsers and cables—were being filled as fast as they could be laid.

Not that Ludwig had wanted the war. He had been in a state of indignation all the previous summer and fall, annoyed by the Jingoes, led in Congress by Senator Lodge and in the War Department by young Assistant Secretary Roosevelt; by the yellow press, which seemed bent on destroying the President whose election it had not been able to prevent, and most of all by the visionary reformers, who thought the Cubans should be freed if it took a war to do it. Ludwig was sure that the President, if let alone, could negotiate with Spain. "He doesn't want a war. He fought in one; he knows what it means. Why should anyone in the country want a war, with no better excuse than a lot of raggle-taggle Cubans?" As McKinley had continued to treat with Spain in spite of the clamor, and had won concessions even to the promise of autonomy for Cuba, tension eased somewhat. However, Ludwig did not cease buying all of the Manila hemp at whatever the price; if a war came and the Philippines were involved, there would be no hemp for the big rope that would be needed. His gamble proved a safe one: scarcely had sober citizens begun to breathe more easily when the battleship *Maine* was blown up, or blew up, in Havana Harbor. After that a peaceful settlement was impossible; revenge for the *Maine* was joined in the minds of Congress, the yellow press, and the citizenry to the cause of Cuban freedom. The President, still endeavoring to negotiate, lost so much influence with the legislators that had he failed in April to send Congress a message asking for a declaration of war, it would have exercised its constitutional right and acted without a request from him.

There may have been a few misgivings on the part of some government leaders as to what other European nations would do, but the war was not expected to amount to much, as wars go, and the expectation seemed confirmed by Dewey's easy victory at Manila Bay on the first of May. Admittedly the Army, previously limited to the size needed to keep order among the Indians in the West, was unprepared and unable to train and fit out the great number of men and boys enlisting; but by mid-June, Cervera's fleet was blockaded in Santiago Harbor, and it began to look as if the Army would not be called on to do much except garrison the towns that were ready to fall into American hands once the fleet had cut them off from Spain.

The war had been little more than newspaper headlines to most of Waynesboro; a number of town boys had volunteered, but had not yet got beyond Tampa. Rodney Stevens, in medical school, had felt the urge to enlist (had not his father and his mother's father been soldiers?), but he had been restrained by his mother, to whom malaria was a dread possibility and yellow fever a worse one. John Gordon, too, had said flatly that he wasn't needed as a soldier, but that he might be as a doctor—to get his degree first, then he might be of some use. When Rodney protested that by that time the war would be over, his Cousin Dock had only gruffed, "So much the better." John, remembering his own bitter helplessness thirty-odd years before, had really little faith in any doctor's efficacy on a battlefield or in camp; medicine had advanced in the last decades, but so far as he could tell from newspaper reports, not against dysentery, typhoid, or malaria, which were proving as deadly in 1898 as they had been in the lines around Vicksburg.

To the Rausches the war was more than the correspondents' dramatic accounts in the papers. Ludwig Junior had enlisted in the Astor Battery. His father had been very angry: he had long suspected that the boy was not single-mindedly devoted to the pursuit of a career on the concert stage, although already he was one of the many violinists in the New York Philharmonic, and so must be submitting to the discipline of long hours of practice and rehearsal. But handsome young Ludwig had been accepted as an eligible bachelor by what Ludwig called "Wall Street Society" through his sister-in-law, Ernest's wife, who had introduced him to her family and friends. His parents knew that he was attending far too many late balls, squiring too many expensive debutantes, perhaps gambling or worse, else why should he be perpetually in debt? In spite of what was surely an adequate allowance and whatever he was paid by the Philharmonic, he was always writing his mother for money, and sometimes, if his need was urgent, coming home for a day or two to present his case in person. He was invariably welcomed by his family with excited rejoicing: Ludwig Junior, boyish, gay, and endowed with the dangerous gift of charm, was almost irresistible, and completely so when, of an evening, he played his violin for them, sometimes solo, sometimes with Paul, with Elsa accompanying them on the piano. All would be moved so deeply as to be convinced of his certain greatness, and he would go of in the morning with his father's check in his pocket and little regard for the admonitions that accompanied the gift.

When he had gone, his father would come down to earth and growl, "He'll never amount to a row of pins. He's playing the part of a millionaire's son to perfection, keeping up with the others in the set he's gotten involved with." Ludwig Senior might not have been so angry at his son's enlisting had he gone into any other outfit than the Astor Battery, but he was still playing the millionaire's son, as the cost of his equipment proved. Whatever shadow of apprehension might lurk in his mother's mind, his father had little fear for his safety, cynically convinced that he would see little or no fighting; but he was grievously disappointed that the boy should find it so easy to give up what should have been dedication to his music.

Ludwig Junior would be the only Rausch to miss his father's house-warming; even the Cincinnati and Burlington families, written to long ago, had arranged to come. It was a good thing, Sally thought, still sitting idly at her desk, that Ludwig had this new house to occupy his mind and give him pleasure. It would not be long now before he had enough family around him to keep his mind off Ludwig Junior. Ordinarily Ernest's wife took their two babies and herself to her family's summer home in Rhode Island, removing them from New Orleans weather, malaria, and possible yellow fever; usually the entourage, nursemaid and all, stopped by briefly in Waynesboro on their way. This year they would delay their departure until Ernest could come as far as Waynesboro with them; they would stay over the Fourth. Charles, too, was bringing his wife and baby. Sally sighed as she contemplated the prospect: the two young women were so different that it would be impossible for them to get beyond a surface politeness with each other. Charles had met his Greta in Burlington through his cousins; she was as German in background as—well, as the Rausches themselves—a calendar-pretty girl who worshipped Charles and would never entertain any ambition for him beyond his own, and Charles seemed perfectly contented to be a kind of glorified shipping clerk in charge of the Kansas City warehouse. Greta took it for granted that it was her part in life to nurse her child, cosset her husband, and be a good wife; her mother-in-law suspected that she felt superior to her sister-in-law, who did none of these things. As for Ernest's wife, there was no doubt at all that she felt superior to Greta. Sally reflected that if, years ago, she could have foreseen what divergent types her two oldest sons, themselves so alike, would marry, she would have expected to have more in common with Emily than with the gentle, unexciting Greta. But she would have been wrong. She made an effort to appear impartial, equally fond of both, but it was Greta for whom she felt genuine affection: she was sweet and good-humored, with no sharp edges. Both the senior Rausches were well aware that Emily was not satisfied with her position, financial or social, in New Orleans. Not when her father, partner in a brokerage house, could so easily find a place for Ernest there. Emily never nagged or criticized Ernest when they were in Waynesboro, but Ernest showed in his deprecating attitude toward his wife the effect of having been nagged. When he gave in—and he would give in—Ernest's parents would find themselves growing more and more out of touch with their eldest son. Poor Ludwig! Four sons, and not one willing or able to take over from him when the time came. Unless Paul— But Paul, like Ludwig Junior, was a born musician, and, they hoped, a more stable character. He certainly lacked the fatal gift of charm. Paul was, at fifteen, a nice boy, his mother thought, but more apt to sulk than cajole when he was crossed. He had been in one of his unresponsive moods ever since his father had refused to let him spend his summer as a bobbin boy in the mill, where he might injure a hand; he was in a state of rebellion against his eternal hours of practice on the violin. Sally, although still determined that one of her sons at least would be a great man, applauded Ludwig's firmness. Besides, his father said, the boy had a keen head for figures, which would serve him if he turned against his violin. Music and mathematics were basically one, Ludwig said, and Sally, not well enough grounded in either to know, accepted his judgment.

Having spent some moments in random contemplation of affairs national, familiar, and personal, Sally again took up her pen with an air of resolution, only to sigh as she looked over the list of names Ludwig had given her. It would be a very informal occasion. The sighing was incongruous: she was reluctant to set about doing what she faced. There were notes to be written to families who were more or less intimate friends of hers and Ludwig's: like Sheldon Edwards and his boys, the Douglas Gardiners and their girls, the Tim Merrills, Dr. Warren and his family; but there were also all the others Ludwig wanted asked, friends of his whom she had never invited to the house in town: Captain and Mrs. Bodien, as well as Stewart and his family from Madison City; all the Rausch Cordage Company office staff, as well as all the bank employees, from cashier down; those solid citizens the Kleins and Hoffmanns, the Thirkields, the Bonner sons and their families—everyone Ludwig could think of, she believed, including Mr. Lichtenstein and his wife and family (and she didn't even know Mrs. Lichtenstein by sight!). But Hillcrest was Ludwig's house, this was to be his housewarming, and if he wanted all Waynesboro there, it was his prerogative. He was not, thank goodness, asking any of his out-of-town political friends—not even Mark Hanna, whom he had forgiven outwardly at least for having forced John Sherman out of the Senate, although he had been bitterly outspoken when, as he had foreseen, the old man resigned as Secretary of State. These "dignitaries," as Ludwig called them, might cast a damper on the enjoyment without restraint that he wanted for his Waynesboro friends.

It was that "without restraint" that troubled Sally. Her husband proposed to have for the children all the firecrackers they would have time to shoot, as well as freezers of ice cream and gallons of lemonade on the side porch, where they could help themselves. For his masculine friends, he planned to have a cask or casks of beer on the back porch. Sally did not suppose that a guest would drink enough beer to make him even silly, but she feared that some of her friends (members of the Woman's Club) would be deeply offended. It was a dilemma that she could not solve, though she would do her best.

She went to work, finally, tossing off in her flowing hand one informal note after another, inviting each guest for the housewarming in the afternoon, with an al fresco supper on the lawn (or on the porch if it rained; she crossed her fingers to ward off any such disaster). After supper, there would be fireworks when it was dark enough, and then dancing. Transportation would be provided by special cars on the Interurban. As for the Woman's Club, she would invite them to a very special thirtieth anniversary dinner to be served in the dining room, with speeches or a history of the Club or something of the sort that would keep them there long enough for all the others to have dispersed and found places for watching the fireworks safely apart from the ladies' reserved chairs on the porch.

She had thought it all out carefully, she had told Anne Gordon a few days before, when Anne had wondered why on earth she wanted to go to all that extra trouble, when her hands would be full enough.

"It would be the oddest dinner party ever given, with only women at the table and all their men picnicking outside. And wherever the ministers and theological professors sit, they will be certain to notice the beery aroma emanating from unregenerates like your husband and mine. And no—laugh if you must—I can hardly write 'Beer will be served' on their invitations, or even let it be whispered about. They would feel duty-bound to decline. I don't want them to do that. We mean to make it a really festive occasion. Think how dull their lives must be. Take the Voorheeses: do you suppose those two unfortunate children have ever been to a real party in their lives? Spin-the-plate and pin-the-tail-on-the-donkey—that sort of thing. As for the men, if we make a point of its being an anniversary with a review of thirty years of Club history and various reminiscences, do you think they will be sorry to miss it?" Both women laughed, thinking of their husbands. Sally concluded, "I'll ask Amanda to write a paper on 'Highlights of the First Thirty Years.'"

Now, remembering that conversation, she began her notes to the members of the Club, longer notes than the others had been, since she had to explain that in addition to the housewarming, for the Woman's Club there would be a thirtieth anniversary dinner meeting. Taking the names alphabetically, she began with Eliza Ballard, thinking as she wrote that at least Eliza, since she had been secretary at Rausch Cordage Company, was hardly the reforming spirit her mother would have liked her to be; Sally doubted whether she even belonged to the W.C.T.U. In other ways Eliza had not mellowed as she approached sixty: her tongue was as caustic as ever. She seemed no older, looked no older, except that, in the common phrase, she was developing "middle-aged spread." In the note to Eliza everything was covered: the special cars leaving the Interurban station on the half-hour, for an afternoon of "visiting" and celebrating the Fourth, the dinner, the fireworks, the dancing. Eliza would not, presumably, stay for the dancing, but she must be asked. There would be others ready to go home after the fireworks, and Ludwig had promised to have a trolley car waiting for them on the siding across the road. Ludwig, still president of the board of the C. & C. Interurban, had had the siding put down, at his own expense, for convenient access to Hillcrest. There were others like the Ballards who no longer drove their own horses and carriages; those who did have them would not willingly take them out on the Fourth at the risk of a rearing or bolting animal, frightened by a torpedo or firecracker tossed at its heels. Stewart Bodien would bring his family up from Madison City in that noisy contraption of his; at least, Sally thought, it wouldn't stand on its hind legs at every bang.

Charlotte Bonner was next on her list; the other Bonners, Charlotte's mother and brothers, would be at one of the outside tables, and would probably have a better time than Charlotte. Poor Charlotte, so plain and lanky, all bones and joints: Sally could not imagine that she would stay for the dancing, unless in her capacity as society editor of the *Torchlight*. But one never knew with Charlotte: she was so unpredictable and so unselfconscious that she might enjoy a lively gallop around the porch. She had been a godsend to the Club, lending a light touch to an all-too-stodgy group. Sally, alone in her sitting room, laughed aloud as she thought of Charlotte in the last Christmas play. The younger members had worked out an actable version of *Alice in Wonderland*, and Charlotte had been the caterpillar, in a tight all-enveloping green garment with caterpillar feet in pairs down the front; she had perched cross-legged on a none-too-sturdy table topped with a linen-covered round cushion to resemble (slightly) a mushroom, puffing, or pretending to, on a hookah—a Waynesboro tobacconist's advertising device that she had persuaded him to lend her.

From Charlotte to Mrs. Deming, who would probably stay for the dancing at least as an onlooker, since Julia would be there and she would not want to go home alone. Mrs. Deming had achieved a certain importance in the Club: she was now its "Author," having successfully completed (and sold, by subscription and through agents) the county history the General had been working on when he died. It had taken a long time and a good many expeditions to the county in question: one did not, apparently, get a book written and published overnight. With reason, Mrs. Deming, when with other Club members, radiated a certain air of importance; you might not like it but you could not blame her: who else among them had written a book?

Sally ticked that name off and went on to the Evanses. Elsa and Gib, who would be house guests, she could skip, but Gib's uncle and aunt, the Reverend Mr. Evans and his wife, must be treated with proper respect. Sally had never been on really confidential terms with Mrs. Evans since the day when they had discussed Gib's and Elsa's relationship; she hoped that now his aunt was satisfied that Gib had made a fortunate choice, and that the marriage was a good one.

Next came the Gordons: Anne, who seemed at last to be her serene and happy self, Dock, Johnny, Julia, and their boy Tucker. One could hardly call Julia "serene," though she seemed contented with her life, and had made a really captivating Alice in the Christmas play. Still Sally could not help but wonder just how happy Julia really was; serenity, she supposed, sprang from something inside a person's mind or spirit. She doubted that Julia was endowed with much in the way of either mind or spirit. Poor Johnny! She could pity him for his blindness, now that Elsa was out of all danger. Johnny would come, and so would his father and the two Evans men. Sophie Lichtenstein would bring her Rudy, who, to be honest, was a presentable gentleman, even an entertaining one, although Ludwig looked askance at his political ambitions. Rudy intended to run as a Democrat against Tim Merrill in the next local election for the office of county prosecutor; Ludwig had no fear of a Democrat's worming his way into the Court House: he was simply unable to understand how a promising and ambitious young man could be one.

From Lichtenstein to Merrill: Tim and Elizabeth and their children. The Reverend Mr. McKinney and the Reverend Dr. Maxwell would come with their wives. Then Amanda Reid. Amanda was beginning to show her age. That stopped her for a moment: after all, Amanda was only a few years older; unfortunately her mind was above such trivialities as her personal appearance. Amanda had been putting on weight, as she herself had done, far too much; but Ludwig liked her as she was, and she was at least firmly and fashionably corseted. Amanda's bulges in the wrong places were unrestrained; her wrists and ankles were incongruously thin, her face lined, her hair limp and graying. She might be a better teacher, Sally thought, if she cared more about how she looked: to her students she'd become "Old Mandy Reid"; however firmly his mother forbade Paul, now in his second year of Latin, to use the epithet, she was sure that her commandment had no weight outside the house. It was a pity, since there was nothing aged or aging about Amanda's mind: she was as acute (and acerb) a literary critic as she had ever been, and there was not a Club essayist who did not await her comments with trepidation.

Disposing of Amanda left Jessamine Stevens, the Traverses, and the Voorheeses. The Voorheeses would not only leave before the dancing began, they would take their young people with them. Sally grimaced as she thought about Blair and Janey: they would not be missed by the other young people, and that was pitiful, somehow. Christina should realize that however well-trained their minds, however spotless their characters, they would never have friends their own age if they were never permitted to mingle with them. Sally could believe that Janey at least might be all that was amiable, but who would ever know? As for the Traverses, Thomasina, bless her, had not changed, beyond growing a little more asthmatic, a little more drooping. And if Sam Travers wanted to stay for the dancing—and perhaps play while the orchestra had supper?—Thomasina would be glad to stay, too, although she had never danced a step in her life and was certainly too old to begin. Then, the Gardiner sisters—and conscience-stricken, she remembered: Miss Caroline Gardiner had finally gone to her reward, having done her best to make Barbara's life a hell on earth for nineteen or twenty years. Not that anyone ever learned that from Barbara, who kept a still tongue. But a still tongue in Waynesboro meant little if there were servants in the house. It had been generally supposed that after Miss Lavinia died, Miss Caroline might be easier to get along with, but everyone knew that she had not been. When the carpet in her sitting room and the matting in her bedroom had been taken up, and the floors painted and varnished, everyone knew it was because Miss Caroline had slipped into a way of spitting on the floor whenever and wherever she felt like it, and carpet and matting were harder to scrub than bare boards. It was strange how character could deteriorate when control weakened. One would have supposed the Misses Gardiner would be ultragenteel to the very end.

When she had finished her notes, she carried them down to the hall table, where she put them for Ben, old Reuben's son and the present houseman-coachman, to pick up and deliver.

In spite of herself, she continued to mull over the guest list as she waited for Ludwig to come home for dinner. She would need to be careful about the seating arrangements. Many of the guests were, like the Rausches, basically *echt Deutsch*, although that had been pretty well forgotten after all these years. Even financial distinctions had been very nearly wiped out: Fritz Klein's

"Fancy Groceries" had certainly prospered; she knew that he had subscribed to a fair number of shares in Rausch and Bodien Coated Paper when they were first offered, and no doubt he had also invested in his brother-in-law's bakery when Mr. Hoffmann had patented his cracker, built a factory, gone into the wholesale business, and succeeded beyond anyone's wildest dreams. The neat brick building on the south edge of town had already been enlarged once, and (sure sign of his threat as a competitor) he had received from bigger companies offers to buy him out. On such occasions he always came to Ludwig for advice, with, Ludwig said, his mind already made up; he only wanted reassurance before he stubbornly refused to sell. Of all that closely related group, only the Lichtensteins were still scraping by on nothing a year, and since the Lichtensteins seemed to enjoy life as much as anyone and more than most, no one held their poverty against them, even though the boys had to make their own way, as Rudy had done, through college and into a profession.

This first generation of Germans presented no problem. Everyone in town knew and liked them and would enjoy their company at dinner. Ernest and Emily could be host and hostess at the table; Charles and Greta could preside over the younger lot. The children would have a table to themselves, with Rose to keep them in some kind of order, while Cassie watched over the babies, sleeping (she hoped) up on the third floor. Sally trusted that Emily would not be too obviously gracious and condescending to Ludwig's friends; if the Gardiners sat close to her and Mr. and Mrs. Lichtenstein as far away as possible, it might be all right. Sally knew that Emily would consider the housewarming an odd social occasion; she would just have to make the best of it. And indeed, when Ernest had arrived with his family and his wife learned what was expected of her, she did not hesitate to say to Elsa that she considered the whole affair "outré"; but it was particularly the honoring of the Woman's Club that astonished her. "Is your mother actually so fond of those women that she doesn't see enough of them in the winter? Very odd and dowdy I thought them, when I first met them at your mother's reception." Elsa said, "She is fond of them strange as it may seem to you. Mamma has been President for so long, it makes a bond. I suppose she feels responsible, in a way, for their enjoying the Club. And they and we all do, you know, even if it is an awful nuisance, every two weeks. It's Papa's friends she's dubious about. But I think you will find them quite convenable. Gemütlich, in fact." (If Emily was going to throw foreign words around, she would too.)

Sally's invitations were received and accepted. Waynesboro folk were not in the habit of going away for summer holidays; the men were busy, and their wives would not dream of taking the children and leaving their husbands behind. Not even Julia Gordon considered it for more than a moment. She had tried to persuade Johnny to go with her, her mother, and Tucker for a few weeks at the seashore, but her suggestion met with a firm "no."

"Julia, I'd like to. I wish I could. But you know I can't get away in the summer. It's our busiest season, with babies coming down with summer complaint every time there's a hot spell. But there's no reason why the rest of you shouldn't go."

"Without you?" She shook her head. "You have no idea how difficult travel would be with an active little boy, and all the valises, and no man to help. If Papa were still with us, it would be different. I suppose I must accept this—dismaying invitation to the Rausches' housewarming?"

"'Dismaying'? I don't see—"

"Johnny, you know it will be horrible. Hot, crowded, and the *noise*—"

"It will be just as noisy in town, with firecrackers popping in every back yard."

"Tucker will be terrified, with all those big boys throwing cannon crackers around. If he isn't frightened, he will be over-excited; and such a long-drawn-out agony: afternoon, dinner with the Woman's Club members that I see quite enough of in nine months of the year, fireworks, dancing, while some colored girl puts Tucker to sleep in the attic."

"'Some colored girl' will be reliable old Cassie, with whomever she brings in to help. And you love to dance. There's even to be an out-of-town orchestra, I understand, not just some Waynesboro piano-player."

"By that time I'll be too exhausted to drag myself around a dance floor. And I didn't know you considered your friend Elsa 'just a Waynesboro piano-player.'"

"Elsa? She's as fine a musician as anyone they can bring in, but you don't expect her to spend her evening playing the piano for others to dance by at her own father's party? Of course not; she enjoys dancing as much as anyone. Don't be cross, Julia darling, just because I can't take you to the seashore. This housewarming is going to be an occasion. Uncle Ludwig's been planning it for weeks: sometimes I wonder if he didn't build the house just so he could warm it. You must write and accept for all of us. Your mother is going?"

"Oh, of course. The Woman's Club, for some reason, is important to her."

"I understand why, and so would you, if you had to deal with as many lonely women as I do. It gives her contacts outside the family, a feeling of belonging: as a member she is connected with something outside herself. With *people*. That's why so many solitary women go in for good works."

"Your mother and father are going?"

"You know they wouldn't miss a Rausch shindig for a pretty penny. Though I expect Pop will spend the afternoon outside with the other men, and give the Woman's Club as wide a berth as possible."

He was quite right about his parents: they never refused a Rausch invitation. Other friends who had often been invited to the Rausches' felt the same way, and those who had never before been asked were atwitter with excitement. The Woman's Club members accepted their invitations, and Amanda, who had been asked to provide the anniversary paper, looked over her wardrobe and decided that she must have a new dress, though it would mean tedious hours of fitting, and expense that she could ill afford.

The only member slow to reply was Christina Voorhees; it was only after a good deal of wavering that she finally accepted. At first she had balked at including her son and daughter: she had heard that all kinds of people had been invited. She did not discuss the matter with Henry until the two of them were lying in bed one night, wakeful because it was so hot. And not even then until Henry had opened the way to the subject. The front windows were wide open, the curtains tucked behind the folded-back shutters. From the Gardiners' front steps, across the street, came the sound of young voices, a banjo, singing, and laughter.

Henry, lying tidily and straight under the sheet, his arms up, his hands clasped under his head, said, "It sounds as if the young people are having fun across the way. Our two ought to be with them."

"What do you mean? They went to bed before we did."

"It's too hot for sleeping. And somehow, they seem to miss the fun they should be having at their age."

"They are not in the habit of going where they have not been asked."

"I doubt if anyone over there was *asked*. Haven't you noticed how the young people make a habit of drifting into the Gardiners', boys and girls both? Tonight some boy brought his banjo, and the others just naturally collected. I wish Blair and Janey had as many friends."

"Are you working up to telling me that I should take them to the Rausch housewarming? You and I must go because it is to be in part an anniversary celebration for the Club and because of your position in the bank. But I see no necessity for taking the children into such a mixed crowd as will be there. And on the Fourth, with fireworks and dancing, the party may easily get out of hand."

"Out of the hands of Ludwig and Mrs. Rausch? That is most unlikely. I feel very strongly that Blair and Janey should go with us. They are too inexperienced in getting along with young boys and girls their age."

"But I don't think—"

"That I realize how left to themselves they are? I had my eyes opened a few days ago. Christina, I have never criticized your idea of educating them at home, and I do not, now: I knew you could take care of that better than any schoolteacher in Waynesboro. But they have missed all the give and take between children growing up together."

"They have friends. They go over to the Gardiners' often."

"Occasionally, not 'often.' Do the Gardiners ever come over here?"

"Well-bred girls do not pursue boys."

"Janey is the same age as one of them, isn't she? Do they ever come to see her?"

"I was thinking of Blair because he—admires—the oldest one."

"Who has been away at college all this past year, and is said to have a steady beau in the Stevens boy when they are both at home. He is a year or so older than Blair and in medical school—almost a man, you might say—and so has an insuperable advantage."

"Henry, where do you pick up these vulgarisms? 'Beau,' indeed! And these bits of gossip?"

"The bank's a great place for gossip. Everyone passes that corner, and not without being noticed." Then abruptly and seriously he said, "Don't you think Blair should go to college?"

"But he doesn't need college. He's ready now to start at the Seminary in the fall."

"Scholastically, yes. But are you sure he feels called to the ministry? Let's send him to one of our Reformed Presbyterian colleges; he can come to no harm there, and it will give him time to decide what he wants. He should choose his own future."

"He has never said the ministry wasn't his choice. What did you mean when you said a minute ago that you had had your eyes opened?"

Henry sighed. "I suppose I shouldn't have mentioned it. But I was in my office the other day, with the door open. There were a couple of boys his age at the teller's cage when Blair went past outside. I suppose they couldn't see me from where they stood."

"What did they say?"

"Blair went around the corner and past my window. He looked seedy. His hair needed cutting. It was down over his shirt collar in the back and looked scruffy. He is stoop-shouldered, and he kind of shuffled along, all loose joints."

"What did they say?"

"At first I didn't notice. Something about his hair, I suppose, because the other fellow said, 'He ought to tie it up with a ribbon, he's such a mollycoddle.' And the first one said, 'Mother's boy, tied to her apron strings.' I'm sorry, Chrissy."

After a stricken moment, Christina said in a strained voice, "Who were they?"

"No one you know. Don't take it too hard. It was a shock to me, too. It's the town's opinion, I suppose."

"I have never felt any compulsion to consider the town's opinion. You know that I kept the children here and taught them myself because I wanted them to be *educated*."

"And you have done it superbly. They are well-informed and well-trained. But somehow, this segregation has gone beyond book-learning; we have been so concerned to keep them from any contact with evil that we have kept them from living full lives." He emphasized the "we" in order to spare her. "Now I wonder whether anyone can be a good minister, even a good man, who has had no experience of good and evil. The line between is so blurred, sometimes. I wonder what your father would have thought."

"Oh, Papa! I was devoted to Papa, as you know, but he condoned much that was evil; at least his friends were men who condoned evil. His taste was catholic, to say the least. I never thought it right."

"Your father was a good man, really good: kind and generous and tolerant.

There is no reason why you should be more inflexible than he was. Do let's loosen the reins a little bit—take Blair and Janey to the Rausch party on the Fourth."

"We'll come home after the fireworks, then." She did not intend to have Blair and Janey undesirably excited by the spectacle of other boys and girls in close embrace on the dance floor. "The Rausches know that we do not dance."

Grateful for what he knew was a concession, Henry told his wife good-night and turned over on his side to go to sleep. Christina was too troubled even to make the attempt. Never before in their married life had Henry so much as suggested how he thought his children should be brought up. If he had believed her in error, he should have said so long ago. (She had no notion of the courage it had required for him to speak now. Henry had always been a "safe" man, a careful one; when he had reached an age he considered right for marriage, he had weighed in his own mind one Waynesboro girl after another; in Christina he had seen so many desirable qualities he doubted he could win her, but did not doubt at all that he loved her. He had married her in the conviction that she was superior to him in every way. However cold and immovable he might be in the bank, when he was at home he deferred to Christina, and accepted her way of doing things as inevitably right.) Christina, who had never deferred to any man except her father and not always to him, had not considered Henry's attitude toward her odd, or unusual: mothers were responsible for bringing up the children unless, as in her own case, a mother died and a father of necessity took over. Lying awake and troubled long after Henry, in spite of the heat, had drifted off to sleep, she went back over their conversation. It was too bad that Blair had let his hair grow so long, but it seemed a minor flaw and one easily remedied. But "mother's boy" and "mollycoddle": those epithets really hurt. She would submit in the matter of the Rausch party; Blair's presence there might help refute them. But college was a different and altogether more serious matter. She was still wide awake and worrying when she heard the very audible good-byes from across the street, a final strum of the banjo, the clang of the Gardiner gate, and the sounds of young footsteps and young voices moving off down the hill.

The invitation to the housewarming at Hillcrest had been very differently received at the Gardiners', where there had been unanimous rejoicing. Lavinia would be coming home from college in a few days; they could greet her with news of the high jinks in prospect. The Gardiner family had always been a happy one; the girls were used to their father's tendency to sarcasm when some solecism in grammar or impropriety had been committed; their mother had managed to keep them largely unaware of any strain imposed by the presence upstairs behind closed doors of the two aunts for many years, and then of one. It was not until Aunt Caroline had died and been buried that they had learned, by being released from them, of the restraints that had existed. They tried, all of them, to grieve; they said "Poor Aunt Caroline."

But Doug relaxed, no longer worried by what Barbara was going through, no longer saying to himself that he should never have married her; and Barbara's burden slipped from her shoulders. When there was no further need to see that her girls' lives should be unshadowed, she herself grew young again, and forgot that at thirty-five she had been middle-aged for a long time. The three girls still at home made up in a month's time for all the years they had been quiet: they called to each other (and Doug did not reprove them) from upstairs down and from downstairs up; they made a clatter with closing doors and running feet; and Mary, who was twelve and really too old to begin such a childish sport, took to sliding down the banisters.

Best of all, the aunts' apartment was done over for the older girls: cleaned, repapered, the woodwork varnished, the floors newly carpeted. As Mary was frank enough to say, the smell was finally gone. Another door was cut into the bathroom, so that it could be entered from both bedrooms—a door made possible by replacing the old zinc-lined, walnut-enclosed tub with a modern porcelain one standing on four claw feet and curved over around the top to offer a handhold. The two girls would have a bathroom all their own, a privilege not to be despised in a household of six, but one that would prove to be illusory after the first week or so, as neither of the younger girls hesitated to use it when the family bath was occupied. The rooms were still unfurnished, awaiting Lavinia's return: she should have some say as to what she wanted.

On the day of Lavinia's return, Doug drove his family to the depot in the surrey: it would be a tight squeeze for six of them, but Lavinia's trunk and valise could be entrusted to Sam Million: he was sure to meet the train with his horse and dray. They scrambled down to the station platform; Doug went to speak to Sam, who was indifferent to Waynesboro's comings and goings, and who said now, "Miss Lavinia's baggage? Yes, suh, cou'se Ah look after it. Yo' sho' got a right pretty lot o' gu'ls, Mistuh Douglas." Doug laughed at him and said, "Pretty is as pretty does, but thank you, Sam." He himself thought that Lavinia and Caroline, black-haired, black-browed, violet-eyed like their mother, were pretty as a picture; fly-away Veronica, if she ever stayed still long enough to be looked at, could be seen to have the fine-cut-features of the Gardiner aunts, their hazel eyes and, alas!, their fine-as-silk, mouse-colored hair. And poor Mary was like her Grandfather Bodien: a stocky build, with nondescript lightish hair and blue eyes, keen but too light for beauty. Douglas looked at her now, bouncing up and down on the edge of the brick platform, watching up the empty track for the first sight of engine smoke, and smiled in self-derision: she would have rejected the "poor Mary" indignantly: her Grandfather Bodien was the favorite person of her world; she would not mind looking like him.

When the train finally pulled in, blowing Mary back from the track, Lavinia was the first passenger off; she could hardly wait for the porter's steps to be put in place. She flung herself first into the embraces of the feminine part of her family, then detached herself and went to her father, who had stood back a little to let Barbara have first chance.

"Papa! It's wonderful to be home!"

Mary said, "We've got a surprise for you."

Doug reproved her: "We have, not 'we've got.'" And Veronica, flibbertigibbet thought she might be, tried to hush her: "Do you want to *spoil* it?"

Lavinia turned back to her sister and mother. "If you mean the Rausch housewarming and ball that's no surprise. Rod wrote me. I hope you won't mind if I go with him? I suppose we're all invited?"

"Of course we're invited—even Veronica and me. But that isn't—"

Barbara clapped a hand over her mouth and said, "Come on, climb into the surrey. Give Papa your baggage check, Vinnie, so he can hand it over to Sam. He'll bring your trunk. What did you do with your valise?"

"Left it to the porter. I suppose he put it off."

"Sam's already got it in the dray."

Doug ignored Mary's "got" this time. He said, "Come along, all of you."

Once home, they all went upstairs together. When Lavinia would have turned to the back bedroom she had always shared with Caroline, they swung her around toward the once tightly locked door.

"Do you mean—? I wondered what you would do."

Barbara threw open the door to what was now the front bedroom. "It's to be yours and Caroline's, a room for each of you—you can decide between you which is to have which. They've both been done over, you see." The room shone so it would have been impossible not to see: sparkling windows, curtained with net and draped with chintz, shutters and woodwork glittering with fresh varnish, a spanking new carpet.

"Oh, Mamma! How lovely! I do thank you. And you, Papa!" She stood on tiptoe to kiss his cheek, a liberty not often taken with her undemonstrative father.

Her mother said, "The other room's just like it, and you can share the bath. You're to draw lots for the bedrooms."

"It really doesn't matter which room. That's why they aren't furnished?"

"Not altogether. We couldn't move the furniture out of your old room: it's to be Mary's now. If you would like one of the fashionable brass beds and a new dressing table, it could be managed. Or there's furniture in the attic."

"Oh, not a brass bed," Lavinia declared emphatically. "You've spent enough already, and besides, I don't really think they are pretty. But not that carved walnut monstrosity of Aunt Lavinia's, either. Aren't there some four-posters upstairs? And chests of drawers? Isn't that what you would like, Carrie? Grandma Bodien's bedrooms are the prettiest I know and that's what she has. Family things, she says, brought from Maryland. I'd like some old Gardiner things, brought from Virginia."

Veronica said, "Vinnie! I declare, you're as bad as the aunts. Papa says they would have been happier if they hadn't always been harking back to Virginia. I'd take the brass bed any day."

"You'll sleep in the bed you've always slept in, young lady; just be thankful you won't have to share it any more. Lavinia, you and Caroline can go attic-searching tomorrow. In the meantime, use your old room—Veronica can put up with Mary, and vice-versa, for a few days more. Unpack in there when Sam brings your trunk, and be sure to get all your soiled clothes out to the laundry for Mitty to wash and iron. Do you have anything you can wear to the Rausches'? Caroline has a good white dress, fortunately. We can look over your things presently. The Fourth's only a couple of weeks off, so if you have to have anything made—"

"I've plenty of clothes from last summer. My high school commencement dress ought to do. Rod says it's an all-day affair, nearly—not a formal ball. How do we get there? Rod may want to take his horse, but Papa won't, not on the Fourth. And I don't suppose Rod will be allowed to."

"I should hope not," her father said emphatically. "The last time Mrs. Stevens had that horse out, they met one of those infernal noisy automobiles, and the horse stood straight up on its hind legs. Fortunately, she can handle horses, or the buggy would have overturned. I hate to think what would happen if a firecracker went off under its nose. No, Mr. Rausch is providing transportation: special cars on the C. & C., leaving every hour on the half-hour, so as not to interfere with the regular hourly schedule. You young people are urged to take the two-thirty car, on the assumption that you can stand a two-to-two A.M. Fourth of July, I suppose."

"It sounds like a great lark."

And so it did to a good part of Waynesboro. There may have been some who thought it unfitting to plan for a gay occasion with the country at war, particularly when, on the first and second of July, the news began to come over the wires of the battle of San Juan Hill, bloody and fruitless, since the Spaniards were still in Havana. Then, late on that Sunday night of the third—or very early, long before the dawn of the Fourth—word came through to the *Torchlight* and thence to every citizen who was awake that the Spanish fleet had been destroyed in Santiago Bay. Like the whole country, Waynesboro was cock-a-whoop: before the sun rose there were not only firecrackers exploding in all directions but bells ringing, even the firebells, and Rausch Cordage Company's steam whistle was going full blast, up the scale and down again. Only a few who put their heads under their pillows on the morning of the Fourth could remain unaware of the victory. To the young this would be the greatest Fourth ever; to their elders, the greatest since Vicksburg and Gettysburg.

Boys and girls and young married couples with their children met at the Interurban Station for the first trolley to Hillcrest, most of them so excited that they could hardly observe proper decorum in boarding the summer car that Ludwig had waiting for them. Its seats were benches that ran from one open side to the other, so that once you had found a place you stayed there, unless like the conductor you were bold enough to walk on the outside running boards. The boys (Rodney, the two Edwardses, a Lichtenstein, and a Hoffmann, with various other high school or college students) were far too excited to remain in their seats: they stood outside, beside whatever girl they had paired off with, and shouted to everyone they passed in the streets: "Have you heard? The *whole* Spanish fleet! That ought to show 'em!"—meaning by "them" not only the Spaniards but the whole world. The small children, squashed safely between their parents, caught the contagion, and shouted "Santiago!" and "Hurrah for the Navy!" with very little understanding of the reason for the cheers.

The car had not reached the edge of town before there was a fusillade of bangs from under the wheels. Some of the children squealed, but Tucker Gordon, hanging on to the seat ahead, showed not the slightest sign of fear. He looked around inquiringly at his father.

"Just torpedoes someone put on the track. Part of the celebration."

"It's going to be a frightful day," Julia sighed, "noisy, I mean; but if he isn't frightened it will be easier. I wish, though, he would sit quietly between us."

"What with your knees and my knees there isn't room for him to fall."

"I still think we would have been more comfortable in the buggy."

"A few firecrackers thrown at the mare and we'd have had a runaway. Besides, Tuck would have missed all the fun he's having now."

"I don't like him to get so keyed up."

There was no doubt that Tucker was excited, but so was everyone else. The car rattled along the track at a great rate; occasionally firecrackers were tossed under the wheels by roadside urchins; the speed at which they were moving created a wind that blew the girls' wide-brimmed, flower-laden hats askew and locks of hair adrift, but who cared? Santiago!

The trip to Hillcrest was a short one. The first-come lot of guests piled out, most of them untroubled by their wind-blown dishevelment. Racing down the slope to meet them came various Rausches: Paul, in the lead, paused to light a giant cannon cracker and toss it nonchalantly to one side. Parents of small children were given pause; older boys and girls ran on unheeding. Ludwig Evans, trailing Paul, rushed headlong to Tucker Gordon's side. "Come on, Tuck! We've got millions of firecrackers!"

Johnny restrained his son. "Hold on, you must make your manners first." And laughing at Ludwig's expression, he added, "That's what we used to be told when I was a boy."

"I know. Cassie says it. But—"

"Tucker must speak to your grandfather and grandmother before he disappears for the afternoon."

Ludwig III turned with them and walked up the hill. By the time the carload of guests had strung out, the younger ones leading as they shouted "Santiago! Have you heard?"

Of course they had heard: the very flag seemed triumphant, high at the top of the pole in the center of the grass plot encircled by the drive, its colors brilliant as the breeze moved its folds in the July sun.

Ludwig and Sally came beaming to greet their guests, completely at ease, no sign of misgivings on Sally's radiant face. She shepherded the girls up the steps to the door, inviting them to find the front bedroom, where Rose was in attendance, to leave their hats, correct any disarrangement of coiffures, and put down where they could find them when needed the dancing slippers that had been carried in velvet bags swinging from their wrists on drawstrings.

Ludwig Evans was dancing with impatience by the time his grandparents got round to shaking hands with the Gordons.

"Come *on*, Tuck!"

The two small boys started off at a run, paying no heed to a wail from the porch where Jennifer Evans had been sitting quietly on her mother's lap; now she was squirming in the effort to break loose.

"No, Jennifer. You can't go. You might get hurt."

Gib unfolded his length in his usual slow motion from the porch chair beside Elsa, reached over, and swung his daughter to his shoulder. Jennifer smiled down at her mother in mischievous triumph. She was at three an elfin child (in appearance, at any rate), with dark hair fine as cobwebs that the heat had curled in tendrils clinging to her damp forehead, and a wonder and a miracle to the blue-eyed Rausches, brown eyes like Gib's that seemed enormous in her small delicate face.

"I'll take her, Elsa. She mustn't miss the fun. I'll see she comes to no harm."

Elsa surrendered. "She'll be cross as two sticks in a little while: she's had no nap. But go along the two of you. Little Tag-along! The boys may not be delighted to see you. Don't spoil their celebration."

Gib made his way down the steps, Jennifer riding his shoulder. Someone on the porch said, "He worships that child, doesn't he?"

And Elsa, smiling complacently, said, "Both of them. He's a very satisfactory parent." "Except that he spoils them," she thought. "Like Papa when I was little. And I have to straighten them out. I hope we won't cross each other the way Mamma and I used to." She looked at the regal figure of her mother at the top of the steps. "I understand better now. And I love her dearly, but there are still some memories that rankle."

By that time the girls had come downstairs, and the boys waiting for them had been led away by Paul to his safely hidden hoard of cannon crackers. The small children had been separated from their parents and dismissed in the charge of Ben and Cassie's grandson Aaron, who would see to it that they shot off their share of firecrackers without danger to anyone. Cassie had taken the small babies upstairs to put them to sleep, or at least to keep them quiet and out of the way. When the last firecrackers had been exploded, the small children could play in the sandpile, or swing in the rope swings (Rausch Cordage's very finest manila rope hung from two or three of the oak trees); the colored boys could swing them, seeing that each got a fair turn. By that time the older children would have worked off their excitement and expended their torpedoes and firecrackers, and they could play croquet or whatever game they chose; for all of them there were freezers of ice cream and tubs of lemonade at the top of the side steps. Parents, even young parents, were glad to sit down, free of responsibility for a while, and joined the group already on the front porch. Johnny found his father and mother already there; Ludwig explained, "Dock thought one of you should have a horse here, in case of a call; you never know what will happen on the Fourth of July. And the old plug he drives these days wouldn't jump at the cannon shot."

Some of the men went with Stewart to see his horseless carriage. Johnny said, "He came all the way from Madison City in it, believe it or not." And he thought to himself, "If a reliable automobile could be made, it might be a good thing to use for country calls."

By the time the rest of the guests arrived (it seemed as though all of Waynesboro was there), the scene was a somewhat less exuberant one. Those already there had, as invariably happens at family reunions or any large conglomerate gathering, drifted into separate groups talking of their very different interests.

The newcomers too were met at the porch steps by Ludwig and Sally and quickly sorted out by their skillful hosts.

All ladies were invited to leave their hats in the front bedroom, and then to find their friends. Mary Gardiner tossed her hat to her mother, and she and Franz Lichtenstein were off like a shot; Janey Voorhees started up the steps behind her parents; her brother hesitated, looking at his mother. It was his father who spoke: "Go find your friends, Blair, and you too, Janey, you don't have to spend your afternoon with us old folks. Don't be so bashful: all your friends are here."

Janey, a thin pale blond edition of her mother, went off slowly in Blair's footsteps. When the ladies had done whatever ladies always need a mirror for and had come down to the drawing room, Ludwig said, "I believe lemonade is to be dispensed, then you are to be shown the house. My wife can hardly wait. The gentlemen can put their hats in the hall and those who would like to see the house can join the ladies. I am afraid our guests who are already here have been sadly neglected—most of their husbands have gone off to admire young Bodien's automobile. Some of you may wish to see it too; if not, you may find some of the men on the back porch."

The hint was clear enough to the beer-drinkers, who drifted off one by one to the group who had got ahead of them, on and above the back steps, close to the keg of beer and the caterer's man who was busy at the spigot. The teetotalers were urged by Sally to join the ladies for a glass of lemonade. "I don't know why it is," she said plaintively, "at a large gathering it is impossible to persuade ladies and gentlemen not to separate into two groups. I often wonder what it is the men want to talk about."

So, for politeness' sake, or perhaps aware of what the other gentlemen were seeking, the more godly among the males went into the drawing room with their wives to leaven the lump of femininity already there. When they had drunk their lemonade and eaten their cookies, Sally started with them on a tour of the house; after all, that was the proclaimed reason for their being there. The ladies were eager to see it; the men, some of them, trailed after; some preferred to sit quietly beside the ice-clinking pitcher of lemonade in the cool room and carry on what conversation they could against the clamor outside.

The afternoon passed, noisily but without accident; the last firecrackers were exploded and comparative silence followed; the swings and the croquet ground were preempted. Mary Gardiner and Franz Lichtenstein gathered the younger children, down to five-year-old Tucker and Ludwig Evans, and half-persuaded, half-coerced them into playing soldier, marching down to the vegetable garden and up and down between rows of gooseberry bushes. Rodney Stevens, hot from swinging the girls, wandered to the back porch, plumped himself down on a step, and asked for a drink of beer. Blair Voorhees had followed at his elbow, and held out his hand, too; two steins were filled and passed to the boys by Mr. Lichtenstein, who was sitting like a fat happy Buddha on the edge of the porch, his feet on the step below, his knees spread to accommodate his belly. Rodney and Blair took the steins; Rodney drank the beer down, but Blair after one mouthful rolled his eyes, clenched his jaws, set the stein down, and sat rigid as a statue, hoping he could swallow it without gagging. Mary Gardiner came up the brick path, hot, her hair straggling from its plaits, her half-grown-up frock crushed and soiled. She appealed to Captain Bodien, sitting well back from the steps, talking business with Stewart. "Gran'pa, will you help us? Franz and I are teaching the little kids to march, but we can't get it through their silly heads they're supposed to be soldiers, going to set the Cubans free." Her glance, even as she spoke, took in the scene. "What are you drinking, beer? Can I taste it? Please, Papa—Please, Gran'pa—just to see what it's like."

Blair, who had finally managed a convulsive swallow, thrust his stein in Rodney's direction. "Here. Maybe she'll like it. I don't." He rose and shuffled off toward the sound of girls' voices, of mallets striking croquet balls.

Rodney, holding the stein out of Mary's reach, consideringly, with all the superiority of the hardened medical student, said, "You know, I doubt if he's ever tasted beer before."

Mr. Lichtenstein said, "Who vaz zat boy? Haf I seen him before?"

There was a muffled snort behind him. His son Rudy said, "That's the Voorhees boy. Let's hope his teetotaling parents don't hear about this, or you've cooked my goose with a good part of the electorate."

"Zose people! Zey vouldn't vote for you anyway."

John Gordon said, "Nothing to worry about, Rudy. It's high time that boy cut loose from the apron strings."

On the lower step Rodney was still holding the stein Blair had thrust into his hand. Mary's grandfather said, "Let her taste it, Rodney. It won't hurt her—she won't like it."

Mary took a good mouthful, glared at Rodney as if he had played a cruel joke on her, and spat it out over the edge of the step, an impropriety her father could not at the moment reprove; he was laughing too hard. "I *don't* like it—I think it's nasty. Gran'pa?"

"Yes, I'm coming." Captain Bodien, always at Mary's beck and call, rose smiling at the wry grimace still twisting her mouth. "Gentlemen, you see an exhibition of the best preventative of any tendency to drink too much: let the children have a taste of beer while they're too young for their palates to accept it." And the stocky, bow-legged Captain went off down the path to the gooseberry patch.

The other men sat on in quiet talk, nursing their steins, occasionally passing one back to be refilled. The croquet game continued until the caterers went out to that one flat space on the top of the hill and asked that it be vacated so that they could put up the tables for dinner. It would be served at six so that it would be finished and cleared away before it was dark enough for fireworks. The young people strolled away, some by twos, some in groups. Rodney, having asserted his manhood, had rejoined Lavinia Gardiner and removed her from Blair Voorhees' silent shadowing.

"I thought you were never coming to my rescue. I can't talk to that boy: what is there to say? And now it's dinnertime, and I must go up and see to my hair."

"Your hair's all right. Let's go look at the horses." Rodney could think of nothing else to look at, where the two of them could be alone. The horses were loose in the pasture beyond the whitewashed stake-and-rail fence that marked the end of Hillcrest's stables, yard, and vegetable garden. As they went down the slope hand in hand, Lavinia said, "Where did you go?"

"I got caught, I'm sorry."

"So I understand. Caught by a stein of beer. Am I to be serious about a *drinking* man? Blair wants to know."

"He tell you he tasted it himself? He didn't like it, so he can go on like his Papa and Mamma, talking about drinking men in that tone of voice. Come to that, your grandfather is a 'drinking man,' and so is your father. You've never seen them drunk, have you?"

Lavinia giggled. "I simply cannot imagine Papa *drunk*. What a lot of nonsense Blair can talk!"

They laughed together, and went on wordlessly, swinging their clasped hands; there was little need for words between them: they knew what they knew, and kept silent about it in the face of parental admonitions: "You're too young to know your own minds" from Rodney's mother; Barbara would not have dared use that argument: she had not been as old as Lavinia when she married. But she could say, "Don't make up your minds until you are through college"; or, "Wait until Rodney is established in his profession." And so when they reached the pasture fence, they were content to lean over it and contemplate the grazing horses until the farm bell's clangor summoned them to supper.

Ernest Rausch at the head of one table and his wife at its foot, and Charles at the second with his wife, waited standing until those who had not already peeked had found their place and cards. Before that the children, served by the colored boys who had been overseeing them all afternoon and now under the supervision of Rose, were well on their way through their fried chicken; they paused, some of them with chicken legs in their hands, to listen in astonishment to the babble from the other tables.

Ernest, when he saw that his company was ready to be seated, said, "A few toasts first, don't you think? Even if we have only lemonade." And he called across to Charles, "Let's all drink together: To Hillcrest, may all its hours be happy ones." Glasses were raised, with some splashing of lemonade, amid cries of agreement. "To our country and its President." A Shout went up from both tables. "To the Navy and its victory!" Redoubled shouts, and then, "To the flag—may it wave forever!" The last toast was applauded so vociferously as to rattle the dishes.

When the shouts had died away, the company at both tables sat down, and were served by the caterers; they fell to at once on standard Fourth of July fare. Ludwig had said firmly to his wife, "Nothing fancy—just fried chicken, mashed potatoes and gravy, and lima beans, and all the trimmings, and strawberry shortcake." And if serving hot food to so many people so far from the kitchen was a problem, it was the caterer's and not Sally's.

In the long dining room inside the house, dinner began more quietly, Mrs. Evans asking the blessing. They bowed their heads beneath the glittering chandelier ("Electric lights all through the house, from their own power plant"—that had been one of the marvels revealed by the afternoon's tour of Hillcrest) and listened to Mrs. Evans give thanks to Almighty God for having vouchsafed a great victory to the country, pray for His continued blessing on the United States and its President; give further thanks for His long-continued benediction on the Waynesboro Woman's Club, which had enjoyed thirty years of striving for the intellectual and moral improvement of its members and indeed of the whole town; and at long last invoke a blessing on the new house whose completion they had come to celebrate, and upon the family for whose hospitality their friends were so much indebted.

Sally, surprised that Gwen Evans was so long-winded, comforted herself with the thought that Mrs. McKinney or Mrs. Maxwell could have dreamed up some things for the Lord to bless that Mrs. Evans hadn't remembered. Once that convention had been taken care of, Sally kept the ladies' attention fixed on reminiscences of Club events, the Club being the one thing all the women had in common.

Anne came to her support, speaking in a sudden lull so that everyone heard her, "Thirty years is a long time—almost a generation, isn't it? And yet, looking back, in spite of everything that has happened, it doesn't seem so long ago: our Commencement at the Female Seminary, and Mrs. Lowrey's summoning us, Sally and me, to a meeting, when we were actually free and no longer had to obey her summons. But I am glad we obeyed and fell in with her plans. The Club has meant something special to all of us, I think."

Eliza Ballard, across the table from her, said, "Thirty years ago! It seems a lifetime to me. Everything has changed so. Do you realize that of those charter members there are only six of us left?"

Eyes turned quickly from one end of the table to the other. It was true: the Ballard sisters, Amanda, Mrs. Deming, and Anne and Sally. It was Sally who said cheerfully, "We were the young members in those days, and we aren't so old now: we should be good for another thirty years."

Everyone laughed, and the conversation became less focused and more diverse as to subject. When the slowest of them had finished the last bite of strawberry shortcake, Sally rose and addressed the table again. "The Club will now hold an informal meeting here, and enjoy the pleasure of hearing Miss Reid's essay on the 'First Thirty Years.'"

Outside at that moment, Ludwig rose from the picnic table to go check the preparations for the fireworks.

"I think everything's ready," he said to John Gordon. "I just want to make sure. I'll supervise this show myself." Then, as he noticed that the guests had risen from all the other outside tables and were heading toward the porch, he said, "One thing you might do, Dock. No telling when the women will be through with their program in the dining room. Can you line up chairs enough for them on the porch, and hold them?"

"I'll see to it." As many chairs as possible had been assembled on the stretch of porch overlooking the long slope, the road, the car tracks, and the canal, and had been arranged in rows. John called out to the men who were following him, "Hey, Johnny, Rudy, Sam Travers—all you married men—snaffle two chairs, each of you, for you and your wives, and hold on to them. I'll take care of the lone females." He went to the back row of chairs to the right of the door, and began turning them up against the wall, muttering as he did so, "Eliza, Amanda, Charlotte Bonner, Jessamine, Mrs. Deming—" He had never been able to bring himself to call his son's mother-in-law "Louisa," in spite of the inevitably close connection. "And Anne and me. That will be enough." It didn't matter in what order the ladies sat. He plumped himself down in the nearest chair and held the next one for Anne, hoping that Amanda would not be long-winded: the twilight was deepening fast, and Ludwig would be impatient.

The free chairs were soon taken by those who had come up from the lawn; they sat quietly, only the mothers of young children worrying a little about their whereabouts. But presently Cassie appeared with them in tow, and sleepy Jennifer Evans in her arms, head on her shoulder.

"Ah done got the leas'es' ones up to bed while yo' eatin'. Miz E'nest's gal took he's and Miz Cha'les's. An' hyah one mo' ready to go. Do I take 'em all up, o' yo gwunna leave 'em to stay up fo' the fi'wuks?"

At that moment, the Club meeting having adjourned, Sally appeared at the door. "Take them all up," she said firmly. "Those who are awake can see the fireworks better from the third floor window than from here."

"An' ef'n any of 'm real scya'ed at the big bangs?"

"If there's any child you can't manage, send one of the other girls down for its mother."

Elsa said "Gib," and Gib stood up quietly.

"You mustn't carry that heavy child all the way to the third floor, Cassie. I'll take her," and take her he did, from a willing Cassie, who felt her age as "de mis'ry in ma back," but would not have owned herself unable to carry a child upstairs. Tim Merrill scooped his youngest from the next-to-the-top step and followed Gib into the hall. Ludwig Evans and Tucker Gordon looked mutely rebellious: they felt themselves as well able to stay up as anyone, but Elsa shook her head. "You heard your grandmother," and Julia said firmly, "Go on Tuck. If the 'big bangs' frighten you, I'll come up and hold your hand."

As Tuck looked at her scornfully, Johnny said mildly to his wife, "Why suggest it?" and to his son, "You won't be frightened, will you? That's a lot of woman's nonsense. You weren't frightened by the firecrackers, were you?"

"Of course not. I *liked* shooting firecrackers." And the two boys, who at five had known each other for a lifetime, went meekly into the house together, letting the screen door slam shut behind them.

By that time all the middle-aged and elderly had found chairs on the porch; the young people, whether by twos or in groups, approached with more laggardly steps, only quickening their pace a little when they came out from under the trees and saw how dark it had grown: fireflies, numerous as the stars overhead, were visible now, above the lawn and gathered under the branches of trees. The stragglers did not bother to look for chairs but took over the steps, or dropped to the grass and sat there, the boys cross-legged, the girls with their feet tucked back under their long skirts.

To call their attention to the glories awaiting them, Ludwig fired a rocket that soared high over the road, bursting with a very "big bang" and filling the sky and the reflecting canal with a shower of falling comets. After that came a constant succession: pinwheels, rockets, Roman candles, red fire that made the canal itself seem to be blazing through clouds of smoke, more rockets, increasingly spectacular until at last the end was reached, the set piece finale, Ludwig's pride, which he came back to the porch to watch: at one end the President, at the other, a warship breasting the waves, with smoke billowing realistially from the stack and the words "Manila" above and "Dewey" below, and in the center, the flag. Before the waving flag was fully alight all except the elderly were on their feet cheering: "McKinley! Dewey! Manila Bay! Santiago! Hurrah for the flag!" with what voice they had left at the end of a raucous day.

When all was dark again, the lights of Japanese lanterns began to glimmer from the lower branches of the trees. Ludwig rose from his perch on a step, and Sally moved from her chair to stand behind him. It was she who spoke: "I am sorry the fireworks cannot go on all night, but I am afraid that is the end. Will you all come inside now for a little while? The chairs must be moved and the floors sprinkled with wax for the dancing. The young ladies I know will want to go upstairs and put on their dancing slippers, and look in the mirror. We should like it if you would all stay—even those of you who do not dance might enjoy watching. But if you feel that you must go, the trolley that brought the orchestra out is waiting to go back to town." The musicians had already climbed the hill, and the street car was standing on the siding. There were no surprises for Sally, or for anyone who knew the town, in the division between those who stayed—all who danced or wanted to watch others dance (and Sam Travers, who would like to play the piano in the orchestra's rest intervals, and Thomasina with him)—and those who departed: the elderly and most of the middle-aged, and all who believed that dancing was an instrument of the devil. They spoke their gratitude for the delightful day, and made their farewells. Of the adolescent young, only Blair and Janey were summoned by their parents.

Henry had stopped to greet one of the bank tellers, then hurried to catch his family, Janey clinging to her mother's arm, Blair following along behind. He fell in with the boy just in time to hear Janey say, "I think you should know, Mamma. Blair drank a glass of beer this afternoon." Christina was so frozen by the words that for a moment she could not move; then, reminded by approaching voices behind her that she was in the middle of a procession, she said, "Not now, please. We will discuss it at home, where we shall not be overheard."

Henry knew from her voice how profound the shock had been. He should perhaps have taken his family home when he became aware of what had drawn the men together; but how could he, without insulting the Rausches, who, after all, held his fate in their hands? He glanced at Blair beside him: the light from the Japanese lanterns hung along the path and its steps hardly gave light enough to see the boy's expression, except that the quivering of the muscles along his jaw showed that his teeth were clenched. Through them he muttered something about "that Janey—" and then, to his father, relaxing his jaws, drawing a long breath, "I only wanted to know what it was like. I just had one swallow. It was nasty."

It was not until the four of them were walking up the street toward home, well away from any other of the car's passengers, that Christina said to her husband, "Did you know what was going on? That *beer* was being served at that house?"

"The innocent!" he thought. "Doesn't know beer when she smells it." He said, "I guessed it."

"We should have left the moment you knew."

"My dear Chrissie: you can't accept someone's hospitality and then walk out because you don't approve of its quality. It would have been insulting. And you don't insult your boss."

"It was an insult to invite us and a number of other abstainers to such an affair. It must have been deliberate."

"A deliberate insult? Oh, no, that would be most unlike either of the Rausches. They were simply giving every guest what he liked."

Later, at home in their sitting room, Christina faced her son and daughter, standing side by side before her as if, Henry thought, they were about ten years old. And instead of simply asking Blair whether or not the awful charge was true, she began like any prosecutor by questioning the witness.

"Now, Janey, if this is true, how did you happen to know it? Were you there?"

"Of course not. When Rodney came back he told us. He laughed and laughed, he thought it was so funny."

"*Funny?* That your brother—?"

"Funny because he didn't like it, I guess, and made such awful faces till he choked it down. Laughed because he thought Blair was a sissy, I suppose. Everyone does—think so, I mean."

Blair, who had been growing whiter and whiter, swung an awkward, half-clenched fist, striking Janey on the shoulder and swinging her around against the door-jamb.

To the speechless horror of her parents, Janey flung out, "And that's why he doesn't have any friends—they know he *hits* people." And she turned, went out and up the stairs.

"Blair! Blair!"

To his mother's horror, Blair reverted to childishness. "And *that's* why she hasn't any friends: she's a sneak and a tattle-tale."

"To think that you would strike your sister!" Shock in his father swiftly turned to anger. "Or any girl! Have you no self-control?"

"The best defense is attack, they say." Christina was cold to the bone now. Henry was hot. "If there were no wrong-doing, there would be no 'tattling' as you call it. I suppose therefore that what Janey heard was true. Was a glass of beer forced on you? Were you dared? Or did you ask for it?"

"Neither." Blair thought it best to forget his outstretched hand. "I was with Rod Stevens. He asked for it, and they just naturally supposed, I guess—Anyway, they filled two steins and handed them to us. We'd just sort of wandered over there—we'd been swinging the girls, and we were hot."

"But you knew what those men were doing. Why 'wander' into temptation?"

"Well, Rod wanted—"

"Surely everyone in Waynesboro knows our position in regard to drinking. Who filled a glass of beer for you?"

"Mamma, I don't know who filled the steins. One of the caterers, I suppose. He wouldn't know me. How could he? It was Mr. Lichtenstein who passed it to me. He wouldn't know me either. I only know him because he's so—so—"

"'Uncouth' I believe is the word. Why did you drink it? Why didn't you put it down?"

"I wanted to know what it tasted like. And I didn't want them to think—they laughed at me, anyway, because I didn't like it. It was so nasty I could hardly swallow just one mouthful. But what could I do? I couldn't spit it out, like a kid. Like Mary Gardiner did, I guess—I had gone by that time, but Rod said that's what she did."

"Do you mean to say they gave little Mary Gardiner a *glass of beer*?"

"She wanted to taste it. No one minded. Her father and grandfather were there. Rodney gave her the stein I'd put down. Mamma," he said desperately, "it was just a kind of joke: they knew she wouldn't like it."

"Ladies don't drink beer. Nor gentlemen, either, for that matter. Who were the men who thought it funny to offer a child an alcoholic beverage? Besides Mr. Lichtenstein?"

"Christina," her husband intervened, "don't ask him that. You pretty well know who, if it matters, and I don't think he should be encouraged to carry tales. I don't like it in Janey. It is a tendency I deplore. Go on to bed, Blair. The experience of having tasted beer will do you no harm if you remember that you don't like it. But get down on your knees and pray for help in controlling your temper."

Gladly Blair made his escape. When the sound of his feet on the stairs came less loudly to the two listening, Henry turned to his grim-faced, silent wife. "Don't make too much of this. Remember that many of those men are of German birth and used to drinking beer from childhood."

"Blair knows it is a sin to drink. But he was unable to resist temptation."

"He has had very little experience of temptation, and he is almost a grown man."

"Too few men can resist that particular temptation. The Anti-Saloon League must work harder for a local option law. But that is not relevant now. You have been regretting that our children have so few friends their own age. I am glad. When Blair starts at the Seminary, he will make more suitable friends than Rodney Stevens."

Henry, who was sick at heart over Blair's reckless display of temper—he had not hurt Janey, but he might have—still thought he should have the give and take of college life before he started at the Seminary, while continuing to live at home. But he had no intention of bringing up that question on this unhappy night.

"How right I was," Christina continued, "to think it unwise to take the children to such a mixed gathering. Every Tom, Dick, and Harry—"

"It was a little like that. But all those men are Ludwig Rausch's friends. Employees, some of them, but friends, too. And anyway, there won't be any more parties like it: housewarmings are not that common."

"I wondered a little about the Club anniversary celebration. I understand very well now. It was an excuse for Sally Rausch to keep her friends separate from his. Did you know—?"

"About the beer? Beforehand? No, certainly not. By dinnertime, yes. After all, beer does have an aroma. I couldn't help wondering if Mrs. Rausch was enjoying herself as much as her husband. I should think it most unlikely that she cares for the Toms, Dicks, and Harrys, or their wives."

In the meantime, back at Hillcrest, no one could have doubted that Sally was enjoying her husband's party. Crumbled wax had been sprinkled on the porch all the way around the house; Japanese lanterns had been hung from the ceiling, to match those still hanging in the trees. The orchestra, having been fed, had taken their places beside the grand piano in the front drawing room, set up their music stands, and were tuning their instruments. All doors and the floor-length windows were wide open, in the hope that the music could be heard on all sides. The caterers had long since cleared away the remains of dinner and in the kitchen were preparing the midnight collation; the beer kegs had been carried off and all the chairs removed so there was a clear way for the dancers on the porch surrounding the house. In the drawing rooms and the library, those who expected to be onlookers at the dancing found chairs arranged inside the windows, whose curtains and draperies had been caught back behind the open shutters. The young people had paired off in the hall, dance programs dangling on silk cords from the girls' wrists; they were waiting for the senior Rausches to open the ball.

Ludwig, struck by an idea that seemed to express the emotions of the day, stopped to speak to the orchestra before leading Sally to the door. "On such a Fourth, we should begin with a grand march around the house. Give us 'The Stars and Stripes Forever,' will you? And Charles, you get all the lazy-bones up from their chairs, and tell them to fall in."

Even without the brasses of a full band, the spirited chords set everyone's feet tapping; Ludwig stepped out, Sally on his arm, the young people tramping two-by-two behind him; as he passed each window he called to those inside, "Fall in! Fall in!" and few disobeyed him. Even Doug's club foot and awkward shoe did not stop him from joining the others. The orchestra played them around the house twice, in all the evolutions of a grand march that Ludwig could remember and that they had room to perform: "Grand left and right—" Then the musicians swung into "When Johnny Comes Marching Home Again," the tempo increased, the elderly and the breathless dropped out, while the youthful forgot their dignity and the march turned into something like a cakewalk. When the leaders came round to the front door again, the orchestra stopped playing and all had a chance to catch their breath. John Gordon said, holding on to Anne's elbow until she was seated, "It's so long since I've done any such prancing, I'd forgotten how strenuous—forgotten my age, I guess."

"Oh, John! What nonsense! Look at Ludwig!"

The orchestra had begun to play "The Blue Danube"; Ludwig had swept Sally into his arms and was whirling her around in the German fashion, turning on every step, so that her skirts twisted about her ankles and fell away again.

"They make a substantial pair, don't they? I wonder the porch floor doesn't creak. It's fun to watch, all that twirling." John grinned at Anne. "But I couldn't do it. I might manage a more sedate waltz, though I thought my dancing days were long over. May I have the honor?" He rose, bowed, and offered Anne his arm. When they had had that one dance and had returned to their chairs, while the orchestra paused just long enough for an exchange of partners, Johnny brought Julia to sit with his father and took his mother out to the porch. Ludwig brought Sally to keep Doug Gardiner company while he danced with Barbara. The young people might be slow to change partners, but Ludwig would make sure that any lady with a desire to dance had her chance to do so. The girls' dance cards were rapidly being filled, and so they were quite prepared to dance the night away; but most of the middle-aged were ready to sit down. When Johnny took his mother back to her chair and went off again with Julia, Anne said she had had enough: she even shook her head at Ludwig when he turned in her direction; she would rather just sit there and watch. She sent John to dance with Barbara, but Barbara's daughters' beaux were dutiful: both Lowrey Edwards and Rodney Stevens approached her ahead of John; he returned to his chair, and he and Anne sat together quite content to watch. They saw Johnny go past with Elsa, and Julia with Gib; Rodney Stevens and Lavinia Gardiner together in a rapt enchantment, dancing slowly and dreamily, their eyes far-away and their faces tender. Jessamine Stevens and Sheldon Edwards danced by, and John said, "Why not—?" and Anne said, "Some day, maybe, for company when the boys are married and gone." Sally remained seated with Doug Gardiner: she had danced all she could, she insisted; one wild whirl with Ludwig would do for the night. And so they and others sat and watched the young people: those in love with each other and those in love with dancing. The short balloon sleeves of the girls that made their thin arms seem so vulnerably young, their full white or pastel skirts swirling about their and the boys' ankles, the sweetness of their faces, the enchantment in their eyes, all in the glow of the Japanese lanterns overhead and the rectangles of light from the open windows: somehow there was something touching about it—about their youth, their happiness.

John said, in Anne's ear, his voice inaudible to others over the music, "They are so young! Were we as young at their age?"

"Thirty years ago? I don't know. (She did know, but would not say: John had never been that young. Not after the war.) I don't feel any older, inside. I'm still *me*."

"I looked around tonight: do you realize that you and I, Ludwig and Sally, are, all of a sudden, the older generation? Remember how it used to be: Judge and Mrs. Ballard, Professor and Mrs. Lowrey, the Gardiner sisters, your old maid school teachers: all gone now. And to those youngsters out there we no doubt seem as old as the dear departed once seemed to us."

"As old as poor Miss Pinney? Or Judge Ballard? Goodness, John! And we're not the older generation! There are the Maxwells and the McKinneys—they were middle-aged when they joined the Club, and Sally and I were still girls."

"I suspect the Gordons and the Rausches—all grandparents, let me remind you—seem to those boys and girls all in the same age bracket as the McKinneys."

"A horrid truth, if it is one. Why so melancholy tonight, of all nights?"

"Melancholy? Not at all. I'm enjoying this thoroughly. But it does give one to think. And what I think is that for Ludwig this is the high point of his life. He has accomplished all he could or ever hoped for. He has years of life ahead of him, but he'll never be at quite this peak again."

"You think that from now on it's 'downhill all the way'? You must be bilious."

"Ludwig and I—maybe even you and Sally—from here on out will be slipping down what I hope will be a long slope. I don't mean that the years ahead won't be good ones, just that we'll be over the crest of the hill. The country won't ever be quite the same, either; this Fourth of July marks the end of an era."

"Whatever do you mean?"

"The war with Spain can't last much longer. But we'll have new problems: Cuba and Puerto Rico, the Philippines—all left on our hands, to do what with? We've already taken on Hawaii. We can't even foresee the complexity of the questions that will come up. And we can't go back, not ever. Can't turn the clock back. America will be different."

"I don't believe it."

"You don't want to, do you? You won't *let* it change."

"Not for you and me, I won't. All the rest—the problems—they won't affect us."

"Perhaps not." He smiled at her. "At any rate, we can remember this Fourth of July as *a* high point if not *the* high point of our lives—as it certainly is of Ludwig's. He has fulfilled his dreams. Which comes of having simple dreams, I suppose."

Anne longed to say, "And your dreams?" She wished he had chosen another time and place to be for once so articulate. At home, at night, in bed. But he was always so tired, too tired for talking, for thinking of what he wanted of life. Perhaps he hadn't any dreams now he was past fifty—had put them away with other childish things. Perhaps it was better not to ask—perhaps that was why what he had said had come so easily: here, now, where he was safe from probing.

At midnight the orchestra put up its instruments for the supper break, a stand-up collation served buffet style on the long dining-room table and the big sideboard. After that, those who had been onlookers at the dancing were ready for home and bed. Ludwig was prepared, and had a trolley car waiting on the siding. Mary Gardiner was collected by her parents, protesting, although she didn't mind too much: she had not yet really learned to dance, and since Franz Lichtenstein had been taken home by his parents after the fireworks, she was sure that anyone who asked her to partner him was being nice to her—a humiliating thought. Veronica truly objected to going, but then, Paul Rausch had been looking after her all evening: that made a difference. Children, half or wholly asleep, were brought down from their attic beds, and slung like meal bags over paternal shoulders. When Johnny

Gordon started upstairs for Tuck, his father said, "You stay, Johnny, you and Julia. I've asked Ludwig to send the horse and buggy around; we can take the boy home with us for the night."

"Oh, do let's, Johnny." Julia, flushed and eager and unlike her usual cool self, laid a hand on Johnny's arm. Johnny looked astonished and—quizzical, his father thought, if one could look those two things at once. Julia went on, "I haven't had such fun for years. And Gib and Elsa will be here, and Sophie and Rudy are staying, so we wouldn't be the only married couple. Papa Dock, could you squeeze Mamma into the buggy, if she holds Tuck on her lap? She hates that trolley, and then you wouldn't have to keep Tuck overnight."

And so Johnny brought Tuck down and transferred him to his grandfather's arms; the four managed to get in the buggy. As they drove off toward town, the orchestra struck up again and the young couples returned with new vigor to their dancing. The tunes were livelier: two-steps from the latest musical comedies, even a Virginia reel, in which the girls were swung around with such abandon, with hard stamping on the boys' part, that the Japanese lanterns were set swaying overhead. The orchestra gave them a chance to catch their breath with another Strauss waltz, and another, then finally moved without warning into "Home, Sweet Home." The dancers slowed to its time and finally came to a halt. The Fourth of July was over. After prolonged good-byes and proper expressions of gratitude to host and hostess, they all made their way down the long hillside path and across the road to the last trolley that would make the trip that night. They were somehow aware, although they hardly shared John Gordon's certainty, that they had enjoyed a Fourth of July whose like they could never know again. And Ludwig and Sally, while Ernest and Charles and Gib went round extinguishing the lanterns, congratulated themselves and each other on a grandly successful social occasion. They had no idea that one family had gone from Hillcrest deeply troubled and unhappy.

After that particularly glorious Fourth there followed a melancholy letdown for the country. The town of Santiago, in spite of the destruction of the Spanish fleet and the more costly but still victorious Battle of San Juan Hill, did not fall like a ripe apple into the hands of the Americans. It was not until the seventeenth of July that the city surrendered. The triumph was but briefly celebrated; by the middle of July the press was beginning to print columns about the sufferings of the American Army, ill-fed, unhealthy in an unhealthy country, falling victim by the scores to typhoid and malaria, all looking forward with horror to the prospect of spending August and September (the yellow fever months) in their miserable Cuban camps. Discharged convalescents confirmed the dispatches. The taking of Puerto Rico late in July scarcely mitigated the gloom. On August third the War Department was informed that the American Army was an army of convalescents that should be transported home at once.

Peace negotiations initiated on July 26 were carried on through the French ambassador during the storm of public indignation over the War Department's ineptitude and mismanagement. The Navy had forced Spain to seek peace; the Army had accomplished next to nothing; it had taken Santiago in the end but never had faced the main Spanish force. Spain was willing to negotiate in the hope of exchanging Cuba for an American withdrawal from the Philippines. She agreed to an armistice on August 12 that entitled the United States to hold the city, bay, and harbor of Manila pending a final peace treaty that would determine the fate of the Islands.

In four months the Americans had captured the scattered remnants of the Spanish Empire; but though citizens could hardly help being stirred by the achievement, millions of them were very doubtful of the wisdom of the course being taken. Furious controversy raged during the fall on two aspects of the war and its consequences: the incapacity of the Quartermaster and Supply Departments and the Surgeon General's Department, all of whom the yellow press was delighted to accuse of worse than inadequacy; and the question of what should be the disposition of the Spanish colonies. The peace treaty would not be signed until the tenth of December, but no one doubted as the negotiations dragged on that Spain would be forced to give up not only Cuba and Puerto Rico but also the Philippines. And what was to be done with them? There was no question of resistance to American occupation of the lesser Islands, but Aguinaldo and his forces were clearly going to fight for independence. Men argued over the alternatives as hotly in Waynesboro as anywhere: in Dock Gordon's middle office, the Thirkield's drugstore, and around the red-hot stove at the rear of Fritz Klein's grocery. The Islands could be sold, one by one, like any other real estate, all except Manila and its harbor, which the Americans must hold on to; it could be turned over to the Filipinos to govern as best they could, or it could be kept by the United States. In the first case, it was agreed, the real estate would be purchased by Germany; if the Islands were freed with no strings attached, chaos would follow and Germany would move in. Germany, coming belatedly onto the world scene, had been seizing colonies when and where she could; since the beginning of the war her intentions had been one of the major worries of the American government. Ludwig Rausch, however gloomy over the possibility of trouble in that direction, was justified in his "I told you so," since he had prophesied at the time Bismarck was ousted that the young emperor was a rash adventurer looking for glory. If Germany moved in on a Filipino government set up by the Americans, that government would have to be sustained. It was easier and less dangerous for the United States to stay there than risk trouble with Germany. Unfortunately it became clearer every day that Aguinaldo and his insurrectos were something less than happy with that solution.

The debate was furious before the peace treaty was signed and after; it continued in Congress until the treaty was ratified on the last day of the Congressional session, and might have failed even then had not the Vice-President's vote in the Senate broken a tie. By that time the Americans on

Luzon had been attacked by the insurrectos. Recriminations followed from all who thought it an unholy departure from American principles, this acquisition of colonies, this sally into imperialism. Those who thought the Administration had been right believed that in the long run it would help preserve peace in the Pacific, and that it would promote trade with the Orient. Even Ludwig, who had been so opposed to the war in the beginning, thought that taking suzerainty over the Philippines was the best of bad alternatives, and granted that it would work to the advantage of rope manufacturers: there would be no tariff on any product (Manila hemp, for instance) from any possession of the United States.

Except as a matter for debate, the question of the Philippines hardly touched Waynesboro. A few families had sons in the expeditionary forces; all connected with Rausch Cordage Company might gain financially. Only the Voorheeses were really involved—tragically involved, as they saw it. Blair had left college in the fall and enlisted in the Army, without so much as coming home first. He had reached the Philippines in time for the insurrectos' attack, and would be caught in whatever fighting might follow. That much Waynesboro knew. The town did not know, and if Christina could help it, never would know, what had led to his enlistment.

Parental discussion of Blair's conduct and his future had begun at once after the dreadful Fourth of July night when he had struck his sister Janey. His mother was concerned for his immortal soul, and Henry was too wise a husband to remind her that she should not worry, since the destination of his soul was foreordained. But he did insist stubbornly that the boy should be sent away to college, should have a chance to prove himself with boys his own age. A Reformed Presbyterian college, of course, whose students would presumably have grown up in godly homes.

"But if he could not resist temptation at home, how could we expect him to resist it away from us?"

"He must experience it before he can resist it." Henry pushed himself up in bed and pulled the pillows higher behind him. These sessions in bed had become the custom; after all, Blair could not be discussed except in private. "I suppose a man's moral muscles as well as his physical need some exercise. And if he slips once or twice, it won't be unforgivable. Most boys do, yet grow up to be righteous men."

"I prefer to keep him out of harm's way. He can go to the Seminary here. Once he is an ordained minister of God he will be safe from temptation."

"Oh, Chrissy! Have you thought how much harm it might do, having a minister who was unprepared to resist temptation telling a congregation how to do it? Besides, are you sure that Blair has experienced a real call to the ministry? That he feels a genuine necessity to devote his life to God's work? Or, if he goes to the Seminary, will he just be following the line of least resistance?"

The argument continued through many hot summer nights. In the end Christina gave way, surrendering finally to the argument that as a Christian she could not be responsible for foisting upon the church so untried and perhaps unworthy candidate for the ministry as her son seemed to be.

Blair was informed of the discussion at the next morning's breakfast table. He accepted the verdict stolidly, with no indication of either pleasure or dismay. His father, who had fought so hard for his freedom, was disappointed and exasperated.

"Well, say something," he snapped. "If you don't want to go, stay here and enter the Seminary."

Blair stared at him coolly. "Of course I want to go. Who would choose to stay in this one-horse town?"

"A number of people do stay, and find life quite pleasant here. However, we'll send in your application at once. We anticipate no difficulty over your admission: although it is late, Aberdeen will find room for Dr. Blair's grandson."

"A church school, then? Better than the Seminary, anyway."

"And a great deal more expensive, what with board and room to pay as well as tuition. So if you don't want to go—"

Christina intervened, hurt though she had been by his contempt for the Seminary. "Of course he wants to go. It's just that he's at the age where it is beneath one's dignity to show enthusiasm."

Once Aberdeen College had agreed to accept him, Christina began to make casual mention of their decision. He seemed a little young, she said, for the Seminary. In some subjects he would find himself ahead of his class in college, in the classical languages, Hebrew, biblical history, English literature; but on the other hand, he might not be as well-grounded as he should be in mathematics and science: "Not my subjects, I fear," with a deprecating smile.

Amanda was surprised; like many others she had heard reports, naturally exaggerated, of the episode at the Rausch housewarming. She had supposed that the maternal reins would be drawn tighter, not that the boy would be given his head. "It must have been a difficult decision for you to make: I know that you have prepared him to go directly to the Seminary. There he won't need mathematics and science. If you thought he needed them," she added with some acerbity, "we have competent teachers of those subjects in the high school." Amanda had always resented a little Christina's assumption that no one else could teach her children.

"It's only that I suppose Aberdeen will expect him to study them, however irrelevant to his needs. He's well-prepared enough for the Seminary, but his father and I decided he needed more experience first, particularly in associating with other young men his own age."

Amanda thought, but of course did not say, that it was a little late for that. She had taught long enough to know that those associations meant the most that began in the first grade and continued for twelve years. Blair had missed much. But she felt sorry for his mother now. As a girl Christina had been overindulged by a father who, however godly and learned, president of a

Reformed Presbyterian Seminary, had nevertheless seen fit to seek out as friends men who could not be called "godly"; and Christina, devoted to him as she had been, had perhaps condemned. At any rate, she had flown to the other extreme. "Who touches pitch"—could Christina possibly have thought her father defiled? Or even herself, intimate as she was with the more worldly members of the Woman's Club?

Amanda brought up the subject of Blair Voorhees one evening when she met Eliza Ballard for dinner at Mrs. Dunbar's boardinghouse. Although she felt nothing like so close to the Ballard sisters as she had when they were young, it had seemed a natural thing for her and Eliza, having met there once by accident, to have slipped into the way of dining there together on Tuesdays and Fridays: they both lived alone, neither liked to cook, and they were used to each other. And so Mrs. Dunbar twice a week set up a table for them in the dining room bay window, where they could talk as confidentially as they pleased, covered as their words were by the babel at the long boardinghouse table so close to them. And so, as they took their chairs and sat down, as they removed their napkins from their rings, Amanda said, "You've heard the Voorheeses are sending Blair away to college in the fall? I feel sorry for Christina: she had such definite plans for his future, and now has been forced to postpone them."

"The most foolish thing a person can do is to plan hopefully for another person's life," Eliza said bitterly. "Most of us learn sooner or later it doesn't pay. What do you mean by 'forced'? By Henry? It hardly seems likely."

"By circumstances, really, I suppose. Blair has shown himself rather unstable, hasn't he? Or at least, too immature to begin studying for the ministry. Although in this case I should think some blame attaches to the one who placed temptation in his way. I never understood why Dr. Blair was so friendly with that ungodly man."

"Are you talking about the Fourth of July and Ludwig Rausch? No need to be so enigmatic—no one can hear. I suppose Mr. Rausch is what you would call 'ungodly' although I have never known him to do a mean or ungenerous thing. And I have never known you, Amanda Reid, to refuse a Rausch invitation."

"I feel a certain obligation to Sally: after all, she is President of the Club, and all the invitations I have ever received have been for Club affairs. As for 'mean' and 'ungenerous,' I call it that, not to have let his invited guests know beforehand that he intended setting up a saloon on the back porch. Numbers of us would have stayed away, including the Voorheeses. And I call it 'mean' to serve an alcoholic beverage to boys and little girls. Don't you? Your mother must be turning in her grave."

"The story seems to have grown as it spread. 'Boys and little girls!' By the dozen, I suppose? And Ludwig wasn't even there—didn't know anything about it until Captain Bodien told us the next morning in the mill office. He thought it was funny enough to pass on. And neither Blair nor Mary Gardiner actually drank the stuff."

"I can believe that Captain Bodien *would* think it funny. But Christina must feel very bitter about it. I doubt if the Voorheeses ever accept another Rausch invitation."

"Then that will be their loss," Eliza retorted sharply.

She reported the conversation to Ludwig the next morning with the perverse satisfaction characteristic of her. "It must be all over town," she concluded, "that you serve alcoholic beverages to children."

"I'm not surprised," Ludwig grinned at her, "knowing Waynesboro."

"I told her the straight of it. Captain Bodien told us, you remember."

"Yes. And you and I believe him. But no one will who likes to think the worst. Leave it alone, Eliza. The less fuss, the sooner it will die down. I'd hate for the story to get back to Sally. She would be upset, after thinking the party such a success."

"The Voorheeses are sending Blair away to college in the fall. I guess, from what Amanda said, in the hope that by meeting more temptation, he'll get so he can resist."

"Then that's to the good, isn't it? It's high time those kids were given a little leeway. But what a storm over a sip of beer! Let's just forget the whole thing."

"The Voorheeses won't." Then remembering that Ludwig was, in a sense, Henry Voorhees' employer, she added, "At least, Christina won't."

"You know, Christina Voorhees isn't awfully important to me. Let her think what she likes. Here's the morning mail: I've been over it. These letters are to be answered—the notes in the margin will tell you what to say."

Eliza resisted the temptation to retort that although Christina was not important to him, she just might be to Sally. If she intended to "Take a Stand," she could enlist not only Amanda on her side but Mrs. McKinney and Mrs. Maxwell—maybe even Thomasina. Then Eliza shrugged it off: there were all those young women ("ungodly" young women, Amanda would say) in the Club now who were most unlikely to be influenced by Christina. But it was a pity—so far the Club had always managed to ignore differences of opinion. But was this just a "difference of opinion"? She did not know.

In September, Blair was sent off to college with enough admonitions to fill a treatise: work hard; write to them frequently, keeping them informed as to how he was getting along and what friends he was making; mind his health, get plenty of sleep and exercise; above all, behave himself according to the principles by which he had been brought up; *avoid alcoholic beverages:* strong drink had been the downfall of many a potentially good man.

For the first few weeks Blair wrote home dutifully if briefly: he was finding his courses easy, except for required math; he did not care much for his roommate but guessed he could live with him the rest of the year; couldn't his mother send him some cookies or something: the meals were terrible. When the letters became fewer, his parents concluded that he was busy studying, making friends, doing whatever boys at Aberdeen could do to amuse themselves.

The letter they received from the president of the college early in November came therefore as a blow that rocked the foundations of their world. Fortunately for Christina the letter was addressed to Henry, and he took it from the bank's box in the morning with the rest of the mail and, sick at heart, bore it home at noon for Christina to read. When the three of them had finished lunch, he followed his wife into the sitting room; he went to the window and stood staring out at the street until Christina, seeing that something was amiss, sent Janey off to the parlor for her usual two hours' practice at the piano. Then he said, "Sit down until I read you this letter about Blair."

"What—? He isn't ill?"

"No. I'll read it. It was addressed to me." He rattled the paper as he unfolded it; his hand trembled. "'I regret to inform you that your son Blair has been brought before the Faculty Committee on Discipline on a charge of conduct unfitting a student of Aberdeen College. He was found guilty by the Committee and suspended for the rest of the year.'"

"*Blair?* Oh, no, there must be some mistake." Christina sat forward on the edge of her chair and held her hand out for the letter.

"There was an enclosure addressed to you. I assumed it contained some explanation, and in the hope that I might be able to soften the blow, took the liberty of reading it. I am afraid there is no mistake. Here—you'd better read it for yourself." He passed the sheet over to her:

My dear Mrs. Voorhees:
My long friendship with and great respect for your late father, who was one of the venerated scholars of our church, forbid that I send your husband this formal notification of our Committee's decision without a word of explanation.

Had not Dr. Blair been Blair Voorhees' grandfather, I fear very much that the sentence would have been one of expulsion rather than suspension. Unhappily, the offense with which he was charged is a very serious one. Under our local option laws this community is "dry," but unfortunately here as elsewhere there are "bootleggers" willing to sell liquor to anyone who knows where to go for it. We have been unable to discover which student smuggled liquor into the dormitory; however, all who indulged were equally guilty.

All the students involved are boys unused to the effects of strong drink. A quarrel began which culminated in a fight between Blair and his roommate, and only concluded when Blair threw a heavy book at the other boy, which struck him in the temple—quite by accident, I am convinced. But it caused him to stumble, strike his head against the corner of the desk, and fall unconscious. The noise and the necessity of procuring aid for the injured boy naturally resulted in exposure. Let me hasten to add that young McClary suffered no lasting damage, and has completely recovered from a slight concussion.

The other boys involved have also of course been suspended. We have been unable to discover from any of them or from the two principals the cause of the fight; in the condition they were in it is possible they do not remember it. I cannot entirely suppress a certain sympathy for Blair: he had not, I regret to say, made many friends among his classmates: he was too superior to them in his academic subjects and in other respects too immature. I suspect that with their tongues loosened by alcohol, they hazed the boy beyond his endurance.

I feel that the college and I as its president are much to blame; we now learn that surreptitious drinking has been going on for some time; we should have discovered it sooner. For this reason, and for the sake of their families, the Committee will make no public announcement of the suspensions; it will therefore not be necessary for you to explain Blair's return home, beyond saying that he was not happy at college—the truth, I am convinced.

We must strongly advise that you do not come to Aberdeen. Your presence here would provoke comment, and no intercession on your part could have any effect on the Committee's decision. If Blair elects to return to Aberdeen in the fall of 1899, we shall be glad to welcome him. I cannot help believing that, with your help, this unhappy occurrence will have a greatly maturing influence on the boy.

This will be a sad blow to you and Mr. Voorhees, I am aware, but I am sure that your Christian fortitude will enable you to sustain it.

This well-intentioned letter fell like a rock on Christina's heart. As she read it, all the color drained from her face; at the end she dropped the pages and swayed forward in her chair. Henry thought he had never seen anyone so white. As he came to his feet, he said, "Put your head down." But she pulled herself together after a fashion, said, "Blair? Our son? I can't believe it. That he might have killed—"

"It wasn't that bad. Dr. Moffett clearly thinks that it was an accident that he hit the boy at all. But how strange that he never showed a violent temper at home! Except that night when he struck Janey."

"No one ever 'hazed' him at home."

"Nor will. Here he can make a fresh start. You were right and I was wrong, Christina. We should never have sent him away."

"What kind of start? He cannot go to the Seminary if it is true that he has taken to drinking and that he struck another boy what might have been a murderous blow. I cannot believe it. If all the boys were intoxicated, how do they know who was fighting? We should go to Aberdeen and investigate."

"Dr. Moffett would have given him the benefit of any doubt. In his mind there is no question. And I am afraid I can believe it, remembering how he struck his own sister in anger."

"Then you think we should not go to be with him in his trouble?"

"Not when Dr. Moffett advises against it so strongly. Don't you read between the lines? The less fuss, the better. If we take it quietly, no one need know. Blair is coming home because he did not like college."

"We should have heard from Blair himself. No doubt he has been too ashamed to write."

"He won't write. He'll be walking in, today or tomorrow."

But his father was wrong: he did not come home, and he did write, to say that he had gone from Aberdeen to Chicago, and there had enlisted in the Regular Army. He had sent his trunks home by express. He was sorry to be a disappointment to them, but it was what he wanted to do. And he was their son, Blair.

This news was almost a worse shock to Christina than his dismissal from college. At home he might have redeemed himself, but never now, "thrown with coarse and ignorant men for *five years*. And to turn *professional killer*. This has been a wicked war from the beginning. But why, why not home?"

"He couldn't face coming home in disgrace. As for the war, it is over, to all intents and purposes. Once the peace treaty is signed, there will only be a temporary need for occupation forces. The Army will soon be reduced to its normal size; he may even be discharged. Or we might get him out—he's only eighteen. Ludwig Rausch might help, he has friends in high places."

"He never got his own son out, or tried to, as far as I know. At any rate, I prefer not to be under obligation to Ludwig Rausch. It was because of him that we are in this grievous trouble."

"Please don't go back to that, Christina. On the Fourth we learned, only indirectly through the Rausches, something about Blair's character that we should have known before. Weakness and temper. And I insisted on the wrong cure for it. Blame me if anyone. At least we can help by not talking about it. I thought that a boy must learn to face temptation and learn to resist it, and I felt sure Blair would overcome his weakness. He would have to if he were to be an example to a congregation. The best thing we can do for the boy now is not to make a secret of this. Janey, for one thing, will have to be told, since we let her know we expected him home. And I suppose there will be times when he has leave, and will appear in uniform."

"Yes. We'll have to make the best of it. He was unhappy in college, and without consulting us decided to enlist."

Blair's running away to join the Army made a louder buzz in Waynesboro than had his departure for college. Those who had disapproved in September now said, "I told you so," and those who had commended untied apron strings said with satisfaction, "She'll never get him home again now." Ludwig Rausch belonged to neither group. He felt sorry for Voorhees, who had clearly suffered a blow to the heart. Henry, he thought, had always been by nature a gray little man; lately he had come to look gray: not that his hair had turned in storybook fashion; it was still mousy-brown and smooth-combed as always, but his face had lost its color and was strained and drawn. Ludwig tried, one day in the cashier's office, to rouse Henry from his despair.

"Can I do anything to help, Voorhees? I know your wife probably thinks this is the end of the world, but there have been other wars, and other soldiers. In fact, most men my age in this town were once soldiers. It didn't ruin us. And now my son."

"I know. But it has been a crushing blow to Christina. She had such hopes and plans, and I ruined them. It was I who persuaded her to let him go to college."

"Don't blame yourself. It is the most natural thing in the world for boys to want to go soldiering, but if there is blame, surely it was your wife who was responsible for his unnatural bringing up."

"It never seemed unnatural to me. Christina is a fine teacher."

"Yes, of course. Sorry, Voorhees. But do try not to take it so hard."

"There is one thing." Henry hesitated; Christina would not like him to ask a favor of Ludwig Rausch. Nevertheless he plunged on. "We have not heard from Blair since he wrote telling us he had enlisted. We don't know what regiment he is in or where he is. Do you suppose you could find out for me? Without letting Christina know I asked?"

Ludwig looked at him with disconcerting keenness; Henry squirmed. The thought, unexpressed, lay there between them: Christina had never forgotten or forgiven that one mouthful of beer. Finally he said cheerfully, "Easiest thing in the world, if he enlisted in his own name, and if I know the place and date of his signing up. I'll write Hanna and he can pass on the inquiry to the proper quarter. You can try our congressman—then, anyway, you can tell Mrs. Voorhees you have written to ask him for it. Just leave me out of it. And for God's sake cheer up, or you'll be driving customers away from the bank."

Christina, "making the best of it," put on a very good show indeed: no one could have guessed the weight on her heart, although the blandness of her expression stiffened and its amiable sweetness came to have a fixed look. She pursued her ordinary daily round, receiving the inquiries of callers with a cool "Yes, he's like all other boys—couldn't resist the beating of a drum." But she could not bring herself to face Sally Rausch: she sent regrets to the next Club meeting and those following. No word, so long as she lived, passed her lips about the disastrous conclusion of Blair's college career; but she could not keep entirely to herself the depths of her despair, and in the need to be absolved of blame permitted two of her friends a glimpse of it: her minister and Amanda Reid. And somehow, among Waynesboro church women, a feeling against the Rausches grew and spread.

And once again, in late November, Eliza Ballard could not forbear attacking Amanda on the painful subject. They were eating together as usual in Mrs. Dunbar's dining room. Eliza asked, "Have you made plans for the Thanksgiving holiday? Or will you dine with me here? I know you usually go to the Voorheeses, but I suppose Christina isn't feeling very thankful this year."

"Don't be flippant. Christina is most unhappy."

"She seems to be bearing up remarkably well, outwardly at least. I suppose she feels no shadow of blame for Blair's defection?"

"Why should she? She never put temptation in his way. Surely any blame attaches partly to the tempter, as well as to the tempted."

"Blair being the 'tempted' and some army recruiting officer the 'tempter'?"

"You know very well that the recruiting officer is the end of the story, not its beginning."

"Surely you are not harking back to the Fourth of July? After all these months?"

"Cause and consequence. At that party liquor was served to boys and even children. Blair did not resist temptation, and Christina had too much conscience to send anyone so unready to study for the ministry; she allowed herself to be persuaded to send him to college."

("Queer," Eliza thought, "Amanda is so tolerant in so many ways you forget that rock-core of Calvinist bigotry.") She said, "And what was the matter with college?"

"He didn't like it. I believe the other boys tormented him. And maybe he expected too much of it—expected more freedom."

"And so he ran away and enlisted. If he expects more freedom in the Army, he will have a rude awakening."

"I am not absolving Blair. He has been very weak, and is certainly not a suitable candidate for the ministry—not yet, at any rate. But had it not been for the Fourth of July incident, he would be safely at home. Christina has not been able to bring herself to attend Club meetings; she is even talking of resigning. After all, the Club has hardly kept to the intellectual standard set in earlier days. It must seem very superficial to Christina, and unimportant in her life."

"What nonsense! How many truly intellectual members have we lost? Mrs. Lowrey, I suppose. My mother, I am sure you would agree. Not little Miss Pinney. Not the Gardiners. We have you still, and your friend Elizabeth Merrill, and Sophie Lichtenstein, who is a real scholar. Surely you agree?"

"Yes. A thorough scholar, German-trained. Now wasting a fine mind on babies and housekeeping." Amanda could never quite forgive the marriage of a woman possessed of a fine mind.

"Charlotte Bonner always writes a good essay. And for that matter, so does Sally Rausch, who is probably the most widely read of us all."

"She has the time for it. At any rate, the emphasis seems different in the Club: frivolous, almost. And if Christina resigns, there may be others."

As she had done before, Eliza relayed this conversation to Ludwig the next morning. He said, leaning back in his swivel chair and looking up at her from behind his desk, "Why do you tell me this, Eliza? Is it just gossip, or do you expect me to do something about it?"

Eliza flushed uncomfortably. "I know you think I am making molehills into mountains. But it isn't I. It's those *dratted* Reformed Presbyterians. And to Sally the Waynesboro Woman's Club is important, though you and I may wonder why. If Christina resigns, there will be others. The Club may break up. I think Sally should be warned, though I don't know what she could do."

"Sally has never heard a word of all this nonsense, so far as I know. She would have served me with an 'I told you so,' since she was opposed to my serving beer to my friends. I asked Elsa and Anne, whose husbands were there on the scene, not to tell her. I didn't suppose anyone else would venture to mention it. If there is trouble coming that can be forestalled, I'll speak to Elsa. She's resourceful. As to my feeling about the Club, although I have had lots of amusement and some very pleasant evenings at Club do's, I wouldn't really care if it blew up with a loud bang. And I've no doubt there are other Waynesboro husbands who feel the same—whose wives go off into something resembling a trance every time they have an essay coming up. But Sally would care. She would feel responsible—and besides, that Club does seem to mean a lot to her."

At that time the Rausches, and Sally particularly, were busy with plans for another gala occasion. Having had the Fourth of July housewarming according to Ludwig's prescription, Sally was preparing now, in her mind, for another celebration that would embody her idea of what a social occasion should be: in the town house, in January, an evening reception and ball in celebration of her and Ludwig's thirtieth wedding anniversary. Their twenty-fifth had gone unnoted except by their children: the hard winter of 1894 had been no time for any kind of extravagance; Ludwig could not in decency (or so he believed) supply his half-time hands with coal and baskets of food, just enough to keep them alive, then turn around and give an elaborate and expensive entertainment for his friends; in fact, he could not afford to spend the money. But the winter of 1898–99 was different: they were under obligation socially to many out-of-town friends. They would ask the party leaders with whom they had been visiting back and forth over the years, their wives, and their sons and daughters of suitable age: Senators Foraker and Hanna, who in spite of their political differences could be trusted to be amiable when brought together in a friend's house (if they could come; Congress was still in session waiting for the peace treaty to be concluded, signed, and presented for ratification). Then there were the Myron Herricks, Governor Bushnell, and various lesser luminaries. Waynesboro couples invited would include no one who would blanch at the sight of a glass of wine: four Gordons, the Douglas Gardiners, Sheldon Edwards and Jessamine Stevens (it was convenient their being a widow and widower of suitable age to be paired off), the Merrills, the senior Evanses, on Gib's account, whom he could advise to decline if they thought it best, and all the young people who would be home for the holidays and any house guests they might have, for the dancing.

In the meantime, while Sally was occupied with her grandiose plans, she had deputed Elsa to act as chairman of a planning committee for the Club Christmas party; she and Ludwig would of course provide the dinner. Elsa had protested. "Mamma, I don't see why you bother, with so much on your mind. There's nothing in the Club constitution that says we have to have a Christmas entertainment and dinner."

"We always have had. I haven't missed a year yet, and I don't want to."

And so Elsa appointed a committee: Anne Gordon and Elizabeth Merrill, and one afternoon in November, when the Club met at her house, she asked the two ladies to stay after the adjournment for a cup of tea and a committee meeting.

When the tea had been drunk and the cups removed, the talk moved from the casual to the purposeful. Elizabeth said, "You wanted me to find out before we made any plans how many members we can count on to take a part. I can tell you very shortly: Elsa here, Charlotte, and Julia Gordon, Mrs. Deming I guess. Sophie's out, of course, since she's expecting again."

"What's the matter with everyone? Mrs. Stevens? Mrs. Voorhees?"

"Mrs. Stevens is willing to sing. She says she can't act and won't make a fool of herself again. We could have a musical program, I suppose. Mrs. Travers is always willing to play. But Mrs. Voorhees won't even attend. She was very cool when I called on her. She says she has heretofore been too lax in condoning what her church condemns. As for Christmas, since the Reformed Presbyterians consider recognition of it a papistical custom, she has set a very bad example by taking part in Club celebrations of the holiday. For a good many years now we have heard all this from her. But this time she sounded quite fierce."

Anne sighed. "It's too bad. She always used to love to shine before an audience."

Elsa, at the same time, blunt as always, said, "How silly! How bigoted! Does she think Blair's running away is the result of our Club dramatics?"

"Not really." Elizabeth spoke consideringly. "She's badly hurt. Blair's defection has been a blow. And like most of us, being hurt she wants to strike out at someone she can hold responsible besides herself. And it's your mother she wants to strike at, Elsa, because she goes back to that taste of beer Blair had at Hillcrest on the Fourth as the beginning of his rebellion. Of course that isn't the way she explains it to herself—that she wants to hurt your mother, I mean. She has persuaded herself that by indulging in worldly activities such as the Club, she has been a stumbling block to the weak. She talked of resigning."

"You mean she is still harking back to the Fourth? Mamma didn't even know about it; Papa hushed me and Paul at the time because Mamma hadn't liked having the beer for his cronies. He said something not long ago about Mrs. Voorhees being on the warpath, but I didn't pay much attention, just thought it was something Eliza Ballard had dreamed up. If Mrs. Voorhees were to resign to get back at Mamma, Mamma wouldn't have the slightest idea what it was all about. Imagine, after all this time! I would have supposed everyone had forgotten about it."

"Not Christina. And I suspect not Amanda, nor Mrs. McKinney, nor Mrs. Maxwell."

"Then that's what Eliza was getting at. She told Papa, and he told me—not Mamma, believe me, although he thought it was funny—that Eliza said Amanda and some of the others thought the Club had deteriorated since

Mrs. Ballard's day—wondered if it was worthwhile. D'you suppose Christina Voorhees has persuaded those women they should resign? Mamma would be so upset! She has prided herself on the Club's having gone for thirty years without any real rift in spite of such diversity of opinion."

"We mustn't let it happen." Anne spoke for the first time since her original exclamation. "Poor Christina! I feel sorry for her. Blair's running away has cost her not only her son but her goal in life. She intended him to be a great minister of the church."

"Aunt Anne, you can be sorry for anyone. Talk about molehills and mountains! He will be out of the Army some day, and probably all the better for having been in it. And if his mother lives to be a hundred, she will never admit to herself that the way he was brought up was the real cause of all the trouble."

"That may be true." Anne smiled at her. "But look at it from his mother's point of view. She was so secure in her assumption that Blair was one of the Elect." Elizabeth Merrill laughed. Anne went on. "That's no laughing matter to Calvinists, my dear, especially the Reformed Presbyterian. Because if he is not of the Elect, then he is doomed through all eternity."

"Have none of the Elect ever slipped up? I thought if you were Elected you could do pretty much what you pleased and still be safe."

"The only way anyone, including yourself, can have any inkling as to whether you are among the Elect or not, is by the way you behave. And Blair— I feel sure that Christina is very unhappy, and probably has been since the Fourth. How do you suppose she ever happened to hear about the beer episode?"

"Oh, that's easy," Elsa said. "Rodney, I'm sure, thought it a huge joke, and regaled his friends with the story, probably with some fancy touches. And Janey could have overheard. She was with the other girls all afternoon."

"Janey is what your Uncle Dock would call 'meeching.'"

"She's a snitch and a tattletale. At least according to Paul, who never goes near her if he can help it."

"I feel sorry for the child."

"Aunt Anne! Not for her, too!"

"She's such a colorless *dank* sort of girl. I can believe that what you call 'snitching' is her only way of making herself felt. No one wants to be a cipher. And that is what her mother has made her. Blair must have had some spark left in him, to be able to break loose. Sometimes the consequences of foolishness—Christina's in this case—are as disastrous as those of downright wickedness. And I don't doubt that Christina sees this as a disaster and is brokenhearted. Of course, Elizabeth's right: she can't be expected to blame herself, or to realize at this late date that a young man who has never been tempted is not very well able to resist. She should have remembered the Milton she must have learned in school, as we did: something about not praising a fugitive and cloistered virtue that slinks from the race, without dust and heat. But all this is beside the point. What shall we do about Christina, and what shall we do about the Club Christmas?"

"Let's give up the idea of a play this year." Elizabeth, having been rebuffed once, did not propose to tackle her fellow Club members again. "Just have a musical evening, with or without Christina. Carols, kind of Dickensy. We've done it before, and it was fun. Carolers going about in the snow in top hats and shawls like Lincoln's."

"Or scarves like my father used to wear, a good six feet long. There must be some still in our attic," Anne contributed. "Hoop skirts for the girls, and bonnets and shawls. It wouldn't be too much trouble to dig up such things."

"It would be fairly easy," Elsa said, knowing how many full trunks were in the attic of her mother's house. "And everyone knows some carols."

"Agreed. But I don't think you should dismiss Mrs. Voorhees' state of mind so lightly. She was serious about resigning."

"Aunt Anne, you said it mustn't happen. Can't you talk to her?"

"I don't want to, but I can, if you think I am the one to try. I have never been intimate with her. Jessamine knows her better, but of course it was Rodney— Very well. I will call and inquire as to her health, on the assumption that I know no other reason for her having missed the last few meetings of the Club. I can also assume that it is an honor to be asked to become a member of the Waynesboro Woman's Club. There are three Reformed Presbyterian members now. Could we stand another one? We have never filled Miss Caroline Gardiner's place. Probably just because there didn't seem to be anyone suitable. It would be nice to have another young member, but Lavinia Gardiner is the only prospect I can think of, and she won't be through college for two or three years. Does anyone know Miss Campbell? You know who I mean: the new R.P. minister's sister who keeps house for him."

The two younger women shook their heads. Elizabeth, who had moved to the "plain Presbyterian" church on her marriage, said, "I saw her in the library one night and asked Ruhamah who it was. After she'd gone, Ruhamah said she was one of the library's best patrons."

"A reader? That's hopeful. I wonder what she reads? Never mind: I'll sound out your mother, Elsa. I'll have to consult her before I suggest to Christina that she put up Miss Campbell's name."

On the following afternoon, having seen Sally, Anne, in her best afternoon costume, including Sunday hat, white gloves, and tortoise shell card-case, went to call on Christina. All the way, as she swept along, lifting skirt and petticoats with the accustomed womanly gesture as she crossed the streets, otherwise letting them swish about her feet unregarded, she composed, discarded, considered possible tactful variants on conversational approaches to one she could hardly help considering on this occasion as an opponent to be won over.

At the Voorheeses' door she was kept standing a long moment. All her rehearsed introductory remarks took flight: when Christina finally opened it,

Anne said, "I thought perhaps you were ill—or dusting the chairs. Remember the time years ago when I called and was kept waiting: when you opened the door, you said if you'd known who it was, you wouldn't have bothered, but you'd noticed how dusty the hall chairs were, and so you sat on each one on your way to the door? Don't you remember? And how we laughed? And I was pleased at the 'wouldn't have bothered,' because it meant we weren't on formal terms. And I had been so in awe of your learning."

"We laughed more easily in those days." But Christina managed a smile. "Come in, won't you?"

"I am glad you are not ill, at any rate." Anne laid a card in the tray on the small table inside the door, and followed Christina into the parlor. "We have missed you at Club meetings lately. I thought I should call and inquire as to your health." She took the straight chair indicated, as Christina sat down on the edge of the narrow horsehair covered sofa.

"No, I haven't been ill. I just hadn't the heart for it."

"I can understand that. There are days, even weeks, when one is out of sorts, and nothing seems worth doing. Fortunately, given time, we recover. I know that you must miss Blair very much, and regret his impulsive act." Then, without awaiting a reply that was slow in coming, she went on. "I hoped you weren't ill, since I wanted to consult you. As you know, no new member has been proposed for the Club in Miss Caroline Gardiner's place; there has been a vacancy for quite a long while that should be filled. Our young people—your Janey, for instance—aren't quite old enough yet. Several of us have wondered whether Miss Campbell would be a good member, and whether she would enjoy the Club? She is new in town, and, I understand, not very young: she must not have many opportunities to meet people outside the church."

"She is pleasant and agreeable. I have had no occasion to test her intellectual capacities. But I doubt whether I am the one to sound her out. Is that what you were going to suggest? I myself have come to question whether membership in the Waynesboro Woman's Club is suitable for Reformed Presbyterians. It has tempted us into frivolity and worldliness. I think that I really must give it up."

Anne thought, "Possibly 'frivolous'—but 'worldly'? The Waynesboro Woman's Club?" She let the adjectives pass, and said bluntly, "Look, Christina, I know you are probably troubled. But you surely cannot blame the Woman's Club for Blair's leaving college to enlist? And you know that our activities have given you a great deal of harmless pleasure."

"I am not sure how harmless. It has drawn me into light-mindedness, and I fear that I have been a bad example to my children. You remember Saint Paul's admonition: 'Take heed lest by any means this liberty of yours becomes a stumbling block to them that are weak.'"

"We all lose our children, sooner or later, one way or another; we have to expect it. But if what they choose to do isn't what we would have chosen for them, must we blame ourselves for having set a bad example? In the end we have to accept their decision, make the best of it and go on. Life can still be full and worth living."

"To lose a child as you did is one thing, as I have, another. Your little girl is at least safe."

" 'Safe'? Somehow that is an odd word for Binny. I believe she is happy, in whatever uncomprehended way immortal souls are happy. But Blair still has his life to live. Just because he has gone soldiering is surely no reason why you should think him not 'safe'? Many men have been soldiers from time to time over the centuries. Surely they have not all been damned?"

"Blair found it impossible to resist temptation before he left home."

"Not so much temptation as pure simple curiosity, if you are harking back to the Fourth of July. Or perhaps, like most boys, he wanted to do what the others were doing. And if you think that someone deliberately shoved a mug of beer at him, knowing his upbringing and wanting to test his principles, you are mistaken, truly. John was there. I am sorry to say that he thought it was funny because Blair was so taken aback by the nasty taste, and made such a face. Little Mary Gardiner spit it out; Gardiner propriety slipped for once. But for Blair, he would have been too humiliated to spit it out—he got it down, finally. And neither the caterer's man who filled the mug nor Mr. Lichtenstein who passed it to him knew him from Adam. I doubt if many of the men there knew him: he has never run around town with the other boys."

"The temptation should never have been put in the way of young people."

"That is what Sally thought," Anne said, twisting the truth a little. "She was opposed to Ludwig's having beer on tap. But his friends are not young people, and many of them are Germans who grew up on beer. It was Ludwig's housewarming, really, and Sally believed the two groups would separate from choice—the Club and Ludwig's friends. I am sorry if you hold her in the least responsible for your trouble, but I really can't see why now you feel that you should leave the Club. You have contributed so much that we can't afford to lose you, and you know that you have enjoyed it very much."

Christina smiled, her most sanctimonious smile, Anne thought, resentfully. "I have been rather forcefully reminded that enjoyment is not the purpose of life."

Anne was so taken aback that she hesitated a long moment before choosing among possible rejoinders. Finally she said, slowly, "Not the *purpose* of life. But do you believe that to enjoy life is sinful?"

"If your enjoyment is someone else's stumbling block."

"But surely you must believe that we are expected to enjoy all that we have been given? Life itself being the greatest gift. You give thanks every day for your blessings. How can you be grateful for them unless you have enjoyed them?" Christina looked so astonished at this outburst that Anne hastened to continue. "I know I am being presumptuous, saying things like that to you of all people. I don't know any theology except the Catechism; that I do know. 'Man's chief end is to glorify God and enjoy Him forever.' It is given to very few men—the mystics, maybe—to enjoy Him directly, as one with Him. Most of us can only enjoy Him, in this life, through His gifts."

"'Enjoy Him forever' I was taught to believe meant not in this life, but in eternity."

Anne looked blank. "Only in another life? No, I don't think I was taught that. Oh, I know as well as you do that, being mortal, we are born to sorrow. No one can live for many years without suffering blows that seem unendurable. But we endure. And life—plain, everyday living—creeps back again, like grass over scorched ground. And we enjoy it. I used to feel sorry to the point of tears for people who died without seeming ever to have lived. Now, I don't know. I wonder if anyone looks at his own life and feels it has been empty for more than a brief despairing moment. The poorest and loneliest of us have at least the world around us for our pleasure. Like—like birds singing early on a spring morning—like lilacs in bloom, and violets or the sweetness on midsummer evenings of petunias that have been in the sun all day. These are not such small things."

"Then you have come to the conclusion that there are no unhappy lives?"

"How silly you must think me. Of course there are unhappy people, born to be unhappy—never satisfied and always sorry for themselves. To me they are the real lost souls, although even they must have moments— And there are lives that are tragic to all seeming, like poor little Ariana McCune. But would anyone at the end rather not have lived?"

"'Never to be born is best.'" Then, pleased by Anne's blank look, "Sophocles."

"Oh? Well, Job cursed the day he was born. But he changed his mind."

"You think it is man's duty to be happy?"

Wondering how she had ever got embarked on this impossible dialogue with one no closer to knowing her mind and heart than Christina Voorhees, she nevertheless persisted. "'Happiness' isn't really the right word. And 'duty' isn't either. I think an obligation is laid on us, even when we may be sad and grieving, to delight in the things that make life good to have. 'Delight' is the Psalmist's word, isn't it? 'In the multitude of my thoughts thy comforts delight my soul.' Life *is* good, and meant to be lived to the utmost, or it is a gift not worthy the Giver. If I didn't believe that, I couldn't believe in God."

"I was taught to believe that life was given us to test our worthiness of Heaven. Not to enjoy."

"And so was I. But unless we can endure our sorrows and really live, are we passing the test? Unless we make the most of life—*face* it—'bear it out even to the edge of doom'—how can we hope—? Oh, Christina, I know how superficial and childish I must sound to you. And you may very well wonder what on earth all this has to do with the Woman's Club. But I believe that having friends is one of the good things to be enjoyed. That is why I hope you won't resign: we may not have much to offer you, but you have much to offer us. I'm sorry if I have touched on a subject so sacred as to be beyond discussion, but I haven't meant to be offensive."

"You might have made a very good preacher." Christina smiled again, for the first time a genuine, unforced smile. "You think that membership in the Club is a sort of obligation, and something I can enjoy without misgivings?"

"Of course. And I think that without misgivings you can join in the carol singing at the Christmas party. Our singing without you these last years has been pretty sad." Anne explained what the Committee had planned, then continued, inventing as she spoke, "Janey, too. We are bringing the young people in so as to have all ages in the group."

"Janey has no voice."

"Very few of us do, so it doesn't matter. Of course Janey will be expected to become a member before too many years. That will make new friends for her as it has for all of us." And that, Anne hoped, would give Christina food for thought. "In the meantime, how about Miss Campbell?"

"I can approach her, I suppose. See whether she would like to become a member. Would *enjoy* it. You would be willing to be a second sponsor for her?"

"Certainly. I was the one who suggested her in the first place."

Anne left the Voorheeses feeling not only exhausted but embarrassed and, somehow, humiliated. To have exposed her deepest beliefs—beliefs she had never put into words before, not to Sally, not to John, perhaps not even to herself—to Christina Voorhees, of all people, was a costly way of saving Sally Rausch a little worry. A naturally reticent person, Anne shrank from the thought that henceforth Christina would in a way be inescapably closer to her than any of those she cared for more deeply.

When Henry Voorhees returned from the bank that evening, Christina told him that Anne had called to persuade her not to resign from the Club and that she had finally agreed. "She seemed almost shocked at my taking Blair's defection so hard."

"I am glad. I haven't liked to say anything—but everyone who has talked to me has said, 'But other boys have gone off to be soldiers before now, don't take it so hard.' I have wondered if before long people wouldn't begin to think there might be something more behind it, something more serious. To go on as we have always done, not to withdraw, is a protection for Blair."

And so Christina attended the next Club meeting and those thereafter; and Miss Campbell became a member. Evidently Christina's misgivings were not shared by the minister of her church. The first meeting Miss Campbell attended was the Christmas dinner and carol singing at the Rausches, her brother having been asked also as the gentleman in her family. Ruth Campbell, in her early forties, looked the born spinster, rather bony as to elbow and shoulder blade; long-faced, mousy as to hair, and dowdily dressed. But she had a gleaming intelligent pair of eyes behind her steel-rimmed spectacles. Those who had not known her up to this time, and who had little chance that evening for more than the usual cordial welcoming words, were left with diverse opinions, depending somewhat on their age: the new member was an old maid who would add little but her presence to the Club; the new member had a good mind; if she would only use it, she would be an addition to the Club.

The carol singing was pleasant as always, the carolers including a number of young people: Janey Voorhees and whomever else Elizabeth Merrill had been able to lay her hands on to save Anne's being made to seem a liar. The evening was enjoyable if not hilarious, the dinner was excellent, and there were no repercussions.

Neither were there repercussions from the Rausch thirtieth wedding anniversary reception. After a good deal of wavering, Sally had decided that the Voorheeses must be asked: to omit them would be altogether too pointed. If she let it be whispered ahead of time that Ludwig had ordered the wine, and rum for the punch, the Voorheeses would decline. As they did.

All that Christina knew of the affair was the account in the *Torchlight*, in which Charlotte had really let herself go, and which Christina read aloud to Henry with self-righteous satisfaction and an occasional interjection. Poor Henry was not really very much interested, but did his best to listen while he waited to get the front page of the paper in his own hands.

> In March of 1869, Miss Sarah Cochran of this city, was united in marriage to Captain Ludwig Rausch, recently of the U.S. Volunteer Army, and at the time living with his family in Burlington, Iowa. The ceremony was performed in the Baptist Church by the Reverend Mr. Evans.
>
> Last evening, after a long, prosperous and happy union, Mr. and Mrs. Rausch were joined by friends and family in celebration of their thirtieth wedding anniversary, at their elegant home on East Market Street.
>
> The reception was a grand social event and no doubt will prove the greatest of the season. There was a general outpouring of beauty and fashion, and the display of magnificent gowns was truly gorgeous.

"I simply can't imagine Charlotte Bonner's writing like that without tongue in cheek," Christina contributed.

> The residence, palatial in its appointments, was ablaze with light and color and exquisite floral decorations, and the host and hostess, who are social favorites, know just how to make a large company at home and at ease, and last evening while receiving the congratulations of their friends they had the appearance of having passed lightly over the thirty years of married life.
>
> Mr. and Mrs. Rausch were assisted in receiving by their sons Ernest and Charles and their wives, and by their daughter and her husband, Mr. and Mrs. Gilbert Evans. An unexpected addition to the company—an addition which must have made the occasion even more thrilling—was the third son of Mr. and Mrs. Rausch, Ludwig, Junior, discharged from his service with the Astor Battery just in time to reach home for the occasion. This young

musician, a great favorite with all who know him, added to the pleasure of the evening by consenting to play the violin for the assemblage, after dinner.

"So *he* is home, safe and sound—and as useless as ever, I don't doubt!"
"Chrissy, would you have had him *not* get home?"
"No. But it hurts—never mind. I'll get on with Charlotte's adjectives."

The hostess looked beautiful in a magnificent gown of buttercup brocade silk *en train*, corsage décolleté and trimmed around the neck with a deep flounce of point lace; the sleeves were large puffs of yellow velvet and the bodice was edged with a deep fringe of pearls; diamond ear-rings and a handsome diamond pendant worn at the throat, the gift of her husband, finished a superb toilet.

Wilson and Reeder of Cincinnati had prepared a splendid collation which was served for the young people in the third story of the house, turned for the occasion into a ballroom; the room with its festoons of pink and green and dainty candelabra and colored wax tapers presenting a veritable fairy-land to the guests; large chrysanthemums graced the center of the tables. In the dining room and library the same feathery flower decorated the tables at which the older guests were seated.

The floral decorations all through the house were richly handsome and were much commented on by the guests. Chrysanthemums, great, large ones, peeped out from the mantels banked in green vines; the effect was indeed beautiful; words are too poor to describe it; it was one of those enchanting scenes that have to be seen to be appreciated.

(But Charlotte certainly did her best!)

Weber's orchestra furnished the dinner music for the occasion, and later the young people enjoyed an evening of dancing.

"'The following is a list of guests attending—' and the list fills a column and a half: all the usual Waynesboro couples, and out-of-town guests—let me see—from Burlington, Iowa; from Washington, D.C., our two senators, from Cleveland the Myron Herricks, from Columbus the Governor, no less, and from Cincinnati, Chicago, Madison City—Mr. and Mrs. Stewart Bodien. I shouldn't have thought they were up to Sally's standard."

"Oh, come! He's a very presentable fellow, and he has helped Ludwig to his fortune."

"Well, I have no doubt it was the social event of the season, considering what Waynesboro's social seasons are, but I am glad we did not go. It was certainly not our kind of affair. Life may be very dull now for Sally: it will be a let-down when she has nothing more to think of than running the Waynesboro Woman's Club."

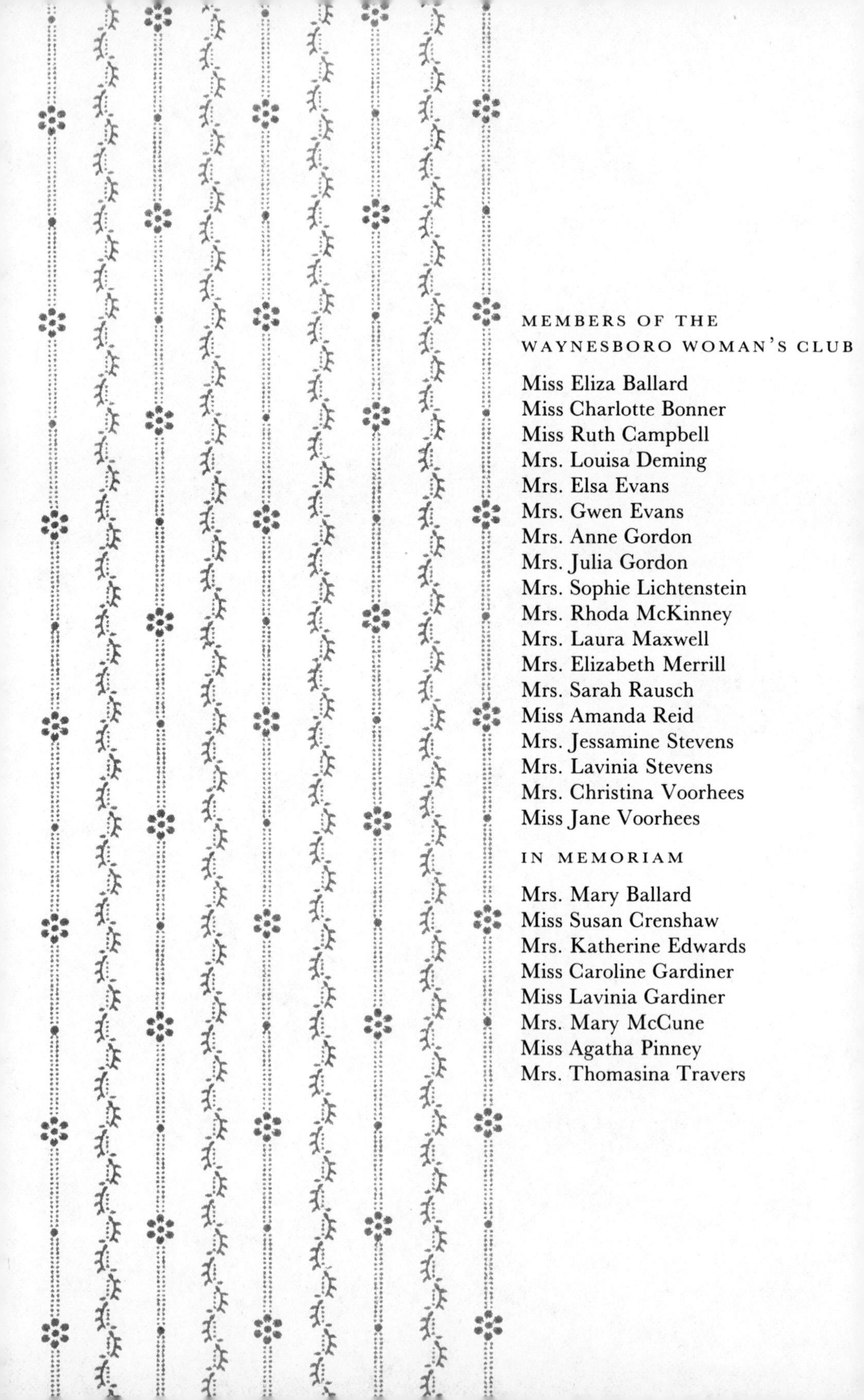

MEMBERS OF THE
WAYNESBORO WOMAN'S CLUB

Miss Eliza Ballard
Miss Charlotte Bonner
Miss Ruth Campbell
Mrs. Louisa Deming
Mrs. Elsa Evans
Mrs. Gwen Evans
Mrs. Anne Gordon
Mrs. Julia Gordon
Mrs. Sophie Lichtenstein
Mrs. Rhoda McKinney
Mrs. Laura Maxwell
Mrs. Elizabeth Merrill
Mrs. Sarah Rausch
Miss Amanda Reid
Mrs. Jessamine Stevens
Mrs. Lavinia Stevens
Mrs. Christina Voorhees
Miss Jane Voorhees

IN MEMORIAM

Mrs. Mary Ballard
Miss Susan Crenshaw
Mrs. Katherine Edwards
Miss Caroline Gardiner
Miss Lavinia Gardiner
Mrs. Mary McCune
Miss Agatha Pinney
Mrs. Thomasina Travers

✻ 1900–1902 ✻

"The turn of the century! The first years of the twentieth century bring changes to the Club: the loss of old dearly loved members and friends; new members, daughters of the Club who have grown up . . ."

The turn of the century. The phrase required definition. As the first of January, 1900, approached, the press became involved in the dispute as to its meaning. Did the nineteenth century end with the thirty-first of December, 1899, or December thirty-first, 1900? Those who maintained that 1900 was required to be counted with the nineteenth century to fill out the hundred years had logic on their side, but everyone who knew how hard it would be to remember to date their checks and letters 19— instead of 18—, felt that the twentieth century should begin on New Year's Day. Regardless of which was right, in December of '99 the press gave pages to the recapitulation of advances to be credited to the nineteenth century—the great inventions that had made more progress possible in that century than in all the others before it: the steamboat, the railroad, the interurban and urban electric cars, and now the automobile; the telegraph, the telephone, the electric light: the catalogue seemed endless. Peace, Progress and Prosperity, said the headlines, marked the end of the 1800s. Of Prosperity in the United States there was no question, and few disagreed as to Progress. Some might wonder about Peace, when every country in Europe was increasing its armaments and the size of its armies each year; if those who shouted Peace could hardly have been expected to foresee the Boxer Rebellion, which would break out in the spring, they might at least have remembered that Britain was fighting the Boer War, and America the Filipino insurrectos.

The prophecies made by newspaper reporters of the inventions to come in the next hundred years were fantastic beyond belief: Marconi had proved that sound could be sent over the air without wires, and his discovery could lead to a whole new system of communication; Edison had invented pictures that moved on a screen; a few inventors had succeeded in staying in the air in gliders; it was not beyond possibility that in another fifty years, man would actually be flying.

No one in Waynesboro longed more intensely than the Gordons' Martha to live long enough to see these miracles. Martha was still reigning in Anne's kitchen; she would not give up and take to her bed, however trembly she felt. And so Anne arranged for Louline's husband, the town's drayman, to bring both the women to the house in the morning and come back for them at night. Louline, to whom the walk to the East End and back was nothing, went home when the noon dishes had been washed, and returned in time to cook dinner, but Martha spent her whole day in the Gordon kitchen, in her rocking chair drawn close to the glowing kitchen range. Anne put down all Louline's complaints—"Don' ca' whut she think, she ain't mah boss"—with a firm "Be patient, Louline. She has been good to us all her life; now it is our turn," and generally managed to spend part of her afternoons with Martha in the kitchen, talking, listening, waiting for the old woman to awaken when she dropped into a doze. They talked inevitably about the past: Anne's past. Martha had never married ("But I wouldn' want yo' to think Ah neve' had me a man."), and she had little in her own life to talk about. But about what had happened in the house she had tended for so many years she remembered details that Anne had long forgotten: the childhood of her brother, Rob, and the years when he and Dock were apprenticed to Dr. Alexander. "An' then they had to go off soldierin' an' thet was the end. Rob neve' came back. They not even good enough to send his body home, an' thet kill yo' Mamma."

"Martha, he was killed in battle and buried where he fell, with all the others. And Mamma died of Bright's disease."

"Yes'm. But she would 'a' fit it off, hadn' po' Rob been killed."

And there was also talk of the poor old Doctor, and poor Binny. Anne felt that she was rehearsing all the sorrows of her life, but there was a kind of melancholy pleasure in the tears she shed in the kitchen in Martha's company. Sometimes she tried to persuade Martha to talk about her own childhood, but she would say, "Ah cain' remembe' " or "Ah don' lak talkin' about it," so that all Anne ever knew was that Martha and her mother had escaped from Kentucky when she was a little girl. It was her vicarious sorrows that Martha dwelt on, until the evening when Anne, after she and John had read the paper, had taken it to the kitchen, and then had heard such a great clacking of tongues that she had gone back to ask what had happened. What had happened was that Louline had read to Martha one of the prophecies that in the new century, men would probably learn to fly.

"Fly!" Martha said. "Ef'n it ain't enough to have those ca'iages whut run widout no hosses. You reckon men gonna fly, Miz Anne?"

"I wouldn't be surprised. They're already trying."

"Mus' be de day of Jedgment a'comin', along wid dis new century eb'rybody talkin' about. Ah sho'ly would lak to be he' to see dat—de graves openin' an' de daid raisin' up."

"You wouldn't like it at all, Martha. You'd be scared to death."

"No, ma'am, not wid de Lawd Jesus comin' down in all his glory."

After that nothing could persuade Martha that the Day of Judgment was not at hand; she talked less to Anne about the past than about the glories to come. She did not live to be disappointed: Anne came home from a Club meeting one January afternoon just as Louline passed through the alley gate and into the kitchen; Louline's uninhibited wail brought Anne on the run, although she knew well enough what had happened; John had warned her, "Any day, Anne." Martha's crumpled figure in the splint-back rocker looked peaceful enough. Anne said, "Quiet, Louline. Can't you see how easily she died, in her sleep? She never knew what happened. You run and get the doctor; I'll stay with her."

The Gordons provided exactly the kind of funeral for their lifetime friend and servant that she would have wanted: in the Zion Baptist Church, which was filled to the last pew by Martha's friends, who had known the servant as long as they had known the mistress; the satin-lined casket open for the last farewells; flowers in baskets surrounding it and on the platform; a long drawn-out eulogy by her pastor; her two Dr. Gordons among the pallbearers. Anne wished she could believe that Martha was looking down from Heaven to see it; and then she thought, "Why not? Such faith should be rewarded; maybe we all get the Heaven we believe in."

The new year, whether a new century or not, saw a change of regime in the Gordon kitchen: Louline was free to take over under Anne's direction, without an intermediary to give her orders. She was in her element, banging around in the kitchen, rushing to answer the doorbell before Anne could get there.

There would be changes, too, in doctors' offices and in the practice of medicine. If any professional men had real cause to congratulate themselves as the nineteenth century came to an end, it was the doctors. The press did not neglect to list medical advances, along with other proofs of progress: the diseases on the way to being conquered through the work of Lister and Pasteur and those who had come after them (at the very moment, Walter Reed and his associates were investigating the causes of yellow fever). The two Gordon doctors were going over these accomplishments in the office one January evening when the last of their patients had been seen and dismissed. His father assured Johnny, not for the first time, that he could have no conception of the state of medicine as it had been in the sixties. Now perhaps further research into the causes and cures of disease was no more important than improvement in the treatment and care of patients; he was glad they had settled in their minds that they, in partnership with Dr. Warren and Rodney, were ready to build their long-dreamed-of hospital. Rodney, having finished his medical school training in Cincinnati, was studying surgery at Johns Hopkins while he interned in the hospital there. The local hospital so far existed only in blueprints; the partners had acquired the land for it, a vacant lot well out on Linden Street large enough for additions to the modest beginning they planned: a one-story brick structure, L-shaped, with offices and a small operating room in the short arm, and ten rooms for patients in the longer wing. Neither the Gordons nor Dr. Warren called themselves surgeons, but they had gone into practice before the days of specialization, and could do what must be done until Rodney's return.

Much awaited the completion of his training. On his twenty-first birthday his mother had turned over to him half of the money the plantation had been sold for, which she had invested and reinvested over the years, well-advised by Henry Voorhees. The other three doctors had for their venture only what they had been able to earn and save: John, who had been practicing for thirty years, had a fair sum, Dr. Warren less, and Johnny comparatively little. Julia was inclined to be a little pettish over the idea of a private hospital. It would be a huge expense; not only would it have to be built and furnished, it would have to be staffed: they would need nurses, wouldn't they? Where would they find them? And no one would think of going into a hospital except those who didn't have homes fit to be sick in, and wouldn't be able to pay a cent.

Johnny tried to persuade her that patients who must have operations (and appendicitis had become fashionable at the turn of the century) would have to have them in a hospital, and that no, they wouldn't all go to Cincinnati to be operated on: Rod was going to be a good surgeon. Patients seriously ill would soon find that it was better to be in a hospital, cared for by professional nurses, with doctors at hand, than at home; and of course other doctors, of whom there were half a dozen or so in Waynesboro in 1900, could send their patients to the local hospital too. The most telling argument with Julia was Johnny's insistence that with all their dangerously ill patients in one place, the doctors would be saved much in time and tiredness. But she was never convinced enough to believe that it was a good way for Johnny to invest his savings. She suggested that he might sell the farm, rather than withdraw his money from the bank, but she was met with an astonished rebuff. "The farm? Oh, no, the farm must go to Tucker some day. It has been handed down from the first Gordon to settle in this county, and Pop has the land grant, signed by President Jackson."

"I thought it was only Southerners who had that obsession about hanging onto land like grim death. But Jessamine didn't seem to mind."

"The Gordon plantation in Mississippi is no older than the Gordon lands here. The brothers left North Carolina together, but Pop's grandfather didn't like slavery, and came on up to Ohio."

"How could she sell it anyway, if it was half Rodney's?"

"It wasn't. Her grandfather made his will leaving everything to her before Rodney was born, and he never changed it. As for her selling it, she did that to get Rod out of a climate that was killing him."

"You mean she didn't have to turn that money over to Rodney? She's very generous."

"There was no legal compulsion, no. But Cousin Jessamine isn't mean; she wanted him to have it while it would mean something to him. She isn't going to starve to death, you know, and it would all go to Rod in the end anyway."

"I call it 'generous' to let him have it now, for such a harebrained project."

Nothing less than a resounding success would prove to Julia that the doctors' plan was anything but "harebrained." Johnny gave up. He said, "I suppose she's glad to have him turn out a responsible citizen, willing to settle in Waynesboro and bring up his children here. Not all parents have so much to be thankful for. Presumably Blair Voorhees is still fighting in the Philippines, and as for Ludwig Rausch, Junior—"

"Oh, Ludwig Junior has so much charm and magnetism he'd land on his feet if his father lost every penny. And look at the marriage he's pulled off."

Julia loved to read about the extravagant affairs of New York society: she would not have cared for that sort of life, she insisted—she even disapproved of it; but one had to read all the accounts to be sure what one disapproved of.

"Marriage or not, the boy has been a bitter disappointment to Uncle Ludwig. He'd rather have him home here in the mill. You must have noticed: there hasn't been any talk lately of a musical career for Paul."

Not even Johnny, who was equipped with a good doctor's perceptiveness, knew how bitter Ludwig's disappointment in young Ludwig was. True, when he was discharged from the Army, he had gone back to New York and his music, playing violin in the Metropolitan Opera Orchestra. But he did not give up his social life, or his carefree attitude toward money. His parents seldom heard from him unless he was in need. After Ernest gave in to Emily's wishes, moved his family to New York, and accepted a position as customer's man in the brokerage firm in which his father-in-law was a partner, the senior Rausches heard more about Ludwig's career. Ernest was no correspondent, except for a postcard occasionally; but Emily was gracious enough, having succeeded in getting her way, to keep in touch with her in-laws by means of long if not very pleasing letters. All was going well with them, she reported, but they had the wisdom not to attempt to break into Mrs. Astor's Four Hundred, as Ludwig Junior had done. He had not had to try very hard: a presentable young single man who never seemed to lack for money was invited everywhere. She often described at length the mad and extravagant social events that Ludwig had attended, but sometimes she just said, "You can read about this in the paper."

Ludwig Senior sighed over every letter. Once he said to Sally, "Our boys would have amounted to more if we had been poor." And again, "Ludwig can't keep this up, you know. He's already had a good part of the share he might inherit. He'd better make the most of his chance to marry a really rich girl."

This Lugwig managed to do. His mother and father went East for the wedding; his father came home more disgusted than ever. He said to Sally, who was still under the influence of Ludwig Junior's charms, and who therefore protested Ludwig's judgment: "That girl's bought herself an amusing and ornamental plaything. It won't last." (He was right. In another year she was ready to discard her toy; Ludwig Junior, still debonair and lighthearted, found himself another millionaire's daughter, who carried him off to Europe to live. His parents, who felt the shame of the divorce, were regretfully relieved that he would not be coming to Waynesboro for a while at least.)

On Ludwig Senior's return from the first wedding, he had told Paul he was to give up any idea of a musical career, and come into the mill: when school was out, he would start at the bottom, like Ernest and Charles, as a bobbin boy. Paul, who had been halfhearted about carrying on seriously with his music, was willing enough, so long as his father allowed him to play his violin when he felt like it. Ludwig would not have dreamed of forbidding him his music: no one could have enjoyed more than he the evenings in the Rausch home, when Elsa and Paul played together.

Ludwig's greatest pleasure in 1900 and the early years of the new century he found in Elsa and her family. At one time he had regretted that Elsa was a daughter: she had the best brain of any of his children, he thought. Now he was satisfied: she was not only a good wife and mother, she was an interesting and delightful woman to be with, and he had no doubt her two children had inherited her brains. If Paul failed him, Ludwig Evans could step into his shoes some day, if only he could hold on that long. It would be a long wait: Ludwig Evans, along with Tucker Gordon, had just entered the first grade that fall.

For the first time in many years, Ludwig was not a delegate to the Republican National Convention in June. He still kept a firm hand on the local Republican organization, but had given up national politics. And anyway, there would be no contest; President McKinley would be nominated for a second term, probably by acclamation, and his reelection was a foregone conclusion. "Full dinner pail" was more than a slogan; it was a fact for most citizens of the country. But Ludwig, like his friend and one-time mentor, Senator Hanna, was not pleased with the party's choice for Vice-President. True, the man who had led the Rough Riders (on foot) up San Juan Hill was still a hero in the eyes of the country, and would attract votes. But Ludwig in his time had known heroic officers who had won renown in battle at the expense of their soldiers. He considered Theodore Roosevelt a show-off who would always be willing to make a grandstand play; he hoped that the man would be buried in the Vice-Presidency, but Heaven forbid that anything should happen to McKinley.

Because of continuing prosperity, the whole country was enjoying an active social life, each town its own kind. Except in the larger cities there was no aping of New York's Four Hundred and its more extravagant affairs; Waynesboro was content with its lawn fetes, garden and tennis parties, and afternoon receptions, and an occasional dance for the young people. The event that set Waynesboro by the ears was none of these, but Janey Voorhees' Coming Out Reception, one afternoon in June. No one in town had ever "come out" before: girls were "out" the first time they paired off with the boys for some high school party. The very idea of a Coming Out Reception (a purely feminine affair) was hilarious to all the town except for a few of Christina's friends, who felt sorry for her, and for Janey, too.

"It's not a bit of use; Christina can't turn Janey into a debutante after all this time—she has scarcely any friends," Sally said to Anne one afternoon when they were together in the Gordon living room, engaged in working on bits of fancy-work for their respective Ladies' Aid Bazaars. "Janey is plainly foreordained to marry a theologue and go off to some God-forsaken place as a missionary's wife."

"And waste all that Greek and Latin? But that's mean of me. Christina's trying—she's trying to do for Janey what she never did for Blair, find some friends for her—friends of her own."

"She's invited all the old ladies in town."

"I know it's an odd way to go about it. But you'll find she's asked all the young girls she knows, too—the Gardiners, for instance—and all the rules of etiquette require that Janey be asked to their houses in return."

"Janey's what—eighteen? And well-educated, certainly. We'll have to ask her to join the Club. And there will be Lavinia Gardiner, too, home again with her college degree, waiting to be married. How long?"

"Until Rodney knows enough, I suppose, to start in the practice of surgery. Not for another year, I should think. She can wait. She's young to have finished college."

The Coming Out Reception was a successful enough social event; but except that Janey stood beside her mother to receive their guests, dressed all in white, with a bouquet of white roses laid carefully over her left arm, it was exactly like any other of Waynesboro's afternoon receptions. On the dining room table, on a snowy damask cloth, little cakes and macaroons were set out, with napkins and plates; a tea urn stood at one end of the table and a coffee service at the other. Those invited for four o'clock were on their way out when those invited for five were arriving: a guest stayed only long enough to chat a moment with the hostess and her daughter, to be passed on to the dining room, where Miss Campbell and Jessamine Stevens were pouring, to drink a cup, to nibble at a macaroon, to exchange a bit of small talk with those at her elbow, to thank the Voorheeses for a lovely afternoon, and to make her way to the door. Some made it in less than an hour. Barbara Gardiner, for instance, and her two oldest daughters: Lavinia, now home to stay, and Caroline, there for the summer vacation.

Caroline considered it the stupidest party she had ever attended, and said so before she so much as reached the gate, bringing down upon her a shocked maternal rebuke. "Caroline, one simply *does not* accept someone's hospitality and then criticize it before one is out the door. I really am horrified at such indecency."

"Sorry, Mamma. But if this is the way adults entertain themselves in Waynesboro, I'm glad I'm out of it for a while longer."

"You and Lavinia are now under obligation to Janey Voorhees, don't forget. I wish I could hope that you would all be a little kinder to her."

This reduced even Caroline to silence; they crossed the street to their own gate without more words. The sisters were not without guile, however; the only real party they gave that summer was a luncheon to be followed by an afternoon of bridge whist; they knew very well that Janey Voorhees would not be allowed to attend; in spite of the written invitation, they did not even bother to await her answer before they were counting noses for four tables of cards.

In the fall Jane Voorhees and Lavinia Gardiner were invited to join the Woman's Club, bringing the membership, if they accepted, to within one of the limit of twenty, a place that Sally considered reserved for Caroline Gardiner. Lavinia had wanted to decline the invitation, since the ladies had never seen fit to invite her mother to join, but Barbara laughed her out of it. "I'd have been a fish out of water: they knew it and I knew it. Besides, the Aunts would have cheerfully blackballed me if my name had come up. But you are educated quite up to their level, I am sure. What do you think we sent you to college for?"

"To enable me to qualify as a member of the Waynesboro Woman's Club, of course. How ridiculous can you be?"

"Seriously, though, Vinnie, you are going to take your place in Waynesboro as Rodney's wife. It won't hurt for you to belong to the Woman's Club." And so Lavinia wrote a properly appreciative note of acceptance to the Corresponding Secretary.

Janey Voorhees acquiesced as a matter of course; she appeared at meetings at her mother's heels, a pale shadow of Christina. The fall passed; the ladies dealt in turn with "Renaissance Artists of Italy." And while they were busying themselves with their papers, election day came and went; McKinley was duly reelected, without much excitement. Cold weather settled in early. There was not often much snow before Christmas, but that year the ground was covered before Thanksgiving.

Thomasina Ballard Travers began to miss Club meetings. Since she had always been a faithful attendant, her friends surmised that she was ill, but all that Eliza contributed in answer to solicitous inquiries was that she believed her sister was suffering more than usual with her asthma. Since all were aware that the doors between the two sides of the Ballard house had seldom if ever been opened since Ariana McCune's death, they stopped inquiring of Eliza. Instead Anne said something to John, who had been the Ballards' doctor for so many years.

"Yes, she has asthma," he agreed. "This devilish weather is no help."

"I thought asthma was worse in hot weather."

"Asthma alone, yes. But any serious bronchial involvement is worse in damp weather. She has developed emphysema, and has a weakening heart."

"Oh, John! Like Dr. Blair?"

"Like Dr. Blair, except that she hasn't his weight to contend with, and isn't so old. On the other hand, she hasn't the resistance, the stamina, he had."

"You mean she will go the same way?"

"Sooner or later. She may pull through this winter. This is between you and me, you understand; don't go spreading it around among those old biddies in your Club. Thomasina has no idea how serious her condition is, and I don't want her to: nervous strain, excitement, could easily bring on a paroxysm."

Anne stared at him in shocked horror. "But I don't believe Eliza has the slightest idea—"

"Eliza knows all about it. I told her myself."

"But doesn't she care?"

"She didn't weep and wail, but I assume she cares. If she hasn't let on, it's probably best. I gave her the same orders I just gave you."

"Shouldn't she stay home and take care of her?"

"Sam Travers is taking excellent care of her. If Eliza went barging in, it would be upsetting all around."

Anne, a good doctor's wife, said nothing about Thomasina's condition to anyone. She was relieved, however, when after Thanksgiving the weather moderated. The snow melted; the ground was soggy but the sun shone; everyone assumed that the season had reverted to normal. Christmas passed without a flake of snow on the ground or in the air, to the disappointment of all the young. But Christmas was no sooner over than Waynesboro was visited by the worst blizzard in the memory of its oldest citizen. The wind began to blow in the morning, a cold, bleak wind out of the northwest, and ominous heavy clouds crept up the sky. When John came home for lunch, he said that it was surely going to snow, and if the wind kept blowing it would be a real storm. He wished that the hospital was built and in service; then he and Johnny could collect their bedridden patients there: it would be so much easier than trying to reach them, scattered as they were. Buy the hospital was not ready; the building had been finished before the bad weather in the fall, but it was not furnished or staffed. Rodney was still in Baltimore, and they wanted him to supervise the fitting out of the operating room; hospital beds had been ordered but not delivered; and as for a staff, there was little hope of finding nurses before June, when new R.N.'s would have finished their training.

Anne, looking out the dining room window, saw that it had begun to snow, and snow heavily, the flakes blowing horizontally across the panes. "Your storm has begun—looks like a blizzard. I do hope if there are country calls to be made, you'll let Johnny take them. You look bone-tired, and he's a younger man than you are."

"I'm always tired. I'm used to it. I thought when Johnny came in with me, the load would be halved; instead of that, he's attracted so many new patients there are twice as many as I used to have. And there are some older people I've attended for so long they consider Johnny little better than an apprentice. But far as I know now, there won't be any country calls. There won't be many patients coming to the office, either, in this. I'll try to get home early."

By two o'clock it was snowing so hard that the outside world was invisible beyond the screen of flakes, but drifts were piling up on the front stoop; a fine sifting of snow had blown under the front door and onto the hall carpet. By four o'clock the front fence was buried, though by peering through the corner of a window, Anne could make out a bare spot in the street, at the corner where the snow was caught up and whirled about like a dust devil. Not long after three John came in, by way of the kitchen, stamping his feet and shaking his overcoat inside the back porch door. When he came into the sitting room, he found Anne trying to revive a moribund fire, shaking the ashes out of the grate and letting what half-burned coal was left fall together in a heap. He took the poker from her, pried the coals apart, thrust in some newspaper from the kindling box, added kindling, and soon had a little flame. She stayed on her knees on the hearthrug, watching; he put a patronizing hand on her head, said, "As a firemaker, you really do take the cake." Then he added, "This is a storm that will go down in history. Already there are drifts head-high, and no sign of a let-up."

"You didn't have to go to the country?"

"It was all I could do to get around town. I had the buggy; I suppose the cutter would have been more sensible, but there are spots as bare as your hand where the wind has swept the snow off. And it is very cold and getting colder, as I found out just walking from the office across the back yard."

"Did you leave Johnny in the office?"

"No. He had a few calls to make, then was going home. Has the paper come?"

"How could the paper boy get through this?"

"That was stupid of me. We'll probably not get a paper. There wasn't a soul on the street uptown. Well, it's a chance for us to get a nap, before someone calls. Wake me if the telephone rings."

He stretched out on the couch, spread his handkerchief over his face, and in a few minutes was snoring. He had had too many night calls lately, Anne thought, vaguely uneasy. Thomasina—all her nights were bad. And there had been others. When Louline came in to say that dinner was ready, she hated to rouse him. But as always, when he was called, he was at once wide-awake. He went to look out the window. It was still snowing as hard as ever. The arc light on the corner shone dimly through the swirl; the wires at any rate were not down—not yet. In the dining room, as he whipped open his napkin and spread it over his knees, he said to Louline, waiting to take Anne her plate when it was served, "How did you manage to get down here this afternoon?"

"When Ah seed whut it was like 'roun' two o'clock, Ah di'n' go home. Not through this, no-suh."

"You can't go home tonight, that's sure. You can bed down in that back bedroom upstairs. Can you get word home?"

"Yassuh. Ah kin call the unde'take' nex' doo'. He let 'um know. Ah sho' glad to stay hyah, night lak this.""

A moment later they heard her in the hall, at the telephone. So neither were telephone wires down, yet. John didn't know whether to be relieved or sorry.

Dinner was over and he and Anne were back in the sitting room beside a now roaring fire when the call came. It was Julia: Did he know that case of Johnny's—the baby that had had so much croup? That baby of the Farneys', out on the Petersville Road? They had just called, the baby was much worse; they thought it had pneumonia. And Johnny had gone to the Traverses'—Mr. Travers had telephoned: he knew his wife was Papa Dock's patient, but for some reason he wanted Johnny. and Johnny when he left said it would be an all-night watch—no point in trying to get home. So Julia wondered if his father would try to get to the Farneys', or would try to telephone them?

John returned to the sitting room to explain to Anne. "Julia. Johnny's at the Traverses' and a patient in the country is worse."

"John, you *can't* go."

"I must try. It's a baby, Anne. They think it is pneumonia."

"At least telephone them first—find out why they think so."

To satisfy her he returned to the telephone. He got no response: the line was down, then, in the country. Lucky the Farneys had got their call through when they did, he said to Anne as he came back from the hall.

"Then at least take Lafe with you. I'd feel safer."

"Why? I know those country roads better than he does. I'll have him hitch the cutter—less chance of getting stuck. Where's my old Army cape? I'll wear it over my overcoat."

"In the hall closet, at the back. Just where it's always been. And your fur cap with the flaps is on the shelf."

He went to the hall, then on his way out stopped in the door for a minute, so wrapped in cape, wool scarf, and cap that little of his face was exposed. "Don't expect me back before morning: this isn't a drive to make twice in one night. And don't worry."

Anne heard him close the back door behind him; beyond that any sound was lost in the roar of the wind. Waiting and listening, she did not even hear the sleigh bells. Perhaps he hadn't bothered to put them on, though if he did get off the road and lost, in the snow and the roar of the wind, the bells might help. "Telling me not to worry!" she thought. "Might as well tell the wind to stop blowing, the snow to stop falling." He couldn't even telephone to let her know he had reached the Farneys if the wires were down. She could at least tell Julia he had gone. She went out to the telephone on the wall outside the sitting room door, took down the receiver, and whirled the handle around; while she waited she thought she could tell the operator—Mabel Drake, wasn't it, at night?—about the wire that was down. Mabel was hardly as appreciative as she might have been. "Wires down all over the county, Miz Gordon. Petersville Road? No, that one hasn't been reported. Repair crews are out, but they can't hardly do nothing until morning, long's this keeps up."

"No, I suppose not. My husband started out that road to the Farneys. I'd just like to be able to get in touch with him to be sure he gets there."

"The doctor? I sure am sorry, ma'am. I hope he makes it. Awful night for a body to be sick, ain't it?"

Anne gave her Johnny's number, succeeded in reaching Julia, and talked with her briefly: the doctor had started out for the Farneys'; she understood that Johnny didn't expect to return home until morning, but when he came in, would Julia please tell him? After the brief contact, Anne was alone with her fear. After a time she banked the fire, almost burned out, hoped that Lafe had not forgotten the furnace (she hadn't heard him shoveling, but would she, in that wind?), and went up to bed. There was no point in sitting up for John. But it seemed to her that she heard the wind all night, through her dreams if she slept at all, and the snow slashing at the window panes. When she dragged herself out of her bed in the morning, she was appalled at her first sight of the outside world. It had stopped snowing, except for a desultory flake or two, but everything was buried deep: the front porch roof had a two-foot-thick overhang of snow that had slipped over the gutter; yard, fence, and sidewalk were indistinguishable one from the other; only in spots was the street bared by the wind. John would never be able to get home until the roads were cleared, and that might take days of shoveling.

While she was at breakfast, crumbling a piece of toast and drinking a cup of coffee, Johnny came in through the kitchen, stamping his feet and brushing snow off his trousers knee-high.

"Don't try to open your front door," he said, "or you'll have an avalanche in the front hall."

"Did you just get back from the Traverses'? You look awful." As indeed he did, unshaven, white, and drawn. "Did you have a hard night?"

"A hard night, indeed. Mrs. Travers died."

"Thomasina? Oh, Johnny—"

"I know. I had to call in Eliza. Thomasina wanted her for some reason she could never articulate."

"Why not? She was her sister. Johnny, your father hasn't had much hope of pulling Thomasina through the winter. Her death wouldn't have upset you as much as—What is wrong? Julia told you your father went out to Farneys' last night?"

"Yes. Have you called there this morning?"

"The line is down."

"Not now. They got it fixed. Lucky you reported the break. It was the linemen found him."

"*Found* him? Then he never got there? He was out—"

"He never got there. The horse got off the edge of the road—nothing to go by, you see—fences buried and a blinding snow. The cutter hit the end of a culvert and overturned. Papa was thrown out."

"And couldn't get up? Then he was hurt—"

"Must have been dazed. Maybe hit his head on something. Yes, he was hurt. The linemen ploughing through the snow saw the horse. Farneys' was closest. They righted the cutter and got him there, somehow."

"How badly was he hurt?"

"Farney thinks he has a broken arm—broken up close to the shoulder. He cut Papa's overcoat and jacket off and got him to bed. But of course he can't do anything about the arm. I must get out there."

"Can you, through this?" Anne was somewhat relieved: a broken arm was a comparatively minor matter.

"In daylight, with the snow stopped, yes. Horseback would be best. Is the old saddle still in the barn? It would be quickest."

"Just where it's always been. Johnny: you are worried about more than just a broken arm. Tell me."

"That's all I know, Mom. But he must have been lying in the snow unconscious for hours. That's a lot of exposure. But don't worry more than you can help. I'll call you from the Farneys'."

When he had gone, Anne paced the floor; she could not sit down for more than a moment, but there was nothing that she could do except wait. She tried not to think "pneumonia"—she thrust it out of her mind. She thought instead of Thomasina, poor Thomasina, who had hardly known all her life what it was to breathe freely. But she had been happy with her Samuel. That Anne was sure of. She wondered whether Sam and Eliza would stay on, each in his own side of the Ballard house, with no communication between them, after the funeral. Funeral? She stopped her pacing briefly to look out the window again. There could be no funeral, not for a while—how could anyone dig—?

When the telephone rang, she was in the hall like lightning. It was Johnny. She tried to control her voice. "How is he? Is he conscious?"

"Yes. I've set the arm. He's feverish, but he wants to be brought home."

"I want him home. But is it wise to try? How—?"

"I think so. We can look after him better there. Farney has a sledge he uses to haul logs when he cuts—he'll hitch his farm horses to it. We can put a mattress on the boards and wrap him up. We'll make it, but it'll be slow. Call Julia for me, will you?"

"How about the baby?"

"The baby? Oh, Farney's baby. Bronchitis, maybe bronchial pneumonia, but she'll be all right."

Anne went back to the sitting room and dropped into her rocker, her knees drained of all strength, now that the suspense had been ended, after a fashion. In a little while, when she thought she could walk to the hall, she went out to call Julia, then to the kitchen.

"You heard me on the phone, Louline? Then you know they're bringing the doctor home. We'll have to get the downstairs bedroom ready—it will be easier for him than trying to get him upstairs. And get some kettles of water on to boil."

Flying about the bedroom, making the bed up with clean warmed sheets, putting clean towels on the washstand, setting Louline to cleaning the bathroom, filling the hot water bottles and putting them into the bed—all those things made the time pass more quickly. When all was done, Anne said, "Do you think you can get home tonight?"

"Yes'm. Mah man come fo' me. Less'n you want me hyah?"

"If the doctor is restless or sick, Johnny will stay. And your children will need you—one night away from them is enough."

When the sledge with its outrider—Johnny on the back of one horse, leading the other—reached the Gordon house, he directed Mr. Farney and his hired hand into the alley, the way he had got into the house that morning. He shouted for Lafe to come help, but even with four of them carrying the makeshift litter—the mattress and its occupant on one of Farney's pasture gates—it was no easy matter to get their burden through the back gate, the length of the back yard, when every step meant sinking knee-deep in the snow. They made it, made the step to the back porch, in through the kitchen to the back hall, and along the bedroom. Anne hovered over their progress from the door, and had the bed turned down ready, and a night shirt laid out for John.

"Don't bother with that, Mom. He can't get his arm in it anyway. We'll just strip off the clothes we didn't cut off, and wrap him up, with hot water bottles. Oh, you've got the hot water bottles already. Good girl."

"There's more water boiling in the kitchen."

When they had got John free of the cocoon wrapping of Farney blankets and between the sheets, surrounded by the hot water bottles and covered by quilts and an eiderdown, Anne for the first time had a real chance to look at her husband. His eyes were closed, his cheekes flushed, his breathing labored.

"I thought you said he was conscious?"

"He's conscious. Just exhausted, eh, Pop."

With tremendous effort, John opened his eyes, murmured "Be all right. Don't worry."

The last was an injunction Anne was tired of hearing. She turned blindly and went into the hall, only to run into Mr. Farney, standing there awkwardly, his knit stocking cap crushed in his hands.

"Oh! I thought you'd gone without my having a chance to thank you."

"It's not for you to thank me, Miz Gordon. If it hadn't 'a' been for us, this wouldn't never have happened."

"Please don't feel that way about it. A sick baby needs help, and John wanted to go. It's too bad he didn't get there."

"The baby's better. Dr. Johnny says she'll be all right. But we was both scared. She's our first, you know, so mebbe we're easy scared. I guess we needn't have—If'n there's anything we can do, lea' me know."

"You've done what was most important—got him home." Then, seeing that the kindhearted young man did not know how to break away, she added, "Please tell Mrs. Farney that we do not blame you in the least, and that we are very grateful to you for bringing him home. And thank her for the loan of all the blankets. You'd better take them and get started back, I expect, or she'll be worrying about you."

While she was urging him on his way, Johnny was at the telephone calling Dr. Warren. She went back to standy by the bed. John gave no sign that he was aware of her presence. He was coughing, lightly but incessantly, and moving his head from side to side. By the time Johnny returned, she had lost the reassurance his earlier telephone call had given her. She said, "Pneumonia, Johnny?"

"I'm afraid so. No man his age can lie in a snowdrift in a roaring winter wind and not suffer the consequences."

"He isn't that old, surely? Sixty? He pulled Miss Gardiner through pneumonia when she was far older than that."

"Bronchial pneumonia. The pneumonia of the very young and the very old. Longer drawn out than lobar pneumonia, but not so—so—"

"So deadly?"

"Mamma, I am not going to try to make this sound better than it is. You wouldn't want me to, would you?"

"No, I wouldn't."

"No one can work as hard as Papa has worked, often under strain, gotten as tired as he has sometimes been, for so many years, and still have the heart of a young man. And the arm is a complication. When the numbness wears off, he is going to feel the pain, and that will tax his strength further. I would suppose Warren will probably give him morphine, unless he thinks it will mask the pain in his lungs that we should know about if we are to make a diagnosis."

Anne left the room when Dr. Warren came in; it seemed an eternity after that before she saw John again conscious and in his right mind. It was arranged that Johnny would spend nights with his father, acting as trained nurse, turning his patients over to Dr. Warren or some other doctor of their choosing; he would sleep daytimes in his old room upstairs where he could hear his mother if she called. Anne would go to bed by night and nurse by day. If Julia objected to the arrangement, Anne never heard of it; she was all solicitude when paths had been shoveled through the snow, and she could get to the house every afternoon, to inquire and to offer any aid in her power—an offer invariably declined with thanks: Anne could not imagine Julia undertaking sickroom chores.

After the first night, John was himself again, though in pain from his broken arm and from his lungs. "What the devil—?" he complained to Anne. "How'd I get here? I remember starting out in the storm, and the cutter going over. Damn' fool horse—gave him his head—I couldn't see—and he landed me in the ditch. Wish I'd had old Molly."

"Don't talk, John." She told him how the linemen had got him to Farney's, and how he had been brought home the next day. "And now you are to lie perfectly quiet until you get over the after-effects of shock and exposure."

"'After-effects' be damned, my girl. D'you think I could practice medicine for forty years and not know pneumonia when it's inside me?"

"Doctors are notorious for not being able to diagnose their own ills. Rather inclined to be hypochrondriac, in fact."

He gave her a sidelong look, a teasing smile. "Have it your own way. I'd as soon not have pneumonia."

"John, you are not to waste your strength talking. Shut your eyes and rest."

"This may be my last sensible moment. Had you thought of that?"

"No, I hadn't. That's nonsense." But she caught her breath and clasped her hands in a hurting grip.

"Just let me, while I am in my right mind—it has been a good marriage, hasn't it, Anne? In spite of—everything, you made a good life?"

"John, it isn't all done with—don't talk as if it were. Yes, we have had a good marriage."

For the first few days, Johnny kept his father shaved, his beard trimmed. Once, coming into the room when Johnny was there, Anne caught her breath. The sunken cheeks, the troubled brow—she had seen John look like that before: thirty-odd years before. Old memories swept her mind, her eyes filled.

"What is it, Mom?"

"He looked like that when he first came home from the war."

"Not so old and troubled, I hope?"

"Old and troubled. Sick at heart because so many boys had died in spite of all he could do. He wasn't going to practice medicine, you know. It took him three years to make up his mind to come back to it."

"By that time I suppose he had got his confidence back." Johnny, who had heard his father's history many times before, was less interested in it than in his patient.

"Every time he lost a patient he felt the same despair. You wouldn't remember, I guess."

"He never had much to say about his practice or his patients. But as far back as my memory goes, he was a happy man. At home, anyway. Remember how we used to laugh at the dinner table at something funny he had seen or heard, or at something foolish Binny or I had done? It was fun, growing up with you and Pop."

"By that time I suppose he had come to recognize that it wasn't his own ignorance so much as it was the ignorance of the profession in general. He grew more resigned, as time went on. But in the beginning—" She couldn't tell Johnny how frightened she had been sometimes, by his despair, lest he take his sister Kate's way out. And how for that reason she had accepted—not happily, but had accepted—his frantic infidelities: she could understand that it was a way of blotting out the *I* short of Kate's way. Poor Kate! She had not thought of her in years—not since Binny—She shut her mind off that path. "You are a great comfort to me, Johnny. All I've been thinking of is myself—if I am left—But you are right: he has had a good life, on the whole, and has made the most of it. For that I am thankful."

Their conversation had been low-voiced; it did not disturb the sick man, who might have been asleep, he lay so quietly. From that day he slipped rapidly from bad to worse; his fever rose; he tossed restlessly, muttered, coughed incessantly. Afterward Anne was not sure how many days passed, with her at the bedside, trying to keep him quiet, swabbing his crusted lips and mouth, catching his murmurs and wondering what he was reliving in his delirium.

One afternoon Louline came to the bedroom door to summon her. John was at the moment lying asleep or in a stupor, only his struggled breathing bearing witness to his condition.

"That Mistah Trave's, he want to see you. Jes' a minute, he says. Ah kin stay with the docto'."

"Oh my goodness, Louline! Thomasina! I forgot about her, even to ask Johnny how they managed—"

"They had a fun'ral se'vice in the chu'ch, then they put he' in the vault in the cemetery twel the snow melt. It was all in the papeh."

"Of course. I just haven't been reading the paper. I'll see him, Louline. You stay here and call me—"

"Yes'm."

Anne went blindly to the sitting room. Sam was not there. Louline had put him in the parlor.

"Sam, do come sit where there's a fire. Sometimes I think that girl hasn't any gumption."

He moved across the hall and stood watching her as she went to her rocker and gestured for him to take the other one.

"I won't intrude for more than a minute. I felt I must come and say how sorry I am. You see, I was to blame." Anne looked so astonished that he hastened to explain. "That was such an awful night when Thomasina took a bad turn—couldn't get her breath—I thought I oughtn't to call Dock out. I called Johnny instead, thinking to spare his father. Somehow, the things I do with the best of intentions turn out all wrong."

"Sam, come sit down, please. I haven't told you how sad I feel about Thomasina, and I am grateful for your consideration of John. It wasn't your fault the other call came. I am sorry I couldn't go to Thomasina's funeral service. I haven't left that bedroom—Thomasina and I had been friends for all our lives, almost—since I grew up enough to be on her level, anyway. I mean in age—maturity. I was never on her level in just pure goodness."

Sam's light blue eyes, red-rimmed behind his spectacles, brimmed with moisture. Anne felt her own eyelids begin to prickle. "Weep, then," she thought, "weep for all of us"—and she made no attempt to stop her tears. "I knew that John was worried about her condition, but I had no idea—did the end come very suddenly? Or would you rather not talk about it?"

"It did, and it didn't. Dock had warned me. He said you couldn't have hay fever when you were a girl and asthma when you grew older, without ending up with emphysema and a failing heart. Please don't weep for Thomasina. If she could come back to me as she used to be, I would wish for it. But I wouldn't wish her back the way she was suffering. For her it was a release, and I think death had no horrors for her. She was a good Christian."

"I am weeping not just for Thomasina, though I shall miss her—dreadfully. Or even for John. Just for mankind in general."

Sam was startled. "You mean Dock—?"

"I don't know. Everything possible is being done. But pneumonia—he's very sick."

"On account of my misguided kindness."

"Put that right out of your head, Sam. What is to be will be, and nothing anyone did or didn't do—You see, sometimes it helps to be a Presbyterian."

Sam Travers was the only caller, besides Julia and Jessamine Stevens, who slipped in and out as members of the family. Sally Rausch did not come or telephone: Anne had asked her not to. "Every time a bell rings he hears it and tries to get up, even when we think he isn't aware of anything. He's been listening for the bell most of his life, and can't stop now. I promise I'll call you every day."

Because of that promise, Sally knew that John grew steadily worse; he was almost constantly delirious; she learned at once when he began calling for Ludwig.

"Would he come?" Anne asked, and Sally at the other end of the line knew that she was weeping. "John may not know him, but he's suffering so from his—dreams, or whatever they are—Johnny thinks since he wants Ludwig, it might quiet him."

Ludwig came as soon as he could get there. Anne led him down the hall, saying, "He may not even know you. Sometimes he doesn't know anyone. And at best, he's confused. When he sleeps it is more like a stupor, but he wasn't asleep just now. Johnny's with him: he's standing almost a twenty-four hour watch now."

Ludwig went in and stood at the foot of the bed. If he was shocked at John's appearance, he managed to keep his face impassive. The sick man's eyes were open, but clouded and wandering. After a moment, Ludwig said, "Here I am, Dock. You wanted to see me?"

John's eyes focused, he frowned, and closed them. "No. It's Cap'n Rausch I wanted. Rausch of the Sixth Iowa." Then he opened them again; he struggled for his breath, but his eyes cleared. "Ludwig! Yes, of course. I wanted—" Then after a long moment while everyone waited, he went on. "You're a friend of John Sherman. Tell him to tell the General—this hospital—boys dying and *I can't help them.* Tell him to move us out of this God-forsaken swamp."

The last words died away to an almost inaudible mumble. Ludwig was silent for a moment. Then he said, "You want me to reach the General through the Senator, ask him to get your hospital out of Duckport. It's as good as done: the Senator owes me something. Go to sleep, Dock, and quit worrying about it."

John murmured, "I knew—you would." And they all watched as he slipped away into what might have been sleep or might have been unconsciousness. Anne and Johnny went with Ludwig into the hall. He said, "I hope that helps. He may forget I've been here, and start going through it all again."

"You at least understood what was on his mind," Johnny said, "in spite of his being so confused."

"I understood. He's lost any sense of time. The years that have gone by don't mean anything. He didn't recognize me at first because he was looking for a young 'Captain Rausch.' Then he knew me, old and stout as I am, but he was still suffering the miseries of that Duckport hospital, 1863, and he's still there, but I was the Ludwig Rausch who was a friend of Senator Sherman—no matter he died last year, and the General in '91." Ludwig's eyes glimmered with unshed tears; he took out his handkerchief and blew vigorously. "Time—" he said, "our youth—it never really goes, does it? It is all held in our minds. But the happy years would be better to remember."

"The war," Johnny sighed. "I suppose no matter how many years, how many accomplishments, events, and changes, it was the biggest thing in the life of everyone who fought in it, and at the end—"

"It was our youth, Johnny. Your father and I have been friends for many years, but most important, we have our youth in common." He gave his nose a final blow, shook Johnny's hand, kissed Anne on the cheek, said, "If Sally or I can do anything—" and took his departure.

"He's right. It should be the happy years that come back to mind," Johnny said, "but in delirium, it's the horrors. The war. He hated it so, and now, burning up with fever, it is all he remembers."

"Never mind, Johnny. You want him to be thinking of me. But at the end of his life a man goes back to the biggest thing in it. And don't pretend that it isn't the end."

And she went back into the sickroom, to take up her watch at the side of the bed.

Johnny persuaded her to go to bed that night with the promise that he would call her at any sign of change. He roused her sometime after midnight; she came quickly downstairs, in nightgown and robe, to find not only Johnny but Dr. Warren standing helpless as John struggled spasmodically for his breath. She went to the other side, knelt on the floor, and took his hand; the uninjured arm had been tossed clear of the bed-covers. At once he opened his eyes and looked into hers, clear for the instant of all confusion. "Anne," he said, and then with a question in his inflection, "Binny?"

"Binny's all right," she said stoutly. "Don't worry any more." She did not weep; her tears were all inside now, like blood draining from her heart. She put her head down on the bed and waited, his hands still in hers. When she felt no further slight response, she sat up, let go of his hand, and reached under the covers to the foot of the bed. "His feet are cold."

"Yes. Hot water bottles won't help now."

It was at that instant that the noisy breathing stopped, after a frighful struggle for air. The silence was shocking after so long a time. Anne sat for an appalled moment, then reached up and closed John's eyes. When Johnny would have pulled the sheet over his face, she stopped him.

"Just leave me here, Johnny—for a little while."

"Mom, Warren and I will take care of—of everything. Don't you—"

"I won't. Just leave me for a little while."

Obediently they left her. When she finally came out of the bedroom, Dr. Warren was waiting for her with a glass of water and a sleeping draught. "Drink it," he said, "however nasty."

She took it and swallowed it down without a grimace. "Not that I can sleep, whatever I take. No, never mind. Johnny, I can get up to bed without your help. I am not going to collapse, or do anything foolish. You stay—do what you must."

The two men watched her up the stairs, before they returned to the bedroom. Dr. Warren said, "You don't really need to do what I know must be painful to you. The undertaker will take care of everything."

"You can call him when you like. But there are some things filial piety demands, and I am glad I can do them. You know—'the last services to the dead'." Johnny stood looking down at his father, the sunken eyes and temples, the hollow unshaven cheeks, the still-black beard. "I must shave him. No one has ever seen him unkept. Queer, isn't it, how old he looks, so suddenly. And he wasn't really old. Sixty-one his next birthday."

"Physicians, real physicians, don't make old bones."

"I know. And he was so used to death. I don't believe it frightened him. I remember his talking to me once when I was beginning to practice, about the great 'enemy death' always in the corner waiting. But I have been with him at so many deathbeds, I know he did not always see death as an enemy, no matter how hard he had fought."

Upstairs, Anne lay down, still convinced that she could not sleep that night, but too spent even to kneel and pray. She had prayed so fervently so many nights, selfishly. However, as the sedative took effect she thought hazily, not even remembering she had taken it, "Now, of course, there is nothing to lie awake listening for. Not the telephone or a knock, not sleigh bells or horses' hooves, or the front door closing. I can sleep forever. But I would rather lie awake, waiting—" And when sleep overtook her, her cheeks and the pillow were wet with the tears she had not shed earlier.

She awoke late the next morning, only half-aware of the leaden weight on her mind and her sickness of heart; it was a heartbeat's instant before she remembered why. The sound of voices came from downstairs, and movement. A bustle. She lay for a moment trying to think why the word had come to mind: it was an Emily Dickinson poem, quoted in an essay read at some Club meeting. She struggled to recall it: it had moved her by its truth when she had heard it, since it put into words her own experiences when her father had died. And Binny. But she could do no better than "a bustle in the house."

She rose finally, bathed and dressed, and started downstairs. Sally and Jessamine were waiting beside the newel post.

"Why do you come down, Anne? There isn't anything you can do."

"Let us do what needs to be done, Cousin Anne. Answer the bells—It's the only way we can say how much we grieve for you."

"I'm all right," Anne said shortly. "And there are things only I can do."

"I telegraphed Rodney," his mother said, "and he wired back. He will take the night train home tonight. I hope you don't mind my taking it upon myself."

"'Mind'? I am glad." Anne looked at her steadily: Jessamine did not shift her eyes. All that had been said in twenty-odd years was in that exchange. "Rodney will be a great help to Johnny, and I'll be glad to have him around. I'm fond of him, you know." Anne broke off to pay attention to Sally.

"Can I send Rosa down to help Louline? To help answer the door? You know there will be a constant stream of callers. Unless you let us stay."

"Thanks, Sally. But Louline and I can manage. I am on my way to the kitchen now to talk to her. I've scarcely seen her since—since the night of the storm."

"It's a blessing the snow's about gone."

"Gone?" Anne went into the sitting room to look out the window. Except in the corners where the deepest drifts had blown, the ground was bare, soaked and dismal. "I hadn't even noticed. How did it go so fast? Come back this afternoon, Sally, and you, too, Jessamine, if you are willing to help receive callers. But I am not going to be pushed off upstairs. John had so many patients you wouldn't know. They may not come, but if they do, I think they would appreciate it if I were there to thank them."

There were not many callers that afternoon. The Reverend Mr. McKinney came, and prayed with Anne; she had grown so accustomed to not really listening to him that she did not mind too much being prayed over. John's obituary was in the paper that night, with the announcement that visiting hours would be at the house the next afternoon. By the end of that next day, Anne was numb with fatigue. She was glad that she had managed to stand beside the coffin through those eternal dragging hours. But it was not until she was back in bed that night that she realized how many hands she had shaken, black and white, how many condolences she had accepted, how many times she had heard, "He was a good friend and a good doctor"; or,

"We'll never forget that he saved our Mary"; or "our Tom"; or, humbly, "I had to come to let you know—we don't see how we can get along without him." Of particular individuals she remembered only Tim O'Reilly and his wife and how she had put out both hands to Tim. Why? She couldn't have said. He wasn't the young Irishman they had helped so many, many years ago: he was portly, silver-haired, and red-faced; and although he was still an engineer on the railroad, in his best blue serge suit, with his air of confidence, he looked as much like a millionaire as anyone in Waynesboro. But she had not been mistaken in her gesture: he had taken her hands in a firm grip, and when she had murmured the phrase that had become automatic, "So good of you to come," he said, "How could we not come? Did you ever once think we had forgotten? He gave us back our self-respect, an' that's more than curin' our ills, though he done that, too." And Mrs. O'Reilly, shier than Tim, put a gentle hand on her arm and said, "We will pray for him, and light a candle." One other individual she remembered: Christina Voorhees. Anne had almost turned and fled when she had seen the Voorheeses coming, but stood fast, and Christina spared her any philosophy; she said, "I can only remember, after all these years, how good a friend he was to Papa, and how much pleasure they had together with their chess." Her eyes—Christina's!—had filled with tears as she had added, quite spontaneously, "If we could only turn the clock back!"

By the next morning, the morning of the funeral, Anne had completely forgotten that she had been groping for a poem in her mind—a poem that she had felt expressed a truth that she needed to hear expressed. She did not think of it again until the funeral was over. She had declined the invitation of Johnny and Julia to go home with them when they were in the carriage returning from the cemetery. "From now on, I'll be alone. I think I would rather start at once in the way I'll be going on. But come in tomorrow morning and we'll look over your father's things. He didn't have many clothes, but some of them are good and I am sure will be useful to someone. The longer it is put off, the harder it will be."

She went into the house, into the sitting room, turned toward her rocking chair and saw at once the sad state of the fire, turning to ashes in the grate. Quite without volition she remembered the words she had thought so many times: "John will laugh at me, but when he comes in he will get it started up. And I can tell him about this afternoon—" Then the first actual realization of her loss swept over her, and she dropped onto the sofa drowned by a wave of desolation. And the poem she had been groping for the morning after John's death came back to her, astonishingly, for she had never memorized it:

> The bustle in a House
> The morning after Death
> Is solemnest of industries
> Enacted upon Earth—

The Sweeping up the Heart
And putting Love away
We shall not want to use again
Until Eternity.

That brought tears: a bitter flood. She could weep over a poem. Louline, just returning from the funeral with Lafe, heard her and came to sit beside her. "That's right, Miz Gordon—you weep twel yo' hea't empty. 'Tain' natural, not takin' on none." She put a sturdy arm around Anne, held her until Anne sat up, dried her eyes, said, "Thank you, Louline. I'm right now. What are we going to do with all the food people brought us? Do take home whatever you want; I can't eat it."

The days that followed were busy, mind-distracting ones, too full for brooding, had Anne been inclined to brood. There were John's personal belongings to be disposed of; unpaid patients' bills, which were for Johnny to deal with, and a not inconsiderable estate to be appraised and administered: a responsibility Johnny declined, since one-third of it, the third that was legally his mother's, was all that she would accept. Anne explained the situation to Tim Merrill: she supposed he thought it odd that a doctor of all people should die intestate, but that was John's decision. She felt no need to tell Tim that shortly after Johnny's marriage, John, in one of his frequent fits of exasperation with Julia, had threatened to make a will leaving everything to Anne. She had dissuaded him: nothing was more likely to make their daughter-in-law resentful. "And remember, I'd be the one to bear the brunt of it." And while Johnny could surely use any money he might inherit, Anne would not have the same need: she would live simply, have a Civil War widow's pension, those good-as-gold W.W. Railroad shares, and the house she had inherited from her father. That would be enough. John was to forget all about making a will; under the law a third of his property would come to her and two-thirds would go to Johnny: a fair enough division, as she explained to Tim. Why bother with a will? But she realized now, sitting in Tim's office and remembering, that they had both been influenced by the instinctive disbelief of all mortals in their own mortality; the months, weeks, years, would go on in the same way they had always gone; but if you thought with your mind and not your instinct, you knew that with the passage of every day the end drew inevitably closer. She had been foolish to have taken it for granted that she and John would grow older together, but so far as his estate was concerned, she knew that she had been right. She wanted Julia to be happy, because only if she were could things go well with Johnny and the boy. And she was still uneasy about Julia.

The first Club meeting she attended after John's death was at Mrs. Deming's. Anne had resumed her normal life, her normal active outward life, almost at once, not only because it was her inclination, but because she knew how much John had disliked ostentatious mourning; she cared little for the opinion of others: Julia and her mother could lift their eyebrows if they liked.

She was not only in her pew in church every Sunday morning, but as always did her own marketing and what errands needed to be done. And when the Club met at Mrs. Deming's, she was there.

She went early, with the intention of seizing upon a chair near the back, and so avoiding condolences, already spoken once. As it happened, she arrived at Mrs. Deming's door so early that Julia had not yet come downstairs. Mrs. Deming, who was seeing Anne not for the first time since the funeral, greeted her cordially, with no reference to her bereavement. "How nice that you came early! Would you like to run up and see what is keeping Julia? She may be having hook and eye trouble. I can't go up now—others may be coming in at any moment."

Anne found Julia in the big bay-windowed bedroom of the apartment. She was, as her mother had guessed, having trouble with the bodice that hooked up the back.

"Mamma Gordon! You have saved my life! Just drop your coat on the bed."

While Anne's quick fingers moved up Julia's back, she looked around at the immaculate bedroom, its white net curtains, white-draped dressing table, white bedspread. Its sterility chilled her bones. There was nothing to show that Johnny had ever been in it. As the two started toward the head of the stairs, Anne glanced into what had been the guest room. Johnny's hair brushes were on the bureau, his pipe rack on the wall, one pipe on its side on the bedside table, ashes spilled out of it as always.

"Johnny has moved in here?"

Julia flushed a little. "It was his idea. He has so many night calls. More than ever, now that Papa Dock is gone. I find it so very difficult to get to sleep again once I'm roused."

(Then Julia did not know, or did not want, the comfort, the security—the all's-well feeling that came even if you were half-asleep when your husband slipped into your warm bed to lie beside you.) "Johnny wouldn't want your rest disturbed, of course."

There had been a sarcastic edge to Anne's voice. Julia gave her a suspicious, sidelong glance. "Johnny is most considerate."

"I am sure he is," his mother retorted. "He considers everyone before himself." And then, as she started down the stairs ahead of Julia, she added, "I wish he could get more rest himself. He seems so tired all the time. And he used to be so lighthearted."

"He has taken the loss of his father very hard. Surely you wouldn't expect him to be 'lighthearted' already?"

"I'd like to think he could laugh—yes, already." Anne said no more, but thought quite a lot. Separate beds, let alone separate bedrooms, were to her mind a sign of no real marriage. What meaning could there be, especially for her warm, loving Johnny, in a marriage that meant little more than shared meals, with a child present? She began after that to study him with an anxious eye on his brief but daily visits—too anxious, she chided herself, since his thin unsmiling face, its drawn look, might indeed be the result of sorrow and of overwork, and not of any—lack—at home.

Through the rest of January the days seemed longer and passed more slowly. Sally Rausch dropped in two or three afternoons a week, not ostensibly to keep Anne from moping, but to keep her in touch with the town's goings-on; not that they amounted to much, really. Anne had never been one to spend her mornings in idleness; it was the late afternoons, the solitary dinner, the evenings that seemed so interminable and so lonely. Reading had always been the chiefest of her pleasures; now she devoured one book after another, thankful that she never felt surfeited.

Then late one afternoon in January, the dark already settling in, Johnny and Tucker came to her front door, Tucker cuddling a butterball of a puppy in his arms and trying to pretend he had not been crying, in spite of his wet, red cheeks, his running nose, and the hiccupping gasps with which he caught his breath.

Anne hustled them inside, said "What—? Is that a new puppy, Tuck?"

"Yes." The tone of his voice was a combination of defiance and sulkiness.

"For goodness' sake, child: let me wipe your face, you'll be all chapped."

Johnny took out a handkerchief that for size put hers to shame, and wiped his boy's cheeks and nose. "It's a fox terrier pup. The Perkins boy gave it to him. It was such good sleighing weather I took him out to the farm with me. Julia wanted eggs and a chicken, but she doesn't like the cold. If she had gone along—"

"He's mine," Tucker insisted. "Father let me take him. We brought him home all wrapped up under the buffalo robe. But Mother says I can't keep him." Tears welled anew, overflowing in trickles from the corners of his eyes. "Father says you like dogs—"

"I see."

"Julia has a point, Mom," Johnny intervened hastily. "An upstairs apartment is no place for a dog: she'd be forever running up and down to let him in or out."

"Since it's the dead of winter and the puppy can't be more than a few weeks old, he won't be wanting to go out much for a while."

Tucker put the dog down in front of the fire, squatted beside it, and with a gentle hand smoothed the still fuzzy hair. "His name is Major. For President McKinley. Father says that's what they used to call him before he was President.

Major wiggled with pleasure, wagged his little rattail, and wet on the hearthrug. Tucker, frightened and aghast, looked up at his grandmother, at a loss as to what he should say.

"Go ask Louline for a wet rag, and come wipe that up."

Tucker ran for the kitchen. Johnny's mouth twitched, but he dared not smile—yet. "Julia doesn't know the first thing about dogs—she never had a pet in her life. I should have had more gumption than to let Tuck have it. To Julia, the idea of housebreaking a dog—"

"Sometimes I think Julia's too fastidious for the everyday world. It's your idea that I should raise it, I suppose?"

"Mom, it's either that or take it back and break Tuck's heart."

The boy came back with a wet rag, and on his hands and knees scrubbed the hearthrug, looking up now and then through his lashes.

"Next time he does that, rub his nose in it, and then put him outside. He'll soon learn."

"Then I can keep him here? Oh, Grandma!"

"How many dogs have you trained in your time, Mom? Remember my first—the long-haired stray that looked like a dirty floor mop when I brought it in? That I named 'Lyss' for General Grant?"

"Indeed I remember. He was a very affectionate dog, particularly when it thundered. Him and Rags and Binny's Dicky. I raised them all. Children always promise to take care of their pets and never do."

"I would, Grandma. Cross my heart."

"Yes, I know: you'll be in school all day now and you live a couple of blocks down the street. You must realize, Tuck: if I take over the training and feeding of the puppy, and play with him, he will be my dog, in his eyes anyway. Dogs are like that."

"So they are," Johnny said. "But Tuck can come when he pleases and play with him, can't he? Teach him tricks? And come spring, the pup can run with him."

"Grandma?"

"Oh, yes, I'll keep him for you. Get him housebroken. But you will have to help. He must learn to mind both of us."

"Oh, Grandma!" Tucker rose to his knees, threw his arms around his grandmother's legs, almost knocked her down.

"Tucker!"

"It's all right. Go, Tuck—ask Louline to find a basket down cellar and line it with some old pieces of blanket for a bed for him. And if he cries all night for his mother—more than one night, anyway—back he goes."

In the days that followed, Anne began to think that perhaps Johnny had planned the whole thing for her benefit, rather than Tucker's: there was nothing equal to a young puppy for keeping you busy and your mind occupied. But she found Major wonderful company: it was better to talk to an ecstatically wiggling puppy than to carry on silent dialogues in your mind; and she saw more of her grandson than she had ever seen before. He came every afternoon after school, played with Major inside or out, according to the weather, and commenced the riotous business of teaching him to return a thrown ball, to beg for his supper, to follow close at his heels.

Anne had thought while the snows were still deep that she really would garden in earnest, come spring: would try all the flowers she had never tried before. But having a puppy underfoot put an end to those ambitions: she would do well if she could keep him out of her usual sweet peas, petunias, snapdragons, asters, and verbenas. After the hard winter spring came early, and for once Anne was able to do what according to garden superstition you should always do: on St. Patrick's Day she got out her sweet pea seeds and set about planting them in the trench Lafe had dug for her. (Lafe had more time for her chores, now that he wasn't hitching and unhitching John's horse all day.)

In the mid-afternoon, when she had almost finished, Sally came down the street and, seeing Anne from the sidewalk, came through the gate and around the house instead of going to the front door.

"What on earth are you doing out here on this wet ground? You're mud from head to foot."

"That's because Major keeps jumping on me. I'm almost through. I've been planting my sweet peas. You know: you're supposed to—"

"Yes, I know: on St. Patrick's Day, at the risk of pneumonia. You gardeners!" Sally, whose gardening was restricted to telling her yard man to set out lobelias and geraniums around the porch, regarded with condescending humor those who willingly got their hands muddy. "Do you plant—or not plant, whichever it is—in the dark of the moon?"

"Don't be a goose. Go on around to the front door and let Louline welcome you properly. I'll go in the kitchen way and be with you as soon as I've scrubbed my hands and changed my shoes."

"And pinned up your hair, too, for goodness' sake."

Anne still had a heavy head of hair, though it had lost the golden highlights it had once had, and was now solid dark brown. She put up her hand to her untidy chignon, said "Oh, heavens," gathered up her gardening tools, and headed for the kitchen door, with Major lolloping along at her heels.

In a few moments, considerably cleaner and tidier, she joined Sally in the sitting room and dismissed Louline, who had been entertaining their guest with East End gossip. "Take the puppy, Louline, and keep him in the kitchen until Tucker comes for him."

When Louline had dragged the dog away, Sally said, "Why on earth you saddled yourself with a pup at your age, I cannot see."

"Do you feel all that old? I don't believe it."

"Not really. But I might with a pet on my hands, they're such a nuisance."

"You and I live in different worlds, now. I can see you wouldn't have time."

"What nonsense! Different worlds, indeed! When you're the only female in Waynesboro I can really talk to. Club members don't count, not when it comes to really getting down to things."

"What do you want to get down to this afternoon?"

"Nothing, really. Everything seems to be going well."

"Only 'seems'?"

"Ludwig's keeping an uneasy eye on this booming stock market."

To all appearances the country had never been so prosperous. Ludwig was kept so busy at the mill, and running down to Madison City at least once a week to check on matters at the Coated Paper Company, that he and Sally had not even gone to Washington for McKinley's second inauguration on the fourth of March. But there was such a thing as unreasoning, even reckless, faith in an unlimited increase in the country's business and in the soaring stock market, which Ludwig thought far too high.

"He's worried about Ernest. He seems to be doing very well as a customer's man in the brokerage firm his father-in-law's a partner in, but we've never thought him the brightest boy in the world. Ludwig's afraid of his burning his fingers in the market."

Anne laughed. She was not in the least interested in the stock market; it would not have occurred to her to sell the stocks she had and invest in something else. And she felt only a mild interest in Ernest's well-being. She said, "Ernest never struck me as the gambling type."

"Fevers are catching." But Sally changed the subject, lest she seem critical of her own son.

As the spring advanced, Ludwig's interest in the market as a puzzled onlooker became real concern for his son, in whose judgement he had little faith. All through April he watched the price of Northern Pacific stock creeping up: on the 22nd, 101; on the 27th, 109; on the 29th, 119.

"The financial experts," he said, slapping his *Enquirer* irritably, "profess not to know who is raiding Northern Pacific." He was with Sally in the library one evening after dinner.

"'Raiding'?"

"Buying up all the stock possible. As an investment it isn't worth 119 dollars a share."

"Then why—?"

"To get control of it, of course. Who has control now? Hill and J. P. Morgan. Who wants it? As a good guess, Harriman, to get hold of the C.B.&Q. for the Union Pacific, with access to Chicago. The Northern Pacific ends at St. Paul, the Union Pacific at Omaha. But Hill and Morgan got control of the Burlington in January."

"So you think Harriman is trying to get the Northern Pacific and the Burlington away from Morgan? Funny, we have ridden that road so many times to Burlington and never given a thought to who owned it. And it doesn't matter to us, now, does it?"

"Not directly, since we haven't stock in any of them. But it is throwing the stock market into a frenzy. Everyone on Wall Street must know that N.P. stock is overvalued; they are selling short intending to buy when it has fallen to a reasonable level. If the fools can't see what is happening, they're going to get themselves out on a limb. Hill and Morgan or Harriman aren't going to let over-priced stock stop them. Selling short when those men are in the market buying is about as safe as putting your hand in one of our heckling machines. Sometimes I think being too close to Wall Street puts blinkers on a fellow."

Sally laughed and then said quickly, "I'm sorry. I wasn't laughing at you, just at your mixed metaphors. I know that it isn't funny. You think Ernest—? Surely his father-in-law would stop him?"

"I think Ernest is just the boy to do what everyone else is doing. I'll send him a telegram in the morning. I don't want to have to bail him out."

The wire was sent: "Don't sell NP short. Can't afford to bail you out." Ludwig was glad he had sent it when by May 6 the price of Northern Pacific had reached 127, and the gamblers and speculators began to move in. That was on Monday; on Tuesday the stock climbed to 143½, and more shares were sold short. By noon Monday's short sellers were in trouble: the price was still rising and the shares they had sold were due for delivery. By night it was evident that the stock had been cornered: shares could not be bought and could only be borrowed at preposterous loan rates. By Wednesday the scramble began; short sellers were trapped: they had to borrow shares at astronomical figures or fail to deliver and go bankrupt. In trying to raise the money to pay loan rates of 35 to eventually 85 percent, owners of other stocks were forced to sell them. By Thursday when it became known who the contending forces were, it was too late: the price of Northern Pacific stock shot to 650, and shares in other companies fell at a corresponding rate. In the midst of the general market crash, 300 shares of Northern Pacific stock sold for a thousand dollars a share.

That afternoon Ludwig received a belated answer to his telegram: Ernest had probably resented being advised, he thought, but at least he had been sensible. The telegram was terse and to the point: "Thanks advice. Sold no NP. Buying steel." Ernest's father breathed more easily; he was even able to chuckle when he reached home and handed the flimsy bit of paper over for Sally to read. "The boy is brighter than I thought."

"Is it bright to buy steel stock now, in the midst of this shambles?"

"Steel's a bargain at the price. The news came over the wire late this afternoon—I stopped at the *Torchlight* office and got the latest bulletin: Harriman has compromised with Hill and Morgan. They will split the board of directors of the Northern Pacific, and they are giving the sellers time to deliver at a price of 150 a share. There won't be many shares to be picked up at that price: it will mean a lot of bankruptcies, I haven't a doubt."

A letter from Ernest, following his telegram, confirmed Ludwig's surmise. Not only were many men ruined, but his father-in-law was one of them: he had lost everything; even the town house and the summer place in Rhode Island must be sold. "And until he gets on his feet again, he and Emily's mother will live in a small apartment in the city."

Ludwig huffed, "And I thought he was one of the *big* operators!" He felt a certain grim and uncharitable pleasure in the downfall of Ernest's father-in-law, but sympathized with Ernest and Emily. At least Emily's parents weren't moving in with them. He wondered about going to New York to look into the situation, but Sally dissuaded him. "For one thing, they probably wouldn't thank you. For another, it won't hurt them a bit, or the children, to feel poor for a while. So long as Ernest still has a job."

"It was a personal bankruptcy: the brokerage firm wasn't involved. Of course the partnership will have to be sold along with everything else, but I see no reason why Ernest should lose his job. He just may come out of this looking like an astute young man."

At the beginning of the summer, Anne again became involved in the affairs of Ruhamah McCune and the Waynesboro Public Library. The institution had grown coniderably since the days of the old Subscription Library, but, with the addition of free-standing steel stacks at right angles to the walls, was exactly as it had always been, crowded into the same upstairs corner room. The Library Board, however, had applied for a Carnegie grant, with every hope of getting one; Ruhamah, always conscientious and exaggeratedly aware of her inadequacy, was frightened by the prospect, much as she hoped for a new building. When she had first been hired by the board of the old Subscription Library and had taken over from the volunteer ladies, she had continued to use their methods. But with tax money to be spent, with many more acquisitions and many, many more patrons (who received their cards free), the old ways soon became time-consuming and inadequate. Ruhamah wanted to know how to run a library in a proper, professional fashion; she had saved her money hoping to go to Albany and study in the New York Library School for a summer. But the Board of Trustees, sure that they were paying her an adequate salary, refused her a leave of absence on half-pay unless she hired a substitute. Ruhamah gave up her dream: there wasn't money enough to hire anyone.

Anne knew nothing of all this. Ruhamah had not confided in her; somehow nowadays there were always too many patrons crowded around the desk to allow opportunity for confidence. Anne was there as frequently as anyone, but she found her own books, let Ruhamah stamp her card with the due date, and departed. it was at the Gardiner-Stevens wedding in June that she learned from Sheldon Edwards of Ruhamah's disappointment.

Rodney and Lavinia Gardiner were married in the Gardiner drawing room late in June of 1901. Rodney was home from Baltimore and ready to begin the practice of surgery. The Gordon-Warren-Stevens hospital was finished, equipped, staffed with nurses trained, or practical but experienced. In the beginning it seemed that Julia's prophecy had been right: only those who could not be taken care of at home had so far been willing to enter. Julia was less of a wet blanket than she had been before Johnny had come into the lion's share of his father's money: she need not worry quite so much about whether a private hospital could make ends meet. No one knew quite what Mrs. Warren thought because no one knew her except casually: she was not only "from away" but also what Waynesboro considered a "homebody," although the Warren children were progressing through the public schools as a part of the town. Anne and Lavinia Gardiner, as much in love with Rodney as she had always been, were enthusiastic believers in the possibility of

Waynesboro's supporting a hospital, and a surgeon to go with it. Rodney had built a house for Lavinia next to the barnlike, one-story unadorned hospital, so that he could always be on call: an unassuming two-story frame house, wide-porched and many-windowed. It had been furnished in great part by the superfluities of the Gardiner and Stevens establishments, and if the old furniture, mostly of the Empire period, sorted ill with the turn-of-the-century house, no one was unduly bothered by the incongruity, least of all the bride and groom.

The wedding was a small one, considering the size of the Gardiner family and the number of their relatives and friends. The majority of the guests were young people, Lavinia and Rodney's friends: Waynesboro schoolmates and a number of boys and girls they had known at college, come to stay at the Gardiner and the Stevens houses. Their effervescing spirits made the wedding a gay one; it was also very pretty. The bride, following her two youngest sisters as bridesmaids and Caroline as maid of honor, came down the broad staircase to where her father was waiting; on his arm Lavinia followed her attendants across the hall to the parlor, where Mr. McKinney, who had married her parents and was now an old man, stood, his back to the fireplace. A restive bridegroom, with Lowrey Edwards as his best man, took her hand as her father withdrew, and in a few moments it was done.

Anne, watching the precession, was inevitably reminded of Doug and Barbara's wedding, particularly since she could not remember having seen Mrs. Bodien from that day to this. She was struck by the alteration in her looks, so thin and sallow had she grown. Doug, too, she studied as if she had not seen him for a long time: he limped more than he had as a young man; sometimes he gave the impression of dragging his bad foot. He had put on weight, too—a stranger might describe him as "portly"—but she supposed if one were as lame as Doug, it would be hard to keep one's weight down. And he had been Common Pleas Judge for so long now that one could only call him—"judgmatical" was the one word she could think of. Only Barbara, however matronly, and her father seemed untouched and much as they had been "once upon a time."

It was not until the necessary words had been spoken that Lavinia raised her eyes to Rodney and Anne remembered the Fourth of July at Hillcrest, and how very obvious even then the two young people had been, the love in their rapt eyes revealing itself there and in the way they touched each other. John had seen it, too, and had smiled at their youth; the recollection caused her a physical pang: she missed him so much and thought it so wrong that he had not been there to see the fairy-tale "happy-forever-after" ending for the boy and girl who had known each other always. The air of enchantment that hung about them was strange and beautiful.

And Lowrey Edwards and Caroline Gardiner had something of the same look in their eyes. Afterward, when the group broke up to stand in a receiving line with their parents, it was the obvious pairing of Lowrey and young Caroline that led Anne to say what she did to Sheldon when they chanced to come together at the reception, balancing plates and teacups in their hands. "I suppose Caroline and young Lowrey will be next? I haven't had a visit with you for so long I hardly know what you and the boys are doing." Sheldon had been kindness itself at the time of John's death; since then she had seen him only briefly, in the store or when he passed the plate in church on a Sunday morning. Now he flushed at her remark.

"Let's push our way out of this crowd and find a place where we can visit now. Doug's study, maybe—"

They found the study empty behind its closed door; it did not disturb them that it had obviously been set aside for a place to put everything that wasn't wanted elsewhere. They found chairs, pulled them to the table by the window, and thankfully put down plates and cups.

Sheldon began where they had left off. "I haven't meant to neglect you. I know only too well how lonely you must be. The days slip by so fast."

"I wasn't reproaching you. I'm all right. I was just explaining why I had to ask."

"About Lowrey and Caroline? I doubt they'll be next: stern parents on both sides say they must finish college first."

"And then?"

"Oh, I think certainly then. Lowrey will come into the store as a partner—his own choice. Heredity is a queer thing, isn't it? Those two older girls are so like their mother: black Irish hair and brows and lashes and amethyst eyes. Though they're not as pretty as she was."

"Still is, at—what? Forty-odd?"

"And they haven't her bounce. They're like Doug in acuteness of intellect, perhaps in character. Veronica is pure Gardiner—that fine small-featured face and all that cloud of flyaway light hair."

"Yes, she isn't really pretty, but manages to give the impression of being so. She is paired off with Paul Rausch today, but I doubt if anything will come of that."

"Anne, they're just children."

"Seventeen, eighteen—thereabouts."

"And then there's little Mary: more character than any of the others, I suspect, but so unfortunately like her grandfather in looks."

"Sandy-haired and stocky," Anne agreed. "It must be painful, with all those pretty sisters."

"You know, I don't imagine Mary wastes much time thinking about her looks. She's too busy-minded."

Anne smiled at him. "You've grown to be a mind-reader?"

"An observer. Don't laugh at me. I've seen a lot of those girls as they grew up. Doug and I have always been close, and Barbara went out of her way to make my boys happy. But to go back to them—it was really their heredity I was going to speak about. Lowrey, in spite of his name, is like me: meek and acquiescent."

"Quiet, maybe, but kind and gentle."

"Thank you. But a stick-in-the-mud. And an Edwards, too. Quite willing to stay here, be a shopkeeper, raise a family in the same old way. And some day, perhaps, be dismayed at how life has slipped by him."

"Oh, no, Sheldon. He will have a happy life, even if—Oh, I suppose all of us somewhere along the way think, when it is too late, 'Is this all there is? When I have only one life to live?' But the moment passes, and we are content enough. I count Lowrey fortunate if he has inherited his character from you. What about Richard?"

"He's like the Lowreys. Like Kitty: spirit enough for two. And when he is through college, he will be off and away. Ever since he was a little boy—remember Dr. Maxwell's lectures about the Holy Land?—ever since then, and since he read about Schliemann digging up Troy, he has set his heart on being an archeologist."

"Oh, my goodness! I can see the fascination. But he's just a boy. Still in high school, isn't he?"

"I know. And it wasn't really to talk about my children or Doug's that I inveigled you in here. I want to talk to you about something else." And Sheldon, who was still on the Library Board of Trustees, told her of Ruhamah's request for a leave of absence. "I commend her for wanting to learn her profession," he concluded, "but it's quite true that the Board, if it gives her a leave of absence with even half-pay, has not the funds to hire a substitute. And she certainly doesn't. It's damnable to see enthusiasm of that kind frustrated."

"The poor child! She hasn't had much help anywhere along the line."

"Not such a child anymore. She must be thirty. She's been in the library since she was fifteen. It's maybe a last chance for her."

"And none of her helpers are capable? No, of course not. I know they're all still in school."

"Anyone taking over would have to be paid a real salary."

"I see what you're driving at, however indirectly. You'd like some volunteer librarians for the summer?"

"You ladies of the Woman's Club took care of the library for years."

"It's rather a different institution now, isn't it? But if the hours could be cut back to something like what they used to be—if your Board would consent to that, yes. I'd be glad to do it myself, just to have something purposeful to do. And I am sure I could persuade someone to substitute for me if anything came up."

And so Anne Gordon had a busy summer. Her daughter-in-law disapproved, thought it only fitting that Anne should live out her days a sorrowing widow. Julia feared, moreover, that the town would think she needed financial help that her son and daughter-in-law begrudged her. That she could not fulfill the role Julia had chosen for her did not bother Anne, but knowing how tongues wagged in Waynesboro, she thought Julia's other objection might have an element of truth in it. She stopped in at the *Torchlight* office and talked to Charlotte Bonner, making it clear that she wanted the town to know that, for the summer, the Library was reverting to the old volunteer system. Julia professed to be satisfied by the notice in the paper, but Anne wondered sometimes, when Julia's pettishness was evident through the screen of perpetual sweetness, whether she was not finding her own role of perfect wife and mother beginning to be something less than satisfying. For one thing, though Anne would have expected Julia to be a possessive mother, she was always willing to let Tucker spend as much time as he liked with his grandmother, and with his dog; or, now that school was out and Rausches and Evanses had shifted to Hillcrest for the summer, to permit him to go there as often and stay as long as he was invited for. Anne suspected that the boy's father missed him more than Julia did, although Johnny maintained that the visits to Hillcrest were good for Tucker, free as he was to range, with companions his own age, over the grounds and gardens, free to fish in the river behind Hillcrest and its meadows, or in the canal beyond the interurban tracks, where the old disused lock made deep water.

Anne enjoyed her hours in the library, however much she felt that she might be bungling Ruhamah's meticulous records. Summer was a slow time, particularly in its earlier weeks when the children had other things than reading to fill their hours, before they grew bored with endless vacation. She spent some afternoons, interrupted by an occasional patron, huddled with the Woman's Club Program Committee—Amanda Reid, Christina Voorhees, and Mrs. McKinney—engaged in exploring the library's resources on the subject of Greek civilization; she occasionally had a chance to visit with one or the other of them who happened to arrive first, or who stayed after the Committee meeting. She attempted to sympathize with Amanda on the loss of her friend Thomasina, but was rebuffed by the sad but final, "Thomasina and I had been growing apart since her marriage. I was never very important to her after that." (As if Thomasina had been married a week or so, when it had been since—well, since very early in the days of the Club. Amanda should have got used to it, Anne thought. Or did one get used to the loss of a friend?) Christina came early one afternoon and found Anne laughing with and at two little Negro boys whose chins came barely to the edge of the desk, and who were responding to Anne's teasing with white-toothed grins. When she had found books for them, she turned to Christina, who said "I see you practice what you preach. You manage to enjoy life."

"Christina, I should never have preached. I'm sorry I did. But yes, I am glad in spite of everything just to be alive." (If she must remind me, Anne thought, I'll remind her.) She said, "I suppose that now Aguinaldo's surrendered there won't be much more fighting in the Philippines. What do you hear from Blair? Will he soon be home?"

"There is still guerilla fighting, I believe. But we don't hear from Blair. We have accepted the fact that he will never come back to Waynesboro. We have ceased to conjecture as to his future."

So that was that? Had the Voorheeses written Blair off, wiped him out?

Their only son? At any rate, Christina had made it clear enough that she preferred not to be asked about him. Anne would not inquire again.

What Anne enjoyed most about the library was her growing acquaintance with what she called "the small fry," who had never been more than names to her, if that: the Merrill children, for instance: Becky, freckled, neat-plaited and demure, ten or twelve years old, with the two little boys in tow, the younger of whom Anne recognized as a hitherto anonymous playmate of Tucker. She was not quite so much at ease with the adolescents, some of whom, girls and boys both, were "paging" in the library for a few cents an hour. The only one she found it easy to talk to was Franz Lichtenstein, who was now working toward college: Rudy and the middle boy, Max, had managed to earn their education; Max, now twenty-three, was half-way through law school, and if they could manage it, Franz said, so could he. Franz had been well indoctrinated politically by his father, and liked to air his views. He amused Anne by his air of condescension; he obviously thought her naïve intellectually, and probably a sentimentalist, ignorant of the world beyond her doors. He set about her education, urging upon her the writings of men of whom she had only vaguely heard, like Karl Marx; the speeches of men like Eugene Debs, whom Anne, like most Americans, looked upon with a mixture of fear and disapprobation. Franz's fiery talk of necessary revolution was rather frightening, unless, as she reminded herself, you could keep in mind how young he was. One day when he was well launched on a diatribe against the rich, against inequality and poverty, and in favor of an equal distribution of wealth, she tackled him.

"How many rich—really rich—men do you know?"

"Well, Mr. Rausch. At least, Papa knows him."

"And does he grind the faces of the poor?"

"He keeps his workmen toiling ten hours a day six days a week. That is how he has gotten rich. And when times are hard, he cuts their work week and their pay."

"Isn't that better than laying them off and shutting down the mill, when it is losing money?"

Franz resorted to juvenile sarcasm. "He's a very charitable man, I understand. He gives his hands Thanksgiving and Christmas baskets. He lets them have coal from the mill stockpile at cost. That is paternalism, and all wrong. They have *earned* what he gives them as charity."

"That's one way of looking at it, I suppose. How about the idle poor? How many of them do you know? Really know?"

"Here, in Waynesboro? I only know they are carted off to the county poorhouse to die."

"Some of them live there for a long while, fed, clothed, and doctored. I know: my husband took care of them for years. And believe it or not, most of them are contented, even though their principal recreation is complaining. But I was talking about the poor who manage to stay out of the County

Home; poor whites who live in the bottoms down along the canal, and who get along without ever doing a hand's lick of work. You can't hire one of them for odd jobs, even. They victimize the churches, Presbyterians as long as the Presbyterians feed and clothe them, then the Methodists for a while. Like old Maggie Mulvaney. She was a town character—before your time, of course. A completely free and independent soul, who didn't give a hoorah in a high wind for what anyone thought. She slopped around town, buxom and bouncing, in a straight up-and-down garment made out of potato sacking tied around her middle with a rope. And barefooted, of course. Once in one of her Methodist periods, she went to beg clothes of the Ballards, not long after the Judge had died. You don't remember Mrs. Ballard, I suppose? She was quite mannish in dress, a Woman's Rights campaigner, among other things. She always wore a felt hat like a man's: a fedora with a led brim on the sides and a crease in the crown. When Maggie called, Mrs. Ballard brought an armful of clothes for her, with one of those hats on top. Maggie took the hat off the pile and threw it at Mrs. Ballard's feet. She said, 'You may be willin' to wear the Judge's old hats. I ain't.'"

Franz obligingly thought the anecdote funny. When he had done laughing, Anne said, "What would anyone like that do in your Socialist Utopia? Will drones be tolerated?"

"There won't be people like that when everyone is educated."

Anne looked at him pityingly. "There won't be any more Maggie Mulvaneys. There aren't now. But I have heard you talk of a 'classless society.' How long do you think it would be 'classless'? After an equal distribution of wealth, the money would soon be back in the hands of its original owners. Or, if the government regulated industry and business so as to make that impossible, soon all power would be in the hands of bureaucrats: they would be the top dogs. No, what you are dreaming of as a Paradise would be impossible to live in. No one could call his soul his own. And if you are planning for the proletariat to take over, I should hate to be governed by any of the proletariat I know. Just who are the proletariat, anyway? Do you think any American would admit to being of that class? Not so long as they can plan for their children to reach a higher level."

"Education—"

"Is the answer to everything? Believe me, Franz: it is an impossible dream. Too many people are uneducable. And when you undertake to educate everyone to want a job—Poverty will not be easy to abolish while there are people who would rather be poor than work. Fifty, sixty, even a hundred years from now, young people will be talking still about ridding the world of poverty."

It was Franz's turn to look at her pityingly. "Women are all alike. You can't think in terms of abstractions like right and wrong: you bring it all down to individuals you have known who probably aren't typical at all. You don't want change, and so you refuse to believe it is coming. But you're wrong. Do you think present conditions will be tolerated for another hundred years? I don't mean to frighten you," he assured her solemnly, "but the Revolution is coming. Marx's Revolution, when Capitalism is swept away, and the fruits of man's labor are his."

"Except what he has to contribute to support the drones."

"But there won't be any drones, rich or poor. No one living on his capital, wrung from other men's labor. No one having to live on what he can beg."

"The drones will be done away with?"

He blinked a little, then said firmly, "Anyone who won't contribute according to his abilityy will be done away with, or put in labor camps."

"You do frighten me, Franz. Are there many young people who think as you do?"

"Most young people don't think." His lip curled scornfully. "I don't suppose the Revolution will come tomorrow. But in the meantime, a fellow can work, like Debs, to see that the working man's condition is improved: higher pay, shorter hours, medical insurance, old age pensions. These are all in effect in Germany now."

"The Emperor gives and the Emperor can take away. You wouldn't call Germany a Socialist state, would you?"

"No. Though it's easier to give than to take away. But I grant you—no, I don't think Socialism has come to Germany. The laboring class's fidelity to the Emperor is bought and paid for by the measures that give them security."

"Do you think security's all that important?"

"For millions who have never been sure of their next meal? Don't you?"

"I value other things more. I know you're thinking I can't judge, since I've always had security. And so I have, if you mean security in a material sense: a roof and food and clothing. But no one is really secure—not against the misfortunes that are more important: illness, disappointment, sorrow."

She had spoken too freely: the reference to "sorrow" had embarrassed Franz. He said, "I suppose—well, I wish you'd read Marx, because I don't explain it very well. Now I guess I'd better earn my ten cents an hour by shelving those books." And he moved away.

Young Franz was such a sobersides when he was attempting her conversion that Anne was relieved to note that in the company of his contemporaries he could be as silly as they were, engaging in the inevitable nonsense that, intended to be *sotto voce* and unnoticed, ended more often than not in fits of giggling, books dropped, and shelves in disorder. She observed also that Mary Gardiner always returned her books and picked up others just before closing time, and that she and Franz went out together. She wondered whether Mary, at fifteen or thereabouts, was a convert to Franz's views, and could not help smiling at the thought of a Gardiner turning Socialist. Still, there was the Bodien blood so plain to be seen in Mary, and Captain Bodien had rebelled against his family, had run away and enlisted in the Army at seventeen. Or so he had told the children in the old days.

At the end of every Library day, however much satisfaction she had found in the work or her patrons young and old (even the critical ones who were never satisfied were sometimes a source of amusement), Anne was thoroughly tired: tired of meeting the public, and rather relieved to be under no further necessity to communicate with anyone except Johnny, who almost always dropped in after office hours in the evenings. For the first time she understood how Amanda Reid could bear to have lived alone for so many years, how she must even find pleasure in going home to an empty silent house after teaching all day. Anne was half-glad and half-sorry when Ruhamah returned from Albany and took over.

By the end of the summer, with life going on much as it had in everyone's memory, most people had forgotten that the new century was expected to be different and much better than the old one. True, year by year more streets were being paved: Chillicothe Street first from the East End to the canal bridge, then Main Street, and now bricks were being laid on Market Street, from above the Seminary, past the Rausches, past the Court House and Opera House, City Hall, past the Presbyterian church and the Gordons'—all the way to the canal. Curbs were put in and trees were sacrificed, but so many were left that the lost ones were not missed by the general public, and it was certainly a blessing to have crossings firm under foot and not ankle-deep in mud. Life on Market Street and one or two others was different in that it was much noisier than it had been: the milkman's clattering of cans, an old familiar sound, was no louder now than the clatter of his horse's hooves on the bricks; the iceman seemed to be driving a much heavier wagon on his daily rounds, rumbling from gate to gate, with the hooves of a team of horses pounding the pavement, stopping at every house, so that pieces of ice chipped off by his pick could easily be retrieved by the children who followed after him. Also, a few Waynesboro citizens, Ludwig among them, had purchased motor cars, and whereas previously they had seemed to most observers not only noisome but noisy, on the paved streets they were much quieter than the horses, whose shod hooves sometimes struck sparks from the bricks.

In September the event occurred that put out of the mind of everyone any idea that the twentieth century would be any better than the nineteenth. Late on the afternoon of September sixth, at the Buffalo Exposition, President McKinley was shot. Since Waynesboro still lived by sun time, the *Torchlight* had an extra on the street almost as soon as the tragedy had happened; housewives, hearing the garbled shouts of the newsboys, came running to their gates to snatch a paper, unable to believe their ears. McKinley, of all people! The kind man, the good man, whom everybody loved, and for whom now the women wept. Their husbands and breadwinners, home later from work than usual, having stopped uptown to see the bulletins in the *Torchlight* windows or to exchange horrified exclamations with their acquaintances on the street corners, came in to supper more cheerful or less realistic than their womenfolk: the doctors' bulletins were hopeful, the President had every chance of surviving. The women, remembering Garfield and his long ordeal, refused to be comforted. By the event they were justified: McKinley died, and even strong men wept. However dreadful other assassinations had been, they had not seemed quite so insane. Even those who had held McKinley in slight esteem had not hated him; to hate him was impossible. He was slain not for anything in his nature or his deeds but simply because to an anarchist he represented government, and government must be destroyed. It was a long while before the shock wore off. Anarchists belonged in the more benighted of European countries, not in America.

And though Theodore Roosevelt, newly sworn in as President, was still a hero to most of his countrymen, there were those who shared the opinion of Mark Hanna: "That cowboy!" Ludwig was one of them, though he chose a different epithet: "That showoff! He'll act on impulse every time he sees another chance to be a hero. Always wrong from the best motives."

"No, Ludwig." Sally tried to smooth him down; she herself had a sneaking admiration for the young President. "He may not be that bad."

"Let's say then—he may want to do the right thing, but he'll have to be spectacular in the way he does it, so it will turn out all wrong."

"You're not exactly clear."

"Wait long enough and you'll see what I mean."

However skeptical Ludwig might be, the new President settled the unease in the country by announcing that he would continue McKinley's policies. The spring's crisis on Wall Street was a thing of the past, only remembered when the compromise over the Northern Pacific and the Burlington had finally been worked out: the Northern Securities Company was launched in November, a holding company taking over the stock of both the railroads and issuing its own in return, with Harriman given three men on the board for his protection. Ernest's father-in-law had after all managed to survive, after a fashion: he was working for the brokerage house in which he had been a partner. He was living unostentatiously, he and his wife, in a New York apartment. Ernest wrote, with unexpected humor, that his father-in-law now deferred occasionally to his judgment, and "I never told him about your telegram: it is you who should have credit for good judgment. But I wouldn't have gambled anyway with what little I have saved. I have seen too many men burn their fingers, selling short." Ludwig was willing to let Ernest have the credit for financial acumen; he only hoped that Emily, who had been the dominating half of that marriage, had also come to believe that Ernest had more insight into high finance than he had ever been given credit for.

While the fall days were passing, Anne had felt them interminable, but when December ended and the paper reprinted articles and pictures of the Big Snow, in celebration of its anniversary, she was startled by the realization that John had been dead a year. She had always understood that as you grow older, the years passed more swiftly, but she was not that old—not yet: in 1901 just fifty-one. With years and years ahead of her, it was perhaps as well that they pass quickly, but it was rather startling just the same, having your life whisked away at such a rate.

She had had Thanksgiving dinner with the Johnny Gordons at Mrs. Deming's table, and, as she had always done before, asked them all to her house for Christmas. Tucker brought a new ball for Major, so that it was livelier than the holiday of a year ago, until Julia declared to Johnny that she could not stand the scrambling through the house a moment longer: either Tucker would have to play outdoors with the dog, or the dog must be shut in the kitchen. Johnny meekly obeyed, seizing Major over Tuck's protests and bearing him away to be company for Louline as she washed the dishes. Anne had rebuked herself often enough for being mother-in-lawish about the Gordons' relations with one another, but she could not help wondering. Tucker obviously adored his mther, but without any demonstration of affection: it was probably her remoteness and her beauty that had enslaved him, as they had Johnny. Anne granted Julia her beauty, greater now than it had been when she was younger: her flat cheeks and aquiline nose, her clean bones like sculpture, her ash-blonde hair like silk and her creamy skin, unlined and smooth. She never frowned, or seldom, though she did occasionally speak sharply to Johnny. It was Tucker's relations with his father that Anne found inexplicable: in the absence of Julia, the boy gave Johnny his open affection, in complete love and trust; if Julia were with them, especially if she spoke pettishly to Johnny, Tucker drew away from his father in what could only be described as fear. Of Johnny! Fear not for himself but for his mother. Anne could not believe that Johnny would ever speak to Julia in anger in the presence of the boy; it was possible, of course that they quarreled sometimes and were overheard. But puzzled as she was, anxious for Tucker to love his father as he deserved to be loved—still, it was none of her business; she refrained from any comment.

The year 1902 was ushered in with the usual hullabaloo, and the cycle of the months began again. It was not, nationally speaking, a dull year. President Roosevelt, however much men like Ludwig Rausch deplored not only his actions but his way of acting, gave his countrymen a certain what-next excitement; he provided them with more entertainment than any president they could remember. There was a constant succession of lively reports in the newspapers: trust-busting (beginning with the Northern Securities Company, which had been so painfully put together to end the Northern Pacific fight); and "malefactors of great wealth," the proposal to build a Panama Canal, negotiations with the government of Colombia. There was always something.

And Waynesboro, kept abreast of national affairs by the *Torchlight*, still went on about its own business much as it had always done, though trying to keep up with the twentieth century by laying sewer pipes and paving additional streets, by taking over the hitherto privately owned water supply, by franchising a locally owned electric power and gas company. And most important for the ladies who had kept the library going for so many years, the foundations of the new Carnegie Library were laid in the vacant lot behind the Theological Seminary, and the laying of the cornerstone was an event of the spring.

The Waynesboro Woman's Club continued to meet fortnightly; Sally

Rausch continued to be reelected President: who else would want to be bothered with it, or could give it so much time and attention? The new members were assimilated: Miss Campbell, who was adequate as an essayist and had a nice turn for dramatics, had also a sense of humor, surprisingly, and was amiable, not surprisingly; Janey Voorhees, whose essays might or might not have been written by her mother—any conclusion depending on the cynicism of the listener; pretty young Mrs. Rodney Stevens, who had undoubtedly inherited her father's brains, but who missed most of the winter's meetings because of her pregnancy, and, in the spring of 1902, the birth of her first child, a daughter, Theresa, named for her great-grandmother Bodien. In another year, after the summer vacation of 1902, her sister, the equally pretty and intelligent Mrs. Lowrey Edwards, was also invited to become a member.

The only stone to stir the town's placid waters was the marriage that same fall of 1902 of Sheldon Edwards and Jessamine Stevens. It was but a minor ripple, really, because the event had been expected by so many of their friends. With Lowrey married and young Richard in college and spending his summers at "digs" in the Southwest, Sheldon was free, and Jessamine had been alone since Rodney's marriage. It was judged, on the whole, to be eminently suitable; although young Mrs. Stevens had caused some lifted eyebrows when she had first come to Waynesboro, she had lived a discreet and circumspect life for many years.

Sheldon called on Anne before there was any announcement of his marriage plans: he had asked Jessamine to let him tell her, he said to Anne, because he wanted to explain.

"But Sheldon, there isn't any need to explain. Why should both of you be lonely when there's no need?" Anne protested.

"I didn't want you to think I had forgotten Kitty, how I felt about her."

"I would never think that. You have put her first for a long time: bringing up her boys and making a very good job of it. She would say so, I know."

"Kitty was always generous. She would understand, I think. She would know that I could not possibly feel for anyone else what I felt for her. Nor Jessamine feel for me what Kitty did. We are both middle-aged, after all. I hope not too set in our ways. I shouldn't be saying these things to anyone, I suppose, but I wanted you of all people to understand."

"I understand. To be alone is sometimes very hard." Then, because she preferred not to seem to be asking for sympathy, she asked abruptly, "Which house are you going to live in?"

"Oh, Jessamine's. I don't feel sentimental about my parent's house. Kitty never lived there; though I have used her furniture—ours—I couldn't expect Jessamine to move in and live with it. Lowrey and Caroline can have it, just as it stands. He has a right to his mother's things. I'll move out with just my clothes."

And that was the way it was done, and all worked out so simply that nothing much seemed to have happened, though members of the Woman's

Club found it difficult for a while to say "Mrs. Edwards" instead of "Mrs. Stevens." Hard for everyone except their President, who was in the first place always eminently correct in her presiding-officer role and, in the second, could not quite forgive Sheldon for remarrying.

Anne scolded her for being silly. "It's been years—Richard was a baby, and now he's in college. Why shouldn't he marry, for companionship, if nothing else?"

"They're not all that old. 'For companionship,' indeed! Would you marry again, for that reason?"

"I? Of course not. But I don't need company. And John and I had so many years together, Kitty and Sheldon so few."

"I wouldn't either. And if Ludwig did, I'd never forgive him. Not that he would be lonely. If I were to die, he would move the Evanses in with him."

Anne laughed. "You can't think how absurd you are. Sitting there talking about dying, when you're the picture of perfect blooming health. Putting on weight, in fact."

"If you weren't my very oldest friend, I should take umbrage, as the novelists say. To you I admit it. I am getting fat. But Ludwig does like a good table, and so do I. So there you are: I am going to be a fat old lady. And you'll be a scrawny one."

"At least, I suppose—" Sally went on, reverting unexpectedly to the Sheldon Edwardses, "there won't be any children. We are always short of Club members because so many of our young women are 'not going out.' Just when I suppose we ought to be thinking of doing something in honor of our thirty-fifth anniversary."

"Who? Lavinia Stevens had her baby a year and a half ago. Is she—? Or Sophie Lichtenstein again?"

"As to Sophie, it wouldn't surprise me. If she is, it isn't obvious yet. But first thing you know, Caroline Edwards—then it will be Lavinia's turn again."

Anne laughed delightedly. "Oh, Sally! How can you have forgotten? There were years when you were continuously in what is called 'an interesting condition.' Aren't you glad to see such nice people having babies—the old Waynesboro families so successfully reproducing?"

"I remember very well all those years when I had to stay home, either because I was going to have a baby, or had one. Elsa had more sense. But yes, I suppose I am glad to have so many prospective Club members appearing on the scene. And if in the meantime Club meetings are too small—well, maybe we should enlarge the membership again and take in some new members. If you would like to make a motion to that effect at the next meeting—"

"I wouldn't," Anne said flatly. "Have you any candidates in mind? Enlarge the membership, and everyone will come up with names to propose. No, leave it alone, Sally. We can worry through this year, and after that, who knows?"

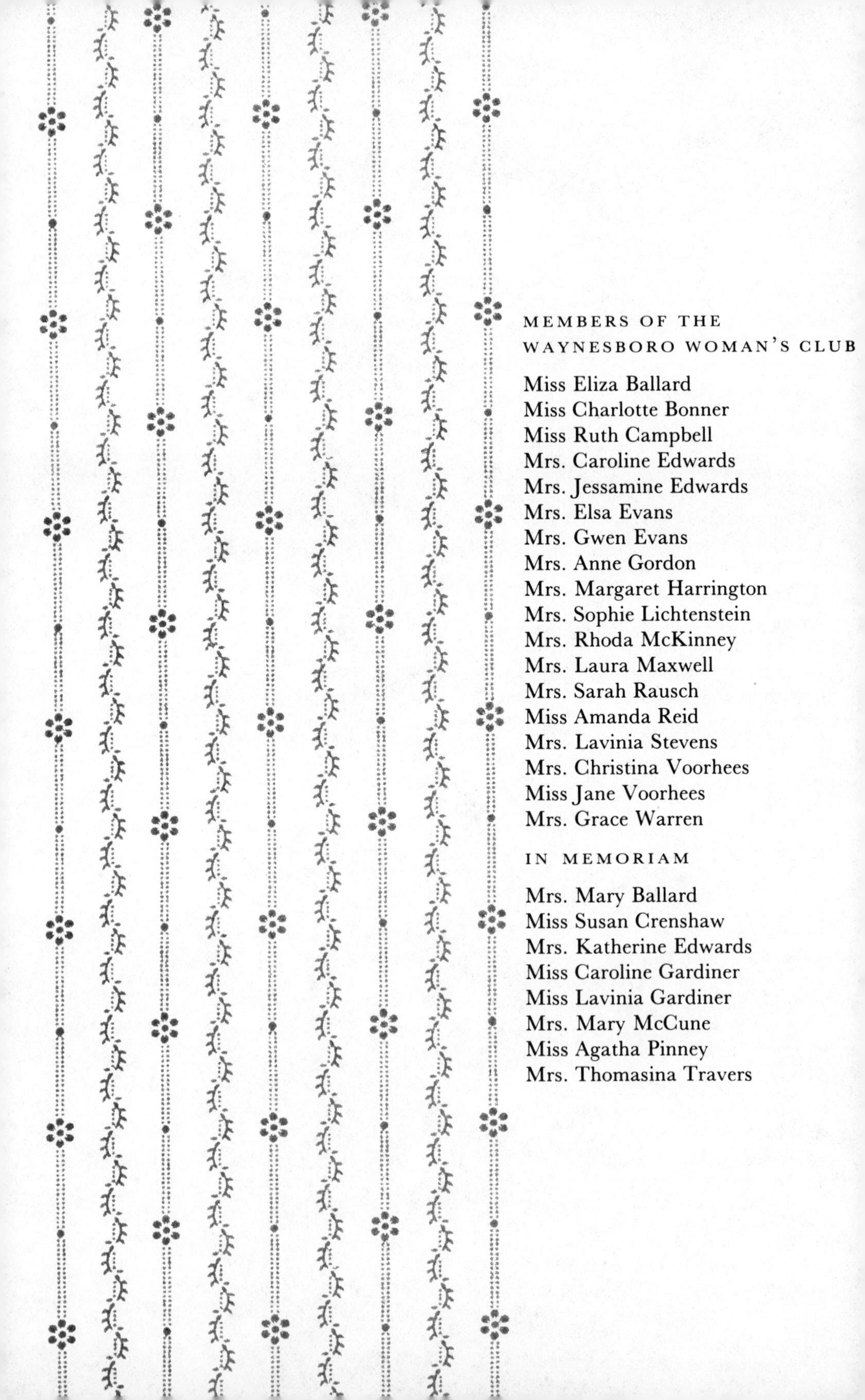

MEMBERS OF THE
WAYNESBORO WOMAN'S CLUB

Miss Eliza Ballard
Miss Charlotte Bonner
Miss Ruth Campbell
Mrs. Caroline Edwards
Mrs. Jessamine Edwards
Mrs. Elsa Evans
Mrs. Gwen Evans
Mrs. Anne Gordon
Mrs. Margaret Harrington
Mrs. Sophie Lichtenstein
Mrs. Rhoda McKinney
Mrs. Laura Maxwell
Mrs. Sarah Rausch
Miss Amanda Reid
Mrs. Lavinia Stevens
Mrs. Christina Voorhees
Miss Jane Voorhees
Mrs. Grace Warren

IN MEMORIAM

Mrs. Mary Ballard
Miss Susan Crenshaw
Mrs. Katherine Edwards
Miss Caroline Gardiner
Miss Lavinia Gardiner
Mrs. Mary McCune
Miss Agatha Pinney
Mrs. Thomasina Travers

* 1904–1905 *

"We lose two of our members to 'Sunny California' . . ."

In the spring of 1904, word came to the Rausch Cordage Company by way of Charles in Kansas City that the wheat crop promised to be so large that there was sure to be a shortage of binder twine: could the mill get out a rush order? The result was perhaps the most spectacular of Rausch Cordage's successes: enough sisal hemp was ordered and delivered, prepared, spun, and twisted, to fill a dozen freight cars lying ready on the siding. On the morning in May when the train was loaded and ready to pull out, the mill whistle was blown, and the hands piled out of the mill to watch its departure. The engineer, joining in the spirit of the occasion, blew his whistle, too, and kept blowing it in triumphant toots, so that idle townsfolk collected where streets crossed the right of way to see the "binder twine special" pull out.

Ludwig was of course pleased: the binder twine would reach the wheat fields in time, and well ahead of that produced by rope factories farther east, which would have a longer freight haul. But he was not unduly triumphant. Indeed, as he said to Captain Bodien when they had watched the caboose round the nearest curve and disappear, he thought they would not see the like again. "The day for binder twine is about over. Except for small farmers with small wheat fields, they won't be using the reaper-and-binder and the steam threshing machine much longer. I remember, decades ago—in the eighties, I think—I saw a photograph of a combined reaper and thresher. I laughed then—it took something like forty horses to pull it, and half the grain must have been trampled from keeping twenty teams in line in the stubble—you couldn't do it. But it won't be long now until some farm machinery company puts an internal combustion engine in such a machine, and there won't be any more binding and stacking of wheat. We'll have to think of something to take up the slack."

Captain Bodien, who in his heart felt nothing but contempt for so rough and cheap a product as binder twine, said, "There'll always be plenty of demand for good rope."

"We hope. Sometimes I think progress is going to put all us old-timers out of business. On the other hand, sometimes new machines mean new demands. Baling rope for the cotton crop never amounted to much. But if they take to baling hay in the field by machine, we'll profit: the hay crop is much greater than cotton."

The two men walked on in silence until they came to the mill, where they prepared to part, Captain Bodien to return to his office in the corner of the rope-laying mill, Ludwig to go on to his more spacious quarters. At that point Ludwig awoke from his preoccupation. "Sorry, Bodien, in the excitement I forgot to ask. How is Mrs. Bodien?"

"Not good." The strong stocky little man shook his head, his expression that of a hurt and bewildered child. "She's having trouble keeping her food down. A touch of jaundice, I guess."

"You have someone staying with her?"

"Barbara, mostly. The girls come in to help when they can, but they both have babies, and Lavinia's going to have another. But someone is there until I get home. Barbara is very good: tries not to let her mother see how worried she is. I guess the jaundice is a consequence, not a cause. The doctor wants her to have an operation."

The word hung in the air for a moment. Ludwig said, "Johnny Gordon?"

"Yes. Of course Rodney would do the operating. But I hate the thought, and she just plain won't have it."

"But if surgery could do something—cure, or help—"

They both shied away from the dread word "cancer" that was in their minds.

"You think she should? Stewart and Barbara are both trying to persuade her."

"I'd want to try anything. If it were my wife" (and God forbid!), "I should try to get her to consent. She can't go on long without food."

"No. I just hope—Johnny's giving her something for the jaundice. And she's afraid of the hospital."

"Anyone would be. But many seem to be finding it better than trying to stick it out at home, if they're awfully sick. It's always nearly full, I understand."

"Every doctor in town sends his patients there, I reckon. But I tell Johnny there's not much point in success if you work yourself to death. He looks mighty tired by the time he reaches our house. And all wound up."

"How is Paul doing?" Ludwig changed the subject abruptly as he saw his youngest son striding toward the door in the rope-laying mill. Paul, through college with an engineering degree at twenty—almost a prodigy—was still by his own choice working under Captain Bodien as a kind of assistant superintendent. He still seemed to Ludwig absurdly young for any such position.

"Paul? He's a bright boy. A lightning calculator."

"Just when adding machines and such are doing away with any need for human calculators. Progress again."

"It will be many a day before adding machines and the like can calculate tensile strength and breaking strength and elasticity and the right twist to fiber and strand to get what you need. Paul's a nice boy, too—he drops in most evenings to spend a few minutes playing for Mrs. Bodien—comes with Johnny, after Johnny's office hours."

"Funny friendship, Johnny's and Paul's. It was a case of extreme hero-worship when Paul had diphtheria. The boy even thought he wanted to be a doctor. Just when his mother had given up on Ludwig, and settled on him to be the family musician. Even now, he thinks Johnny can do no wrong."

"As I say, he plays his violin for us often, though without accompaniment the violin is kinda thin. None of us are piano-players, except Barbara, and she's gone home by that time. And we've got a perfectly good piano, too."

"I'm glad to know Paul's so obliging. He's been the family's spoiled baby all his life; it's to his credit that he is thinking of other people."

Not long after that, Mrs. Bodien was persuaded to go into the hospital for surgery. She might just as well have stayed at home in her own bed. Rodney operated, found far-advanced cancer of the liver, and sewed her up again. On his advice and Johnny's, Captain Bodien took her home as soon as she could be moved.

"You never can be sure with cancer of the liver." Rodney was not one to mince words. "She may be ill for quite a long while. I suppose Mother Gardiner will continue to spend days with her. Vinny and Caroline can take turns relieving her—they can always dump their babies on each other or on my mother. But Grandmother Bodien must have a night nurse: you can't stay up with her and work too."

"But Lavinia—" Lavinia Gardiner Stevens was pregnant for the second time, when the little Theresa was not yet three.

"I know—she'll be incapacitated for a while when the baby is born. But they can manage the days between them. A night nurse you must have."

If Captain Bodien resented his grandson-in-law's dictating matters to him, he let no sign appear. He said, "That cousin of Stewart's wife—what's her name—Norah—you know that family of O'Neills? Kathleen's rather disreputable cousins? The oldest daughter has finished her nurse's training."

"I know. She applied for a position at the hospital, but we've all the staff we need." Since Norah O'Neill was almost a connection of his, the cousin of his wife's aunt-by-marriage, he refrained from saying that although the hospital in Cincinnati had recommended the girl without reservations as to her nursing skill, it had been rather more than ambiguous as to her character. But after all, what mischief could she get into at the Bodiens'? And there was so great a gap between the West End and the rest of Waynesboro that no one who mattered would be watching her off-duty conduct.

Norah O'Neill was duly installed as night nurse at the Bodiens'. She started her nights late, leaving Captain Bodien alone with his wife through the supper hour, so that she could stay until nine o'clock in the morning, giving Barbara time to have breakfast with her husband before she came to take over. Norah never saw the Gardiner daughters, although she knew that they were there almost every day until Lavinia went into the hospital to have her baby. Norah was an excellent nurse, cheerful, even amusing, deft and strong, brimming with vitality. The Bodiens saw her in no other light. They thought nothing of the fact that Paul and Johnny no longer arrived together of an evening: Paul came earlier, the doctor bringing Norah with him after his office hours. It was a long walk from the apartment she had taken, and only natural that Johnny should stop by for her and give her a lift. As often as not they entered the house to the sound of violin music and the sight of Paul standing at the foot of the stairs, whence Mrs. Bodien, her bedroom door open, could hear the music.

On one warm evening, when the doors and all the windows were open, Paul heard between phrases of the music, the voices of Dr. Johnny and Norah as they came up the path. Until then Mrs. Bodien's nurse had been little more than a wax figure to Paul, but there was something—some note of warmth, a relaxed closeness—in their voices that made him drop his bow and watch the door. The two came in together, decorously apart. Still, there hung about them an aura of satisfaction, content—repletion? (Paul had no words for what he saw.) At twenty-one he could still blush, although he was experienced enough to recognize—Could *Johnny*—? But Johnny was married to an iceberg, and Norah—She was not a pretty girl, in spite of her black Irish hair and blue Irish eyes, but she had a full figure, revealed by her nurse's uniform, clipped tight as it was around her waist, and her face was aglow with life and the enjoyment of it. In the moment it took the pair to reach the newel post, Paul's mind had compassed these thoughts. He and Norah exchanged a direct, revealing look.

With no quiver of embarrassment in her voice she said, "Good evening to you, Mr. Rausch. And do go on playing. Though I must say it would sound better with a piano accompaniment."

"There's no one to play the piano."

"You should try my little sister. She's home from school now. The sisters have taught her to play very well. Along with a lot of other accomplishments, useless for an O'Neill. I'll bring her along with me tomorrow night, and you can see for yourself."

Smiling she went past him up the stairs, Johnny following after. Paul, standing with his bow loose in his hand, could hear them in the hall above: Johnny's tense "Why that unnecessary complication?" and her reply "Not a complication. A distraction. Didn't you see? He knew at once. Ellen will take his mind off—"

That was all he heard. It was enough. He put his violin in its case and slipped out the front door. He wished desperately he had not seen, did not know. There would be Hell to pay if the two were as obvious to everyone as to himself. But of course, he thought, only those at the Bodien house would ever see them together, and the Bodiens had no thought for anyone or anything but the dying wife and mother. A lingering doubt remained in his mind: little happened in Waynesboro that all Waynesboro did not know sooner or later, and anything like this—he had heard enough masculine gossip in cigar stores and barber shops to know with what pleasure such a tale would be seized upon.

A mixture of revulsion and excitement that he could not control took him to the Bodien house again the following night. Norah, unaccompanied by Johnny, brought her sister. Paul forgot both nurse and doctor. He caught his breath at his first sight of young Ellen, slim as a willow wand, pretty as a picture: his mind tumbled through his collection of boyish clichés and found nothing worthy. She was lovely, she was beautiful—no use trying to think how lovely: she had the same gray-blue eyes and long lashes as her sister, the same black hair, but a saucy nose and a laughing mouth and a clear pink and white skin that flooded with color when they were introduced.

"Miss O'Neill says you will play my accompaniments. You understand: I come to play because poor Mrs. Bodien seems to like it. It would sound better with a piano, but I don't suppose it's been tuned in years."

"If Captain Bodien kept his promise," Norah threw over her shoulder, "it was tuned today. Try it."

There was no light in the Bodien parlor. Match in hand, Paul investigated: a wall-bracket gas lamp hung inside the hall door, and a kerosene one, its wick floating in a full bowl, had been placed on a stand by the piano. Paul lighted them both and spread some sheets of music open above the keyboard. When Johnny came in a half-hour or so later, the two musicians were absorbed, working their way through the Irish airs that were Mrs. Bodien's favorites.

In a little while Johnny stopped on his way out to look into the parlor. "Mrs. Bodien's asleep. You're excused, unless," he grinned at them, "you are playing for your own pleasure."

They stopped at once. Ellen said, "Oh, no—I don't mean it wasn't a pleasure, but it is time I was getting home."

Paul said, "I'll drive you home in my motor car: it's out front." He laid his violin in its case on top of the upright piano. "I'll leave this here. I don't have the time to practice, anyway. You'll come again tomorrow, won't you?"

"Unless Captain Bodien would rather we didn't. He may think it's heartless, the playing of such tunes when his—when he is so full of sorrow."

Captain Bodien had in fact a stomachful of troubles. Sick at heart over his wife's suffering and his prospective loss after forty-odd years of a happy marriage, he had in addition to submit to the constant attendance of the priest, whose presence at her side seemed to mean more to his wife than having her husband there. "Forever stumbling over Father Halloran," he complained to Barbara. "Home's not my own anymore." And then, to add to his distress, his granddaughter Mary—the granddaughter he had loved and laughed at all her life, and the only one of the four Gardiners that was like him, unfortunately plain but unmistakably a Bodien—came home for the summer from her first year at college not for the fun of a Waynesboro vacation with all the other young people, most of whom liked the world very well as it was and enjoyed it to the fullest, but fired by the desire to remake, determined to improve the condition of Labor with a capital L. She unfortunately decided to begin her crusade at once, and with the Rausch Cordage Company. She marched boldly into her grandfather's office one day with Franz Lichtenstein, also home from college, at her heels. Since she had been a small child, Mary had been familiar with that crowded office, whose thin walls vibrated to the roar of the big rope-laying machines. She was not in the least bashful about tackling her grandfather, though Franz at twenty felt some trepidation at confronting the fierce-looking like Captain. Mary was not even taken aback to find Paul Rausch at a smaller desk that had been squeezed into the cubicle. She knew him too well as one of Veronica's high school beaux; she looked upon the light-minded Veronica with something like contempt. Perhaps Paul did, too, now that he was grown up: she hadn't seen him around all summer. (And Veronica, whose aim in life was to get away from Waynesboro forever, had somehow attached to herself her roommate's brother, a Clevelander.)

"So this is where you work," she said. "I want to talk to Gramp in confidence. Can't you take your papers somewhere else?"

Paul did his best to look down his nose at her, difficult, since, trying to rise as politeness demanded, but hampered by lack of space, he was bent awkwardly over his desk. "As it happens, these are fairly important calculations. If I'm interrupted. I'll have to start all over again."

"You've been interrupted. And I have no intention of discussing the matter I've come to discuss in the presence of the boss's son."

"Oh, Lord! What are you up to now? Some of your Socialistic nonsense, I suppose. I'll move over to the other office and prepare Pop." He began scrabbling his untidy spread of papers together.

"Not a word to your father, till I'm ready to talk to him."

Paul went out, his nose definitely in the air once he was clear of his desk.

"What in the world, Mary? What are you up to?"

"I want to talk to you about labor conditions in this mill."

"What's wrong with them? A ropewalk isn't a very clean place to work, but they're used to the tar—and even the de gras, smell though it does. They're satisfied, far's I know."

"What do you pay them?"

"Mary, it isn't any of your damn' business. An' most of 'em would say so, if you asked them. But in case you found some who didn't, I might as well tell you. The spinner girls, six dollars a week. Unskilled labor, mostly niggers, seven. Skilled labor, the men who lay the rope, it depends: eight to ten dollars a week. Anything wrong with that? A dollar a day is a good wage, even for skilled labor."

"It's abominable. How many hours do they work?"

"Fifty-four, since we've been shutting down Saturday afternoons. Unless there are orders we have to finish."

"And they don't realize they are being exploited?"

"If they don't like their wage and pay, they can always quit. Tell the truth, the niggers oftener than not lay off in summer—with garden truck and fishing they can make out all right without working—working's the thing they'd least rather do, given a choice."

"If they were paid more, they mightn't mind working. Gramp, you don't realize how unfair it is? These are the ones who produce the goods. But you are paid a big salary. Even that whippersnapper Paul Rausch, I suppose."

"Paul earns every cent he's paid. D'you think the hands could run this mill without us?"

"And as for Mr. Rausch: he has grown rich, exploiting his workers."

"'Exploiting!' You don't know what you're talking about, you ungrateful young ninny. How much of your father's income—and it's sending you to college—comes from his fees as attorney for the Rausch interests?"

"But he's been Common Pleas Judge for years. How can he—?"

"He's held on to his practice, of course—as much as he has time for."

"If that's the way the law works, I'd rather be poor." She stared at her grandfather defiantly. Captain Bodien too was getting hot under the collar by now. They were amazingly alike, glaring at each other: the man in his sixties, the fringe of hair around his bald head well sprinkled with gray, and the stocky, square-jawed young girl.

Captain Bodien let out a held breath when he thought he could safely speak. "And what is the purpose of this interview, may I ask? Did you think you could come here and tell us to increase our workers' pay and shorten their hours, and that we would say 'Yes, of course. Anything to oblige'?"

"I am not so naïve as to expect anything except under compulsion. We came, Franz and I, to ask you to let us organize a union, and to warn you that if you say 'No,' we'll do it anyway."

"A *union*? There isn't a unionized rope company in the country. Unions mean nothing but trouble: higher wages mean higher prices—you price yourself out of competition, and first thing you know, you're out of business. Union, indeed! This Cap'n Rausch must hear. Come along." He stamped out ahead of the pair, crossed the yard to the company office, threw the door open, and motioned them in.

"Sorry, Cap'n, if I'm interrupting something important. But I want you to hear what these young people are up to."

Ludwig was in the middle of dictating letters to Eliza. He said, "It's all right. Eliza knows as well as I do what to say in acknowledging these orders. Just so you get the hemp orders in the mail—leave the other things on my desk. I'll sign them. Close the door behind you, will you? And tell Paul he can get back to his own desk. Now, what is it that is so important?"

"These infant anarchists—"

"Not anarchists, Socialists," Franz corrected emphatically. He had left her grandfather to Mary to handle; he was ready to take on this more formidable but (he hoped) less irascible, antagonist himself, logically and rationally.

"Ah, you are the Lichtenstein boy? Of Course. Your father is a very old friend of mine. I know he is a Socialist, has been for years. Naturally—"

Franz caught his implication. "A theoretical Socialist. We mean to act, Mary and I."

"Mary Gardiner? Mary, I haven't seen you to know you for years, not since you were a little girl." He smiled a little, remembering a certain Fourth of July. "How does your father feel about your views? Does he know?"

"He ought to. We've argued about them often enough. But he didn't know we were coming here today, if that's what you mean."

Ludwig tilted his swivel chair back, put his elbows on its arms, and locked his fingers together under his chin. "Now, as I understand it, Socialists believe all industry should be government owned and operated, and government should be in the hands of the workers. Where are you going to find men of the laboring class who know enough to run the industries?"

"They needn't be of the so-called laboring class, if they were willing to work for the government."

"Industry in the hands of bureaucrats, under a government in the hands of the workers? H'mph. I believe the catchword is 'To each according to his need, from each according to his ability.' Who is to decide need and ability? Government in the hands of the workers? Who is to pay the bill? When everyone is to receive according to his need, whether he works or not, there will be a bill, believe me."

"We are not so cynical. We think men feel a need to work."

"So long as it's work or go hungry, yes."

"Do even the drones go hungry in Waynesboro? You know they don't. They're taken care of: alms, or the poorhouse. It's degrading."

"And when you do away with alms, and the government takes care of the drones and unfit, who pays the bill?"

"There won't be so many drones when men are better educated. The unfit will have free medical care. The bill will be paid by taxes on the profits of industry, of course."

"What profits, 'of course'? Prices of raw materials will rise, to pay the wages of their producers; prices of finished goods will rise; unless consumers are paid more, too, they won't be able to buy. If everyone is paid more, you will soon have inflation running out of control. And even if your workmen running the government find managers who can manage, there won't be any profits to go back. As for tax revenue, which makes the wheels go round, the government can hardly tax what it owns."

"All private property will be taken over by the state. There will be rents."

"Rents! Not a drop in the bucket, any more than residential property taxes are here. In this town the biggest taxpayer is the railroad. The government will of course own the railroads."

Franz nodded. "First of all."

"Then bang goes that source of revenue. Rausch Cordage Company is the second biggest taxpayer, I suppose, and next, your Uncle Hoffmann's bakery. Without them the town could not pay its police, its firemen, its schoolteachers."

Franz shifted uncomfortably in his chair. He knew the answers to logical arguments, if Ludwig's were logical, which he doubted, but the points he wanted to make seemed to be buried beyond reach in his mind. "We know that Socialism is a long way off, government ownership and all. It won't come tomorrow, but it will come, and all these problems will be worked out. But the condition of the exploited workman can be helped now, with the means at hand. That is what we came to talk about. Will you let us organize a union in your mill? Captain Bodien doesn't think you will of your own accord raise their wages or shorten their hours."

"They are being paid the going rate. Their hours are shorter than many, now we're giving them Saturday afternoons off. And except for the bobbin boys, they are paid by the week, not the hour. If they are not satisfied, they can quit. Labor is a commodity like any other: its cost depends on supply and demand, and the supply is adequate."

"'Labor is a commodity,' but workmen, even mill hands, are human beings."

"Workmen become human beings when they are treated as indivduals. This is a small plant. I not only know my men as men, I know their problems, domestic and otherwise. They are always free—and feel free—to come to me or Captain Bodien with their troubles. But if they don't like working for us, they can be replaced."

"Not so easily, when there is a union: scabs would be driven out. As for their coming to you with their problems—what do they call you?"

"'Boss,' ordinarily."

"You see: do you think that means they regard you as their friend?"

"I have always thought so. We have had a friendly, free-and-easy feeling in this mill. Do you prescribe to the pernicious theory that the boss and his workmen must be antagonists?"

"A capitalist and his workmen are naturally antagonists, since their interests are opposed."

"What nonsense! Their interests are identical: to keep an industry running at a profit, so that all can earn a living. You've been reading some pretty one-sided stuff. That jailbird Debs?"

"I would vote for him if I were old enough to vote."

"Then your vote would be wasted."

"Marx says—"

"To the devil with Marx! Look: you didn't come here to explain Socialism to me. What did you want?"

"To ask you to let us organize a union."

"You expect me to say 'Bless you, my children: assemble the workmen out there in the yard and organize a union'? No. Unions have caused enough trouble in this country already. Let's not have any of that nonsense here in Waynesboro."

"We were sure that was what you would say, but believed we should ask you—warn you—before we took action. We mean to go ahead. If we can't speak to your workmen here, we'll hire a hall."

"Try the Opera House," Ludwig said drily. "It belongs to the city—that is to say, the government. You would only have to pay for lighting it, and janitor service."

"That's a good idea. Thank you, sir." Franz rose, and the silent Mary with him. "You'll hear from us again." And with that parting shot he ushered Mary out of the door.

"The impudence of the rascal!" Ludwig couldn't help laughing.

"You kept your temper better than I did."

"Don't think I didn't feel angry. Those chits! Not dry behind the ears."

"Do you think they can make trouble for us?"

"God knows. Unions have made trouble enough for other companies. But I doubt it. Our labor force probably doesn't know the meaning of the word, and we could replace them easily enough anyway. We could train a new lot of spinners, if need be. It's the skilled labor, the men who have to know rope and how to lay it: if they went out on strike, they would be hard to replace. On the other hand, they have but the one skill, and there are not so many ropewalks in the country. They might hesitate to run the risk of losing their jobs."

"You would let them strike, then, and fire them if they did?"

"I'll fight this nonsense, of course. A union, indeed! And an end to friendly relations with the hands. I'd give them a chance to come back—twenty-four hours, maybe, or forty-eight—before I started firing."

The next afternoon, when the five-thirty whistle blew and the gates of Rausch Cordage Company were crowded with departing workers, they were met by Franz and Mary with armloads of dodgers to pass out. ("Better when they are leaving," Mary had said. "It would be just like their bosses to stand at the doors and collect them if the workers were going in. Besides, we'd have to be there at six-thirty. Imagine having to be at work at six-thirty.") The dodgers invited all Rausch Cordage Company mill hands to attend a meeting at the Opera House on Thursday at eight (the next evening but one, so as to give them forty-eight hours to mull it over) to discuss the organization of a union, and to air any grievances they might have against their employers. No foreman, superintendent, or officer of the company would be admitted: all could speak freely.

Of course copies of the dodger were dropped at the gate, and equally of course found their way into the hand of Ludwig and Captain Bodien.

"I see we aren't invited," Ludwig said, when the two got together.

"Did you think we would be?"

"No. I'd like to hear, if they have real grievances to air, but I won't stoop to looking for a spy among my men."

The *Torchlight* reporter (one of the Bonners) had insisted that the movement would be helped by publicity, and had attended the meeting. He was almost as good as a spy: a full account was printed in the Friday evening paper. By that time, however, Ludwig knew all that he wanted to know: he was visited by a delegation of workmen—"Union representatives"—in his office on Friday morning. Two were white men from the preparation room, and one was one of the spinner girls. The spokesman informed him of the organization of the union, of which he had been elected president; of the collection of dues, which would keep the union members going if they had to strike; of their decision to demand certain things of the company: first, recognition of the union and the right to strike; second, an increase of a dollar a week in everyone's—man's, woman's, boy's—wage; and third, a shortening of the work week by four hours.

Ludwig heard him out in silence. "Before I answer these demands, let me ask you this: did anyone take advantage of the chance to speak of any particular grievance against the company? I should like to know if there is anything I can set right, if the complaint is a reasonable one."

"Only Ji—" The spinner girl started to speak, was sternly silenced.

"No names, woman. D'you want him fired?"

"Have I ever fired anyone without just cause? Did it take only one evening of haranguing by those half-baked kids to turn you against me? You yourself have worked here fifteen years or so; you know that in good times we make money and that in bad times I put you to work making all kinds of junk rope and practically give it away, so there will be work for you."

"They showed us how we have been—what's the word?—been used, anyway—to make you rich. You owe us work in bad times."

"Good God, Pat Flannery! Never mind—What was the anonymous complainer's complaint?"

"That when the weather's bad and those of us as brings our lunches can't eat in the yard—an' them cobbles is damn' hard anyway—we got to squat around the machines."

"I always thought, from the horseplay I heard out there, you rather enjoyed that hour on the cobbles. But I agree: in bad weather it wouldn't be so much fun." Ludwig was a little taken aback. "Why didn't someone of you bring this up before? It is what I do call a reasonable complaint: you should have somewhere inside. When the new binder twine mill is finished, the old one can be made over into a lunch room, instead of being torn down. But as for the requests—demands?—you were delegated to make, the answer is 'no' all along the line. No union. No raise. No shortening of the work week. These are demands being made at the point of a gun—I suppose you are threatening a strike? Even if I thought them reasonable. The answer is no, and no, and again no."

"Then we strike on Monday morning." The union representative sounded half-scared at even the threat of such a step.

"I don't know how many of you voted for this nonsense. The whistle will blow as usual on Monday morning. Anyone who is not back at work on Tuesday will find his place has been filled."

"You can't run the mill with scabs."

"Then we'll close it down till you come to your senses. You're all thinking of Captain Bodien and me as men who have grown rich as the result of your toil. Try asking yourselves whether we may not be rich enough to get along very well without making any more money here. To whom is this mill indispensable? Now, if that's all you have to say, get on back to work. The Captain and I haven't any more time to waste on you."

Three crestfallen laborers went out, sheepishly, but stopped outside the door and put their heads together. Ludwig and Captain Bodien watched them through the glass in the office door.

"I'm afraid you've made them mad, now, 'Boss'."

"They made me mad. One should know better than to expect gratitude, but I honestly thought they felt friendly."

"They do, really. Most of them won't go out, you'll see. I could spank Mary Gardiner for her nonsense."

Her grandfather was not the only one who felt such an inclination. That evening Judge Gardiner drove out to Hillcrest, where the Rausches and Evanses were spending the summer, to apologize for his black sheep daughter.

Ludwig took him inside to his den, leaving his womenfolk and various children to spend the evening on the porch. (Ludwig had put a strong rope swing there. On that particular evening two Evanses, Tucker Gordon, and the youngest Merrill were swinging as high as they could swing; inside, with all the windows open, the men's talk was punctuated by the sound not only of their laughter but of the thumping of their feet against the porch ceiling, which would in a short while display a curious exhibit of footprints leading nowhere.)

Ludwig got his caller seated, with a stein of beer at his elbow, and Doug plunged into his subject. "I came to tell you that I tried to put a stop to Mary's nonsense before it got started. But my children are too grown-up now to pay much attention to paternal advice."

Ludwig laughed. "That time always comes. They will choose their own paths, nor will Hell nor high water stop them."

"It used to be Veronica I worried about: she seemed to me to be growing up with all the nonsenical prejudices cherished by my aunts: she's light-minded, no doubt about it, and determined to marry a rich man and get away from Waynesboro. That's all she needs to live happily ever after. And seemingly she's found a likely prospect in her roommate's brother. And now Mary goes off the rails."

"I'm not sure I wouldn't prefer her type of nonsense to her sister's. She may outgrow it, and at least she is thinking of other people."

"She won't outgrow it," Doug said pessimistically. "And she'll probably marry that Lichtenstein boy and devote her life to Causes. What I want to know is, how much trouble is that couple making for you?"

Ludwig smiled rather grimly. "I've no way of knowing until I see how many hands join a picket line Monday morning instead of coming to work. But at best I'm afraid it will take a while to erase the notion that they are being downtrodden and exploited—to restore our old easy relationship."

It did not take as long as Ludwig feared. A boom of laughter cleared the air. He had gone into town very early on Monday morning, with Paul, in order to reach the mill before the six-thirty whistle blew, even, he hoped, before any pickets would be in line. The two Rausches, with Captain Bodien and various foremen arriving at the same time with the same intention, entered the mill by way of the office door when Ludwig had unlocked the street door; they all made their way to the second floor of the hemp warehouse, whose windows were near enough and high enough above the mill gate, still padlocked on the inside, to give them a vantage point for their observations. The solid board gate, ten feet high, was the only opening in the equally high board fence that surrounded the mill except at the ramp down to the canal. The fence was also presumed to be solid, but Ludwig noticed that boards were loose here and there: it must be mended if there was really going to be trouble.

Before anyone else turned up, well before six-thirty, a dozen or so pickets, wearing sandwich boards or carrying crudely printed signs—"Strike! Higher Wages!" or "Strike! Union Recognition!"—had collected in a shambling group outside the gate. Then Mary and Franz appeared, Mary having managed to be on hand at that unheard-of-hour; they lined the pickets up and set them marching past the gate and back again. Six-fifteen came. A flock of Negro men collected and watched the parade, shuffling their feet and muttering. Six-thirty came, but no whistle blew. "No fireman for the boiler," Bodien muttered, looking at his watch. "That's bad."

"They must all be somewhere in that crowd," Ludwig replied. "I don't think we've got that many hands. All the loafers in town must be here."

"Looking for excitement. They all want to know what's going to happen. Even the spinner girls." For there were some familiar rather frowsy looking girls and women in aprons milling about among the men, moving together into one clot.

And then the spinner girl known to the whole mill as "Big Liz" came striding across the canal bridge. She was a brawny Irish woman, nearly six feet tall and big-boned to match, and really the boss of the spinning room, although there was a foreman supposedly in charge. Big Liz crossed the bridge, came to the narrow path that ran alongside the mill on the canal bank, and hardly breaking stride, reached out and pulled off one of the loose fence boards and began swinging it around her shoulders. She yelled at the pickets: "A strike, is it? You'll see a strike if yez don't get out of me way. I dast any lily-livered coward to try to kape me from me job." She threatened a sign-carrying workman with the ten-foot board she was swinging as easily as if it were a lath. He dodged, dropped his sign, and retreated. The next man in line, hampered by his sandwich board, did not wait for her next swing but bolted. So did the next in line, and all the others. She paid no attention to Mary and Franz: they just stood to one side, looking more than a little crestfallen. By the time Big Liz had chased the pickets away, the watchman had the gate open; she went and stood by it and shouted: "Now, all you damn' fools git in here an' git to work. An' if there's any ain't here, they'll come when the whistle blows, soon as that good-for-nothin' Les Flood gits some steam up."

Ludwig and Captain Bodien doubled up with laughter as the shamefaced workmen dodged away from the angry woman. As Ludwig told his family at the Hillcrest dinner table that evening. "In the first place the niggers never had any intention of striking: they were bewildered by the whole thing, but scared to cross the picket line. They were glad to scuttle through the gate when Big Liz had cleared the way. Then the others, all of them, went following after, with Big Liz standing herd on them. When they were all inside, she tossed her board aside, brushed off her hands, and turned to the two kids. She said. "And don't you be mixin' in anybody else's business till you know what it means to have a job that saves you and your kids from starvin'."

Sally laughed at his tale, but she was still troubled. "You think that will be the end of it?"

"It will be the end of it. You never saw such a sheepish collection of men. I'm only sorry Gib had to go to Chicago and miss it."

"Mary Gardiner ought to be turned over her father's knee."

"The girl is grown up. As I told Doug the evening he was here, a time comes when you can't antagonize your children without losing them. He'd better not even argue with her. He isn't going to change her opinions—not now, anyway. She is determined to make the world over: no more poor, no more rich, no more this and that."

"'The whirligig of time'," said Sally, "surely does 'bring its revenges.' I remember very well when Doug's aunts almost refused to join the Woman's Club because the Ballard women were members: those unfeminine, crusading *Reformers*. Does Doug think she will outgrow this phase? I suppose the Bodien side was bound to crop out in one of the children."

"Sally! Still thinking Doug married beneath him? Waiting all these years to see it proved? You don't really believe it. Barbara has been just the wife Doug needed, and I don't know a happier couple. If you do believe it, then there's worse to come, in your eyes. Doug thinks Mary will wind up marrying Franz Lichtenstein."

"Good Heavens! The Gardiners have a positive bent for *mésalliances*."

"Don't exaggerate, Geliebte. The two oldest girls have observed all the conventions, and are, I believe, honored members of your Club. And there's nothing off-color about Franz, except his wild ideas."

"There's nothing wrong with the Lichtensteins, Mamma." Elsa spoke for the first time. "Their father's brought them up to think as he does, just as you and Papa have brought us up to vote the straight Republican ticket were the devil himself running. Rudy's a nice fellow, and he and Sophie are perfectly happy, raising their children on less then nothing, and keeping them happy and healthy, too. And you know we don't have a more intellectual Club member than Sophie." Then she changed the subject. "Where is Paul keeping himself these days? He comes home nights after I'm in bed and is up and gone so early I never see him. You should never have given him that automobile, Mama."

"He's old enought to be independent. When we're in the country, he can't be expected to come and go with his father. Or stand around waiting for the trolley. Of course he wants to spend his evenings in town with the young people."

"He isn't spending them all with the young people," Ludwig said. "He goes often to the Bodiens of an evening, for a while, anyway, and plays the fiddle for Mrs. Bodien. Captain Bodien says she counts on it—it's the only pleasure she has left except what she gets from her religion."

"Ludwig! But how *morbid*, spending his evenings with a dying woman! You should have told me. Paul's too young."

"Not *with* her, Sally. Downstairs in the parlor, where the piano is."

"Who plays the piano for him?"

"How should I know? Some friend of the Bodiens, I suppose."

If Sally felt any misgivings about these musical evenings, she said nothing more. But when the blow fell on the Rausches, in the early fall, after they had returned to town, she was glad she had not said anything to anyone about any possible Gardiner *mésalliance*, considering the trouble she and Ludwig had to face. The bad news was brought to her by Ludwig, who had caught the full brunt of it in person, in his office, near the end of the working day.

Captain Bodien had ushered in the Catholic priest from the yard just before time for the whistle to blow, and as he introduced him, grimaced over the black-jacketed shoulder what Ludwig took to be a warning.

Ludwig rose, shook hands, said, "What can I do for you, Father?"

Captain Bodien said, "He wants to talk with you in private."

"In private? Then sit down and we'll talk about the weather until closing time. If I were to shut the door between this office and that one—" He inclined his head to indicate the room beyond, the front entrance vestibule, whence came the clacking of typewriter and adding machine. "The door is never closed: they would be consumed by curiosity. They'll all be gone in a few minutes."

When Eliza brought the last of Ludwig's letters to be signed, the two men—Captain Bodien had slipped away quickly once he had made the introduction—were talking about Mrs. Bodien, whether anything could be done to make her more comfortable until the expected end came. Eliza looked at them curiously, but made a prompt exit. When the whistle blew, she put on her hat and gloves and took up her purse; she was first out of the building, followed at once by the bookkeeper and his accountant-assistant, and by Gib Evans, who was in town that week to go over his orders with Ludwig. He paused only long enough to say good-night to his father-in-law, who dismissed him with a "See you tomorrow, Gib." When the outside door had closed after the last of them, Ludwig said again, "What can I do for you, Father?"

"I am not sure what you can do," the priest said slowly. "Or whether you will want to do anything. It's about your son Paul."

"Paul?" The wild idea crossed Ludwig's mind that perhaps the boy wanted to turn Catholic.

"Yes. I hardly know how to put this—perhaps bluntly will be best. I am sure you have no inkling—The boy has seduced one of my young parishioners, and she is with child."

"*Paul?*" Ludwig got to his feet slowly, flushing with anger. "I don't believe it. I mean, you must be mistaken. Wait—" He went to the door, called to the watchman already on duty, "If Paul hasn't gone, tell him to wait for me. I want to see him in my office presently." He returned to his desk. "Now—let me have it. Who is the girl?"

"Ellen O'Neill. Norah O'Neill's younger sister.

"Norah O'Neill? Mrs. Bodien's nurse? But she's well-known—" he bit off the rest of the sentence: "to be carrying on with Johnny Gordon." It wasn't the sort of thing one let slip about a friend, and anyway, gossip—how could one be sure it was true?

Father Halloran said, "I have nothing to say about Norah O'Neill. She is a lapsed Catholic. I know her reputation. But the youngest daughter is just out of convent school and has always been devout. I have wondered why she hasn't been to confession all summer. And now this. Norah came to me with the tale this afternoon."

"You mean she came to confession? But if it is her sister—"

"No, no. Had it been a confession, I could not be here telling you. She came to the rectory to tell me about it because she wanted me to do something."

"Go on."

"Ellen was graduated in June from the Ursuline Academy in Cincinnati. Her education was made possible by Stewart Bodien's wife, who I believe is fond of her young cousin, and wanted to give her a chance to escape from her family. I don't know whether you know the Dan O'Neills."

"I know him. He does occasional labor in the mill, when he's sober. You mean to say Paul and his daughter—?"

"Don't judge Ellen by her father. She's an innocent who fell head over heels in love."

"According to Norah?"

"According to Norah, who is feeling guilty, or pretending to, because she brought them together. It seems she suggested Ellen as an accompanist for Paul's violin when he goes to play for Mrs. Bodien."

"Then this has been going on since last spring?"

"I believe so. When Norah took this job as night nurse for Mrs. Bodien, she moved into an apartment—she calls it that—two rooms and an outside entrance in Mrs. Sullivan's house; she had to have a place where she could sleep in the daytime, which was impossible at home."

"And the youngest girl had permission to use it? At night, after the musical sessions? Are you asking me to believe that Norah didn't know what was going on? What would happen? Possibly planned it?"

"I am not asking you to believe anything except that Paul is the father of Ellen's unborn child. I have no idea what Norah's plans were. I hold no brief for her. But she came to me in great distress because when she wormed Ellen's secret out of her, Ellen said she had not told Paul, would not tell Paul, and if Norah told him, she would run away."

"What did she plan to do?"

"Return to the Ursuline sisters and throw herself on their mercy."

"I think we had better hear Paul's side of the story." Ludwig went once more to the door, called to the watchman, "Did you stop Paul? Then send him here, will you?"

Paul came in, tall, slender, dark except for his gray eyes, utterly unlike all the other Rausches. At the moment he looked more than a little frightened.

"Yes, Papa?"

"Paul, you have never lied to me in your life, far as I know. I want the truth from you now. Did you this spring—this summer—seduce young Ellen O'Neill?"

Paul stopped short, still several feet from the desk where his father sat in judgment. His cheeks flushed. "That's a—a horrible word. It sounds as if I started out intending—as if I planned it. It just happened. We fell in love."

"You became her lover. Were you the first?"

"Please, Papa, don't make it sound so nasty. It wasn't—and of course I was the only one. She was just out of school or she probably wouldn't have looked at me twice."

"And you took advantage of her sister's having an apartment that was empty every night?"

"We—we went there, yes. Sometimes. Sometimes we just went riding."

"She is carrying a child. Is it yours?"

The flush and all the natural color drained from Paul's face; he went to his father's desk to steady himself against it.

"Good God, no. I mean, I don't believe it. Why didn't she tell me? Of course if it's true, it is mine. There's never been anyone else. Why didn't she tell me?"

"Wanted to spare you the consequences, no doubt. What do you propose to do about it?"

"Do? Marry her, of course." His expression was defiant. "Tomorrow—the day after—as soon as possible."

Ludwig looked slightly less grim. "Then I shan't be compelled to coerce you. As I would have done, believe me: there will be no Rausch bastards in this town. But—I take it from your vehemence—you are willing?"

"Willing? Papa, from the moment I first saw her I wanted to marry her." The color crept back into his cheeks. He even looked elated. "Papa—I have your permission? I was afraid. I'm not of age."

"You should have told us."

"I know. But there would have been such a row—I couldn't screw my courage. Mamma—And I didn't know about this—"

"I'll take care of your mother. She won't like it, but—Never mind. You go ask your Ellen if she will marry you, and make your arrangements with Father Halloran. At the rectory, I suppose, Father?"

"Since Paul is not a Catholic, yes. With the usual conditions."

"Children raised Catholics, no doubt. There is no end to consequences, is there? Well, I'll go break the news to my wife. Paul, you'd better go out to Elsa's for dinner. Give me a chance to talk to your mother. And Elsa may help."

Ludwig was in such distress of mind that he was halfway to his automobile parked outside the mill gate before he remembered Father Halloran. He turned and called to him.

"Can I take you home, Father?"

"I haven't a long walk. Thank you and God bless you."

"Not even the respite of a few blocks out of my way," Ludwig thought. He cranked the automobile with such fury that it almost shook him loose when the engine caught. That woke him up. He must keep his emotions under control; he knew that a stormy interview was ahead: better wait till dinner was over and the servants out of the way. He drove with tears in his eyes: there would be no son to follow him, to take over the mill when he was gone. Paul could not live in Waynesboro with Dan O'Neill's daughter for a wife. He garaged the motor and went into the house by his usual route, called to the cook that he was home and ready for dinner and that Paul would not be there, washed, changed his shoes, and went to find Sally. He was astonished, somehow, to find her composed as usual, sitting in the library with the evening paper. He bent to kiss her cheek. She folded the paper to hand to him.

"I declare, there's less in the *Torchlight* every night. There's not even much about the campaign this year."

"It isn't very newsworthy. If Hanna hadn't died—but Roosevelt is popular, showing his teeth and waving his big stick. And who ever heard of Judge Parker?"

"Where's Paul?"

"He went out to Elsa's for dinner."

"He should have let the cook know. Honestly! He's thoughtless as a child."

"I told her as I came in." Ludwig shook out the paper and hid behind it. Sally did not really see him face to face until they sat down opposite each other, at the table reduced in size now to its smallest, all the leaves put away. But had it been as large as it once had been, Sally would have known at once that something had happened to upset her husband, something serious.

"What is it, Ludwig? Is it Paul? Has he been in an accident?"

"No. Ever since you gave him that automobile you have worried about his having an accident. I told you, he went out to Elsa's for dinner."

"Then what? Not more trouble at the mill?"

"No, no trouble at the mill. Leave it, will you Sally? I'd rather not discuss it until we are alone."

What with dread on Ludwig's part and apprehension on Sally's, they both toyed with their dinner in silence, only making some pretense at conversation when Rose came in to change the plates. Once safely back in the library, Ludwig went to stand by the still-covered fireplace. When Sally came up to him, he turned and said, "Better sit down."

"It's that bad?" She returned to her rocker.

"It's bad. And I don't know how to tell you. Except with the most vulgar of common phrases. Paul has got a girl in trouble."

"*Paul?* Not Paul! Of all the boys the most unlikely! How *could* he! What a worry that will be for you, and expense. But—" She drew a long breath. "I thought someone had died, at least. This is something that can be taken care of. You frightened me so."

"There is only one way it can be taken care of. One honorable way."

"What do you mean? Surely Johnny must know of someone—"

He looked at her in horror. "An *abortion?* Oh, Sally! And the girl's a Catholic."

"Then send her away somewhere until it's over. Who is this girl?"

"One of the O'Neills. Norah's sister. I can't even think of her name—but I will say to you what I said to Paul: I will have no Rausch bastard running around this town for fingers to point at. And don't say no one need know. Everyone would know. Her family would see to it. There is only one possible decent solution. He will marry her."

"*Marry!* A boy's light-of-love." Sally's voice turned to ice, to stone. "Over my dead body. You mean you would coerce him into it? He isn't even of age."

"There is no question of coercion. He wants to marry her. He is in love. He didn't know about the child until today. He wouldn't have known at all if Norah hadn't gone to the priest."

"Norah O'Neill! Johnny Gordon's—If Johnny brought them together, I'll never forgive him. Never. How can we be sure—how can anyone be sure—it's Paul's child?"

"It's Paul's child. The girl—Ellen, that's her name—just finished convent school in June. She's never known any boy but Paul."

"You can't be sure. Anyway, no doubt she was ready and willing. A rich man's son."

"She's so young—just eighteen—she probably never gave that a thought. The sister may have, if she threw them together. Do you think it is so unlikely that a young girl should fall in love with Paul?"

"Oh, calf love! What is the use of money if we can't use it to get out of mistakes like this? Give the girl a settlement and some good Catholic will be glad to marry her."

"Sally—" Ludwig groaned. "I have gone about this all wrong. I should have told you to begin with that Paul's in love."

"I could have put an end to nonsense of that kind, believe me."

"That was what he was afraid of, your opposition. That is why he didn't tell us how much in love he was."

"I won't have it, Ludwig. It must be stopped. Paul married to one of those O'Neills!"

"You can't stop it. I gave Father Halloran authority to publish the bans. They will be married as soon as possible."

Sally was silent for a long moment. Then she said, "I may be able to forgive you some day, but I swear—"

"Don't say anything irrevocable, Sally, please."

She rose and went close, stood facing him. "This I mean to be irrevocable. Never will Paul's wife, if this girl becomes his wife, enter my door. Never will I recognize her."

"Banish her and you banish Paul. Could you bear that?"

Tears filled her eyes; she breathed heavily. "We spoiled him. He's always had anything he wanted, and never had to suffer the consequences of any mistakes. Like renouncing his musical career. This whim he will have to pay for. If he prefers this—this Irish washerwoman's child to his own mother, then—"

"Don't say it, Sally, I beg of you. Think. Haven't you the pride to see you through this? By our attitude we can stop the town's talking."

"If you think so, you don't know this town. I will not countenance this marriage. If that gives the gossips food for talk, let them. That is the least of it."

"You will countenance it to this extent: you will go with me and Elsa and Gib to the priest's house to see them married. I cannot force you to invite anyone here against your wish. This is your house. Paul and his wife and children will be welcome at Hillcrest."

Ninety-nine times out of a hundred she had her way with Ludwig—until she came up against something of importance to him. This was one of those times when he gave the orders.

"Ludwig—" Sally was suddenly frightened by the threat of a gulf between them. Between her and *Ludwig*! She was living in a nightmare. She said, on a little different note, "I suppose you sent him out to Elsa's to win her over to his side."

"I sent him out there to spare him what you and I have just gone through. I may have been wrong. The boy is very much in love. He might have moved you."

"Never."

Ludwig knew that that was true. Poor Elsa, he was sure, had been maneuvered into a loveless marriage, which as it happened had worked out well, but only because Elsa had determined, with all her strength of character, that it would. He was sure that she would sympathize with Paul, but would get nowhere with her mother.

"Sally, I am not happy about this either. Believe me, an O'Neill would not have been my choice for Paul. But we must do the decent thing, even to the extent of accepting it without recrimination. At least outside this house let us keep silent."

"You say that when I have no doubt you have already talked it over with Captain Bodien."

"I have talked it over with no one except Paul and the priest who came to me. Bodien, I'm sure, had no idea of what was going on. Of course he heard them playing down in the parlor, the piano and the violin, but when he is at home he is thinking of nothing but his wife. She is dying by inches. Let me ask you just this one thing: do not—please do not say anything of what you feel outside this house. Don't even discuss it with Anne."

"Anne is the last person I would discuss it with. I consider Johnny responsible."

"Johnny? You don't know that Johnny had anything to do with it. I don't think he did."

"If he did not bring them together, he certainly set them an example."

"How can you be so sure? I didn't know you had heard that particular bit of gossip."

"I'm sure. He's looking sleek as a cat full of cream. Julia never made him look like that. It's a pity. Paul has always thought Johnny could do no wrong. If he could go to bed with one sister, why not Paul with the other?"

"Sally, Sally! How can you be so—"

"Vulgar? It's a vulgar situation. One thinks so when it is someone else's, why not when it is your own? What do you propose they do after they are married? Settle here, where Paul will be intimately associated with the O'Neills? His in-laws?"

"No. I cannot stomach that any more than you can. I was thinking about it on my way home. I'll ask Stewart Bodien to find him a place in the paper mill. They can live in Madison City. Paul is a bright boy—Stewart will find him useful. And his wife will be good to her cousin Ellen. It was she who put her through convent school."

"I always knew that in the end no good would come of the Bodiens. I wish you had never heard the name."

"Oh, come! If it hadn't been for the Captain at the rope mill and Stewart in Madison City, we wouldn't be where we are today. You have enjoyed those profits as much as anyone."

"We could have managed without them. Ludwig, I have had enough tonight. I can't face Paul. I am going to bed."

"That's sensible. In the morning you may feel better. I'll wait for Paul and then I'll be up."

She went upstairs, slowly dragged her clothes off, and got in bed. She did not sleep. She was not a woman who wept easily, and she did not weep that night. She lay on her back, in despair and in a fury. It would have been so easy for Ludwig—She could not say, even that night, that she would never forgive him: she had loved him too long. But whether her absolute trust in him would ever be the same—She had known him to put his foot down before, and successfully, but she had never contested him seriously because it had never happened over anything important to her, not as this was important. And although she knew that for himself he held to the strictest code of morality, he had always seemed indulgent in the masculine way toward the diversions of others of his sex. Who would have expected him to be such—such a *Puritan?* And at what cost to himself: she knew very well how pleased he had been to have Paul go into the mill, with every chance of his taking over one day. Now, none of his sons—But she felt no pity for him because what he was doing seemed to her so unnecessary.

She heard Paul come in and go into the library. He and his father must have talked for a long while: she heard no voices, but it was late when Ludwig came up to bed. When she heard him coming, she turned over on her side, away from his pillow, and pretended to be asleep. He probably knew that she wasn't, but he said nothing and went into his dressing room to prepare for bed, so as not to disturb her. And she could not turn over and give him the comfort he no doubt needed. She could not do it. And so for the first time in all the years they had been married, they lay side by side but estranged.

In the morning when Ludwig rose at the usual time, she said, "I am not coming down. Have Rose bring me some coffee."

She stayed in bed until she was sure that the men had gone and then forced herself to get up and dress. Elsa would soon appear, if she knew Elsa, and she preferred to be on her feet for the interview. She had not quite finished with her hair when she heard Rose go to open the front door, and Elsa's voice. She opened her bedroom door to listen.

To some soft-voiced query from Elsa she heard Rose say: "Yo' Mamma is po'ly, Miss Elsa. Ah neveh knowed he' not to come to breakfas' with the miste' onless she sick."

"I'll go up."

Sally returned to the dressing table and watched the door in the mirror. When Elsa came in, she was busy with her hairpins.

In that same mirror, Elsa could see her mother's face. She was shocked.

Her mother had aged overnight. Elsa had come intending to do battle for her brother; now she softened, realizing for the first time what grief her mother was feeling. Paul had been the Benjamin of the family, the spoiled but lovable and much-loved boy. She had herself, until now, thought only of what he was feeling, had known the anger, the opposition, the estrangement he must face, and had hoped to help him. Now—

She said, "Mamma, I have come to talk about this miserable situation."

"I prefer not to discuss it."

"It can't just be swept under the rug. I know how you must feel, but we have to accept it and put the best face possible on it."

"I cannot bring myself to accept it. I have no intention of trying. Your father has made the matter impossible, insisting on this marriage. There were other ways out."

"No other way, once Paul found out his Ellen was pregnant. Or do you think she could have been whisked away somewhere out of town before he knew it?" Then seeing by her mother's face that she had hit upon the truth, she added, "Mamma, can't you look at it from Paul's point of view? He is in love and ecstatically happy, now that he is to marry her. Don't you—can't you remember what it was like, being in love?"

"Sit down, Elsa. Don't stand hovering over me." Then Sally herself got up and began to pace the floor, her dressing gown sweeping the carpet behind her. "Love! He doesn't know the meaning of the word. He's only a boy."

"You gave him an automobile so that he could be independent. You didn't think of him then as a boy, did you?"

"I didn't want him tied to my apron strings, like Blair Voorhees. Queer. Tie them, and they break away. Untie them, and they escape you just the same."

"Children grow up. Please, Mamma. Paul doesn't want to 'escape' you. He just wants you to accept and forgive him."

"For what? Not telling me in the beginning what was going on? He wouldn't have dared: he would have known I would put a stop to it. The daughter of a poor-white family, with a—a designing harlot of a sister!"

"Mamma! Let's leave the sister out of it. Paul says he fell in love with Ellen the first time he saw her. And she with him."

"I really blame Johnny Gordon."

"Johnny had nothing to do with it."

"Hadn't he? I suspect he thought Paul was closing in on what he believed was a secret, but what everyone in town knows, and threw him the girl to distract him."

Elsa's sympathy was fast ebbing away. "Don't say that, for Heaven's sake. Gossip—and you accept it. You never used to believe gossip, you were above it. And whether it is true or not, if Julia ever heard it—"

"How fortunate you did not marry him."

"Johnny has never cared for anyone but Julia."

"May I say again, how fortunate for you! The Gordon men are womanizers. If Anne had had more spunk, years ago—Never mind that. Isn't there some way of stopping this madness of Paul's and your father's? The girl is a mere child with her life before her: one slip need not ruin her, especially if she had a settlement of some sort. Some nice Catholic boy could be found to marry her, then."

"Mamma! Please! I can't believe my ears. There are some problems that money cannot solve. As for Ellen's being a child: she is eighteen. I seem to remember hearing that you were eighteen when you met Papa, and fell in love at first sight."

"Girls of eighteen were older in those days."

"Nonsense. Mamma, you have been used to managing your family. But you couldn't manage Ludwig Junior. And you had better admit that you cannot manage Paul. Do you want to lose him too?"

"If he marries this girl, I will consider him lost. I told your father last night that she will never be welcome here!"

"You can't mean that!" With sinking heart Elsa realized that she did mean it. "You have always been an awful snob. But I never thought pure snobbery would make you break with your favorite son. I mean to have Ellen to dinner Sunday so that we can meet her. Won't you even give her a chance?"

"Paul and your father may go. I thank you, but I decline. I have no desire to meet her. Your father says we are going to the wedding, but after that—" She made a brushing away gesture with her hands as she stopped for a moment facing the window. "I promised your father—and after all I have some pride—that not a word of how I feel about the matter will be uttered outside the house."

"That's something, anyway. It would be dreadful if the whole town damned Paul's wife just because you did." She knew that this concession was the only one her mother would make. If she kept her promise, it might save Johnny from trouble. In her heart she too was sure that it was somehow through Johnny that the two young people had come together.

"It wouldn't matter much whether the town damned her or not. Your father is planning to move Paul to Madison City. But I do not care to have anyone saying the Rausches have had their comeuppance. I will at least appear to accept the marriage."

"Do you think the town hates us that much that it would gloat? That is nonsense. Papa is liked and admired. You are liked."

"Human beings are human beings. Envious of anyone who gets his head above the rest."

"You don't believe that, really. You couldn't be so cynical. Think how many friends you have. Don't let this unfortunate affair change you from what you have always been. Gracious and generous and liking people."

Elsa left her mother with a heavy heart. Time might perhaps soften her attitude. But Elsa wondered whether she was getting cynical herself: how many of her mother's friends would secretly rejoice at this blow to Rausch pride? And she remembered all too well how, just a few years ago. Christina Voorhees had blamed the Rausches for Blair's defection.

That evening the *Torchlight* printed a brief notice on its society page. Sally had not expected it; her heart stopped when the Rausch name leaped out from the column she had merely glanced at, and caught her eye: "Mr. and Mrs. Daniel O'Neill announce the engagement of their daughter Ellen to Mr. Paul Rausch, son of Captain and Mrs. Rausch of this city. The wedding is planned for mid-October." For the first time Sally really believed the unbelievable must inevitably happen. And Ludwig was of course responsible for that announcement: it was beyond the capacity of the O'Neills to have composed it or even thought of it.

In spite of her continued anger and despair, in spite of being sick at heart, Sally was as good as her word: she suppressed and concealed her emotions when she appeared in public. Elsa, who had held her breath, could not but admire the usualness of her mother's demeanor when she presided over the next Club meeting. But when the meeting had adjourned and the ladies were collecting their wraps, her hands-off stiffness showed plainly enough that she preferred not to discuss family affairs. Only one member—Christina, of course—dared broach the subject. She said, "You are about to lose a son, I see. It must have distressed you very much to have him choose a Roman Catholic."

"Paul is not of age, you know. But he is very much in love. We put no obstacles in his way." (Which, she thought, is only the truth, regrettably.) She looked over Christina's shoulder to Janey, hovering behind her mother. "It will soon be your turn, I suppose, Janey? I hear that a certain young seminarian is very attentive, and this matter of marrying is contagious." She immediately regretted having made so coy a remark, so out of character, to Janey Voorhees, of all people. She walked away without waiting to see Janey's unbecoming blush. That girl, she told herself savagely, must be at least twenty-two—she was older than Paul; she had better make the most of her opportunities: she would soon be older than the theologues.

In the hall she picked up Elsa, said a polite good-bye to Anne; with Elsa as protection she went on to the door; Elsa provided a diversion by bending to kiss Anne on the cheek and say, "We don't see enough of you—come spend the afternoon with us soon," and her mother escaped without having to exchange any confidences with her oldest and dearest friend. Anne, who knew Sally so well, was not as bewildered as she perhaps should have been: she concluded rightly that Sally was very unhappy, and wrongly, that she would hear all about it sooner or later.

The marriage took place as planned, in the presence of a few unhappy people, Rausches and Evanses, and several happy ones, the O'Neills, who considered Ellen very lucky, and hoped that the luck would rub off on them.

The *Torchlight* dealt as simply with the wedding as it had the engagement: "At ten o'clock this morning at the rectory of St. Barnabas, Father Halloran officiating, in the presence of the immediate families of the bride and groom, Miss Ellen O'Neill was joined in holy matrimony to Mr. Paul Rausch. Mrs. Rausch, daughter of Mr. and Mrs. Daniel O'Neill of this city, was educated at the Ursuline Sisters' Academy, Cincinnati, Ohio. Mr. Paul Rausch received his engineering degree from Case in June, and after the honeymoon will take up his new position at the Rausch and Bodien Coated Paper Company in Madison City, where the young people will reside."

It was after the adjournment of the next Club meeting that Sally was exacerbated beyond all caution, stung into speech by Mrs. Deming. Only a few words slipped out, but they could not be called back, and by them the damage was done.

Elsa was in the front hall, bidding her guests good-bye. Only Anne had the courage to mention Paul to her. "I am sorry not to have seen him, to congratulate him myself. Tell him I hope he will be happy 'forever after'."

"Thank you, Aunt Anne. Paul is ecstatically happy. As usual, he has got what he wanted, regardless."

"Don't worry. If his wife makes him happy, your mother will forgive her for snatching her ewe lamb." And Anne went on to the front door, leaving the next in line to shake Elsa's hand and thank her for her hospitality.

Eliza Ballard, Sally, and Mrs. Deming had lingered in the bedroom. Mrs. Deming was in front of the mirror, adjusting her hat, and Sally was awaiting her turn: hats that year were so wide and so burdened with fruit and flowers that the strongest hatpins would not long keep them straight. Eliza, who cared nothing for fashion and wore the same clothes as long as they held together, was beside the bed, slipping into ther coat, quite ready to go, except that she was curious.

Mrs. Deming moved and Sally took her place; their eyes met in the mirror, linked, and held. Mrs. Deming said: "I suppose you miss Paul very much, you and your husband alone in that big house. Boys are unaccountable creatures, aren't they? One never knows whom they will meet, nor where. How did Paul and his bride ever come together? The O'Neills are hardly in your social circle."

"Your son-in-law brought them together."

"Johnny? Whatever do you mean?"

Sally turned and left the room without ever hearing the question. Eliza was still there.

"I suppose she meant that she blames Johnny for introducing them." Eliza enjoyed creating a sensation, and was delighted with the startled question in Mrs. Deming's eyes. She sympathized with the Rausches, but by the evidence she had seen, the fragments of gossip she had heard, and some inspired guessing, she had come to the truth. "Oh, didn't you know? Johnny is a friend—an intimate friend—of the older sister."

"Oh, nonsense. She nurses some of his cases. That doesn't make them intimate."

She brushed off the innuendoes, but when Eliza had gone out, she stood rigid, staring at herself in the mirror. She had long ago heard that Johnny's father—but Johnny wasn't his father. If he were straying, Julia must take him in hand. She had no doubt of Julia's being able to deal with any such problem.

When she went into the hall, she found that Julia had accepted for herself and her mother young Mrs. Rodney Stevens' offer to drive them home, along with her mother-in-law Jessamine Edwards, who could be dropped off at her gate. The carriage was waiting; Rodney must have sent his man with it. As in a number of families in that decade, the horse and carriage had been turned over to the wife for her use when the husband bought an automobile. So long as the weather permitted—unless Rodney would have to put his motor car up on blocks in his converted half of the stable— Lavinia had the use of his horse.

As the four women climbed into the carriage, the talk was of horses and motor-cars. Jessamine was being very emphatic on the subject, and as always when emphatic, very southern: "Neveh, neveh, will I change my ho'se fo' one of those abominable contraptions. They a' a menace on ou' streets." The two younger women laughed at her: if her horse would quit standing on his hind legs every time he encountered an automobile, she wouldn't hate them so much.

Mrs. Deming let them rattle on, glad for their nonsense; she was planning what she would say, and how much, to Julia. When the horse was stopped at the Deming carriage step, she came to with a start and thanked Lavinia for the ride home. It *was* a rather long walk from the Evanses' and she was grateful; she waited for Julia to follow her. Once inside the gate she said, "Don't go upstairs until I have a talk with you."

"What is it? You sound portentous." But Mrs. Deming said no more until the two of them, having discarded cloaks, hats, and gloves in the hall, were settled before the fire. Then Julia asked again, "What is it?" and her mother, for all the planning on how to conduct the interview, was at a loss as to how to begin.

"Julia, some disquieting innuendoes were tossed in my direction this afternoon. Have you heard any gossip about Johnny?"

"Of course not. Who is gossiping?"

"Never mind that. What matters is whether there is anything behind it."

"What kind of gossip?"

"That he is intimate—perhaps too intimate—with that nurse who's taking care of Mrs. Bodien at night."

"*Johnny?* How silly! Who—? Of course it isn't true. Do you think I wouldn't know?" She stopped short. She really saw very little of Johnny these days, except at mealtimes, and even then he was often so late that she and Tucker did not wait for him.

"They say the wife is always the last to know. And even if it isn't true, Johnny should be warned that people are talking."

"*Talking!* As if that were important!" Julia was beginning to look pinched about the nostrils.

"Julia, I have this to say, whether you like it or not. I warned you before you were married, you may remember. If Johnny has—looked elsewhere—it may be partly your fault. Husbands have certain marital rights. And I suspect that you have denied Johnny, banishing him to another bedroom."

"Men are beasts sometimes. I cannot see that that gives them any right to make their wives behave in beastly fashion. If Johnny has a wandering eye, as you so delicately put it—or in plain English, if he has committed adultery—I will divorce him."

"Oh, Julia! Don't be ridiculous! Divorce! People of our sort don't get divorced. All you'll need to do is warn him." Mrs. Deming was so horrified that she regretted having said a word.

"I mean it, Mamma. I will not live under the same roof with an unfaithful husband."

"But to be a divorcee in this town—"

"Here? No. We'll go to California, you and I and Tucker."

Mrs. Deming was suddenly and astoundedly aware that the idea of a divorce was not repugnant to Julia. "You seem to have it all planned."

"I haven't enjoyed being married all that much. Yes, I have even thought how pleasant it might be to be free. Johnny can be so tiresome."

"Then you will be rather pleased then otherwise if you find you do have grounds?"

"No!" Julia came to her feet, her eyes blazing blue fire. "How can you say that? It is humiliating enough to know your husband is being gossiped about, but to discover you have lost him to another woman—it is disgusting that he can come to you and pretend that he wants—it is degrading." She dropped back into her chair. "Though come to think of it, it is a long while since he has knocked at my door. Maybe it is true."

As if on cue, the street door opened and closed; both women listened to firm masculine steps on the stairs. "He's home early. I may as well go and have it out with him. One thing, Johnny won't lie to me."

"Where's Tucker?"

"Where he always is, I suppose. At his Grandmother Gordon's, playing with that dog. Or running wild somewhere with Ludwig Evans and the other boys. Johnny insists he must have his freedom. Telephone his grandmother, will you, and ask her to keep him for dinner? If he isn't there now, he will have to take the dog back."

In the hall Julia scooped up coat, hat, gloves, and purse, and went firmly and steadily up the stairs. Still carrying her wraps, she went in to the sitting room, where Johnny had settled down with the evening paper.

"Oh, there you are. I forgot this was your Club afternoon. I got through my patients early, and thought we might have an extra hour together. What's the matter, Julia?" She was standing close, looking down at him accusingly.

"I may as well tell you without beating around the bush. The whole town is gossiping about you. You and the O'Neill woman. The Woman's Club—even those *ladies*, it seems."

He could only stare at her in silent shocked appeal, as the color drained from his face.

"Well! Say something. Is it true? She is your—mistress?"

After a long dismayed silence he said. "I'm sorry, Julia. She really doesn't mean anything to me. Nor I to her." He got to his feet, but as he approached, she withdrew.

"Then it is true?"

"Yes. It's true, I am ashamed to say. But it was just something that—happened—between two warm-blooded people."

"What an excuse!"

"It's no excuse. But I hope you will forgive me. You know very well that I have never cared for anyone else in my life—that I have loved you with all my heart since we were children."

"I did think so. Now I know that your love, so-called, hasn't stood any real test. It has just faded away, or your conscience would have you sick."

He groaned, dropped heavily into a chair, put his head down on his supporting hands. "Forgive me, Julia. Of course my conscience makes me sick. But she has had nothing from me that you ever wanted. I do love you."

"I want a divorce. I am going to have one."

He lifted his head and looked at her in shocked horror. "A *divorce?* Over this—this *nothing?*"

"I am not the complaisant wife your mother was. Oh, I have heard—your father—"

"Leave my parents out of this. Whatever he may have done wasn't important in the long run, either. If he did anything that called for forgiveness, she forgave him. Love forgiveth all things, remember? You can't really mean it, that you would divorce me? What about Tucker?"

"He's at your mother's. Don't worry about his overhearing. But if you mean afterward, of course when I go, I'll take him with me. The court will give me custody, considering the grounds."

"Go! Where are you going?"

"California. I hate this town; I hate this climate; I hate the gossiping hags in the Woman's Club."

"You just heard about Norah O'Neill this afternoon, yet you have your plans all made. Since when—?"

"Since you used to pester me so. I thought then, how pleasant—"

"You have been wanting to get away all that time? Julia, Julia! Then you never loved me, did you?"

"I have put up with a lot because divorce seemed to me so degrading. Now it would be more degrading to go on, with you chasing after—harlots."

Johnny flushed with anger. "So be it, then. Go see Tim Merrill—I won't contest a divorce. The case be heard in Judge Gardiner's chambers: no point in making a public show of it. I'll pack a bag and go stay at Mamma's. If you change you mind, for Tuck's and all our sakes, let me know."

"I won't changed my mind."

Johnny left the house knowing that she meant it; by the time he reached his mother's, he had persuaded himself that she might possibly be moved by the thought of Tucker, by the recollection of his long years of single-minded devotion. Yet he felt as though he were living through an earthquake: fences swayed and the pavement heaved under his feet; he clung to the gate at his mother's a moment before he opened it, straightened his shoulders, and went inside. He dropped his valise and his doctor's bag in the hall and walked into the living room, where he found his mother with Tucker, the dog lying beside him on the couch. She was reading the paper—inevitably, at that hour; Tucker, even while he played with the dog's ears, was reading the book open on his lap.

He said, attempting lightness, "Can you feed another guest? Julia isn't feeling very well."

Startled by his look of dazed shock, she said, "Is she really ill? She seemed to be all right at the Woman's Club this afternoon."

"No, no. She'll be all right."

Tucker studied him gravely. "Did you hurt her, Father?"

"Hurt her! Of course not. I never hurt her in her life."

"Tucker!" his grandmother said to the boy, who was looking at his father dubiously. "Whatever gave you such a notion? Surely you know your father better than that! Run tell Louline, will you, that there will be a third for dinner?" And when he had gone, "What is it, Johnny? Something has happened."

"Later—when Tucker has gone home."

The three of them ate a rather silent meal. Tucker's attention, fortunately, was diverted by Major, who sat close to his knee, begging. Ordinarily he was forbidden to feed the dog at the table, but that evening no one seemed to notice. When the adults had finished their pretense of eating and were leaving the dinning room, Johnny said, "Run on home, now. Keep Mother company. Hey—" as the boy obediently picked up his cap and raised his face for his grandmother's kiss, "Kiss me good-night, too, son. I am spending tonight here." The boy squirmed a little in his father's tight embrace, but kissed him and submitted to being kissed before he broke for the front door.

"Now, Johnny—" Anne pointed to his father's rocking chair and took her own at the other end of the hearthrug. "Out with it."

"It's a shameful story. Mom."

"What have you done that you are ashamed of?"

"You haven't heard any gossip, then? Julie implied the whole Woman's Club was talking."

"You've got yourself mixed up with some woman? Oh, Johnny, how could you? No, I haven't heard a word. I suppose mothers, like wives, are the last to hear. Poor Julia! She is so proud she won't take it lightly. It isn't something any woman takes lightly. But I knew no good would come of that separate bedroom business."

"Don't blame Julia. Whatever her—whims, I should have been more patient. And God knows I have been ashamed."

"Stop talking in bits and pieces, and tell me—is the woman one you will have to support, or are supporting?"

"Lord, no. Nurse O'Neill. It hasn't meant a thing to either of us, really. It's just—we were there."

"Mrs. Bodien's nurse. Sister of the girl Paul Rausch married? So that's why Sally—"

"What about Aunt Sally?"

"Hasn't confided in me about that marriage. Probably blames you for bringing them together."

"I didn't. It was Norah. I doubt if she had an ulterior motive. Paul's violin needed a piano accompaniment. But never mind the Rausches. Right now they aren't important. What is important is that Julia is determined to have a divorce."

"Divorce! Oh, Johnny! She couldn't! It's unthinkable."

"Not to her, it isn't. She seems to have been thinking of it for a long while—even before this gave her justification. She expects to take her mother and Tucker and move to California."

Anne leaned forward a little to stare at him in dismay. "California! Oh, she couldn't."

"She can, and will. I told her I wouldn't contest it. How could I? Better it should be done quietly, with as little scandal as possible." He rose abruptly; he could talk about it no more. "You won't mind if I move back into my old room, beginning tonight?"

"Don't be foolish. But don't give up hope, either. I'll go talk to her tomorrow."

"I'd rather you didn't."

"Johnny, someone should remind her: you have never cared for anyone else in your life, and you never will."

"No. It's too old a habit, I never will. But there's no use your appealing to her, and it might be—unpleasant. Now, I must go deal with my office patients as best I can, and those in the hospital. And Mrs. Bodien. If there's nothing else, there's always work."

"How is Mrs. Bodien?"

"Dying. A few more days at most. Father Halloran will be on one side of her bed and Captain Bodien on the other, glaring at him."

"That nurse, Johnny: she won't expect you to marry her if you are free?"

"Good God, no! Mama, it just happened because she was there, and I was there, and both of us at loose ends, shall we say? I wasn't her first, believe me—she didn't even pretend it was so. And she hates Waynesboro and private nursing. She has already made her plans to go back to her Cincinnati hospital."

"That's something, anyway. I'll go up and make your bed for you. I'm sorry for your unhappiness, Johnny, even if you did bring it on yourself." She let it go at that: no use saying to your child that his grief was yours, that you too were shaken. "But I'll be glad to have you home."

In the morning, in spite of Johnny's warning, she went to talk to Julia: she could leave no stone unturned. She rang the bell for the upstairs apartment; the maid came down to admit her, but before she reached the stairs, Mrs. Deming came to the sitting room door. To the maid she said. "Go tell your mistress that Mrs. Gordon is here, and will be right up. Come in, Anne, for just a moment. You have come to talk to Julia? It won't do any good."

"You don't approve, surely?"

"Of *divorce?* Of course not." All concerned except Julia uttered the word in horrified italics. "Unfaithfulness is hard to forgive in a husband, but it is partly Julia's fault, and I told her so. There are always two sides. Not that I am condoning Johnny's—"

"No, nor I. I am ashamed for him. But I must ask her to forgive him, or afterward I might think 'If I only had—'"

Julia was waiting for her in her sitting room; she was wearing her most beruffled dressing gown; her beautiful fair hair was piled high on her head, so that her bared neck gave her a vulnerable look, like a child's. Her expression was one of sadness, wistfulness. "The Betrayed Wife," Anne thought.

"Mamma Gordon, isn't this a dreadful thing that Johnny has done?"

"Dreadful, yes."

"No one can say that I have not been a good and faithful wife and mother. Kept the house, seen to the meals, waited for him till all hours, without ever letting him see how exasperating it was."

"It takes more than a housekeeper to make a good marriage."

"If you are going to say I drove Johnny to this misbehavior, you are wasting your breath."

"No, I am not going to say that."

"Or if you have come to ask me to forgive him and take him back fresh from another woman's embraces—" She shuddered in revulsion. "The answer is 'No'."

"Have you no feeling left for him at all?" Anne could not bring herself to use the word "love" to this woman, so suddenly a stranger.

"After this? You may have been willing to overlook unfaithfulness. I am not. Forgive once and you will be expected to forgive seven times seven and more. I am not going to be whispered about in this town as a complaisant wife."

Anne turned on her heel; feeling as if she had been struck in the face, she went blindly down the stairs, out the door, across the porch and through the gate and home. Safely there, she went to her room, and threw herself on her bed, tossing her hat aside carelessly. So that was why Johnny had told her not to go: no doubt Julia had taunted him about his father—and she had always thought Johnny had never known. The town, it seemed—and

Waynesboro was her town and she had no desire to leave it—the town knew everything, and never forgot. How could she have believed—? Gossip was carried by an underground system: Mrs. A's cook knew all about Mrs. A, and unless she was remarkably loyal, told all to Mrs. B's cook and Mrs. C's cook and right on through the alphabet. Hadn't Louline said to her a long while ago, now. "Ah hyah Mistuh Johnny been moved out o' Miz' Julia's bedroom. Thet ain' no way to treat a husban'. He git tiahed o' thet some day." Anne had stopped her short, with a reproof; she never listened to Louline's more dramatic comments, but not everyone was so scrupulous. Since then no doubt Louline had heard that Johnny had got tired of it, but had had better sense than to report it to his mother. As for the Woman's Club, she wouldn't have called any of them real gossips, except Eliza Ballard. And why should Eliza want to make trouble for Johnny? He and his father, too, had done their best for the Ballards—particularly when Thomasina had died, and before that, Ariana McCune.

Eliza had not, in fact, thought of any trouble she might be making for Johnny. She had felt sympathetic with Sally Rausch, and indignant with Mrs. Deming, and had impulsively said what she had. But if Sally hadn't spoken first, she would not have been drawn into it. She was horrified when she read of the divorce: a small notice tucked away under "News of the Courts," grounds not mentioned, custody of the child to be shared. Ordinarily the "News of the Courts" column went unread by leading citizens, but that item was well noted. The town was shaken: members of prominent families had never been divorced before. It was unheard of. Johnny was held at fault; there was some speculation as to whether it would cost him his practice. On the whole, the judgment was that it would not: his patients swore by him, and there was no question that he was a good doctor; his wife had never been well-known, or where she was known, had not been particularly liked. While his patients were making up their minds that he was still the doctor for them, Johnny, except when he was actually with one of them, went through his days like a sleepwalker; he kept an iron control over his outward being, but it was as if he were bleeding to death inside.

He allowed himself to be drawn into the matter of the divorce only when it was impossible to escape. Tim Merrill had called at the office after Julia had interviewed him. "She said you told her to come to me, and so I accepted the case. But you must be represented. She is now my client, and I must do my best for her, but unethical or not, I must warn you that she intends to strip you of everything you have."

"Let her have it by way of reparation. I can earn a living."

"Look, Johnny. I know as well as you do what your father left you. Probate court records are not secret. But I suppose you have sunk a lot of that capital in the hospital. Do you want to lose that? Or the farm? For God's sake, if you don't care for yourself, think of the boy."

"He must have the farm—it's been Gordon land for generations, and Julia wouldn't care about that. She would sell it. Very well, I'll see a lawyer. Rudy Lichtenstein? I know him better than any of the others."

"Rudy's a good lawyer, in spite of his damn-fool politics."

And so Johnny went to see Rudy in his office across the hall from the upstairs room where his father was still content to act as notary public. Rudy was so surprised to see him there that it made it difficult for him to begin.

"I'm glad to see you, Johnny. I guess the last time was at the Woman's Club Christmas party. I never seem to be home when Sophie calls you in for the children's ailments. Do sit down. What can I do for you? I know any law business you may have goes to Gardiner and Merrill."

Johnny studied his old schoolmate before replying, and saw him as he had always been: slight, very dark as to hair and eyes, hawk-faced, with a thrusting nose—much more Jewish looking than his father.

"In this case Tim is representing my wife. She is suing for divorce."

"*Julia* is? I knew Julia in school, same as you. I thought her the most unexcitable, coolest person I knew, and I have never seen any reason to change my mind. What has happened?"

Johnny told him the whole miserable story, concluding with Tim's hint at what Julia wanted from him. "I said, 'Let her have it.'"

Rudy grinned, and interrupted. "Thanks to your being such a good friend of his, I have a client?"

"He said he was duty-bound to do his best for her, and so I should be represented—presumably by someone who could block him. I wouldn't have agreed. I'd gladly have let her have all the worldly goods I endowed her with. I make a good enough income to live on. But it would mean losing the farm and what I have invested in the hospital, and I don't think Rodney or Warren or both of them together could pay for my interest. And there's Tucker: I should manage to keep something of what the Gordons before me have been able to accumulate, particularly the farm, to pass on to him."

"She wants a settlement, then? And you don't trust her to live on the income and pass the capital on to the boy?"

"She doesn't care a rap for the farm; she would sell it." He flushed. "Mrs. Deming is a prudent woman, but I doubt whether she could hold Julia in check—Julia likes nice things, and to be comfortable and the equal of anyone she knows."

"I'll fight for alimony instead of a settlement. It's the sensible thing for you. It may have to be a big one, but if she marries again, you won't have to pay it."

"She won't marry again."

"What makes you so sure? She is young, and a very handsome woman. And I understand the hills and canyons out West are full of bachelors."

"She didn't care very much about—being married."

Rudy wondered at the power of love not to blind its victims but to make them acquiescent. Johnny saw his wife quite clearly as a cold, selfish, extravagant woman, but he would have given her the coat off his back.

"Just the same, I'll fight for alimony rather than a settlement. How about the child? You would like shared custody?"

"Of course. I'd like to have the law say I could have him summers, here with me and my mother. But I don't believe you will have to fight very hard for that."

An indifferent mother, then—that too. "I'll do my best for you. I don't believe it will be a very hard fight. Judge Gardiner is a fair and reasonable man."

"Thanks, Rudy. I won't have to appear in court? I couldn't bear that." Johnny rose to go, and then, as an afterthought, rebuking himself for being so entirely concentrated on his own thoughts, he said, "I hope you are getting along well, Rudy? I see your name in the paper often enough, defending this one and that one—mostly poor devils who can't pay you much, surely. Why did you ever think you wanted to be County Prosecutor?"

"Some of them," Rudy laughed, "need for the town's sake to be prosecuted. And as you have guessed, most of my clients are not very good pay. But I have steered clear of corporation law. I don't mean to criticize Gardiner and Merrill. I just happen to feel, thinking as I do about corporations, my hands would be dirtied by that kind of practice. I make out, and since I have a contented wife and a brood of healthy, lively children, I count myself blessed."

"I am glad for your good fortune." There was something so sad about the way it was said that Rudy caught his breath.

"I'm sorry. I apologize—I know it is not time for me to be boasting to you."

"On the contrary, I am glad to hear of an old friend's good fortune."

The two men shook hands. Johnny went away feeling a little better: it had been true that he was glad that things had turned out well for Sophie and Rudy.

The only time after that that Johnny came close to showing any emotion was when, after the divorce had been granted, Tucker came to say good-bye. The child was still bewildered by what had happened, and even at eleven, unashamedly grief-stricken. He did not want to go to California. He did not want to go anywhere. He wanted to stay at home with his mother and with his grandmother and Major—with his father. And his friends. When his worst fears were realized and he was told that he could not take Major to California with him, he made no pretense of being what his mother told him he must now be: the man of the family. His weeping was so uncontrolled, his rebellion so vehement, that his mother sent him to his room in disgrace. "I cannot stand another sound out of you. It is not a happy situation for any of us, but we must make the best of it." Tucker had never asked his mother what his father had done, although she was quite prepared to tell him if he did. "You never know," she said to her mother, "what goes through the head of a boy that age: they pick up all kinds of gutter knowledge at school, and I don't doubt Ludwig Evans is full of information."

"I don't believe Elsa and her husband would discuss the matter before the children."

"If she did, all her sympathy would be for 'poor Johnny'."

"It was only yesterday I heard you on the phone, telling her you would send an address as soon as you were settled, and begging her to write."

"Naturally I want to keep in touch, know what is going on here where I have so many friends."

Preparations for their leaving were not lengthy or delayed. The furniture the two women wanted to keep was packed and sent to the freight depot to be shipped; the rest of it sold to a second-hand dealer; the house was put in the hands of a real estate agent. Johnny took out of it just what he had taken in when he was married: his clothes, his books, his doctor's bag. Mrs. Deming's reactions to being snatched away were confided to Anne, and to Anne only: she felt that her daughter's behavior had been most distasteful; Waynesboro was their home after all these years. Yet Julia, who had cared more for her father than anyone in her life, could see his house sold without a qualm. She could not be permitted to go off to California alone; her mother, willy-nilly, had to go with her. The house was Mrs. Deming's, but since Johnny was to pay alimony instead of making a settlement, they would need the lump sum the house would bring if they were to buy another home in California. Anne wondered a little whether Mrs. Deming's financial situation had not as much to do with her willingness to move as her concern for Julia: she had of course her Civil War widow's pension—presumably a good one, since her husband had been a general—and some capital; but Julia had been awarded what Anne considered an outrageously large alimony, besides support for Tucker, and would be a fairly well-to-do grass widow.

Early in the evening before the date set for their departure, a very teary boy came to his grandmother's to say good-bye.

"We're ready to go, I guess." He stood on the living room threshold, turning his cap in his hands, looking at no one, not even Major, who had gone to grovel at his feet, tail wagging, tongue lolling. Anne rose from her chair, went and got down on one knee beside him, and took him in her arms.

"Don't feel too bad about it, Tuck. You will like California. Time goes so fast, too—you know you will be home to spend the summer with us, come June."

"I know. Good-bye, Grandmother." They looked squarely into each other's eyes, a long, loving interchange. Finally he threw his arms around her, kissed her, and turned to his father, who had come to stand in the door.

"Good-bye, Father." The child's eyes brimmed with tears.

"Ready to go, are you?" Johnny put his hands on Tucker's shoulders, drew him close, looked down on the ash blond hair so like Julia's, which he would never again touch, spread on the pillow, a great golden fan. Johnny kissed his son hard, abruptly, turned away. Tucker dropped to the floor, said, "Good-bye, Major," and burst into a flood of tears. Johnny left the room, heading for his refuge, the office. Anne said, "Major will miss you, but I'll take care of him for you. Here, take my handkerchief—you're too big a boy—"

"Do you think he will know me when I come home?"

If the word "home" touched her, his grandmother gave no sign. "Dogs never forget. If you were gone ten years, he would know, and my goodness, it'll only be a few months. Wipe your tears. You don't want your mother to know that you don't want to go with her, surely?"

"I want to be with her, but I want her to stay here."

"It's a little late for that, isn't it? Railroad tickets bought and everything packed. You'll love that long trip, Tuck, across the plains and through the mountains."

He obediently mopped his eyes, nose, and cheeks, and returned the handkerchief. "Yes, maybe that part of it will be fun. Just so you're sure Major will remember me."

"I'm positive." She kissed him again and went with him to the door, with the inevitable admonitions: "Be a good boy. Write to us often. We'll miss you, you know. We'll want to hear what you're doing."

Mrs. Bodien died that same week. Johnny, who had been with her most of the night, came to the breakfast table drawn and exhausted, and reported to his mother that the long-expected death had occurred.

"And you had to be there? And her family? And the nurse—?"

"Not the nurse, Mom. The priest was there to administer the final rites. Rather horrible, I thought. And I know the Captain did. Everyone, maybe, except Stewart and his wife. The poor soul was so full of dope she couldn't possibly know what was happening, but Father Halloran pretended that she made the right responses, gave extreme unction, guaranteed her admission to Heaven—after, I suppose, a spell in Purgatory. But they'll pray her out of there in no time."

"Johnny, I've never known you to be so hard."

"All that mumbo-jumbo, and none of it any comfort to Captain Bodien. It was a blessed release for her and a blow for him, although he knew it was coming, and thought he had accepted it—even wanted it for her."

"Yes. Death is so final."

"But the natural end for all of us. It must be easier to bear than other kinds of separation."

"I never heard you say anything so selfish before. You aren't wishing that Julia had died?"

"Of course not. She is young and has a long life ahead of her to enjoy. I just meant I might have accepted her death more—philosophically."

His mother said, "You'll get over it," although she knew he never would. "What is foreordained to happen, happens; it is wise to accept it. And time does heal our scars, thought they're still there, to ache on rainy days."

"You're too philosophical for me this morning." He smiled at her, a smile that wrenched her heart. "I don't know whether you consider yourself a Calvinist or a Stoic."

"Oh, a Calvinist. Of sorts, anyway. I wonder what ever became of Kitty Edwards' Marcus Aurelius? She gave it to your father when she knew she was dying—said Sheldon was a Christian and didn't need it. But your father never cared for it: said Marcus Aurelius was always looking at himself to see how well he was bearing up, but that there wasn't any time in his life for that sort of thing."

Johnny laughed. "Sounds like Pop." But he knew there had been times when his father had needed help, Marcus Aurelius or another. "He must have left the book among his others in the office. I'll look for it some day. Now," and he pushed his chair back from the table, "I must go. I'm due at the hospital this morning. You'll go with me to Mrs. Bodien's funeral?"

"Yes, if you think you must go. I didn't know doctors went to see their patients buried."

"Mom, you can't make me feel guilty about Mrs. Bodien's death. No one could have saved her—not the best doctor in the country. We know nothing about cancer—not the cause, and certainly not the cure, unless it is caught in the very beginning and cut out. And yes, I must go to the funeral. I have been a friend of the Bodiens—the Captain, at least, and Barbara—since I was a boy."

The solemn high requiem mass for Mrs. Bodien was celebrated with all the elaborate rites of the church. There were a few other Protestants there besides the Gordons; some of them Anne was sure had (like herself) never been to a Catholic funeral before. But some of those she recognized she suspected of being there out of curiosity. Perhaps she was uncharitable, but she was glad Johnny had told her that Norah O'Neill had already returned to Cincinnati.

The Woman's Club met the next week for its regular fortnightly session. Anne would have like not to go, but one must show oneself unflinching in the face of curiosity: if her fellow members wanted to know how she was taking the blow that had fallen upon the Gordons and broken a family, she would show them. Perhaps—and she straightened her shoulders—there was something of the Stoic in her after all.

Sally presided at the meeting, businesslike as always, urging the members quickly through the preliminaries. No one had business, old or new, to lay before the members. Sally said, "I believe the Corresponding Secretary has a communication to read to the ladies. Mrs. Merrill?"

Elizabeth rose, with a sheet of notepaper in her hand. "Madame President: Ladies of the Club. I received this note last week: 'Dear Mrs. Merrill; It is with real regret that I submit my resignation and that of my daughter Mrs. Gordon from the Waynesboro Woman's Club. Of all the ties that must be broken as we depart for a new home in the Far West, this is the one I most regret. I have been proud of and enjoyed being a member since the day in 1868 when the formation of the Club was first proposed, and my daughter, one might almost say, grew up in its circle. I leave Waynesboro with the sincerest good wishes for the continuing success of the Woman's Club in providing intellectual stimulation for its members.—Yours very truly, Louisa Tucker Deming.'"

Anne, in her defiant "let-them-satisfy-their-curiosity" mood, had taken a front seat. Only the President and the recording secretary faced her; she held her rigidly fixed eyes in their direction. But she could feel herself flushing. "Of all the ties that must be broken"—how cruel of Louisa! Dimly she heard Sally making her conventional pretty speech: "As she had reminded us, Mrs. Deming was a charter member of the Club, and that must make us even sadder at having to lose her: there are but a few of us left."

("Eliza, Amanda, you and me," Anne thought, "but after all, it's been"—and she subtracted hastily—"thirty-six years.") "And," Sally continued, "Mrs. Deming has contributed very much over that stretch of time to what she calls 'intellectual stimulation'." (Anne would have liked at that point to wink at Sally: did she remember how, when they were school girls, they had called her 'Teapot Tucker'?) Sally swept on without catching Anne's eye: "And none of us will forget, I am sure, the charm and beauty of her daughter as 'Alice in Wonderland' and in many of our other Club dramatics. But I fear that we must, however reluctantly, accept these resignations. Do I hear a motion?"

The motion was made, seconded, and passed. Louisa Tucker Deming and her daughter Julia Deming Gordon were no longer members of the Woman's Club. When the matter had been dealt with, Sally said, "These resignations of course leave two vacancies in the Club. I should like to suggest that we approach the question of their replacements with due and unhurried consideration. Never yet have we chosen an unworthy member; I should dislike now to do something in haste, without full knowledge of a candidate's potentialities. Now I call upon the Secretary to read the program of the day."

And while the secretary read the program—and indeed, halfway through the essay of the day—Anne tried to think who it could be that Sally hoped to block. Sally, to her at least, was pretty transparent. Probably some ministerial or theological wife; the president had not been too pleased at the admission of Miss Campbell, swelling the Reformed Presbyterian ranks. But Ruth Campbell had been a good member. Anne gave it up, but her ruminations had at least diverted her mind; she had forgotten to be self-conscious.

When she was preparing to leave, Sally called to her from the door of the big living room, where the chairs were in disarray after the adjournment.

"Wait, Anne, I'll drive you home. Just a minute until I finish what I was saying to Mrs. Merrill. I told Ben to bring the carriage, it's too bleak a day for walking."

In the carriage Anne thought, "It's a long time since Sally has wanted to talk to me, and even now there's Ben." And so she said, "It was an interesting meeting, wasn't it? But I don't quite understand why you want to delay choosing new members."

"Don't you think the theological element is rather large already? I understand some other Seminary wives besides Mrs. Maxwell are worthy of consideration."

"You don't mind Miss Campbell being a member, do you? I rather forced her on you."

"As it turned out, no. She has a sense of humor, which is more than can be said for most of the R.P.'s. And she is not nearly the bigot that Christina has turned out to be. Sophie Lichtenstein's committee for the Christmas play has persuaded her to act the lead in *The Admirable Crichton*." They both laughed: Miss Campbell, all bone and awkward joints, wearing her invariably mannish hats, dressing always in tailored suits whose skirts reached only to her insteps (no mud-bedraggled hems for her), was not a very feminine figure at any time.

"She doesn't mind being laughed at."

"She and Charlotte, who will play Lord Loam, are enough in themselves to carry the play." Then she dropped her voice. "I am glad you had the spunk to come today. It's easier, after the first time. Who would ever have thought our sons would shame us this way?"

"I feel sad, not exactly shamed. Though I knew everyone would stare to see how I was taking it. Sad for Johnny. Of course he was to blame—I don't deny it. But he will never get over it."

"He always loved Julia. But 'never' is a long time, and he's young still. Just be glad he didn't *marry* that woman, as Paul had to."

"Don't be so bitter."

"I feel bitter. It was so unnecessary. But Ludwig—"

"I suspected you blamed Johnny."

"Yes. In a way I did. I don't think he deliberately threw that little girl in Paul's way. The sister was responsible for that, I'm sure. But you know Paul has always thought Johnny could do no wrong, and he wasn't exactly setting a good example."

"He was behaving abominably."

"But since Paul insisted to Elsa and his father that he had fallen in love at first sight, I can hardly blame Johnny. To show that all is forgiven, I'd like the two of you to have Christmas dinner with us. Elsa may be joining us and may not."

"If I can persuade Johnny. It would be good for him. He's brooding too much."

As it happened, Elsa and her family were at the Rausches for Christmas. She had held off accepting her mother's invitation, although it was traditional for the four Evanses to dine there that day: she had invited Paul and his bride to come and stay with them over the holiday. Paul had declined. "We are expected to have Christmas with Stewart and his family, where we will be welcomed by all." In a way, Elsa was relieved: she would have given anything to bring Paul and his mother together, but was glad that he, or his Ellen, or both, had spirit enough not to come crawling. As a consequence, there were eight to sit down around the Rausch turkey, and all tendency on the part of the adults to be even a little melancholy was controlled and suppressed for the sake of Ludwig III and Jennifer.

Anne and Johnny had had one letter from Tucker since he had gone: school was all right, he guessed. It was warm and not like winter in Los Angeles and the flowers were in bloom, but he thought that palm trees were ugly. There weren't any real woods anywhere. His grandmother reported the substance of this letter to the Evans children.

"I guess he misses the woods around Hillcrest," young Ludwig said. "If he were here now, we'd be looking for the last persimmons. And for walnuts."

"D'you know what he calls me?" Jennifer, as slim and dark a child as her brother was sturdy and fair, thrust out her lower lip. "Tag-along. So does Ludwig."

"Well, you do, don't you?" Her father teased her. "Small chance they would have of gathering walnuts without you."

Johnny said, "D'you mind? I used to call my sister 'Little Me-Too.' So did your mother. Remember, Shaney?"

"I remember."

And Jennifer said judiciously, "I don't really mind, because they don't really care if I go along. I guess. But I wouldn't let anyone else call me that."

Elsa, catching Johnny's eye, wondered a little sadly whether history could be going to repeat itself. But Tucker was gone—until summer, anyway.

After Christmas, things were better. Johnny made a pretense, at least with his mother, of having adjusted to his life with her, although she knew it was really his patients, in and out of the hospital, that he was giving his mind and spirit to. She was glad when Dr. Warren's son finished his residency in a Chicago hospital and returned, with his bride, to join his father: it would take some of the load off Johnny. The year moved slowly through the early spring, with its miserable, off-and-on-again weather. The Club as always met every two weeks, and that gave one something to think about; Anne forgot to be self-conscious with her old friends, and enjoyed seeing them; the Club meant more to her than it ever had done before, and to Sally, too, she thought: both of them were more alone and had more time on their hands than they had had when they were younger. But it was Elsa, not Sally, who told her in March of the birth of Paul's daughter, named Kathleen for Stewart Bodien's wife. "She has done so much for Ellen, and now for both of them," Elsa said half-apologetically. "But I must say 'Kathleen Rausch' is as incongruous as 'Ludwig Evans'."

By early June the Gordons were ready and waiting for Tucker to come; Johnny would meet him in Chicago, where he would have to change trains. Before that Ludwig and Sally and the Evanses had transferred themselves to Hillcrest. Elsa had told her mother with more than a little bitterness that she needn't worry about having to entertain Paul and 'that girl.' "'That girl' is not going anywhere she knows she will not be welcomed by all of us. What I am sorry about is that the children will be out in the country when Tucker comes. He will miss them."

"Surely he has other friends his own age?"

"Dear me, yes. Like Ludwig, a gaggle of them: Merrills and Thirkields, Bonners and Lichtensteins. But Tucker loves to be out here, and I don't suppose his father and grandmother will want to let him out of their sight."

About that she was wrong: what his grandmother and father most wanted was for Tucker to have a happy summer. When his father brought him in from the train, he seemed at first strangely stiff and shy: he shook hands with Anne instead of embracing her. Of course he had grown out of all knowledge, and perhaps felt himself at twelve too old for kissing, but she could not help wondering whethering his mother, regretting the necessity of turning him over to them for almost three months, had influenced him. Before she could finish thinking it, there was a tremendous burst of barking from the back hall door, Louline opened it, and a black and white streak of fox terrier launched himself at Tucker, alternately wriggling his hindquarters over the floor, and leaping at the boy with eager cries and ready tongue. Tucker dropped to the floor to squeeze him. No nonsense about being too old to be kissed by a dog.

"He didn't forget me, did he? You said he wouldn't."

"I knew he wouldn't. Now he's got you back, he won't let you out of his sight. Johnny, take Tucker and his suitcase upstairs to his room, and see that he gets washed for lunch. Then he can come tell us about everything."

"Everything" to begin with was the wonder of the train trip: in a Pullman car all on his own, what he had seen, what he had eaten, whom he had talked to. A good many sentences began "There was this man on the train; he said—" Tucker, who had never been a talkative child, gave way completely to his excitement. It was a while before Anne could even ask, as politeness required that she do, how he had left his mother and his Grandmother Deming.

"Oh, they're fine. They *like* California."

"I suppose they hated to see you go? They will miss you."

"They won't miss me. They are going to the Islands on a cruise."

"'The Islands'?"

"Hawaii. And if I hadn't been coming here, they would have had to take me."

"But didn't you want to go?"

"All those grown-ups? No. I wanted to come here, and see you and Father and Major." The dog was sitting close to his knees; Tucker was fondling his ears with one hand as he ate with the other. "And Ludwig and Tag-along and Charley Merrill—"

"Tucker, you really shouldn't call Jennifer by that ridiculous name. She's ten years old. They are out at Hillcrest, and can hardly wait for you to come out."

"But we'd like to have you here with us a few days first," his father said. "We want to hear all about school, and what you do with yourself when you're not in school—and whether you get to the beach, and are learning to swim."

"I already know how to swim." Tucker was surprised at such ignorance on the part of his father. "Didn't I ever say so? I learned in the canal, out at Hillcrest, with the other kids. The beach isn't much fun. The ocean is too rough for swimming, and the salt water's mucky, I think. Los Angeles isn't much fun, either. You can't do anything all by yourself or just with other boys. It takes so long to get anywhere, and there always has to be a grown-up with you, for fear of snakes and tarantulas and things like that, and there aren't any real woods—just dry brown hills with sagebrush and cactus."

"Well, in the circumstances"—and Johnny looked so relieved that his mother knew he had been worried—"I can see you might have more fun here. Just so you let us know in a general sort of way where you are going and when you will be back. I bought you a bicycle, so you could get around on your own. It isn't really very far to Hillcrest. Three or four miles."

"A bicycle! Oh, Father, thank you. That's simply swell. Do you think it will take me long to learn to ride it?"

"No, All the boys have bikes now. Get one of them to show you."

Learning to manage the bicycle was not a long-drawn-out process; in a few days Tucker, with Major panting after, was riding with the other boys to Anderson's Fork for a swim in the deep river water, or alone or with others out to Hillcrest, where sometimes Tucker spent the day, sometimes stayed overnight. On the whole, it was a good summer—particularly for Tucker, for whom the high point came with a spectacular Fourth of July at Hillcrest. Perhaps for his father and grandmother, those weeks were shadowed by the recognition that they were going all too fast. For them the three months passed with unbelievable rapidity: they missed Tucker sadly when he had gone—when Major, listless and lonely, searched through all the rooms every little whipstitch, as Anne said, and would then come to sit at her feet and look up at her dolefully. Days in the quiet house stretched out interminably, yet the fall months slipped past in rapid succession in the routine she and Johnny followed.

The Woman's Club met as usual. Lavinia Stevens brought a guest to one fall meeting: young Mrs. Dr. Warren. She was an attractive girl, charmed the members, and, most importantly, Sally Rausch; and before the fall was over, she had been invited to become a member. "At least," as Sally said, "no clerical taint." Having had her way so far as one member was concerned, she did not oppose the election of the Methodist minister's wife for the other vacancy—a Mrs. Harrington. "Methodist ministers aren't allowed to stay long, anyway," she said to Anne.

Before it seemed possible, Christmas was looming again on the horizon, and it was time to get a box packed for Tucker, and mailed. After Christmas, when the *Torchlight* printed a summary of 1905's notable events before the new year began, Anne wondered to what purpose she had so faithfully read the paper all year. She remembered little about the year's disasters—the inevitable mine explosions, fires, tornadoes, and shipwrecks. It was as if her mind had been numbed by all that had happened to her and hers. Even the Russo-Japanese War was a matter of seeing Tucker on summer evenings, leaning over his father's shoulder, in spite of her reproval of such rudeness, trying to puzzle out the headlines, demanding not only an explanation of what was happening, but the pronunciation of the Japanese and Russian names, and Johnny patiently wrestling with them himself. As for the peace negotiations carried on at Portsmouth, and the treaty signed in September: of course she had known about them, as much as any newspaper reader could; but when she thought about it all afterward, what she remembered, and laughed at, was Ludwig's fulmination at the Christmas dinner table, where the Gordons were once more present. Someone brought it on by expressing gratitude for peace on earth, and Ludwig let loose his denunciation of the President. Everyone knew that in his eyes Roosevelt could do no good, and doubted that he really believed what he was saying: that it was none of the President's business, or ours, America's; why should we intervene to save the Japs from what in the end, considering Russian population and resources, must have been a defeat? Roosevelt had made a world power of Japan. He might live to be sorry. Russia would never be a threat to our trade overseas, "but those little yellow devils just might be."

Sally had remonstrated with him. "Just be thankful that men have stopped shooting at each other. Let us hope that 1906 will be peaceful. I think I am getting old: all that I ask of a new year is that it be uneventful."

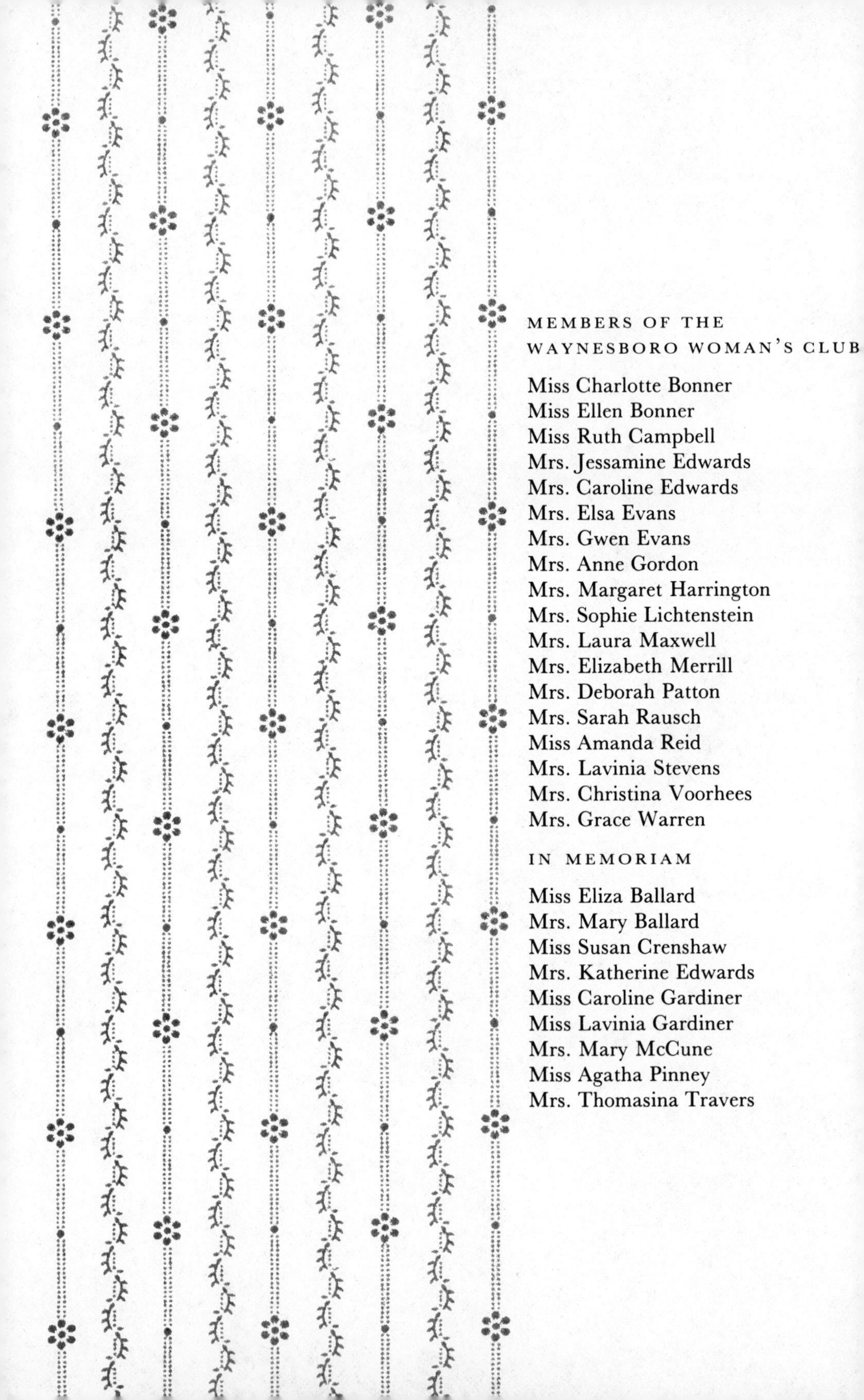

MEMBERS OF THE
WAYNESBORO WOMAN'S CLUB

Miss Charlotte Bonner
Miss Ellen Bonner
Miss Ruth Campbell
Mrs. Jessamine Edwards
Mrs. Caroline Edwards
Mrs. Elsa Evans
Mrs. Gwen Evans
Mrs. Anne Gordon
Mrs. Margaret Harrington
Mrs. Sophie Lichtenstein
Mrs. Laura Maxwell
Mrs. Elizabeth Merrill
Mrs. Deborah Patton
Mrs. Sarah Rausch
Miss Amanda Reid
Mrs. Lavinia Stevens
Mrs. Christina Voorhees
Mrs. Grace Warren

IN MEMORIAM

Miss Eliza Ballard
Mrs. Mary Ballard
Miss Susan Crenshaw
Mrs. Katherine Edwards
Miss Caroline Gardiner
Miss Lavinia Gardiner
Mrs. Mary McCune
Miss Agatha Pinney
Mrs. Thomasina Travers

* 1908 *

"Old members depart, death takes another charter member, but new members are added to our roll . . ."

On an afternoon in the late May of 1908, the members of the Waynesboro Woman's Club began to disperse from the Stevenses' house. The last meeting of the year, it had been longer than usual, so that it was almost five o'clock when the ladies adjourned. Sophie Lichtenstein had been the essayist of the day, and Sophie developed any subject assigned to her with true Teutonic thoroughness: she had dealt at length with the "Works of Thomas Hardy," and when the President called for a discussion of the paper, Amanda Reid delivered a well-reasoned but not brief critique, mingling praise with a tart questioning of some of the essayist's conclusions.

At the opening of the meeting, there had also been new business to be laid before the members: the corresponding secretary read a note from Mrs. McKinney, submitting a request that her resignation from the Club be accepted. "As you are aware," she said, "Mr. McKinney has retired and we plan to leave Waynesboro." This announcement surprised no one, since Mr. McKinney's resignation had been duly reported in the *Torchlight.* But that the McKinneys, who had lived in Waynesboro for so many years, should now be planning to move away startled the ladies. Sally competently put an end to the many-voiced murmur, saying, "This is an unexpected blow to you all, I know. It was to me, when Madam Secretary told me of Mrs. McKinney's note. We had all supposed that of course the McKinneys, who have been a part of Waynesboro for so long and who have so many friends here, would spend their days of retirement among us. But Mrs. McKinney has explained that her husband"—and Sally found herself crossing glances with Anne—"has long cherished a hope of going home, to the town where he grew up. They are planning to return to Pennsylvania as soon as a successor to Mr. McKinney has been chosen. I fear that we must therefore accede to Mrs.

McKinney's request, though with the provision that the resignation not take effect until her actual departure. Madam Secretary, have you any other communication to read to us?"

"Yes, Madam President, one similar in content. 'Dear Madam Secretary: As I expect to be married and on my way to India before the next meeting of the Waynesboro Woman's Club, I must ask you to accept my resignation, tendered with the greatest regret, believe me. Yours very truly, Jane Voorhees.'"

This note brought forth no murmur: everyone knew of Janey's plans (her triumph, if you could call it that), since her parents had announced her engagement to a graduating seminarian at a dinner for his class, the Seminary professors, and their wives. The only subject for wonder was what the prospective missionary could be thinking of: any picture of Janey taking on the duties of a missionary's wife was beyond imagination. As Caroline Edwards said to Lowrey disgustedly, "She's as near *nothing* as a human being can be. I know. I grew up across the street from her, and was always having to be nice to 'poor Janey'."

This second resignation was also accepted, after Sally had expressed the Club's conventional regrets and hope for her happiness in the new walk of life to which she had been called. After the opening preliminaries and the reading of the minutes, the program for the day was read, and the essayist, Sophie Lichtenstein, rose murmuring, "Madam President and Ladies of the Club," and with an uncertain shaky voice plunged into her work on Thomas Hardy. Sophie knew perfectly well that her mind was as competent and probably better trained than any in the room; nevertheless, there was always that first shaky moment.

When the meeting stood adjourned, there was still the necessary amount of social intercourse for the members to express their regrets to Mrs. McKinney and their hopes for her and Mr. McKinney's continued health and happiness, which she accepted with the familiar deprecating smile and tucked-in chin. Then all the same words had to be spoken, perhaps more perfunctorily, to Janey Voorhees. Lavinia, acting the gracious hostess, knew that by this time her mother must be exhausted by tending the two small Stevens daughters and still smaller son; they had been deposited at the Gardiners' by Rodney after lunch, so she felt sure by this time that he would be watching from his office window to see the ladies depart. She accepted graciously the ladies' thanks for her hospitality, but urged only her sister Caroline to linger, saying, "Can't you stay for a good gossip? Rod will be home when he sees the coast's clear."

"You know very well I can't. It's late, and dinner can't be started until I take the children off Romie's hands. I'm sorry. But I will take time to go to Mother's and pick up your children and bring them home. Save Rodney a trip."

Caroline bustled past the ladies who were straggling down the Stevens path by twos and threes, and threw herself into her new little electric runabout, Lowrey's latest gift to his wife. None of the others were in such a hurry; clusters formed so the ladies could say what they had on their minds. Charlotte Bonner was close on the heels of Mrs. Rausch and Mrs. Gordon. Over Sally's shoulder she said, "Does Mr. Rausch think it is true that the President is grooming Mr. Taft to take his place? Is he going to the Convention in June?"

Sally turned to smile at her. "Looking for news nuggets? No, he doesn't plan to go: says it will be cut and dried. Taft will be nominated, which suits Ludwig. He says he is a sound man, and anyway the Tafts are a Cincinnati family. He will be glad to get that 'Wild Man' out of the White House. He is confident of the result nationally, and will confine his politicking to the state and district tickets. Personally, I have enjoyed the President: he keeps things stirred up, and gives us some excitement, at least. But we're just getting over our last depression—the worst in so long—and Ludwig blames the President for that: undermining the country's faith in its financial and industrial leaders—you know—'malefactors of great wealth'—and he hasn't liked all this interfering in other countries' affairs. Especially now Japan is trying to take over Korea, he is saying 'I told you so.' But if you want to *print* anything of what Ludwig thinks, go interview him. Don't you dare quote me."

Charlotte laughed. "Cross my heart. I was just wondering about the Convention." She said good-bye to the older women at the gate and went striding off alone, up the hill.

Sally said to Anne, "You are expecting Tucker for the summer, of course. When?"

"In a couple of weeks. I wonder if he will have grown as much as Ludwig Evans? I just might not know him."

"Ludwig's big for his age. I hope he hasn't altogether outgrown his pleasure in childish amusements, if you call fishing and swimming childish. Anyway, the boys and Jennifer have had two perfect summers. 'Halcyon' I believe is the word."

"Any reason to think this summer will be different?"

"I hope not, but those boys are thirteen, and young Ludwig, according to his grandfather, spends all his after-school time at the mill. There isn't much for him to do, now they don't use bobbin boys any more, but he runs errands and follows Captain Bodien around, watching how everything is done. His grandfather is pleased as punch. But it may be different when school's out and we're in the country. The young people are looking forward to having Tucker back. We'll be at Hillcrest after next week. Be sure to tell Tucker he'll be welcome any time."

Behind those two, Eliza Ballard and Amanda Reid had fallen into step; they might have much to say to each other when they dined at the boardinghouse, as they customarily did after Club meetings. At the moment they were silent.

Not so Elsa, Sophie Lichtenstein, and Elizabeth Merrill, coming down the path on their heels.

"Amanda's wonderful, isn't she?" Elizabeth murmured under her breath. "No one could have made a more complete criticism of your paper, and all *ex tempore*."

"It got a real going over," Sophie said ruefully. "She scares me to death—always has since she taught me Latin in High School. But yes, she's wonderful. After all these years, still in the classroom. Could you have kept it up, Elizabeth?"

"If Tim hadn't come along—I don't know. I liked teaching."

"You don't teach your own children."

"Heaven forbid! We've all seen what comes of that."

They reached the gate and paused a moment: Elsa would turn left to go on out Linden Street, the others would go the other way. Elsa, her hand on the gate, looked at the two older women as they started slowly uptown and said, "Miss Reid's all right. She has her idiosyncrasies, but she's healthy enough. I wonder some about Miss Ballard."

"Eliza Ballard! Surely—"

"Look at her, Elizabeth." Eliza's figure bore a certain resemblance, seen from the rear, to a pregnant woman; it was obvious even under the loose black silk coat.

"I know, but she's been like that for a long time. Admittedly getting worse. How can she go on like that?"

"You mean she hasn't been to a doctor?" Elizabeth was startled.

"D'you think a doctor worth his salt wouldn't do something? It can't be cancer, or she would have been dead long ago, but still—"

"It couldn't be—" Sophie asked a little sheepishly—there was no denying that Eliza's figure was approaching the grotesque—"it couldn't be just middle-aged spread?"

"Sophie, in some ways, really! No, it couldn't. Elsa, your father must have some influence with her: couldn't he suggest—?"

"I asked him. He said he'd as soon tangle with a buzz saw. Her private life and what she chooses to do with it is none of his business."

"So we stand by and watch and do nothing?"

"Would you say anything to her?"

"You know I wouldn't. Sophie?"

"Himmel! No. Come on, Elsa: we're holding up the Voorhees'. We'll meet again in the fall?"

"You'll be coming out to Hillcrest, both of you. With your children, mind. I'll telephone some day when we're settled."

Rodney's mother was the last to say good-bye to Lavinia; she lingered for a moment at the door to ask about her grandchildren. The gate had hardly closed behind Jessamine when Lavinia, back at the window, saw Rodney approaching almost as if on tiptoe. Like Agag, Lavinia thought, and had begun to laugh even before his cautious entrance from the kitchen. He said in conspiratorial tones, "Coast clear?"

"As if you hadn't been watching for them to go. What a goose! And you could have come in to speak to your mother."

"There might have been another straggler or two in the front hall. My respect for the Woman's Club is such that my knees quake at the thought of breaking in. Want me to go for the children?"

"Caroline said she'd bring them. She had her little electric out today. The children will love that."

"Tell me about your meeting. Was it worth all the dislocation?"

"I wonder if all Club husbands splutter the way you do. It was all right. Sophie Lichtenstein exhausted her subject, as usual. The Works—and I mean *Works*—of Thomas Hardy. And Miss Reid took her to pieces afterward. Two resignations: the McKinneys are going back to Pennsylvania when he retires; Jane Voorhees is going to be married and go to India with her missionary."

"No great loss, either one, I should think. Nothing else?"

"Have you seen Eliza Ballard lately?"

"I never see her. Why?"

"Everyone was looking at her and at each other. She's growing larger and larger below the waist. Looks about eight months gone."

"Don't be vulgar, my girl. You've all made up your minds it's a tumor? Could be just plain fat. You've been commenting on her appearance for a long while, but she's apparently well. Still working, isn't she?"

"Yes. But it isn't fat. At least, her arms and ankles are bony enough. I wonder if she's seen a doctor?"

"Haven't a notion. Why? You don't care all that much for Miss Ballard, to be so exercised about her."

"I hate to see anyone doing nothing when doing something is possible. Would have been in the beginning, anyway. Couldn't you—"

"Vinnie, my love! You know perfectly well that I couldn't. Hasn't she a friend who could speak to her?"

"Either they have, and she doesn't pay any attention, or they don't dare. If anything happens to Eliza, I wonder what will become of that house?"

"You're a great crosser of bridges, I must say. Half of the house is hers to dispose of as she likes and half of it is the little music teacher's?"

"Yes. The queerest will. Papa drew it up for the old Judge—couldn't persuade him it might lead to trouble. He had faith in the bond between his daughters."

"Has Eliza made a will?"

"How should I know? She wouldn't go to Papa, anyway. They have never been exactly friendly, you know. Not since he fired her after her father died. Caught her snooping in his office files or something. Though I oughtn't to say that. I never really heard what it was all about."

At that point the children came bursting in: Theresa, six; Barbara, four; and two-year-old Gardiner Stevens, all overflowing with words bubbling on their tongues: Aunt Caroline's new electric automobile, and the bliss of the ride home wiping from their minds any lesser events of the afternoon. Speculation as to Eliza Ballard's condition and testamentary intentions were forgotten, the parents' being overwhelmed with children climbing over them, clamoring for attention. When they had quieted a little, Lavinia said, "Tess, please run tell Cindy we're all here—she can serve dinner whenever she's ready. I suppose you have to go back to the hospital, Rod?"

"Yes. Some post-operative cases. None serious, I'm glad to say." Rodney, with Gardiner astride his ankle, was playing ride-a-cock-horse. He didn't even look particularly tired, Lavinia thought: he looked scarcely older than the handsome boy she had married seven years ago. Probably all his women patients fell in love with him; secure Lavinia was not worried.

When Theresa returned, her mother asked if she had seen her Grandpa Bodien that afternoon.

"No. He didn't get home before Aunt Caroline came for us."

"So you didn't hear any more about his Big War?"

"No. But he's coming here for dinner Sunday, you said. To tell about the bad mans that hit him with a hatchet."

"Indians," Rodney corrected her. "And a tomahawk, not a hatchet."

"He said it was like a hatchet, with feathers tied to it."

"And you are not to monopolize him while he's here."

"History goes on repeating itself," Rodney said. "Last summer it was Ludwig Evans and Tucker and their friends, and now it's Theresa. But don't worry about her being a nuisance to him. You know very well he loves an audience."

Captain Bodien, after living alone in the big house in the West End for several years after his wife's death, had finally been persuaded to move in with the Gardiners. Barbara had worried about him, not because he was not perfectly capable of taking care of himself, but because she was persuaded that living alone was bad for him: his life had been reduced to his work in the mill and his memories of the past; he was not so old—not sixty yet—that he should cut himself off from the world, particularly the world of his family. And after all, there was that apartment upstairs that had been first the aunts' and then the girls'. She had broached the subject to Doug tentatively and with some hesitation, but he agreed that his father-in-law was becoming too withdrawn, and of course he wouldn't mind: after all the house was too large for the two of them. Moreover, he was fond of his father-in-law. It wouldn't be like—

"He may get very childish, Doug. You know he's strong as an ox physically."

"If he gets very old, he'll no doubt get very childish. Don't we all? It doesn't matter. Barbie—after what you put up with for so many years, why should I mind a little childishness?"

Captain Bodien, who would have scoffed at the word "withdrawn" (after all, there were still boys who liked to hear about the Civil War, and a constant succession of workmen at his door who wanted this or that), was persuaded by the assurance that in the upstairs apartment he could be perfectly independent: eat with them or not, as he pleased; come and go at his own hours (an important point, since he still went to the mill when the six-thirty whistle blew); and could have whatever guests he wanted. The girlish fripperies were removed from the apartment; the Captain transferred his most cherished pieces of furniture, his books, and various mementoes like his gun and saber, gave all else to Stewart and to Barbara's married girls, sold what they did not want or could not use, and moved in with the Gardiners', to be drawn at once into the close family circle, with not only his granddaughters but his five small great-grandchildren coming and going.

If Mary had had any intention of coming home to live after her graduation from college, her grandfather would have refused to take the apartment that should now be hers. Mary, however, had made her intentions quite clear: she did not expect to marry the moment her diploma was in her hand, like her sisters; she did expect to go to work—in New York, however, not in Waynesboro. She would come home with her parents after Commencement, and favor them with her presence (not that she expressed herself so, but her attitude spoke for her) until fall; then she would go to New York and engage herself in some kind of social work, probably in a settlement house. She was not, in her letters home, more expansive than that. She feared being laughed at if she said she meant to make the world a better place to live in: nevertheless, it was her intention. Nor did she confide on paper her expectation of marrying Franz Lichtenstein when he could afford a wife; he was already at work as a labor union organizer, but for a negligible salary. Mary was no coward: she knew that her family would not like it, and it seemed to her fairer to oppose them face to face.

Her mother and father went East to her Commencement. Franz was also in attendance: a disquieting matter to Doug and Barbara. It was not that they considered the boy inferior; he undoubtedly had brains, like all the Lichtensteins, and he was a nice-looking, well-mannered gentleman. But his views were well known in Waynesboro, and there was more chance of his turning their world upside down than there had been of his father's doing it. The Gardiners objected to what they considered Franz's unacceptable if not crazy ideas.

The three Gardiners had hardly settled themselves in the Pullman in Boston's South Station before Doug began to probe.

"You didn't tell us that we were to have the pleasure of Franz Lichtenstein's company at your Commencement."

"I suppose it wasn't much pleasure for you—having him there, I mean: it kind of divided my attention. But you couldn't have been surprised. Franz and I have done everything together for years. You never objected."

"There is nothing objectionable about the boy, so far as character or personality are concerned. His judgment I question. He is old enough to have outgrown his father's crackpot ideas. An out-and-out Socialist?"

"Then you must also doubt my judgment. Because I am an out-and-out Socialist too."

"Oh, Mary!"

"But you'll outgrow it," her father said comfortably. "One expects young people to believe in utopias."

"I won't have time to 'outgrow' it. I didn't intend to tell you this until we got home, but this seems as good a time as any. I intend to marry Franz and help him in his work."

"Marry! But—" Then her father stopped short. "Is Franz aware of your intention?"

"Oh, Papa! I—I put it awkwardly. Franz and I intend to be married when we can afford it."

"Do you care for him? Or just for his ideas?"

Mary's plain face was transfigured; her clear blue eyes, so like her grandfather's, deepened in color as the pupils dilated. "Care for him? Yes. Since I was about fifteen. Before I even knew about his ideas. It's just luck we think alike because I'd marry him in spite of his ideas if need be."

"Well, well! It never ceases to amaze me, the people that people fall in love with. I saw nothing so extraordinary about the boy as to inspire these raptures."

"Doug, don't tease her." Barbara, sitting next the car window with Mary beside her, leaned forward to touch her husband's knee. "Remember what we—I never understood what it was that induced you to choose me. I was nothing but a goose of a girl."

"It was your beautiful face, my dear." Doug's eyes twinkled. "It took me a while to appreciate your sterling character." Then he sobered. "Don't worry, Barby. I am not going to play the Victorian papa. You and I have suffered enough for several following generations."

"Oh, Papa! I thought you would be so angry—and cutting."

"You mean I have an inclination to be cutting when I am put out? With my family? I suppose it is the influence of the court room reaching into the domestic scene. No. I'll go no further than this: say nothing of your engagement while you're home this summer. If you are of the same mind in September, we'll announce it."

"Can't I even tell Gramp and the girls?"

"Your grandfather, if you dare. He will respect your confidence, although he won't approve. He had never forgotten Franz's and your attempt to unionize the mill. But the girls would tell their husbands, and first thing you know, it might as well be in the *Torchlight*. Has Franz told his family?"

"I haven't an idea."

"I'll go see old Lichtenstein when I have a chance after we get home. In the meantime just try to have an ordinary summer at home, Mary. And you mustn't blame me if I hope you find out you're wrong. About what you have been feeling. Is that too bad of me?"

Mary grinned. "Compared with what you might say or do, it's positively magnanimous. I—I guess I didn't realize how much you and Mother had suffered from the aunts."

"'Suffered' is a strong word, considering how happy your mother and I have been, having each other, and you girls. But I certainly have no intention of making their mistake, and exhibiting an antagonism that can be avoided."

The train had passed through Boston's suburbs. With the first call for dinner, Mary rose. "Let's eat right away."

The porter was standing in the end of the Pullman waiting for a chance to begin his evening's work. Doug said, "If we go now, we'll come back to find our berths made up and nothing to do but get in them."

"I'm ready. I'd no idea Commencement would be so exhausting. All those functions, but mostly all those good-byes. I hadn't realized how fond I'd grown of my friends in four years."

When they had eaten, Doug and Barbara dropped off in the lounge car, and let Mary go crawl into bed. Barbara said, "You were very good with her. I know how much you must hate the idea, but I don't think she even realized how you felt."

"I—yes—I hate the idea. But being a judge teaches you how to conceal your reactions if need be. I couldn't let her see how I feel about having a daughter take up crackpot Socialistic ideas. However idealistic. Like old Mrs. Ballard. She was the laughing stock of the town."

"Some people laughed at her, I know. But she was greatly respected just the same. And it is only natural that one of our four children should be a rebel, and refuse to lead the life she is expected to live. You have always said Mary took after Papa. He was a rebel—against the Catholic church and all its works, and against his parents when they wanted to make a priest of him. He ran away from home, you remember."

"I remember very well." He refrained from commenting on how many times he had heard the story. "And I am not sure that Mary's idealism, however ill-founded, isn't better than Veronica's materialism. Oh, I know, she married a nice boy, and seems to be happy. But why? Because young Hunter could give her whatever she wanted, and some more sophisticated spot than Waynesboro. At any rate there will be no estrangement in our family if I can help it. Paul Rausch is an example of what can happen. I've known Sally Rausch since I was a boy—she's one of my very old friends—but she acted the fool about Paul. And the breach seems unbridgeable now."

"They don't even pretened, do they? Just never see each other."

"Never. When Paul comes to talk business with his father or with us—Tim or me—he goes out to Elsa's to eat or sleep, not home."

Mary's father had been quite right in supposing that if Franz had written his family about his engagement, it would be impossible to keep it from the ears of all Waynesboro, however tentative he had endeavored to make it. The first time that Mr. Lichtenstein encountered Ludwig after he had heard the news from Franz, he stopped him where they met on the path up to the Court House.

"You haf a minute you can spare? I need maybe just reassurement." He looked about: lawyers, taxpayers, clerks, and other citizens were coming and going on the Court House steps. "Iss not so private here. Could you—?"

"My automobile is there at the curb. If we sit in it, we can be private as you please. I can talk for a few minutes."

With some difficulty the obese old man climbed into the front seat of Ludwig's touring car. He had never been inside an automobile before, but he was intent only on his problem.

"I vass on my way to talk to Judge Gardiner, but it iss maybe better I should talk to you first."

"Judge Gardiner is in court this morning, anyway. So out with it."

"You don't know, I sink, my boy vants to marry his girl."

Ludwig started to whistle, choked it off. "There is only one Gardiner still not married. You mean the little one, Mary? And your Franz?"

"She iss not now so little. She iss finished vis her collitch."

"I did see something about the Gardiners going to her Commencement. Just got back, I think. So your Franz wants to marry her. How does she feel?"

"She feels ze same. Engaged yet. Zoze kinder."

"Then if it's mutual, what's the problem?"

"How iss her parents going to feel? A daughter married to a Lichtenstein—a Socialist Lichtenstein?"

"You brought those boys up to be Socialists. That's hardly Franz's fault, is it?"

"Neffer—neffer do I vant him to forget his brinciples. He iss a labor union organizer, you know?"

"So I heard." And let him stay away from Waynesboro, Ludwig thought.

"Mary iss also a Socialist, vill vork for ze cause. Zat iss not vot vorries me." The old man sighed, clasped hands between his spread knees, under his gross belly. "Vy couldn't he haf chosen one of us—a Klein, a Hoffmann. Like Sophie and my Rudy. Zen no-vone sinks twice. Vill Judge Gardiner disown her?"

"If they are in love and agreed on how they want to spend their lives, why should he? You were right, though, in intending to talk with him. Go when he is free some time."

"Zen you sink I should not put down my foot?"

"Putting down the foot when two young people are in love never gets you anywhere. Except," Ludwig added, "into trouble. Family quarrels. No. Go see what Doug has to say—and if he doesn't like the idea, he'll have to lump it."

Before Mr. Lichtenstein could find Judge Gardiner free, Doug came to him, up the dusty stairs to his notary public office. The two men agreed that however much they might wish matters otherwise, there was nothing to do but make the best of the situation. And if Doug concealed his distaste behind the sarcasm with which he dismissed Mary's political, social, and economic views as an aberration of youth, a childish disease with a hopeful prognosis, Franz's father could accept it: he knew Judge Gardiner's views on those subjects. He could understand that point of view as he could not have accepted the concealed repugnance that Doug felt at the thought of being in any way connected with the gross old man.

Mary's Grandfather Bodien was furiously angry, and swore (to her father, not to Mary) that he would never forgive her. Doug soothed him as best he could, but the Captain could not forbear letting off steam to Ludwig the next morning. And Ludwig, seeing that the engagement was becoming generally known, told Sally of it when he went to Hillcrest that evening. He had waited until they were alone in their big bedroom; with the Evanses there, and Charles's children come from Kansas City for their holiday in the country, you could not count on privacy anywhere else in the house, big as it was.

Sally stopped short in the act of undressing when he told her. "I remember you foresaw this years ago, but is it actually going to happen? A Gardiner and a Lichtenstein? You mean to say her parents are permitting it? A boy who's starting a career of making a nuisance of himself about the poor laborer? The Gardiners have a talent for stooping: first Doug, now Mary. Of course he couldn't put his foot down, could he?"

Ludwig, thinking he had heard all too much lately about feet being put down, said, "Douglas Gardiner is a lawyer and has been a judge for many years; he has more than a fair acquaintance with human nature. I doubt if he will risk estranging his daughter. That is what 'putting a foot down' generally comes to in the end," he concluded bitterly.

Sally understood the reproach, and was cut by it; she knew that Ludwig had not really, in his heart, forgiven her treatment of Paul, though he never alluded to it. At the risk of his saying more, however, she insisted stubbornly, "She'll never be received in Waynesboro as Franz Lichtenstein's wife."

"Don't be foolish, Sally. Sophie Lichtenstein is 'received', isn't she?

"Well, within limits. But Rudy's only a Democrat, which is bad enough. Franz is a Socialist."

"At any rate, they don't plan to be in Waynesboro, 'received' or not—and I can't imagine anything that would trouble them less. They expect to live in New York, where Franz has a job, and carry on the good work there."

"The farther away the better."

(And does she wish, Ludwig thought, that Paul and his *fröhliche Kinder* were far away, so that she would not be stabbed by the thought: so close, but never here?)

"The time may come," she continued, "when you don't speak so lightly of the 'good work'."

"It may indeed. Not that I think labor unions are all bad. Some laborers, where there is a constant flood of immigrants ready to take any job, are certainly underpaid, overworked, and all the rest of it."

"You didn't like it a little bit when those two tried to unionize the mill."

Ludwig laughed. "Of course I didn't. That's what sticks in Bodien's craw. Here, it was nonsense. We don't have so many hands that they can't come to me or Bodien with any grievance. They don't need a union. But that was a pretty amateur effort that Mary and young Lichtenstein put on. I'll never forget Big Liz laying about her."

Sally laughed too. But she went to bed a deeply troubled woman. She had not realized—she could no longer bear the shadow that lay between her and Ludwig. Who was she to say the Gardiners were stooping: it was the pot calling the kettle black. A few nights later, as they lay in their bed together, she said, "Ludwig, you have been right about Paul, and I have been dreadfully wrong. Life is too short for family estrangements to go on and on. Is it too late? Or do you think that if I wrote Ellen and invited them all for the Fourth, she would come?"

"I don't know. It has been a long time. But Liebchen." he turned and took her in his arms, "try it. Paul will welcome it, I think."

He said nothing more, but took an opportunity to warn Elsa not to be too surprised if her mother really did write such a letter—to take it as a matter of course that she was bound to soften in time. And Elsa thought, "One good thing the Gardiner-Lichtenstein engagement has done," though she was never quite sure how it had brought her mother around. She had been from the first day she heard the news a partisan of Mary and Franz: she was fond of Rudy, and accepted his half-brother as of like caliber. The engagement, after everyone knew of it, was announced briefly in the *Torchlight*, with the note "No date for the wedding has been set." The town for the most part refused to be surprised: it was just what might have been expected of that wild pair; Mary had shocked them before and would again, no doubt, but at least she would not be in Waynesboro. What she might do in New York could be overlooked by her native town.

So far as the younger people were concerned, the summer began much as usual. Tucker Gordon arrived in June to spend the summer with his father. At fifteen he was considered responsible enough to change trains in Chicago by himself. His father and grandmother met him at the Waynesboro depot; he leaped from the Pullman steps and hurled himself toward them. Had he not done so, they might not have recognized him: he had reached the age when boys grow fastest and change the most; since the previous summer he had added inches to his height and was rather scrawny, with awkward elbows and knees, and he was wearing steel-rimmed spectacles. When embraces had been exchanged and greetings spoken, his grandmother said, "My goodness, Tuck! You're so big I scarcely know you. And you never wrote us that you had to wear glasses."

"They're new, nearly." He fingered the bow resting on his still immature nose. "They're a nuisance, kind of, but I do see better. Let's get my things and go home. Is Major—?"

"Major is fine. Getting a little fat. You'll have to run him a lot this summer."

Johnny went off with the check for Tucker's trunk, and collected his hand baggage when the porter had lined it up at the foot of the Pullman's steps: a suitcase, a tennis racquet, and a case with a fishing rod in it and a reel in the pocket.

"This looks like it must be a mighty fine rod, Tuck." Too fine by far, Johnny thought, judging by the maker's name, for a fifteen-year-old boy who would never take care of it. How could his mother—?

Instead of showing a proper pride in it, Tucker said scornfully, "It's no good for here. Who could use a fly rod in the old canal? It's too deep for wading and too narrow to cast from the bank. But I had to bring it: it was a present." Then, suddenly fearful, "You haven't lost my bamboo pole, have you?"

His grandmother reassured him. "We haven't lost anything of yours. Your bicycle and your baseball and your fishing rod are all in the woodshed just where you always leave them."

Tucker relaxed. "Gee, it's good to get back. I s'pose Ludwig and Tag-along are out at Hillcrest."

"Along with a half a dozen or so cousins. From what their mother says, they are tired of playing nursemaid and are eagerly awaiting your arrival."

At the dinner table that evening, Johnny returned to the subject of the expensive rod and reel that Tucker had stood in the corner of his room and promptly forgotten, what with the fox terrier leaping on him, and his grandmother's polite inquiries as to the health of his mother and his Grandmother Deming, as to his school, his sports, his friends, his hobbies: all the things grandmothers insist on knowing.

Johnny, when the plates had been served and Louline had retired to the kitchen, said, "How come you didn't tell your mother that wasn't the kind of rod you fish with?"

"Mother? Oh, she didn't buy it. She would have thought it silly. I told you it was a present. From Uncle Robert." As the boy pronounced the name, his face stiffened, became expressionless.

"And who the devil," said his astonished father, "is Uncle Robert?"

"That's what he tells me to call him. I can't help it very well: Mother says I mustn't hurt his feelings."

"But who—?"

The frozen face broke into a gamin grin. "He's Grandmother Deming's beau."

"Tuck, what a vulgar expression!"

"Your grandmother's—?"

"That's what Mother calls him. I—it doesn't seem vulgar when she says it. Because she's just kidding. I guess."

"But who is he? Why your grandmother—?"

"Oh, he's old," Tucker said. "An old, old man. Older'n Grandmother, I guess. He was on that cruise to Alaska they took last summer. They go somewhere every summer. I guess they're glad to get rid of me. Just so they don't make me go along. Anyway, he's been hanging around ever since. Dinner here and dinner there and dinner at our house. And trips on his yacht weekends. Just short trips," he added reassuringly as he read his father's stunned expression. "He hasn't any family of his own, he says. That's why he likes me to call him Uncle Robert. And the fishing rod doesn't really matter, because he's filthy rich."

"Tucker!"

"It that vulgar, too? I'm sorry, Gran. It's what Mother says when she is teasing Grandmother Deming."

"Well—" Anne looked at Johnny, who shook his head. "It's nice that they have a friend who can afford to give them pleasure. I thought your grandmother might be lonely in California."

"Oh, no! They have lots of friends. They belong to a bridge-whist club and—and that sort of thing. It's only that I don't really like Uncle Robert much. He *tries* too hard. You know what I mean?"

They knew what he meant. His grandmother said comfortably, "You won't have to think about him all summer. By fall he may have vanished from the scene."

Tucker was young enough still to feel the summer stretching ahead of him for an almost infinite time; anything could happen. He turned his thoughts to tomorrow and the next day and the next. When tomorrow came, he dug his bicycle out of the shed, cleaned and oiled it, slung his bamboo pole over his shoulder, and started out for Hillcrest. Major trotting beside him. In late afternoon he returned, soaked with perspiration, his hair wet and tousled, a string of crappies and bluegills swinging from his handle bars. His grandmother rejoiced with him in his fisherman's luck, but warned him that if he wanted to eat the fish he would have to clean them: Louline would draw the line.

Louline sent him scatting out to the neighborhood of the garbage can for the cleaning operation, after sniffing at the size of the fish.

"Now, you catch a good big *cat*, that *be* something."

"Oh, Louline! We threw the catfish back."

"Boy, yo' out o' yo' mind. Don't know good eatin', fo' sho'. I reckon the' isn' no catfish in Califo'ny?"

"I reckon not. Next one I catch that's any size at all, I'll bring it to you."

"Yo' do thet, an' Ah clean the measly panfish fo' yo'. But watch them ho'ns—them's poison."

Tucker said, "I will" meekly enough, though he had known all his life, it seemed to him, to be wary of catfish.

One evening when he came in to dinner, he announced that the New York Rausch children with their attendant nursemaid had gone home. "They could hardly wait. Can you imagine? They only come because their mother and father make them, so as not to hurt Uncle Ludwig's feelings, and Aunt Sally's."

"I hope they don't say so to their grandparents, or that you don't."

"Oh, Gran! Nobody wants to hurt anybody's feelings. It's funny, though. They keep talking about their cottage at Watch Hill, right close to the shore, where they can go in the ocean every day if they want to. They don't like swimming in the canal. Silly kids. Sea water's horrid to swim in—all sticky with salt. And you can't really swim in it, anyway, unless you're a lifeguard or something. It's too rough. All you can do is paddle around and pretend."

"How about the Kansas City cousins?"

"They've got more sense. They like Hillcrest. Only Aunt Sally thinks they're too little to go swimming in the canal with us."

"How fortunate—then you don't have to worry about pulling them out." She remembered that Ludwig III, Jennifer, and Tucker had haunted the canal lock and the water behind it long before they were as old as Charles's children.

So far as the young people were concerned, it was a peaceful and rather uneventful summer, if it could be called so when every day offered its own delight. Fourth of July at Hillcrest, with the Paul Rausches present for the first time ever. Although Sally and her young daughter-in-law would never really be happy with one another, the breach had been at least outwardly repaired. Elsa had been stunned when her mother had told her they were coming, but held her tongue, saying only, "Papa will be pleased." But she was amused when Ellen (the only Rausch Paul's wife really knew) confided in her that she thought maybe it was all for the best that Paul's mother had helf off for so long: as a bride, ignorant of the world as she had been, she might have been overawed "by all this," but she had grown accustomed at Cousin Kathleen's to the way people with money lived.

After the Fourth, there was the harvesting of the wheat at the Gordon farm, where the boys were allowed to make themselves more or less useful, shocking the bundles of wheat, carrying water, stuffing themselves at the harvest hands' dinner, going back to town in the evening so tired their bicycles wobbled, and often Ludwig stayed overnight with Tucker because he couldn't face the extra few miles to Hillcrest, and the two of them tumbling into bed, leaving the grains of wheat that fell out of their clothes scattered over the floor that Louline tried to keep clean.

But the boys were growing up. Young Ludwig, who seemed to have put aside for the summer his fascination with the cordage mill, telephoned Tucker one evening at suppertime: his grandfather, just come in, said they would be laying hawser the next day. Ludwig wanted to see it, and wouldn't Tucker like to, too? Then, meet him at the mill at six-thirty. Tucker agreed, but returned to the dining room with the question, "What's so different about a hawser? Lud wants me to go with him to the mill to watch them make one tomorrow."

"'Lay' is the word, not 'make.' Dear me, when I was your age I knew the mill inside out, and all the scores of different kinds of rope. And you live close to the ocean and go yachting, but you don't know what a hawser is?"

"I know it's what they tie a ship to the wharf with, but I didn't know it was different from any rope, except it's bigger."

"A hawser is three right-laid ropes twisted together in a left lay. Never mind: they'll explain it to you tomorrow. Captain Bodien will be only too glad."

When Tucker came in for lunch the next day and was asked as to his morning, he admitted that it had been "kind of interesting." "I learned about hawsers, anyway. I never knew there were so many kinds of rope. Oil well ropes, for rigging and drilling, a dozen different ones. Lariat rope. Climbing ropes, for lumbering." He paused, struck by a sudden thought. "I wonder if Uncle Robert's lumber company buys Rausch rope."

"I thought you said he was an old man. Surely he doesn't go lumbering?"

"He's retired. But I guess he still owns the company. He thought I might like to spend the summer at the camp in Oregon. But I wanted to come home."

"To watch the Cordage Company lay rope?"

"No. I don't really care much about machinery. I am going to be a doctor."

"Oh! You are? Needless to say I would be delighted. But have you told your mother?" She doesn't hold the profession in very high esteem."

"Well, no. I thought there was plenty of time for that. But Uncle Ludwig says that long before you were as old as I am, you were working with Gran'pa rolling bandages and things. Going with him on his calls. Can't I start with you, now?"

Johnny put down his knife and fork to study the boy. Tucker returned his gaze steadily.

"You're really serious about this, aren't you? Well, we don't have to roll bandages any more—they come already rolled and sterile. But you could be useful in the office, sterilizing instruments, that sort of thing, and if nothing else, doing some reading in medical books. I wouldn't mind taking you with me on my country calls, some of them: there are old men, and women too, with broken bones, or anyway, housebound, who enjoys nothing more than a new face. I could explain you were learning."

And so the summer of 1908 turned out to be different from earlier summers. Much time was still given to swimming and fishing and roaming the woods, but more to the serious business of life, as the boys saw it anyway, with Ludwig going to the mill and Tucker to his father's office or into the country, or even, rarely, to the hospital. Jennifer complained so bitterly at their desertion of her that Tucker gave in and asked his father to take her too on his country visits. "Aunt Elsa won't mind, if there's nothing contagious."

"Your 'Tag-along' must take after her mother, who resented being a girl and having to behave like one. I don't mind, Tuck, either, if a call happens to be out that way. I'm too busy to go round by Hillcrest if a patient lives in the other direction."

The summer passed in this preparatory fashion that the boys took earnestly. And although it was in truth uneventful and his duties soon became routine, it brought Tucker and his father closer than they had ever been as they discussed Johnny's cases and treatments, when he felt free to do so.

For the older generation the summer was humdrum enough except for Janey Voorhees' wedding: in the evening in the Reformed Presbyterian church, with a reception at the house afterward, so that a number of Waynesboro husbands, grumbling and resisting to the last, were forced to don dress suits and dress shirts on an evening so hot that wilted collars and buckling bosoms were a certainty. Janey, if not a pretty bride, was at least a transparently happy one. The only jarring note was Eliza Ballard's inquiry as to whether Janey expected to see her brother in the Philippines on their way to India. Janey looked utterly blank for a moment and then said hastily, "Oh, we don't expect to go by way of the Philippines," leaving all who overheard to wonder whether the Vooheeses had the slightest idea as to Blair's whereabouts.

Anne, with Johnny escorting her, had walked to the church; the Rausches insisted on driving them to the reception and, afterward, home again. A few conventional remarks on the wedding were exchanged, and then Anne said, "Poor Janey! I don't suppose she has the slightest idea of what will be expected of her. If ever a child was unprepared to face up to life—"

"I declare, Anne." Sally, in the back with her, clicked her tongue in exasperation. "You have the biggest bump of commiseration of anyone I know. And so unnecessary, in Janey's case. The Reverend Mr. Simpson will be lord of all he surveys. They will be waited on hand and foot, have servants by the dozen, and transfer to the mountains for the hot season."

"You've been reading too much Kipling. You're thinking of British army officers. I don't believe missionaries live like that."

"I do. You don't think Janey and her children, if any, will be allowed to pine away in Lahore through tropical summers? I've been thinking about it and have come to the conclusion that a man's most dangerous choice of profession—dangerous to his immortal soul—is missionarying. Being a minister is next, and teaching school next after that. Teachers and ministers deal with their inferiors. They come to feel that they always know best, and get so they lay down the law to everyone. But missionaries are the worst, because they deal with inferiors not only in godliness and knowledge, but in the color of their skin. Missionaries slip into a Godlike I-can-do-no-wrong assumption that should condemn them to the lowest circle of Hell. 'By that sin fell the angels.' You can laugh, Johnny Gordon, but isn't it true?"

Johnny, in the front seat where she could see his shoulders shaking, said,

"You have a point, Aunt Sally. And what a pleasant thought: Heaven without ministers—all of them in the pit with Lucifer."

"Johnny!" his mother reproved him. "Don't blaspheme."

"And don't be too cocky, either," Sally said. "Doctors are in only slightly less danger. They play God, too; do this, don't do that, or suffer the consequences."

"But we don't feel that our patients are our inferiors. And we don't threaten the disobedient with eternal damnation."

"Our new minister isn't like that at all," Anne protested, "He's an intelligent, agreeable gentleman, who doesn't feel superior to anyone, I'm sure."

"Wait until he moves to Waynesboro and settles down. What is his wife like?"

"I haven't the slightest idea." Anne knew Sally was thinking of the Club. "She wasn't with him the times he preached as a candidate. Too busy to come, I suppose, with two children of her own and a step-daughter."

"Something odd about that marriage." Ludwig, attentive to his driving, spoke for the first time. "Something his last congregation objected to. Maybe your church is more broad-minded."

"More broad-minded that the Reformed Presbyterians, anyway. What did you hear, Ludwig? And how on earth—?"

"How d'you suppose? Eliza. She and that female newshawk in the Post Office put their heads together. Miss Christy knows somebody in the town he is leaving and got the story. She wrote and asked, wondering why, if he was as good a preacher as everyone seemed to think, he was leaving. And according to her friend—mind you, Anne, there may not be a word of truth in this—it had leaked out that he had been a Reformed Presbyterian minister originally, but after his first wife died, he married his cousin. That is an unforgivable sin, apparently, to the R.P.'s, and he was excommunicated. So he moved to this town in Pennsylvania, after having been ordained as a Presbyterian minister. But when the congregation found out, they too turned against him. His oldest daughter—there was no blot on her, of course—went to the Reformed Presbyterian Sunday school and church, where she explained the family situation."

"Oh, Ludwig! Trouble before he even gets here. Is Eliza spreading this tale?"

"You know Eliza. Your church doesn't excommunicate a good Presbyterian just because he married a cousin, surely?"

"Not that I ever heard of. But what chance do they have of being happy here? I wonder whether the Session knew all this when they invited him? Sheldon's an Elder now, I'll ask him. How old is the stepdaughter? It might be—Oh, dear! I'd like to give Eliza a piece of my mind. But better the whole story come out and *nothing* be made of it. Because it isn't worth making trouble over. It's just that Eliza does love to stir things up."

"Think what a dull life she would lead otherwise." Sally teased her: "Can't you find it in your heart to be sorry for her?"

"No, I can't. Not yet, anyway," she added, thinking how gaunt and ill Eliza had looked at the wedding, in spite of her size.

The conversation ended there: Ludwig had stopped his car at the Gordon gate; Johnny alighted and came to open the door for his mother; thanks and good-nights were spoken, and Ludwig drove off.

The next day Anne went up to Sheldon & Edwards' to see if she could have a moment in private with its owner. The street was dazzingly hot and bright, the store's interior so dark by contrast that she stopped inside the door for a moment. The great fans whirred overhead, stirring the voiles and lawns and dimities spread on the counters. There were one or two customers toward the rear; she could hear voices. Before she could locate a clerk who might tell her where Sheldon was, young Lowrey came hurrying, his hand outstretched to take her elbow.

"Mrs. Gordon! Are you all right?"

She smiled at him. No doubt in his mind she belonged to the category of helpless elderly widow. "Good-morning, Lowrey." How much the boy—boy?—looked like his father at that age! "I am quite all right, thank you. For a moment, coming in out of that sun, I couldn't see. Now my eyes have adjusted, and I can admire your enticing display of yard goods. But I must apologize—I didn't come as a customer this morning, but to have a word with your father. Is he here?"

If Lowrey was curious he gave no sign of it. He said, "He's in his private sanctum, up on the mezzanine. I'll show you. This way."

"If he's busy—"

"You may be sure he isn't too busy to talk to you."

She followed him down the center aisle to the broad curving stairs, up them, and to the partitioned-off corner at the rear of what Lowrey called the "mezzanine," though to Anne it had always been the "balcony" where cloaks and suits and corsets and other intimate garments were fitted behind closed cubby-hole doors. The office, once on the ground floor, was up here, in more spacious quarters. Lowrey opened the door, poked his head in, said, "Mrs. Gordon to see you, Pop," and smiling at her took his departure.

"Anne! What brings you out on a hot morning like this? Is something wrong?"

"I hope not. I just thought— Can we be private here? I should have gone to your house, but I knew Jessamine would wonder; and if what I heard hasn't a word of truth in it, it need not be spread."

"Sit down, Anne, and spit it out. You terrify me."

He was laughing at her, of course. And how easy it was to pick up the young people's slang! "Spit it out," indeed!

She took the chair he offered her, smoothed her skirt over her knees, and then the wrinkles out of her gloves.

"What I've come about is really none of my business. I'm interfering again. And it may not be important. Johnny thinks it is just funny, and nothing to make a fuss about. So if I overstep the line, don't answer, and I'll not feel rebuffed." And then she began more hurriedly. "When the Session interviewed Mr. Patton, did he tell you the story of his life?"

Sheldon, who had stopped smiling, sat perfectly still for a second. Then, "I think so. What have you heard?"

She told him, concluding, "There isn't anything in our church laws, is there, about not marrying cousins?"

His lips twitched into a half-smile. "No. Nor in the Pentateuch, so far as I know. He told us, yes. We promised him—"

"To keep it quiet? Sheldon, you might have known."

"I suppose so. Who ferreted it out?"

"Eliza Ballard, of course."

"It's no concern of hers. She's a Methodist."

"Everything is Eliza's concern. Surely you know that. How much damage will be done, do you think?"

"I don't know," he said slowly. "I suppose he will be ostracized by the Reformed Presbyterians, and it is the strongest church in town."

"And the most bigoted."

"Not so bigoted, I hope, as the Pennsylvania presbytery that excommunicated Mr. Patton. He told us how shortly before his own trouble he married an elderly couple, widow and widower, who had been engaged when they were youngsters, but had been separated by their parents because one family were 'New Light' Convenanters and one 'Old Light'."

"How ubelievable! But there are no more bitter quarrels than those that split a congregation. I suppose Old Lighters and New Lighters hated each other even more than they hated Roman Catholics. But it's a pity that Mr. Patton couldn't have found a church in town where there were no Reformed Presbyterians."

"I suppose so. Yet, you heard him preach, Anne—you met him. Do you think we should at this late date tell him we have changed our minds? How difficult is it going to be?"

"I don't know. But don't give in to the nay-sayers even before they say nay. I just hoped you could think of something to do that would ward off trouble for him and his family."

"It might have been better if we had told the congregation all this at the meeting where they voted to invite him. Then anyone who couldn't accept the situation could have voted 'No.' But after all, they're only second cousins. It's ridiculous."

"Second? You mean it was their grandparents who were brother and sister, or however it was?"

"Yes. I wish he could have brought Mrs. Patton with him to Waynesboro. She is delightful. But I'm prejudiced: something about her reminded me of Kitty. But the step-daughter may be difficult."

"I hope no one will be reminded of the McCunes."

"Why the McCunes?"

"You wouldn't remember, I suppose. A second marriage that was perfectly proper, but a daughter who ran away."

"I always understood McCune was a bigot of the worst kind, and Ariana, everyone liked her, didn't they? I mean Johnny and the others her age? This girl is different—as different as Mr. Patton and Mr. McCune. I saw her only once, of course, but she's plain, unattractive, sullen, and at the most difficult age, too—thirteen or fourteen. Of course Ariana must have been difficult, too, but not sullen. With her friends she wore her heart on her sleeve, as they say. Or so I always believed."

"Yes. Quick to laugh, quick to weep. Affectionate."

"This girl showed no sign of having a heart. And if she really stuck to the Reformed Presbyterian Church—was that part of Eliza's story?—then if so the R.P.'s here will be waiting and watching." Then Sheldon added with sudden resolution, "I think I will go talk with Mr. Campbell. He's a decent enough fellow—narrow, of course, but—"

"I am sure you will do whatever is best. Don't involve me if you don't have to. I am breaking a longstanding vow never to interfere in anyone else's life again. I only came because I thought you should know there might be trouble ahead."

"It's as well we should be prepared. I am truly grateful to you, Anne."

When she had closed the office door behind her, Sheldon returned to his desk chair, sighing and lamenting the day he had permitted himself to be chosen as Elder. And Anne went down the stairs thinking that Sheldon was much too easy-going to prepare for the worst before it happened. At any rate, she had done the only thing she could do.

As for Eliza Ballard, she had thrown her last stone into the Waynesboro pool to see how far the circles spread. One morning a couple of weeks or so after Janey Voorhees' wedding, she was late in getting to work; and when she did come into the office, she dropped into the chair behind her desk and stayed there. Ludwig, waiting for her to go over the mail with him, heard someone in the other office say, "What's the matter, Miss Ballard?"

He rose at once and went to he door. Eliza was sitting bolt upright, gripping the edge of her desk so hard that the tendons of her hands stood out like heavy cords.

"What is it, Eliza? Do you feel ill?"

"Just a touch of indigestion. But more, maybe, acute this time—"

She gave up her valiant attempt to conceal her agony, bent double over the desk, with her hands pressed hard, one over the other, at the end of her breast bone.

"You shouldn't have come. But since you didn't stay home and call the doctor like a sensible woman, I'll take you to see him. Hand me her hat, someone, and help me get her into the auto."

"I'm not going to the doctor. It will—pass off—it does."

"You are going to the doctor. Especially since it would seem this isn't the first. Johnny Gordon, I suppose?"

The frightened little bookkeeper helped Ludwig get her into Ludwig's automobile, doubled over with pain but still rebellious. With some difficulty they got her into the back seat. Ludwig said as he cranked the car, "Go call Dr. Gordon's office. If he isn't there, I'll take her directly to the hospital. If he is there, tell him we are coming."

Through white lips Eliza insisted. "Not the hospital. I absolutely refuse."

Fortunately Johnny was reached on the phone and was reported to be in his office. Ludwig climbed in behind the steering wheel.

"First time," Eliza muttered, "ever rode in one of these."

"And whose fault? I've offered any number of times to take you home." If Eliza could even attempt to be conversational, he thought, the pain must have eased a bit; he was sure of it when he stopped at the Gordon office and helped her down to the running board and over to the curb. Nevertheless, he was thankful to turn her over to Johnny.

Johnny took her into the back office, telling Tucker to skedaddle as they passed him reading in the middle room; he knew very well how Eliza would feel at having the boy there. Once the door had closed behind them, he bade her loosen her clothes and lie down on the couch. Thankful to get her belt off, her skirt band unbuttoned, her corset unhooked, she said, "Fuss about nothing. Indigestion. Better already."

"Lie down. Flat on your back."

Lying so, her abdomen was mountainous. Johnny said, "Can you look at that and not know what is the matter with you? You may indeed have indigestion—your stomach and intestines haven't room to function."

"A tumor, I suppose. But that's nothing to get upset about. If it had been malignant—"

"You would have been dead long ago. I know. But serious damage may have been done."

He took his stethoscope and went over her chest, inch by inch. "Miss Ballard, that wasn't indigestion. It was a heart attack."

"Heart?"

"No doubt about it. You must have that tumor out. Without waiting."

"An *operation?* I absolutely refuse."

"I can't force you, of course. And I can't promise it isn't too late. Your internal organs have been squeezed together like a sponge, and there is definite heart damage. But I can promise that if you don't have it out—"

"Days numbered? Then why not let me die in peace?"

"You can call it 'peace,' what you suffered this morning? There would be more and more of it. Besides, you have more spunk than that. I would expect you to take even a hundred-to-one-chance." Without waiting for a reply, he went to the phone, called the hospital, told whoever answered to prepare a room and tell Rodney they were coming. He then told the operator to call his mother and ask her to send Tucker back to the office to answer any calls there might be, but if he wasn't handy, not to worry. Then he turned back to help Eliza. "Leave that damnable garment off," he said. "Carry it under your arm."

"But—stockings—indecent."

"Forget it. My automobile is out back. No one will see you. At the hospital orderlies will bring a stretcher."

"A stretcher!" Eliza's lips quivered. "Will—will Rodney want to operate right away?"

"This afternoon, for instance? Hardly, after this morning's attack. We'll have to get your heart settled down first. Don't worry about the operation. You'll be under anesthesia—you won't know anything about it." She kept silent. After a moment he went on, "We have known each other a long while—been through a lot together. I know how much courage you have."

"You remember, then, Ariana?"

"Remember Ariana? Of course I do. We grew up together. And after she came home, to your house, I saw her almost every day."

They drew up at the rear door of the hospital. Two Negro youths in white were waiting with a stretcher; they got her inside to the room that had been prepared for her. A nurse was standing by to undress her, get her into bed. Johnny said, "I must go consult with Rodney, if he's finished in the operating room. We'll be back, but if you have that pain again, tell the nurse. She will call me." He went out, leaving a wild-eyed Eliza.

She said to the nurse, "He'll give me something?"

"For the pain, if you have another attack? Yes, of course. But lie down and rest quietly and it may not come back."

Eliza rested, if not quietly, for what seemed to her an eternity. Rodney came in with Johnny, eventually, and they proceeded to examine her with and without their stethoscopes; their only remarks were enigmatic ones, directed at each other. "Treating me like a wax dummy," she thought rebelliously. When they had done, she smoothed her hospital gown down as far as it would go, pulled the sheet up under her chin, feeling that she had endured the ultimate in humiliation. She said, "Well?"

"Johnny and I will have to sort this out, and decide. But I can say now that what Johnny has told you is correct. Your only chance is to have that tumor out. The sooner the better."

"Then I must stay here? But no toothbrush, no comb, no decent gown—"

"We are prepared for emergencies. New toothbrushes. New combs. The gown you must put up with. Makes it easier for the nurses when a patient is helpless."

"So I am going to be helpless. I see. Let Ludwig know, will you please? And Amanda Reid. We were to have dinner together tonight. Tell her I want to see her."

Outside in the hall, Johnny said, "What are the chances?"

Rodney shrugged his shoulders. "Not good. Too much damage done. These damnfool old maids won't consult a doctor in time."

Then at the look on Johnny's face he added, "Sorry, I didn't mean to sound heartless. She's a friend of our mothers, isn't she? But I get so frustrated with these *idiots* who wait until it is too late!"

Johnny went off to make his telephone calls: to Ludwig, to his mother, who might perhaps reach Amanda Reid at noon, and to his office, to ask Tuck if anyone had called. He was well aware that by nightfall everyone in town would have been informed that Eliza was in the hospital. His and Rodney's estimate of her chances he kept to himself, knowing full well that if she died there would still be some to say, "I told you so. You go into the hospital to die." It made no difference that many more patients recovered than were lost. He hoped that his mother and Ludwig would not be the only ones to say, "What a pity she waited so long!"

Amanda came to see Eliza that evening. She had never been in the hospital before, and she entered with quaking knees and a sickish feeling in her stomach. It helped that the receptionist at the desk was a former pupil: Amanda at once was in control of the situation.

"Miss Ballard sent word that she wanted to see me. If you will tell me which is her room?"

"I'll have to check with the nurse. I believe the orders were 'No visitors'."

"Do that, please." The nurse came to report that the order did not apply to Miss Reid—that she might see Miss Ballard for ten minutes. "He says you are to keep her from talking as much as possible." The nurse started down the hall, Amanda following, despising herself for the way her knees were behaving. Once inside the room, however, she recovered her composure. Eliza, although in bed, looked as well as she had looked any time in the last year or so.

The two friends greeted each other noncommittally, under the nurse's eyes. Eliza waited for her to go; when she showed no sign of doing so she asked her to leave in no uncertain terms.

"I wish to speak to my friend in private." she said.

"But the doctor said only ten minutes."

"Miss Reid is very conscientious. But if she fails to notice when the ten minutes have passed, you may return."

The effort required for that speech left Eliza white of face and short of breath. The nurse left saying only, "No more talking than necessary. Doctor's orders." She closed the door firmly behind her.

The effect on Eliza of her brief dialogue with the nurse frightened Amanda. She said, "I'm sorry you—I came as soon as I could. Is there anything I can do for you?"

"Just don't say 'I told you so.' You were right about this. I admit it." With a listless gesture she indicated the mounded bedclothes.

"Don't waste words on such foolishness. The doctor said you were to talk as little as possible. I was to do the talking. So tell me as briefly as possible what I can do for you."

"Nothing. I want to ask you a question. I have no family, as you know. You are my oldest friend. How are you fixed?"

"Fixed?"

"Financially. Have you enough saved up?"

Amanda drew herself up, antagonized by Eliza's blunt approach. "I am quite capable of taking care of myself, as you should know by this time. I need nothing from you. Besides, why think of such things? You aren't all that badly off. Once that growth is removed you will be all right—live to spend your money."

"The doctors haven't much hope. I can tell, though they don't say so. Do you want what little I have, or not? Don't be too proud to say so."

Amanda was too proud. And besides, she knew Eliza so well. If she really wanted to leave her what she had, she would not have bothered to ask her: asking was just a recognition of a lifelong friendship.

"At this point or any other, Eliza, I can take care of myself, as I have always done."

Eliza sighed, closed her eyes. Lying so, she looked to Amanda both very old and ill.

"Eliza, isn't there anything—?"

Eliza lifted her hand from the folded-back sheet, gestured in negation. "That's what I wanted to know. I intend to make my will tomorrow. I hope you understand."

"I promise you—if it comes to reading your will, as I hope it won't, I shall understand. That is all? There is nothing I can bring you? Then my time isn't up, but I think I had better call the nurse."

She opened the door and motioned. As the nurse made her swishing approach, Amanda looked back at the bed. "Good-night, Eliza."

Eliza, spent but firm, said, "Good-bye Amanda. Thank you for coming."

The next day she asked Johnny for a pencil and paper. She was more like herself, had had no more pain, and was intent on carrying out her intention.

"Paper and pencil? Why not just rest?"

"After I make my will. Should have done it before. It will stand, though, if it is handwritten, and witnessed by you and Rodney. And if you say my mind was clear."

He brought her paper and pencil, helped her to sit up, turned the bedside table so that she could write on it, and waited while she scrawled a few lines, folded the paper over so that there was space for him to write his name without being able to read what she had written.

"There," she said. "Short and clear."

He signed in full: John Alexander Gordon. "I'll tell Rodney you want him to sign, though he may not be out of the operating room yet. The nurse would do."

"The nurse! She hasn't the slightest idea that I am *compos mentis*. Doesn't act like it, anyway." Rodney was summoned, came, and signed his name. Eliza said, "Mail it to young Merrill, will you? If I get up and about again, I'll do it in proper form."

Eliza survived the operation two days later. (A *forty pound* tumor was the awed whisper that circulated in the town, though how its citizens could have had any notion of its size when the doctors and a tight-lipped nurse passed on no information, no one could be sure. It was a case of "I heard—Could it be possible?")

She survived the operation, recovered consciousness, and was hideously sick; then, two days later, she had another more severe heart attack and died of cardiac failure. She was buried from her church with all the showmanship of the Methodists, all members of the Woman's Club, according to their natures, suffering through it or accepting it with a kind of pleasure in its perfection.

Johnny said to his mother when they sat down to dinner that evening, "I thought you and Aunt Sally would be more upset about Eliza Ballard."

Anne unfolded her napkin slowly, thankful that Tucker was at Hillcrest for the night: she could speak freely. "Of course she was a charter member of the Club, and I have seen her every two weeks in the winter for years, besides having known her in a sort of way all my life. She will be missed." Then when Louline, having passed the vegetables, returned to the kitchen, she said, "I never heard such a eulogy. How the minister could have had the *face* to say what he did about her. Of course there was more about her parents, and her being 'the last of one of Waynesboro's distinguisshed families.' It all made me slightly sick. The only suitable text for Eliza's funeral sermon should have been taken from *Julius Caesar*."

Johnny looked blank for a moment, then laughed a little. "You mean 'The evil that men do'? I have never heard you so uncharitable."

"She caused a lot of unhappiness in her time." Surely he must suspect that it was Eliza who had gossiped to Mrs. Deming?

"What I remember best about her is her care of Ariana through that long, hopeless illness. She was capable of a selfless devotion."

"Yes, she was. I'm sorry, Johnny. She loved that child and the old Judge, and has been a good and loyal friend of Ludwig. The good must not be interred and forgotten."

"Uncle Ludwig won't forget it. He admits to the hopelessness of finding her equal as a secretary. He paid her hospital and funeral expenses. I told him I thought there was no need: she made a will just after she entered the hospital, and she wouldn't have bothered if she had had noting to leave."

"Her half of the house, I suppose, at least. Who is to have it? She has no family, and she wouldn't leave it to Sam Travers. He wasn't even at the funeral, didn't you notice?"

On the day after the funeral, Tim Merrill telephoned Ruhamah McCune at the library and made an appointment with her for late that afternoon; he also called Amanda Reid after school. Amanda said tartly that if it was about Eliza's will, she had said not to leave her anything, and if she had, he could tell her over the telephone. Tim, relieved that he was not to have to face disappointment, said, "Only her books, and her half of her father's library." And Amanda said, "Thank you for saving me a trip uptown. I expected nothing."

When Ruhamah entered the Gardiner & Merrill office at the appointed time, she was confused and frightened; she could think of no possible reason for the summons except that she must have done something wrong at the library—the bookkeeping? She said to the receptionist at the desk that had once been Eliza's, "Mr. Merrill? He made an appointment with me." She picked at the frayed finger-tips of her gloves.

"Yes, I know. Come inside." She pressed the catch that released the gate in the railing. "I'll tell him you're here."

The young woman smiled. Imagine being nervous because of Tim Merrill, even if he was now County Prosecutor! "It's not bad news, believe me."

Tim, having heard their voices, came to the door of his office. "Come in, Ruhamah." His superior age and the fact that his wife had once taught her brought the use of her first name easily to his tongue, although his children, devoted patrons of the library as they were, stood in awe and were a little afraid of Miss McCune. He said, "Indeed, it is good news for you. Come take a chair by the desk. I have a document to read to you." He studied her for a moment before unfolding the sheet of paper on his desk: the severely dressed, flat-chested, stooped little figure, the plain square bespectacled face, the hair parted in the middle, combed flat and knotted on the back of her head. She looked so exactly suited to the life she led—it seemed inappropriate, in a way—Eliza's will. He cleared his throat and said again, "I have a document to read to you." He could see the heartbeats in her neck above the tight collar; she had not been reassured. Best get it over.

"You knew Miss Eliza Ballard, of course? This is her will, written in the hospital and witnessed by her doctors. 'I, Eliza Ballard, being sound of mind, do declare this to be my last will and testament. I direct that all my debts be paid, and my funeral expenses'—and by the way, there were no funeral expenses: Mr. Rausch paid for those. 'Since I have no surviving kin, I give and bequeath my estate to Amanda Reid and Ruhamah McCune, spinsters of this town. To Amanda Reid, my books and my share of my father's library. to Ruhamah all the residue: my savings account at the bank and my half of my father's house. I do this not only in rememberance of her deceased sister, who was dear to me, and would have had everything of mine had she lived, but out of admiration for her courage and her resolute independence, and the way in which she has conducted the Carnegie Library of Waynesboro. Signed, Eliza Ballard; witnessed by John Alexander Gordon and Rodney Stevens.'" He looked up when he had finished reading to find her staring at him—in confusion? Or in consternation? "You had no idea Miss Ballard intended this?"

"No. I—" Ruhamah smiled doubtfully. "I wonder if she did intend it? Or if she couldn't think of anyone else? Why not to Miss Reid? They have been friends—"

"Time out of mind, I know. But this is what she intended. Johnny says she wrote it down in one motion, almost, as if she had learned it by heart. And when I called Miss Reid to invite her to come listen, as one of the heirs, she said, 'Eliza promised not to leave me anything,' and was surprised even about the books. So you need have no qualms."

"But what did she think I would do with that house? Even half of it?"

"There are several things you can do. Live in it for one."

"All alone, as she has all this time? And so far from the library?" Ruhamah shook her head.

"You could sell it. There is nothing in the law to prevent that, though it might be difficult, with Mr. Travers still living and giving music lessons in the other half. Or you could rent it. You will have plenty of time to think it over. The will must be probated, and an estate is not settled overnight. The court will take care of any debts, or I will as executor, and pay the taxes as they fall due, and see that necessary repairs are made out to the savings account. Allow me to congratulate you, Ruhamah: you are bewildered now, but soon you will realize it means you won't have to worry about the future."

In due time the will was published in the *Torchlight*'s Court News. Since no one had expected anything from Eliza Ballard, there was no disappointment; there was in some quarters (mostly Methodist) regret that there had been no deathbed reconciliation with her brother-in-law, but not among those who had been familiar with the situation over the years and knew Eliza and Sam Travers. He might seem a mousy little man—a nonentity to some people, but not to his music pupils (a large proportion of Waynesboro's population, adult and juvenile). Few had escaped having their knuckles rapped for their careless mistakes, and quite a number of them had been refused further lessons because they would not or could not learn to play the piano at least passably. He was not the man to have accepted largesse from the sister-in-law who had never pretended not to despise him, and her sister for having married him.

For once at least the recipient of good fortune was not envied. No one begrudged Ruhamah such a stroke of luck: she deserved it. There were some, however, who wondered what on earth she would do with half of that gloomy, huge, old-fashioned house—the house that had been Judge Ballard's pride when it was built, and Waynesboro's showplace.

After Eliza's death, one other event of the summer engaged the attention of at least some Waynesboro adults: the arrival and installation of the new Presbyterian minister. Mr. Patton came alone for the occasion: he intended to ensure that the scandal that had followed him from one Pennsylvania town to another would not make Waynesboro impossible for his wife. If there were clouds on the horizons, he intended to resign the charge before he took it. He therefore called on Sheldon Edwards promptly, once he had left his valise with the McKinneys, his host and hostess for the weekend. The long session with Sheldon was in part disquieting: his situation was known; in another way, it was reassuring. Sheldon had talked to the Reverend Mr. Campbell, minister of the Reformed Presbyterians, who had made it quite clear that he considered the private life of the Presbyterian minister a matter only for the church considering him, not for him or his congregation.

"'When he was excommunicated from our church, we were left with no jurisdiction. I believe he is a good man who has done nothing against his conscience,'" Sheldon quoted the Reverend. "Mr Campbell didn't say—couldn't. I suppose,—that he thought his church acted with unnecessary conformity to outworn rules."

"Thank you, Mr. Edwards, for making our path smoother than it might have been." Mr. Patton's smile was tentative. "How about the women? They could still make Deborah unhappy."

"The sister who keeps house for Mr. Campbell is not without force, or influence, I believe, over the ladies of the Missionary Society and the Ladies' Aid."

"That sounds hopeful. But there is one other thing." He looked uncomfortable. "I hate to bring this up, but feel that I must. As you have doubtless heard, my oldest daughter Naomi has never forgiven my second marriage. She has helped to make things difficult. I do not understand it: Deborah has tried valiantly to win her confidence and affection. Naomi was but four when her mother died, six when I married again. She was older than that, of course, at the time of our troubles. She was already a member of the church, which gave her grounds for saying that *she* had not been excommunicated, and would continue to belong to her mother's church. I suppose I should have taken a firm stand. But how could I? If she thought hers was the only church, who was I to tell her differently? Now she is thirteen, a very difficult age to deal with. But I want my family to be united in one church. Do you suppose we could see the Reverend Mr. Campbell about this?"

If Sheldon thought Mr. Patton a little weak in confessing his helplessness, he did not say so. "Certainly. He is very approachable. We may as well go at once. I'll telephone first."

"There is one other problem I should like to bring up, before we go—oh, a lesser one, let me reassure you. As you know, the McKinneys have kindly taken me in for the weekend. I have had a good chance to see the house. Mrs. McKinney takes it for granted that it will continue to be the manse. But I understand from the financial arrangements we made that the house is but rented, with the church paying the rent?"

"Yes. We have never thought it wise to own a manse: after all, ministers' families come in different sizes. The McKinneys have been here for so long, however, that I suppose everyone takes it for granted. You don't like the house?"

"It is a pleasant house. But it is small and there are five of us."

Sheldon frowned, drummed his fingertips on his desk. "Unfortunately, there is very little rental property in Waynesboro—nothing very suitable that I can think of." Then his face cleared. "One possibility occurs to me. The result of a recent death." He summarized the facts briefly: Eliza's death, Ruhamah's newly inherited property. "Of course the estate has not been settled yet. But the court would permit the church to rent it, I feel sure. You understand: it would be only half of a very large house, with a music teacher living in the other half. Could you stand that? The walls are no doubt thick, but even so."

"At this point, that seems minor." Mr. Patton smiled, more genuinely this time. "Could we see it?"

"I'll call the executor. I believe there is a caretaker."

Sheldon made his two telephone calls, and they set out on their errands. Armed with a note from Tim Merrill, they went out to view the Ballard house. Eliza had lived so entirely in her bedroom, dining room, and kitchen, that the other rooms were almost exactly as Mrs. Ballard had left them: the furniture dust-covered upstairs and down, the drawing room and front hall chandeliers tied up in bags.

"The furniture—" Sheldon was stopped for a moment by the sight of the massive sideboard, the big mahogany dining table. "Of course it can't be sold until the estate is settled. If the house suits you, could you live with it for a while?"

This time Mr. Patton actually laughed, thinking of their battered pieces. "It is so much better than ours. Deborah would be delighted. And yes, I like the house, and so would she. The best thing about it is its being on the edge of town, with all that huge yard: a wonderful place for children."

They could hear the tinkling of the piano next door in a muted way. "If that piano geets to be too much, you could always use the study in the church for writing sermons. Mr. McKinney has used it. I'll see Merrill and find out what can be done. Now for the Reverend."

Sheldon, who had been congratulating himself and his congregation that Mr. Patton was not painfully ministerial of speech, found that he inevitably slipped into it, once he had been introduced to Mr. Campbell.

"It is kind of you, sir, to spare me a moment."

"Not at all. It is good of Mr. Edwards to allow me this opportunity to meet and welcome you. Come into the study, won't you?"

Once they were seated in the study, Mr. Campbell looked his fellow Calvinist over with a keen and not particularly indulgent eye. "What can I do for you? I have already assured Mr. Edwards that you will not be persecuted by me or, if I can help it, by any member of my congregation."

"He told me. I cannot express how grateful I am. More even for my wife that for myself. I hope that here I shall be able to preach the word of God, and do what good I am able, free from harassment. However, one problem remains." He explained about his recalcitrant daughter Naomi. "Here in Waynesboro, where we dare hope to start with a clean slate, I should like all my family to be in the minister's pew on a Sabbath morning. Would it be considered proselyting if I asked you not to receive Naomi into your church? She will bring you her letter, I know, and ask that it be accepted."

The Reverend Mr. Campbell, childless, looked at him pityingly: a minister of the gospel who could not control his own family! "I cannot refuse, nor can the Session, to accept into my flock one who brings us a letter from her former church. I am sure you will agree. However, if she comes to me, I will do my best to dissuade her. I agree with you: it is fit and proper for a minister's family to sit united at his feet."

Mr. Patton felt that even so much showed a broad-mindedness on the part of a Reformed Presbyterian minister that was unexpected and reassuring. After thanking him, he and Sheldon rose to go.

"I should like you to meet my sister before you take your leave. She is my help and mainstay."

He took them into his parlor and introduced them to Miss Campbell, who was busying herself hemming napkins. Mr. Patton was a little disconcerted by her quizzical appraisal of him, head to toe; he felt the truth of what Mr. Edwards had said: if she were an ally, she would be a formidable one.

These visits and decisions were made on Saturday; on Sunday Mr. Patton was formally installed as the new Presbyterian minister; on Monday he returned to Pennsylvania to pick up his family and such belongings as were worth bringing to Waynesboro. What remained they would sell to a secondhand dealer for what they could get; their linens and things of that sort could be packed in trunks along with their clothes. They were in Waynesboro and settling into Eliza Ballard's house before it seemed possible.

Anne gave them a little time to recover from their move, and then, armed with her card case, a fan, and a parasol, went to call. Johnny had taken Tucker as far as Chicago on his way to California, since there was a medical meeting there he wanted to attend. The ineffable, eternal summer, had, after all, come to an end. Anne was glad to leave her empty house and a woebegone Major for even a little while, although the prospect of calling on Mrs. Patton was a rather daunting one in view of the circumstances.

Mrs. Patton came to the door herself, aproned, her face flushed, her hair escaping its bounds in damp tendrils. "A pretty woman," Anne thought, surprised—and wondering at her surprise, remembered Sheldon's comment, and said to herself, "But she isn't in the least like Kitty."

She said, "I am sorry. I seem to have come at an inconvenient time. I had hoped you were all settled." She entered the door held open for her, laid a card on the table in the hall, and continued, "I am one of your husband's congregation—Mrs. John Gordon. I wanted to welcome you as soon as possible."

"Mrs. Gordon? How kind of you. Do come into the drawing room." Mrs. Patton untied her apron, dropped it on the newel post, and led the way. "I suppose you know this room well? We have changed nothing. I understand the furniture cannot be sold until the estate is settled, and so we are living with it." Unexpectedly, she laughed, a laugh of pure amusement. "It is so—so incongruous—for the Pattons."

Anne took one of the stiff chairs, looked about her, and said, "I was familiar with it once. It is years since I have been in it. But I can see nothing has changed." She could almost conjure up a long-dead Mrs. Ballard, standing in the fireplace angle and presiding over Club meetings. "Miss Ballard was a business woman; she had no leisure for exchanging calls or entertaining the Woman's Club. I suppose you have heard the story of the Ballards from everyone you've met?"

"We have heard it," Mrs. Patton admitted cautiously. "Mr. Travers has called. We found him most kind."

"He is a thoroughly kind and good man. It was not his fault—I suppose he or someone has told you of the old Judge's will that split the house? I hope the music lessons won't annoy you too much? And of course I should have known: Eliza never opened up these front rooms, and the cleaning job must have been monumental. You couldn't possibly be ready for callers."

Mrs. Patton shook her head vigorously; more blond trendrils escaped. "Not at all."

She was interrupted by a crash of broken glass or china from the rear of the house. She started up, then ruefully sank back. "Something broken. I hope not too valuable an item belonging to the estate. Miss McCune did tell us to use everything as if it were our own. I think she hopes to sell it to us eventually."

"I did interrupt you, then, in your settling in. I'm sorry. But surely you don't have to wash all that—"

"All that china?" Mrs. Patton laughed again. "It seemed such a blessing to have the use of it. If we can find two glasses that match among our own things, we are lucky. But it did have the dust of ages on it."

"Of course. I don't suppose Eliza used more than a plate and a cup and saucer. No doubt it is the same next door. The two girls divided their mother's china and silver."

The wide blue eyes of her hostess widened further. "There must have been enough to have served the—the President."

"It may *have*. The Judge was a great friend of the Hayeses, but I don't remember whether they entertained them after he was elected President."

"That should impress the children—make them more careful. I left the two oldest in the kitchen when the doorbell rang. Thankfully, Davie is still small enough to sleep in the afternoon."

"I am wasting your time, then. You'd better get back," and Anne rose. "If you'll lend me an apron, I'll help. I would be more reliable than the children."

She followed Mrs. Patton from the room, thankful that no self-conscious protest had been made. At the threshold of the kitchen, the two women paused. The smaller girl, the image of her mother, blue eyes, curling golden tendrils that had escaped from their plaits, was stooped over holding the dust pan, while the older one swept into it pieces and shards of shattered porcelain. Both stopped still at the presence of the two women. The little one gave them a sidelong mischievous glance as she said, "We hoped we could get this swep' up before you came. So you wouldn't know."

"What an idea! We could hear it all the way to the parlor. This is Mrs. Gordon—Melissa, Naomi. She was kind enough to call to welcome us, and now has come out to help with the dishwashing. I won't scold you, though you might say you are sorry."

The older girl had not spoken. Now she said, without looking at them, "We're sorry."

"Never mind—just get it swept up and go somewhere else. Mrs. Gordon and I will finish. But get an apron for her first, will you, Naomi?"

In the kitchen, washing dishes together, dialogue between the two women became more spare but easier, any dead spots covered by their picking dishes up, washing and wiping and putting them away.

"I don't believe we'll ever miss whatever was broken," Mrs. Patton said. "The appraisers may. But mercy me, if they take their time over that estate, there will be more than one piece gone. Maybe we shouldn't use it, after all."

"Oh, do use it. What's the sense—? It has been sitting on those shelves since Mrs. Ballard died, doing no one any good. Children are just naturally destructive. But I'll say one thing for those two: neither accused the other."

"Talebearing is the one thing I will not put up with, and they know it. It was doubtless Melissa who dropped it: she is still a butter-fingers at six."

Any slight discomfiture Mrs. Patton might have felt over the incident had dissipated. She asked about Waynesboro and Waynesboro people and her husband's new congregation as if there were no shadow on her mind, as if she felt no misgiving as to their welcome. Anne was sure that she was happily confident of her welcome. Mr. Patton must have convinced her—probably not a difficult task; she would be easily convinced. Her resemblence to Kitty Edwards: Anne put her finger on what Sheldon had been unable to express; like Kitty, Deborah Patton had a merry heart. Over the years Anne could hear an old man's voice uttering those words like a benediction. Old Mr. Edwards, Sheldon's father, on the night Kitty died. She brooded a moment as they put the last dishes away on the shelves, a pleasurable melancholy, after all these years. If the young woman beside her had Kitty's gift, she was well-armored. She would need to be. That older girl, the stepdaughter, had not smiled once while she was still in the kitchen. She was a very plain child:

glasses over clear but unrevealing gray eyes, a high knobby forehead, hair parted in the middle and braided in two tight plaits; but none of this would have mattered if her face had not been so frozen, as if in reaction to some blow. Being a stepchild after having her father to herself for so long?

On the following afternoon, her stepmother's reluctant permission having been granted, Naomi Patton, the precious letter in hand that guaranteed her to be a genuine and faithful member of the Reformed Presbyterian church, went to call on the Reverend Mr. Campbell. The doorbell was answered by his sister.

"My name is Naomi Patton. I have come to see Mr. Campbell."

"Come in, won't you. He is in his study. I hope he is not too busy to see you. Have a chair, while I ask."

Naomi sat down on the stiff hall chair beside the hatrack, feet flat on the floor, knees together, hands in her lap, one clutching the letter.

Miss Campbell returned at once. "He will be glad to give you a few minutes. And do stop in the drawing room on your way out for a visit with me, and a glass of lemonade. I always have a chat with my brother's callers, if they can spare me the time."

Naomi went down the hall; the door to the study had been left open. She entered, closing the door behind her. It would be a painful interview for the minister, his sister knew: for once in his life he was honor-bound to discourage one who wanted to join his church. She went to the kitchen, took a pitcher of lemonade from the icebox, chipped some pieces of ice and dropped them into the pitcher and put it on a tray with two glasses and a plate of cookies and returned to the parlor. With the refreshments ready she went to her sitting room for the napkin she had been hemming and her work-basket, and hurried back to the parlor to await the opening of the study door. When she heard it, and her brother's farewell, she put down her sewing and went at once to the hall. Naomi hesitated at her appearance, then came on reluctantly; quite clearly she had intended to slip out the front door without any more visiting.

"You haven't forgotten your lemonade, have you? And your visit with me? Do come in and take a seat on the sofa—it's comfortable, and you can use the stand there for your glass." When she had got Naomi settled, letter in one hand and lemonade glass in the other, she said, "I hope my brother was able to help you?" As the child remained silent, she continued, "Did you have a satisfactory talk?"

"No."

"No?" Miss Campbell's only knowledge of children was derived from her many years of teaching a Sabbath school class, where communication was largely restricted to repeating by rote the Westminister Shorter Catechism. She was at a loss before that immobile face, those clear unrevealing eyes. She could not assume any of what she thought of as childishness in that child; could not talk down to her. She said, "I'm sorry if you were disappointed. You came to ask him to admit you to the fellowship of our church?"

"Yes."

"We had heard that you were not a member of your father's church back in Pennsylvania. But my brother happens to believe very strongly that the strength of a church lies in the strength of its families, united in worship as in all other ways. Do you find it so impossible to become a member of your father's church? 'Honor thy father and mother,' you know."

"Yes. But I know that 'The Lord thy God is a jealous God, visiting the iniquities of the fathers upon the children.'"

"But, my dear—!" She stopped the word "child" on her tongue, knowing it would be a mistake. "If you believe that, how can you believe you would avoid it by joining our church?"

"By being one of the Elect."

Torn between acute exasperation and a desire to laugh, Miss Campbell said, "You will know on the Day of Judgment whether you are one of the Elect, and not before. The things is to live as if you were and don't blaspheme by taking if for granted. No—don't interrupt. I haven't finished. Have you not forgotten 'Judge not, that ye be not judged'? By what authority do you accuse your father of iniquity? His church judged him, rightly or wrongly, and has punished him. God will one day judge him. Let that suffice. The Presbyterians believe that he is a good man, and have called him to be their minister. Accept that, and be a loyal daughter and member of his church."

"How can I, while Cousin Deborah is his wife?" The hitherto rigid mouth curled scornfully, nostrils flared.

Miss Campbell, enlightened, stared at the girl for a long moment. "So that is it. How old were you when your mother died?"

"Four."

"Then you cannot have any clear recollection of her. How long has your father been married to the present Mrs. Patton?"

"Seven years. Since I was six."

"So you had your father's undivided attention for two years. You would have resented his marrying anyone. Her being his cousin has given you a handle to use against her. No, wait—I still haven't finished." She gave Naomi credit for having sat still through her interrogation, and for having answered her questions as well as for having kept her eyes upon her, without evasion. "I do not believe that anyone with such a clear steady look is incapable of being honest with herself. Try it for a moment, will you? Look at yourself. When you want to join our church, are you making your religion a weapon to use against your parents? That would be blasphemous. Is it concern for your immortal soul, or because you know it hurts your father? You do not deceive the Lord: 'I the Lord search the heart.' Ask yourself whether you are being 'righteous overmuch,' as the Good Book tells us not to be. Is it because you do not want your parents to be happy?"

"They are happy."

"And you do not want them to be? For a young girl you know your Bible well. Do you remember 'Love is strong as death, jealousy is cruel as the grave'? Whom does jealousy hurt? The one who is jealous." She saw that the tight mouth was beginning to tremble: she had gone as far as she could.

Naomi, who had said almost nothing, now burst out, "They love each other. Not me."

"You have not exactly encouraged it, have you? But I think if you gave it a trial, you would find that they have stored in their hearts what you have so far rejected. I cannot believe that you could say, even feeling as you do, that you have been mistreated?"

"No. Oh, no"—reluctantly—"unless you would call taking care of the children sometimes—and washing dishes—and helping to clean the house and run errands."

Miss Campbell could not help laughing; the resentment in Naomi's voice had increased with each abuse enumerated. "My dear child!" This time she used the word, feeling it permissible after Naomi's outburst. "There's not a minister's daughter in this country who grows up without doing some or all of those things, or even worse. And it is particularly the sad fate of the oldest. Now, I have said my say, and I hope you will forgive me for having done so. Preaching is my brother's prerogative, not mine. And I really did ask you to stop for a visit with me: I had not intended to speak as I have done. Finish your lemonade and let me fill your glass, and tell me how you think you will like Waynesboro? Although I suppose you can't really tell until after school begins."

A few minutes later, as Naomi rose to go, Miss Campbell thought "She will never want to see me again. But she needn't, and I can do without her, too, if only she will take my words to heart."

Naomi left the manse seething with anger, thinking, "How dared she! I hate her, hate her!" But she was frightened as well as angry, wondering if she seemed to others as she did to Miss Campbell, a jealous little girl. If so, they were wrong. All she wanted to be or to seem was a faithful Christian, according to the doctrine of the Reformed Presbyterian church. She feared God, as the Bible commanded, and sought to serve Him in all things; He alone knew, and would judge. But there was a certain discomfort in that conclusion. She could almost hear Him speaking the words Miss Campbell had used: "Jealousy is cruel as the grave'." Could it be that she was *jealous?*

She reported on her return home that Mr. Campbell thought it was her duty to join the Presbyterian church; she would stand up with her family when their letters were read. Her face was so set and stony that her father said only, "Good. It would be best for all of us. Thank you, Naomi."

She was silent through the evening meal, but she was always that. Her most notable departure from the ordinary came when she rose voluntarily to clear the table, and offered to wash the dishes. "Meliss can wipe them. You will remember, Meliss, that it isn't our china? And Cousin Deborah can put David to bed."

On the day after Labor Day, the children of Waynesboro trooped back to school. Among them were two Pattons: Naomi to enter the eighth grade, Melissa the first. In the same eighth grade in that fall of 1908, along with the oldest of Rudy and Sophie Lichtenstein's children and the youngest Merrill, and standing out from all the others, was Jennifer Evans, known as "Jenny" to all except her mother, her teacher, and her brother. And Tucker Gordon, who still called her "Tag-along." Jennifer at thirteen was queen of all she surveyed: top student among the thirty-odd in her class, dictator on the playground and in after-school games. Delicate-featured, brown-eyed, with a mass of black hair that she wore in the fashion prevailing among the young that season: caught with a bow on the crown of her head and again with another at the end, and in between, falling loose down her back. She was a striking-looking child, who gave promise to being more than that; she was hardly even pretty at thirteen: her face needed filling out, thin as it was, her long pointed chin unhappily emphasized. But no one ever gave thought to her beauty or lack of it: her face had not the same expression two minutes running, so alive was it.

Naomi noticed her at once—how could she help it?—and marked her as one of those like Melissa, to whom all things were given without their having to seek them. Naomi, tall for her age, was assigned a back seat; she could sit and stare at that waterfall of black hair and nurse her determination to "show her"; she knew she wasn't pretty, but she could at least excel at her lessons.

She was, as it happened, quite wrong about Jennifer, to whom it would not have occurred that all she could desire would be hers by some law of nature, with no effort on her part. She had always worked at her lessons to keep at the head of the class, but after a couple of weeks in the classroom she became quite aware that she had a rival in the big homely girl in the back row. She reported at home: "The new girl in our room—Naomi something—is smarter than I am. But she is queer."

The Evans family was at the dinner table at the time. Her brother Ludwig, sitting across from her, spoke up around the large piece of beefsteak he had just taken in his mouth. "Good: knock the conceit out of you."

"I'm not—"

Her mother laughed. "It won't hurt you a bit to have a little competition. I suppose that's the new Presbyterian minister's daughter. I never heard of another Naomi."

"A minister's daughter? That explains why she's so homely. D'you s'pose they make her wear her hair scraped back into tight plaits?"

"Personally, I consider tight plaits preferable to all that loose hair floating around. In your food, most likely. However, be nice to her, Jennifer. Her mother died when she was a little thing. Her stepmother—everyone likes her, says she is good, but she has two children of her own. I doubt if she has time to spare to help Naomi with her hair."

"Make friends with her, Jenny." Her father's kind face was troubled. "If she's homely as you say and smart to boot, it may not be easy for her at first. And remember, please, that I was brought up by a minister and his wife, along with their own boys, and I don't believe I was queerer than most. I don't often hear you say unkind things, and I don't like it."

Jennifer was the apple of her father's eye and seldom rebuked by him. She said. "Oh, Father! I didn't mean it like that. I'll be friends with her if she will."

Her father was wise enough not to say "she will" as he might have, since he considered Jennifer irresistible. "She may be stand-offish, you know. In a strange place and—and all," he finished lamely. He and Elsa never gossiped at the dinner table, nor anywhere in the presence of their children.

He might not have been entirely pleased with the spirit in which Jennifer set about her conquest, as she did the following day: not out of kindness but because she felt that any rival (and so far as books were concerned, Naomi was assuredly that) would be more endurable as a friend than as an enemy. She took the first step at recess. Instead of joining the rowdy games of the other girls, Naomi had previously spent those precious moments sitting on a corner of the stone steps, reading. On that day she went to the same place and sat down with a book on her lap. Jennifer came to the edge of the gravel at the foot of the steps, and spoke to her. "Hey, Naomi! I like to read too, but recess is for *playing*. We're going to play Blackman, and I choose you on my side."

"I don't know how to play Blackman."

"Oh, heck! I thought—oh, well, do you know how to play tag?"

The immobile face cracked almost into a smile. "Yes. But—"

Jennifer turned to the girls gathered into a knot behind her. "Hey, kids! We're gonna play tag. You count out for It, Ruby."

No one cared much what she played, so long as it called for running and shouting. The game of tag was in full swing, once the counting out was done; a circle of girls danced jeering around the unfortunate It. "Can't catch a flea! Can't catch a flea!" The bewildered Naomi was not very quick; she was soon tagged, and was unhappily unable to catch anyone else. When she had enough of the mockery, she turned away and walked toward the steps.

Jennifer darted after her. "Hey, where you going?"

"I'm quitting. It's a silly childish game."

"You can't do that! Catch me—I'll be It. I don't mind." She darted in close, Naomi lunged. Jennifer danced away, but not in time. "I'm It." she proclaimed. "Who says I can't catch a flea?" But Naomi continued on her way to the steps and her book.

When the bell rang to summon a lot of breathless girls (and breathless boys from the other side of the building), Jennifer took Naomi's arm, leaned close, and said, "Look, don't you want the kids to like you? You can't get sore every time you're It."

"I'm sorry. I guess I just don't care for such silly games."

Jennifer was provoked into warm speech. "Look, if you'd rather be by yourself all the time than run the risk of being tagged, I guess it's up to you. But you won't have any fun that way."

"It seemed like very silly fun to me."

They came up to the top step where Miss Carter stood with the handbell. Conversation ceased as they joined the stream of children crowding into the hall. The rest of the morning dragged; two shame-faced girls had time to regret their brief angry exchange. Jennifer realized that she had not exactly advanced herself in Naomi's opinion; Naomi was determined not to take back what she had said, but she could not remember that anyone had ever cared before whether she joined in a game or not, however silly it might be. She bent her head over her book, ashamed even to look at Jennifer's back and the now tangled mass of black hair.

When classes were dismissed at noon, she found Jennifer waiting for her at the tall schoolyard gate.

"Look, Naomi: I wasn't very polite, when you're new and all. I guess at your old school you didn't play silly games at recess time."

Naomi smiled, her set expression relaxed. "I was silly to get so mad just because I couldn't catch anyone and they yelled at me. I'm sorry."

"Then we can be friends?"

"If—if you still want to."

"Sure I do. Look, when you get home at noon ask your mother if you can stop at my house this afternoon after school, to play with the gang. You'll prob'ly think our games are silly—Hide and Seek, most likely, or Run, Sheep, Run. But we do have fun."

"Cousin Deborah," Naomi corrected her automatically. "She won't mind unless she wants me to take care of the children."

"There are others besides Melissa?"

"David. He's two."

If she expected Jennifer to commiserate with her, she was disappointed. "You mean you have a baby brother? Oh, I envy you. I should love above all things to have a baby in the family. But Mother says I'll have to wait till I have my own: she has her hands full now. Is David cute?"

"Yes." All of a sudden Naomi realized that he was cute. "They are both cute. And Cousin Deborah doesn't often ask me to take care of them. Only when there's a church meeting."

"Next time let me help, will you? I'd love to."

Naomi stopped at the Evanses' that afternoon for a rowdy game of "Run, Sheep, Run." At her Cousin Deborah's suggestion she invited them to come the next afternoon to her house for the game.

"You know where she lives," Jennifer said, to the startled boys and girls, with an unpardonably proprietary air. "In the other half of Mr. Travers' house."

Even those who had never taken music lessons from Mr. Travers knew where he lived. They looked at Naomi with something like awe; one spoke for all of them: "You mean you've got all that *great, big, yard to play in?*"

"Well, the half that's on our side." She did not feel compelled to add that her Cousin Deborah had made it a condition that they stay away from Mr. Travers' windows, lest they disturb him.

The games of Hide and Seek and Run, Sheep, Run transferred themselves to the Pattons' wide expanse of lawn, shrubbery, trees, and empty stable. The noise stopped Mr. Patton's sermon-writing in the late afternoon; without complaint he went to the church study. He and Deborah did not pretend to understand the change in Naomi, who laughed occasionally, now and then, even when only her family was present. She talked to her stepmother, not in any intimate way, but still she occasionally had something to say. They did not scold her, or even express particular surprise when she came home one afternoon from the Evanses' with half her front hair chopped off in bangs. She faced them somewhat fearfully, but ready to be defiant.

"Jennifer thought I'd look better if I hid some of my forehead."

"I'm not sure but that you do," Deborah said judiciously. "But I didn't know bangs were in style these days."

"Neither are plaits, I guess. But," she hastened to add, "I wouldn't want my hair down my back, like the others'. It would be a nuisance."

"How did your friend happen to suggest that you have—too much forehead? It sounds a little rude."

"Oh, no. I started it, wishing I was pretty like her. She doesn't think she is pretty, and she said if I wore my hair different—and she got out some old photographs of her mother when she was a girl, and she had bangs. You don't mind if I'm not in style, do you? If it looks better?"

The long bangs came almost to her eyebrows, mitigating the bony forehead, emphasizing the clear hazel eyes. Naomi would never be pretty, but with the change in her hair and—as she did not realize—in her more responsive countenance, she was far less conspicuously homely than she had been. She was reassured by her parents, who told her that if she didn't mind being out of fashion, the different way of wearing her hair was certainly becoming to her. But how did it happen Jennifer's mother permitted her to do it?

"Oh, we did it upstairs in Jenny's bedroom. When we came down, her mother was scandalized. Said we should have asked you first. But I was afraid I'd never have the courage again."

That night, in the privacy of their bedroom, the Pattons discussed the metamorphosis of their eldest child.

"This Jennifer Evans has Naomi under her thumb. Do you know who she is, Andrew?"

"Haven't you met her?" Her husband was startled; it was a mother's duty to know her children's friends.

"Of course I've met her. She's here half the time. She's a nice-mannered child and she is good with the baby, but I'd like to know something about her people."

His wife, Andrew thought, had got her confidence back: instead of worrying about her own acceptance in the town, the shoe was on the other foot. He thanked God wordlessly, saying aloud only, "Ask Naomi. Or I will."

And so he did, the next morning at breakfast. Jennifer Evans seemed like such a nice young girl. Did Naomi know anything about her family?

For a moment her face froze into the old stubborn blankness. Then she said, "I only know her mother and her brother. He's an awful tease, but her mother's nice. I've never seen her father. He works, travels a lot. His uncle—he was an orphan and his uncle raised him—his uncle"—and she held her breath—"is the Baptist minister. Well? Is there anything wrong with that?"

Her father's lip twitched; he restrained a smile. "Of course not. They are good Christians, the Baptists. Of course," he added solemnly, "it might have been better if you could have found a Presbyterian to chum with."

Late that afternoon, when he came home from sermon-writing in the church study, he went smiling to the kitchen in search of his wife. He took her in his arms, spattered apron and all, kissed her gently, and said, "Luckily, in pursuing your inquiries it was Mr. Edwards I ran into uptown and asked, 'Who are the Evanses?' He knows how to hold his tongue, or we might be a laughing stock. Because even after we've been here a while we still had to ask. It seems Mrs. Gilbert Evans' father is our Waynesboro millionaire. And more important, according to Edwards, she is all one can ask of a woman. Her mother is something of a snob, he says, but Mrs. Evans never has been, is not, and never will be."

"The child certainly puts on no airs, I'll say that. She's a natural-born manager but not because of who she is or what her family has."

"Edwards says she hasn't a notion, probably, of the importance of her grandfather."

"And they don't mind us being—? Do they know, I wonder?"

It hurt him to see her so ready to be rebuffed. "My dear girl, I told you everyone in this town knows about us. At first I took that as a bitter blow, but now I think I am glad. No need to worry over what ostensibly friendly people might do when they found out."

At the age of thirteen intimate friendships can develop with the speed of desert flowers in that rainy season; they can also wither away as quickly. But Jennifer and Naomi found a bond that held them more surely than any good intentions on the part of either. Games might pall, but they were both readers, almost compulsively addicted to the printed word. The first time Elsa, on a rainy Saturday afternoon, came upon them in the living room, each curled up with a hook, she protested vigorously.

"Jennifer! Is that a courteous way to treat a guest, sitting there reading? Can't you find some way to entertain Naomi? Checkers or something?"

"But she'd rather read, Mother. Honestly. And it's fun, doing it together."

"Together? You aren't even reading the same book."

"She's read lots of books I haven't, and I've read lots she hasn't, like *Lady*

Jane and *Master Skylark* and *Lorna Doone*. All the books you and Father have given me."

"But surely you could lend them to her—let her take them home?"

Utter silence showed Elsa that she had said the wrong thing. Finally Naomi stammered, "I—I don't know—about stories. I never asked because until we came here I thought it was wicked, a sinful waste of time, to read stories."

"That was when you were a Reformed Presbyterian?" Elsa smiled at the solemn child. "But now you are a Presbyterian, I understand. That is one of the comfortable differences between the churches: Presbyterians read stories with a clear conscience. And of course it is a waste of time—but when you're young, you have time to waste—lots and lots of time. Let her take something home with her Jennifer, and ask her father."

"Oh, we have lots of books," Naomi assured her. "At least—I like to read history, and we have some. There are all those books locked up, too," she added, "that were the Ballards that we can't read."

"Law books, I suppose?"

"Yes, But others too. You can see them through the glass doors. All of Scott. All of Dickens and Cooper."

"That's too bad—but you can save those for later. Read Jennifer's now, or use the Carnegie Library, if your father has a card." But Elsa remembered the child's wistful face as she spoke of the books behind locked doors.

The Woman's Club held its first October meeting at its President's house. After adjournment Elsa made her way quickly to the side of Amanda Reid, who had paused for the usual polite little speech to Mrs. Rausch, thanking her for her hospitality.

"Miss Reid! Please—just a second. It is true, isn't it, that Eliza Ballard left you her share of her father's books?"

"It is true." Amanda's smile was ironic. "Coals to Newcastle. I haven't room for any more books."

"Then have you made any provision—?"

Amanda's eyebrows went up. "You don't want them, surely? I have made no provision, no, but I had thought rather vaguely about disposing of them: the law books to Gardiner and Merrill, or the Law Library in the Court House; the rest to the Carnegie Library. When they are turned over to me to dispose of."

"And in the meantime, there's a book-starved child pressing her nose against those glass doors."

For the first time Amanda looked interested. "That oldest girl of the Reverend Mr. Patton? She has the reputation of being an odd child: the reputation she would surely have in Waynesboro if she likes to read."

"She isn't odd, really. Just, up until now, frozen in on herself. She and Jennifer are great friends, and Jennifer doesn't find her odd. But of course Jennifer is a reader too."

"There's not a bit of sense in those books being locked up, then. I'll speak to Tim Merrill about it. But you know, the law may forbid—Tim can ask the Judge about it."

The judge of the Probate Court could see no sense in it either. "The books are Miss Reid's in due time. If she realizes some may turn up missing or damaged, and doesn't care, I'll see that you get the bookcase keys and you can pass them on, and let the Reverend's children have free run of the shelves. There won't be anything to hurt them in Judge Ballard's collection, but I'd expect them to be rather dry reading for a child."

And so in time the bookcases were opened and the books read, not only by Naomi but by her father and her Cousin Deborah, in such spare time as they had.

Elsa had not been permitted to leave her mother's house at once that afternoon of the Club meeting; after she had spoken to Amanda, her mother stopped her.

"I want to talk to you, Elsa. You too, Anne. Don't go just yet. Sit down somewhere until I have said good-bye to the last of the ladies."

When Sally had closed the door after the last departing member, she returned to the drawing room; fanning herself vigorously with a palm leaf fan, she went to the chair that had been hers during the meeting.

"Is it always this hot in October? I don't remember it so."

"If you'd take off some of that weight, Mamma—but never mind. You didn't keep us here to talk about the weather."

"No. It's that Memorial Meeting for Eliza Ballard a fortnight from today. I have asked Amanda for a formal tribute. Christina will oblige with some music—psalms, I suppose. But when I ask whether some other member would like to speak—whether someone hasn't some cherished memory of Eliza that she would like to share with the ladies—what will happen?"

"There will be an utter, profound, and embarrassing silence," Elsa laughed. "Must you?"

"We always do."

"Then," said Anne, "you are asking us to spend the next two weeks thinking of some spontaneously and suddenly recollected instance of great virtue on Eliza's part. I must beg to be excused."

"Now, Anne."

Elsa intervened hastily. "I am perfectly willing to recollect how good she was to Ariana, and how devoted. Of course Amanda may cover all that."

"Can't you think of something not everyone knows?"

"Her devotion to Rausch Cordage Company? The good and faithful servant?"

"That would do. It would be true, too. I can remember what a fool I thought your father was to hire her, but he never regretted it. I suppose she was grateful—no one else would have given her a place when she needed it.

At any rate, she was efficient and trustworthy. Never passed on a word of what she heard there. Anne, can't you think of something?"

"Nothing suitable to the occasion, believe me."

"You and I and Amanda are the only ones who remember her as a girl."

"Then let someone who hasn't known her quite so long think of something." Anne picked up the gloves she had worn during the meeting but had taken off when ordered to sit down and wait.

"No, don't be in such a hurry. That isn't the only thing I wanted to talk over. What about these vacancies in the Club? Our members are dwindling sadly, and I don't like it. Janey Voorhees, now Eliza, and soon, Mrs. McKinney. They are moving next week. Can't you suggest any possibilities?"

"The Bonner girl," Elsa suggested promptly. "Charlotte's niece—William's daughter."

"But I thought when she got her B.A. she went to New York and found herself a job?"

"You're slipping, Mamma. With Eliza Ballard gone, the communication system has gone to pieces. Mrs. William isn't well, and Esther is needed at home. Charlotte says she will find life dull, even if they give her some job on the paper."

"What's wrong with Mrs. William?"

"Charlotte didn't say, but from her tone I suspect nothing but her imagination and her age."

"Would the girl be a good member? How well do you know her?"

"I've known all the Bonners for a good many years. Esther isn't another Charlotte. A little stodgy, like William. But no more so than some of our other members. Yes: I think she would contribute."

"Suppose you propose her name then at the next meeting. Charlotte can be a second sponsor. The other lady I intended to sound you out about is Mrs. Andrew Patton." That her two auditors were surprised would be putting it too mildly; they kept a startled silence. "Well? You know her, don't you, Anne? She is your minister's wife."

Anne, who recognized Sally's suggestion as a challenge to Christina, said, "Yes. I know her slightly. I called on her once, and have spoken to her at church. I like her very much, but—"

"Elsa?"

"Mamma, I don't know her at all. Why should I? They've been here for such a short time."

"D'you mean to say you let Jennifer be intimate with the little girl without even calling? To see what the stepmother is like?"

"That's exactly why I haven't called. The poor woman has had troubles enough without exposing her to what she would surely consider parental inspection. I know Naomi, of course. She isn't half so difficult as people seem to think. She's been through some emotional upheavals, but she just needs a little more time."

"That doesn't tell me much about her mother."

"Yes it does," Anne said. "That child made life miserable for her father and his wife before they came here. You remember what Eliza said. The day I called, Naomi struck me as impossible to deal with: frozen face, blank eyes, responses restricted to a word or two. If as Elsa says she is beginning to resemble a normal young person—with all due credit to Jennifer, she couldn't have done it all. It speaks worlds for her stepmother's wisdom and patience and naturally loving and happy nature. But all that doesn't matter, does it? What's she like? After all, considering the way the Reformed Presbyterians in Pennsylvania treated the Pattons, wouldn't our R.P. ladies blackball her?"

"Now, Anne, you know I would sound them out before her name was proposed. There'll be no blackballing if I can help it. But it was Miss Campbell who suggested her name to me."

"Miss Campbell! How does she happen to know her?"

"Just by calling on her, like Anne. I got the impression—she was careful not to put it into words—that Mrs. Patton, after what she had been through, needed reassurance. And that it should come, if not by the hands of the R.P.'s, at least with their approval."

Anne said, "So the world does move! Imagine in the McCunes' day! But how about Christina?"

"I asked Miss Campbell about Christina and Amanda and Mrs. Maxwell. She said that Mrs. Maxwell was too old to put up any kind of fight, and she was sure Amanda wouldn't. She had talked to Christina, who was inclined to be obstructive, but she told her the time for that kind of nonsense was past."

Both Anne and Elsa laughed, and Elsa said, "I should like to have heard that."

And indeed the interview would have been worth hearing. Christina was scandalized by the idea of having to consort with an excommunicated sinner. Miss Campbell said, "But you exchange common courtesies with many who do not profess even to be good Christians. Do you feel contaminated? After all, Mr. Patton was excommunicated for what no other church would so much as blink at."

"But he and his wife were Reformed Presbyterians. It was their duty to obey the laws of the church."

"I thought Protestants of whatever denomination were free within limits to follow their consciences."

"Within the limits laid down by the church. Why are you so set on this. Do you know Mrs. Patton?"

"I have called, yes. I felt I owed her an apology for having given the girl Naomi a piece of my mind, but it wasn't necessary: I very soon discovered that my lecture had not been reported at home. I found Mrs. Patton a pleasant, intelligent young woman, and I am suggesting her for the Woman's

Club because I feel that the Reformed Presbyterians owe her some recompense for the trouble they have caused."

"No doubt that is one way to look at it. But the Pattons brought their trouble on themselves."

"And so deserve it? But very few of our congregation are still as narrow as that, you know. Some of them now sing hymns, I understand, and all have organs and choirs."

"I am glad my father did not live to see the day. In some ways he was what you would call broad-minded, but he did observe church discipline."

"Your father has been dead many years, I understand. Had he lived until now—"

Christina reluctantly gave in. "If the ladies wish to invite Mrs. Patton to become a member of the Club, I shall do nothing to prevent it. As you say, there are those who do not see eye to eye with us, and I have found that Club meetings do not necessarily involve intimacy with other members. There have been times, though, when I have had qualms about giving so much time to so wordly an organization, however intellectual."

In the course of the next two weeks, Sally herself approached the possible objectors to either proposed candidate, and finding their acceptance would be unanimous, gave Elsa and Miss Campbell the nod: at the next meeting the two names were presented, to be voted on a fortnight later. At that time they were duly elected to membership in the Waynesboro Woman's Club, and were welcomed at the next meeting, their hands shaken, the necessary pleasant words spoken.

"All these strange faces," Sally complained to Anne after that meeting. "Mrs. Andrew Patton. Miss Esther Bonner. And I haven't got used to the last new members yet. Mrs. Harrington, who so seldom appears. The Methodists keep her busy, I suppose. I never thought to say it, but I miss Eliza."

"Give them a month or two," and Anne smiled at her, "and you'll love them dearly. Don't you always?"

"As President," said Sally at her haughtiest, "I feel a certain obligation." And Anne thought, Sally minds teasing more than she once had; she had ruled her small world for so long that she had begun to take herself seriously.

Without Waynesboro's paying much attention to events as they happened, life went on there and in the country. In October, Mary Gardiner and Franz Lichtenstein yielded to family pressure and came home to be married, as her sisters had been, in her father's parlor, but on her insistence without all the fuss and bother of a large wedding: only members of the two families were present. Grandfather Bodien was noticeably absent, but Uncle Stewart and family were there. Once married, the bridal couple took the first train back to New York and their chosen work.

As Ludwig had predicted, the presidential campaign caused little excitement; no one questioned that Taft would be elected by a comfortable margin, with that wild man Bryan running against him. Life would be duller with

Roosevelt off the front pages of the papers, but for the country four years of Mr. Taft should be smooth sailing. Everyone in Waynesboro seemed to be prospering: Sheldon & Edwards, Drygoods; Thirkield's Drugs, where Billy had taken over from his father; Fritz Klein & Sons, Fancy Groceries. The time had passed when the cordage mill was the only industry in town: Waynesboro boasted a new shoe factory and a tobacco stemmery, which competed with Rausch Cordage Company for Negro hands. And there was Mr. Hoffmann's bakery, enlarged twice since he had started as a wholesale dealer in crackers. There were apparently enough laborers to keep all plants working; everyone said Waynesboro must be growing, although the last census had not shown much increase in population.

Mr. Hoffmann not only made his crackers in quantity, boxed them, and shipped them around the state, but also carried on his local bakery and shop, in the same block as Klein's, where the ladies who believed in doing their own marketing stopped on mornings when they knew there would be not only fresh bread but pastries of all kinds, plain rolls and sweet rolls, cinnamon twists, thinking a stop at Hoffmann's worth the trouble just for the pleasure of inhaling the various warm scents drifting in from the ovens behind the shop. Mr. Hoffmann was prospering to so great an extent as to find himself in a quandary. As he had done once before, he went to Ludwig Rausch. He was greeted, the evening he rang the doorbell, as cordially as always, taken to Ludwig's study, provided with a stein of beer, and invited to unburden himself. Although, as Ludwig said, it was difficult to believe that he could be in any kind of financial difficulty.

"No. All goes smoothly yet. My boy does ze baking for ze shop. And my wife and my girl sell vot he bakes. And ze crackers—I myself overlooking ze help—you vouldn't believe. That iss vot brought me to zis—zis—crossroad, and I come to you again for advice. The American Biscuit Company vould like to buy me out."

"Then you are stepping on their toes."

"Vielleicht—yes. It iss a very gut offer. The question iss, should I accept? I could quit vork altogether, venefer I liked. The uptown shop zey do not vant. I could occupy myself zere. But vot vould zey do vis ze cracker factory?"

"Close it down," said Ludwig, with the bitterness of experience. "They want to end the competition."

"Zey offer to guarantee to run it for a year."

"Which clearly shows their intention."

"I feared so. Zen all vould go for nossing, except for ze money in ze bank."

"As I remember, one reason you started that factory was because you thought Waynesboro needed more than one employer of labor. Those are nice girls that work for you—where would they go?"

"To ze shoe factory, maybe? Zey hire some vomen. But I—no—I vould not like it, no. It vould be like turning out my own family. But if I say 'no' to zat big company, zey vill fight me, no?"

"Probably. Bring pressure to bear on your customers, cut prices, maybe. I don't know enough about the American Biscuit Company to judge how far they would go."

"Big corporations like zat, ze left hand doesn't know vot ze right hand does. Who knows vot might happen should I say 'no'?"

"I don't belive they could destroy you. Your business might be hurt, but the cracker recipe—formula—whatever you call it—would still be yours. And you have a good local business. You're not too old to fight it out. Unless you think the business would come to an end anyway, when you retire?"

"Ven I die, you mean. Zat iss ven I retire. No, it vould not end; my Anton vould go on." Mr. Hoffmann laughed. "He iss a good baker; he sinks he iss ready today—tomorrow—any time."

"Then your family isn't asking you to sell?"

"No. Zey vant me not to sell. Zey are so proud ven zey go into a grocery and see boxes of Hoffmann's crackers. Ven zey go to Zinzinnati, zey look in all groceries. But I tell zem, here iss zis big money, like picking it off a tree. Enough for us all, for all our lives, so long as ve don't get big ideas, you know? And if ze cracker bakery vas ruined, zen ve go back to vot it vass like before: ze bakery uptown, me driving ze horse, ringing ze bell."

"Nevertheless, they want you to hold on?"

"Yes. But I am afraid zey do not realize—zey might be sorry."

"You should have more faith in them. They are made of good sturdy stuff. My advice, for what it is worth is, if you are tired of making crackers and want to sell, then sell. If you don't want to, tell the American Biscuit Company 'no,' and let then do their worst."

"Danke schön. It iss gut to be advised to do vot you already made up your mind, almost, to do. I vill say 'no'."

"You didn't want advice. You just wanted your courage bolstered. Good luck, Hoffmann." Ludwig rang the bell to bring Rosie with more beer, and the two men settled down to comfortable male talk about the town and its people (men do not have a reputation for gossiping, but information spreads among them at a remarkable speed), about the state of the country, the election and the elimination of Roosevelt from the national scene. They enjoyed themselves thoroughly, and Sally in her comfortable chair by the fire in the library, wondered what earth-shaking crisis Mr. Hoffmann was having to face up to.

Sally was confronting her own far from earth-shaking problem, which did not seem a trivial one to her. What should the Woman's Club do for a Christmas entertainment for the gentlemen? When there were so many new and still unknown quantities to be dealt with? The committee for the Christmas play, as printed in the Club Calendar, included Charlotte Bonner, Chairman; Mrs. Lavinia Stevens and Mrs. Caroline Edwards, with Mrs.

Elizabeth Merrill as director. Could they be trusted to produce something that more straitlaced members would not object to? Elsa had laughed at her worries: "They aren't children, Mama. After all, Charlotte is a year older than I am, and I am getting close to forty. The Gardiners came into the Club as unmarried girls. You forget how time passes. They are settled-down wives and mothers and have belonged to the Club for years."

In spite of Elsa, Sally was pleased when Charlotte telephoned to ask whether their choice of *She Stoops to Conquer* (scenes from) met with presidential approval. Sally had heard one of the Gardiners say to the other Gardiner, "We're two to one on that Committee. Let's be firm with Miss Bonner: *not* Shakespeare again," and had wondered whether they might be thinking of Ibsen or Chekov. Since Charlotte's sense of humor could be relied on, Sally explained why she had possibly sounded relieved. Charlotte had been amused: "Of course to them everyone over thirty-five is a stick-in-the-mud. I must have surprised them: I said I was getting a little tired of reaching for the stars, myself, and I thought Goldsmith was more nearly within our capabilities, although I just might have plumped for *The Rivals* in the hope of persuading Miss Campbell to do Mrs. Malaprop." Sally hastened to agree that *She Stoops to Conquer* would do nicely, and she ceased to fret about what attitude Amanda and Christina and Mrs. Maxwell might take: whether they would disapprove of their pastor's sister acting in a play, or would think since she did that they could hardly express disapproval.

Parts were assigned, rehearsals began almost at once, and lines were more or less learned. The cast began to meet at the Rausches', so that its members could accustom themselves to points of entrance and exit, the use of screens, and all the other necessary makeshifts attendant upon parlor dramatics. Sally reveled in the activity; she came to know very well the new and almost-new members of her Club. Bright-eyed Mrs. Warren and Mrs. Patton, who was not only pretty but displayed an unsuspected flair for dramatization. It was all very silly and a great deal of fun, and for the cast, rewarding in that they became intimate in a fashion that would not otherwise have been possible.

Sally had not forgotten that 1908 was the Club's fortieth anniversary; the occasion was recognized: the older members were seated, with their menfolk, if any, at the table in the dining room, the other "younger members" at tables for four in the double parlor. They were served one of Sally's elaborate dinners. The younger people finished first: they had fewer recollections of previous Club functions and a smaller store of anecdotes to be brought out at the dinner table. By the time the older men and women left the dining room, they found that under Elizabeth's direction the small tables had been cleared and removed and the chairs set up in rows. For once Sally had prevailed upon Anne instead of Amanda to "say a few words" to honor the anniversary; Anne was brief indeed, since she did not consider introduction of the Christmas play a time for reminiscences. Briefly she exhorted the younger members to believe that their elders had also enjoyed dramatics and Rausch hospitality; that husbands of those years had laughed as hard as she was sure the young men present on that evening would do. And even as she returned to her seat, she wondered whether Johnny could laugh; he had seemed not to do so for months. She had insisted on his coming: "You get out far too seldom. You are invited as my escort," she had said, "and I expect you to take me, just as you have been doing these last years." But when she caught his eye as she was speaking, his quick smile seemed to her so sad as to be almost unbearable.

But even Johnny could bring himself to laugh, not only at Goldsmith's lines, but at the risible aspect of ladies masquerading imperfectly, as was inevitable, as men. They romped through the chosen scenes, with Elizabeth summarizing those omitted, not often missing a cue or fumbling a line, but sometimes so overcome with laughter themselves that the audience, not knowing the cause, still laughed with them. It was one of the Club's better Christmas celebrations, Anne thought, and said so to Sally as she and Johnny spoke their farewells.

Hard upon the Christmas play came the school holidays, frantic preparations, and finally ("finally" at least in the eyes of the children), Christmas itself. Adults without young people passed it quietly; it was celebrated without restraint in such families as the Gardiner-Stevens-Edwards connection. Captain Bodien had gone on the Interurban to Madison City to spend the day with Stewart and his family (including the Paul Rausches); otherwise all even loosely a part of their family spent the day at the Gardiners' with Doug and Barbara, including even Richard Edwards, home for once from his archeological graduate studies. At the Rausches were gathered in not only Gib and Elsa and their two, but the senior Evanses and Anne and Johnny Gordon. The only family to whom all the to-do about Christmas was new and strange was that of the Reverend Patton, who had hitherto accepted the Reformed Presbyterian view that the Roman church had taken over a pagan holiday with the intention of keeping newly converted Christians happy, and that as a papist festival it was to be ignored by true Christians. It had come therefore as something of a surprise to Andrew Patton when Naomi on an afternoon after school had stopped in his study in the church to consult him as to his feeling about Christmas giving. "Jennifer," she explained, "is making presents for all her family; she has only money enough to buy something for her mother. I felt funny when she asked me what I was going to make for all of you and I had to say 'nothing.' Father, if you don't think it is wrong, I would like to try. I think I would like to give something, even if it is botched. I am not very good with my hands."

"You can give any time of the year, you know: it doesn't have to be Christmas. But I don't see any real reason why it shouldn't be then. What had you thought of?"

"Whatever Jennifer can show me how to do. I've already learned to hemstitch. I thought a hemstitched handkerchief for Cousin Deborah." Her throat almost closed on the words, she was so embarrassed; her father's astonished expression forced an explanation from her. "I've been trying," she said, and in despair, "Haven't you even noticed?"

"Of course we have noticed, my dear child. Home has been a happier place here in Waynesboro, but—"

"She has always been nice to me, even when I wasn't nice to her. I was horrid; I guess I wanted you all to myself." She blushed unbecomingly; with a quick gesture to hide the tears in her eyes, she brushed the long bangs aside and exposed her high forehead. "It has taken me a long time to really *feel* sorry, and I can't—I can't say it. But a Christmas present, wouldn't that say it?"

"That would say it, and I think a hemstitched handkerchief would be most suitable. And the children?"

"I'll think of something."

"Would a dollar help? I can spare that much, I think." He reached into his pocket, jingled his coins, pulled out a silver dollar, and passed it over. She examined it curiously, both sides. "I don't think I've ever had one of these before, to spend as I please. Thank you, Father. I can go to the Famous Cheap Store: they have the little dolls Melissa likes, and I can find something for David. Imagine!" She turned the bright coin over in her palm. "Imagine! I can go Christmas shopping just like everyone else!" Then struck by a frightening thought she went on, "Father, you won't say anything to Cousin Deborah? About Christmas? Or anything I said about being sorry? Please. Because I know I'm the one to say it—and I can't."

"Not a word. I promise. The time will come perhaps when you can—meanwhile, say it with that hemstitched handkerchief."

The sewing, such as it was, was done at the Evanses' in Jennifer's company, and so too the present for her father; the toys were bought at the Famous on a Saturday afternoon after much vacillation; four presents, rather untidily wrapped in white tissue paper and tied with narrow red ribbon, were arranged on the dining room table early Christmas morning before anyone else was down for breakfast. There was no more surprised family in Waynesboro than the Pattons that morning, nor a happier one. Deborah, picking up the little package, knowing no adult hand had wrapped it, looked at once at Naomi.

"For me? A Christmas present? How nice."

"It isn't, really. Very nice, I mean." Naomi was flushing, the unbecoming color running up her neck to her cheeks. "I'm no good at sewing, and I got it so *dirty*—I don't know how—I always washed my hands. But I could hardly get it clean when I washed it."

"But—" Deborah had the package open, the handkerchief unfolded. "All that work! For me! I—I don't believe I ever had a hand-hemstitched handkerchief before. Thank you, Naomi, with all my heart."

They were saved from lapsing into undue sentimentality by their husband and father's nonplussed look as he waved on one finger by the cord that dangled from it a round object, a ball six or eight inches in diameter, made of a myriad of circular pieces of pale green tissue paper, each folded twice and strung together into what was a not quite perfect ball. "It is a very pretty thing, Naomi, but—what—?"

"It's a shaving ball. Jenny says she has to make one for her father every Christmas, he likes them so much. Mine isn't as good as hers—it bulges. You hang it by the mirror in the bathroom, and when you've finished shaving, you jerk out one of the pieces of paper to wipe your razor on."

"Well! How very ingenious! And useful. I'm always groping for something."

"And have been known to cut a towel. So I'm grateful for that, too, Naomi." Their mother looked at the two younger children, both absorbed. "The little dolls are presents from Naomi, Melissa—say 'Thank you.' You know, Andrew, I was thinking at the Rausches' the other night, the Christmas tree was so beautiful, from the angel at the top to the creche underneath. Is there any real reason—?"

"Now that we are plain Presbyterians, none in the world. How very foolish some prohibitions seem, when you get away from them. Like not singing hymns. Thank you, Naomi, for everything—and for opening our eyes. There are pleasures in this life that rejoice the heart and harm no one. Now, before we eat the porridge that is probably cold, let us ask the blessing." Part of the Reverend's prayer was silent: he thanked his God for his wife, whose patience and forbearance seemed to have been rewarded, and for a daughter who had shown a capacity to love, and for whom there seemed now the possibility of a happy, useful, and normal life. "Amen, Amen," he said in his heart with all the fervor of a truly religious man.

MEMBERS OF THE
WAYNESBORO WOMAN'S CLUB

Miss Charlotte Bonner
Miss Ellen Bonner
Miss Ruth Campbell
Mrs. Jessamine Edwards
Mrs. Caroline Edwards
Mrs. Elsa Evans
Mrs. Gwen Evans
Mrs. Anne Gordon
Mrs. Sophie Lichtenstein
Mrs. Laura Maxwell
Mrs. Elizabeth Merrill
Mrs. Deborah Patton
Mrs. Sarah Rausch
Miss Amanda Reid
Mrs. Lavinia Stevens
Mrs. Christina Voorhees
Mrs. Grace Warren

IN MEMORIAM

Miss Eliza Ballard
Mrs. Mary Ballard
Miss Susan Crenshaw
Mrs. Louisa Deming
Mrs. Katherine Edwards
Miss Caroline Gardiner
Miss Lavinia Gardiner
Mrs. Mary McCune
Miss Agatha Pinney
Mrs. Thomasina Travers

* 1909 *

"We lament the passing of still another charter member, although she died far away from her old home, which she had left a number of years ago."

Christmas passed, the new year, 1909, began. The holidays came to an end. But winter was never dull for the young, if they were accommodated with either ice or snow. Adults returned to their various routine duties and pleasures. For a few select females there was the fortnightly break provided by the meetings of the Waynesboro Woman's Club.

The first meeting of the new year was held at Mrs. Andrew Patton's, and for most of the ladies it was the first time in that house since Mrs. Ballard's death. Those who had known the room in her day and had had no occasion to call on Mrs. Patton were astonished to find it exactly as it had been all those years ago. The more practical among them thought, "But of course Eliza had no use for this room; it has been shut up all this time." Anne Gordon was not particularly practical-minded. She was moved to a profound but pleasurable melancholy by the evidence that human life is brief and is long survived by the material things it had believed itself to possess. For one brief bitter moment she wished that they were all back in an ealier year, with Mrs. Ballard presiding. But Sally was on her feet to bring the meeting to order: after the roll was called, the afternoon's essay was embarked upon by one of those members who had certainly never been in the room before. At any rate, Anne thought, the Club has survived: in institutions, at least, there can be unbroken continuity. But it was strange to be meeting in the Ballard parlor, with all the Ballards dead and gone. With the best will in the world, she could not keep her attention on the paper being read. She was disquieted, and as she thought of it now, she realized that her disquiet went all the way back to that afternoon in the early fall when she and Elsa had stayed after the meeting at Sally's, and had then walked down Market Street together.

Anne remembered every word of that seemingly unimportant conversation, which Elsa had introduced by saying that Tucker's father and grandmother must miss him very much, now he had returned to California, but she supposed they heard from him frequently.

"Not really. And you know the kind of letters boys write. A polite note to me, no doubt dictated by his mother, thanking me for the summer's "hospitality." Not Tucker's word, I know: he thinks of our house as home. His father has had one letter, written on the train, almost indecipherable, but longer, telling about the trip, his fellow travelers, and so on. Nothing since."

"He does better by Jennifer. No doubt it's easier to write to her. She had a long letter from him this morning. Rather a lugubrious one. He said that when he got back his mother said he'd gotten out of hand, running wild in Waynesboro, and Uncle Robert thought military school would be the making of him. You know about Uncle Robert?"

"Grandmother Deming's 'beau'? Yes, he told us."

"So off he goes to military school. Poor Tuck! He hates the idea; he doesn't like 'Uncle Robert' and he wishes he were here, going to school with his friends."

"Do you think there is anything to this relationship of 'Uncle Robert' and Louisa?"

Tuck quite honestly thinks so, but no, he is too old a man for her. How old do you suppose he is? Tuck says as old as Louisa Deming. But however old—no, I don't think he would choose anyone his own age. But do you suppose—Julia? Johnny has been so sure she would not marry again: that she was escaping from matrimony as much as from him. Tell me, did you think Tuck got 'out of hand'?"

Elsa laughed. "No more than my two. Of course they have always run wild, all of them, out at Hillcrest, but this summer they weren't there as much. Do you suppose Tuck told his mother he spent most of his time with his father, in his office and on his rounds? She never liked the profession of medicine—wanted Johnny to give it up, of all things. So she might consider Tuck's activities as getting 'out of hand.' And I suppose she would like to get him out from underfoot, away at school."

"I wish that were so. Then she might—"

"Turn him over to Johnny? You know better. She isn't going to let go of anything she has that someone else wants. Especially to her ex-husband."

When Anne reached home, she found Johnny in the sitting room with the *Torchlight*; for once there had been no house calls to be made after he had ushered out his last office patient at four o'clock. He had looked so tired and sad in the instant before he laid the paper down and smiled at her that she decided not to repeat what Elsa had told her and perhaps distress him unnecessarily. But before she had a chance to sit down, he had asked her whether there had been nothing in the afternoon mail from Tucker. Forced into a "Nothing," she went on. "Perhaps the boy can't bear to write us. Jennifer had a letter from him this morning, Elsa said." And she had repeated their conversation.

"A military school? Because Tuck had got 'out of hand'? What nonsense. He couldn't have told her much about this summer working in my office and making calls with me. I suppose she doesn't know what to do with a boy his age. But she can't afford a good military school, and a second-rate one—"

"Wait and see, Johnny," she had said. "We'll hear from him sooner or later. It may not turn out to be as bad as he thinks."

In January, sitting in Mrs. Patton's parlor, Anne went back over all that had been said on that afternoon. Until after Christmas they had not heard from Tucker again. He had then written them a thank-you note for the presents they had sent, and had said that military school was not so bad. But there was something—stand-offish? was that possible?—about the letter that worried Anne. Her experience of men and boys told her that they withdrew into silence when things went wrong. As she tried to keep her mind on the Club meeting, she was still worrying, even so many days later.

After the meeting, as the ladies were dispersing, Elsa Evans contrived to go through the door and down the front steps with Anne. "Are you walking? So am I. I feel the need of fresh air, cold as it is." The two started out together, waving off invitations to ride with those who had carriages or motor cars waiting. For a moment they were silent; then as they went through the iron gate to Main Street, Elsa said abruptly, "I had a letter from Julia this morning."

Anne caught her breath; she hoped her agitation did not show in her voice. "I didn't know you corresponded with Julia."

"Oh, sporadically. We keep up the fiction of girlhood friendship. She likes news of Waynesboro people, and for Johnny's sake, I like to know what she is doing. Not that he ever asks. But once in a while I can toss him a 'Just heard from Julia: she seems to be fine.' He still—"

"He has loved her all his life, Elsa, preposterous as it seems. And always will."

"I know. I accepted that long ago. There is nothing in this letter really. She says Tucker is fine, and likes his school. Her mother has not been very well—complains of pains in her side, but her doctor can find nothing wrong. Julia thinks there isn't; that she is sick of chagrin."

Anne was silent for half a block; finally she said, "That means Julia is going to marry Mr. Armstrong."

"I am afraid so."

"It doesn't sound in the least like Louisa Deming. She is a proud woman. And the last person I know to turn hypochrondriac. Unless she has changed very much. Of course she is an old woman now. After all, your mother and I went to school to her; she must have been in her thirties when she married, maybe more."

"Do you think Julia is lying? I mean that her mother is really ill, and she doesn't want to admit it?"

"I think Julia has an infinite capacity for self-deception. Especially if it means avoiding expectation of trouble."

"Has she ever cared for anyone in her life?"

"Oh, yes." Anne turned her head to look at Elsa in surprise. "Her father, who thought she was perfect. It was the fault of the doctors that he died—John, Johnny, Dr. Warren, let him die. They were never completely forgiven. She was kind and loving with poor Binny, and Johnny never forgot it. I always thought she liked being adored."

"I hoped she cares—really cares—for Tucker. He's as nice a boy as I know."

"She should. I hope she does. Tucker, so far as I know, still thinks she is perfect: however hard it is for him to understand everything, he sees no flaw. And I hope he won't until he is grown up enough to see her as she is but can be tolerant enough to accept and still care for her."

"You want him to care for her?" Elsa was bitter. "I should think the best thing would be for him to break away."

"In time, yes. But it would be a dreadful thing for a boy not to be able to love his mother."

Elsa said no more; they parted at her gate on Linden Street talking of other things. Anne reported to Johnny part of what Julia had written to Elsa: that Tucker was enjoying his school; that her mother complained of not feeling at all well, but her doctor could find nothing wrong. Johnny acknowledged the information with a grunt, passing on at once to say that he must go to Cincinnati the next day to consult a specialist about a case that bothered him. "I could get him up here for a consultation, but it would cost more than the Mortons could pay, and she isn't able to go down there."

Johnny went off for a couple of days in the city, and when he returned nothing was said about Julia or her son or her mother. It was in February that Elsa called to say that she had another letter from Julia, one that she preferred not to read over the telephone: was Anne going to be at home if she came around with it?

Anne thought she knew what the letter would contain. With a heavy heart she kept watch from the glass in the front door and greeted Elsa with "It is true, then, what we suspected? It isn't Tucker? I mean, there isn't anything wrong with him?"

"Oh, no. I'm sorry if I frightened you. It isn't Tuck you need to worry about; it's Johnny."

"Come in and sit down here by the fire—which is still burning, for a wonder. Put your coat down here, then read me the letter and get it over with."

"It is Julia at her worst." Elsa sat down and took the letter from her purse to read:

Dear Elsa:

You will be surprised to hear from me again so soon. But when I wrote you before, my fate was suspended in mid-air. Now all has been decided, and I can report to you, for all Waynesboro to hear, if anyone there has a thought to spare for me. I am going to marry Robert Armstrong. A simple ceremony at the minister's house will take place in a few days.

I suppose you will have heard about his "Uncle Robert" from Tucker. From the beginning of our acquaintance Robert has been very good, very indulgent to Tucker, even when we thought it was *Mamma* he was interested in. Of course I have known for a long while, as any woman would, that it wasn't *Mamma*. But she never did come to, until I showed her my diamond. Since then she has been in a state of hysteria (if you can imagine Mamma distraught!). I fear she is beginning to show her age. She accuses me of having stolen Robert from her. She is really ridiculous, and I have to keep telling her not to make such a fool of herself—I am so afraid she will say something to him. I keep explaining that Robert is really quite shy: he has never been around women much, never been married before, has been too busy making money (he says he knows why now—for me!) and so he approached me by way of Mamma. He says I was so unapproachable at first that I frightened him, but from the moment he saw me he wanted to hang me with diamonds!! But Mamma will never forgive me, never. She says he is much too old for me! If I were romantically inclined, I might think so myself, as he is as old or older than she is. But I tell her, *young men* are much too demanding. There won't be any of that *horrid business* with Robert—you know what I mean—he is much too old for it. I really don't know why he wants to marry me, unless it is to add one more beautiful possession to his collection (he thinks I am beautiful!!).

I am looking forward to years of life when I'll never have to worry one minute about *stretching my income* to the end of the month. Johnny's alimony seemed quite adequate at the time of the divorce, and it might have been if I had stayed in Waynesboro, but in Los Angeles, where my friends are all well-endowed, it has seemed hardly more than *pin money*. You can tell Johnny (though Robert has asked his lawyer to get in touch with Mr. Merrill, so that all will be done *officially* and *legally*) that he need not pay it any longer. I expect he will be glad to be relieved of his *burden*. He can free himself of the necessity of contributing to Tucker's support, if he will: Robert, having no children of his own, would like to adopt Tucker and have him take his name. Johnny probably won't like the idea, but he must be generous enough to consider the advantages to Tucker, who would, along with me, be Robert's heir.

Robert would of course be glad to support Mamma, but she is in no mood to accept anything from him. She plans to remain in this apartment and live on her Civil War pension, what she got for the Waynesboro house and invested, and the driblets that come for her from the sale of those county histories. Isn't it incredible that people still buy them!

I will send you my address when we have decided whether we will live in the city or on Robert's ranch (both, probably!). You would like the ranch: it was an original Spanish land grant, owned by the *same family* since those days until the last impoverished Don sold it to Robert. The house is very old, very Spanish and picturesque, but I don't know *how comfortable*.

Let me have the news of Waynesboro and that quaint institution the

Woman's Club. I can't say I shed any tears over the demise of Miss Eliza Ballard, which someone wrote Mamma about.

Yours as always,
Julia Deming Gordon
(soon to be Armstrong.)

Elsa folded the letter with a sharp crackle and thrust it in her purse. Anne, who had heard Julia out, as conveyed by Elsa, without interruption, but growing increasingly rigid and tense, white with fury, now burst out, "I could kill her! The—the—effrontery! The indecency! I could kill her!"

"Oh, so could I. Curious how she reveals herself in a letter. As she never did in person. She was always too conscious of the impression she was making."

"Some of it was meant to be insulting. All that about her alimony, when she has been bleeding Johnny all these years. I wonder if she knew quite how indecent she was: making fun of her mother, admitting she was marrying for money, and that bit about the old man not bothering her. She may be surprised," Anne concluded viciously.

"Yes. But so may he be." Elsa looked at Anne consideringly, spoke tentatively. "You agree with me that Julia is a completely frigid woman? I know that ladies are not expected to discuss these things, but I have always been convinced that Johnny, feeling as he did about Julia, would never have gone off the rails if she had been warmer."

"She never cared for him, really. She wanted to be married: any woman who isn't is a failure. And Johnny was there for the taking. But all this is water under the bridge. Now it's Johnny's peace of mind. He has been so sure of her delight in her freedom, her being spared—importunities—as if she were Diana, or the Snow Queen. He was satisfied that she had not rejected him personally, just the—obligations of marriage. Of course Johnny will never consent to let a stepfather adopt Tucker. Never."

"Has he ever refused her anything?"

"This he will refuse. The boy is all he has. Oh, Elsa! How much unhappiness that woman is responsible for! Johnny, you, now her mother, perhaps Tucker—"

"Leave me out, Aunt Anne." Elsa spoke quickly, rather coldly. "I have not been nursing a broken heart all these years, believe me. Gib and I have had a good marriage; we have a happy family life. I know that you saw or realized that I fancied myself in love with Johnny once: I considered him mine. Any man would have walked away from that, Julia or no Julia."

"I'm sorry I even remembered it. You have shown real character in making a good life." (And if the young Elsa was somewhat diminished, eagerness and zest lost in the model wife and mother, that was the price exacted of her; and if she had foreseen, she would have accepted it.) "I would have forgotten the circumstances long ago, if it had not been so regrettable for Johnny. It is all past and done with, anyway."

"You will break the news to Johnny? Do you want to keep the letter to read to him?"

"Heaven forbid! If he can preserve any illusions, let him."

Elsa took her leave. Anne spent the rest of the afternoon in torment of mind, rehearsing how best to tell Johnny. The hours dragged out; five o'clock came and went. His office hours often did not end at four: he stayed until he had seen all the patients in the wating room. Then there might still be house calls and hospital visits. Johnny was working too hard (his mother's mind escaped its burden long enough for that thought); he was working as hard or harder than his father had done, in spite of partnerships and the hospital. She had never protested because, except for the few months when Tucker was with him, his work was what he had to occupy his mind; she did not even remonstrate with him over his sitting up half the night, when he hadn't been called out, studying new medical books and piles of medical journals. Better he should not have time to think.

It was nearer six than five when he came in. One glance at his strained face told her he knew; she needn't have imagined all those possible improbable dialogues. Her face must have been just as revealing, for even as he came into the sitting room, he said, "You have heard from Julia?"

"Not I. Elsa had a letter. I don't believe she had the courage to write me. How did you hear?"

"It shouldn't have needed courage. She was perfectly free to marry again if she chose."

('Ah, but Johnny! You were so sure she wouldn't!') She asked again, "Who told you?"

"Rudy Lichtenstein. I've been with him and Merrill the last hour. The old man's lawyer got in touch with Tim, naturally, since he acted for her before."

"And what did his lawyer have to say?"

"Just what I suppose Julia told Elsa, only in longer words. Julia is to be married almost immediately. Tucker has been sent to military school, where he will associate with boys of his own social standing, boys who will one day be his business associates. If I accede to his and Julia's desire and permit him to be adopted, he'll take the name 'Armstrong'."

There was such concentrated bitterness and contempt in his tone that Anne was startled, almost frightened. "Sit down, Johnny, for goodness' sake. Don't get so worked up: they can't take Tucker from you against your will. He is still a boy: you would have to give your consent."

"I know." Johnny dropped onto the edge of the couch, his shoulders bent, his hands clasped between his knees. "It made me so angry I could hardly—the condescension—the unmitigated gall! I mustn't react immediately and obstructively, the lawyer's letter said. I must consider the advantages to Tucker—advantages that I could not afford, he assumed, since my payments for his support had never been exactly lavish—and Tucker would in time be the old man's heir, along with Julia, since he had no children of his own."

"He didn't dare! Oh, Johnny! What did you say?"

"I said, 'Over my dead body!' Regrettably, I said if the old man wanted a son let him beget one: Julia is not past child-bearing age."

"One of the things Julia said to Elsa was that he is so old there won't be any of that 'horrid business' to put up with, leaving us to guess what 'horrid business'."

"She may find out that men don't get that old. Not too old to try anyway. And Julie—" he looked at his mother with anguished eyes. "Julie was always so *revolted*. I thought she wanted out—that she would never, never—I must have been too insistent in the beginning. Maybe the old man will be wiser in his approach."

"You don't know what you are saying. Don't talk like that. Julia will not let him in her bedroom, never fear."

"But why? Why marry a man old enough for her mother, according to what Tucker told us? I wonder how Mrs. Deming is taking it?"

"According to Julia, with hysterics and accusations. I suppose when Julia teased her about her beau, she let herself be persuaded to believe it. Julia says he never was interested in her mother. It was just an indirect approach. She positively gloated over her mother's having made a fool of herself."

"Oh, Mamma! Julia isn't like that; she is devoted to her mother. I suppose by the time you'd heard that much of her letter you were so angry you could read anything into it. I hope for poor Mrs. Deming's sake this story doesn't spread."

"You know Elsa better than that. And me, I hope. If it spreads, it will be because Louisa Deming is angry enough to spread it. I don't know whether she still has correspondents here or not."

"It doesn't matter. I still don't see why Julia—"

"The money, Johnny. The money. I suppose Mr. Armstrong is really very rich?"

"His lawyer's letter indicated as much. But Julia was never mercenary. Oh, she liked nice things, but—"

"The sight of enormous riches dangled in front of her might very well tempt her."

"I hope it doesn't tempt Tucker."

"But you know he said he didn't like his 'Uncle Robert.' And he idolizes his mother; he may very well be as—as horrified as you are."

"A boy that age? What does he know? I am afraid they will persuade him."

"If he wanted to be adopted, would you give your consent?"

"I don't know. I don't think so. But I don't want him to turn against me, either. I—I just can't believe it of Julia. She is so beautiful, so remote—but not cruel. Not emotional, even as a girl. But not cruel either."

Anne might not agree with his judgment, but she did not say so. She kept silent, remembering how hysterical Julia had been over her father's death. In a moment Johnny went on, in a disjointed sort of way. "Shock," she thought. "If I were a doctor, I would say 'shock'."

"I can't imagine—and I can't help imagining—Julia in another man's—

picturing it. It makes her leaving me a personal rejection. I never believed it was. I just thought that she wanted to be free—in possession of herself—aloof—not pestered by a husband's insistence. But if she can marry again, then it was me she wanted to get rid of. She never did like my being a doctor, but—Excuse me, Mom—I'll go wash my face, pull myself together."

Anne, who had known so well how he would feel, could only sit and wait in acute misery, hoping that he would not remember the things he had been saying: he would be so humiliated. After a time he returned, white to the lips but washed—even his hair had been doused. He was in control of himself.

"I apologize, Mamma. What a spectacle for a grown man to make of himself! After all, Julia has been gone for four years. I should be used to it. There was never any hope of her coming back. I won't do this again, I promise you. I suppose Louline is holding dinner until you give her word?"

"No doubt. Can you eat dinner?"

He managed a smile. "I'm even hungry, impossible as that seems. I had had a hard day before I went to Rudy's office."

The next day Johnny's worst fears were allayed by a short letter from Tucker; it was a curious letter, but perfectly clear to his father:

Dear Father:

I am at this Harvey Military School. Did you know? I like it well enough. How is Grandma and Major and Ludwig and Tag-along? Write to me. By this time you know it was Mother and not Grandmother Deming that Uncle Robert wants to marry. They have plans for me, I guess.

But I keep remembering what a good time I had in Waynesboro this summer. With you. And at Hillcrest. All the fishing. And when it was too hot to fish just lying in the grass, teaching the Kansas kids the silly rhymes we used to say when we were little. Like "What's your name? Puddin' Tane. Where do you live? Down crooked lane." Do you remember that? I always said "My name is *Alexander Tucker Gordon.* I live on West Market Street, *Waynesboro, Ohio, U.S.A, the World.*" And that rhyme we said on kids' buttons. "Rich man, poor man, beggarman, thief, *doctor*, lawyer, merchant, chief." Silly isn't it, that I can't get those ding-dong rhymes out of my head. This is a silly letter. That is because we have to write our parents in a study hall period, and when the bell rings they collect them and mail them for us because there isn't any way we can buy stamps. But I don't mind. Lessons are all right, and I kind of like drill. That is all I can think of to say. Give my love to Grandma and Major.

Your *loving son* (don't forget)
Alexander Tucker Gordon.

Johnny bore this letter home to his mother, smiling as he handed it to her. "See what you make of this."

She read the painfully neat, correctly spelled missive, and handed it back to him with a laugh. "What a relief! What I make of it is that the boys' letters are read, and he preferred not to say too much. After all, I suppose 'Uncle

Robert' is paying the school bills. Tuck definitely does not want to be adopted, and I hope that settles that. He considers this his home, and he intends to come back and be a doctor."

"Bless the boy! There's no reason why he shouldn't be a doctor, Julia or no Julia, if he sticks to it until he's of age and free to make a choice. He would do all right: he learned a lot this summer, and is an apt pupil."

But if they thought Tucker's unwillingness to be adopted would put an end to that project, they underestimated the "old man," as Johnny persisted in calling Julia's bridegroom. A week or so later, Rudy Lichtenstein called Johnny and made an appointment to meet him in the Gardiner & Merrill office as soon as he was free. "Mr. Armstrong," said Rudy, "has sent his lawyer to persuade us yokels to let him have his way with Tucker. All you have to do is say 'no.' And 'no' and 'no'. But I think you'd better see him."

And so Johnny appeared at the Gardiner & Merrill office at something after four. He was seething with anger, but had it well under control. He had had long experience in concealing his emotions in moments of crisis. He shook hands affably with Mr. Armstrong's emissary. The western lawyer was older than the three Waynesboro men, immaculately clad, suave in manner, iron-gray hair cut short and a pair of beetling (no other word would do, Johnny thought, however trite it might be) eyebrows over a pair of keen light blue eyes. As Johnny studied him, so he studied Johnny, who could read the verdict in the flick of those eyes from him to Rudy to Tim: a country doctor and two country lawyers, middle-western to the bone, and bourgeois types to boot. Even Tim, who in his middle fifties was rather impressive. The four men sat down, Tim behind his desk, Mr. DeCourcy beside him, the other two opposite in the stiff visitors' chairs.

Tim could be suave enough himself if occasion demanded. He said, "I believe Mr. Armstrong's residence is Los Angeles. Your card says you are from San Francisco."

"That is so. Mr. Armstrong has financial interests in San Francisco and as far north as Oregon, although he has lately lived in Southern California because he prefers the climate. I have represented his interests for many years, and he has sent me to you because he believes Los Angeles lawyers lack the—er—sophistication, shall I say?—to deal with his problem."

Rudy spoke for the first time since he had acknowledged the introduction. "There doesn't seem to be anything very sophisticated about this problem. Let's get on with it, shall we?"

Mr. DeCourcy eyed Rudy up and down. "Your name, as I understood it, is Lichtenstein? There are many Germans in this section of the Middle West, I believe?"

Rudy grinned. "And a good many of them are of Jewish descent. Has that anything to do with the issue?"

The heavy eyebrows were lifted. "Nothing whatsoever. Except that I have never known anyone with Jewish blood who did not understand the value of money. Perhaps you can persuade your client—"

His three listeners laughed. He threw his head back and up, looked down his nose at them.

Tim felt it incumbent upon him to explain. "There isn't a Lichtenstein in Waynesboro who has one penny to rub against another or cares. Rudy here could have gone into corporation law like my partner and me, but instead he chose criminal law and has made a career of defending the underdog, however penniless. His youngest brother, just out of law school, is beginning to work as a labor organizer in New York."

"Oh? His name?"

"Franz. Why?"

The older man smiled frostily. "Franz Lichtenstein. I must remember. We keep a list of potential trouble-makers, have since the organization of would-be revolutionaries into the I.W.W." Then he cleared his throat. "However, I have not come all this way to discuss labor problems, but to deal with one far more simple. So simple that the trip seemed to me unnecessary, but Mr. Armstrong wanted me to come. He has set his heart on adopting your son, Doctor, and believes that if you realize all that is involved you cannot deny the boy the advantages that would accrue to him as his son and heir."

Tim lifted his hand to stop Johnny's protest, said, "Suppose you outline those advantages to us."

"You realize—or perhaps you don't—that Mr. Armstrong is a very wealthy man?"

"We have been assuming as much, since the former Mrs. Gordon is about to marry him."

Mr. DeCourcy was plainly taken aback. "But you are, or have been her lawyer. I expected your support."

"I was her lawyer in the divorce action, at her husband's request. That began and ended any connection between us. Do please continue: those advantages for Tucker?"

"Why, the best schools, here or abroad, foreign travel, and in the end an enormous fortune."

"Just as a matter of curiosity," Rudy intervened, "where did all this wealth come from?"

"Not from grinding the faces of the poor, if that is what you are suggesting. In the beginning, lumber. Then mining, and later various allied interests."

"I see. Not grinding the faces of the poor, but raping the country's resources."

"Cut it out, Rudy," Johnny said abruptly. "What difference does it make to us? Let's get on with it. Boiled down, the advantage to Tucker would lie in his being a rich man's son. Would he be any happier for it?"

Mr. DeCourcy smiled that frosty smile again. "Money isn't everything, I agree with you. But it makes life easier and more pleasant. And the best possible education is surely desirable."

"It does a boy no good, having an easy and pleasant life. We are not without experience in this town, unsophisticated though we may be, of rich men's sons. They don't always amount to much."

"The power that goes with great wealth enables a man to do or be anything he desires."

"You and Mr. Armstrong have an exaggerated idea of the power of wealth. A man who trusts to that power has been corrupted by it to the point where he cannot see there are limits to it. You have come up against one of those limits now. Go back to Los Angeles and say the answer is 'No'."

"If I tell you it is what the boy wants?"

"Did he tell you it is what he wants?"

"He is in school. I have had no opportunity to discuss it with him. His mother told me that if she wanted it, he would want it."

"He has always, up until now, been devoted to his mother. On this question she is wrong." Johnny reached into his pocket and brought out Tucker's letter. "Here—read this and tell me whether you think he wants it."

Mr. DeCourcy read it and smiled. "It is a very childish letter, isn't it, for a sixteen-year-old boy? Immature as he must be, how can he know what he wants?"

"It is not childish. It is a very astute letter from a boy who knows it will be read, perhaps reported, by school authorities." (Imagine censoring letters written by sixteen-year-old boys!) "He must be attending a very rigid school. He managed, however, to get into it his name, his home—what he considers home—his hope for a future profession. If his mother does not want to retain him in her custody as Tucker Gordon, she can return him to me. I perhaps can do more for him, now that I do not have to pay alimony. Go back and tell the old man the answer is no—most emphatically no. But you must not give him the impression that we are wild-eyed radicals, prepared to subvert my son. Mr. Lichtenstein is an old friend, but politically we do not see eye to eye: Merrill and I are as rock-bibbed Republicans as any millionaire—and are quite willing for him to keep his millions: in return we expect to be let alone. I regret it if my friends and I have seemed hostile to you. I know that you are simply carrying out a mission. As it happens, an unsuccessful one." Johnny rose, picked up Tucker's letter from the desk, shook hands with Mr. DeCourcy, touched Rudy's shoulder on the way to the door, saluted Tim, and departed, Rudy after him. Poor Tim was left to decide whether he was obligated to take a high-powered San Francisco lawyer home to dinner, Elizabeth all unprepared; he was consequently relieved when Mr. DeCourcy pulled his watch from his pocket and said he had time to catch the late afternoon train to Chicago.

And that was that, as Johnny reported to his mother. Julia did not give up easily; the old man was obviously accustomed to having his own way; they might still try to work around his "no," but the law was on his side, and Tucker. "I must write the boy this evening and tell him I have not forgotten his name, home, or profession."

When the *Torchlight* carried the notice of the marriage of Mrs. Julia

Deming Gordon to Mr. Robert Armstrong in a simple ceremony at the home of the bride's mother in Los Angeles, Johnny, who had not mentioned Julia since Mr. DeCourcy's visit, stared at it a long time. Concealed from his mother as he was by the open paper, Anne could see only his knuckles, whitened by his clasp on a crumpling news sheet. Finally he drew a long breath, let the paper drop into his lap, said, "Seeing it in print makes you realize how final it really is. That's that, then."

He said nothing more, on that evening or later. Anne, however, knew how deep the wound was, how slow to heal. She worried about him: he was never at home except for meals and at night, after evening office hours. He spent his days in his office, in the hospital, or making his round of house calls. His mother was usually in bed when he came in, but not asleep: sometimes she would slip into the hall to lean over the banisters and call good-night to him before he went into the sitting room to read, or pace the floor. There was no way in which she could help; he refused to talk, obviously preferred to be let alone. She could do nothing but pray, often wordless prayers, on her knees by her bed; without words the God to whom she prayed would know that she wanted peace of mind for her son.

Not long after that Elsa had another letter from Julia, in which she made no reference to her earlier assertion that there was nothing really wrong with her mother. Mrs. Deming was gravely ill: wasting away and in constant pain unless doped. The doctors had decided it must be cancer of the pancreas, and, Julia wrote, "It seems that although there are organs in the human body which can be spared, the pancreas is not one of them." There were no plans for even an exploratory operation; the best that could be hoped for was that the coming end would be quick and soon, for her mother's sake and that of everyone concerned. Julia concluded, "Mamma has made me promise to take her body back to Waynesboro and bury it beside Papa's. And I am anticipating my first and I hope my last return to my home town."

The letter was written in April; it was mid-May when word came of Mrs. Deming's death: a period that perhaps seemed infinitely long to those awaiting the end in California, but was shockingly brief to Waynesboro friends who had enough other things to think of and had been deceived into believing "But it was just the other day we heard—"

The undertaker in Los Angeles made all the necessary arrangements with Mr. Crawford in Waynesboro. There would be a simple service at the Methodist church before the burial. Mr. and Mrs. Armstrong would go directly from the cemetery to Madison City, where hotel reservations had been made for them; they would be in Waynesboro just long enough for the funeral.

Anne wanted Johnny to go away somewhere—anywhere—just so he would not have to be in town. "She will be curious—her husband will be curious—"

"I will be curious, the whole town will be curious. There will be a lot of people at that funeral who weren't friends of the deceased." Johnny smiled, creasing the deep lines in his cheeks. "I cannot run away. My mother-in-law was always a friend to me, and in a crisis she was worth ten of Julia. Of course I must go to the church service at least."

If he had hoped to avoid the cemetery and the necessity of speaking to Julia, he was due to be disappointed: the undertaker called to say that Johnny was among those designated by Mrs. Deming as pallbearers; Julia hoped very much that he would consent, since her mother had so few friends left in Waynesboro. Although an acceptance would mean that he must attend not only the church service but go with the hearse to the cemetery, he could not refuse: that was one obligation that only serious illness would permit one to avoid.

The church, as Johnny had foreseen, was full, not only of Mrs. Deming's friends, like the members of the Women's Club sitting together in a forward pew, and of the women of the Methodist church with whom she had been associated in so many endeavors, but also of those who wanted to see the ex-Mrs. Gordon's new multimillionaire husband. Johnny went through the ordeal expressionlessly. But he was not to escape. As the handful who had followed the hearse to the graveside turned to leave, the last prayer said, the last handful of dust tossed on the coffin, Julia intercepted him, turning back the black veil that until then had shielded her from the curious.

She held out her hand. He did not see it. The impact of her living presence blinded him. Julie—Julie—more beautiful than ever, exquisitely turned out in her crepe; no California sun wrinkles around her eyes or criss-crossing the flat cheeks that gave her that look of fragility.

"Johnny," she said, "aren't you even going to shake hands with me?"

He saw her hand then, took it, dropped it.

"I wanted to thank you for this last service. It was kind of you."

"Your mother was always kind to me. I am sorry for your loss."

"Johnny, you have no idea what an ordeal it has been! For her—but for us too. Thank God Tucker was spared, being away at school."

"But she did not live with you?"

"No. She refused. Of course we had nurses for her, but I was there every day." She shuddered. "If it had not been for Robert—I'd like you to meet my husband. You will want to wish us happiness, I am sure."

He kept her name from his tongue, lest it sound like a cry of agony; the muscles rippling along his jaw showed how hard he had clenched his teeth. He looked up, saw over her shoulder, with a sense of shock, a tall but stooped old man with thinning white hair, cut long enough to blow in the May wind, with a white beard and mustache. This man was really old, then. Tucker had said so, that summer when he had first mentioned "Uncle Robert," but to a boy of that age anyone over forty has one foot in the grave. He must be older than Mrs. Deming had been—just seventy, according to the *Torchlight*. And Julia—Johnny dropped his eyes to the hand clasping her elbow, a big hand, heavily veined and brown-spotted: one that once and for a long while had done heavy work. Then Johnny lifted his gaze from that possessive grasp to the eyes: red-rimmed but still coldly blue and arrogant.

He managed "How do you do, sir?" and received a curt acknowledgement. He could read the old man's mind and felt suddenly not only insignificant and countrified but worn—worn to the bone—and knew the question in the other's mind: "What could she ever have seen in him?" Mr. Armstrong said, "Don't forget, my dear, you have a favor to ask."

Johnny shut his eyes, drew a long breath. No longer was there any impulse to call out to her from his heart.

"What is it, Julia? You have never been backward about appealing to me."

"My appeals haven't always been answered, have they?" Then more gently, "Robert and I plan a trip around the world. In the summer so that, if you permit it, we can take Tucker with us, without keeping him out of school. It would be such a very broadening experience for him."

"Still trying. Never give up, do you? Believe me, you and Mr. Armstrong both: what I decide about Tucker, insofar as I have any power to make decisions, is for his good and not for my pleasure, or yours. I have no doubt that a trip around the world would be educational. If Tucker wants to go and if I have a letter from him that I am sure is a real expression of such a desire, without influence having been brought to bear, I will let you have this one summer." Then aware, with some amusement, of Julia's taken-aback expression, he lifted his eyes again to the man still standing behind her. "This was your idea, sir, I imagine?" Johnny hoped that sirring the old man would annoy him. Perhaps it did: he said, "The offer could hardly come from Julia." ("The money, after all, is mine.") "I suppose you are confident that he will prefer to come here?"

"I am confident of nothing," Johnny snapped. "To a boy that age the uses of money can have an undermining effect. And belittling a cherished person or place to the point where it seems shameful to still cherish it, that is easy enough. Tell Tucker that this is a countrified small town, that its inhabitants are yokels, that he is meant for higher things: if he believes you, I shall be disappointed but not surprised."

He turned on his heel and strode away across the uneven grass of the cemetery, not heeding the "But, Johnny—" that he heard as he walked off, relieved, when he finally looked back, to see that only the gravediggers were left around the hole in the ground. And in the road, the undertaker's carriage. Waiting for the Armstrongs, of course. He took a side path, preferring not to have them pass him plodding along the stony road to the cemetery gate.

The letter from Tucker reached his father some ten days later; it was delivered with the office mail, and Johnny took it home with him for his mother to read. Tucker hoped that they would understand if he asked permission to go around the world with his mother and his Uncle Robert (so he still clung to the "Uncle"). There were a lot of places he would like to see. And anyway, Ludwig Evans was going to spend the summer working in the mill again, and Jennifer was being taken by her mother to spend July at her Uncle Ernest's summer place on the seashore, so he guessed there wouldn't be much to do in Waynesboro. He would miss wheat harvest on the farm and the Country Fair and being with his father and his grandmother and Major, but particularly he would miss going on house calls with his father; but a year wasn't so awfully long, was it? This was an opportunity he might not have again and he should make the most of it, so could he please go? He would see them all the next summer, and in the meantime he was his father's loving son.

When Anne had read the letter and handed it back to him, Johnny said, "So I have lost the last round."

"I'm sorry—we'll miss him. But he'll be back. And a year passes quickly."

"I doubt whether he'll ever be back. I won't force him against his will."

"Don't be such a pessimist. I know this is a blow, but I give Tucker credit for more strength of character than you do."

"He's too young to have developed strength of character enough to resist, on the one hand, his mother, and on the other, his stepfather's generosity. The funny thing is, Julia looked so surprised when I said he could go if he really wanted to. I thought for a moment she had counted on my saying no."

Anne held her tongue: it would not help matters to say she was sure that Julia would prefer not to have a big boy like Tucker underfoot, revealing her age. She only said, after a moment, "We'll just have to make the best of it. A long, quiet summer all to ourselves. Unless—wouldn't you like to go somewhere for a vacation? You need it."

"I couldn't possibly get away; it would mean turning my patients over to the Warrens, or someone. There aren't so many doctors in town that they are not all busy, even the quacks. Or especially the quacks."

As the summer began, Johnny carried on his exacting routine: morning house calls and the hospital; afternoon office hours and house calls again; after-dinner office hours and hospital rounds—in addition to emergencies that often kept him out for most of the night. Anne was sure that he could not be attending patients all those hours he spent in his office; indeed, when she asked him, he said there was more sickness than usual: "summer complaint" among the infants, hay fever and kindred troubles among the adults, and the usual number of accidents on farms and among daredevil boys who at any other season would be in school under guard.

It was not until August, after the County Fair, that anything unusual turned up. Then one evening after he had come home for dinner, he was called to the telephone just as he and his mother were about to sit down at the table. He was at the phone a long while—so long that Anne thought as she sat waiting that dinner would not be fit to eat, a dinner that he liked in hot weather: baked ham, fresh corn on the cob, fresh lima beans, watermelon.

When he did return to the dining room, he sat quickly, flipped his napkin open, and set about carving the ham. "Sorry, Mamma, I must eat and run. That was Dr. Collins calling: he has a patient, some ten-year-old child, he thinks has poliomyelitis." His mother looked so blank that he translated.

"Infantile paralysis. Collins wants him in the hospital. The right place for him, of course. I phoned to tell them to set up an isolation ward in the south wing. But I must get there to see to it."

"'Isolation ward'? You mean infantile paralysis is contagious?"

"All the evidence points to it. Epidemics and so on. Not extremely so—not like scarlet fever. Remember years ago: one child in a family got scarlet fever, they all got it. Poliomyelitis seldom hits more than one child in a family, but—I never thought to say it, but I am glad Tucker isn't here this summer."

"Don't you think this could be just an isolated case? There's never been an epidemic of infantile paralysis in Waynesboro."

"Depends on where the child got it, and how many it's already been passed on to." Between bites of ham and an ear of corn eaten so hastily that butter ran down his chin, he enlightened her further.

"Baffling disease. No one has been able to isolate a causative organism, though all the research fellows think it's there. It must be small enough to go through filters, and too small for microscopes. It's one of the worst childhood diseases—most deadly, most crippling." He tosed his napkin down on the table, said, "Don't wait up for me," grabbed up his hat from the hall, and was off to his car.

Because the town had never experienced an epidemic of infantile paralysis, Anne could not help feeling that Johnny's fears were exaggerated. But soon there were a couple of additional cases; still not Johnny's, but since they had been taken to the hospital and put in the section from which all post-operative patients had been removed, he felt more or less responsible. Then one evening during his office hours, Tim Merrill telephoned. His boy Charley had been out of sorts all day and now was running a fever, was restless and complaining of aching head, back, and legs. Did Johnny think he had beeter see him? Johnny did, and so urgently that he dismissed waiting patients with a hurried "Emergency call. Better not wait unless you feel that it is absolutely necessary to see me," and was out into his automobile, left at the curb for just such a need. Inside an hour Charley Merrill was in the hospital, in a room in the isolation section, his mother and father with him, waiting and getting in the way of doctors and nurses.

Tim and Elizabeth were frightened speechless. Their three children had always been almost abnormally healthy, and to have the younger son stricken with so dread a disease had reduced them to inarticulate terror: they could only cling to each other's hands and look on. When Johnny had completed his examination, written a hasty prescription, left the boy to the nurses and turned to them, he congratulated them quickly, to reassure them, on having called him so promptly. The dose of hexamethylenamin administered as an antiseptic in the early stages might possibly prevent lasting effects. "It can't hurt him—a preparation of formaldehyde—and may do some good."

It was Elizabeth who finally found the courage to ask the question: "Johnny, will he be paralyzed?"

Johnny could only shake his head. "We may know in a day; it could be three days. But catching it early is a help."

"And to think," Tim said, "I was reluctant to call you—it didn't seem like anything much. But Elizabeth knew about the cases you had here. I didn't even know it was contagious."

"Infectious, we think. Otherwise, why the epidemics? I suppose that Charley, like every other boy in town, went to the Fair?"

"Of course," Elizabeth said sadly. "You think—"

"It's possible. All an infectious disease needs to turn epidemic is a moving crowd of people." He somehow managed to usher them out before him into the corridor, pulling the door with its "Do Not Enter" sign closed behind him. "Tim, take her home. Both of you get what rest you can. Nothing's going to happen to the boy tonight, and you'll need your strength later. And you must think of your other children. It doesn't seem likely you could carry the infection to them, but it might be wise—"

"Can I come tomorrow and stay with him? All the time, I mean, with a cot in there? I know he's a big boy now, but I think he might feel safer. Becky can cook for the others for a few days, and I could report to Tim out of the window, couldn't I?"

Johnny said, "I think it could be managed," and he smiled, "if Tim can bear it."

Anne was shocked and startled when Johnny finally got home and reported to her. "Somehow I never thought of anyone we knew catching it."

"That's because you're used to connecting infectious desease with poverty and filth, since medical men decided they were spread by living organisms. But it doesn't necessarily follow. A whole town's drinking water can be contaminated by typhoid germs. And unfortunately poliomyelitis is apt to strike just the people we do know, healthy young ones, for the most part. We don't know why. It can be guessed that adults and the children of the poor have met this particular microorganism some time, without being sick, and have built up an immunity. We just don't know."

With that weary admission, he stooped to kiss his mother good-night, a rare gesture, and went on upstairs.

Elizabeth Merrill moved into the hospital, where her principal activity, aside from moving out of the way of attendant nurses, was reading aloud to Charley, though he was too restless and miserable to pay much attention. Late on the second day, when Johnny came in on his evening visit and threw back the covers to examine the boy's legs, his face turned so rigid that Elizabeth knew at once what had happened.

"Johnny?"

"Don't frighten him. It isn't too serious. One leg. You can't move it, can you, Charley? Never mind, it won't stay like that. There are all sorts of things we can do, like massage, and warm baths, and sandbags to keep it from getting twisted. Just a minute, Elizabeth, till I find a nurse." He was out and back in a moment, with a nurse in crackling white, to whom he dictated his instructions; when he had finished, he said to Elizabeth, "Outside." In the corridor he continued: "I am so sorry. I had hoped—" And he said it so sadly and wearily that Elizabeth was moved to comfort him. "It isn't your fault—we don't feel guilty, for goodness' sake. But how bad is it?"

He could only shake his head. "It may pass off entirely. On the other hand, he may be crippled permanently, slightly or seriously. A lot will depend on therapy. Do you think you can manage? Massage, warm baths, exercise?"

"Of course I can. I can learn. Anything. And if he is lame the rest of his life—lots of people are lame. I won't let him grow up feeling sorry for himself, or bitter. Like Doug Gardiner. Doug told us once that he grew up hating his club foot so much that it was easy to hate the whole world, and that only falling in love with Barbara had saved him."

"That's very enlightening. It explains—he can still be very sarcastic, you know."

"I know. He unburdened himself in a moment of confidence. I probably shouldn't have said anything. But Doug, as he is now, can be an example for Charley, if he must be lame. Lameness needn't spoil your life." She broke off as the nurse at her desk at the end of the corridor rose and came hurrying toward them.

"You're wanted on the telephone, Doctor. The phone on my desk."

"Oh, Johnny! I hope not another one!"

"Lord knows, so do I. Try not to worry, Elizabeth. I'll stop in again this evening."

The Reverend Mr. Patton was on the phone, a parent so shaken that his words tumbled over one another. "Dr. Gordon? Andrew Patton speaking. Can you come? We have a sick child. Very sick, I'm afraid. She's—"

"I'll be right there. Don't waste time trying to tell me over the phone." He replaced the receiver, snatched up his bag from where he had put it down at his feet, and went through the hospital's south wing door, blessing the man who had invented the automobile: even if his was stubborn in responding to the crank, it would be quicker than any horse.

But when he was taken into Naomi's bedroom and had his first look at her, he knew that it was too late for his haste to have made any difference. Mr. Patton had escorted him to the bedside; his wife was already there, standing with one hand on Naomi's shoulder, quiet, but with fear in her eyes. Faced with what he saw, Johnny forgot that when he had left Elizabeth Merrill he had felt that he had reached the limit of exhaustion. At the bedside, with no preliminaries, he tossed back the bedclothes.

"Let me see you lift your legs, one at a time, slowly."

No sign of movement followed. Naomi whispered. "I can't."

"Try your best—No, if you can't, don't cry about it. How about your arms."

Naomi moved her head from side to side on the pillow.

"Neither one? Well, never you mind, we'll cart you off to the hospital with the other children—see what we can do." He drew the bed covers up, indicated that he wanted her parents outside in the hall; they followed him. "Just a minute while I call the hospital. Where is your telephone?" He made his call; asked for an ambulance, and for a room to be prepared; returned to the shaken parents, still standing at the bedroom door. Ariana's old room, he remembered with a pang. "How long has she been like this?"

Deborah Patton shook her head. "We honestly don't know. That's what makes it so dreadful." She was shaken by a dry sob like a hiccough. "Maybe we did do wrong, Andrew. And Naomi is being punished—the sins of—"

"No, don't say it. I cannot think that Divine Providence is so cruel."

"Divine Providence," Johnny said, "had nothing to do with this, You must have known there were cases of infantile paralysis in town. How did you fail to notice she was ill?"

"We knew about the Merrill boy, of course; they belong to my congregation. But we never expected danger to one of ours. And when we wondered, she denied feeling ill. Said she was all right. Then last night she began vomiting. Deborah put her to bed. We thought—bilious attack—then this morning—"

"I brought her breakfast. Her hands kept twitching, but she wouldn't let me feed her. When I came for her tray, she hadn't touched it. The same at noon. It wasn't until I came up with some supper that I found she couldn't move. Andrew has been trying to get you ever since. I should have kept a closer watch, but I thought she just wanted to be left alone. She—she turned her head away."

"Don't feel guilty. Getting me sooner probably wouldn't have helped. Where could she have picked it up? She didn't go to the County Fair?"

"Oh, but she did. You see, the Presbyterian women served the meals in the dining hall, and the high school girls let her help wait on tables. But what—?"

(Of course. His mother had helped with the cooking.) "In every case that has developed, the child went to the Fair."

"Then you think this is a contagious disease?"

"I'm quite sure. It's a blessing the Fair's over and done with; there shouldn't be more cases from that source. No comfort to you, I know. Well, the thing to do is to get her to the hospital at once.

"What are her chances, Doctor?"

Johnny had been postponing the question as best he could. Now he looked at them, one and then the other, and said slowly, "I can't be very hopeful. This general paralysis, if we can't stop it, it will advance upward—digestive organs—speech—in the end, lungs. I'm sorry if I seem too pessimistic, but the prognosis is not good. You must be prepared."

"You mean—" Deborah's whisper was like a cry of agony. "I thought at the worst she might be lame. You mean *she will die?*"

"We can always hope. And"—he looked at Naomi's father—"pray. I am a skeptic, but you have faith—it may move mountains. The thing now is to get her to the hospital, where there are facilities for doing whatever can be done."

"Can I stay there with her? Andrew can manage the little children."

"Yes. Of course. If you think it will help her. Either one of you can stay—whichever she wants. Let's go back."

They returned to the bedside. Naomi said querulously, like any sick child, "You were gone a long while."

"Trying to decide where you could have picked up whatever germ has laid you low. Your father says you went to the County Fair."

"Oh, I did. I never had so much fun before. The sideshow barkers—if we could get them a second slice of watermelon or a piece of pie, they let us in free. And the merry-go-round, the Ferris wheel. All we had to do was wear our aprons."

The long outburst left her breathless, but she had not finished what she wanted to say. "All year has been fun. I am so glad we came here. If I were to die tomorrow, I would have had this year, anyway." She was so obviously far from believing that she would die that breathless as she was she went on to ask, "Is Jenny home yet?"

"No, she isn't." (Thank God! He must get word to Shaney to not let her come back yet.)

"When she does, tell her—" Naomi fell silent, exhausted. What he was to tell Jenny couldn't possibly matter, anyway.

"Go pack your bag, Mrs. Patton, with whatever you will need at the hospital, and put in Naomi's things." Mrs. Patton turned back from the window, where she had been standing to hide her tears from Naomi, and went out of the room. "Now, we'll get you rolled up in your blanket ready for the ambulance."

Naomi opened her eyes, a question in them. "But Cousin Deborah?"

"She wants to stay with you. Would you like that?"

"Oh! yes, I would. But Meliss and the others?"

"Your father can manage for a while. We'll carry you down to the ambulance, and follow along in my car. Unless you'd rather have your father stay?"

Naomi looked from one to the other of them for a long while, and then decided. "No, I don't think I would. Men aren't—aren't—Tell Miss Campbell something for me, Papa?"

"Miss Campbell? I didn't know you knew her, even."

"Yes. I do. Tell her I honor my father and my mother, but when I'm sick it's my mother I want."

"I'll tell her. You think she will be pleased, is that it?"

"Yes. Once—" But she felt far too ill to go into a long explanation. "She can explain."

Johnny said to her father, "Do you want to go with us to see her settled?"

"How can I with two small children in the house?"

"There isn't anyone—?" Johnny frowned. "How about Travers?"

"He's been neighborly. But we can't impose on him."

"In an emergency you can. I'll go explain to him." Johnny went to the door in the hall that had been unlocked for a while, so long ago, when Ariana lay ill in the bed where Naomi was now. He knocked; the knock was answered almost immediately.

"Johnny. I saw your car. Is someone ill? Can I help?"

Johnny slipped through to the other side of the door to explain, and then returned with Mr. Travers.

"Show me the little ones. We'll manage fine. I can play the piano for them, or something."

In a few moments it was arranged: Mr. Travers led the two children through the separating door and closed it behind them; the ambulance came clanging up to the porte cochere, and a bundled up Naomi was carried downstairs on a stretcher and lifted into it; Mrs. Patton threw a few essentials into a valise, and the three of them crawled into Johnny's motor car. They were silent: Johnny intent on his driving, Deborah wiping away her last tears, Andrew Patton sunk in gloom.

Then Deborah began to speak; partly as a result of shock and partly to relieve her mind of its burden. "That's the first time Naomi's ever spoken of me as 'mother.' It came so easily, though, she must have thinking of me so, but found it too hard to change from 'Cousin Deborah'—such a habit, now. And someone might have been tactless enough to comment. Naomi has been a different child since we came here—oh, it wasn't easy—she struggled. She was so sure no one cared for her that she cared for no one. Or pretended so. When she gave up the pretense it was easier. She learned what most of us never have to learn. Most of us just naturally grow up caring. I don't know why she got so twisted a start. I tried—I really did. But here she changed. I don't know why. Partly Jennifer Evans, I guess. And maybe something Miss Campbell said? Jennifer was nice to her without ever being patronizing. I mean, they were equals, and enjoyed being together, and she helped Naomi to make other school friends. I had come to believe that she would grow up to be a happy woman, after all. She had a fine mind, you know—she might have done something great, even. But now this—and you don't think she is going to grow up at all. She is just fourteen. That's too young."

"Yes. Far too young. Someday medical science will lick this plague, as it has smallpox and diphtheria. But that doesn't help much today."

"Remember," Andrew said, "and thank God—she did have this year. One happy year. A great blessing. She might, if one could ask, say that this year made up for all the others. Perhaps even for the years she may miss: she would have had sorrows to endure like all the rest of us."

After they had looked in on Naomi in her hospital bed, the two men went into the corridor, the father so reluctantly that Johnny, who had stopped for a minute with Charley Merrill, called after him. "Look, Mr. Patton, if you would like to stay too, I'm sure my mother would spend the night at your house, look after the children. I must call her anyway to say I won't be home."

"That is too much to ask. I know your mother well enough to know she would say yes, but—"

"She would never forgive us if we didn't ask her, and you weren't free to stay tonight."

"You think—tonight?"

"No. Not really. But I don't know."

"There isn't anything I could do. But—but—Naomi—You see, I cared deeply for her mother, as deeply as for Deborah now, and I have been much troubled about having failed the child."

"You must stay. Or rather, come back. It might be well if you were there to introduce my mother to the children."

"And give her the key. But I'll wait until you have talked to her."

Johnny strode down the corridor to the telephone on the nurse's desk and returned to tell Mr. Patton that his mother would be ready. After that matter was settled, he went to visit Charley Merrill as he had promised, told Elizabeth, who had heard the bustle, that she was lucky, dashed off to the already darkened kitchen, poured himself a cup of strong stale coffee, found the makings of a sandwich, swallowed it down, and returned to the bedside he had left. Mrs. Patton was leaning forward from the straight chair she had drawn close to the bed, and was holding Naomi's limp hand.

"Any change?"

She shook her head. "She hasn't tried to talk, so I don't know how she feels, or if she feels. Is she aware at all? She doesn't respond to my touch."

"I think so. That she's paralyzed doesn't mean that she has lost her tactile sense." He bent over, said gently, "Naomi, are you awake?"

She opened her eyes, looked from him to Deborah and back again, even managed the hint of a smile.

"Can you talk? Tell us how you feel? Then, touched by her struggle, he went on, "No, don't try, if your throat is stiff. Can you nod your head?"

She managed that. "And you can hear?"

She nodded again. Johnny flashed a warning look at Deborah: it was easy to assume that one who could not move or speak must also be past hearing, and he did not want Naomi frightened. "Then you heard what your mother said. She wasn't sure you knew she was here, holding your hand. Tell me—just nod—does it help, having your hand held?"

The wide hazel eyes flew open, in them terror and pleading. She nodded; they could read the unvoiced "please" formed by her lips.

"That is what we wanted to know. Your mother will stay right there beside you, and I will be here, too, watching to see how you do. And presently your father will be back." He threw an explanation over his shoulder to Deborah: "My mother will go spend the night at your house, see to the children." And again to Naomi, "So we'll all be right here with you, and you can rest easy."

After what seemed a long while, but was not, Mr. Patton slipped in quietly and, taking in the scene, stopped at the foot of the bed and stood clutching the rail.

"Pull up a chair—you can't stand all night."

"Is she worse? Is she unconscious?"

"No." And Naomi answered wordlessly by opening her eyes to look at her father and smile. "Just now she is having trouble speaking, and so we haven't tried to talk."

He understood all too well. He turned blindly away, went to the window, and stood staring out at the dark. The nurse came in with a glass of water and a pill; Johnny lifted Naomi on his arm; she obediently opened her mouth for the pill and a drink, but both were rejected. The water ran down her chin. Johnny felt in her mouth for the pill. "Can't have you choking—that wouldn't help a bit." He laid her back on the pillow, said to the nurse, "One drop of tincture of opium in a hypodermic—"

Naomi's father, back at the foot rail of the bed, said, "Her throat, now?" Johnny nodded. "Then the opium—"

"Just to make her more comfortable."

The vigil lasted all night, the nurse coming in at intervals, the others going out at intervals, briefly. Johnny watched the rise and fall of her chest, saw at once when the final struggle began. He said, "Now her chest muscles—"

Deborah, still holding the limp hand in hers, said to Johnny, "Can she hear now?"

"I hope not. I gave her the opium to spare her. For a child to be frightened—"

"Just the same, I'll try. Naomi—Naomi—" Then she shook her head, the tears running down her cheeks again. "I hope she realized—"

Her husband put his hand on her shoulder. "She realized, my dear." Then he went to his knees beside the pillow and bent his head. Johnny, the child's wrist in his fingers, was at least thankful that the prayer was silent. At last, when there was not the slightest flutter in the pulse he held, he rose. Deborah looked up. "That is it," and he disengaged the hand that was still in Deborah's, and pulled the sheet up over Naomi's arm and shoulder, over her face. Her father murmured "Into Thy hands, Oh, Lord, I commit my child—" and struggled to his feet.

Outside the window the dawn was breaking; the shaded lamp in the corner was hardly necessary. In the queer light, Johnny looked worse than either of the Pattons: drained, utterly exhausted.

"I'm sorry. It is hard to lose a child. My little sister died at just about that age. I can't tell you—I did all I know."

"Don't blame yourself, Doctor. It was hopeless from the beginning. Our fault, if any, not to have seen—Now we must accept it. The Lord giveth and taketh away."

The two parents stood helpless, not knowing what to do next. Johnny made one final effort.

"You can go home now. The nurse at the desk will call a cab for you, and will telephone whatever undertaker you like. You would prefer to have the funeral at home? Mamma had better take the little children to stay with her."

Obediently and silently, they went out into the corridor. Johnny kept on his feet until they had gone, then fell back into the chair where he had spent most of the night, assailed by a pain in his chest he believed he could not survive. Unimaginable pain. He had seen others struck by it—angina, of course—only angina. Every doctor should have angina just once, so he would know. Wracked as he was, he managed to reach the bell to summon the night nurse. When she came, he cut short her inquiries. "Nitroglycerine. Out of my bag."

Thoroughly frightened by his white-lipped, tortured aspect, she stood stock still for an instant. "Hurry—bag—in corner."

Since she had often replenished the drug supply he carried, she moved quickly, found what he wanted at once, brought it, crushed it under his nose. They waited until the pain had subsided somewhat; then she said, "I'll call Dr. Stevens. When I dare leave you."

"First, help me to an empty bed."

"You should stay still until I find a doctor."

"Do—as I say."

"Don't move, then, until I get back. There's a wheel chair in the corridor." She flashed out the door, was in again instantly with the chair. "Can you lift yourself enough for me to change chairs?" She helped him up, whipped one chair out from under him, pushed up the other. "Now." She lowered him, turned the chair, and pushed him out the door and along the corridor. "You won't want to be in the isolation ward. I'll take you to the central wing."

"I just need to rest for an hour or two."

She did not answer what she considered an absurdity, but wheeled him to the desk where she said to the nurse on station, "Call Dr. Stevens—emergency—he's closest. It's Dr. Gordon, tell him." Having settled him on the bed in an empty room, she proceeded to undress him, not heeding his feeble protests. She was a strong girl, quite capable of handling so slight a man as Johnny. She had him quickly between the sheets, exhausted in the extreme, but relaxed with the lessening of the pain. She had hardly managed it when Rodney came in, stethoscope swinging from his hand, looking as he always looked, freshly shaven, completely dressed, to his tie and the handkerchief in his pocket. She was not surprised: surgery began early in the morning, and it was—she stole a look at her watch—not yet seven. She was astonished: it seemed that endless time had passed since the bell had summoned her.

Now Rodney dismissed her. "Thank you, Nurse. If I need help, I'll ring. The day staff should be here soon—you go and get your sleep. Last night was a rough one, I understand, and tonight may be another."

She slipped out, but at the desk she was stopped by the universal desire to be first with the news, particularly bad news—and of course Nurse Weldon was curious.

"What is it? You said, 'Emergency, get Dr. Stevens.'"

"For Dr. Gordon. At first I thought maybe a cerebral or a coronary—but nitroglycerin helped when he asked for it, so I knew."

"Angina, then." The two nurses looked at each other, shocked and frightened, until Mrs. Weldon said, "Oh, well! Lots of people have angina attacks and live for years and die of something else."

Back in the room where Johnny had been put to bed, Rodney tried to conceal his dismay, bending his head to hide his face as he moved his stethoscope about.

"Rod, no point in that. You know—I know—it's angina."

Rodney hung his stethoscope around his neck. "A pretty severe warning, if you don't mind my saying so. Of coronary trouble. It's not my department—you should have called one of the Warrens. But you know as well as I do that after one attack, you're always liable—What have you been doing to yourself, Johnny? How long since you've had a night's sleep in bed?"

Johnny smiled and shook his head.

"I can believe you: you don't even remember. Don't know when you last had a meal, either, I bet. Well, here you stay until Warren says you can get up."

"But that's—"

"Impossible? Indeed it isn't. The Warrens can look after your patients. The poliomyelitis cases are getting along as well as can be expected, I understand."

"The little Patton girl—"

"I know. Not your fault. And what did you accomplish sitting up with her all night?"

"For her, nothing. For her parents—"

"It isn't your profession you're dedicated to, it's the people you get involved with. You might be a better physician if you weren't so damned sympathetic."

"Like my father?"

"I suppose so. But Cousin Dock, however he may have bled inside, outside he was pretty rough and tough. He'd grown a protective shell. Anyway, here you stay. I'll call your mother."

"Oh, Lord! I told the Pattons she would take the children until after the funeral. Don't frighten her, Rod. Just tell her that I've gone to bed here after being up all night—couldn't sleep at home with those kids there. And that I'll spend my nights here until things quiet down a little. Promise?"

Rodney studied him doubtfully. "She'll have to know, and the sooner the better."

"Just stop her from coming here. Tell her I'm in quarantine. Tell her anything, but stop her. When I'm all right. When she can be convinced that I am not going to die on the doorstep."

They left it at that. When Johnny was up and about again; when the Merrills were allowed to take Charley home, and other similar or slighter cases had been dismissed; when no new cases were reported and the isolation ward was not needed as such, Johnny went home to his mother.

She embraced him as if she had not seen him for a month, then held him off to look at him. "You don't look as tired as I was afraid you would. Have you had any chance to rest?"

He laughed. "The last few days I've had plenty. My colleagues put me to bed and kept me there after I had what may have been an attack of angina."

"*Angina*!"

"Don't fuss, Mom. I'm all right. I was tired, and the Patton child's death was hard to accept. But I couldn't save her."

"You can't save them all. No doctor can. If anyone could, you could."

"How are her parents?"

"It was a blow. But they are faithful Christians, and are accepting it as the will of God. It wouldn't surprise me if you took it as hard as they did."

"Because I don't think it was the will of God? You're right: I don't. I don't believe in holding God responsible for man's stupidity, or, a better word, his ignorance. By this time we should know what causes poliomyelitis, and have a preventive vaccine. But for this summer at least, the epidemic has run its course. Are Shaney and Jennifer home? It's safe enough now. Have you heard from Tuck?"

"Postcard from London. By now they're on their way back to California by Canadian Pacific. He said he had seen a lot of interesting places but didn't specify what."

"I'm glad he wasn't here."

"Next summer will be here before you know it." Then, struck by something lost and sad in his expression, she continued, "Johnny, are you sure you're all right?"

"Quite sure." He smiled at her. "Surely you remember how Pop used to say no one lived so long as the person who had a touch of heart trouble, and learned that he had to take care of himself?"

"I remember that, but I don't remember his ever calling angina 'a touch of heart trouble'."

"Ah, but it was just a touch of angina. And I intend to be careful. Can't be anything else, between you and Rod."

Oddly enough—at least to Anne it was odd—Johnny seemed more cheerful after his brush with disaster than he had all summer. But one morning when it was raining, she went in his bedroom to close his windows and saw that on his bedside stand, beside the lamp, lay the old copy of Marcus Aurelius' *Meditations* that Kiddy Edwards had so long ago given to John. It troubled her: he was looking for something to hold on to, she thought. When she knew that he was safe in his office for the afternoon, she walked out to the hospital to talk to Rodney, whose consulting rooms were there. She went hesitantly through the front entrance: inside the doors the smell of ether was all-pervading, and made her feel slightly sick. She was never squeamish about illness at home, but often as she had been to the hospital to visit friends, it still frightened her a little. She stopped at the reception desk to ask for Dr. Stevens and was at once shown to his office. He was at his desk working on records, still in his surgeon's gown; he looked up frowning at the interruption until he saw who it was. Then he got to his feet at once.

"Cousin Anne! What can I do for you? You aren't feeling ill, I hope?"

"Not at all." In these surroundings Anne saw him without being reminded of his boyhood, of the bitter memories. She thought only, "He doesn't look like Johnny any more, except his eyes. He's more formidable." For one thing, he was taller than Johnny; his face was narrower, his profile more aquiline. She refused to be daunted, however, by this sudden unfamiliarity.

"I'm worried about Johnny. I hope you will tell me the truth about his condition. He told me about his attack of what may have been angina, and I know what angina is, however he belittles it. But I thought it was only old people who were liable to angina. Johnny isn't forty. It seems impossible."

"A man's physical age doesn't depend altogether on the number of years he has lived, unfortunately."

"How bad was the attack? How likely—?"

"To recur? There his age is in his favor. If he takes care of himself. It was a hard summer for all of us. Things are quieter now, but whether anyone can keep Johnny from driving himself, I don't know."

"He has been working as hard as ever since he came home, answering every call and studying half the night."

"It was the polio epidemic that brought him to the breaking point. But it isn't hard work alone that did the damage. You don't mind my being frank? He has never been a happy man since the divorce. Those who are close to him here have known that, and the passage of time hasn't helped. All this year he has seemed to me—not to others, I am sure, he is so controlled: but I know him so well—to be a man bereft of all he had to live for. Except for his profession."

"He has been bitterly unhappy since Julia's remarriage." (Now *I* am being frank. Betraying him, perhaps. But he needs help.) "After Julia had left him, he comforted himself somewhat by the belief that it was marriage itself rather than anything he did: that she was glad to escape from the—demands. He was sure that she would never remarry. When she did, his last feeble defense was gone. And when Tucker chose to go round the world rather than spend the summer here, it seemed to him the end, as if he had lost everything. Of course he never said so, but I knew. You think his domestic troubles are partly responsible for that attack?"

"I am sure of it. Julia is—" He could have told her in a few strong words what he thought of Julia: of her frigidity, of her reasons for marrying a man old enough to be her father; he refrained, afraid of shocking Johnny's mother. "Never mind what Julia is. He fell in love with her so long ago he will never see her with a man's—perception, shall we say?" Rodney thought fleetingly of his own warmly loving, sometimes fiercely passionate wife, of the merriment that bubbled in her and the children, and of what happiness it was to be husband and father when all was well in the house.

"But he has been more like himself since the polio epidemic is behind him," Rodney went on. "Possibly because Tucker is sound of limb and might so easily not have been. That makes him seem rather selfish, maybe, when there are youngsters in town who will be lame for life, but Johnny isn't that. He suffered over all those children, and particularly over the Patton child. But it is human nature to rejoice when your own do escape. I know I did. Johnny must learn to be more objective with his patients. And to forget Julia."

"That he will never do. As to being objective, his father took decades to achieve that, if he ever did. It there anything I can do besides keep in touch with Tucker—make sure he doesn't forget his father?"

"Spoil Johnny. Persuade him to rest. Give him his favorite dishes to eat."

Anne laughed. "Louline does all the spoiling that is necessary in that direction. We'll just have to see what can manage. Well, I mustn't take up any more of your time. You are like all doctors: talk a lot and say nothing. Evasive. How bad was that attack of angina?"

"I haven't meant to be evasive. I wasn't here, you know—they had to send for me. It was so early in the morning. By the time I got over here, the attack itself was over; at least he had responded to the medicine he told the nurse to give him. What he was suffering from then was post-angina exhaustion. And so I can't tell you how bad it was. Now he checks with Warren. After all, angina isn't my department. I suppose there is no use telling you not to worry?"

"If it were you, would your mother worry?"

He laughed. "She would worry herself and me and everyone else to a frazzle, demanding that I give up the hospital, my work, everything. But that is one thing you mustn't do if you want to help Johnny. Lead your normal life. If you must worry, don't tell him; and above all else, don't try to persuade him to give up his practice. It is all he has left."

Anne rose. "Thank you, Rodney. I shall remember all that you have said and try not to imagine what you might have said and didn't. I know that you will watch over Johnny."

"Like a brother, Cousin Anne. Few people means as much to me as he does."

When she had gone, Rodney sighed in relief, mopped a damp brow, and wondered whether he had been wise. He had told her nothing that was not true, but he could still hear Johnny saying that morning in the hospital, "Another one like that will kill me."

Once again on the street, at the top of the hill, Anne wondered how much of the truth she had heard. Rodney at least had been emphatic about not letting Johnny see that she was worried. She was to lead her normal life. That certainly she would try to do, however apprehensive she might be.

And she could begin at once, since the afternoon was not half over, by making some calls. Not formal calls, since she had no cards with her, but she could go out to the Evanses': she had not seen Elsa since her return from the East, delayed as that had been by the epidemic. She turned about and walked down the hill and out Linden Street.

Elsa was at home and glad to see her, ready to commiserate with her over Waynesboro's dreadful summer, rejoicing that Jennifer had not been in town and that Ludwig had spent his time in the mill, sleeping, he and his father both, at Hillcrest, and seeing little or nothing of his contemporaries. "It is selfish, I suppose, to be thinking of your own escape, rather than sympathizing with those who didn't. Poor Elizabeth! She and Tim are so troubled about Charley, even at the same time they are rejoicing that his life was spared."

"How bad?"

"He'll be lame. He is still having massage and therapy, and she says Johnny thinks he won't have to wear a brace. At any rate, he is alive. Elizabeth says she is ashamed every time she says that to herself. Charley was in the room next to where they put Naomi Patton, so they heard when they brought her in. How is Johnny? She says there were nights in succession when he didn't so much as lie down."

Anne resisted the temptation to unburden herself to Elsa. "He is exhausted, of course. But he got some rest when the worst was over. And like you, he was glad Tucker wasn't here. How is Jennifer? I thought she might be crushed by Naomi's death."

"She will miss her. Last year they were constantly together. But I think actually she didn't feel the loss so much as she was shocked at the realization that a young person can die. Death was a very remote possibility in her mind—inevitable, but not something that had to be faced for an infinitely long time. She has still not got over being terrified."

"Did she tell you all this? Admit it, I mean?"

"My dear Aunt Anne! Does any girl that age confide in her mother? No. I can just surmise. I have never seen her look frightened before: now she does, occasionally, when she is pretending to read but it really staring into space. She'll get over it, and maybe it is good that she has learned something about the uncertainties of life."

"Does she still hear from Tucker?"

"Oh, indeed. Postcards from every port. She is very envious, as no doubt he intends her to be. She has always been the enviable one. He loves being in Waynesboro, but it wouldn't be natural for a normal boy not to show off a little about all he has seen."

Anne asked about Elsa's summer, and how Ernest and his family were; Elsa in her turn asked about Waynesboro friends. They agreed that with Sally at Hillcrest and Eliza gone, reported gossip was scarcer.

They chatted a few minutes longer: the senior Rausches would soon be back in town; Club meetings would resume shortly, and the ladies would slip into the autumn routine. Anne, when she took her leave, remarked upon the swiftness with which the months passed, unnoticed; the thought remained with her on the long walk home. Six years since Julia had left, and Tucker was now a boy of sixteen. It was unbelievable.

Summer came to an end, having lingered as it always did well into September. Anne attended church services on Sunday, did what was expected of her in the matter of the Ladies' Aid and the Missionary Society, received afternoon calls and returned them, went to all Club meetings—and watched Johnny. She had grown used, as one does, to his drawn look, his thinness. But he seemed untroubled, and was more companionable when at home than he had been for a long while. Long before she had begun to think of Christmas, he brought up the subject of a present for Tucker, when they were at dinner one evening. Anne said she supposed she could ask Ludwig Evans what the boys liked that year: she hadn't a notion herself. Johnny refrained from suggesting that no doubt Tucker's stepfather kept him supplied with all a boy fancied in this fall of 1909.

He said, "Would you mind if I sent him Papa's old set of surgical knives? The ones he used in the war?"

If Anne felt a pang, she did not show it. "They are yours, to do with what you please. But don't you think he's a little young?"

"To appreciate what they mean? After all, he loved to listen to Captain Bodien's tales, just like the other boys. And they may just remind him—"

"That he wanted to be a doctor?"

"Don't put it in the past tense. I hope he still does."

"There will be pressure brought to bear."

"I know. That's why I want him to have them."

"Julia will throw them out."

"She wouldn't dare." His jaws muscles tensed, his chin set hard and firm. "But just to be sure, I'll write a letter to go with them: tell him that if he has changed his mind, or ever does, he must send them back. That we value them, and when we're gone they can go to some Civil War or medical museum."

Anne said, "That should take care of it. Julia will have to respect your wishes in that matter, anyway." She was taken aback by Johnny's having spoken as though he and she were contemporaries: "when we're gone." It was upsetting, somehow.

A few days later he brought over from the office the worn case and the shining knives that had been in the drawer of John Gordon's desk since the beginning of his peacetime practice of medicine. The letter to be enclosed was with the case.

"You can do it up fancy, tissue paper and all, and mail it with whatever you send when it's time to get it off."

Through November the younger memberes of the Club were planning their Christmas play: scenes from Lessing's *Minna von Barnhelm*, by way of a change from the standard English fare. Those who had children left them with nursemaids or husbands while they wasted afternoons and evenings (in their husbands' eyes, at least), rehearsing, gossiping, or just having fun. But however much time they were taking up with nonsensical chatter, they would be ready to perform on the fifteenth of December, at the home of the President, who as usual expected them and their husbands or other menfolk to dinner before the play.

Anne took it for granted that, as had been the custom over the last few years, Johnny would be her escort to the Rausches; but when she told him the date, he said he could not possibly go: he planned to attend a medical convention in Cincinnati. He was sorry to have to miss a Rausch blow-out, and she could say so for him. Rodney, he knew, would be glad to take her, along with his wife. Or the Sheldon Edwardses.

"I don't have to be taken, goodness gracious! I am perfectly capable of walking those few blocks. But I am sorry you'll miss it. Are you sure you feel equal to a medical convention? Is it important?"

"It is important to me, and, yes, I am sure I feel equal to it. There is to be a symposium on infectious diseases of children; I'd like to hear about the latest research and discoveries, if any. No one yet has found the causative organism of not only poliomyelitis, but measles, scarlet fever, and whooping cough."

And so on the thirteenth Johnny packed his bag and took the train for Cincinnati, not without reminding his mother to get Tucker's Christmas presents in the mail. She did so promptly, although she found it hard to believe the mails were quite that slow.

Before the fifteenth, Jessamine Edwards telephoned to say that she and Sheldon would pick her up on their way to the Rausches', so that she did not have to walk after all. The Rausch house was lighted, front to back, upstairs and down; there were wreaths in the windows, garlands of evergreens around the stair rail, poinsettias and chrysanthemums where there was room for them, and the usual magnificent Christmas tree in the front parlor. There was also all the high-hearted bustle that accompanied a Rausch "blow-out": a double line of guests on the stairs, going up with their wraps, coming down without them, slowly moving lines, because of the pauses for greetings and good wishes; Ludwig and Sally in the front drawing-room door to salute their arriving friends, and urge them to join the babel in the double parlors. For dinner Anne was as always at the long table in the dining room, with Ludwig and Sally, Gib and Elsa, and the older members of the Club: she found her place card without really having to look for it.

All was just as usual through dinner, until the very end. After she had served the coffee, the waitress returned, leaned over Elsa to murmur something in her ear. Elsa's reply was audible. "At the back door? Very well, I'll come at once. Find Dr. Stevens, will you?"

The guests finished their coffee hurriedly after Elsa had gone out. A call for the doctor was not so unusual, but still, ordinarily for this annual occasion any doctor invited had usually arranged for someone else to take his calls. It was too bad, they thought: Rodney would miss the play, and the gentlemen did so love to see their women playing the fool. It must be some kind of emergency. They rose, dismissing the matter from their minds, and started for the back parlor, where rows of chairs awaited an audience.

As Anne reached the hall, Rodney went past on his way to the back door, caught her eye, looked away, and quickened his step. She stopped short; everything stopped: her heart, her breath. Somehow she knew. It was Johnny. Rodney wouldn't otherwise have noticed her so particularly and then avoided her eye. Instead of crossing the hall, she turned left and followed him. In the kitchen corridor, just inside the back door, she came upon a group of three: Elsa, Rodney, and Tim O'Reilly. She couldn't think why Tim—she blurted out, "What is it, Tim? Is Johnny—?"

He looked frightened. "I don't know, Miz Gordon. I hated to bust in on a grand party for mebbe nothin', that's why I come to the back."

"Quit apologizing. Tell us what brought you." Rodney was impatient.

"Johnny was on the train I just brung up from the city. I seen him get off while I was still in the cab. He was staggerin' like, an' I never seen Johnny the worse for drink. I swung down to help him, but he'd got across the platform to the hack waitin' there. When I seen his face, I knowed he was sick—mebbe awful sick. Sorry, Miz Gordon. But while I was gettin' out of my overalls, cleanin' up, I remembered the party tonight. You wouldn't be home. I went highballin' after him to your house. To see if he'd got in all right. There was a light on, but nobody answered the bell. The door was locked an' the inside shutters closed so's I couldn't see in. I knew you'd be here an' mebbe a doctor, so I run up the hill fast as I could. An' it's mebbe crazy I am to be scarin' you—"

"You did quite right, Tim." It was Rodney's quiet voice, reassuring now that he knew. "Johnny has had at least one heart attack that I know about; he may have had another. Can you go back with me? I may need help. We can go in my car—it's at the curb."

"I'm coming, Rodney," Anne protested. "You can't leave me here."

"Get a coat, then—quickly."

Elsa went to the back hall closet, brought out old cloaks. "Put this on. I'll see that you get your own later. I'll wear the other one. No, of course I'm coming. I wouldn't let you—Is your key in that bag?"

Anne was clutching in both hands her beaded evening bag. When she nodded, Elsa went on, "Let's go, then. Rod will have his car started." She said to the wide-eyed waitress, who was still standing a few feet away, "Explain to Mamma, Linny. But where no one can hear you. Tell her I'll phone her later if I don't come right back."

The two women went out the back door and down the path to the side gate. Rodney had left his car there; he had the motor running, so that it was easy to find him. He had already put the car in gear; when the women (whom he wished anywhere in the world but there) had got in the back seat, he let the clutch out and turned the corner into Market Street. As they started down the hill, he said to Tim, "I don't see how you knew where everyone would be."

"Easy. My youngest girl works for Bachman, the florist. She ain't talked about nothin' else for a week but the decorations Miz Rausch ordered for tonight."

"How lucky for Johnny. You did right to come."

Anne was not listening; she was noting their progress: houses passed, and the Court House. It was not a minute's drive down Market Street, and they were out at the Gordon gate and up on the porch, with Anne handing her bag to Elsa and saying, "You find my key. My hands are shaking."

Elsa found it, unlocked the door. They stepped into the dark hall, lighted only from the half-open sitting room door.

Rodney said, "You wait here a minute," and strode toward the door. Anne said, "I'm coming," and followed, Elsa close behind. Tim stopped on the threshold. From the door the far side of the room, with the couch under the window, was half-hidden by the big library table, piled as always with books, magazines, and newspapers. But Rodney was looking down, not at the couch but at the floor. Anne went around the table to stand beside him. Tim, in the door, crossed himself.

Johnny lay there, his head back, his face frozen in agony, his eyes open, glazed, one arm outflung. His mother went down on one knee beside him, laid her hand against his cheek, said matter of factly, "He's getting cold." Rodney, wondering at her control, thought, "She's been expecting this." Anne closed his eyes gently, and spoke again in a wondering sort of voice, "He was such a happy little boy," and, over her shoulder, added, "You remember, Tim?" Then Rodney thought, "Shock."

He put a hand under her elbow, helped her to rise, felt the tremors that shook her rigid body.

"I'm sorry, Cousin Anne. I wouldn't have had this happen—I can't tell you—"

"Would it have made any difference if I had been home?"

At the door Tim made a choking sound. "I should 'a' broke the window in."

"It wouldn't have made any difference." Rodney's voice was heavy with sorrow, regret. "One angina attack too many. If he looked ill when you saw him at the station, he must have had one on the train, managed to get home, and had another before he could so much as sit down. If you will help me, Tim, we'll lift him to the couch. Then I must do some telephoning."

As Tim came into the room, Anne said, "Rodney—you are sure about the angina? I mean—he didn't—didn't—take something?" Elsa could see how she was shaking, and took her arm to steady her.

Tim, horrified, looked over his shoulder as he straightened Johnny's legs on the couch. "Oh, Miz Gordon—Johnny do away with himself? He wouldn't never."

"He wasn't very happy."

Rodney stooped and picked up from the rug an ampoule that had been under Johnny where he had lain on the floor.

"Cousin Anne, look at this, don't you see? He was trying to get the nitroglycerine, and didn't have the instant it would have taken. That's why it's on the floor. No, Tim is right. However unhappy he wouldn't, ever—not so long as he had you and Tucker to think of, and even one patient who needed him. Johnny was a strong man. He wouldn't have given way even to despair."

"Will there have to be an inquest?"

"Certainly not. I can't sign a death certificate, since I wasn't his physician, but Warren can. I must call him. Elsa, can you get Cousin Anne to bed—away from all this?" He lowered his voice. "Stay with her. She is in shock. Use hot water bottles and blankets. Call if you need me."

"I'll stay the night. I'll call Gib and Mamma later. The party won't be over yet."

Anne protested: she was used to being alone. Elsa's family would be upset.

"They can do without me for one night." As Anne turned to the door, she said to Rodney, "You will give me something to make her sleep?"

"I was out for a social evening, remember? I'll ask Warren to bring something."

Tim, still standing awkwardly at the foot of the couch, said, "I'd best be goin', Miss Elsa. I'm just in the way, now."

"Oh—and no one has thanked you! I know Aunt Anne will, when she is more herself. If you hadn't done as you did, she would have come in from the party alone and found him. That would have been unspeakably awful." She put out her hand to Tim.

He shook it awkwardly, saying, "Thank you for sayin' that. An' it's the truth of it: it would have been dreadful. Poor Johnny! But he wouldn't never—"

"No. He wouldn't." Elsa's eyes glimmered with tears; she could reassure Tim, who had turned to go; she was not sure herself. At least, she would take Rodney's word for it that he hadn't. For the first time she stepped close to the head of the couch and, as Anne had done, laid the back of her hand against his cheek. "Good-bye, Johnny." She turned away blindly as Rodney returned to the room; with tears on her cheeks she said, "He *was* a happy boy, you know. And no one else in the world called me 'Shaney'."

Rodney, looking after her, thought, "And Johnny never realized. How unbearably sad life can be, just through ordinary human blindness." Until Dr. Warren came, there was nothing more he could do here; he followed Elsa to the stairs and went after her and the now steadier Anne, who had rejected Elsa's support. At least, he thought, I can deal with shock.

Anne stayed in bed the next day, kept there first by Elsa, then by Sally. She did not rebel, beyond refusing to let them call the doctor. Johnny was gone; let someone else take over the preparations for the funeral. She saw no one except Mr. Patton—one couldn't deny one's minister; she submitted in silence to his consolatory sentences and his prayers. She did not rise, go downstairs, and receive those who called. Elsa, Jessamine, Sally—they would probably tell Johnny's friends that his mother was "prostrated." And, she thought, with surprise, perhaps she was; perhaps that was the word for what she felt. She did not leave her bed until time to dress for the funeral. Not much of the service reached her, not even Mr. Patton's reference to Johnny's attendance on his daughter Naomi, which had been such an example of the good physician's devotion to a patient. She was withdrawn and tearless, taciturn with all who tried to speak to her.

After the funeral, there was first the matter of a letter to Tucker, containing a more complete account of his father's death than could have been incuded in a telegram: then, the reading of Johnny's will. Rudy Lichtenstein made an appointment with her by phone, and then came down to the house one afternoon.

When she had taken him into the sitting room and indicated a chair, he said first that he had not had a chance to offer his condolences at the funeral, and did so now: "I was a lifelong friend of Johnny's, and I feel the loss. I don't know why he came to me to draw up his will—I know that Gardiner and Merrill have always acted for your family except in the divorce case. I suppose Johnny figured that whatever my fee amounted to, it would mean more to me than to them." Rudy smiled. "And of course that is true. At any rate, here it is." He took some papers out of his brief case. Everything was to be put in trust for Tucker until he was twenty-one: money, farm, partnership in the hospital, with a place kept open for him there if he ever cared to claim it. "He was sure," Rudy said, with a rising inflection, "that you were provided for."

"Yes. I shall be all right. It should go to his boy."

"You and the bank are to be trustees. If he needs to pay for his own college and medical school, he is to have the necessary money. Johnny seemed to think the boy's stepfather would be unwilling to pay for medical training. And—" Rudy smiled, "having encountered the gentleman's lawyer, I guess he was probably right. Well, I think that's it. I'll file the will in Probate Court, then we can go about finding just what his assets were." Then he continued, in a less lawyer-like vein. "I was troubled, you know. I wanted him to appoint a younger trustee than you—after all, so far as I knew, he had years ahead of him. He was so stubborn about it, I couldn't help wondering—I didn't know until afterward about his heart trouble."

"He expected to go first, I am sure. Although he kept insisting he was all right, and I really believed he was better—at least more at peace with himself than he had been. And he was stubborn about my being trustee because I knew how much he wanted Tucker to study medicine and come back and take his place here. And how much Tucker wanted it, once. Now I don't know. But I'll do what I can."

After that began the dismal business of clearing up all that Johnny had left: in the house, clothes that could be given away, letters and papers that could be destroyed; in the office, his desk. Dr. Warren and Rodney went through his files at the hospital, and the books and charts and records in the office on Chillicothe Street. Only the desk there was left for Anne to go through, as she had asked; she had missed the Marcus Aurelius from his bedside table, concluded he had taken it to the office, and for some reason wanted to find it herself: he had marked passages in it, she had noticed, and knew that Johnny would prefer not to have it fall into the hands even of Rodney. If she found it, she would take it home with her. She wavered as to whether to rent the offices to some other doctor and add a little to the estate, or whether to just lock up the three rooms as they were, in case Tucker ever did return; she had come to think that most unlikely, now. Nevertheless, that was what she finally decided to do, perhaps because she could not face the turmoil that moving out would involve; perhaps because she was so emotionally exhausted that she could not bear to think of what had been: her father, her husband, her son. As for Tucker, she thought of him almost with indifference; he was so far away now in every sense: in time, in space, and, she believed, in alienation. Sitting in the middle office, at the old desk, now dust-covered, she felt bereft and alone.

Then, emptying one of the pigeonholes to go over the papers jammed into it, she found the letter, along with Marcus Aurelius. A letter to her: "To be given to my mother in the event of my sudden death." With trembling hands she slit the envelope, pulled out the sheets covered with Johnny's beautiful small neat writing, taught him so long ago by Miss Pinney. Her heart was beating so hard that she postponed the reading for a moment's recollection of Miss Pinney and the children's naughtiness. Then resolutely she smoothed out the sheets on the desk:

> Dear Mama:
> You may never see this: who knows but that I may live longer than I think? But in case I don't, there are a few things I want to put down that I could never bring myself to say.
> Last summer I lived through days and nights of despair. Engulfing despair, so that I forgot what reasons I had to go on living. This is not telling you anything you did not know: I could guess from the way you looked at me that you could read my mind as well as you had always done when I was a boy. If I were not sure of this I would not confess it now, since I am deeply ashamed of having had so little power to reason with myself. But there were evenings when I had cleared the office of patients, that I swung the desk chair around and stared at the poison cupboard. It could have been so easy and so quick, and I had nothing to make me want to go on. And I am not sure now that it was not pure lethargy—the inertia of melancholy—that kept me in my chair.
> Then came the poliomyelitis epidemic, the pressure of work, the fighting, the defeats. I had no time to think of myself. The only despair I felt was when I saw that I could do nothing to save Naomi Patton; I found a purpose, then—to save children where possible from the deadly infectious diseases. My profession, for which I had cared so much and which I had been feeling had betrayed me, became all-important again.

Then—the angina attack—the indescribably shocking pain. It lasted but a few moments, but for some reason—I don't think I can explain it—everything looked different. Perhaps it was that having had a close brush with death, its finality—life however hard seemed better than extinction. But I think rather it was that the decision had been taken out of my hands. In a way. No more "To be or not to be." The end was coming, perhaps soon. I have done nothing to invite it; I have done my best to obey Warren's orders, but I feel—shall I say—insecure? It has not always been easy to go on, in spite of my change of heart, and so—you will be able to smile about this, I hope—I dug out the old Marcus Aurelius from among Papa's books. And learned something from him in spite of Papa's contempt. He is talking to himself: I wonder whether he even meant the Meditations to be made into a book (a scroll?). Skipping all the maxims about how to be a good man—too late for me—I found and was stiffened by his ability to put a man's life in perspective in relation to the universe: "Nothing can happen to thee which is not incidental unto thee, as thou art a man." And "Within a while the earth shall cover us all, and then she herself shall have her change"; and "What a small part of vast and infinite eternity it is, that is allowed unto every one of us, and how soon it vanisheth into the general age of the world." And he wrote much about the unimportance of death: perhaps to reassure himself. Who knows? I, who so shortly before had considered death preferable to life-in-despair, but who had somehow been resored to my rational mind, found that reassurance great comfort. "Thou hast taken ship, thou hast sailed, thou art come to land, go out, if to another world, there also shalt thou find gods, who are everywhere. If all life and sense shall cease, then shalt thou cease also to be subject to pains and pleasures"; and "Death is a cessation from the impression of the senses, the tyranny of the passions, the errors of the mind and the servitude of the senses." And finally, "If in this kind of life the body be able to hold out, it is a shame thy soul should faint first and give over."

So think of me without grief, as "one that has ordered his life; as one that expecteth nothing but the sound of the trumpet, sounding a retreat to depart out this life with all expedition."

If you can, keep in touch with my son. Tucker loves you, I know. But whether there is iron in him to resist the kind of pressure being brought to bear—he is so young—how can we know?

Just one more line from Marcus Aurelius, for you. You don't need reassurance: that you find in your faith and in the Bible, but this line made me think of you: "To live happily is an inward power of the soul." You have always had that power; because you were happy you made us happy: Papa, and Binny and I when we were children, and in his turn, Tucker. For that we have all loved you. When—and if—I go before you, I shall die believing that you can still be so.

Anne folded the sheets, replaced them in the envelope, and slipped it into the book. Then for the first time, she completely broke down; alone in the office she wept without restraint: for Johnny, who should have had a happy life all his years, not just as a child; for the brevity of his life and all human lives, for Binny, for John, for herself who had lost them all. Except Tucker. Whom she must keep, as Johnny had asked her to do. The thought stopped her tears, restored her to life, put an end to her detachment, her insulation. She must write Tucker again: a warmer letter than her first painful account of what had happened. She must explain about his inheritance; she must say that the office would be waiting for him; and, she realized suddenly, she must say something about his father's Christmas present to him. She had forgotten to mention that present before, and now he would be opening the package in a couple of days. She dropped her sodden handkerchief into her handbag, pushed the papers aside that she had taken from the pigeonhole, found a pad of unused prescription blanks, and set about writing.

The death of her son had meant for Anne almost unbearable pain, but as time passed she began to feel (and was ashamed to admit to herself) a certain beyond-emotion relief and release from tension. She would no longer be worried: there was no one to be worried about. She would do what she could to obey Johnny's "Keep in touch with Tucker," but he was too far away for her to be concerned about. He would be kept in California, now that Julia would be under no compulsion to share him with his father. "I have lost him," she thought: "Julia and her husband, with all that money to tempt the boy, will have their way with him." She would write to him, but he was no longer to be her responsibility. From now on she would be simply living, unconcerned, with no one to care about.

As the months passed, what had seemed unendurable became endurable and ordinary everyday routine: home, church, Club, and visiting with friends seemed no longer just a matter of going through the motions, but rather a succession of days, which brought, each one, some pleasure to be enjoyed. Even such an ordinary thing as a sunny winter day.

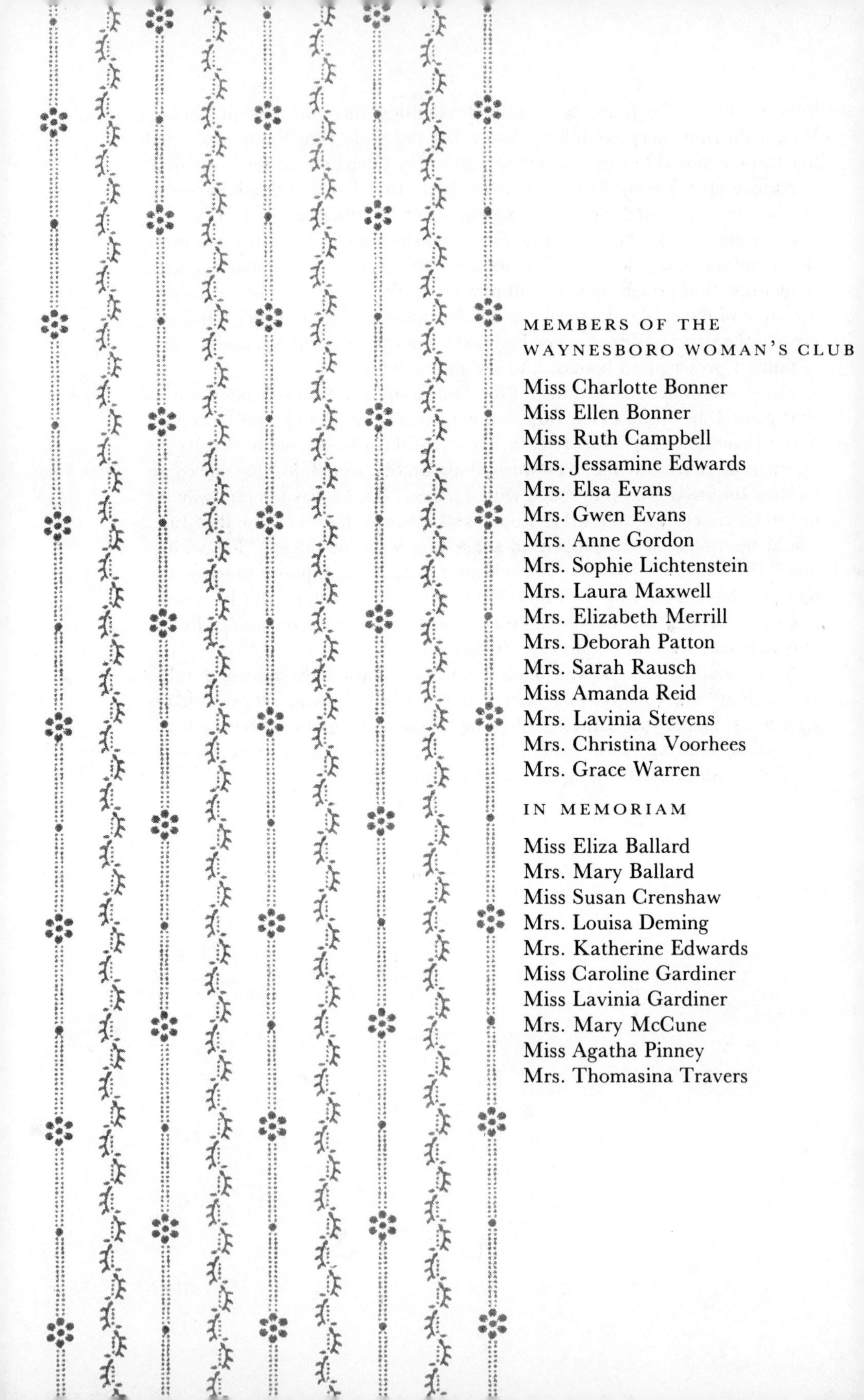

MEMBERS OF THE
WAYNESBORO WOMAN'S CLUB

Miss Charlotte Bonner
Miss Ellen Bonner
Miss Ruth Campbell
Mrs. Jessamine Edwards
Mrs. Elsa Evans
Mrs. Gwen Evans
Mrs. Anne Gordon
Mrs. Sophie Lichtenstein
Mrs. Laura Maxwell
Mrs. Elizabeth Merrill
Mrs. Deborah Patton
Mrs. Sarah Rausch
Miss Amanda Reid
Mrs. Lavinia Stevens
Mrs. Christina Voorhees
Mrs. Grace Warren

IN MEMORIAM

Miss Eliza Ballard
Mrs. Mary Ballard
Miss Susan Crenshaw
Mrs. Louisa Deming
Mrs. Katherine Edwards
Miss Caroline Gardiner
Miss Lavinia Gardiner
Mrs. Mary McCune
Miss Agatha Pinney
Mrs. Thomasina Travers

* *1913* *

"Waynesboro and the Woman's Club strive to meet the crisis of 1913 . . ."

Waynesboro, like most of southwestern Ohio, was used to "high-water season" in the spring, when streams rose beyond their banks, overflowed roads and bottomlands, and even low-lying streets and houses. In due course the waters receded, mud was cleared away, chuck-holes filled, fences and bridges mended. Only towns along the Ohio had real floods, when the river went on a rampage and water swept into every town along its banks. Although March of 1913 was cold and wet and streams ran bank-full, since the ground was still frozen and water drained away into creeks and rivers, few in Waynesboro or in other towns along minor streams expected real disaster. The bad weather merely served as a distraction from the troubling fact that a Democrat had just been inaugurated as President, an event that most of Waynesboro deplored. Even Ludwig Rausch stopped muttering about "that traitor to his party" and changed to "a damned schoolteacher in the White House."

On Easter Sunday record-breaking rains began; in forty-eight hours the torrential downpour measured between five and ten inches; eventually three thousand square miles were covered with water. By Monday there were some in Waynesboro who were apprehensive: those who lived in the small one-story houses on Canal Street, facing the towpath. Those on the other side of the river, on Front Street, in the same kind of houses, felt safe behind their levee. All this was West End territory, beyond any constant awareness on the part of the rest of Waynesboro, safely uphill from the streams; the cottages were the dwellings of laborers: the cordage mill hands, railroaders, and various others. On Sunday these householders watched the rising waters from their windows. There was a driving rain, but even then they felt no real panic: their attitude was rather one of "Here we go again" as they looked forward to clearing mud and debris from their yards and porches, perhaps from their floors. The men went to work as usual on Monday.

Two did foresee calamity on that morning. Ludwig Rausch and Captain Bodien stood together on the canal bridge and watched the current roaring past under their feet. The rain continued without slackening; debris was borne tumbling along in both canal and river; water was lapping at the low-lying banks of the mill site between them. On their left the old towpath made a barrier of sorts that was still keeping the water out of Canal Street, but it was creeping up the ramp to the mill yard that was once used for loading and unloading barges. It could not rise much higher without reaching the mill buildings and the office; the machine shop and warehouses clustered around the cobbled yard would still be safe.

The same thought was in the minds of both men: the reservoirs seventy or eighty miles north, constructed many years earlier as feeders for the canal. At that time no money had been wasted cutting down trees: they had been left to drown when the valleys were flooded; their skeletons lay or still stood, submerged in the reservoirs. If the floodgates were intentionally opened or torn apart by the force of the water, the dreadful effect would be felt downstream as far as Waynesboro. Already the water came to within a few inches of the flat span of the canal bridge. As the two men watched, a dead tree branch swept down by the swirling current was caught and held by the underpinnings of the bridge.

"That could have been washed from the bank of the canal," Ludwig said, "but if it came from the reservoir, we're in real trouble. We must get it away from there before more debris piles up, and backs the water into the mill. Get some of the hands, Captain, and enough rope to haul it away. Better stop all mill operations. Send the spinner girls home, and collect the men in the yard where I can tell them what must be done."

Ludwig crossed the bridge and went into the office, where the clerical staff was gathering, silent, dismayed by the situation, waiting to be told what to do. He made short work of it: the women secretaries were to go home; others of the office staff, under Gib's supervision, were to ready everything that could be moved—records, correspondence, typewriters, adding machines—for carrying across to the second floor of the big warehouse on the other side of the preparation mill: he would send someone to help with the carrying. Outside in the yard Captain Bodien had collected the hands; there Ludwig gave them their instructions: a few to help the office staff, a number to get all fiber, all spun strands, all finished twine and rope, to the same warehouse; when that had been done, they could busy themselves greasing the mill machinery to preserve it from muddy water and any consequent rusting, use the barrels of de gras on hand for lubricating hemp. The mill would stink like a sheepfold, but nothing was more water-resistant than a thick layer of wool fat.

As Ludwig finished, there was a dismayed reaction from the assembled laborers. The spinner girls had already slipped away, anxious to be home. The men knew well enough that a flood could not be warded off; but until they realized that the boss thought the mill would be flooded, they had not foreseen that their homes might be in danger of anything worse than a foot or so of water on their floors.

One of them spoke up, addressing Captain Bodien rather than Ludwig. "Cap'n, you think this flood's gonna climb past the doors of the mill buildings?"

It was Ludwig who answered. "This isn't very high land, and it looks like a really bad flood this time. I hope I'm wrong, but I want to be prepared."

"Then our houses gonna be under water to their ridge poles."

Ludwig was startled. "So they will. You'd better move out, all of you who live along the canal or the river. Take your families to stay with friends; don't wait till it's too late. Get out before nightfall."

"Go an' leave everything? All our furniture? All we got?"

"No," Ludwig said slowly. "It might not be there when you get back. I hadn't thought. But—look—the top floor of the warehouse there by the railroad siding is empty, since we've shipped out so much binder twine. All of you that live on Canal and Front streets—warn your wives and children—get them out of the house—then you get your furniture together, and pile it up outside. Zeb! You know where the draymen live. They'll be home, a day like this. Send every one of them down to Canal and Front streets to haul that furniture to the warehouse here. Tell 'em I'll pay for the haulage. Be off with you—don't waste any time." Then he turned to the men who were edging toward the yard gate. "I know how it will be with your womenfolk. They won't want to go. You make 'em. The river will surely top the levee. We'll do our best to save their furniture, and they must save the children."

"Where kin we go? Our friends an' kinfolk is all in the same fix."

"Send them to the Court House basement until some kind of arrangements can be made. I'll see to it. Go along now, at once—and pray, all of you, that it won't be as bad as I think." As they edged away, he turned to the remaining hands, mostly the Negroes who lived high in the East End. "Now, the rest of you—you'll have double work to get everything done here that must be done, so you'll have double pay. Take their names, will you, Bodien, and get started. Have one of the boys watch the canal bridge, and let us know if brush piles up against it, or if the water looks like going over. We don't want to be cut off from town. The river bridge will be all right: it's higher and stronger."

After what seemed like a long time but was really, in the circumstances, very soon, all the ramshackle drays from the East End came rattling and slashing through the creeping water, with loads of furniture, each with its owner perched somewhere on the load, furniture looking as it always does on movers' wagons, more shabby and dilapidated than in its accustomed corners. It was unloaded from the drays, piled on the creaking freight elevator, and carried to the top story of the warehouse. Somehow before dusk, when water was a few inches deep over the canal bridge and in the mill yard, all that could be done had been done. Captain Bodien and Gib had worked alongside Ludwig all afternoon through the driving rain helping to move everything movable. Finally the remaining workers were dismissed. Before he followed them home, Ludwig made an attempt to telephone Paul. In Madison City, river and canal, separated by half a dozen or so blocks, crossed the central business section, the river winding its way, the canal straight as an arrow. If the two overflowed, the flood would not be confined to the edge of town: it would engulf not only shops, but the city hall, the fire houses, all the seats of community authority. The paper mill was not very close to either stream, but all the city lay on flat ground. And Paul had built himself a one-story house, not very far from the mill, because, he said, any of the paper company's workmen must feel free to ring his doorbell when they had reason to see him out of working hours; he did not want them awed by an ostentatious show place. It wasn't a small house—it spread over a lot of square feet, but it was not intimidating, as Stewart Bodien's mansion, behind its iron fence, might very well be; besides Stewart was the Big Boss, and laborers would be far more likely to take their troubles to Paul. Ludwig had time to think of all these things and of Paul's sympathy for the mills hands before he got him on the telephone. Then Paul refused to take him seriously: there were levees to protect the city, along both river and canal; no flood had ever gone over them. And anyway, his house and the mill were not close to either stream. Ludwig could not persuade him to at least take the precaution of moving his family out. He hung up the receiver just as Captain Bodien came in the office door; he said, "Paul thinks I'm an old fuddy-duddy; he won't listen. You better try to get Stewart."

"After we get home. I came to tell you: the canal bridge isn't going to hold much longer—wood piling up against it—and the yard is inches deep. We'd best go."

"The workmen are cleared out?"

"All clear: gone uptown to see to their womenfolks. Front Street people were afraid they'd be cut off from town—and so they would be, before long."

Ludwig locked the door on an empty office; they splashed across the cobblestones to where he had left his car, and Captain Bodien got in beside him. "Thank God for the self-starter," Ludwig said. "I don't believe I'd have the strength to crank the damned thing. I tell you, Bodien, a day like this, and I feel my age."

"Some of the younger fellows are going to have stiff muscles tomorrow. But we did what we could. Now there's the women and children that were pried out of their houses to think of."

"I doubt if we pried them all, knowing how they feel about their homes. But there'll be most of them, and more tomorrow, at the Court House, I suppose. We'll let the women take over: your Barbara and my Elsa and her mother, to start with. There isn't a church in town that hasn't a Sunday school room that could house a few families for a while, even if they have to sleep on the floor."

His confidence in Waynesboro women was not misplaced. His wife, having heard his automobile come in, met him at the back door, half-angry, half-fearful, because he had not called to say he would be late.

"Where on earth, Ludwig? It's seven o'clock—" Then struck by his haggard face, she said, "You were right, then? There is going to be a flood?"

"There is a flood already. The mill yard is under water, and we haven't got the run off yet from upstream." Still in the back hall, shaking off his raincoat, pulling off his boots, he told her about the displaced women and children now presumably collected in the Court House. "Call Elsa, call your friends. See if you can't get the churches to open their Sunday school rooms. Find mattresses for them to sleep on. Get some food into them. The churches all have kitchens of a sort, don't they, for their social do's?"

"I'll see to it. First, we'll have to find out how many there are."

"Call Barbara Gardiner. Bodien will have told her what is needed."

"Go along to the kitchen, Ludwig—get your dinner. It's in the oven, keeping hot. I'll eat something later." And she went off to the telephone, thinking, "First Barbara. Then Elsa. Gib will have got her started, maybe. Then Anne and Jessamine, for the Presbyterian church. Then Christina and Miss Campbell and Amanda for the R.P.'s. If that isn't enough, there're the Methodists. And the Catholics. Call Fritz Klein—get him to open up so we can get food for them, if it's nothing but canned soup."

She only just caught Barbara, who was preparing to start for the Court House. "They were beginning to turn up while Doug was still in his office. He called the County Commissioners to get their permission, so it's all right. But before we can start moving them, there'll have to be a count. I'm ready now to go do it."

"Will you let me know as soon as you can? In the meantime, I'll call the good church women I know, to see if the churches can't take them in."

As it turned out, some twenty-odd families with their more than seventy children had gone to the Court House on their husbands' orders. A confused night followed: they were divided up among the churches, Catholic as well as Protestant, so there was space enough for all; mattresses, cots, and blankets were collected and delivered by Sheldon and Edwards trucks, some from the store, some from the hospital, some from friends. Fritz Klein not only opened up his store, but collected canned soups from his shelves and from those of other grocers and delivered them to the specified churches in the specified amounts; he called his brother-in-law the baker and asked for bread. By ten or eleven, children had been fed and bedded down; their parents had been fed, and were sitting on their makeshift beds, wondering dolorously whether they should really have left their homes. In the morning they were convinced: husbands who had spent the night in rescue work in the still pouring rain hunted up their families to tell them that the houses they had left were under water—water flowing with murderous swiftness, so that all who had refused to get out the day before could only be rescued by the linking of a human chain, each link of which clung with one hand to the belt or jacket of the man next, and with the other hand passed along the women and children. If any were left in those houses now, they could not be rescued until boats could be brought in, and not then unless their ridgepoles remained above water, or were close to big trees they could climb into. All able-bodied men had stayed at the scene as long as they dared; when they left, it was all they could do to save themselves from being swept away. The water-soaked rescuers brought the miserable women and children they had saved to whichever church still had room; they were all voluble, if not hysterical, relating over and over again their narrow escapes. Only boats could be of any use now, and Waynesboro, in whose daily life the river had so little part, was singularly boatless; ordinarily the river was too shallow to move a boat; there were a few canoes belonging to the more sporting members of the community, but no canoe could be trusted in that torrent with its burden of old boards, tree branches and trunks, and matted islands of cornstalks.

The same church women who had settled and fed the refugees the night before returned in the morning to make coffee for the adults, to pour milk for the children, to pass the plain bread and butter, which was the best they could manage on such short notice. School had not been suspended: no school building was in any danger; things were quieter when children who had been moved out in still dry clothing had been sent off to a hopefully ordinary day of lessons. No man was willing to sit around in a church basement when he could perhaps be of help, or at least could watch the exciting disaster. Their women, left alone or with small children, drooped pathetically on the hard pews. The church women collected and washed the dishes, cleaned up the kitchens, and began to think of the mid-day meal.

Ludwig went almost before daylight to the edge of the water at the foot of Chillicothe Street; he was joined at once by Captain Bodien.

"Risin' fast." Captain Bodien preserved an imperturbable demeanor, but he was chewing a wad of tobacco at a ferocious rate.

"Yes. The canal bridge will go soon. Look at it."

The bridge was completely under water; only the pile of debris showed where the waters were blocked, so that they swirled angrily, swept into the millyard, against the river bridge beyond, itself almost out of sight. As they watched, a great mass of boards swept down, was broken up and piled behind the other debris.

"Either a barn," Ludwig said, "or a covered bridge. Enough to do it."

The canal bridge gave way, and water and boards and the accumulated trash swept through with a roar. At the same time the old mill—the original ropewalk—collapsed; jagged boards piled up and went into the current slowly.

"Not much loss," Captain Bodien said comfortably.

"No, but I kind of hate to see it go. That's where we started. But if that's the worst damage—"

They fell silent. Both knew that there would be other losses, and were only too aware that there was no such thing as insurance against floods. They watched the water climb. In half an hour it had risen three feet, and watchers had been forced back past two cross streets, beyond the railroad tracks.

"Those folks were a little late getting out," Captain Bodien said finally. From the corner where they stood but from which they would shortly be forced to move farther up Chillicothe Street, they looked at the side street, already flooded; men were carrying out women and children on their crossed hands or slung over their shoulders.

"There are going to be more refugees than we bargained for. The mayor's standing over there—think I'll go talk to him. There ought to be a committee. Then I'll try to call Paul, see if the damn fool boy took my warning seriously."

With the mayor, Ludwig's intervention was unnecessary; he pulled a prepared list from his pocket and unfolded it.

"This here's the committee I'm appointing. Your name's the first one on it, along with Judge Gardiner and Lowrey Edwards and Rudy Lichtenstein and Father Halloran."

"O.K. We'll do what we can. But first I want to see if I can get in touch with my son in Madison City. I'll be back."

After a time a troubled Ludwig returned. "The telephone people thought I was crazy. Lines are down everywhere. Madison City is cut off: no trains running or interurban cars—tracks under water everywhere. A lot of passengers are marooned at the depot here; I reckon we'll have to feed them, too, once the dining car and the depot restaurant have been cleaned out."

He and the mayor found their committee members in the crowd; no one was pretending to do any business that day. They agreed to meet in the mayor's office after lunch. When Ludwig went home for his meal, it was to tell Sally that the water was now at least ten feet deep where he had stood early that morning; he could tell by gauging it against the corner buildings and the lamp posts. "But it won't come much farther this way; the hill rises too steeply; it will spread out over the lowlands."

"The reservoirs?"

"I don't think so. The rise has been fast, God knows, but gradual. There would have been a solid wall of water, so I suppose those dams are holding. You know, Sally, Waynesboro is only being hurt on its fringe. I can't imagine what Madison City's like. And we might as well be on the moon so far as finding out is concerned. No communication lines, no trains or interurban."

"You can't reach Paul?"

"No. And I can't spend the afternoon trying." He explained about the mayor's committee. "Waynesboro is my first responsibility. But I can't deny I'm worried. I talked to Paul yesterday—I told you—but he laughed at my warning."

"How about Hillcrest?"

"It's high enough, but it will be an island in the middle of a sea of water."

By evening all Waynesboro refugees had been sorted out and settled in the various churches and were being fed by Ladies' Aid Societies; a master list of families and their locations had been compiled. But by that time a draggle-tailed lot of women and children from Madison City were being brought in, those who lived on the same side of the river as Waynesboro; a train had been sent from Columbus by roundabout routes as close as it could go, to pick them up. By the time they had been dispersed, settled, and fed, it was seven o'clock; exhausted Waynesboro citizens drifted home to late dinners. Ludwig and Sally were halfway through the dried up and overdone meal that they were too tired to do more than pick at, when the telephone rang.

Ludwig tossed down his napkin. "Du lieber Gott! Paul—?"

"Sit down, Ludwig. It can't be Paul. Linny will answer it."

Linny, who had replaced Rose as waitress and maid, had not acquired Rose's equanimity in times of stress. When she came to the dining room door, she looked frightened. "Fo' yo', Mistuh Rausch."

"Who is it, Linny?"

"Dunno, suh. Di'n git the name. Tain' Mistuh Paul, thet Ah know fo' sho'." She rolled her eyes until the whites showed. "Sorry, suh."

Ludwig went out. Sally sat waiting, gripping the edge of the table. When he returned, his ruddy color had faded, making visible the network of capillaries in his cheeks. He came to stand beside Sally. "Not news of Paul, anyway. I was afraid—"

"But bad news?"

"Yes. At least—It was Barnes—you know—he has a farm on Fishhook Road, on the other side of the canal from Hillcrest. On the edge of the flood. He can see a fire in that direction. Thought he should tell me."

"Hillcrest! Oh, Ludwig! And there's nothing can be done?"

"No. Water all around it. But I'm going out to Barnes's to see for myself."

"Call Gib. You're too tired to drive out there, and on a night like this. I know Gib's been working all day, too, but he's younger."

"You call him, will you? While I find my binoculars."

When Gib drove up to the gate and sounded his horn, Elsa was with him. Sally snatched up an old cloak and a shawl from a hook in the back-hall closet, and went down to the gate with Ludwig. The drive out the Fishhook Road was not an easy one: in places the car splashed through water, or bumped over boulders that had been washed bare. Mr. Barnes was waiting at his gate; Mrs. Barnes, head covered with an old jacket, was down at the fence corner watching the red glare in the sky, reflected widely by the low-lying clouds.

"It might be the barns," the farmer said, offering what hope he could. "It may not be the house. But there isn't anyone else's place in just that direction."

"I'm obliged to you for calling me. I know there's nothing to be done, but I wanted to see for myself. It's the house, no question."

The two Rausches and Gib and Elsa, disregarding mud and water, hurried with Mr. Barnes down to the fence. With unsteady hands Ludwig pulled the binoculars from their case, and after shaking the caps from the lenses, lifted them to his eyes, adjusted them, and said again, "It's the house."

"But Papa, how? The electricity wasn't on, was it?"

"No. Maybe some tramp seeking shelter built a fire. What does it matter, how? There's an end to Hillcrest. By morning there'll be nothing left but chimneys."

"It meant so much to you, Papa—to all of us. Fifteen summers."

"That doesn't seem so long when you're over seventy. I had thought it would pass along to the next generation."

Sally handed the binoculars to Gib, saying, "I can't bear to watch. And I can't bear to hear your father talking like an old man, either. You can rebuild, Ludwig. There will be insurance, won't there?"

"Fire insurance, yes. But I can't—no—I won't rebuild. I'm too old. And the insurance money will help with the mill, when we can get in and assess the damage there." He took the binoculars when Gib turned them over, and stood watching the fiery glow. All stood and stared, silent. A burst of flame was briefly visible, and after a moment subsided. Ludwig lowered the glasses. "That was the roof." He put the binoculars in their case. "There's noting more. Let's go home. You'll all catch your deaths in this wet." He strode back to where they had left Gib's automobile, opened the rear door for Sally, and climbed in beside her. She put her hand on his. Not even Elsa had known as well as she what Hillcrest had meant to him; she was too choked up to speak. It was left to Elsa to try with words to console him.

"When everything is straightened out—the business, I mean—you will find you'll want to build—oh, not another Hillcrest, maybe, but another summer place."

"No. When I built Hillcrest I thought it would be for all the family. But only Paul's children are young enough to care about it now. The other grandchildren: Ernest's never really did like coming; it was just something they had to do. Charles's liked it when they were little, but they have outgrown such simple pleasures. Even Ludwig and Jennifer—no, Elsa. It's all right. Better Hillcrest should go this way than be sold because none of you wanted it, only to slip downhill, shabby and tumbledown because no one cared enough or could afford to keep it up. We'll call it the end of a chapter in all our lives."

Finally Elsa replied, turning to look over her shoulder at her father. "All right, Papa. But it has been a lovely chapter. And whether you think so or not, Ludwig and Jennifer are going to be brokenhearted. All those summers, running free in the country." But she knew as well as her father did that her children—Jennifer still in high school, and Ludwig in college—really preferred to spend their summer days in town, where there was always something stirring in the circle of their friends. She said nothing more. The ride back to town was finished in silence.

The flood passed its crest that night. The rain had stopped, and by morning the water had begun slowly to withdraw. Ludwig set out to search for Paul and his family. He could only go by a circuitous route: on a W.W. train that had brought supplies of food from Columbus and was returning, then by the Big Four on a train going to the help of devastated Madison City. He never admitted to Sally how long and hazardous his search had been, nor how hopeless he had been made to feel by the estimate poured into his ears of the number of drowned. Coast Guard boats had been brought to the western edge of the flood from Lake Erie; no ordinary row boat could have withstood the current. Ludwig managed to find a place in one that was preparing to carry food from the train through the city to its western fringe, where every schoolhouse and church had its quota of refugees, and was cut off except by boat from every nearby town. He made himself as small as possible, squatting among the bags of flour and other supplies; he held his breath when the boat reached deep water and was caught by the current until it had fought its way across what had been the river bed and got into what should have been familiar streets, where the globes of the street lights were only just above the roiling, muddy flood. The rain had given way to snow; it seemed cold beyond belief, and desolate; all Madison City, as he had foreseen, was under water: court house, city hall, library, schools, shops, post office, firehouse—all with ten or twelve feet of water swirling about them, and sections of the business district still burning where fires had broken out the night before. In time the boat reached the far shore, where Red Cross headquarters had been set up at the West Side High School. So far, it had been impossible to bring order out of the chaos: all community offices were under water so deep as to make them inaccessible. The Red Cross had no master list of refugees; all hands were busy dispatching meals to every refuge: the numbers of those to be fed at each point were known with some certainty, but not their names. Ludwig looked over those queuing up in the soup line at the hospital; Paul was not among them, nor his wife nor children. He succeeded in getting a list copied of those schools and churches where refugees had been taken, and set out on foot to find his son. It was not until afternoon, after he had walked for miles, that he was successful: in the crowd outside the Covenant Presbyterian church Paul was ladling out soup to a row of children. He saw his father before he was seen.

"Pop!" He dropped the ladle into the kettle, for someone else to take up, brushed children aside, and went striding across the playground.

"Paul—thank God!" The two men embraced, tears in their eyes. Paul had never seen his father weep; Ludwig had not seen Paul do so since he had been a small boy; neither was ashamed that he could not speak for a moment. Then Ludwig, withdrawing a little, put his hands on his son's shoulders, said "I was afraid—"

"I was a fool not to pay attention when you warned me. But we thought the levees—"

"You are all all right? When I heard how bad it was, I knew your house—"

"Only the roof was out of water." Paul smiled wryly. "We climbed out the scuttle and sat on the ridge pole yesterday when the water was coming up three feet an hour. There wasn't anything else to do—but yes, all of us, even Kathie's pup. Finally a boat came along and took us off. We weren't the only ones. Some of our neighbors were in trees, even."

"Gott sei dank—Paul, your mother said, 'Bring them home—' "

Paul pulled away from him. "That's impossible, Papa, and you know it. Since you managed somehow to get over here from east of the river, you must realize we daren't try it, with small children."

"The water is falling. Slowly, I admit."

"I know. When it has fallen far enough we'll go camp at Stewart's, where the Bodiens are living on their second floor. Until we can get home and clean the mud out. Now I'm helping here, and Ellen is trying to keep order among the women and children."

"I want to see them all—see for myself."

Paul laughed. "The kids are enjoying it." He turned to look back at the line before the soup kettle. "Kathie!"

One little girl reluctantly detached herself and started toward them. As soon as she recognized her grandfather, she ran to embrace his knees. "Grandpa! I'm in the breadline!"

"A rare privilege," her father said, "to be in a breadline. Where are the others? Why aren't they with you?"

"Inside with Mother. She got their soup for them, they're so little and so cold."

"We'll go in, then. You go back where you were, or you will miss your soup."

Inside the church front pews were covered with blankets and pillows; other blankets were around the shoulders of huddled women and children.

"The minister and his congregation have been awfully good. There's too much water in the basement to light the furnace or the cooking stoves, so the ladies collected blankets for the women and children, and we cook outside—so it has to be mostly soup."

Small children were enjoying the situation, as they do any novelty: running up and down the aisles, up and over the platform with its carved chairs and pulpit.

Long before Ludwig had heard the story again, from Ellen and the babies, of how they had sat on the ridgepole waiting for a boat, it had grown dark. Ludwig, who had not given a thought to his return home, knew that he could not, by night, go back the way he had come. He sent a message to the Red Cross headquarters, which the messenger promised to get through, although it would have to go by boat back to the switch where relief trains were coming; Ludwig wrote, "Paul, Ellen and children safe. Impossible to get back tonight; will stay with Paul. Water falling. Home tomorrow."—and could only hope that somehow it would go by telegraph to Sally.

The children were all of them eventually put to bed on the front pews; the chandelier and side lights were put out except for candles in a few sconces lighting the auditorium dimly. Ludwig thought the stooped rows of woebegone women, the hopeless attitudes of the men crowding the austere room, made as dismal a scene as he had ever looked upon, unless (and his mind went back fifty years) it was soldiers on a retreat, resting by the way on a rainy night, huddled just so. It was that memory that led him to say to Paul, "Don't worry about me; I'm an old campaigner," when Paul suggested he find an empty pew and try to get some sleep. "Besides," he added, "there is much to tell you, and we can't begin planning too soon." So the two men talked far into the night: the loss of Hillcrest, the damage done to Rausch Cordage (the amount conjectural, of course), the destruction of the canal bridge, and perhaps even the one over the river, the damages, perhaps destruction, wreaked on the mill hands' houses, and of the godsend the insurance money for Hillcrest would be. "We may be able to get the mill in shape without borrowing. I'll get it done, even if I have to sell all the securities I have accumulated."

"Not your stock in Rausch and Bodien Coated Papers, I hope. We'd lose control."

"No. Nor my holdings in the C. & C. Interurban, which will have to be almost completely rebuilt—new track put down. For those two companies I feel some responsibility. But they are open companies: the board of directors will have to decide how much to borrow and on what terms, whether or not to skip June dividends. Until the water is gone and we can get in to clean up, we'll have no real idea of what must be done."

They left it at that. Both stretched out on the hard pews to try to sleep in spite of cold, damp, and worry. In the morning Ludwig stood with his grandchildren in the breadline and accepted gratefully a bowl of thin oatmeal and a cup of coffee. The flood waters had fallen, slowly but enough so that he was able to reach the railroad and a train to Columbus; from there he could get home on the W. W.

In Waynesboro the work of cleaning up followed the withdrawing flood; families whose houses had withstood the current were in them, keeping the last of the water stirred up in the hope that as it went it would take the mud with it. To help those whose homes had been badly damaged or swept away, Ludwig called the towns' carpenters and builders to meet him in the bank, and promised to back any loan made to one of his workmen, if reasonable contracts could be made, and if the bank would charge reasonable interest. At that point everyone still wanted to help, and workmen could afford to sign contracts on the terms offered. The work began at once.

One of the builders had asked about the mill; its restoration promised to be more lucrative than rebuilding small cottages.

"My workmen can clean it up, I think. And they need to earn money to pay you fellows. We took what precautions we could. The railroad spur trestle bridge is gone. I'll have to have help—an engineer—to replace it. But I'll let you know."

For the next few weeks and all through the summer, Ludwig worked harder, he thought, than he had ever worked in his life. The cordage mill had to be brought into production as rapidly as possible, or there would be no binder twine for the northwest's summer wheat; there were orders for rope that had come in before the flood; it was Gib's responsibility to ask their customers for time to fill their contracts; machinery had to be cleaned, water-soaked fiber dried or even replaced. Worst of all, the current had torn away a corner of the solidly built office; bricklayers and plasterers had to be brought in. A thousand things. And the Rausch and Bodien Coated Paper Company was in worse shape: raw material ruined and machinery damaged; some buildings ripped open. The Interurban had lost miles of track, and many of its stations had been under water. Ludwig went from board meeting to board meeting, planning for the future of those two corporations.

His daughter Elsa believed that she was the only member of his family who saw his intense weariness, and was concerned about him. Gib was on the road much of the time; Paul, when he saw his father at the paper mill, was as busy and harried as the older man. And her mother would not admit to Elsa that there was cause for uneasiness.

"Your father is strong as an ox," she scoffed. "He revels in hard work. Of course if he would slow down, I'd see more of him. I'll be glad when all is put straight and everything is running smoothly again, because he'll not be satisfied until some of his losses are made good. But he will be all right."

Elsa unburdened herself to Anne Gordon one late spring afternoon. She had gone ostensibly to pay an afternoon call, but she did not waste much time on the airy chit-chat appropriate to such occasions. She hardly gave Anne a chance to get her into a chair before she came to the point.

"Have you seen Papa lately, Aunt Anne?"

"I don't think anyone has seen anything of him since the flood. Isn't he busy?"

"Too busy. He's exhausted. Worse than that: he's broken—he's an old man."

"Let's see—he and John were the same age. He must be seventy-three? He has never seemed old. Being married to your mother has kept him her age."

"It did, I think. Not now. The loss of Hillcrest—you know how he loved that place—and the worry over money. He told me the flood had cost him half a million, and he's determined to get it back for Mamma and all of us. It's so *silly*. Mamma has enough, and the rest of us can manage. The money doesn't matter, he does."

"I suppose you have more influence over him than anyone."

"Not more than Mamma. But she can't see that he's killing himself. I thought maybe if you could tell her how awful Papa looks. You can do more with her than anyone else."

Anne smiled. "Not as much as your father. And if she thinks he's doing what he wants to do—I wouldn't want to frighten her, Elsa."

Elsa brought her gloved fists down hard on her knees; tears came to her eyes, but did not quite fall. "He's killing himself. And it's so needless."

"Don't, Elsa. If I can bring the subject up naturally the next time I see your mother, I will. I suppose he would like to keep on going until your Ludwig is ready to go into the mill? Take over?"

"My Ludwig has three more years at Tech before he is even a fledgling engineer. Of course he knows the mill inside out. He's spent his summers there since he was a child, and he loves everything about it, even the smell. More than my brothers ever did. But he isn't ready to step into Papa's shoes. He knows nothing about finances, I'm sure."

"Does he still hear from Tucker? I have a dutiful letter every month, which never says anything." She added indulgently, "Of course you don't expect any confidences from a boy in college."

Ludwig is no hand with a pen, certainly. Of course he was home briefly for his spring vacation when things at the mill were at the worst. He wanted to stay, but his father and grandfather both vetoed that: he would lose too much time. He's written since, a postcard occasionally, that's all. Strangely enough he felt worse about Hillcrest than about the mill. I thought he and Jennifer had outgrown summers in the country. But they took it hard. The end of a chapter for them, too. I think Jennifer still hears from Tucker now and then."

"Little 'Tag-along'? If he were to see her today, Tucker would do the tagging."

The two women smiled at each other, the picture of Jennifer-at-eighteen in their minds: the slight figure, the fine aquiline features, the soft dark hair, the black eyes. "Jennifer is a throwback to some Welsh ancestor," her mother said. "No one would ever guess she was related to the Rausches. Now she's about to finish high school, and will be off to college next fall. We'll miss her and the trampling hordes of adolescents that have been hanging around the honey-pot. There's no chance of Tucker's coming for the summer, I suppose?"

"No. His stepfather is still trying to persuade him to follow in his footsteps. Though I don't think that after his years at Stanford he is any more interested in business than he ever was. He did write me once that he was taking as much chemistry and biology as he could squeeze in with the courses he had been ordered to take. This summer he is being sent to Oregon, to one of Mr. Armstrong's lumber camps. He can't make his own decisions until he is of age. Another year. By that time he may have given way under the pressure."

"There's more iron in him than there was in his father. Fond as I was of Johnny, I'm glad that Tucker is no more to be bent than Julia ever was."

"I haven't written him yet about the flood and Hillcrest. I couldn't bear to. Hillcrest was his idea of heaven on earth. I just bundled up the *Torchlights* and sent them on."

When Elsa had gone, Anne went to her desk to write the long-postponed letter to her grandson. Before she began she took out of the pigeonhole where she kept it the letter Tucker had written her after his father's death. Nothing written since had told her as much about the boy's feelings, and so she still kept it, ill-written and spattered with tear stains as it was, and reread it once in a while:

> Dear Grandma:
> Thanks for your letter. I feel better about Father, now I know he had already had one heart attack, and didn't kill himself because I didn't come home last summer. Mother thought on account of her, because she divorced him. I didn't really think he would do a thing like that. Because he wouldn't want to leave you and me. I suppose he thought maybe he would have another attack, or he wouldn't have sent me Grandpa's knives and things. Mother wanted to throw them away, she was afraid I would scratch myself and get blood-poisoning or something. But Uncle Robert wouldn't let her, he put them in his safe. I can have them when I am twenty-one. If I don't want them I can give them to some museum. Imagine. I am glad he has some sense, if not much. Now that Mother is my only guardian I don't guess I'll be let to come home summers. But no matter what, I'm coming back to Waynesboro some day to live and practice medicine.

Four years after that letter had been written, Anne hardly believed he would ever return. And, still emotionally uninvolved as she strove to remain, she was not sure she wanted him to. She felt she could speak of his intention to return quite safely, convinced as she was that by this time he must have become the Complete Californian. And so she wrote a long dramatic account of the flood and the burning of Hillcrest, and concluded, "You will miss it when you come back to Waynesboro. Ludwig and Jennifer feel very sad, their mother says, even if they are too old to enjoy doing all the things they used to do. Your Uncle Ludwig took its loss very hard, and your Aunt Elsa is worried about him. The flood was a disaster for him financially, and he is working far too hard to get things back in running order."

Soon after that Anne bundled up the bedspread she was crocheting and went up to spend the afternoon with Sally. The two old friends spent many such afternoons together, and were so sure of each other, after all the years, that they could be outspoken: they often argued and disputed to the point where anyone overhearing would think them the deadliest of opponents.

Anne had hardly got her crochet needle in her fingers before she said, "How's Ludwig? I suppose you don't see much of him these days. I should think he would be tired to the limits of exhaustion."

"Of course he's tired. Elsa thinks I should try to slow him down. Did she put you up to speaking to me? I wish she would mind her own business. Elsa is a fool about her father, always was. But come right down to it, I understand him better than she does, though she thinks I am blind to his well-being. That I refuse to worry, when really I just refuse to show that I am worrying. I worry every minute—every time he's late getting home, every time I don't know where he is."

"Then can't you slow him down?"

"No. And I wouldn't if I could. He would fret himself into a fever. He has set his heart on seeing the mill restored to what it was, and the Interurban and the paper company. I won't fuss with him about it. And if you think it's the money I care about, you're a bigger ninny than I thought."

"But why don't you explain to Elsa?"

"I don't want her to know I'm worried. She would go straight to her father. And don't you say anything to her. At this point I refuse to be a drag on him. He needs some ease of mind while he does what he thinks he must, and home is where he finds it. He tries to forget business problems here just because he doesn't want me to be concerned."

"You would think a shared worry—but I know men are funny: they insist on sparing the women and children." Anne knew it would do no good to try to persuade Sally to confide in Elsa: there had always been a certain antagonism between them.

"When we were young, Ludwig and I shared our problems. But then he was sure he would succeed in the end. Now I suspect he wonders whether he will have time, whether his end is far enough off."

"Oh, Sally!"

"There's nothing to be gained by denying the facts. He is seventy-three and working like a man of thirty. But if he must, he must. I prefer not to discuss it again."

The long dismal spring drew to a close. In June, Jennifer Evans' class was graduated from the high school, Jennifer standing out among forty-odd others like a thoroughbred in a pasture of plow horses. She was showered with benedictions and presents by her grandfather, as well as by other members of the family, but once the event was over he forgot her. The Club year concluded with a luncheon and play, Sally Rausch presiding. Never at any meeting had she given any sign of being worried or preoccupied, but she was for once glad when the last meeting of the spring had adjourned. Ludwig Evans came home from Tech, ready for his summer education in all aspects of the cordage business. As the hot months passed, he was taught by his grandfather and Captain Bodien not only every process involved in making every kind of twine and rope (which he was confident he had learned long ago) but also the when and how and what of purchasing fine manila for good rope, sisal for cheaper brands and for binder twine. Once Ludwig Senior said, "You will have to look forward to the end of the bonanza the binder twine business has been. When the new combines take the field, there won't be any sheaves of wheat to bind. Watch for something to take up the slack. Maybe twine for hay-balers."

"But you'll—"

"Oh, I expect the demand for binder twine to outlast me. But not by much."

The summer ended. Young Ludwig returned to college, and Jennifer went down to the University of Cincinnati. (No woman's college for young Jennifer!) The tracks of the Interurban had been relaid; the Coated Paper Company had resumed operations, and Rausch Cordage was as it had been before the flood, with some improvements: a new bridge across the canal, built by the town, and a new trestle for the railroad siding; a new office building, larger than the old to accommodate an expanded staff: a traffic manager, secretaries, and accountants. By fall all was finished and the mill running smoothly, as if, Ludwig thought, he need not even be there.

He himself realized how much the year had taken out of him; for the first time in his life he rose reluctantly in the morning, and he went home too tired in the evening to care whether he ate dinner or not. Reluctantly but of his own accord, without a word to Sally, he concluded that he must do what he had never done since the war: consult a doctor. If only Dock Gordon, or even Johnny—There were a dozen or so doctors in Waynesboro in 1913; of them all he knew only Dr. Warren; there was young Dr. Warren now, too, he remembered, a tall raw-boned young man whose red-blond hair made him conspicuous, with the one long lock forever flopping down over his left eye, just like his father's. When Ludwig went into the Warrens' office one afternoon, it was the young doctor he found free. In the consulting room Ludwig said belligerently, "It's been a tough summer. I'm tired. Maybe a tonic or something?"

"Something, maybe. We'll see."

Ludwig submitted wordlessly to a wordless examination. When told to put his clothes on, he did so, still awaiting the verdict in silence. Finally he was forced into a reluctant "Well?"

"Not very well, I am afraid. You have noticed how your ankles are swollen?"

"Couldn't help noticing. Heart?"

"You have been asking too much of it for a man your age. You must lay off, take a rest. I can give you medicine that will help, for a while at least."

"Things are in shape now, so I can relax a little. Can you put a name to it?"

"What's in a name? There's some valvular trouble—failure of compensation. What to expect depends on how you behave. No tobacco, no alcohol, a light diet. Rest in bed, if you can bring yourself to it."

"Sounds a happy life," Ludwig laughed shortly.

"And tell your wife. Don't try to spare her: you will need her cooperation." Ludwig obediently went home and told Sally. She had just returned from the first fall Club meeting, and was taking off her hat as he came in, as usual by way of the back door and corridor. She was astonished. "You mean you actually left the office early?"

It gave him the opening he needed. As they walked into the library to their accustomed chairs, he admitted he had gone to the doctor, and told her of young Dr. Warren's verdict. She said, "I haven't said anything all summer, but I have worried. I am glad you had the gumption to go—and to tell me." She rose from where she was sitting with some difficulty; she had begun to suffer from what she called scornfully "just a touch of rheumatism," and arthritic knees did not respond quickly to the demand that they lift Sally's weight. She went to Ludwig, leaned over his chairback, put her hands on his shoulders. "We'll do exactly as the doctor says, and you will be all right. Did he tell you to go to bed?"

"He recommended it," Ludwig admitted sheepishly. "He wants to see what complete rest will do for me. He's stopping by in a few days. Also, I'm to eat pap, throw away my pipes, pour out any beer that's around—"

"Then you'll go to bed at once and get started resting. I must say it's about time. Take the paper and go along with you, while I tell Linny what to carry up for your supper."

Sally was frightened, but she would not let Ludwig see it. She kept him in bed as long as she could, but he was up and about before the doctor thought he should be, and back in his office; his only surrender to his weakness was the hiring of a chauffeur to drive his big car. He thought scornfully that he could have managed the little electric that Sally used for running around town, but he considered that strictly for females. In spite of his activities, he knew that not much time was left him; he showed that he knew by the slow cautiousness with which he moved. His family—Sally, Elsa and Gib, Paul when he came to Waynesboro to talk business with his father—sometimes hoped that he was being more careful than he need be, but sometimes with terror weakening their bones watched him, Ludwig Rausch, moving like an old, old man. He spent his winter arranging his affairs, while Elsa and her mother busied themselves with Club meetings and plans for the Christmas party, which that year would be held at Jessamine Edwards'. He did not feel really needed at the mill; it got along very well without his concentrated attention; he accepted the banal truth that no man is indispensable. If he were to die the next day, rope would be made and sold, and in another few years young Ludwig would be ready to take over. But there were certain other matters to be worked out: the bank of which he had so long been president, for one. To Elsa he said, one Sunday when she had come up to spend the afternoon with him and her mother, that he would like it if she could be president in his place. "You have more financial sense than anyone I can think of, unless it's Paul, and he isn't here."

Elsa, disbelieving, laughed at him. "Don't talk about anyone taking your place. And besides—remember?—I can't even add without counting on my fingers."

"Plenty of others to do the adding. The president of the bank concerns himself with policy."

"You know very well no one would trust a bank with a woman president. All our depositors would go to the other bank."

The "other bank" had been in operation successfully for twenty-five or thirty years; Waynesboro had grown large enough and prosperous enough to support two banks, but the second one was still in some quarters regarded as an upstart.

"I don't think so. That's a silly prejudice. Either one has money sense or one hasn't. And Paul is on the board of directors, anyway."

"But Henry Voorhees has been in the bank so long. Won't he think he should be president?"

"He's too insignificant. No force. He would be frightened by responsibility into excessive caution. He is better off where he is. And so is the bank."

"Papa, you may outlast us all."

"Schöne Elsa! Do be realistic. You and Paul will outlive your mother and me by a generation—or you should."

It was with Paul that Ludwig discussed the future of the C. & C. Interurban. Now that the tracks had been relaid, fallen poles and wires replaced, its cars were running on schedule again and carrying the usual number of passengers. But Ludwig was foresighted enough to see that it would not always be so.

"With every Tom, Dick, and Harry buying one of Mr. Ford's automobiles, there will have to be roads for them to run on. Hardsurfaced roads like city streets. Give the traction lines another ten-fifteen years and they'll be as outmoded and useless as the canals. Unload my stock when its value gets up to what it was before the flood. Gradually, of course. Sell it all at once and you'll force the value down."

"I do realize that." Paul laughed. "I know how large your holdings are. And I think you're probably right about the interurban lines. But there won't be decent roads for a while. Good Lord, Papa, the road up from Madison City still has thank-you-ma'ams up the Darbytown hill, to rest the horses that have to drag wagons and carriages up it."

"It may not be as long as you think. When did you last see a horse and carriage on that hill?"

Ludwig sold the site of Hillcrest, where only the great chimneys stood above a cellar full of ashes to show where the house had been: in the hands of its new owner it would revert to farmland, only the old barn and the stables usable still. It was when he and Sally had finished signing the papers and were being driven home from Gardiner and Merrill's offices that Ludwig said to her, "I should like the boys and their families home for Christmas. D'you suppose they would come?"

"Such a houseful would be too much for you."

"I don't think so. I am really feeling better now everything's in order. There is nothing left for me to do but enjoy myself."

"Ludwig, please! Of course you've every right to enjoy yourself, but you mustn't kill yourself doing it. Besides, you may think you're dispensable, but to me you're not."

There were tears in her eyes. He put his hand on her gloved ones, folded quietly in her lap; he refrained from saying, "A useless hulk of an old man for you to take care of." He did say, "I'm being as careful as any hypochondriacal female. Don't worry. Remember:—it's in *Hamlet*, isn't it?—'If it be now, then 'tis not to come' and 'The readiness is all'."

Sally thought, "He's been reading some pretty gloomy things, but maybe there's some comfort in them." She made no more protests against his desire for a family gathering at Christmas, but wrote to Ernest and Charles, who had been kept informed of their father's condition, letters that they could not fail to respond to: "He doesn't say so, but I am sure your father thinks it will be his last Christmas." She also wrote to Ludwig Junior in France, to the last address she had for him; he still, being occasionally in need of money, kept in touch with her. And to Paul. Although for appearance' sake, the difference between her and Paul had long since been smoothed over, at least on the surface, and his family had been often at Hillcrest, he had not since his marriage brought his family to his mother's house; she urged him now for his father's sake to come home and bring them, and compassion moved him to accept. Christmas in 1913 fell on Thursday: they were all to be there at least by Wednesday and stay over the weekend, and Ludwig Junior, whom they had not seen for many years, longer if he would. That errant son sent his mother a cable: he would be there.

Ludwig was at home when the Western Union messenger came. He said, "You wrote to Ludwig too?"

"I thought if we were having a family reunion all the boys should be home."

"I'm glad you did. I wouldn't," he admitted, "have known where to write. I send his quarterly allowance to a Paris bank. It probably doesn't keep him in the style to which his wives accustomed him. Too bad he couldn't have kept one of them."

"Well, maybe. I do send him money when he asked. I am glad for anything that keeps him in touch. I've always told you when I've heard from him."

"But never given me the letters to read. Never mind—you have been afraid I would say 'don't.' But I have never tried to stop you from spending your money as you liked."

Elsa was horrified when she heard about the plans for the Rausch Christmas. "It will kill him, Mamma. Why, even this big house hasn't bedrooms enough."

"He wants it. And we can put the grandchildren up on the third floor, in the old ballroom, even if they have to sleep on mattresses on the floor. They won't mind."

"Some of them are getting pretty big to consider it fun to sleep on mattresses on the floor. Let me take at least one lot of them."

"Not Paul's. I'm trying to make amends for his sake and your fathers. Even if—and I never thought to see the day—Ellen and the children have to go to Mass. When? Christmas Eve? Christmas morning?"

"Paul's are sweet children, no matter what their church. Much nicer than the young snobs Emily has brought up. I'll ask Ernest's to stay with me. I'm sure his lot would prefer not to sleep on mattresses."

All the preparations were made: extra help brought in, beds made up for the younger grandchildren on the top floor. There was a good deal of turmoil, and Sally and Elsa had both been grateful when Jessamine Edwards had offered to have the Club Christmas dinner. Since she had the help of her daughter-in-law and step-daughter-in-law, Rodney's wife and Lowrey's, she was quite equal to the occasion. (Not that anyone felt that it was quite the same, without Ludwig Rausch and Sally to receive them as host and hostess.)

Once the Christmas party was over, the Rausches were ready. Ludwig Junior, whose time was his own, was the first of the sons to reach Waynesboro. At thirty-six Ludwig looked a middle-aged man: dissipation had left its mark; his thin face was lined, his eyes puffy; there was gray in his hair. But he retained his charm: the adults forgave him all his shortcomings once he was present, and the younger generation was completely won over not only by his personality but by his aura of expatriate sophistication. Jennifer Evans, home from the university for the holidays, fell victim at once; she told her mother flatly that he was the most fascinating man she had ever met: "and I had somehow got the impression he was the family black sheep."

"The family grasshopper. He's never done a useful thing in his life."

"Oh, useful! It's what a man is, not what he does, that matters. The other men in this family are real stick-in-the-muds."

"Are you by any chance including your father?"

"Oh, Mother! I meant the Rausch uncles. Father is Father. I wouldn't want him to be different. But Uncle Ludwig says if I can come to France next summer he will show me Paris."

"I can think of better chaperons for a young girl in Paris."

"I've always understood no one was as strict with the women of his family as an old roué."

"Ludwig isn't all that old," Elsa said wryly. "He's a good eight years younger than I am."

Like most of the very young, Jennifer considered her parents aged, or at least ageless. She looked slightly astonished, said hastily, "Oh, I never think of you or Father as old. I didn't mean—but what about it? Can I go? I'm as old as you were when you went abroad to study."

"Strictly chaperoned by your grandfather's German aunts, uncles, and cousins. No, I don't think so. Things are too unsettled here at home."

"Maybe by that time they'll be settled. But if I can't, I suppose I can't." She shrugged her shoulders and rose from the table where she and her mother had been dawdling over their morning coffee, more or less waiting for Ernest's wife and children to come down. Elsa smiled after Jennifer as she left the dining room; she knew her daughter: she would persist; she would bring up the subject morning, noon, and night, with seeming casualness, until the repetition would become as unbearable as a dripping faucet. And Gib would not be able to resist.

The Rausch Christmas turned out to be all that Ludwig wanted it to be: a spectacular tree, piles of gifts, clamourous overexcited children. Their parents, reunited, found it easiest to talk of what they had in common: their childhood memories. Ludwig senior rejoiced in their presence, as he listened to their recollections of their earlier, happier days; he was sure they were together for the very last time. And they were all enjoying themselves, their diversities forgotten. If Sally was less casual and at ease with her daughter-in-law Ellen than with the other two, there were too many in the house for it to be noticeable, and she was willing victim to the children's spontaneous delight in being there. Elsa provided beds and breakfasts for Ernest and his family; they were at the Rausch house so briefly in the daytime, for lunch and again for dinner, that Sally found it possible to be cordial to Emily and Ernest's children, even to pretend to a liking she did not feel.

Once Christmas was over, the excitement subsided. Ludwig had had enough. He had been so completely his old self that his sons, after the first shock of seeing how thin and old he looked, began to wonder what all the fuss had been about. But once they had all gone (and Sally had not urged even Ludwig Junior to stay on), he reverted to the near decrepitude those who saw him day in, day out, had grown used to.

"It was a grand reunion," he said to Sally when they gone to bed for the first time in a house empty except for themselves. "But company is wearing for old people like you and me. I'll take the rest of the week off and rest up."

For a few days he kept up the pretense that he would soon be back at the mill; then he decided that he would turn his den into an office and operate from there. "Gib," he said, "can bring whatever matters are pending for my decision. And Judy Crawford can bring the mail here and go through it with me before she goes to the office. She's a capable enough secretary; she can write letters that are correctly spelled and passably grammatical. But she isn't as good as Eliza Ballard. I still miss that woman: she knew as much about the business as I did."

"Your business and everyone else's. Of course the Crawford girl isn't in the position to know everything about everybody, and keep you informed." Sally spoke lightly, dismayed as she was; she would not let Ludwig know of the weight that had settled about her heart. "I don't see why you don't turn the mill over to the next generation, anyway. It's time you retired."

"Oh, I couldn't do that."

But, in effect, he did. For a while his secretary came in the mornings with the mail, and he dictated replies. Then he slipped into the way of saying, "Just turn that over to Mr. Evans" or "To Captain Bodien"; in a short while he told her she needn't come: the mill could be operated by those in charge; if questions arose needing his decision, they could be referred to him. Before winter was over the doctor told him not to attempt to go up and down the stairs. A small elevator was installed at the end of the hall where the coat closet had been. He used it for a while, but soon took to staying in his room until dinnertime, and then presently did not make the effort to go down: he and Sally had dinner together in the bedroom, with trays brought up by Linny, who did not complain, since there was the elevator she could use. Ludwig resigned himself first to the limits of the second floor and then to the bedroom he had shared for so many years with his wife. Further steps in his decline followed inevitably and rapidly: he could not sleep in bed; although he determinedly dressed every morning and undressed at night, he spent most of the twenty-four hours of the day in the wing chair beside the fire, propped at night by pillows so that he could sleep, while Sally lay wide awake in bed, keeping watch over him. She would not leave him alone: if Elsa could not be with him for a turn, Sally stayed, no matter what she missed of meetings or calls. As a consequence, Elsa spent much of her time with her father; she and her mother took turns attending Club meetings. Elsa finally protested, to him, not to her mother.

"This acting as nurse is too much for Mamma. Can't you see? I doubt if she gets more than two or three hours of sleep a night."

He submitted to the final indignity: Dr. Warren provided a night nurse. Sally, under protest and only after exacting from the nurse the most solemn of promises to call her if so much as his breathing changed, moved her night clothes into the bedroom across the hall. To him that change marked the end of their time together. He did not put that certainty into words, but one afternoon when she was sitting with him, he did say: "We've had many years given us, Liebchen, and a good life."

She did not reply brusquely, as she sometimes did, "Don't talk like that," but put her hands on his, bent, and kissed his cheek. "It has been a good life, and I am grateful to you."

On another day, when Elsa was with him, he drifted off the sleep, then wakened with a start to stare at her in bewilderment.

"What is it, Papa?"

He shut his eyes, shook his head a little, opened them again, said, "It must have been a dream. But so real. You know I have never been one to live in the past—not even lately. Or to remember the war. As so many old soldiers do when— Those were not the most important years in my life. And when it comes to dying words, mine will be for your mother. But just now—"

He had spoken slowly, catching his breath between sentences. Elsa tried to stop him: "Don't talk so much, Papa. Forget about your dream."

"No, let me tell it while I remember. It was night, and there was a river. Black dark, and only the noise of the water. I was loading my company into rowboats, trying to get them in quietly. Before Chattanooga—the night before the battle—it was like that: pitch dark, the men moving up, the sound of the water." He fell silent for a moment: when he resumed, Elsa did not know which he was recalling, the event or the dream. "Then Sherman was there. I told the boys 'It's the Old Man.' Most of them had never heard his voice, but he got off his horse to come close to them and tell them to move quietly. It made all the difference. You always knew where Sherman was, everything would be all right." After another silence he added, "That was in sixty-three. Better than fifty years ago. Absurd that I should dream of it now. I've had a full life since then, and a happy one."

Ludwig had no opportunity to play the scene with Sally that he had anticipated. Early one March morning the shaken nurse went in to waken Sally. "I never had a chance to tell you. He just put his head back against the chair and gasped once for breath—and that was it."

All Waynesboro had known that Ludwig Rausch was dying, but nevertheless the end came as a shock. He had long been recognized as the town's leading citizen: not only because he had made himself rich and in doing so had become the biggest employer of labor in Waynesboro, but also because he was a leader as well as a maker, potent in politics, a tower of strength in time of trouble. Crowds passed through the Rausch parlors for the "viewing," some curious, but most of them friends. Sally, overwhelmed not only by grief but by the crowds, retreated to the upstairs, and would allow no one to see her but Anne Gordon. Anne had little of comfort to say. By Sally's loss she was reminded of her own, so long ago. "At least," she said, "the weather is better. No blizzard." Sally did not ask what she was talking about, but supposed vaguely the flood of the year before. It was true that on the day of the funeral weather was better than in the spring of 1913: if it was not warm, it was at least sunny, with high clear skies and a crisp wind. The day was recognized by the whole town: not only the mill but the banks, the shops, the other factories, closed down to do Ludwig honor. Of his old political friends few were left: Myron Herrick was still in France, the United States Ambassador; John Sherman, Hanna, and McKinley were long gone. But the leaders of the party in the state and even the Democratic governor, in recognition of his help at the time of the flood, all came, Captain Bodien, grim-faced, organized an honor guard of such local veterans as were still able to walk to the cemetery, and enlisted a firing squad of volunteer militiamen from the local National Guard company. Few beyond the members of the family, their closest friends, the notable citizens, the Cordage Company staff, and representatives of the labor force could be accommodated in the small Baptist church, but the streets were lined with those who wanted to see the funeral procession. Elsa thought unhappily, "As good as Decoration Day," and protested her mother's conventional mourning, on the ground that her father would have hated it. Sally was to some extent comforted by the crowds, by the honors showered on Ludwig; she even took pride in the military show, in the closed shops and banks. Following the hearse in the first carriage, she managed to see it all. "You see," she said to Elsa, "how right it was to wear this veil. Not because it is right and proper, but because all these people will be staring to see how I am 'bearing up.' At least such a crowd shows that your father was appreciated. I wish he could have known." And Elsa compassionately agreed with her, though she thought privately that her father would have had little patience with such a show.

If Waynesboro citizens were fittingly sympathetic, regretful, and respectful, they were no less eager to know how the Rausch fortune had been disposed of. The will was duly reported, at least in its main provisions, in the *Torchlight*, along with the evaluation of the estate. The report did not altogether satisfy the general curiosity: Judge Gardiner used his influence to suppress the details of Paul's father's instructions to him, who was to be executor of the estate, and to Merrill, who was to be trustee. All was to be put in a trust, the income going to Mrs. Rausch during her life, and then the whole divided among his children on her death. That much any readers of the paper knew, and most thought it a foolish will: "That old lady has plenty of her own. All her father's bank stock, this house—everything Cochran had." They did not know of the restrictions on the trust; the directions to Paul were explicit: the controlling number of shares in the Rausch Cordage Company were to go to Ludwig Evans on his coming of age and completion of his education; the minority interest was to be divided at that time between son Charles in Kansas City and Gilbert Evans, son-in-law. The Rausch shares in Bodien and Rausch Coated Paper Company were to be Paul's on his mother's death; in the meantime he was to vote them, but not sell. Ernest and Ludwig Junior, neither of whom had ever shown the slightest interest in the rope business, were to have securities equal to the value of the shares turned over to those who had worked for it, except that from Ludwig's share there was to be subtracted the amount supplied him over the years as quarterly allowance. Elsa was to have the bank shares her father owned. During the life of the trust, Paul was to use his judgment in the buying and selling of stock (the C. & C. Interurban, Paul knew) except that he was not to let control of the paper company slip out of his hands and Stewart Bodien's. Elsa was to have at once the house she had lived in all her married life. After his wife's death, what securites were left in the trust were to be divided equally among his five children. It was obvious to Judge Gardiner that if his estate were to be divided immediately, there would be little or no residue: his father in drawing up the will was clearly relying on Paul to build it up to what it had been, or would have been a year earlier. Townspeople were surprised that the sum total of the Rausch estate was no larger than the amount given in the paper: "I would've thought he had more than that, the way they lived. I supposed he was a millionaire for sure. I don't believe it's all accounted for in the paper." The estimated half-million the flood had cost Ludwig—the number of securities sold for the capital to restore the cordage mill and help restore his other properties—outsiders did not of course know about. Whether or not at the time of Sally's death there would be a larger residue to divide would depend on Paul's financial judgment.

However close a family may be, if there is a large estate to be inherited it is unlikely that all the heirs will be pleased with the will that disposes of it. Ernest was hurt, his wife angry: he as oldest son should have been named trustee, and the handling of investments was after all his business. Paul endeavored to placate him. "I'm here, you see, to keep an eye on things."

"And the idea of putting Rausch Cordage in the hands of that young whippersnapper!"

"Young Ludwig has been brought up in that mill; he will manage."

"And what will happen to the bank? Who will succeed Papa as president?"

Paul looked at him curiously. Was it possible he thought of himself? He dismissed the idea: Ernest's wife would never leave New York, nor would he, probably. Nevertheless he took his time in answering, pausing to light a cigarette, making a business of shaking out the match. "What Papa planned, I suppose. He wanted Elsa to be president and me to be chairman of the board."

"Elsa! A female bank president! How preposterous! Of course she always was his favorite, and I suppose she had a lot of influence at the end."

"Don't be like that, Ernest. Papa had good judgment: Elsa has the best head of any of us."

"Will the depositors share that opinion?"

Paul smiled wryly. "Those who don't will assume she's taking orders from me. Quite erroneously, of course."

"By the time Mamma dies her bank shares won't be worth a nickel."

"Oh, nonsense: it will work out all right." "So that's it," Paul thought. "He's looking forward to his share of Mamma's estate." And he added aloud, "Anyway, Mamma's good for another ten or fifteen years at least. And if things go wrong, we can always make a change."

(And so far as anyone could see, it did work out "all right." Elsa was made president of the bank and Paul chairman of the board, and if Henry Voorhees felt any humiliation at having been passed over in favor of a woman, he gave no sign of it.)

Ludwig Junior was not there to show his resentment, if he felt any. It had been impossible for him to reach home from Paris in time for the funeral, and at any rate he had said good-bye to his father at Christmas, and by him had been warned. "It wouldn't be fair to the other boys not to make some distinction between you. They have, none of them, had money from me, except an occasional loan, always repaid. Not since they left home and went to work. Gib Evans has had nothing from me but his salary, which he has earned. I believe in justice—unlike the father of the Prodigal Son."

"The trouble is, I'm not really that. I intend returning to my accustomed wicked ways. And I can manage." And so Ludwig Junior at that point had taken it well—partly because he did not believe that his father's end was as near as the frightened womenfolk feared: he seemed, allowing for age, very much as he had always seemed, enjoying to the utmost the noisy houseful of youngsters; and partly because Ludwig knew that in any case his mother would continue his allowance; and again partly, because he was not really mercenary, had no desire for great sums of money, and never asked for more than he needed to live like the lilies of the field, giving no thought to the morrow.

Ernest may have nursed his indignation for a while. The other Rausches accepted their father's decisions amiably, spending more emotion on their loss. The will as published was the subject for speculation among the town's citizens for a few days, and was then forgotten. The widow was considered to be "bearing up well," as she returned to her various activities, showing no intention of moving from the big house on the hill, where she and then her children had grown up, although it was considered to be a lot of house for just one lonely woman.

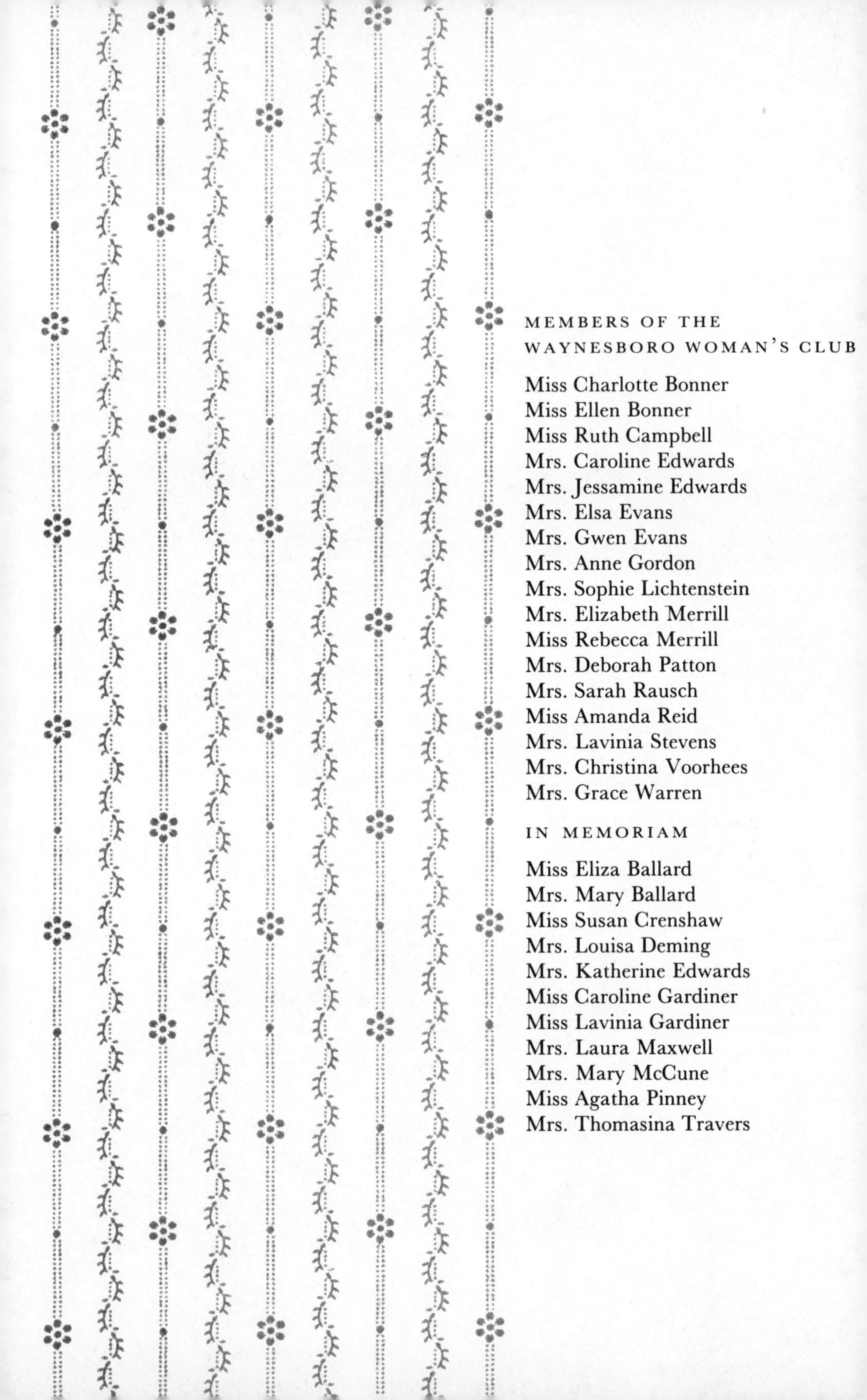

MEMBERS OF THE
WAYNESBORO WOMAN'S CLUB

Miss Charlotte Bonner
Miss Ellen Bonner
Miss Ruth Campbell
Mrs. Caroline Edwards
Mrs. Jessamine Edwards
Mrs. Elsa Evans
Mrs. Gwen Evans
Mrs. Anne Gordon
Mrs. Sophie Lichtenstein
Mrs. Elizabeth Merrill
Miss Rebecca Merrill
Mrs. Deborah Patton
Mrs. Sarah Rausch
Miss Amanda Reid
Mrs. Lavinia Stevens
Mrs. Christina Voorhees
Mrs. Grace Warren

IN MEMORIAM

Miss Eliza Ballard
Mrs. Mary Ballard
Miss Susan Crenshaw
Mrs. Louisa Deming
Mrs. Katherine Edwards
Miss Caroline Gardiner
Miss Lavinia Gardiner
Mrs. Laura Maxwell
Mrs. Mary McCune
Miss Agatha Pinney
Mrs. Thomasina Travers

* 1914–1916 *

"The Waynesboro Woman's Club continues its quiet way while the Great War rages, and we knit and roll bandages"

Jennifer Evans did indeed succeed in securing her father's permission to go abroad in the summer of 1914, not to be footloose in Paris or on the Riviera under the supervision of an irresponsible uncle, but with a group of her college classmates chaperoned by a couple of their instructors. Gib and Elsa went with her to New York to see her off; her brother Ludwig, home from Tech for the summer, stayed with his grandmother and practiced at managing the mill in his father's absence, accepting suggestions from those who had been there long enough to know more than he, particularly old man Bodien. Young Ludwig suspected that he was laughed at behind his back when he came forth with some notion they patently considered absurd; he did not mind: he had another year of college in which to learn more, and besides, his father had been acting manager of the mill since his grandfather's death, and the company was doing very well in his hands; it would no doubt continue to do so for another while.

Gib and Elsa went from New York and the departure scene to spend a couple of weeks at Ernest's Rhode Island summer place. While they were there, the heir to the Austro-Hungarian throne was assassinated at Sarajevo. Gib was apprehensive; he easily became so when one of his children seemed to him threatened. He wished Elsa had put her foot down when he told Jennifer she might spend the summer in Europe; he was ready to go home at once, though what difference it could make to Jennifer whether they were in Ohio or Rhode Island Elsa could not see. "She might cable us," he protested.

"Whatever for? Oh, Gib: don't worry so: it's just another of those Balkan upsets, and Jennifer is not going to the Balkans. They're going to Italy first. If Austria gets all stirred up, they can skip Vienna and go directly to Germany. Our cousins there will look after her."

Nevertheless, the Evanses packed their bags and went home. Their son was surprised at their return, and scoffed at their fears. "Jenny's perfectly capable of looking after herself. She isn't a little girl any more. If you have to worry about someone, worry about Grandmother." This at the breakfast table the morning after their return.

"What's the matter with Mother?" Elsa was startled.

"Maybe you don't realize how bad her arthritis is. In her knees. She oughtn't to be alone in that big house with only servants. I know she has Rose's Portia stay nights, but even so—"

"I know she must be very lonely; she's always been used to a full house."

"That's not the point. Portia's a good enough girl—devoted and all that. So is Linny, there daytimes. But did you know Grandmother's knees are so bad she doesn't try to get up in the morning until someone comes to help her?"

"I did not. I suppose by the time I see her she's walked the stiffness off. She's never said a word to me. I know she's still driving that electric runabout of hers. It was silly of her to give up the big car and Papa's chauffeur, but she got into a penny-pinching streak after he died. It's lucky they put in that elevator for Papa! Of course I knew she never uses the stairs any more. But what if she has to get up in the night?"

"I asked her. She keeps a sheet knotted around the bedpost so she can hold on to it and pull herself up. But what if she should fall?"

"Oh, Gib!" Elsa turned to her husband ruefully. "I've always known we'd have to move in with Mamma some day, but I hoped not yet. People don't get any easier to get along with as they grow older. And we've been so contented and happy here, just the four of us."

"Thank you, Mrs. Evans! What a nice thing for you to say! But I've always got along fine with your mother."

"You have a nicer nature than I have: you're so easy to get along with. But day in and day out—"

"It's our responsibility; we may as well face it. And after all, here you and I are, two of us in a house that's too large, now the kids are away most of the year, and your mother rattling round alone in that mansion."

"Of course it's what we must do. If she wants us. I'll ask her. She's probably just as happy bossing those colored girls around as she would be with us. She would refuse to listen to me too."

"We could rent this house until Ludwig is ready to set up housekeeping."

Ludwig snorted. "That'll be a while yet. There's no girl I know I'd want to be married to." He crumpled his napkin, dropped it beside his plate. "I must go. I can't wait for Father; the office staff don't keep the same hours as us common laborers. Just think it over—Grandmother, I mean."

Troubled over this domestic complication (though the evil day was postponed by Sally's tart "When I need you here, I'll let you know."), the Evanses put out of their minds any thought of possible trouble in Europe, especially when Jennifer's first letter, written on shipboard but with a postscript added in Genoa, made no mention of the unfortunate archduke.

With every transatlantic mail after that there were postcards to her parents telling them what she was doing and seeing, with no suggestion that the Italians were uneasy. On the fifteenth the party moved on from Venice to Vienna. At home the papers had dropped the subject of the assassination; hints from foreign correspondents of trouble brewing were dismissed as of little consequence: reporters could always find or invent something to be excited about. It was accepted in the United States that a general war in modern times with modern weapons was unthinkable. Jennifer's first letter from Vienna supported the conclusion that there was no calamity threatening: the city was as gay and lighthearted as it was reputed to be; the Austrians seemed to Jennifer a light-opera kind of people who could only wage a light-opera kind of war, should it come to that. If there was in the Austrian capital a dance-of-death, last-fling-of-the-old-order atmosphere, Jennifer was too young and inexperienced to sense it.

By the time that letter reched Waynesboro, the prospect had altered; black headlines called Americans' attention to foreign correspondents' cables reporting Austria's intransigence toward Serbia. Some editors were convinced that Serbia must give in; others that she would not; in either case she was bound to be swallowed by the Austro-Hungarian empire. Readers of these predictions thought only that should they be true there would be one less Balkan country; over the last decades they had grown weary of reports of wars in that section of Europe, peppered as they were with unpronounceable names of unknown men and places. But there were those who wondered with horror and disbelief whether calamity waited in the wings while Americans occupied dress circle seats and, uninvolved, could only look on and hold their breath. For this minority the arrival of the evening paper was of importance. In Waynesboro, as in most towns of comparable size, hot July afternoons were spent, at least by the women, on their shaded front porches. By the third week of July they were not sitting relaxed in their swings or rocking chairs; they were waiting and watching for the paper boy's appearance. On July 28 the headlines indicated the first of the irrevocable events to follow: Austria had declared war on Serbia. Only July 20 Jennifer had cabled home from Zurich, of all places: "Safe in neutral Switzerland. Letter follows." The cable was almost as terrifying as it was reassuring. What was happening in Europe? The omissions from the brief message were enumerated, wondered at, and debated. The party was to have gone from Vienna to Dresden, where Jennifer would spend a few days with her Rausch cousins while the others stayed at a pension. Why then Switzerland? Had they not gone to Dresden at all? Did the change of plan mean that Germany was going to become involved?

Before Jennifer's promised letter reached Waynesboro, what was going to happen had happened: on July 29 the Austrians bombarded Belgrade; on the thirtieth, Russia, which already had troops massed on the Austrian border, ordered full mobilization. Germany then issued the ultimatum to Russia:

demobilize within twelve hours, and when the ultimatum was ignored, on the first of August declared war on Russia.

By that time America had turned into a nation of avid newspaper readers. Much of Waynesboro, knowing that the "little Evans girl" was somewhere abroad, felt a personal interest in the whirl of events. Gib reported that men he wouldn't have supposed knew he had a daughter stopped him on the street to ask her whereabouts. He gave them all the same comfortable answer: "She's safe in Switzerland. If she can't get home, she can sit out the trouble in Zurich. It can't last but a few months."

Elsa had a different idea of what was possible. "From the Kaiser down, the German military have been spoiling for a fight. As long ago as when I was there, in the nineties. The people may have more sense, but they have nothing to say about it. I remember how they used to get out of the way—step off the sidewalk, even—when a couple of those arrogant Prussian officers came swaggering down the street. Let's just hope it won't be the walkover they expect."

Jennifer's letter from Zurich was delivered in Waynesboro on July 31. Her parents, her grandmother, Gib's Aunt Gwen (old Mrs. Evans) read it almost to pieces. Charlotte Bonner heard of it and succeeded in persuading Elsa to let her copy a few paragraphs for the *Torchlight*, omitting Jenny's insulting remarks about her mother's cousins and the Germans in general. After that Jennifer was often quoted as "Our Correspondent in Europe." Jennifer's letter, including the paragraphs not given to the press, was vivid and indignant:

> The whole world suddenly just went crazy. Vienna at first was just what you had led me to expect. Then all at once the Viennese seemed to realize what their government was up to, and what had been all fun and pleasure wasn't any more. So we decided to go on to Germany. It was a long unpleasant trip from Vienna to Dresden by way of Prague (I wished we could have stopped there—everyone says it is such a fascinating city—but of course we couldn't). We thought once we were in Germany it would be all right, but it wasn't. It was worse. Your cousin Heinrich, the one your age that you used to be so fond of, met us at the station. I could see right away he wasn't a bit glad to see us, really, though he was very polite—found cabs to take our party to their pension, and put my bags in another one and took me off to his house. He asked after you, of course, said he was glad to meet me, but it was "unglücklich" that I had chosen this summer to come. When we reached his house, he introduced me to his family: his mother, the widow of Grandfather's uncle who was so good to you, his sister and her children. It turned out his two sons and his sister's husband were all officers in the German army; they were not there, of course: had been called up. His mother was warm enough in her greeting, but it was a teary one: If only I had come any other time—the best thing to do was to get away home while we could. I was astounded. I said you don't think this Austrian-Serbian business is going to amount to anything, surely? I guess I was flippant; anyway they weren't pleased. Cousin Heinrich said, "Russia will not permit the conquest

of Serbia without a fight." And he explained Weltpolitik from the German point of view. "We have a treaty with Austria; if Russia intervenes we cannot stand aside. It is best to leave Germany." I could see they were frightened—honestly frightened—at my being there, so I said, "Of course if you think it wise, I'll get in touch with my party right away and we can leave for Paris tomorrow." And *that* made them positively *blanch*. "Ach, nimmer!" seemed to be the reaction. Train travel to the French border, or Belgian or Dutch—anywhere in a westward direction—was out of the question: the trains would be carrying troops, we'd never get there, etc. I said stupidly "But Russia is in the other direction." I said the wrong thing. Cousin Heinrich said darkly "Germany has other enemies, those bound to Russia by treaties. We cannot turn our backs to the West." So then I knew the Kaiser and his merry men were reaching for another slice of France. (I'm sorry, Mother, but I *can't like them*. They think the earth belongs to them, or should. I know Grandfather left Germany when the '48 Revolution failed, but I am sure that they—the Prussians—have grown even more arrogant than they were then. Even since you were here.) Heinrich's mother said, "It might be very uncomfortable for you and your party, Liebchen. Your German is passable, but you might be taken for *English*." "And that would be bad?" I said. "*England* isn't involved in this hurly-burly." Said she, her mouth a thin straight line, "We do not love the English. I would not be sure there would not be unpleasantness." I thought for goodness' sake why should they hate the English? But I knew they were frightened, too. I suppose they believed they might be suspected of harboring an "Engländerin." So I said, "If you are right, I must go at once to prepare the rest of my party. I'll spend the night at their pension and we'll be off somewhere else tomorrow."—"Switzerland would be best." The relief in the room could be *felt*. "Zurich by way of Munich. There will still be passenger trains going that way, though you may be held up at junctions." So I took my departure, having had a *very* brief visit with your cousins. We got off for Munich the next morning, but were we held up! At every station we stopped for troop trains, and were hours in Munich before there was a train for Zurich—full, by the way, of other stranded Americans trying to get home. All nearly penniless because like us they couldn't get their letters of credit cashed in Germany. What a mess! And I have seen enough of these stiff-legged, stomping, booted *Pickelhaube* to last me a lifetime. We reach Zurich at last and relaxed— after a fashion. The problem now is to get out of here: Switzerland is a kind of dead end road. Most of the party, including our chaperones, are divided between wishing to stay until this "unpleasantness" is over—if they can get their letters of credit cashed—and wanting to get home by way of Genoa, as we came. I have no intention of doing either. To sit here with folded hands would be unendurable, and I am not going home without seeing Paris and Uncle Ludwig.

On the first of August, the day after the delivery of Jennifer's letter, Germany declared war on Russia. Gib said, "So the Germans are going East, not West." Just the same he wanted Jennifer home; he cabled to her at the Zurich pension, only to receive the report in return that Miss Evans had left, address unknown. Elsa could not reassure him, knowing her daughter as she did. "She hasn't sat in Zurich all the time it has taken her letter to get here. She's probably in Paris by now. I hope Ludwig is there to help her. Or that she remembers that Myron Herrick is a friend of the family."

In a day or two they had another of those disquieting cablegrams—from Jennifer in Paris. "Arrived roundabout way. Staying Uncle's pension. Will write." It aroused the usual conjectures: what was Ludwig, who usually spent his summer in Biarritz, doing in Paris? Had Jennifer known he would be there? How had she found him, and how had she got the money to traipse around France? These questions remained unanswered for a long time.

On the evening of August first, as reported in American morning papers, the German army had crossed the frontier of Luxembourg; by the end of the next day the Grand Duchy was entirely overrun and occupied; on the same day an ultimatum was deliverred to the Belgian government: let the German armies pass through the country without hindrance; on the third the Belgian government said flatly "no," and on the morning of the fourth the Germans crossed the Belgian frontier. The American reaction was one of shocked disbelief; up to that point, in spite of all the ultimatums and declarations, except for Austria's attack on Serbia no guns had been fired. Now a courageous small nation was attempting to resist the German juggernaut. Belgians were being killed. Admiration of Belgium's heroism knew no bounds. If France and England had not kept their sworn word and in their turn declared war on Germany, they would have been despised. Headlines were big and black the next few days: "France Declares War on Germany"—"England Declares War on Germany"

The first news of combat brought cheers from Americans: the Liége forts were holding out; the French were attacking successfully in Alsace and Lorraine. Then the Liége forts were battered to pieces, the Belgian government and army retreated to Antwerp, Brussels fell without resistance, and the French were pushed back from their advance at the far right of their line. American correspondents, forbidden to visit British and French headquarters and armies, flocked to Brussels; their reports horrified an already shocked America. The Germans, having expected no resistance from the Belgians, were dealing savagely with the opposition they met: villages were burned in reprisal; civilians were collected in town plazas and shot by the scores; leading citizens were held as hostages, and in their turn executed; roads were flooded with refugees fleeing with what possessions they could manage to take with them.

Gib came home from the mill one evening to find Elsa in tears over one of these reports. Mopping her eyes as she handed the paper to him, she said, "I never thought to see the day when I would say 'I am glad Papa isn't here.' But this would have broken his heart."

"These reports may be very much exaggerated."

She shook her head. "I don't believe famous reporters like Richard Harding Davis, Will Irwin, Irvin S. Cobb, would be taken in. I can't see why the

Germans are such fools as to let the correspondents go along with them and see what they are doing."

"To impress neutrals with their omnipotence. Or it could be that they expect it all to be over so quickly it doesn't matter what neutrals think."

"Or," Elsa was bitter, "most likely they really think they're justified and aren't expecting criticism. I don't imagine that after the things American reporters have cabled home, our newspapermen will be allowed to go far with them."

Not all Waynesboro (nor all America) was as convinced as Elsa was of the truth of the atrocity reports, nor as ready to accuse. Young people argued interminably and angrily on front porches in the evening, those of Irish or German descent denouncing "British propaganda!", while those who had grown up thinking of Great Britain as the source of everything good in America were outraged and said so. The young could afford to argue, however hot their tempers grew: they had plenty of time ahead of them in which tempers could subside, and indeed they were friends again when they met the next day.

Their elders, so many of them of German origin, dared not argue, and could not bear to hear their children doing so. They were afraid not of physical violence but that they would be expected to be ashamed of their fatherland, and of losing old friends if they were not. The women, particularly the grandmothers, stayed at home with drawn blinds, preferring not to show their faces abroad. Their menfolk carried on their businesses, tight-lipped, avoiding any reference to the war. Most midwestern towns were as divided as Waynesboro: pro-Ally sentiment was the strongest, but many, even non-Germans, scoffed at the newspaper stories, saying, "English propaganda to persuade us to help them out." Waynesboro citizens who had once been German subjects felt the hurt of discovering that their old friends could believe such things of a civilized people.

Sophie Lichtenstein stopped to call on Elsa late one August afternoon, and Elsa, as was customary, seated her on the front porch and went inside for glasses and the pitcher of lemonade kept full and in the icebox all summer, and a plate of cookies. When she put the tray on the wicker table, Sophie said, "Are you sure you wouldn't rather go inside, where the neighbors won't see you entertaining me?"

"What on earth are you talking about?"

"Mamma won't sit on our porch until after dark. She is afraid that women who have been her neighbors for years will go past without speaking."

"Sophie! How ridiculous! But how awful, too. Does she think my mother—? Why, they've lived across the street from each other as long as I can remember. Does she feel that guilty? Or that bitter? Good heavens! Why should she? She and your father have been American citizens for some forty-odd years."

"That isn't it. She hasn't any idea of what Germany is like now. She doesn't believe the stories that are coming out of Belgium, and doesn't want to. She's afraid of an argument with those who do. Because how could Germans, so *gemütlich*—and her brothers and nieces and nephews are still there—do such things? No. Somehow the British have managed to persuade the newspapermen to tell these lies. And though Papa shakes his head at her, she maintains that the invasion of Belgium was justified; it should not have resisted. It is wonderful what one can persuade oneself to believe. I can't argue with her, and won't. Elsa, how much do you believe?"

Elsa hesitated. "Do you remember—as long ago as when you and I were studying in Germany—how the German army officers behaved? Even in the nineties they were taking perfectly nice Geman boys and turning them into wooden soldiers with no will of their own. Goose-stepping down Unter den Linden. Those officers, those soldiers, are ruling Germany now. Yes, I believe the stories. Unhappily, many German-Americans—and plain Americans—find it impossible to think that ordinary normal boys can be trained out of their humanity to the extent that they can commit these atrocities when ordered. Or that German officers think nothing of giving such orders. On the other hand, far too many of us are ready to believe that all Germans are savage monsters, and can't forgive German-Americans the loyalty they feel for their fatherland. I can understand that loyalty: they are kind and decent people; they left kind and decent people behind them, and have warm and affectionate memories of their childhood. Don't worry, Sophie. All this animosity will die down if the war is over as quickly as people seem to think."

"If it is over quickly, it will be because the Germans win it quickly, and I can't see how that will improve matters." Sophie changed the subject abruptly. "What do you hear from Jennifer?"

"We had a letter from Paris yesterday, the first and I hope the last from there. It was dated the fifth, the day after fighting had actually begun. Her Uncle Ludwig is doing his best to get her off to England, where she can take a ship for home, along with thousands of other stranded Americans. He wasn't pleased to see her, I surmise. He had sent her his Paris address before she ever left home, so she took a cab to his pension from the station. His greeting, according to her, was "Good Lord! What the devil are you doing here?" He was in uniform; he had managed to join a French ambulance unit as a stretcher-bearer, so he won't be in Paris long, to look after her. Mamma cabled him to come home. Imagine Ludwig turning his back on a war! But he's being very protective of Jennifer so far, taking her to see the American Ambassador to try to get money for her trip home. Her American letter of credit is no good right now, not on the Continent, anyway. Mr. Herrick was a great friend of Papa's when he was an Ohio politician, and Papa helped him get elected governor. He hadn't forgotten. He cashed her letter of credit for her, gave her French and English money, and somehow managed to reserve a place for her on a channel ferry. They seem to be running still. She wasn't at all anxious to go, but she had been ordered to leave the next day for London. I suppose she got there. She hasn't cabled, but Mr. Herrick got word to

Mamma: he and Ludwig had seen her off for Cherbourg, Calais being a bit close to the war zone, and the port of entry for the English army. It was closed to ordinary transport. Mr. Herrick gave her a note for Ambassador Page in London. Her letters home are very slow. That is the last we have heard. She did say she was in Paris on the first of August when mobilization was ordered: she and Ludwig were in the Place de la Concorde when the reservists were marched off to the Gare de l'Est, with their bundles and their bunches of flowers, the crowds all waving and cheering. In the Place one group of conscripts stopped to tear black crepe off the statue representing Strasbourg, while the crowd wept and cheered. Jennifer can be graphic enough, given a subject that moves her."

"As the German soldiers didn't, obviously, from her letter in the *Torchlight*."

"No, they didn't. They were so arrogant, so grimly eager to be given a chance at those they had decided were their enemies. And in the railroad stations, where she saw so many troop trains, they must have been at their worst. At any rate, she is finally on her way home, though I don't know when we'll hear she had actually landed."

When Sophie had gone, Elsa remembered sadly those days when Mrs. Klein had called them all in from their games to have milk and her brother the baker's crackers. But Elsa hadn't been in the Klein house since Sophie's marriage, and she probably would not be welcome now, if Mrs. Klein was shutting herself away from people. There was nothing she could do to reassure or to comfort: she could only hope that with the passage of time, in a Waynesboro continuing in its accustomed ways, the poor woman's mind would be eased. Certainly when the Woman's Club resumed its meetings in September, there was no indication that anyone remembered that Sophie's parents were immigrants or her doctorate a German one.

Jennifer reached home on the twentieth of August, the day the Germans began their bombardment of Namur. She was in a strange state of mind, restless, abstracted. She was glad to be home, she insisted; of course she was glad to be with them. But somehow the sleepy tranquility of the town was impossible for her to adjust to. She lived for the arrival of the papers: the *Cincinnati Enquirer* in the morning, the *Torchlight* in the afternoon; for most of the time she was silent, but occasionally broke out with long accounts of what she had seen of gathering armies. She had come home sure of a French victory; her spirits plummeted as day followed day and the German advance on Paris looked irresistible.

One evening at the dinner table, her mother said, "We must spend next week looking over your clothes: what you have already, what you need new. The University opens in a couple of weeks, and you haven't given it a thought."

"I have given it a lot of thought," and Jennifer braced herself: "I'm not going back."

"Not going back? What do you mean?"

"I'm going to train to be a nurse. I've sent in an application to Cincinnati General's Nursing School. Mother," she pleaded with a shocked-into-silence Elsa, "can't you see this is the biggest thing that will ever happen in my lifetime? I must have a part in it."

Her brother Ludwig, half-envious, faced as he was with another year at Tech, and half-derisive, grinned at her and said, "Still little Tag-along. Much good you would be."

"That's what Mr. Herrick said when I wanted to stay in Paris, only he was kinder about it. He said I'd be just another mouth to feed, unless I was trained for something useful. I can't think of anything more useful in wartime than a trained nurse."

"Jennifer—"

Ludwig broke in again. "Nursing is hard work, you ninny. You've never done a lick of work in your life."

Their father intervened. "Never mind, Ludwig. Let her start nurse's training. If it's too hard for her, or if the war ends soon, as it looks like doing, she can always go back to the University."

"You have always said it would be a short war," Elsa admitted, "and it looks now as if nothing could stop the Germans."

With that slightly comforting, wholly horrifying thought, that the war would be over long before Jenny could finish her training, they gave way, though not without another protest from Gib: "I don't see why you think you have to have a part in what America isn't involved in."

"Not *yet* involved in, you mean."

Ludwig unexpectedly supported her. "Father, you can't believe we should stand aside and let those booted Germans trample all Europe underfoot?"

"I don't know about *should*," Elsa entered the argument, "with that *schoolmaster* in the White House always lecturing us on neutrality. Thank God Roosevelt isn't President."

"Mother! I can't believe you're that wishy-washy."

"Jennifer, my dear, I doubt if anyone has ever called me that before. But it's what happens when you're frightened for your children."

"You don't need to worry about Jenny. She'll be safe enough in some hospital, if she sticks to the training. And I am planning like a good boy to go back and get my degree, then come home and help in the mill."

"You'll be more useful to the Allies in the mill than anywhere else, swamped as we are with orders. We've got to speed up production, though getting raw material is already a problem."

Any remaining doubts as to German ruthlessness were settled for most Americans by the six-day sack and burning of Louvain. The event could not be questioned, officially reported as it was by the American legation. Only die-hard pro-Germans, accepting the reports of atrocities first committed by Belgian civilians, believed that retaliation was justified. At the other extreme were Americans who thought the country should join the Allies without delay, and in the middle were those convinced that Germany must not be allowed to conquer Western Europe, but who still hoped that England and France could prevent such a calamity. (Although it was good that Russia was also fighting, since many German troops were held on the Eastern front, no one really hoped for much help from that quarter, especially after the Russian defeats at Tannenberg and the Masurian Lakes.) Since it had become quite clear that England and France could not do what they must in a matter of days or weeks, the hope that the war would be short was slowly dissipated; it had become the kind of war that could not be negotiated: only a military victory on one side or the other would end it.

When the time came they drove Jenny down to Cincinnati and at the hospital gave her their reluctant blessing. Ludwig too went off to his last year at Tech. His father missed him sorely: he was needed at the mill. If it had not been for old Captain Bodien, he reported at home, it would have been hard to keep up with the orders. By example and exhortation the Captain pushed the production of every laborer to the limit. "He's grimly determined to stay on till the thing's all over. He's in his seventies if he's a day, but as capable as ever. He keeps saying 'Our War was a picnic compared to this one.'"

At home, in the sitting room of his apartment at the Gardiners', Captain Bodien had fastened a huge map of the Western Front on the wall; after reading the evening paper, he would move the thumbtacks to mark the opposing lines, always, it seemed, advancing Germans and retreating Allies. The Stevens and Edwards children spent what time they could in that room learning about the war from him. Theresa Stevens, who was twelve in 1914 and had heard his reminiscent stories so many times and with such attention that she knew almost as much about the Civil War as he did, was the only one of his great-grandchildren old enough to understand what he was telling them now, and rejoiced with him when the German tide was stopped at the Marne. "The French success was nothing less than a miracle," he said, "but they haven't the strength to push the Germans back. They may hold them, if they dig in, but that will be Petersburg all over again. Trenches, revetments, bombardments, sorties. But Petersburg only lasted half-a-year. Far's I can see this could go on forever. Unless we get over there with the manpower they need." And Theresa became on the spot a noisy if negligible advocate of American intervention.

Jennifer Evans was so overwhelmed by her relief over the result of the Battle of the Marne that she telephoned home just to be able to say exultantly, "I told you so," and "You see, it isn't going to be over before Christmas, as you kept saying. I'll get there yet."

At the Woman's Club meetings that fall, the war was seldom mentioned. For one thing, except among intimate friends, no member could be quite sure of the neutrality of another member, well as they knew each other by the fall of 1914. The membership of the Club had changed very little in the last few years. Mrs. Maxwell had died in the spring of 1913, her death going almost unnoticed when the whole town was so busy cleaning up after the flood, although of course she had been duly memorialized. Miss Rebecca Merrill had been invited to become a member in her place. Rebecca, the Becky whom Anne Gordon had come to know as a real bookworm that summer when she had substituted in the library for Ruhamah McCune, was now a budding medievalist. She dreamed of going to France for graduate study once the war was over. Meanwhile, she had applied for a position in the high school and had been lucky enough to be appointed to the post for which she was best fitted: she taught ancient history to the freshmen, and medieval and modern history to the sophomores. It had been Amanda, oddly enough, with whom she had come into contact first and most closely. Amanda remembered with pleasure the year when Rebecca's mother had shared her home; and besides there was a certain relationship between Roman history and Caesar's Commentaries and Cicero's Oratories. Rebecca did not agree with those of Amanda's younger colleagues who thought it high time she was replaced. It was true that Amanda, approaching seventy-five, had begun to show a certain lack of concern for such trifles as dress and other conventions, but there was nothing the matter with her mind. And that, Rebecca thought, is what should count in a teacher.

She and Amanda usually attended Club meetings together since both of necessity had to arrive late, often missing much of the first essayist's paper.

One afternoon when they entered, Mrs. Evans was halfway through her paper. To Rebecca, Mrs. Evans seemed very old and frail. But for that matter, so did a goodly number of "the ladies." True, Mrs. Rausch still presided over meetings but she had to use a cane to lean on when she had to stand: her weight was far too great to be supported by her increasingly arthritic knees. Miss Campbell was looking the perfect dried-up, raw-boned old maid. Charlotte Bonner had ceased to care what people thought. She was always a law unto herself, they tell me, Rebecca thought. Now she came to meetings in the mannish tailored suit and grey fedora hat that had long been her uniform as a newspaperwoman. Mrs. Sheldon Edwards was still a handsome woman with her sleek black hair, aquiline features, and dark eyes, but she was distinctly a dowager.

Mrs. Gordon she found she could not judge objectively: she would always remember her as she was the summer when Miss McCune had gone off to some library school, and Mrs. Gordon had substituted for her. She had been so much less the disciplinarian and had laughed so easily. Miss McCune was not much given to laughter. (But, Rebecca thought loyally, she really knew more about books than anyone.) Mrs. Gordon had retained her sense of humor: however old she might be now, she could still laugh, or at least smile, if you caught her eye when an essayist revealed some odd quirk in her personality by a phrase or two.

At this point, Rebecca gave her attention to the essayist of the day. As the meeting adjourned, she noted one guest, a washed-out blonde who was a stranger to her. She was introduced: Mrs. Lane, the daughter of Mrs. Voorhees. Everyone else knew Janey Voorhees, in this country with her husband and two children for his Sabbatical year. Janey was at her mother's for a "brief visit," Christina explained: she had left her family with Mr. Lane's people, and would return there very shortly herself. "She thinks the schools are better: it is a very well-to-do suburb of St. Louis. Of course I should have been glad to teach them this year," and her most complacent smile, "but Janey insists on sparing me."

Those who heard her mother wondered at Janey's spunk—they wouldn't have expected it of her. Someone asked, "The *public* school?" and Janey with a smile rather like her mother's said, "Oh, yes, certainly. You wouldn't expect poor missionaries to be able to afford a private school, would you?"

Members of the Club dispersed, imagining with relish the scene that must have taken place between her and Christina; not a voice-raised scene, of course, but a bitter one, nevertheless, over what amounted to a repudiation of Christina's ideas on the education of children. But those who felt that courtesy demanded of them an afternoon call at the Voorheeses while Janey was home became a little more doubtful of the wisdom of her methods: she had no worries, she said, about the children being a burden on their Lane grandparents. "We have an excellent ayah, devoted to us all. We brought her home with us. That is why I can spend this time at Mamma's. She promised solemnly that she would take them to school every morning and meet them when school was out." The general verdict was, "Just one step better than her mother."

Only Elsa, when she called, had the temerity to mention Blair, and then only when Christina had gone to the kitchen to put the teakettle on to boil. She said, "You came home by way of the Philippines, did you not? Did you have a chance to see Blair? The last anyone here has known anything about him, that's where he was."

Janey's reply was repressive, to say the least. "I believe that he is still in the Army, and out West somewhere. We have made no attempt to get in touch with him. He chose the way he wanted to go, and it wasn't our way; his name is never mentioned in this house." And Elsa, thinking of her brother Ludwig, still loved and forgiven his misdeeds, could only wonder at the implacably hard hearts concealed beneath such bland exteriors.

As the weeks went on, Christmas passed and 1914 became 1915, so recognized by calendars distributed by butcher, baker, and grocer. The war continued, but through the winter attracted less attention from newspaper readers. As Captain Bodien had foreseen, the opposing armies settled down to trench warfare; bloody attacks were made and repulsed, with no advantage gained and the stalemate unbroken. The hostile armies faced each other from battle lines elaborately entrenched and fortified. There were spurts of activity; the slaughter continued, but Captain Bodien could never move the pins on his map more than a fraction of an inch. Waynesboro women who had the leisure now spent hours knitting for the Red Cross or attending bandage-rolling sessions in the Court House basement. On the whole they did not talk much about the war. The sinking of the *Lusitania* in the spring blew up a storm of public opinion, but when it became clear that the President would do no more than exact from the Germans a promise not to do so again, it gradually died down, leaving a residue of wrath and a country less neutral.

Tucker Gordon's stepfather died that late spring of 1915, when the boy was a senior at Stanford. As he wrote his grandmother,

> Uncle Robert was an old, old man, but he knew what he was doing when he settled his affairs: he sold his interest in all his businesses and industries, put the whole shebang into a trust fund, the income to go to Mother for the rest of her life, so long as she doesn't remarry; after her death it is to be divided among a lot of California and Oregon institutions: universities and so on. Mother earned it, I guess. It can't be easy to live with an old man, but she always made him happy. Of course it had been made clear to me a long while ago that I might inherit a good-sized chunk of it if I would go into one of his companies and eventually run it as his son. I knew how much I would hate it, so I refused. I didn't really want all that money, anyway. Now that I am over twenty-one I suppose Father's trust could be dissolved, but I would far rather the trustees kept on looking after it for me. I intend to write and ask them. I will start next fall on my first year at med school here at Stanford, and I can manage on the income from the fund. It was enough to see me through college. When I finish med school here (or should I transfer to Cincinnati?) I'll be coming home *at last*. I don't worry a bit about Mother. She has always been dead set against my studying medicine, and has tried even harder than Uncle Robert to persuade me to give up what she always called a silly notion. But she won't miss me. I haven't spent enough time with her for that. She will have all the money she wants, she can travel or stay here and play bridge, as she likes. She is still beautiful and dresses like a queen—cuts quite a dash—but I don't think she will ever marry again, when she has all that money to spend if she doesn't. I don't mean to sound critical: she doesn't care for money for its own sake, she just likes to have fun, and is at her nicest when she is enjoying herself. Like all the rest of us, I guess. But what a way to spend your life—playing bridge!

He concluded his letter with love to her and greetings to his old friends, and a request that she tell Jennifer he would write soon.

Anne was shaken by the letter, the longest and most informative she had received in a long time. She applauded Tucker's determined resistance to the pressure of parents and the temptation of great wealth, but nevertheless, now that it was quite clear that he did intend to return to Waynesboro, she felt it something of a jolt. She would inevitably be involved emotionally, as she had thought she would never be again. She told herself that it would be five or six years before he would be ready to come back as a full-fledged physician, and in that length of time anything could happen. Then she caught herself up: what kind of woman had she become that all she wanted was just to be left alone? "I care for nobody, no not I, and nobody cares for me." And since the "anything" of "anything could happen" might just include being sent to fight in a bloody war, she shied away from that extreme to thought of the demands sure to be made on her long-suspended capacity to feel deeply, to love profoundly. What a way for her to carry out Johnny's injunction to keep in touch with Tucker! And she was not an old lady; she was just sixty-five, and in vigorous good health.

Shaking herself mentally, she went to call Elsa to ask her to relay Tucker's message to Jennifer, only to be told in turn that Elsa had had a letter from Julia, reporting her husband's death, her financial situation, and her son's stubbornness, when he could have been really *rich!*

"'If he had only been reasonable,' she says, 'but no!' And she blames you and Johnny and Rodney and all the Evanses, especially Jennifer. She prefers to believe that no one, unless influenced, could possibly *want* to be a doctor."

"Johnny has been dead so long now," Anne said bleakly, "she's put any memories of him right out of her mind—deliberately forgotten him. I don't like to think of her, either. What's all this about a message to Jennifer? I remember once you said they corresponded."

"They corresponded. I don't believe they write very frequently these days; if they did, he would know she isn't home. I don't pry into Jennifer's private life. I never liked mine pried into, as it was, of course. So far as the pair of them is concerned, they haven't seen each other for years, and if they ever meet again, they might not like each other at all."

"No one can help liking Jenny." Though, Anne thought, she is a watered-down version of you and her grandmother, with some more easy-going quality inherited from Gib? "Why?" she said, "would you rather they didn't?"

Elsa laughed. "That depends on how much Tucker is like his mother and his Deming grandparents. He must be, to some extent, to have resisted so stubbornly the presure brought to bear. Johnny was always so—so manageable."

"But," Anne thought, "Johnny resented being managed, and that was one of the reasons—" She said, rather sharply, "Tucker never seemed to me in the least like his mother. But it is of little consequence at this point; it will be years before he can come back and be a practicing physician."

The year 1915 passed into history. Events on their own side of the Atlantic, in spite of war headlines, attracted more American attention than what was going on across the Atlantic: the near-completion of the Panama Canal, and the conquest of yellow fever; the social reforms enacted by Congress at the request of the President; the brouhaha with Mexico following their revolution, with the consequent occupation of Vera Cruz by American forces. The following year was much like it, with the added excitement of a presidential election in wartime. Waynesboro like the rest of America was divided between those who though a wishy-washy President should long ago have challenged Germany, and those who rejoiced that he had not. Old ladies, who seldom become less prejudiced politically as they age, grew quite fierce on the subject, and spoke vehemently as they agreed that Wilson must go. The middle-aged, with perhaps as strong convictions, had less to say: heated arguments could lead to lasting estrangements.

In the fall of 1916 Jennifer Evans finished her nurse's training, became an R.N., cap and all, and applied to the Red Cross to be sent to France with some hospital unit. Gib scoffed: "They want experienced nurses. And I hope middle-aged and homely ones. They won't want to be bothered by a chit like you over there." And when she was accepted and assigned to the American Hospital at Neuilly, he was sick at heart. Elsa was more resigned, having expected it, and was only relieved that Jennifer was being sent to what would surely be a safe berth. She comforted Gib in his fretting, but like him was relieved when they finally heard of her safe arrival in France. She had sailed on a hospital ship, but after all who could be sure, with all those German submarines haunting the Atlantic?

And so "little Jenny Evans," to the wonder of Waynesboro, became the first American whom they actually knew to become involved in the Great War. (Unless you counted her Uncle Ludwig, after so long a time almost forgotten in his home town.) Jennifer's letters home were frequent but hardly more than notes: she was full of admiration for her wounded poilus, and what anecdotes she had time to write were printed in the *Torchlight* under the heading "An American Hospital in Paris." She occasionally saw her Uncle Ludwig when he was in the city, and her admiration for his devil-may-care courage grew by leaps and bounds; regretfully she wrote that he was looking old and exhausted. Elsa could have wept: Ludwig, not yet forty!

Late in the fall of 1916, Ludwig's ambulance, leaving the battle area with a load of French wounded, was struck by a German shell. Word reached Jenny through an officer on that section of the front who was a friend of her uncle's, and it fell to her to send the news home. She regretted in her letter to her mother that kind Ambassador Herrick had been replaced (those damned Democrats!); he had known both Ludwig and his mother, and would have written a better letter than she could manage. She admitted having given way to cowardice, in writing to her mother, but would she break the news—?

Elsa received the letter in the morning's mail; having read it, she went at once to her mother. Shaken by her own grief and fearful of how her mother would take it, she felt too weak in the knees to walk the long way to her mother's; she backed her little electric runabout out of the garage. This in itself was so out-of-the-ordinary as to bring her mother struggling to her feet from the wing chair in the drawing-room window, where she had been casually watching the comings and goings of her neighbors. The delay caused by Elsa's sitting in her car to take time to pull herself together gave Sally time to hobble to the front door and get it open.

She waited until Elsa reached the steps, then called to her, "Good morning! What brings you out in such style?" Then, seeing her daughter's face, she said, "What has happened? Jenny? Ludwig?"

"Not Jenny."

Sally leaned for support against the door frame. Elsa came to help her, but was told, "Don't fuss. I can take bad news as well as anyone. Is it Ludwig?

Not—killed?" And she limped back to her chair, Elsa close behind her, a hand ready to give support.

"We have all had Ludwig on our minds, haven't we? Knowing the danger—Here is Jennifer's letter."

Sally pulled her reading glasses from the button pinned below her shoulder and took the letter. When she had finished reading it, and was holding it in a trembling hand in her lap, she said, "There's nothing official about this. It's just gossip. Ludwig has always managed to get out of his scrapes."

"I don't know what official news we could get. Ludwig was with the French Army, not the American Red Cross. The friend Jenny mentions made a point of going to Neuilly to tell her."

"Whatever her source, it could still be a mistake. I'll write to Myron Herrick for verification."

"Mamma, Mr. Herrick hasn't been in Paris since 1914."

"I haven't lost my memory, Elsa, whatever you may think. I know he isn't in Paris. But he will have kept in touch with his French friends."

"Oh, Mamma! Don't cherish a false hope! It would be better to accept it—face it now—than to add suspense to your grief. I know what a blow it is. Ludwig was always—" she stopped herself from saying "your favorite" and went on instead "a favorite of all of us. But we have seen so little of him—he hasn't been home since the winter Papa died. You can't believe you are going to miss him."

"Of course I shall miss him. There hasn't been a day that he hasn't been in my thoughts."

"I know." Elsa might have doubted her mother's statement, but a day has twenty-four hours, and a thought can pass through the mind in seconds.

"He was the most talented of the boys."

"Perhaps. Certainly the ablest at winning our hearts. We all loved him. But he wasted his abilities. Threw them away. Then the war gave him a chance to redeem himself. And he did. He has done what I suppose none of us expected of him: made a noble end. Sacrificed himself for something he loved." Elsa was moved to uncharacteristic eloquence. "We can weep for our loss, but don't weep for him. He knew what he was doing."

"'It is a far, far better thing', you mean," Her mother snapped at her. "That's all right in books, but not—" Tears began to run down her cheeks, and she added, "I wish you weren't so sure."

"Write Mr. Herrick, if you want to. But don't cherish any false hopes: it will be harder in the end. I will telephone the other boys tonight, when I can catch them at home."

"I wish his body could be brought home."

"Mamma," Elsa said, again pleading with her, "you lived through the Civil War. How many who died in battle were brought home for burial? All those thousands of graves all over the South. And how many French boys, and English, have had to be buried where they fell?" Elsa's eyes filled, her tears dropped, whether for Ludwig alone or for all fallen youth, she hardly knew.

Once home again, she waited for her husband and son to come in for lunch, then gave them Jenny's letter to read. Neither had seen enough of Ludwig to feel the grief she felt, but they sympathized with her and expressed concern for her mother in her stubborn refusal to believe. They suggested that Elsa call Charlotte Bonner and let the news of Ludwig Rausch Junior's death be printed at once: it would be weeks before Mr. Herrick could verify Jennifer's letter, if ever. "If she sees it in print, it may seem more real—may convince her. And if by the hundredth chance it proves to be a false report, think of the rejoicing!

"I'll call Aunt Anne first. She mustn't read it in the paper without having heard from us."

Her mother had already called Anne, who proposed going to the Rausch house that afternoon to condole with Sally. Elsa was relieved. "She has come to accept it, then. Tell her, will you please, that I am calling Charlotte for the *Torchlight*?"

Elsa telephoned the newspaper office, talked to Charlotte, and read parts of Jennifer's letter. It was too late for anything more than for a stop-press notice on the front page. "Word has been received . . . "; but on the next afternoon the *Torchlight* printed a tribute to Ludwig first among its obituaries: a full biography, covering his musical career, making much of his service in the Spanish-American War when he was hardly more than a boy, and of his courage and willingness to sacrifice his life for the country where he had lived so long. Quoted in full was Jennifer's admittedly hearsay account of his death.

Ludwig's mother proudly and characteristically pulled herself together, and presided with her usual mastery over the next meeting of the Woman's Club. Before that day most of the members had called on her, or written notes, so that she did not have to face the ordeal of accepting and replying to many expressions of sympathy.

Ludwig Evans, who had been shaken by his uncle's death, was one of the young people who had felt bitterly about the reelection of President Wilson. "We ought to have been in there doing our share of the fighting since the *Lusitania* was sunk, and that's a year and a half ago," he said one noon at the luncheon table. "I should have gone into the National Guard then."

"And spent the summer chasing Villa around Mexico? You're better off right here in the mill."

"I'm of half-a-mind to go to Canada to enlist." Ludwig was in normal times a peaceable young man, if not phlegmatic youth; but his parents had been listening to his opinions for some months, and had ceased to expect him to act on them. They suspected that his attitude could be in part at least attributed to his resentment of Jenny's being, as she had said two years ago, a part of "the biggest thing that will happen in our lifetime" while he stayed tamely at home. But the threat to enlist in Canada was a new one. Gib crumpled his napkin petulantly, dropped it beside his plate.

"Canada, indeed! It's time you were growing up, boy!"

Ludwig was naturally indignant: since he had taken his engineering degree, he had worked steadily and sensibly at the mill, taking hold of the manufacturing end under the unobtrusive guidance of Captain Bodien. His father had assured him constantly that he could not be spared. Now, before he could now assert his adulthood, he heard it again: "We can't do without you at the mill. It is your responsibility. Your grandfather saw to that."

"Right now, as you know very well, the mill is no problem and won't be while the war lasts. All we have to do is turn out our orders fast enough. Captain Bodien can see better than I can that the quality of the product is maintained. He knows more about rope than all the rest of us put together."

"He's getting old."

"In his seventies, I suppose. But a sturdy specimen and plenty keen enough mentally."

"That I grant you. But old men in their seventies can't be counted on to last indefinitely."

"Father, whether you like it or not, we are going to be in this war, in spite of that pusillanimous—*pedagogue*—in the White House. Personally, I think it should be sooner, but I confess I'd prefer to fight under my own flag. So forget Canada. I'll join the National Guard company here. That will take me away from Waynesboro only for a few weeks' training every year. And I may be ready when we get into it ourselves."

MEMBERS OF THE WAYNESBORO WOMAN'S CLUB

Miss Charlotte Bonner
Miss Ruth Campbell
Mrs. Caroline Edwards
Mrs. Jessamine Edwards
Mrs. Elsa Evans
Mrs. Anne Gordon
Mrs. Jennifer Gordon
Mrs. Sophie Lichtenstein
Miss Renata Lichtenstein
Mrs. Elizabeth Merrill
Mrs. Deborah Patton
Mrs. Sarah Rausch
Mrs. Ellen Richards
Miss Amanda Reid
Mrs. Lavinia Stevens
Mrs. Grace Warren

IN MEMORIAM

Miss Eliza Ballard
Mrs. Mary Ballard
Miss Susan Crenshaw
Mrs. Louisa Deming
Mrs. Katherine Edwards
Miss Caroline Gardiner
Miss Lavinia Gardiner
Mrs. Laura Maxwell
Mrs. Mary McCune
Miss Agatha Pinney
Mrs. Thomasina Travers

1916–1924

"The Woman's Club survives the Great War . . ."

Long afterward, when time had played its tricks on memory, it was hard to recall that in 1916 a war was being fought in Europe, that an American President had been reelected on a "peace at any price" slogan, even while a program of what was called "preparedness" was getting under way. The trivial daily events that had somehow affected a person's life were in the end what were chiefly remembered. The year 1916 was thought of not as the year of Verdun, Ypres, and the Somme, but as the year when this friend was married, this or that member of the family was ill or died, or a son or daughter was graduated from high school or college.

Ellen Bonner married the advertising manager of the *Torchlight*, Harry Richards; neither of them was in the first flush of youth, but it was presumably a happy occasion, and Ellen would at least remain in Waynesboro and continue to occupy a chair at Club meetings, producing papers that were suspected to have come at least in part from the pen of Aunt Charlotte.

Caroline Gardiner Edwards gave birth in the summer to her fourth and last child, having succeeded in doing for Lowrey what Kitty had not been able to do for his father: given him a brood of healthy children. The whole Edwards family counted 1916 a good year since the war in Palestine and Mesopotamia made archeological expeditions to the Middle East impossible, and brought Richie Edwards home for a visit. He was too thin and so sun-wrinkled that his face in repose showed white where the lines were deepest. Communication between Richie and his father was still difficult, although perhaps easier than when he had been still at home: he was such a stranger that it was possible to treat him as an honored guest, and for him to behave as one, since his brother's house was so full, what with three growing children and a new baby, that he stayed with his father and Jessamine. About the war in Mesopotamia he was laconic to the point of brusqueness, seeing it only as an annoying interruption of his work; about his digging he was willing to talk, and talk with eloquence. He would not stay in Waynesboro to be "fatted up," as his family begged, but was soon off to Yucatan, leaving several young Edwardses and Stevenses thinking archeology must be the most fascinating pursuit in the world, perhaps superior even to soldiering.

The oldest members of the Club had less to be happy about than the younger ones. Amanda Reid was untouched by the war personally, having no family to be concerned about, although it became increasingly harder for her as she read the news to believe that all the slaughter had been foreordained. Sally Rausch would never forget that 1916 was the year of Ludwig's death. For Anne Gordon it was the year that Tucker left medical school when he was halfway through to join an American ambulance unit and depart with it to France without being able to stop in Waynesboro and bid her good-bye; although she had not been in very close touch with the boy for a number of years, the thought that he might be lost as Ludwig Rausch had been wrenched her heart.

For the senior Mrs. Evans, 1916 was the year when her eyesight had deteriorated to the point where she could no longer live alone. Gib and Elsa begged her to move in with them, or at least let them find someone to move in with her, but she was stubbornly determined to go live with the son who was a Baptist minister in some small unheard of Kansas town. She had, she said, accepted enough from Gib; it was true that she would be leaving all her friends—she would miss them—but be dependent on her nephew now she would not. As she thought but did not say, his was a marriage that against all her expectations had turned out well, but who knew what the effect might be of having an aged relative in their house?

Her departure left another vacancy in the Club membership. Elsa said to her mother that two vacancies were too many; they could not let the Club dwindle away.

"I suppose you have a name to suggest?"

"Yes. Sophie's Renata finished college last June."

"Another Lichtenstein? Sometimes I wish we still had the Seminary wives we used to have. They may have been bigoted, but at least they had *background.*"

There was no use in Elsa's saying one more time "Don't be such a snob." Instead she said, "Renata may not have what you call 'background,' but she has the family brains. And it would be a convincing reassurance to Sophie. Renata's staying home on her account, I suspect: Sophie's been having a hard time, what with being so over-sensitive to her own family's pro-German prejudice, and the Lichtenstein brothers' ways of being troublesome." Elsa had no trouble in securing the acceptance of Renata as a Club member, since the groundwork had been done. Renata was unanimously elected to membership.

Sophie that fall did need reassurance; she had felt torn to bits. Brought up to love Germany and its people, she sympathized even into the third year of the war with her parents, who could not believe that all Germans were "Huns." On the other hand, she and Rudy were having trouble persuading their son Frederick to stay in law school; he wanted to apply to Plattsburg for officers' training; they suspected that he longed to prove that he was American without a hyphen; Sophie could not help wondering whether he had been made to suffer at college, though he had never said so.

Matters were complicated for her by the behavior of her now well-known brother-in-law in New York. Franz and Mary Lichtenstein, labor leaders and radicals, were making themselves conspicuous not as pro-Germans but as anti-war agitators, by their pacifist speeches and writings. When the senior Mr. Lichtenstein died very suddenly just before Christmas of a stroke, Franz and Mary of course came home for the funeral.

That funeral was an unmitigated horror to Sophie. Sitting in the first row with the family, she could almost have touched the open casket, placed just below the Lutheran altar; only by closing her eyes could she avoid seeing Waynesboro's public school children, an endless line marching past the coffin and that stony frozen face—some of them reflecting its stoniness, teeth clenched, others unable to conceal their awe and terror.

"It was barbarous," she said to Elsa, who made her condolence call after the family had once more dispersed. "He deserved to be honored for his service to the schools, but not at the expense of those poor children. Anyway, it was a big funeral—a lot of old friends paid their respects—at the end it didn't matter how German he was."

"It never mattered, beginning, middle, or end. Sometimes I could shake you, Sophie. You're so foolish about your German blood, yours and Rudy's. My father was as German as yours, and I don't worry about it."

"That's different: he was brought over as a child in time to grow up and fight in the Civil War. And you yourself are only half-German. Your mother belonged to an old original Waynesboro family. But what I was really afraid of was that Franz and Mary might meet with some unpleasantness when they were here for the funeral."

"They didn't. No one here would mar such a solemn occasion. Franz's father hadn't minded his being a pacifist, surely?"

"No. He brought up his children to be Socialists and pacifists. And the Gardiners seem to accept it as natural, too. I was talking to Lavinia Stevens the other day—she said, 'Why be upset about what you're not responsible for? We washed our hands of Mary long ago.' Then she hurried to explain she didn't mean that they had cut off relations—theirs was too close-knit a family for that; but they'd just accepted the fact that Mary would go her own way regardless. Only her Grandfather Bodien, apparently, has turned against her. Mary was always his favorite, maybe because she is so like him. He won't let Mary's name be spoken in his hearing. That's why she and Franz stayed with us and not the Gardiners when they were home. D'you suppose it's true, that after all these years at Rausch Cordage Captain Bodien is still a 'soldier at heart'?"

"I'm sure he is." Elsa was emphatic. "When we were little—but that's neither here nor there. I saw Franz and Mary at the funeral. And Max. I haven't seen Max Lichtenstein in years and years."

"He's the one Father Lichtenstein would have found it hard to forgive. A fashionable lawyer in Cleveland—he's done his very best to shake loose from his background. Married a rich a girl, has grown rich himself. Rudy and I think he was responsible—partly, anyway—for his father's stroke. Did you know he's changed his name? Anglicized it? He's 'Lightstone' now—went to court and had it made legal. We tried to keep it from Papa Lichtenstein, but he read it in the *Plain Dealer*. We always thought he took that paper just so he could keep up with Max. Rudy will never forgive his brother—half-brother, really—for forgetting all his father should have meant to him."

"How about your Frederick? Ludwig thinks—"

"What Ludwig thinks is doubtless correct. Fritz is itching to get into this cataclysm. So far Rudy has persuaded him to stay in law school—at least until he is needed."

"Ludwig is still at the mill, just biding his time, and doing some training with the National Guard. Rudy thinks then that the country will get into the war?"

"Sooner or later. Don't you?"

"I don't know. Wilson has been so superior about being 'too proud to fight.' But lately he has been forceful enough about Germany's resumption of submarine warfare. I find myself torn. I despise Wilson, but I don't want Ludwig to have to go."

In contrast to 1916, the following year would be remembered not for any small town or family incident, but for the United States' long-delayed entry into the war. It was perhaps the relief of tension after nerves had been stretched too tight for too long that made the war seem to Americans a crusade to be undertaken with uplifted hearts, even gaily, with songs and bands and martial music. Only the old ladies, with vague feelings of guilt because they too had been wondering 'What the country was coming to,' and saying 'We usen't to be so cowardly,' now remembered the years of the Civil War with grave misgiving, thinking of the changes that had then been wrought in brothers, lovers, and husbands, even those who had come home safe and whole physically.

Before the Waynesboro National Guard unit (and Ludwig Evans) had been called up with the rest of Ohio's Thirty-seventh Division and sent to train at a camp in Alabama, Frederick Lichtenstein had enlisted in the local company, along with several other Waynesboro boys who would have considered it ignominious to wait to be drafted, among them the older Merrill boy, Frank. Charlie, lamed by polio as he was, was left at home, to become increasingly bitter. His mother said to Elsa one day when they had been talking of their sons in the army, "I never thought to see the day when I would be glad Charlie is crippled. But he is taking it so hard he is impossible to live with; no boy his age can be philosophical about being physically handicapped. You'd think he'd be used to it. I'm glad he's through college and ready to go on to law school in the fall."

The rest of 1917 was to those living through it a dismal stretch of time. Allied attacks on the German lines were bloody disasters. The American Regular Army was taken to France in July, only to be broken up and sent to various parts of the Allied front for training, and so performed no newsworthy exploits. The Rainbow Division sailed in October, but saw no fighting until spring. In the meantime, at home, thousands of socks and sweaters were knit, meatless days were more or less observed, government bonds were bought and sold, bands continued to play, and Irving Berlin tunes were sung everywhere.

In Waynesboro concentration on the war gave way briefly to notice of one change that in normal times would have been considered an Event. The Theological Seminary had been for several years in a decline: the Reformed Presbyterian denomination was decreasing in numbers and produced few sons to study at Waynesboro; three or four aging professors taught all the classes; its president, the widowed Dr. Maxwell, was growing increasingly feeble physically if not mentally. After having graduated just five theologians in the summer of 1917, the board of trustees, foreseeing the end, voted to merge with the United Presbyterian seminary in Pittsburgh. To Christina Voorhees the decision seemed a tragedy and a betrayal. She unburdened herself one Sabbath morning after church to Miss Campbell, lamenting that her father's life work had come to nothing.

Commonsensible Miss Campbell said, "That's nonsense, Christina. His life work was the educating of hundreds of young men for the ministry, and that is work that cannot be undone."

"He gave up many years of his life to the building and strengthening of that institution." Christina was not to be consoled. She was the exception. Since by that time there were no Seminary wives in the Woman's Club, the only ripple caused there by the removal was among the oldest members, who remembered it as it had been in its heyday, and wondered now what would become of the buildings that had housed the Female College before the Seminary had taken it over. Even Amanda Reid, who had been closely associated with both institutions, and strict Reformed Presbyterian though she was, was not very sympathetic with Christina. "Those boys who left—or did not apply for admission—could have claimed exemption from the draft, had they so chosen. As ministers or conscientious objectors. But Calvinists have never been pacifists: they have always been all too ready for a fight."

"The Seminary could have ridden out the war. But it had to end sometime."

In the early winter of 1917 and the spring of 1918, it did indeed look as if the war might be over—disastrously—before Americans in any number had reached the battle lines. By late in the spring, the English and French armies were barely hanging on, after their bloody and unsuccessful battles of the winter. The Italians had been defeated, and Russia was out of the war. In 1917 the first Russian Revolution had been hailed in America as the end of a despotism, and any misgiving that had been felt over an alliance with the Czar gave way after his abdication to enthusiasm for the new government. The Bolshevik Revolution in the fall had been a shock; the peace of Brest-Litovsk at the beginning of March had made it certain that the German armies on the eastern front could be moved to the west; it became more terrifyingly possible that the French and English could no longer hold their lines. The race to get American soldiers to France accelerated, but when the great German advance began in March, there were still but few American divisions dispersed among the Allied armies. As week followed week, the Germans were not stopped. Newspapers were picked up with apprehension; pessimists predicted that the channel ports would fall in a matter of days; the third German attack in late May drove the French back to the Marne, where they had not been since 1914.

The Thirty-seventh Division crossed the Atlantic in June, and was sent to a quiet sector for more training. From the day of the soldiers' arrival in France, families were kept in ignorance as to where they were or what they were doing: letters were so censored that the boys gave up trying to be informative, and no one at home knew more than he could read in the newspapers. Happily, Jennifer could write that she had seen Ludwig and Fritz Lichtenstein when they had been briefly in Paris; she hoped that their next leave would come when Tucker Gordon was in the city. Her family inferred that if she was not seeing Tucker frequently, she was at least in touch with him. With the arrival of the Forty-second Division in France, Tucker's ambulance unit had been taken over and inducted into the American army, including him as a medical corpsman.

The last German assault began in the middle of July, but ran its course in three days. When the first counterattack was successful and the Germans were pushed back from Soissons and the Marne, and from south of the Somme, Pershing was at last given permission to collect his scattered divisions and put them together into an American army. The Thirty-seventh was one of the massed divisions that attacked along the Meuse-Argonne in September.

Except for newspaper reports of the drive by American troops, Waynesboro folk still had no notion of exactly where their sons were, or, in any detail, of what they were doing, except that they were certainly "In It" at last. Not until the day when Elsa took from the Western Union boy at the front door the telegram from the War Department. Before she summoned courage to open it, she had time to think, "This will kill Gib; I'll have to hold him up while he thinks he's holding me up." She stayed where she was in the front hall behind the closed door. She was trembling so that she could scarcely close the door and tear the envelope open. It read, "Private First Class Ludwig Evans missing in action before Montfaucon, believed captured by the enemy."

Her relief was so great she feared for a moment that she would fall, and put her hand for balance on the stand behind her, knocking off the silver tray kept there for the reception of calling cards. The clatter it made brought Ravenna from the kitchen to the door at the end of the hall.

"Never mind, Venny," Elsa said as she stooped to pick it up. "Just my awkwardness." Then, abruptly she continued, "Ludwig is reported missing in action." She returned to the living room and sat down, the telegram in her hand.

Timidly, the colored woman said, "Po' Mistuh Ludwig! Miz Evans, you want I should call Mistuh Evans fo' yo'?"

Elsa roused herself. "No. I'd rather tell him face to face when he comes home at noon. It will be a blow."

"Yas'm. He sho' dotes on that boy. Maybe I'd oughta hold lunch back a little."

"If you will, Venny. Give us a little time."

Elsa sat immobile when she was alone, thinking, "Gib cares more for his children than most fathers," wondering, "Could he have known?", going on to "But we have had a good life all these years, and I do love him for his goodness and gentleness. And now I'm afraid for him."

When she heard the gate clang shut at noon, she went to the door, telegram still in her hand. He looked at her as he came up the porch steps, said, "Something has happened." The color drained from his face. "Ludwig?"

"Bad news, but not the worst. 'Missing in action, believed captured'." She handed him the telegram and, as she thought afterward, saw him age before her eyes.

"I have been afraid from the first," he said finally, "that we'd never see Ludwig again."

"Oh, Gib! Of course we'll see him again. He'll be put in a prisoner of war camp, where he'll be safe even if he's miserable."

"'Missing in action' can mean anything. They just may not have found his body."

He brushed past her, went into the living room, dropped heavily into the nearest chair, his hands between his knees, still holding the telegram. Slowly he read it again, looking for hope he did not find.

Elsa came and stood beside him, leaning against his chair. "I don't believe for a minute—and you mustn't either—that he wouldn't have been found if he'd been left on the battlefield. The Waynesboro boys—Fritz, Frank Merrill—all the others—they would have looked for him."

"They were fighting a battle. How could they stop?"

"The Germans are retreating. They're not dragging any seriously wounded prisoners with them. Certainly not any—dead bodies. And our ambulances must come up quickly."

"It is dreadful not to know. To try to keep hope alive for weeks maybe or until the war ends. I don't think I can bear it."

"It won't be weeks. The Red Cross in Switzerland gets lists of prisoners of war. And Fritz will write home."

"When? He's busy on the firing line."

"I'll call Sophie this afternoon. And I'll do what Mamma threatened to do when Ludwig Junior was killed: I'll write Myron Herrick. He's a close family friend, and he must still be able to do a little wire-pulling. That might hurry the Red Cross—or someone in a position to learn something."

Time passed—an eternity, it seemed to Elsa, watching Gib suffer, seeing him turn into a gray-faced, shrunken old man at fifty. The answer to her appeal to Herrick came first: Ludwig had been captured, after having been gassed. He was still, at the time the information had been obtained, in the prison camp hospital. His family could communicate with him through the Red Cross. And Mr. Herrick had added an encouraging note: it was true that the German armies had behaved like barbarians in the beginning, but so far as prisoners of war were concerned, they were observing the Geneva Convention, and were permitting Red Cross representatives to inspect their camps.

A little later the Lichtensteins had a letter from their Fritz. It was only as informative as the censors permitted: in fighting the retreating Germans, they had run into a gas attack; Ludwig was with a patrol ahead of the line, and had caught the gas first, had been captured with the rest of the patrol when they stopped to put their gas masks on. Fritz had not seen that small flurry of action, but knew that Ludwig had not been left among the dead in front of the German trench because after the Krauts had retreated he had been one of the burial detail, and they had not found Ludwig.

Even after that letter—even, finally, after a note from Ludwig himself, saying that he wanted *food* and *wool socks*, even the kind his mother knit, and that he was OK—still Gib worried and had to be told over and over again that gas was not necessarily or even probably fatal, that the war would soon end, and that a country facing defeat would certainly take care of its prisoners.

Gib was provoked even at Jennifer because she did not lament Ludwig's misfortune as a calamity; she had had a letter from Fritz Lichtenstein that had convinced her that Ludwig was not only safe, but "safely out of it for the duration." She wrote cheerfully of having seen Tucker Gordon in Paris, when he had brought a load from field hospital to base hospital and had then been given a few days' leave. She had had dinner with him, and he had told her his strange tale about having run into Blair Voorhees "up the line." Blair had a cushy job, Tuck had said, chauffeuring some general, and not many generals got hit. This one had turned up to inspect a field hospital and had left his car and chauffeur outside. Someone came out to give the chauffeur a message, and had hailed him as "Voorhees." Tuck had never known him—he was a kid when Blair disappeared from Waynesboro—but he'd heard of him, and when he caught the name he wondered if he was the same person, and asked him. And sure enough. "He's been in the Army all these years, and that's as far as he's got: chauffeur to a general. Looks as if he was a hard drinker, Tuck says: tough and ugly, like most of the Regular Army enlisted men. He wasn't in the least interested in Waynesboro or his family. I guess the Army's his whole life. I don't know whether you should pass this on to his folks or not. His mother might be glad to know he's all right and in a good safe place, but not the rest of it."

"Jenny never knew Blair Voorhees, for God's sake," her father complained, "and she's more interested in him than in her own brother."

"She isn't worrying about Ludwig. Why should she? He's out of it. And whatever-became-of-Blair-Voorhees has been a Waynesboro mystery for almost twenty years."

"How does Tucker Gordon rate all these Paris leaves she writes about, when there's fighting going on?"

"He's transporting wounded, and I suppose manages a day off now and then between trips. I suspect she's more worried about him than about Ludwig—after all, he's doing what got her uncle killed."

"Why the devil should she—? Do you mean she's *interested* in Tucker Gordon?"

Elsa could have said, "Remember she's living in an atmosphere of here-today-and-gone tomorrow"; but she controlled her tongue and contented herself with, "They've been friends for a good many years."

Gib did not for a moment suspect that Elsa was indifferent to the welfare of her children, but he considered her unreasonably optimistic, not realizing that in large part her optimism was assumed for his benefit. She worried silently but fearfully about Ludwig's having been gassed, wondered whether he was being properly treated. She managed to hide her worries, and few of her friends realized how she was struggling against them.

Anne Gordon was one who did see it, first on an afternoon when the Club had met at her house and Elsa lingered afterward to speak of Jenny's news about Tucker, suspecting with reason that she knew more about him than his grandmother did.

"I don't think you need to worry about him, Aunt Anne. He's carrying wounded back to base hospitals from the forward ones. And anyway it can't be long now: the Germans are retreating everywhere, and the British have broken the Hindenburg lines."

"I don't hear from him often, and then only briefly. He did write me about seeing Blair Voorhees—I suppose Jennifer told you? I don't know whether to mention it to Christina. But I'm sure you're right about its not being long now. I'm glad our boys haven't had the long years of fighting that the British and French have had. I don't believe we'll find them much changed when they get home. I remember all too well, fighting can stamp a boy. If only they all come through whole."

"If! Ludwig's whiff of mustard gas—I don't know. Gib is reading everything he can find about what gas can do. I try to stop him, but—He's worrying himself sick, and I have to pretend to be unconcerned just to keep him sane."

Anne thought how the tempestuous tomboy that had run free with Johnny had grown into this strong woman: years of marriage to a man she had not been in love with—a marriage that she had determined to make a happy one—had been the discipline that had made her what she had become. And if those who had known her as a girl regretted the loss of fire and spontaneity, they should not: the serenity achieved far outweighed any loss. And yet, she mourned the young Elsa: the fierce little girl who had refused to let anyone but Johnny call her "Shaney."

When the war's end came, expected yet unexpectedly sudden, the country rejoiced hysterically and noisily. No more fear. No more boys shot. They would be brought home as rapidly as possible. And then the influenza epidemic struck, and the rejoicing was muted. Ironically, after all the slaughter, it was the young people who were dying, particularly the boys still in training camps. In Waynesboro the railroad station platform was piled high with crated caskets waiting trans-shipment to Camp Sherman.

The epidemic had begun in Europe; hospitals were filled with its victims, as well as with wounded soldiers; except for troops in the Occupation Army, those in the medical or nurses' corps would be the last to reach home. Prisoners of war were freed at once.

Ludwig Evans was returned on a hospital ship, since the medical officer who examined him did not consider him in need of hospitalization. After the delays caused by military red tape, he was given his discharge papers and sent home. His parents were waiting for him on the station platform when he alighted from the train, exhausted, white, and drawn. His father wept unashamedly while Ludwig embraced his mother. He made his own welcome brief.

"We have the car waiting. Do you want to go to bed at home or in the hospital?"

"Pop, for God's sake! Neither one. I'm all right. A whiff of gas—I made the most of it, just to get home quicker. They didn't keep me in bed on the ship. I don't think they were fooled. But the Thirty-seventh was in Belgium toward the end; now they're trying to restore normal conditions there, and Lord knows when they'll be back."

In spite of his protest, they insisted on calling "young" Dr. Warren, who came at once, looking more disheveled and rawboned than usual, run off his feet as he was by a hospital full to overflowing and patients in bed at home, victims of influenza. He went over Ludwig with his stethoscope, said he thought not much damage had been done, but told him to come into the hospital the next day for chest X-rays.

"I didn't get a bad dose. We were patrolling ahead of the company. We knew the Germans were retreating, and like fools we weren't wearing gas masks. We got too close to them—they weren't retreating—not yet—they gave us a dose of mustard gas and grabbed the lot. They put us in the hospital in the prison camp till we were OK. Only thing the matter with me is I'm starved to death."

"D'you mean the Germans didn't feed you?" Gib cut in. He had been an anxious observer of the doctor's examination.

"They couldn't even feed themselves, there toward the end. I'm sure they did the best they could. The doctor was an old duffer, fifty years behind the times, but he did all right. Of course their first-rate medical men were with the Army."

Dr. Warren departed; Ludwig was persuaded to lie down, went to sleep, and had to be awakened to go to his grandmother's for dinner. She lamented his gaunt appearance, muttered something about "Andersonville all over again," fed him hugely, and then began her questions, which were answered in as few words as possible: yes, he had had a Paris leave and had seen Jenny—hadn't she written?—and yes, she was fine: working like a dog, but enjoying it. It would be a while before she could get home: the hospital at Neuilly was still full. And no, he hadn't seen Tuck Gordon, but thought he would be home soon: there was little need for ambulances now, and although the M.D.'s might have to stay awhile, surely some of the ambulance drivers could be spared. And no, he didn't know anything about Fritz Lichtenstein and the other Waynesboro boys; presumably they were still in Belgium, and they might be unlucky enough to become part of the Occupation Army.

After that first day, when Ludwig's family had him to themselves, the telephone rang incessantly, always, it seemed, when he was sleeping. (For the first week he didn't do much but sleep.) Anxious Waynesboro parents wanted to ask what Ludwig knew about their sons, and he had to tell them, "From the day of my capture, nothing." "Don't those fellows write home?" he grumbled. "Some of them I never saw after I got over there. Some of them I never knew even here in Waynesboro. But I might as well go see all these people, and stop this telephoning. Then I am going to work: catch up with what is going on in the mill. I'll be there Monday morning."

"We need you. It's going to be tough sledding for a while, what with orders being canceled and a carry-over of raw material purchased at wartime prices. And the government has a stockpile of rope it will throw on the market at reduced prices. We can keep running if we cut costs: fewer hours and lower wages."

"Don't be such a pessimist, Pop. Any depression we have now will be short-lived—there's too much unsatisfied civilian demand—must be—stands to reason. And we must have been building up our capital reserve these last years. I think we should build a new mill—modern, with new machinery run by electric power. All we have is pretty old now."

"A new mill! Captain Bodien is only waiting for your return to quit; the old man must be pushing eighty: he's getting pretty shaky, and in some ways downright childish. But he's trained young Henderson to take his place as mill superintendent."

"If he's past planning a new mill, I'll get Stuart to help with his advice. Anyway, I'll be there Monday morning."

It was not until nearly Christmas that Jennifer Evans came safely home, and Gib's worry over his children was relieved at last. His ordeal had told on him: he looked and moved like a man twenty years his senior, and was in his relief inclined to be querulous. Jennifer was more shocked (more perceptive, perhaps) than Ludwig had been. Son and father were opposing each other over the matter of building a new rope mill, but since Captain Bodien and Stuart agreed that it was high time the factory was modernized, and since, after all, Ludwig was now in control, there was little Gib could do except utter dire warnings. Plans were drawn up, contracts signed, the matter of up-to-date machinery run by electric power was investigated, and Ludwig was eager to get started on his first project as head of the corporation.

Her experience had left its mark on Jennifer as well as on her brother. She gave the impression, at first, of a highly sophisticated young lady—an impression for which Parisian styles were largely responsible, and the bobbed hair like a black cap, which her father deprecated but forgave: after all, it would grow in again. The whole effect was enough to make her old friends feel out of touch with her and reluctant to renew school-girl intimacies. It took a while to realize her maturity; she had grown into a quiet, capable young woman, willing to talk about her experiences in answer to questions, but not forcing anyone to listen to them. She slipped easily into the role of daughter-of-the-house, but since she refused to permit her mother to present her name as candidate for membership in the Woman's Club, to fill the vacancy that had been held for her so long, Elsa concluded that Jennifer's plans did not include a permanent stay in Waynesboro.

She did accept her grandmother's invitation to attend the Christmas meeting of the Club—dinner and play, and a celebration of its fiftieth anniversary, postponed from the exact date in the fall first by the war and then by the influenza epidemic. Sally as usual gave them one of her elaborate dinners, much appreciated by the husbands and other males invited. Amanda read a paper about the fifty years of the Club's existence, and they all then thoroughly enjoyed Elizabeth Merrill's choice of the entertainment of the evening: scenes from *East Lynn* done as the broadest kind of farce.

The evening was an unqualified success, particularly in Sally's eyes; she did love for her parties to be enjoyed, and she rejoiced to have the house full of young people again; not only the young Club members like Renata Lichtenstein, but also her own two Evans grandchildren, and others home from the war, like Fritz Lichtenstein and Frank Merrill.

Shortly after Christmas, Tucker Gordon turned up unexpectedly at his grandmother's. The doorbell caught her with her hands in the dishpan, suds to the elbow. After all the years she still did not trust Louline with the best china, and she had had Sunday dinner the day before for Sally Rausch and the Evans family. It was a task requiring no thought, and she had let her mind wander: the war was over, but Gib Evans would never go back to being young again. And from Gib her thoughts went back to her own father, who had never been the same after Rob had been killed in action in the South. She was startled by the doorbell into a jerk of fear, a suspension of action, rather as a consequence of the point to which her idle thoughts had brought her than by so commonplace an occurrence. But as she lifted her hands from the dishpan and brushed the suds from her arms, she remembered: "It was like this before—I was washing dishes when the bell rang and it was the message about Rob. Summer vacation, and I was helping Martha, or thought I was, wash the dishes, and the bell rang and I wiped my hands and answered it—"

Before she had finished wiping her hands, the bell rang again insistently. Unreasonably, her heart thudded. She shoved blind old Major out of her way with her foot and started to answer it. From the kitchen she could see the length of the hall, and through the net curtains covering the glass in the door. It was not a Western Union messenger boy outside. She didn't know what she could have been expecting, but she relaxed, her heart quietened.

She opened the door to a tall, spectacled young man, deeply tanned, in a rumpled uniform and untidy puttees, and looked at him inquiringly. "What—?" Major, who had followed at her heels from the kitchen, began to quiver, whimpered, and tried to pass her.

"Gran'ma! Don't you know me?"

"Tuck! Bless my soul! It's been so long—and you've grown so!" (Taller than any Gordon had ever been.) "But do come in and let me look at you—make sure you're real."

He came inside, laughing, but before he embraced her he stooped to pet the ecstatic dog. "You knew me, didn't you, boy? Poor old Major! You never told me he was still alive. And imagine his remembering!"

"Dogs always remember. I guess I just didn't think to mention him in my letters, I'm so used to his being underfoot. But he's been a world of company for me. I'd thought of—I really should have had him put to sleep. He's blind with cataracts, he bumps into the furniture and falls off the porch; but I couldn't bring myself to do it, and now I'm glad I didn't. It's such a blissful moment for him." Having thus bridged the awkward transition from non-recognition to welcome, she said, "Come in the sitting room and find a chair, and tell me about what you've seen and done."

"Oh, let's not talk about that."

Anne was reminded of another medical man who had not wanted to talk about his war. She said, "Drop your satchel there, and your cap, and come on in. I hope you can stay for a while."

"I'm coming home soon, to stay where I belong. But right now, it can only be overnight. I've got to go back to California to get out of this uniform and see my mother."

In the living room Anne took her rocker and he dropped on the old sofa, where Major could lie beside him, head on his thigh. So many possible things to say racketed through Anne's mind that she said none of them, only studied him: rough blond head, bony face, broad shoulders, and only the dark eyes behind the spectacles to show him Johnny's son.

Tucker, taken aback by the silent scrutiny, said, "Don't you want me to come?"

"Oh, Tuck! It's only that I never thought you would, really. I can hardly believe it. Does your mother know?"

"I've told her often enough; she wouldn't believe me either. I'll tell her again when I see her. She'll try to stop me, because if I go it will mean she couldn't keep me. A defeat for her, kind of. But she won't really care. She's leading exactly the kind of life she likes: all the money she can spend, trips, parties with other rich Los Angeles widows, bridge games day in and day out." He sounded so contemptuous that his grandmother reproved him.

"Tuck, don't. You always adored your mother."

"When I was a little boy. She was so beautiful it seemed she couldn't ever be wrong. But we all grow up. I learned a long while ago that she is a real snow-queen. Cold all the way through. Uncle Robert didn't mind—he just wanted her to be hostess for him and that sort of thing. Another beautiful possession. When we left here and went to California, I couldn't see how father could have done what he must have done. Now I'm grown-up, I understand."

Anne was shocked. "She's your mother, and what your father did was wrong. She could not condone it," she argued against her heart.

"I wonder." His dark eyes searched his grandmother's face. He thought, "You would have condoned and forgiven. You were a warmhearted—passionate?—woman." And he remembered the moment of revelation when he had learned about his parents. Back in college he had taken a girl for a ride and, as he knew she expected, an evening of petting. She had been submissive, even eager, when they parked the car on a lookout spot on a hill road and moved to the back seat, eager enough to stir his blood: fondling, kissing, his hand on her breast. But when he unfastened his trousers, put his hand beneath her skirt, it was "Don't—don't—no, Tuck, stop it. I'm afraid of being hurt." He had stopped. The outcry had taken him back to the dreadful nights of his childhood, long forgotten. Instead of "Stop, Tuck," he heard "Stop it, Johnny—stop! You're hurting me—" and the moans from his mother that had taken him out of bed to stand trembling behind the door, wondering whether he dared—and not daring—afraid of his father, afraid for his mother, but standing there until all was quiet in their bedroom. At the moment when the block was removed from his memory, he knew the cause of those tortured nights, and felt more than a little nauseated. He had said to the girl, "Be quiet. I'm not going to do anything you don't want. Straighten yourself up and we'll get out of here." He had fastened his own clothes, moved to the front seat, and driven away from the clifftop parking bay with an angry scattering of gravel. He had said nothing in reply to the girl's pleas—"Don't be mad, Tuck."—and to her farewell "I don't suppose I'll ever see you again" only a gruff "It hasn't anything to do with you." As it hadn't, when in his mind he was reiterating, "So that was it—that was it all the time."

In his grandmother's living room he returned to the present, after what had perhaps been a rather long silence (how long did it take the mind to remember and dismiss a memory, really?). He sighed, moved his hands, which he had clenched between his knees, and said, "She didn't want me to go into medicine. You knew that."

Anne thought, "She has made it hard for him," interpreting so the grim expression, the white-knuckled hands.

He continued, "I've told her all along I was coming back to Waynesboro and be a doctor. She will only believe it when I get out of uniform, pack up my belongings, and leave. I still have two years of medical school. I'll take them at Cincinnati, like Father and Grandfather. If they'll accept me. Then I'll come home and start practice in their old office." Then suddenly afraid he was taking too much for granted, he added "You haven't sold it, have you?"

Anne shook her head. "It wasn't mine to sell. It's part of your inheritance, along with your father's partnership in the hospital. It's rented, of course—your trustees have seen to that—but you won't want it for a while."

"To another doctor? He'll have plenty of time to find another place."

"You're all right for money?"

"Yes. You know it's still in trust—I fixed it with the bank when I was twenty-one because I knew I would be enlisting or something. I had managed two years at Stanford on the interest. Now I'll want some of the capital. I hope the bank or Judge Gardiner will take care of that—let me have the stocks and bonds or whatever, but still look after the real estate while I'm in Cincinnati. Because—Gran'ma," he drew a long breath, "I'm going to be married."

"Married! but—"

"I'm grown up, Gran, even if I haven't finished school."

"Some California girl?" Anne asked. ("Poor little Tag-along!" she thought, "I'm sure Elsa thinks she—") "Or someone you knew in France?"

Tucker grinned. "I knew her in France all right. But long before that. Surely you know, or should, that I have never cared for anyone but Jenny."

"You mean—Oh, Tuckl You mean you and Jennifer Evans? How wonderful! A novelist couldn't have worked things out better. I can hardly believe it." Then, more doubtfully, "You've fixed it all up? Jennifer has been home for a month, and I'm sure hasn't said a word even to her mother."

"Jenny promised not to tell anyone—not even Aunt Elsa—until I got home to ask for her hand properly. But I should think they might have guessed. Yes, we have it all fixed up. Her family won't object, do you think?"

"Not her parents. She's always had her father in the palm of her hand. But her grandmother may."

"Old Mrs. Rausch? Aunt Sally? She isn't in the picture, surely?"

"She's not all that old. No older than I am." Inwardly she was chuckling: imagine Sally Rausch being "not in the picture"—any picture.

"Then—" Tucker had a moment's compunction. He had been thinking that his grandmother, whom he had not seen for so long, was beginning to show her years. Not many gray hairs in the brown, no network of wrinkles, but the hollows beneath her cheekbones would be there for the rest of her life. He felt a pang that surprised him: he had not yet learned how saddening it is to see the first marks of age, irreversible, on someone you care for. He said, "I know that, of course. And if she has held her own like you, I suppose that she will have to be reckoned with."

"She has always considered the Gordon men a little unstable. But Jennifer's mother can cope with her. How soon are you planning to be married?"

"As soon as I get back from California. There's no reason for waiting. We'll take an apartment in Cincinnati while I'm in medical school, and if Jenny wants to, she can go on nursing. She is good, and she likes it."

"You take my breath away. You have it all planned?"

"Oh, yes. We even know where we are going to live when we come back. In the old Gordon house. Build something new and convenient for the tenant and restore the original house. It can be beautiful, that old brick."

The house that had had unhappy associations for John. But Tucker probably had never heard about his great-aunt Kate. She said, "But for a doctor—out in the country?"

"It's only a few miles from town. With a car, it will be nothing. And it will be a wonderful place for children. I always loved the farm, and Hillcrest. Remember?"

He was startled to see tears on his grandmother's lashes. "What is it, Gran? Have I said something wrong?

"Of course not. It is just—I didn't know how much you remembered, or how much you cared. I know you kept saying—but at longer and longer intervals."

"And you couldn't take my word for it. If I could have got home in those years—but until I was twenty-one, I—there was always some good reason."

"I'm sure there was," Anne said, thinking of Julia. "And anyway, that's all water under the bridge now. Somehow, when you did write about coming back some day"—she faced him squarely—"I always shrank a little. You see—I don't suppose you can, but try—I hadn't anyone left here to be concerned about. I was so detached and—and free I didn't want to be dragged into *caring* again."

("And 'caring,' for her," Tucker thought, "has always ended in grief.")

"I can't believe it of myself, but it was true. I couldn't admit that to be alive, no matter how easy, with no one to care for was hardly to be alive at all. Now, with you actually here, on that sofa, fooling with that poor old blind dog, I'm as glad to have you back as he is. I couldn't say more."

The sound of the kitchen door closing gave Tucker a chance to cut short what had become an emotional scene.

"That's Louline? Come to get dinner? I must go speak to her. Unless you've got a new girl?"

"It's Louline. Tell her you will be staying for dinner."

He hesitated. "Well, I'll call Jenny to tell her when to expect me." He swung the dog to his shoulder the way he had always carried him, Major's feet dangling, his hind feet clawing for a hold on the khaki, and went out.

Anne did not go with him. She listened, smiling but not quite dry-eyed, to the noisy greetings in the kitchen. She needed a moment to catch her breath. "Those young-uns," she thought, "and all their elaborate plans." But they were not children, and what they had seen and experienced in the last years had made for a quick maturity. Besides, Jennifer after all was five or six years older than she herself had been—she looked back at the young girl who had been so completely and enduringly in love, and so afraid that, in the old phrase, her love was unrequited. In a way, looking back, it seemed a long, long time since she had been eighteen, but in another way her memories were so clear and vivid that it seemed like yesterday. Time was an accordion, all the air squeezed out of it as you grew old. And how strange that in your mind you did not feel any older. You were the same person, but where had the years gone?

After dinner Tucker left for the Evanses'. He was visibly nervous, perhaps even a little frightened, of Gib Evans, of all people! But his grandmother smiled only inwardly: it was, after all, rather an intimidating ordeal, whoever the father of whatever girl.

As Anne had foreseen, Tucker met with no opposition from Gib, nor from Elsa when she had been invited into the parlor to join in the interview. They did not even seem surprised. "After all," Gib said, "She never wrote a letter home without mentioning you."

As they moved from the front room to join Jennifer and Ludwig in the family living room, Gib was making his only protest. "I wish you wouldn't be in such a hurry. Jenny's been home such a little while. Can't you wait until you have your M.D.?"

Ludwig, who had obviously had an explanation from Jenny, said as he rose to shake hands with Tucker, take him by the shoulders and shake him a little, "Life's too short. Too short to be wasted waiting when there's no reason for it. Always and forever *waiting*."

"You had more of that than most of us," Tucker grinned at him. "But I'm not sure you weren't lucky."

"*Lucky?*"

"To be out of it. The Thirty-seventh took some heavy losses. Fritz and Frank Merrill: they came through OK? They're home, I suppose? And the other fellows from Waynesboro? What you need now is to stop waiting—find the girl, get married, and settle down. To just plain everyday living."

"I'm settled down without a girl. In over my head at the mill. And I haven't seen a girl I want. I'll have to let the young sprigs grow up, and see how they turn out. And as for my being lucky: the whole American Army was lucky in a way. Lucky that we didn't have to fight very long."

Jennifer said, "This country has no idea what real losses are."

Tucker agreed. "No. You and I know because we were there before America was involved. France and England—Germany too, for that matter. They've lost their best and bravest: the men who would have been their leaders in another fifteen, twenty years."

Jenny murmured, "'The flowers o' the forest are a' wede awa'."

"Don't lament now about the state of the world twenty years from now." Elsa cut them short. "I want to know your plans. Like her father, I think it would be nice to have Jennifer home for a while."

"We'll be married in June. That will give me almost six months in California. A simple wedding. Then we'll go house-hunting in the city, and get settled before the start of the fall term at med school."

"No honeymoon trip?"

"We've traveled enough lately. We're ready to start housekeeping."

Ludwig laughed. The idea of Jenny at a stove seemed ludicrous. "Start cold? You don't know the first thing about cooking."

"I admit. But I can learn between now and June."

The young people had their way about all their plans except the "simple wedding."

Sally Rausch, who was still, in spite of her physical handicaps, occasionally driving her little electric runabout, called Elsa the next morning to ask her company on an errand to the country. Elsa, who knew her mother would consider it an insult if she offered to drive, agreed, thinking, "A good chance to break the news," and obediently got herself cloaked, hatted, and gloved. Never one to postpone what might be difficult, she had hardly closed the car door behind her before she announced Jennifer's engagement to Tucker. Her mother's reaction was what she had expected.

"With your permission, no doubt?"

"Tucker came last night, all proper, to ask for her hand."

"I hadn't heard he was in town. Why didn't Anne—?"

"He got in late yesterday afternoon, and left for Los Angeles this morning."

"Gordon men do not make good husbands, as you very well know."

"Tucker after all is only one-quarter Gordon. Anne is faithfulness itself, and he has inherited some of his mother's single-mindedness."

"Imagine! Teapot Tucker's grandson marrying into our family!" But Sally's agitation was revealed less by what she said that by her erratic driving. Down Chillicothe Street she kept to the center, on the interurban track. Elsa clamped her mouth shut, although one of the big traction cars was not far behind them, spitting sparks from the overhead lines. When they came to the old towpath where the road turned, Sally kept to the tracks.

Elsa could not restrain herself. "Mamma! What on earth do you think you are doing?"

"This will be a short-cut," her mother said, outwardly composed, unwilling to concede her error. Her children were always after her to give up her driving and her independence. By the time they had passed the far edge of town, road and track were separated by a high grassy bank; the interurban car was but a few feet behind them, its bell incessantly clanging. But Sally at that point could not possibly get back to the road.

"He has no need to make all that racket. We know he's there, and he must know who we are." She let her fright work itself out in indignation. "Has he forgotten your father built this line?"

"Mamma! For goodness' sake! How many years ago? Watch for the next crossing and get off the track."

"He wouldn't dare run into us." But Sally was thoroughly rattled, and in her agitation moved the steering bar just beough to drop them from the rails to the ties, which fortunately were buried their full depth in mud and gravel. Nevertheless they bump-bumped their way to the first crossroad, where Sally succeeded in getting off the track and on to the rutted gravel.

Elsa breathed a sigh of relief. The trolley picked up speed and swept on its way. "Do watch where you're going. I swear this is the last time I ride with you."

"Nonsense! This road is much rougher than the track was, and that motorman had no business making such a din. Your father—"

"I know. Papa built the interurban line." Elsa relieved herself in sarcasm. "A mere twenty years ago. But we haven't even been stockholders for four or five years. I don't suppose that motorman ever heard of Papa, much less knew his wife. Mamma, you really are—"

"Of course he knows me. Now what were you saying about a 'simple wedding'? Jennifer will be married properly in the Baptist church, as you were and as I was. The wedding reception will be at my house, of course."

Elsa was past arguing. Tucker and Jenny would have to fight their own fight, or submit. They should submit, and be glad that her Grandmother Rausch made no real objection to the marriage.

"And Jenny will of course come into the Club."

"In time, I suppose. Tuck still has two years of medical school and a year of internship."

"But they are coming back? Tucker will take over the hospital?"

"Hardly 'take over.' After all—" But what was the use? "He inherited a partnership from his father, and will take his place."

"They can come live with me. My house is too big for one person."

"We've been telling you so for years. Any time you want us, Gib and I will move in with you. Jennifer and Tucker are going to restore the old Gordon place and live there. Ludwig can have our house when the time comes."

"The time *has* come. The time for him to marry and settle down. I hope he will be discreet enough to choose wisely."

"And that," thought Elsa, "is something he will do for himself, however much you look around for an appropriate bride for him." She said only, "I hope so," and dropped the subject. The two women drove home in comparative silence. Elsa alighted at her gate, hoping that her mother would get home safely, and determined to get that runabout out of her hands. In spite of Sally's affectation of nonchalance, however, she had seen for herself that she must give up driving and her independence; the electric was sold and for the rest of her life, as long as she was able to get out at all, she was chauffeur-driven in her big limousine.

Tucker and Jennifer were married in the summer of 1919, the wedding a "June event," according to the *Torchlight*, made so by Sally Rausch's determination. Rausches gathered in force: Ernest and Charles and their families from East and West, and Paul and his wife and children from Madison City. Elsa's house was full of Jennifer's out-of-town friends, Sally's with her sons and their families; in consequence it became incumbent upon Anne Gordon to offer hospitality to Tucker's mother. (Jessamine had offered her guest room, but agreed that it "wouldn't look right," since Tucker was staying with his grandmother.) Julia had not returned to Waynesboro since she had come to bury her mother. Her one-time friends agreed that she was still a very handsome woman, fine-drawn and exquisite, sophisticated and expensively clad, with gorgeous jewelry, but agreed that the southern California sun had finally ruined even her complexion.

To Anne, Julia was graciousness itself: the condescending great lady (a role she had been playing for so long that it had become second nature, Anne thought). And as such, she was not going to admit by word or sign that she was less than delighted with the match, nor that as things had turned out, Gordons and Rausches had triumphed in a contest that she now refused to acknowledge.

The young Gordons set up housekeeping in a Cincinnati apartment. Jennifer nursed for a while in the hospital where she had trained, but stopped in late 1919 to have her first baby: a girl born early in 1920, whom they dutifully named Sally Anne. In due time a couple of years later, Tucker finished his training and with his family returned to Waynesboro to live in the old Gordon house, restored under the knowledgeable eye of his grandmother: the walls stripped of layers of paper down to the original walnut paneling; the five-foot stone fireplace in the living room opened up and made usable, the whole furnished in large part with superfluous antiques that had been moved to the Rausches' barn loft when they had been replaced in the house. The Tucker Gordons moved in, gave a housewarming for their families and such friends as the Stevenses and the Edwardses, the Gardiners, and the two Dr. Warrens. There was general rejoicing in Waynesboro among their own group of friends, but especially on the part of Rodney Stevens, the two Warren M.D.'s, and the rest of the hospital staff. The load had grown too heavy. The senior Dr. Warren had begun to dream of retirement, and it would be necessary soon to build an additional wing to relieve the crowding.

Gib and Elsa had in the meantime moved in with her mother, who had had one jolting fall, and had thereafter been persuaded that she must no longer live alone, however devoted her servants might be. Ludwig stayed on in the house where he had grown up, preferring bachelor housekeeping, with Ravenna to "do for him," to a matriarchy.

Through the early twenties, the Woman's Club continued on its uncontroversial course, omitting by consent any discussion of Wilson and the League of Nations and even what touched the emotions and convictions of its members more sharply, the two new amendments to the Constitution: the Prohibition Amendment, which some members had worked for heart and soul and others thought preposterous, and the Woman Suffrage Amendment, which all members of the Club, strong-minded old ladies or breezy young ones, considered long overdue. Nor was there much debate about the 1920 election: it was unanimously considered by the ladies that it was high time the Democrats were turned out, and Harding, who was Senator from Ohio, was a worthy candidate: naturally, any Senator from Ohio could take over the Presidency.

One event in the fall of 1922 was considered news and gossip-worthy. Henry Voorhees retired from the bank and announced his and his wife's imminent departure for Florida, where they would live their remaining years in warmth and sunshine. His assistant was appointed cashier in his stead, and bank affairs continued to run smoothly with Elsa as president. When she had first been chosen to fill her father's shoes after his death, there had been some covert smiles in Waynesboro: everyone knew that Elsa had a better business head than her husband. It was natural that some member of the family would succeed to that position; after all, Rausch holdings of bank stock gave them control. And since first Mr. Cochran and afterward Ludwig Rausch had managed their own money wisely, and their customers' as well, it was assumed that Elsa as president, with Paul as chairman of the board, would do as well. The bank lost no depositors.

There was some conjecture as to why Henry Voorhees had stayed on as cashier after he had been passed over. (But that was what bank jobs were like: safe for a lifetime, but with little chance of promotion. Once a cashier, always a cashier.) Had he expected that Elsa would come a cropper, and that he would at last become president? If so, by 1922 he had given up hope; that seemed the only logical reason why, after staying as long as he had, he now decided to retire; after all, he was not all that old.

What was not general knowledge, since the Waynesboro Woman's Club eschewed publicity, was the fact that Christina in her turn had been passed over when Mrs. Ludwig Rausch resigned as President of the Club. That resignation really shook the organization, although it had become very difficult for Sally to attend any meetings except those at her own house, and Christina had presided in her stead at more meetings than not. Perhaps the ladies had found Christina lacking as presiding officer: too stiff and formal, too inflexible, her firm control not balanced by the unfailing ease of manner, cordiality, and graciousness that Club members had become accustomed to. At any rate, at the meeting for the annual election of officers, Christina, with her usual bland smile, called on the secretary to read the communication she had received—Sally's resignation as President—and called for nomination of candidates for the office. Instead, Charlotte Bonner rose, proposed that the Club make Mrs. Rausch, "who had served so well for so long," President Emeritus, and that then, instead of bothering with written ballots, they take a *viva voce* vote on the election of her daughter Mrs. Gilbert Evans, as president in her stead. The motion was made, seconded, discussed (a shocked Elsa protesting vehemently), voted on, and carried with only Elsa's single vote against it—all conducted by Christina with no twitch in her smile. She was the first to congratulate Elsa. And Elsa was convinced that she would always think that it had been a put-up job.

Very shortly after that the Voorheeses announced their intention to move to Florida, and Christina wrote her letter of resignation to the Club secretary. It was regretted and protested to no avail; a farewell tea honored her at the conclusion of the program at the home of Mrs. Sheldon Edwards; Jessamine said, having remembered in time her long-ago first year in Waynesboro, "Christina was the first friend I made in Waynesboro, except of course for Cousin Anne. It was Mrs. Voorhees who proposed my name for membership in the Club." During the tea hour a great deal was said to Christina about her various and valuable contributions: her ever-ready willingness, when she was young, to sing and act for the members. Those old enough to have known Christina as a girl looked at her and wondered what had happened in the years between to have changed her so; younger members found it hard to believe that the intellectual, inflexibly moral, and serious-minded Mrs. Voorhees whom they knew had ever been young, let alone given to frivolous pursuits.

Anne and Sally Rausch had their own theories, confided only to each other, as to one motive for the Voorheeses' removal from the scene, in addition to the humiliation of having been passed over, both of them, in favor of Elsa Evans. Shortly after Tucker's return from France, Anne had tried to tell Christina that he had encountered Blair overseas. Christina had cut her off, saying, "That name has not been mentioned in our house for many years. I prefer not to hear it." The shocked Anne reported to Sally, "I can't believe there's a woman on earth who wouldn't be delighted to hear her long-lost son was alive and well. But to her he's dead and buried."

"She must know," Sally said, "that all Waynesboro knows that Tuck saw Blair in France. She has heard about it too often. I spoke to her, too, and got the same rebuff; so I suppose did other Club members. And who knows how many have spoken about him to Henry in the bank? Chauffeur to a general: she wouldn't like that. So now she or both of them want to go where no one has ever heard of Blair Voorhees."

Jennifer had been elected to Club membership when the young Gordons had returned to Waynesboro, Tucker ready to begin the practice of medicine. But Jennifer was absent almost as much as she was present—pregnant in 1922 with John Alexander, and with Belinda in 1924.

There had been an argument with her grandmother about the baby's name one summer morning when Jennifer had dropped in to see her mother. Elsa was out, and the baby's great-grandmother seized the opportunity to protest: she turned off the radio and gave Jennifer her full attention.

"Belinda is a name so old-fashioned as to be ridiculous: lace-paper valentines and croquet on the lawn. And besides, it's an unhappy name. Anne will feel sad every time she hears it."

"It's a pretty name. Old fashions come into style again, you know."

"I wish they would," Sally said, feeling contrary and critical. She had been listening to the radio report of the Democratic National Convention and was a little annoyed at the interruption. "Skirts to your knees, rolled stockings, belts around your thighs, bobbed hair, and those ridiculous tight hats—cloche?—that are like blinkers on a horse."

"At least they stay on, without our using hatpins like lethal weapons."

"When you first came home from Paris with your skirts half-way to your knees, I thought you would come to your senses. Instead of that, now all you young things are making yourselves hideous."

"It's the style. I suppose you never made yourself look ridiculous, wearing some outlandish fashion?" As that was unanswerable, Jennifer swept on: "As for Gran, she's pleased to have her little girl remembered: she's happy about it."

"Was there anything special you wanted to see your mother about?"

"Yes. I'd like to suggest Melissa Patton as a member of the Club. We're below the number the Constitution allows, and we need more young people."

"Melissa! That baby!" (Anne Gordon would have agreed with her "That baby!" Babies did grow up, but it was unbelievable that Melissa—!)

"She has finished library school, and accepted a position here as Miss McCune's assistant."

"And we have never even considered Ruhamah McCune as a member! Of course she has had little formal education, but she probably knows more—

However, I see no objection to Melissa. Mrs. Patton has been a valuable member. I'll tell your mother."

"O.K., Grandmother. And thank you. Don't be cross with me, please, just because I look freakish in 1924 clothes. Do go back to your Convention—I'm sorry I interrupted you."

Sally, when she had gone, turned her radio on again. For the first time in history a Democratic Presidential Nominating Convention was being broadcast, and all over the country good Republicans were laughing themselves sick as they listened to the opposition party tearing itself to pieces. As Sally heard for the umpteenth time the roll call of the states, and Alabama's stubborn vote for Oscar W. Underwood, she forgot Melissa Patton. The only shadow on her enjoyment of the program was the fact that Ludwig was not alive to share her pleasure.

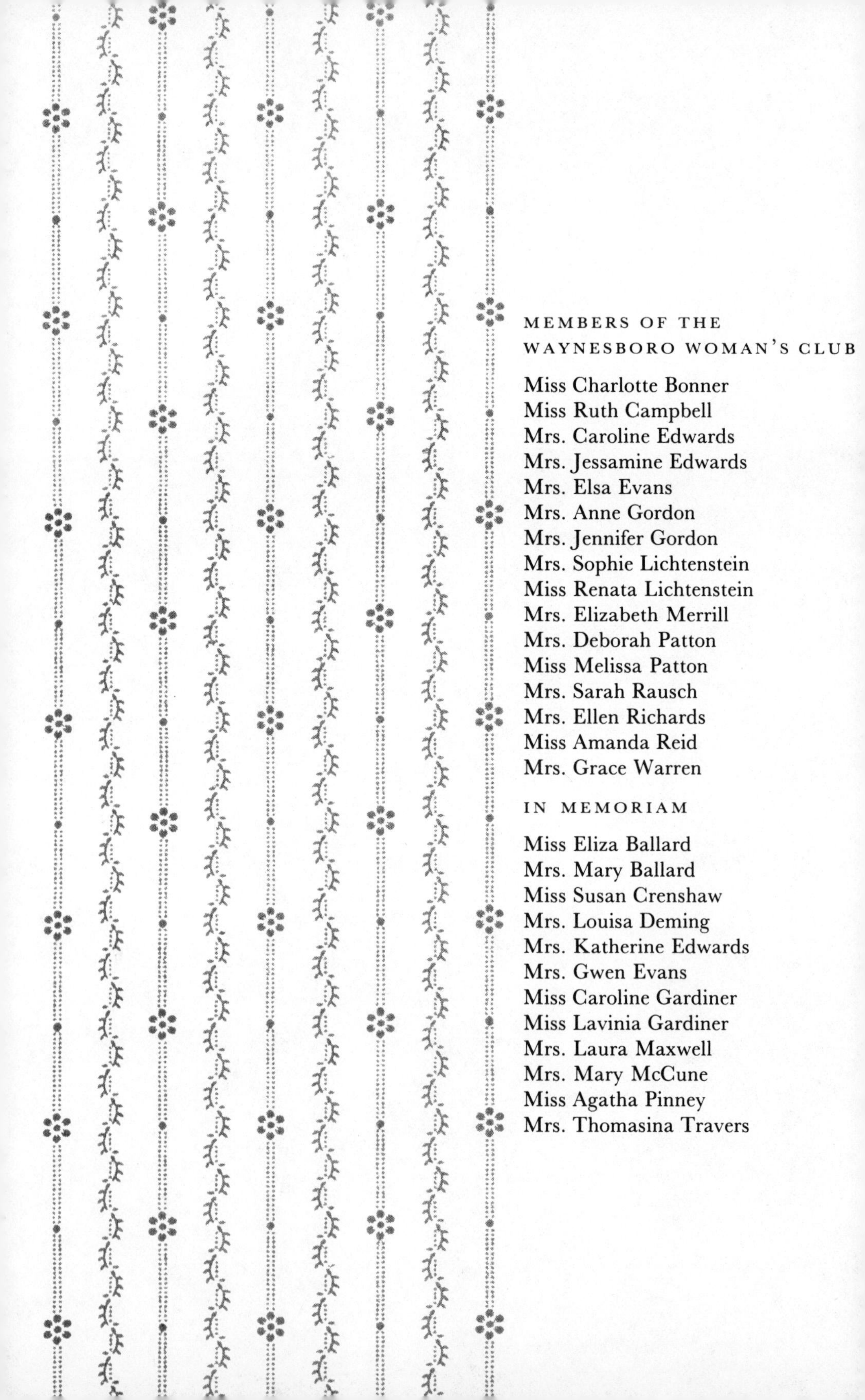

MEMBERS OF THE
WAYNESBORO WOMAN'S CLUB

Miss Charlotte Bonner
Miss Ruth Campbell
Mrs. Caroline Edwards
Mrs. Jessamine Edwards
Mrs. Elsa Evans
Mrs. Anne Gordon
Mrs. Jennifer Gordon
Mrs. Sophie Lichtenstein
Miss Renata Lichtenstein
Mrs. Elizabeth Merrill
Mrs. Deborah Patton
Miss Melissa Patton
Mrs. Sarah Rausch
Mrs. Ellen Richards
Miss Amanda Reid
Mrs. Grace Warren

IN MEMORIAM

Miss Eliza Ballard
Mrs. Mary Ballard
Miss Susan Crenshaw
Mrs. Louisa Deming
Mrs. Katherine Edwards
Mrs. Gwen Evans
Miss Caroline Gardiner
Miss Lavinia Gardiner
Mrs. Laura Maxwell
Mrs. Mary McCune
Miss Agatha Pinney
Mrs. Thomasina Travers

1925–1929

"The Club congratulates its new bride . . ."

Captain Bodien retired from the Rausch Cordage Company shortly after the completion of young Ludwig's new mill, professing himself baffled by the modern machinery. Ludwig was reluctant to let him go, less for the mill's sake than for that of the old man, fearing that when he had nothing to do he would go to pieces. But it was 1925 before he gave up, took to his bed, and stayed there. The doctor—"young" Dr. Gordon, whom the patient more often than not confused with his father or even his grandfather—could find nothing vitally wrong with him except hardening of the arteries. As Tucker said to Barbara,"He's just had enough. He's ready to quit. After all, he is ninety."

"Eighty-seven."

"Near enough. It will be tough on you, unless you can find a nurse. But not so tough as it would be if he were one of those old men who wander away, and have to be watched or hunted for. I suppose you do have someone to carry trays for you?"

"He doesn't eat much, although all he seems to think of—all he has to think of, I suppose—is his next meal. Don't worry, Tucker: I have two daughters here in town, and various granddaughters: we can manage." She stood for a moment looking across from the hall door to the dozing old man. "It's strange, isn't it? He still looks like himself, not like a dying man. He has the barber in every morning to shave him and keep his mustache in order."

"Still a soldier, and looks it." Tucker wondered whether she had not noticed how thin the old man was, just skin and bones. But he reminded himself Barbara might not have noticed his day-to-day decline.

"Should he have company? I wonder if Mary—"

"Why not, if the company is someone he wants to see? It might rouse him from this lethargy—keep him interested in staying alive."

Her mother wrote that night to Veronica, and to Mary Lichtenstein, the

Gardiner daughter who had once been so close to her grandfather. Barbara's note said, "You were always his favorite, and his memory has grown so bad he may have forgotten your unforgivable ideas."

Before her mother heard from Mary, she had cause to wonder whether she had been right: some prejudices had been so long-rooted in her father's mind that they had become a part of it, ineradicable. Answering the doorbell one afternoon, she found the Catholic priest on the front step. Not Father Halloran, who had known her father so long he would have had better judgment, but his young successor.

"I have come to see Captain Bodien," he explained when she had ushered him into the hall. "I consider him one of my congregation. I know he is a lapsed Catholic, but he is a Catholic. As they near the end, most old people want the consolation of their religion, however long they have turned their backs on the church."

"I know that happens occasionally. But my father—"

"I have had a note from your sister-in-law asking me to make this call. It would make her and your brother very happy if he would receive me. Will you ask him if he will? He may want to, even if he hasn't admitted it. You wouldn't deny him—?"

"No, I wouldn't deny him." Barbara knew her father better than did her sister-in-law. Damn Katherine, anyway! "Sit down, Father, and I'll run up and see what he says."

When she entered her father's bedroom, she closed the door firmly behind her. The brick partitions of the old house were so thick that only the faintest murmur of voices drifted down the staircase. What did reach the priest's ear was an unmistakable bellow of rage. Sighing, he picked up his hat and stood waiting, one hand on the newel post.

When Barbara reappeared and was halfway down the stair, she said,"You heard?" And when the priest nodded, she continued,"I apologize for him, Father. But he has not changed his mind about the church. I am sorry you had your long walk for nothing."

"Perhaps not for nothing. How about you? You were born into the church. Doesn't this unsanctified end trouble you?"

"No, it doesn't." (Damn and double-damn that sister-in-law of mine!)"I am sorry to seem brusque, but no. My father has led a good and useful life, and I am not in the least troubled about his end."

He said,"Some day, perhaps. At any rate, thank you for letting me try."

With a polite but cold exchange of "Good afternoon," the priest left. Barbara waited in the living room for Doug's return from the Court House. She met him at the door, lifted her face for his kiss, said,"Before you go upstairs—" and took him into the sitting room.

Doug saw that she was worried; she looked worn out; her black hair was getting gray streaks in it. He thought,"She has had a hellish married life: always old people on her hands." He said only,"What now, Barbie?"

"Papa has really been outrageous. The *Catholic* priest called this afternoon, hoping for a death-bed repentance—confession—absolution—all the rigamarole. The least I could do was go ask Papa. He not only wouldn't see him, he wanted his 'carbeen' beside him on the bed. He wasn't going to be pestered by priests the way Mamma was, forgetting that she had wanted Father Halloran close at hand. So I got his gun down, and he's going to keep it there beside him, in bed."

Doug thought it funny, this latest quirk of the old man; reluctantly Barbara joined him in laughing. Finally he said,"It's not loaded, I hope?"

"Give me credit for a little sense. I got him to agree, finally, that just pointing it would serve his purpose. I don't think he's strong enough to lift it, actually." She did not confess that what had annoyed ber most was her sister-in-law's interference.

When Doug went upstairs to spend a pre-dinner hour with his father-in-law, he opened the door to face the wavering barrel of a gun. He threw up his hands in the time-honored gesture."It's only me, Pop."

"Doug is it? Takes me a minute to be sure. It's all that white hair."

"He still sees me as a young man," Doug thought. Doug had been Judge for so many years that he had grown to look the part in spite of his limp; staid and dignified, sometimes stern and implacable. The white hair contributed to the picture. Aloud, he said,"I'm getting on in years, along with my contemporaries."

"You an' Barbie—you been married—lessee—you had four girls, didn't you?" And then, almost fiercely,"Where's Mary?"

Since that was the first time in ten years or so that he had mentioned Mary's name, Doug was astonished: the old man had dropped a long span of time out of his memory. The years he preferred to forget, no doubt. Mary's father said,"Mary is coming home soon, we had a letter from her this morning."

"Seems's if she ought to be about through college. Best of the lot, Mary. Got some spunk. The others were properly brought up young ladies."

His granddaughters Caroline and Lavinia were helping every day, one spending an hour or so with him while the other was taking Barbara out for a ride and on errands. Their grandfather's contemptous dismissal of them was unjust, although Doug doubted whether he recognized them most of the time.

The old man fingered the gun he had dropped on the bed.

"Did Barbara tell you why—?"

"Yes. You needn't worry. She won't let him in if he comes again."

"Never can tell with those fellows. They can creep through keyholes. I'll keep this handy. Not an artillery man's gun—artillery weapon was the saber, for hand-to-hand. I took this off a dead cavalryman. At Gettysburg?—I guess. Wonder whether I ever showed it to Tess."

"Undoubtedly," Doug thought. Theresa Stevens, Doug's oldest grandchild, had spent more time with Bodien than all the rest of them put together. Always had. Doug remembered the World War map on the wall, and

Theresa an entranced listener to the lectures and reminiscences. At twenty-three, through college and home again, for a while at least, she was giving her time to the old man in his stuffy bedroom, listening to stories she must know by heart, waiting when he drifted off to sleep, and when he wakened, giving him the cue that would start him off again. Doug could not understand why a young girl should spend her time so, but he was grateful, since it made Barbara and the Captain happy. What he did not know, nor did anyone else, was that Theresa went home from the Gardiners' and made notes of what she had heard. As a child she had determined she would write books when she grew up, and was not bashful about saying so. When she was in her teens, she had decided that her great-grandfather Bodien's life would make a good subject, but she had grown reticent about her writing, lest after all she couldn't do it; she would say nothing to anyone until the book was done. It did not bother her that Captain Bodien seldom knew her as Theresa, and called her indifferently Barbara, Lavinia, Caroline.

Doug felt close to his granddaughter Tess: he had a partiality for brains. Poor Theresa, like her Aunt Mary before her, had not been a pretty child and was not a pretty girl: mousy brown hair so fine it always looked windblown, thin cheeks, and a jaw slightly asymmetrical; but she had one redeeming feature: her Grandmother Barbara's beautiful violet-blue eyes. Doug had not gone unmindful of the fact that when she was little her father and her Grandmother Jessamine had found it hard to forgive her childish homeliness, especially when her pretty little sister Barbara had come along, and the two pretty daughters of her Aunt Caroline. Her father had got over it, when the grade cards she brought home from school proved her intelligence, but it was taken for granted by her family and friends that she would live and die an old maid: she was quiet, reserved, plain and intellectual.

In the minds of those who knew them, she was in the same category as Renata Lichtenstein, who had gone off to Yale as soon as her mother had recovered her equanimity once the war was over, or as Rebecca Merrill, who had finally had her two years at the Sorbonne and had achieved a French degree in addition to her American Ph.D., and who was now back at Oberlin as an assistant professor. She still spent most of her summers abroad, doing research and writing learned articles for scholarly journals. Although highly respected, she was judged to be a hopeless bluestocking, an old maid more interested in Charlemagne than in any living man. To Doug it seemed an honorable career—even an enviable one. Although he enjoyed having Tess around, it surprised him that she should be content to stay in Waynesboro, doing nothing but listening to a senile old man.

Veronica dutifully came home to see her grandfather, spent a weekend with her sister Caroline and her noisy brood of young Edwardses, and was off again, home to Cleveland. When she had gone, her grandfather complained to Barbara, "I can't keep people straight in my mind anymore. Who was that pretty highfalutin young lady that was just here? One of yours?"

"Yes. Veronica. Came specially to see you."

He closed his eyes, but he was pondering, not asleep. Finally he said, "I know. She married that stuffed shirt from Cleveland. She happy?"

"As far as I know. She has what she asked out of life."

"All anybody can expect, I guess."

When Mary arrived shortly afterward, to stay at home for "a good visit," there was no doubt in her grandfather's mind as to her indentity. She looked and dressed like the social worker she was: her heavy sandy hair combed back and wound into a coil on the back of her head, and her plain dark dress at least six inches longer than anyone else was wearing that year. But when she came to his bedside and roused him by demanding "What's the gun for?" he knew her at once.

"For the first priest comes stickin' his nose in here."

It was so obvious that he could not lift the heavy carbine that, even as Mary laughed, she grieved for him: it was all gone, the strength he had once had. "Never mind, Gramp. I'll keep 'em out."

"Been a long time, Mary, Still in college, are you?"

So the intervening years had been wiped out. Better so. She said, "I was always slow."

"Should say so. That girl of Lavinia's—Tess, they call her—she's already graduated. Sits with me some days. Humors me, listening to the story of my life. Isn't sick of it, like all the rest of you."

"I was never tired of listening." Mary thought, "Eight years or so in the Army, and after that, all the rest of his adult life spent making rope, and it is still the Army years that mean most to him." She wondered rather bitterly whether that was true of all old soldiers: they lived briefly on the razor's edge and nothing else in life afterward seemed so worth remembering. Was it futile to work hard for peace, as hard as she and Franz had? She felt again the despair she had felt when the Senate had refused to let the United States join the League of Nations. But she would say nothing to remind her grandfather of her pacifist activities. Instead she stayed a moment chatting about the family, then rose to go.

Captain Bodien opened his eyes, said "I'll see you again?"

"I'm staying a week."

"Good. But no more monkey business trying to start a union at the mill, hear me?"

"No more monkey business at the mill, I promise you."

Later she said to her father, "I suppose the Cordage Company still isn't unionized?"

"No. Casual labor like that, what would they need a union for? Their hours have been shortened since Rausch Senior died; they are paid a fair wage."

"The time will come."

"Oh, I suppose so," he said agreeably. "But Ludwig Evans would be a hard man to fight. Like his grandfather, he knows every laborer in the mill as a person, not just as a hand. Very competent fellow, Ludwig Evans."

"And young enough to keep up with the times."

"Oh, very innovative, I believe. A new mill building, the latest in machinery, run by electricity, instead of steam power."

"Innovative in every respect except dealing with his labor force. I suppose the company is doing well?"

"Nothing to worry about."

"I remember Ludwig Evans when he was a little boy. He always seemed gentle, amenable."

"Exactly like his grandfather, is my guess. Amenable enough over unimportant things, but when he puts his foot down, it's down."

"Heaven help his wife. I suppose he's married?"

"No."

"Odd. No one to carry on the dynasty."

"He can't be much over thirty. Plenty of time."

Though no one realized it, not he himself, much less his family, Ludwig was even then falling headfirst in love—not even knowing the girl. He knew her name, Melissa Patton, only because he had asked his family about the "new girl" in the library.

He had gone there one evening to look for some technical material and had found a young girl behind the desk instead of Miss McCune. She looked so young that at first he hesitated to ask for what he wanted; how could anyone who looked like that—oval face, intensely blue eyes, short hair, not quite red, more golden—know anything about technology?

Her hair curled in tendrils about her forehead left her neck bare, giving it a look of vulnerability. That slender neck reminded him of someone—someone he had sat behind somewhere, but he couldn't remember where. Her wrists looked too fragile to be handling all those heavy books, he thought. And then it came to him. He had been with Jennifer at the Fiftieth Anniversary dinner and program of the Woman's Club. It had been at his grandmother's, and after dinner they had sat in rows of straight-backed chairs to listen while the ladies gave the program. The girl had been sitting in the row in front of them, and he had noticed how vulnerable that young neck looked. It was the year he got home from the war—1918, he reminded himself. When the program reached its end, they had left, and he had never thought of that childish figure again.

But now there was no doubt about it. He knew this was the girl he wanted to marry. When he asked his family about her, he was told that she was Melissa Patton and that she was now Ruhamah's assistant. She had gone off to a college that prepared young women for various professions, had graduated with a degree in library science, and had then returned to work in the library she was so familiar with. Without his asking they told him that the Patton family lived in half of the old Ballard house, where Sam Travers had lived for so many years.

Head over heels in love or not, Ludwig's courtship was a very formal and conventional one. While Waynesboro watched, he spent as much time as he could with her: her evenings off, as frequently as he thought decent, he called at the Pattons, where the two of them spent the time like two decorous Victorians in the parlor that had once been the Ballards'.

After a while, thinking that such evenings must be very dull for her, he invited Jenny to have them to dinner and for the evening.

But before this could be arranged, there came an evening when Tuck called to ask him to go around to the Gardiners. "The old man is asking for you," he told him, "will you come?"

"Of course. He may not know me when I get there. He didn't the last time."

"I think he will. One of those last-minute lucid intervals."

Ludwig covered the back street blocks at a good pace. As he stood by the bed, there was no doubt that Captain Bodien knew him. He said, "Young Ludwig, you've taken over at the mill."

Ludwig looked down with real grief at the gray-faced, sunken-eyed, little old man, still with his artilleryman's mustache. "Yes. I'm not exactly filling Grandpa's shoes, but—yes."

"The—company—doing all right?"

"Yes. Of course things don't run as smoothly as when you were there, but business is better than it was right after the war."

"Depression?"

"No. Business is fair enough. But I've given up some rather grandiose notions about further expansion. Better a small plant that pays its way than a big one heavily in debt. Business boomed so during the war, and now the stock market is sky-high, out of all reason. There is bound to be a reaction."

"You don't remember the seventies, do you? Those were bad times. Your grandfather kept the hands working making oakum, bedrope, anything, even if it couldn't be sold."

"I've heard about those days."

"Hard times come again. Always do. Ninety-six. Nineteen and six. Do like Captain Rausch. Don't let—hands—starve."

Tucker, who had stood at the foot of the bed during the brief interview, shook his head at Ludwig. "That's enough."

Ludwig put his strong hand on the heavily veined one still lying on the butt of the gun. "I promise, Captain Bodien. As long as I am running the mill, I'll keep it coming. Our workers will have their jobs."

On the way out, as he passed the living room door, he paused to speak to the Gardiners and to Stewart Bodien and his wife. Doug and Barbara rose to see him to the front vestibule.

"How did he seem to you?"

"Weak. But his mind was perfectly clear. Didn't call me 'Cap'n Rausch' once."

"I'm glad. He wanders so. But he's had the mill on his mind. Thank you for coming. Tucker thinks it won't be long now. Stewart and I—Kathleen—are just waiting. We wouldn't let the girls come, or the children. I don't believe in these deathbed scenes, with the whole family around the bed. So Irish Catholic—and Papa would have hated it."

"I'm glad you let me come. I may have deprived you of the last clear moments. Thank you, Mrs. Gardiner."

When he had closed the front door behind him, he thought, "She's so exhausted she babbles. But she is right: deathbed scenes are a relic of Victorian barbarism."

But Captain Bodien had his deathbed scene, even though a limited one. When Ludwig had gone, Tucker took the gun from under an unrestraining hand, stood it in the corner, and called down to Barbara. "Mrs. Gardiner, you'd better come."

Barbara led the way upstairs, actually hoping her father was not conscious: the clicking of Kathleen's rosary would have annoyed him so. Hoping still for repentance and salvation? She had been forbidden in no uncertain terms to call the priest. Barbara need not have worried. Her father's eyes were open, but blank. He murmured, "Cap'n Rausch? Here—a minute ago."

"He's gone, Papa." No use trying to explain.

"Did I ever tell him—can't remember—Antietam? General Gibbon serving a gun himself? Middle of the road—gunners all shot down? Watch—cornfield—Rebs coming back through—smoke—" His voice died away. His finger picked at the quilt; his right hand crept out to where the gun had lain. He slipped into unconsciousness without realizing its absence.

Tucker said, "It won't be long now. Stay if you like, but it won't mean anything to him. Antietam! How often, when Lud and I were boys—"

Stewart said gruffly, "How queer it is! I guess they all go back to their war at the end, however long ago."

"Not so queer," Tucker replied. "You're never as alive as when you are aware that in a minute you may not be. It stays vivid in the memory. I know."

He fell silent then, listening for the scarcely discernible breath until it stopped. He took the old man's fragile wrist, felt for a pulse, and after a moment drew the sheet up over Captain Bodien's face. "The death of an old soldier," he said.

Not long after the funeral, Theresa Stevens went to Tucker for the details of her great-grandfather's dying moments. She waited in his outer office one afternoon until it was cleared of patients and, when he came to the door, asked if he had time to talk to her. She wasn't there because of "anything the matter."

He grinned at her. "I must say you look in the pink. Sure, come inside."

He led her to the middle office that had been the scene of so much of his father's and grandfather's lives, and motioned her into one of the low slant-backed leather chairs. Instead of relaxing in it, Theresa sat on the edge, reluctant to speak, after all.

"Now, what can I do for you?"

"Tell me," she said abruptly, "about Grandpa Bodien's death. Mother wasn't there, and I can't ask Grandmother Gardiner: it would be cruel."

"Aren't you being a little morbid?" He studied her curiously. Not a beauty, certainly, except for the dark-lashed violet eyes. In spite of her being Rodney's child, a cousin in some remote degree, he did not know her well. Having been away from Waynesboro for so many years, he had missed seeing her grow up.

"No. I just want to know how he died, what he was thinking of."

"You couldn't call it 'thinking.' His mind was wandering."

"Please, I want to know. 'Wandering' where? I didn't want to be there watching him die. I was much too fond of him. But I want to know what he said." And though her eyes were damp and her lower lip trembled, she fumbled in her handbag not for a handkerchief but for a notebook and pencil.

Tucker thought, "What an odd girl! Does she want to record his deathbed ramblings for posterity?" Theresa had never been very forthcoming, but what little he had seen of her during the past few years, she had seemed to be perfectly normal.

During his long silence Theresa made up her mind. She did not want him to think her queer, and Cousin Tuck would be easy to confide in, even the secret she had kept from everyone else.

"I'll tell you why I want it, if you will promise not to laugh or think I'm silly—or being presumptuous to believe I can do it. Or tell anyone else."

He smiled at her. Tucker had a heartwarming smile. "I promise. You wouldn't believe how practiced doctors are in keeping secrets."

"I'm writing a book about Gran'pa Bodien, and I need to know."

"Of course. I see." Tucker was relieved. "A biography?"

"Well, only sort of. Mostly what he remembered and talked about. To generations of children."

"I see," Tucker said again. "You'd better call it 'Pied Piper.' I was one of those children, you know. Ludwig Evans and I and sometimes Jennifer used to go down to the mill when we were small, just to walk home with him and listen."

"That's a picture I didn't have: even your generation, then. Thank you. But you won't tell anyone, will you? No one knows. Oh, of course Mother and Dad know I'm trying to write something: I spend all my days in my room scribbling, and they heard me say often when I was little that I was going to write books when I grew up. But they don't know *what.* I couldn't bear having them tell me what to say, and perpetually asking how I'm getting on. And I would feel pretty silly going around Waynesboro saying, 'I'm writing a book.' It would sound so conceited—and I may not be able to do it anyway."

"That I can understand, too." Tucker knew that she could not be more than nine or ten years younger than he, but seeing her there, leaning back in the old chair, her light-brown hair ruffled and windblown, her face lighted and eager, she hardly seemed to him "grown up." "Cross-my-heart-and-hope-to-die: I won't tell a soul. Now take your notebook, and I'll tell you his last words. It wasn't a tragic death, you know—it was sad only in that a long full life does have to come to an end."

In a few moments he had dictated the Captain's last words as he remembered them. When she had taken it all down, he said, "You were right, you see: he was the old soldier to the end. Your grandparents were there, and your Uncle Stewart and his wife, rattling her beads and praying, but he never saw or heard any of them."

"That must have been hard for Grandmother."

"I don't think it was. He would have been so angry at Mrs. Bodien, telling her beads. I think your grandmother was relieved when it was all over. Well, good luck, Theresa. And if there's anything else I can tell you, let me know."

Tucker kept his word: he did not even report Theresa's call to Jennifer. He did tell Ludwig the next time he saw him that after he had left Captain Bodien's bedside that last evening, the old man thought he had been talking to Captain Rausch. "You do look something alike, you know. In fact, you're very like him."

"Not half the man, and never will be. I don't have his drive."

Tucker thought Ludwig very abstracted, indifferent to casual conversational exchanges, and wondered whether the affairs of Rausch Cordage Company could be going badly. When he said something of the sort of Jenny, she laughed at him.

"He's head over heels in love with Melissa Patton. I told you before."

After the first dinner and evening at the Gordons', calls at the Pattons' were interspersed with visits to Jenny and sometimes Tuck; sometimes an evening spent in the company of Fritz and Renata Lichtenstein and various others. Then Ludwig branched out: he took her for one whole day and the evening to Cincinnati, where they wandered through the zoo and the art museum and dined at the Gibson House. He refrained from showing her through Rausch Cordage Company, lest that be too obvious. They did go down to Madison City more than once, to dine at a restaurant or with his Uncle Paul and his family. All this in the mid-twenties, when other young people were hunting out speak-easies and roadhouses where they could eat, drink, and dance. When her parents saw that the affair was becoming serious, and reminded her that the Rausch family was a very worldly one, she could say quite truthfully that Ludwig had never taken her anywhere her father would not have gone.

"Except that I couldn't afford it," the Reverend Mr. Patton reminded her. "Melissa, you would feel like a fish out of water if you married into that family."

"I don't see why. I've known Jennifer as long as I can remember. I know his mother and his grandmother in the Club—so does Mother. Besides, who's talking about marrying? He hasn't even asked me." And she left the room abruptly.

Not long after that he did ask her. On a beautiful evening in early spring, when budding leaves in the trees made them faintly green in contrast to the emerald of growing wheat, he took her for a drive in the country. He stopped the car on a hilltop whence they could see light dying in the west, the dusk coming on, the stars coming out. He turned to her and dared to do what he had so long so wanted to do: put out his hand and brushed the fine curls back from her forehead.

"Melissa. Oh, Lissa! Do you know me well enough now to know whether you can think of marrying me?"

She was laughing at him a little, but her eyes were tender; gently, then, he took her in his arms and, when she lifted her face, kissed her. And once was not enough.

"You mean you will? Oh, Lissa, I love you so much."

She nodded her head against his shoulder. "Yes. I will. I love you, too. And come Hell or high water, I intend to marry you."

He laughed at her choice of oaths, but put his arms around her again; their second embrace had nothing of the tentativeness of the first. They were two young people passionately in love.

When they finally pulled apart, Ludwig said, "What did you mean, 'Hell or high water'? Will your family object?"

"Not really. It's just that they'll think I am venturing into another world—one I may not feel at home in. As if I wouldn't wherever you were. But how about your family? If I weren't welcome—I admire your grandmother, when we have Club meetings at her house—like an empress in her big chair. But I'd be afraid of her, too, if she disapproved. Even if she isn't President any more, everyone does what she wants and plans."

"If you mean she's an old tyrant, I guess she is. Always has been, I suppose, but it's grown on her since Grandpa died. Or it's old age. Haven't you noticed how faults are exaggerated in old age? Maybe the controls slip that conceal how difficult people really are, underneath. But people do love Grandmother, you know: it isn't hard."

"I have never known any old people really well."

"You will—believe me, my darling, you will."

"Ludwig, wait. How about your mother and father? I couldn't bear it if they—"

"They've been hounding me for years to get married—afraid I was getting too old, I guess: turning into a real bachelor." ("The most eligible bachelor in Waynesboro," Melissa told him.) He went on, "Haven't you felt that I'm old and dull? If I were more lively, more of a kicker-up-of-heels, I could understand better why you—you do love me?"

"Indeed I do, Ludwig," she assured him. And I don't want a 'kicker-up-of-heels.' How foolish can you be? That my parents really would object to. But I can't marry you right away. I must keep my job until my brother is through school. My parents spent everything they could scrape together on my education, so I must help with my brother. I owe them that. He has another year in college, and then the Seminary."

"But I'm getting older every day! Of course we must get married now. The money for your brother can be managed. A loan, if you like."

"No. That would be all wrong. To marry you, and then at once take money from you."

"I can see," he said slowly. "Pride. I respect that my darling. But couldn't you, if you wanted to, keep on working after we were married?" (And be-damned to what his grandmother would think!)

"You wouldn't mind?"

"Darling, I'd like it better if you'd just let me lend you the money, but I'd far rather be married to a working woman than not be married at all, if you're the working woman."

They embraced again, laughing, then she withdrew to say, "Of course I'll have to find out whether the Library Board will hire a married woman."

"Who's on the Board?"

"Mr. Merrill. Mr. Rudy Lichtenstein. Miss Reid. The senior Mrs. Gordon, Miss Bonner."

Ludwig laughed again. "Unless it's old Mandy Reid—Lord, she was ossified when she taught me Latin—I'm sure all the rest of them are fair-minded believers in marriage: no one in town is more completely a married man than Mr. Rudy Lichtenstein, unless it's Merrill. Surely you can be certain of the other women. So if you're sure that's what you want, it's all settled. We'd better go before your father's off to bed, so that I can ask him for your hand, like a proper gentleman."

"Oh, Ludwig!" Melissa's quick laughter rang out. "You are a proper young man! After all, I'm a responsible adult, earning a salary. I can even vote. We'll just go in and tell them we're going to be married. When?"

"As soon as we can get the license."

"Ridiculous! We have to have time to get ready. In June."

"All right. June. Maybe I can manage to get away from the mill for a few weeks. Are you interested in rope? Making it, I mean?"

"I never was until you started coming to the library for all that technical material. But since you are, I'll learn to be."

"There's something romantic about it to me—all the different uses and the different places we ship it to. Lucky I feel that way, since it's the way I earn my living and all the family's, in a way. It was my whole life until the first time I saw you. I'll take you through the mill some day soon."

They embraced again, slowly, and drew apart reluctantly. Ludwig started the car.

There remained the, to him, formidable ordeal of telling the families concerned. What astonished him was that no one seemed surprised. Not the Reverend Mr. Patton, who gave them his blessing and was not so ministerial as Ludwig had feared. Not Mrs. Patton, who was candidly delighted. Not Jennifer, who called her brother an old slow-poker who might have died for want of the courage to propose.

"I know. But you and Tucker have known each other all your lives. Lissa and I haven't. I wanted her to be sure."

"And you too?"

"I've always been sure. But you can't ask a girl to marry you the first time you see her."

"That isn't the way you talked at first, after your first encounter. You were being very cautious."

Tucker, beside her on the davenport, pinched her so hard she yelped. "Don't tease him, Sweetie. He didn't tease you, as I remember. We're truly glad for you, Lud, and are sure you'll be happy. She's a thoroughly nice, charming girl. Bring her around soon, so that we can say the same to her."

"Tomorrow night," Jenny suggested. "A celebration dinner. I'll go call her this minute. Tuck doesn't have office hours Saturday evenings."

"O.K. Just so you don't call Mother. I haven't got round to telling them, and it's too late tonight."

Since the mill closed at noon on Saturday, he was free to go up to the Rausch house the next afternoon. He found the three members of his family sitting as usual in the library. Elsa and Gib were no more surprised than Jenny had been: they congratulated him and wished him happiness. And his grandmother, on whom he had kept a wary eye, said only, "An announcement all Waynesboro has been waiting for, I believe. Of course I wish you happiness."

It was not until the next morning when she was alone with Elsa that Ludwig's grandmother voiced her opinion.

"I suppose you are not putting obstacles in the way of Ludwig's marriage?"

"Why should we? She's a nice girl, and he's in love with her."

"And she with him? Or with his money and his position in this town?"

"Ludwig hasn't all that much money of his own. He puts most of what he earns in dividends back into the business as capital reserve and only keeps his salary. And as for position, who had a higher position in this town than the Presbyterian minister?"

"A minister who married his cousin. No, never mind—don't protest. I realize that has been forgotten, since the children grew up to be normal. But you know very well what I mean. Once Ludwig is married, he should assume his grandfather's position. Not only in the mill, but as a public man. And what would that child know about entertaining distinguished guests? The menus, the wines, the service—for men in government and their wives—a little church mouse like Melissa Patton?"

"Ludwig is grown up. He knows what kind of life he wants. In some ways he is like Papa, but he hasn't the slightest interest in politics. And where are there any 'men of distinction' in government these days? Conditions have changed, believe me."

"Mr. Cooper is a gentleman. He just might beat that Vic Donahey for

Governor in the fall. However, as you say, Ludwig doesn't seem to care for politics. And I realize that Ohio is not so important in the scheme of things as it used to be." She brushed off the subject and entered upon another. "The Pattons are poor, I am sure. I suppose it will be up to you and me to have an announcement party. Maybe Mrs. Patton doesn't know the bride's parents should do it."

"Mamma, really! You speak of Melissa's family as if they were poor whites. Mrs. Patton has been a member of the Club for years: have you ever found her ignorant of the conventions? The amenities? Of course they will announce it."

And they did, in the *Torchlight*, without any party: "The Reverend Mr. Andrew and Mrs. Patton announce the engagement of their daughter Melissa to Mr. Ludwig Evans, son of Mr. and Mrs. Gilbert Evans of this city. The marriage will take place in June."

After the announcement there was the usual rush of entertaining. Tucker had protested when his grandmother first proposed a Sunday after-church dinner, with all relatives on both sides to be invited. He did not remind Anne that she was an old lady, but after all, she was approaching her seventy-sixth birthday in that spring of 1926.

"That will make thirteen in all."

"Not at the table," she said quickly. "I'll put the little ones at a table of their own. Your nursemaid will come, won't she, and oversee them?"

He laughed at her. "You know I'm not superstitious. It's just that it might be too many for you, that's all. Louline isn't as young as she used to be, either. And I suppose, beforehand, you'll insist on having all the best china washed and the silver polished."

"It will seem funny," Anne said, "to have a party without Sally Rausch. I'll ask her, of course, but she seldom makes the effort to go out these days."

"You mustn't belittle her difficulties, Gran. She doesn't like to admit to her aches and pains, but no one can be as crippled with arthritis as she is and not suffer."

"That's just like her: she'd rather we all thought her fat and lazy than admit to any physical difficulty. She loves Club meetings when we go there because she can be present."

"And fortifies herself for the meetings with a double dose of pain pills."

"Oh, dear! I had never realized that. I am sorry."

"Not a word, then. If she hasn't told even you, she doesn't want you to know."

"It's sad, Tuck—age does contract your life into smaller and smaller circles. Once Sally and I were in and out of each other's houses practically every day, and now sometimes weeks go by. Anyway, as for my having a family dinner party—I'm not feeble yet, and Louline can get one of her nieces to come help cook and wait on the table."

Anne had her dinner party exactly as she wanted it, with help not only from Louline and her niece but from Jenny, who came in to wash the good china, and did, in spite of a jealous Louline, who kept muttering, "She think Ah cain't tak ca' mah Miz Gordon jes' lak Ah done all these yea's. Who she, takin' ovah in mah kitchen?"

It was at that dinner party, when plans for the wedding were under discussion, that the subject of the choice of churches came up.

"Sometimes I think," Melissa said, "and I know Ludwig feels the same way, that it would be better to be married at home, with just the family."

"It's Mamma," Elsa explained to Anne. "She was married in the Baptist church, so was I, so was Jenny. So why not Ludwig? That Melissa's father happens to be the Presbyterian minister makes no difference. But she can't always have her way. Melissa wants her father to marry her, and where but in his own church?"

"For some reason," Anne said slowly, "many more young husbands these days transfer to their wives' churches than the other way around. It didn't used to be so. It was considered right and proper for a wife to go to her husband's church. But I suppose now a woman takes her church more seriously than a man. Not only its doctrine, but all the associations. Like Tuck turning Baptist."

Jenny laughed. "He hasn't exactly 'turned Baptist.' He goes to church with me if he hasn't the excuse of a patient he just must see. But he won't join because he would have to be baptized again, and he says he would feel a fool being immersed in that tank in the basement. But the Presbyterians have lost him, if they ever had him. He's a heathen, really. And now they'll get Ludwig, so they'll be even."

Anne thought, "They're all heathen, these young people," a little shocked at Jenny's flippancy. Then she caught herself: after all, John had been an unbeliever, and so had Johnny, in spite of the years of Sunday school and of learning the Westminster Catechism. And as for herself, church-going was a habit, but how much did she actually believe, so far as doctrine was concerned? Only the bred-in-the-bone bits, like foreordination, and the church organization bits like "No bishops." As for all the rest, she let it go, and read her Bible before she turned her light out at night because she loved and found what she needed in the beauty of its poetry.

Ludwig and Melissa were married on a sunny June afternoon in the Presbyterian church. Since Ludwig's grandmother had given in with good grace on that question, they let her have her way as to the size and grandeur of the wedding; everyone they knew in Waynesboro, including, on Ludwig's insistence, the officers, superintendents, and foremen of the mill, assembled in the flower-bedecked church for a ceremony that lasted a few minutes. "There were some very odd people at the wedding," Sally said to Elsa afterward. "I'm not sure I would have wanted to receive some of them in my home."

"I'm quite sure you wouldn't. Those were Ludwig's friends from the mill. Don't blame the Pattons for them."

Ludwig and Melissa went off on their honeymoom, and Waynesboro settled down to its usual lethargic summer.

For another year young Mrs. Ludwig Evans continued to work in the library; then her brother was through college, and would go to the Seminary on a scholarship. Melissa resigned from her position; and, as she told Ludwig, they could start now having babies. The first, a boy, was born early in 1928, and the second, a girl, in the late summer of 1929. The boy they named David; Ludwig put his foot down when his womenfolk suggested "Ludwig Junior." "It's too confusing, two of the same name, and besides I've always hated it." The little girl they called "Deborah." "I hope you won't mind," Melissa had said, before the baby was born. "It's old-fashioned, but it's my mother's name."

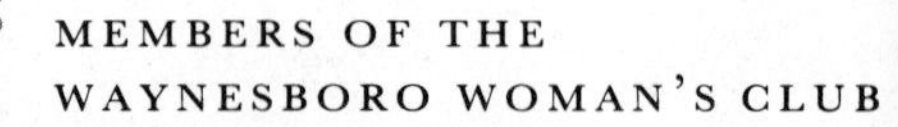

MEMBERS OF THE
WAYNESBORO WOMAN'S CLUB

Miss Charlotte Bonner
Miss Ruth Campbell
Mrs. Caroline Edwards
Mrs. Jessamine Edwards
Mrs. Elsa Evans
Mrs. Melissa Evans
Mrs. Anne Gordon
Mrs. Jennifer Gordon
Mrs. Sophie Lichtenstein
Mrs. Elizabeth Merrill
Mrs. Deborah Patton
Mrs. Sarah Rausch
Mrs. Ellen Richards
Mrs. Lavinia Stevens
Miss Theresa Stevens
Mrs. Grace Warren

IN MEMORIAM

Miss Eliza Ballard
Mrs. Mary Ballard
Miss Susan Crenshaw
Mrs. Louisa Deming
Mrs. Katherine Edwards
Mrs. Gwen Evans
Miss Caroline Gardiner
Miss Lavinia Gardiner
Mrs. Laura Maxwell
Mrs. Mary McCune
Miss Agatha Pinney
Miss Amanda Reid
Mrs. Thomasina Travers

✻ 1929 ✻

"We grieve over the loss of another charter member, but rejoice with our youngest on the publication of her first book . . ."

By 1929 Elsa had become in actuality what she had been in name for several years: President of the Waynesboro Woman's Club. Her mother, like a smiling Buddha, was always in her wing chair when the Club met at her house, as it generally did, since it was so very difficult for her to get out. Elsa thought, "This is wrong": after all, as she told her mother, the Club Constitution said, "Meetings to be held fortnightly at the homes of members." It must seem as though she and her mother had taken over the Club. She went back to an earlier custom: at the conclusion of each meeting, she asked if any member would like to invite the Club for the next meeting; it was only when no one volunteered that she said "You know that the President Emeritus and I are always glad to entertain the ladies."

Elsa took upon herself the responsibility of seeing that every member was transported to meetings. Some were getting too old to walk, and with traffic growing heavier all the time, the street crossings were not as safe as they once had been.

Their insistence that they could do so still was perhaps a reassurance to themselves; what they could do at forty, they could still do at seventy.

Anne Gordon and Amanda Reid laughed. They had walked all their lives and still did their errands on foot. Nevertheless, they gave in and agreed to be transported.

Amanda was increasingly showing her age. She was past eighty and looked it: her stockings were often wrinkled around the tops of her high-laced shoes: her skirts were long and hung crookedly, her white hair was too thin to hold a hat straight; her face was paper-white and network wrinkled. But happily she had kept her wits; she was never muzzy or bewildered.

The younger members of the Club accepted Amanda as an eccentric, but a painfully intelligent one. They would not have thought of worrying about anyone who was always completely assured. Older members, who knew something of her circumstances, did worry—once a fortnight, at least. What did she live on? She had inherited a little from her mother, but that must have gone long ago; she had retired before teachers were pensioned; she had certainly not bought any new clothes for years (how long had it been since high-laced shoes had disappeared from shop windows?). Her friends could only suppose that she was managing still on her life's savings; her name was never on the delinquent tax list. They hoped she could buy proper food. Occasionally one of them, when the man of the house was to be away (for no one could inflict Amanda on a husband), would invite her to dinner. Otherwise, she managed, but Caroline Edwards' story about her boy Rob and the grass-cutting, funny as it was, indicated the narrow margin she lived on.

The Lowrey Edwardses were feeling the economic pinch in the late twenties—the first in Waynesboro to do so—all because of better roads and more numerous automobiles. Sheldon & Edwards, Drygoods, had fallen upon hard times: no one sewed at home much; dressmakers had gone out of business, and yard goods were not very saleable; as for ready-made clothes, it had become too easy to get to the city for more sophisticated garments than Sheldon & Edwards could afford to carry. For small things—notions, hosiery, ribbons, and gloves—Waynesboro still went to the local store, but the profits shared by Lowrey and his father were not large. Sheldon hopefully assumed that things would get better sometime; Lowrey knew that the day had passed for a store like theirs; expensive elegance was very nearly a thing of the past. But he felt helpless; he was too sorry for what his father would feel even to suggest selling out for what they could get. The store, still as beautifully kept as it had always been, remained a fixture in Waynesboro; but Lowrey, supporting his big family on his salary as manager, had little left for the education of children. Katherine, the oldest, was through college, married, and gone to Cincinnati to live; the next, a boy, was in the State University on a football scholarship. That left the younger girls and Robert, the very youngest, who earned what he could toward his education by passing the paper and by yard work in summer and shoveling snow in winter. One of the trials of his summer was the mowing of Miss Reid's grass. She never had it cut until the grass was long and full of weeds and she feared her neighbors would complain. When the time was reached, she would summon Robert by means of a neighbor's phone and he would walk out Linden Street, armed with a sickle as well as a lawn mower, for he knew he would have to cut her grass twice: once with the sickle, and after that with the lawn mower; then he had to rake it with Amanda's rake. When he had finished, and went to the back door to say so, Miss Reid would drop a fifty-cent piece in his hand, invariably saying, "It looks a little ragged, but I guess you have earned your money." Once home again, sickle in hand, lawn mower dragging behind him, he would grumble to his mother, and kindhearted Caroline would remonstrate: "Just remember, Rob: She's old and alone and poor, as any of us may be some day." And Rob would be ashamed. But Caroline, kindhearted though she might be, thought it funny, and entertained her sister and various friends with the story, so that Amanda's fifty-cent lawn-mowing amused much of Waynesboro.

Fortunately, Amanda was not self-conscious about her clothes (more decent than most, she probably thought); at any rate she never missed a meeting, even before Elsa arranged a "transportation scheme" for the ladies and asked Melissa to bring her mother and Anne and Amanda. Ludwig and Melissa, with their two babies, were living in the house on Linden Street where Sally and Ludwig Senior had begun their married life. It would be no great task for her to call for the three ladies.

Usually on Club days Amanda was ready, watching, through the glass in her front door for Melissa. But one bitter February afternoon, she was not visible when Melissa stopped at the front gate.

Assuming that she wasn't ready, Melissa rang her bell. Amanda's door had an old-fashioned twirl-around doorbell, thumbpiece on the outside and the bell on the inside. Melissa twirled and twirled, but the bell was not answered. She finally gave it up, and returned to her car looking both perplexed and somewhat troubled.

"Either Amanda isn't there or she is sick," she said to Anne and her mother, whom she had picked up first. "Perhaps she had lunch with another of the ladies and went on with her to the meeting. She has no telephone so she wouldn't be able to let me know. We'd better go on. If she isn't there, we'll stop on our way home."

"This is one meeting neither Amanda nor I could have walked to," Anne said smiling. Even though they did go on, they were all somewhat troubled.

Amanda was not at the meeting, nor when the roll was called did anyone volunteer "Miss Reid asked me to express her regrets." At the close of the program, Anne said to Melissa, "You go on and take your mother home. I want to stop to speak to the children. Jenny won't mind driving me home, and we'll go by way of Miss Reid's. If we can't rouse her, we'll call Tucker. If she is sick and alone, it isn't a young person's problem." Jenny too, though older than Melissa, was still young, but she had been a trained nurse and must have had to deal with other difficult situations.

There was no more response to Jenny's attack on the Reid doorbell than there had been to Melissa's. Anne, who had been told to wait in the car, instead came to the porch where Jenny stood hesitating.

"You should have stayed in the car, Gran, out of the wind. But since you're here, keep on ringing the bell while I walk around the house to see if anything's open. Thank goodness there's no snow."

In a few minutes she was back, and reported no door unlocked, no window unshuttered. "Could she have gone away?" she wondered.

"I doubt it. We'll go to the nearest neighbor with a phone and call Tucker." Anne did not feel as unshaken as she managed to sound: there had been that awful time, long, long ago, when Miss Pinney—that death still represented to Anne the worst that could happen to the old and alone. But however trembly she felt, she managed to walk with Jenny past several vacant lots to the nearest neighbor's. There she let Jenny telephone her husband while she asked questions, and got little satisfaction: no, the Grovers hadn't seen Miss Reid go by that day. They weren't surprised: it had been so dreadfully cold. And no, they hadn't noticed whether there had been smoke from the kitchen chimney. The other taller chimneys never smoked, since Miss Reid used little portable coal-oil stoves to heat the house, one upstairs and one downstairs. However, Mrs. Grover had seen her the day before coming home from the library with an armload of books. So if she was sick, it couldn't have been for long.

Jenny came back from the phone. "Tuck is coming right away." They thanked the neighbor; it was not until they were outside that she added, "He is stopping to pick up a policeman, in case we have to break in."

The two women sat in Jenny's car, out of the wind, saying nothing, but each thinking that only death could make a house look so desolate. In a few minutes Tucker drove up, accompanied by a large youthful policeman whom neither of the women knew. He was not very sure of himself, or of what should be done: he wanted them to stay in their car while he and the doctor investigated. Tucker vetoed the suggestion: "If Miss Reid is ill in there, to have strange men break into the house would frighten her to death. Besides, my wife is a nurse, and my grandmother is Miss Reid's oldest friend.

The policeman walked around the house, and in his turn found no means of entry. He came back to say, "Reckon this is the best place to get inside. You're sure she hasn't just gone away for a visit?"

"We're sure," Anne said. "There's no one for her to visit out of town, and if she were in town, and able, she would have come to the Club meeting today."

The young officer broke the glass in the door with his billy, pulled out enough of the jagged points to get his hand inside, unlocked and opened the door. Anne called from the threshold, "Amanda?" but did not go on. Once the door was open, they had been assaulted by the powerful stench of coal oil. They entered on tiptoe, even after the crash of breaking glass. The hall was deathly cold—"like a sepulcher," Anne thought, shivering.

"You go first, Doctor. I don't want to frighten her."

If Tucker thought it was the policeman who was frightened, he did not say so. "Which way, Gran?"

"The sitting room is on the right—that door down there."

They all stood close behind Tucker as he opened the door. The coal oil smell washed over their heads. On the floor close to the big center table lay the stove, overturned—a smallish iron cylinder with an ornamental top, and a bail for carrying it. On the floor and across the stove lay Amanda, face down on its cold iron, her winter coat on, her hat still pinned to her scant hair but knocked grotesquely to one side. Under her and around her, the old worn carpet was soaked with kerosene.

Tucker went in quickly and knelt beside her to feel her pulse. In her hand he found a match. He held it up. "She's gone. Been dead about twenty-four hours at a guess. You can see what happened: she came in from outdoors and started to light her stove before she even took her wraps off. Upset the stove when she keeled over, before she could light the match, fortunately."

There were some sharply drawn breaths in the room. Tucker, feeling the carpet around her, said, "Yes, I'd say twenty-four hours. Officer, open the shutters, will you? Open the windows, too—clear the air in here."

"Twenty-four hours," Anne said slowly. "Right after the neighbors saw her." With the shutters open and more daylight in the room, she could see on the table a pile of library books. It was then that she began to shake uncontrollably: she backed against the door frame for support. "How fortunate this was Club day or she might have lain here—"

"Who was her doctor, Gran? I can't sign a death certificate."

"I doubt if she could afford one. She was never sick, anyway. But to make sure, I suppose you could look through her desk for bills."

"If she didn't have a regular physician, that means an autopsy."

"Oh, Tuck," Jenny protested, "you know she died from natural causes."

The policeman, looking everywhere except at Amanda's body, said, "Better get the old lady out of here. Looks like fainting. Bound to be a shock, finding a friend this way."

Tucker looked over his shoulder, saw his grandmother white as a sheet, got up and went to her. "Jenny, get her out of here into the parlor. Get her head down between her knees. When she can make it to the car, get her home to bed, treat her for shock."

Anne protested. "It's just the awful smell. And—autopsy. The thought—"

"The law is the law, Gran."

When the two women had gone, Tucker said, "Good thing my wife's nerves are strong. She can take care of my grandmother. Now, son, help me turn this poor old body over, so I can see."

The young officer obligingly helped, looking away from the aged gray waxen face. "The book," he said, "tells a corpus shouldn't be moved."

"Before the arrival of the police. You're the police, aren't you? That law is to prevent any concealment of unnatural death. There's no possibility of that in this case."

"Then, Doc, what d'you think it was?"

"Could have been a coronary, a heart attack. But it has all the marks of a massive cerebral hemorrhage. Now, suppose you get down to that neighbor's and phone one of the undertakers to come move the body to the hospital for an autopsy."

The policeman, now choosing to pretend that he had not been shaken, became suddenly talkative. "Damn' lucky she didn't get that match lit, or the place would have gone up like an election-night bonfire, and we'd a had a burnt-up corpus to deal with. Which undertaker?"

"Doesn't matter, I guess. She hasn't any family to ask. Oh, Pottingill, I suppose. He buries most of the R.P.'s. Then you come back and stay till he comes. You don't have to stay in here, but just don't let any curious neighbors in. I must go check on my grandmother."

Once in Jenny's car, Anne recovered her composure, outwardly at least. She still shivered: the cold, or the shock, had got to her bones. Jenny reached for the robe on the back seat and tucked it around her. Anne was surprised to see that Jenny was weeping: at least, tears were running down her cheeks.

"My dear child! A death like that is bound to be a shock. But don't grieve for Amanda—please don't mind so much. Think instead how fortunate she was to go between one breath and another, without having suffered. And she might have fallen with a lighted match in her hand."

Jenny shuddered. "It doesn't bear thinking of."

"She was spared that. And after all, she had had her full quota of years."

"I know. That isn't what makes me so—I'm sorry, Gran. I must get you home." But even as she started the car, she went on talking. "To die alone, like that, after all those many, many years, without ever having really lived. That seems so sad: year in and year out, and never anything. And now, this."

Anne looked at her, startled. How long ago—? How many years ago? She said, "You mustn't feel like that. What can we know about Amanda's life? What it meant to her? My husband taught me, when I was young like you and wept for what seemed to me to have been an empty life: there isn't any way we can really *know*—we can't get that close to one another. I suppose nine-tenths of one's life is lived inwardly. And I don't believe Amanda would have wanted to be anyone other than Amanda."

Jenny, as they drove up the Linden Street hill and approached a busier part of town, dabbed at her eyes and smiled at Anne. "I guess you're right. She had a sort of intellectual arrogance, hadn't she? She enjoyed knowing that her mind had a wider, deeper range than any of ours."

"That is very astute, Jenny. In a sense, she lived eighty-odd years without any experience. In another sense, she had experienced everything."

"But, Gran, you must admit that there are unhappy lives."

"Oh, yes. I only meant that we can't really know. Except for those people who have unhappy natures, or those whose religion demands that they think of life as a vale of tears, something to be endured in order to arrive at Heaven. But I have never known one of them to say with the Greeks 'Better never to have been born'."

"No," Jenny agreed absently, diverted to what she had sometimes thought before: the old—really old—whom she knew were better educated than those who had come afterward. Who would have expected Gran to come out with 'the Greeks'?

Jenny got Anne home, paused long enough for a word of explanation to Louline, then took her upstairs and, in spite of her protests, got her into bed with blankets and hot water bottles, saying only, "Doctor's orders. Tuck will be in soon: you can complain to him."

Anne was quite herself the next day, and attended Amanda's funeral a few days later. The service was held at the Reformed Presbyterian church, in the presence of members of the Woman's Club and of the congregation, and a handful of the hundreds of Waynesobro citizens whom she had taught.

The next meeting of the Club began with the planned program for that day, then continued with a memorial tribute to Amanda: charter member and faithful and valuable contributor to its programs for sixty years; it concluded with a vote to contribute memorial volumes to the library.

Elsa had asked Anne to write the formal eulogy, to be read and inserted in the minutes. When she rose, her hands were trembling so much that she fumbled with her reading glasses, trying to get them on; before she had read a page her eyes were wet, her voice shaking. Younger members, embarrassed for her, pretended not to notice (the old ladies always wept on such occasions), but Jenny Gordon stared in amazement, remembering what had been said on the afternoon they had found Amanda. But Anne's conclusion explained:

> "We can only rejoice in the swiftness of Amanda Reid's going, without suffering, between one breath and the next. We cannot grieve for her. But those of us who are old will understand when I say, 'We grieve for ourselves because we have lost her.' She was not only in herself all that I have said: she was a lifelong friend of some of us, and there comes a time when there are very few left who knew you as a girl, and the sudden breaking of such a tie is indeed a matter of sorrow. But those of us who grieve for the loss of one who had completed her span of years must endeavor to see it in its true perspective. And I quote from the philosopher Marcus Aurelius: 'What a small portion of vast and infinite eternity it is, that is allowed unto every one of us, and how soon it vanisheth into the general age of the world.'"

As Anne returned to her seat, Jenny, Melissa, and Theresa, in the back row and safe from observation, looked at each other with lifted eyebrows. Marcus Aurelius, indeed! And Miss Campbell was plainly restive: she could hardly wait for the President to open the meeting to other members who would like to add a few words. Miss Campbell was tolerant, but she was the sister of a Reformed Presbyterian minister, and there were limits.

"We all acknowledge," Miss Campbell began, after a quick nod in Elsa's direction and a muttered "Madame President and Ladies," "that Miss Reid was the most learned among us in the Greek and Roman classics. The quotation from Marcus Aurelius is therefore not inappropriate. But she was also a devoted Christian, no less familiar with the Bible than with the classics. I submit that even more appropriate would have been a quotation from the New Testament, the book on which she based her faith in eternal life; she would like us to remember her today with 'Let not your heart be troubled: ye believe in God, believe also in me. In my Father's house are many mansions; if it were not so I would have told you; I go to prepare a place for you.'"

Miss Campbell sat down. The silence was unbroken until Sally Rausch, in her wing chair by the hearth, commenced her struggle to rise. With cane in hand she managed it, waving away offers of assistance from those near her.

"Madame President and Ladies: Miss Campbell will I hope forgive those of us who are not members of her church if we tend to forget how devoted a Christian Amanda was. We remember rather how when we were girls, and I dare say reprehensibly light-minded, she set her heart on a college education, then no common ambition among females, much less often an achievement. And by her own efforts secured it. She was tied by family responsibility to Waynesboro; with her B.A. degree she came back to teach Latin, first at the Female College, then in the public high school. She devoted the rest of her long life to teaching young people all that she could persuade them to learn. There are few citizens, male or female, who have better served their community." With a that's-that sigh, Sally lowered herself into her chair. No other member felt inclined to contribute further remarks. The ladies dispersed quietly without the usual few moments of conversation.

Jennifer conducted her grandmother-in-law to her car. "No one else going with you?" Anne asked, when she had been assisted into the front seat. "Then I can express my feelings? I was well and thoroughly rebuked, wasn't I?"

"Well, yes." Jenny laughed. "But why Marcus Aurelius, Gran? There are verses in the Bible that say the same thing, like 'As for man, his days are as grass; as a flower of the field so he flourisheth. For the wind passeth over it, and it is gone, and the place thereof shall know it no more'." Her voice ceased on a melancholy but appreciative tone, then more briskly she added, "And don't look at me like that, Gran. After all I went to the Baptist Sunday school when I was little, and we memorized and memorized."

"I think that is one of the most beautiful passages in the Bible, and certainly the most forlorn. But I don't think it does say the same thing, exactly. It isn't quite so—all encompassing?—as 'vast and infinite eternity.' There is space in those words as well as time."

Jenny said, "Marcus Aurelius must be a favorite of the Gordons. Tuck has a copy of the *Meditations* on his bedside table. An old book, with somebody's name in the front in a crabbed, aged handwriting. He told me once you gave it to him."

"But not why?" There must be some griefs that Tucker had not shared with his wife. "It's a long story." Anne hesitated. "The book was Professor Lowrey's, when he had the Female College here. You know: he taught Amanda and Sally and me, among others. When he left here, he gave the book to his daughter Kitty. Kitty married Sheldon Edwards. You know that, of course; she was Lowrey Edwards' mother. When she lay dying, she gave the book to John. My husband, not Tuck's father. Thought it might help him over rough spots, and Sheldon, she said, was too good a Christian to need it. John was her doctor."

"She was the first Mrs. Sheldon Edwards then. I never heard much about her. Would Mother remember her?"

"Certainly. Johnny and his friends were having a taffy pull in our kitchen the night she died. Elsa was there."

"You were fond of her. I can tell by the way you speak her name. Fonder than of the present Mrs. Edwards?"

"Jessamine has made Sheldon a good wife: they are congenial companions. She's been his wife longer than Kitty was. But Kitty—yes, I was fonder of Kitty."

"And the Marcus Aurelius?"

"John didn't find it much to his taste: said the philosopher was always looking at himself to see how he was bearing up. Not fair of John, really. But John was no philosopher. He kept the book among those in his office, and after he died it went to Johnny. Then after Johnny died I came upon it, clearing things out. He had liked it—had marked a lot of passages. I copied some of them out for Tucker. Then when he came home to stay, I gave him the book. I am glad to know he's kept it."

Jenny brought the car to a stop at Anne's gate, got out, and went around to help her out.

"I suppose you can't come in for a little while? The only chance we seem to have for a visit, just you and I, is riding back and forth to Club."

"I'm sorry. But the children will run young Dorina ragged by this time, and she doesn't like to stay after dark. I'll have to get her home, then do something about our dinner. I can't find any colored girl willing to work in the country in the evening. I'll drop by soon."

Tucker, who seldom got away from his office as early as five-thirty, came in the back door as Anne, in the front hall, was stripping off her gloves. "Just home, Gran? I suppose you all had a lovely teary meeting?"

"Believe it or not," and Anne was a little sharp with him, still feeling shamefaced over her own embarrassing display of emotion in front of all the ladies, "no. It was not. Very few of those present really cared; for them I imagine Memorial meetings are unmitigated boredom."

"Probably spent the time wondering who will take her place."

"Probably. There's a kind of unofficial waiting list of course. It would have been Katherine Edwards, but she married and went to Cincinnati to live. Barbara Stevens, maybe. Or Mrs. Frank Merrill. She's from away, but everyone seems to like and admire her."

"Rod isn't happy about Barbara. She's running around with Charlie Merrill. He's not only too old for her but he's drinking like a fish. That Country Club crowd! Frank, on the other hand, is steady as a rock, practicing law with Gardiner and Merrill, married to a nice girl, and thinking about going into politics."

"I never have understood how doctors know so much that they feel free to tell."

"Rod unburdens himself once in a while. Anyway, about Charlie, it isn't any secret. And there's at least one member of the Stevens family who is happy. Theresa stopped by for a moment before your meeting."

"Theresa? What's the matter?"

"Nothing. She's in seventh heaven. She's found a publisher for her book about Captain Bodien."

"*What* book? I didn't know she was writing one. How did you know about it?"

"Good Lord! Then she really did keep it dark." Tucker explained. "I don't suppose it's awfully good, really. She's such a child."

"She's twenty-six or seven."

"I guess the publishing business is like all businesses in these high-flying days: anything sells, so why not gamble?"

"The country has gone crazy. I hope you aren't doing any stock exchange gambling?"

He grinned at her. "You may not believe it, but I have reached the age of discretion. Anyway, I'm far too busy to follow the stock market. If you give it your full attention, I suppose you can gamble—everyone seems to be doing it: buying today and selling tomorrow. I couldn't be bothered. And besides, the market has gone up beyond all reason. The Evanses—Ludwig and his father—are worried for fear that Ernest will lose his head, now that his father isn't there to restrain him. He lives and breathes Wall Street. Lud says business isn't really all that good: the salesmen work hard but don't get many orders. Small companies like Rausch Cordage are being snatched up willy-nilly by holding companies. Of course the company here is a close corporation, with Lud in control. Just the same, he is glad he bought Ernest's shares. Ernest inherited what seems to me a whopping lot of money, so he might take a flier, but he hasn't any Rausch Cordage to put up as collateral. Grandmother Rausch is sitting tight on her bank stock and W. W. Railroad shares."

"As I am sitting on mine. It's funny, really. Papa bought as much as he could of that railroad stock when the company was first organized, just to help Waynesboro get a railway. That was the fever in those days. And it turned out to be as smart a thing as he ever did."

"I only hope I do as well by my family."

"What I have will be yours some day."

"A far-off 'some day,' I trust. Well, having had this illuminating discussion of high finance, I must go. Better not say anything about Theresa's book until the news leaks out. I expected all you Club ladies to know about it."

"I still find it hard to believe: that intellectual young girl and Captain Bodien! As unlikely a subject for her as one can imagine."

"Anyone with real talent can make something of any subject, I guess. We'll just have to wait and see."

Waynesboro waited quite a while before Theresa's book reached its publication date, but at last a copy was in the author's hands: *Old Soldier*, by Theresa Stevens.

By that time, late in the fall of 1929, the stock market had crashed. Most of Waynesboro said, "I told you so"; those who had got their fingers burned kept quiet about it. Ernest Rausch came home to visit his mother. He hadn't exactly been wiped out, he told her, but he could use a loan. To hold onto the stocks he'd bought, he must put up more collateral.

Ernest looked old and haggard. Sally's oldest son, but not all that old. She was not without sympathy, but she needed to make an effort not to seem contemptuous.

"Of course, you bought on margin. Not through your own firm, I hope."

"No. Through another broker. But we're asking for more margin from our customers. I couldn't have bought a tenth of what I have if I had paid for it. And they're good stocks. If I can only hold on, the market will bounce back in a week or two."

"The eternal optimist, aren't you? Have you forgotten the depression of the nineties? I haven't. Nor that of the seventies, when no one had money and bills were paid in kind or not at all. If it hadn't been for the churches and their charities, and your father's keeping the mill running no matter what it cost, there would have been starvation right here in Waynesboro. A 'week or two,' indeed! This may go on for years. No, I am not going to throw money away just for it to be lost when the market keeps on falling."

"But it's just the market. The country is fundamentally sound. Business shouldn't be affected."

"What do you think caused the crash, beyond the fact that gamblers kept bidding the market higher and higher? According to Gilbert and young Ludwig, business hasn't been good for a long while."

"Do you mean to tell me that Rausch Cordage Company is in trouble? Of course those stuffed shirts haven't Papa's touch. I always thought it was foolish to trust it to them."

"'Stuffed shirts'! Just because they happen not to be gamblers. I remember that your father warned you once. I wish you had never gone to New York. As children you and Charles were so alike you might almost have been twins, but not now: imagine Charles gambling on the stock market! No, Rausch Cordage is not in trouble, but much of it may have to be used to keep the mill running, making what there's little sale for."

"For God's sake, why? Why not keep the money, if things are really that bad, and close the mill down? If young Ludwig had had any financial sense at all, he could have persuaded the Cincinnati cousins to sell; and they could have sold out to some holding company a few weeks back and now be sitting pretty."

"*Sell* Rausch Cordage Company? Ernest, you really—don't you know that there are things in this world worth more than money? Your father left the mill to Ludwig for him to run, not for him to sell. And as for closing it down even temporarily, only necessity would force that on Ludwig. He will keep it running even if there are no dividends to be passed out to the family."

"That is pure damned foolishness, Mamma. I'm glad I sold him my few shares."

"Like your father, Ludwig and Gib are compassionate men who consider the mill hands as a responsibility. Do you think they want to close the mill gates in their faces, and let them starve or live on charity? It isn't a huge corporation like Bodien and Rausch in Madison City, where the top men don't know their hands. I don't know what Paul and Stewart will do. But, here, hours may be cut, even wages, but there will be work enough to keep the hands from starving, at least."

"Call me an 'optimist'! And what is wrong in being optimistic. The country is fundamentally sound. You're the kind of pessimist that is frightening everyone into backing off and selling out."

"As I say, I have lived through depressions before. In the long run, of course we'll pull out of it. But it may take years."

"I wonder if Paul shares your views? I know that he and Bodien have made a big thing of that paper company. Its shares are traded on the Big Board."

"I see very little of Paul. I know he has done well. If you want to borrow money from him, go ask him. but don't say I sent you."

Elsa returned from a Club meeting just as Ernest was coming down the stairs, valise in hand.

"Oh, Ernest! Not leaving so soon?"

"I must get back." He did not say whether or not he intended to see Paul in Madison City. "Mamma wasn't very helpful. She hasn't exactly mellowed with the years, has she?"

"What do you expect, only coming to see her when you want help? But no, age has not had a mellowing effect. But remember: she is seventy-nine—eighty on her next birthday—and in constant pain from her arthritis. Tuck prescribes pain pills, and tells her not to try to be a hero, but she is reluctant to dope herself. She wants to know just how bad the pain really is."

"Making it harder for you, of course. I'm sorry. I thought when I first saw her she was looking much older—really old, in spite of—"

"Her weight? That's half the problem. But you know her well enough to be sure that she still says, 'I like a good table.' And this is her house and eating is one of her few pleasures."

"I soon found, when she told me off, her mind hasn't weakened. But she always managed to be generous with Ludwig Junior."

"That was a long time ago. She isn't ungenerous now, in her own way. She wouldn't let you starve. But to throw good money after bad, as she sees it, no. I'm sorry I can't help, even if I would. But we may need all we have to keep the mill running."

When he had said good-bye and the front door had closed behind him, Elsa dropped her gloves, hat, and cloak over the newel post and went into the parlor where her mother so habitually sat nowadays: she was comfortable in the wing chair that was too big to be easily moved, and she could have a small table at hand for books, papers, magazines, and a glass of water and her pills.

"You saw Ernest? I heard you talking. No doubt he thought me hard-hearted. But if I bailed him out now, he would just get in deeper and deeper.

What a way to spend your life! I thought he looked awful—strained and twice his age. I suppose he is worried frantic. But anything I gave him would just be swept away in this market collapse. The slump is going to last longer than he thinks. 'A week or two' is the way he sees the situation. He should let the stocks go that he's bought on margin. Then when the market reached rock bottom, I would let him have some of the money that will be his eventually, and he could start over."

"That seems generous enough to me. But I suppose it would be dismal to see what amounted to a fortune for a few days just go down the drain."

"He'll probably go try Paul."

"Paul has better sense. Thank Heaven that the bank is absolutely safe in his hands; that is one thing we needn't worry about."

"And in your hands, too. I give you credit for that, Elsa. How was the Club meeting, and where is the next one to be?"

"They're coming here. We decided that, don't you remember? The publication date of Theresa's book is next week, so we'll have a celebration of sorts. Tea, at least."

"How that child found enough to say about Captain Bodien to fill a book I cannot imagine."

"We'll soon see. The book store here will stock it, and I have ordered a copy."

Anne Gordon had also ordered a copy, and aside from Theresa's own family, who had author's copies before the publication date, she was probably the first in Waynesboro to read it. She had more time for reading than most.

She settled herself that day in her rocker, and stared at the slender book in her hands. *Old Soldier*, she mused. That was certainly Captain Bodien. She pressed the cover and first few pages back and ran her hand over the first page of Chapter One, where she saw the title, "Antietam." With a small sigh, she thought, "I cannot possibly read another book about the Civil War." But the first page was not about the war:

> The Saturday night band concert had brought many of the townspeople to the Court House square. They had come to enjoy the soft spring evening: the green young grass, the honey-sweet fragrance of the locust trees in bloom somewhere nearby, the encounters with friends, and the music. The band played mostly military tunes: half of its members were veterans of the Civil War, over and done with now for so many years that they remembered it sentimentally with "Tenting Tonight," "John Brown's Body," and "Just before the Battle, Mother." These martial airs were interspersed with Stephen Foster tunes and other old favorites, and once or twice with something more ambitious, like the "Anvil Chorus."
>
> The older members of the audience sat in disordered rows of camp chairs, leaning forward at intervals to talk across drawn-back knees to some friends close by. Younger couples strolled about over the grass—if married, arm in arm, if youths and maidens, sedately apart. Romping children raced about

among them, sometimes dashing off to skin-the-cat on the Market Street hitching rail.

In one corner of the square a group sat close to the Civil War memorial cannon; around it a bare patch of ground showed where the grass had been trampled to dust by boys playing on it. Around the edge of that bare spot a circle of children sprawled on the grass: several boys and one girl, who had "made a pudding" by whirling around in her full skirts and petticoats and then squatting quickly so that as she sat cross-legged she neither showed her pantalettes nor soiled her frock.

Anne thought, "Pantalettes still in the seventies?" And then, with dismay, "I can't remember."

The children were listening spellbound to the man who sat before them on the bench backed up to the cannon. He leaned forward over the dusty patch of ground: a stocky, short, broad-shouldered man, bald except for a fringe of hair around the edges of his skull, but with a full, flowing artillery man's mustache. He had about him no suggestion of the Pied Piper, yet the children hung on his every word. In the dust he drew lines with a stick one of the boys had found in the gutter.

"Here," he said, "is the Hagerstown Pike, where we marched into battle that morning. Here was a rail fence, and behind it, both sides of the pike, were cornfields, the corn higher than a man's head. It was September, and the fence was all grown up with brambles and goldenrod. Way back over here there was a woods, and on the other side, another one, both crawling with Stonewall Jackson's men, as we soon found out. The Iron Brigade was in line in front of us, to protect the guns. We had unlimbered facing the cornfield, one gun in the middle of the road to sweep it clear of Rebs should they attack, and two guns on the right in a pasture with haystacks, the other three on the other side in a farmyard with barns and outbuildings. The Iron Brigade attacked through the cornfield and cleared the Rebs out, but they got reinforced and came back. Three times that happened—through the cornfield and then back—with our guns still shooting until the Rebs were so close we couldn't lower the guns enough to throw canister at them.

"Was it a hard fight?"

"A tough, stand-up fight. Murderous! Captain Campbell was wounded and Lieutenant Stewart took command. Cannoneers fell right and left—some able to crawl away, some dead."

At that moment the band started to play "Marching Through Georgia." The fair-haired little girl lifted her head to listen. "Captain Bodien, did you march through Georgia? My Papa did."

A vague sense of recognition tugged at a corner of Anne's mind, but it only momentarily disturbed her concentration as she continued to read.

"I know. And Johnny's. And they came home from the War thinking Sherman was the greatest general of them all. Maybe he was. But they didn't see

> our General Gibbon that day at Antietam. When there weren't enough men left standing to serve the gun in the middle of the road, he went out there and acted as gunner and cannoneer both—sighted the gun and fired it. He was in his general's uniform and must have been in full view of the Reb gunners back in the woods."
>
> There was a moment's held breath—then, "Did they *hit* him?"
>
> "No, by a miracle."
>
> "Go on, *please*. And don't interrupt again, you goose of a Shaney!"

Jolted alert, Anne read the line again. "That's Johnny!" she thought. "And Elsa—and their friends! How could I not have realized?" Memories flooded over her as she recalled those years of her life—the way the town had looked then: the trees, the hitching rail, the bumpy brick pavements, the higgledy-piggledy granite curbstones. "I haven't thought of Waynesboro as it was then for years," she said to herself, with some surprise. "But how did that child Theresa know?" She pondered this briefly, her eyes fixed, but not seeing, on the thumb restraining the cover and the first few pages. She sat quietly for a moment as her mind roamed backward in time, but then, with interest now, she returned her attention to Theresa's book.

Absorbed, scouring the pages for signals less obvious than the absurd nickname that Elsa had reserved for Johnny's use alone, she forgot entirely that she had begun to read the book never expecting to finish it. She reached the last page of chapter one:

> At that moment the opening chords of "The Star-Spangled Banner" sounded from the bandstand. Captain Bodien rose with alacrity, and the children reluctantly scrambled to their feet. They and all the others in the Court House square stood stiffly until the final notes died away. Then the circle around the Captain dispersed, and the crowd slowly drifted away. The band members put up their instruments and came down from the stand. Soon there were only far-away voices to be heard, under the clatter of camp chairs being closed and collected. Stronger than ever the scent of the locust trees hung over the deserted square.

Anne, dropping the book to her knee for a moment, said to herself, "That's the way it was." She wondered how Theresa could imagine it so vividly—so rightly? Those years in the seventies, early in the eighties. The war had been over for a long time, but what a man might be doing to earn a living was still less important to him than having been a soldier. How secondary seemed Captain Bodien's years spent working in the rope mill.

But as she read on, she discovered that Theresa had set down those years too. She heard in her mind the clang of horseshoes in the cobble yard and saw the firelit figures at work in the tarring shed. Nostalgia washed like a tide across her mind. She savored the gentle melancholy for a moment, as the old are wont to do, and then brusquely thrust it aside.

Occasionally, one of the Captain's tales was familiar to her, as she recalled

Johnny's dancing excitement and breathless retelling of it when he had returned home from one of those sessions at the Captain's feet.

She came to Theresa's description of the snowball fight, when Barbara Bodien and Kitty Edwards had stood off the attack of the children's artillery brigade in front of the Rausches' house; she remembered, sadly, that the story was first told to her by Barbara that night at the Edwards house, when Kitty lay dying.

"How long ago it all was," Anne thought.

The first section of Theresa's book ended with Barbara's wedding, attended by Captain Bodien's two heroes, General Gibbon and Major Stewart, their presence ending the suspicion on the part of some that the Captain's stories were more than a little stretched. And the children—even Binny, Anne remembered with a pang—had been more interested in the soldiers than in the bride.

The second section began with the date:

> On a summer afternoon in 1892, Captain Bodien, on an iron garden bench against a big tree that shaded the side yard, sat in the midst of a circle of children.

"The next generation," Anne thought, "Barbara's girls, Kitty's boys, and Rodney."

The afternoon waned as Anne read with steady absorption. She relived the gaiety of the Fourth of July housewarming at Hillcrest; the dark time of the flood, when Anne and other Club members and church women had worked endless hours at the churches feeding and comforting those who had been driven from their houses.

Theresa's story edged forward in time until, near its close, she herself had joined the circle at the Captain's feet. And so she came at last to the old man's death, when his mind wandered back to Antietam—to comrades and generals who had perhaps been killed in battle, or who had died in the years between, or who were themselves old, old men, awaiting the end.

Anne closed the book, holding it in both hands, and let her eyes wander over the dancing shadows on the carpet of the naked branches of the tree silhouetted against the late afternoon sun. A chill shook her, and she darted an anxious glance toward the fire in the grate. She heard the back door open and close: Louline come to prepare dinner.

The book was kindly reviewed in various papers by the critics (some in condescending tone), but it did not exactly set the world afire. In Waynesboro it was a nine-days' wonder. Other natives had written and published books, but not until after they had left the town; no actual citizen had accomplished as much since the days of General Deming's county and regimental histories. That "little Theresa Stevens" had produced a book that was as much about the town as it was about her great-grandfather made a brief sensation; she spent one afternoon in the local bookstore, signing her name to copies bought by friends and acquaintances, and by men and women whose faces were familiar but whose names had been forgotten or never known to Theresa, and by totally unfamiliar people who claimed to know her. Charlotte Bonner reviewed the work in the *Torchlight*, seeing nothing in it that was not praiseworthy; and, being reminded of her father's months in Andersonville, she contributed some reminiscences of her own, to bring her article to a full column length.

The Woman's Club, meeting at the Rausches', honored the author with additional reviews and comments and an elaborate tea, set out on the dining room table, stretched out to its full length. Since the days when Mrs. Ballard had written stories for Sunday school papers and Mrs. Deming had helped with the General's histories, the Club had had no author on its rolls, so that much was made of the occasion. Young Mrs. Jennifer Gordon had been assigned to write the formal review. When Jenny had finished the "literary" criticism, she added spontaneously that she had once been among the children who had listened enthralled to the Captain's stories. "One thing that struck me, reading it, is how in the comparatively few years since then, children's activities have been curtailed. It seems to me now that we were free to come and go as we pleased, just so we left word at home when to expect us back. There were few cars in town, and no lurking dangers, so far as we knew. We could follow the 'Pied Piper'."

Elsa, presiding, complimented her daughter on her essay and the author on her book; then added that her own childhood had been brought back to her mind, as no doubt had happened with other listeners: it was perhaps that nostalgic effect that had moved them all so much. But the reviewer who had spoken (Jenny) had had no experience of real freedom: she should have been a child in the seventies. And Elsa went on to speak briefly of the robust games she had enjoyed, so many of them based on the Captain's stories.

When she had concluded, she threw the meeting open to members who had comments to add. Various ladies wanted to speak of their memories; and Captain Bodien's two granddaughters, Mrs. Lavinia Stevens and Mrs. Caroline Edwards, told of the enchantment of the Old West as they had learned of it, in that circle of children under the maple tree in the Gardiner side yard. Caroline added a word in praise of her niece, who she thought was rarely gifted, a tribute that came more becomingly from an aunt than from a mother.

Club members were slow in taking their leave after tea had been served, each feeling that it was only right and proper to compliment the author, at length and fulsomely. When Theresa, her mother, and grandmother Jessamine Edwards finally got away, Lavinia said to her daughter, "How did all that make you feel? Proud?"

Theresa, occupied in backing her mother's car out of the driveway, did not answer until she had turned safely into the street. Then she said, "Like a fool, if you must know. I can never think of anything to say except 'Thank you'."

"I wondered. You've always set your heart on being famous, but you just looked embarrassed."

"Don't be silly, Mother. Famous, indeed! If ten people outside Waynesboro read that book, I'll be surprised. It isn't all that good."

Jessamine spoke from the back seat. "I think it is a real *tour de force*, putting in the children as well as Captain Bodien. People love to be reminded of what the world was like when they were young. Of course I had a very different childhood in a very different kind of place, but even I can remember being happy now and then when some old comrade of my father's would come to the plantation to talk about their battles and what a brave man he had been. Grandfather Gordon hated it but had stuck it out, a Union man to the end. I loved it: they made my father, whom I couldn't remember at all, seem so grand and heroic. Grandfather Gordon never forgave his son for being what he considered a traitor to his country, but he was too polite to tell the visitors that. Some of them even remembered my mothers's father, who had been killed too. He was in a Lousiana regiment."

"It sounds very sad," said Theresa, who had never heard much about her grandmother's life in Mississippi. "Somehow, with Uncle Remus and *In Old Virginny* to base your judgment on, plantation life has always seemed so carefree."

"Not after the war, it wasn't."

That remark of Jessamine's put an end to the conversation; it was not until they had left her at her door that Lavinia spoke again, the reluctant-to-put-it-into-words utterance of a reserved if loving woman: "You know without my saying so, of course: your father and I are very proud of you, and think you succeeded in doing exactly what you set out to do: bring an epoch back to life. Now what next? You aren't going to stop, are you, because you felt like a fool today?"

"Oh, Mother! I can't stop. Writing is all I've wanted to do all my life. But I don't know what next. I've been thinking so long and hard about this that now my mind is a blank."

"Don't worry about it. It will come. In the meantime, why not keep your hand in by writing some short things? I'll try to make it easier for you to work—stop interrupting so much."

And so Theresa, during the rest of the winter of 1929–30, spent her days in her bedroom, making a show of getting some work done, but spending a lot of time sharpening pencils and looking at blank pieces of paper, and thinking of what a clamorous household she lived in. As long as she had been working on *Old Soldier*, she had been able to concentrate; it had all been so alive to her that she hadn't even minded interruptions; she had known so certainly what she wanted to say next that she could always pick up where she had left off. Now she couldn't think for the incessant ringing of the telephone and the doorbell, the noisy comings and goings of her brother and sister and their friends; even her mother, whose intentions had been so good, did occasionally come to ask Theresa's advice about something important, like what to have for dinner, and Theresa loved her far too much to rebuff her; in fact, since she was getting nowhere, she really welcomed such interruptions as an excuse for wasted time.

And she was humiliated by the smallness of her royalty checks, in spite of her insistence to herself and others that she expected nothing of her book in the way of sales. Here she was, grown-up, a published author, living on her family as if she were still in high school. She should really find herself some kind of a job. But jobs were not easy to find that winter, as she knew very well, and if she found one, it might be depriving someone who needed it worse. She stayed at her desk.

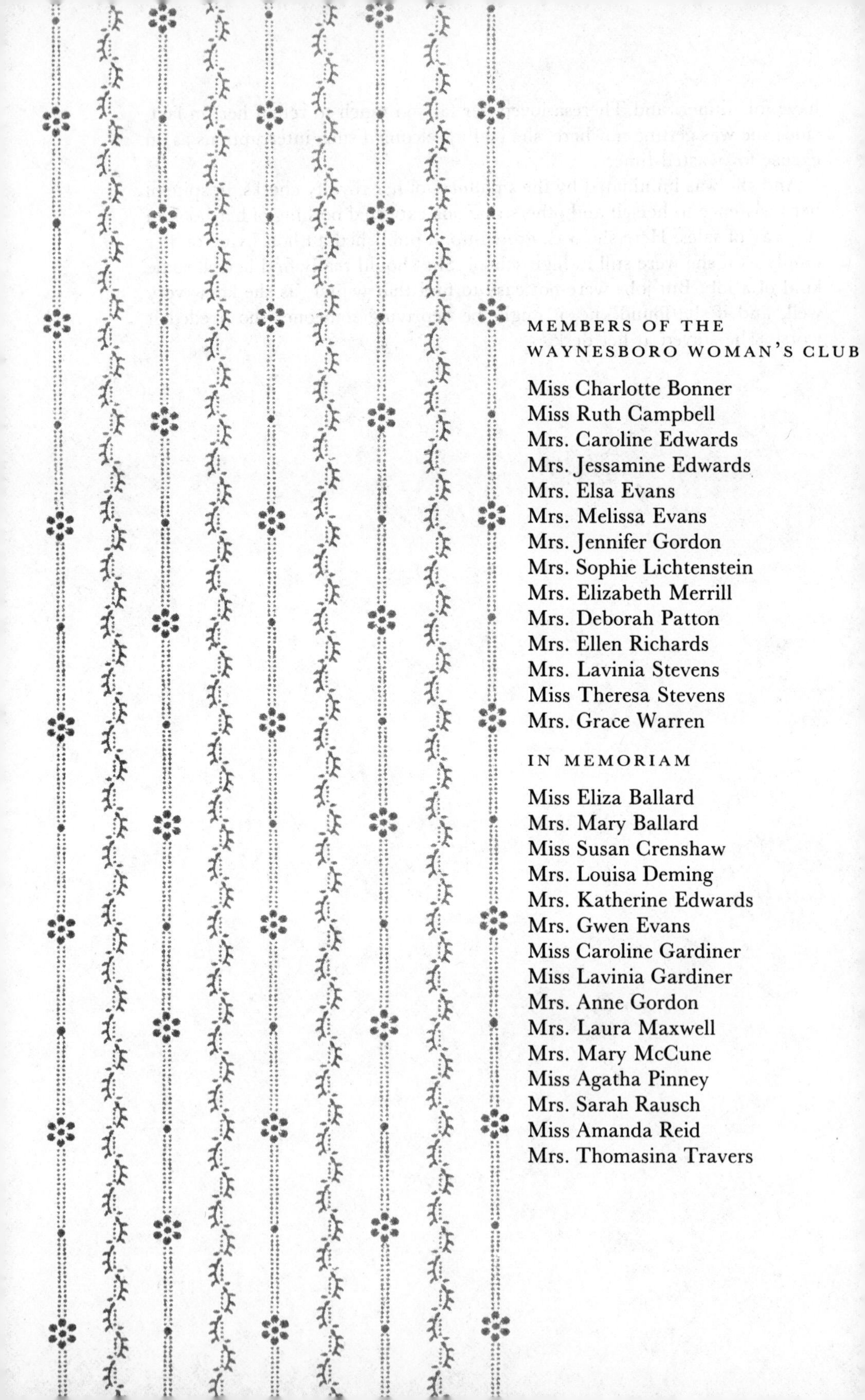

MEMBERS OF THE
WAYNESBORO WOMAN'S CLUB

Miss Charlotte Bonner
Miss Ruth Campbell
Mrs. Caroline Edwards
Mrs. Jessamine Edwards
Mrs. Elsa Evans
Mrs. Melissa Evans
Mrs. Jennifer Gordon
Mrs. Sophie Lichtenstein
Mrs. Elizabeth Merrill
Mrs. Deborah Patton
Mrs. Ellen Richards
Mrs. Lavinia Stevens
Miss Theresa Stevens
Mrs. Grace Warren

IN MEMORIAM

Miss Eliza Ballard
Mrs. Mary Ballard
Miss Susan Crenshaw
Mrs. Louisa Deming
Mrs. Katherine Edwards
Mrs. Gwen Evans
Miss Caroline Gardiner
Miss Lavinia Gardiner
Mrs. Anne Gordon
Mrs. Laura Maxwell
Mrs. Mary McCune
Miss Agatha Pinney
Mrs. Sarah Rausch
Miss Amanda Reid
Mrs. Thomasina Travers

* 1930–1932 *

"The end of an era: we lose the last of our charter members . . ."

During the early months of 1930 and afterward, Rausch Cordage Company fought to keep the mill running. Ludwig called the hands together one noon and explained the situation. The factory must either close down for a while or run part time, with reduced pay for everyone, from top executive down to unskilled laborers. He intended to keep the mill operating if at all possible, but orders were very hard to get. If worst came to worst, they would do what his grandfather had once done, in equally hard times: make any kind of hemp produce, down to oakum, and store it until the depression was over. The company could help make up for the lower wages; although the plant no longer operated on steam power, except for the whistle, it could buy coal by the carload and sell it to the hands at carload rates. He asked the men to choose a representative who would come to him in his office and tell him what the workman were willing to do. The verdict was what he expected: they would work on reduced pay and hours. They knew very well that men were being laid off everywhere, and that there would be little chance, particularly for the unskilled, and for the comparatively well-paid rope-makers, to find jobs anywhere else. Ludwig asked the hands' spokesman to thank the men for their loyalty. He said, "No one knows how long this depression will last, but I promise you that the mill will run as long as our capital reserves hold out; until then no one will be fired except for cause."

Ludwig's decision was hard for Gib to accept; he was as fretful about it as an old man. In fact, Ludwig thought sadly, at sixty his father was an old man, broken by his anxiety for his children a dozen years ago. His son tried to buoy him up. "One good thing: the price of hemp—manila and sisal both—is dropping fast, and will drop lower: we can stock up—fill a warehouse, maybe. We haven't a great supply on hand; haven't had since we got rid of the war surplus in the good years. We haven't a big inventory, either: for some time we have made no more than enough to fill orders.

"I know, boy, I know. But to make a lot of trash you can't sell may ruin us."

"I don't think so. There'll still be some demand for binder twine, in spite of the combines. And twine for hay-balers. Ship's fenders. It's too bad," and Ludwig laughed, (he could still laugh) "that bed rope is a thing of the past. I'm sorry, Father, if you are upset. But what Grandfather did he would expect me to do. And Captain Bodien." With some muttering about the weight of dead hands, Gib dismissed the subject.

Neither man took his troubles home from the office. Ludwig still felt protective toward his warm, loving, and happy wife, who was completely wrapped up in her family, her house, and her freinds. But Melissa read the newspapers, and she knew that Ludwig was troubled. She taxed him with it one evening after dinner, when she came downstairs after getting the children to bed.

"Ludwig, I'm not a child. I'm your wife. How bad are things at the mill? I see you looking worn-out every evening when you come home from the office."

"They're bad enough. As you know, we're running only part time. It was that or let our laborers go. So far, as least, we haven't actually *lost* money: we have good salesmen on the road. And these hard times can't go on forever."

"But if they last, you will lose money?"

"I'm afraid so. We'll have to dip into our reserves. Or borrow from the bank. Father and I and all the other executives cut our own salaries before we cut wages."

"Then we should cut our expenditures. Let's sell my car and let Mirella go. After all, I was brought up to cook and keep house."

"And what would Mirella do? She supports her old father and mother, doesn't she? Without her wages they would go to the poorhouse. We have a responsibility to her as well as to the mill hands."

"Yes. I'm sorry, darling. I was only thinking of us. But the car?"

Ludwig thought, "I was thinking of you, partly: this house, the meals, the babies." But he knew he was right about Mirella. And as for the car—"We'll hang on to the car a while longer: it would be hard for you to get around without it. You can use it only when you need to get—to get my mother and grandmother, or get to your father and mother's, or have errands to do."

"You know, until I married you, I walked. I think my legs are still useful."

He laughed at her. "I'm sure they are. But we'll keep your car."

At a time when other women were self-righteously or of necessity letting the hired help go, there was criticism of the Rausch family and others: "Things may be going badly at the mill, but the Rausches and all their connection hang on to their servants. Catch any of them doing their own work. Even the Dr. Gordons, living in the country, can keep their hired girl and a nursemaid, and a chauffeur for the doctor. That family never did give a rap what anyone thought."

It was unfair, as so much criticism of the supposedly wealthy is. It came finally to Gib's ears; he was contemptuous, and responded as Ludwig had: "If we turn the servants off, they'd wind up in the poorhouse, even it they've saved a little." But like Ludwig, he was thinking not only of the servants but of his wife.

Gib no longer talked business at home, as he had always done, unconsciously acknowledging that Elsa knew as much about it as he did, and perhaps, had better business judgment. But Mrs. Rausch had become a constant worry to her daughter, and he was not going to pile anything more on her shoulders.

Elsa could see that her mother was failing, and failing fast. For some reason—the stimulation, perhaps—she was able to be perfectly herself when there were callers at the house, or the Club met there, following the essays as they were presented and commenting on them without fumbling for words. Other times she was showing her age. When Anne Gordon came to spend the afternoon with her, as she often did, Sally, who was at ease with her, did not make so much of an effort. She often paused to grope for the word she wanted, putting her hand to her mouth, or, if she didn't pause, coming out with the wrong one. Then she would laugh at herself and say, "Drat it! I think of the word I want, and hear myself saying something entirely different."

"I'm just the same," Anne would reply. "Half the time I talk to old friends without daring to call them by name." But she knew very well that she was not so bad as Sally about words; common, everyday words still came readily to her tongue.

Elsa, one afternoon when Anne was with her mother, went to Tucker's office to consult with him. Being herself roubustly healthy, she had not had occasion to go there since Tucker had begun to practice; their relationship was entirely familiar. But when she did go, and Tucker took her into the middle office, she dropped gratefully into the deeply curved seat of the old leather armchair.

"You know," she said, "your father and I did a lot of our growing up in this office. There was something about it—a feeling of mysterious miracles being perfomed—and for a gruff man, Uncle Dock was kind to us, never hinting we might be in the way. He just took his patients on through this room." And then, abruptly, "I've come to talk about Mamma. It's hopeless to try to get her to let me call a doctor to come see her."

"I know Aunt Sally." His eyes twinkled behind his glasses. "I've known her all my life, and now I see her at last once every two weeks." The Tucker Gordons and the Ludwig Evans went every other Sunday to have a big midday diner with Jenny's parents and grandmother. "She has known me too long—she can't think of me as a doctor, except when she wants pain pills."

"She won't let me call any doctor. Insist there's no need."

"She must be eighty. I know she's Gran's age. The years are beginning to tell."

"You must have seen, trying to talk to her: her mind is clear enough, but her speech isn't. She so often comes out with one word when she intends something altogether different; or she waits and waits, with her lips working, while her mind struggles. It is so unlike Mamma. I know she hates it." Elsa's eyes filled. "She was always so—so on top of the world—so ready with the right word."

"Of course I've noticed it. It's a mild form of aphasia common among the elderly. Anyone your mother's age is bound to have some hardening of the cerebral arteries."

"There's nothing that can be done about it?"

"If she has high blood pressure, that can be treated. But how could any doctor prescribe without an examination? And she probably wouldn't take anything, anyway."

"I know, Tuck. She's hopeless to deal with. What are the prospects?"

"With no more to go on than what you have told me, and what I have seen, I can't possibly make a prognosis." Then he added abruptly, "She won't get any better, you know that."

"She could have a stroke? I mean a massive cerebral hemorrhage instead of these little ones?"

"If I am right, yes."

"Mamma might live to be helpless? She's the last person in the world to suffer such a fate."

"Try to persuade her to see a doctor. There are several very good ones in town now."

"It isn't that she questions your or any other doctor's qualifications. She just wants to go on pretending to herself that she is all right."

"I commend her spirit. I wish more of my old ladies were like her. If you can't persuade her to have professional advice, don't worry any more than you can help. All I have said is guesswork. She probably won't have a stroke."

But when he went home finally for his dinner, he told Jenny that her mother had been in to see him and that he had given her more than a hint of what he feared. "I know you have been insisting that I mustn't because she wouldn't have another easy moment. But she begged me to be honest."

"She will worry herself sick. Funny. Because she and Grandmother have always rubbed each other the wrong way. Too much alike, I suppose. How did she take it?"

"How would you expect her to take it, honey? Your mother is a woman of character who faces up to things. And I could honestly tell her that I could make neither diagnosis nor prognosis without an examination."

He was glad afterward that he had taken the stand he had, for Sally Rausch was spared the paralysis that he and her family feared. One morning in late spring of 1930, she fell when she was trying to get out of bed. The maid, there to help her up and dress, ran terrified to call Elsa from her room across the hall. Gib unfortunately had already gone to the office. The two women could not have lifted Sally back to her bed, even had they dared try to move her. If she had been unconscious at all, it was not for long. She said, wih characteristic impatience, "Can't you two ninnies help me up?"

"Not until we get the doctor. You may have broken a bone. Pull the covers off the bed, Portia, and put them over her, while I go call Tuck and Gib."

"My arm—I think—I had it around the bedpost. Get Tucker. This isn't—isn't—" She fell silent, her eyes closed, her mouth working. Elsa could not tell whether she was trying for a word, or, hopefully, had fainted.

The doctors, not only Tuck but Rodney too, were there before they could have been expected; Gib and Ludwig were close on their heels. Rodney went to one knee on the floor beside her. He found her right arm broken in two places, and one broken rib, but so far as he could tell, no other serious damage. She opened her eyes before he had finished, said, "Rodney, get me up off this hard floor."

"It will be painful. You have broken your arm. I'll give you a bit of morphine before we move you."

When the hypodermic had taken effect, the four men managed to lift her to her bed, with Elsa, beside them, holding the broken arm across her body. They put the covers back over her, and Elsa, at Tucker's bidding, went for more blankets."She's bound to suffer from shock." And while Rodney and he set the broken arm and splinted it, and taped the rib, he said as she returned, "Did you find her unconscious?"

"No. She was talking to us quite sensibly—asked for you and called Portia and me 'ninnies.' Before you came I think she fainted for a minute."

"Then if it was a stroke, it was a light one. I can't see that her face is distorted."

Rodney agreed, but said, "She should be in the hospital. For X-rays. We could call the ambulance and take her down on a stretcher in your elevator."

"Impossible." Elsa was firm. "The elevator isn't that big. And she would never forgive me."

"Traumatic pneumonia is always a possibility with anyone her age, and her weight is against her. When the morphine wears off and she is in pain, do try to persuade her. We could keep her more comfortable."

Elsa promised, but added, "I have never had much luck at persuading Mamma of anything. Tuck, maybe—You will be back, Tuck?"

"Of course. And I'll call Jenny: she's a good nurse, you know."

"I'll need her more later on. If Mamma recovers consciousness."

Elsa sat by her mother's bed all day, even asking Portia to bring her some lunch on a tray. As the afternoon passed and the anesthetic wore off, she worried about the clearly increasing discomfort and dangerous restlessness. When her mother opened her eyes and, after a moment of orientation, said, "Elsa? I broke my arm?" Elsa repeated the doctors' findings, told her what they had done, and said: "An arm broken in two places, a broken rib—You need X-rays and a hospital bed."

The suggestion was emphatically rejected. "X-rays! These newfangled notions!" When she had caught her breath, she snapped, "I intend to die in my own bed. And be buried from my parlor."

"But no one has suggested you might die of a broken arm."

Sally was suffering too much to consider the remark worthy of comment. "When Tucker comes again, he can stop the pain. What time is it?"

"Very nearly five."

"Too late then. I want you to call Anne and ask her to come see me tomorrow."

"The doctors said 'no visitors.' I didn't even let Jenny come. She wanted to do the nursing."

Sally's lips worked as she struggled for words, finally got them out.

"'The doctors say'—'the doctors say'—and what does it matter? I want to see Anne."

"She telephoned when she heard you had fallen. You know she will come when you are able to see her."

"I wish to see her before it is too late. To ask her to forgive me."

Elsa wondered if her mother's mind was confused, though up to this point she had seemed lucid."Mamma? Forgive you for what? You have been bosom friends since you were girls, and never any hint of anything wrong."

"No trouble—because Anne didn't know. It was I who hinted to Louisa Deming about Johnny's—" The word "involvement" was lost beyond recall. Elsa waited. Her mother resumed. "About Johnny and that nurse."

Elsa was shocked. Finally she said, "Mamma, you couldn't have! It was Eliza Ballard."

"I did though. I never supposed—divorce. I was so angry about Paul—with him, with your father, but particularly with Johnny, who got him into that—trouble."

Of what use to say now that it wasn't in the end "trouble," that Paul and his wife had been happy all their married years?

"You think I'm wandering? No. I blamed Johnny—and just struck out."

"And now, after all these years, you want to be forgiven for what Aunt Anne never knew you did."

"I should like to die with a clear conscience."

"In the first place, you aren't going to die. What if after you had confessed, Aunt Anne didn't forgive you? And if you are determined to die, why do you want to clear the slate at Aunt Anne's expense? So many years since the divorce, and since Johnny died. Water under the bridge long ago. Aunt Anne is happy now, with Tuck and Jenny and their children to take his place. Why recall that old heartbreak to her mind?"

"It was your heartbreak too, wasn't it?"

Elsa drew back as if she had been struck. "Mamma!" At last she admitted,"In a way, yes. I wanted Johnny to be happy, and I'll never believe he would have died when he did if he hadn't been torn to pieces emotionally. But what I felt was nothing compared to what Aunt Anne—"

"Are you going to send for her?"

"Not until Tucker says I may. And not at all unless you promise solemnly not to say a word about Johnny."

Sally's mouth worked again; she moved her head on the pillow in mute rebellion until her white hair was a thin scattering of tangled locks. Then she murmured something about being so old she must submit to her own child's bossiness. Elsa kept silent. Finally her mother gave in. "Very well. I promise. I cannot go without seeing her. Our friendship—"

"When you are well enough for visitors, I'll call her. You're in no fit state now. And I've let you talk far too much."

Elsa had grown increasingly uneasy during that too-long argument. When Tucker came in for a moment before he went home for dinner, she told him her mother was sure she was dying. "I can't understand it. Mamma was always a fighter." She wanted him to scoff. He didn't.

He said, "If she has made up her mind to it, it could happen. Shock, age—and perhaps a feeling that she has had enough." And when the two of them came downstairs together after he had examined her mother, he did not reassure her. "I can't say I feel very hopeful. Her lungs have begun to fill up, lying flat as she must, with her bruises, broken rib, and her arm in a cast. One thing—I don't believe that now she is in much pain: a cerebral hemorrhage may have mercifully deadened some nerve centers."

"She wants to see your grandmother."

"Send for her, then. Tomorrow. It can't hurt your mother as much as fretting would do, and I know Gran would want to come."

"You think—?"

"Call her in the morning. I'll ask Jenny to bring her up."

Elsa had stopped on the bottom step, hand on the newel post.

Tucker for a moment laid his on it. "You must know how it grieves me to see her like this. She was so good to me those summers at Hillcrest. And she was such a—such a *person*."

"That she always was," and Elsa smiled a little, watching him out the door. Then she went out to the kitchen, fixed a tray and took it up, and held a cup of soup while her mother drank it. Later Jenny came, wanted or not, to spend the night beside her grandmother; she sent her mother off to bed. In the morning she reported that her patient was certainly not improving. Elsa brought up some breakfast, fed, washed, and combed the panting old lady, and propped her up on plumped pillows so that she could breathe more easily. When Elsa heard a car stop in front, she went to the top of the banisters; at the opening of the door she called down, "That you, Jenny?"

"And Gran. How is Grandmother?"

"About as she was when you left. Will you wait in the library, Jenny? She wants to see Aunt Anne."

Elsa watched Anne come up the stairs, one hand on the banisters. "And she's old, too," she thought, seeing how slowly the long flight of stairs was mastered. She went into her mother's room and drew a chair to the beside for Anne.

Sally cut short Anne's expression of regret, snapping at Elsa: "There's no need for you to stay. I'll keep my word."

When Elsa had gone out, closing the door behind her, Anne said, "Keep your word about what?" She was shocked by Sally's appearance and her breathlessness.

"Not letting you tire me out. As if it mattered at this point."

Anne took the chair that had been placed for her. For a moment she found nothing to say in reply: after all, Elsa could shoo her out when she showed signs of staying too long. Finally she ventured, "But they say you're getting along."

"Doctors!" Sally's contemptuous vehemence not only made her gasp but beads of perspiration came out on her face and under her chin. "What do they know?"

"I like to think Tucker knows what he is doing."

"Anne—" Sally was through with small talk. "It's been a long time—"

"That we have been friends?" It seemed better to finish what she thought Sally meant to say than to let her make the effort.

"Since we were little girls. Remember?"

"When we first went to school to Miss Pinney. Pantalettes and pinafores. And all the way to graduation from the Female College." "And," Anne's thoughts went on, "what bright blue eyes you had. I had forgotten that direct blue gaze. I have seen them faded as they are for so long a time. But not quite like this: she's not looking at me now, but beyond me."

"Commence—Commencement. Couldn't think of the word—so maddening. You remember?"

"Of course. The first time you ever laid eyes on Ludwig Rausch."

"And Dock came to see you—graduate. A long time—"

"Better than sixty years. It doesn't seem possible. Where has the time gone?"

"Always the question. Where—all the years—? But—always friends."

"Sally, of course. So many years, good and bad."

"And now we have—grandchildren."

"And great-grandchildren—in common. If only we could have known it was to be so." And she thought, "If I could have known, when Johnny—I might not have grieved so."

"Predestined? Calvinist—still—aren't you? Anyway, it ends happily."

"I hope so." She took her handkerchief and wiped Sally's face and neck. "We haven't reached the end."

"I have. And you—you can't hope—to live forever."

"My mind knows that. But instinctively, I suppose, I expect next year to be like this year, and the next after that."

"If you want it—I hope so. But as for me—" Sally was struggling so for breath that Anne had to lean close to hear her. "I wanted to say—good-bye—while I had my senses."

Anne stood up. "I have been here long enough. Elsa won't like my tiring you out. I'll say 'good-bye' if you want me to, just to ease your mind. But I'll be back to see you again." She bent to kiss Sally's cheek, then turned blindly to the door and went out.

Elsa was in the hall. She took one look at Anne, went in to see that her mother was comfortable, straightened the covers, gave her a drink, and said, "I'll see Aunt Anne out, then be back."

In the hall she found Anne still standing at the top of the stairs, clinging with one hand to the banisters.

"Aunt Anne, what is it?"

"Nothing, except I was trying to remember a line of poetry. Archibald MacLeish maybe? In a Club paper not long ago—"

"Yes. Elizabeth Merrill."

"I don't remember poetry as I used to. But something about hearing for the last time a familiar hand closing the door and going—It moved me at the time: the poem, I mean. And now—"

"So you think Mamma—?"

"Yes. I hate to say it—but yes. She has that look in her eyes. Blank. Far-off. She sees the end coming. But don't grieve too much. As she said to me, we have had many good years, and have come to a happy end. No, Elsa, don't go down with me. Jenny is waiting in the library to drive me home. She will come back, I'm sure, if you want or need her."

"No. No reason to call on her, unless the doctors say 'night nurse.' Then she can hunt up one of her uniforms. Thank you for coming, Aunt Anne. Mamma was determined—"

"She just wanted to say good-bye. There is no one else left who has known her for so long." Starting down the stairs, blinded by her tears, Anne cautiously crept around the curve of the banister and on down.

By the next morning there was no doubt that Sally had pneumonia. Her sons were sent for and came at once. A few days later she was dead. The funeral service, attended mostly by family, members of the Woman's Club, and a scattering of Baptists, was held as she had desired in the parlors of her own house: the big rooms filled, the coffin banked with flowers, the air filled with their unmistakably funereal scent.

The *Torchlight* printed a long obituary article, reviewing the antecedents of Mrs. Ludwig Rausch, her marriage to the man who had become Waynesboro's leading citizen, naming their children. What the paper did not tell, and what Waynesboro citizens were inquisitive about, was how she had disposed of her wealth.

The President Emeritus of the Waynesboro Woman's Club and "one of the last of its charter members" was memorialized at length at its next meeting, the vice-president presiding. In due time the *Torchlight* printed in its News of the Courts column the terms of her will. Ludwig's estate, so much of which had been held in trust for his wife for so long as she lived, was to be divided as he had directed. What she had inherited from her parents was disposed of, as all agreed, very sensibly; to Elsa, the house; to Elsa and Paul, share and share alike of her bank stock and railroad shares; to Ernest and Charles her stock holdings in other corporations and government bonds, equal in value to those stocks that would go to Paul and Elsa; fair-sized amounts were willed to Jennifer and Melissa because "a married woman should have money of her own"; smaller bequests to the servants, and substantial sums to the Baptist church and to the Waynesboro Public Library. The residue was to be held in trust for her great-grandchildren, if there was a residue. Gilbert Evans was named executor and Douglas Gardiner trustee for the great-grandchildren.

For Elsa the time that followed as spring became summer was a rather difficult period of adjustment: much as she had sometimes resented her mother's dictatorial ways, she had loved her dearly; just how much she discovered belatedly when the big house without that pervading presence seemed so desolate and empty, and only she and Gib were left to rattle around in it.

Nevertheless, by fall she was able to initiate the Club's season with her usual calm aplomb. The first order of business was the choice of a new member in her mother's place. Elsa had previously consulted Lavinia and Theresa Stevens privately as to whether Barbara would like to be a member. The Club never asked anyone to join without first making sure that the invitation would not be declined. Barbara's reaction to her mother's and sister's sounding-out was considerably more vehement than they had expected: she did not feel in the least inclined to give up an afternoon every two weeks to "those women," particularly now that she had finished business school and taken a position in the advertising department of the *Torchlight*. How could she ask for all that time off? The Stevenses' report to Elsa was toned down to a more acceptable phrasing, and the Club's President turned to look elsewhere. In due course, Elizabeth Merrill's daughter-in-law, Mrs. Frank (Eunice) Merrill, was chosen to replace, however inadequately, President Emeritus Sally Rausch.

One morning in November, Anne Gordon, waking early, as old people are likely to do, lay meditating drowsily as she waited for the hall clock to strike a reasonable hour for rising. She had awakened as she usually did, thinking of the day ahead, and how she was going to fill the hours. It was not a Club meeting day, or Ladies' Aid, or Sunday, that she must go to church. Nothing was left to be done at the house in preparation for winter. Lafe had finished tidying up the yard. Windows had been washed inside and out after the screens had been taken down and the house had had its fall cleaning. It would be a day for reading or knitting. (Tucker's children could not have too many sweaters.) Or perhaps for entertaining a caller, although afternoon calls seemed to have become a thing of the past.

It was curious: hours and days could seem infinitely long, either looking ahead in the morning, or living through them. Then, once over, they dropped into the void of the past, and before you knew what had happened, you had reached the end of another year. And the more years you put behind you, the shorter the present one became. "Here we are now," she thought, "already in November. It is only a little while since Christmas, and we are almost there again."

And as always, for as far back as she could remember, she saw the shape of the year: not round, like a clock's face, but a kind of irregular polygon. Clock hands moved, but you did not: you simply noted their position. Days and weeks were printed on calendars: you sat at your desk and turned the pages. But you yourself moved around the misshapen circle of the year. You thought, "It is Tuesday," or "It is the twelfth," or "It is four o'clock"; but you said to yourself or another, "In June," or "In October." She saw herself a lonely figure moving around the many-sided face of the year: up the steep slope of November; December rising sharply to a peak, Christmas the high point of the twelve months; January sloping in a long slow downward line, the longest month; February shorter, dropping more steeply; March, another long line, falling almost vertically to April; April and May turning backward and slanting down; June dropping more swiftly to the other high point of the year, or low point: the Fourth of July. These two holidays points had been fixed immutably in her mind by their childhood delights. July itself was another almost horizontal line, merging into August, the next to the longest month, rising only slightly to September's outward slant; then three months of climbing back to the beginning again, through October, November, and December to another Christmas.

This diagram of the year was so firmly imbedded in her mind that the name of the current month, thought or spoken, meant seeing herself on that polygon, sliding down to spring and summer, climbing again to Christmas. Poets talked about the "circling years," but it was not the years that circled, it was you, going round and round and round, again and again and again, the circle being large enough, like the equator, that your head did not swim. And the most astonishing thing about Time was that when you had made the circuit and the year was over and done with, it collapsed like a burst balloon: it was nothing—it was over, and you started in again on January's long, long line. There were so many years gone—Time's dustheap—that long-ago and not-so-long-ago were almost indistinguishable, and there was nothing left but memories. Johnny had been dead for more than twenty years. Twenty years! And his death seemed no longer ago than Sally Rausch's in the spring. Anne's mind paused on that thought: why had she not grieved more over the loss of her oldest and dearest friend? Had Sally's death come forty years ago, it would have been felt as a deep and continuing affliction. One of the consequences of growing old was that you felt nothing as keenly as you would once have done: it was as if one's emotions were at least partially anesthetized. The circle of your friends became more and more circumscribed: like a snail you drew in your horns. Not that she did not feel affection for her friends and a deep love for Tucker and his family, but there was a realized difference between what she felt now and what she would have felt once upon a time.

Aging, she decided, was a process of erosion—of one's emotions—probably of one's personality—and certainly of one's faith. She still thanked God for the days that were His gift: she rejoiced that she lived in enjoyment of them. She kept to her lifelong habits: read a chapter in the Bible every night before turning out her light; went to church on Sunday, where she sang "Faith of Our Fathers" along with the rest of the congregation as an act of filial piety, but she could no longer join in the recital of the Apostles' Creed. It contained too much that a rational mind could not accept. The Heaven that she had once believed in now seemed to her preposterous: it was impossible to imagine her husband and her son strumming harps in golden streets, or even, without the harps or the street, being eternally happy singing the praise of the Lord. She remembered with crawling shame the night she had presumed to try to comfort old Mr. Edwards: the night Kitty Edwards had died and he was of an age when even his sturdy faith might have been eroded by the years. An impossible Heaven, an impossible personal immortality. What God had ordained no mortal mind could comprehend: that she accepted, even as she remembered how as a child sometimes on a starry night she slipped from being Anne Alexander, had almost known and been one with—what? God? The universe? Light, all-encompassing? Words were too small—But just grow old enough and you brushed the questions from your mind, reconciling yourself to the belief that when the end came, then at last they would be answered and you would know.

From that consideration her thoughts slipped to mundane matters—what she must still do before she died, and to what had been a transient worry to her for a long time: the attic that had not been weeded out for three or four generations. Tucker and Jenny would probably never live in this house, but someday they would own it and she must not leave the accumulation for them to have to deal with. It was not really an attic: the old brick house had three full floors, with the stairs curving onto the second floor hall and then climbing again, the second flight a repetition of the first, to the third floor hall and the three rooms opening from it. All full. She had not been up there since she had gone with Tuck and Jenny to look for old furniture they might like to have. Any other climb up those stairs had been to add to the collection, not subtract from it. There were trunks of clothes, most of them female, back to hoop skirts; among them somewhere were John's captain's uniform and his old army cape, as well as his frock coats, his broadcloth coat, and discarded picture frames and unframed pictures tilted against the walls. What troubled her most deeply was the thought of all the family papers. Furniture, clothes: Jenny could dispose of those; the clothes might even be useful for Club plays as they had sometimes been before now. But the papers: she could not bear the thought of Tucker and Jenny going through them before she had read them and burned what should be burned.

"Today," she said to herself. At seven-thirty she rose, and by eight was ready for breakfast. When Louline brought the coffee pot into the dining room, she said, "There's a job I'd like to get at this morning. We'll go up to the attic and look around. I want to bring down all the family papers and go through them."

"Now, Miz Gordon—them papehs been up theh, 'long wid a mess o'otheh junk, since Ah fust come hyah. What call you got distu'bin' 'um now? Ain' doin' no hahm."

"It's a job I don't want to leave for Tucker. It isn't his reponsibility."

When breakfast was over and the dishes washed, the two women, one old and the other aging, climbed to the attic, Louline ahead, dragging behind her a clothesbasket to put loose papers in and grumbling all the way. Anne, following more slowly, paid no attention to the mumbled complaints, conserving her breath, or trying to. When she reached the third-floor hall, she clung for a moment to the banisters and in blind instinctive terror made for a horsehair-seated chair with a broken back, and sat down, white-faced and trembling, panicked by the sensation that everything—floor, house, the ground itself—was dropping away from under her.

A frightened Louline scolded her. "Ah done tol' you. You got no call to come trippin' up them staihs lak yo' sixteen yeahs ol'. Now how'm Ah gon git yo' down again?"

Anne caught her breath. The floor was once more stable under her feet, although her heart pounded in an off-again, on-again fashion. "Don't be foolish. Just took my breath for a minute." She fixed her eyes on her father's saddlebag dropped in a corner of the room where she sat, thought, "Tuck might like to have those," then said, "Somewhere, front room, I think, there's a sort of box, leather-covered, with Dr. Gordon's Army papers. Find it."

Louline eventually brought it back to her: a small chest whose leather covering was cracked and peeling away from the design of the brass nails and the old-fashioned lock in front and the handle for carrying it in the middle of the lid.

"He had that chest with him in the war. Just take it down to my bedroom, will you? And come back."

By the time Louline returned, coming upstairs one foot at a time to indicate her displeasure, Anne's heart had settled down, or at least was not skipping beats so often, and a little color had returned to her face.

"Now: empty my father's desk drawers, over in the corner, into the basket. In the cupboard here are old newspapers; take them. In the other back room, in a trunk, are letters—old ones to my mother, some to her mother. Some of mine. Bring them."

"Less jes' throw 'em out the window? Ah go down an' collec' um an' make a bonfiah."

"I am not going to burn a scrap until I have looked at it. Just bring everything that has any writing on it.

Louline, somewhat recovered from her fright, was more ready to humor her mistress. "Yas'm. Yo' jes' set an' Ah'll look." But when she glanced into the cupboard at the pile of old *Torchlights*, she rebelled again. "Who wants them ol' papehs? They so dirty no one could read um, should they want to."

"They can be dusted. Put them in the basket and I'll look them over. There might be something—" "Obituaries," she thought, "weddings."

The clothes basket filled up: newspapers, loose letters, letters tied in bundles, legal documents, old deeds, diplomas, all saved for no good reason, as well as those that might be interesting or important. When all that could be found had been piled into the clothes basket, Anne said, "Now, the photographs: on the shelves of the front room cupboard: some albums and a box of daguerreotypes. Bring them, all of them."

When Louline came back with albums piled on the box that she held with both arms under it, she said, "Yo' don' expec' me to ca'y that basket an' all these hyah down them staihs?"

"No, of course not. You can let the basket slide down. You'll have to come back for the pictures. Just put them down now. Drag the basket to the head of the stairs and get behind it and hold the handle so it won't go too fast. Drag it into Binny's room."

"Liable to break mah neck. Pu' foolishness in yo' haid today. But yo' set still an' Ah'll come back fo' them when Ah get shed all this truck."

Anne was quite content to sit. She could follow Louline's descent by the thump-thump of the basket. Near the bottom of the steps she must have lost her hold: there was a rushing and a scratching sound, and a crash. Finally Louline was back.

"Ah got it down an' drug in Binny's room. Some of ut spilled, but Ah pick ut all up. Di'n he'p the steps none. Scratch um everywhe'."

"That's easily mended. Now all these pictures. In my bedroom."

Louline again piled albums on box, laid the collection across her arms, her nails whitened by pressure where she curled her long black fingers around the bottom. "Ah kin ca'y this. Yo' come afteh me an' ketch holt if yo' gonna fall."

"I'm not going to fall. I'll hold on to the banisters. If you put the little chest in my room, I'll get started on those Army papers."

She could not bear to admit to Louline that all she wanted was to lie down on her bed. Her heart had calmed down, but not so much that she was not aware of it and the occasional missed beat. Disquieting, at the least. But the sort of thing to be expected at her age.

Although her Miz Go'don was apparently all right at lunchtime, Louline's fright had been too great for her to be completely reassured. Instead of going home for the afternoon, she waited in the kitchen for Dr. Tucker, who almost always came in that way to spend a few minutes with his grandmother between his office hours and his house calls and hospital rounds. If he was distressed by Louline's story of the morning, he was noncommittal with her, saying only, "She's too old to climb all those steps. I'll check her out, but don't worry, Louly. If she will take care of herself, I expect she will be pretty good for a while yet."

Anne, who had heard their voices, was prepared when he came into the living room swinging his stethoscope. She said, "That Louline! She's been telling tales. Did she roll her eyes and throw her arms around? She has a fine sense of the dramatic."

"She was frightened. It's a good thing you have her. How bad was it, Gran?"

"I was out of breath when I got up those stairs."

"Be honest with me."

"There was a second when my heart quit beating. Or it felt like it—then began going lickety-split. A little palpitation, I guess."

"We're not going to guess. We're going to investigate. Any pain with it?"

"Not the slightest. My heart skipped a bit now and then. It was beating so hard I could tell."

"Not really, it didn't. Just an occasional beat too weak for you to feel." He examined her with the stethoscope and took her blood pressure. "A bit irregular," he said, as he returned his instruments to his pockets. "A small dosage of digitalis should put that right. But no more expeditions to the attic."

"Oh, Tucker! I wanted to get those rooms cleaned out and put to rights, not leave it for you and Jenny."

"If you take care of yourself, you needn't worry about that for a while."

"Papa—and John, too—used to say none lived so long as those frightened into good behavior by a slight heart attack."

"Right. Go slow and you'll keep going. First thing: move to the downstairs bedroom."

"But I've slept in that upstairs bedroom since I was first married. I can't bear—"

"There comes a time when we can no longer do the things we've always done. A change of scene will do you good. Get Louline to move your traps downstairs."

"This very day?"

"You won't need anything before tomorrow except your night clothes and toilet things."

"We got your grandfather's Army papers just that far, still in his campaign chest. I intended going over them, but I think there isn't anything in there but lists of drugs: duplicates of what he had requisitioned. And his diary and discharge paper. Maybe some letters. If you want them, I guess I won't have to go over them. Take the chest."

"Of course I want them. Civil War papers?"

"The insufferable hospital in Duckport, Louisiana, where he first knew Ludwig Rausch, and then after he had finally got his complaint as far as General Sherman and it was evacuated, the siege of Vicksburg. It's all in his diary."

"Good God, Gran! I hadn't an idea! I'll get the chest before I go."

"And just remember, if you ever want to sell this house, the attic is still full."

"Just quit worrying about the attic. I wouldn't dream of selling this house.

One of the children might want it someday. Forget it. And relax. I'll ask Dick Warren to look at you tomorrow morning. Don't get up until he's been here."

"You won't take my case? If it is a case?"

"You have lived with doctors long enough to know that wouldn't do. Unethical. Besides, you will tell him things you wouldn't dream of telling me."

When Tucker had taken his leave, his grandfather's chest in hand, and gone out to his car by way of the back door, Anne went to the kitchen to scold Louline. "All that fuss about me," she said, "and you've just made yourself more trouble. You can go up now and bring down my nightclothes and brush and comb and toothbrush. Tomorrow everything will have to come down."

"Lawd o' mussy! All them papehs? 'Sides yo' clothes? Ah seed Tuckeh taken the li'l chest."

"I gave it to him. The other stuff I must look over, and if I can't go up there, it must be moved down here. And the old albums and the daguerreotypes: I'd like to look at them again. Maybe some of them can be thrown out. Bring down as many of my clothes as will go in the old wardrobe, and everything out of the chest of drawers: underwear and so on."

"Yas'm. Once ut's done we'he through traipsin' up and down them stai's, an' twel be easieh to keep'n mah eye on yo, ef'n yo' stay down heah. That boy got right good sense. Di'n' he leave you no medicine?"

"Don't fuss, Louline. I'm all right."

Tucker was not as optimistic, reporting to Jenny when he got home that evening. "Not a bad attack, so far as I could tell, but the beginning of a failure of compensation. Senile myocarditis."

"It will get progressively worse?"

"Digitalis will help for a while. But yes. Oh, nothing immediate. But I don't like her spending her nights alone in the house. Louline has to go home to tend to her own family."

"You couldn't persuade her to move in with us? I'd kind of hate to move into town, when the children are so happy here—but I would, willingly: you know how fond I am of her."

"Bless you! But there's no question of either move. Having three lively children under foot wouldn't help a bit."

"If we could only think of some single friend of hers who would be willing. Or one of your nurses?"

"We're understaffed now—can't afford to pay as many nurses as we need. We may have to close the new wing. A lot of people are too proud to come to the hospital when they know they can't pay. As for Gran, a nurse wouldn't be a good idea. She would imagine herself worse than she is. Don't worry, Sweetie: we'll find a solution. Her house could easily be made into two apartments and we just might find a nice couple who would live upstairs, keep an eye on her, and take care of the house and yard in return for a rent-free place to live, now that times are so hard."

Times were indeed hard and getting harder. The Rausch Cordage Company was still operating, though day by day Gib looked more worried and Ludwig thinner and more gaunt. Like everyone else, doctors were suffering: the hospital was half empty because people could not afford to be ill except at home; even small bills for house calls were going unpaid. Emergency cases, at home or in the hospital, were taken care of; some would be paid for in time, some never.

As Rodney Stevens said to Lavinia one evening when he had finished reading the paper and had laid it down, it was a bleak outlook for their son. Gardiner at twenty-four was halfway through medical school: a couple more years and he would be ready to come to a hospital that did not need him. "If things don't improve, I'll advise him to apply for a residency when he finishes his internship. I know that is several years away, but—"

"He'll be all right. Let him start with a struggle: it won't hurt him. It is not always good for a boy to step into a place being held for him." Gardiner's mother was not so hardhearted as she sounded. "If worst comes to worst, you could sell some of those stocks your mother turned over to you on your twenty-first birthday."

"Sell perfectly good stock at today's market prices? Only as a last resort. And there aren't so many left. I sold some, you remember, to cover my third of starting the hospital."

Theresa, present at this living room conversation, seemed to be intent on the book she was reading, off in a corner. But she listened and was ashamed, abysmally, that she was not out earning a living. The good opinion of her father was important to her; she remembered all too well the days when she had not had it: when her feet were too big, her elbows awkward, her face nothing to rouse pride in a parent. He had forgotten that phase of growing up: she had not; she could not bear for him to think her useless now. "I must try to find a job," she contributed to the conversation. "Teaching or something. Maybe the library. Miss McCune has lost another assistant."

"Tess, my darling," her father said, "we're not going to the poorhouse. We may wear old clothes, but we won't go hungry. Besides, teachers are a dime a dozen: everyone who can't find anything more remunerative to do thinks he can at least teach. And as for the library: just when everyone out of work wants to read, the town has cut the library's budget. Miss McCune is working for peanuts. She would work for nothing, as she did during the war, rather than close the library. But there's no money for another assistant, not right now."

"She didn't! Work for nothing?"

"She did during the war." Tess's mother was emphatic. "Of course she couldn't have, if she hadn't had the rent from the Ballard house she had inherited. Don't worry, Tess. We like having you around."

Theresa thought, "I know, my dear mother. I love you with all my heart. But how can I get any work done with so many interruptions. I know you try not to bother me, but there are errands to be run and my advice about having the curtains cleaned to be given. I guess you and your sisters lived in each other's pockets, although one would never guess it now, when only Aunt Caroline is around, in and out." She said, "If I'd been sensible, I'd have gone to business school like Barb."

Rodney, who was not so unsympathetic as Theresa feared, said, "Nonsense. You're well started on what can be a distinguished career. Barbara is frittering her time away waiting for Charlie Merrill to propose or reform, I don't know which."

"Even if he reforms—and I don't suppose he is an unsalvageable alcoholic yet—" Lavinia said reflectively, "he wouldn't be an easy man to live with. Bitter and cynical. Like my father."

"Like Grandfather! Grandfather Gardiner!" Theresa was astonished. "Why, he never drank, did he?"

"No, not that. It wasn't against the law then, so there was no challenge. No, I just meant that club foot—just like Charlie's bad leg. He must always have been conscious of it when he was a boy. He was hard to live with, or at least to grow up under. I never heard him say a sarcastic word to Mamma, but at least until we learned table manners and how to speak grammatically, with us he was pretty caustic. And the dinner hour was never much fun, he was so cynical. Oh, I know that's hard to believe, since he has turned into an indulgent grandfather. But believe me, he has mellowed. He was saved by being married to Mamma."

"And so might Charlie be," Rodney said, "if Barbara cares as much for him as your father's Barbara did for him. Don't take your mother too seriously, Tess. The Gardiner house was a good place to go—the gathering point for all of us, and we were welcome there, even if the old aunts didn't like the hubbub. But Charlie's excessive drinking is something else. His parents are worried sick. And he's too old for Barbie anyway."

Theresa said, "Barbara isn't a fool, even if she is beautiful. And because she is beautiful, he may be enough in love to straighten up. If he was a young boy, it would be worse. How are Gardiner and Merrill doing, anyway?"

"No doubt they feel the pinch, like everyone else. I don't know whether Charlie could keep a wife on what he is earning. The real threat of suffering for the whole town lies with Rausch Cordage: whether it can keep operating. Tucker says Ludwig insists on keeping the mill running, making rope and twine he can't sell—and will, until the capital is used, no doubt. But then? The smaller industries in town—the handle factory, the lumber companies, the ice plant—are all in trouble."

"And the Hoffmann bakery?"

"Doing better. People manage to eat, if only stale loaves of bread for a penny."

"To make bread you need flour." Theresa was being logical. "And for flour you need wheat. I should think Rausch's could sell binder twine."

"Except that the price paid for wheat is so low that the farmers may just quit raising it. On which cheerful note I must leave you for a look at my patients." But in a moment, hat and bag in hand, he thrust his head around the door post. "I almost forgot to tell you: Tucker says his grandmother is beginning to have heart difficulties. He's trying to find someone to live in the house with her: he doesn't like her being there alone at night." And he proved that he was more aware of Theresa's difficulties than he had ever shown by adding, "There's your chance, Tess, if you want peace and quiet—out from under too much family."

When he had gone, the two women looked at each other in dismay. "Poor Cousin Anne," Theresa said. "To be alone and old and ailing, that's the saddest—"

"Not quite," her mother was quick to answer, remembering Amanda Reid. "At least she isn't poor. And Tucker stops to see her every day, and Jenny is constantly in-and-out. So she isn't altogether alone. And she will never feel sorry for herself: she will make the most of what years she still has; I don't know anyone who has had a sadder life, yet she has always been—more than serene—she has always been able to laugh—to love life in spite of sorrow. Oh, I'm no good with words: you could say it better. But I admire her, and I am fond of her."

"Who isn't? I don't know her as well, of course, but she was awfully nice about my book. And really understood what it was all about. Mother, how big is the upstairs of that house?"

"As big as the downstairs. Let's see—five bedrooms, I think, and a bath, and a balcony between front and back bedrooms on the east side—you know: that recessed two-story porch."

"Plenty large enough for an apartment, even if you turned the back bedrooms into kitchen and dining room. There isn't any reason, is there, why I shouldn't go live there? Except money, dammit. I never expected to care whether I had money or not."

"But Tess, your father's Cousin Anne by marriage isn't your responsibility. Your father didn't mean it. There's no need for you to sacrifice yourself taking care of an old lady."

"I don't think Father meant she needed taking care of—and anyway, she has Louline daytimes. It's just that she oughtn't to be all alone at night."

Theresa said no more. She could not hurt her mother—not for anything she could possibly gain by it. But she had an opportunity to speak to Anne herself at the next Club meeting at her Grandmother Edwards'. She and Lavinia were the last arrivals: Elsa was already standing in front of the fireplace, preparatory to opening the meeting. Lavinia dropped into the last empty chair in the back row; Theresa perforce squeezed her way down to the front and tucked herself into a space on the davenport under the nose of Elsa, who waited for her to get seated before asking for the roll call.

"The most comfortable seat in Grandmother's parlor," she whispered to Anne. "I feel guilty taking it."

Anne's eyes twinkled. "I was the shameless one: I got first choice. Yours is the last."

The secretary rose, and whispering was suspended up and down the rows of chairs as she took over. Anne pretended to listen, but was thinking of the girl beside her while she kept her attentive gaze on the presiding officer. Theresa was blood kin to her husband, a cousin in some remote degree, whatever other closer ties there might be. Theresa, however, had no look at all of the Gordons, except the level set of her eyes: short brown hair that always managed to look windblown even under a hat, a slightly out-of-line triangular face and long jaw, all redeemed by the amazing long-lashed amethyst eyes, her grandmother Gardiner's over again. "Not pretty," Anne concluded, "but what a nice child she is." When the meeting was adjourned, she held Theresa with a hand on her knee. "I don't suppose you like to talk about it, but I'd love to know. How is the next book coming?"

Theresa grimaced. "Not very well. Oh, I have an idea and a sort of outline and various characters in my mind. But I can't seem to get down to *writing*. I need long stretches of time. I can't do it in snatched minutes, between interruptions. One's family feels so free! I'd love an apartment where I could be alone. But I haven't any money."

"My dear child, I can imagine. A family would find it impossible to believe that what one is trying to do can be of the least importance. Could I tempt you to come live with me? The whole upstairs is unused, you know. All it needs to make it into an apartment is a kitchen. And I wouldn't interrupt you. Tucker says I mustn't climb stairs."

"Cousin Anne, do you mean it? You wouldn't mind having your house torn up? And the expense? Of course I'd have to persuade Mother that you really need someone. Maybe you could say you don't like living alone?"

"But I don't mind that, myself: I am used to it. But Tucker, although he keeps assuring me I haven't a serious heart condition, admits he doesn't like me to be alone at night. He would be delighted with such an arrangement. And of course if you were to come to live with me for my sake, there wouldn't be any question of rent."

Anne wondered a little if she were the victim of a plan worked out by Tucker and Rodney, but if so she didn't mind: it would be a pleasure to have the ardent young woman living upstairs. Her suspicions were confirmed by the alacrity with which the arrangements were made. The smaller back bedroom, overlooking the side street, was made into a kitchen, and modern fittings replaced the old-fashioned ones in the bathroom. The furniture was moved out that had been hers and John's, and sold, whatever pangs it cost to part with it. The front bedroom was refurnished as a living room with a heterogeneous collection from various attics. The bedroom across the hall was left as it was; Johnny's old room opening on the upstairs porch, became the dining room, and the small spare room over Anne's bedroom downstairs was to be used as a study. Theresa had demurred: the typewriter would drive Cousin Anne crazy. Anne laughed at her: the floors in the old house were as thick as the walls, and anyway she was not in her bedroom except to sleep, dress, and undress.

Theresa moved in when all was done: that is, she put her clothes, her typewriter, notes, a supply of paper, and a number of books into her mother's car, and transferred them from one house to the other. She did not leave without a stern admonition from her father: "Cousin Anne won't accept one cent of rent because she thinks you are doing this for her. I'll pay half the coal and utility bills: Tucker and I have agreed to that. But even if you are there, as Tucker sees it, to look after her at nights, you are still under obligation to her. Help whenever you can. She has always been a great gardener, so when spring comes do the planting and such for her. She's past doing all of it for herself. We owe Cousin Anne more than we can ever repay: she made Mamma and me welcome when we first came here from Mississippi, and introduced us to her friends. And Johnny and his father, I can't tell you how much I owe them. So do what you can for her."

"Oh, Father! As if I wouldn't. You know I'm fond of her, and I know how fortunate I am to be given a place of my own, rent free."

"I understand, Theresa," he smiled at her, "even if your mother doesn't, quite. It's a little difficult being a member of a family when you need to be alone."

"Jane Austen could do it, but I'm no Jane Austen."

"I think that in Cousin Anne's house you will find you have plenty of time to yourself. Make the most of it, but don't forget: help whenever you can."

"Yes, Father." No daughter of twenty-eight really likes parental strictures like Rodney's: Theresa's "Yes, Father" was so meek as to be almost a mockery. Rodney obligingly laughed. "Just remember: we are proud of you and expect great things."

No doubt Theresa was missed at home, especially by her mother, but the move was a happy one for her, for Anne, and for Louline, who had grown reluctant to leave her mistress for the afternoon, and particularly after the dinner dishes had been washed in the evenings. With Theresa upstairs, she often said something to Anne like "They's a-plenty o' thet roas' beef lef' fo' yo' to get tiahed of. Di'n Ah betteh call Miss Theresa down fo' suppeh?" Theresa began to feel that Cousin Anne was feeding as well as housing her.

She was at first rather reluctant to sit down after dinner in Cousin Anne's sitting room, lest she be asked how the writing was coming, and she could not bear to talk about it. But Anne, who grew fonder of her day by day, was well aware of her sensitiveness and—perhaps "insecurity" was the word—or "modesty": she sensed that she would not want to talk about what might never be accomplished. The typewriter clacked away steadily all day (and of course it could be heard downstairs), but it was pleasing rather than bothersome, because it was evidence that Theresa must be making progress. The house had been empty and silent for so long that even the light footfalls overhead were a pleasure to Anne. Her friends had never really neglected her: in addition to Tuck and Jennifer, Elsa, Jessamine and Sheldon Edwards, and Barbara Gardiner came fairly often for brief visits, Melissa and her mother occasionally, and Mr. Patton rather too frequently. Anne never had relished being prayed over and for: it embarrassed her, but she could not quite bring herself to say so to him. She did go to church (and since Dr. Warren thought she should not walk, Jenny became a more faithful attendant at Sunday services than she had ever been before). With the same chauffeur she managed to get to most Club meetings, and to Tuck's or Elsa's for Sunday dinners.

She would have said before Theresa moved in that she had been leading a fairly active life, all things considered; but with Theresa there, the house became altogether livelier. Working hours were respected by Tess's family and friends, but after four-thirty they felt free to drop in; occasionally Theresa invited two or three of them to stay for dinner, and the sound of young laughter dropping down the stairs and echoing along the hall was a delight to Anne.

In the interval since she and Louline had brought the family papers downstairs, Anne had gone through them and sorted them out, tying the letters into bundles: those to her mother from her family, recounting vicissitudes, misfortunes, and dull, comfortable domesticity, but nothing shameful; those to her father and to her from Rob and John from camps and battlefields; John's to her were letters to a child. It had taken him a long time to realize that she was growing up, but that was no reason to destroy them. There were no letters at all that she felt must be burned before someone read them. Documents she tied up and put in a stout manila envelope: old deeds, the original land grant to the Gordon farm, signed by Thomas Jefferson, copies of wills, receipts, her father's and John's medical school diplomas, and her own from the Female Seminary. When she had gone over everything, she put all, including the old *Torchlights*, the photographs, and the daguerreotypes, into the drawer at the bottom of her wardrobe. Tucker could do what he pleased with them when the time came: burn or keep.

Months passed while Anne was so employed, interrupted by various social obligations that she could not quite neglect. Christmas of 1930 was celebrated by the Club as always; Elsa followed her mother's established custom, with no relaxation of standards: dinner to feed the gentlemen, a play to entertain them. Elsa was not quite so positive as her mother had always been that they were really entertained, but like her, thought it was good for the family men to have to dress once a year in their tuxedoes and stiff shirts.

The play—an original one, written for them by a reluctant Theresa—was built around a group of choral singers, which gave the Club members' small fry a chance to show off; they saw little of the festivities, however, fetched as they were by their fathers when dinner was over and the drawing room being rearranged. And when the play was over and they had had their ice cream and cake, they were whisked off again and turned over to nursemaids, aunts, or grandmothers at home. Even so, like other generations before them, small Gordons, Evanses, Merrills, Lichtensteins, and Warrens felt they had taken part in an occasion.

New Year's Day of 1931 found the country sinking deeper into hard times; it was not a season of jubilation. The people grew restless, the unemployed turbulent. Only those like Anne Gordon, who had lived long enough to have experienced earlier depressions, thought the threat in the atmosphere portentous: all that was required was patience; the economy would recover as it had always done. In the meantime there was no one actually starving: surely the really poor were being taken care of.

Winter slipped into spring, and for some at least of Waynesboro folk the state of the country, which had weighed so heavily on the spirit, became secondary to the pleasure of getting the flower beds ready for planting, and the delight of seeing daffodils again and violets and lilies of the valley; then the lilacs, and before Memorial Day, the wisteria and peonies and syringa. Anne was not very willing to let Theresa pull the weeds and plant the annual seeds, protesting that she was supposed to be upstairs at her typewriter. Theresa brushed off such remonstrances, saying, "I have to take an hour off now and then. Besides, I've almost finished this bed." Anne gave in, although the urge to kneel and get her hands in the soil was almost irresistible. She had some unforgettable association with almost everything in her yard, which Theresa listened to and stored away in her memory: the plantain lilies just coming up had been her mother's; so too the garden heliotrope and the yellow rosebush; Binny had brought violets from the woods and planted them and now they had taken over the place.

Then one summer morning Anne went out with Louline and Theresa to enjoy the air and to watch, from a kitchen chair they had brought out for her, while they picked the cherries: Louline from a stepladder and Theresa from well up in the tree. Without thinking, Anne rose and reached for a full branch just overhead; with arms lifted, she felt a bit tottery, but surely, she told herself, she was equal to so undemanding a chore as picking the cherries she could reach. When Theresa looked down from her perch at some unexpected sound—an audible choke or half-gasp, half-cough—Anne was clinging to a cherry bough, struggling for breath. Theresa dropped to the ground and helped Anne to reach her chair and sit down. Louline by that time was beside her.

"Look over the fence, Louline: see if Tucker's car is there."

But Tucker's car was not there, Louline reported.

"Then you stay with her while I call the hospital; one of the doctors is sure to be in."

Anne was able to protest. "Just one of those momentary things. I'll be all right."

Theresa paid no heed; she ran into the house to the telephone in the hall. She returned to say that Dr. Warren was coming, and meanwhile couldn't she and Louline make a chair with their hands and carry Mrs. Gordon inside and get her on a bed?

They got her into the house, Theresa's strong young hands and Louline's old and stronger ones crossed in a wrist-grasping square that Anne could sit on. She was still protesting. "I never felt such a fool. I can still walk, for goodness' sake." They paid no attention. By the time Dr. Warren arrived,

Anne was lying on her bed with her shoes off. She had apparently recovered, but he scolded her, blue eyes twinkling at her fractiousness. After applying his stethoscope, he said, "A stronger dose of digitalis, and if that doesn't work, a little nitroglycerin with it. In the meantime, take this. Louline, bring a glass of water, please. I'll give Tucker a prescription and he can bring you the pills this afternoon." He pushed back the lock of sandy hair that had fallen into his eyes when he stopped. "Better stay on the bed the rest of the day," he said. "We aim to keep you well for a long while, you know."

In the hall he told Louline and Theresa, "Try to keep her quiet. But if she very much wants to do something, I'd let her. She has really done very well this last year, and at her age, what do a few months more or less matter? Better a few happy ones than many spent as an invalid."

Theresa stopped what would have been a lamentation from Louline by a firm hand on her shoulder. "She'll hear you: do be quiet." As she saw the doctor out, he said, "I'll look in again tomorrow. Sooner if she needs me, or if Tucker thinks I should."

Theresa returned to the bedroom, where she found Louline helping Anne get her dress off, straightening her out on the bed, spreading an afghan over her.

"Now—yo' jes' lay theh, lak the docteh tell yo', while we go finish with them cherries. Ah bring yo' bell off'n the dinin' room table: yo' ring does yo' want us."

Anne smiled, thanked her, and was asleep before the kitchen screen had closed behind them, wondering, as she drifted off, whether young Warren (as he would always be to her) had not fooled her into taking a sleeping tablet.

After that unsettling incident, on the stronger medicine Anne seemed normal enough, though hardly as brisk as in other years. She spent a good part of her time reading. Dickens and Jane Austen mostly, but some new novels too, just for the sake of keeping up with the times. When her eyes tired, she took up her knitting, although she considered it a last resort.

Theresa finished her novel and sent it off to her publishers. "They won't want it," she insisted to Anne one evening when they were together, after dinner. Theresa was forlornly at loose ends now that her book was in the hands of her publishers. "Everyone now is writing about the depression—at least everyone who is published—and being pessimistic and cynical about America, saying only a revolution can save it. I don't believe all that nonsense. Besides, I can't write about conditions, only about people."

"People past or present?" Anne ventured to ask.

"Both, as a matter of fact. Like this: a young woman—oh, thirty or so, not too young—comes back to her home town after twenty years. It brings back to her mind a sad love affair she had seen acted out when she was too small to comprehend what she was watching. She tells the story from the child's point of view as she remembers it, with a—a slant that shows how, as a grown-up woman looking back, she thinks it must in fact really have been. At least, that is what I meant to do. It is a short book."

"Funny," Theresa thought, "how much easier it was to say all this to Cousin Anne than it would have been to my family." The family would never know what she had been working on unless she could put a published book in their hands.

Anne said, "You remember very well, astonishingly well, how the world and people look to a child. *Old Soldier* was proof of that. You must have a good memory."

"Oh, total recall," Theresa laughed. "But I'd like to go back beyond what I remember and do a long book about the 60's, 70's, and 80's. Trouble is, I don't know anything about those years, really, except for what has got into books. Not what they felt like to people when they were living them."

"There are all those old letters I put in the wardrobe drawer. Read them, if you like—they're far too old to be personal and private. All the persons concerned are long gone, except me. They would tell you how their writers felt; they might give you background and atmosphere. And in the attic there are those huge old volumes of bound *Harper's Weekly* for those very years. I didn't ask Louline to carry them down: they were much too heavy. But you could manage one at a time."

Theresa was delighted by the offered opportunity. She could not settle down to actually beginning another book until she had done with the second one; even if the verdict on her manuscript was favorable, there would still be the ordeal of proof-reading before she could put it behind her. For the rest of the summer, most of the long afternoons were spent companionably with Anne on the sofa, handing letters one by one to Theresa on a stool at her feet, with the necessary explanations: "Eleanor was my mother's older sister, who went with her minister husband to his charge in Kentucky. She died young, of consumption. But for some reason, this one letter from her survived: all about what she thought of Kentucky."

As the long-dead Eleanor had written, she was shocked and sickened by what she had seen for the first time in her life: a coffle of slaves, chained together, on their way to the auction block, "like animals. Or worse. They don't chain cattle together when they drive them to slaughter."

Theresa took the letter in hand and scanned the spidery handwriting on the faded blue pages. "Those days seem so long ago until you read something like this, and then it becomes immediate: this is how it seemed to be alive in the fifties."

After school began in the fall, little Sally Anne Gordon joined them more often than not. She was eleven in the autumn of 1931, and ready for the sixth grade; her parents had decided it would be wise to send her in town to school, where she would grow up with all kinds of children, especially those who would presumably be her adult friends, instead of to a one-room school attended by only farmers' children. It was just possible she might learn more than in a one-room township school, although her mother was doubtful about that, having herself gone through the Waynesboro schools. Her father brought her every morning as far as the hospital, and let her walk the rest of the way; or, if he was unavailable (as doctors so often are, at any hour of the day), her mother delivered her. After school, on the nice days of early September, she often walked the few miles out to the Gordon place; when the weather turned bad, she went to her father's office to await the end of his office hours, and if he had been called out, she would cross the back yards to her great-grandmother's, knowing that he would stop there before he went on home.

Anne loved her three great-grandchildren dearly, but had loved and spoiled them as a bundle of three rather than as individuals. Now she came to know Sally Anne very well. She was an ingratiating child, eager to please and be loved. She was also a pretty one, who resembled no one member of the family in particular but had certain reminiscent features: not her oval face, but the dimples like Johnny's; not the color of her eyes, but the way they were set, like all the Gordons', full and heavy-lidded. Anne regretted that the child had inherited what she considered her own worst feature: the too-wide mouth. She failed to see that the little girl also had hair like hers: hers that had so long been dark brown but now was lightened by gray. But a trace of its babyhood gold still showed when the sun shone on it. Sally Anne's was still more fair than dark, soft and heavy; it was unmanageable even by plaits, combs, or ribbons. Her mother was constantly threatening her with bangs (in a year when no little girl wore bangs) if she could not keep it off her face and out of her eyes. By the time a school day was over, the uncontrollable hair was her most conspicuous feature, but her great-grandmother did not demand tidiness: she had grown to love the child for herself, not just because she was her great-grandchild, and always welcomed her when she dropped in.

Happening in one afternoon when Anne and Theresa were in the sitting room looking over letters, Theresa reading them aloud while Anne put in some explanation, all duly noted, Sally Anne was caught up, entranced and filled with awe by the dates, the pale blue paper folded over and addressed without benefit of envelopes, the fine delicate handwriting, sometimes covering a page in two directions. Anne, seeing that Theresa was being completely distracted, said to the child, "Wouldn't you like to come back to my room and look at some pictures of your ancestors? I can show you what I looked like at your age, pantalettes and all."

Theresa, troubled at the thought of Anne's opening the heavy drawer and dragging its contents out, said, "Let me bring them in here. I know where they are. And if you don't mind, I'll take this bundle of letters upstairs."

And so Anne and Sally spent a completely happy hour looking at daguerreotypes. In the beginning they sat side by side on the sofa under the window, while Sally Anne picked one after another out of the box at her feet, but in a little while she slipped to the floor and laid the daguerreotypes, the ambrotypes, the Civil War *cartes de visite* of soldiers in uniform in rows in front of her knees, and surveyed the grim faces with concentrated attention. Finally she said, "They all look so sad. Living in pioneer times must have been very hard."

Anne laughed with pure delight. "Bless you, child! These were taken long after 'pioneer times' were over and done with. Here, anyway. Not out West, of course. And they only *look* sad. I suppose they were like everyone else: sad sometimes and happy sometimes. But in daguerreotypes and ambrotypes they all look solemn because they had to hold still so long: for a whole minute, maybe more. Nobody can hold a smile that long without moving or looking silly. You sat with your head in a clamp on a tall tripod behind you where it wouldn't show, so you couldn't move or blink. No such thing as a snapshot. In that daguerreotype of my mother—your great-great-grandmother—she looks sad and wistful, doesn't she? But the way I remember her, she was full of fun—happy as a lark until she got sick, and my brother Rob went off to war."

"You can remember when she was full of fun? How old were you?"

"When she died? Eleven, just like you. Certainly I remember her. Wouldn't you remember your mother?"

Sally Anne's eyes widened with horror. "But she isn't going to die, is she?"

"Of course she isn't, honey. She's young—hardly more than a girl. My mother was older: my brother Rob was ten years older than I." No need to mention the babies in between, who had died in infancy: she regretted having upset the child, and would say nothing to make matters worse. "See those two solemn-looking little boys? One was my brother Rob, one was your Great-grandfather John Gordon, who grew up and married me—and all that solemnity was for the picture-taking: no one ever saw them looking like that." Each daguerreotype showed a glowering boy of ten or eleven, standing with one hand on a truncated Ionic pillar, clad in long loose trousers down to his high boot-tops, and short roundabouts that showed a great deal of white cuff and wide white collar spread over the jacket, and an extravagantly flowered and flowing bow tie. "Of course, that was a long while before John came to stay at our house and learn medicine from my father. When these were taken, though, they were already friends, going to the Reverend Mr. McMillan's School for Boys. And mischievous young—" She paused as she heard the kitchen door open and Tucker speak to Louline.

"Tell me, Gran."

"Some other time, Sweetheart. There's your father come for you. Pick them all up, will you, and put them back in the box."

Sally Anne was still trying to arrange them so that the lid would go on when her father came in.

"I hope you haven't been wearing your grandmother out. Gran, you shouldn't let her. She's insatiable."

To divert him, Sally Anne lifted a daguerreotype from the box. "Daddy, do you know who that is?"

Tucker studied the little girl in round comb and pantalettes, and said,

"Gran, of course." He looked down at his daughter's mischievously smiling, dimpled face. "You know what? You look something like her. And by golly, *her* mother had the hair problem licked."

"She looks something like Alice in Wonderland, doesn't she. But no one wears combs like that nowadays."

"I might suggest it to your mother. Now you must get those pictures put away and back in the wardrobe drawer." When she had staggered out, he added to his grandmother, "I must get her home: I have house calls to make before dinner. And Gran, don't let her tire you out. You could tell her stories all day, and she'd never have enough."

After that, the collection of old pictures was brought out with fair frequency. Sally Anne demanded stories about the bad boys; her favorite was the Halloween exploit conducted when they were fifteen or sixteen, and John was spending the night at the Alexanders'. They were out early, lifting gates and tipping over privies, but had come in at bedtime, as they had promised they would, and had gone upstairs. In the middle of the night, Dr. Alexander answered a peremptory knock at the door, and opened it to be confronted by a wrathful constable. A farmers' wagon had been taken to pieces and part by part carried up the Court House stairs to the roof, where it had been put together again straddling the ridgepole. Dr. Alexander indignantly insisted his boys had gone long since to bed, and could not have been guilty. The constable was equally sure that they had been involved. When Dr. Alexander had taken him upstairs to the boys' bedroom to prove his contention, they found Rob's room empty. The boys had climbed over the porch railing, slid down a post, and made their escape. Having assured the constable that he would take care of the miscreants, he waited up for them, caught them as they were about to shinny up the post, made them return to the scene of the crime, disassemble the wagon, carry the parts down several flights of stairs, put it together again, and return it to the barnyard where they had found it. The first time Sally Anne heard the story, she went to the door to the recessed porch, studied the height of the post to the second floor. "I don't believe," she said, "that I could do that. I'm not very good at shinnying up a tree. Petticoats get in the way. I'd be scared of falling."

"I should hope so. I told you they were very naughty boys."

"Did they ever do that again?"

"Slide down the post, you mean? Oh, I think when they were a little older and John was living with us except for Saturdays and Sundays, that was their favorite exit. Even when there was no reason why they shouldn't go out the front door like Christians—as they did when they were sparking the girls and didn't want to rumple their Sunday-best clothes."

In this fashion the weeks passed: September became October; October, November. As December approached, Sally Anne spent less time with her great-grandmother: she was making Christmas presents at Jennifer's urging, as Jennifer herself had done as a child, passing on what she had been taught: that presents made by loving hands meant more than presents bought. Her mother met Sally Anne at the schoolhouse most afternoons and took her home.

Anne reluctantly started to work on her Club paper. It was due shortly after New Year's: "Realism in the Twenties: Dreiser's *American Tragedy*, Anderson's *Poor White*, and O'Neill's *Anna Christie*." None of them appealed to her greatly; she wondered whether the Program Committee had been influenced by a misplaced sense of humor, assigning such a subject to an octogenarian. Nevertheless, she tried very hard to see why younger readers admired them.

By late November, Theresa's book was printed and bound and the publication date set: December 10, in time for the Christmas trade. Theresa felt that she had done with it and put it behind her; she scarcely glanced at her author's copies, although she autographed one for Anne and one for her parents. She felt ready to go to work on the book she had set her heart on writing: a long one, covering several generations of life in a small midwestern city: the sort of thing that had been popular a few years back, like *Jean-Christophe* and *Remembrance of Things Past* and *The Forsyte Saga*. She laughed at herself ruefully: she was no Galsworthy, much less a Rolland or a Proust. But she would like to write an answer to Sinclair Lewis, whose *Main Street* had made her so angry that after a decade she seethed when she thought of it. She set about planning the new book with stubborn concentration. She hoped that times would be better when she had finished, or no publisher would look at it, nor anyone have the patience to read it. But there was a chance that, after the depression had somehow been dealt with, some readers might still be interested in what she felt compelled to do: Old America changing, while New America seemed to be tumbling about one's ears. For comfort and encouragement, in the first weeks of 1932 she had the better-than-moderate success of the newly published novel; it was well reviewed, and although it never reached any best-seller list, her royalty checks enabled her to take over, for the time being at any rate, the half of the coal and utilities bills her father had been paying; she even dared spend a part of her checking account (her first ever, and naturally a source of pride) on a couple of new dresses for church and Club meetings.

The usual Christmas festivities, including the Club party, interrupted both authors, and Anne at least found it difficult to finish her paper, even any-old-how. She was much more interested in what was going on in the country, now that it was warming up for a presidential election. In the midst of the depression it made her both sick and angry to read in the papers or hear over the radio the denunciations of poor President Hoover as the sole cause of the trouble. He had become the villain of the day. The young people—even the middle-aged ones—seemed not to react as she did: she missed Sally Rausch more than she had done in the months past. Sally would have agreed with her and would have expressed herself forcefully: together they could really have let themselves go. As the months passed, she felt this more and more keenly. It came to be generally acknowledged, even by Republicans, that the

Democrats were bound to win the 1932 election: the party in power was always blamed for hard times. Anne refused to admit that it must of necessity bo so this year. When summer came, and the Democrats assembled for their nominating convention, she listened on her radio, remembering others more satisfactory to Republicans. The convention of 1932 was to her wholly dismaying: even she would have admitted that there were some fairly sensible Democrats in the country who would not send it headlong to ruin, but the delegates could not have done worse: that bland, patronizing demagogue Roosevelt!

To some extent both Theresa and Tucker, along with his wife and in-laws, shared her feelings: after all, they were bred-in-the-bone Republicans. But they did not encourage her to hope, and said, however glumly, that they guessed the country would survive: it had survived Wilson, hadn't it? Anne, listening to campaign speeches, wishing for Sally Rausch to listen (and mutter) with her, felt that there was a world of difference between Wilson the schoolmaster, who had wanted his country and other countries to be guided by his wisdom, and this man, who was promising everything to the poor and benighted: his schemes for sweeping reforms to bring about recovery—unemployment relief and made work, new laws for the stock market to save the country from another panic, lower tariffs, legislation to protect agriculture, help for the one-third of the population "ill-housed, ill-clad, ill-fed," all summed up in the phrase "a New Deal for the forgotten man." Anne was aware, as she put it to Tucker one day when she exploded to him, that they were "some starry-eyed idealists who really believed there would be no poor, if everyone had work to do and was paid for it. But not that Roosevelt. I don't suppose he's ever known a poor man in his life, and he's no idealist: he knows very well that there are many who would rather be poor than work, and he's promising that the government will take care of them. It sounds like the decline of the Roman Empire to me: bread and circuses. And once the people get the idea that the government has an obligation to support its citizens, there'll be no end to what they will demand. America will be on a long toboggan slide downhill to Socialism. I remember long ago Franz Lichtenstein, when he couldn't have been more than fifteen or sixteen, assuring me that in time we would have a Socialist government. I suppose he's delighted with all this, and is expecting to join in the redistribution of wealth. I've always liked Franz, and Mary, too. But imagine them in positions of authority."

"A couple of your 'starry-eyed idealists.' That was quite a speech, Gran. But I wish you wouldn't get so worked up—it isn't good for you. You're all out of breath. Can't you take it more calmly? Because it's going to happen, and our votes won't stop it. One of Rodney's patients told him the other day that she would pay her bill when she got back the thousand dollars Hoover owed her."

"But how—how could she believe—?"

"I suppose she had her money in some bank or building-and-loan that has folded. There have been a number of them. Thank the Lord our Waynesboro banks are sound."

"Poor President Hoover! I know: it's all his fault."

"He's going to take the punishment, his fault or not. So take it calmly. Remember: even if Roosevelt becomes President, Congress may not give him everything he wants."

But in spite of all the warnings, and her attempts to take it calmly, the election came as a profound shock. She and Theresa listened to the returns as reported on the radio; in spite of Tess's remonstrances, Anne sat up far beyond her bedtime into the small hours, hoping that somewhere across the country the tide would turn. It never did, and she finally went to bed in despair muttering, "Where did all those votes come from? Poor white trash must have crawled out like worms from under stones."

It was small comfort to her to read in the paper the next day that more than fifteen million Americans had preferred President Hoover to Roosevelt. The country had survived other Democrats, true, but they had not in her eyes been the threat to America that this one was: the country would outlive Roosevelt, but it would not be the America in which she had grown up and lived her life. No matter how she argued with herself that, after all, government did not impinge much on real life—loving, bearing children, bringing them up, growing old and dying—she was still depressed and full of foreboding. She was too old, she supposed, to adjust to what young people could take in stride.

On the Sunday after election day, at dinner at Elsa's, Anne brought down the house with the remark that showed how she felt.

Since Sally's death, it had become the custom for the senior and junior Evanses and Tucker and Jennifer to take turns having the family for Sunday dinner. Sometimes they were all there; sometimes Ludwig and Melissa with their children went to her parents'; often Anne felt unequal to so many people and the turmoil necessarily created by the children. On that particular Sunday though, they were also there with Gib and Elsa; Ludwig's family, and Tucker's, with Anne. For dinner the children were at their usual small table, with Sally Anne old enough to keep them in some kind of order. As Gib was carving the roast and all the adults were watching him with that concentration so unnerving to the carver, Anne spoke suddenly into the silence, in a meditative tone of voice: "I hate to think of dying and leaving the country in the hands of the Democrats."

A second of speechless astonishment was followed by a chorus of laughter. After a moment Anne began to laugh with them. "That must have sounded ridiculous. As if my being alive could make any difference. It's just that I'd like to live long enough to see what happens—know that the country is safe."

"Why not?" Gib reassured her. "It's only for four years. By 1936 the country may be fed up with the Democrats."

Elsa said, "Do let's forget the election and talk about something else. It's done: nothing can change it."

After dinner, when the children were playing in what was still "the library" and the adults were gathering in the drawing room, Anne said that she had better go on home, if Tucker was free to take her. He came at once to put on his overcoat while Elsa went upstairs for Anne's cloak and hat. While Anne waited, leaning against the newel post, alone except for Tucker in the far reaches of the hall, Sally Anne, alerted by all the good-byes, came out of the library to stand close to her great-grandmother at the foot of the stairs.

"I heard what you said at dinner. I didn't see why everyone laughed."

"Because I said something very silly." She knew what troubled the child. "Don't worry, Sweetheart. I'm not thinking of dying: no one enjoys being alive more than I do. I'll keep going as long as I can. But when you are as old as I am, the years begin to pile up: I've already had twelve years beyond the three score and ten allotted to men. So you mustn't be surprised, nor grieved when—Read the Book of Job, and you will see that dying is not something to be afraid of. Verses like, 'He discovereth deep things out of darkness, and bringeth out to light the shadow of death.'"

Tucker came up behind her as the conversation concluded, took her cloak from Elsa at the foot of the stairs, held it for her, and waited while she adjusted her hat. Sally Anne said, "Good-bye, Gran. I'll remember," and returned to the library. As Tucker helped his grandmother down the porch steps and the long walk to the gate, he said, "I never knew before that Job could be resorted to for comfort."

"I don't suppose you have ever read Job through in your life," Anne said tartly. Thereafter she saved her breath until she was safely in his car, beside him, and then she added, "Job looked at reality and still had faith. Not easy to do. I'm sorry I made such a stupid remark at dinner. I upset Sally Anne. I never thought of the children listening."

At home, after she had been persuaded to lie down on the sofa with the afghan over her, and Tucker had built up the fire in the grate and gone, she immediately rose and wrote a note for him to find in her desk some day. "Please see that Sally Anne gets my Bible. I'll put a bookmark in the twelfth chapter of Job with a note telling her what I think it means." On another sheet of paper she wrote, "I think this verse means that God, if you trust Him, can bring from darkness, where your mind has buried it, the fear of death, to the light, where you can face it. At the end when you have passed through that shadow, there will be Light. All-encompassing." She was not satisfied with what she had written, but after staring at the paper for a while, decided it was the best she could do. She moved a buckram bookmark cross-stitched with the words "Bless God" to the Book of Job, chapter twelve, and felt that she had made all the preparation she could to spare the child she loved so much.

After the Gordon children were in bed that night, Jennifer came downstairs. Tucker was preparing to go out again to check on his hospital patients, but he stopped for a few minutes' conversation with her.

"Gran really has been shaken up by the election," she said. "You would think an old person so near the end wouldn't be so upset."

"I have found that old people tend to become more prejudiced as time passes, rather than less. Old ladies, particularly, can be venomous about politics."

"How far is Gran from the end, do you think?"

"You must see, darling: she is failing. Her heart is worse than she admits—or knows, perhaps."

"I've been afraid of that. Can't we stop her doing so much?"

"To what end? You know how much she has meant to me: I would keep her alive forever if I could. But she loves life so much—ironical, isn't it—that it would be cruel to deprive her of whatever she can still enjoy."

"After you'd gone this afternoon to take her home, Mother said Gran had proposed resigning from the Club. She has missed several meetings this fall, with various excuses, but until she spoke to Mother, no admission that she didn't feel equal to the meetings."

"What did your mother tell her?"

"That of course she couldn't resign. What if she did miss an occasional meeting? After all, she is the last of the charter members: how could she think of resigning?"

"Good for your mother. Your Club members are all grown women, and if she had a heart attack at a meeting, you could cope, Jenny."

"You think it could happen any time." Jennifer caught her breath.

"Any time. Any hour."

"I was afraid of it. That is why I have kept Sally Anne so busy after school making Christmas presents. Now it will have to be music lessons or dancing lessons, or something. It would be a frightful shock to the child, if she were alone with Gran, even with Louline in the kitchen and Tess upstairs. But Gran must miss her. Do you suppose she realizes what I am doing?"

"I shouldn't be surprised. She did her best this afternoon to prepare Sally Anne." He reported the colloquy he had overheard in the hall.

"Sally Anne is young to experience death so close at hand. But Gran is old, and old people's deaths are never really unexpected. I don't think she felt any shock at my grandmother's death, though of course she was younger. But when you are a child and someone your own age dies, it's different. I remember when Naomi Patton died. We were at Uncle Ernest's at the time, until the epidemic here was over, but her death shook me to the roots of my being, even after we came home and stayed at Hillcrest. You never knew, did you? That was the summer you weren't here. I wasn't much older than Sally Anne. I hadn't realized, actually, that children as well as old people could die. I was terrified. I spent nights lying awake, trying to imagine what it would be like. I frightened myself into a premonition: I absolutely *knew* my turn would come next. There wasn't a thing the matter with me—I wasn't sick—so it would have to be an accident. I wouldn't sit in the swing out at

Hillcrest, for fear of the rope breaking. Remember, Tuck: the footprints on the porch ceiling? I didn't put any there that year. And I didn't want to go riding with Grandpa in his automobile, and I had always loved to drive with him. He couldn't understand it. But it was Naomi's being my own age. I really don't think children feel the deaths of old people in that way. But just the same—"

Tuck, seeing the tears in her eyes, took her in his arms. "Poor little Tag-along! I'm sorry I wasn't here. And there was never another summer for me at Hillcrest." He released her. "But of course you are right: we must see that Sally Anne isn't alone with Gran. But whenever possible, you or I must take her there. We can't keep them altogether apart—not after they have enjoyed themselves so much."

They need not have worried. The end came not long after that Sunday, on the next Club meeting day. Theresa had gone off with Jenny and Melissa to Mrs. Lowrey Edwards' house, after Anne had assured her that she was all right, and that Louline would be in shortly to get dinner. When Theresa had gone, after having shaken up the fire and laid on more coal, Anne struggled from the couch where she had been lying and moved, afghan and pillow in hand, to her rocking chair by the hearth. She was cold, and grateful for the fire, thinking it was a good thing it hadn't been left to her ministrations. How John had used to laugh at her unfailing bent for putting out a fire! She turned on the radio: there was always good music from the State University in the afternoons. Then, spent by the effort, she dropped into the chair. She had not admitted to anyone that it was difficult for her to breathe lying down and a little easier sitting up, nor that she spent her nights, after she had been seen into bed by Tess, sleeping in the low cane-seated rocker in her bedroom that, as she always remembered, she had sat in to nurse her children. If Tucker or Dr. Warren knew that was where she spent her nights, they would likely insist on a night nurse, and she didn't want a stranger fussing over her.

Because her nights were so uneasy, she often dozed in the afternoons if she was alone. On that Wednesday afternoon she had hardly got herself arranged when she fell into a doze, her head dropping forward.

A jolting tumult in her chest wakened her; she lifted her head, struggling for breath, and her blurred gaze went to the dining room doorway. Framed in it stood Johnny, as he had come in so many afternoons: smiling, dimpled, tossing an apple high over his head with one hand and catching it with the other. For one brief flash of a second, as she tried to speak, she thought, "Johnny, home from school. I have been asleep—but what an odd dream: me an old woman, and all those years—" Then she heard the radio. It brought her briefly to the present. She had not dreamed those years: they had passed—unless that was what life was—a dream. Johnny was gone from the door. But he had been there, just as he had been once upon a time—a happy child. So after all there was something—something—John, too. She put her head back, gasped once for breath, and suddenly was aware of nothing—nothing in all the world but a great blaze of light. In a last flicker of consciousness, words came to her mind: "Out of the darkness He bringeth out to light the shadow of death."

Louline found her there only moments later when she came to prepare her dinner. At the dining room doorway, she stopped short upon sight of the oddly tilted figure, the hands palms up, fingers loosely curled: she knew at once what had happened. With a gnarled hand she clutched at her mouth to stifle a low anguished moan; but then, before she could give way to welling grief, she heard in her mind the voice, quiet but firm, say once more, "Don't fuss, Louline."

Suddenly solaced, she moved forward and looked down at the serene face. A wisp of hair had come loose and hung down across the forehead. "She done seen the light," Louline said quietly, and reaching, she brushed the lock back into place, the back of her hand grazing the smooth brow as she did. "We all be togetha 'gain soon," she said softly. Then, blinking back her tears, she moved from the now shadowed room to the telephone in the hallway.

She waited by the front door, and almost at once, it seemed, opened it to Tucker.

"She die easy, Mist' Tucker—praise the Lawd fo' His goodness."

Tuck's hand gripped convulsively at Louline's for a second, and then, straightening, he strode past her through the dining room. Beside the huddled figure in the rocking chair, he hesitated, then placed two fingers at the wrist of the nearest upturned hand, only to remove them a moment later.

Tenderly, then, he lifted her from the chair and laid her on the sofa, covering her with the afghan after one final look at the beloved face. Behind him Louline stifled a sob, and he turned. "We mustn't grieve, Louly: any of us. Didn't you see how untroubled she looked? No pain, no fear."

Anne's funeral was a simple one, at home in her own parlor, where the same service had been held for all her family: present were only those who were closest to her: Louline of course; the Evanses—Gib and Elsa, Ludwig and Melissa; Doug Gardiner and Barbara; the Stevenses and the Sheldon Edwardses; Tuck, Jennifer, and, because she had insisted on it, Sally Anne. Her mother had protested, but Sally Anne said, "She wasn't afraid. Why should I be?" And Tuck said, "Let her go: Let her look reality in the eye. Everyone in this country is getting so they don't want to do that: the moment breath is out of the body, whisk it away to a funeral home, and forget all about it as soon as possible. Gran—" Tucker's voice broke. "We can't treat Gran that way." Inadequate, but he could not express what he felt. "We'll have the casket closed; then Sally Anne and all of us will remember her as she was, before. It will be all right for you to go, Sally Anne, and tell her goodbye."

Those who wept at the funeral were Elsa, who had so many fond memories, and Theresa, who had so much imagination. At the cemetery, as the small group was turning from the desolate hole in the ground, Theresa found herself walking with Jennifer and a subdued Sally Anne, clinging to her mother's hand. Theresa, to explain her tears to the tearless, said, "I'm not weeping because she died: there wasn't much left for her—she would soon have been helpless. I am weeping over the relentlessness of time."

"'Within a time the earth shall cover us all.'" Jennifer continued, perhaps to explain her dry eyes, "Remember when Gran quoted Marcus Aurelius at the Memorial for Miss Reid? Since then I have sometimes picked up Tuck's copy when I have been in bed waiting for him to come in from a night call. So much of it applies to everyone, but some of it to Gran particularly. I have heard people wonder how she could be so cheerful after so many tragedies. She wasn't cheerful: she was happy. And Marcus Aurelius would have understood: 'To live happily is an inward power of the soul.' That she made hers not only a good life but a happy one is what I most admired in her."

The next meeting of the Waynesboro Woman's Club was a Memorial meeting in honor of Anne Alexander Gordon. It was duly recorded in the minutes by the secretary: "The Club met on the afternoon of November 30th at the home of our President, Mrs. Gilbert Evans, who presided. The program of the day was preceded by a Memorial for the last of our charter members, Mrs. John Gordon. The principal tribute was delivered by our President, who reminded us that as far back as she could remember, she had known familiarly the late Mrs. Gordon, whom she had called by the courtesy title of 'Aunt Anne,' since she was the most intimate friend of her mother, Mrs. Ludwig Rausch. She spoke of Mrs. Gordon's loyalty, kindness, indomitability in the face of grief, her capacity for living life to the full, illustrating these qualities by reminiscences of her childhood. On the conclusion of this brief tribute, other members of the Club also spoke: Mrs. Jessamine Edwards, who claimed kinship with Mrs. Gordon's husband, but who knew no one else in Waynesboro when she came here as a stranger, and was taken in, with her small son, by Mrs. Gordon and made to feel truly a member of the family and of the community: Mrs. Tucker Gordon, wife of Mrs. Gordon's grandson, also spoke, as did Miss Theresa Stevens, Mrs. Ludwig Evans, and Miss Charlotte Bonner, who had already written an obituary for the *Torchlight*. When the tributes were concluded, the Secretary was asked to read the program of the day, and two fine papers were read by Mrs. Patton and Mrs. Merrill.

"The Secretary believes that all members concur with her in feeling that today's Memorial Program marked a very sad occasion for us. Mrs. Gordon was the last of that small band of courageous women who defied convention and organized the Waynesboro Woman's Club. An era has ended. Another begins, which we hope will be as fruitful, however much the familiar faces are missed."